I0819879

ROXANÂ ROMANCE

ROŠANAK NÂMEH

e-nû-ma eliš la na-bu-û šâ-ma-mu...

When above was not named...

Šu-qu-ra-a…

… There were no gods… and there were no destinies… time had no meaning…

Then Apsû and Ti'âmat joined together, the sweet water and the salty sea… and created gods, in the midst of Heaven.

Two turned into many…

The thirdborns were the great gods who first gathered in council…

Seven of the great gods of council became the gods who decreed destinies…

Six generations of gods and goddesses born and reborn…

Mu-um-mu…

Lahmû and Lahâmu…

and Qi-in-gu and Ištar…

Anšar and Kišar…

Anu, Enlil and Êa…

Adad, Nânna, Šamaš, Nêbiru, Nânâ and Ninlil…

… each generation more powerful than the one before…

….

The young gods danced and feasted and disturbed the peaceful sleep of Apsû.

Apsû raged at Ti'âmat, "I will destroy them all, I will! So I can sleep again in peace!"

Ti'âmat wept. "How could we destroy those we have created ourselves?" She loved Apsû and she loved her children. She could not choose one or the other.

Then Êa, the son of Anšar and Kišar, having heard it all, divined the intention of the first father. He stole away into the depths of the sweet fresh water and drew a magic circle around Apsû and chanted a powerful spell.

Apsû fell into eternal sleep.

Êa took the crown and the divine splendor and the realm of the first father and begot Marduk, the warrior god, with his consort, Dam-ki-na, in the Chamber of Destinies, over the remains of Apsû.

Marduk was the first of his kind of the seventhborn gods. All were warlike and powerful, but none as splendid and strong as Marduk.

When Qi-in-gu, the great god of the thirdborn gods and the favorite of Apsû, discovered the fate of the first father, he raged at the mother goddess Ti'âmat. "The first father shall not go unavenged. Let us wage war against those who have sinned!"

And Ti'âmat consented. She missed her hâ'iru, her bed was empty. No other was equal to the sweetness of Apsû in her heart.

She said to Qi-in-gu, "If you prevail, I shall exalt you over all of my children. You will be the greatest of all the gods and goddesses." And then she gave Qi-in-gu the power to do battle against Êa and the great gods who stood with him. She gave him the Tablet of Destinies to wear as a shield and said to him, "Dupšîmâti. Words from your lips will be written on the Tablet of Destinies. You will decree the destinies of all others."

She then forged monsters for the coming war: Anzû and girtablilû and ugallu demons... mušhuššu and nêšu and bašmu and zuqaqîpu... dragons, lions, snakes and scorpions bedecked with fearsome beauty. She filled their bodies with poison and their hearts with fire.

But Êa heard it all and became fearful. He knew the heart of Qi-in-gu was against him. And so with his older brother, Anu, he went to his father, Anšar. "Ti'âmat, our first mother, has planned evil for us! Many gods have joined forces with her and they are planning war! No one could confront the great mother goddess and escape her wrath with their lives!"

"Has our fate been written in the Tablet of Destinies?" Anšar asked.

"Not yet," Êa replied.

"Go, my son," Anšar commanded Anu, his firstborn son. "Humble yourself before our first mother and talk to her and make her heart merciful."

"My son, send for Marduk, your son." Anšar commanded Êa.

Then Anšar called the Assembly of the great gods of council in Ub-šu-ukkinna, the divine assembly hall. Lahmû and Lahâmu, Kišar, Ki, Enlil and Ninlil, Ištar, Amurru, Nânna, Šamaš, Adad, Melqart, Nânâ and the rest gathered...

Of the seven great gods who decreed destinies, all came, except for one... the great god Qi-in-gu.

They kissed one another and took their seats. Anunnakkî, the old gods, sat on one side of the Assembly. Igîgî, the young gods, who served the old gods, sat on the other side. They ate bread and kukku and drank sesame wine and bittersweet beer.

Anu said to the Assembly, "Now that our first father, Apsû, is in eternal sleep, Ti'âmat, the great mother goddess, means to exalt Qi-in-gu to have dominion over all the great gods and goddesses. Her anger over the death of Apsû, has no bound. She repelled my offer of peace. Her command is mighty... no one alone could resist her."

And Anunnakkî, the old gods, became crestfallen. None knew how to do battle; they were peaceful gods.

But Igîgî, the young gods, were delighted and called for Marduk, the warrior god, having heard of his immense warlike powers.

Êa summoned Marduk. The young god entered the Assembly and took his place among the great gods. Êa said to him, "End is near!" and Marduk understood.

"Which god is it, who has dared to bring battle against the great gods who decree destinies?" Marduk asked the Assembly.

"Not a god— a goddess," Êa said to Marduk. "Bêlet ilî, Ti'âmat, the mother goddess, plans evil against us all. None among us could transgress the boundary of her powers—"

"It is you who has brought the wrath of our first mother upon all of us!" Enlil interrupted. Êa was known for his mischievous magical spells, but this time his younger brother had gone too far. "You should have gathered us in council before you unleashed your magic on the first father!"

The great gods of council murmured in agreement. They had heard it all before; another spell of Êa's gone wayward. But Êa would never admit to doing anything wrong.

"We are blameless. The first father desired to sleep peacefully. We fulfilled his desire—" Êa said to the Assembly in his own defense.

"What is done is done! It cannot be undone!" Anu said.

"It is you she wants!" Enlil shouted back at Êa, ignoring Anu. "We should hand you over to Ti'âmat to do with as she wishes and make the heart of the great mother goddess merciful toward the rest—"

"Who stood by you, when you seduced the virgin Ninlil and begot a son out of wedlock?" Êa shouted, pointing at Ninlil and Nânna. "When our mother wished to banish you and make an example of you? Ha? Who?"

Ninlil started to glow red.

"I took the punishment that the great gods decreed for me!" Enlil stood up in anger, yelled across the Assembly, "I love Ninlil! Nânna is a love child!" and readied himself to strike Êa. "You are one to talk! You have bedded half of the Assembly!"

Anu, their older brother, got to his feet.

Anšar, their father, cleared his throat.

Êa looked around the assembly hall and smiled.

Young goddesses started to glow.

Êa was the most handsome of all the great gods.

"Can this wait?" Ištar stood and said to Êa and Enlil. "Armies of gods and monsters are heading this way to shed our blood and the two of you fight like newborn gods!"

The Assembly turned quiet.

Êa and Enlil cooled.

Ištar, the luminous goddess of love, was so beautiful that most gods forgot their own names when she spoke. She was one of the old Anunnakkî goddesses; she was born to love and nothing else except for war. She had initiated both Êa and Enlil when they were young gods and if angered she could unveil their love secrets in front of the great gods of council.

"And if I accept to be your protector," Marduk rose to his feet and broke the silence, addressing the Assembly. "If I vanquish Ti'âmat and give you life?"

"What do you desire in return, my son?" Anu asked.

"To be the one above all... To sit supreme in Ub-šu-ukkinna and to decree destinies... that whatever I decree will not be questioned, changed or revoked by the great gods of council... ever!"

The great gods murmured and deliberated among themselves. Then they decided.

"So be it... You will become the supreme god in the Assembly of all the great gods of council. Your utterance shall decide destinies... words of your lips shall never be changed nor ever be disobeyed. Speak and your command shall be fulfilled, to destroy and to create... command and create a lumâšu and let it vanish, and speak the words again and let the lumâšu reappear!"

Marduk conjured up a splendid lumâšu with his words and then destroyed it with a wave of his hand. Again he commanded it, and again the lumâšu reappeared, as if it had never vanished.

And the great gods were pleased with his powers. They gave Marduk a bow and a quiver with one arrow and gave him šâr erbetti, the Four Winds: the South wind and the North wind and the East wind and the West wind.

And so Marduk agreed and went to do battle with Ti'âmat, Bêlet Balâti, the great mother goddess, the goddess of creation, the Lady of Life...

Ti'âmat cast her spell.

The young warrior god trembled at the sight of her awesome glory. But he stood fast. Bow and quiver hung at his side. His feet were set by the great gods on a path from which there was no return.

Marduk tried and failed and tried and failed again...

Šeššišu...

Marduk knew his powers, though immense, were no match for the powers of the great mother goddess of creation and her fierce army. And so he challenged her to a single battle.

"Bêlet ilî! Stand! You and I! And we will join in battle to decide the destiny of the great gods!"

All the gods gave way and stood aside, encircling them, holding back Qi-in-gu from going to the side of the great mother goddess. All were curious to see if Bêlet ilî would accept the challenge of the young warrior god and give battle.

Monsters mingled with gods.

"Sakâtu!" Qi-in-gu shouted angrily, struggling to free himself. "How dare you challenge the Lady of Life? You are not even allowed to address the Assembly of the great gods who sit in council!"

"Amâru!" Marduk said and conjured up a blinding rainstorm, without Adad, the great god of rain and lightning.

It poured.

"Dabâbu!" Ti'âmat said, "Speak! You have our permission."

"Bêlet ilî—"

"ê!" Ti'âmat raised her hand. "Do not try our patience. Mannu? Who are you?"

"Anâku... AMAR.UTU... Bukru of Êa, Nudimmud."

Wrath and rage swept over Ti'âmat like a wave from the salty sea.

"Marduk? Firstborn son of Êa? The one begotten over the remains of Apsû?" Ti'âmat screamed, "May a mad uridimmu bite his ušâru!"

Êa heard the words of the great mother goddess from the far side and shuddered.

"Anîna Bêlet Balâti! Great gods sat in council—"

"Those gods of council have sent you, have they? Those ungrateful fools? To fight rather than to humble themselves and kneel at my feet and beg my forgiveness and plead for my mercy?" Ti'âmat raged in fury, full of wrath, standing in the stormy rain.

"Bêlet ilî! Šemû! Return to the salty sea! Let there be peace! Or I must do as bidden to do by my fathers!"

"Sît libbi, you are the son of my sons, but you do not understand my powers... If you spill the blood of your mother," Ti'âmat warned, "there shall be Išutu, in my image! She shall avenge my blood! Every drop of it!

"I have many names... my names shall all be written in the blood of mar'utu. Ânâhatâ... Arûru... Ahurani... Dingir-ma... Mamma... Mammîtu... Nânâ... Nanaya... Ninhursaga... Ninmah... Ninmena... Nekhbet... Omorka... Pârvatî... Šassuru...Tabšut ilî...

"It will take more than wind and water to destroy my memory!"

Marduk stood before her, drenched in rain, while she spoke to him like a mother to a son.

"Mother, let mê—" Qi-in-gu screamed, fearful of the worst. Howling rainstorm drowned his voice and fury.

"Lû!" Ti'âmat was too angry to heed and listen. "Let it be!"

They drew closer, Ti'âmat and Marduk.

Ti'âmat cast another spell, "Drink water. Hussanni!"

Marduk pointed up and spoke and thunder and lightning swept across the air.

Ti'âmat became distracted.

Marduk then created imhullu, the Evil Wind, mixing the Four Winds with the tempest, the hurricane, and the whirlwind, into one colossal wind which had no equal. He sent forth seven of the seven-faced wind.

Ti'âmat opened her mouth to cast the most magical spell she knew, "ra'âmu—" but her body filled with the force of the seven evil winds. And then Marduk swiftly drew his arrow and pierced her heart.

The blood of Ti'âmat flowed into the winds and turned into Ku-li-li, the Dragonfly. Marduk commanded the North wind to gather and carry every drop of her blood into secret places.

Her armies scattered... her forces vanished...

He cast down and stood upon her body, looking down at it wondering what to do next.

Once freed, Qi-in-gu came to claim the body of the great mother goddess. But Marduk captured him, took the Tablet of Destinies and wore it on his chest as a sign of his victory.

He thought and it was written on the Tablet of Destinies and he was amazed at his own godly powers. The glow from the tablet clouded his eyes and Qi-in-gu fled from his grasp.

When his sight cleared, Marduk split the body of Ti'âmat like a flat fish.

He made her upper half into the sky and created the Sun and the Moon and the stars and clouds and the heavenly bodies, and he commanded Nêbiru, son of Anu, to set their paths. He created time and year and month and day, and divided the year into twelve months and each month into thirty days. He decreed Nânna, the Moon-god, son of Enlil, to rule over night and decreed Šamaš, the Sun-god, the other son of Anu, to rule over day. He set Ištar, the goddess of love, to rule over both, and he set Ninurta, the god of war, the other son of Enlil, to watch over her.

And then he created the Earth from the lower half of Ti'âmat's body. Her eyes became River Diglat and River Purattu to cry till the end of the Earth and her hair became the tall reeds that grew in the lands between the twin rivers of tears. Her head became the mountains and her breasts became the hills.

Marduk caught the rest of the rebel gods in his net and took them all to the Assembly, bound in godly fetters.

The great gods of council hailed Marduk as the supreme god and gave him a scepter and a crown and a throne and a ring. They called him *Bêlu* and gave him fifty divine names to exalt him above all gods... Aranuna, Asarluhi... Marukka, Marutukku, Meršakušu... Bêl ilâni, Bêl mâtâti... Lugal-Dimmer-an-ki-a, Lugal-Šuanna...

This done, Bêl Marduk called on all the great gods to deliver unto him the great rebel god, the one who had incited Ti'âmat to turn on her children. "Give up the rebel god you protect!" And the great gods reluctantly offered up Qi-in-gu.

The great gods wiped the Tablet of Destinies clean of Ti'âmat with sweet water and washed away her memory in the sea of salt and forbade the name of Ti'âmat from ever being spoken again in the Assembly. Such was the destiny of Bêlet ilî, the Lady of Life, the first mother of all the great gods, undone by the hands of her own offspring.

Bêl Marduk bathed, washing off the blood of battle and presided over the Assembly with a mušhuššu dragon curled at his feet. They made Enlil the keeper of the Tablet of Destinies, as he alone among them all could write. All the rest of the great gods and goddesses could do was to eat, drink, divine, decree, intrigue, love, and speak and scream and sneer and sleep... in whatever order that pleased them most.

Then, Bêl Marduk demanded and the great gods of council swiftly passed judgment on Qi-in-gu, their son, brother and father. He did not kneel before them and they showed him no mercy. They bound him and Êa cut him and Qi-in-gu bled like a great god...

"I am forever!"

Qi-in-gu screamed defiantly with wrath and fury, feeling the pain of death, never felt by a great god before.

"Mother! Where are you? Why have you forsaken me?"

His godly blood dripped on common clay as he raged.

The great gods spit on Qi-in-gu and drew out his breath of life and broke it into bits and pieces and tossed it into the bloody clay. He was and he was not... he was a great god and great gods were granted death and rebirth. But he was arrogant and the great gods were glad to be rid of him, knowing well that he could not be killed, but that he could be tormented. So they all spit on him...

The rest of the rebel gods were banished to Earth.

Zarpânîtu, consort of Bêl Marduk, sat by his side. At the sight of her divine beauty, the heart of Bêl Marduk remembered the last words of the first mother, the goddess of creation. He opened his mouth and unto the heart of his father, Êa, he spoke: "Great gods shall be free... to feast and decree destinies and send omens!"

Êa formed Man out of the blood of Qi-in-gu mixed with common clay and proclaimed, "Amêlûtu... I make Man so he may live on Earth, that he may serve the great gods, and build temples to worship us." He paused; "I will make Woman—" but he did not know why.

"Let Man remember this day!" Bêl Marduk said in all his glory and it was day five of the month Nîsannu, the first month of the year.

All the great gods and goddesses gathered and feasted and drank and made merry on that day.

In gratitude for their lives, the great gods of council built E-temen-an-ki, a splendid house for Bêl Marduk on the foundation of Heaven on Earth. They covered its walls with gold and lapis lazuli and gave it winged lions and guardian bulls and mušhuššu dragons... and they gave it many names, Bâbil... Bâb-ilani... Bâb-ili... Bâb-ilim... Bâb-ilu... Bâbiruš... Bêl-êpuš... KÂ.DINGIR.RA.KI... all with one meaning: the Gate of Gods.

Mankind were small and noisy and blackheaded and there were too many of them. They disturbed the peaceful sleep of the great gods. But Êa was proud of his creation and stood for them in the Assembly and sent them seven apkallu to teach them the ways of the great gods.

"They are not mine!" Enlil warned the Assembly. "I will not be their god!" and he vowed to destroy all of Man one day.

And the great gods took sides... some favored Enlil and others favored Êa. Bêl Marduk decreed the fate of the gods in the Tablet of Destinies; the fate of Men, he left to the great gods of council decreed in the Book of Heaven.

Thousands and thousands of years passed...

Time now had meaning and its meaning was death, which was meaningless to the great gods. So whatever it was, there was less and less of it as time went by...

Great gods and goddesses aged...

Êa aged...

Man became as troublesome as gods... some said even more...

Êa came to regret mixing of the blood of Qi-in-gu with common clay. Mankind had turned out rebellious like Qi-in-gu and there were as many Women as Men and they were all as fiery as the first mother, Ti'âmat.

If he had known at the beginning of the creation what he knew later, he would have mixed his own blood with the common clay, but it was too late. The great gods of council no longer mentioned his grave error whenever they gathered in Assembly.

He was the father of Bêl Marduk and they were all fearful to offend Bêlu and find their unwritten šimtu quickly written in the Tablet of Destinies and themselves banished to some outer heavenly body where there was no Man to worship them and bring them food... the children of Man went hungry before gods did.

The Anunnakkî gods of council had disparaged Bêl Marduk for creating time, and half of them had turned into white ashes by a quick angry glance. But that was all before Bêl Marduk had learned to master his temper, and there were so many young Igîgî gods eager for a seat at the Assembly that the burnt Anunnakkî gods were hardly missed.

Then the wrathful Enlil opened the floodgates of Heaven and unleashed a Great Flood to destroy Man, as he had always threatened to do.

And he was amazed at how the small noisy creations of Êa survived, no matter what the great gods decreed for their own amusement.

Êa rescued Man. He went down to the lands between the twin rivers wearing a purple robe and walked among what remained of his blackheaded creations after the Great Flood. He gave Man whatever they needed to survive, should Enlil and the great gods of council impose any other calamities on his children. He gave them fire... kings... duppu šarrute... law... a piece of his own wisdom and cunning, and seventy kinds of beer.

Thousands and thousands of years passed...

Warrior gods took the place of peaceful gods in the Assembly and became the great gods of council. But still only Bêl Marduk decreed destinies of gods...

Bêl Marduk was worshiped in the Temple of E-sag-ila in Bâb-ilim. He remained indifferent to Man, as long as they kept faithfully to serving gods, so that the young Igîgî were free from serving the old Anunnakkî.

And Man honored Bêl Marduk for the first eleven days of the month Nîsannu, the first month of the new year, in the ritual of Akîtu. On day five of Akîtu, the kings of Man were humbled before Bêl Marduk, never knowing why. But Bêl Marduk knew and if Man ever forgot, the fury of Bêlu had no bounds.

Then came Gilgâmeš, the splendid two-thirds divine King of Uruk.Ki, the son of goddess Ninsûna and the mortal king, Lugal-banda. He rejected Ištar when she desired him and said to her, "Which lover have you loved forever?"

To soothe her fury, Anu gave Ištar the Bull of Heaven to destroy Uruk.Ki.

And when Gilgâmeš killed the Bull of Heaven and called Ištar a leaky wineskin, Ištar descended to Earth in shame and passed naked through the Seven Gates into Arallû, the house of Ereškigal, her sister, in the Land of No Return.

Ninlil left Enlil... Gods and goddesses slept alone... Men and Women slept alone... Love lost...

Enlil threatened to destroy the above and below to get Ninlil back. The great gods of council besieged Bêl Marduk to appease Enlil and to avenge the honor of Ištar and decree a fate for Gilgâmeš that would never be forgotten. Ištar had initiated the Bêlu too when he was just a young warrior god, so he decreed the death of Enkîdu, the lover of the King, to make him suffer bitterly. But Bêlu could not bring back Ištar, as she had chosen her fate of her own free will.

Ištar soon tired of the Underworld and missed the Heaven and called to Bêl Marduk, "Save me, Bêlu, restore me to myself again! Let me return to your divine light!"

And Bêl Marduk sprinkled Ištar with the Water of Life and commanded Nergal, the god of the dead, to clothe her in luminosity and release her from the Seven Gates of Arallû.

Love reborn... Ninlil returned to Enlil... the heart of Enlil became merciful.

The great gods of council received Ištar with every mark of honor and placed her in the heart of the Assembly and decreed the ritual of sacred marriage of the love-goddess and the kings during the ritual of Akîtu.

Again Gilgâmeš defied the will of the great gods and said, "Man is just the shadow of a bleeding god. But a divine king is the mirror of all the great gods!"

He washed and anointed the body of Enkîdu with sacred oils and left it unburied, so that his lover would rise up again.

This angered Bêl Marduk and brought his wrath upon all kings. He sent flesh-eating maggots to consume the one-third divine body of Enkîdu.

And then he revoked the immortality of the part-divine king and all the kings who were to come after and said, "Let no king or man defy a great god or goddess and live."

Gilgâmeš buried Enkîdu and wandered high and low on Earth and over the deep Waters of Death, like a hunter in search of his lost immortality... he saw all and experienced all... and finally weary and worn, he wept.

"Hear me, Bêl Marduk, the great god of my fathers! Let me not see the death which I fear! Darkness is empty! Will a dead man ever see the sun again?"

He begged and cried and pleaded for immortality. He built the splendid Temple of E-an-na in Uruk.Ki to honor and worship Ištar.

Ninsûna pleaded on her knees with Bêl Marduk and the great gods of council for the life of her only son, but what Bêl Marduk had decreed could not be set aside, even by Bêlu himself.

Gilgâmeš suffered the fate of all Man and went to the Land of Dust and Darkness, from which no dead man had ever returned.

No king ever denied the luminosity of the goddess of love again, knowing the fate of Gilgâmeš, whose story was told and retold by the Scribes of the Book of Heaven in all the courts of the mortal kings.

Bêl Marduk began to prefer the taming of his mušhuššu dragons to attending the Assembly of the great gods, and became more desirous of his heavenly solitude.

"Let the future be like the past," he decreed and it was so written in the Tablet of Destinies and the Book of Heaven.

Then he sent his only son, Nabû, to sit at the Assembly of the great gods of council.

Nabû liked Man, who worshipped him as the patron god of all the scribes who toiled faithfully in the temples of the great gods.

Man and Woman drank the sweet water and remembered the mother goddess... she was worshiped by many names all through the lands, no matter how hard the great gods of council tried to steer them away from her.

Years and years passed...

Êa aged more...

His dark beard turned long and white...

He left the Heaven and lived on Earth, desiring to be closer to his first mother and to his last children.

Years passed...

Êa became sleepless.

He walked around the wet marshes with a tall walking scepter night and day and listened to the many voices of Ti'âmat still mourning and wailing and weeping among the tall reeds whenever the winds blew this way and that way... lamenting the loss of Apsû... not knowing the fate of Qi-in-gu...

At last, Êa relented.

He knelt and called unto her tearfully with all his heart, "Bêlet Balâti... Bêlet ilî... Bêlet Šamê... um-mi... Ama.Ka," and begged for her forgiveness and pleaded for her mercy.

Earth gave in and opened up and took his divine body and wept tears of joy for reuniting with her lost son.

A sycamore fig tree of life grew and spread wide over the remains of the great god who had created Man and Woman.

Ištânu, the North wind, breezed around the splendid tree and golden ku-li-li danced around it.

The great gods of council wept in sorrow and their tears poured on Earth.

River Diglat and River Purattu swelled up with the tears of the great gods and made their way into the Lower Sea.

Sweet waters mixed with the salty sea... again...

Ra'âmu ahriatiš...

ROXANÂ ROMANCE
ROŠANAK NÂMEH

A. J. CAVE

TUP-ŠARRATU

PAVASTÂ

Published by Pavastâ
San Mateo, California, U.S.A.

www.pavasta.com

For information regarding permission, please contact the publisher,
publisher@pavasta.com

ISBN 10: 0-9802061-0-3
ISBN 13: 978-0-9802061-0-4

Printed in the United States of America

First hardcover edition, January 2008

To Bâb-ilim

𒆍𒀭𒊏𒆠

The Gate of Gods...

In the name of My Lord,

Who ordered Nêbiru to set...

... and Ninurta to rise...

... and then said to Šamaš: Eclipse Nânna.

CONTENTS

CELESTIAL OMENS \ 1

One

TIE that BINDS \ 10

Two

EDGES of the HEART \ 180

Three

AXIS of EMPIRE \ 286

Four

MURMURS \ 309

Five

ECLIPSE of the SUN \ 381

Six

SON and FATHERS \ 458

Seven

LANDS without KINGS \ 554

MOON and the PEACOCK \ 618

Glossaries

Fragments \ 721

GODS and MEN

PERSIANS

UPLANDERS

PEACOCKS

TIMELINE

WORDS

SOURCES

Scribe's Note \ 801

CELESTIAL OMENS

1

Celestial Omens

E-TEMEN-AN-KI TEMPLE. ROYAL CITY of BÂB-ILIM. BÂBIRUŠ
YEAR 5 of the THIRD DÂRIUŠ, MONTH 6, ULÛLU
NIGHT

"Here it is, Master!"

Bêl-rê'ušu anxiously rushes into the candlelit room waving a small clay tablet in his hand.

"Careful with that!" Kî-Nabû yells. "It is not a damn army standard you are waving over your head! You want to get kicked out of Bît Ṭuppi like Aia-râm for dropping one of the tablets of the *Book of Heaven*?"

Bêl-rê'ušu swallows hard and catches his breath. "Sorry, Master!" He bows his head and with trembling fingers quietly puts the clay tablet on the wooden table in front of his old master. "Aia-râm said Demon Šakku bit him in the arm—"

Kî-Nabû gives him a sharp look.

"A demon in the Great House of Bêl Marduk?"

Bêl-rê'ušu takes a quick step back and hides his red face in the darkness.

Kî-Nabû shakes his head and takes a deep breath and holds it for a short moment.

If the North wind had blown during the eclipse, gods would have had mercy upon the King of the Lands…

Kî-Nabû reluctantly leans forward in his tall worn chair and pulls the flickering candle closer. He reads the latest entry in the *Book of Heaven*.

E-NÛ-MA ilu ANU ilu ÊA ilu BÊL…
When the great gods Anu, Êa and Bêl
established the bounds of Heaven and Earth in council…

Year 5 of Artašatu who is called Dâriuš, Month 6, Ulûlu
Day 13: Sunset to Moonrise: 8°
There was an Eclipse of the Moon.
Nânna was covered at the moment when Nêbiru set and Ninurta rose.
During totality, the West wind blew.
During clearing, the East wind blew.
During the eclipse, there were deaths and plagues.

His old eyes betray him. He pulls the flickering candle and the hardening clay tablet closer. He carefully reads the words again, rubbing his fingers on words pressed hard into the wet clay, every word. "Amurrû… West wind… then Ṣitân… East wind… no wind from the north." He mumbles to himself, shaking his head. "No ištânu? Are they sure?"

"Yes, Master."

"Ninurta, god of war—" He looks up and narrows his eyes, searching for the boy. "Bêl-rê'ušu?"

Bêl-rê'ušu quickly takes a step forward into the light of the burning candle. "Father?"

Kî-Nabû opens his eyes wide. He considers his young son under his white brow for a long moment, shaking his head. He then scorns him impatiently.

"I am your father at home. Here, I am Ummâni dannuti and you are my šamallû and no more, until you have mastered the art of your fathers."

"Yes, Master." Bêl-rê'ušu gathers himself quickly.

Kî-Nabû shakes his head and takes a deep breath slowly. "Did you forget to bring the commentary again?"

"No, Master!" Bêl-rê'ušu quickly bows and puts another small clay tablet in front of his father, the chief diviner and scribe of the royal court in Bâb-ilim.

Kî-Nabû rubs his tired eyes and lifts the second clay tablet, bringing it closer. He reads the commentary under his breath.

ŠUMMA NÂNNA INA TÂMARTÎŠU MÂ...

If the Moon is observed, then...

The omen foretells the eclipse of the Persian Empire.
The Eclipse of the Moon took place in Zibbâtu, close to Saguš, in month 6, ulûlu, which is unfavorable for the Great King of the Lands.
Western wind at the beginning of the eclipse foretells that doom is to come from the West.
Nêbiru, which could have taken away the evil of the Eclipse of Nânna, had already set.
Ninurta, the god of war, has risen.

Kî-Nabû puts down the clay tablet and strokes his short brittle white beard.

Something was missing... what was it?

Total Eclipse of the Moon on the day 13, in month 6, Ulûlu, in the last year of King Nabû-Na'id had only meant that the Moon-God wanted a new high priestess of royal blood, the daughter of the king, to tend to his service in Bâb-ilim.

He looks up and narrows his eyes again at Bêl-rê'ušu lingering quietly before him. "Anything else?"

Bêl-rê'ušu hesitates for a long moment, fearful of offending the ears of the gods with carelessly chosen words and attracting the attention of the dark spirits who roamed at night. He finally leans his head forward and points with his finger toward the open window and utters in a hushed voice, "The moon—"

Kî-Nabû leans back a little and looks at his son impatiently and grunts.

"Do I have to pull every word out of your mouth? What about the moon?"

Bêl-rê'ušu looks around the dimly lit room and touches his right arm, feeling the sacred Amulet of Lamassu tightly tied around it.

"Moon turned the color of clotted blood, Master." He brings his hands to his lips to hide his words from Šakku, the seven-headed demon serpent, lurking in dark shadows, always ready to strike and cause pain.

Kî-Nabû closes his eyes and shifts slightly in his tall worn chair. "Ah!"

He leans back further and rests his old bones on older wood.

"That is the missing piece!"

For thousands and thousands of years, since after the days of the Great Flood that had swept across the Lands and purified the Earth, his priestly ancestors had been the Watchers of the Heavens, observing the skies faithfully from the crowns of the high mountains and the platters of the lowlands.

And from the Crown of E-temen-an-ki, the Foundation of the Heaven on Earth… a duty and an honor that was bestowed upon them by the kings who had descended from the heavens… sent by the great gods… in former days… before the living memory… long ago…

Everything was foretold by the heavenly movements of the sun and the moon and the heavenly bodies and the little stars.

And the secrets of the great gods and the great heavens had been faithfully passed down to Tupšar E-nû-ma Anu Eâ Bêl… Scribes of the Book of Heaven…

…father to son, man to man, generation to generation… from time immemorial…

Nothing was ever new except for what was forgotten from the living memory of men.

Precious Arabâya incense smolders slowly in the fire altar, scenting the warm room.

Kî-Nabû takes a deep breath. He shifts his bones again and leans back deeper in his old chair.

The moon…

Moon was the heavenly sign of the Persians.

His old face creases and folds in pain.

Men were flawed… created by the great gods from kneading of common clay with the blood of a rebel god who had been slaughtered by the great gods for his arrogance… lowly clay mixed with the shattered bits and pieces of the condemned soul of the rebel god to make him serve the great gods and suffer endlessly… till the end of heavens… till the end of time… trapped and caged eternally in tombs of dying and rotting mortal clay.

Men were forgetful… but the great gods made men remember… that men were servants of the great gods and no more. And when men forgot… and when the rebel god stirred again restlessly in his clay tomb, remembering who he used to be, the great gods who had spilled his godly blood struck back, struck hard, and struck fast… reminding the rebel god of the first sin…

Great gods spit on the mortal clay…

Great gods spit on the rebel god…

But the rebel god was still powerful… even in bits and pieces.

He was once one of the great gods of council… one of the seven who decreed destinies… he wanted to be free… wanted to be a great god again… wanted to rule over other great gods… wanted to spill their godly blood as they had spilled his… his dark wrath endless… his blood thirst insatiable…

And when clay turned to dust… men forgot… men always forgot… and now they were stirring again…

"Well, it looks like the great gods have sat in council again and have deliberated what is to come. They have planned another colossal calamity for men. What would I give to be a little kakkubu in the Vault of Heaven where the great gods of council gather to hear Enlil plot—" Kî-Nabû says to himself looking at the commentary. "Bêl-rê'ušu, when was the first of such calamities?"

"It was the Great Flood of the former days, Master, when men had disrupted the restful sleep of the great gods again. Great god Enlil—"

"Yes," Kî-Nabû interrupts and nods. "Great god Enlil has already written it all in the Tablet of Destinies, fate that cannot be changed. Now the heavenly bodies are whispering in my ears, revealing what little I am humbly permitted to record of their godly intentions in the Book of Heaven." He points to the sky and says, "As I always say, Bêl-rê'ušu, evil in the sky above is a sign of evil on the earth below." He starts rubbing his eyes mindlessly, his eyes close restlessly.

"The moon of the mighty Persians has eclipsed and has turned bloody."

The age of the splendid Great Kings, sons of A-ha-ma-ni-iš and the worshippers of the U-ra-ma-az-da of the Persians, had come to pass… just as the times of Šarru-kîn and Ha-am-mu-ra-pi and Gilgâmeš and Aššur-bâni-apli and Nabû-Kudurrî-Ûṣur before them…

The doom was coming from the other side of the stormy seas. Clay armies of the Lord of Darkness, servant of the rebel god, were coming, sheathed in full metal arm and armor. The King of the Race of Wrath was leading the armed armies of the Lord of Darkness into the Lands and Waters of the Persians… and the Sun of Bâb-ilim too was fated to share the fate of the Persian Moon…

The age of chaos was to be unleashed upon the dirt of earth… it was written in the stars… it had been foretold for generations…

For six thousand years the Wise Lord of gods and the Lord of Darkness were to join in battle across the Lands of the Persians, fighting with words and swords and spears…

And their battle was for the souls of the men. For the whole soul of the rebel god… collected bit by bit, piece by piece, released from the broken clay vessel tombs… freed from the clay servants of the great gods…

… turning into truth in the hands of the great gods…

… turning into lies in the hands of the rebel god…

And what was to come of it too was foretold by the lips of the heavens.
Great gods had bestowed their divine glory unto the Persian Kings.
Bêl Marduk had called Ku-raš the Elder to Bâb-ilim and had made him the truthful guardian of the restless blackheaded clay mortals.
The Persian Kings had become powerful and they had gathered all the Lands and all the People under their kingly powers… they had become the Great Kings, the Kings of Kings, the Kings of the Lands, the Kings of the Lands Across-the-River and the Lands Beyond the Sea too… the Kings of all the Lands and all the People…
… the first Empire Builders…
And they had grown arrogant and had forgotten the ways of the great gods.
Ka-ši-ar-šâ, son of Da-ri-a-muš, had taken the golden statue of the Bêl to Û-pe-e on River Diglat to punish Bâb-ilim and that had angered Bêl Marduk.
In the year he was born, nearly seventy years ago, the Royal Son of the House, the Younger Ku-raš, had cursed his Royal Brother with his last dying breath when his royal blood had been spilled and splattered by his royal brother, the Great King, on the Lands at Kuišta, not that far from the other side of Bâb-ilim.
The King of the Lands, the Second Ar-tak-šat-su, had lived a long and fruitful life and the bloody curse of his Royal Brother was all but forgotten.
But the heavens had a long memory… stretching forward and backward and in every other direction… and they never forgot the dying curse of a wronged Son of the Royal House of ancient royal blood. The warm winds of Ulûlu and Karbašiyaš and Belilit that had bathed the dead body of the favored Royal Son remembered and guarded his memory whenever they blew hot and restless across the highlands and the lowlands and the flatlands of the Lands and Waters of the Persians.
Û-ma-su, the bastard son of the Second Ar-tak-šat-su, had treacherously put to the sword or to the poison almost all the Royal Sons of the Royal House of Hakhâmaniš to secure his royal throne.
Royal blood had been spilled to keep the royal crown…

Bêl-rê'ušu leans slightly forward into the dim light.

"Master? The Persian pirradaziš is waiting impatiently!" he says in a worried voice. "What shall I tell him?"

Kî-Nabû opens his eyes and looks out the open window for a moment, gathering his thoughts. He sees the night stars. Great gods and stars move this way and that way in his eyes. He shakes his head and slowly leans forward in his chair and asks quietly, "How old is Mâr Bît Šarri, the Persian Crown-Prince Tiršata? You were six when he was born."

"Master, Mâr Bît Šarri will turn seven in the next cycle of the sun."

Kî-Nabû closes his eyes again and leans back in his chair. The lines around his olden eyes sharpen and deepen with pain. He opens his eyes again and the bloody sight of the headless young royal body drenched in his own royal blood still haunts him.

He shakes his head from side to side.

"Well, well, nothing lasts forever, after all!"

Persians were the first, but they were not the only ones... great gods were not fools!

More empires were to come, bigger and mightier, and they too were to ebb and flow like the waves of the deep watery oceans...

... wax and wane like the cycles of the silvery moon...

Their powers rising and setting like the mighty sun of the heavenly skies...

An Eastern Empire setting like the moon...

A Western Empire rising like the sun...

... knotted together in the battle of the great gods... for the fate of all the heavens.

But at a distance, another Eastern Lion was rising and an Eastern Dragon too knotted with a Phoenix...

And a three-legged bird to soar majestically over the eastern skies of the Land of the Calm Mornings on the other side of the Land of the Phoenix and the Dragon.

And suns set,

And moons rise... again...

... by and by...

"Well, at least the royal blood of the rightful Younger Ku-raš, born to Persian Purple, will be avenged from the descendants of his bloody wrongful vanquishers. Bêl Marduk is finally holding the feet of the Persian Royal Sons to the burning sins of their Royal Fathers. May the great gods and goddesses known and unknown have mercy."

Kî-Nabû draws another deep breath. His old body fills with new pain again. Every bone hurts.

He had lived far too long... the life of a court scribe was not an easy life... and it had become much harder after death had taken his beloved wife after a long illness.

The great gods had given him a son and had taken his wife in return.

He prays quietly under his breath, "My Lords, Bêl Marduk and Nabû, in all my years, I have served you well. My life is written before you. When I was sleeping, death crept quietly into my bedroom and took her and set her feet toward the Gates of Arallû from which she shall not return. My life is finished. What can I do without her, who will take care of me? Please be merciful to your old faithful obedient servant! Do not abandon me!"

A cool breeze lazily fills the warm room.

A great golden dragonfly suddenly flies into the room and crashes carelessly into the burning flame of the flickering candle and flies out again with a burning wing.

Kî-Nabû's eyes chase after the dragonfly. He bites his lip and mumbles under his breath, "Ku-li-li, are you taking my prayer to the great gods of destinies on your fiery wings?"

He takes a deep breath and mumbles to himself.

"My Lord, let there be truth in my words... Who really knows the will of the great gods?"

He nods to himself and then leans forward in his chair, turning the clay tablet over in front of him and starts writing on the other side of the commentary.

BÂRÛTU
Divination

The Royal Son of the House of A-ha-ma-ni-iš who is called Hakhâmaniš will become purified for the Persian Throne but his dark head will not be golden crowned.
A king has come with the armies of the West.
There will be abundance and riches on his path.
For eight years he will exercise kingship. He will defeat the Persian Royal Army. He will relentlessly pursue his enemies.
Ninurta, the god of war, with the hands of a lion and claws of an eagle, will favor him for eight unbroken years.

Kî-Nabû puts down his tablet marker on the wooden table, pushes the hardening clay tablet and the flickering candle away from him, looking out the window at the darkening heavens.

All the great gods and goddesses were sleeping, Anu and Êa and Enlil…

Bêl Marduk and Nabû and Šamaš and Nânna and Ištar…

A long moment passes in silence.

Sounds of life and living from the Royal City of Bâb-ilim float in the room.

Then he chants an ancient prayer to the stars, the gods and goddesses of the night, under his lips.

"*ilî Mušîti,*

"veiled is the night, the holy places are quiet and dark. I call to you, all the stars, gods and goddesses of the night, the bright ones, whom Bêlu has created. Stand by me in this night, on this side of me and on that side of me. Take my prayers to Šamaš, the Divine Judge, the Father of the Fatherless, beg him to undo the evil. Let the evil pass by the King of the Lands in the night."

He opens his hands and prays to Ištar, the great goddess of love.

"O Ištar, the glorious one, who reigns among the Igîgî, who soothes the angry gods,
iltu Ištar, šu-pu-u-tum la-ab-bat ilu Igîgî mu-kan-ni-šat ilâni šab-su-ti,
forgive my transgression, accept my prayer,
mi-e-ši hab-la-ti-ia li-ki-e un-ni-ni-ia,
say the words, so at your command, may the angry gods have mercy…
ki-bi-ma ina ki-bi-ti-ki ilu zi-nu-u li-is-lim…
let your mercy be upon me, be my life.
ta-ai-ra-tu-ki rab-ba-a-ti lib-ša-a eli-ia, um-ma lu-u a-na-ku-ma.

Kî-Nabû mindlessly rubs the deep lines on his forehead and continues.

"My goddess, lay thy punishment on he who is sinful, be merciful that the innocent not be destroyed."

"My goddess is queen."

iltu bêlti-ma šar-rat.

He then points with his old finger to the clay tablets and says quietly to his young šamallû, "Take these to Kênu-nâ'id and tell him that Kî-Nabû said that these tablets should be kept in the royal archives forever, after they are fully baked. Do not drop them on the way!"

"Master, I will be careful! But— what shall I tell the Persian pirradaziš?"

Kî-Nabû leans back again in his chair. His body disappears in the darkness of the night. His voice writes on the skin of a woeful heart.

"Tell the Persian pirradaziš to tell the following to the Persian King:

"To the King, My Lord Dâriuš, from his loyal subject, Kî-Nabû:

"Good health to Your Majesty. May the great gods Marduk and Nabû bless Your Majesty. May U-ra-ma-az-da and all the gods whose names Your Majesty has invoked bless Your Majesty a thousand times more. Seven times and again seven times more I kneel before Your Majesty and kiss the ground at your feet.

"As to Your Majesty asking me: *Kî-Nabû, what is the meaning of the Eclipse of the Moon on day 13 past the beginning of the month 6, Ulûlu?* This omen is not like the others. It is a fair warning the great gods have given to Your Majesty.

"Total Eclipse of the Moon on day 13, the Day of Darkness in the month 6, Ulûlu, is inauspicious for Your Majesty. The hainâ has come for the blood and crown and gold and lands and women of Your Majesty. On the day of the battle, Your Majesty must array the Royal Army facing the setting sun. Your Majesty must avoid facing the rising sun. May he who plans evil against the King of the Kings receive the punishment of the great gods and die a shameful death.

"Your Majesty should invoke all the great gods who have your Lands in their keeping and pray to them with your hands raised to the heavens and perform sacred sacrifices to avert the coming evil.

"I pray to Bêlet Arba-ilu, Nânâ, the daughter of Nânna, the Moon-God, who dwells in the City of Arba-ilu and watches over the Land of the Black Eagle, to bless Your Majesty who holds fast the hem of her gown.

"Let Nânâ, the thirdborn goddess, hear my prayers and accept your offerings and fulfill your desires.

"My Lord, the great gods have given you the world from the rising of the sun to the setting of the sun. May the great gods extend your rule forever."

One

TIE that BINDS

FORTRESS of SUGHUD. SATRAPY of SUGHUDA
YEAR 10 of ALEXANDER, MONTH 6, XANDIKOS
YEAR 3 of ALEXANDER, MONTH 12, VIYAXANA
3 YEARS LATER
SUN RISING

"Wings!"

"Men with wings!"

Anxious screams pierce through the veil of silence of the early dawn, echoing off the sleepy walls of the ancient mountaintop Fortress of Sughud and the mountainous caverns cresting massively above it.

Rošanak opens her sleepy eyes. It is still dark outside.

Silence.

She pulls the soft warm blanket over her head, closes her eyes and drifts back to sleep.

Just another bad dream…

"They have wings! Bastards!"

"They can fly!"

Loud screams seep through the heavy windows of the ancient didâ, shut tight to keep out the cold mountain air of late winter. Silence splinters and shatters and falls on the stony floor like a delicate piece of thin green Persian kâsaka.

Rošanak quickly opens her eyes.

No… not a bad dream. A bloody nightmare.

The ancient didâ starts to awake and murmur with the sounds of feet running in all directions.

Rošanak jumps out of her warm bed, pulling the thick wool blanket around her, and rushes into the dimly lit hallway, blindly running down the dark stony steps, caught in the midst of a wave rolling and rushing into the middle courtyard of the massive ancient didâ.

Cold air brushes against her face like fine grains of desert sand. An eagle screams. She looks around.

She was swimming in a sea of elders and women and children. Everyone in the ancient didâ had poured like water out of a broken vessel and into the cold courtyard, crowding all around her…

… some hurriedly wrapped up in warm wool night blankets… the rest shaking and shivering and shuddering in the late winter cold… all anxious and scared and stunned… and tongueless and wordless.

No one left inside but the newborns and the very young… and the very old.

Itâna, her brother, and a few other young boys who have been up on night watch duty, excitedly point with their whole bodies to the crown of the high mountain that hangs silently over the ancient didâ.

"Look up! There! Up on the ice-covered ridge!"

All eyes, young and old, roll and hurriedly follow the directions of the hands pointing upward.

The pale winter sun is slowly rising from behind the old mountain ridges, its rays shooting like arrows into searching eyes.

Rošanak shades her eyes with her hands to see better into the sun.

The multitudes around her start to murmur with sheer disbelief and panic and terror.

High over the ancient Fortress of Sughud, on a snow-covered ridge below the crown of the high mountain, a row of armed and armored enemy warriors stood victoriously, waving pieces of their scarlet standards in the cold wintry morning air. It was hard to see how many enemy warriors in arms stood high over their heads ready to do battle and shed blood; their bodies were sheathed in the pale rays of sun rising behind them.

"Impossible!" Some voices murmur in disbelief.

"God help us!" Other voices murmur in sheer terror.

Other voices plead and pray desperately.

Cries of children fill the fearful ears.

Mothers are too terrified to be of any comfort to their children.

"It cannot be!" Rošanak mumbles to herself as she stands there motionless, utterly stunned. She forgets to breathe.

The ancient didâ, high on the crown of the sheer-faced Rock of Sughud and bigger than a town, was impenetrable, so they said. The King and all his kingsmen and warriors had sent their women and children and elders there for safe-keeping during the war. When an azdâkara had come from the enemy camp a few days earlier asking the ancient didâ to surrender in return for mercy and safe passage, the boys who were given the task of guarding the impenetrable ancient didâ, Itâna being one of them, had arrogantly laughed and shouted back:

"Only if you can fly!"

And the enemy warriors had grown wings overnight and had flown… high above them.

And now here they all stood in the icy morning mountain air looking up at the enemy warriors, standing over their heads with their sharp naked swords glinting in the early snow-golden rays of dawning winter sun, eager for the taste of their blood.

"Death or slavery!" An old woman standing close to Rošanak cries out bitterly in fear.

"Death." Rošanak utters quietly under her breath, grinding her teeth, shaking her head.

When the old Fortress of Âriâmazda, perched on top of another sheer-faced rock, had fallen into the hands of the enemy army, the old Âriâmazda and all his sons and his kinsmen and his elders and all the warriors defending the old didâ had been put to the sword.

All their women and children had been taken and raped and sold in the slave markets in the Lands Beyond the Sea.

"Barefoot? Again? In this cold? Have you lost your mind?"

Rošanak's thoughts are torn by the voice of her blood mother who pushes her toward the inside of the ancient didâ.

"Go inside before you catch your death in this cold!"

Rošanak turns her head toward the familiar voice.

"But Mother—" She pleads with her blood mother, pointing with her trembling fingers upward toward the row of enemy warriors standing high above them.

"All of you! Go inside and get dressed! You all look like a flock of fleeced sheep waiting to be slaughtered!" Aššat Šarri Farânak, Rošanak's mother, raises her voice above the multitudes.

Toth Totote!

The unexpected shattering sound of the enemy war trumpet blowing.

Everyone jumps, startled. Then, the loud accented voice of the enemy azdâkara breaks over their worried heads, asking for their surrender to the winged warriors.

Chaos and fear and panic pour down like snowflakes.

"Itâna, send a messenger to your father and the elders," Aššat Šarri Farânak orders Itâna calmly.

"But—" Itâna protests loudly.

Aššat Šarri Farânak pushes her way through the murmuring multitudes and grabs Itâna by the shoulders. "But what, Itâna?" She speaks calmly, with her royal air taming his youthful pride, simmering with fear and anger and uncertainty under her skin.

"Nothing," Itâna mumbles quietly, hanging his head low, looking aimlessly at his feet. "We told them we would surrender, if they could fly!"

"The blame is not yours, Itâna. These men would have found a way in, somehow. These are the same men who got through the Persian Gates in the middle of the winter."

"NO? Was he not the same idiot who yelled: *Grow wings and we will surrender!?*" Rošanak yells mockingly from the other side of the stony courtyard, still lingering in the frame of the massive door, carelessly wrapped in her warm blanket.

All eyes turn and lock mercilessly on the young boys who are all now looking down at their feet, ashamed, defeated and utterly humiliated.

Aššat Šarri Farânak lets go of Itâna and turns around. She gives her a sharp look and yells, "Rošanak!"

Rošanak shrugs her shoulders. "I am going inside," she yells back, "but if Utâna were here, he would have taken a barbed branch to Itâna and the rest of those idiot boys and bleed their bloody backs for good measure!"

Her voice echoes and hangs in the cold air, and then haunted silence. She turns and walks inside the massive doorway quickly to avoid the scornful gaze of her blood mother.

How could her mother be so calm and forgiving?

They were to become captives of murderous merciless ruthless enemies…

Life was over…

And her blood mother was screaming at her instead of choking that idiot Itâna.

Aššat Šarri Farânak looks at Rošanak, shaking her head as her daughter disappears inside the ancient didâ. She looks around and narrows her eyes.

The multitudes start to quickly head back inside the fortress, feeling her commanding eyes on their trembling backs.

LATER that DAY

Uxšiyârta, tall and weathered and weary, Itâna's blood father, followed by Oštana, his middleborn son, and a few elders walk into the middle courtyard of the ancient didâ and into the midst of the anxious murmuring throng.

Cloudy skies hang low over their heads.

"We have surrendered the Fortress of Sughud to the enemy army in exchange for free passage. You can all leave in safety and return to your homes," Uxšiyârta declares with authority. "They will garrison the didâ. Do not stand around! Go! Take your belongings and leave! Go!"

The multitudes murmur anxiously.

"Alexander has given quarters to all the women and children and elders, everyone!" Uxšiyârta softens his voice, trying to sound more comforting and reassuring. "He will honor his words! He just wants the damn fortress!"

More anxious murmuring.

No one moves, neither this way nor that way; all stand rooted in fear of death.

Uxšiyârta nods with guarded confidence and says, "We will host a feast for Alexander tomorrow night at my house. You can all come," pointing to the other elders standing by his side who nod uneasily in agreement under their proud old brows.

Murmurs.

"What are you all still waiting for?" Uxšiyârta loses his temper and growls impatiently. "Stand where you are and die when Alexander and his men march into the fortress!"

The multitudes grumble. They finally relent and begin to scatter with heavy hearts.

Uxšiyârta looks around his fortress.

The stony courtyard slowly becomes empty.

Winter wind blows and howls.

"Do not be too hard on the boys!" Aššat Šarri Farânak says quietly to Uxšiyârta, her blood brother, as she gently puts her arms around him.

"My fault! All my fault! I should not have left a bunch of boys in charge. I should have told them, I should have warned them not to bait these men.

"Who would have thought they would climb a sheer iced rock, in the middle of a moonless night, no less?" Uxšiyârta says, shaking his head, grinding his teeth quietly, and blaming himself. "Alexander has been blazing with endless wrath ever since he crossed into the Lands, with Aešma, the Demon of Wrath and Fury, going by his side, bending grown men to his unbending will. He is not a man to match wits with boys."

"Maybe it was all meant to be—" Aššat Šarri Farânak says quietly, taking a deep resigned breath.

"The Wise Lord has forgotten us." Uxšiyârta mumbles bitterly under his breath.

"Watch your words, Brother! Lord is Wise. His eternal will unfolds beyond our mortal lives. Do not lose hope!"

"Do you blame me?" Uxšiyârta grunts and closes his eyes in white anger. "My Utâna, all your blood sons, your husband, your eldest daughter and her husband, all dead."

Mournful silence.

Wind howls.

Winter sun breaks through low clouds.

"Life and death are by the favor of the Wise Lord," Aššat Šarri Farânak says, pushing back tears, breaking the silence. "Some good will come out of this. You still have Oštana and Itâna, and I still have Rošanak and the little ones—"

"Itâna, Ha! The boy is useless. He cost me our old ancestral fortress. This ancient didâ would have held two more years under siege, maybe longer!"

"The boy is young, and we all would have lost all reason and gone mad if we had to stay here two more years." Aššat Šarri Farânak says, "I know you miss Utâna. We all do. Rošanak— well—" Aššat Šarri Farânak pauses, takes a deep breath. "Those we love live in our hearts. If the Wise Lord had truly abandoned us, he would have taken our sweet memories of our loved ones instead, so we would suffer living without remembering why—"

"Forgive me!" Uxšiyârta gently holds Farânak's hand and quietly pleads.

"What is there to forgive?"

"I should have given my blessing to Utâna to wed Rošanak, but her blood father had just died and I just could not think of a wedding in the middle of a war. No one thought this cursed war would go on for so long."

Regret and sadness cloud Uxšiyârta's face. "I could have had a grandson by now."

"Oštana will make you a grandfather soon, he is handsome and girls favor him in abundance, and Itâna too," Aššat Šarri Farânak says tenderly, "when he grows up into manhood. Wise Lord bless their mother."

"Will you come to the feast tomorrow night?" Uxšiyârta asks hurriedly, hopefully, changing the subject.

His sister knew the truth but was forever hopeful…

Itâna was an idiot and no one had ever seen Oštana chase after a girl!

"Oh, no," Aššat Šarri Farânak says as they start walking back inside, "we leave for Baktra as soon as the maids pack everything."

"Ah!" Uxšiyârta grunts, his eyes become cloudy.

"What?"

The wind blows colder.

"The Hadiš at Baktra," Uxšiyârta says in a low voice.

"Has my home been destroyed?" she asks worriedly.

"No. But Artâvazda, the old satrap was living in the small hadiš by the gates and Alexander in the other when Baktra fell into their hands. I hear a new satrap, one of the men of the enemy army, is to replace the old bastard soon!" Uxšiyârta says with a voice loaded with guilt. He fidgets with embarrassment and steals away his eyes. "I did not want to grieve you needlessly, so I did not mention anything."

Not offering bad news was not lying.

Just delaying… and hoping for better news to replace bad news…

Aššat Šarri Farânak stops and turns half way and looks at Uxšiyârta, startled. Her eyes narrow with pain. "Artâvazda?" She lets go of Uxšiyârta's arm. "Then Rošanak, the little ones and I are without a home, while a traitor lives in our house?"

"Your own properties are still yours, and you are still my sister. You can have any of my homes. My needs are few these days."

"I just never thought of someone else living in my home, Artâvazda no less, the man who betrayed my husband, caused his wretched death." She speaks with a faint voice as if coming from the bottom of a waterless well in the heat of Bakhtriš summer. "All my children were born there. Parânak was married there. Rošanak keeps telling me I am getting old. I am already old and forgetful."

"Come to the feast tomorrow night. Ask Alexander! They say he willingly grants favors to women who approach him directly. He forgave a woman who had killed one of his own men for raping her," he says with guarded confidence. "Forget Artâvazda! The old bastard is ancient. They say even the Wise Lord does not want his wretched old carcass and so he goes on living while the royal and the noble and the good die young all around him. His family still lives in the Satrapy of Sparda. He trails Alexander because he speaks his tongue and Alexander trusts the traitor."

Uxšiyârta drops his voice and whispers wickedly with half a smile, "They say his eldest daughter, Barsine, half-Hellene, twice mothered, twice widowed, was the woman who initiated Alexander before Setâreh."

Aššat Šarri Farânak raises her eyebrow wordlessly and gives a disapproving glance at Uxšiyârta.

He straightens quickly. "Ah, well, he is leaving and I can see no reason why the new satrap cannot live in the small hadiš and return the main hadiš into the hands of the rightful owner.

"How much room does one bloody invader need?

"He should be out sacking and burning and looting and killing somewhere, not living comfortably in a stolen palace!"

"I…" She hesitates, wonders, worries. "What if he declines my request?"

"Then we think of something else, no use worrying about it now," Uxšiyârta shrugs his shoulder. "As the wife of the old king, you can always offer to marry the new king and then kill him in bed!"

Aššat Šarri Farânak shakes her head with dismay.

No wonder Itâna had turned out this way… he clearly had taken after his own father.

"It is settled then!" Uxšiyârta puts his strong arms around Aššat Šarri Farânak without waiting for her response and lets out a sigh of relief. "You all come down to my house tonight. Once you charm Alexander out of your own hadiš, I will take you down to Baktra myself!"

Aššat Šarri Farânak takes a breath and relents and nods her head agreeably.

Her face and fingers had lost all feeling… it was just too cold to keep arguing with her brother. He always wanted to have the last word!

HOUSE of UXŠIYÂRTA. SATRAPY of SUGHUDA
FOLLOWING DAY
AFTERNOON

"How can a gown shrink so much in one year?" Rošanak asks Mâr'at Bani Âriyânnâz, biting her lower lip. She looks at her gown again in the looking glass and straightens the heaving seams with the tips of her delicate fingers.

"Tell me! I want to know!"

When she had left the Hadiš at Baktra so long ago, they said it was only to pass the heat of summer in the coolness of the mountains… then until the war was over. So, she had only brought one of her royal silk gowns, the one in blood red crimson embroidered with golden lions. It was the one Utâna loved the best.

Summer had slowly turned into Autumn and then into Winter and then into Spring, Summer, Autumn and another Winter…

Why was happiness always no longer than a half blink of an eye and misery stretched forward and backward into eternity?

Utâna had died in battle in the first winter.

When she was told, she had worn this gown and had lain down on her bed in the ancient didâ day after day, waiting to die too. Utâna had sworn that he would come back for her and she wanted to be ready when he did… she did not want him to see her in an ugly old gown and lose his love for her.

When death had not come as beckoned, the gown was stuffed in an old wooden cedar chest to ward off gown-eating moths and then painfully forgotten… and now the once rose-scented gown smelled like old dead wood and had shrunk in half.

"The feast hall will be dimly lit, no one will see the rough seams," Mâr'at Bani Âriyânnâz says, needle in hand, rubbing her fingers on the side seams of Rošanak's gown to make them obey, without much luck.

"This is not a splendid palace feast of the Great King in the Royal Persian Court."

"Âriyânnâz, Look!" Rošanak points down to the hem of her gown. "It is shorter too! It fit perfectly just a year ago!" She holds in her breath, standing straight, trying to make the unyielding gown fit her small breasts. "Well, at least there are no holes from hungry moths."

"Rošanak, the gown has not shrunk. You have grown," Mâr'at Bani Âriyânnâz says, smiling, "shapely like a beautiful virgin, ripe for womanhood."

"This is not the time for flattery!" Rošanak grumbles and pulls on her gown again. "It still feels tight here and there is no more cloth to let out. If I take it off, I can never force myself back in!"

"You can wear one of my gowns."

Rošanak turns her head and looks at Mâr'at Bani Âriyânnâz's gown: big and flowy, perfectly hiding her round body underneath a thousand folds, looking like a royal tent with a head.

She would rather die!

"You are not going to the feast!"

Rošanak and Mâr'at Bani Âriyânnâz turn their heads toward the voice of Aššat Šarri Farânak, who is standing in the doorway, watching them.

"But," Rošanak says, "this is the first feast in two years with music and dancing—"

"No." Aššat Šarri Farânak dismisses Mâr'at Bani Âriyânnâz tactfully and sits on the edge of the bed.

Mâr'at Bani Âriyânnâz gets to her feet and bows her head. She quietly leaves the room and closes the door behind her.

"Rošanak, there will be other feasts, this one is just for men to make peace among themselves."

"But you are going, right?"

"Yes, but not for feasting."

"You are going to the feast, not for feasting? Then why are you going?"

"Rošanak!"

"Mother, please! I am seventeen!" Rošanak sits down on the bed next to her blood mother, disappointed, brooding, sulking.

"Sixteen!" Aššat Šarri Farânak says, shaking her head.

"I will hide under a table. No one will see me. I promise."

"No."

"I will hide in one of Âriyânnâz's gowns."

"No!" Aššat Šarri Farânak says and then softens her voice.

"These are enemy barbarians who have invaded our Lands, not Persian royals and nobles of the Lands, worthy of the pleasure of your company."

"What pleasure? Who will take notice of me? I am not fifteen anymore! I am an old maid, no one will even look at me. Uxšiyârta has invited everyone. Even that idiot Itâna is going."

"No. The boys will not be there, just the men," Aššat Šarri Farânak says while gently caressing Rošanak's hair. "I am going because—" she hesitates, "our home, the Hadiš at Baktra is— well, we have not been there for a while, and in our absence, the new satrap and the invaders have made themselves at home there. It was to be expected, I guess. Where else would they live?"

"Nooo!" Rošanak moans. "Where will we live now?"

"The old satrap, Artâvazda, lived there for a while," Aššat Šarri Farânak says quietly.

Rošanak eyes her blood mother under her long, dark, rolling lashes.

Her blood mother was getting old… she always repeated what everyone already knew at least once or twice. Sometimes more…

"I know, Mother. The bloody traitor who abandoned my father. A blood kinsman no less. Hell will be too good for him!"

"Rošanak!" Aššat Šarri Farânak says scornfully, taking a deep breath. "Uxšiyârta told me to go to the feast and ask Alexander myself for our home. So, that is why I am going. Men are more eager to grant favors to women when they are softened with wine and song." She gets to her feet hesitatingly and then straightens up. She looks out the small window. "It is getting dark…"

The feast would start soon… she should get there before the men got too loaded with strong wine.

"If it all goes well, we can leave for Baktra tomorrow. If not, then we stay here with my brother." She takes a deep breath longingly, "It will be good to be home again for the Festival of No'rouz."

"Yes. Can I go to the feast with you?"

"No!"

"Mother!"

LATER that NIGHT

Alexander sips his strong wine and looks around the crowded banquet hall. Musicians are playing dancing drums. Wine and food flow freely among the multitudes, mostly his own men. Most of the Bakhtrian and Sughdians guests sit comfortably on carpets spread around the hall, while the Makedonians uneasily sit on chairs hastily arranged around the feast tables.

He preferred lounging couches for drinking wine with his kingsmen and his close companions. His chair was uncomfortable, but at least the wine was cold.

He did not intend to stay long.

They had been spending the last two campaigning seasons up and down the furthest satrapies of the Persians on the other side of Ecbatana.

Plagued by bitter snow, blistering sun, scanty food and filthy water, chasing ghostly rebels and faceless enemies, and this was all he had to show for it.

He knew how to win a pitched battle!

The Battle at Granikos had started late one evening and had ended in victory by the end of the following day.

The Battle at Issos had lasted one day… from sunrise to sunset… dawn to dusk.

The Battle at Gaugamela too had only lasted a day… a long bloody dusty day.

He was victorious in all the pitched battles.

He knew how to win sea battles on land too. He had captured or razed all the landports of the Great King, denying his ships access to land… and to provisions.

Like any army, the navy too moved on its belly.

The Great King was long dead and he was now in possession of all the gold and silver in all of Persia.

The heads of most of the rebel leaders had been cut off and handed to him. Still the region remained unconquerable and undefeated and untamed… caught in a circle of surrender and rebellion… and worst, his own men, the toughest warriors anywhere, were beginning to show signs of restlessness and weariness.

His enemies were as faceless and unpredictable as shifting desert sands.

He had broken his Royal Army into units to take every village and town and fortress.

What was taken had to be retaken over and over and over… another town and village and fortress rebelled against him for every town and village and fortress he defeated and destroyed.

How could such an enemy ever be conquered?

Even his own birth mother was hiding the sons of Makedonian nobles in the royal palace in Pella. He had to write to her and order her to hand over the young men to his kingsmen so they could be brought to Baktria to join his Royal Army.

He had given Amyntas, the new Satrap of Baktria, ten thousand Foot and three thousand and five hundred Horse and thousands of Hellene mercenaries to settle and secure the region— the largest force he had left behind anywhere on his path since he had crossed into Asia years ago…

He sips his strong wine slowly.

Bessos executed…

Spitamenes beheaded…

Satibarzanes killed…

Mazæos dead…

Oxodates replaced…

Erigyios dead…

Parmenion and Philotas dead too…

Philotas tortured by his kingsmen and stoned to death by the Makedonian Royal Army… Parmenion beheaded in Ecbatana by Kleandros, Brother of Koinos, the kinsman of Parmenion… both by his orders… by his wishes…

One more of Philip's kingsmen and his dangerous blood were eliminated when no longer needed.

He was prepared to forgive Philotas, even with all his arrogance and all his annoying boastfulness since the surrender of the Two Lands. If only he had proven himself absolutely loyal to him.

Why had he not even once mentioned to him that some Makedonians in the Royal Army were plotting to kill him? How could he have had such a careless disregard for the safety of his King? Was it not because Philotas would have benefited from the death of the King, even if he himself was not the one wielding the treacherous naked dagger of an assassin… just as he himself had benefited from the death of his own father at the hands of an assassin?

Well, at least most of his kingsmen around him now were his own men and not those of his father… men he could trust and as capable as Philotas and Parmenion. Krateros had served under Parmenion and had proven as good if not better… Perdikkas was leading some of the Horse now…

He had meant to rid himself of all the kingsmen who were still loyal to his father sooner or later and now only a handful of them remained under his command in his royal court. Last year when the Sogdian rebel Spitamenes, the old kinsman of Bessos, had besieged Marakanda, he had sent two thousand and five hundred mercenaries under the command of the Makedonian Karanos and Andronikos and Menedemos along with the Lykian interpreter, Pharnuches, to negotiate a peace agreement, and the Sogdian Spitamenes had massacred them all… something he had kept from the Royal Army…

His Makedonians never fell in battle! And no one cared much about what happened to the Hellene mercenaries.

It was at a drinking feast after the royal hunt at Basista, where his kingsmen had hunted and slaughtered all the wild beasts in the Great King's royal hunting grounds, some four thousand animals, when some of his kingsmen had criticized the command of the fallen Makedonians… the Black Kleitos, loaded with strong wine, had risen to the defense of the defeated… the fool!

Yes… the Black Kleitos was dead too… they were all heavy with pure wine and the Black Kleitos had dared to exalt his father, Philip, and to criticize him, the Lord of Asia, by quoting Euripides at the drinking feast:

"Alas! Warriors shed their blood, so that their king can claim all the glory!"

And so he had run the Black Kleitos through with a spear in a moment of drunken rage. Even sober, it would not have mattered much… he had hurled the spear like a thunder-wielding Zeus.

Afterward he had shown remorse openly, since Lanike, the sister of the Black Kleitos, was his own wet nurse during childhood, and Proteas, her son, was one of his kingsmen. Proteas had renounced the Black Kleitos quickly and had remained faithful to him and was drinking deep somewhere close by.

The Royal Army had turned a blind eye to the murder; they had declared him justified in killing the Black Kleitos.

"Whatever the King does, is his right to do!" they said.

The King was always right… even when he was murderously wrong!

It was not his golden Persian Purple clothes or the bended Persian knees in his royal court that had turned him into a Persian King… it was the tongues of his own men who extolled everything he did! Men like Anaxarchos, and all the rest…

"The King could do no wrong!"

"The King is godly!" Anaxarchos had declared in front of the royal court.

Uxšiyârta fills up Alexander's wine cup again and says something with a courteous smile. His words drown in the beat of the drums.

Old Artâvazda leans forward and interprets for Alexander, "Oxyartes says the wine is local. He says he is pleased that you do not taint your wine with water, as the ignorant Hellenes do."

Alexander nods and forces a smile and takes another sip of his wine.

He had captured another unconquerable fortress on a sheer rock in the cold of the late winter in the early morning dawn and he was praised for how he drank his wine!

Drums play loudly.

He looks around the banquet hall again.

His father, Philip, would have taken all the Persian gold at Sardeis and the long hands of one of the tall Royal Daughters in a marriage alliance with Darius and would have gone back to Pella, declaring himself victorious… the new kinsman of the Great King!

Not him!

He wanted it all… he wanted to be the Great King, not just another one of his many kinsmen… and the more he wanted, the less remained in his tight kingly grasp.

Alexander turns his head. A beautiful woman approaches his table and generously bows her head, in a courtly manner indicating her noble birth. He eyes her for a moment and then slowly gets up to his painful feet.

His leg was still healing from a month-old arrow wound. The pain of it he could ignore during the day… but at night, the pain was searing… strong wine helped it…

Uxšiyârta smiles and introduces his blood sister.

Artâvazda grabs his tall walking stick, gets up to his old feet and interprets in Attik, slightly bowing his head to the woman. "Alexander, this is Princess Faranak, Sister of Oxyartes."

"I am Alexander," he says with an easy smile.

Another beautiful older highborn woman…

He had always found it easier to bond with such women since he had crossed into Asia over six years ago.

He knew well how to be a Royal Son. Even Kallisthenes had made much of his relation with the old Persian queen-mother when he had written home about his bond with Queen Sisygambis, the Royal Mother of Darius. He had felt genuine affection for Sisygambis. She had the royal blood of the Great Kings. She was his adoptive Persian Royal Mother. She cared for him more than she cared for Darius. She was kinder to him than his own birth mother and she did not keep snakes in her royal room.

He hated snakes! Snakes belonged on coins and in temples, not in beds.

Uxšiyârta bellows again and Artâvazda interprets faithfully, "Princess Faranak used to live in the Baktra Palace."

"Baktra Palace?" Alexander looks at Artâvazda. "Is that not the old residence of Bessos?"

"Yes, Alexander," Artâvazda nods and adds quietly, "Princess Faranak was the wife of Bessos."

Alexander looks back at her quickly. His eyes brighten. He forgets the pain in his leg. He orders one of his royal guards. "Bring a chair for the Princess."

Alexander considers Aššat Šarri Farânak while a chair is quickly brought for her.

It was easy for the Persians to bow to him so gracefully. It came to them naturally.

It was an old custom of the Persian Royal Court, a mark of highest honor due the Great Kings.

He had not understood it before the Battle of Issos. Then after his victory, he had visited the Royal Women of Darius in their royal tent and after they had all bowed to him, it had all become clear, understood, desired.

It was not a sign decadent royal opulence; it was a sign of absolute royal power.

Men who mocked the Persian Royal Court customs were not Great Kings.

He had to crack the hard heads of his Makedonians to get them to show him the same royal honors.

She bows her head again and sits down graciously between Alexander and Artâvazda.

Uxšiyârta pours some wine in a cup and puts it in front of his blood sister. Aššat Šarri Farânak picks up the wine cup and takes a sip to quiet her trembling nervous body. Alexander eyes her sharply, slightly amused.

This was the first time he had seen a Royal Woman drinking wine with the men.

Alexander glances over at Hephæstion who is also watching them with amusement. He looks at her. She smiles graciously and utters a few words quietly, muffled by the beat of the drums.

"The Princess," Artâvazda says, "wishes to return to her Palace in Baktra."

"Her palace," Alexander says, eyeing Aššat Šarri Farânak intently, "I see." He leans back into his chair, picks up his wine cup and slowly takes another sip.

After the Battle of Issos, he had come into possession of the Royal Women of Darius… and now, with the surrender of the Sogdian Rock, he had come into possession of the Royal Woman of Bessos.

The capture of the damn rock had been more rewarding than he had first realized; he now had all the Royal Women of the Persians in his royal grasp!

Alexander smiles to himself with satisfaction.

He leans toward Artâvazda. "Artabazos, you should be heading back home to Pergamos to your family soon, and Amyntas, the new satrap, can take the house of one of the Baktrian nobles. I prefer to stay in my royal tent anyway, close to my kingsmen," Alexander says smiling, looking at her intently.

"The Princess can return to Baktra Palace, as she wishes, with all her privileges whole. I will order Harpalos to provide for the Baktra Palace expenses from the royal funds."

"Alexander bequeaths the Baktra Hadiš to you," Artâvazda says, adding, "with all your royal privileges, funded with gold from the Royal Treasuries."

"What does the King expect in return for such generosity?" she cautiously asks Artâvazda.

"Nothing."

Aššat Šarri Farânak looks at Artâvazda, stunned. She narrows her eyes and then looks back at Alexander discreetly.

She had come fully prepared to hate the man who had ordered the execution of her king-husband and caused the death of all her blood sons… but in person, Alexander seemed boyish, generous, pleasant and eager to please…

Alexander smiles and nods his head.

Aššat Šarri Farânak relaxes. She smiles, gracefully rises and bows her head. She pushes back her chair and walks away without a word.

Uxšiyârta leans back smiling, satisfied with the outcome.

His beautiful blood sister could charm a snake out of its hole.

Alexander gets up to his feet slowly, looks at Aššat Šarri Farânak walking away and thinks about calling her back to him for a moment.

He wished she had stayed longer, but she surely would be more grateful to him when he visited her later in Baktra Palace. She was almost the same age as Queen Stateira, and almost as beautiful and not as tall.

Alexander slowly sits back down.

Hephæstion walks over with his wine cup and sits to the right of Alexander with half a smile. "Who is she?"

"Wife of Bessos, Sister of Oxyartes."

"Ah!" Hephæstion smiles mischievously. "Is she adopting you too?" He asks with the intimate familiarity of old friends and lovers, not expecting a response.

Alexander gives Hephæstion a sharp look and then sips his wine.

Hephæstion could be annoying at times… especially when he was loaded with wine.

But he was still sober and there was no hint of malice in his voice yet.

He had ordered his men to remain sober during the feast in case the Baktrians and Sogdians had treachery at heart… for the surrender of their fortress…

"Most kings take the wives of their enemies as theirs." Hephæstion ignores Alexander's gaze and continues undaunted. "You collect their mothers. You have more mothers than wives."

"I have no wives!" Alexander grunts with annoyance.

"No, just three Queen-Mothers, Olympias and Ada and Sisygambis. Four, counting this one." Hephæstion continues teasing and laughing.

"Olympias will be happy to find out that she now has to share you with your new Baktrian mother, the wife of a former sworn enemy, no less!

"Do not tell Olympias how beautiful your new adopted mother is. She will send her Makedonian ropes to hang herself!"

Alexander ignores Hephæstion and looks around the hall. Someone catches a corner of his sharp eyes.

He leans forward and looks intently at the other side of the hall close to the tall entrance doors, behind the rich standards hanging from the high ceiling.

"Hephæstion, look over there, by the doors, there, by the fire altar." Alexander points with his finger.

Hephæstion looks in the direction Alexander is pointing. "You mean the girl leaning against the wall?"

"Yes."

Hephæstion shrugs his shoulders. He leans back and sips his wine. "Well, it looks like these Baktrian girls are used to going to these feasts with their men. There are a few others too, mostly among the locals though. I think Ptolemaios and a few others have brought their Hellene mistresses with them too."

"Is she not the one who passed us by yesterday, with her long hair flowing in the wind? The one who was following closely behind Oxyartes?"

Hephæstion narrows his eyes and says, "I cannot tell. She is too far away and it is not all that bright in here." He shrugs his shoulders again with marked indifference and sips more of his wine.

Alexander beckons Artâvazda.

"Artabazos, who is that girl standing all the way in the back, by the fire altar?"

"Alexander," Artâvazda smiles and shakes his head, "at my age, I am lucky to see my own feet."

"Ask Oxyartes!" Alexander says eagerly.

Artâvazda takes a deep breath. "Very well." He leans over and whispers into Uxšiyârta's ear.

Uxšiyârta narrows his eyes. He looks around the hall. His eyes find their mark, the figure of a young girl, standing discreetly in the back by the fire altar. He curses under his lips and grunts. "No one!"

"Who?" Artâvazda leans closer to hear above the beat of the drums.

"Nobody!" Uxšiyârta mumbles again with a tone not eager for more words.

"If the King wants a girl to pass the night with, there are some dancing girls." Uxšiyârta points with his hand to the girls dancing on the other side of the hall, close to the drums.

Artâvazda looks at Uxšiyârta, who has turned away from him, talking to the Bakhtrians sitting behind them, completely ignoring him. He leans back and interprets for Alexander. "Oxyartes says the dancing girls are here for your pleasure."

Alexander looks at Artâvazda and then at Uxšiyârta with marked displeasure.

Did they think he was blind?

That he did not know a highborn woman from a dancing girl?

The arrow had torn into his leg, not his eyes. She was wearing a royal color.

He beckons one of his royal guards, points toward the girl and commands, "Bring her to me."

The royal guard looks in the direction Alexander is pointing. "Sir? Who?"

Alexander turns his head and looks around the hall. The pain returns to his leg.

The girl had vanished in the thick air of the feast.

"I am going back to my tent." Alexander grinds his teeth and slowly gets up to his painful feet and heads for the doors.

Hephæstion puts down his wine cup and rises to follow Alexander.

Royal guards follow them.

Uxšiyârta takes a deep breath, relieved, savoring his cup of pure Bakhtrian wine as he watches Alexander and his men peacefully leave the feast.

She will be well forgotten by sunrise, if not sooner!

ALEXANDER'S ROYAL TENT. FOOT of ROCK of SUGHUD
FOLLOWING DAY
MORNING

"Who is the girl?" Alexander sneers at Uxšiyârta.

Artâvazda interprets.

"Who?" Uxšiyârta grunts.

He knew.

And the knowing pained him noticeably…

"The girl who was at the feast last night. The one in the blood red dress. I know he knows who she is! I can see it in his eyes! She was walking closely behind him when his old fortress was emptied and surrendered to me!" Alexander growls at Artâvazda.

"He knows you know who she is." Artâvazda interprets.

Uxšiyârta eyes Artâvazda suspiciously and sneers back, "What does he want with her?"

"He wants to know what you intend to do with the girl," Artâvazda asks Alexander tactfully.

"I just want to talk to her!"

"The King just wants to talk to her."

"Talk to her? Nonsense! No man ever wants to just talk to a woman!" Uxšiyârta says with all the subtlety of a charging ox. "Would you trust your own women with him?" He grunts, immediately regrets his careless question, but it is too late.

Artâvazda takes a deep breath and thinks about his own daughter, Barsine, for a moment. His dark eyes become darker.

Barsine was captured in Dimašqa after the Battle at Issos along with the rest of his family, when the traitorous Governor of Dimašqa had betrayed the Great King and delivered all the noble wives and daughters in his charge to Parmenion in return for gold.

Parmenion had taken them all to Alexander afterward, as captives and not as friends… none was spared… and they all knew what that meant… women were to be treated as Hellenes and Makedonians as conquerors had always used captive women… for pleasure.

He had been heading to the Royal City of Bâbiru with Dâriuš at the time, else he would have never allowed it… even though his entire family knew Alexander from the days he was in exile in Pella as a guest of Philip, Alexander's father. Even seeing the bloody head of the Governor of Dimašqa delivered to Dâriuš in Bâbiru for his treachery had not eased his pain. He would have killed all his women rather than let them fall into the hands of the invaders…

"Is she your daughter?" Artâvazda asks sympathetically in a low voice.

"No!" Uxšiyârta grunts.

"Then why not tell him who she is and be done!"

"Well?" Alexander interrupts impatiently.

The Persians always talked on beyond what was necessary.

If Oxyartes was not going to tell him who the girl was, he would just order Laomedon to question him. Laomedon was in charge of all the Persian prisoners and spoke two tongues. Laomedon and the rest of his kingsmen could break any man under torture… tougher than hammered metal, battle-hardened Philotas had not lasted more than three days in their skilled hands.

Artâvazda feels Alexander's anger rising like the heat from the embers in the sacred fire altars. He leans forward and speaks in a firm concerned voice. "Uxšiyârta, do not be deceived by his young looks and easy manners. He chased after Dâriuš for three years, and Bayasa for another year afterward. He is a hunter and a good one and he is smelling blood. He will not let go of his prey until he has had his fill of blood!" Artâvazda breathes down Uxšiyârta's neck.

"What kind of a fool do you take me for? Ha? With four dead sons, one of them my firstborn, do you think I do not know that, Artâvazda?"

"Uxšiyârta, I know you know. But, the King is not mad either, nor a man to disregard his gods. He is forgiving to those who beg his mercy."

Tempers flare like fire.

"Beg his mercy? Why should the girl beg his mercy? Because men like you and I failed to keep our women safe from these barbarians?"

Artâvazda relents.

"Uxšiyârta, now that her face is caught in his eyes, he will search every town, village and fortress in the Land of a Thousand Cities to find her. Tell me and let me decide. I swear by the Wise Lord that I will not betray your trust!"

Uxšiyârta narrows his eyes at Artâvazda.

What good was the word of a traitor to the Great King?

But from the fiery look in Alexander's eyes, he knew Artâvazda was right.

It was too late.

He relents and grinds his teeth. He forces the words out of his throat harshly.

"She is the daughter of Bayasa. The lastborn child of my blood sister still living. That is who she is." Uxšiyârta takes a deep breath. He leans back and continues with sadness rippling through his throaty voice. "She is more precious than a daughter, she was betrothed to my firstborn son, Utâna, who died in battle last year at the hands of these barbarians."

Artâvazda takes a deep breath and straightens his back.

He felt old… all spent…

"I honored the words of my lastborn son and surrendered my own fortress to this man, when he met the terms my foolish son had declared aloud so carelessly. I want nothing more than for him to go and leave us in peace." Uxšiyârta loses his temper and says angrily, "But I made him no gift of our women! I will die protecting them if I have to!"

Artâvazda looks at Alexander guardedly. "Alexander, will you pledge the safety of the girl?"

Alexander sneers at Artâvazda. "Artabazos, you have known me for many years, since I was a Boy-Prince in the royal court of my father. Have you ever known me to ill-treat women?"

Artâvazda thinks about his Barsine at once. He bites his lip and considers Alexander for a long moment.

Dâriuš had ordered the Royal City of Pârsâ to surrender peacefully to Alexander to avoid the needless slaughter of men and shameful rape of women. He was with Dâriuš in the Royal City of Hagmâtâna when news had come that Alexander's Royal Army had sacked Pârsâ and had raped and killed most of the Persian women.

Some Persians had killed their own women and children and had set fire to their own houses in Pârsâ, fearing the worst…

But Alexander himself had not been known for taking and raping captive women. Neither was he known to have a taste for women… he was always surrounded by men. He was not the sort of a man who had women on his mind… only war…

Barsine had known Alexander since childhood and had given herself to him freely, hoping to become the wife of the new Lord of Asia. Foolish girl! She was half-Hellene. A Persian Royal Daughter would never have done what Barsine had done!

"Artabazos!" Alexander yells.

"Alexander, the girl is the daughter of Princess Faranak," Artâvazda says formally.

Alexander looks at Artâvazda and then at Uxšiyârta. The unexpected words fall like rain on fire. His anger cools.

"Daughter of Bessos. Oxyartes is the brother of her birth mother," Artâvazda adds in a quiet voice.

"Daughter of Bessos?"

"Yes," Artâvazda says quietly, nodding his head.

"I see. Where is she now?"

"Where is she?" Artâvazda asks Uxšiyârta warily.

"They left this morning for the Baktra Hadiš." Uxšiyârta grunts quietly.

"She is on her way to the Palace at Baktra with her birth mother," Artâvazda tells Alexander guardedly.

Alexander slowly sits down. His anger leaves, curiosity returns.

He had only glimpsed her for a short moment, but her memory still lingered in his eyes and now his curiosity had grown even more.

She was not just another girl! She was the daughter of a hated enemy… an enemy who had declared himself the Great King after the death of the Third Darius… a man whom he had executed himself.

And he was the Lord of all the Asia and more!

"Tell Oxyartes to go after them and bring them back. They cannot have traveled all that far on icy roads, if they left this morning in carriages."

"Alexander wishes to have them brought to him for an audience," Artâvazda says to Uxšiyârta. "He can send his own men, but it is better if you bring them back yourself. They will be sent on their way, once his curiosity is satisfied."

Uxšiyârta narrows his eyes at Artâvazda and then shows him his hands. "Artâvazda, I have killed ferocious lions with these hands. I will kill you too with the same hands, if he treats my daughter like a captive woman! Make no mistake, old man! I am not Bayasa and you are no kinsman of mine! I do not care if the entire royal blood of Kuruš the Elder himself irrigates your rotting ancient body!"

Artâvazda looks Uxšiyârta straight in the eyes. "I am a father too, Uxšiyârta. The dishonor of such an act, brought on a Royal Daughter by my own words, would be more painful than punishing death!"

Uxšiyârta looks at Artâvazda and then at Alexander. He reluctantly stands up, bowing his head slightly and leaves the royal tent with heavy feet.

"Does he know all his kinsmen are hostages until he returns with the girl?" Alexander asks Artâvazda.

"He knows."

ROAD to BAKTRA

"The King just wants to talk to her, ha!" Uxšiyârta grudgingly mumbles to himself, riding his horse past the carriages and horses of the multitudes heading back to Bakhtriš. "The same way he talked to Setâreh?"

He catches up with the covered carriages taking his blood sister and her family back to Baktra.

It was cold and the road was crowded… the carriages had traveled slowly on the still icy rough roads from Sughuda down to Bakhtriš.

Abi-Samar, the faithful Bâbiruviya eunuch in charge of protecting the Royal Women, pulls the carriages slightly off the dirt road and stops them at the sight of Uxšiyârta.

Horses neigh.

Aššat Šarri Farânak pushes her head out of her carriage.

Uxšiyârta pulls his horse alongside his blood sister's carriage and calls to her, "Farânak, I need to speak with you," while dismounting his horse.

Gently pushing the small boys out of her lap, she gets out of her carriage. She bites her lip. Intense feelings of disquiet and distress pour into her.

Had the Makedonian King sobered up in the light of the sun and reconsidered his generous gift to her?

"Good news, I pray?" she asks in a cloudy tone, not eager to hear bad news.

Uxšiyârta leans closer to her face and whispers quietly, "Alexander wants to meet Rošanak."

"What?" Aššat Šarri Farânak pulls back startled and her eyes widen. Unguarded fear pours into her. "Rošanak?"

Uxšiyârta nods, confirming without uttering a word.

"Why?"

"He saw her at the feast last night."

Anger seizes Aššat Šarri Farânak and reddens her face.

This was even worse than taking back the hadiš.

She turns around quickly and walks back toward the carriage behind hers and yells, "Rošanak!"

"Yes, Mother?" Rošanak jumps down from her carriage quickly. Her belly quickly fills up with buzzing bees.

"Did I not order you *not* to go to the feast last night?" Aššat Šarri Farânak sputters in anger and frustration.

Rošanak looks at Uxšiyârta and then at her blood mother, embarrassed. She nods, casting down her eyes. "Yes." Her voice drowns in the noises from the other carriages and horses going past them, slowing down, eyeing them with curiosity.

"And did you obey my order?"

"Ah, yes— no—" Rošanak looks down at her feet, wondering how her blood mother had found out. Her face reddens with shame.

Being caught was horrible… but lying about it was evil… her mother would forgive the one… eventually… but not the other… ever…

"I was there for less than the blink of an eye. No one saw me, I swear by Divine Ânâhitâ!" Rošanak says with a trembling voice. "I was there just for a moment, my gown forced me to go!"

"Your gown? Ha? It cried out to you: *Rošanak, take me to the feast. Display me like a whore to the barbarian invaders heavy with wine!*"

Rošanak casts her eyes down again, looking at her feet, biting her lower lip.

No use arguing with her blood mother… she always prevailed.

"Little Star!" A young Bakhtrian yells out her name, slowing down his horse as he rides past them, trying to catch her eyes.

"Flicker a kiss to my lips!"

Rošanak turns bright red. She bites her lip again and smiles shyly, stealing away her eyes, embarrassed and flattered.

Uxšiyârta turns his head and gives the young man a sharp look, reaching for his sword.

The young Bakhtrian laughs, speeds up and quickly passes.

"It was fated!" Uxšiyârta says, glaring at the rest of the young Bakhtrian riders. He says distractedly under his breath, "Rošanak, Alexander, the Lord of Asia, wants to meet you."

"Meet me? Why? I have done nothing wrong! All women go to feasts! He cannot punish me for that!" Rošanak pales and pleads with Uxšiyârta.

"No need to worry needlessly. He is probably just curious. He has seen all the Royal Women of the Lands. He is after all, the new Ruler of the Lands." Uxšiyârta turns his head and speaks with firm authority.

Aššat Šarri Farânak and Rošanak both look at Uxšiyârta scornfully.

He shrugs his shoulders. "He is known for his benevolence and generosity toward the Royal Women. They say your grandmother Dukšiš Sisygambis treats him like her son and he treats her like his own blood mother!"

"We have all heard the royal court rumors, Uxšiyârta. What else is the poor Ummi Šarri supposed to do with all the sharp swords pointing at the royal throats of the young Crown-Prince and the Royal Daughters? What would any mother do?" Aššat Šarri Farânak says, shaking her head. "Ummi Šarri Sisygambis would have danced with the Lord of Darkness himself on the edge of a sharp Persian blade to save the lives of her royal grandchildren!"

Uxšiyârta looks down at his feet feeling guilty, avoiding their eyes and taking a deep breath. "It is best if you let her come back with me and not read too much into this. He is not known for ill-treating Royal Women. Dâriuš offered him his choice of his Royal Daughters and he did not touch either of them. The sooner he meets with Rošanak, the sooner you can head down to Baktra."

Setâreh… well… the benevolent Lord of Asia was still a man…

"Very well," Aššat Šarri Farânak shakes her head with dismay and utters quietly, accepting the inevitable.

Setâreh… well… she was the key to the royal crown…

But it was too late now; not much else could be done at the moment.

"You still remember how to ride a horse, Rošanak?" Uxšiyârta asks with a smile, teasing her.

Rošanak pulls up her heavy winter gown and shows him her Persian sarbalâ and riding boots. "Of course, Abû!"

"Good." Uxšiyârta nods, smiling. "You can ride back with me then, on my horse. When you meet him, just be well-mannered and answer his questions and no more! Do not look at him. Do not talk to him if you are not spoken to!"

"Abû! I am a Royal Daughter!" Rošanak says proudly, looking at her blood mother, seeking her approval.

Everyone knew what that meant.

Aššat Šarri Faranak nods approvingly, but worriedly bites her lip.

"Abi-Samar!" Uxšiyârta bellows.

"Yes, My Lord?" Abi-Samar steps forward and bows his head.

"We are heading back to my house for the night. Rošanak will ride with me. Turn around the carriages and follow us back to my house."

"Yes, My Lord."

ALEXANDER'S ROYAL TENT

LATER that DAY

"Sir!"

A royal boy on first watch guard duty walks into Alexander's royal tent and stands at attention.

Alexander is reviewing his military plans with his kingsmen and commanders, all Makedonians. He interrupts Krateros and looks at the royal boy.

"What is it?"

"Alexander, our host from last night, the Baktrian Warlord, is here with a girl, requesting an audience. One of the royal guards says that you are expecting them."

Alexander narrows his eyes and looks toward the royal tent flap.

"Fetch Artabazos and when he gets here, bring him in with the girl. Tell Oxyartes to wait outside."

"Yes, Sir." The royal boy nods his head and leaves quickly.

"Shall we continue later, Alexander?" Hephæstion asks formally.

"No. This should not take long." He says, looking at his kingsmen, "I have summoned the daughter of Bessos."

The kingsmen exchange glances, curiously, but no one speaks.

Alexander had never summoned a woman for an audience before... he had gone to see the Royal Women of Darius in their royal tents after the Battle at Issos and afterward...

"Wife and Daughter of Bessos were among the people of the Fortress of Sogdiana," Alexander says, "I gave them leave last night to return to the Palace at Baktra."

"Alexander, is that wise?" Krateros asks cautiously. "We still have not crushed the rebellion. Both Baktrian and Sogdian Satrapies remain faithful to Bessos, and the rebellion is spreading fast among bordering satrapies."

"That is why Alexander has summoned this girl to see if she could be used to reconcile the region and the people," Hephæstion sneers at Krateros.

He had no idea why Alexander wanted to see the damn girl, but if Krateros thought it was unwise, then it must be wise!

Alexander looks at them both with displeasure.

Hephæstion and Krateros had hated each other as long as he could remember... like two lions always clawing at each other...

Both had shown up in armor ready to do battle… one day he would have to separate the two before they killed each other in hot blood!

They only hated Philotas more and had joined forces to destroy him.

Afterward they had gone right back to hating each other… even torturing Philotas together had not made them bond.

Before any further words are spoken, old Artâvazda walks slowly into the royal tent, leaning heavily on his walking stick, and bows his head to the young king. "Alexander."

"Where is—"

Before Alexander finishes his words, the royal tent flap opens again and Rošanak walks gracefully inside. She takes a few steps and stops and looks straight as a Persian arrow at the men before her.

Everyone turns their heads, eager for a glimpse of her.

The large tent full of men goes quiet. It becomes small. A colored rainbow paints and stretches slowly from one side of the tent to the other.

The slight young girl, dressed in travel clothes, was plain and simple and free of splendid jewelry and luxurious gown, and yet no man could look away…

Her skin was pure ivory… her long black hair carelessly fell around her face… and her eyes, gazing straight at them, was the color of the ancient forests of the lands of their ancestors far away, shaded by the longest lashes, stolen shamelessly from the feathers of a raven…

Her knees were unbent and unhurried… somehow secure in knowing even the god of time knelt in wonder before such heavenly beauty… before rushing forth like a hungry lion to devour it whole…

"I am Rošanak," she says simply. Her soft womanly voice pours like drops of rain into parched manly ears.

Artâvazda turns around and looks at her. Time bridges longingly into the fragrant Persian garden of youth.

Her name was a beautiful ancient Persian name, Rauxšanâ, the name of many Royal Women at the Persian Royal Court that had softened over the years… Rošanak…

The Karka Herodotos had already done the deed and translated her older name to Roxana in his Book of Histories.

And she was the daughter of Vîsa Puça Bayasa… another Son of the Royal House… his brother of different father and mother.

The girl was not just a Royal Daughter…

She was pure Persian Poetry wrapped in purple prose…

Now he understood why Alexander was so bent on finding her, after just a fleeting glance.

The girl was not just the daughter of the enemy, a prize of war and conquest.

She was heavenly beauty made flesh… the reason why the moon waxed and waned… a woman poets could write volumes about…

Like the stolen Helene of the ancient tale of Ilias who had unleashed the glorious Trojan Wars…

Why was the Wise Lord showing him such youth and beauty in his old age?

Was it to finally punish him for all his wrongful deeds?

Artâvazda regains his reason, walks back to Rošanak and introduces himself with the golden tongue of the Persian Royal Court. "Rošanak, I am Artâvazda, Son of Pharnâvâzda, Grandson of the Second Artakhšaçâ. I knew your father."

"Mâr Bani Artâvazda." Rošanak slightly bows her head and speaks quietly, standing straight, unbending.

Yes, the damn traitor knew her father… the man who had betrayed her royal father to the enemy invaders after her father had assumed the golden Persian Purple and had worn the Persian Crown…

Artâvazda turns toward Alexander and his kingsmen and points graciously to Rošanak. "Alexander, this is Princess Roxana. Her name means *Little Star* in Baktrian and *Luminous* in Persian."

She was as easy on manly eyes as she was to manly ears… even her name like her beauty was easy to translate for the conquering king.

The Hellenes and the Makedonians had no tongue for Persian names; they changed and twisted them into names even the Persians did not recognize themselves. The Persian birth mothers did not know their own blood sons and daughters in their twisted Hellene names. Mercifully, Hellene names were simple enough.

"Rošanak, this is Alexander, the Lord of Asia." Artâvazda graciously points to Alexander. "His name means *Protector of Men.*"

Rošanak slowly turns her head toward all the men staring at her and considers them for a short moment.

All the warriors were wearing tunics, decorated with bits of gold from the Persian Royal Treasuries, their legs bare.

Unlike Persians, the enemy invaders did not wear trousers.

The man the traitor Artâvazda was pointing to was a full head shorter than the rest, with unruly hair, tangled like the mane of a golden lion, the color of a field of golden wheat, flying around his face. His white tunic was pinned and strapped with heads of golden lions. He was not much taller than she… just half a head… with his eyes locked on her… like a Persian arrow finding its target… like a lion gazing at his prey… and his head bent slightly to the side… right… no… to the left side…

More fierce and warlike than handsome…

He was not what she had expected. She had thought one of the taller, older ones, standing close to him, shining in burnished armor, was the conquering king.

"My Lord." Rošanak bows her head slightly to Alexander.

Artâvazda interprets.

Alexander stares at her, searching for words.

His royal tongue had left the royal tent as the Royal Daughter had entered…

"I am Alexander," he finally says quietly, mumbling slightly.

Artâvazda looks at Alexander curiously.

Earlier he had been ready to kill Uxšiyârta with his bare hands if he had not revealed who the girl was and now here she was standing right in front of him, and he and all his kingsmen had lost their tongues like royal prisoners.

"Alexander?"

Breathless silence.

Alexander looks at Rošanak, lost for words.

Artâvazda looks at Alexander intently. His silence speaks to him.

Alexander! The greatest warrior king on battlefields, who had cleverly unraveled the Gordian Knot by pulling out the wooden peg, was now all coiled up in a Gordian Knot over a Persian Royal Daughter!

They were all men.

And kings and men, Persian or not… they all bent to beauty in the same way…

Artâvazda turns his head back to Rošanak and asks kindly, "Rošanak, did you just arrive? Would you like something to drink, My Daughter?" trying to make gracious talk, until reason returned to Alexander, the fierce tongueless Lord of Asia.

"How well did you know my father?" Rošanak asks softly, ignoring his polite offer completely.

How dare he call her 'Daughter'?

"Ah!" Artâvazda is caught off guard, but glad to talk. "Your father, Bayasa, was the only child of Dukšiš Amastris, the sister of Dukšiš Apâma, my mother. Your father and the Third Dâriuš were second brothers. Dukšiš Sisygambis is the Royal Daughter of Vîsa Puça Ostâna and Amastris was the Royal Daughter of the Second Artakhšaçâ. Vîsa Puça Ostâna was the brother of my grandfather, the Second Artakhšaçâ, of another mother. Your father was raised at the Persian Royal Court by my sisters since his royal mother died after birthing him."

Rošanak listens graciously, patiently, taking it all in, word by word, and looks at Artâvazda intently.

"I am curious, Mâr Bani Artâvazda," she says softly.

"About?" Artâvazda asks cautiously, narrowing his eyes at her.

"By your own words, you and my father were brothers, the grandsons of the Second Artakhšaçâ, and the bloodline of my father is as royal as your own blood and that of the Third Dâriuš. Yet you dishonor my father, by not recognizing his blood claim to the Persian Crown and calling him by his throne name."

Silence.

Air leaves Artâvazda's brittle old bones.

He gasps for a short breath in shock.

She had the royal tongue of her father.

He had boasted foolishly and had made much of his royal bloodline to impress her, and in exchange she had swiftly cut him to size with just a few words.

Well-spoken in perfect Persian, as softly as the Persian Royal Women had spoken into the ears of Great Kings for generations.

His own Persian wife had divorced him immediately when he had raised an army against the Great King, refusing to come before the Third Artakhšaçâ when he had summoned him to Persian Royal Court, and he had fled the Lands of the Persians in fear for his life.

That was the same year Alexander was born to Philip.

The Persian Royal Women were the guardians of the royal bloodlines and never faltered.

And this girl, no matter how young or how beautiful, traced her bloody bloodline to Dukšiš Purušâtu, the famous royal wife and sister of Second Dâriuš and the mother of the Younger Kuruš… from her to Dukšiš Atossâ, the legendary Royal Woman of the First Dâriuš… the Royal Daughter of Kuruš the Elder… the first Royal Daughter…

Dukšiš Purušâtu had put to the sword all those who had a hand in the death of her most beloved Royal Son, the Younger Kuruš…

And why not?

What else was there?

The Lands of the Persians were all that mattered.

Persia was the World.

Persians were the Masters of the World.

And the Great King, the King of Kings, was the only king who mattered…

Alexander had not renamed the lands he had won by his spear 'Lands of the Makedonians'. He was obsessed with Persia since childhood. He had claimed himself the heir to the Persian Kings of the Royal House of the Hakhâmanišiya Clan.

Persia was all that mattered to Alexander and what eluded him the most.

He had proven himself worthy of the Persian Crown on the fields of battle, but what he lacked was the ancient royal blood of Persian Kings flowing through him… what the girl had in abundance… the royal blood that freely flowed in her royal body!

King of the Persians had to be Persian… and connected by the blood of the Royal Women to the Royal Hakhâmanišiya…

"Artabazos?" Alexander asks quietly, interrupting, carelessly tearing the thread of his old thoughts.

"She asked me about her father, Alexander," Artâvazda utters quietly, trying to regain his reason.

"I see." Alexander twists his lips. "Ask her if—"

"If what, Alexander?"

Alexander turns around and looks at his kingsmen who are minding his every word.

"We can continue later. You are all dismissed for now."

This was not something he wished to speak of in front of his men… not even his kingsmen.

Long gone were the days when he would run around naked putting wreaths on ancient tombs to declare his love for an old lover…

What suited a young warrior king once was now unbefitting the Lord of Asia.

The kingsmen acknowledge with their eyes and leave one by one.

"You too, Hephæstion."

"Yes, Alexander." Hephæstion lingers for a blink of an eye, considering Rošanak, and then leaves, following the rest.

The royal tent empties.

"Ask her if her mother is here yet."

"Did your mother come back with you?"

"My Lord, I came on horseback with my father, Uxšiyârta. My mother was to follow in her carriage."

"Not yet, Alexander. But she is on her way back."

"Good. Tell Oxyartes to take Roxana and her mother back to his house. I will join them for the night meal tonight. You will come with me to interpret."

"Yes, Alexander."

"Bring Oxyartes in for an audience now," Alexander commands one of the royal guards.

"Artabazos, you can tell her she may leave."

"Yes, Alexander."

Artâvazda smiles politely at Rošanak and points toward the royal tent flap. "Alexander will have his night meal with Uxšiyârta and your mother tonight. You may retire to the house of your father for now."

Rošanak eyes Alexander discreetly for a short moment and then bows her head slightly toward him. "Thank you, My Lord," she says politely, then turns around and leaves the royal tent.

"Oxyartes," Alexander says in a pleasant tone as Uxšiyârta enters the tent, "would the Princess be interested in a marriage alliance?"

Artâvazda turns his head and looks at Alexander, startled. "Marriage?" he mumbles faintly under his breath.

"Yes, Artabazos, ask him," Alexander says cautiously without hiding his eagerness.

Artâvazda's brow folds in pain. He loses his words and pales. He shifts his walking stick to the other side and leans on it painfully.

A few moments pass.

"Artabazos!" Alexander raises his voice.

Artâvazda slowly masks his face and takes a deep breath.

"The King wants to know if your sister would think agreeably about a marriage alliance."

"He wants to marry Farânak?" Uxšiyârta asks. His eyes widen in surprise.

"Alexander, Oxyartes wants to know if you wish to marry Princess Faranak?"

"My mother?" Alexander looks surprised. "No, I wish to marry Roxana!"

Artâvazda looks at Alexander. Dark clouds cross his heart and drift to his eyes. The face of his daughter runs back into his mind.

"You," he asks Alexander in a hushed voice, "wish to marry?"

"Yes," Alexander says nodding his head.

Silence.

Words stop and pour back into Artâvazda's throat. He looks down at his feet and hesitates.

Had Alexander forgotten that he was the father of Barsine?

Had he meant to dishonor him like this?

He had not even thought of marrying Setâreh when she was heavy with his child.

He bites his lip, trying to gather himself without losing honor.

As a man and a kinsman of the Great King, he knew well that when Barsine was left behind, she was no longer in favor… but as a father, he had chosen to remain ignorant of reality.

Barsine had not listened to his counsel and had not told Alexander when she had gotten with his child… wishing to be beckoned back to the royal court when she was missed by Alexander and then present him with his son… hoping Alexander would marry her afterward. She had not considered that the gods might have other plans for Alexander.

Now it no longer mattered…

Alexander had known Barsine most of his life. They were both raised in the same Royal Court of Makedon.

Nothing in a royal court ever remained a secret for long. Alexander was told Barsine was heavy with his child and he had ignored her all the same.

Now Alexander had finally chosen a woman for a wife… a girl who had caught his eyes for no longer than a blink at a feast in his honor in Sughud…

Like most men, the King seemed to have fallen for a woman when least expected… on the edges of the empire… in the middle of a brutal campaign of conquest…

Hellene gods had a Persian sense of humor.

"Artabazos!" Alexander raises his voice higher. "You are not yourself today. Are you feeling well?"

"Rošanak— the King wishes to marry Rošanak," Artâvazda says faintly, hiding his pain.

"Rošanak?" Uxšiyârta says unguardedly in a low voice loaded with surprise.

Alexander nods his head.

"The King will have night meal with you and Aššat Šarri Farânak tonight to discuss terms."

Finally, relenting and calling the wife of his dead royal brother, the Wife of the King.

Uxšiyârta notices, making a note of it in his ears. He rises to his feet and considers Alexander for a moment. He then bows his head slightly and quickly leaves the royal tent without another word.

"What do you think, Artabazos? Will she agree to it?" Alexander asks hesitantly, as soon as Uxšiyârta leaves.

Silence.

Artâvazda eyes Alexander discreetly under his old brow. His eyes fill with the question his lips are too proud to ask.

Alexander looks at Artâvazda. Their eyes meet and speak.

Alexander looks away.

Artabazos knew better than anyone that Barsine was not in his heart.

Artâvazda hears the answer to his question spoken in the silence of the King.

Alexander did not mean to dishonor him.

Barsine was not loved as a woman and she was not sought as a Royal Woman.

He casts down his eyes. His old heart beats faster with anger and pain.

Rošanak had come as a total surprise to him.

She had the ancient blood of Persian Royal Women flowing through her.

The Persian Royal Women were the golden fetters the Persian Kings used to hold their vast Empire in peace, through creating blood ties with the worthy, mostly Persian nobles. The famed nobles of the Seven Persian Families were all not just kingsmen but kinsmen of the Great Kings through the blood of their Royal Daughters. But he doubted these Bakhtrian nobles desired such a marriage alliance with a man who had slaughtered their men and their kinsmen and had devastated their lands.

There was no denying that she was beautiful; her beauty favored her Persian ancestors. But marrying her lawfully was an entirely different matter than bedding her for her beauty… She was a captive Royal Woman honored with an offer of lawful marriage with the King, while his own daughter had been dishonored. Any son of hers will be an heir to an empire and Barsine's son was now a bastard unworthy of a crown.

"Artabazos!" Alexander raises his voice again, without looking at him.

Artâvazda shakes his head, "I do not know Alexander," he says truthfully, "but you are the King, the Lord of Asia. What you wish, will come to pass."

"Getting married came so naturally to my father." Alexander fidgets and mumbles. "He had seven wives! The last one was his undoing!"

His father Philip would have taken the offer of Darius after the Battle of Issos and would have married one of the Royal Daughters of Darius. He would have gone back to Makedonia with thirty thousand talents of golden gift; he would not have gone up country past Issos.

Everyone knew that the Persian blood spilled at the Battle of Issos had more than avenged the Hellenes for the burning of Athenai by Xerxes.

"I know, Alexander," Artâvazda says as his mind wanders, sinking into the memories of the former years, trying hard to gather himself honorably without angering the King.

Philip was a true-born Makedonian… he had forged Makedon out of nothing.

But he was a practical man as well… he had worked hard to bathe the Makedonian Royal Court in the civil waters of the Hellenes. He had spent loads and loads of silver to attract and keep cultured and learned Hellene MainLanders at his barbaric court.

Philip would have accepted the royal gift of Dâriuš after the Battle of Issos and would have married one of Royal Daughters and would have gone back to Makedonia with thirty thousand biltu of daraniya… pure gold.

Everyone knew that the fury unleashed against the Persians after the Battle of Issos had by all accounts nothing to do with avenging the Hellenes for the burning of Athenai by the First Khašâyâr, more than eight generations ago…

Hellenes and Persians had long since made their peace. An uneasy peace at times… but peace nonetheless… signed and sealed and guaranteed with glittering Persian gold. If Hellene lips spoke ill of the Persians, Hellene hands eagerly took their gold.

For Philip, it was all about the Persian gold… and about keeping peace at home by making war elsewhere. He cared nothing for the troublesome Hellenes spread across the edges of the Lands of the Persians by the Middle Sea.

But for Alexander, it was all about his own glory. He did not just want the Persian gold of the Great King… he wanted to be the Persian Great King!

And now the warrior king was finally thinking about begetting a rightful Royal Son and heir… and like all the Great Kings before him, he had desired a Persian Royal Daughter…

He loses the battle with himself. His thoughts return to his daughter.

Barsine…

Barsine had the same royal blood as Rošanak, but she was not a Royal Daughter, just the half-breed daughter of an old satrap, a kinsman of the Great King.

He had kept faith with Alexander after Dâriuš was put to the sword. He had always hoped and prayed that for his loyalty, Alexander would marry Barsine one day, or at least make her a woman of his royal court. But now that day was not to come at all.

He himself would have never married a Hellene if his Persian wife had not left him.

Bayasa was right after all: when he claimed the kingship after Dâriuš, that had made his daughter a Royal Daughter, the Daughter of the Great King.

This was his just punishment for betraying his own royal brother.

The daughter of his brother was to become a queen, while his own daughter was to become forgotten.

Alexander breaks the silence. "This will be my first, but I do not wish her to be my bride and in my bed, if she is not willing." He says wistfully, "I want her to marry me, not the king."

"Alexander," Artâvazda gathers himself and says, bowing his head painfully, "the man is the King and the King is a man. The Lord of Asia."

… and a true-born Persian Royal Daughter would never marry a man whose head was not worthy of a royal crown… ever… they married the noblest and the bravest of the Persians… they were the golden Persian ropes that held the vast Persian Empire together, tied in a golden Persian knot.

Great Kings could not rule without their Royal Women.

Royal Women were the splendor of the royal court of the Great Kings.

CAVE of LIONS. HOUSE of UXŠIYÂRTA
LATER
SETTING SUN

"Marry her?"

Aššat Šarri Farânak looks stunned. She leans back in her comfortable chair collecting her thoughts, tossing and turning the words on the tip of her tongue.

Alexander had taken away all her men and now he had come for her last daughter.

"Yes," Uxšiyârta nods, biting into an apple, distracted.

"Huh…"

"My fear was that, well, he could just claim her, like a captive woman," Uxšiyârta says. "Who can tell with these bloody invaders, not bound by the Laws of the Great Kings, nor by the Laws of the Wise Lord. Men who want to rule the world without wearing trousers. Fools! They must not know how cold and windy the Lands can get! Tying their manhoods to their waists will not help!"

Aššat Šarri Farânak gives him a look.

"Farânak, you remember when they used to be vassals of the Persians? Now they claim kingship over our Lands, trying to outdo the Persians in Persianness!

"As the old proverb says:

> *"Once the potter's dog crawls into the warm potter's shop, he bites the potter and steals his food!"*

He takes another bite of the apple, shakes his head side to side and mumbles. "Following in the footsteps of the damn Persians, will not make them Persian!"

Aššat Šarri Farânak gives him another look.

Uxšiyârta shrugs his shoulders and leans toward the cool window frame, looking outside. He wrestles with a painful thought for a moment.

The moment passes.

Like most men, he did not like to think about memories of old wounds.

He and his blood sister hailed from the noblest Bakhtrians. Their blood was mixed with Persian royalty since the beginning of the Empire. Even their names were Persian.

The Satrapy of Bakhtriš was the most important satrapy of the Empire, not just for the fierceness of its warriors, but because Bakhtriš was the adopted land of the blessed Zarathuštra, the Holy Prophet. All the Persian Kings of the Royal House of Hakhâmaniš and the Persian Royal Court had been the followers of Zarathuštra since the days of Kuruš the Elder.

And there were still more fierce warriors left in Bakhtriš and Sughud than in the armies of the satraps from the other side of the Empire by the seas… more warriors than there were at the Battle of Granikos.

His sister Farânak had married Mâr Šarri Bayasa, the grandson of the Second Artakhšaçâ, and he had married ša ekalli Parmys, a second sister of Bayasa, to ensure the continued loyalty of the Satrapy of Bakhtriš to the Great King.

The beautiful Parmys had turned out to be the love of his life. She had died at childbirth, while giving birth to Itâna.

Itâna was the son he both loved and hated, a constant reminder of a love lost many years ago and a son gained. Oštana was the forgotten middleborn son and Utâna was his firstborn, the son he had loved and lost to the bloody war.

Aššat Šarri Farânak takes a deep breath. Her mind races.

"He was not what I had expected."

Alexander was the man responsible for the death of all her men… her king-husband and all the Sons of the Royal House.

Uxšiyârta looks at her and takes another bite of his apple.

"What did you expect?"

His sister was kind-hearted, and everything had a hidden meaning in her life… coming to her from the Wise Lord or Divine Ânâhitâ or Divine Mithrâ… or some other guardian angel!

That was how she had survived the bloody death of all of her men: it was all fated by the Wise Lord for some higher purpose.

None had died… they all had gone to the Land of the Eternal Light.

As much as he was devoted to the worship of the Wise Lord, he had always preferred bathing in a cool stream he could see with his own eyes to bathing in the Eternal Light he had never seen. A loving wife in his bed was better than promise of ten in Heaven…

She bites her lip.

"I thought he would look like a giant fire-breathing beast, a man who could kill hundreds of thousands and thousands. He got to his feet when I approached him; he smiled at me. He seemed eager to talk. He sounded kingly confident as if he could charm a falcon down from the heavens and make it kneel at his feet and bend it to his will and let it eat from his hand!"

"I see—" Uxšiyârta takes another bite of his apple. "A mighty falcon who thinks all the Great Kings are his small prey!" He shrugs his shoulders. "He only breathes fire on battlefields; otherwise, he seems like any other man."

"Rošanak is blossoming. The sooner she marries the better. Young men were riding by our carriage yesterday, calling to her. Now that she is no longer kept hidden in a fortress, the men will all start hanging around wherever she is. But marrying a man who is not of our faith, even though he is a king? How will he treat her?"

"Men are men!"

BEHIND the DOOR

"What are they saying?" Rošanak whispers anxiously into Itâna's ear, as they both press their ears hard against the thick doors to Uxšiyârta's Cave of Lions.

"I cannot hear anything with you screaming into my ears!" Itâna whispers back, pushing her away. "Something about someone getting married!"

"Who?"

"Not you!" Itâna whispers back wickedly taunting her. "No one will marry an old bony girl with no breasts!"

Rošanak lightly hits Itâna on the head.

"Ouch! No one will marry an old bony girl with no breasts and a hot temper!" Itâna says, rubbing his head in pain.

"What are they saying?"

"I cannot hear, there is a ringing in my ear!"

"That is because you were dropped on your head when you were born!"

"You were the one who dropped me on my head!"

Rošanak hits Itâna on the head again.

"Ouch!" Itâna rubs his head again. "Honestly, I do not know what Utâna ever saw in you! He must have been blind as a cave bat!"

Rošanak hits Itâna on the head harder.

"OUCH!" Itâna yells out in pain.

The thick door opens suddenly and they both go crashing into the room, rolling on top of each other. Mounted heads of golden lions Uxšiyârta had hunted over the years stare down at them.

"Come in!" Uxšiyârta thunders at them, with his hands on his sides. "Even the dead standing on the Bridge of Chinvât can hear you two idiots spying behind closed doors!"

Rošanak gets up to her feet quickly and straightens.

Itâna stands up quickly and tries to makes his way back out of the door unnoticed.

Rošanak grabs him firmly and pulls him back.

"I was helping Itâna find his favorite frog!"

Itâna shrugs his shoulders, stealing his eyes, looking down at his feet.

He was already in heaps of trouble for forfeiting the ancient didâ of his father to the enemy without any help from his troublesome sister.

"The damn frog is lost again?" Uxšiyârta grunts.

Rošanak nods boldly.

"You will make a fine queen!" Aššat Šarri Farânak says, shaking her head with dismay.

"Me?"

"HER?" Itâna says loudly with disbelief, forgetting his pain and shame.

"Me?"

"Alexander wants to marry you."

"ME?"

"Her?"

"No!" Rošanak says, tightening her grip on Itâna without thinking, her fingers digging sharply into his shoulders.

"Ouch!" Itâna grunts and tries to loosen her hold.

Uxšiyârta pulls Itâna out of Rošanak's clutches and pushes him out of the door.

"Go look for your lucky frog in the hallway!" he bellows, and closes the door behind him.

"He can listen from behind the door. It will improve his hearing for hunting. You cannot hunt, if you cannot hear!" he says, pointing to the heads of lions on the walls.

"Sit down!" Uxšiyârta points to Rošanak. "What did Alexander tell you today?"

"His name."

Uxšiyârta narrows his eyes and leans into Rošanak.

She falls into a chair and pulls back from him.

"His name? That is all?"

"Yes."

"What else?" Uxšiyârta asks impatiently.

"I talked to Artâvazda."

"About?"

"His bloodline."

"Damn Persians and their cursed bloodlines!"

"Uxšiyârta!" Aššat Šarri Farânak says disapprovingly.

Uxšiyârta straightens.

"What else?"

"Nothing—" Rošanak casts her eyes down and avoids the piercing direct stare of Uxšiyârta.

"Well, I just told Artâvazda it was unworthy of him to dispute the blood claim of my father to the Persian Throne."

Uxšiyârta turns his head and looks at his blood sister, who is looking at Rošanak with a hint of admiration.

She was every bit her father's daughter since the day she was born to her mother…

She had inherited her arrogant feverish Persianness whole from the seed of her father.

"I said nothing more! I swear!" Rošanak shakes her head confidently. "I loved the Third Dâriuš, the King of Kings. Utâna told me that Dâriuš lost, not because he was a bad commander, but because Alexander was better. And omens were unfavorable for the Great King."

She pauses, waiting for his reaction.

Silence.

She continues.

"After the Eclipse of the Moon, rumors had circulated in the camps of the Persians before the Battle at the Black Eagle that the Persians were cursed by the dead at Kuništa. They said the Third Dâriuš had a dream and woke up cursing. In his dream, he saw the ghost of Younger Kuruš standing over Alexander, holding up his eagle standard. Utâna said to me even the Land of the Black Eagle was unlucky for Dâriuš as eagle was the royal sign of the Younger Kuruš!"

And all the Persians knew about the curse of the Younger Kuruš…

"My father could have pushed Alexander back to the land of his birth, if he had not been betrayed by his own men. And I believed Utâna. He always spoke the truth, he told me what was in his heart." Her voice quivers.

"And what else does Utâna tell you?" Uxšiyârta says, leaning into her, forgetting for a moment that Utâna was long dead.

"He says: *Defeated in some damn battle does not mean Conquered!*"

Uxšiyârta straightens again.

He missed Utâna bitterly.

The Lands had been at peace during most of his life.

In peace, he had buried his noble father… in war, he had buried his warrior son…

Uxšiyârta takes a deep breath and crashes down into a big chair. "A royal wedding. But, he has none of his women with him, just a half-wit brother, they say—"

"Good! Someone to sit with Itâna at the Bride's Table!" Rošanak says mockingly, glancing back toward the closed doors.

Aššat Šarri Farânak gets to her feet and walks over to Rošanak and gently caresses her hair.

Rošanak puts her arms around her blood mother and holds on to her, slightly trembling with fear. Her eyes well with tears.

"But I have no desire to marry Alexander. I will not marry a man who is responsible for the death of all my men, my father, my brothers, my Utâna—"

"Rošanak," Aššat Šarri Farânak whispers quietly, pushing back tears.

"Your father and all your brothers died honorably, as fated by the Wise Lord. No death is more honorable than dying in battle!"

"You do not have to!" Uxšiyârta says with a defiant tone. "Warriors are pouring around us as we speak. When Alexander told me he wanted to meet you today, I assumed the worst and sent secret word out calling to arms all the Bakhtrian warriors who are bound to me. We will fight Alexander, if he forces himself on you without your consent."

"There has been enough blood spilled. It is time to bring peace to the Land of a Thousand Cities. My own marriage to your father was to ensure the political alliance between the Bakhtrians and the Great Kings was continued," Aššat Šarri Farânak says, firmly pushing back tears.

"Noooo!" Rošanak cries out, disbelieving her own ears.

"Our marriages and the mixing of the bloodlines has been within the royals and the nobles of the Lands, the Seven Noble Persian Families, not with the bloody enemy invaders!" Uxšiyârta yells at Aššat Šarri Farânak.

Aššat Šarri Farânak gives him a sharp look.

Her blood brother could be really annoying sometimes even with the best of intentions.

She then gently pushes Rošanak away, walks and opens the heavy door, grabs Itâna and pulls him back into the middle of the room by his ear.

"You want to see your lastborn die too?"

Itâna stands there shamefacedly looking at his father, biting his lip in pain.

"I do not fear death!"

Aššat Šarri Farânak lightly hits Itâna on the head.

"Ouch!"

LATER that NIGHT

"I wish to marry Roxana," Alexander says impatiently, doing away with the usual pleasantries as he sips his sweet wine.

Even though he had expected a night meal, there was no sign of a meal to be had.

It would not be wise to execute the kinsmen of his wife-to-be for not obeying his royal orders before winning her hand in wedded matrimony!

Well, at least there was pure wine.

"The King—"

"Why?" Uxšiyârta interrupts Artâvazda, without waiting for all the words to be interpreted.

"If I asked a Great King that question, my head would roll on the floor in front of his royal feet for my insolence."

"And for good measure!" Uxšiyârta says with a forced smile. "Now, why Rošanak? He has the Royal Daughters of Dâriuš in his grasp at Çûšâ Hadiš."

Aššat Šarri Farânak interrupts seamlessly into the conversation. "Is the King interested in my daughter, or a peace agreement secured by a marriage alliance?"

"Alexander, is the marriage an alliance to secure peace?" Artâvazda asks cautiously.

Alexander hesitates.

That was what Hephæstion had told the others. But he just wanted the girl.

The peace would come sooner or later, at the point of his sharp sword… even if he had to raze the entire region to the ground and put everyone to the sword himself!

"Will marriage bring peace?" Alexander asks without expecting much.

"What are your terms for peace?" Artâvazda asks Uxšiyârta cautiously.

Uxšiyârta glances over at the closed doors.

No doubt Rošanak and the useless boy were listening in behind them… although they had taken more pains this time to be quiet.

"Mercy for Bakhtrians. All warriors can return home to their families and they will not be hunted, or punished, or killed," Aššat Šarri Farânak says softly with firmness before Uxšiyârta speaks.

Uxšiyârta raises an eyebrow and then nods half-heartedly, not eager to disagree with his blood sister in front of the bloody invaders.

"Quarters for all the Baktrian rebels, still fighting, if they peacefully return to their homes," Artâvazda interprets.

"Agreed." Alexander eyes his new mother, nods and speaks quickly without hesitation.

"The King grants your wishes," Artâvazda says quietly.

"Is the King willing to marry my daughter according to the customs of the Wise Lord?" Aššat Šarri Farânak asks quietly.

"Alexander, are you willing to marry Roxana according to the customs of the Persians?" Artâvazda asks cautiously.

Alexander considers Aššat Šarri Farânak for a moment and then nods. "Yes."

ALEXANDER'S ROYAL TENT
LATER

Alexander sits alone in his royal tent, sipping wine late at night.

When Persepolis had fallen into his hands without a siege and all its vast royal funds had lain wide open at his feet, he had thought he was victorious… that he had finally conquered the arrogant Persians.

He had stood on the lofty terrace of Persepolis and yelled:

"Men of Makedon, see how the mighty Persians have fallen to our swords!"

But the powerful Persians had not been conquered, they had either died or had simply disappeared… vanished into the highlands of Persis…

And nothing had come painlessly since the sack of Persepolis.

That cursed night that had made his men rich beyond their wildest dreams had also broken the unbroken string of favorable omens for him.

Aristandros, his diviner, had been artfully covering up one ill omen after another and he had overlooked it for the sake of the spirits of the Royal Army. But dreadful fortune was becoming more difficult to explain and disguise and remedy… and now this… on the furthest edges of his Empire…

He takes a deep breath and drinks more wine.

All he ever wanted was to be famed for his glorious deeds.

Achilleos had broken the Trojans and he wanted to conquer the Persians!

Persians had ruled over the world and he wanted to rule over the Persians and the world of the Persians and more!

He was raised on stories about the Great Kings…

All his life he was so worried that his father would leave him nothing to conquer and would rob him of all his fame and glory.

Then his half-breed father had married a pure Makedonian and had tried hard to get her with a son… a better son than he was… more Makedonian… all Makedonian… pure Makedonian.

He had seen the eyes of Pausanias, the young man who had killed his father… his hatred was drawn on his face in plain view. He was unarmed for the wedding ritual of his younger sister, but he could have done something. He had hunted and killed a lion on foot at the royal hunt at Basista with no one around him. But he had done nothing to stop the murderous blade that had killed his father.

The murder of the King-Father meant immediate kingship of the Son-Prince… he had wanted to be a Great King all his life…

Now the shade of Philip was arrogantly mocking him… again.

Was it not bad luck to take an arrow from mischievous Eros… straight in the heart no less… in the middle of a luckless campaign?

He had not thought seriously about getting married for years… not even when the Third Darius had offered him the hand of one of his daughters in royal marriage alliance.

When his father had arranged a marriage between Arrhidaios, his dim-witted brother and the daughter of the Karian Satrap, Pixodaros, his mother had persuaded him to secretly offer up himself to the Karian as the Groom, fearing Philip meant to make Arrhidaios his heir. Philotas had told Philip, who had chastised him royally, in front of Philotas, no less, and had banished all of his loyal advisors into exile for encouraging his youthful thoughtless deed. Philotas had always been quick to remind him with his arrogant eyes of this humiliation by his father…

That had been the end of his desire to get married… to anyone… until now.

He had not even considered wedding Queen Stateira when she was heavy with his child, as she was still wedded to Darius.

Hephæstion walks in quietly and pours himself a cup of pure wine and sits across from Alexander, looking at him, searching without asking. He slowly takes a sip of the wine.

Unlike Hellenes, they drank their wines pure, unmixed and untainted by water, since they were old enough to recline in the presence of their elders, once they had all killed wild boars with their bare hands.

But when they had first crossed into Asia, they had no gold to buy wine. So they had started to water their wine to make it last longer… until they had entered Babylon as conquerors. In Babylon, an old eunuch had summoned up enough courage to tell Alexander that Persians drank their wine unmixed and only one old queen in living memory had ever mixed her wine with water for health reasons, and with special permission from the Great King himself. And the sacred water from River Choaspes had been added to the old queen's pure wine. The old eunuch had said:

"Men who drink watered wine are not worthy to wear the Persian Purple."

… right before he had been run through with a spear for his insolence by one of the Makedonian royal guards. But afterward Alexander had thought better of it, and Alexander was never a man to back down from a challenge! Now that they had all the gold in the world, they could drink the best of wine… pure and strong, as they had in their former days.

Hephæstion eyes Alexander and finally breaks the silence. "Not bad, but not as splendid as the pure wines from the storehouses of Persepolis, where cellar doors were made of gold!"

"I have told the Princess that I wish to marry Roxana."

Hephæstion sips his wine. His face creases invisibly.

This was fated… it would have come sooner or later, but that knowledge did not ease the cutting pain of losing the Beloved.

When young passion had cooled long ago… love had lingered and deepened and remained.

"Wines from Babylon were good too, or was it the taste of Babylonian women drenched in young wine?" with a voice breaking on the words.

Alexander gives Hephæstion a deliberate glance from the corner of his eyes.

He knew they were busy counting the gold of the Great King in the Royal Treasury of Babylon to pay the Royal Army, appeasing the Babylonian temple priests with pledges and planning and negotiating their next conquest with the Babylonian Satrap of Susa.

"I told her only if Roxana was willing too."

Hephæstion takes another sip of his wine, trying not to think.

"There is another fortress not that far from here, much bigger, much higher. The locals call it the *Birdless Rock.* It sits too high on the mountain even for the birds and the legend says that not even Herakles himself could conquer it."

The legend said that about every piece of rock in the region.

"The bride price is quarters given to all the Baktrian rebels."

"Have you eaten?"

"Just wine, no food."

Hephæstion calls out and a royal boy runs inside and stands to attention.

"Go wake up the cook and tell him to make something for the King, a chunk of bread with some eggs, perhaps."

The royal boy nods and disappears out of the royal tent quickly.

Alexander looks at Hephæstion.

Hephæstion looks down at his wine. "Makedonians will not like it."

"And you?"

The loaded question hangs in the air for a moment between the old lovers.

Hephæstion leans back in his tall chair, runs his finger on the rim of his wine cup and takes a deep breath, avoiding Alexander's piercing gaze.

"You turned down the hands of the Royal Daughters of Darius in marriage alliance along with a dowry of thirty thousand talents." Hephæstion sips his wine. "You own most of the Empire now, without a handout from the Great King, but you still can marry one of his Royal Daughters, if you wish."

"Bessos was the cousin of Darius, neither of them had a direct blood claim to the throne; both had equal blood claims. The Royal Daughters of Darius and the Royal Daughter of Bessos have similar royal bloodlines. Bessos was the last Persian King, making the claim of his Royal Daughter closer to the Persian Throne."

"Are you going to publicly recognize Bessos as the Fifth Artaxerxes?"

"No!"

"Then why care about his bloodline?"

"Because—" Alexander takes a deep breath. "Roxana is beautiful."

"They are all barbarians."

"Hephæstion!"

"Makedonians will not like to see you marry a barbarian. Persians are being rolled into the Royal Army too quickly. The kingsmen love the Persian horses and accept the Persian horse-riding nobles. It is easy to mix along the love of horses and horsemanship.

"But you know well that the Foot are pure Makedonians to their bones and think of the Persians as defeated in battle.

"It is hard for them to see Persians as equals, harder yet to see Persians exalted over them in all manners. You push them too hard, they will not bend to your will. They will break."

Alexander leans back in his golden chair. He takes another sip of his wine.

"I see myself as the Great King of all the Lands and all the People, just like Kuros. Makedonia is just one of my many lands. Persians like Makedonians and Hellenes are my subjects. Makedonians have to get used to them."

Alexander leans forward. "Philip tamed these men just a generation ago. The Persians go back many generations, they were civilized even before the time of Kuros. You saw Persepolis, before we burned it. Those magnificent palaces were built by magnificent kings, they did not just grow out of the plains of Persis like trees."

The royal boy returns with a plate of food.

"Anything else, Alexander?"

"No. Thank you."

The royal boy leaves quickly.

Hephæstion leans forward and tastes Alexander's food and then leans back in his tall chair.

Alexander starts eating with a distracted mouth.

What they ate did not matter all that much… what they drank mattered more… wine was the rope that tied them all together in a bonded bundle of power.

"Marry a Makedonian first and get her with child, and then marry anyone you please. No one cares much about minor wives, except for minor wives and their bloody sons killing each other for the kingship."

"Whom shall I marry?" Alexander looks up and tilts his head to the side.

Silence.

"Queen Stateira is dead. My mother Queen Sisygambis writes that my sisters, the Royal Daughters of Darius, have grown as tall as their mother, towering over me. The daughters of Antipatros look hawkish like him with bent noses and fiery hair. My mother will choose a snake-crazy Molossian from the groves of Epiros. You have no sisters—" Alexander pauses and smiles broadly at Hephæstion. "Any girl from Makedonia will throw all the noble families of Makedon into a frenzy at each others' throats, and mine. I need Makedon in peace while I secure the rest of the world."

"A Hellene maybe?" Hephæstion offers cautiously.

"Right! And the LowLanders and the HighLanders have such great love for the MainLanders." Alexander laughs. "No matter whom I marry, I will displease someone. Makedonians will be insulted if I marry a Persian, the Persians will be insulted if I marry a Baktrian, and no one will please Kallisthenes, other than a virtuous Athenian who has been locked away all her life in the house of one of the nobles of the noblest eleven families in Athenai."

Alexander shakes his head.

"I will marry Roxana, if she agrees to it, and I will please myself."

ROŠANAK'S BEDROOM
NIGHT

"I will not!" Rošanak lies in her bed late at night, crying softly.

Aššat Šarri Farânak gently tries to console her. "Rošanak, you are a Royal Daughter. With privilege of royal birth come royal duties. If your father were here, he would have accepted the offer of political alliance, secured by a royal marriage. Empires rise and fall and rise again. For thousands of years past, it has been the way and for thousands of years hence, it will be the way."

"My father would not have forced me to marry a barbarian. I was to marry my Utâna!"

Aššat Šarri Farânak pushes back a tear.

"I am not forcing you either. Choose for yourself. But no matter whom you choose, Utâna is dead and he is not coming back to you."

"No!" Rošanak cries. "None of the sons of the Seven Persians will ever come near me, if I marry a barbarian."

"He is a king and marriage is sacred. A wedded woman is meant to keep herself for the bed of her husband, and not worry about other men."

Mâr'at Bani Âriyânnâz had filled her daughter's head with stories of the Royal Daughters who took Persian lovers when their marriage alliances were not agreeable.

Aššat Šarri Farânak pauses and softens her words.

"He could have just taken and raped you after the ancient didâ fell into his hands, but he has asked for your hand in lawful marriage. He said to me himself that he only wished it if you were willing yourself. Is it not what he said himself? Did Artâvazda not interpret rightly?"

"How would I know?" Rošanak stubbornly hides her face in the pillow.

"Were you not listening behind the door?"

"No!"

"Right." Aššat Šarri Farânak plays with Rošanak's hair tenderly. "Well, then we can ask him to come back tomorrow and ask you again directly himself."

"No!"

"Your bride price is mercy for all the men of the Lands still fighting and hiding in the mountains. There are thousands and thousands of men, men like Utâna and your blood brothers, still living and fighting and dying, who could return safely to their homes to the arms of their beloveds."

Aššat Šarri Farânak takes a deep breath and lets it out quietly.

"If Utâna was one among them, would you not have wanted your lover returned to your sweet arms, by the sacrifice of a benevolent Royal Woman?"

"I would give anything to have Utâna back!"

Aššat Šarri Farânak takes another deep breath; her heart folds. She speaks quietly to Rošanak. "With privilege comes duty. Accept the bride price and marry the Barbarian King and return all the men out there to their beloved women."

Sacrificing the lastborn daughter to end the unending bloodshed…

Some hundred thousand Bakhtrians and Sughdians had died since the start of the war… and more dying every day. The enemy army had started to put to the sword all the men who were caught in their nets… without quarters… young or old… warrior or not… it mattered not… soon, there would be no one left… no one!

The Land of a Thousand Cities was bleeding cities here and there… on this side and on that side of the mountains and the deserts and the rivers.

Instead of bathing in the light of the God, the land of the prophet was now bathing in the blood of the faithful…

A lot worse could happen to her Royal Daughter than marrying the Lord of Asia… a man who had turned down the Royal Daughters of Setâreh and had asked for the hand of her Royal Daughter in a lawful marriage alliance.

And there were her grandsons to protect… with breath of life…under pain of death…

Who knew what such a fire-breathing king was capable of if his fair offer of marriage alliance was slighted by a Royal Daughter?

Could he not just breathe fire and burn the whole world?

Who among men had ever taken lightly to rejection from a woman?

Who among kings had ever taken peacefully to a refusal from a Royal Woman?

Rošanak cries.

"I have written to your royal grandmother and have left the marriage offer of the Lord of Asia in the hands of his mother. She will make the final decision. Alexander will listen to whatever Sisygambis would say about this."

HOUSE of UXŠIYÂRTA
FOLLOWING DAY

"Where is she?" Alexander says impatiently as he paces around the room.

Word had come early that day from his Princess-Mother inviting him to the mid-day meal. He had arrived early with Hephæstion and Artabazos in tow.

This time there was food. The table in the middle of the room was set generously with an abundance of food and wine.

Uxšiyârta sits at the head of the table, watching Alexander walk nervously round and round the room, and fills up with pain.

The love his firstborn son had for his lastborn sister had been passed on to the care of a total stranger, an enemy invader no less… Utâna had loved Rošanak her whole life and Alexander had only seen her once… or twice… or three times… and no more…

Hephæstion and Artâvazda stand by the door, all waiting for the Royal Women, who seem to have ignored all requests to come any sooner than they had intended.

Artâvazda leans harder on his walking stick and starts to speak, but he is interrupted by the doors opening and two small boys bursting into the room followed by Aššat Šarri Farânak and Rošanak and a couple of old nursemaids. The boys run noisily and sit by Uxšiyârta, with their nursemaids following closely behind them.

Aššat Šarri Farânak smiles graciously and bows her head slightly to Alexander and beckons them to sit down at the food table.

Alexander eyes Rošanak, wearing a big, flowy dress, concealing her slight body under folds and rolls of cloth.

He was certain she was wearing a crimson gown, the color of his royal standard, with embroidered golden lions to the banquet… well, at least the rest of her looked like her. Her hair flowed freely around her face, down on her shoulders. Her face sparkled in the bright light of the mid-day sun pouring into the large room through high windows.

"My Lord," Rošanak says softly to Alexander, slightly bowing her head.

Bathing her eyes all morning in icy scented water mixed with tea leaves had magically removed all traces of puffed up and red crying eyes.

"Roxana, I am glad to see you again." Alexander smiles and tilts his head slightly more to the left.

Artâvazda interprets.

Rošanak discreetly eyes Alexander.

He was now wearing the Persian Purple around his head, the strip of royal purple cloth edged in gold as the sign of kingship, but narrower than what the Great Kings usually wore… and a Persian tunic edged in royal purple…

Hephæstion considers Rošanak carefully.

She was smallish… shorter than Alexander… more to his liking… not like Stateira, a full head and shoulder taller than Alexander. He did not have to pretend to be taller than he was around her, as he had with Stateira, wearing the tall padded boots of the Great Kings.

He steps forward, looking straight at her and introduces himself.

"I am Hephæstion."

"This is Hefesteyon, companion of Alexander."

Rošanak bows her head slightly and acknowledges him politely. "My Lord."

"Good. Everyone is here. Let us eat." Uxšiyârta says pointing to the food, with a voice eager to rid himself of the unwanted guests after a quick meal.

His rough manners, a carefully crafted mask, were refined over years of dealing with the Persians. Bakhtrians were simpler than Persians in their manners, but no less shrewd and scheming.

Everyone sits at the food table, with Alexander taking his seat across from Uxšiyârta, flanked by Hephæstion and Artâvazda.

Rošanak discreetly looks at Alexander from the corner of her eyes.

Maids serve the food and pour the wine.

Aššat Šarri Farânak leans forward and quietly speaks to the small boys flanking Uxšiyârta, tactfully pointing with her eyes.

The small boys, about six and seven years of age, look at each other mischievously and then eagerly jump up and run to the other side of the food table.

The maids bring more chairs and the boys sit down flanking Alexander and start eating from his plate.

Aššat Šarri Farânak then whispers into Rošanak's ear. Rošanak obediently gets to her feet, follows the boys and points to them.

"Nimâ and Dârâ, children of my late sister, Dukšiš Parânak."

Artâvazda interprets.

"Dara and Neema, the children of Princess Paranak, the late sister of Roxana."

Rošanak leans over gracefully and picks up Alexander's wine cup and takes a sip. She then puts down the wine cup and goes back and sits down next to her blood mother.

Alexander eyes Rošanak intently.

She was scented with jasmine. And she had tasted his wine fearlessly.

The mid-day meal finishes wordlessly. The maids clear the table and bring bowls of fruit, Persian sweets and cold sweet wine.

Silent tension lingers in the air, mixed with the aroma of the food.

The boys cannot contain themselves any longer and start making faces at each other. Then a food fight suddenly breaks out noisily, the two boys throwing pieces of fruit at each other.

A couple of pieces of fruit hit Alexander and Hephæstion, finally breaking the tension in the room.

Hephæstion wipes a piece of fruit from his face. Alexander laughs unguardedly.

"NIMÂ! DÂRÂ!" Aššat Šarri Farânak sternly yells at the boys.

The boys stop for a brief moment and look at their grandmother at the other side of the food table and then start again, undaunted.

Alexander reaches and grabs the boys by the collars of their tunics, trying to keep them from continuing their fight. The boys are undeterred. Their old nursemaids quickly step forward and lift up the boys and start taking them away.

"We want to stay!" Dârâ yells.

"We will be good!" Nimâ yells louder.

"Mammanie!" Dârâ yells.

"Mammanie!" Nimâ yells louder.

The sounds of the boys pleading and yelling start to fade in the hallway. Doors are closed behind them and the room becomes momentarily quiet.

Aššat Šarri Farânak bites her lip, looking slightly embarrassed.

Rošanak and Uxšiyârta burst into laugher, glancing at Alexander and Hephæstion, still cleaning bits of fruit from their tunics.

Aššat Šarri Farânak gives a sharp look and Rošanak stops laughing and straightens. Uxšiyârta too.

Alexander looks at Rošanak, smiling with a boyish grin.

He had sacrificed generously to Zeus and Hera earlier, asking for their blessings, and what was to gain by waiting any longer?

He gets to his feet and takes out his dagger, cuts the sweet cake on the food table in half and takes a half to Rošanak.

Rošanak takes the sweet cake from Alexander politely and takes a bite graciously, eyeing her mother under her dark lashes.

Alexander smiles broadly.

Hephæstion and Artâvazda look at Alexander in stunned silence.

Alexander looks at Hephæstion, uncertain of what to do next.

Hephæstion eyes Alexander and then quickly gets up to his feet and picks up his wine cup. "To your health, Alexander, and to yours, Roxana."

Artâvazda pushes himself up, picks up his wine cup and interprets.

The Makedonian Boys did not know what they were doing.

And the Bakhtrians knew even less.

The Wise Lord had perfectly matched up the fools!

Uxšiyârta gets to his feet and lifts his wine cup. "May the Wise Lord look favorably upon his humble servants."

Aššat Šarri Farânak and Rošanak both stand.

"I have written to her grandmother, Dukšiš Sisygambis. If she agrees to the wedding, then it will be after the Festival of No'rouz. The day and the month of the royal wedding will be decided by the royal star-charter," Aššat Šarri Farânak says softly, bows her head to Alexander and heads for the door with Rošanak following.

Artâvazda thinks about telling the Aššat Šarri that her daughter was already married as far as Alexander was concerned. Then he thinks about interpreting Aššat Šarri's last words for Alexander, and then he thinks of his own daughter and he keeps all his words to himself.

They both were soon to find out… and the rest was no longer any concern of his.

He was finally going back home.

ALEXANDER'S ROYAL TENT

LATER

Alexander beams as he enters his royal tent.

His kingsmen were all here… Hephæstion right behind him… Krateros, Perdikkas, Ptolemaios, Leonnatos, Lysimachos, Medeios, Koinos and others were standing around the long silver-footed Persian table waiting for him.

These were his kingsmen… some friends since childhood, most with bonds to him forged during years of bloody battles. His invincible legend had been hard won with the honor wounds these men had been collecting and wearing with pride on their hard bodies.

His victories had made them all rich beyond their wildest dreams and had made him the one above all others… the Lord of Asia.

"I have married Roxana, Daughter of Bessos."

Stunned silence.

The royal tent quickly empties of all breathable air.

"Married? A captive girl?"

"Are you sure, Alexander?"

"To the barbarian girl who was here, just the other day?"

"Alexander, we all want to see you beget a son, but an illiterate barbarian bride from Sogdiana who—"

"You may call her the Queen, the Persian, the Baktrian, or simply Roxana. But if you ever call her a barbarian, I will hand deliver you to Hades myself!" Alexander growls.

"But, Alexander—"

"You want to be first, Krateros?"

Krateros gathers himself quickly. "No, Alexander, we are just wondering when, where, how—"

"Today, at the feast prepared for mid-day by Noble Oxyartes, Father of the Bride. I cut a loaf in half and gave her a half and she took a bite."

All the kingsmen eye each other utterly stunned.

"And you did not see fit to have us there to wish you well?" Ptolemaios says guardedly.

"Hephæstion was there. There will be a big royal wedding feast. Hephæstion will see to it, when we return to Baktra, after we capture the other rock on the way."

"Joy to the Bridegroom!"

"I have given quarters to all the rebels still fighting. The marriage alliance guarantees the peace agreement."

"Quarters to all the rebels?"

"To the men who have killed our men?"

"These rebels will not honor a marriage alliance."

"You have a better idea, Krateros, short of wiping out the multitudes living in Baktria and Sogdiana?"

"No, Alexander."

"Eumenes, send word out to the entire region declaring the Royal Marriage Alliance and the Peace Agreement. Quarters to all warriors, if they lay down their arms and return to their homes peacefully."

"Yes, Alexander."

CAVE of LIONS. HOUSE of UXŠIYÂRTA
FOLLOWING MORNING

"They are gone!"

"Who?"

"The Barbarians!"

"WHAT? WHERE?"

"Trail of horses and feet say they are heading east toward the rising sun."

"Rising sun? Are you sure?"

"Yes, Father!" Itâna says confidently. "Oštana told me this morning before he left with them."

"East? What is in the East? Nothing is in the East, just the old hermit Sisimithrâ and his didâ and all his kinsmen and clan—" Uxšiyârta narrows his eyes and rubs his forehead.

"The damn Makedonian has never heard of diplomacy or common sense. If Kuruš and Dâriuš had spent all their time chasing down every piece of rock in the Lands, the Persians would still be rounding up wild horses and smelly goats around Pârsâkata!"

"Yes, Father."

"Well, good! They have been in the satrapy for two years eating everything like vultures, even sacred animals in sacred groves and their own horses and mules. They killed and ate four thousand beasts in the Royal Paradayadâ of the Great King! There is nothing they have not slaughtered and eaten! Worse, they have drunk every drop of wine, ripe or ripening, in all the satrapies! If they do not all leave or die soon, we will all starve to death, or die of thirst, whichever comes first!"

"Yes, Father."

A maid enters the room quietly. "Master, there are some men here to see you."

"Who?

"Men of the enemy."

"Show them in."

A Makedonian Envoy from Alexander enters the room, followed by a pair of men carrying a heavy silver-hemmed wooden chest.

"Oxyartes, Alexander, Lord of Asia, sends you greeting," the Makedonian Envoy says in heavy accented Bakhtrian.

"Greetings to Alexander too."

"King Alexander has sent," the Makedonian Envoy says pointing to the wooden chest, "gifts for his bride, Roxana," as the men set the heavy chest in front of Uxšiyârta.

"Bride? Rošanak?" Itâna says rolling his eyes with surprise.

Uxšiyârta gives a sharp look to Itâna.

Itâna grunts quietly, biting his lip so hard he tastes his own blood in his mouth. He swallows hard.

Uxšiyârta hides his own surprise. "Yes, thank you."

The Makedonian Envoy hands a folded parchment to Uxšiyârta.

"King Alexander has given quarters to all the Baktrian warriors, as he has agreed to. They can now all return home under the protection of the Lord of Asia himself."

Uxšiyârta takes the parchment and holds it in his hands for a moment and considers it. He raises his eyebrow, surprised.

The soft parchment was sealed with the Royal Seal of Dâriuš.

He looks at the Makedonian Envoy, then breaks the royal seal and unfolds the royal document. He brings it to his eyes and looks at it closely.

Huh!

The decree of the Lord of Asia was written in Aramaic, one of the written tongues of the Persian Royal Court, on precious parchment no less, by a royal court scribe… just like any other kingly order from the Great King himself.

He reads the document.

From King Alexander, Lord of Asia, to the people who are in the Satrapies of Bakhtriš and Sughuda.
In Month 12, Viyaxana, 24 days passed, in Year 3 of Alexander:

I send you much greetings of peace and prosperity. Now that there is peace here with me, may there also be peace with you.
I swear by Zeus-Ammon and by all the gods and goddesses of the Lands, that I shall stand by this Agreement and that I shall not break this Agreement, nor shall I bear arms against those who shall stand by this Agreement.
Thus shall it be known to you that there shall be peace if...
... do not attack my Royal Army...
Accept my rule and that of my sons and sons of my sons... it is my desire that... shall pay tribute to the royal funds in the amount of...

Uxšiyârta looks closer.

The ignorant scribe had mixed Persian and Aramaic words together to impress his new master.

Some of the Persian words he had used had died long ago and were no longer remembered by the living.

He tries in vain to guess the meaning of some of the ancient words.

"Hmm…" He finally gives up and skips over them and reads the rest of the royal document.

... as was paid to the Great King... any disputes shall be judged by us in our Royal Court... there shall be a garrison of adequate size supplied... by... Alexander, the Lord of Asia.

By the order of King Alexander, Eumenes of Kardia wrote this.

Uxšiyârta folds the parchment and looks at the Makedonian Envoy.

"Where is your King going?"

"Heading East, toward the Rock of Sisimitres."

"I see."

LATER

"Royal gifts from your husband, the Lord of Asia," Uxšiyârta says, pointing to the silvery wooden chest in the middle of the room.

"Mostly stolen loot from Pârsâ and other Persian Palaces, returning to the hands of its rightful royal owners."

"Husband?" Rošanak goes pale.

"*But*—" Words fly quickly out of the gates of her lips.

"The wedding will be after the Persian New Year, if my royal grandmother agrees to it, as my mother said!"

"He thinks you are already married!"

"But we told him—" Aššat Šarri Farânak bites her lip nervously.

"Artâvazda must not have interpreted properly. I think the old goat goes deaf whenever it suits him, or he is deaf and only chooses to hear what pleases his goat ears." Uxšiyârta grunts. "I should have broken his old neck, when I had a chance, just to avenge the massacre of old Âriâmazda and all his kinsmen and clan. It was the cursed Kophen, his bastard half-breed son from his Hellene whore who caused all those deaths with his broken tongue! I just could not bear to touch his rotting traitorous carcass with my clean hands—"

"Do not worry, Little Sister, he is already gone!" Itâna says with certainty, not waiting long enough for his father to finish his words.

Uxšiyârta looks at Itâna sideways and shakes his head.

"Gone? Gone where?" Rošanak asks faintly.

"Gone, yes, flown away, to capture the next Birdless Rock, and kill all the poor birds!" Itâna gestures like birds with his hands.

"His envoy said this morning that the word about the Peace Agreement guaranteed by the Royal Marriage Alliance is going out to everyone. He gave me a copy of the Decree of the Lord of Asia on royal parchment."

"Maybe it is the will of the Wise Lord to have peace now rather than later," Aššat Šarri Farânak wonders out loud.

"It is better this way." Uxšiyârta rubs the lines on his forehead. His fingers slightly tremble. "We will see how the men respond to the news. If they start honoring the peace agreement, then we can have a wedding, that is if Alexander insists on it. If the peace agreement does not hold, then we can refute the marriage alliance and continue fighting as we have done"'"

"Who knows, maybe he falls off the next Birdless Rock and becomes food for the damn birds and never returns, by the favor of the Wise Lord!" Itâna says quickly.

Everyone ignores Itâna.

"What if Sisygambis declines the marriage alliance of her granddaughter?" Aššat Šarri Farânak says, quietly wondering.

"Then, there will be no wedding!" Uxšiyârta says with certainty and scratches his head and takes a deep breath.

"That would be a matter between the mother and the son. Meanwhile, we should get you back to Baktra Hadiš and get you settled there as soon as possible. I will send for the Zarathuštra Athravan to purify the hadiš, before you set foot in it again."

Color returns to Rošanak's face.

This was the will of the Divine Goddess Ânâhitâ. She must have heard her desperate teary prayers.

Maybe her father was right and Alexander will leave her in peace… maybe all he really wanted was just the pretense of a marriage to forge an alliance and no more…

LATER

"I told you Little Sister, no man will ever marry you!"

Rošanak raises her hand to hit Itâna on the head.

Itâna dodges quickly.

She misses.

He smiles victoriously.

"Dârparna and I went to the camp of the Persians yesterday. No one stopped us! There are lots of Persians in his Royal Army now, all with better pay, some have been promoted to high ranks. He has bought the Persians with their own damn gold. More Persians than Makedonians in his Royal Army now. Some Bakhtrians too, but not that many. Bakhtrians are smarter than Persians!"

"Itâna!"

"You have nothing to worry about, Little Sister! He just wanted to stop fighting and quietly leave the Land of a Thousand Cities without anyone taking notice of it, so he married you to become a kinsman in name and left quickly. His men have already eaten everything they could find; as father always says, not much is left for them to get their hands on. They soon will have to start killing and roasting and eating each other!

"He is not coming back for the rest of you! There is not enough flesh on your bones to even feed a small falcon, let alone a small king— that much I am certain of!"

Rošanak takes a deep breath and looks at Itâna with dismay.

"And even if by bad fortune he does come back this way, he has no interest in women. That is probably why he chose you as his bride."

Itâna pulls away from Rošanak quickly, but she sits motionless, resting her head on her knees.

"Persians told us that he has no women now, no wives, no mistresses, no whores. There was that old half-breed Hellene daughter of the traitor Artâvazda after the battle of Issos that fell into his victorious lap, the wife of the dead Memnon and before him, the dead Mentor, brother of Memnon. He claimed his right of conquest a few times and then left her behind somewhere, who knows where, the Persians did not know.

"They said she was heavy with child, a bastard. He must have thrown her away in the middle of the night when no one took notice of it! He probably thought that miserable old woman had brought enough bad fortune to two dead husbands already! He did not wish to be the third dead husband!"

"Itâna!"

"Well, at least he might be smarter than he looks, being shorter than all his kingsmen!" Itâna dodges quickly and continues wickedly. "Then there was Dukšiš Setâreh who died at childbirth! So, she is dead now!"

"Itâna, have you nothing better to do than to sit here and torment me?"

"No!"

Itâna shrugs his shoulders and continues undeterred. "They said that he prefers the company of men. His old lover from the land of his fathers, and a scrawny sickly half-Bâbiruviya eunuch who pretends he is pure Persian and the old beloved of the Third Dâriuš."

Itâna shakes his head.

"No one cares that he pretends he was the whore of Dâriuš. The Great King was ancient; he could not satisfy his Royal Woman any more, so he bedded palace eunuchs. But the damn eunuch should be beheaded for pretending to be a Persian! Even a dumb mule knows that all the eunuchs are from the rebellious satrapies— punished for their insolence. I would have cut out his lying tongue myself, if he had claimed he was Bakhtrian!"

"Itâna!"

Itâna leans forward and continues wickedly in a hushed voice, making a forbidden sign with his hands.

"The Makedonian was probably curious about the damn eunuch, he wanted to see for himself what a man cut into the shape of a woman felt like!"

"Itâna!"

"Ah! And the Persians said that the Mudrâya had said he had another lover, a young son of one of his kingsmen, who drowned swimming in the Great River of Pirâva in the Two Lands before he got here, so he is dead too. That is why the Makedonian has no rightful sons. Try making a son between the legs of a—"

"ITÂNA! If your father ever heard you talk and sign like this, he would cut off your fingers and rip your tongue out and then strangle you with his own bare hands and cut off your little head and hang it in the Cave of Lions."

Itâna ignores Rošanak and weaves the tale with excitement.

"Well, everyone knows Bakhtrians have no taste for boys. We love our women and our wine and we keep our swords sharp to keep our women and our wine to ourselves."

Rošanak eyes Itâna for a long moment and thinks about telling him about their blood brothers, but she thinks better of it and keeps her tongue.

Oštana, and her blood brother, both born between the firstborn and the lastborn sons, nearly the same age, were lovers since youth and even after they had passed into manhood.

Oštana had broken his leg falling from his horse playing chogân the month before they both had been summoned to the Royal Army of the Third Dâriuš.

Her blood brother had gone as ordered and Oštana had remained behind and her blood brother had died in Issos and that had broken Oštana's heart…

One was long dead and the other long tormented, keeping to himself mostly.

If Oštana had not broken his leg that year, he too would have died at Issos either by the thrust of the sword of the enemy or by his own sword after her blood brother had fallen. Neither would have wanted to live after the death of the other… they were devoted to each other…

… both were kind to her when she was a child and had let her ride their horses…

Their love for each other was forbidden, as unions that produced no children were against the Laws of the Wise Lord… no… some secrets were better kept to the grave…

As Sisygambis, her royal grandmother, always said:

"… a Royal Daughter must guard her tongue to keep her head!"

"Rošanak, are you listening to me?"

"I am not deaf! Let me see now, you love your women and wine? Ha! You do not even have a beard yet!"

Itâna ignores Rošanak. "Have you seen those ugly asses they ride?"

"No."

"Dârparna says that is why these Makedonians are so bloodthirsty and wicked. They have no good women and no good wine and no good horses!"

"Itâna!"

"Ah! And they do not wear Persian sarbalâ. It must be painful sitting on those short shaggy mules all day, with their naked manhood tied with a—"

Rošanak swiftly hits Itâna on the head, hard.

"Ouch!" Itâna yells out in pain, rubbing his head.

"He deserves a wife like you to make his life miserable for all the misery he has brought on everyone else!"

Rošanak hits Itâna on the head, much harder.

"OUCH!"

Itâna screams.

"And you! You deserve a short ugly husband like him, to make your life miserable!"

HADIŠ at BAKTRA. SATRAPY of BAKHTRIŠ
A MONTH LATER
NIGHT

Cold cloudy night.

Knotted sounds of horses and men.

Alexander, Hephæstion, Perdikkas, a few other kingsmen and royal guards and a pair of royal boys drop their weary horses at the guarded gate with the palace grooms and head for the small palace, inside the fortified walls of the Palaces at Baktra.

Alexander eyes the small palace. It seems empty.

They had arrived ahead of the rest of the Royal Army which was slowly crawling back toward Baktra.

They had been riding steadily for the past week from the Rock of Sisimitres, which had finally surrendered, when Oxyartes, Roxana's father and his new kinsman, had shown up and had talked the old warlord holding down the fortress into providing two months of rations for the Royal Army in exchange for being left alone on the crown of the mountain. The old Sisimitres had agreed to the terms and had given them rations for two months and had sent him and his men eagerly on their way.

He wanted to get back to Baktra, where Roxana and her mother had returned and taken up residence in their old palace… word had finally come from Queen-Mother Sisygambis, agreeing to the marriage alliance with Roxana. He had kept his pledge to the Princess-Mother and had ordered Amyntas to find himself another place to live and empty the palace and deliver it to the Princess-Mother whole.

But he was the Lord of Asia and he and his kingsmen needed a warm place to sleep for the night.

"All I need is a warm bath, a flagon of pure wine and a hard bed." Perdikkas says stretching his legs.

"And a soft woman of easy virtue."

"Or one of the handsome royal boys."

Men laugh.

By all accounts, the peace agreement had strangely been holding, since it had become known that Alexander had married Roxana.

The mood of the kingsmen and the men had lifted, as peace had started to take root and grow branches in the jagged mountains and the flatlands and the deserts…

Alexander points to the small palace. "You can all sleep here tonight, until your tents arrive."

"Sir, look!" one of the royal boys says, pointing with his hand in the direction of a dark shadow moving through the fragrant gardens of the palace. "A rebel?"

Men turn their heads.

Peace was too new and suspicion still prevailed.

They all had stayed in and around the palace for months before pursuing rebels all around the area and their eyes were as sharp as the edges of their swords.

"Maybe the news of the success of the peace was just another trap?" Perdikkas grunts tiredly.

The royal boys quickly unsheathe their swords and start heading for the dark shadow.

"Wait," Alexander commands calmly. "Follow him quietly from a distance, like hunting a deer, to catch the whole herd."

The royal boys acknowledge his command and walk away fast and quiet, following the dark shadow.

"Hephæstion, Perdikkas, you two with me!"

Alexander points to the residence, "The rest of you secure the main palace."

They all nod in agreement, heading for the palace.

Alexander looks around and takes a deep breath resignedly. He starts after the royal boys, with Hephæstion and Perdikkas following him silently.

The dark shadow leaves the palace walls and walks watchfully in the dark streets, turns a corner and enters an old broken temple.

The royal boys quietly follow him inside.

It is dark and cold.

The shadow wipes clean a tree branch, stirs the sleeping embers in an old silver fire altar and slowly fans the low flames with his hand. Fire flares up and dimly lights the middle of the temple. The shadow then removes the turban wrapped around his head and rubs his hands over the fire altar for warmth.

Long dark hair falls and flows around the head of the shadow.

The royal boys get a good look in the dim light of the fire altar.

The dark shadow was a young girl with dark hair.

She looks around and then kneels down next to a broken statue on the ground in the middle of the old cold temple.

"Tell Alexander, it is just a girl!" one of the royal boys whispers in the ear of the other one, gripping his sword firmly. "I will stay here and watch her."

The other royal boy leaves quietly and reports to Alexander outside.

"Sir, he is just a girl!"

Alexander raises his eyebrow with curiosity. "Stay here and secure the door."

"Yes, Sir."

Alexander enters the old broken temple, followed by Hephæstion and Perdikkas. In the dim light of the fire altar, they all see Rošanak's face.

Hephæstion quietly whispers into Alexander's ears. "This is the ancient temple of the local goddess."

Rošanak reaches for her bag in the darkness, pulls something out of it, opens it and holds it up to the dim light.

A golden gossamer fringed shawl that Alexander had gifted her as his bride.

Abandoned stillness hangs in the air.

Rošanak looks around with utter sadness.

The sacred âyadana was utterly sacked and except for the broken pieces of the statue of the goddess and the old silver altar, not much of anything was left.

The men who had sacked the sacred âyadana had taken away all the golden gold and had left behind the sacred silver and the broken goddess.

She grabs her turban and lovingly dusts the broken statue, looking abandoned and aged and forgotten. She drops the turban and wraps the golden shawl around the statue.

She reaches and grabs her bag again and takes out the golden wreath, another gift from Alexander, and throws the bag on the ground next to her feet. She gently places the wreath on the goddess' fallen head. The statue is almost life-size and the wreath fits comfortably on its broken head. She looks beyond the statue and bites her lip and takes a deep breath.

A tear falls in the dim glow of the fire altar.

Her goddess was broken too… just like her heart… and her world… the world was broken…

She had wanted to come sooner, but she was too ashamed to face her goddess.

She wipes her tears with her cold fingers, gets to her feet and spreads a handful of fragrant Arabâya incense over the sacred fire.

Fire crackles and the scent of sacred incense fills the old âyadana.

Rošanak takes another deep breath and fills up with the scent of incense, then kneels back down, gazing loyally at the broken statue for a long moment. She clasps her hands and casts her eyes downward and starts to pray quietly:

> *"I worship the Wise Lord.*
>
> *"Divine Ânâhitâ, the Mother Goddess, who makes the seeds of all men pure, who makes the womb of all women pure for bringing forth…"*

"She must be praying." Hephæstion whispers quietly in Alexander's ear.

None of them knew a word of Persian. And they collectively knew even less Baktrian than Persian.

She sighs and takes a deep breath and continues with a teary voice, praying with all her heart and soul.

> *"My father, the Great King is dead. The Lands of the Persians still have no king. The holy words of Avesta have been burned. Your sacred âyadana has been sacked and desecrated by the enemy armies.*
>
> *"I am a captive woman bound to the conqueror of the Persians who worships unknown gods… my prayers are not worthy to be heard…*
>
> *"So, I offer you a prayer from the lips of my beloved blood mother, who worships the Wise Lord freely:*
>
> > *"Divine Ânâhitâ, I pray thee to hear my voice and strike those who have desecrated your sacred âyadana… those who worship the Lord of Darkness and do not obey the laws of the Wise Lord…*

"Divine Ânâhitâ, I pray thee to let the holy earth sleep and not hear the footsteps of the conquering armies. I pray thee to let the holy earth awaken when the Divine Mithrâ has expelled the enemies of the Persians from the Lands of the Persians and when a new Persian King sits on the Persian Throne and wears the Persian Crown and the sacred Persian Purple Robe."

Rošanak looks down at the broken statue, then picks up her turban and shakes the dust off.

The dust flies around her head and makes her sneeze. She utters a blessing under her lips.

Alexander takes a deep breath in the darkness and kisses the tip of his fingers and raises his hand to heavens. Hephæstion and Perdikkas do the same.

A good omen sent by Zeus!

She waves away the dust and wraps her head and face again warmly, gets to her feet and picks up the empty bag and heads for the broken door.

Alexander and his kingsmen pull further into the darkness and wait for her to leave the temple unnoticed.

"Shall we follow her?" the royal boy asks quietly in a hushed voice.

"No. You are dismissed. Go back to the palace. Tell the others to go back to the small palace too."

"Yes, Sir." The royal boy leaves the dark temple quickly.

Alexander steps out of the darkness and stands in the middle of the cold temple looking at the broken statue in the dim glow of the fire altar. The golden wreath and golden shawl glints in the light of the flickering golden fire. The gold he had gifted his new bride now adorns the statue of the goddess.

He smiles to himself.

His bride was generous with her gods and goddesses.

"We closed most of the temples when the rebellion broke out in the satrapies provoked by the temple priests," Hephæstion says quietly.

Perdikkas pulls a sleepy old man, dressed in a white robe, into the middle of the cold old temple. "I found him sleeping in one of the chambers in the back. He must be a temple priest or a mage. I cannot tell the difference! He understands a few words of Attik—"

"I am a mage and a follower of Zoroaster," the old Zarathuštra Athravan says in broken Attik.

Alexander peers into the eyes of the athravan and points to the broken statue. "Tell me about your goddess."

The old Zarathuštra Athravan mumbles in broken accented Attik, mixing his words here and there with Persian and Bakhtrian. "Divine Ânâhitâ is an ancient goddess. She is the Mother Goddess, hallowed and holy, sacred to all Bakhtrians and Persians."

He points around at the sacked âyadana with his old brittle fingers.

"This temple used to be so rich that it was plundered by many old kings who needed the Bakhtrian gold to make war upon their enemies.

"It was looted last by—" The old Zarathuštra Athravan pauses and eyes the men with disdain, "—by your army. It was closed and abandoned by the order of that last cursed satrap, Artâvazda. He closed this most holy of all temples of the Lands until he got around to see to its restoration. Curse of the divine goddess on him and on all his cursed blood!"

Alexander walks around and eyes the old broken temple in the dim light of the fire altar.

This was the sacred temple of his Queen.

"Hephæstion, I want this temple to be restored before my wedding."

"Yes, Alexander."

"Tell Eumenes to send out instructions to the Satraps in Baktria and Sogdiana that all the temples are to be opened again for worship by my order as long as the peace keeps."

"Yes, Alexander."

"Perdikkas, tell all my commanders to tell my men that they are to return anything that has been taken from this old temple.

"No one will be punished, as long as they freely return what they have stolen from the goddess. Everyone will be punished, if the temple goods are not returned."

"Yes, Alexander."

"Hephæstion, talk to this old mage and make a list of whatever should be here and then have Harpalos send gold from Babylon by the royal messenger, to replace what is missing."

"Yes, Alexander."

Alexander takes another look around and then turns and leaves and heads back for the palace. Hephæstion and Perdikkas follow.

MAIN HADIŠ
FOLLOWING DAY
MORNING

"We arrived late last night," Alexander says politely to Aššat Šarri Farânak. "I hope we did not wake you."

A young Makedonian translates in thickly accented, nearly unrecognizable Bakhtrian.

Aššat Šarri Farânak narrows her eyes trying to understand the tongue of the new uštiâmu, but his thick words are unheard in her thin ears. She smiles tactfully and discreetly beckons her maid forward. "Go fetch Polydoros, quickly!"

The young maid runs away.

A few awkward moments pass in silence.

Alexander eyes the mother of his bride with affection.

As Euripides had said in Andromache:

"Choose the daughter of a good mother!"

The gentle woman was so unlike his own fiery mother… she was good, and she was now his mother too.

Aššat Šarri Farânak reads Alexander's eyes and reddens, and casts down her eyes modestly.

A short fleshy old man wearing a Hellene cloth walks mindlessly into the room and rushes to the side of Aššat Šarri Farânak. He takes her hand and speaks robustly in accented Persian. "My Dear Queen, you are not well? The maid told me to come quickly. More headaches? Back pain? Belly ache?"

"I am well, Polydoros." Aššat Šarri Farânak takes a deep breath, relieved, and speaks kindly, pointing to Alexander and the translator. "This is the Lord of Asia and his new interpreter. I have difficulty understanding the poor man. Would you be kind enough to interpret for me?"

Polydoros straightens.

"Ah! Yes! Of course, My Dear Queen, but why not ask—"

"But you have such a nice soothing voice, tempered with such knowledge and wisdom!" Aššat Šarri Farânak interrupts Polydoros and flatters him generously.

"Quite right, My Dear Queen! Youth is not a substitute for worldly knowledge and wisdom!" Polydoros smiles and walks up to the taller man and introduces himself. "My Dear King, I am Polydoros of Athenai. The family healer."

The young translator discreetly points to Alexander with his head and says in a hushed horrified voice, "Not me! Him!"

"I am Alexander, Lord of Asia."

Polydoros turns his head toward the shorter man and bows his head and quickly corrects himself. "O Yes! My Dear King! I am Polydoros from Athenai. The family healer." Polydoros gets a little closer to Alexander and whispers, eyeing the young translator. "The Queen summoned me, because she cannot understand your man over there!"

The face of the young translator reddens. He looks offended and embarrassed in front of Alexander. "But my Baktrian is excellent, Alexander. I have been in Baktria for two years now."

Alexander looks at the young translator. "You are dismissed. I will summon you if I need you later."

Alexander then smiles at Polydoros, "Old Artabazos left for Pergamos when we headed for the Fortress of Sisimitres." He points to Aššat Šarri Farânak. "I was telling the Princess that my kingsmen and I got here late last night and I hope we did not disturb the Princess and the household."

"The King says he hopes he did not wake you up in the middle of the night when he and his men crashed recklessly into the palace grounds, raising the dead!" Polydoros interprets.

"I heard you, My Dear King, and my living quarters are all the way in the back of the palace!" Polydoros says, pointing with his hands without waiting for a response from Aššat Šarri Farânak.

"So, she must have heard you too, she is not deaf, My Dear King, I assure you! I am her healer! She hears quite well, but the Queen is too highborn to say so."

"I see." Alexander smiles.

"We did not hear anything." Aššat Šarri Farânak says agreeably.

"There! See! She says she did not hear anything!" Polydoros nods knowingly.

"We will move to tents outside of the palace walls, once our tents arrive with the rest of the Royal Army. We got here ahead of the baggage train."

"That certainly will be good for the gardens. Having so many men with heavy feet carelessly trampling all around the royal gardens coming and going at all times of night and day will give My Dear Queen a bad headache, and worse, will ruin our beautiful gardens."

Alexander smiles and looks at Polydoros curiously.

"Ah! Yes. I should tell the Queen." Polydoros says absently and turns to Aššat Šarri Farânak. "The Lord of Asia says he and his men will move to tents outside the palace, once their tents arrive."

"That is very considerate of the Lord of Asia."

"She says, *Good!*"

Polydoros counts with his fingers.

"When are your Camp and Court expected, My Dear King? The Persian New Year is coming and it would be good if you could move to your tents before the New Year. The palace and the gardens must be flawless for the Persian New Year!"

Alexander laughs. He is not quite sure what to make of Polydoros.

Was he a Persian-Hellene, or a Hellene-Persian?

"Polydoros, how long have you been here?"

"I used to be the healer of Prince Bessos and other princes when they all lived in the Royal City of Susa. When the Great King gifted Bessos the Satrapy of Baktria and Sogdiana, I came with him. There was a healer from the Two Lands in the court who begged the Great King for the position, but Prince Bessos picked me. He hated the TwoLanders.

"Here he married the pretty princess. Yes, Prince Bessos was given Princess Faranak when he was given the satrapy by the Second Artaxerxes."

He starts counting on his fingers again. "Let me see now, twenty two, no, twenty three years ago, maybe twenty four, yes, twenty four, maybe—"

"I see." Alexander smiles. "Is Roxana still sleeping?"

Did her mother know she was out late last night?

"Our Roxana?" Polydoros narrows his eyes at Alexander for a short moment.

What did the Lord of Asia want with their girl?

He then shrugs his shoulders and laughs. "Oh! No, My Dear King, she is probably in the stables or riding her horse out in the back somewhere."

"He is asking about the whereabouts of Roshanak," Polydoros tells Aššat Šarri Farânak.

"Roxana can ride a horse?"

"O Yes, My Dear King!" Polydoros laughs. "This is Baktria. Everyone can ride a horse here, before they can even walk! The babies are thrown on the backs of the horses right after they are born, and before they are born, they ride horses in the bellies of their mothers! She is better on a horse than some of your companions." He nods and smiles to himself proudly. "The Baktrian boys can shoot an arrow straight before they can walk. If you tell a Baktrian to shoot a man in the eye with an arrow, ten stadia away, do you know what he is going to ask you?"

"No."

"Right eye or left?" Polydoros smiles wickedly.

Alexander narrows his eyes at Polydoros, feeling the pain in his leg.

He knew who Baktrians were. He had been chasing them high and low for nearly three years. He had an arrow wound in his leg that still hurt!

Some archer had asked his commander, "Which leg, Sir?" and the commander had said, "Left."

"Rošanak is sleeping." Aššat Šarri Farânak says with a smile, as soon as Polydoros pauses.

"See! She says Roxana is sleeping, because the girl looks no better than her horse in the mornings and she would be embarrassed if you saw her daughter like that. She just rolls out of her bed and goes to see her horse, no bathing, no scenting, no face paint, no fancy gowns or splendid jewelry."

Polydoros shakes his head side to side with dismay. "A sad case, if you ask me, nothing like her blood sister who was perfection before she died.

"Roxana would have been lashed and whipped by the order of the Great King, if she lived at a proper Persian Royal Court. Here, her father was too indulgent with her, he indulged her, yes, spoiled to the bone, truly! Being the lastborn to her birth mother, she got away with everything. I feel sorry for her poor husband. She will drive him mad!"

"I am her husband!"

"Huh? Ah!" Polydoros goes quiet for a short moment, stunned. He looks at Alexander keenly and then collects himself and turns toward Aššat Šarri Farânak.

No one had told him anything about this.

"The Lord of Asia says he is married to our Roshanak."

"Not yet. We told him if her royal grandmother gives her blessing for the wedding, then our holy man will pick a blessed date after No'rouz."

"She says," Polydoros says cautiously, "that you are not married yet."

He had heard of Alexander's fiery reputation.

Alexander looks puzzled.

"We got married at the House of Oxyartes, after the Sogdian Rock surrendered," he says, nodding his head.

"I cut a loaf of bread in half and gave her a piece and she took a bite. It was not the ceremonial bread though," he mumbles.

"Ah! The Lord of Asia says he cut the bread in half, gave her a piece and she took a bite."

Aššat Šarri Farânak looks confused. She looks at Alexander, eyes widen, mouth slightly open, skin paling.

"My Dear Queen, these Makedonians are UpLanders. They are not refined like the Athenians and the rest of the Hellene MainLanders. They have a drunken feast, cut a loaf of bread in half with a sword, I think a loaf of olive bread, or maybe a sweet cake, who knows, and drink pure wine until they all pass out on couches or on the floor and they consider themselves married. Totally barbaric, if you ask me!"

Aššat Šarri Farânak pales, becomes white as a ghost.

"It was just a small loaf of honey sweetened sesame cake, served after the mid-day meal with sweet wine—"

Alexander looks at Aššat Šarri Farânak, sensing her anguish.

He should have brought Hephæstion with him. He was good at fixing this sort of trouble.

"My Dear King, of course a union between the Lord of Asia and our Princess could bring nothing but good to us all. The wedding ritual itself is more symbolic, but—"

"But what?"

"The sacred Persian wedding ritual is rather obligatory, if you want to bed your bride. Do you wish to bed your bride, My Dear King?"

Silence.

Alexander narrows his eyes at Polydoros.

He hated weddings.

During the last wedding feast he had attended, the wedding of his sister to his uncle, his father was assassinated.

And the one before that was the wedding feast of his father to Kleopatra, during which Attalos had called him a bastard and his lame father, loaded with wine, had tried to kill him! It was the night he had taken his mother and left Pella in sheer anger and hatred and rage. The night that had broken his bond with his father forever.

His father had deliberately dishonored him in front of his entire royal court.

And he had never cared to ask about the wedding customs of the Persians.

Alexander looks back at Aššat Šarri Farânak. "I have never seen a Persian wedding. Herodotos said—"

"Herodotos! O Yes, the teller of tall tales!" Polydoros says, shaking his head side-to-side with dismay.

"Forget Herodotos, My Dear King! The man was kicked out of Halikarnassos by the Persian Satrap of Karia. He must have written his whole book somewhere in the back woods of Alinda, without ever setting foot in the heartland of the Persians.

"If he ever got as far as Babylon, he probably fell into the first brothel on his way and never left it! Or he was kicked out when his gold ran out, if he had any! Or he was blind, like Homer!" Polydoros says confidently. "He wrote: *Even the greatest kings lose everything*. Are you planning to lose everything, My Dear King?"

Polydoros pauses and catches his breath and eyes Alexander intently under his old brows.

A maid offers Alexander a cup of wine. He takes the cup and takes a sip, eyeing Polydoros.

Hellenes!

They always envied the good fortune of others and resented those stronger than themselves! Themistokles, the victor at Salamis, was rewarded by Athenians to a life in exile. He had fled Athenai and had ended up in Susa in the service of the Son of Xerxes and had finally died in exile. Hellenes never allowed him to return to Athenai… the city he had saved had banished him without pity!

But the Spartans… they were equally arrogant and greedy and corruptible. But they were great warriors… they used to be the greatest of all the warriors… that was all they knew how to do!

They could have sent twenty five thousand to fight the Persians at Thermopylæ, but thinking it was a lost battle they could not win, they only sent one of their kings with 300 men who had already fathered sons.

What was 300 to a real royal army? A thousand of his best warriors guarded him even before the battle from the time of answering the call of nature before arm and armor.

Well, the 300 were ordered by their king to die at Thermopylæ and they did! And there were two thousand and one hundred helots, seven for each Spartan, as Spartans were not raised to do anything else but fight… win or die… and seven thousand Boeotians too. Spartans always fought separately from others and were not in the habit of counting anyone but themselves… they did not have enough fingers among them to count!

Afterward, the Spartans had gladly taken Persian gold and slaughtered Hellenes for it. After the Battle at Granikos, he himself had sent 300 golden Persian arm and armor to Athenai to be dedicated to the Goddess Athena, with his words written on them:

ALEXANDER, SON OF PHILIP, AND THE HELLENES,
EXCEPT FOR THE SPARTANS, DEDICATED THESE.

And everyone in Hellas knew what his words meant.

Spartans had failed the Hellenes again, but this time they no longer mattered.

It was now the sun of the Makedonians that shone over all of Hellas.

Makedonians were the best of the great warriors!

Polydoros continues, shaking his head.

"Ha! They should have carved on their stone grave markers:

GO TELL THE SPARTANS, WE TOLD THE PERSIANS
TO COME AND GET OUR ARMS IF THEY WANTED THEM
AND THEY DID.
AND SO HERE WE LIE DEAD, BECAUSE
EVERYONE ELSE HAD GONE TO THE OLYMPIC GAMES
TO WIN AN OLIVE WREATH.

"The only wreath those fools should be crowned with is one given for dim-witted stubbornness!"

Alexander narrows his eyes and looks at him curiously. He silently sips his wine.

Like all Hellenes, he hated the Spartans too! They had not joined the League of Korinth and Philip had rightly ignored them. The time of their glory was long behind them, their sons had grown unworthy of their fathers. They had been defeated by the Theban Sacred Band and the Sacred Band had fallen to his own sword.

From a total of 300, 254 Theban of the Sacred Band had been cut to pieces by him and his men in the Battle of Chæronea; the rest were captured alive, before they could kill themselves. Their grave marker read:

HERE WE LIE DEAD, SO HELLENES CAN BE FREE.
OUR GLORY WILL NEVER FADE.

Well, Spartans were not the only dim-witted Hellenes.

It was only his glory that would never fade.

And yes… Hellenes could be free, as long as they were his obedient subjects.

Nothing was free!

Still… He had been rash when he had said: Antipatros had won a Battle of Mice when he had defeated the Spartan King, the Third Agis, and his men who had taken arms against Makedon with Persian gold after he had left for Asia.

He knew Spartans had no fear of death on the fields of battle, it was how they achieved their glory. They were either victorious or they were dead. And now they were mostly dead.

Spartans were not mice… they were lions who had feasted on rats for far too long.

"I—" Aššat Šarri Farânak tries to get the attention of the men.

Polydoros rambles on, after catching his breath. "Herodotos probably had a green beard, a pot belly and smelled like a goat. Skulls of the Persians are soft because they wear a cap! Absurd! Really! I would have liked to crack his damn skull to see how hard his head was! Now Xenophon, My Dear King, he was a noble Athenian, like me!"

"Polydoros!" Aššat Šarri Farânak finally interrupts and rises to her feet, smiling graciously.

"Please tell the King I will send for Uxšiyârta and we can entertain the Lord of Asia tonight for the night meal."

"She says Oxyartes will be here tonight. You should come back then."

Alexander looks back at the Aššat Šarri Farânak.

She bows her head slightly.

Alexander smiles. He puts down his half-full wine cup and turns around and leaves.

Next time he will come with Hephæstion. He was good with Persians… and with Baktrians.

HADIŠ HORSE STABLES

LATER

"She rides a horse," Alexander mumbles as he walks down the steps and heads right toward the royal stables behind the main palace.

His horse, Bukephalas, was there and it was a perfectly good reason to visit the stables unannounced.

Royal grooms had taken good care of Bukephalas when he had stayed in the palace before, feeding him green horse food and brushing and washing him daily.

A pair of royal boys follow him. He stops.

He was always followed.

"I am just going to the stables to check on Bukephalas! You are dismissed."

The royal boys look at each other. "But, Sir!"

Alexander gives them both a sharp look and they both step back. "Yes, Sir!"

Alexander dismisses the royal guards too and then turns and heads towards the stables. He walks into the stables and the royal grooms all bow and point to the stall where Bukephalas was being kept. He looks around.

No sign of Roxana!

If that Hellene fool was making light of him, he would put him on the Makedonian rack!

"Ah!" Rošanak walks out of one of the stalls, pulling a white horse behind her without looking and runs right into Alexander.

"Roxana!"

Rošanak quickly takes a step backward, surprised, and stops in her tracks motionlessly.

Alexander stares at her with frustration and twists his lips.

He should not have dismissed the damn interpreter.

How was he going to talk to her now?

They both look around wondering what to do next.

Rošanak steps forward and tries to go around Alexander, but Alexander blocks her way. Rošanak steps backward and bites her lip and then tries again. Alexander blocks her again.

Awkward silence.

White horse neighs.

Rošanak finally relents. "This is my horse," she says slowly and cautiously in accented Attik.

Alexander is surprised to hear her speak Attik. "You speak Attik?"

"Not well!" She hesitates. "Our family healer, Polydoros, is from Erchia, a small village close to Athenai. He has been tutoring me." Rošanak speaks slowly, minding her every word, carefully stringing them together like beads on a golden chain.

"I see." Alexander eyes her intently.

Polydoros had not mentioned Roxana could speak Attik.

"We were at the Fortress of Sogdiana in the middle of nowhere for almost two years, with not much else to do. My mother told Polydoros to teach me his mother tongue."

"I see." Alexander eyes her more intently.

The Princess-Mother had not mentioned Roxana could speak Attik.

"Polydoros is short and fleshy and has never been too popular with Persian women. Ah! Or with any woman! So the first story he read to me in his tongue was the story of the first woman, Pandora, created by Hephæstos by the order of Zeus, and her mysterious jar filled with all the troubles gods could unleash upon men."

She pauses and eyes Alexander, who is listening to her patiently. She smiles and continues with more confidence. "Polydoros says that all the troubles in the world are unleashed by women upon poor unsuspecting men. He says even his gods are not beyond the mysterious spells cast by troublesome women!"

Alexander relaxes and smiles.

True!

The old Hellene spoke his mind.

He had stacks of letters from old Antipatros complaining about all the troubles his own birth mother was making for him, trying to tell him what to do.

He also had stacks of letters from his birth mother, complaining about old Antipatros acting more like a king than a regent.

"He probably has heard of my mother."

"Polydoros says I speak Attik as well as the barbarian slaves in the marketplace of Athenai."

"I would have him lashed for insulting you."

"No! Polydoros speaks the truth. I know my tongue is flawed. I come here and force my poor horse to listen to me practice." Rošanak caresses the mane of her horse and rests her head on his neck. "Even my Persian is accented, I am told. I speak Persian with a Baktrian accent, speak Baktrian with a Persian accent, and I am not quite sure what I sound like in your tongue," she says, shaking her head.

Alexander stares at her, captivated.

Polydoros was right about her clothes but he could not see paint improving upon her wondrous beauty. She looked even more beautiful than he remembered.

She was generous with her gods and goddesses and she loved horses and she was beautiful... beyond words.

Alexander narrows his eyes at her.

"Why did you not mention you could understand me?"

"I do not trust myself with your tongue. I have no talent for other tongues besides my own mother tongue. I do not speak anything all that well," she says, "and I do not understand your tongue completely, especially when you speak to your own men, I am totally lost."

"My native tongue is Makedonian."

He pauses and wonders if she understood what he meant.

Rošanak looks at Alexander intently.

"My kingsmen, the ones you have seen, are all Makedonians," he says, speaking slowly.

"Hephæstion is half-Makedonian, but he was born in Makedonia of a Makedonian mother and speaks Makedonian like his mother tongue. So we all speak Makedonian. But Attik is a more common tongue. Everyone speaks a little Attik, even the slaves in the Agora of Athenai. Artabazos and other interpreters speak Attik. So, we speak Attik, when it needs to be interpreted."

"I see."

"Your Attik is good enough though." Alexander steps closer and caresses the mane of Rošanak's horse. "Is this your horse?"

"Yes, this is my horse. He is called: Saiyma Aspa, Silver Horse. But I call him Šâru. It means *wind* in Babylonian. He is faster than all Baktrian horses. He rides like the wind!"

"Magnificent horse. A white pure-bred Nisæan steed."

"Yes, he is pure-bred, not a half-breed like me! My father, the Fifth Artaxerxes, was the second brother of King Darius. And my mother is a Baktrian Princess. So, I am a half-breed by birth, one-half Baktrian and one-half Persian. Some days I am more Baktrian, other days I am more Persian, never whole. One foot on this side, the other foot on that side."

Alexander smiles.

"I am a half-breed too, half-Makedonian and half-Molossian. My father, Philip, was half-Makedonian and my mother, Olympias, is a princess of Epiros bordering Makedonia, from the Royal House of Molossia."

Rošanak looks at Alexander admiring her horse.

"Utâna was my oldest brother of a different mother and father. This is his horse. My brother Utâna loved this horse. Šâru came back to the stables after Utâna was killed in the battle, in the mountains of Baktria."

"The horse found his way back, all this way?"

"Yes! The soul of the dead roams the earth for three days after the death of the body. I think the soul of my brother rode his horse back home and left him in my care.

"They told me when I was at the Fortress of Sogdiana. I have been taking care of him ever since I got back. I missed him bitterly when I was staying at the Fortress, knowing he was here at the stables."

The grooms had hidden her horse well so he would not fall into the hands of the enemy invaders.

Alexander points to the stall housing his horse.

"The Thessalian Philonikos offered Bukephalas to Philip, my father. But no man could ride him. I wagered thirteen talents that I could. I saw that Bukephalas was afraid of his own shadow, so I kept him facing the sun, to keep his shadow behind him. He has been mine since I was thirteen."

Rošanak has seen his horse.

He obviously loved his horse, as she did hers. But his poor horse was no bigger than a Persian mule, much smaller than hers, a real horse.

Someone should have gotten him a proper Persian Nisâya horse.

No wonder Persians had not taken to him. Royal Sons of the House only rode pure-bred horses from Nišaya, on the other side of the Royal City of Hagmâtâna.

Other horses were not worthy of the Great Kings… or the Royal Sons.

They said he had threatened to annihilate an entire tribe of horse thieves when they had stolen his favorite horse and he had killed a few of the thieves he had caught to show the rest of them his resolve. Those idiot horse thieves should not have wasted their worthless blood stealing a little mule! They should have been hanged for their stupidity!

Only magnificent Persian Nisâya horses were worthy of being stolen!

Rošanak's horse neighs and pushes her forward with his head. She bows her head slightly. "Ah! Well, it is time for my morning ride. Good day, Alexander!"

"May I ride with you?" Alexander asks cautiously.

Rošanak is surprised. She considers him for a moment and then says in a low voice, "The marriage alliance is to stop the bloodshed. You do not even have to lay eyes upon me after the marriage ceremony. Nor I, on you."

"I wish it to be a real marriage," Alexander says quietly, keeping his eyes locked on her intently.

"A real marriage?" Rošanak says faintly and eyes Alexander, startled.

Stunned silence.

Rošanak tosses and turns the words on the tip of her tongue.

Attik was a difficult tongue… too direct for Persians…

In Persian tongue, nothing spoken in words quite meant what was heard.

Every Persian word had multiple meanings, only decipherable to Persians in the context and tone and manner spoken. An art not mastered by the men who were not from the Lands, who were not Persians.

What did he mean by a real marriage?

She stares back at him, not knowing what to think.

Was he mocking her?

They were in the middle of the horse stables. She was wearing old worn out clothes of her brothers and the mane of her horse looked better than her hair.

"Does the King demand as a conqueror, or ask as a lover?"

For a moment neither speaks. Both eye each other intently.

"If as a conqueror, then take me here and now and be done!"

"I do not want a sacrificial offering. I want to see desire for me in your eyes when I take you into my arms as my wife. Conquering king can command marriage but not pleasure, and pleasure forced by the tip of the sword holds no interest for me." Alexander eyes her carefully. "Just having you is not enough!"

Rošanak narrows her eyes at him and interprets his big words in her small head.

"A lover then. Tell me, why should I make a gift of myself to a man who has killed my father and my blood brothers and my other brothers, and has made the sons of my sister fatherless and motherless?"

Alexander is taken back.

This was not courtship… this was war!

But this was a tongue he understood completely!

This small enemy had baited him with eyes the colors of the young trees of ancient forest groves of the LowLands and the HighLands and with the sweetest voice she had lured him into her fold. True to his nature, he had rushed carelessly straight into the center of the small enemy line and she had effortlessly rolled her flanks on both sides, left and right, and encircled him. And now she was daring him to a single battle.

Alexander looks around him.

He was totally cut off from the rest of his men. No one was following him.

Did she think he was not up to the challenge by himself?

"Roxana. By the gods. I ask you as a man who is a king. The undoing of your father was by his own hands. Bessos executed King Darius and declared himself King Artaxerxes, King of Kings. He warred upon me. At the end, his men betrayed him and delivered him into my hands. He did not repent, he did not ask for my mercy. What was I to do with him then?"

Rošanak narrows her eyes at Alexander again. She only half understands his swift words. "My Attik is not that good. Could you please speak a little slower?"

Alexander takes a deep breath. "There can be only one King of the Persians!" He says a little slower, "As the rightful King of the Persian Empire, I had to avenge the death of Darius. I cannot undo what is done. But, by Zeus, I will protect you and yours from further harm."

He had not known Bessos had the most beautiful daughter in all his lands.

"Ask me for anything and everything you wish, for I shall grant them, and whatever else you can persuade me to give you, is yours!"

"What of the sons of my sister, Dârâ and Nimâ? Will you demand them as hostages to ensure my loyalty?"

"No! They can remain here freely with our mother!" Alexander says without hesitation.

"And my brothers, Oštana and Itâna. Itâna is just a boy."

"The oldest can stay in my Royal Army and proves himself, if he wishes. The younger boy can stay with his father."

"And what of the Palace at Baktra?"

"Yours."

"And what of the fate of the Baktrians?"

"If they honor the peace agreement through the hands of their Queen, then by gods, I will treat them as I would the Hellenes."

But not as well as the Makedonians.

Rošanak bites her lip.

There must be something that he will refuse her.

"Two years of bloody battles has left the satrapy with thousands and thousands of sons with no fathers. How will fatherless sons become men and take their place among honorable men?"

Even though she thought Itâna was an idiot and would never amount to anything, even with a father breathing down his neck day and night.

Alexander considers her for a moment.

Why not?

"I will take all the best of the Baktrian fatherless boys into my Royal Army. I swear by Zeus-Ammon, that they will be trained the same as any Makedonian boy."

Rošanak eyes him.

That was not a bad bargain. After all, Persians had lost a few battles to this man and the Bakhtrians could do well to learn something from the victors.

"It is the duty of the king to provide a rightful heir for the Lands. Kings have many wives and some have many women of the court to ensure many sons are born to the king, but the king has only one queen consort." Rošanak looks him in the eye. "What will I be to you? A woman of the court, a wife, or a Royal Woman?"

"You will be my Queen."

Rošanak's knees go weak. She cannot think of anything else to ask for.

"My tongue will never flatter you!"

"There is an army of men flattering me day and night and in between!"

The whole world, it seemed, either fought him or flattered him.

She pauses and then relents. "If I can bear no sons for you, then I will release you of your oath to me, so you can father sons by another wife."

"By my honor, I accept your terms."

"Very well then, my dowry will be the peace agreement."

"And the bride-price will be the Palace at Baktra, the Baktrian fatherless boys and the freedom of your kinsmen, and quarters for the Baktrian warriors."

Rošanak takes a deep breath and stands there stunned.

"Now, may I ride with you?"

"Will you honor your words even if I die?" she asks quietly.

Alexander looks at her, surprised. "You said," checking to see if he had heard her correctly, "die?"

Rošanak nods guardedly.

"As your king and husband, I order you not to die!"

Rošanak narrows her eyes at him intently.

"I will bargain with Hades. He can have anything he wants in exchange for your life. I am the Lord of Asia. I have everything that is to be had by a king and more."

Rošanak looks at him blankly.

Who was Hades?

Ah! The Lord of Darkness… the Dark Lord of the Hellenes…

Why would he bargain with the Lord of Darkness for her life?

"Will you or not?" She ignores his words and demands an answer of him.

Alexander considers her for a short moment.

She looked serious enough.

"Yes. I am not fickle like the gods. What I agree to, I agree to for eternity." And he means it.

"Now may I ride with you?"

Rošanak stares deep into Alexander's eyes, considering him for a moment, and then points with her fingers.

"Your eyes are odd! This one is the color of the early morning dawning sky and that one is the color of the late night darkening sky."

Alexander is taken off guard. He smiles sweetly. "No one has ever said that to my face!"

"How do you see the world with eyes of different colors?"

"As I have always seen the world."

A moment of silence passes between them.

"Well, come then!" Rošanak says with her hands, "Do you play Chogân?"

"Show… gaan?"

"Ah! No? I will show you!"

Rošanak puts a weathered oxen skin saddlecloth on her horse.

Alexander brings out Bukephalas from his stall. A palace groom rushes over and puts a blanket on the horse.

Rošanak stops. She looks at Alexander's horse.

The smallish noble horse was branded with the mark of his ancestry on his forehead.

Dark as the darkest night, the horse looked proud and noble, not ashamed of his size, facing her bigger, light as day, white horse.

She steps over and stands before Alexander's horse and lets him smell her and take a good look at her.

Bukephalas smells Rošanak and then nuzzles her neck gently.

Rošanak raises her hand and gently strokes his newly brushed mane, cleaned and washed just like her Šâru.

She loved horses… all horses… size did not matter… much…

Alexander eyes Bukephalas.

His horse had just fallen in love with her too.

Rošanak turns and walks up to an elaborate wooden closet and opens the carved doors. A row of long wooden sticks with beautifully carved mallet-heads were hanging on a wooden rack, waiting obediently to be called into service.

She pulls one out and hands it to Alexander.

Alexander takes the wooden stick and looks at it curiously.

The head of the mallet was an ornately carved lion.

Rošanak takes another one for herself and picks up a round ball from the shelf on the bottom of the wooden closet and closes the closet door.

"Follow me, Alexander. This way." Rošanak pulls her horse's bridle and leaves the hadiš stable. "Šâru, come."

Alexander follows her, holding the wooden stick in his hand, pulling Bukephalas behind him.

Rošanak crosses a long dirt path overgrown with old berry bushes, opens a weathered ornate metal gate and walks into a vast lush field. "This field is not kept well these days, as my father and brothers—" Rošanak bites her lip and does not finish her words.

No one had played on this field after her blood brothers had died years ago… A few old goats used to graze on the overgrown field before they were eaten by the invaders.

Alexander follows her without asking any questions.

He had seen this field before, but had not examined it too closely. It was a large flat field obscured by trees and overgrown thorny bushes. He had thought one day it could be cleared and used for Royal Army Foot and Horse races.

Rošanak stops and points to an old inscription on a stone marker next to the chogân Field.

"It is written in Âryâ, the royal tongue of the First Darius. It is a royal honor and privilege for the satraps to use the royal markings of the Great Kings of the Persians."

Alexander's eyes follow her around.

She steps closer and rubs the tips of her fingers on the carved markings.

[illegible]
[illegible]
[illegible]

And then she interprets:

Let others play other things.
The King of Games is still the Game of Kings.

Rošanak proudly declares, "Chogân is the game of kings!" and points to the lush overgrown field stretching before their eyes, under the golden rays of the mid-morning sun. "The chogân field is about nine hundred arašni long from this side of the field to the other side and two hundred seventy arašni wide from that side to this side and at each end the stone bâji posts are fifteen arašni apart."

She had no idea how to measure and then translate those measurements into his tongue.

She only knew how to measure everything with her own eyes and hands and feet.

She could not count in his tongue either.

She eyes Alexander intently, not certain he understands her words, and then shrugs her shoulders, walks toward the middle of the field, stomps on the grass, places the rounded ball in the center of the field and starts walking back.

She points to the ball.

"This is a simple war game. It starts with the ball placed in the middle of the battle ground. The two opposing armies charge each other from the opposite sides. The one throwing the highest number of balls into the stone bâji posts in the land of her enemy wins!"

"Very well." Alexander nods in agreement.

Rošanak jumps on her horse, grabs the bridle and rides to the other side of the field.

Alexander smiles, mounts Bukephalas and arrays himself opposite Rošanak on his side of the field.

Rošanak calls out loudly to Alexander from the other side.

"Stay as you are, Alexander, and there is peace between us. Move forward or backward and there is war!"

Alexander raises his eyebrow and half-smiles to himself.

Her Attik was better than the barbarian slaves in the Agora of Athenai.

She knew Xenophon.

"The view of the King is the same as yours," he taunts her loudly. "Stay as we are and there is peace. Move and there is war!"

"WAR or PEACE?" Rošanak demands again louder.

Alexander smiles and waits and baits her.

"Which is your pleasure, Alexander?"

Sun waxes warmer, a cool breeze blows.

Alexander stirs forward on Bukephalas.

Rošanak nods and smiles and calls out to Alexander.

"Very well, then, Alexander. So be it. War it is!"

Rošanak gallops to the ball first and hits it into Alexander's land.

After all, her horse was a splendid pure-bred Nisâya, bred and raised on fields of pure luscious asp'asta, not a puny mule bred and raised on tasteless dry hay.

TEMPLE of DIVINE GODDESS ÂNÂHITÂ

FOLLOWING NIGHT

Sleeping sky.

"Ah!"

Rošanak fumbles in the darkness of the night, searching for the familiar crack in the door to the Temple of Divine Goddess Ânâhitâ. The old broken door feels new and solid, the old crack is gone.

"It was right here. Where did it go?" she mumbles to herself.

... of all nights... why tonight? How will she get in now?

She runs her hands over the new wooden door, searching for the mayûxa. She must get into the âyadana!

"Ahhh!" she sighs in pain, feeling a sharp wood splinter piercing through the soft skin in the palm of her hand. "Damn Artâvazda to Hell!" she curses under her lips and then immediately regrets it.

This was a hallowed place, the home of the divine goddess, not to be desecrated with curses or words of evil.

"Forgive me, Divine Ânâhitâ!" she utters quietly under her breath, still searching. She finally feels the smooth and rounded mayûxa and smiles to herself.

Her goddess must have heard her and forgiven her, guided her fingers and given her passage inside her sacred temple.

She slowly opens the door and cautiously steps inside, not knowing what to expect. She is immediately awed and amazed. "Ah!"

In the dim light of a few candles burning and glowing in the old stâna carved into the walls, the âyadana almost looked as it did before it was sacked by the Makedonians.

She was just here days ago and had seen for herself how the sacred âyadana had been desecrated, but now it was swept up and clean and fragrant... warm and holy again... the way it looked the last night she was there before leaving for sanctuary in the Rock of Sughud.

The once broken statue of the Divine Goddess Ânâhitâ stood tall and divinely in the middle of the âyadana, resting whole on its solid stony base.

She steps closer to the statue and looks up with delight and wonder.

All the broken pieces were mended and the missing stone chunks were filled in by expert hands.

The offerings she had brought days ago looked even more splendid... the golden wreath crown sat divinely on the head of the goddess and the golden fringed shawl wrapped wonderfully around her.

Not one, but two new silver fire altar flanked the statue of the goddess on each side, with fragrant incense crackling among the smoldering sacred fire embers.

Had angels come down from Heaven to mend her broken goddess?

The familiar scent of precious incense dances into Rošanak's body. She looks beyond the statue.

Tall new white linen curtains embroidered with golden stars hung from the ceiling to the ground behind the statue.

Behind the curtains were small chambers used mostly for storage, now hidden from view, quietly guarding their old secrets.

Rošanak looks at the palm of her hand and pulls out the wooden splinter with the tip of her nails in the light of the fire altars and her eyes turn back to the statue. Something new catches a corner of her eyes.

New words were carved on the stony base of the goddess in front.

She steps closer; it was in Attik.

She rubs her fingers on the carving, sounding out the words that were hard to see in the dim light of the âyadana.

She reads out the dipî quietly under her breath.

ALEXANDER, THE LORD OF ASIA,
RESTORED THIS SACRED TEMPLE
FOR THE LOVE OF HIS QUEEN, ROXANA OF BAKTRIA.
WHOEVER DESECRATES THIS TEMPLE,
THIS GODDESS WILL SEE TO HIM.

"Ah!" Rošanak sighs, stunned, and her heart sinks to the bottoms of her feet.

Alexander had ordered the restoration.

How did he know?

She had said nothing to him about her sacred âyadana.

She rubs her fingers once more on the carving and then steps back. Tears stream silently on her face. She clasps her hands in front of her, bows her head and starts praying:

> *"I worship the Wise Lord, the Lord of all the Lands and all the Great Kings.*
>
> *"My Lord, remember my good words and my good deeds… forgive me my evil words and my evil thoughts and my evil deeds…"*

She stops and her mind wanders.

Alexander had repeated the terms he had agreed to in front of her blood mother and her father, interpreted and translated twice by Polydoros and herself. All written down and signed properly and sealed with the King's signet ring, and in return they had agreed to the wedding to be held as soon as possible.

The diviners and the seers and the charters had all agreed on the first day deemed 'favored by the stars' and the wedding day was set for seven days hence.

And the whole hadiš had flown into a wild frenzy preparing for the wedding. A row of young girls had been brought in to weave the virgin white ceremonial silk carpet. The Chief Gardener was frantically running around the gardens with a small army of gardeners, fixing and pruning and planting.

She had thought she had more time… she had thought her blood mother would not agree to the wedding before the Festival of No'rouz.

No'rouz was coming in a few weeks… and No'rouz was her favorite time of the year… she wanted to see No'rouz again… celebrated like the olden days one last time… But she had run out of time.

She takes a deep breath and looks up at the divine goddess through the blur of her teary eyes.

Her goddess knew!

Divine Ânâhitâ was an ancient goddess… older than the living memory…

They said that one could only pray for the Persian King of Kings and the Lands of the Persians to the Wise Lord.

So women prayed to the Divine Ânâhitâ for things more near and dear to their hearts… for love and for sons and for healthy babies and for safe birthing… and for handsome lovers and for faithful husbands and for beauty to keep their husbands faithful…

Even men prayed to the goddess for what was near and dear to their hearts… for honor and for loyalty and for bravery… and for the favor of the Great King… and for sons and for love and for devoted wives and for strong bodies to keep their wives devoted to them…

She was standing in the same place praying as she had that night in former days.

She had felt familiar loving arms wrapping around her, and the scent of him she had loved with every breath…

"Rošanak."

"Utâna."

"Are you praying for me?"

"No!"

"Liar!"

Utâna showers her neck with sweet kisses.

"Not here… the old athravan will see us!"

"I gave the old man a handful of silver archers and told him to go buy incense and flowers for the âyadana. He will not be back until morning. He well remembers his own young days when he was in love himself."

"I am worth only a handful of silver coins to you?"

"No! I think I paid too much!"

"Utâna!" she says with displeasure and jabs him in his side with her elbow.

"Ouch! Yes… way too much!"

"Someone will walk in to pray!"

"I have locked the front door!"

"Utâna! This is a holy âyadana!"

"Holy Temple of Love. No one prays late at night like you. They are all home tending to their husbands in their laps!"

"Utâna!"

And he had closed her nervous mouth quickly with a sweet kiss.

Rošanak pushes back tears and thinks about another inscription on the back of the statue.

She slowly walks around the statue and kneels down and touches the stony base lovingly.

The dipî was still there… still remained sweetly carved on the back of the stony base…

She knows it word for word by heart.

She had scorned Utâna for spoiling the statue of the divine goddess with a love poem in her name and Utâna had laughed and said:

"Even angry gods are moved by the sweet words of love!"

She reads it again.

Rošanak,
Emerald-eyed,
Ruby-lipped,
Yâsmin-haired,
Moon-faced,
Willowy,
Heavenly beauty,
What is day without sun?
What is night without moon?
What is life without love?
What is land without water?
… Heaven without little stars?
… Man without woman?
… eyes without tears?
… lips without kisses?
You pour your sweet wine,
And I drink it all…
And the more I drink…
… the thirstier I become…

Utâna
𐎢𐎫𐎠𐎴

She kisses the cold stone and utters a prayer for Utâna. Then she gets to her feet and walks toward the edge of the tall white curtain behind the statue and slips quietly behind the snowy linen.

It was dimmer behind the curtains, but her eyes were now used to the dim light of the âyadana. The doors to all the small rooms were closed.

She quietly knocks on the first door.

Silence.

She knocks again and then she slowly turns the mayûxa and opens the second door.

The room, the largest among all the small rooms, once occupied by an old Zarathuštra Athravan, was now all empty.

She slowly closes the door and walks toward the third door and stands motionless.

Âyadana was empty.

She then leans forward and slowly opens the door, hesitating for a moment not knowing what to expect, but the third room is also empty.

She steps inside the room.

The old silver altar that used to guard the statue of the divine goddess sits quietly by the high window, catching rays of the silvery moon.

A beam of moonlight dances and sways in the darkness and wraps around her body.

She takes a deep breath and does not hesitate. It takes less than a passing moment and is nearly painless. She looks at her wrists. They look ivory pale in the light of the silvery moon. Then blood, looking purplish, almost the color of royal purple, starts to flow from her wrists, falling silently to the ground. Her eyes track the blood drops, losing them in the darkness by her feet.

They said the precious royal purple from Şurru was the color of the blood of the kings… not purple but purplish red and they were right. They said when Şurru was captured by Alexander, the waters around the island were the color of royal purple, from the blood of all who were slaughtered by the Makedonians… they said some eight thousand men and women and children had bled to death into the waters around Şurru.

She rubs her fingers lovingly on her gown, a Persian purple royal gown, embroidered with golden lotus flowers, a wedding gift sent to her from the Royal City of Çûšâ by her royal grandmother who had agreed to her marriage alliance.

She had always wanted one… but she was never old enough to have one and then the war had come…

She gently puts the small Persian dagger in the basin of the old silver altar. Her blood drips into the ancient holy altar. She utters quietly under her lips. "Divine Ânâhitâ, forgive me."

She looks up at the moon shining through the window and then sits down. The floor under her body feels cold and damp. Her mind wanders back to that blessed night.

Utâna had pulled her by her hand to this very room.

Her heart had skipped a few beats when he had opened the door.

Inside the light of small candles flickered all around the room… a thick silk snow white blanket was spread on the floor, over another thick blanket, nearly covering the entire room, the cool white silk linen cradling fragrant yâsmins and orange blossoms from this end to the other end…

A wedding bed…

"I picked the yâsmins from your gardens and the orange blossoms from my gardens," Utâna had whispered sweetly in her ear.

It was early summer…

The small room smelled like the sacred fire, anointed generously with white yâsmins and orange blossoms, mixed in with the sweet night air coming through the window from the high mountains. It was quiet too… a night just like tonight…

Utâna had embraced her from the back, holding her tightly, resting his head on her shoulders, and whispering sweet love words in her ears, while tying a silky shimmery white thread around her right wrist… his hands trembling… his voice quivering…

"In the name of the Wise Lord, take my hand and take my love and grant me yours."

Rošanak closes her eyes. Her heart races just as it did that night. She opens her eyes and looks down at her wrists. Her tears fall on her wrist and mix carelessly with her blood. She closes her eyes again and rests her head back against the cold wall and remembers more.

The room begins to smell like fragrant yâsmin and orange blossoms.

Almost all of the men who had gone to war had died… all her blood brothers and her blood father… only her Utâna had come back and he was returning to fight more too. What use was waiting?

So, in this room, in the house of the sacred divine mother goddess, she had made a gift of her virginity to Utâna and he had showered her with all his love and had promised her a big wedding when he returned.

Her blood mother had told her blood sister the night before her sister's wedding… she had said the first union would be awkward and painful…

But she had felt no pain… just a slight pressure at first and then filled with heavenly pleasure.

The pain had only come when they had to part before dawn. She was meant for him and he was meant for her… she had loved him as long as she could remember… their lives were knotted together since childhood… brother and sister of different fathers and mothers.

She had hoped and prayed every day for a child… a son…

But it was not meant to be.

He had died in battle in the middle of the winter.

The divine goddess had blessed her that night only with the pleasure of love because she knew of the pain that would come with Utâna's death.

"What are you doing here?" Uxšiyârta grunts scornfully. "I have been looking for you everywhere!"

Rošanak opens her eyes in stunned silence.

Her memories break into pieces, shatter like kâsaka.

"Baktra is swarming with godless enemy invaders!" he yells at her.

"Do you know what these men would do to a girl wandering the streets alone in the middle of the night?"

Rošanak pulls away from him, edging closer into the darkness.

"Get up! Your mother is waiting for you. She is worried sick!"

"Nooo!"

Uxšiyârta bends down and grabs her hands to pull her to her feet. He smells the blood before he feels it on her wrists. He sinks to his knees next to her in horror and pulls her wrists into the moonlight.

Fresh blood. Still dripping from her fresh cuts.

His eyes widen with fear and fright.

"What have you done to yourself, Daughter? Why?"

Rošanak tries to pull away without answering.

Uxšiyârta holds on to her firmly and asks again more forcefully, "Why?"

She cries harder.

Uxšiyârta lets go of her wrists and without hesitating pulls out his dagger from his belt and slashes the hem of her precious gown. He pulls one of her wrists and starts wrapping it with the strip of royal purple cloth.

Tyrian royal purple wraps tightly around Persian royal blood.

Royal red hemmed in by royal purple…

Rošanak resists and tries to pull away.

Uxšiyârta tightens his hold on her.

She moans in pain. "Please! Let me die!"

"Be still, child! You shall not die by your own hands and condemn your immortal soul to eternal darkness!"

"Abû, please!"

Uxšiyârta slashes another piece of her precious gown and starts wrapping the other bleeding wrist. He softens his voice. "Rošanak, getting married is nothing to fear!"

"Please!" Rošanak pleads, sobbing quietly.

"The Makedonian does not look like a rough man in bed." Uxšiyârta tries to console her. "Are you scared of the wedding night?" he asks gently.

"No!" And she means it.

"Then why?" Uxšiyârta thinks for a moment. "Did he already—?"

"No!"

Uxšiyârta shakes his head with dismay and takes a deep breath and finishes wrapping her bleeding wrist, frustrated. His hands are marked with her blood. He rubs her blood between his fingers, thinking.

"You are marrying a man who has agreed to all you have asked. He is a king. He will make you his queen. The union is meant to bring peace to the satrapies."

"I do not feel like a queen!"

"Being a queen is not a feeling! It is a divine duty! It is bestowed upon you by the favor of the Wise Lord!" Uxšiyârta growls.

He touches her wrists. He feels her royal blood seeping through the royal purple and blending seamlessly.

"Your cuts are not deep, but they need to be looked after by the old Hellene wound-healer."

Rošanak pulls back into the darkened wall.

Uxšiyârta looks at her with frustration.

"What would you have me do? Huh? What would your blood father have done?" He rubs his forehead. Her moist blood smears on his forehead. He wipes his forehead with his arm and then he stands straight.

"Get up!" He raises his voice, starting to lose his patience.

"I am not a virgin!"

"WHAT?"

Rošanak pulls back into the darkness.

Uxšiyârta is not sure what to do or say. He rubs his bloodied hands through his hair trying to think.

"Who?"

Silence.

"WHO?"

Silence.

"WHO?" He yells at her angrily.

"Utâna—"

"Utâna?"

Rošanak bites her lip and nods in the darkness, crying.

Stunned silence. Then night air fills the small room.

"Utâna, my son?" his voice softens.

"Yes."

Uxšiyârta takes a deep breath and kneels down on the floor next to her, not sure what to say.

"Were you willing? Or did he—?"

"I loved Utâna. I would have died with him, if I could, if you would let me."

Uxšiyârta sinks down next to her and leans against the wall, silently soaking up her teary words.

"Utâna—"

Utâna had begged him to let him marry her.

He wanted his father's blessing and his God's blessing. But he had not agreed to it and he had regretted his decision ever since. And now he felt a sweet guilty satisfaction in what she had just told him.

Utâna had died well… and well-loved…

Uxšiyârta turns his head and looks at Rošanak.

"He did not get you with child?"

"No," she moans miserably.

"It was not meant to be then," he says, regretfully consoling himself. He soaks in the moment for a while longer and then he gets up to his feet.

"What shall I do?" she pleads quietly.

"Nothing!" he says firmly. "You will marry the Makedonian and this will all be forgotten."

"The wedding night—" she moans.

"If it was not for the mark of honor, most men would not know if they are bedding a temple virgin or a whore of Babirû on their wedding night, especially if they are drunk!"

"I care nothing for him!"

"Then?"

"My mother, she will die if she finds out."

"Ah! That is what this is all about?" Uxšiyârta lets out a deep breath, relieved.

"No! My sister is a woman! She will not die! But she will kill you!"

"Abû!"

He bends and takes her shoulders and starts pulling her up gently to her feet.

"Get up! Leave your mother to me!"

MAIN HADIŠ at BAKTRA
YEAR 10 of ALEXANDER, MONTH 7, ARTEMISIOS
YEAR 4 of ALEXANDER, MONTH 1, ADUKANAIŠA
DAY 7: AMURDÂD, DAY of IMMORTALITY
WEDDING DAY
DAWN

Light dawn chasing away the dark night.

A beating heart. Fast.

Rošanak steals quietly into the kitchen barefooted right after sunrise.

She had not slept much, tossing and turning all night long and her eyes betrayed her secret easily.

Her blood mother and Mâr'at Bani Âriyânnâz and the cooks and the maids were already cramming into the kitchen preparing for the wedding feast.

The aroma of Persian sweets made especially for the day fills the air.

"Rošanak, oh, my beautiful bride!"

The old cook, Thukrâ, swaggers as she walks over and puts her loving arms around Rošanak and kisses her face with tears in her eyes. "I prayed to the goddess to let me live long enough to cook for your wedding feast."

"Thukrâ."

Rošanak kisses her soft and kind face wordlessly with deep affection.

Thukrâ had been the head cook of their kitchen as long as Rošanak could remember. She had come from the Royal City of Çûšâ with her father when he had married her mother. She hennaed her hair to a fiery red to cover the snowy white and her father had started to call her Θukrâ, Red, and that had become her calling.

Thukrâ pulls Rošanak toward the table and pushes a piece of sweet noghl, sugared sliver of almond, into her mouth.

"Here. Eat this. Sweet noghl to sweeten the taste of the bride for the groom in the wedding bed."

Women laugh heartily.

Rošanak blushes and reddens bashfully.

"Your mother was so nervous on the day of her wedding feast that she ate a whole plateful before the ceremony. She must have tasted really sweet that night!" Thukrâ says with a wink and a smile.

"Telling tall tales again, Thukrâ?" Aššat Šarri Farânak says with a smile.

"Come, Ladies. Sweeten your mouths and say a prayer for the souls of the dead, who are all coming today to witness the wedding. It will rain tears today, if the souls do not hear their names remembered by their kinsmen and kindred and their beloveds, and think themselves forgotten by the living."

The women flock toward the plate of the sweet noghls and all take a few and utter the names of their dead under their lips.

Fathers and mothers, brothers and sisters, sons and daughters, lovers and friends…

… all their kinsmen and kindred…

Rošanak takes a handful and whispers names under her breath.

She had gone to the Âyadana of Divine Goddess Ânâhitâ last night and had taken a full plate of freshly baked Persian sweets for the living and a full bag of precious Arabâya incense for the remembrance of her dead… and had begged for Utâna's forgiveness with her tears… on her knees…

Rošanak glances over at the two golden crowns that were quietly sitting on the kitchen table.

Mâr'at Bani Âriyânnâz starts weaving the flowers around the gold crowns, chanting under her breath:

"Baby's Breath for pure heart,
Yâsmin for grace and elegance,
Orange Blossom for fidelity and fertility,
Pink Roses for love and perfection,
And Rosemary— Rosemary for remembrance."

Rošanak watches as the crowns of gold slowly turn into wreaths of blessed flowers.

Aššat Šarri Farânak walks up to Rošanak and examines her face in the lucent early morning light.

Rošanak's face was bare. Her eyebrows were threaded to perfection a few days ago and the redness and swelling had finally healed in time.

"You did not sleep last night. Did you?"

"I tried!"

"Thukrâ, cut a cucumber and give me two slices for her eyes." Aššat Šarri Farânak sighs and eyes Rošanak, mumbling to herself, "It is your wedding, Rošanak, not your funeral!" with a voice praying for one and not the other.

Thukrâ brings over a plate of cucumber slices and says kindly, "Virgin Bride! She is just nervous, My Lady."

Aššat Šarri Farânak pushes Rošanak into a chair and closes her eyes with cooling slices of cucumber, nodding, her hands shaking slightly. "Virgin Bride. Yes, that must be it." She steadies her hands, and her heart, and utters a silent prayer.

If she knew this then, when the Makedonian King had asked for her daughter's hand, she would have never agreed to it.

The day was going to end in a wedding or in a killing…

It was now too late… it was all in the hands of the Wise Lord…

Rošanak wonders nervously, resting her eyes.

Did her blood mother know?

What had Uxšiyârta told her?

Her face reddens with the thought of her blood mother knowing about her and Utâna, her heart beating nervously, her belly full of fiery fireflies.

"Just close your eyes, child, and let him have his way," Thukrâ says kindly.

"The goddess willing, it will go quickly. Hellenes are not like Persians, they do not last that long!" Thukrâ laughs and winks.

"Speaking from experience, Thukrâ?" one of the women asks light-heartedly with a laugh.

"Yes. I had a Hellene lover once, when I was in the Royal City of Çûšâ. He was a mercenary. Sadly, he was too small for me." Thukrâ sighs remembering. "He could not fill me up, no matter how hard he tried."

"Thukrâ!" Aššat Šarri Farânak says scornfully, eyeing Rošanak.

"She will find out soon enough!" Thukrâ shrugs her shoulder and takes a deep breath and goes back to her cooking.

Aššat Šarri Farânak looks around the kitchen.

Everyone was busy with cooking and preparing for the wedding feast, not minding Thukrâ too much.

Mâr'at Bani Âriyânnâz was almost finished with the wedding crowns.

"Shall I add more roses?" Mâr'at Bani Âriyânnâz asks loudly, wondering.

Rošanak peels the cucumber slices from her eyes and looks at the flower crowns.

"Maybe more rosemary—" Aššat Šarri Farânak says, considering.

"Rošanak, why are you sitting around here? Go take your wedding bath. Thukrâ, make her something small to eat while she is in the bath. Do not make her a full plate or she will not fit into her wedding gown!"

"I will make your favorite." Thukrâ says lovingly.

It was as if her own daughter was getting married.

Rošanak looks at her blood mother and gets to her feet slowly, her eyes bathed in the juice of cooling cucumber, loaded with worrisome questions.

"Take these with you." Aššat Šarri Farânak pushes the cucumber plate into Rošanak's hands, ignoring her eyes.

....

Rošanak soaks into her warm and fragrant wedding bath.

The maids had threaded her body of unsightly hair and had drawn her a soothing bath, warm water mixed with goat milk for softness and yâsmin oil and rose petals to seduce the senses and a few threads of precious red za'farân to take away the pain.

She rests her head on the edge of the bath basin, as a maid gently washes her hair. Her mind drifts.

Last night, when she had left the âyadana, Alexander was waiting for her alone. He had walked her back to the hadiš through old groves of fragrant pistachio and sweet mulberry trees, without too many words, just holding the tips of her fingers in his hand. Then suddenly and unexpectedly he had taken her into his strong arms and had kissed her passionately in the middle of the fragrant gardens and then had turned around and left her without a word... He had taken her breath away.

And had returned for one more kiss...

Utâna was tall and rugged and handsome.

Alexander was a good head shorter, light skinned with hair the color of golden wheat, catching all the rays of the sun… he was rugged and strong and sure of himself, filled with kingly confidence.

She takes a deep breath as a maid puts slices of cucumber on her eyes. Her heart races.

She had tossed and turned all night long, wondering.

She tosses away the cucumber slices and opens her eyes and looks at her wet wrists. The cuts looked more like faded red lines drawn on her wrists.

Uxšiyârta had taken her to Polydoros that night and the old wound-healer had cleaned her wounds of dried blood, covered them with foul-smelling thick layers of brownish waxy salve and had wrapped them tightly with clean strips of white linen, all done with eyes loaded with questions but with silent lips.

In the expert hands of Polydoros, her cuts had bonded and scabbed and healed quickly. The visible scars were to be hidden under multitudes of lovely golden bracelets, with heads of lions, guarding her secrets like ancient protectors of Royal Daughters.

Her stomach becomes full of worrisome bees, buzzing around.

Uxšiyârta had taken her blood mother into the middle of the blossoming gardens the following day and had talked to her away from the eyes and ears of the palace. Neither of them had said anything to her afterward. It was as if it had never been…

She soaks further into the warm bath basin. The maid rinses her hair and rubs yâsmin oil through its dampness. The fine delicate scent fills her senses.

Alexander had told her that he wanted a real marriage and she had agreed to it, thinking she would not live long enough to worry about the meaning of that. But here it was, her wedding day… followed by her wedding night… and she was still alive!

She closes her eyes.

"Open your mouth!" Aššat Šarri Farânak says, kneeling on the floor by Rošanak's bridal bath.

Rošanak opens her eyes and her mouth and takes a bite of food obediently. She cannot taste anything. "Mother, your dress is getting wet."

"It does not matter. I have to change for the wedding anyway."

"Mother?"

"Yes?"

"Tonight—"

"Take another bite."

Rošanak takes another bite obediently and swallows quickly.

"Tonight—"

"Did you not go to the âyadana last night?"

"Yes."

"Did you not pray to the Divine Ašaivanuhî, goddess of marriage and giver of happiness?"

"Yes."

"Whatever happens tonight is by the favor of the Wise Lord."

"Yes, but—"

"But what?"

"What shall I say? What shall I do?"

Aššat Šarri Farânak puts down the plate of food, reaches to take Rošanak's face into her hands tenderly and takes a deep breath.

Rošanak's eyes were wide and searching. She looked younger than her years in the huge water basin, like the little girl who used to come back to the hadiš, all bruised up from falling off horses and trees and whatever else she had taken a fancy to climb.

Her father had said that if she ever cried like a girl she could not tumble like the boys, and so she had never cried. When Rošanak was young, she was always covered with dirt and mud and muck and smelled like the horses and dogs she loved so much.

She had such high hopes for her blood daughters when they were born to her. She wanted to see them wedded to the nobles of the Seven Persian Families.

She had always worried that Rošanak would break her face or bones or body and become utterly unmarriageable… but except for cuts and bruises here and there, on this side or on that side of her body, her face had always been protected by the favor of the divine goddess and had escaped lasting harm. She finally had turned out soft and womanly and graceful, once Utâna had taken an interest in her.

Rošanak had cried a river when Utâna died and had refused to eat or drink for days. She was so worried that her lastborn daughter might just die of a broken heart, like her firstborn daughter. She had sacrificed to the divine goddess and had prayed night and day that her lastborn would be spared and so she had been… she had finally healed…

"Do and say what comes purely from your heart to your lips, and no more and no less and leave the rest to the Divine Goddess Ašaivanuhî."

"But—"

Aššat Šarri Farânak leans forward and kisses Rošanak's face and softens her voice. "I wish you were to marry the man you loved today. But that was not to be." Aššat Šarri Farânak speaks quietly into Rošanak's face. "Alexander will not be Utâna, but he is the Lord of Asia and he is eager for your love and has asked honorably for your hand. Dâriuš offered him his choice of your royal sisters and he took none." Aššat Šarri Farânak pauses and takes a breath.

"I will not counsel you to hold your breath until he is done with you. I know he will not force himself on you. His mother has raised him well."

And that was the best she would say of any man…

"He is willing to take from you what you are willing to give him freely. When he claims you tonight and if you find pain in his arms, it will not last long. And if you find pleasure in his embrace, there is no shame, as the union will be blessed by the Wise Lord and any pain or pleasure from it is within the sanctity of the blessed marital bed."

Rošanak closes her eyes, wondering.

"Now get out of the bath, before you turn into a shriveled old prune on your wedding day!"

"Farânak!" Uxšiyârta bellows into the bath room, through a small crack in the door. "You better come see this!"

"Ayyyy!" Rošanak yells and sinks into the bath basin.

Aššat Šarri Farânak gets up to her feet. "Uxšiyârta, close the door! Rošanak is naked!"

"Tell her to get out and get dressed. Her guests are rolling in!"

"What?" Aššat Šarri Farânak rushes to the bath room door.

"Come and see!" Uxšiyârta pushes the door open and walks in and pulls Aššat Šarri Farânak by the arm to the window and points with his fingers, "There!"

Aššat Šarri Farânak pushes the window open and looks outside.

As Uxšiyârta had said, the palace gardens were covered with men and women and children. Noble Bakhtrians in their finest clothes, walking freely around her gardens.

Rošanak, dripping wet, covered up in a thick linen sheet, pushes against her blood mother, trying to see for herself.

Men… nobles and warlords and warriors… most who had not been seen since the war had started, were pouring into the gardens below and they had brought their wives and mothers and sisters and beloveds and children, bedecked and dressed in their finest clothes for the wedding feast. And not a sword or dagger or knife in sight!

"I have already ordered more lamb and oxen to be roasted in the back," Uxšiyârta says excitedly, rubbing his hands together.

There had not been such a big feast since the war had started.

"And they have come unarmed?" Rošanak asks, stunned.

"They have honored the peace agreement and have come for the first royal wedding feast in the satrapy in almost five years. I had sent word out but I did not think many would come—"

Children laugh and run around playing noisily in the Persian gardens.

"Why have they come without their swords? What if the Makedonians turn on them for revenge?" Rošanak asks worriedly.

"These men do not need swords to defend themselves. Some have torn lions and wolves apart with their bare hands. Most have been fighting the Makedonians for some five years, and will die to the last man defending the Lands if they have to. They have not come defeated in battle with their heads in their hands seeking quarters, they have come with their honors to be persuaded for peace," Uxšiyârta says with words dripping with admiration. "I will go down to greet them."

Uxšiyârta nudges Aššat Šarri Farânak in the elbow. "Go get dressed and come down and see to your guests, Sister!"

Uxšiyârta stops in the middle of the bath room and takes notice of Rošanak, standing by the window looking like a drowned rat and then turns to his sister. "She will not look like this tonight, right?"

"Abû!"

"Uxšiyârta!" Aššat Šarri Farânak says bitingly and pushes him out the door.

SMALL HADIŠ
MID-DAY

"How many men are taking Baktrian wives?" Alexander asks Hephæstion.

"About a thousand, maybe a few more. Harpalos is sending gold for them from Babylon, as you have ordered."

"Good," Alexander says and nods, distracted. He looks away and takes a deep breath. "I got a letter from Barsine," he says quietly, leans back in his chair and taps gently on the wooden table.

"Barsine?"

"Yes," Alexander nods, looking at Hephæstion. "She said she has borne me a son."

Hephæstion's eyes narrow. He leans forward in his chair and quietly asks, "A son?"

"Yes." Alexander looks away. "She has named him Herakles, in honor of my ancestors."

"Did she have your leave to give him a royal name?" Hephæstion asks under his breath.

"No."

Hephæstion tries to reckon the months in his head and then on his fingers. "How old is the child?"

"She did not say. Artabazos, her father, had told her that I was to marry a Persian Royal Daughter and the news had upset her."

"Is it— yours?"

"I was with her only a few times after the Battle at Issos. That was a long time ago, before claiming Stateira, and then a few times after Stateira died."

Why bed a half-breed Rhodian, when you can bed the beautiful Persian Queen?

"Will you acknowledge the boy?"

"No." Alexander sips his wine. "He is a bastard born out of wedlock."

Parmenion was the one who had brought her to him, when she had fallen into his hands at Damaskos. Artabazos and his kinsmen were at Philip's court after Artabazos had fled to Makedonia. He knew her as a child. She meant nothing to him anymore.

She was comely, but no great beauty. No Helene to tempt Paris… not even Andromache to bed Hektor… her face could not launch a thousand ships…

She was not Stateira of Darius… nor Roxana… or pure Persian…

The Persian Royal Women were the ones who tormented his eyes with their beauty.

"She is older than I and half-Rhodian, not an ideal wife, acceptable neither to Makedonians nor to Persians. She has a daughter, as old as Roxana."

Hephæstion picks up his wine cup and takes a sip. "You know how I feel about her."

"You were right," Alexander nods. "I heard rumors that she had eyes for Philotas, from her days in Pella. I think Parmenion sent her to me to get a half-breed barbarian away from his own son."

Hephæstion takes another sip of his wine.

"When we tortured Philotas, he knew things about you that he should not have known, things she must have told him in confidence."

Alexander's eyes lock on Hephæstion's eyes.

"What happens in the bedroom of a king, must not become crude gossip among his men," Hephæstion utters quietly.

"Do you think Philotas told her about what happened at the Battle of Granikos?" Alexander asks quietly, changing the subject.

"Philotas had a big mouth and never missed an opportunity to talk about his own greatness, or that of his father." Hephæstion shrugs his shoulders with indifference and speaks mockingly, sipping his wine.

"It does not matter any more, what really happened at Granikos is already buried with the dead. Kleitos was the last one who could have brought it up to my face, and he rests in the House of Hades now."

Alexander points with his head toward his Royal Army Camp on the other side of the palace walls. "They are loyal to me and more eager to forget anything that would shame them publicly and cast a shadow over their honor. We won at Granikos and that is all that matters. The rest is forgotten and buried with the dead as it should be."

"What will you do with her?" Hephæstion asks, changing the subject.

"She is going to Pergamos with her son. I will see to her comfort. One-eyed Antigonos will see to her safety and will watch over the boy."

Hephæstion looks at Alexander with disapproving eyes. "Why?"

"Artabazos is a good man and a loyal subject and an honorable adviser. I see no need to insult him by refuting Barsine openly. Persians take to such insults no different than the Makedonians. Parmenion and Philotas are dead—" Alexander plays with his wine cup. "I will care for her as long as she does not meddle with Roxana."

"Do you really care for her?" Hephæstion asks in a hushed, brooding voice.

"She is the most beautiful woman in the whole of Asia!"

"We have not seen all the women in Asia!"

"We have seen enough." Alexander sips his wine. "The only ones who matter are the Royal Women of Darius. His Royal Wife is dead and his Royal Daughters are growing up tall in Susa. The girls are as beautiful as their mother, I am told. But—"

Their father had fled from him on the fields of battle and had refused his commands afterward to come before him and submit to him as his vassal king.

And they were both so damn tall.

"But what?"

"There is a fire in her that burns my fingers—"

"Burning fingers of desire is not a reason to marry! Marriage is just to beget sons and no more!"

"You know well that I had no plans to marry. Philip took a wife with each of his campaigns. If I had followed his ways, I would have had more wives than kingsmen!" Alexander laughs and then takes a deep breath. "But Roxana, she—"

"Ah! And Roxana. You walked into those forest-green eyes and have not found your way back out yet, eh?" Hephæstion says dismissively.

"Bessos was betrayed by the cowards around him, otherwise we would still be running up and down and around these rugged mountains and parched deserts trying to capture him!"

"He was a worthy enemy." Hephæstion nods in agreement.

"And that is the blood and bones Roxana is made of."

"Still, there is no need for you to marry her and anger the Makedonians. You can just claim your right of conquest upon her body, and satisfy your desire for her."

Alexander shakes his head. "I will not take a woman to bed who is not willing and she is not willing without being married, nor will her mother ever allow it!"

"Would you have married her, if she was not the daughter of Artaxerxes?"

Alexander hesitates.

She was so beautiful…

Then he nods. "Yes."

Hephæstion leans back in his chair.

"Is she not very beautiful?" Alexander asks suddenly.

"Yes," Hephæstion says quietly, looks away and closes his heart.

"You better get ready. The wedding ritual will start at sunset. May the marriage be a lucky one."

A royal boy runs in and interrupts and points excitedly. "Sir, you should come and see this!"

"What?"

"The Persians, Alexander!"

"What about the Persians?"

"The Persians! Sir! The Persians are coming!"

"What?"

Alexander and Hephæstion get to their feet quickly and walk up to the window.

"Baktrians, not Persians."

"Yes, Sir! They are unarmed, Sir! A few hundred so far! They have all brought their women and children as hostages!"

Alexander looks down at the multitudes walking around the gardens below and then looks at Hephæstion.

"What shall we do, Alexander?" the royal boy asks with uncertainty.

"What do you think?" Alexander asks Hephæstion.

"I think it will be a big wedding feast!"

Alexander smiles and looks at the multitudes. "Is there enough food and wine for the feast for all the men?"

"Yes, Alexander. Cooks have their orders. Everyone in the camp will have a good meal tonight and plenty of good wine to drink," Hephæstion says calmly.

"Good!"

"You have any orders, Alexander?" the royal boy asks.

"I am ready for my bath."

"Yes, Alexander."

"Hephæstion, tell my kingsmen they can come to my wedding in ceremonial armor, but not in arms."

"Yes, Alexander." Hephæstion nods and turns around heading for the door.

"Hephæstion?" Alexander calls him quietly.

"Yes?"

"I—"

"I know."

And that was all that was needed to be said between two old lovers.

"Sir." The royal boy returns in haste, interrupting again.

"What now?"

"A Polydoros of Athenai to see you, Sir! Shall I turn him away?"

"Polydoros?"

"Yes, Sir."

"Bring him up."

"Sir!"

Alexander looks at Hephæstion wordlessly. Hephæstion obeys and lingers and waits.

A few moments pass in silence.

"Ah! My Dear King, Greeting!" Polydoros enters the room warmly. "Ah! Hephæstion, a fellow Hellene. Greeting!"

Hephæstion eyes him with annoyance. "Polydoros."

He was half-Makedonian… born and raised in Pella of a Makedonian mother…

… as much as he loved his father, he did not like being called a Hellene in front of a Makedonian King.

"My Dear King, I bring greetings from Queen Faranak. She has sent you a wedding robe."

"A wedding robe?"

"Yes. White. Zoroastrians wear white for their wedding rituals, the bride and the groom, that is. It is edged with golden purple as mark of royalty. I left it with the royal boys downstairs. Hephæstion, you can wear anything you like, as long as it is clean and scented."

Hephæstion glares at Polydoros, raising his eyebrow.

"My Dear King?"

"Yes, Polydoros?"

"Do you wish me to interpret the ceremony for you? Or your own man has improved his tongue?"

"Roxana can do it."

"She is the bride, My Dear King!"

"Ah! Right!" Alexander looks at Hephæstion.

"Or I can tell you now what will happen. I have been to many Persian and Baktrian weddings. I know all the words by heart, there were lots of weddings before the war, yes, lots. Persians love weddings, Baktrians too, yes, everyone loves weddings! When her sister got married, there was a big wedding, everyone still talks about—"

"You can translate."

"O My Dear King, I can only interpret. Baktrian is similar to Persian. Translation from Hellene to Persian and back is impossible. Persian is a simple tongue to learn, but to master it is impossible for one not born to it. Each word has a thousand meanings and none but one is meaningful to the ear of another Persian, depending on—"

"Very well, Polydoros, you can interpret."

"I will be honored, My Dear King! You will not be disappointed! My Baktrian is flawless! For the ceremony, just observe Roxana and do as she does!"

"If all Hellenes start talking like him, we will have to kill them all!" Hephæstion breaks into Makedonian tongue.

Alexander laughs.

Polydoros eyes Hephæstion discreetly and then turns to Alexander. "My Dear King, for the ceremony, the bride and the groom kneel in front of the High Priest to receive the sacred blessing of the Wise Lord." He asks carefully in a low voice, "would that be a problem?"

"Kneel? I am the Lord of Asia!"

"Yes, My Dear King, but even the Great King knelt before the Wise Lord. Persian Kings are the servants of their Wise Lord, they rule by the favor of their god."

"Who attends the ceremony?" Hephæstion asks calmly.

"Anyone the King commands of course, but usually just the kinsmen of the groom and the bride and elders of other clans and benefactors and anyone sent by the Great King, yes, everyone!"

Alexander and Hephæstion look at each other undecided. Alexander takes a deep breath. Lines appear around his eyes.

"However, when the King kneels, My Dear King, everyone kneels behind him, only the high priest of the faith stands in front of the bride and the groom and he is smallish, not too tall, no—" Polydoros adds, discreetly advising Alexander of the Persian court customs. "No head will be higher than the head of the King!"

Persian Kings were taller than Alexander, much taller, but there was no need to mention that… no need at all… the head of the bride will be lower… as she was slightly shorter than the King! And she was the only one who will be in his eyes anyway.

A few silent moments pass in contemplation.

"Will the King not yield to the gods?" Polydoros asks carefully.

"Did you not kneel when you consulted the Oracle at Siwah, Alexander?" Hephæstion breaks into their mother tongue again.

"Yes."

"Did you not kneel on the sands of the Two Lands and draw the city of Alexandria with your own hands?"

"Yes."

"Then this is no different. By your order, we will only allow your closest kingsmen and no other! I will talk to all before the ceremony. They do not have to come if they do not wish to kneel!"

And who would dare to not want to be close to the King and Court?

"Hephæstion."

"Yes?"

"Tell them that I do not desire any of them to make a toast during the feast."

Hephæstion nods in agreement.

A dishonorable drunken toast from Attalos during the wedding of Philip to Kleopatra wishing for a legitimate heir to Philip thus calling Alexander a bastard had caused all of them to flee into exile.

The memory of it after all these years was still painfully fresh.

"Very well," Alexander relents, speaking in Attik.

Polydoros considers Hephæstion carefully.

The Hellene was clever and cunning like the Persian foxes!

"Hephæstion, may I have a word with you, if the King gives us leave? I have a message for you from the mother of the bride."

Hephæstion and Alexander exchange curious glances.

"Maybe she wants to adopt you too!" Alexander says with a smile.

Hephæstion gives Alexander a look from the corner of his eye.

Alexander shrugs his shoulders.

"Very well," Hephæstion says quietly, taking a deep breath.

MAIN HADIŠ
ROYAL WEDDING
SETTING SUN

Wall to wall…

Fragrant flowers… Flickering candles… Looking glass…

Tables filled from one end of the hall to the other with Persian sweets.

Guarded happy murmurs, and roses, red roses, heaps of red roses.

The entire hadiš glitters for the Wedding Ritual and the Wedding Feast later.

Stench of wretched war chased away with the blessed scent of sacred incense burning low in silvery fire altars.

A wedding was a blessing from the Wise Lord.

Mourning could come back another day.

Alexander, wearing the white tunic bordered with Persian Purple under his white wedding robe, clasped with heads of lions and burnished bronze leg guards, followed by Hephæstion, Ptolemaios, Perdikkas, Lysimachos, Seleukos and a few other kingsmen and royal guards wearing their scarlet Makedonian cloaks, makes his way to the main hadiš through the Persian gardens heaving with guests. He is greeted and treated courteously by Uxšiyârta and Polydoros and a few Bakhtrian elders and then guided through the public audience hall into a smaller private hall in the back.

A few long moments pass with nervous guarded anticipation.

Rošanak, dressed in a long flowing white gown, decorated with precious and semi-precious stones and the royal markings of her family, embroidered with golden thread around the hem, enters the small private hall through a side door.

She is followed by Aššat Šarri Farânak and the noble women of the Satrapies of Bakhtriš and Sughud. Her wrists are bedecked and bejeweled with multitudes of golden lion-headed bracelets, loaded almost half up to her elbow, all glinting and glittering.

Her face dusted with a fine powder from crushed pearls from Varkâna Sea. Eyes drawn with black fine lines, cheeks dusted with pink powder, lips lined and filled with knotted wax and red powder, like a scented rose from a heavenly Persian garden.

Alexander loses his words.

His bride was breathtakingly beautiful…

Like a goddess of the heavens…

Rošanak looks nervously around the small private hall and her eyes find Alexander. Her heart races and her hands tremble slightly. She takes a deep breath and then glides graciously toward the old Zarathuštra Athravan, kneels down in front of him on the silky white virgin carpet and clasps her hands in front of her.

Polydoros quietly whispers in Alexander's ears and Alexander walks up to Rošanak's right, with Hephæstion following closely behind. Alexander eyes the old Zarathuštra Athravan whose life he had spared that night in the old temple.

Alexander slowly kneels down next to Rošanak on the soft carpet.

Hephæstion immediately bends his knees and kneels down behind Alexander and everyone in the small private hall lines up and kneels behind them on hard floor.

A generous gift to the beloved…

And to the King… Lord of Asia…

Alexander hears the shuffling of the bodies bending and folding and kneeling behind him, eyes Rošanak by his side and relaxes and smiles to himself.

The old Zarathuštra Athravan crowns Alexander and then Rošanak with the golden flower wreaths.

Faces shine and jewels sparkle in the flicker of dancing candles.

The room murmurs quietly with the sound of sacred blessings.

Aššat Šarri Farânak and Mâr'at Bani Âriyânnâz and the noble women unroll a shimmery white gossamer cloth over the heads of the Bride and the Groom, filled with fragrant yâsmin, bountiful rice, golden coins, and sweet noghls and kneel down around them, holding up the edges of the virgin cloth.

"I give the hand of my daughter, Rošanak, in blessed marriage," Uxšiyârta says with a trembling voice and Polydoros interprets.

The old Zarathuštra Athravan nods and starts the sacred wedding ritual.

Alexander and Rošanak look up at the old Zarathuštra Athravan.

"Alexander, Son of Philip, King of Skudra, do you accept Rošanak, Daughter of Artakhšaçâ, of your free will as your wife?"

"Alexander, Son of Philip, Lord of Asia, do you accept Roxana, Daughter of Bessos, of your free will as your wife?" Polydoros interprets.

"Yes."

"Yes!"

"Rošanak, Daughter of Artakhšaçâ, do you accept Alexander, Son of Philip, King of Skudra, of your free will as your husband?"

"Roxana, Daughter of Bessos, do you accept Alexander, Son of Philip, Lord of Asia, of your free will as your husband?"

"Yes."

"Yes!"

"May the Wise Lord grant you a progeny of sons and grandsons, prosperity, heart-ravishing love, bodily strength and long life."

"May Zeus grant you sons and grandsons, prosperity, loyalty, bodily strength and long life."

The old Zarathuštra Athravan brings Alexander's left hand and Rošanak's right hand together and wraps a delicate white, long, soft, sheer silk thread around both their hands loosely seven times and ties a knot, tying their hands and their lives together. Both hands tremble slightly.

And thus the sacred religious ritual was finished and Alexander married Rošanak, a Royal Daughter, according to the customs of the Persians.

Aššat Šarri Farânak and Mâr'at Bani Âriyânnâz and the noble women get slowly to their feet, carefully rolling the shimmery wedded cloth away from the heads of the wedded Groom and his Bride.

Rošanak leans forward and takes a small sweet noghl from a silver plate in front of their feet and brings it to Alexander's lips. Alexander smiles and takes her sweet offering into his mouth and leans forward and takes a sweet noghl and puts it into Rošanak's mouth.

He then takes Rošanak's hand tied to his hand in his hand and gets to his feet and pulls her up to her feet along with him.

All men get to their feet first. Then all rise.

The sun has set and the torches all around the hadiš are lit.

Uxšiyârta signals to Itâna standing at the door of the small private hall and the sound of Bakhtrian drums announcing the completion of the sacred wedding ritual fills the air.

Sounds of cheering and laughter break all around the Bride and the Groom.

Hephæstion steps forward and bows his head and is the first one to offer his blessing. "Joy to the Bride and the Groom."

Uxšiyârta walks up and embraces Rošanak, slightly trembling, and then speaks to Alexander, words breaking.

"Oxyartes wishes you many sons," Polydoros whispers.

Alexander smiles and nods.

Alexander and Rošanak are swept up by the crush of guests, taking them to the wedding feast and seating them at the Bride's Table.

The large hall is filled with the happy crowd spilling over into the gardens. Roasted meats and pure wine and honeyed sweets start to flow freely in the large hall and in the gardens. The drums start to play dancing music. The crowd clears the center with loud cheers and the women rush toward Rošanak and untie her hand and pull her with them and they all start dancing, with their men clapping and making a circle around them.

Alexander's eyes follow Rošanak around.

The Makedonians circle around Alexander, drinking and cheering, some loaded with true happiness, others loaded with forced politeness.

After a few dances, Rošanak starts heading back to the Bride's Table and runs into her brother. "Itâna."

Itâna looks down at his feet, avoiding her eyes wordlessly, slightly loaded with forbidden wine.

"Come and dance with the Bride, Little Brother."

"I hate you!" Itâna says quietly and hangs his head low and walks away.

Rošanak bites her lip and watches Itâna walk away.

"Forget him. He is sulking like a wounded lion cub." Oštana says gently.

Rošanak turns toward Oštana and smiles. "Do you want to dance with your Little Sister, Oštana?"

"No—" Oštana smiles and points with his head toward Alexander. "Not in front of my new Framâtar."

"He said you did not have to stay in his Royal Army, if you did not wish to!"

"I know—"

Oštana leans over and kisses her face kindly. His eyes darken for a moment. "I am a warrior. What else would I do? Stay behind again?" He pauses in remembrance of old lost love. "I will talk to Itâna. Now, go back to your husband, Little Sister. His eyes are on you."

"Oštana?" She calls him back to her hesitatingly.

Oštana looks back at her warmly. He is merry with pure wine.

Her eyes ask him the dreaded question.

He bathes her with the generosity of his heart and his love for his sister.

"Life is for the living, Little Sister." Oštana leans over and kisses Rošanak's face again. "He would have taken another girl to his bed, if you had died."

Rošanak sighs with relief, as Oštana walks away.

She was happy with his kind forgiving words, even though he himself had not taken his own counsel and had not given up the memory of her dead blood brother.

Rošanak blesses Oštana under her breath, "May you find love again, my good brother!" She then looks back at Itâna hoping to catch his eyes, but his back is turned in her direction. She hangs her head low and turns around and starts walking toward the Bride's Table.

Dârâ and Nimâ play noisily with other children in the corner of the large hall.

Thukrâ rushes over and embraces her tightly and kisses her face with teary eyes and whispers a mother's blessing into her ears, then lets go and disappears into the crowd.

Rošanak takes a deep breath and finds her way back to the Bride's Table through the dancing multitudes. She sits down quietly next to Alexander and picks up the blessed silvery thread laying carelessly on the table and ties it around her right wrist again.

Alexander is talking to Uxšiyârta and the elders, telling them about training the Bakhtrian boys for his Royal Army, with Polydoros interpreting faithfully.

"No! Not hostages! They will be paid and kept and promoted if they prove their bravery and courage and honor and loyalty to their new king!"

Rošanak takes a sip of her sweet wine.

Aššat Šarri Farânak makes her way to Rošanak and puts her arms around her and whispers a mother's blessings gently into her ears, runs her fingers through her hair and then kisses her face tenderly.

Rošanak lowers her head and kisses the hands of her blood mother and watches her as she is pulled away by the women, dancing and laughing and talking.

She knew it was the life her blood mother had missed. Unlike her, her mother was tightly knotted with her Bakhtrian kinsmen and kindred and liked having them all around her in happy times… and all the times in between…

Rošanak looks around the large hall. Her heart fills with old memories and new feelings, both happy and sad, bitter and sweet, and then quite unexpectedly Alexander leans over and reaches and takes her fingers into his hand and pulls her closer to him and smiles, while still talking, watching her from the corner of his eye.

The Bakhtrians see his tender gesture and look among themselves and relax.

Alexander was no longer a loathed enemy… he was now their kinsman, married to one of their women… a Royal Daughter of the Lands no less… and for that, he was to be treated as such until he broke with his words… and broke faith with them.

Not lasting peace… but at least a lasting truce throughout the blessed wedding night.

Aššat Šarri Farânak returns to the Bride's Table, carrying a loaf of bread. She puts it in front of Alexander and looks at Hephæstion and smiles.

Hephæstion quickly gets to his feet.

"Pelignas, your Molossian cook, baked the ceremonial wedding loaf at the request of the Mother of the Bride," Hephæstion says formally, pointing to the loaf of freshly baked bread.

Alexander smiles at Aššat Šarri Farânak and rises to his feet.

Aššat Šarri Farânak remembers what she has forgotten in her haste and bites her lip with embarrassment.

"Ah! I forgot to bring a knife to cut the bread!"

Polydoros elaborately interprets.

Clank, clank, clank, clank, clank, clank, clank...

The Bride's Table is suddenly covered with small knives and daggers and short stabbing swords of all shapes and sizes. Unsheathed.

The Bakhtrians had come armed and prepared after all... wearing Persian trousers had its advantages.

Hushed silence quickly rolls over the large hall, leaving only the sounds of nervous tense beating hearts.

They all eye Alexander carefully, Makedonians and Bakhtrians alike, and eye each other. Hands and feet prepare for trouble.

But Alexander smiles again brightly and leans over and looks through the knives and daggers and swords. A sharp blade catches his sharp eyes. He picks up a jewel-encrusted gold-handled Persian dagger ending in double lion heads, cuts the loaf in half and offers half to Rošanak.

Rošanak takes half of the wedding loaf, takes a bite and offers the rest to Alexander.

Tension breaks. Sounds of cheers and blessings fill the air.

Alexander smiles and takes the half wedding loaf from Rošanak, takes a bite, and puts the golden dagger and the rest of the ceremonial wedding loaf back on the Bride's Table in front of him.

A Bakhtrian elder seated next to Uxšiyârta speaks in Bakhtrian, pointing to the golden dagger.

"You will honor your kinsmen, My Dear King, if you accept the golden dagger as a wedding gift." Polydoros interprets loudly, pointing proudly to the Bakhtrians.

Alexander smiles and takes the golden Persian dagger and slides it under his belt.

The Bakhtrians smile and nod approvingly at their new kinsman.

Hephæstion hesitates for a moment and then leans over to Alexander and whispers in his ear.

"It is time!"

Scented gardens.

Flickering candles.

Gold coins and white rice scattered everywhere like dirt and dust.

Alexander walks up the steps to the small palace, still holding Rošanak's hand in his hand. Fragrant incense burns slowly in the small stony basins, resting lazily on the sleepy steps.

The steps leading to the small palace were covered with petals of fragrant flowers, like the processional path leading to the Gate of Gods the day he had marched victoriously into Babylon.

They look up, holding on to their flower wreaths, and they are showered with fragrant rose petals falling on them from the top of the small palace. Alexander stops and fills his body with the memory of his first true glory.

A wedding gift and a blessing from Hephæstion…

Rošanak follows Alexander into his dimly-lit royal bedchamber on the second story which had been reborn into a royal wedding chamber with more roses and candles.

The massive royal bed, a wedding gift from the Third Artakhšaçâ to her father, stood majestically in the center of the bedchamber, patiently awaiting new memories…

The exquisite snowy soft Mudrâya linen covering the royal bed was generously spread with sensuous petals from the reddest roses and long red threads of golden za'farân… all brought for the wedding from Aspâdâna…

No sign of fragrant white yâsmin or orange blossom anywhere…

Rošanak gasps.

A wedding gift and a blessing from her blood mother… her mother knew…

Rošanak's heart pounds nervously against her chest. She invokes the divine goddess under her anxious breath.

He would either love her or kill her in a few moments.

Alexander removes his wreathed wedding crown, lays it down on a small table and steps toward Rošanak, taking her hands, spellbound.

Her wondrous beauty warmed his senses and burned the tips of his fingers and the rest of him with burning desire. Reading her green eyes was like star gazing in an ancient forest grove.

He takes her golden hands, brings them to his lips and kisses them, and sweetly whispers, "I choose you and with you I stand before my gods and accept whatever pleasure or pain they have schemed for me."

A tear falls on Rošanak's cheek.

She leans forward and looks deep into his eyes and she finds nothing but sweetness and desire for her in both his eyes, light and dark, and then her heart softens and she drops her unseen arm and armor on the floor and surrenders freely.

Alexander too, drops his hidden arm and armor on the floor, along with all he is wearing and stands there clothed in the light of the heaven.

Muffled knotted sounds of drums and santoors and laughter dance in the night air through the open window.

"Roxana," Alexander whispers her name and removes her flower crown and puts it next to his and then cups her face into his hands and draws her nearer to him. His hands are slightly trembling.

Rošanak looks at Alexander.

Like Utâna, his naked body was marked with battle scars all over… everywhere… sword cuts and arrow wounds and stone marks. His head slightly bent in the opposite direction from a large faded purplish mark on his neck and shoulder.

Rošanak reaches and gently caresses the blood mark, her fingers trembling. "Does it hurt?"

"No—" Alexander turning his head into her hand and kissing her palm gently. "I only feel pain when my heart is marked, not my body," he says quietly.

Rošanak fills up with tenderness for him. She slides her golden bracelets and armlets off her hands. They fall all around them on the floor soundlessly. She holds up her wrists to his eyes.

Alexander sees the healed cut marks in the dim light of the flickering candles. He gently caresses her wrists and looks searchingly into her eyes.

"I opened my wrists when the day of the wedding was set."

Alexander's light eye darkens. He looks at her with questioning eyes.

"I am not a virgin—" She gasps and looks into his light and dark eyes and then slowly continues, "I gave my virginity to my lover before he went to war—and died."

Alexander holds on to her wrists and takes another look and then looks into her eyes again, his hands slightly trembling.

"Do you still love him?"

"Yes." And she means it.

"Who knows?"

"No one." And he willingly believes her.

"Why did you not tell me before?"

"You did not ask."

"Why do you tell me now?"

"They said you had no taste for women. I never thought you would want to—"

Alexander's eyes darken more, both eyes.

The battle had not even begun and she wanted him to think his flank was already turned.

"There will be no mark of honor if you claim me. No one will blame you if you cast me aside. I ask for no mercy for myself. All I ask is that you kill me instead and not shame my mother by displaying an unmarked sheet."

Alexander pulls her into his arms suddenly and kisses her tenderly and then lets her go.

"I did not force you to marry me! Did I? You kissed me. Have you changed your mind? Do you wish me to release you from your wedded oath?"

"No," she catches her breath and says softly.

Alexander narrows his eyes at her.

He had sacrificed generously to the gods in the morning to appease them for his good fortune.

He had pledged that he would stand by her and take whatever they were sending his way… and his gods had taken notice… all too quickly.

The old Chaldæan had warned him of the Persian Royal Women: Even the sweetest of them were bitter… and stay away from the last of the Royal Daughters if he meant to keep what he would conquer.

He had said a Royal Woman would come between him and his kingdom and his kingsmen. The old Chaldæan did not know the Makedonians; he and his kingsmen were bound and tied to each other by war and wine and words… unbreakable ties forged by blood of battles… and gold of enemies.

Alexander looks at her intently.

The gods were not virtuous, neither Zeus who had married his sister Hera and had seduced any mortal man or woman who had caught his fancy, nor Apollo or Ares, nor Aphrodite or the rest of the Olympians. Even Athena was raped by Hephæstos…

The gods were powerful…

Damn Pandora and her jar! Had anyone anywhere ever understood damn women?

Half of his subjects were women. Where men were simple and predictable, women were creatures like locks with no keys… totally unpredictable.

It was good he did not have to face the cursed creatures in battle, he could never guess what they were going to do or why!

He cared nothing about her virginity… his ancestor was Molossos, the son of Neoptolemos and Andromache, the widow of Hektor, who was his prize from the sack of Troia… and Andromache was not a virgin either.

He cared that she loved another…

He had been offered more women than gods were offered precious incense…

Makedonians, Hellenes, Egyptians, Babylonians… Scythians, Amazons… Persians.

The Royal Daughters of Darius and all of his women and whores. But the one he had finally chosen for himself loved another.

And she was not the Royal Daughter of the Last Persian King before him… it was his throne that her father had claimed unjustly…

So she had to be conquered… won… taken… just like the Lands of the Persians.

He bends down to his knees and searches through his clothes on the Bakhtrian carpet. "Ah!"

He gets to his feet, holding the golden dagger he had cut the wedding loaf with in his hand and smells it.

It smelled sweet. The scent of the wedding loaf still wrapped around the cutting blade.

Rošanak stands there motionless, holding her breath, eyeing him… her heart beating faster, her feet planted firmly, unable to move.

Was he going to kill her with no mercy, even though she had asked for it with her own lips?

Alexander runs his finger on the edge of the golden dagger. The sharp edge turns reddish with his warm blood. He drops the dagger to the floor and walks with a slight limp to the wedding bed and rubs his bloody finger in the middle of the white linen sheet.

"There! The bloody mark of honor!"

Rošanak stares at him, stunned.

Alexander sits on the edge of the bed and beckons her to him. "Come here!"

Rošanak stands rooted to the carpet.

"I said: Come here!"

Rošanak looks at him, daring him with her silence.

He eyes her for a long moment.

The knowledge that he, Alexander, the Lord of Asia, was coming upon his enemies, was often too much for them, and they would abandon their strongholds and flee or surrender to him…

Now, he was upon his Queen-Wife and had ordered her to surrender her arms and armor and find what royal mercy she could in the bed of her King-Husband and she had stood her ground and said wordlessly:

"The victor never lays down her arms and drops her armor!

Come and get them, if you desire me!"

And there she stood, as Persepolis had stood before him, majestic in the midst of blazing fire, secure in her own knowledge of her beauty and timelessness. Even the flames of the candles around the royal wedding chamber had grown longer in their desire to flicker toward her heavenly royal body.

She was motionless and in motion at the same time… the tips of her breasts pushing through her white wedding gown, beckoning him to her… for a single battle…

She must not have heard how he had broken Tyre to his will. He had sieged Tyre mercilessly for seven months, pounding on its indestructible walls until the walls had finally cracked. He had filled the sea with stones to break Tyre to her bloodied knees…

This too… was sweet war!

He would lay siege upon her… until she opened the double gates to her heart and let him in… and then he would show mercy and give her quarters and all that she desired of him and more.

Alexander gets to his feet and walks over to her.

"I have chosen you and I mean to keep you."

Alexander leans over and pulls the white wedding gown from her body and stands back for a moment, dazzled by her naked beauty.

Rošanak stands shamelessly naked, her heart beating visibly under her ivory skin like the Bakhtrian drums at her wedding feast. The shadows of the flickering fire of the candles wrap around her, hurriedly trying to seduce her first before the flame of the King claims her.

Alexander reaches and grabs her hand and pulls her with him onto the bed.

Red rose petals fly, some lightly landing on her naked face and naked body.

Alexander unhurriedly removes the soft petals one by one from her face and body, replacing each petal tenderly with a kiss. Rošanak rolls her fingers on the rose petals and collects a handful and showers her face and body with them. Alexander smiles and leans over and kisses her mouth and showers her body with more kisses. The pain in his body fades.

A kiss for a rose petal was fair royal gift exchange between king and wife…

This… was what it meant to be a man!

Sun overtakes the Moon at the base of the heavens.

FOLLOWING DAY
BEFORE DAWN

Fragrant air.

Stillness of the night.

Alexander opens his eyes. He is wrapped around Rošanak, warming her naked body with the heat of his naked body in the coolness of the night, his head buried in her yâsmin-scented raven hair. She is sleeping with her head resting on his arm, breathing quietly.

The last of the candles flicker in the dance of death in the early dawn morning breeze, unwilling to abandon the new lovers. He moves his head and kisses her bare neck and she stirs back into him gently without waking.

His birth mother was so worried about his lack of interest in women that she had sent a Makedonian girl to his bed once to initiate him and had urged him to bed her.

No man he knew had ever bedded a girl who was sent to him by his birth mother!

But he had never given it much thought. His destiny was war, not women… and there was always Hephæstion.

But he had always known that gods would send him a woman wrapped in perfect Persian beauty and he had patiently waited, shunning all others. Achilleos had Patroklos… but it was the soft bed of Briseis, a captive Trojan girl, his share of the spoils of war, that had comforted Achilleos at night. It was for the loss of soft Briseis to hard Agamemnon that Achilleos had sulkily withdrawn his men from the field of battle and had planned his return to Hellas.

The whole Trojan War had started with the abduction of Helene by his namesake, the Trojan Prince, Alexander Paris…

But now it was Achilleos who finally had Helene in his bed… and no matter over what else Gods and Kings and Warriors and Heroes waged wars, they would first and forever fight over the beautiful Persians.

He had claimed her three times and finally she had breathed his name sweetly and had gasped with pleasure from his body.

… Ah… Alexander…

And hearing her uttering his name with pleasure was the sweetest sound his ears had ever heard… even sweeter than his warriors shouting the ancient battle cry of their ancestors and beating their swords on their shields ready to do battle to win glory!

A sweet sigh meant for his ears only…

He kisses her neck again and whispers sweetly, "Roxana."

Rošanak rolls gently within his tender arms on her back and pulls him back into her.

Alexander smiles and steers smoothly into her.

The Makedonian ship had at last found a safe Persian harbor to anchor for the rest of his mortal nights.

SUNRISE

Dawn comes.

Sweetness of the morning. After.

Birds singing noisily in the Persian gardens. Lovesick nightingales pleading feverishly for the favor of the fragrant roses.

Rošanak slowly opens her eyes.

The royal wedding chamber was filled with the rays of the golden sun. The curtains swayed soundlessly in the early morning breeze.

Her naked skin remembered Alexander before the rest of her. Her body felt different. She felt awakened… alive… she had been loved and she had been loved well…

She takes a deep breath and closes her eyes again.

Utâna had consumed her passionately like a sweet roaring fire.

But Alexander…

A king impatient for glory on the fields of battle had seduced her slowly, like the smoldering embers in the fire altar burning inside of her all night long.

He had gifted her generously with heaps of kisses and had sweetly persuaded her to open the hadiš gates to the enemy conqueror…

A Conqueror had turned into a Lover…

A King into a Husband…

"Rošanak."

A gentle hand pulls the soft linen sheet on her body covering her nakedness. Rošanak opens her eyes again. "Thukrâ."

Thukrâ caresses Rošanak's hair lovingly, eager to find out what had gone on the night before. "Beloved, how are you feeling?"

"Alexander?"

"The King is not here."

Rošanak closes her eyes. A sharp pain travels through her heart.

Why had he left her?

Where had he gone?

Was he coming back?

When was he coming back?

"We have prepared you a nice warm bath. Get up, come with me. I have brought you something to eat too!"

"My mother?"

"She sent us."

Rošanak opens her eyes and pushes herself up on the bed.

Thukrâ wraps a scented clean sheet around her gently, covering her naked body. Wilted rose petals and za'farân threads are stuck to her ivory skin, here and there, silently bearing witness to a night of wedded passion. She slowly gets out of bed.

"He did not hurt you? Did he?"

"No."

Thukrâ glances back at the wedding bed with guarded eyes and then smiles, relieved. She puts her loving hands around Rošanak and kisses her and walks her toward the door.

She had stayed up all night long worrying and praying and crying. An unmarked sheet would have brought such shame to the House of her Royal Woman… and to her beloved daughter.

A pair of maids are waiting outside the room.

Thukrâ nods her head and gently tells them, "Take the bridal linen to the Queen-Mother."

TERRACE OVERLOOKING the GARDENS
MAIN HADIŠ
MORNING

Unspoken silence.

Anxious moments.

Aššat Šarri Farânak paces back and forth on the hadiš terrace, while Uxšiyârta taps his fingers on his dagger, trying not to think. Both weary from a restless sleepless worrisome night. Neither dares to break the silence first.

Maids are still cleaning up the remains of the wedding feast.

"My Lady, here is the bridal linen," a maid says brightly, handing the folded sheet to Aššat Šarri Farânak. "Thukrâ told me to bring it right over!"

"Dukšiš?" Aššat Šarri Farânak quietly asks and takes the sheet with trepidation.

"Old Thukrâ is giving Dukšiš her bride's blessed bath, My Lady. She sent me over with the bridal linen. Thukrâ said you wanted to see this first!"

Aššat Šarri Farânak clenches the soft white linen in her hands worriedly; her delicate fingers turn the color of the linen.

"Well?" Uxšiyârta looks at her with dreaded anticipation. "Are you going to hold on to it for dear life for the rest of the day?"

Aššat Šarri Farânak hesitates for a moment and bites her lip. And then she opens the linen and searches it with guarded eyes and then sighs with relief. She hands the marked linen back to the maid.

The maid takes the open linen and runs back into the main hadiš smiling, waving the bloodied linen in the morning air like the standard of a victorious army.

Aššat Šarri Farânak collapses exhausted into a couch.

Happy and sad.

Her little girl has crossed over to womanhood… and with honors… but to a man who… Well, at least he seemed eager for her…

"I wonder how she did it!" Uxšiyârta bristles with admiration.

"Maybe Utâna did not— really— and she was a virgin and did not know the difference—"

"Are you doubting my son's manhood?" Uxšiyârta sneers at her, with a voice too tired to be polite.

"No, Brother—" Aššat Šarri Farânak catches her breath and gathers herself quickly.

"Well, she is the great granddaughter of Purušâtu. Purušâtu pulled the Younger Kuruš right out of the murderous clasp of his Royal Brother and sent him away to safety."

"True. Still— he left early this morning, too early—"

"He is a king, he has a big army under his command— which is eating our lands clean like a plague of armed and oiled locusts!"

"I wonder if—"

Uxšiyârta starts to lose patience with her doubtfulness and grinds his teeth. "Wondering is fruitless, Farânak. They are both alive. What matters is that he keeps to his word and to his wife, and peace keeps!"

LATER

"Mother—"

Rošanak walks on the main hadiš terrace, bathed and scented and dressed after her bridal bath, and collapses on the floor before Aššat Šarri Farânak, hiding her head in her mother's lap crying, ignoring the lavish meal her mother has prepared for her.

"He left me!"

Aššat Šarri Farânak strokes Rošanak's hair and tries to console her.

Innocence of youth…

She did not want any part of him at first… and now she could not live without him.

"He will be back, and when he does, he should not see you crying over him!"

"If my father was alive, he would have killed him for mistreating the Royal Daughter!"

"Did he mistreat you?"

"He left me!" She sobs.

Aššat Šarri Farânak caresses Rošanak's hair lovingly. "Did Thukrâ not talk to you?"

"Yes."

"What did she tell you?"

"Love more than you are loved and it will all come back to you."

Aššat Šarri Farânak closes her eyes and takes a deep breath.

No one had ever said womanhood was as pleasant as walking through a Persian Paridaiza… even for the Royal Women…

Dukšiš Sisygambis had told her once that to be a Royal Woman of the Persian Royal Court, one must learn to dance bare-footed on the sharp edge of a Persian sword… and enjoy bleeding…

But the prize was the eternal love of the Persian Great Kings and Royal Sons and the mighty Nobles of the Seven Persian Families for their Royal Women… Masters of the Lands and the Waters… committed unto their noble hands by the Wise Lord… bathed in everlasting glory…

The guardians of the sacred flame, forever flickering… timely and timeless…

What else was there?

NIGHT

Alexander walks into the small palace. It is deserted, except for a pair of young maids bowing nervously and wordlessly by the doors. He dismisses the royal boys and the royal guards.

"Roxana." He calls for her.

Silence.

"Roxana!" He calls for her again and rubs the cut on the tip of his finger.

Silence.

He beckons one of the young maids forward.

"Where is Queen Roxana?"

The young maid looks at him with wide eyes. She does not understand his strange words. The King babbles like an idiot.

"R O X A N A," he says louder and slower.

The young maid looks at him blankly.

"ROW… SHA… NAAK…"

The young maid smiles and points toward the main palace.

Alexander takes a deep breath and looks down at his feet and smiles.

"Come, Peritas. Let us go find the Queen!"

Peritas wags his golden tail and follows Alexander obediently.

Starry night.

Alexander walks up the small steps of the quiet main palace.

Rošanak is sleeping on a couch on the terrace overlooking the gardens.

Mâr'at Bani Âriyânnâz is quietly watching over her. She stands up and bows and quickly leaves at the sight of approaching Alexander.

Alexander kneels down in front of Rošanak on the terrace and whispers her name sweetly.

"Roxana."

Rošanak opens her eyes.

Her body fills and spills over with happiness at the sight of him.

He was back, as her blood mother had said, and while she was waiting a silvery crescent moon and heaps of little stars, stretching splendidly as a silky Persian carpet from this end of the heavens to the other end, had filled the skies above…

Woof!

"This is Peritas!" Alexander points to his hound.

"Peritas." Rošanak extends her hand to Peritas and lets him smell her. Her golden old spaka that Utâna had given her as a child had died when they were at the Fortress of Sughud.

Peritas sniffs her hand eagerly. He noses her face and wags his golden tail approvingly, and then drops on his four legs and settles down and stretches on the terrace floor peacefully.

Alexander smiles.

His wife was generous with her gods and goddesses and she loved horses and dogs.

He rubs Peritas' ears and playfully scorns his hound with half a smile. "Peritas, where are your manners? You cannot laze down like this, before the Queen has given you leave."

Peritas rolls over eagerly.

Alexander smiles and shakes his head.

"He is showing off. He is normally better mannered."

Rošanak extends her hand and runs her fingers into Alexander's unruly hair.

Alexander smiles and takes her hand and kisses it. "Missed me?"

"No!"

Alexander laughs.

"Makedonians call me *King*, Persians bend their knees to me, Egyptians call me *Son of Ammon-Zeus*, Baktrians call me *Kinsman*. Everyone calls me the *Lord of Asia*, and my Queen ignores me!"

"She must have a very good reason, like being seduced and abandoned by her Kingly-Husband after her wedding night."

Peritas rolls over again and snores.

Alexander smiles and leans over and shows her the dagger cut on his finger as a sign of his affection for her.

Rošanak smiles.

He kisses her and whispers intimate words into her ears.

She blushes and laughs quietly.

Alexander gets to his feet, bends down and takes her hand, pulls her up to her feet and puts his arms around her.

"Peritas!" Alexander calls his dog.

Peritas stretches and yawns and lazily gets on his four legs and obediently follows them back to the small palace.

SMALL HADIŠ
FOLLOWING DAY
SUNRISE

Full rays of the calm morning sun.

"Roxana."

Alexander reaches out searching for Rošanak with eyes closed; his bed is empty. He calls her without opening his eyes. "Roxana."

Silence.

He opens his eyes and calls her again. "Roxana?"

Silence.

He raises his head from the soft pillow and looks around.

It must be mid-market time… the room full of rays of the sun.

He calls her again louder. "Roxana!"

Where was she?

Silence.

"ROXANA!" He calls louder.

Hellenes were right to lock up their women in their houses; at least their husbands knew where their wives could be found… when desired…

He throws back the soft bed linen and gets out of the massive royal bed and goes to the window and looks outside.

A handful of old gardeners were busy working the gardens. One was floating lotus flowers on top of the water basin in the center of the Persian garden.

He leans out of the window and yells, "ROXANA!"

His voice carries over the gardens. The old gardeners look up at him and at once all bow down to their knees. A younger man points in the direction of the stables.

Alexander mumbles under his breath and turns back into the room.

"Peritas."

Silence.

There was no sign of his hound either.

He grinds his teeth, strides toward the door and pushes it open and heads downstairs.

A pair of royal boys jump to their feet and follow him quickly.

Alexander growls at them. "Did you see the Queen?"
"Sir! Yes, Sir!"
"When?"
"After dawn, Sir."
"And she got past you?"
"Ah! Yes."
Alexander growls wordlessly.
"Sir, were we supposed to detain her, Sir?" one of the royal boys asks timidly, embarrassed at not knowing.
"Detain her? She is the damn Queen!"
"Yes, Sir!"

HADIŠ GARDENS

Alexander races through the garden paths, straight as a Persian arrow toward the horse stables.
Everyone bows to their knees, shielding their eyes.
Alexander runs right into Polydoros, almost knocking him down.
"Ah! My Dear King!"
Polydoros bows his head quickly as he regains his balance. And then he looks at Alexander.
The King was naked and bare-footed, his body marked with honor wounds all over… and even so, his body, toned and muscled, bathed gloriously in the sun. With that body, he could have his pick of any boy.
Polydoros sighs.
"The Queen must be instructed in proper Persian Royal Court ways!" Alexander growls.
"Roxana?" Polydoros asks, startled.
"Is there another queen in this palace?"
"Ah! Well, yes, My Dear King, Queen Faranak *is* the Queen-Mother. But she shuns the title, she thinks it makes her—"
Alexander growls and pushes Polydoros out of his way with annoyance and heads for the stables.
He was looking for his wife!
He was not looking to debate the Hellene wound-healer early in the morning!
Polydoros stops talking and follows Alexander nervously. The royal boys follow them a few steps behind.
"Queen Roxana is well-schooled in the ways of the Persian Royal Court, My Dear King! All royals are careless of observing the royal rules themselves! Royal rules are for royal subjects!"
Polydoros continues cautiously. "Lady Ariana from the Seven Families was gifted by the Great King himself to the King— I mean Bessos. She is— she was directly accountable to the Great King for the tutoring of the Royal Daughters.

"The Persian Kings value their Royal Sons, but they value their Royal Daughters as no other. The Persian Royal Daughters are the guardians of the royal bloodlines."

"Well, she knows nothing about how to treat the King!"

Alexander ignores Polydoros and walks into the stables.

The grooms bow quickly, shielding their eyes and point away.

"She is probably riding her horse, My Dear King," Polydoros says miserably, trying to keep up with Alexander.

"Ah! The game field—" Alexander grunts under his breath and heads toward the chogân field.

Polydoros follows him worriedly.

The King looked seriously committed to pursuing the poor girl.

What had she done to him?

"My Dear King," Polydoros runs after Alexander, panting. "Has she refused you?"

A serious offense indeed!

"No!"

"Ah! Has she offended you?"

Another even more serious offense!

"No!" Alexander grunts with a commanding tone, not eager for more words from anyone. He hastily navigates through the overgrown berry brushes on the path. Sharp branches scratch his skin as he passes through recklessly. They reach the chogân field.

Rošanak is riding her horse, wearing old faded sarbalâ and the weather-worn oxen skin tunic of a Persian horse rider. Peritas is noisily chasing after her.

Sun waxes warmer.

"Roxana!" Alexander thunders.

Rošanak rides her horse toward them, Peritas trotting behind, wagging his tail.

Alexander stands there naked, flanked by Polydoros and the royal boys. He walks up to her and takes the bridle of her horse and starts pulling the horse toward the stables.

"You are not to leave my bed, unless you are ordered by the King!"

Rošanak bends down and whispers playfully, "My Lord, you missed me?"

"*No!*" Alexander grunts.

"Mammanie!"

A frightened scream shoots straight like an arrow through the clear morning air.

Alexander lets go of the horse bridle and runs toward the scream, even before the rest have heard the echo. Peritas bolts after him, barking madly.

Polydoros and the royal boys rush after Alexander.

Rošanak hurls down her horse quickly and runs after them with trembling knees.

"Nimâ! Nimâ! Nimâ!"

Dârâ is standing by the water basin in the middle of the garden, jumping up and down excitedly.

"O! Dear Lord! No!" Rošanak screams. "Alexander!"

Alexander's head emerges from the water basin and then the rest of him, pulling the limp body of Nimâ out of the water and shaking him vigorously.

He had found the boy floating in the bottom of the water basin, even before the nearby gardeners had heard and minded the young cries for help.

Polydoros quickly grabs Nimâ from Alexander and puts him on the flower bed and pushes down on his belly.

Rošanak bends to her knees.

Heavens sink into utter silence… Øakata… an eternity passes slowly…

Nimâ gasps for air and throws up a belly full of water and starts crying.

"Nimâ! Nimâ! Nimâ!" Dârâ jumps up and down excitedly.

"Mammanie!" Nimâ cries, frightened.

Polydoros sighs with relief and picks him up and scolds him.

"Neema, your grandmother told you not to play around the water! Did she not?"

"Mammanie!" Nimâ cries noisily.

Rošanak wipes her tears and takes a deep breath. A long one.

Heavens fill with sacred utterances of the divine mother goddess…

Maids rush out of the main hadiš and take the small boys back inside.

Rošanak turns around and looks at Alexander, dripping wet, standing on the ledge of the water basin. She rips the Hellene cloth off Polydoros and quickly wraps it around Alexander.

"Ah!" Polydoros grunts as he coils around himself, awkwardly covering his naked old body.

Alexander pulls the chiton around himself carelessly.

Peritas rubs against Alexander's legs, happily barking and wagging his golden tail madly.

"Go tell the kingsmen of Alexander that the King is resting today," Rošanak tells the royal boys.

The royal boys look at her and then back at Alexander.

"You heard the Queen," Alexander nods his head and commands them.

The royal boys look at each other with twisted faces.

"Yes, Sir!"

"Go prepare a warm bath for the King!" Rošanak orders one of the maids in Bakhtrian.

"Yes, My Lady."

Murmur of running water.

The floor of the bath room was tiled with designs of golden lotus flowers resting on a blue background, resembling floating flowers on the deep waters of the sea. A huge black marble sunken water basin sat firmly in the middle of the room.

The Bath was being filled by golden pipes with golden spouts shaped like the mouths of mythical griffins, pouring warm waters from natural spring sources in the mountains. Steam rose from the bath as the warm water poured into it.

Alexander drops the chiton, steps into the water basin and immerses himself in the warm bath water.

The water basin fills quickly. The maids start pouring various liquids from small bottles and jars into the bath water. Heavenly aromas of amber and orange fill the room. The bath water turns golden as precious healing threads of red za'farân are added.

Alexander sinks deeper into the warm water and closes his eyes. The pain in his body starts to fade.

Rošanak steps quietly into the bath room and dismisses the maids. She kneels by Alexander's head and starts wetting and washing his unruly hair with a potion that smells like musk.

Alexander lingers with closed eyes and relaxes.

Rošanak leans and kisses the new scratches on his face and whispers softly, "The Queen-Mother has sent greetings to the King and all her blessings for saving the beloved son of her eldest Royal Daughter."

Alexander smiles with eyes closed.

"She also begs the King not to wear the light of the heaven outside of the royal bedroom."

Alexander opens his eyes.

"What?"

Rošanak laughs.

"My mother says do not walk around the palace naked as the day you were born!"

Alexander grins.

"Did she see me?"

"Who knows! But my father used to say my mother had a thousand eyes and ears, just like the Divine Mithrâ! And that is why he never strayed."

"How many eyes and ears do you have?"

"Two!"

Alexander grins brightly.

"Good! You would look scarier than Medusa with more," and pulls her into the water basin.

SMALL HADIŠ
FOLLOWING DAY
DAWN

Alexander opens his eyes. Rošanak is sleeping wrapped around him.

Good! She had obeyed his command!

He smiles to himself and goes back to sleep.

His wife had taken to him like a rose bush to the summer sun.

SUNRISE

Rošanak opens her eyes. Alexander is sleeping wrapped round her.

Good… He had understood her words…

She smiles to herself and goes back to sleep.

Her husband had taken to her like fish to the water.

TERRACE OVERLOOKING the GARDENS
MAIN HADIŠ
2 NIGHTS LATER

"Give me 4 and 2!" Rošanak tosses the dice in her hands and rolls them.

"4 and 2!" Rošanak declares excitedly, sitting crossed-legged on a Persian carpet on the main hadiš terrace, playing takh'teh nard with Itâna. She leans over the board and says wickedly, "Fortune always favors the Royal Women!"

Itâna gives her a sharp look. And rolls his eyes to the back of his head. And grunts, "Girls!"

He had finally given up his anger and had decided to rejoin his kinsmen and clan and companions. After all, his sister was now married to a king… even a barbarian king kinsman was better than nothing.

And Dârparna, his best friend in all the heavens, was telling everyone that the Lord of Asia himself was consulting him on all matters of great importance to the Lands.

Aššat Šarri Farânak and a few close kindred and Mâr'at Bani Âriyânnâz are sprawled comfortably on couches talking and laughing.

A woman plays soulfully on her Persian santoor.

"That is the man I told you about!" Itâna says quietly and deliberately, pointing with his eyes.

"Who?" Rošanak says distractedly, eyes searching on the wooden board, considering her next clever move.

"The old lover of your King-Husband!"

Rošanak sits up and looks at Itâna and then slowly follows the gaze of his eyes. A familiar face approaches and stands in front of the terrace steps, looking up at them.

"Roxana." He slightly bows his head.

"Maybe the King thinks you need instructions in bed!?" Itâna says wickedly, leaning toward her and whispering in Bakhtrian.

Rošanak looks back at Itâna. Her eyes narrow and darken.

"Itâna! Go to Hell!"

"And forfeit the game to you? Ha! Not on your life, Little Sister! You are losing and you know it! I can already feel that silver šiklu of yours obediently jumping into my winning hand!" He rubs his hands together eagerly.

Hephæstion takes another firm step forward and waits patiently to be acknowledged.

"My Lord." Rošanak turns her attention to him briefly and utters quietly.

"Alexander sent me. He is still busy with the new recruits from the HighLands. He asked that you wait up for him."

"Yes. Thank you, My Lord," Rošanak says without looking at him.

Hephæstion looks at her and lingers for a long moment and then sits down on the stone steps calmly.

He knew Alexander.

The message from Alexander was not an order from a King to a Queen… a Conqueror to a Captive… more like a plea from a Lover to a Beloved.

Queen or not, she was just a girl and Alexander would soon tire of her. Olympias would see to it, she would tell Alexander to leave the barbarian campaign wife behind in another month. Nothing less than an Olympian goddess would do and not even then.

But still… the girl had unknowingly taken what was once his.

And he was curious too… Was Patroklos not curious about Briseis?

Peritas, stretched out on the cool surface of the stone-covered terrace, senses Hephæstion's scent, raises his head and wags his tail in old familiarity to him and goes back down to sleep.

Hephæstion looks curiously at Peritas who looks like he has claimed the palace whole as if he was born to it.

His father had always told him: "Dogs can see into the hearts of men… and probably women." Although he himself was not entirely sure women had hearts.

Peritas never left the feet of the new woman of Alexander… lazy old hound!

"Hephæstion."

"My Lord?"

"My name is Hephæstion!"

"Yes, My Lord," she says with a quick tone of voice, dismissing him distractedly.

"No. Not *My Lord*. Hephæstion!" He insists politely.

Itâna rolls the dice. "5 and 1. I have you now!"

Hephæstion narrows his eyes at Rošanak trying to catch her gaze and then taps Itâna on the arm.

Itâna looks at him insulted and his temper rises. His blood quickly rushes to his ears and turns them bright red.

Rošanak glances at Itâna's red face.

"Game!" Rošanak suddenly forfeits the game to cool Itâna's temper and puts a silver šiklu on the ledge of the takh'teh nard board.

Itâna looks back at Rošanak and frowns with marked annoyance.

"Itâna!" Aššat Šarri Farânak calls him, beckoning him to her.

Itâna looks back at Hephæstion and then back at Rošanak, takes the silver šiklu and reluctantly joins his mother.

"Go home, Itâna, before your father sends for you again."

Itâna shakes his head in protest. "But he is neither a kinsman nor a eunuch. He will bring shame to us all!"

"Itâna!"

"Very well. Just fair warning, Dear Mother! Do not blame me if he takes your daughter and has his way with her right here under your roof in front of you!"

"Itâna!"

Itâna shrugs his shoulders and grabs a couple of figs from a plate on the table and heads out, mumbling under his breath and shaking his head. "Men know such things!"

Hephæstion looks amused.

Rošanak looks back at him intently. "You dismissed my wealthy opponent, My Lord. I was planning to empty his treasury!"

"How old is the boy?" Hephæstion asks nicely, smiling.

"Itâna? Fourteen. But he tries to act older since his first blood brother died, My Lord."

"Hephæstion!" Hephæstion tries again, undaunted.

Rošanak eyes him intently for another moment and then relents.

"He-fes-tea-oon."

Hephæstion laughs outright.

Her Attik was not as good as Alexander had been bragging about.

Rošanak blushes and reddens, slightly embarrassed. "Hellene names are hard. They do not roll off the tongue like the Persian names!"

Hephæstion eyes her and then looks back at the gaming board.

Row-Sha-Nakk… Persian names were not that easy either!

"It looks similar to an Egyptian board game," he says out loud, thinking to himself.

Rošanak looks at him scornfully, insulted.

"Takh'teh Nard? A board game? Egyptian?" she mocks him politely.

Hephæstion hears her dismissive words and looks at her for a moment and then reconsiders the game board intently, not giving up easily.

"How is the game played?"

Rošanak eyes him for a long moment.

Was Itâna right?

Everyone knew about the old customs of the Hellenes and the love of their men for each other. Hellenes always made much of how they had taught Persians their old ways…

It was not forbidden to them as it was among the Persians… it was why Oštana had felt more at ease among the Makedonians than among his own kinsmen and clan…

She had seen Oštana, loaded with wine, quietly leaving with a young handsome Hellene mercenary from the Royal Army on the night of her wedding from the corner of her eye. Weddings always made the unwedded lonelier than ever!

And everyone knew that even the Younger Kuruš had a lover in his younger days, even though it was forbidden… and only Royal Women bore heirs to the Persian Crown and the Throne…

But why had Alexander not sent a royal boy to deliver his message?

"Each game is one gold archer!" She breaks the silence and dares him.

Hephæstion's eyes widen and then he laughs quietly, shaking his head.

A gold darik was a month's pay for a common foot warrior!

The life in the palace was so far removed from the lives of the multitudes.

That was why Alexander had taken refuge in her… she was his sanctuary to mend and heal… he always knew what he needed to survive the brutality of war.

"A gold darik a game? A princely sum for a lowly board game!"

Rošanak raises her eyebrow and considers him for another long moment.

A golden archer was reasonable.

Dukšiš Purušâtu, her great grandmother, had played a hand with her Royal Son, the Second Artakhšaçâ, for a court eunuch. And when she had won the battle, she had demanded and the Second Artakhšaçâ had faithfully handed her the same eunuch who had cut off the head of his Royal Brother and her beloved Royal Son, the Younger Kuruš. She had buried the eunuch alive… he was eaten alive by flesh eating maggots. The damned and doomed eunuch had the blood of a Royal Son of the House on his bloody hands… it was not something a Royal Woman could ever forgive or forget!

Rošanak smiles and baits him. "Then perhaps you should visit the quarters of your Royal Army for loftier games that will not sack your treasury!"

Hephæstion smiles and relents and takes the bait willingly.

She had played with the boy for a silver coin… still, a gold darik was a fair price for a glimpse of what Alexander saw in her.

There had been so many women Alexander could have taken to bed or even married… Why her?

Everyone knew Alexander put his trust in the thrust of a sharp sword, not on a marriage alliance… he was not like his father to seal his hard conquests with soft brides!

"A gold darik it is."

Rošanak smiles with her eyes, shakes the dice and rolls, and points, "Takh'teh Nard is a war game of strategy. Each queen—" she pauses, "or king, pursues and attacks the warriors of the hainâ, the enemy army, mercilessly, and kills and forces them off the battlefield and moves her own warriors around the field into safety away from the path of her enemy army according to the roll of the dice and then removes them all before her enemy rescues his warriors."

Rošanak leans forward and counts and moves one of her wooden warriors.

"3 and 1. Like this. And to the conqueror go the spoils of war!"

Hephæstion eyes her and smiles.

That was a game he knew how to play… well…

"Very well." Hephæstion nods and Rošanak resets the board and rolls the dice.

Rošanak moves her wooden warriors around the board.

Hephæstion rolls the dice.

Rošanak laughs and points. "Ah! 5 and 4! Not good!"

Hephæstion counts and moves his wooden warriors around the board.

Rošanak rolls the dice. "6 and 6! Good!" Rošanak smiles and continues softly, "Are you related to Alexander by blood?"

Hephæstion looks up, caught off guard. The dice fly out of his hand distractedly.

"Ah! No. I am half-Makedonian. My family originally hails from Athenai. We moved to Pella after my noble father and his father fell out of favor in Athenai. He was in favor of an alliance with the Great King and against the Spartans. My mother was a highborn Makedonian HighLander."

He pauses and then continues, "Alexander is a LowLander, from a long line of warrior kings, half-Makedonian, half-Molossian. I have been with him from the beginning. He is destined to be the greatest conqueror roaming the known world, always in search of his next big conquest."

He pauses again.

Alexander would go to the ends of the earth to do his father one better.

Wounded, Philip had fallen from his dying horse fighting the mutinous Hellenes, and it was Alexander who had rushed over and protected his father from a certain death with his own shield and sword… but Philip had never acknowledged or honored Alexander publicly for that… unwilling to admit that he was indebted to his own son for his life… and that had turned Alexander bitter toward his father.

The venomous words of Olympias had done the rest.

And then he adds, "I have known Alexander since childhood. I am a year older than he. We have been together since he was fourteen years old. We both were tutored by Aristoteles. He is the most brilliant commander on the fields of battle, and… a good friend!"

Rošanak eyes him discreetly.

Dauštar?

A good friend?

She then points to the dice and smiles and taunts him. "Ah! 2 and 1! Fortune is not favoring you tonight!" She rolls the dice. "6 and 6 again! Not even your gods can come down from their heavenly mountain to help you win now!"

Hephæstion rolls the dice. "1 and 1! I surrender!" He raises his hand in the air, showing his palm, signaling defeat.

Rošanak smiles, grabs a fig hungrily and takes a bite, and considers him discreetly.

He was taller than Alexander, as tall as Utâna, and more slender… more Persian in manners… with hair the color of harvested wheat in autumn… eyes the color of the deep sea…

Hammered metal bones underneath muscled flesh and smooth skin… but wrapped in grace and gentleness… like a superbly sharpened Persian sword resting peacefully inside a splendidly jeweled scabbard, fully aware of his deadly powers, without a desire to flaunt it… calm like the cool skin of a deadly sea… ebbing and flowing silently underneath…

It would be hard to tell him apart from Utâna from a long distance… maybe even from a closer distance…

Hephæstion picks up a fig and takes a bite and looks at Rošanak intently.

"Who were you to marry, before Alexander?"

Utâna! "Many years of bloody wars. Not many kings and princes left." Rošanak says carefully, "I would have become a temple virgin instead."

He eyes her with disbelief, "Hmm…" then shakes the dice in his hand. "Another game?"

Rošanak shakes her head side-to-side. "No!"

Hephæstion rolls the dice and baits her. "4 and 4. Then I shall go back to my lonely quarters and open my wrists, for being rejected by a beautiful woman."

Rošanak touches her wrist unconsciously.

Uvâmaršiya… taking his own life?

Had Alexander betrayed her secret and told him about her?

"You will be banished eternally to the dark underworld, the Land of the Endless Darkness! Better to wait and die honorably on the battlefields at the hands of the Persians, your mortal enemies!" she whispers.

Hephæstion laughs unguardedly. "You are heartless!"

Rošanak smiles and nods and straightens and eats another fig. "I am a Royal Woman!" She takes a deep breath. "After the death of my lover, I thought about running away to the shores of the Hyrkania Sea to marry a fisherman."

Hephæstion's eyes widen, startled.

She had a lover before Alexander?

Did Alexander know?

"Huh! A fisherman?"

"Yes! I would feast all day long on precious golden khav'jar seeds harvested from ancient huso'husos, captured by my sweet fisherman-husband."

Then Rošanak straightens again. "But, my mother told me marrying your King Alexander was a noble sacrifice to bring peace to the Lands. With privilege comes duty, my birth mother always says."

Hephæstion narrows his eyes and carefully considers her.

Hmmm… duty… sacrifice… marrying Alexander?

What about love?

Aristoteles was right. "True love was only among men!" Women were imperfect… useful only for bearing sons and no more!

Nimâ and Dârâ, the sons of Rošanak's blood sister, enter the terrace noisily and run and throw themselves at Rošanak from both sides in an all-out attack, tickling her madly.

"Rošanie!"

"Rošanie!"

Rošanak grabs them both, laughing and kissing them.

Hephæstion recognizes the small boys. He sits back and watches.

Rošanak rolls on the carpet, laughing and defending herself from the attack of the boys. "Dârâ! Nimâ! Sons of my sister! They are in the care of my mother, as their mother, my sweet sister, died a few years ago of a broken heart when her beloved husband was killed at the Battle of Issos."

Hephæstion eyes Rošanak.

The boys leave Rošanak and run to their grandmother, Aššat Šarri Farânak.

"Mammanie!" Dârâ screeches with laughter.

"Mammanie!" Nimâ pulls on Aššat Šarri Farânak's gown for her attention.

Aššat Šarri Farânak picks up one of the boys and gets to her feet.

Everyone stands up.

"Rošanak, it is time to retire for the night!" Aššat Šarri Farânak says graciously, glancing at Hephæstion and walking inside.

This was not the Persian royal court. A wedded woman should not entertain a handsome man who was neither her wedded husband nor a kinsman.

Rošanak hears her mother's unspoken words from the tone of her voice and gets to her feet. Peritas stretches out lazily, raises himself up, moves next to Rošanak and rubs against her, affectionately wagging his tail.

"Ah! Bedtime for the Boys!" She bends down and scratches Peritas' ears.

Hephæstion stands up and bows his head slightly to Aššat Šarri Farânak. "Shall I tell Alexander that you will wait up for him?"

"Tell Alexander to come and get me when he gets back. He knows where to find me."

Hephæstion slightly bows his head. "I will give him your message."

"Hephæstion, you owe me three golden dariks! Come back anytime you wish to lose more of your Persian booty to me."

Hephæstion acknowledges with a smile. "Good night, Roxana." He turns and starts walking down the steps.

Torches flicker on the terrace.

"Hephæstion?" Flawlessly.

Hephæstion stops and turns around. "Yes, Roxana?"

Rošanak steps down. She looks at him straight in the eyes.

Was he a friend to her or her enemy?

He was the one she had first noticed among the men of the enemies when she had left the Fortress of Sughud following Uxšiyârta and her blood mother.

"May I beg a favor of you?"

Hephæstion looks into her eyes.

Words spoken carefully, scented with sweet intoxicating jasmine…

Beg… a favor?

From a Persian Royal Woman? From the wife of Alexander?

The Royal Women of Darius had asked for nothing when they had been captured, just that they would be allowed to bury Darius with honors due a Great King.

Had he already been weighed and measured… that quickly?

"A favor?"

"The sacred Festival of No'rouz is coming— the beginning of the Persian New Year."

"Yes?"

"Yes…" Rošanak looks uncertain. "Alexander gave me a golden crown, a gift."

"Yes?"

"Probably from Persepolis or Susa Treasuries."

"Yes?"

"He wants me to wear it for No'rouz."

"Ah." Hephæstion straightens and nods.

The golden crown she had offered to her goddess that night…

She had gotten close to Alexander and now Alexander was testing her loyalty to him… as he did with all those close to him. Alexander always loved passionately but demanded absolute loyalty in return. Now he had set his deadly trap for his first wife and was waiting to see what she would do.

"Yes?" he asks.

"I offered it to the Divine Anaitis, the Mother Goddess!" she confesses.

Hephæstion taunts her. "You offered a wedding gift from the King to a goddess, a golden crown?"

"Yes."

"I see."

Silence.

"Would the King himself not freely give to a goddess of his own faith?"

Silence.

"What shall I tell Alexander?"

Hephæstion looks deep into Rošanak's eyes and considers her for a long moment.

There was no fear in her eyes… just clouds. She was not afraid… just loath to displease Alexander…

A gap had opened all too quickly in the line of his enemy… all he had to do was to ride straight through it and destroy her.

But Alexander needed a rightful son and an heir and he had not taken to any other woman after Stateira and the girl was so young.

He did not want the blood of a young girl on his hands. His father would disclaim him for a lot less. Alexander would tire of her soon enough.

The peace had been keeping because of her and like the rest of the Royal Army, he was tired of marching and fighting and killing.

"The truth." Hephæstion takes a deep breath and softens. "Tell him the truth. Alexander will understand."

Rošanak looks deep into Hephæstion's eyes… watery waves ebbed and flowed on the shores of their calm, deep sea.

If Itâna had spoken the truth, she could see why he was what he was to Alexander… he was truthful.

Alexander was far from the land of his ancestors with no blood kinsman to watch over him and kings had no friends.

Hephæstion was like the beclouded moon… like Nânna… the ancient Moon-God of the Bâb-ilim… measured and deliberate… aware of his immense quiet powers… secure in his own place and position… watching faithfully over the man who was his king.

Not like Alexander, pulsating with raw power like Enlil, the Bâb-ilani god… driven to dazzle… demanding to be worshiped…

No… Nothing like Alexander…

"Who restored the blessed Temple of Divine Goddess Anaitis?"

"I did."

"Why?"

"Alexander ordered it."

"And the new inscription on the statue of the goddess?"

"That too."

Hephæstion bows his head slightly and turns around and leaves quietly, as Rošanak and Peritas watch him disappear from sight in the dark of the night.

Peritas wags his tail with familiarity after his first master, then drops on the cool terrace floor and falls back into deep sleep.

HADIŠ GARDENS
FOLLOWING NIGHT

"Tell me, what is your age?"

"Nine and twenty years." Alexander thinks for a moment and eyes Rošanak curiously.

It was not a question he was asked often.

Everyone knew.

"Why?"

"Twenty nine— that makes you older than my oldest blood brother, born to my birth mother. You are ancient!"

Arf!

"Peritas thinks you are old too!"

"You have spoiled my hound. I will send the damn dog to Hephæstion to beat some obedience back into him."

"Why? The clever dog is agreeing with his master!"

"I am his master!" Alexander narrows his eyes at her and says with authority.

"Hound of the King is agreeing with his Queen!"

Alexander grabs Rošanak tenderly. "An Evil Persian Queen!"

Rošanak laughs and taunts Alexander.

"My Lord, you should keep your royal strength for the royal bed. You should not spend it all on your way getting there." She smiles as they walk under the stars toward the small hadiš.

Alexander pulls her closer to him and brags, "Thalestris, the Queen of the Amazons, came down from her kingdom to see me after having heard about me. She desired a child begotten by *me*. If the child was a girl, she would keep her and if the child was a boy, she would return him to his father, *me*. I kept her in bed for thirteen days, night stretching into day, day stretching into night, satisfying her endless desire. She did not think of me as old. She begged me for more every time I withdrew from her warm body."

Rošanak tosses and turns his big words in her small eyes.

"Thirteen days? My Lord must have been exhausted considering his advanced years!"

"Jealous?"

Rošanak raises an eyebrow and smiles wickedly.

Only another Royal Woman with more royal bloodlines was worthy of her jealousy. Sakâ women were savages who did not even bathe or shave and smelled like the horses they rode and probably tasted like soured goat milk.

No man she knew would even think of Sakâs as women… more like landless savages from beyond the Lands and Waters… who cut off their right breasts, so they could more easily stretch their bows.

"My Lord, all that the nomad Amazon Queen could offer you is the shaggy old mule she rides and a patch of parched land between her legs that took Your Majesty thirteen days to irrigate." She pauses and eyes him tenderly. "This Evil Persian Queen, on the other hand, holds the keys to the most desirous kingdom in all the Lands."

Alexander laughs.

"But— if My Lord, the Lord of Asia, prefers a one-breasted, unwashed, unkempt HighLand Scythian from the other side of the frozen deserts, to his scented wedded Persian Royal Woman of the noblest ancient royal blood, then the Royal Immortals should be dispatched at once to bring the Amazon back to his royal bed!"

"You are an Evil Persian Queen!"

Rošanak laughs and frees herself from Alexander's arms and runs away from him in the darkness under a silvery waxing moon.

Alexander runs after her and they both fall into a fragrant flower bed close to the water basin in the middle of the Persian garden.

Rošanak laughs quietly and tries to push him away.

Alexander holds her down and kisses her hard and his hands start moving intimately down her soft body.

Woof!

"Go away, Peritas!" Alexander commands with a voice of absolute power.

Peritas hears and obeys and disappears quickly.

"Hyacinths!" Rošanak whispers softly. "We are in the middle of the hyacinths!"

"Good! If you did not run like a girl, we would have landed right on top of the rose bushes!"

"You would not have thrown me into the thorny rose bushes."

"Oh yes I would have!" Alexander's hands start pulling up her gown and caressing her body more intimately.

Whispers…

"Not here!"

"Why not?"

"The royal boys—"

"Banned from inside the royal palace!"

"The royal guards—"

"Them too!"

"The kingsmen—"

"Gone! All of them!"

"The ground is wet and muddy and the King is ruining the Queen's beautiful gown!"

"I will gift you a thousand more gowns."

His body finds hers and takes her, another kingdom won by spear.

Rapture.

"Ah!" She arches her back and sighs.

He comes back to himself and catches his breath.

"So, you think the King is old?"

"Yes, utterly ancient!"

He stretches back over her.

The night was long and the hyacinths smelled heavenly… and there was an advantage to not wearing Persian trousers.

Her body quickens and she moans softly again and holds her breath and then lets out another sigh.

"Ahh…"

HADIŠ GARDENS
FOLLOWING DAY
MID-DAY

"Greetings, Your Royal Highness, Dukšiš Rošanak!" the old gardener calls out as he runs after Rošanak, bowing and panting, out of breath and almost in tears.

Rošanak stops reluctantly and looks at him hesitantly. Peritas stands in front of her keeping the old gardener from getting any closer.

"Greetings to you, Master Frâda," she says in a low voice.

"Your Highness, the hyacinths!"

"Yes?" she says faintly.

She knew!

He points to the gardens nearly choking. "The hyacinths are— dead! All dead! Crushed! By some wild beast last night!"

Rošanak looks guilty. Her face warms and glows. "All of them?"

"Yes! A mountain lion must have stomped through them!" He shakes his head side-to-side with painful grief. "The entire garden is ruined! Paridaiza lost!"

"Does my mother know?"

"Yes! She told me to speak to you about them—"

"Me?"

"Yes! The Aššat Šarri said that the affairs of the hadiš are now in your royal hands, being the new wife of a king who is still alive!"

Rošanak bites her lip.

"No'rouz!" The old gardener cries out. "Heaven on Earth! Lost!" He points, "Come with me, Your Highness, let me show you the terrible tragedy that has befallen on us!"

Rošanak hangs her head low and takes a deep breath. "Very well. Let us go and see."

The old gardener points the way and bows his head. "This way, Your Highness!"

Rošanak follows him with Peritas walking by her side. Her heart beats faster approaching the bed of hyacinths.

The sun is getting warmer, turning morning into day.

Rošanak reddens and looks at the wilted and crushed hyacinths, bearing silent witness to a long night of wild passion. Peritas runs around and sniffs the crushed hyacinths. Rošanak looks toward the main hadiš, bending her neck to the side trying to see.

Could her mother see that far in the dark of the night?

It would be hard to see anything… that far away… but her blood mother… she must have the legendary Cup of Kuruš to gaze into.

"See, Your Royal Highness. See. Here! Look! Only a wild mountain lion could do this much damage! A deer would have eaten my beautiful flowers."

He shakes his head with sheer misery and points with his hands. "The ferocious mountain lion must have just dropped right here and then rolled around there and back here and then this way and then that way and crushed them all!"

"Yes… you must be right."

"They survived the heavy feet of the invaders and the dancing feet of all the wedding guests to be destroyed by a lion. No robbers either. There were no buried treasures hidden under the poor lovely hyacinths."

Rošanak starts walking around the garden, evaluating the battlefield grounds.

"Master Frâda, you may hire extra men to help clean up and mend the royal garden."

A smile brightens the old gardener's face. "Yes, yes, Your Highness." He points to the young boy. "Record the words of the Aššat Šarri, boy! Word for word!"

The young boy writes quickly, as Rošanak speaks.

"This garden came to be many, many years ago."

"Yes, yes, Your Highness. My father's great niyâka was the Master Gardener then, too."

"No'rouz?"

"Yes! The garden paridaiza will be back to its original splendor for the arrival of the Persian New Year! Yes!"

"This garden is our favorite garden. My mother would love to have more fragrant spring flowers."

"Your Highness, for a few extra golden archers, I can build the most splendid of Persian gardens here! My father and the fathers of my father before him were not as well-traveled as I am, Your Highness. I have seen the royal gardens in the Royal Cities of Pârsâ and Çûšâ. And the beautiful hanging gardens of Bâbiru, falling straight from Heaven down to Earth!

"These exotic gardens… Heaven on Earth… truly… having four rivers and four quadrants, representing the four corners of the heavens, and with water canals running through each of the four gardens to connect to a central water basin, like this one!" He points to the water basin.

"Such a splendid garden will cost more than a few golden dariks."

The old gardener bows, rubbing his hands together. "Yes, yes, Your Highness! But you are the Persian Aššat Šarri and your gardens must reflect the importance of your stature in the Lands!"

Rošanak laughs. "Ah! Master Frâda. You attempt to rob my treasury of precious gold, while tempting my senses with flattery."

The old gardener protests politely. "Ah! No! Your Highness! I am certain that if your Royal Highness had seen the splendid gardens that I had seen in Royal Çûšâ and Royal Pârsâ, you would have ordered me to dig up the entire royal garden myself with my own hands. One must move with the times, Your Royal Highness."

"I have seen the gardens in Pârsâ," and she bites her lip.

They were the loveliest gardens on the driest lands before Pârsâ was sacked and razed and burned…

"I can bargain with the Hinduya traders for a fair price for the royal rose bushes."

"Royal rose bushes?"

"Yes, yes, Your Highness! The rose bushes that decorate this sad patch of dirt here are old!"

"Ah! Master Frâda. A rose bush is a rose bush. Who will pay precious gold for these ancient dried-up rose bushes?"

"No, Your Highness! A rose bush is not a rose bush! And these are not mere lowly rose bushes! No! They are the royal rose bushes, from the royal gardens of the Hadiš of Baktra! The Hadiš where Persian Kings and Queens have resided! They will make a fine addition to any noble garden!"

"Aye! You are indeed clever, Master Frâda."

The old gardener is pleased with the praise. "Yes, Your Highness! I will plant white lilies of the valley and red tulips from Skudra over there, a few rows of hyacinths right here, and line the garden with fragrant lavender bushes and night blooming yâsmin from Hinduš. Your royal garden will be in bloom from the first days of the spring till the first snow flakes of the winter. From the Spring Festival of No'rouz to the Winter Solstice of Day'ghan."

"Very well, Master Frâda. But with no more than twenty golden archers."

"Yes, yes, Your Highness! Write down twenty golden archers, my boy!"

The young boy bows and presents the order on soft clay to Rošanak.

Rošanak checks the order and makes a correction.

"The garden expenses will be paid from the royal funds of Alexander, Lord of Asia, not from the gold of Dukšiš Rošanak."

The young boy bows, quickly makes the correction and represents the order back to Rošanak, bowing his head.

Rošanak checks again, smiles and then presses her ring with her royal seal into the soft clay, thus sealing the order. She beckons the young boy. "Battiš, come with me." She turns and heads in the other direction, with the young boy following her obediently.

"Peritas, come."

Peritas follows her obediently too.

POLYDOROS' QUARTERS. MAIN HADIŠ

Rošanak reaches the quarters of Polydoros and knocks politely and enters.

"Greetings, Polydoros."

"Princess, I mean Queen."

Peritas spreads like a well-worn carpet on the floor.

"Polydoros, please write a letter for me in Attik."

"But you can write well yourself, as I have taught you."

"Yes— but this is an official letter. I can only scratch a few lines about the matters of little importance and my handwriting looks like the mad footprints of a crow on wet clay."

Polydoros shrugs his shoulders and sits at his table and gets ready.

"Ready?"

"Yes."

To King Alexander, favored by the heavens, who is in my prayers,
In Month 1, Adukanaisha, 14 days passed, in Year 4 of Alexander:
Roxana, the Queen, says that Master Fraada, the palace gardener, spoke as follows:

A ferocious mountain lion destroyed a beloved patch of fragrant hyacinths, a much valued portion of the royal gardens in the Palace at Baktra last night.

Polydoros stops abruptly and looks up startled. "A mountain lion? Here— in the palace?"

"Yes."

"But lions are too smart to come down from the mountains!"

"Write. Please."

"But lions eat people, not flowers!"

"Please! Write!"

"Ah! Yes!"

Roxana, the Queen, requests twenty gold dariks from the royal treasury of the Lord of Asia to be provisioned for the restoration of the gardens to Master Fraada.
Please give the gold dariks to Battish, the son of Master Fraada, the bearer of this note, to bring to the Queen.

"Twenty gold dariks?"

"Yes."

By the order of Queen Roxana, Polydoros of Athenai wrote this.

"Done."

"Let me see."

Rošanak looks at the parchment and then nods and folds and seals the letter with her signet ring and gives it to the young boy. "Battiš, take this to the King. Do not leave his presence until he gives you the gold archers. Understood?"

"Yes, My Lady!" The young boy eagerly nods his head and takes the letter and runs out the door.

Polydoros gets up to his feet and walks over and looks at Rošanak. Her ivory skin is bruised with love marks turning faded purplish on her body.

Lion was the mark of the Lord of Asia…

And the lion had pawed her ferociously… and had written his love marks with purple ink all over her ivory body.

"Mountain lion, ha?"

Rošanak reddens and smiles and bites her lip. "Yes, an old mountain lion."

ALEXANDER'S ROYAL TENT

LATER

"Sir!"

Alexander looks up.

"A barbarian boy from the palace brought this, Sir! It has a royal seal. He is waiting outside."

Alexander takes the letter from the royal boy and reads it.

"Hephæstion."

"Alexander?"

"Take this and see to it."

Hephæstion takes the letter and reads it. "A mountain lion in the palace? Shall I post some guards inside the palace walls to capture it?"

"No! Just give the boy the gold dariks."

Hephæstion considers Alexander for a moment. He thinks of the days when they were boys together.

Memories of the meadows at Mieza, where they were tutored by Aristoteles.

The nights they had looked up at the starry skies and had planned their glorious conquests together… it all seemed so far in the past now…

"Twenty gold dariks? For a garden?" Hephæstion gives a long look to Alexander.

This was why he always had to borrow from everyone… he cared nothing for gold beyond paying for the Royal Army and whatever else that pleased him.

"Give him thirty!" Alexander says, avoiding Hephæstion's eyes.

"Mountain lion, ha?"

"Yes—" Alexander looks up and smiles and then looks back at the documents on his table and busies himself. "An old mountain lion, as the letter says."

"The letter says, *ferocious mountain lion*."

"Yes. Her Attik is not good. She meant, *a ferocious old mountain lion*."

TEMPLE of DIVINE GODDESS ÂNÂHITÂ
FESTIVAL of FRAWARDIGÂN
3 NIGHTS before the PERSIAN NEW YEAR

Sacred murmurs knotted with the scent of sacred incense.

The âyadana is crowded with a sea of Bakhtrian women, gathered to honor the Festival of Frawardigân, the Festival of All-Souls, at the end of the old year and before the beginning of the new year.

Aššat Šarri Farânak and Rošanak enter the âyadana and are swept up by the multitudes of women all around them.

The statue of the Divine Goddess Ânâhitâ is covered with offerings, incense, sweets, flowers, and coins offered along with sacred prayers to the souls of the dead.

The old Zarathuštra Athravan makes his way to them. "Aššat Šarri Farânak."

Aššat Šarri Farânak smiles and nods.

Rošanak looks at the old Zarathuštra Athravan and smiles shyly. His kindness had given her one blessed night with her lover.

"For the Divine Goddess Ânâhitâ, in remembrance of our loved ones. My father and all my brothers and my sister and her husband," Rošanak says quietly, extending a small skin bag to the old Zarathuštra Athravan.

All the extra gold Alexander had given to her.

The âyadana too was a part of her paridaiza.

The old Zarathuštra Athravan takes the skin bag and looks inside. A handful of golden archers smile at him brightly.

"The dead are always blessed when they are remembered so generously by their living."

Aššat Šarri Farânak is swept away by her kindred.

Rošanak leans forward and asks the old Zarathuštra Athravan quietly, "Do they know?"

"Who knows what, My Daughter?"

"The dead… do they know… what the living do… every day?" Rošanak asks hesitatingly, dreading the knowledge.

The old Zarathuštra Athravan considers her for a moment.

She was newly wedded to the Lord of Asia.

He was the one who had wedded her to the Lord of Asia who had restored the blessed âyadana, in her name… and punished his men who had desecrated the old temple.

And her name was carved on the statute of the goddess along with a love poem dedicated to her by a lover long dead…

"Only the Wise Lord knows everything. Only he sees what cannot be seen by the eyes of the mortals."

Rošanak breathes out a sigh of relief and relaxes. "Good!"

Her body feels warm all over.

Her bedded wedded secrets were safely hidden.

SMALL HADIŠ

DAY BEFORE the FESTIVAL of NO'ROUZ

DAWN

"Wake up, Alexander!" Rošanak shakes her King-Husband and starts pulling him out of the massive royal bed. "Alexander! Wake up!"

Alexander stirs and slowly opens his eyes, still heavy with deep sleep.

"No'rouz is tomorrow and there is much to be done today!"

"Penalty for disturbing the King from deep sleep is death!"

Rošanak ignores him and pulls a tunic over his sleepy head.

"Penalty for sleeping through sacred No'rouz is a year full of unbroken dreadful fortune!"

Rošanak offers him a pair of Persian trousers.

"I die before slaving my thighs into one of those!" Alexander grunts, still half-asleep.

Rošanak shrugs her shoulder and tosses the sarbalâ toward the royal bed. She grabs a white robe and clasps it around him with golden lion fasteners. She pushes him into a chair and hands him his sandals and then looks around.

Alexander pulls on his sandals grudgingly.

He wanted to crawl back into bed and pull her with him and sleep wrapped around her through the whole day. And through the night.

She hands him a pair of weatherworn leg guards.

"Wear these… they make you look more kingly."

Alexander takes the old leg guards and grimaces.

Rošanak looks at Alexander's hair and then shrugs her shoulders.

There was not much she could do with the golden mane of a sleepy lion without the lion taking a good bite out of her arm in gratitude!

Rošanak grabs his arm and pulls him behind her down the steps.

Peritas, banished from the royal bedchamber, and sleeping on the cool stone in the doorway entrance downstairs, jumps up excited, wags his tail eagerly and trots in front of them.

The royal boys jump to their feet and start following them quickly too.

MAIN HADIŠ

Rošanak pulls Alexander into the main hadiš and into the kitchen and pushes him down into a chair behind a large table.

The royal boys stand by the door. Peritas makes his way into the kitchen and lies down at Alexander's feet.

The maids, scurrying around the kitchen, turn white in fear and all kneel down and bow their heads.

"Get up, Ladies. The No'rouz table will not set itself." Rošanak orders the maids happily.

They all bow their heads and get to their feet and return to work, casting down their eyes.

"Thukrâ! Bring the King something to eat!"

Thukrâ turns around, goes pale and quickly drops to her feet and bows.

"Thukrâ! Hurry!"

Thukrâ gets back up to her feet and walks over, bowing. "Your Majesty," she says timidly in accented broken Attik, shielding her eyes, looking at her feet, "what is your pleasure this morning?"

Alexander looks at her for a brief moment.

Rošanak walks around the kitchen, humming like a bird under her breath.

Alexander's eyes follow her around the room.

Thukrâ looks from the corner of her eye and then speaks gently in a low obedient voice, holding her hands, shielding her mouth, head bowed. "Your Majesty, Festival of No'rouz is her favorite. Since she was a little girl, she would go into a frenzy for a whole month. It is in her royal Persian blood. She hears her kingly ancestors calling her unto them."

Alexander turns his head and looks back at Thukrâ. "Where did you learn Attik, Mother?"

"At Susa, Your Majesty! I was working in the royal kitchen. I was gifted by the Third Artaxerxes to Prince Bessos, when he was sent here to Baktria."

Alexander's eyes follow Rošanak. "Did all the cooks in Susa speak Attik, Mother?"

"No, Your Majesty. I had a Hellene lover," she says shyly.

Alexander looks back at Thukrâ and smiles unguardedly. His bright smile charms Thukrâ. She blushes and lowers her head.

"Some eggs and a cup of wine, Mother."

Thukrâ bows quickly and walks backward and then turns and starts cooking. Rošanak pours a cup of wine and takes a sip and hands it to Alexander. She bends and kisses his face wordlessly and walks away.

Thukrâ approaches, bowing, with a plate full of cooked eggs and a chunk of fresh barley bread.

Rošanak sits down next to him and takes a silver spoon and tastes Alexander's food. The heavy taste of cooked eggs lingers on her tongue.

Thukrâ returns with a plateful for Peritas. The hound licks Thukrâ's hands and gulps his food down fast as usual.

Rošanak slides off her sandals and sinks her bare feet into Peritas' soft fur. Peritas licks her feet.

"Thukrâ, bring me some figs and sweets."

"You should eat some eggs and bread!"

"No… just some figs and pits… and lots of sweets."

Thukrâ approaches, bowing, with a plate full of figs and pits and Persian sweets. "You should eat something more, beloved. Pits and sweets will not keep you strong for the King!" she says gently in Persian.

Rošanak smiles and eats a fig whole, erasing the taste of eggs from her tongue, and leans into Alexander. "Eat faster, My Lord! We do not want to be late to the goddess!"

Alexander looks at her, smiling, finally beginning to wake up.

He did not need urging from his wife… he always started his days with sacrificing to the gods and then a seated meal at the table.

"Thukrâ! Feed the royal boys! Give them some bread and wine and something sweet."

Thukrâ obeys and takes two plates of eggs for the royal boys.

The royal boys look at her and then back at Alexander.

Alexander nods and they take the bread from the plates and the cups of wine.

Alexander reaches and takes Rošanak's hand and pulls her close to him. "You are ruining my royal boys too! They are supposed to be hard as hammered Makedonian metal, not soft like pampered Hellene mistresses!"

Peritas snores on the floor with a belly full of food and happiness.

"You have absolutely ruined my hunting hound beyond mending!" Alexander points down with his eyes to Peritas.

"But it is No'rouz, Alexander!" Rošanak whispers back softly and kisses his face.

TEMPLE of DIVINE GODDESS ÂNÂHITÂ

LATER

Sacred silence.

Alexander enters the ancient temple. He looks around.

The temple was quiet… what was old and broken was now new and mended and bathed in glory. Fires burned in the silvery twin altars flanking the statue of the goddess.

The golden crown and the gossamer shawl still adorned the sacred statue.

Hephæstion had done a good job of restoring the Queen's Temple.

The Queen should be pleased!

Rošanak stands in front of the statue of the divine goddess, with her hands clasped, whispering quietly in Persian. She finishes and empties a small skin bag full of incense into each of the fire altars. She turns around and looks at Alexander who is watching her intently.

He steps forward and puts a handful of incense into each of the fire altars and turns and stands next to her.

She points to the golden wreath with her finger. "My goddess used to have a golden crown with rays of light and a hundred golden stars before her sacred temple was sacked."

She pauses and points with her eyes, "I told the divine goddess that her sacred temple was restored by your order and that the golden crown and the golden shawl were your offerings to bless our marriage and I asked for her blessings for the generous Lord of Asia."

Alexander looks at her smiling, his head tilting slightly more to the left.

His wife was generous with her gods and goddesses and she loved horses and dogs and she was his… and she was more beautiful than all the goddesses in the heavens…

"Good. One should not be stingy with the gods and goddesses!"

Rošanak smiles and leans over and kisses him sweetly.

"I am glad you are not too tall. I can kiss your face anywhere without climbing on a ladder."

Alexander smiles brightly.

"I am glad the Persian Queen is satisfied with her short and old mountain lion."

Rošanak kisses him again.

"Utterly satisfied, My Lord."

MAIN HADIŠ

LATER

"Hephæstion."

"Alexander," Hephæstion says as Alexander and Rošanak and Peritas and the royal boys walk on the main palace terrace.

Alexander dismisses the royal guards and the royal boys.

"Roxana." Hephæstion bows his head slightly.

"Hephæstion."

Peritas trots and barks at Hephæstion and wags his tail side to side. Hephæstion kneels down and scratches Peritas' ears. "I can see you are growing fat and lazy in your old days, Peritas. My father told me you had Persian blood."

Rošanak laughs and calls on her dog. "Peritas!"

Peritas runs back to her and lies down at her feet obediently.

"Then Hephæstion, I am grateful that you have returned Peritas to his rightful Land and unto the hands of his rightful master. We do not care if our dogs are old and lazy, as long as they are obedient to our commands."

Hephæstion stands up and looks at Alexander curiously.

Alexander shrugs his shoulders. "He does not mind me anymore either. If he was one of my men, I could have had him hanged for disloyalty."

Rošanak laughs unguardedly and bends her knees and scratches Peritas' ears.

The maids are busy setting up the No'rouz table inside the palace.

Rošanak straightens and heads inside the palace.

Peritas jumps up and follows her.

"Alexander." Rošanak calls him.

Alexander turns and follows Rošanak inside.

Hephæstion follows Alexander.

"No'rouz, the New Day, the day of the renewal… vernal equinox will start at sunrise tomorrow, when the first rays of the rising sun hit the center of this palace hall."

Alexander and Hephæstion look around.

The maids bow and continue their work under the watchful eyes of Rošanak.

"And we will eat splendid sweets prepared specially for this splendid occasion all day long!" Rošanak walks toward one of the tables and points.

"Yes, there will be exquisite Persian sweets, made with sugar and almonds, pistachios and rose water, dried fruits, nuts and berries."

Alexander and Hephæstion follow her around, caught up in her excitement.

"It is the day when all the kings and satraps and governors from all the Lands of the Persians brought magnificent gifts and tributes for the Persian King in Persepolis!" she says. "Alexander, as you are the new ruler of the region, your subjects will come to this palace, bringing you tributes and gifts. Baktrian gold. And silk from Qin, spices from India, ivory from Parikanioi, pearls from the Hyrkania Sea, and goats and—"

Alexander interrupts ruefully. "No one came to see us when we were in Persepolis."

"They will come, Alexander. We are married. Baktrians came to the wedding and they will come for No'rouz. Everyone will come to give their blessings to the King and his Queen and wish us well for the start of the New Year."

Rošanak smiles and points to the table. "My favorite is the setting of the table with sacred offerings, each corresponding to the Seven Creations and the Seven Holy Guardian Angels protecting them."

She points excitedly to each item on the table and counts and mumbles under her breath.

"Wheat and barley seeds growing in a golden platter for rebirth and renewal,
the sweet paste made from wheat germ for riches and wealth,
the dried fruit of the oleaster tree for love,
garlic for healing,
apples for beauty and health,
summâq berries for the rising of the sun,
sour wine for patience and wisdom,
fragrant hyacinth flower for the coming of spring…"

Her face reddens and she steals her eyes and continues,

"sweet wine for remembrance…
… and golden archers for prosperity and wealth."

She looks around, tapping her fingers on her chin, counting to see if she has forgotten anything.

"And on this table, there will be lit candles for enlightenment and for happiness, a looking glass, colored eggs, one for each member of the family for fertility…

"On that table, a bowl with a golden fish, sign of life, a bowl of water with an orange in it, symbol of sun floating in sky, and rose water for its magical cleansing powers, and a few books of prayer and poetry."

"Ah! Finally a place to display your worn-out copy of the *Ilias*, Alexander."

"*Ilias* ?"

"Yes. Alexander's favorite book. The *Ilias* by Homer. He carries a copy with him everywhere."

"Aristoteles, my teacher, gave it to me."

"Ah! Aristoteles. Yes. Polydoros knows of him. He forced me to read *Ilias*."

Rošanak eats a sweet and mumbles to herself lightheartedly.

"Tale of the fighting in the last days of the siege of Troia, a Land on the edge of the Lands of the Persians. Helene of Sparta. Men died to gain her favor. A great love story of the ancients. Helene, Daughter of Zeus, Wife of Menelaos, seduced by Paris, the handsome Prince of Troia."

Hephæstion shakes his head side to side. "It is not a tale of love, it is a tale of honor and loyalty and bravery. About Achilleos, not Helene."

"It is about Helene!" Rošanak insists.

"Achilleos!" Hephæstion insists too.

"Sing goddess, the wrath of Achilleos, the son of Peleos, the destructive rage that sent countless pains on the old Hellenes," Hephæstion declares with open arms. "The opening lines of *Ilias*. It took me months to memorize these lines."

Rošanak shakes her head in disagreement. "Helene! Named after Helene, Hellenic Goddess of Light, with a face that launched a thousand ships! Helene wept and said: *Hektor, tamer of horses, I weep for you and for myself.*" She sighs.

"I wish I was so fair that men would wage battles over me!"

Alexander looks at Rošanak. "But Roxana, you are the most beautiful woman in my whole Empire!"

Rošanak asks guardedly, "You have seen all the women of the Lands?"

"No, but—"

Hephæstion interrupts and utters passionately. "Wrath of Achilleos is the heart of *Ilias*."

"When Agamemnon, the commander of the forces of Hellas at Troia, takes Briseis, a captive woman given to him as a prize of war, he dishonors Achilleos. Achilleos becomes furious, and withdraws from the battle. Without Achilleos, the Hellenes are nearly defeated by the Trojans," Alexander says. "As without me, my men would fail!"

"When Patroklos, a close friend of Achilleos, is killed by the Trojan Prince, Hektor," Hephæstion says, "Achilleos comes back to the battlefield, where he kills Hektor and desecrates his body. Priamos, father of Hektor, ransoms the body of Hektor, with the help of the gods."

"It all ends with the funeral of Hektor." Alexander finishes.

"Poor Hektor," Rošanak utters quietly, masking a sad memory.

"The Makedonians desecrated the body of my father, King Artaxerxes. They tore his royal body to pieces. There was nothing left for us to bury," she says, without thinking.

Alexander and Hephæstion are caught off guard and exchange glances.

Alexander had ordered it and Ptolemaios had tied Bessos to the bent trees and then released the trees… some pieces of his body were never found.

Rošanak bites her lip and shrugs her shoulders and pushes the memory out of her mind.

As her blood mother always said: Her royal father had died honorably by the favor of the Wise Lord…

And now he was in the Land of the Eternal Light with all her brothers and sister and the other blessed souls of his royal ancestors…

"A dead body— is nothing but an empty vessel. It is the soul that matters. The soul lingers on earth for three days after death and then after the First Judgment on the fourth day, the Wise Lord takes the soul to the Land of the Eternal Light…"

… or to the Land of the Eternal Darkness…

Thukrâ brings new trays of Persian sweets, freshly prepared.

Tension breaks.

Rošanak takes a couple of pieces and offers them to Alexander and Hephæstion and says, "But I prefer Persian tales… tales dripping with blood, knotted with myths and legends and heroes… lovers and swords and sorcerers… God and Kings… blood and wine… old legends passed lip to lip… lip to ear… from mother to daughter… father to son… lover to lover… generation to generation…"

SMALL HADIŠ at BAKTRA
YEAR 10 of ALEXANDER, MONTH 7, ARTEMISIOS
YEAR 4 of ALEXANDER, MONTH 1, ADUKANAIŠA, DAY 21
FESTIVAL of NO'ROUZ
BEFORE DAWN

Fragrant night.

Rošanak slowly opens her eyes.

Quiet. It is still dark outside. A small candle still flickers somewhere in the bedchamber, hanging stubbornly to dear life. She feels a little unsettled.

Thukrâ was right… she should have eaten something more yesterday… but she was caught in the excitement of No'rouz and her fancy took to nothing but figs and sweets…

She turns and lies down on her back. Alexander is still sleeping. She turns toward him and watches him sleep and listens to him breathe.

… when he slept, he was oblivious to the world around him, but still kept the golden dagger from their wedding night under his pillow.

She was a light sleeper… she could hear every sound… feel every move.

This was to be the first real No'rouz celebration since the war had started.

Her heart feels full and empty, empty for the loss of Utâna and full for the gain of Alexander.

Her life felt so certain when she was a child… she was a Royal Daughter… she was going to marry and have many sons and serve the Great King and the Wise Lord… but when the war had come, she had become used to living day by day.

Silent tears fall on her pillow.

She feels uncertain.

Alexander lay just a few fingers away from her heart and yet it felt like they were separated by a river wider than the River of Sands…

Did he love her?

… or was she just a captive woman, soon to be left behind and forgotten from his heart when he returned to the lands of his ancestors…

He had left her royal sisters at the Royal City of Çûšâ and they were both far more beautiful than she and they both had learned his tongue and the ways of his ancestors from the tutors he had sent to them himself.

Had he claimed Setâreh, the Royal Wife of Dâriuš? They said she had died before the Battle of Black Eagle… he had mourned her death… Did he think of Setâreh when he was lying in her arms? She had prayed for years to look like Setâreh… Setâreh was so splendidly Persian… tall and curved and brown-eyed and milky-skinned and rose-scented and utterly beautiful… She looked like a bag of bones compared to wondrous Setâreh…

Did she love him?

… or was it just the fleeting desire of her body responding to the touch of a new lover and nothing more… How could she love a man who had destroyed the world and all that she was born into? Why was it so easy to love him in spite of all he had done?

She had cursed the enemies of the Persians all her life, thinking them evil, wretched, fire-breathing, two-headed monsters… but Alexander and his kingsmen were just men… men like all other men.

She was so worried that yielding to Alexander would lessen her love for Utâna, but nothing in her heart had changed much. It was like the ancient tale of creation about the Earth expanding three times and then three times more to make room for all the newcomers… or like a new Great King ascending to the same Persian throne and building himself a new palace in Pârsâ, leaving older palaces of former kings well alone.

She takes a deep breath and turns around and slowly gets out of bed.

The hadiš was quiet… the night was quiet… the world was quiet… in breathless anticipation of the coming new year…

She hesitates for a long moment.

The royal boys were probably falling asleep at the door or chasing fireflies in the garden, trying to stay awake… boys awash in a strange rough sea, far from the lands of their fathers, and the tongue of their ancestors, yet seeming so sure of themselves…

Then she wraps a silky sheet of linen around her nakedness and quietly heads down the steps.

She felt like taking a warm bath… washing away the old year and the bad memories… making herself clean and new and ready for the New Year…

The new year lion was returning faithfully to devour the old year bull… like the lion consuming the bull on the walls of Pârsâ… not like a predator feeding on a prey… but like a lover claiming the beloved…

Lion and the Bull… two lovers… forever bound to each other, locked in an eternal embrace of birth and death and renewal.

And they said women were not carved on the walls of Pârsâ… Men were blind!

To barbarian eyes, Pârsâ was motionless, caught in tiresome repetition… to Persian eyes, Pârsâ was the Empire at peace… with the Great Kings and their kinsmen and kingsmen keeping the proper balance of Good and Evil… Truth and Lie… everything peacefully in its proper place as it was always meant to be… life as it should be… serving the Wise Lord as ordained by the Wise Lord…

Candles burn around the hadiš, lighting her path.

She was glad for the candles… Persian palaces were never dark… always bathed in the light of the sacred flames… never extinguished… but for the death of the Great King.

She utters a quiet prayer under her lips for the sacred flames of the candles and makes her way into the kitchen. She smiles and walks to the table and sits down on a chair and wraps the soft sheet loosely around her.

On the table, Thukrâ had left her plates full of freshly made Persian sweets and figs.

She hungrily eats a couple of figs; they settle her grumbling belly.

She pulls a plate of sweets toward her and puts one in her mouth; sweetened almond paste melts like sweet butter in her mouth. She eats another.

Thukrâ never forgot her… she always took care of her…

She looks around.

The small hadiš was not smaller than the main hadiš, and was built the same…

… and both palaces… no, indeed the palaces and the gardens at Baktra were fashioned after the palaces and gardens in Pârsâkata… it was always the desire of the Great Kings to have their satraps live as nobly as the Great King himself.

The small palace was mostly used by her father to entertain royals and nobles and warlords and envoys of the Great King.

When her brothers had passed into manhood, they used to bring their beloveds to the bedrooms upstairs…

The love tales those walls could tell…
The love songs those walls could sing…
The love scenes those walls could paint…

And then the war had started and the men of the house had gone to war and the small hadiš had become the dwelling of the forgotten ghosts… and then occupied by the barbarian armies of the invaders.

But it was to the kitchen in the main hadiš that everyone flocked day or night.

Ladies and maids and eunuchs… and men… it was the heart of the palace where news from the Lands and stories and rumors were passed on along with plates of sweets: Thukrâ's specialty.

She eats another sweet.

She loved Thukrâ… and Thukrâ loved her, as if she was born to her own body. Thukrâ loved her as she was… When no one else was around, she called her 'My Sweet Daughter'.

Old Thukrâ was not much older than her blood mother, just two seasons. She had come with her father from the heartland. Mâr'at Bani Âriyânnâz was her tutor, a gift from the Great King… the one who had taught her how to be a Persian Royal Daughter.

Her blood mother had given her life and she loved her blood mother…

But Thukrâ was her memories… Thukrâ knew more about her than she knew about herself. Thukrâ remembered her as a child… the memories of which had been lost to her long ago. It was Thukrâ who always had a plate full of sweets for her and kind kisses when she would come home battered and bruised and bloodied… fallen off horses and trees and whatever else she could climb…

She eats another sweet.

She was the lastborn to her mother. They said after she was born, the passion of her blood mother had cooled for her blood father. Her father loved her mother and had not taken another wife nor a mistress…

But her father was a man… and he had taken comfort in Thukrâ's generous body. Her blood mother knew but had turned a blind eye.

Thukrâ had never uttered a word to anyone and had always been respectful to her blood mother.
Her blood mother was willowy and beautiful and had borne three Royal Sons to her father.
Thukrâ was barren and short and fleshy, with a kind face… and glad for the use of her body late in her years.
She had found out when she had stolen away late one night into the small hadiš to spy on her brothers… and had found her father and Thukrâ joined together…
Her blood mother did not have a thousand eyes…
She takes a deep breath.
She and her blood mother had not been close when she was growing up… she always followed her father and chased after her blood brothers and her other brothers. Her blood mother and her sister of the same mother were close… almost like blood sisters. She had grown close to her blood mother after her father and her blood brothers and her blood sister had died…
She had Thukrâ when she was growing up. Her Hellene lover was not too small for her, as she had claimed publicly… he had not followed her when she was sent to Baktra and that was her bitter heartbreak… the reason her hair had turned all white…
Thukrâ had cried a river when her father was executed… not even her blood mother had poured out that many tears for her father. Thukrâ said it was because her blood mother had spent all her tears when her blood sons had died at war.
Utâna had told her that it was Thukrâ who had made them the wedding bed in the âyadana… and it was Thukrâ who had waited and had bathed her in the small hadiš, after she had returned home that early dawn. She had rubbed her with healing za'farân paste and anointed her with sacred oils and the love bruises on her body had almost vanished by the next day… and she had fed her a full plate of Persian sweets.
Thukrâ had taken to comforting Uxšiyârta after the death of her father; Uxšiyârta was a man too and he had not wedded after the death of his Persian wife. And it was Thukrâ who had told Uxšiyârta where he could find her the night she had gone to the âyadana to offer up her life, and she was the one who had held her in her arms and let her cry a river over her pending doom when Uxšiyârta had come for her and had dragged her back to the hadiš…
She eats another sweet and thinks of Alexander.
It was Thukrâ who had taken away all her fear of Alexander.
She had told her to treat Alexander like a lion… never let him smell fear in her, unless she wanted the lion to make a meal of her…

"Be a lion if you want to conquer a lion!"

It was a tongue she had understood well…
She had gone on hunts with her fathers and all her brothers when she was younger… and had watched them hunt golden lions…

Uxšiyârta was the fiercest hunter in all the satrapies on this side of the Royal City of Hagmâtâna. His left shoulder was marked with the claws of a ferocious lion from long ago. He always waited until the lion got so close to him that they looked at each other eye to eye and breathed into each other's faces before Uxšiyârta pierced the underbelly of the noble beast, straight to the heart with a Persian dagger… preserving the full beauty of the skin of the golden lion… without unsightly marks of killer arrows or spears or swords…

She gets up to her feet and pulls the sheet loosely around her and makes her way to the bêt rimdi. She opens the golden spout and the water basin starts to fill with warm water.

LATER that NIGHT

Alexander radiates with kingly glory.

The Persian New Day, marking the beginning of the Persian New Year had come to pass.

He had sat on his royal throne… and unlike Persepolis, his subjects had come.

They had come to pay tribute to Alexander, the Lord of Asia, and his Queen, Roxana, in the audience hall, filled with the rays of the dawning sun… decorated by his Queen, filled with hyacinths and tulips… flanked by silvery fire altars and slow smoldering sacred fire spiced with heaps of precious incense…

First, Roxana had knelt before him and uttered softly in Persian, as Polydoros interpreted quietly in his ears…

> *"I worship the Wise Lord…*
>
> *… who made the light and the dark, the morning, the noon and the night, who keeps the sky from falling…*
>
> *'May the Wise Lord keep the Lord of Asia and the Lands and Waters of the Persians…*
>
> *'May the Divine Goddess Anaitis bless the Lord of Asia with a progeny of sons…*
>
> *'May the Divine Mithres watch over the King and the men of the King in battle…*
>
> *'May the kingly glory remain with the King and the Lands in the New Year…*
>
> *'May the Lord of Asia accept the love of his Persian Queen as the first tribute of the people of his Lands on the New Day at the start of the blessed New Year…"*

And then she had leaned over and kissed his right hand… and had looked up and smiled at him… waiting…

The words had come to him, as if he had done this a thousand times…

> *'May the Lord of Asia remain worthy of the favor of the gods and the loyalty of his brave warriors and the love of his Persian Queen."*

Roxana had gracefully gotten to her feet and had smiled and walked and stood by his throne where the Persian Queens had stood for countless generations… a body's width behind the King… in his blind sight… not visibly seen… but utterly felt…

Then, Princess Faranak and Prince Oxyartes and all their kinsmen had come forward and kissed his face.

Followed by the noblest Persians and Baktrians and others from neighboring satrapies… all bowing and bending rightfully to their new king… bringing everything from precious golden coins to horses, to goats and singing birds!

Small children had brought him handfuls of fragrant spring flowers…

And it was bittersweet…

His first Persian New Year… three years after the Death of Darius… four years after the Battle of Gaugamela… five years after the Siege of Tyre… six years after the Battle of Issos… seven years after the Battle of Granikos… it had felt magical and sacred.

Three years ago, he had sat on the throne of the Great King in Persepolis, the sacred and ceremonial seat of the Persian Empire, his throne by conquest, won by blood and spear…

… waiting and waiting and waiting…

He had commanded Darius to come before him as a vassal king and relinquish his crown to him in Persepolis according to the customs of the Achæmenids… and he had not come before him… no one had come. He had waited for four months… then Persepolis had flamed and blackened and burned in his drunken anger and rage and wrath.

If not him, then no one else would ever ascend to the throne of the Great Kings in Persepolis… No one!

He had not conquered Persepolis by the grace of the gods of the Persians, but by the will of his own gods… the gods of the Persians had not called unto him to come to Persia, as the gods of Babylon had called to Kuros to go to Babylon… and so he had sacrificed Persepolis to his own gods and for his own glory.

Achilleos' wrath had burned Troia, the City of the Trojans… his wrath had burned Persepolis, the City of the Persians.

And when the wine had drained from his body, he knew in his bones that all was lost… but now… he finally had been given a small taste of the true splendor of the Persian Kings… Persepolis would have been truly glorious, but magical no more.

Even his close kingsmen had come… First, Hephæstion, bowing and proclaiming:

"Health and prosperity to King Alexander."

And all the favored friends of the King, and then his companions, and all the kingsmen… and a handful of his common men too.

Some had bowed and paid him tribute and some had not… some had given him their blessings and some had cast evil eyes upon him… and he had made a note of all.

Rošanak crawls into bed and looks at Alexander. She does not have to ask. Alexander's happiness is carved on his face, like a kingly declaration on a splendid palace wall.

He wraps his body around her naked body and holds her tightly; his desire for her grows long and strong.

He had worn the royal Tyrian-purpled robe… he had sat on the tall jewel-crusted thrones… he had slept under golden-embroidered skies with the jeweled Tree-of-Life guarding over him… he had drank pure unmixed wine from golden cups.

But the eternal glory and grace of the Persian Kings that had finally poured into his blood… had come through the jasmine-scented words and sweet kisses of his Persian Queen…

The Oracle of Zeus-Ammon at Siwah had told him that he was to become immortal… and the Oracle had spoken the truth.

ALEXANDER'S ROYAL TENT
DRINKING FEAST
2 NIGHTS LATER

"Alexander! Do not let him kiss you!" one of the kingsmen bellows indignantly across the royal tent. "Kallisthenes did not show you the Persian mark of honor!"

Hushed silence.

Alexander stops mid-sentence talking to Hephæstion and turns his head and his eyes toward Kallisthenes.

Kallisthenes stands before him, holding the Persian rhyton in his hand, waiting to kiss him like a kinsman.

Alexander reclines further on his silver couch and waits for a few moments and considers him.

Kallisthenes stands boldly, knees unbent, head unbowed.

Alexander narrows his eyes at him and waves him away.

"I go away poorer for one kiss!" Kallisthenes quips as he walks away and hands the Persian rhyton to another kingsman.

Alexander turns back to Hephæstion and grinds his teeth angrily, glaring at Kallisthenes. "The fool mocks me!"

"I talked to him, Alexander. He promised!"

Alexander looks back at Hephæstion with blazing eyes.

"My Queen of royal blood kneels before me and kisses my hands, and this son of a filthy Hellene whore dares to dishonor me with a silver tongue in my royal court in front of my kingsmen."

Hephæstion looks back at Kallisthenes and marks him with his eyes.

Every one… Perdikkas, Lysimachos, Medeios, Ptolemaios… even Leonnatos who had laughed foolishly once at a Persian noble for bowing low to the King and bending his knees… and all the rest had sipped pure unmixed wine from the golden Persian rhyton and had bowed before Alexander, as all the Persian nobles had before them. All but Kallisthenes, who had agreed when he had invited him to the royal court drinking feast.

Krateros, the pure Makedonian, and old Polyperchon would have done it too, if they had been there.

Kallisthenes had bargained far too long with his token of kinship with Aristoteles…

And the token was now all spent!

And lately he had been boastful about how he had made the legend and the myth of Alexander… and how easily he could unmake him… all the same… with his lofty words about freedom and tyrants…

Idiot Philosopher! The Men of the Words were so ignorant of how their fates danced carelessly on the cutting blades of the Men of the Sword.

POLYDOROS' QUARTERS
DAYS LATER

"Thukra tells me you have been eating nothing but figs and Persians sweets." Polydoros narrows his eyes and speaks in a scornful tone.

"Not true! I have also been drinking sweet wine." Rošanak sweetens her voice. "It is No'rouz, Polydoros, lighten up. You know I always crave sweets this time of year."

"I see."

"Ouch!"

Rošanak steps back and puts her hands on her breasts.

"The tips of your breasts are tender too? This time of the year?"

Rošanak makes a face. "Polydoros! I am a married woman now! I can order your fingers cut off for touching my breasts! Or have your manhood removed!"

"You can, but neither will change the fact that you are with child."

"With child?"

"Yes."

"Are you certain?"

"Yes."

"But I have no taste for sour pomegranate! That is what my blood mother craved whenever she was with child!"

"I am a healer! I know!"

Rošanak embraces Polydoros and kisses him and puts her hands on her belly.

"A son!" she says happily, beaming.

"Do you think Alexander will be pleased?"

"Maybe about begetting an heir— but—"

"But what?"

"I do not know about Makedonians, but Hellenes will not touch a woman who is with child, until the child is born."

"Why?"

Polydoros shrugs his shoulders. "Bad fortune!"

Tears rush into Rošanak's eyes.

"I do not know how to sleep without Alexander. I crave him like air—"

Polydoros counts on his fingers. "Crave him a little less!"

"But—"

"Soon, it will be hard to hide your swelling belly from him. Even if he was blind, his wandering fingers will betray your rounded secret. Your own mother will forbid you to bed your husband, according to your faith."

"Swear by one of your gods that you will not tell anyone!"

Polydoros looks at her, puzzled. "Why not?"

"I want to be certain of it!"

She had eaten whole trees of figs after her one night of love with Utâna… but his seed had not taken in her…

Polydoros shakes his head.

Women!

"Swear it!" Rošanak insists.

"Oh, very well. I swear to Asklepios that I will not tell anyone that you are with child, even if your belly swells up to the size of a Persian melon! I will just say that you have swallowed watermelon seeds— and now one is growing in your belly! They will have to kill me first to get to the truth!"

"Good!"

"Women!"

MAIN HADIŠ
DAYS LATER
AFTERNOON

"Gaugamela." Alexander says, pointing down at his feet.

"Gau Gamela. The Land of the Black Eagle. In the Lands Across-the-River," Polydoros interprets.

The terrace floor of the main hadiš is covered with small wooden toy warriors and horses and chariots.

Polydoros, Itâna, Nimâ and Dârâ are sitting on the floor along the edges, waiting eagerly to hear the tale of the famous battle from the King who had carried the day himself.

Nimâ and Dârâ laugh with excitement.

Large platters filled with summer fruits are spread across the terrace within easy reach of all.

Aššat Šarri Farânak and Uxšiyârta sit on a couch, pushed back against the wall.

Hephæstion stands back further, leaning against the wall and watching intently.

Rošanak walks onto the terrace and sits down next to the boys, with Peritas following her obediently and lying down at her feet.

"The Battle of Gaugamela!"

Uxšiyârta shifts uncomfortably.

Alexander smiles and points to the false battlefield at his feet and speaks as Polydoros interprets eagerly.

"This is how I crossed into the land called the Land Between the Two Rivers, having the River Euphrates and the mountains of Armenia on my left. When I started from the River Euphrates, I did not march to Babylon by the direct road." Alexander pauses and asks the boys, "Why?"

The boys shrug their shoulders.

"Because Hephæstion said," Alexander points to Hephæstion, "that finding hay for our horses and provisions for our men was easier going the other way, and the heat was more tolerable too.

"We took some of the men from the Royal Army of Darius, who were scouting the area, prisoners! They told us that Darius was encamped near the River Tigris to prevent me from crossing that river. The prisoners also told us that Darius had a much larger Royal Army than the one he had at the Battle of Issos.

"When I heard this, I marched as fast as I could towards the River Tigris—but when I reached the river, I found neither Darius himself nor any of his Royal Army. The damn prisoners had lied to us!"

Everybody laughs.

Rošanak looks around and eats a slice of a sweet Persian melon.

Boys and men alike were all captivated by the tale of the bloody battle. They were seeing warriors, arrayed for battle in countess numbers, they were hearing the sounds of clashing of men and neighing of horses and clanking of swords… and smelling the blood pouring, as Alexander spoke… the men felt the battle in their bones… they were not seeing wooden toys…

They were all standing next to Divine Mithrâ, the Sun-God, watching over the Persians where the Great King had led the Royal Army, with the Kingsmen of the Great King arrayed in countless numbers summoned from all the Lands.

They were all gods looking down from the crown of that Mount Olympus in heavens, deliberating over the fortunes and misfortunes of pitiful mortals…

….

Alexander pauses and points up at the skies. "Then, a total Eclipse of the Moon occurred!"

"Ahhh!"

"I offered sacrifice to the Moon, the Sun and the Earth. Aristandros thought that this Eclipse of the Moon was a favorable omen! It meant that I and the Makedonians would be victorious in a battle occurring in that month!"

"Ahhh!"

"So, I marched my Royal Army from…"

….

"… there were 40,000 Horse, 1,000,000 Foot, and 200 scythe-bearing Chariots in the whole Royal Army of Darius—"

"The whole Royal Army of Darius had 40,000 Horse, 1,000,000 Immortals, and 200 knifed-chariots," Polydoros translates cautiously.

Uxšiyârta stirs on the couch and grunts. "Alexander, there were only 55,000 Foot and 35,000 Horse, in the whole Royal Army of the Third Dâriuš!"

Even though cowards did not count in battle… they just got in the way of the brave…

Nimâ and Dârâ point at Alexander and laugh.

Rošanak translates carefully.

Alexander eyes Uxšiyârta and then points to the toy elephants and continues undaunted. "There were only a few elephants, about fifteen, belonging to the Indians who live this side of the River Indus."

Uxšiyârta shakes his head side to side.

....

"My men stood tall, shoulder to shoulder, shields joined, all as skilled as their commanders. I took my place before the royal standard and told my entire Royal Army that this battle they were going to fight was not as before, either for the Lands Across-the-River or for the Lands by the Sea or for the Two Lands, but for the whole of Asia!" Alexander continues loudly and proudly, with his arms open wide: "I said: *This battle would decide who were to be the Masters of Asia!*"

His voice echoes.

"Ahhh!" Nimâ and Dârâ cheer loudly.

Alexander asks mysteriously, "Why did I say that?"

The boys shrug their shoulders.

"Because, it was necessary for my men to keep discipline during the dangerous moments of the battle! *And* to take care to obey their orders quickly, and to pass on the orders they had received to the ranks as fast as they could, each man remembering that absolute victory or defeat was in his own hands!"

"Ahhh!"

....

"The Royal Army of Darius was drawn up in the following manner: his left wing was held by the Baktrian Horse, on his right again were the Medes, next to them the Parthians, in the center, was Darius himself, with the Persian royal guards carrying spears with golden apples—"

"Pomegranate!" Rošanak says loudly.

They were the Arštibara… the Royal Bodyguards… the first One Thousand of the Ten Thousand Anauša… where all her brothers had served the Great King…

"On the left, opposite of my right, was the Scythian Horse, about 1,000 Baktrians and 100 scythe-bearing chariots."

Rošanak eyes Alexander and smiles.

The Amazons again?

"In front of Darius' Horse stood the elephants and 50 chariots. In front of the right flank were the Armenian and Kappadokian Horse with 50 scythe-bearing chariots. The Hellene mercenaries stood right opposite the Makedonian phalanx, in two divisions close beside Darius himself and his royal guards, one division on each side—"

Rošanak calmly interrupts, one eyebrow raised.

"Alexander, how do you remember such tedious details?"

Alexander smiles. "I am a military genius!"

Rošanak eyes him. "Ah! And so modest!"

Alexander grins.

"My Royal Army was commanded as follows: the right wing was held by the Makedonian Horse, in front of them were the Makedonian Foot, commanded by the Black Kleitos…"

Rošanak looks around. Boredom slowly wraps around her. Her ears start to fall asleep. Alexander's words fade in and out.

Alexander pauses for a moment and remembers the dead Kleitos with blood pouring out of his spear wound and then continues, "Near them was the squadron of Glaukias, next to it that of Aristo, then that of Sopolis, son of Hermodoros, then that of Herakleides, son of Antiochos. Near them was that of Demetrios, son of Althæmenes, then that of Meleagros, and last one of the royal squadrons commanded by Hegelochos, son of Hippostratos. All the Horse were under the command of Philotas, son of Parmenion—"

Alexander pauses for another moment and looks at Hephæstion.

"—of Makedonian Foot, nearest to the Horse were the hand-picked troops of shield-bearing guards, and then the rest of the shield-bearing guards, under the command of Nikanor, also son of Parmenion. Next to them were the men under the command of Koinos, then the men under the command of Perdikkas, then those under the command of Meleagros…

"Then the men under the command of Polyperchon… Krateros commanded the left flank of the Foot.

"Next to him was the Hellene Horse under the command of Erigyios. Next to them, towards the left wing of the Royal Army, were the Thessalian Horse, under the command of Philippos. The whole left wing was under the command of Parmenion, with the Pharsalian Horse, who were both the best and largest of the Thessalian Horse—"

Alexander catches his breath and thinks about old Parmenion for a moment. "Yes!" he nods. "I commanded 7,000 Horse and about 40,000 Foot! When the Royal Armies drew near each other, I carefully watched Darius and his kingsmen…"

….

Setting sun.

Alexander waving a sword in the air.

"I led them with a quick charge and a loud battle cry straight towards Darius himself! Ailalalala!"

"Ohhhh!"

Aššat Šarri Farânak sighs on her couch.

Rošanak opens her eyes and interrupts.

"Alexander! You are frightening my mother!"

Alexander lowers the sword.

"Then for a short time, men fought hand-to-hand. Then I commanded the Makedonian Horse. We pressed on forcefully, thrusting against the Persians and striking their—" Alexander pauses and glances at his Princess-Mother and then at Rošanak and the boys and mumbles the rest under his breath, "—faces with our spears. When the Makedonian Foot, arrayed tightly bristling with long sarissas, attack the Persians, Darius panicked and he was the first to turn and flee."

He glances at Rošanak and the boys. "The Persians fled and the Makedonians followed them—" he mumbles the rest quietly, "—and put them to the sword—"

. . . .

"Then the most dangerous Horse fight in the whole battle happened!" Alexander says confidently. "The Horse of the two Royal Armies clashed powerfully, every man trying to break through what stood in his way— they struck and were struck without quarter, about sixty of my Horse fell— Hephæstion, Perdikkas, Koinos and Menidas were all wounded."

Rošanak eyes Hephæstion discreetly, whose face had wrapped up in the darkness of the falling night.

Alexander continues. "Then I pursued Darius until the sunset— first I marched towards Arbela, with the hope of capturing Darius there, together with his royal funds and the rest of his royal property. But Darius had not stopped at Arbela. All I found on the way was his royal chariot and his golden spear and bow, just as I had after the Battle of Issos."

Alexander boasts, making much of his words. "100 of my men were killed and more than 1,000 of my horses were lost! 300,000 of enemy were killed and far more were taken prisoner!"

"Ahhh!"

Rošanak interrupts again. "Alexander! Uxšiyârta says only 90,000 in the entire Persian Royal Army! 55,000 Foot and 35,000 Horse! 200 Chariots and a handful of war elephants! He knows. He was there with my father!"

Alexander smiles and opens his arms wide. "I prefer the glorious to the truth!"

Rošanak shakes her head.

Boys laugh.

"Such was the result of this battle, which was fought in the archonship of Aristophanes at Athenai, in the Makedonian month of Hyperberetaios, making the prediction of Aristandros come true! I both fought a battle and gained a victory in the same month in which the moon was seen to have eclipsed!"

Even though he had to rename two months the same to make the prediction come true.

Twilight has completely surrendered to the night.

The boys are beginning to fall asleep on the carpet.

"Immediately after the battle, Darius marched through the mountains of Armenia towards Media, with all the Baktrian Horse, and what was left of his kinsmen and his royal guards."

Maids light the torches around the terrace.

Alexander continues, "About 2,000 of his Hellene mercenaries also followed Darius towards Ecbatana, because he thought I would take the road to Babylon and Susa immediately after the battle, because the lands were inhabited and the road was not difficult for the passage of baggage." He straightens and says quietly, "Royal Treasuries of Babylon and Susa were the prizes of the war."

Alexander looks around. Hephæstion is still faithfully watching over him. He looks around for Rošanak. She has fallen asleep, with Peritas snoring, sleeping soundly at her feet.

His faithful hound had switched sides just as easily as some of the men had on the battlefields!

Alexander looks at the darkened horizon. The dusty Battle of Gaugamela unfolds again vividly before his eyes.

What he had told Kallisthenes to write of the account of the battle was the bloody story washed and cleaned in the cold waters of a mountain stream. Not even he knew the full account of what had happened… all that was ever certain was the dust and chaos and confusion of the battle.

It was also certain that instead of fighting to the last man, the Royal Army of Darius had abandoned the battle once Darius had left the battlefield wounded by his spear…

Fortunes of kings were always betrayed and reversed by the treachery of their men.

Alexander grinds his teeth and mumbles to himself, "The prize of the war was capturing and killing Darius!"

TERRACE. MAIN HADIŠ
FOLLOWING DAY
MID-DAY

"Damn fool!"

Uxšiyârta grinds his teeth, crushing a wooden toy warrior mindlessly in his hand, kneeling down by the wooden toys, utterly lost in his thoughts.

Rošanak walks across the terrace of the main palace.

The false battlefield was in disarray as the real one must have been, with wooden toy warriors and toy horses and toy arms spread haphazardly around the terrace floor.

A bloody mess… even the maids had not yet attempted to clean up.

"Good Day, Abû," Rošanak says with a warm smile. "May your morning be blessed."

Uxšiyârta turns his head and looks at her. His eyes are heavy with tears, but he makes no attempt to hide his pain.

Rošanak is stunned.

This was the second time she had seen tears in the eyes of her father.

The first time was when he had come to the Sughud Fortress to tell her that Utâna was dead… they said he had cried for days when the dead body of his son had been brought back to him by his men.

Uxšiyârta considers her for a moment.

It was all his fault… He should have let Utâna marry her and get her with child.

He had thought about killing her at first, when the Makedonian King had asked for her, instead of letting her fall into the hands of the invaders. But he loved her like a daughter… the children of his blood sister and his own children had grown up together. He could rip lions apart with his bare hands, but could not bring himself to harm a hair on her head…

He looks up at the peaceful skies and mumbles to himself, pointing with his head. "There was a total Eclipse of the Moon… after the sunset… we all stood there in utter silence and watched the moon turn the color of clotted blood and then become utterly dark."

He looks back down at his feet and mumbles, "The Chaldæans sent word to Dâriuš that the Eclipse of the Moon on the day 13 of the Bâbiruviya month 6, Ulûlu, meant disaster for the King of the Persians. They foretold of the victory of the enemy king. They said for eight years he will exercise kingship… he will defeat everyone… he will find wealth and riches on his path and he will pursue his enemy relentlessly. They said there will be no end to his good fortune for eight years, until—"

Uxšiyârta closes his eyes in pain of remembrance.

"The Persians knew the old curse from the days of the Younger Kuruš… the rumors spread quickly through the whole Royal Army… everyone knew the fate of the Great King was already sealed."

Uxšiyârta looks up at Rošanak with teary eyes.

Yes… all the Persians knew the old curse, when the Younger Kuruš had cursed his older brother, before he had died at his hands… on a day not of his fate…

"My blood will be avenged… remember me in Hell!"

The Second Artakhšaçâ had cut off the head of his brother, the Younger Kuruš, and had held up the dripping bloody head to the horrified eyes of his men as proof of his victory…

Brother killing brother… cutting off his head with no mercy… sealing the fate of all the Lands in royal blood…

Blood begetting blood…

Treachery begetting more blood…

Uxšiyârta looks back down, his eyes wandering.

"The Persians had heard his legend too, how he had destroyed Ṣurru and Gaza, and they had seen him at Granikos and Issos. The brave satraps had charged Alexander fiercely at Granikos— his horse was killed under him, one satrap had hit him with his spear but was killed by king's own spear pushed right into his face—

"Another had smashed Alexander's helmet and had grazed the top of his head. As he moved to deliver the final blow, his arm had been cut off by one of Alexander's royal guards and his head cut off afterward.

"At Issos, Alexander had killed the kingsmen of Dâriuš by his own spear and sword and had survived a deep thigh wound in single battle with Dâriuš.

"He was invincible, protected from the deadliness of arrows and stones and swords and spears that killed mere mortals… Men were convinced by words and eyes that Alexander was protected by the tormented soul of the Younger Kuruš. There was nothing that could kill him. When he survived a death chill at Kissuwadna, after bathing in the River of Ice, everyone was convinced that the soul of the Younger Kuruš was his shield. Kissuwadna was the old satrapy of the Younger Kuruš— and the River of Ice was the same River of Ice the Younger Kuruš used to bathe in after hunting—"

Uxšiyârta shakes his head side to side.

"All the nobles of the Seven Persian Families went among the men, day after day. They told the men that there was no curse… no wicked magic… that moon was just passing behind the earth, that it was just wicked rumors spread by superstitious Hellene mercenaries, descendants of the Eight Thousand who had marched up country after the Battle of Kuništa under the watchful eyes of Tišafârnâ. Damn Artakhšaçâ had beheaded his own Royal Brother with no mercy and had mercifully spared the damn Hellenes, and in their ignorance they had thought the mercy of the Great King was weakness."

He takes a deep breath. "The Hellenes hated the Persians, but their sons and the sons of their sons had returned again and again to serve the Great Kings of the Persians in the Royal Armies. The Persian Gold was the cure for whatever ailed the Hellenes! There was not even one Hellene who had ever turned down the gold of the Great King. The Persian gold archers had always been stronger than the Hellene bronze shields!"

Uxšiyârta pauses.

"Honor! Ha! What honor? Hellenes fight other Hellenes for gold and glory! No Persian has ever fought another Persian for gold!" He shakes his head. "Name one Persian who had to escape to the Hellenes in disgrace because he had faithfully served the Great King!"

He draws a deep breath.

"Meanwhile, the kingsmen of Dâriuš had convinced him to wait for a season and starve the enemy army. We paid the farmers for their crops and then we burned the rolling wheat fields all around by the order of the Great King.

"Then a cursed eunuch escaped from the Makedonian camp and brought words that Setâreh had died at childbirth the month before."

"Ah!" Rošanak's knees fold under her. She sits down on the terrace floor. "They say she died of exhaustion… she was delicate…" she says quietly, trying to convince herself. Her face masks over in denial. "They say he showed her the greatest honor that could be shown to a Royal Woman!"

Uxšiyârta looks at her.

She was so young…

Who among mortal men could walk away from a heavenly beauty like Setâreh?

No one! Hearts pounded in the chest of men and their manhood grew long with desire at the mere mention of her name…

"Yes— she was shown the honor of lying naked in his bed while he got her with child!" he says, nodding his head mockingly.

"No!" Rošanak moans softly.

He shrugs his shoulders and looks back down at his feet.

It did not matter what he said… everyone was blind to the true nature of a lover or a beloved. Alexander had gone from enemy-king to king-husband in the eyes of his daughter… Women…

"The Great King had sent envoys offering 30,000 biltu of gold he was holding at Dimašqa to ransom his Royal Family, but Alexander had flatly refused and said to tell Dâriuš, what he had lost and what he still had were prizes of war.

"The eunuch said Alexander mourned her death for three days… he did not eat or drink or sleep… he even had refused to return her body to Dâriuš for burial even though Sisygambis had begged and pleaded with him. He had buried her himself… with full marks of honor, the damn eunuch said…"

Rošanak wells up with tears. She puts her hand on her belly unconsciously.

"Dâriuš cried throughout the whole night… Hukhšaqra, his Royal Brother, and his closest kinsmen and kingsmen kept watch over him for days. He loved her… the most beautiful woman in all the Lands, the most Royal Woman— A Persian Queen— had died the most horrid death to avoid bringing more shame to her king and husband."

Air leaves the terrace.

It could not be true!

She had heard the hushed rumors but that was before she had married Alexander…

Did he think of Setâreh when he was bedding her?

Uxšiyârta picks up one of the toy chariots and looks at it intently.

"Those most intimate with Dâriuš had almost convinced him not to use those worthless knifed-chariots, they had proven useless at the Battle in Kuništa and everyone knew it. Men just broke formation and stepped away and let them pass.

"And the Hellenes had told Dâriuš that leading from the center was fruitless against the Makedonians. They had to be out-flanked! Both right and left!"

Uxšiyârta takes a deep breath and carelessly throws the toy chariot back on the floor in front of him. He grinds his teeth. "But the treacherous rape and the wretched death of his beloved wife had beclouded his mind.

"He changed his battle formation to what his grandfather, the Second Artakhšaçâ, had arrayed before the Younger Kuruš and his Royal Army.

"He said that the Wise Lord had guided his grandfather to victory against the wrongful claim of his brother, using the same formation, and he too would be victorious against the wrongful claim of an enemy who had raped his beloved wife and had gotten her with a bastard child that in the end had killed her!"

Uxšiyârta clenches his teeth in anger. His eyes blaze in the color of blood.

"No one dared tell Dâriuš that his cursed grandfather had all but lost that cursed battle, saved by a mysterious treacherous arrow of a lowly Karka that had hit the Younger Kuruš in the face right below his right eye."

Uxšiyârta slowly gets to his feet and looks up at the heavens. "The night before the battle was an almost moonless night, but not dark… just haunted… no one slept, guarding against a night attack. On the morning of the battle, Alexander raised his standard.

"The two Royal Armies arrayed and clashed and attacked each other… their flanks swung hither and thither as they pushed forward and backward… there was enemy in the front and more enemy in the back.

"Men fought hard, hand to hand, sword to sword… man to man… on a hot day with dust storms raging on the dusty fields on the Land of the Black Eagle… and when they finally separated, each thought they had gained the victory and had carried the day.

"Dâriuš on his chariot, Alexander on his horse— both Kings were surrounded by their most noble warriors… careless of their own lives… if their king was to die, their men did not wish to live, nor could they. If they were to die, they all wished to die before the eyes of their Kings… both knotted so thick that the archers held back their arrows in fear of slaying the Great King himself. Warriors died on both sides. The fields were covered with dead bodies drenched in a sea of blood…

"There was so much dust in the air that no one could see their own hands… there was no air to breathe… just dust… both Royal Armies were confused… almost joined as one… impossible to tell friend from enemy… Persian from Makedonian… in an ocean ebbing and flowing with men and arms and armor and horses—"

He rubs his forehead, distracted.

"Then a rumor started to go from man to man… a black eagle had been seen flying over the head of Alexander all day… floating high in the air… not even the thick dust had diverted it from its mark. Men lost their reason and started to flee… Eagle was the mark of the Younger Kuruš… the golden sign on his standard. They all knew… they were not fighting men… they were fighting ghosts of wronged men… they were doomed by ancient curses."

He catches his breath for a moment.

"In the chaos of the dust, Alexander saw Dâriuš with the eyes of the black eagle… just as Younger Kuruš had marked his brother, the Second Artakhšaçâ.

"Alexander charged for Dâriuš… the charioteer of Dâriuš fell dead by a spear through his neck… the tip of the spear marked and wounded Dâriuš and he fell backward as his horses were pierced by spears too and bolted in the air with the pain of dying.

"Everyone thought the Great King was dead… killed by the enemy…"

"Ah!" Rošanak covers her mouth with her hands.

"But by the favor of the Wise Lord, your father and the faithful, some of the men most loyal to the Great King, pulled his wounded body off his golden chariot and rescued him to safety. With the Royal Immortals protecting their backs, the rest of the royal kinsmen and kingsmen fought bravely to protect him from falling into the hands of Alexander and his murderous men who fiercely followed the Great King in hope of capturing him alive or killing him. They all died to the last man in front of the Great King."

He narrows his eyes in pain.

"It was late in the day when Dâriuš was finally carried away to safety, someone sounded the retreat… we stopped… they continued… the battle turned into a bloody massacre… and finally the men opened their ranks and started falling. They all saw with their own eyes their sons and fathers and brothers and kinsmen dying all around them and still no one flinched from their sacred duty to save the Great King… they all died to the last man…"

Uxšiyârta takes a deep breath and straightens. "More than 100,000 died that day… Persians and the men from all the Lands… many more… only the Wise Lord knows how many…"

He closes his eyes with sorrow.

"It was unthinkable to let the Great King die by the swords and spears of the barbarians. The Divine Mithrâ saved our Great King that day from dying in the hands of the son of a snake-worshipping sorceress who could bring down the Moon from heaven to kill the Earth!"

Uxšiyârta looks back down at Rošanak. She is softly crying.

"Womanish!" Uxšiyârta thunders. "The bastards call us *Womanish*. The Persians and Bakhtrians and the people of the Lands fight bare-headed with no shields… these barbarians are honorless filthy sons of whores who massacre women and children with no mercy and sell what they do not kill in slave markets. They are so scared of the Persians that they encase themselves in a mountain of metal to summon up courage to face us!"

Rošanak's ears hurt. She softly moans.

Uxšiyârta grinds his teeth.

"Liberate the Lands from the Persians! Ha! How could they be fighting for the cause of the Hellenes, when they slaughtered to the last man, woman and child, the poor wretched Branchidæs, the descendants of old Hellenes living on the other side of River Bakhtruš, who had gone to greet the Makedonians with open arms?

"There were more Hellenes in the Royal Army of Dâriuš than in the Royal Army of Alexander. Alexander had no more than 7,000 Hellenes… Dâriuš had 25,000… everyone knows that Alexander has killed more Hellenes than Persians since the war started… he butchered 18,000 Hellenes at Granikos with no mercy."

He shakes his head angrily.

"No, they have not come to liberate the people of the Lands… the greedy bastards have come to liberate the Persian gold from the Great Kings!"

"Abû—"

Uxšiyârta is startled. He has forgotten all about her for a moment. He looks down at her and his heart softens for her.

"An old curse— royal blood of a Royal Son and Brother drawn by another Royal Son and King, brought disaster for the Persians on the fields of battle… an older curse is now upon all the men— Barbarian and Persian alike, who did not protect Pârsâ with their last dying breath, who burned the sacred words of the Wise Lord kept in sacred storehouses and plundered the forbidden gold of God kept in the royal treasuries.

"The names of the Persian traitors are cursed by the Divine Mithrâ and will be all but forgotten… the earth will swallow their bones and their sons and their women and their lands… nothing of them will remain… nothing… by their own bloody deeds they have cursed their own bloodlines… all for the sake of a handful of gold and their honorless titles and worthless lands and shameful whores…

"May their own lands open up and swallow them whole and become their own graves! May all that they hold more dear than their honor and duty to the Great Kings become their grave goods!" Uxšiyârta curses under his breath.

"Mazdâyâ, the cursed Satrap of Bâbiru, who turned on Dâriuš and sold his soul for gold and power and opened the gates of the Bâbiru to the invaders, has already been sent to Hell… Abulites, the cursed Satrap of Çûšâ, the Bâbiruviya pig, who betrayed the Persians, is marked too…

"Tiridâta, the Keeper of the Royal Treasuries of Pârsâ too… he is the most wretched of all, as the sacred words of the Wise Lord were burned in Pârsâ when Pârsâ was treacherously put to the torch. He is not just cursed by men, he is cursed by all the Guardian Angels of the Wise Lord… may he burn in the pits of Hell till the end of time.

"Artâvazda is a walking dead man… not even the Lord of Darkness wants his stinking corpse." Uxšiyârta takes a deep breath. "How wretched can you become, when you cannot even die and go to Hell?" he bellows.

"When Persians talk about the whores of Bâbiru, they are not talking about the Priestesses of Ištar, they are talking about the Persian traitors who easily opened up their sinful legs to Alexander and his army! May they all rot in Hell until the Day of the Final Judgment! May all their blood rot in Hell with them!"

He bites his lip hard. He tastes his own blood.

"Not all in war is fair. The barbarian Makedonians are not praiseworthy warriors… they are blood-thirsty butchers. The Wise Lord will punish them for their evil deeds… for burning of his godly words and for needlessly shedding the blood of the innocent. They too will all leave their bones on the Lands of the Persians… they will never see the lands of their blood fathers again… their names too will be forgotten. What they have done, will be done to them."

Uxšiyârta pauses and catches his breath and then takes a deep breath.

The other prophecy…

Well, that one might never come to pass, as the Makedonian had turned down the Royal Daughters of Dâriuš…

Ah! Sometimes the best prophecies were the ones that did not loosely dance on the lips of careless men… the best prophecies were the ones that came true without making much of them!

Rošanak cries softly.

She was with child, begotten by the King, son of a snake-worshipping sorceress.

She was forsaken… one of the damned and doomed!

"Men can change…" she moans softly.

"Men never change!" Uxšiyârta bellows and closes his eyes and takes another deep breath.

It was all his own damn fault…

He kneels down by Rošanak and caresses her hair sadly, remembering her when she was a little girl running around carelessly after her blood brothers and his blood sons.

Like all men, he liked the sweetness of peace… the hunts and the feasts. The Lands had been peaceful for generations after the Battle at Kuništa… men had forgotten the art of war… the taste of blood. What was forgotten in peace, had to be learned anew.

And like all men, he knew this peace would not last… that the Persians and the Bakhtrians would never yield to the men from the Lands Beyond the Sea…

Bakhtriš was the Land of Zarathuštra… the First Land where the Wise Lord had sent the Sacred Fire.

The Second Kuruš had not sent a Royal Army to conquer Bakhtriš; he had come himself unarmed bearing magnificent gifts. He had left behind his second Royal Son, Vîsa Puça Bârdiyâ, who had built the sacred temple for the Divine Ânâhitâ.

His daughter's marriage to the Makedonian had provided a lull in the business of war… some breathing space… and soon they all had to return to the bloody fields of battle… and do the work of men.

There was not even one family in all the Lands who had not lost fathers and sons and brothers and kinsmen to the sarissas and spears and swords of the wretched invaders and worse… not even one family who had not lost mothers and daughters and sisters and women to death and rape and shame of captivity.

Of the eight years foretold for Alexander's kingship, four years had been already burnt and spent… the rest was a blink of an eye… time to seed the alliances and the women and let them both bear fruit and grow… ready for the coming wars…

To war for a peace that was earned by the tip of the sword… not one that was bestowed by the benevolence of the invaders…

No one was in need of being liberated from themselves and their kinsmen and no one was in need of a gifted peace by an enemy… by men who not only did not worship the Wise Lord, but mocked him and their ancient ways and burned his sacred words in roaring fires…

The enemy invaders had killed not just the warriors, but women and children and elders too… would that not make every man and woman and child a warrior?

When no one was spared, would everyone not fight to the death to rid themselves of the faithless invaders? Even if it took thousands of years?

What was thousands of years? Just a single thread in the cloth of eternity…

"Utâna was right, defeated in battle does not mean conquered," Uxšiyârta says quietly and then he gets up to his feet.

Utâna was always right.

"Marathon and Salamis were avenged a hundred years later. Mudrâya was reclaimed after sixty years. This too will come to pass… after a year or after a thousand years or after thousands of years. The men of the Lands of the Persians are masters in waiting… time has no meaning in reclaiming of the ancient ancestral lands from enemies of the Wise Lord.

"The Great Kings cannot fall as long as their royal blood runs through the bodies of their Royal Women… all the Nobles of the Seven Persian families are connected by the blood of their women. We are all one tree, root and branch, worshiping the one god, the Wise Lord, fighting the one demon, the Lord of Darkness… there will be peace if the Wise Lord wills it and there will be war, as long as the Wise Lord commands it."

He turns around and leaves in silence.

Rošanak coils into herself in pain.

TERRACE. MAIN HADIŠ

MID-DAY

"Thukra tells me you have been crying for two days! And not eating anything, not even pits!"

Polydoros frowns, holding a plate full of figs in his hands.

Rošanak sobs quietly, sprawled on the carpet, buried amidst large cushions.

"Are you in pain?" Polydoros tries again.

Rošanak shakes her head sobbing.

"Are you— bleeding?"

Rošanak shakes her head side-to-side.

Polydoros grinds his teeth exasperated.

He should have become a horse-healer. Horses were so much more dignified than women… and had a lot more sense! No horse was ever caught sobbing for any reason!

It was all Ktesias' fault… if Ktesias had not written about the intrigues in the Persian Court when he was tending to Artaxerxes, he himself would have never thought of becoming a healer.

Thanks to Ktesias, every young Hellene healer wanted to become a healer to the Persian Royals… even after Apollonides of Kos had been kept in heavy chains by the Great King for months and then buried alive for bedding a Royal Daughter… bedding a Persian Royal Daughter or a Royal Son was worth dying for!

Where else could healers tend to highborn women? Hellenes locked away their women in their homes in their own private quarters. How hard was it to remain virtuous, when all the Athenian women were kept locked up in their rooms?

The slaves were seen more freely in Athenai than the highborn Athenian women… their names were not even mentioned by anyone!

Were they alive, while they were living?

He kneels down next to her on the carpet and puts away the plate of fruit and takes a deep breath and softens his voice. "I cannot cure you, if you do not tell me what is wrong with you!"

Rošanak sobs. "Uxšiyârta… told… me…"

"What?"

More sobbing.

"Oxyartes told you *what*?"

More sobbing.

Polydoros gives up in frustration.

"Very well! I will send for Oxyartes and when he gets here I will ask him myself what he has told you to make you cry like this!"

Rošanak relents and gets a few words out amidst sobbing. "He said… that I am… with the child of the… son of a—"

"What?"

"—a… a snake-worshiping… sorceress…" Rošanak hides her face in a big cushion, sobbing.

Polydoros sits down next to her on the carpet, and takes a deep breath.

"I see!"

Women!

They could bear the pain of birthing… time and time again, no less… but one wrong word falling into their small ears and there was no bound to their monstrous madness…

Poor Athenian Women! Their husbands had them locked up in their houses because of the Persian Women who ran around and intrigued and caused all sorts of trouble for the Persian men.

Solon from Athenai, who had no use for women even on a good day, had declared any woman seen in public a whore!

"What shall I do?"

Polydoros looks at her and scratches his face. "The unborn inside of you is begotten by a king—"

"—who is the son of a—" Rošanak sobs.

"A king who is the son of a king!" Polydoros says confidently with utter conviction.

Rošanak lifts up her head and looks at Polydoros through a veil of tears.

Polydoros straightens.

He was a Hellene… Alexander and his men were Makedonians who had brought the Hellenes under their sway… they had razed the holy city of Thebai to the ground.

But he was also a man of science. He could not fault the Makedonians for the foolishness of the Hellene politicians… and he himself admired Philip, the father of Alexander, for collecting the Hellenes all into one league… something the Hellenes themselves had never seemed to accomplish from time immemorial. They only knew how to talk… and talk… and kill each other when they stopped talking.

Yes… Hellenes hated the Persians… but they hated each other as much! If not more! And they hated the Makedonians too! Hellenes hated everyone!

And those idiot Spartans were of no help either! They hated everyone too and everyone hated them!

"Well—" Polydoros thinks.

At least she had stopped sobbing. He had seen inside the skulls of men cracked by battle axes… but never inside the skull of a woman. He had always wondered if the gods had put self-renewing waterskins behinds the eyes of women… flowing obediently on command like the water spouts in the Persian gardens…

"Your King-Husband is the son of Philip, from a long line of Makedonian Kings. Ancient Aryas who found their way into the Lands of the Middle Sea and mixed with ancient Hellenes!"

"Yes, but his blood mother… her bloodline—"

"She, too, is a Royal Woman, like you—"

Rošanak pushes herself up and sits and wipes her tears. "But—"

Polydoros bites his lip.

Philip had a big appetite! He was not as particular as the Persian Kings in choosing wives… even less particular in choosing lovers. He had taken a wife with each of his campaigns… a great source of entertaining gossip among the citizen-males of Athenai and elsewhere. There were easier ways of finding wives than starting wars!

Alexander was the son of his fifth wife, Myrtale, a Molossian Princess, who had taken the royal title of Olympias after Philip's horse had won in the Olympic games the year Alexander was born to her.

But Alexander was the royal heir to the throne of his father and had proven himself well worthy of it.

Even though his royal mother was a snake-worshiping priestess of some outlandish NorthLander Dionysos cult…

"Your unborn is begotten by a king of the Royal House of Argeads from the old bloodline of the Kings of Makedon, an unbroken royal bloodline to their ancestral father, the First Perdikkas."

Rošanak wipes her face with the tips of her fingers and looks at Polydoros more attentively.

He pushes the plate of figs into her lap. "Eat!"

She takes a pit and bites into it.

"The history of the Royal House of Argeads is wrapped in mystery. They claim their ancestry to Argos, descendants of Temenos, kinsman of Herakles—"

"But their women—"

Polydoros narrows his eyes at her.

Well, she was raised a Royal Daughter…

Polydoros takes a deep breath and continues in a low voice, "They say— that Amyntas, father of Arrhidaios, father of the Third Amyntas, father of Philip, father of your Alexander— was begotten by Xerxes when Xerxes crossed Hellespont into the Lands of the Middle Sea."

Rošanak swallows the rest of the pit. Her eyes widen with hope.

"They do?"

Polydoros smiles and nods and continues, weaving a tale of intrigue and mystery.

"They say the wife of the First Alexander was sent to Xerxes as a hostage to ensure the absolute loyalty of her husband to Xerxes, when he came for Athenai."

"Really?" Rošanak eats another fig ravenously, her tears now forgotten.

Polydoros nods again.

Nothing better than a captive listener to make a tale grow longer…

"Xerxes was the most striking man any mortal had ever laid eyes upon, tall, handsome and kingly, clean shaven, and scented with precious oils, clothed in finest silks bejeweled with gold and precious stones— unlike the smelly, rough, bearded men of the Land of the Middle Sea."

Rošanak smiles wickedly.

Most of the Makedonians had not changed much from their ancestors… but the ones she had seen were mostly clean-shaven by Alexander's orders… he said he did not want their enemies to grab his men by their beards to pull them forward to stab—

"They say the wife of the First Alexander fell in love with Xerxes and Xerxes took her to bed for one night and got her with child— a prince called Amyntas."

"Ah!"

She knew the legend well…

She had always thought it was just another fantastic tale about the First Khašâyar… Khašâyar was so splendidly handsome that during and after his death, the legend of his prowess with women had grown infinitely.

If he had bedded all the women he was storied about, the poor Great King must never have left his royal bed! And he was the one who had built Pârsâ after the death of his father, the First Dâriuš.

Yet, all the Royal Daughters had prayed for generations for a lover like Khašâyâr… divinely handsome and moody and sensual… utterly perfect in every way.

"What happened to her?"

"Who knows! No one even knows her name.

"After Xerxes left the Lands of the Middle Sea, the First Alexander tried to cover his shame and the heavy belly of his wife with tall tales about how he had murdered Persian envoys.

"He spread tales about how he helped the Hellenes during the Battle of Salamis by Xerxes, but the Athenians knew better. I am an Athenian, as you know! Yes!"

Rošanak eats another fig and nods.

Yes… Polydoros never failed to mention that… at least once or twice a day, he reminded everyone of the land of his fathers. He was a proud Hellene-Persian.

"Did Xerxes love her?"

"No! By Zeus! He spent just one night with her. He sent her back to her husband when he went back to the Lands of the Persians! They say he never touched another Makedonian woman as long as he lived. You could soak a woman like that in a basin full of mare's milk for a month and she still would not become silky like a Persian Royal Woman! Xerxes was used to the splendid Persian Royal Women in his bed. I am sure the royal court eunuch bathed and shaved and scented her before they took her to his bed, but still, what can a woman like that offer the Great King?!"

Rošanak smiles and puts her hand on her belly. Hope returns.

All was well again…

Her unborn had the blood of the First Khašâyâr…

The Royal Son of the First Dâriuš… The Royal Son of the legendary Queen Atossâ, the first Royal Daughter… the Royal Daughter of the Kuruš the Elder.

She leans over and kisses Polydoros' face.

The old Hellene wound-healer blushes unguardedly.

Women!

SMALL HADIŠ

NIGHTS LATER

"Alexander?"

Rošanak opens her eyes and looks around the dimly lit bedchamber and calls again quietly. "Alexander?"

Silence.

She sees a shadow by the open window.

The curtains sway in the night breeze.

She calls again quietly. "Alexander."

Silence.

Rošanak gets out of the bed and walks toward the shadow and embraces him.

Alexander smells heavy with wine.

"Alexander."

Silence.

She holds him tighter.

"Alexander, come to bed."

Alexander takes a deep breath. He leans back a little into Rošanak and puts his hands on her arms holding him. He caresses her arms gently.

He rambles remorsefully, heavy with guilt, loaded with wine.

"When we arrived at Persepolis, I saw the glory that was the envy of every king who had heard of it! With its majestic audience halls and ceremonial palaces! The Palace of Darius, the Gate of People, the Palace of Xerxes, the Audience Hall, the Throne Hall, the Royal Treasury, the Royal Storehouses. Splendid columns, made of the largest cedars of Lebanon and teak trees of India— at the sight of such riches, my men went into a frenzy! They started to plunder and kill and loot the city."

Rošanak starts to tremble. She starts to pull away.

Alexander holds on to her tighter.

"Persepolis was the wealthiest city we had ever seen. The private houses were filled with magnificent riches of every kind.

"My men rushed into the city, killing all the men and plundering all the houses— dragging the women away with their jewels and precious gowns, woven with crimson and with gold. Prizes to the victors! They even killed each other with madness of greed!"

Rošanak's eyes fill with tears of utter sadness. "Alexander."

"I did not stop them! It was what I had been promising my men. It was why they had followed me for years. For the promise of riches beyond their wildest dreams! I had promised Glory to the Makedonians, Revenge to the Hellenes, and Persian Gold to all the rest."

Alexander pauses and takes a deep breath.

"I took over the Palaces of Persepolis! I went up to the citadel and took possession of the royal treasures stored there— gold and silver, collected from the time of Kuros… 2,500 talents of pure gold! The rest in silver. It took 20,000 mules and 5,000 camels to carry it all away.

"I decided to keep the Palaces of Persepolis for myself! I declared them Royal Property."

He pauses.

"I had a vision of Kuros, the night before reaching Persepolis. He was standing on the steps of the palace, 10,000 Immortals were standing in perfect formation behind him. He was holding the royal scepter. A dove was flying over his head."

"Alexander—"

Tears fall on Rošanak's face. Words fail her.

"I wanted to stand on the steps of Persepolis, where Kuros was standing— to have all the Makedonians see me! I, Alexander! I was the one who had become the Lord of Asia, the King of all the Lands! Not Philip!

"I was the one who had brought the Persians to their knees! I, Alexander! Every one from the four corners of the world would come to see me! They would walk up to the Gates of Xerxes, bringing me tributes! They would all kneel down before me, worship me, treat me as their Great King!"

Alexander closes his eyes in pain. The memory haunts him.

"The burning was an accident, by Zeus! When I reached Persepolis, I offered magnificent sacrifices to Zeus and the gods! We were favored by our gods!

"Then for four months, every night, we feasted for our glorious victory over the Persians. One night, we were drinking in the Palace of Xerxes, on the highest terrace. The walls of the royal palace were tiled and decorated with images of lions and bulls.

"My father, Philip, had a dream before I was born. In his dream, he sealed my mother's womb with the seal of the lion. Aristandros proclaimed that I would have the character of a lion!

"Persepolis was built for me! Heads of lions everywhere! Lions devouring the bulls!"

His voice quivers. Wine loosens his tongue, unties his shame, bathes his dishonorable deeds in the light of the heaven.

"I commanded Darius to come before me as a vassal king and to crown me in Persepolis according to the customs of the Achæmenids, and he ignored my command. He did not come, no one came.

"I waited patiently for four months— My kingsmen, Hephæstion, Perdikkas, Krateros… Philotas, Kleitos. Ptolemaios, Medeios, Leonnatos, Lysimachos and the others. We were drunk with wine. The Hellene flute girls were playing and the Hellene dancers were entertaining us.

"We were the glorious conquerors, the heroes. And we were all heavy with power." He pauses and closes his eyes for a moment.

"Hephæstion and Krateros, loaded with wine, were quarrelling as usual. Krateros said something and Hephæstion charged at him and pulled him off his silver couch and they both landed on the floor. One of them accidentally fell against an incense burner and the entire row of the incense burners came crashing down! Ten… twenty… thirty… all crashing down one after another. That horrid noise still rings in my ears."

Rošanak moans.

"They say some Hellene whore set the fire to avenge the burning of the Temple of Athena—"

Alexander opens his eyes.

"Thaïs, mistress of Ptolemaios, drunk with wine, picked up a torch and threw it at the curtains and laughed. What had horrified us, had excited her.

"The silk curtains caught fire and the fire spread quickly to the wooden columns. Even the largest columns burned like dried wood in a fireplace.

"Persepolis was in flames, by gods!" he shakes his head. "I can still smell the cedar burning. We all stood there in a drunken daze, watching the fire. The earthen roofs started to collapse when the columns burned to the ground. Then we all joined in and the fire spread. Fire devoured all.

"I told everyone afterward that I had intended to burn Persepolis for the arrogance of Darius. To completely destroy the beloved Palace of the Great King who had ignored me… who had dishonored me.

"If not me, then no one else would ever ascend to the Throne of the Great Kings in Persepolis— no one!

"If men thought that Persepolis had burned by accident during a drunken feast, I would have looked like a drunken fool, not a glorious hero in command of himself." He takes a breath of pain. "Wrath of Achilleos had burned Troia. My wrath burned Persepolis."

"No!"

Alexander's voice trembles with anger.

"Hephæstion and Krateros! One loved by a man, the other loved by a king, by Zeus. If I had not been that drunk and if I did not love them, I would have run my spear straight through their hearts. They destroyed my most splendid prize!"

He says remorsefully, "Persepolis burned for days and nights, we all sat and watched it burn, it was razed to the ground. Consumed by the demon of fire. Swallowed in flames."

Alexander trembles.

Rošanak cries quietly.

Their burning hearts repel the cool breeze from the open window like a bronze shield.

Grief and regret scent the night air.

A few moments pass silently.

Rošanak swallows hard.

"What happened was the will of the Wise Lord. My mother always says Empires rise and fall and rise again!"

Persians were a young Empire, only ten generations old.

The TwoLanders and the Chaldæans and the Aøuriya and the Bâb-ilani and the Elam-tu and the Mâda, had been around for thousands of years before the Persians had gathered them all under the absolute rule of the Great Kings…

If it was the will of the Wise Lord, Pârsâ would be rebuilt… or… it would stand in ruins as a witness to the ancient glory of the Masters of the Persian Empire and a haunting reminder to those who will follow.

Rošanak closes her eyes.

She was heavy with child, begotten by the King… who had burned Pârsâ… son of a snake-worshipping sorceress… who must have brought down the Moon-God, the protector of Pârsâ, the night her Son-King had set Pârsâ on fire…

She was forsaken… one of the damned and doomed.

"I am seeded with your child," she whispers softly, trying to wash away evil with good.

Alexander turns around startled, looks at her for a moment and then embraces her tightly.

He was favored by the gods again…

KINGSMEN'S QUARTERS. ROYAL ARMY CAMP
FOLLOWING NIGHT

"Gods have returned our Alexander back to us!" Ptolemaios nods and smiles triumphantly to Hephæstion and winks. "I knew that the illiterate barbarian would not hold his interest. Alexander likes his pleasures manly. Three months, though! I did not even think it would last this long!"

Ptolemaios mumbles to himself. "The thrill of the hunt is in the chase, not the capture."

Hephæstion looks at Ptolemaios and then looks away and says quietly, "She is with child."

"With child?" Ptolemaios raises his eyebrow, surprised.

"He wrote to Olympias yesterday."

Ptolemaios takes a deep breath.

"A half-breed barbarian child. No doubt Queen Olympias will be thrilled. She will no doubt counsel him to smother the child immediately after birth!"

"Alexander's child!" Hephæstion sneers at Ptolemaios.

Ptolemaios gathers himself quickly.

"Well, good! It is about time! Old Parmenion was right! Even a half-breed son of a rightful barbarian queen is better than no sons at all. He will beget a proper pure-breed Makedonian heir after we return to Makedonia." He nods and continues, "Now he can leave her behind and we can move on to conquering the rest of the world."

Hephæstion takes a deep breath and lets it out.

"He has ordered Arrhidæus to make a special carriage for her, one that does not jar too much on the road, like a bier suitable for carrying a dead royal body."

"He is not planning to leave her behind?"

"No."

"Why not?"

Hephæstion looks away.

Ptolemaios shakes his head with disbelief. Stunned.

"After all these years… he has finally fallen for a girl."

ROYAL ARMY CAMP
DAYS LATER
MID-DAY

"Arrhidæus has added more support in the bottom of the royal carriage," Alexander says proudly, pointing to the carriage. "I rode in it myself."

Rošanak eyes Alexander curiously. She does her royal best not to laugh.

"You— are going to ride in a wagon to war?" Rošanak asks wickedly with half a smile.

Old age, no doubt.

"Not me! You!"

"ME?"

"YOU!"

The smile immediately disappears from Rošanak's face.

She puts her hand on her belly without thinking and eyes the carriage again and then looks at Alexander. He has a big smile on his face.

He must be suffering, no doubt, from whatever ailed Arrhidaios, his dim-witted brother from a different mother.

"I ride a horse. Why would I ride in a carriage?"

"You are coming with me!"

Rošanak eyes Alexander and then breaks into laughter unguardedly.

He was taking his revenge on her… for calling him Ancient.

"I take it back, Alexander. You are not that old!"

Alexander shrugs his shoulders.

"Arrhidæus is preparing two more, just like this, for the Women of the Queen."

Rošanak goes pale.

"Alexander, surely you do not wish your wife heavy with child to follow you in a carriage in your campaigns."

"Yes! I do!"

Rošanak goes paler.

"But— Alexander—"

"The tent of the Queen has arrived from Susa too."

"Alexander—"

"Snow has melted in the passes. We leave in two days."

Rošanak turns alabaster white.

LATER

"Tell your men that they can bring their wives with them when we leave for India," Alexander says to all his kingsmen summoned to his royal tent.

Stunned silence.

The kingsmen eye each other uncomfortably, but they all keep their tongues fiercely under their command.

The memory of the dead Kleitos with a spear straight through his body was still bleeding in their eyes.

Krateros eyes everyone and then breaks the silence cautiously.

"Alexander, we already have close to forty thousand camp-followers, almost as many as the number of Foot we had when we crossed into Asia."

Alexander considers Krateros and his kingsmen for a moment. He then eyes Hephæstion.

"I am bringing Roxana. As I always treat my men as myself, they can, too, bring their wives, if they so choose."

Uneasy silence.

Kingship was in their blood…

All of Alexander's kingsmen wanted Alexander to beget an heir… even a half-breed son of a barbarian was better than no son.

But none wanted the trouble of having men bringing their women with them to armed campaigns.

There were some wives who were tough enough to follow their men and there were multitudes of Hellene mistresses and common whores who were already traveling with the Royal Army. But they were all overlooked… they could all be left behind, when needed…

But this was a new rule, one that was foreign to their nature.

Makedonians did not take their women to wars with them and for good reason.

When the wife of Darius had died at birthing, Alexander had gone mad with grief. They were relieved when the Royal Women of Darius were finally left behind at the Susa Palace.

Now they were getting not just another carriage load of a Royal Wife, but the formal recognition and addition of thousands and thousands of barbarian women their men had collected on their way through Asia… a logistical nightmare for any army.

They never understood how Persians had ever taken their wives and children with them on armed campaigns… but they were barbarians…

Alexander eyes his kingsmen.

They all look at Hephæstion cautiously.

He was the one responsible for the Royal Army logistics and provisions and for all the Royal Army camp followers…

Silence.

Perdikkas finally and cautiously breaks the silence.

"Alexander, your rule impacts Hephæstion the most. He is the one who now has to feed the multitudes of women our men will bring with them and has to look out for their safety and transport, all by the order of the King."

Alexander looks at Hephæstion again, his eyes asking.

"Whatever Alexander decides," Hephæstion says quietly.

Alexander smiles.

Two

EDGES of the HEART

ROŠANAK'S TENT. ROYAL ARMY CAMP. HINDU KUSH
YEAR 10 of ALEXANDER, MONTH 10, LOIOS
YEAR 4 of ALEXANDER, MONTH 4, GARMAPADA
NIGHT

"Oh, no!"

Rošanak wipes her tears from her face and from the face of the precious parchment and starts writing in the middle of the night by the light of a small candle.

> *A letter from Rošanak to my beloved mother, Farânak,*
> *In the year 232 after Kuruš the Elder, in Month 4, Garmapada, 9 days passed, in Year 4 of Alexander:*
> *May the Wise Lord and Divine Ânâhitâ bless my mother and keep her in good health. May my mother be well and her heart be happy.*

Then she puts her hand on her belly and pushes back another tear.

She needed her mothers more than ever and her mothers were so far away on the other side of the mountains.

And she missed her horse!

Traveling in a carriage day after day was horrid. Bakhtrian women could ride their horses well close to birthing and she was half-Bakhtrian. Her blood sister rode her horse until a few days before the birth of her sons.

Alexander would come to see her whenever the Royal Army camped for the night… but he would not spend the night with her. He had stopped touching her intimately and bedding her after she had told him she was with child… as if she was infected with some incurable sickness of the body.

Old Polydoros was right after all. She had been utterly abandoned.

Days stretching into nights… nights stretching into days… sunrise to sunset… sunset to sunrise… without any sign of Alexander.

Bukephalas saw more of him than she did.

She takes a deep breath and looks down and tears well up again.

Peritas was snoring on the ground, sleeping deeply at her feet.

She shakes her head with dismay.

No! Alexander was not coming to see her! But he would come to see her dog!

He had done everything short of stealing Peritas in the middle of the night like a common thief to persuade her dog to go with him and Peritas had remained faithful to her and had refused to go with Alexander.

She bends over and caresses Peritas' furry skin, then straightens and blows her nose and continues writing:

Mother, I miss you! My life in Bakhtriš now seems like a dream in former days. We have been moving bit by bit through the mountains for the past month since we left Baktra.
I think about writing often, but being married to Alexander and traveling in a carriage with a large army of men on treacherous lands on snow and mud covered roads is hard.
It took ten days to cross into Hinduš across Khâwak and Kaošân passes in the high mountains of Hindu Kush. We have camped on rich well-watered grounds around the City of Alexandria, which Alexander founded here two seasons ago. His city is filled with old men and the wounded and those who cannot fight any longer.

She pauses.
Days after they had left Baktra, most of the carriages that contained the private belongings of the Royal Army had caught fire and burned to the ground, and the fire had spread to some of the carriages carrying extra rations for the Royal Army.
The smell of burned supplies was unbearable.
Alexander said he had ordered the fire himself because having only necessary supplies for the campaign made for a faster and more inspired Royal Army.
She looks around her bare tent.
He had burned most of her belongings too.
She sighs and starts writing again:

Mother, I am sending you a list of some of my belongings that were lost to a fire. Most of my royal gowns were destroyed. There are no splendid banquets to attend on battlefields of Hinduš, so I will not be in need of splendid gowns until I return to the Lands of my beloved Persia.
By the favor of the Wise Lord, I will replace some of the things I have lost when we reach Gandâra. Until then, If you could please send me some Persian sweets with the next shipment of the Royal Mail, I would be grateful.
Please tell Abû that Oštana is well. He comes to see me whenever he can.
May the Wise Lord and Divine Ânâhitâ bless Dârâ and Nimâ and keep them in good health. Thukrâ, too.
May the Wise Lord and Divine Mithrâ bless Abû and Itâna and keep them in good health.

ROYAL SEAL of DUKŠIŠ ROŠANAK

Rošanak closes her eyes and remembers her blood mother, tears rolling down her cheeks.

Her blood mother had stood silently on the terrace of the main hadiš, pushing back her tears.

She had begged Alexander herself to leave her daughter in her care.

Her blood mother was holding Dârâ and Nimâ's hands for comfort. They were all crying. She had kissed her mother softly on the cheeks and knelt to her knees and had kissed Dârâ and Nimâ. Dârâ had put his arms around her neck and had given her a big kiss. Nimâ had turned away hiding his head in his grandmother's flowing gown. She had run her fingers through Nimâ's hair… but he had not turned his head to look at her.

Old Polydoros had stayed with her mother… he had told Alexander he was too old to ride in a carriage all day and so an old Persian wound-healer had come with her to care for her. The old Hellene wound-healer was lost without her blood mother… so was she… they had never been separated.

She had not told her mothers that she was with child… her blood mother would have never let her leave with Alexander, if she knew!

Thukrâ knew somehow that she was with child… and she had kept her secret… she had cried a river for two whole days…

HEPHÆSTION'S TENT. ROYAL ARMY CAMP. HINDU KUSH
YEAR 10 of ALEXANDER, MONTH 11, GORPIAIOS
YEAR 4 of ALEXANDER, MONTH 5, TURNABAZIŠ
MID-DAY

"Kallisthenes, it is the wish of Alexander that you tutor the Queen in Attik."

Silence.

"Kallisthenes!" Hephæstion says louder.

"I? Tutor a barbarian, and a woman no less?" Kallisthenes stands up indignantly. "What have I done? What crime have I committed? Which god have I offended— that Alexander wishes to exact such a punishment on me?"

Hephæstion eyes Kallisthenes with contempt.

"My uncle Aristoteles says rightly that women are imperfect by nature and barbarians are no better than slaves, created to serve the Hellenes. They should be treated like animals or plants. Now, one does not teach Attik to an animal or a plant, does one?" Kallisthenes points with his hands. "I am too busy with the education of the royal boys who guard the King. My knowledge is not wasted on them, as it would be on a barbarian woman!"

Hephæstion looks at Kallisthenes intently and then dismisses him politely.

"I will tell the King that you declined," he says formally, hiding his anger.

Kallisthenes shrugs his shoulders indifferently and leaves the tent.

Hephæstion looks down at the parchment in front of him.

Because of the old Aristoteles, Alexander had decided to give Kallisthenes one more chance to redeem himself in the royal court and the arrogant fool had failed again.

How could a man understand philosophy and be so ignorant of reality?

He raises his head and looks around.

Alexander had forbidden him to ask Anaxarchos, the other philosopher who had found his way to the royal court. His Hellene tongue, loaded with flattery and irony, had always pleased Alexander, but Anaxarchos loved lavishness and women and kept a naked slave girl in his tent to serve him his wine. He was not a man to be trusted around a beautiful woman.

He leans back in his chair and looks around his tent. He picks up a book from his table and considers it for a moment.

Why not? He himself could teach her Attik. He had a stack of old books that could be put to good use. His father always sent him books he had read himself and wrote notes on the edges of the pages for him.

He puts the book down, leans forward and starts writing.

Kallisthenes was guilty of disobeying the King. He had made light of the King's wishes for observing proper Persian Royal Court customs and was now guilty of insulting the Queen. Alexander was well within his kingly powers to punish Kallisthenes.

He finishes, looks up and leans back in his chair.

Alexander was not a man to take lightly to such charges.

ROŠANAK'S TENT. ROYAL ARMY CAMP. HINDU KUSH
YEAR 10 of ALEXANDER, MONTH 12, HYPERBERETAIOS
YEAR 4 of ALEXANDER, MONTH 6, KARBAŠIYAŠ
NIGHT

Rošanak writes late at night.

> *A letter from Rošanak to Farânak, my beloved mother:*
> *In the year 232 after Kuruš the Elder, Month 6, Karbašiyaš, 23 days passed, in Year 4 of Alexander:*
> *May the Wise Lord and Divine Ânâhitâ bless my mother and keep her in good health. I received your letter yesterday. From the date, it appears that it took two months for your letter to reach my hands. Beyond the Lands of the Persians, mail seems to travel slowly. Even Royal Mail travels slower than a land turtle.*
> *Alexander conquered some nameless town last month. He was injured with an arrow during the battle, but by the favor of the Wise Lord, he has now fully recovered. I now constantly worry when he leaves for battle: in what shape and manner he will return to me at night? The knowledge that life and death are by the favor of the Wise Lord does not ease my mind.*
> *Traveling in a carriage is horrid! I miss my bed and my bath in the Baktra Hadiš! But above all, I miss you and Dârâ and Nimâ and Thukrâ.*

She pauses and looks up.
Should she tell her blood mother that she was with child?
She bites her lip undecided and then decides against it.
Her blood mother would kill her if she ever found out she had lied to her when she had asked her if she was with child before leaving Baktra!
She pushes back a tear and continues writing:

> *Hephæstion has been tutoring me in Attik. He says I have much improved. He said to tell Polydoros that I can now speak Attik as well as the shopkeepers in the marketplace of Athenai. He knows. He has been to Athenai.*
> *Please tell Abû that Oštana is well. He took an arrow in the shoulder, but he is healing up fast. He told me it was a small arrow and showed me the wound to prove it.*
> *May the Wise Lord and Divine Ânâhitâ bless Dârâ and Nimâ and keep them in good health. Thukrâ, too. May the Wise Lord and Divine Mithrâ bless Abû and Itâna and keep them in good health.*

ROŠANAK'S TENT. ROYAL ARMY CAMP. HINDU KUSH
YEAR 11 of ALEXANDER, MONTH 1, DIOS
YEAR 4 of ALEXANDER, MONTH 7, BÂGAYADIŠ
MID-DAY

Silence.

Then earth rattles and shakes and trembles under Rošanak's feet.

Men running.

Rošanak worriedly pushes herself up to her feet from her bed. She puts her hands on her sides and wobbles toward the tent flap. A young maid quickly opens the tent flap for her.

"Rošanak, wait!" Mâr'at Bani Âriyânnâz calls after her hastily.

Men are running toward the banks of the river. Calling, shouting, yelling…

Coarse and barbaric sounds she did not understand… like the sounds of hungry wild beasts… filled with bloodlust… chasing after their wounded prey in the frenzy and fury of hunt…

She follows the men without thinking.

Close to Alexander's royal tent, a group of six or seven young boys, some of the royal boys who guarded Alexander's royal tent and tended to him and his horses, were facing a shouting angry mass of Makedonians…

She recognizes one or two of the young boys.

Alexander and Hephæstion and the rest of Alexander's kingsmen were standing in front of Alexander's royal tent.

Men running past her on both sides cloud her sight. She gets closer, her sight clears. She sees blood stains on the tunics and the bodies of the royal boys. Her knees weaken.

Shouts get louder and angrier.

THUG!

A stone hits one the royal boys square in the face and he screams in severe pain. "Ahhhhhh!"

"Ah!" Rošanak jumps, startled.

A hail of watery stones collected from the banks of the river pours down on the royal boys, stones not from the skies, but from the hands of the Makedonians.

"Do not look!" Mâr'at Bani Âriyânnâz says in terror. "Close your eyes!"

But Rošanak cannot look away. Her heart sinks into her chest and then quickly rolls down to her feet. She stands rooted with fear and shock, unable to do or say anything, as the royal boys are swiftly stoned to death. Bloody bits and pieces of them fly in the warm still air. Her eyes look up, mindlessly chasing after flying blood and flesh.

The sky becomes bloody red.

Rošanak's blood starts to run hot with fear, her heart beats like a restless drum in her throat. The sound of death fills her ears, warm water runs down her legs, then warmer blood. She reaches and grabs her heavy belly with her hands. Her legs fold under her and she starts to go down on her knees. Excruciating pain shoots down her back, as her body starts to purge the unborn.

"Noooo!" She moans in pain.

Abi-Samar quickly steps closer and lifts her in his arms before she totally collapses and rushes her bleeding body back to her tent.

LATER

The Old Persian Healer wraps the tiny newborn in a clean white linen edged in royal purple and hands him to Mâr'at Bani Âriyânnâz.

....

Alexander is pacing backward and forward in his royal tent.

"Alexander, you have a son," the court chamberlain announces formally, without further words.

Alexander quickly turns around and leaves the royal tent and heads for Rošanak's tent.

....

Rošanak lies in her bed, unconscious. Her bed is soaked with her blood. Mâr'at Bani Âriyânnâz is gently washing the birthing blood off her limp body.

Peritas is whimpering silently by her bed, guarding her faithfully.

Alexander looks at the blood-soaked bed and remembers the death of Stateira. He calls on Hephæstion who is quietly standing by the tent flap.

"Find a new bed for Roxana. Burn this one." Alexander says quietly.

Hephæstion nods silently and leaves the tent.

It becomes quiet.

LATER

Rošanak is sleeping in a new, clean bed. She opens her eyes. The tent is quiet and dimly lit. Alexander is sitting by her bed, gently wiping her forehead with a cool piece of clean linen.

"I had this dream... I was standing on high ground watching a bloody battle raging down below. I saw the men killing my blood brothers. I just stood there watching like a mute... their blood rose from their bodies and covered me... I was drenched in their blood... I was drenched in my own blood..."

Alexander leans over and kisses her face tenderly. "Just a bad dream. Go back to sleep."

Rošanak closes her eyes and drifts for a moment and then opens her eyes again and grabs her belly in panic.

"My baby— where is my baby?" Rošanak moans in fear.

"He is resting with the wet nurse."

Rošanak hears Alexander, her eyes tear up.

"We have a son." He tenderly kisses her hand.

"Where is my baby? What have you done to my baby?"

"Roxana, by Zeus, I swear he is resting with the wet nurse!"

"Please! Show me my baby! Let me see him!" Rošanak moans.

Alexander signals the royal guard. "Tell the wet nurse to bring my son."

Rošanak cries. "Those boys… they took my baby with them…" she mumbles under her breath faintly. "Why… Why did you kill them? My brothers… where are they?"

Rošanak fades in and out of reality.

Alexander dries the sweat from her face. "Roxana."

The wet nurse brings in the sleeping royal newborn baby all bundled and wrapped and gently hands him over to Alexander.

Alexander holds his newborn son in his arms and whispers quietly, "Roxana, here is our son."

Rošanak has almost passed out again.

Alexander gently takes her hand and squeezes it. "Roxana."

Rošanak opens her eyes again. Alexander gently lays the newborn over her heart and then tucks another pillow behind her back. Rošanak cradles her tiny baby boy in her arms and looks at him intently and starts to tear up again.

"Forgive me!" She gently touches the face of her newborn boy. The tiny baby sleeps quietly in her arms.

"Where is Âriyânnâz?" Rošanak asks in Persian.

Mâr'at Bani Âriyânnâz steps forward quietly from the shadows, holding back her tears. She whispers quietly, careful not to wake up the newborn, "I am here, Rošanak."

Rošanak asks softly, "Did you see my baby?"

Mâr'at Bani Âriyânnâz bows her head, whispering, biting her lip. "Yes, Rošanak. He is favored by the Wise Lord."

"Alexander, he is so little!"

Alexander caresses Rošanak's hands holding his newborn son. "He is…"

Rošanak brings her newborn baby boy closer to her face and kisses his tiny head. "He smells like the fresh air of the Baktrian mountains. Has he eaten?"

"The wet nurse is taking good care of him."

ROŠANAK'S TENT

FOLLOWING DAY

Hushed dim tent.

Soft hum of an ancient lullaby, sung in the ears of the Persian newborns from time immemorial… calling all guardian angels to protect the newborn from all evil demons…

Rošanak is sitting on the floor of her tent, gently rocking her newborn baby boy in her arms, back and forth… humming an ancient lullaby… humming…

Mâr'at Bani Âriyânnâz is quietly crying in the corner, hidden from sight.

Alexander is sitting on the floor next to Rošanak, wrapped around her.

Hephæstion is quietly standing back, out of sight, watching Alexander and Rošanak.

Stateira had never woken up after the birth of Alexander's firstborn… his firstborn had died right after birth…

And now this…

Alexander quietly pleads with Rošanak. "Roxana… Please…"

Rošanak brings her newborn baby boy closer to her face and kisses his little head. "Sssss… He is just sleeping… He is so small…" Rošanak whispers.

"I will give him an honorable burial, befitting of my son." Alexander's voice quivers.

"He is just sleeping… what shall we name him?"

Alexander rests his head on her shoulder. "Roxana— Please— Let go of him."

"Surely the Wise Lord will not take him from me. He knows how much I love him."

Her firstborn was dead…

Her heart had cracked and blood was pouring out…

Her world was broken…

She had failed as a mother…

… she had failed as a woman.

And she had failed as a Royal Woman.

She had utterly failed…

Alexander lifts his head and kisses Rošanak's head and then slowly pushes himself off the floor and stands up. He lingers for a few moments watching Rošanak cradling and rocking his dead son in her arms. He then turns around and quietly leaves her tent. Hephæstion quietly follows him.

"Make sure she has whatever she needs." Alexander says quietly to Hephæstion, his eyes darkened with mourning.

He had been favored by fortune…

Gods had become envious…

They had taken his sons… his first-born first and now his second-born next.

They had extracted their price for his good fortune…

Had he not sacrificed to the right gods for the life of his sons?

Could the son of Zeus-Ammon not have a son of his own body?

Hephæstion quietly nods and follows him back to the royal tent.

The Old Persian Healer is waiting for them inside, summoned by the order of Alexander. "There was nothing I could have done!" he says remorsefully at the sight of Alexander.

His Persian words are quietly interpreted.

Alexander walks in silence and slumps in his golden chair.

Hephæstion puts his hand gently on the shoulder of the Old Persian Healer.

"He knows!"

"The baby was born too early— too small to live—"

Hephæstion eyes Alexander and takes a deep breath. "The Queen— she has lost her blood— will she heal?"

"She is young and strong. By the favor of the Wise Lord, she can have many more sons."

Hephæstion eyes Alexander again and then nods and dismisses the Old Persian Healer. "Attend to the Queen!"

Words are interpreted.

The Old Persian Healer nods in sorrow as he leaves the royal tent and mumbles under his breath. "My poor Dukšiš… she so wanted this child…"

ALEXANDER'S ROYAL TENT

FOLLOWING NIGHT

Painful silence.

Alexander is slumped in his golden chair in his royal tent, intently studying a cup of wine in his hand.

Rošanak painfully walks in the royal tent and slowly lowers herself and uneasily kneels on the floor in front of Alexander, her belly all wrapped in clean linen, hidden by a flowy gown, covered by a royal robe.

Hephæstion gets to his feet quickly and stands in the back of the royal tent, out of sight.

"Alexander, please! You cannot burn my baby on a pile of wood," she utters quietly, pleading with him in tears.

"My son will be given an honorable burial, a glorious funeral pyre." Alexander's voice quivers with the pain of loss.

"*Alexander, please!* The sacred fire cannot be desecrated with the body of the dead— not even with my son!" Rošanak bleeds more tears. "Please, Alexander! A dead Royal Son is of no use to his King-Father. Please. Let me take my son home and bury him in the tomb of my ancestors."

"No!" Alexander looks away.

Rošanak leans on Alexander's knees, pleading with more tears.

"Alexander! Please! I beg of you! Please do not burn my baby!"

"Leave!" Alexander swallows his wine.

"Alexander! Please! I beg of you!"

Painful silence.

"Alexander!"

Silence.

Hephæstion silently walks over and bends down and helps Rošanak up to her feet. Her gown is stained with more blood.

LATER

MIDDLE of the NIGHT

Dark night.

Hephæstion is walking back to his tent on the other side of the royal tent. The air is still and the sound carries far and wide. He hears a familiar mourning and wailing sound in the distance from the middle of the army followers' camp.

He asks one of the night guards coming from the direction of the sound, "What is that noise?

"Nothing unusual, Commander. Just a bunch of camp women mourning the death of a baby."

Hephæstion nods and turns and walks into his tent. He starts to take off his clothes. His warm bath is waiting for him in the corner of his tent. He looks at the bath for a moment and then throws on a simple tunic and leaves his tent quietly, heading in the direction of the crying and wailing sound.

The mourning sounds starts to die down.

He finds a camp woman rubbing the body of a small dead baby with sacred herbs and oils, next to a small camp fire. The woman is dressed like a Hellene.

"Are you a Hellene?" he asks her.

"Yes."

Hephæstion kneels down next to her. "When did your child die, Mother?"

"Yesterday! He was deadborn."

"Where is the father?"

"Dead."

"Was he a fighting man?"

"Yes. A Hellene mercenary, Mæandros, son of Kabelios from Kardia."

"Give me your child, Mother, and I will burn him with honors and bury his bones as his father would have done."

"May gods give you their blessings."

"I will send you extra food rations for a month for your pain."

"May gods give you their blessings!"

ROŠANAK'S TENT

LATER

Hephæstion approaches Rošanak's tent on the far side of the royal tent under the cover of night, with a small bundle under his arms.

Abi-Samar, armed to the teeth, bars him from entering her tent.

"I have business with the Queen," Hephæstion says in a low voice.

"Come back tomorrow, Commander. The Queen has retired for the night," Abi-Samar says in accented broken Attik.

"It is urgent business. Let me talk to Lady Ariana."

"I said: Come back tomorrow!"

Hephæstion reaches for his sword and then curses under his breath.

Damn! He was unarmed!

He lingers for a moment, but Abi-Samar does not move and puts his hand on his sword. Hephæstion grunts and turns around and starts to head back to his tent. Then he hears a soft voice behind his back with words he does not understand. He quickly turns around and sees Mâr'at Bani Âriyânnâz, standing next to the troublesome eunuch. He turns back and walks up to her.

"Lady Ariana, I have business with the Queen."

Abi-Samar grudgingly translates for her.

Mâr'at Bani Âriyânnâz beckons him to enter the tent.

Hephæstion brushes against Abi-Samar and enters the tent following her. Inside, the tent is dimly lit with candles. Mâr'at Bani Âriyânnâz turns around and looks at Hephæstion. He walks to the table, puts down the small bundle carefully covered with Hellene cloth, and starts unwrapping it.

Mâr'at Bani Âriyânnâz looks at the dead baby wordlessly with wide eyes and steps back, uncertain, then turns around and disappears into the private back of the tent.

Hephæstion stands there motionlessly for a moment, wondering what to do next. He hears a soft shuffling sound and looks up and sees Rošanak walking into the antechamber, followed faithfully by Peritas, with her body tightly wrapped and a robe carelessly pulled around her.

"Hephæstion?"

Rošanak looks down at the body of the deadborn baby. Her eyes widen in pain. She steadies herself on the edge of the table.

"This newborn was deadborn yesterday—" Hephæstion says quietly.

Rošanak narrows her eyes and looks at Hephæstion wearily.

What did he want in the middle of the night?

Why had he brought her another dead baby?

Was one dead baby not enough?

Peritas walks over and rubs himself against Hephæstion's leg and wags his tail.

Hephæstion looks down at Peritas and then looks at Rošanak and says in a calm comforting voice, "All newborns look the same, to me anyway—" and then points, "We can replace this deadborn for your son. Alexander will honor this one in the funeral tomorrow and you can send the body of your son to the tomb of your ancestors. Both you and Alexander will do what needs to be done."

He takes a breath. "There is enough death, let there be peace between us."

Rošanak understands in a blink of an eye and her heart fills with gratitude. She turns around and whispers quietly to Mâr'at Bani Âriyânnâz.

Mâr'at Bani Âriyânnâz looks at Hephæstion and then at the deadborn baby, stunned, and turns around and leaves the tent quietly in haste.

Rošanak turns and looks at Hephæstion. "Lady Ariana has gone to fetch the body of my son," she says in a mournful quiet voice.

"The eunuch— is he bound to you?" Hephæstion asks pointing with his head.

"Yes— he is sworn to protect me with his life."

"I can take him on my horse to the village up the road tonight and give him some gold dariks. He will have to find his own way back to Baktria from there."

"He knows the way and he has a horse, no need for you to risk your life any further," Rošanak says gratefully in a hushed voice.

Hephæstion nods quietly. "Very well."

Mâr'at Bani Âriyânnâz quietly enters the tent with a bundle wrapped in royal purple linen and gently lays the bundle on the table next to the other deadborn and starts to unwrap it.

Rošanak starts to walk back toward her dead son, but Hephæstion puts his arms around her and holds her firmly in place. "Roxana— there is not much time—"

Rošanak softly moans. "Please let me see my baby… one last time…"

Hephæstion holds her firmly in place. "Roxana, please. Wait until the deed is done."

Rošanak buries her face in his arm, her warm tears falling on his skin.

Mâr'at Bani Âriyânnâz quickly exchanges the two bodies and wraps the deadborn in the royal purple linen and takes him swiftly out of the tent.

Hephæstion slowly lets go of Rošanak. She wipes her tears and walks back to the table quietly and gently touches the dead body of her firstborn. She pulls the robe tighter around her and walks slowly to a small chest. She bends down painfully, takes out a simple white linen sheet, brings it over to the table and lovingly wraps her dead baby, quietly uttering a sacred prayer under her breath.

Hephæstion walks to the table and gently picks up the small wrapped body.

Rošanak puts her hand on her dead baby and softly pleads with Hephæstion.

"Please let me go with you."

Hephæstion thinks for a moment and then relents. "Very well. Beckon the eunuch inside and instruct him as you wish."

Rošanak swallows hard and takes a deep breath and calls, "Abi-Samar."

Abi-Samar walks in with his hand on his dagger, suspiciously eyeing Hephæstion.

"Abi-Samar, he is holding my son. Take my son and bury him in the tomb of my ancestors," Rošanak says quietly, pointing to the bundle in Hephæstion's arms.

Abi-Samar's eyes widen, he lets go of his anger and dagger. "Yes, My Lady. As you wish!" he says in a low voice, stunned.

"If you see my mother… do not tell her of my misery… tell her I am happy… and well and well-loved…"

"Yes, Dukšiš!"

"Roxana—" Hephæstion interrupts in a low voice, "we must go now."

Rošanak nods quietly.

Hephæstion swiftly leaves the tent, leading the way, with Rošanak and Peritas and Abi-Samar following quietly.

He guides them away from the night guards and into the stables.

They wait outside, as Abi-Samar fetches his horse.

Hephæstion then expertly guides them to the edge of the Royal Army Camp.

"Walk straight on foot until the light of the army camp disappears, then mount your horse and ride away as fast as you can. Do not stop for anything. May your gods light your path in the darkness," and gives him a small skin bag full of gold dariks.

"Yes, Commander. I hear and obey."

Hephæstion gently hands the royal bundle in his arm to Abi-Samar.

Rošanak steps forward and rests her head gently on the bundled body of her firstborn and prays under her breath.

"Divine Ânâhitâ..."

Hephæstion gives her a moment and then gently and silently pulls her away and holds her back firmly. She trembles in his arms. They stand there quietly watching Abi-Samar walking away, pulling the bridle of his horse behind him and disappearing into the dark of the night.

Rošanak clasps her hands and continues to pray quietly.

"Divine Sraoša, I invoke you who watches over the dead..."

Hephæstion lets go of her and stands quietly listening to her words, words that he does not understand, in a grief-soaked tone that needs no interpretation.

"I worship the Wise Lord... My Lord, please give safe passage to my Royal Son and guide his path to the lands of my royal ancestors."

Rošanak stands there quietly for a few moments, unable to move her legs, and then finally turns around and slowly walks back toward her tent, bracing her sides, passing by Hephæstion without seeing him.

Peritas quietly lingers by Hephæstion.

Hephæstion bends his knees and scratches Peritas' ears. And then he gets to his feet and turns around and looks at Rošanak for a long moment.

Rošanak stops and turns around and slowly walks back to Hephæstion.

Hephæstion looks at her bare face.

Her face was covered with tears, glistening in the moonless night.

Her eyes, the color of spring, had deepened into the color of autumn.

Rošanak reaches and takes Hephæstion's hand into her hand and kisses it gratefully without uttering a word and then turns around again and slowly disappears back into the camp.

Peritas follows her faithfully.

Hephæstion looks up at the night sky.

In Baktria, she had casually mentioned that a dead body was just an empty vessel.

Tonight, she was bleeding tears for the empty vessel that was born to her three days ago.

Hephæstion takes a deep breath and runs his fingers on the gifted kiss mixed with warm tears on the back of his hand, bestowed upon him by a grateful grieving mother.

It was a royal gift well worth what he had risked his life for.

They say…

To Alexander, the death of his secondborn son was like another honor wound from a battle. It soon scabbed over and healed and just left a soul mark, right next to the mark left by the death of his firstborn, like all the other battle wound scars on his body.

India beckoned him and there was no time for wasteful grieving and matters of little importance, and he was never a man to waste time.

To Rošanak, the death of her firstborn was a wound in her heart that never healed… just a constant throbbing pain she learned to live with…

How could a mother ever forget the death of a child she had held in her arms?

She had tasted the cruelty of a loved husband…

And the kindness of a stranger…

And that had marked her heart forever…

But her body, unlike her wounded heart, had not only healed, it had grown more beautiful. Her belly had tightened, like the string of a Persian bow once the arrow had been released; the string had snapped back with relative ease into its usual place.

The thin body of a young girl had blossomed into the sensuous body of a young woman, like a rosebud opening into a luscious Persian rose in the golden rays of Hinduš summer sun…

ALEXANDER'S ROYAL TENT
NIGHTS LATER

"My Lord, if it pleases you, I wish to return to Baktria to my mother." Rošanak bows her head and asks quietly in a formal tone.

Alexander narrows his eyes and grinds his teeth and grunts. "No! It does not please me— it does not please me at all!"

Rošanak goes pale with pain.

"Please!"

Alexander shakes his head with dismay.

Rošanak sinks to the ground on her knees and pleads with what is left of her broken heart.

"Alexander, the Baktrians have revolted— the peace agreement is broken— our son is dead," she says with tears in her voice, "what use is our marriage alliance any more?"

"Baktrians will be subdued!" Alexander grunts.

"You said you will grant me whatever I ask for!"

Alexander narrows his eyes and stands up and kneels down on the ground next to her.

"Roxana— I told you ask me for anything and you shall have it and I meant it— but not this."

"Please!"

Alexander puts his arms around her tenderly, pulls her close gently and kisses her face.

"This too will pass. We will have another—"

Rošanak tears up and pulls away.

She felt nothing… for him… or for anything…

Thoughts of him having ever touched her sickened her soul…

He cared nothing for her… or for her son…

"Roxana—"

She closes her eyes in pain.

It was godly justice that she should be treated like a captive woman… she had freely married a man who had ordered the death of her father… and his men had killed all her brothers in battle.

Worse! She had come to care for him… and he had abandoned her heartlessly when she had gotten with his child… and the unborn had not grown strong within her… when he had felt that his father was no longer desirous of his mother.

Unborns were like delicate flowers… once seeded in their mothers, they needed to be loved and watered by their fathers to take root and grow…

What kind of a woman loved a man like that?

Alexander whispers and caresses Rošanak's body more intimately.

"Ask me for anything else, and I will grant it!"

Rošanak pushes him away and slowly gets up to her feet and wipes her tears with her fingers. Her voice hardens.

"Do not summon me to your tent and do not come to visit me in mine!"

"Roxana—"

"Do not come near me!"

"Roxana!"

Rošanak turns around and leaves the royal tent.

"ROXANA!" Angered, Alexander rises and calls her at the top of his voice.

Kings usually did not execute their wives for refusing them… they just banished the disobedient wife and took another to bed!

He could have any woman in his kingdom… any woman…

Alexander grinds his teeth and his heart softens.

But he knew himself… he had no taste for another woman…

This would pass… it was too soon for her… she would come back to him…

She was in his blood… and he knew it…

ALEXANDER'S ROYAL TENT

FOLLOWING MORNING

"Hephæstion." Alexander dismisses everyone else and beckons Hephæstion.

"Yes, Alexander?"

"I am sending Roxana with you and Perdikkas."

Hephæstion eyes Alexander disapprovingly.

Alexander had split the Royal Army earlier that day and had given him and Perdikkas half of the Makedonian Horse, all of the mercenary Horse and three brigades of Makedonian Foot… and all the troublesome baggage train to move in advance of the main Royal Army to reach River Indus, secure the lowlands and make preparations to span and ford the rushing river.

The multitudes of Royal Army camp followers had now grown larger than the size of the Royal Army… all the merchants, wives, children, mistresses, whores, servants, grooms, cooks, scribes, wound-healers, plant-gatherers, land-mappers, scientists and philosophers. Well, one less ignorant troublesome philosopher in the baggage train these days…

Alexander was to take all the rest of the Royal Army under his own command and march through the mountainous passes and secure the highlands above while the rest of the Royal Army marched along the lowlands below the mountains under the command of Perdikkas and himself.

It would be best to get Roxana with child again and then send her back to Baktria to have the child in safety, away from the marches and campaigns and battles… Alexander should not have brought her in the first place… following a campaigning Royal Army was not a place for a Queen…

"Alexander, you should get her with child and send her back to Baktria."

"No!"

ROŠANAK'S TENT. HEPHÆSTION'S ROYAL ARMY CAMP
YEAR 11 of ALEXANDER, MONTH 3, AUDNAIOS
YEAR 4 of ALEXANDER, MONTH 9, ÂÇIYÂDIYA
A MONTH LATER
NIGHT

"They say the King is warming his bed with a pretty eunuch these days!"

"In this heat? He should bathe in his icy queen instead!" The Bakhtrian girls whisper and laugh.

Rošanak rolls the dice and ignores the chatter of the girls behind her.

"3 and 1," she says distractedly.

The chatter and laughter behind her continues.

"He needs a real woman in his bed, not a queen who does not yield to his command and keeps the palace doors closed to the King."

"A queen who opens up the double gates of the forbidden city to the conquering enemy."

"A woman who flows wet like a spring river, not like a treacherous mountain pass, iced up eternally in deep winter."

Rošanak ignores them. "5 and 2."

"A goddess who lets a mortal worship inside her sacred temple."

"He can worship inside my temple with his sword drawn night and day."

More quiet cutting laughter in the back.

"Enough!" Rošanak grunts. "Get out of my tent!" She turns her head, yelling at the Bakhtrian girls angrily, and throws the dice at them.

Mâr'at Bani Âriyânnâz quickly gets to her feet and pushes the Bakhtrian girls out of the tent, picks up and brings back the dice.

"Lowborn wenches! They will not be allowed back to bother you with their mindless gossip and vicious rumors," she says, shaking her head.

"What were they saying?" Hephæstion asks curiously.

"Nothing!" Rošanak says without attempting to mask her anger and rolls the dice. "5 and 4!"

Hephæstion eyes Rošanak. "Ha! Nothing— right!"

Anger burned and smoldered like fire in the forests of her eyes…

"Play or leave!" Rošanak says annoyed.

Hephæstion rolls the dice. "1 and 1."

In FRONT of HEPHÆSTION'S TENT
LATER

"Peukestas, they say you speak the tongue of the Persians better than anyone under my command."

"Yes, Hephæstion. Like I was born to it." Peukestas says proudly.

"Did you know it beforehand?"

"No, Hephæstion. I learned it from my wife after the sack of Persepolis."

"How did you master it? Was it difficult?"

Peukestas thinks for a moment.

"Hephæstion— Persian is not a tongue to be mastered, if you are not born to it. It is a tongue to be loved and if you love it well, it will reveal its secret treasures to you, like a bride offering up her hidden beauty to her husband on their wedding night. It is the sweetest tongue, after Attik, of course."

"Attik is not sweet!" Hephæstion grunts.

Peukestas eyes Hephæstion under his brow and then starts elaborating. "When we were sacking Persepolis, I ran into this magnificent house, in search of golden treasures. What I found was the most beautiful girl I had even seen in my life. Eros must have shot me with his arrow, just as I laid eyes upon her, just to save her life."

"And?"

"She was standing in the middle of the entrance hall pointing a sharp dagger at me and yelling words I did not understand, but she was so beautiful! Hair like the feathers of a raven, skin more luminous than Korinthian marble, lips made for kissing, breasts like—"

Hephæstion interrupts impatiently. "Peukestas!"

"Yes, Hephæstion! Well, I had a choice of either killing her or kissing her! I am not fond of killing highborn women, they are more useful alive. Nor am I fond of raping them, women are much sweeter if they give themselves freely—"

"Peukestas! I am not interested in your strategy toward women, just in your mastery of the Persian tongue."

"Yes, Hephæstion! I am getting to it. Where was I? Ah! Yes, well, I decided to kiss her!" He nods and smiles. "She must have liked my kisses too, although she denied it later— after I married her—"

"Peukestas!"

"Hephæstion, you cannot be impatient like this, if you wish to learn Persian!" Peukestas says with a polite tongue. "Where was I? Yes! Well, for a few months, I would listen to her whispering sweetly into my ears. Her words filled my ears and spilled all over my pillow at nights. I did not understand a word of it. I was not sure if she was sweetly plotting my demise, or if she was asking for more loving. So, I decided to learn her tongue. Leaning a tongue is so easy when it is poured softly into your ears resting on soft pillows under starry skies."

"I see." Hephæstion eyes Peukestas with annoyance.

"Yes. I know a Persian word that has seventy-eight different meanings!"

"Peukestas, starting tomorrow at sunrise, you are to teach me Persian. Come to my tent."

"At sunrise, Hephæstion?"

"Yes, at sunrise! Unless you prefer to share my pillow at nights and whisper Persian sweetly into my ears all night long?"

Peukestas takes a step back. "No, Hephæstion. Sunrise it is!"

ROŠANAK'S TENT. NEAR the CITY of LOTUSES
YEAR 11 of ALEXANDER, MONTH 4, PERITIOS
YEAR 4 of ALEXANDER, MONTH 10, ANÂMAKA
A MONTH PASSES
NIGHT

"Roxana," Perdikkas says as he enters Rošanak's tent and sits himself down at the meal table.

The siege of Peukelaotis had finally ended after a month. The town had been razed to the ground and Raja Astês had perished along with the town people.

And he was hungry enough to eat his own horse!

Rošanak smiles nicely at him. "I had lost all hope that you and Hephæstion would join me for a meal tonight."

She was glad for his company… traveling with a smaller part of the Royal Army away from the trappings of the King and Court had been easier… her Persian cook was becoming skillful at making sweets, as Thukrâ had taught her, and Hephæstion and Perdikkas came to her tent most nights to share food at her table.

Perdikkas puts a book he is holding in front of Rošanak.

"This book just arrived today for Hephæstion, along with communications from Makedonia. A book by Euripides— I am sure he has read it and has no need of it himself. I thought it might help along your mastery of Attik."

Rošanak picks up the book and flips through the pages. "*Medea…*"

It was written on common papyrus, but the handwriting was clear and easy to read and had some notes written neatly along the edges of it.

"Hmm… Euripides… Was he not the one who said some Hellene god was born in Baktria?"

"Yes, Dionysos, Son of Zeus, God of Wine."

"Ah! Do you not wish to read it first yourself?"

Perdikkas shakes his head, "No," and eagerly starts filling up his plate with food.

Hephæstion always made sure she was well cared for and well provisioned and she always invited the kingsmen of Alexander to join her table for the night meal.

And the food at her table was better than anywhere else in the army camp.

Her cook knew how to cook!

"No!" he says again. "It is an old book. I read it when I was young and I know it by heart and I only read accounts of heroic battles now. I have not much time or use for soft tales—"

He points with his head to the book in Rošanak's hands. "Euripides was an Athenian writer who was born on the day of the Battle of Salamis, but he had the good sense to die in Makedonia in the court of Philip."

Rošanak looks through the book. "Do not believe all of what Herodotos wrote in the *Histories*," she says suddenly.

Perdikkas raises an eyebrow. "You have read Herodotos?"

Rošanak shakes her head side to side. "No, not all of it. Polydoros, the family healer, gave me an old copy to read, when he was teaching me Attik. It was full of lies. Lying is the source of evil. I gave the book to my dog. Lies must have tasted horrid. Even my dog did not like to chew on it. He took it and buried it somewhere outside the fortress along with some old bones!"

Perdikkas laughs. "I see! But this is not tiresome history, it is a play."

"Is *Medea* a play, like *Persians*, by Aischylos?"

"Yes."

Rošanak makes a face. "Hephæstion made me read *Persians*."

"Did you like it?"

"No! Hephæstion said the *nameless woman* was the wife of the First Darius and the mother of Xerxes! Well, everyone knows that Queen Atossa, the Royal Mother of Xerxes, died after her lastborn— when Xerxes was just a boy.

"Hephæstion said she was an imaginary woman, created by Aischylos to make a point about the Persian Royal Women."

She leans forward and whispers, "It is utterly evil to put lies in the mouth of a dead Royal Woman— and even worse, desecrate the memory of dead Great Kings by writing lies about them. I do not think Aischylos liked Persians or women. No wonder his play did not win a prize. Even Hellenes must have realized that Aischylos was just lying about the Persians for the sake of winning a worthless leafy wreath."

Perdikkas shrugs his shoulders and eats.

Rošanak starts reading a page:

"Let no one think of me,
As humble or weak or passive.
Let them understand.
I am a different kind...
Loyal to my friends,
Dangerous to my enemies,
To such a life glory belongs."

Rošanak closes the book and puts it down on the table.

"Sounds like Alexander."

"Medea was a barbarian princess from the Land of the Golden Fleece. But your Attik is getting better everyday." Perdikkas says with a mouth full of food.

Rošanak blushes lightly and smiles, pleased with his kind words.

Perdikkas, like Hephæstion, was not like the other kingsmen around Alexander, always trying for his attention... and he had never tried to flatter her. He had come with Hephæstion one night and more nights afterward... he enjoyed the Persian food served at her table... he said few words but he ate a lot.

"Ah! Thank you Perdikkas. Hephæstion is a patient teacher. The fault is with the books he forces me to read. I would learn much faster if I could read poetry or tales of love."

Perdikkas nods with a full mouth.

"But at least he writes notes for me on the edges of the books he has me read!" She points to the book. "Can I write on this book?"

Perdikkas nods and forces a few words out through a mouthful. "The book is yours. Do with it what you like."

She looks toward the tent flap. "Shall we save some food for Hephæstion? I can send it to his tent."

Soon, nothing would be left for Hephæstion, the way Perdikkas was devouring the food!

Perdikkas nods, putting some more food on his plate. "Hephæstion is sick. He was feeling feverish for a few days and after the siege ended yesterday, he collapsed. It is this horrid heat."

Rošanak is surprised.

Hephæstion had not sent her any words…

"Hephæstion is sick? Has your Army Healer checked up on him?"

"Yes— but he says it is fever caused by the weather, or something else— we have had many sick men lately, some have died of it."

Rošanak becomes alarmed. "Perdikkas— shall we send word to Alexander?"

Perdikkas thinks for a long moment.

News had come from the main Royal Army earlier. Alexander had just conquered the formidable Fortress of Massaga. The Chief of Massaga had died in the attack and the fortress had been taken by storm. Seven thousand Indian mercenary troops had tried to flee in the middle of the night after they had agreed to join the Royal Army and Alexander had them slaughtered for breaking faith with him. The envoys said that Alexander had taken Kleophis, the wife of the dead Massaga Chief to bed, to punish the Massaga Tribe for resisting him.

Perdikkas takes a deep breath and then shakes his head.

"Hephæstion is strong as an ox. Those who died from the fever were mostly wounded men and weakling women and young children. The Army Healer is waiting to see if he takes a turn for worse, before alerting the King. If we tell Alexander and Hephæstion dies, Alexander will punish the wound-healer— if Hephæstion is cured in a day or so, everyone will laugh at us for acting emotionally like women— that, Roxana, is worse than death! It is best to wait and see who wins the battle: Hades or Hephæstion."

"But Hephæstion could die of it?"

"Hmmm… then he is dead, by Zeus and we will burn his body and bury his bones honorably and hang the Army Healer to appease Alexander!"

Perdikkas looks at the food on the table. "Although, he is responsible for feeding the Royal Army and everyone else. No one is better than him in securing provisions. He can even talk mice into giving up grain for gold."

Rošanak eyes Perdikkas for a moment and then looks at the food on her table with dismay.

She had not thought much about food before… she had never gone hungry… not even at the Sughud Rock…

Perdikkas points to the wine on the table.

"Following Alexander means better wine at the table; following Hephæstion means better food. He has been giving most of his own provisions to you and some of mine too, since we eat at your table a lot. He always makes sure you get your share first— even before he provisions the men."

Rošanak eyes Perdikkas for a moment and tosses and turns his words in her heart.

She had been such a fool!

The army camp was full of women and children… and she was fed before all of them… just because she was still married to a man who cared nothing for her these days and was bedding the wife of a conquered enemy.

Nothing Alexander did remained a secret for too long.

"Perdikkas— may I visit him with my Persian healer?"

"I see no problem with that, Roxana. I do not think he is contagious. I have visited him and I feel no worse for it!"

Rošanak pushes a plate of sweets toward Perdikkas. "Perdikkas, my cook baked these today especially for you, knowing how you enjoy Persian sweets."

Perdikkas takes the plate with a smile.

"Roxana, eating at your table is dangerous— Alexander warned me to stay away from it, if I wanted to remain a pure Makedonian, and well— I see no harm in enjoying Persian food, even if I have to exercise more to keep in good form for campaigning. I carry my own sand with me for wrestling."

Rošanak laughs.

What a fool!

There was plenty of sand in Asia!

HEPHÆSTION'S TENT

LATER

Perdikkas and Rošanak and her Old Persian Healer enter Hephæstion's tent, lit by a few candles.

Hephæstion's old attendant is standing over him by his bedside, wetting his body with a damp piece of linen. He stands back as Perdikkas and Rošanak and the Old Persian Healer approach Hephæstion's bed. Hephæstion lies naked and unconscious in his bed, burning up with fever.

The Old Persian Healer starts examining Hephæstion.

Rošanak interprets for Perdikkas.

"His blood is running hot… Dark demons are ravaging his body…" The Old Persian Healer scratches his beard, thinking carefully.

"What shall be done for him?" Perdikkas asks.

Rošanak interprets for the Old Persian Healer.

"Healing comes from a knife or from a plant or from words… his cure will be by the mixed juice of ancient plants and utterances of sacred words."

Rošanak eyes the old healer and takes Hephæstion's hand.

"His body is so warm… Do you have the plants that can cure him?"

When the old man did not know what to do, he always left the cure in the hands of the Wise Lord.

"No… not all the plants that I need… it is too warm and damp to keep some of them. But I still have enough Haoma leaves, which is the most important one. He will get worse before he gets better, as he cannot have any water or food… or he might die… I cannot say with any certainty…" The Old Persian Healer scratches his beard thinking absently.

Rošanak interprets without elaborating.

Perdikkas beckons the old attendant and gives him an order.

"Go and fetch the Army Healer who was here earlier today and bring him here."

The old attendant puts down the wet linen and quickly leaves the tent.

Rošanak picks up the damp linen and dips it in the bucket of water next to the bed and wipes the sweat from Hephæstion's face.

The Old Persian Healer looks at the bucket of water for a moment and then takes the linen from Rošanak's hand, smells it and throws it with disdain into the bucket and mumbles, pointing to the bucket of water. "Any water coming in contact with the sick Makedonian has to be boiled first."

The Army Healer followed by the old attendant enters, looking disheveled and tired. "Commander, you sent for me?"

"Check Commander Hephæstion. Is he any better than the last time you saw him? Or not?"

The Army Healer walks up to Hephæstion and starts examining him.

"His fever is worse— two men and some women and children died of this fever today. I am not sure what more I can do— it is not the kind of fever I have seen before— it is like an evil rising from the swamps."

Rošanak translates for the Old Persian Healer.

"What are the symptoms?"

"Hot fever, cold chills, headache, sweats, tiredness, and purging—Commander was tired and feverish for a few days and he passed out yesterday."

"What remedy have you given to Commander Hephæstion?" Perdikkas asks worriedly.

"The same remedy I prescribe for snake bites."

Rošanak translates for the Old Persian Healer.

"He was not bitten by a snake!" the Old Persian Healer says with certainty.

Rošanak takes Hephæstion's hand. "My Persian healer is willing to take on the responsibility for the Commander."

They all look at her.

"Shall we send a messenger to the King and let him make a decision?" she asks cautiously.

"Can you cure Commander Hephæstion?" Perdikkas asks the Army Healer.

"I cannot be sure. No one has survived the fever yet."

Perdikkas takes a deep breath and looks at Hephæstion for a moment.

"Roxana— this is worse than I thought— if Hephæstion dies under the care of the Persian healer, I cannot be certain how Alexander will react… sending a messenger to the main army camp for a decision from Alexander can take no less than five days— maybe even longer!"

Rošanak takes Perdikkas' hand in her hands. The two healers look at them intently. "Herbs are no stranger to us. We seek them and we revere them to fight sickness from evil demons who attack our mortal bodies—" Rošanak says persuasively. "What would Hephæstion do, if it was you laying in your sick bed? He would know that I would never allow anyone to harm you!"

Perdikkas eyes her for a moment and then relents. "Very well— May gods help us!"

"The care of Commander Hephæstion is given to the Persian healer by my command— and with the blessing of the Queen," Perdikkas tells the Army Healer.

Rošanak lets go of Perdikkas' hands.

The Army Healer looks at Hephæstion and then nods, relieved. "Very well, Commander."

"The Commander is under your care now," Rošanak tells the Old Persian Healer quietly.

"But— I am the royal healer— and the Makedonians are barbarians— I hear that they kill the poor healer if the sick dies!" he says with dismay.

Rošanak gives the Old Persian Healer a sharp look.

"Commander Hephæstion is the dearest friend of the King. As such, you are now responsible for his care!"

"Oh, very well— but I can cure only royal sickness— not the strange diseases of ordinary men!"

Perdikkas interrupts and commands the Army Healer. "You are dismissed. Get some rest. Report to me tomorrow morning with the list of all the dead and the sick."

"The Queen and the Persian wound-healer will care for Commander Hephæstion. Do as they command you, or I will have you hanged," Perdikkas tells Hephæstion's old attendant.

"I will walk you back to your tent," Perdikkas says to Rošanak.

"Thank you, Perdikkas. I will stay here for a short while. My eunuch would conduct me back."

"Very well. Good night, Roxana."

"Good night."

Perdikkas looks at Hephæstion for a short moment and then turns around and leaves the tent.

It becomes quiet.

The Old Persian Healer scratches his beard, thinking. "I will go and mix an herbal remedy for him. Please have his servant boil some water… he can wipe down his body with the cooled boiled water, after I feed him the Haoma…"

"Would you boil a bucket of water for your Commander? We will wash down his body when the water cools," Rošanak tells the old attendant politely. The old man nods and quickly leaves the tent.

The Old Persian Healer checks on Hephæstion once more and notices an old long sword scar above his manhood. He looks closer and then looks up and points. "We should not waste Haoma on this man. He will probably never have sons."

Rošanak is startled. She looks at the scar on Hephæstion's body and then pulls the corner of a linen sheet to cover his manhood and shakes her head.

"It makes no difference. Do what you can!"

The Old Persian Healer shakes his head and then leaves the tent wordlessly.

The tent becomes quiet again.

Rošanak looks at Hephæstion. The light of a candle by his bed flickers on his burning face. She see that he is still unconscious and unaware of what is going on around him.

She reaches and gently touches his forehead. His body feels like a burning furnace in the middle of a cold night. She walks around his bed and pours some drinking water from a jar on the small table next to his bed into a small hand bowl. She looks around for a piece of clean linen.

This was the first time she had been in Hephæstion's tent. Unlike the royal tent, his tent was simple and unadorned, with few luxuries. His military arm and armor was neatly arranged in one corner of the tent and a small table covered with books and stacks of parchment and a pair of chairs sat in another corner.

The only luxury in his tent was a Persian water basin for bathing, no doubt from one of the former royal palaces in Pârsâ.

She notices a small wooden chest by his arm and armor. She walks over and opens it. Inside the wooden chest, linen and clothes were folded neatly, next to each other. She takes a clean white linen, closes the chest and walks back to Hephæstion's bedside. She dips the clean linen in the water bowl and gently wipes the hot sweat from his face and his body.

She knew so little about him… other than being a reckless takh'teh nard player, who spoke a few words of Persian, had helped her in her moment of need and had been giving her his own food rations.

What kind of a man was he truly?

What lay within his magnificently muscled, perfected body, undiminished even in evil of sickness?

Her thoughts are interrupted as the old attendant enters the tent carrying two large buckets of water and empties them into the large Persian water basin.

Steam rises from the hot water in the basin.

He takes the empty buckets and leaves the tent again.

Rošanak continues wiping Hephæstion's body with the drinking water.

The Old Persian Healer returns after a while, carefully holding a small jar in his hand like precious golden jewelry.

"We have to get him to drink the sacred Haoma… it will make him worse first… causing visions and illusions and delusions… then his body should start repelling the demons, by the favor of the Wise Lord."

"Are you sure of this?"

"No… not completely sure… relatively sure… but… no… not entirely sure… No!"

Rošanak raises her palm and cuts off the rambling of the Old Persian Healer. She puts down the damp linen, wipes her hands on her gown, grabs Hephæstion's shoulders and starts calling him gently.

"Hephæstion, Hephæstion."

He smelled feverish…

There is no response.

Rošanak holds Hephæstion's shoulders harder and starts shaking him gently. "Hephæstion! Open your eyes! Hephæstion!"

Hephæstion slowly opens his eyes, totally disoriented.

Rošanak grabs the Haoma jar from the Old Persian Healer and brings it to Hephæstion's lips. "Hephæstion, drink this! It will drive the evil from your body— it will make you better!"

Hephæstion closes his eyes and starts to fade again. The Old Persian Healer puts his hand on Hephæstion's back, pushing him upright.

"Hephæstion! Please hear my voice! Drink this!"

Hephæstion slowly opens his eyes again and Rošanak forces the golden milky drink down his throat. Hephæstion drinks half of the Haoma mindlessly without tasting it and passes out again.

Rošanak and the Old Persian Healer gently lay him down on his bed. The Old Persian Healer takes the Haoma jar from Rošanak and looks at what remains inside. "Good… he drank most of it…"

"What now?"

"Now, we just wait… Haoma is most effective with the utterance of sacred words," the Old Persian Healer says, eyeing Rošanak and then continues. "If the fever does not break… well…" He touches Hephæstion's forehead and points to the old attendant.

"You should tell him to keep rubbing down the body of the Makedonian with boiled water, to cool off his body."

Rošanak turns her head and sees the old attendant standing silently behind them, watching them. Rošanak turns her back and looks at Hephæstion. She sees no change in him. "How long before we know?" she asks impatiently.

In all the old legends, the dying hero was always cured at once by the first golden drop of sacred Haoma reaching his lips.

"I cannot say… it depends on how evil are the demons who have taken hold of his body. I will bring him more Haoma in the morning. Just tell his servant to force the rest of the Haoma down his throat, if he wakes up. Do not give him any water, no matter how much he begs for it."

"No water—" Rošanak repeats under her lips.

The Old Persian Healer continues. "And no food, until his fever breaks!"

"And no food—" Rošanak repeats.

"You should go to bed yourself, Your Highness. His servant can stay up with him. A Royal Woman should not attend to a barbarian."

Rošanak touches Hephæstion's feverish forehead. "Yes… A Royal Woman should not attend to a barbarian," she repeats faintly.

The Old Persian Healer bows low and leaves the tent.

It becomes quiet again.

Rošanak stands motionless by Hephæstion's bedside. The old attendant walks up quietly, stands next to her, and takes and holds Hephæstion's hand for a moment. He then walks back to the water basin, fills a jar with water and fills up the bowl with boiled water, dips the linen in the water and starts wiping Hephæstion's body, without a word.

Rošanak turns and takes a few steps toward the tent flap. The buried memory of the night he had come to her so generously, helping her at his own peril, saving her dead firstborn son from the flames of Alexander, heaves and rushes like a meandering wave, bathes her in remembrance and beckons her back to him.

She stops and utters a quiet prayer under her lips for her firstborn. Then she turns around and walks back to Hephæstion's bedside and puts her hands on the shoulder of the old attendant. "You can rest for a while. I will stay with the Commander. I will wake you before I go."

The old attendant hesitates.

"Go. Go rest."

The old attendant bows his head awkwardly and hands the linen to Rošanak and leaves the tent quietly. Rošanak takes the linen and wipes Hephæstion's forehead. The tent flap opens quietly and the old attendant enters, spreads a small blanket on the ground close to the side of the tent, and curls up on it and goes to sleep.

Rošanak soaks the linen in the water bowl and wipes Hephæstion's body.

He starts to twist and moan in pain in his sleep.

Rošanak soaks the linen again and folds it and leaves it on Hephæstion's forehead. She walks over and picks up a small chair from the middle of the tent and brings it back to Hephæstion's bedside and sits on it. She takes Hephæstion's hot hand and rests her head on the side of his bed and quietly prays.

"I worship the Wise Lord.

"Divine Mithrâ, Protector of the Warriors… this man is not the Persian King… and he is not a Persian, but he is a warrior… He defied his king at his own peril, just to bring peace to the heart of a Persian Royal Woman, much grieved by the death of her firstborn son…

"For his act of kindness and mercy toward the dead Royal Son of the King, please take him under your protection and rid his body of the demons of the Lord of Darkness."

"My Lord, grant me this blessing…"

Ahurô Mazdâ… auuat aiiaptəm dazdi mê…

Rošanak closes her eyes and starts to drift away in the warm tent.

MIDDLE of the NIGHT

Rošanak's hand shakes suddenly and she is awakened violently. The tent is dimly lit, with just one candle still burning on the center table. Hephæstion is tossing and turning around in his bed unconsciously. She quickly gets to her feet and touches Hephæstion's forehead. The Book of *Medea* in her lap falls carelessly on the ground.

Hephæstion's body has become warmer, burning up like the midday sun. He moans in pain.

"Water…"

Rošanak grabs the wet linen that has fallen off Hephæstion's head onto his pillow. Her hand brushes against his pillow; it is soaking wet. She touches the linen on his bed; it is all soaked through with his sweat, feeling clammy and soggy and watery. She looks around and sees his old attendant curled up sleeping quietly by the door. She walks quickly, gently shakes the old attendant and wakes him up. He jumps up quickly and follows her to Hephæstion's bed.

"He is flaming! Let us get him into the water basin to cool him down. Then you can change the dirty linen on his bed."

The old attendant nods and the two of them try to lift Hephæstion from his bed. He is delirious and heavy as a sack full of gold coins. They finally manage to pull him down from the bed and drag him into the water basin.

Rošanak kneels down by the water basin, exhausted, and holds Hephæstion's hand. Hephæstion sinks into the water basin and the cooled water comforts him. The old attendant quickly replaces the wet linen of his bed with fresh, dry clean linen. Rošanak washes Hephæstion's face and rinses his sweaty wet hair with clean water.

Night ends. Dawn breaks.

Hephæstion has been soaking in the water basin most of the night. Rošanak and his old attendant have fallen asleep, Rošanak on the edge of the water basin and the old attendant on his blanket by the tent flap.

Hephæstion slowly opens his eyes. He looks around trying to remember. He sees Rošanak's head coming into focus, resting on the edge of the water basin. He does not remember how he got into the basin. His head hurts and he feels extremely thirsty.

"Water…" Hephæstion asks faintly.

Rošanak hears Hephæstion's voice in her sleep and opens her eyes and sees him awake in the water basin looking at her. She lifts up her head. Her neck feels sore from resting on the ledge of the basin. She reaches and gently touches Hephæstion's head. His forehead feels cooler to her touch.

"Hephæstion… how are you feeling?" Rošanak asks quietly.

"Where is… Philippo?" Hephæstion asks faintly.

"Who is Philippo?"

"My attendant."

"He is sleeping by the door. He does not talk… much…"

"He lost his tongue somewhere on a battlefield long ago."

"Ah!"

"Thirsty— water— please—"

Rošanak achingly gets up to her feet. "I will bring you something to drink."

Rošanak walks back and grabs the small Haoma jar and puts it to Hephæstion's lips.

Hephæstion takes a sip and spits it out immediately and pushes the jar from his lips. "This is not water— it tastes like poison!"

"It is Haoma… ancient Persian remedy… Drink it… It will heal you."

She takes a small sip of Haoma herself. "See… it is not poison!"

Hephæstion pushes away the Haoma jar, pleading. "I am thirsty! I want water! Please get me some water!"

"Hephæstion, please… drink this… my healer said you cannot have any water!"

"Get me some water or go away!" Hephæstion grunts angrily.

"Hephæstion, please! I know you are thirsty, but you have a demon fever! Haoma will chase the evil demon out of your body."

Hephæstion tries to push himself out of the water basin, but he is too weak and sinks back into the basin.

"Roxana… I am dying of thirst… please have mercy… please give me some water…"

"Hephæstion, drink the rest of Haoma and I will grant you any wish, in place of giving you water."

"Any wish?"

"Yes. Any wish!"

Hephæstion eyes Rošanak with his feverish eyes. "I wish… to be loved," he says, without hesitation.

Silence.

Rošanak takes a deep breath and pauses, and then says quietly, "Then, I will love you."

Hephæstion closes his eyes for a moment and then opens his eyes and looks at Rošanak. Rošanak gently puts the jar back to his lips and he drinks the rest of Haoma and swallows it hard.

Rošanak puts the jar down on the floor. She looks up and Hephæstion has passed out again. She prays under her breath:

> *"O Green One, I invoke your healing power for the whole body… I ask you to grant me this blessing… health for his body… I ask you to grant me this blessing… long life for this warrior…"*

DAYBREAK

Rošanak and Philippo lift Hephæstion out of the water basin slowly, with the aid of Abi-Samar, drying him off first and then laying him down gently in his clean bed.

Philippo empties the water basin with buckets and refills it with freshly boiled water.

Hephæstion sleeps quietly in his bed, with Rošanak sitting by his bedside.

The Old Persian Healer enters the tent and is surprised to see Rošanak there. He bows. "Your Highness?"

Rošanak touches Hephæstion's forehead. "He drank all of Haoma… his body feels cooler."

The Old Persian Healer approaches Hephæstion and touches his forehead and holds his hand.

"He woke up at dawn… he was thirsty… I gave him no water…"

"Hmmm… he is still feverish… the demons are still feasting within him. He needs to drink more Haoma."

"He extracted a heavy price for drinking the rest of Haoma when he came to at dawn!" Rošanak says quietly, tired from the night watch.

"Hmmm… he will not remember any of it."

"Good."

NIGHT

Perdikkas enters Hephæstion's tent.

Hephæstion is sleeping and Rošanak has passed out on the edge of Hephæstion's bed. The tent flap is open, allowing some air to enter the tent freely.

Philippo sits quietly by the door. He stands up quickly as Perdikkas walks in.

Perdikkas walks to the bed and stands over Hephæstion, whose naked body is covered with a thin white linen sheet. Hephæstion slowly opens his eyes.

"Hephæstion."

"Perdikkas." Hephæstion says faintly.

"Good! You know who I am!" Perdikkas says, sounding relieved.

"How long?"

"You collapsed three days ago on the banks of the river. Roxana put you under the care of her Persian wound-healer, when I told her that you were sick with fever.

"I was— worried about a Persian Healer caring for you— but by gods you are still alive."

Hephæstion closes his eyes.

"Roxana has been sitting by your bedside, tending to you. She must know what you mean to Alexander."

"That must be it."

"Ah! I almost forgot!" Perdikkas puts a folded parchment on the small table, next to Hephæstion's bed.

"Here is a letter for you from home. It looks like the handwriting of old Aristoteles."

"Thank you."

Perdikkas continues, shaking his head. "I still think that old windbag put Kallisthenes on the path of treachery to Alexander. All that philosophical nonsense a world away about how kingsmen and warriors should or should not treat their king, who has made them rich beyond their wildest dreams. I say Alexander should summon the old man here, drag him on a battlefield, shoot an arrow into his leg, give him a marker and a piece of parchment and see how many treatises he writes on the actions of the King and his men, when life is pouring out of him!"

He points to the letter. "The fools who cannot wield a sword are always the ones to tell the warriors how they could do it better."

"Perdikkas, can you give me some water?"

"Ah! No! There is an order attached to your tent, sealed by the Persian Healer that prohibits giving you any food or water. On pain of death, no less! If I give you water and you die of it, Roxana will tell Alexander and Alexander will do to me what he did to Kleitos."

"I am feeling much better."

"You look like Hades." Perdikkas says truthfully and then points to Rošanak. "Do you want me to get her out of here?"

"No…"

"Well, then recover quickly. I am starving to death. I miss eating at her table. And the construction of the bridge has slowed since you have gotten sick. And the ships Alexander has ordered will not build themselves."

"Yes…"

"Ah! I sacrificed to your health this morning," Perdikkas says as he starts to leave, "an ox and a full jar of pure olive oil! That is probably why you are feeling better!"

"Thank you, that must be so—"

"Ah! I almost forgot! Your father had sent you a copy of *Medea* and I gave it to Roxana. You are in no shape to be reading."

"Good," Hephæstion says under his breath, "it was meant for her."

Perdikkas nods and leaves the tent.

Hephæstion beckons Philippo to approach him. He points to the small Haoma jar next to his bed.

"Philippo, help me drink the rest of this vile potion."

Philippo quickly obeys and puts the Haoma jar to Hephæstion's lips. Hephæstion drinks the rest in one swallow and closes his eyes, trying to forget thc taste.

"Go on to your wife. I do not need you for tonight."

Philippo stands hesitantly, unsure whether he should leave his commander against their ancient customs.

Hephæstion reads his face. "Go on! I am bloody thirsty and if you deny me water again, I might just kill you!"

Philippo takes a step back and then nods his head and turns around and leaves. Hephæstion looks at Rošanak who is still passed out on the edge of his bed. He reaches and gently caresses her hair.

No one had sat by his bedside, taking care of him in sickness, since he had left for Asia… he had forgotten the sweet comfort of it… knowing he was not all alone in a strange land…

Rošanak reaches and takes Hephæstion's hand in her hand and holds it tightly, in her sleep, without waking.

Hephæstion closes his eyes, as Haoma starts to run through his body again.

EARLY DAWN

Rošanak opens her eyes. She has been in Hephæstion's tent for two nights. She feels a gentle hand on her shoulder. She looks up and sees Mâr'at Bani Âriyânnâz.

"Rošanak, I can sit with the Makedonian. You need to bathe and eat and rest!"

"I am bound to him for his kindness. It is my debt and mine alone."

"Can I at least bring you something to eat and drink?"

"No! He cannot eat or drink, until his fever breaks for good. He will smell food and water on me and will suffer more for it."

"Rošanak… He is just a barbarian, after all."

"He is not a barbarian. Please go and take your rest. Do not worry about me. I am well enough."

Mâr'at Bani Âriyânnâz bends and kisses Rošanak's face and lingers for a moment, undecided, and then she turns and leaves the tent quietly.

Rošanak gets to her feet and stretches. Her body is sore from napping here and there in odd positions. She walks to the door and takes a quick look outside, then closes the tent flap and walks over to the water basin and looks at it longingly.

She smelled ghastly… she had not bathed since she had entered Hephæstion's tent.

She takes a deep breath and then walks back and stands by Hephæstion's bedside. The Haoma juice was all gone. She reaches and gently touches Hephæstion's forehead. He slowly opens his eyes and looks at her.

"Hephæstion."

"Go back to your tent and rest for the day. I am well!"

"You are still feverish."

"I will live…"

"You wish to rid yourself of me, so you can drink down a jug of water to quench your thirst."

"I am not thirsty anymore."

"Liar!"

"I am not lying!"

"Then swear by one of your gods!"

Hephæstion starts to shiver uncontrollably and wraps his arms around himself. "I am so cold!"

Rošanak feels Hephæstion's forehead. His body is burning up. She quickly grabs a linen sheet and wraps it around him. Hephæstion continues to shiver and quiver. "I am so cold!"

Rošanak quickly grabs a blanket from the small chest and wraps it around Hephæstion's body and holds him in her arms for a while. Hephæstion stops shivering and curls up in his bed. She lets go of him.

"Go! I have no need of you!" Hephæstion says faintly and closes his eyes in pain.

"But I am in need of you! Who else I can find who so easily parts with his gold dariks, playing my favorite board game?"

All men were ill-tempered when they were sick!

Hephæstion points to the letter with his head.

"Then be useful! Read me my letter."

Rošanak looks at the folded parchment by his bedside. "Is it a love letter from one of your beloveds?"

"It is from Aristoteles, my old teacher."

"Ah!" Rošanak picks up the letter, breaks the seal, opens it and starts reading: "Aristoteles to Hephaistion, Greeting." She shows the letter to Hephæstion. "Is this the way your name is written?"

"Yes…" Hephæstion says, his body trembling.

"Hephæstion, I am saddened by the news of the death of my nephew, Kallisthenes."

Rošanak looks at Hephæstion, startled. "Is Kallisthenes dead?"

"Yes…"

She continues reading: "It is well within the authority of Alexander and the Assembly to execute the traitors. But I assure you my nephew, Kallisthenes, was not one of them."

Rošanak looks at Hephæstion again. "Alexander killed Kallisthenes?"

Hephæstion pulls the blanket tighter around him. "No… I did…"

"Oh!"

Silence.

She eyes the trembling Hephæstion for a short moment and then continues reading: "Kallisthenes was politically dim-witted, but he was a good philosopher. Everyone liked his eloquence in the *Deeds of Alexander* he wrote. But truthfully he had no taste for the practice of pro-sky-nee…"

"Proskynesis."

"Ah!" She continues reading: "Proskynesis— what does it mean?"

"The Persian act of bowing to the king and offering him kisses."

"Ah!" She eyes Hephæstion and teases him. "The Makedonians do not kiss their kings?"

"No!"

"Pity. Persians must love their kings more than Makedonians love theirs."

"Read!"

She continues reading: "But he would never have plotted against Alexander. He was not that heroic. He was terrified of his own shadow."

Rošanak starts mumbling to herself, "Kallisthenes never liked me. He said to me I was an illiterate dancing girl— not worthy of Alexander. But, I did not wish him dead. Ignorance is a high enough price extracted from a historian. He did say I was beautiful— but not as beautiful as Queen Setâreh…"

She pauses and then shrugs her shoulder. "I would have taken more pity on him, if he had at least corrected the name of my father when I told him of his error. But he said I was a barbarian and no one would care who my father was. I told Alexander and he said he would see to him. I should tell Alexander to have the writings of Kallisthenes corrected with the true name of my father—"

Hephæstion shivers. "He knows."

"Then?"

"Deeds of men are recorded by men for men. Women are not of any importance."

"But—"

"Read the letter!"

"King Artaxerxes was my father, not Oxyartes! Oxyartes is the blood brother of my birth mother and my guardian after the death of my father. It is the custom of my faith. Everyone knows that!"

"Read!"

Rošanak shrugs her shoulder again and continues reading: "I have written to Alexander, inquiring about the evidence that caused him to believe in the guilt of Kallisthenes and I have assured him of my faithfulness to him. If Kallisthenes had provoked the royal boys who were stoned to death, then he too deserved death for his treachery."

Rošanak looks at Hephæstion. "The royal boys who were stoned… had plotted against Alexander?"

"Yes… they had planned to kill him in bed while he slept."

"Why?"

"Because Alexander thinks of himself as a Great King and acts like one."

"Oh!" she sighs, surprised, and then continues reading: "In the private matter you had confided in me—" Rošanak looks at Hephæstion. "Do you want me to read the rest?"

Hephæstion closes his eyes and grunts. "Read it…"

Rošanak continues reading: "It is not a matter about which a philosopher can guide you to the truth. But speaking as a man, passion and reason do not flow in the same river, when it comes to love of a child. That is why boys here are raised entirely by their mothers. Their fathers do not lay eyes upon their sons until they reach the age of seven, so they do not grieve needlessly if their sons die young. Your compassionate act lessened the burden of the wife of Alexander—"

Rošanak stops for a moment, thinking, and then takes a deep breath and continues reading: "… although I have no regard for her myself, and Alexander is no worse off, since his son died with no historical consequence. Although, a dead son indicates the maleness of Alexander's seeds. As long as you repent and sacrifice to the gods, your act is forgiven." Rošanak stops again and looks at the letter and then looks at Hephæstion, biting her lip. Her eyes darken.

"Do you regret— what you did for me?"

Hephæstion looks at her.

"I regret nothing! What I did, I did freely. My actions create no debt of gratitude on your part. Swear you will not speak of this again," he says irritably.

Rošanak looks at Hephæstion searchingly and then looks back at the letter and reads the rest: "Women are simple beings. To know what is in the heart of a woman, a man must first know what is in his own noble heart.

"Farewell." She finishes reading and folds the letter and puts it back on the small table.

Hephæstion starts to toss and turn and forcefully pulls the blanket and the linen off himself and moans. "It is so hot!"

Rošanak gets to her feet and picks up the linen and soaks it in the water bowl and silently wipes Hephæstion's face and body.

Hephæstion looks at her and faintly says, "Say something!"

"You cannot have any food or water until your fever breaks."

Hephæstion reaches and grabs her hand fiercely and holds it tightly in his grip. Rošanak bends and kisses Hephæstion's hand. He loosens his grip and she finishes wiping his body. Hephæstion moans faintly. "Roxana…"

Rošanak holds back a tear. "I am not repaying you my debt of gratitude… my debt to you is a debt that cannot be repaid…

"I care for you… hoping that when my blood brothers lay dying on the dusty muddy bloody battlefields years ago… some kind arms held their dying bodies near their hearts, and they did not die alone."

Hephæstion closes his eyes and softly moans. "Roshanak…"

At Issos there were so many dead and dying that they had crossed a bridge of corpses with their horses to chase after Darius…

Dying on a battlefield was a horrid lonely death…

NIGHT

Perdikkas walks into Hephæstion's dimly lit tent.

Philippo is sitting quietly by the door.

Perdikkas is surprised to see Rošanak again, passed out on the ledge of Hephæstion's bed. He shakes his head with dismay. He walks over and stands next to her and gently puts his hand on her shoulder, shaking it lightly.

Rošanak wakes up and looks at Hephæstion. He is sleeping deeply. She looks up at Perdikkas. "Perdikkas."

"Roxana, go back to your tent and rest. Hephæstion is not deserving of all your attention. Your Persian healer cares for him and that is enough. Not even Alexander can expect his Queen to hold a constant watch over his best friend with such devotion." Perdikkas speaks kindly, sounding concerned.

"Perdikkas, this is not for Alexander. It is for me. Hephæstion deserves what little I can do for him and more."

"Roxana?"

"Hephæstion is the only one among all the kingsmen of Alexander who has treated me fairly. He took me under his protection from the first time you all laid eyes upon me in the royal tent after the fall of the Fortress of Sogdian Rock. He saw me freely. He did not see the invisible chains that were wrapped around my captive hands that fateful day."

Rošanak takes a deep breath.

"Men think war is easy on women, because they are spared their lives. They see women bury their dead, pack their cooking vessels and iron cauldrons and the rest of their belongings and go live with the victors and bear new children. Men do not take notice when captive women bury their hearts along with their dead."

She pauses and then points with her head. "Alexander told me. When everyone advised him in private to just treat me as a prize of war and claim the right of a victor upon my body, Hephæstion supported a lawful marriage alliance, even though he too did not approve of Alexander marrying a Persian.

"Because of his support, Alexander married me and I was not shamed by my captors in the eyes of my mother and my noble ancestors… and the Wise Lord."

Perdikkas takes a deep breath.

Hephæstion is awakened by the voices and lay quietly listening, with his eyes closed. Her frankness startles him. He realizes that she knew all too well how much the Makedonians disapproved of her.

Rošanak continues, her voice rippling with sadness. "Not even Alexander himself has treated me that well, as I was cast aside for failing as a mother to produce a strong child worthy of his King-Father. And his kingsmen took no notice of my pain when I lost my child— all too glad that a half-breed son did not live long enough to become an heir to their Alexander."

"Roxana— Alexander has not cast you aside. You are safer with us than with a campaigning Royal Army. You will have another child by Alexander. Most of the babies born to a fighting marching army die. It is a fact all too well known and understood among the men of the sword."

Rošanak gets up to her feet, pointing to Hephæstion.

"Hephæstion is suffering not just from the demons causing him his fever, but from extreme thirst and hunger. His pain drives him to needless cruelty. He will plunge the knife kept under his pillow into anyone denying him what he desires the most— but not even madness will provoke him enough to kill a woman. He will take his death before his dishonor."

Perdikkas eyes her intently for a moment and then quietly points to Hephæstion with his head. "We are equals in rank and strength. I can stay with him tonight. Go rest and come back tomorrow well rested."

Rošanak soaks a fresh linen in the bowl of water and starts wiping Hephæstion's body.

"Perdikkas— you are not a nursemaid. You are the Commander of all of us and we rely on you to keep us safe from harm. Go to your tent and get your rest.

"I am just a woman and a Persian no less, traveling with a wound-healer, a cook, a maid and a eunuch, among a sea of men of the sword… thousands and thousands of them… all my sworn enemies… all capable of killing me with the slightest force of their bare hands—" She takes a breath. "So it is possible that I am truly ignorant of your Makedonian heart, but you eat at my table, not motivated by making you think well of me, but because I can see that underneath all that Makedonian metal, you are an honorable man.

"I will never break bread with Ptolemaios who killed my Kingly-Father and spilled royal blood. Your unkind words long ago were motivated by your devotion to Alexander and the bloodiness of the war, not by your true hatred of me. I forgave you your harsh words long ago. Go in peace."

Perdikkas looks at her intently and takes a deep breath and then nods and heads for the door. He stops halfway and turns around. "Persians fought honorably on the battlefields of Issos and Gaugamela. Hephæstion and I were both badly wounded at Gaugamela. No one left the battlefield without a wound.

"In the chaos of the battle, I got careless and took a wrong turn. A Persian chariot, with sharp blades secured to its wheels, tore into the legs of my horse.

"I fell. My dying horse fell upon me right in front of the charging Persian chariots. Hephæstion saw this and hurled off his horse and pulled me away from the weight of a certain death. He was stabbed as he was shielding me."

Perdikkas looks intently at Rošanak.

"On my honor, Roxana, like Hephæstion, I too will extend you my protection from now on. I will protect you with my last dying breath."

Rošanak watches Perdikkas leave the tent. She quietly beckons Philippo forward.

Philippo rushes and stands in front of her quietly.

"Philippo, your commander is sleeping. His body is cooler tonight. If he gets warmer, I will have the guards and my eunuch carry him to the water basin. You go back to your wife and rest. Come back at early dawn."

Philippo nods and bows his head awkwardly, then turns around and leaves.

Rošanak puts down the wet linen on the small table and longingly gazes over at the still water in the basin. She resists the temptation and gently touches Hephæstion's forehead. He is burning up again. She finally relents and fills up a small glass with drinking water and pours it on the ground around Hephæstion's bed and quietly starts to pray and utter the sacred words.

Hephæstion wakes up again and quietly listens, as Rošanak's Persian words softly fill his ears and spill over onto his pillow.

Rošanak whispers softly:

> *"I worship the Wise Lord.*
>
> *"The Lord and Master of all the Seven Corners of the World. The wisest of all beings, the brightest of all beings, the most glorious of all beings.*
>
> *"The perfection of holiness!*
>
> *"I invoke Divine Mithrâ, Angel of the Sun and the Heavenly Lights and of Bread and Wine… and of Butter and Milk, sleepless and ever awake, loved by the Wise Lord… who resides in the brightest mountain guarded by heavenly stars, where there is neither night nor darkness, neither cold nor hot, and no deathful sickness made by the Lord of Darkness and his demons.*
>
> *"Here lies a warrior, brave and strong, sickened by the demons of the Lord of Darkness.*
>
> *"Divine Mithrâ, may you hear my voice and be pleased with my prayer and grant me my wish which I beg of you… destroy his demons by your heavenly light… pour your glory upon earth made by the Wise Lord… increase the shining sun…*
>
> *"For your brightness and glory, I offer you this water, a sacrifice worthy of being heard, as I have neither drunk nor eaten for two days…"*

Rošanak finishes and takes a deep breath. She puts down the empty glass of water and then sits back down on the small chair by Hephæstion's bedside. She leans forward and takes Hephæstion's hand in her hand and rests her head on the edge of his bed.

"Hephæstion, when I was a young girl, my sister and I used to lie down by the water basin in the middle of our Garden of Roses on hot Baktrian summer days. She used to interrupt my sweet dreams of marrying a handsome Royal Son with her rose-scented words about the moon and heavenly stars. I was forced to listen to her reciting the latest poem she had memorized by heart."

Rošanak closes her eyes, remembering her murmuring water basin amidst her Persian gardens. She sighs and continues. "My sister, Parânak, died the year after the Battle of Black Eagle. She was older than me and when her beloved husband died at the Battle of Issos, she withdrew into herself, she was never the same. She told me once I did not understand how it felt to lose a lover… how she longed for his kisses in the dark of the night… that life without her lover and husband was not life at all… just a never-ending bad dream…"

Rošanak takes a deep breath. "Her face is beginning to fade from my memory, but I still remember how much she loved poetry… I will always remember the one she used to utter over and over and over. She said she wrote it herself… but I think she heard it somewhere or found it in an old prayer book and she liked it so much and read it so often that in the end she believed it was entirely her own creation… like all splendid love poems… the murmuring heart feels it was written in its own blood on its own skin by its own pulsating beat and not by the hands of a poet…"

She remembers lovingly.

"She would whisper sweetly as if she was uttering sacred words meant only for the ears of the Wise Lord and his Guardian Angels…"

She whispers sweetly in remembrance:

"Why does the Moon wax?
Why does the Moon wane?
For fifteen days the Moon waxes…
For fifteen days the Moon wanes…
As long as her waxing, so long is her waning…
As long as her waning, so long is her waxing…
Who but you, My Lord, makes the Moon wax and wane?"

Rošanak's voice starts to fade into sleep.

Hephæstion squeezes Rošanak's hand faintly, doubting she would notice. She has fallen asleep on the edge of his bed again. He starts to fall asleep himself.

Peukestas was right. Persian was the sweetest tongue, whispered softly in hard ears resting on soft pillows, and spilling over into the night.

SUNRISE

Sun breaks and starts to make the day.

Rošanak stands by Hephæstion's bedside, touching his forehead and holding his hand. Hephæstion is sleeping peacefully.

The Old Persian Healer enters the tent, no longer surprised to see Rošanak there. He bows his head low. "Your Highness."

Rošanak touches Hephæstion's forehead. "His body is cool… his fever is broken. He slept peacefully all night long, without waking."

The Old Persian Healer approaches Hephæstion and touches his forehead and holds his hand. "Yes, his fever is broken. The demons have left his body," he says, utterly relieved.

"He no longer is in need of me," Rošanak says, sounding exhausted. She gently lets go of Hephæstion's hand.

Thump!

Rošanak and the Old Persian Healer look in horror as a small black snake falls on Hephæstion almost out of nowhere, coils carelessly and rests motionlessly on his naked chest.

Rošanak steps back mindlessly and utters a short, loud scream without even hearing her own voice. "Ah!" Her knees fold under her.

The Old Persian Healer stands still, cold with fear.

Abi-Samar, guarding the tent, hears Rošanak's scream and rushes into the tent with his dagger drawn and runs to Rošanak's side.

Rošanak's face is as white as pure fallen snow.

"My Lady?" Abi-Samar says in haste, looking around.

Rošanak, voiceless and wordless, points to Hephæstion.

Abi-Samar walks quickly toward Hephæstion's bed, pointing his dagger at him. He then notices the black snake, curled up on Hephæstion's bare chest.

The Old Persian Healer points upward with his head looking terrified.

"It just fell from the sky!"

Abi-Samar looks at the black snake and then at Hephæstion who is peacefully sleeping, oblivious to the snake resting on his chest. Abi-Samar sheaths his dagger and slowly and fearlessly extends his arm in front of the black snake and orders firmly.

"Şerru."

The black snake moves and slowly coils itself around Abi-Samar's arm.

"This is a favorable omen… if a snake falls on the bed of a sick man, the sick man will get well," Abi-Samar says in a quiet voice and then turns around and slowly leaves the tent with the black snake wrapped around his arm.

Rošanak finally fills her lungs with air and then lets it out, relieved but slightly shaking. She walks over to Hephæstion's bed and takes his hand. He is sleeping deeply, unaware.

The Old Persian Healer gets closer too and examines Hephæstion's naked chest. He sees no snake bites or marks, takes a deep breath and regains his reason, and mumbles to himself.

"This wretched land crawls with vicious snakes and scorpions and spiders!"

Rošanak lets go of Hephæstion's hand, slowly walks toward the tent flap and disappears without a word.

LATER

Hephæstion wakes up. His tent is filled with air and light coming in from outside through the opened tent flap. He looks around the room, searching for Rošanak, but there is no sign of her. He tries to sit up.

The Old Persian Healer is sitting at his table writing. He hears the creaking sound coming from Hephæstion's bed and looks in his direction. He stands up and quickly walks up to Hephæstion.

Philippo runs to Hephæstion's bedside.

"Your fever is broken, but your body is still weak—" Old Persian Healer mumbles without expecting to be heard.

"I need to bathe—" Hephæstion says faintly under his breath.

The Old Persian Healer looks startled.

The Makedonian spoke broken Persian…

Hephæstion turns his head and asks Philippo faintly, "Is my bath ready?"

Philippo nods and points with his hands to the water basin with a smile, happy to see Hephæstion feeling better.

Hephæstion slowly gets to his feet. His head spins, he steadies himself on the edge of his bed. "Can I drink some water now?" he asks faintly.

"Yes, but only boiled water from now on. No drinking from the rivers, and you can eat too. Your servant can make you something to eat, nothing raw, only well-cooked food, in small amounts. I would better ask the Queen to send over some proper food." The Old Persian Healer instructs him slowly in Persian.

Hephæstion quietly asks, "Where is the Queen?"

"She went back to her tent right before you woke up. She must be deadly tired. She nursed you well!"

"What was my sickness?"

"I cannot be sure… a fever I have not seen before!" the Old Persian Healer says truthfully.

"How did you— heal me?"

"None of the remedies of your own wound healer had worked, so I gave you the juice of Haoma, the most sacred plant. Haoma is not just a healing brew, it is used in acts of worship. If Haoma could not have cured you, nothing else would have."

Abi-Samar politely enters Hephæstion's tent, followed by a young maid with a tray of food. He bows to Hephæstion and points to the tray, as the maid sets it upon the wooden table. "Commander, My Lady has sent you something to eat, prepared by her own cook."

"Eunuch, tell Queen Roxana that I thank her for her kindness."

Abi-Samar eyes Hephæstion for a moment.

His name was a proud name… his father had named him after an ancient Bâb-ilani king. He had served a king… he was the Protector of a Royal Woman… he was a proud man. He was not marked on his forehead as arad-šarrûtu… slave of the crown… he was marked on his wrist as the protector of the Royal Women.

He slightly bows his head. "Commander, my name is Abi-Samar of Babylon. I was entrusted with the protection of the Royal Women of the House of the King at the age of thirteen, since the first Royal Daughter of the King was born."

"Thank you, Abi-Samar."

The young maid approaches Hephæstion's bed with a plate of food.

Abi-Samar bows his head and points to the maid. "Commander, My Lady said the girl can stay and tend to your needs— whatever they may be."

Hephæstion eagerly takes the plate of food without taking notice of the girl.

"Thank you, Abi-Samar. No need for the girl to stay."

Abi-Samar bows and speaks to the young maid. The young maid bows low and leaves the tent. Abi-Samar bows again and starts heading toward the door.

"Abi-Samar…"

Abi-Samar stops and turns around. "Commander?"

"The Queen— is she well?"

"Yes, Commander." He thinks for a moment and then adds, "I was guarding your tent, while the Queen was tending you."

"Ah! Did I—? I thought I heard a scream—"

"No, Commander. I would have killed you, if you had laid your hands upon her without her permission."

Hephæstion eyes Abi-Samar. "Right."

Abi-Samar bows again and starts heading toward the door.

"Abi-Samar."

Abi-Samar stops and turns around. "Commander?"

"I would never harm her! I—"

"No, Commander. Not even the Makedonians—" Abi-Samar pauses and points, "Your dagger was under your pillow the whole time. She did not allow me to remove it. She said her life rested in the hands of the Wise Lord, not on the tip of your sharp dagger."

Hephæstion stops eating and considers Abi-Samar for a moment.

Abi-Samar bows again and leaves Hephæstion's tent.

BRIDGE of BOATS. BANKS of RIVER SINDHU
YEAR 11 of ALEXANDER, MONTH 5, DYSTROS
YEAR 4 of ALEXANDER, MONTH 11, SAMIYAMAŠ
MID-DAY

Warm and breezy.

Alexander stands on the Bridge of Boats stretching over the River Sindhu.

Spring has finally come and all the omens are favorable!

New rays of sun float like leaves of pure glinting gold on the skin of the River Indus…

Alexander looks around.

Wide planks of wood were bound together, lying flat on top of the wooden boats, all securely roped together.

The bridge was bound to the river banks by gangways… strong and sturdy and secure to bear the weight of tens of thousands of men and horses and carriages…

Hephæstion stands close by, followed by Perdikkas, Krateros, and the rest of the kingsmen of Alexander.

Alexander smiles.

His Royal Army was whole again and spirits were high.

And Hephæstion had built another great bridge, worthy of his standing.

Never disappointing… dependable as usual!

Alexander turns around and smiles at Hephæstion.

Knowing well that his wordless smile was all the recognition Hephæstion desired.

KINGSMEN'S QUARTERS. ROYAL ARMY CAMP. SATRAPY of GANDÂRA
YEAR 11 of ALEXANDER, MONTH 6, XANDIKOS
YEAR 4 of ALEXANDER, MONTH 12, VIYAXANA
NIGHT

"So Hephæstion, they say the barbarian queen breathed life back into you when you were dying from fever. Does she taste as sweet as she looks?" Krateros, heavy with wine, makes a comment within the earshot of Hephæstion, taunting him.

Alexander and his kingsmen are gathered for drinking. They are all heavy with wine. Hephæstion is reclining close to Alexander.

"Krateros! Watch your bloody mouth!" Perdikkas sneers at Krateros.

Hephæstion jumps up angrily and rushes for Krateros before anyone can stop him. He grabs him and pulls him off his couch and pins him down on the floor and threatens him. "How dare you?! I will pull you apart limb by limb for insulting Alexander!"

"Get off me! I will pull you apart limb by limb for insulting me!"

Tension builds.

Perdikkas and other kingsmen, friends of Hephæstion and Krateros, jump up and try to pull them apart and keep them from quarrelling again.

Alexander eyes them, heavy with wine himself.

Perdikkas pushes Hephæstion back. "Ignore him! He is just jealous of your closeness to Alexander! He is trying to provoke you into another fight!"

Hephæstion yells at Krateros, ignoring Perdikkas. "Go ahead and make your accusation to Alexander, if you dare!"

Tempers fly.

"Krateros, be careful of the words coming out of your mouth!" Perdikkas sneers.

Alexander commands, "That is enough! Both of you leave my sight at once and do not return until you have made peace between you!"

"I will not make peace with this pig!" Hephæstion grunts.

"Neither will I! Alexander, I demand to avenge my honor—" Krateros growls.

"I said: *Enough*!" Alexander screams at them. "One more word out of either of you and you will both pay the price of my wrath!"

ALEXANDER'S ROYAL TENT
LATER that NIGHT

Alexander is getting ready for bed in his royal tent.

Hephæstion enters and reclines on the couch, looking angry. He notices the young eunuch preparing Alexander's bed and dismisses him sharply. "Leave us!"

Alexander looks at the young eunuch and nods for him to leave.

The young eunuch leaves quietly.

"He is a slave of the Persian crown. You know he means nothing to me," Alexander says with indifference after the young eunuch is gone.

"He is a whore!" Hephæstion sneers at Alexander.

They both knew what that meant.

Alexander looks at Hephæstion, irritated.

"Have you made peace with Krateros?"

"No! I said I will not make peace with a pig!"

"Do not assume that I will not punish you, as I have said so publicly!"

"Do away with me as you wish."

"Is there any truth to his words— about you and Roxana?" Alexander asks, burying his pain in his voice.

Hephæstion replies calmly, his anger simmering underneath his words; not denying… evading… "You left your Queen in my care when you split the Royal Army and sent me away. I did not ask for the privilege!"

"Hephæstion!"

Hephæstion takes a deep breath, and says more calmly, "How would you have me treat your Queen when she is in my care? Huh?" Hephæstion grunts. "Would you have me tie her to one of the carriages and drag her behind the baggage train to please the Makedonians— or shall I treat her as a Queen should be treated to please the Persians?"

"Hephæstion!"

"I treat your Queen no better or worse than you treated the Royal Women of Darius when they were taken captive after the Battle of Issos. Did you ravish the wife of Darius? His daughters? His mother—" Hephæstion stops abruptly.

Well… Alexander had taken the wife of Darius to bed.

Alexander eyes Hephæstion for a moment and then says quietly, "Queen-Mother Sisygambis is almost seventy years old!"

Silence. Then a quiet laughter.

Tension breaks.

"Hephæstion, please do it for me! If Krateros formally accuses you, I will have no choice but to refer the charges of treason to the Assembly of the Makedonians."

"Has she left your heart? Do you not love her any longer?"

Alexander takes a deep breath.

"You know well that I do! As I love—" Alexander pauses and then continues, "Please make peace with Krateros and let the rumors die. Facts are of no relevance to the truth. Krateros has the loyalty of the Horse. Everyone knows your father is a Hellene. The Assembly will not vote in your favor, no matter how much your friendship means to their king! And they will be too eager to rid themselves of the Persian Queen, no matter how much their king loves her."

Hephæstion shakes his head.

"She cared for me selflessly— nursed me back to health when I caught the black fever at Paropamisadai in the midst of building the bridge on the River Indus. She stayed with me night after night, when I was burning up with fever.

"I would have died without her healing hands and sacred words. And for her kindness, Krateros wants her dishonored."

Hephæstion softens his voice.

"Let her share your bed. Take her with you. She is lonely and homesick and the death of her firstborn weighs heavily on her. You and I were born to the sword— we live the lives of our own choosing. She is only eighteen and lives a life forced upon her by the death of her father and the might of our army! Your Royal Army Standard is older than she is. There is a reason why men do not carry their women with them into battle—"

Alexander looks away.

"She is the one who shuns my bed. She cannot even bear to look at me. Her body goes cold when I touch her— the love I once saw in her eyes has vanished. It pains me to think of all the misery I have brought on the only woman I love— her eyes blame me for the death of our son—"

"No, Alexander— she blames herself for losing your son. Maybe you should send her back to Baktria to her mother. She will heal there. You can go back to her once you conquer India— or summon her back to the royal court."

"No! I will never force myself upon her, but I want her close to me. She loved me once and she will love me again. Women of Darius survived two years trailing my Royal Army. She too will get used to traveling with us, given time."

Hephæstion shakes his head and pleads for her.

"Alexander— By Zeus! Have mercy on her! The wife of Darius died of exhaustion during childbirth— after two years of being dragged from the battlefields of Issos half across Asia!"

Alexander leans back.

"Roxana is not Stateira! There is metal in her bones!"

"She is fragile like glass!"

"No!"

Hephæstion finally relents.

He knew all too well that arguing with Alexander was fruitless, once his mind was set.

"If I am to extend my right hand to Krateros, command me as a king! Do not ask me as a friend."

"Very well, then. I command you as your king."

"Then I will make peace with Krateros, as the King has commanded."

"Good! I will talk with Krateros in private and persuade him to accept your offer of peace. Stay away from him."

OUTSIDE the PALACE of RAJAH ÂMBHI. TAKŠIÇILA. SATRAPY of GANDÂRA
ROYAL ARMY CAMP
YEAR 11 of ALEXANDER, MONTH 6, XANDIKOS
YEAR 4 of ALEXANDER, MONTH 12, VIYAXANA
MID-DAY

Breezy air.

"Roxana!"

Rošanak stops and turns toward Alexander slowly, her heart beating faster.

Mâr'at Bani Âriyânnâz and Abi-Samar discreetly step away and fade among the multitudes shopping in the Hindu market outside the Palace of Rajah Âmbhi.

"Alexander." Rošanak quietly responds.

Alexander eyes her tenderly.

She was clothed like the women of Raja Omphis, sheathed in a sheer silk gown, in the color of the Bitter Sea.

He had missed her… five months had passed since the last time he had seen her.

She looked even more beautiful than he remembered… her hair longer… her body fuller… beckoning him to her from under the shimmery wrapper…

Memories of love outflanked the bits and pieces of loss…

A moment passes silently in the midst of the loud and lively noises of the crowded market.

Alexander steps closer, almost touching her body, breathing her in. The scent of her yâsmined hair fills his body.

"My Lord?"

Rošanak stands motionlessly, looking at Alexander. His familiar scent pours back into her.

She had missed him… it had been five months since the last time she had seen him.

His hair looked longer and more golden in the rays of the sun… the tips of her fingers begged her to caress him.

He had done as she had asked and had stayed away from her.

He should have known better than to listen to her.

Alexander lingers and hopelessly searches for words.

Silence.

Rošanak relents and breaks the silence and points upward with her eyes.

"They say, My Lord, that before reaching here, you and your men, wreathed in ivy and clothed in the light of the heaven, were singing and drinking and feasting in the old forest groves atop the mountains on the other side of the river for ten days."

Alexander relaxes and smiles and gently takes her hand into his hand. And starts playing with the tips of her fingers.

"The old forest groves were the color of your eyes."

Rošanak smiles.

"Could you hear us all the way down there?"

Rošanak shakes her head and smiles again.

"No. I saw Hystanes, my brother. He told me!"

Alexander smiles and starts walking and gently pulling her fingers along with him. She follows him.

"Did he tell you that before the sacred ritual, I conquered the Rock of Arnos? The Rock was two hundred stadia wide and no lower than eleven stadia at its height, with only one narrow path to the top cut by the hands of men. They say not even my ancestor, Herakles himself, was able to capture this Fortress!"

"Fortress of Âvarana? The Sanctuary of the Heavens? No, he did not say," Rošanak says softly with a playful smile.

Everyone in the Lands and beyond had heard of this by now.

Well, almost everyone… but the hard of hearing.

Alexander's smile widens as he talks in a low voice into her ear, walking her back toward the palace through a sea of people— enjoying the sprawling market with multitudes of merchants in the scented spring air.

All of the Royal Army had finally crossed over the River Indus on the Bridge of Boats and had made their way to the great city of Taxila, the center of the Satrapy of Paropamisadai, after Omphis had proven peaceful and had submitted to him willingly.

"Krateros made camp at the foot of the rock to capture anyone who passed by me undetected— then my men filled a ravine with cut trees and made a mound high enough for our arrows to reach the fortress.

"I did not sleep for four days myself until the mound was raised high enough. When the Indians saw my men approaching the fortress, they offered to surrender the fortress at first— but later they tried to flee in the middle of the night and we put to the sword all of those we captured! The rest surrendered quickly!"

"Roxana!"

Alexander pauses. They both stop and look in the direction of the loud voice rushing toward them.

Arrhidaios, Alexander's brother, makes his way through the thinning multitudes and stands before them smiling. "Look, Roxana! Look!" He waves a wooden toy monkey in his hands excitedly.

Rošanak smiles at him kindly.

Arrhidaios was a man-child who had never grown into manhood.

"Arrhidaios, you did not give that man all your coins, did you?"

Arrhidaios smiles mischievously, like a small boy. "I told him I was the brother of the King! He gave it to me for only one shiny gold coin!"

Rošanak smiles and shakes her head.

"Do you want one too? Come! I will buy it for you! Over there! I have lots of shiny coins left! Alexander gave them to me." Arrhidaios points to the rows of merchants and takes Rošanak's hand, pulling her toward him.

Alexander locks his fingers with hers and holds her firmly in place. Rošanak stays locked with him.

"Arrhidaios, go find Hephæstion and show him your new toy!" Alexander orders him kindly. "Go with him! Tell Hephæstion I sent him!" Alexander orders the royal boys following him.

"Yes, Sir!"

"Tell Hephæstion that Arrhidaios paid a golden darik for the toy monkey," Rošanak says under her lips.

Hephæstion knew what to do with merchants who stole from the weak and cheated the rest who did not know how to bargain.

"Come, Arrhidaios." One of the royal boys takes Arrhidaios' hand.

Peritas squeezes himself into the small gap opened between Alexander and Rošanak and rubs himself affectionately on the leg of his old master and wags his tail side to side excitedly.

Alexander smiles and bends down and scratches Peritas' ears. He straightens and says, "Take Peritas with you!"

"Yes, Sir!"

"Come Arrhidaios! Come Peritas!"

Peritas looks at Rošanak and wags his tail, waiting for her command.

Rošanak eyes Alexander and then points with her hand.

"Go Peritas! Go with Arrhidaios!"

Arrhidaios smiles and follows the royal boys. Peritas follows them, wagging his tail.

"Hephæstion will want one of these too!" Arrhidaios says, eagerly shaking the wooden toy monkey in his hand.

Alexander relaxes his fingers and starts walking back toward the palace, pulling her fingers gently along with him; the rest of her follows him too.

"I garrisoned the Fortress and left Sisikottos, the Indian, in charge."

"Sasiguptâ?" Rošanak asks quietly.

Sasiguptâ, 'Protected by the Moon', was an honorable warrior from the Hindu Satrapies at the Battle of Black Eagle, who had joined her father afterward and had remained faithful to him until his death.

"Yes."

"He is a good man. He kept faith with my father to the end. He will be loyal to you."

Alexander nods and smiles, "Yes, he will."

They reach his quarters in the Palace of Rajah Âmbhi.

Rošanak lingers for a moment, not knowing what to do, and then starts heading for the quarters of Rajah's women on the other side of the palace, where she has been staying since they had reached Takšiçila.

Alexander gently pulls her fingers back toward him. Rošanak hesitates for a blink of an eye and then follows Alexander into his quarters— obediently.

Alexander waves his hands and dismisses the royal guards following them.

Doors to his bedchamber close behind them quietly. Tall silky curtains dance in the quiet breeze from the open windows, guarding and shielding the room from meddling light and sound.

Alexander walks over to a large ornate table, pulling her along with him. He lets go of her fingers and picks up a small jeweled silver casket. He opens it and takes out a golden emerald necklace and whispers in a low voice:

"These look like you!"

Omphis had gifted him the splendid golden encased emerald necklace and earrings along with the elephants and oxen and sheep and talents of silver… he had said they were royal gifts from the Great King to his father, when he had become the Satrap of Paropamisadai many years ago.

The emeralds were the color of forest groves… the color of her eyes… a gift that had pleased him and had clothed Omphis in the magnificence of his generosity later…

He clasps the necklace around her neck and then picks up the golden emerald earrings, the color of her eyes, and puts them in the palm of her hands.

He pauses and watches her intently for another sign.

She would wear his royal gift if she had forgiven him… almost every gift he had sent her since he had seen her last had been offered to various temples along the way, he had been told.

Generosity to the gods had kingly limits… munificence to his beloved Wife-Queen was limitless.

Rošanak secures the earrings on her ears effortlessly with her delicate fingers.

Alexander smiles and takes a deep breath and continues. "Omphis has given me his own private quarters in the palace to honor me. He gifted me two hundred talents of silver, three thousand oxen, ten thousand sheep and thirty elephants— in return, I gave him a thousand talents from the Persepolis Treasury, gold and silver vessels, splendid Persian robes and thirty horses I have ridden myself. I am sending some of the oxen back to Makedonia."

"You do not have cows in Makedonia?" Her voice glinting and teasing in the air with old familiarity.

Alexander smiles and puts his face into her hair and whispers softly, gently caressing her neck with the tips of his fingers.

"Have you missed me?" whispering wistfully…

"No…" whispering faintly… lying…

"I have missed you!" he whispers longingly, as he kisses her face tenderly and touches her intimately and murmurs love words into her ears.

He had kept his words to her… he had not summoned her to his bed and had not gone to hers… and she knew he would never stay away from her… too long…

"I missed you a little when I heard you had taken an arrow in your shoulder."

His men as usual had maddened with anger and had razed a nameless town to the ground and had put everyone to the sword… she had cried for days…

"All healed." He drops his tunic and stands sheathed in the light of the heaven and proudly shows her his newest honor wound on his shoulder.

She leans forward into him and softly kisses his latest scar. Her body warms all over lightly touching his naked body. Her heart beats faster in anticipation.

He pulls her tightly into his arms and unwraps her shimmery saree and pulls her into the scented bed and wraps her in his desire.

The adoring Wife-Queen had returned to the bed of the adored King-Husband, Lord and Master of Asia and the Queen… and beyond…

Just as she was in his blood, he was in hers…

ROYAL ARMY CAMP. TAKŠIÇILA
FOLLOWING DAY
AFTERNOON

Sunny and breezy.

"I am Rošanak, wife of King Alexander. I am told that the Hinduya Sage is not eating well. The King is concerned for his health and well being. He asked me to come and see to him. These are Persian sweets that my mother has sent me for the celebration of the Persian New Year that is coming next month."

Rošanak slowly kneels on the ground under an old shady sycamore fig tree and puts a plate of Persian sweets in front of the old Hinduya Sage and looks around.

Alexander had asked a number of Hinduya Sages living in Takšiçila to join his Court and Camp and Campaign. Only one sage had answered his call freely and had come along with a younger man to interpret his words.

Peritas lies down on the ground next to Rošanak and falls asleep.

Rošanak takes a deep breath and waits for her words to be interpreted.

Hinduya words were first interpreted into broken Persian and then into broken Attik for Alexander and his words were interpreted into broken Persian and then into broken tongue of Hinduya. Results were uncertain in any tongue.

And so, he had sent her to speak to the old Hinduya Sage in her Persian tongue.

Alexander had offered the old sage worldly comfort and he had refused it all. All that the smallish sage owned was a wooden food bowl and a piece of cloth that covered his manhood and no more. At his late age, the old man walked straight as a Persian arrow without a walking stick, sat cross-legged under shaded trees or blazing sun or pouring rain, and slept on the dirt or greens or palm tree leaves.

Alexander marveled at him!

Hindu camp women came by wherever the old sage was and brought him food and lay flowers at his feet.

"My teacher, Kalyana, is a Hindu Brahman. He thanks you for your kindness to him," the young Hinduya Brahman says in accented Persian.

"Is there anything else that your Brahman teacher desires?"

"My teacher, Kalyana, asks for something to write on and something to write with and he will write down the answers to the questions in your heart. My teacher says that you should come back after three setting suns."

Rošanak narrows her eyes at the old Hinduya Brahman and considers him for a moment and then slowly gets to her feet. "Three sunsets? Very well. Tell your teacher that if he desires anything before then, he can send for me. I am staying at the Palace of the Rajah Âmbhi in the royal quarters."

"My teacher, Kalyana, thanks you for your kindness."

"Come Peritas!" Peritas wakes up and jumps up to his four feet and follows her obediently.

3 DAYS LATER
SUNSET

"I have come back as your teacher asked of me."

Rošanak is kneeling before the old Hinduya Brahman on palm leaves on the ground under open skies.

"Tell me, what does your teacher desire at the Gate of the King?" she asks eagerly, knowing well the answer would please Alexander.

Peritas quickly drops to his belly and spreads on the ground next to her.

The young Hinduya Brahman shyly puts a small bundle wrapped in silky orange cloth, the color of the rising sun, in front of Rošanak and says modestly in accented Persian, "My teacher, Kalyana, says that the King will need to be loved softly on his torn body."

Rošanak narrows her surprised eyes at the old Hinduya Brahman and considers him for a moment, then leans forward and picks up the orange bundle and looks at it.

Peritas moves his head eagerly and smells the bundle in her hands and then rolls back on the ground uninterested. There was no food in the useless bundle.

Rošanak slowly opens the bundle. It is a small k^{e}tâb made of neatly cut and sewn pieces of the precious parchment she had sent to the old Hinduya Brahman at his request. She opens the small k^{e}tâb and takes a look and blushes and quickly closes the k^{e}tâb and puts it down, slightly embarrassed. Her face and ears turn blood red and her body warms.

This was not what she had expected from the old Hinduya Brahman.

She had come for a list of what the old Brahman wanted to ease his mortal life following Alexander around behind the Royal Army… a tent and some furnishings and servants and garments and food and other useful things…

Instead, he had given her an illuminated k^{e}tâb with delicately drawn patikara of a man and a woman joined together in various intimate embraces…

"My teacher, Kalyana, says that he does not know Persian or the tongue of the King… he has written these love instructions for you and the King in his own tongue which he knows well…" the young Hinduya Brahman says shyly.

Rošanak blushes and reddens more. She mumbles shyly under her breath. "The King is well-loved."

"My teacher, Kalyana, says that the art of love is sacred and divine… these are the ancient teachings of Kâma, the ancient Hindu god of mortal desire… passed on from lips to lips since time immemorial. They were written first by Bull Nandi, when he was moved to sacred utterance when he overheard Great Lord Šiva making love to Goddess Pârvatî, his wife… my teacher says pleasing the desires of men is the highest calling of women… as is pleasing the desire of a woman by a man…"

Rošanak reddens more. Her heart beats louder. She loses her tongue. "I…"

"My teacher, Kalyana, says that love awaits you on the banks of River Vitastâ, one of the seven holy rivers of the Land of Seven Rivers… when the red blood pours on the red mud of the sacred river… red upon red… my teacher says… fulfillment of earthly desire is sacred, overflowing with earthly beauty…"

"I am— well-loved by the King!" Rošanak whispers in a hushed flickering voice, while quickly rewrapping the small k^{e}tâb in the sunny orange silk cloth. "What does your teacher desire for worldly comfort from the King?" she asked distractedly.

The young Hinduya Brahman points to two small wooden bowls and says modestly, "My teacher, Kalyana, and I desire nothing of the material world— just enough food to fill these wooden bowls, once a day… and no flesh of dead animals… just some cooked rice, sacred herbs and vegetables."

"Surely there must be something that can be of comfort to your teacher— a tent, a bed, some furnishings, garments, books, servants. The King will grant anything your teacher desires."

"My teacher, Kalyana, says that comfort is an illusion of the weak mind. His Master will provide him with all he desires in the old City of the Elam-tu. My teacher says Kâma, the ancient Hindu love god, grants heart-felt prayers of lovers uttered under the old sacred wishing tree."

Rošanak slowly gets to her feet. "Your teacher talks in riddles." She starts walking away with reddened face and ears. "Peritas!"

"My teacher, Kalyana, says life is infinite… love is truth… in the sea of darkness, search for the light!"

"Peritas!"

"My teacher, Kalyana, says that Lord Brahma creates the universe when he wakes up each morning. My teacher says marigolds, as golden as the rays of the sun, grow where the blood of your brothers flowed on the fields beyond the lands between the two ancient rivers… my teacher says your brothers died well and are higher reborn to a second life more agreeable to their desires!"

"Ah!" Rošanak stops. She turns around and bends to her knees and picks up the small bundle of the illuminating sun and hurriedly walks back toward the palace. Peritas trots in front of her, wagging his tail.

ROŠANAK'S TENT. ROYAL ARMY CAMP. SIND
YEAR 11 of ALEXANDER, MONTH 7, ARTEMISIOS
YEAR 5 of ALEXANDER, MONTH 1, ADUKANAIŠA, DAY 21
EVENING

Has it been already a year?
Tears fill Rošanak's heart as she writes.

A letter from Rošanak to Farânak, my beloved mother:
In the year 233 after Kuruš the Elder, in Month 1, Adukanaiša, 21 days passed, in Year 5 of Alexander:

May the Wise Lord and Divine Ânâhitâ bless my mother and keep her in good health. May my mother be well and her heart be happy.
Today is NO'ROUZ! I miss you! This is the first year that I am not in Baktra, celebrating the New Day with you! I promise, by the favor of the Wise Lord, that I will be in the Lands of the Persians next year to spend the No'rouz with you!
I ate the whole plateful of Persian sweets you sent to me for No'rouz.
I hope my gardens are in full bloom for the New Year. Nowhere on earth smells as sweet as my gardens, as written in Master Frâda's account of my gardens that came last week.
Please increase the budget for the gardens, so Master Frâda can plant more exotic flowers! As long as they are fragrant as well as beautiful.
Alexander has promised that once he reaches that Ocean that lies on the other edge of the world, we will return to Persia.
May the Wise Lord and Divine Ânâhitâ bless Dârâ and Nimâ and keep them in good health. Thukrâ, too.
May the Wise Lord and Divine Mithrâ bless Abû and Itâna and keep them in good health.

ROYAL SEAL of DUKŠIŠ ROŠANAK

BATTLEFIELD. BANKS of RIVER VITASTÂ. SIND
YEAR 11 of ALEXANDER, MONTH 9, PANEMOS
YEAR 5 of ALEXANDER, MONTH 3, ØÂIGRACIŠ
NIGHT

Hellish night of mud and blood…

"How do you wish to be treated?"

"Like a king!"

"That I will do for my own sake! What else?" Alexander asks again as rain pours.

"Everything is contained in those words!"

Rajah Parvataka twists in pain as words are spoken and interpreted and interpreted again between him and Alexander three times. Blood still pours out of the nine arrows and spears that have pierced his royal body. He has lost a river of blood and still he is as fierce as ever. His fighting war elephant lies dying close by, covered in blood… his body too pierced by more arrows and spears that can be counted in the dim light of the dark night, with half of one tusk hacked away… and his trunk brutally mutilated… an arrow blinding one eye…

Sweltering heat…

Never-ending rain…

Un-breathable air…

Death everywhere…

Alexander looks around.

After a month of preparing and posturing in blazing heat and monsoon rains no less, it was finally over in a black, stormy night.

Even his beloved Bukephalas had not survived the night of death.

….

Alexander, Hephæstion, Krateros, Perdikkas and other kingsmen ride around the muddy, bloody battlefield which is thickly covered with the dead and dying bodies of Indians and Makedonians and others.

The Makedonians and the Indians had finally stopped the futile fighting… no higher price for victory had been extracted from the Makedonians on any other battlefield.

More than 4,000 Makedonian Foot had been killed and some 8,000 more wounded or dying…

12,000 Indians had been killed too and another 9,000 captured…

A muddled blood bath…

Alexander looks at the sea of blood and then eyes Hephæstion discreetly.

Hephæstion had no taste for pure blood butchery and it screamed silently in his troubled eyes… his nose was refusing to breathe in the repugnant stench of death and dying.

He himself could tolerate what was necessary to be victorious…

Every bloody victory bound his men closer to him and struck utter fear in the hearts of his enemies.

"It is done! Hephæstion, take your men and head back to the main Royal Army Camp. There are enough men here to do what needs to be done."

Alexander turns to Krateros and Koinos.

"Let the Indians come and claim their dead. We will bury our dead tomorrow with honors after giving them their due death rites."

"Yes, Alexander."

Hephæstion signals one of his men and relays Alexander's command, then turns his horse around and rides back toward the main Royal Army Camp across and down the river.

LATER that NIGHT

Hephæstion and a handful of his men approach the main Royal Army Camp after riding hard for most of the night in heavy rain, having crossed the rushing River Vitastâ in two places.

A few torches are lit around the main camp, still flickering in the rain.

He removes his helmet and the guards recognize him; he makes his way toward his tent undisturbed.

His body was sore and aching and tired and the sword cuts on his arms and legs were throbbing. The monsoon rains continued but at last he was far away from the horrible death stench and the horrific deadly sounds of the death grounds…

… sounds of swords clashing and cries of men dying…

Mad elephants and maddened horses…

The main Royal Army Camp is nearly empty with almost all of the fighting men still engaged in the battlefield up and across the river and the remaining are either asleep in their tents or trying to keep out of the rain.

He reaches his tent and dismounts. He releases the care of his wounded horse to a young guard, pointing to the arrow wound on the horse's flank and then enters his tent.

HEPHÆSTION'S TENT

Philippo comes rushing in.

Hephæstion, drenched, removes his arm and armor and hands them over to him.

"Philippo, fill up the water basin so I can wash away the death from my filthy body."

Philippo quickly puts Hephæstion's helmet and arm and armor on a small table and runs back out into the monsoon rain.

Hephæstion drops the rest of his blood-soaked clothes on the ground and pours a rhyton full of pure wine. He drinks it whole and drops the rhyton on the ground too. He stands naked in the middle of his tent and checks out his wounded body. Some of the deeper sword cuts on his body have reopened and fresh blood is dripping and streaming on the ground.

Philippo comes back with couple of buckets of rain water, followed by two slaves carrying a couple of buckets each and the water basin starts to fill up with clean rainwater.

Hephæstion grabs a full bucket from one of the slaves and empties it on his head. Philippo and the slaves make two more journeys and the water basin fills up quickly. Hephæstion steps in the basin and dismisses Philippo.

"Go to your wife. I do not need you for the rest of the night. Do not wake me in the morning. The King will not return for a few more days. I will sleep until I awake."

Philippo nods and leaves the dry clean linens nearby on a chair, then leaves the tent.

It becomes quiet… just the sound of the monsoon rain pounding on the tent, trying to flatten it to the ground.

Hephæstion closes his eyes and sinks lower into the water basin. The water is warm, same as the rain, and the air even in the middle of the night is warm and misty. He takes a deep breath, exhausted.

It was good that Alexander had relieved him and had sent him back ahead of the others.

Alexander knew that he tolerated the battles, but he had no real taste for bloodshed like the rest of the Makedonians. He had the blood of his father. Alexander had always been careful not to give him any command that demanded absolute bloodshed and slaughter.

Any army moved on its belly and he was the man who fed the Royal Army.

Let them try to fight on empty bellies…

Another deep breath. Warm wine and warm water slowly ease the pain in his aching bleeding body. The rain bath water reddens with his blood… he drifts…

Alexander had finally perfected the art of war and the killing of multitudes, by all accounts… and tonight was his crowning achievement…

Deadly destruction had slowly become his second nature…

He no longer felt the horror of it… it was just the price of unbroken victory he was willing to pay to the gods… spilled blood was worth the glory!

He had started to demand formal acts of submission from all the rulers in his path, after the stoning deaths of the disloyal royal boys and the death of his Royal Son.

His heart had blackened and hardened… any disobedience of his royal orders was now an act of war ending in utter destruction! So many men left behind in garrisoned towns and cities had been murdered by the natives that bloodshed and slaughter had become preferred by Alexander even over peace and submission… dead men did not rise again to take up arms against them after the Royal Army had passed through their lands.

Victory was all that mattered to Alexander now.

He had said to Parmenion before the Battle at Gaugamela that he did not want to steal his victory, by attacking the Persian Royal Army at night unexpectedly.

But he had stolen his victory at River Hydaspes against Raja Poros by an elaborate deceitful night crossing of the ferocious river. He knew well that Indian chariots would run aground in the muddy fields and Indian archers would be useless in the rain with wet bowstrings… which only left the Indian elephants and he had ordered the archers and the spear-throwers to aim for the eyes of the giant beasts and for their riders… and for others to hack the trunks and tusks of the elephants with battle axes.

Hephæstion immerses his head in the water basin, washes his hair, then pushes himself up and gets out. He grabs the sheet of linen and starts to dry off. He checks his leg wounds and thinks about summoning an army wound-healer to see to his sword cuts, but the thought of additional pain repels him and he decides against it.

Most of the Royal Army wound-healers were probably still on the battlefield seeing to the wounded and dying…

He rubs some soothing balm over his wounds, cuts off a piece of linen with his dagger and wraps his large leg wound tightly. He eases his naked body gently onto his bed and relaxes his head on a soft pillow.

The tent gets dimmer as a couple of candles burn out. He closes his eyes and starts drifting into sleep.

LATER

Soft shuffling sound.

Almost asleep, Hephæstion opens his eyes and sees a shadow standing by his bed. He quickly grabs his dagger from under his pillow with one hand while seizing the shadow with the other hand and swiftly puts the sharp dagger at its throat. The shadow, clad in Athenian himation gown, does not move. The blade of the dagger slides and rests above the hollow of the shadow's throat for a long moment.

"Ah!" the shadow moans softly.

The candle flickers on the shadow.

"Roshanak?"

Hephæstion slowly moves his dagger away from Rošanak's throat and drops it. The dagger falls silently on his bed. He runs his finger on her throat checking for blood and then breathes, relieved.

"Roshanak! What are you doing here? Why are you dressed like this? I almost killed you!" Hephæstion speaks quietly in accented Persian.

"Kill me now! I want to die!"

Hephæstion sits up on his bed, slides the dagger back under his pillow and reaches for her hand. She pulls away.

She is wet from the rain. Tears fall on her wet face.

"I had a dream… the same dream I had before my son was born… I was standing on high ground watching a bloody battle raging down below.

"I saw the Makedonians killing my brothers. I just stood there watching wordlessly… their blood rose from their bodies and covered me… I was drenched in their blood and I did nothing… no tears from my heart, no sound from my soul… and now my beloved son is waiting for me by the Bridge of Chinvât, to be judged by the Wise Lord and share the same judgment as that of his wretched mother. He cannot cross over into the Land of the Eternal Light alone, as he died so young and innocent—"

She pleads tearfully with Hephæstion, "Kill me. Let me go to my son. Let me deliver him to my brothers who will love him as their own in the Land of the Eternal Light."

Hephæstion takes a deep breath.

Rošanak rises from his bed and sits down carelessly on the damp ground, leaning against the bed, and covers her face in her hands, crying softly.

Hephæstion gets out of bed, pulls Rošanak up from the ground and sits her on his bed. He walks to his chest, pulls out a tunic and brings it over and sits next to Rošanak. "Roshanak, you need to get out of those wet clothes. Here—you can wear this. I will get dressed and take you back to your tent myself."

Rošanak pulls away and lies down on his bed and curls up crying.

Hephæstion puts the tunic down next to her, walks over and grabs a dry linen from his chair and starts patting off the rain from her wet skin.

He speaks gently. "It is still pouring outside. We can wait for a break in the rain or we can leave now. You just had a bad dream… that is all… you will feel better after a good night's rest—"

"A good night's rest… awaits me in my grave…"

Hephæstion touches her forehead. "You are running a fever… it is this bloody heat… this bloody land…"

"Kill me or let me be!"

"Roshanak, please! Stop this talk! This bloody heat, this savage rain is what is causing your madness! Let me care for you as you did for me, when I caught the black fever."

"Why should you care if I live or die?"

"How can I not care? I—"

"You… neither love me… nor leave me… Do you take pleasure from torturing me with your affection?"

"Roshanak!"

"Stop calling me that! Only those who love me call me by my Persian name!"

"Roshanak…"

"You kissed me tenderly and then you abandoned me! Why?"

"I— You— belong to Alexander—"

"Yes… I belong to Alexander… we all belong to Alexander… Bukephalas and Peritas and I… a horse and a hound and a half-breed, all marked and branded on our foreheads like slaves of the crown with the seal of Alexander…" She looks at him with teary eyes. "And you… do you belong to Alexander too?"

"Bukephalas died tonight!"

Tears fall on Rošanak's face. "Lucky horse! Perhaps I am already dead too! Death does not come by the forgiving tip of a sharp sword… it comes heartlessly when one becomes utterly useless to those she loves…"

Hephæstion finally relents and says sweetly, "You are useful to me…"

"Liar!"

Rošanak pushes Hephæstion away, gets to her feet and starts walking toward the tent flap.

Hephæstion forgets his painful torn up body, stands up quickly and goes after her, grabbing her hand and pulling her back toward him.

Rošanak pulls away her hand and continues walking.

Hephæstion catches up with her quickly and locks his powerful arms around her and holds her still. She struggles and tries to free herself of him, but Hephæstion holds her tightly until she stops moving and then releases her.

Rošanak runs toward the tent flap and Hephæstion, utterly annoyed, claws at her, misses, and grabs her gown forcefully. Her thin wet gown rips easily and the clasp on her himation opens; the rest of her wet gown rips and falls to the ground. She stands motionlessly and tries to cover her nakedness instinctively… but then she just stands there and her hands fall to her sides.

Hephæstion stands unmoving for a moment too and then slowly steps back and looks at her utterly naked back… ignorant of the blood that seeps through the white linen on his leg.

Shaped like a goddess of the heavens…

Her naked body was more beautiful than the statue of the Aphrodite of Knidos, carved in pure Parian marble by the masterful hands of Praxiteles of Athenai…

If Hellenes were right about the soul shaping the mortal body, then she must have the finest soul in the Empire…

He orders his eyes to look away, but his eyes ignore him. He orders his body to step back and withdraw from the enemy rear before he is discovered and his body disobeys him too. He loses control… his body empties of searing pain and fills with burning desire for her body. He reaches and gently caresses her naked shoulders. Her skin is soft to his touch. He steps closer to her, moves her wet hair aside and kisses the back of her neck… and her naked shoulders…

Rošanak stands motionlessly without resisting him… she feels his strong hands lovingly caressing her weak body… she feels his lips marking her shoulders with kisses…

He puts his arms around her and caresses the front of her neck. His hands glide down her neck and his fingers caress the deep hollow of her throat and then glide gently down and caress her sensuous ripe breasts… the tips of his fingers feel the nervous beat of her heart under her wet skin…

Her heart pounds faster and faster under the touch of his beating fingers… like a hollow Persian drum beating under the drumming fingers of a Persian drummer… her knees weaken… she leans back into him.

He gently turns her toward him, pulls her close and caresses her naked back… the hardened tips of her breasts push into his hard chest.

He starts kissing her face. Her tears taste salty in his mouth. He looks into her glinting eyes…

Her eyes beckon him to her seductively.

Your fate awaits you in my embrace…
The Moon who rules the night,
Surrenders her shield to your sword…
Draw forth your sword…
Make use of all your strength…
My kingdom is yours… do with it what you will…
May the light of the Moon illuminate the path of your Sun…

He grows stronger… he kisses her mouth once and then once more and picks her up and carries her back to his bed and lays her down on it.

The monsoon rain is still pouring all around the tent outside.

He bends down and kisses the deep hollow of her throat… she moans softly…

He stretches over her like a stormy night rain cloud stretches over a shimmery wet Persian Moon…

She wraps her soft arms around his hard body, closes her eyes and surrenders, and sighs as his body finds hers.

He waxes and she wanes…

The sharp sword had finally rasped in its splendid scabbard…

… waging war for the kingdom of the little shimmering star…

LATER

Hephæstion slowly opens his eyes and starts to sober up. Wine and passion and madness slowly evaporate from his wounded body.

Just a dream…

His tent is dark… the candles have burned out. It is still raining outside.

Night or day?

He moves and Rošanak moves with him… she is sleeping softly, perfectly nestled within his strong arms on his simple bed.

Not a dream… sheer madness…

What had he done? Was he mad?

He had lost control of his desires…

He had broken faith with Alexander! He had bedded his wedded wife!

Patroklos had betrayed Achilleos!

Dishonor and shame!

Alexander had stolen the Persian Empire… he had stolen the Persian wife of Alexander… both wrong and both right…

Hephæstion orders his body to leave hers and his body disobeys him again and scorns him. He holds on to her tighter.

Keep your honor… Leave, if you wish!

Go! But leave her for me… I am staying right here, with her!

She is mine! She is my prize of war and victory!

I will not give her up to you!

I will not give her up to anyone!

He takes a deep breath.

She fitted so perfectly within his arms, as if on a lazy summer afternoon he had fallen asleep under a shading Persian tree of life, and Zeus had come upon him and ordered a heavenly goddess to be made of flesh and bones just to fit his arms so and the rest of him too…

His familiar scent from the pillow fills Rošanak's body. She opens her eyes… feels Hephæstion sleeping wrapped around her. His quiet breathing caresses her bare neck and shoulders.

Except for the monsoon rain still pelting its roof, there is no other sign of the existence of a world beyond the tough cloth of the almost empty tent.

Rošanak closes her eyes. Her body is happy and languid and warm from his hot love.

As if Goddess Ânâhitâ herself had finally bent her divine head and whispered the secrets of womanhood into her body… in the tender embrace of Hephæstion, she had found answers to questions she had longed for all her life.

She was driven to him, not knowing why… and now she knew.

What Utâna had started, Hephæstion had finished… all the old stories about lovers… all the old poems about love, all the stolen glances and the sighs and the tears and the laughter…

… all that was lost after Utâna had died, had come back to her now and more…

She takes a deep breath.

The damn old wound-healer was wrong.

A man who could love her body like that, could surely father many sons.

Voices whispering softly in the dark of the rainy day…

"Come away with me," she says in a warm and golden voice. "We can go to Bakhtriš, my people will protect us, we will disappear in the mountains, no one will ever find us."

"Alexander will find us. And his wrath will have no bounds, betrayed by the ones he loves most."

Alexander had left ten thousand Foot and three thousand and five hundred Horse in Baktria… her mother and the sons of her sister and all Baktrians were safe, under the protection of the Lord of Asia!

And thirty thousand Baktrian boys were hostages to ensure the peace would keep in Baktria… and that the Queen would remain bound to the King…

"We will live a happy life, blessed by sons I will bear for you."

A few drops of rain finally break through the seams of the tent and fall on Rošanak's bare shoulder.

Hephæstion's lips disobey his direct orders and gently lick the raindrops off her soft scented skin in the dark.

The raindrops mix with her scent and taste sweet in his mouth.

"Alexander will forget us… we will disappear in the shadows… there are so many around him, pleading for his favor…"

"He will not forget—"

A haunted pause. Whispering murmurs of an older love.

"I first met him at school at Mieza, in the forested foothill of the mountains, when my father sent me away from Pella to be tutored by Aristoteles. His father had ordered it— Philip wanted Alexander to be surrounded by the sons of his kingsmen. He wanted their sons to be bound to his son-prince, as their fathers were to him.

"He was small for his age and mindful of his size, tormented by the quarrels of his royal parents and envied by the ambitious sons of nobles. But he had the claws of a lion and all of its courage and the eyes of a fox. I was tall and strong and half-Hellene and had no desire to be a king— Makedonians would never accept a half-Hellene lording over them.

"So, I pledged to support his kingship with my blood until my last breath and initiated him into manhood… he is bound to me, as I am to him by my oath of honor… it is an oath that cannot be broken…"

"And what about me? What am I to you?"

Hephæstion's face creases and folds in torment. His heart and his words disobey and betray him too. He is left without arm and armor flat on his back at the mercy of the conquering enemy. "You are my reward for being born a man… and my torment for having lived like one…"

"Do you not love me?"

"… it can never be…"

"It can be! Alexander loves me not… I am just his wife… and they say he is sharing his bed with others… and if he loves you as they say… he will forgive your love for me."

"He will not forgive your love for me and mine for you! He was bound to you from the moment he laid eyes upon you in the foothills of the Fortress on the Sogdian Rock. He had seen all the women to be seen from Makedonia to Persia and only the sight of your beauty stirred his blood… as it does mine."

"Setâreh…"

"He did not love her— she was his by right of conquest! He used her to break Darius."

"He mourned her death."

"He mourned his loss."

Hephæstion takes a deep breath.

He knew Alexander!

She had always thought that Alexander had left her because she was heavy with child… but the truth was that Alexander always left her when he was heavy with war… what he cared most about was either kill the bravest or command them…

"The true love of Alexander is war! The beauty and the terror of war excite him more than any mortal who occasionally shares his bed. And he can count all his true friends on the fingers of one hand and still have fingers left over! He will notice a missing friend and a missing wife!"

A couple more raindrops fall on Rošanak's bare shoulders and Hephæstion drinks them up from her wet skin with hunger.

"What will become of us?"

"I will love you with my last dying breath—"

"And I will curse you…"

Pain stabs Hephæstion right in the heart with the sharp blade of her harsh Persian words. "How can you say such cruel words to me?"

"I came for you in the blinding heat and unforgiving rain tonight. I heard you calling me… I knew that I had to come to you… and now that I have tasted your love, how can I go back? How can I ever go back to a life that is no longer mine?"

"Roshanak—" Hephæstion pauses and takes a deep breath. "You must go back to Alexander— or he will unleash his wrath upon the world…"

"I am not afraid to die for loving you!"

"And I want you to live… Alexander will not kill me… but he will make me kill you or worse… he will make me watch you being tortured to death, so I can remember it for the rest of my days… and he will raze the whole of Baktria to ashes… Just tell me that you love me and that will be enough to fill my heart with you!"

Rošanak pulls away from Hephæstion. "I hate you! Fill your heart with that!"

Hephæstion fills up with more pain. Desire and madness pour back into him. He kisses her neck and pulls her toward him and tries to kiss her mouth. She turns her face away. Hephæstion bends his head and kisses the hollow of her throat.

"Look into my eyes and tell me how much you hate me," he whispers quietly.

Rošanak bites her lip and tears fall away from her eyes and into the pillow.

"I hate you…" she whispers back, lying, even though lying was evil… the source of all evil…

Hephæstion covers her face with kisses and more kisses and she finally relents and turns her head toward him and lets him kiss her mouth, as his sober body conquers her kingdom again.

Her sweet wine was the purest of all the wines he had tasted and he had tasted enough. He was a man who could hold his wine well and better than any man… one more cupful made no difference.

He would stop drinking love wine after the night of love was over.

PALACE of RAJAH PARVATAKA. SIND
YEAR 11 of ALEXANDER, MONTH 11, GORPIAIOS
YEAR 5 of ALEXANDER, MONTH 5, TURNABAZIŠ
2 MONTHS LATER
AFTERNOON

Soft murmurs of cooling water in the water basins…

Heat lingers mercilessly in the air… even in the shades of giant palm leaves…

Rošanak and the wives and the women of Rajah Parvataka's court are cooling off in the shade of the palace's inner courtyard.

Rajah's youngest son enters the courtyard and announces cheerfully that Rajah Parvataka and the Makedonians were returning and that they would be arriving before the setting sun.

Excitement fills the air and the Hinduya women hastily jump up to ready themselves to welcome back Rajah Parvataka to his palace.

Bhârati gently pulls Rošanak's arm. "Come! I will help you get ready!"

Rošanak looks at her with trepidation.

Bhârati pulls her arm and says in Persian with a smile, "Chandrâ will talk to Rajah about you! You must look like a bride, not a wilted basket of old flowers!"

"But…"

"What?"

"What if the Rajah does not agree to the union?"

"Why not? My father hates the invaders! They killed his eldest son and my brother. And he thinks Chandrâ is meant for greatness, protected by the gods, since the sacred tiger spared his life."

….

Rajah Parvataka and Hephæstion ride toward the glittering palace, Rajah on his elephant and Hephæstion on his horse.

Rajah's wives and women stand in front of the palace, with all the children standing behind them.

Rajah Parvataka speaks to the interpreter, who quickly interprets for Hephæstion in Persian, pointing to the women.

"The wives and children of the Great Rajah are waiting to welcome him back. You are most welcome to join the Great Rajah as the envoy of your king, but your men should not approach Rajah's family."

Hephæstion turns to one of his men and orders, "Dismiss all the men. Give them all three days off with pay. Send a messenger to Alexander's Camp and tell the King that we have completed our charge and we are ready to reunite with the main Royal Army."

The man nods and turns his horse around and signals, and the rest of the men follow him, eager for a much needed rest after two months of hard campaigning.

Hephæstion turns back and looks at the assembly of women waiting for them.

His heart sends a secret message to his eyes: *"Where is my Roshanak? Find her for me quickly!"*

Rajah Parvataka's elephant stops in front of the women and bends his front legs and Rajah Parvataka dismounts with some difficulty; his wounds from the hellish battle are still healing.

Hephæstion dismounts his horse right behind the giant elephant and gives the bridle to a servant approaching him.

It had taken awhile to get the horses to ride with the elephants; the unfamiliar smell of the giant beasts frightened them.

Rajah Parvataka and Hephæstion walk toward the waiting women.

Hephæstion looks at the brightly colored gathering, his eyes still discreetly and unconsciously searching for Rošanak.

Rajah's wives approach him with fragrant flower wreaths. Rajah bends with a smile, and his neck becomes covered with the fragrant wreaths. He is a full head taller than Hephæstion. His children run toward him and surround him noisily, asking him about his latest battles. One of Rajah's middle sons, a handsome young man, approaches and kisses his father's face and stands next to him.

Rajah Parvataka was still blessed with many young sons… even though his eldest and bravest had died in the battle with Alexander.

Rajah's Chief Wife steps forward and Hephæstion sees Rošanak standing a step behind her and his knees go weak. She is wearing silky sheer Indian clothing, in the color of deep green forests, embroidered with golden thread, bare-footed, holding a few flower wreaths in her hands. Her hair, parted in the middle, is adorned with a ridge of precious rubies, ending in a large tear-shaped emerald sparkling in the afternoon sun, making her eyes even greener. Her arms, decked and jeweled with golden bangles from her wrists almost to her elbows, sparkle in the light of the late sun.

Aristoteles, who always spoke to them of the value of moderation in everything when they were young men at Mieza, had never seen a woman like Roshanak.

Beautifully standing there, her midriff naked, with a gold belt falling on her Indian skirt, her long silky raven hair falling on her shoulders, almost to the middle of her back… the tips of her breasts peeking through the sheerness of the cloth barely covering them… she was the very definition of excess in every way.

He feels her smile, but it is not meant for him.

Her eyes were gazing at a young Indian Prince standing next to Raja's young son… the Prince Alexander had ordered Raja to keep in chains for his insolence.

He discreetly glances over at the Prince, who whispers something in Raja's ear, looking directly at Rošanak. His body warms with anger. He puts his hand on the handle of his sharp sword without thinking.

Were they gone that long?

Was he already forgotten?

Had she taken another lover?

Rošanak follows Rajah's Chief Wife and offers one of the flower wreaths to Rajah. Rajah bends down and she puts the wreath around his neck on top of the other wreaths and smiles, glancing sideways at the young Hindu Prince.

Rajah smiles back at her and straightens, hiding the pain in his body.

Rošanak then steps toward Hephæstion and her sweet voice fills his angry ears. She graciously offers him a flower wreath without looking him in the eyes.

"Commander, I trust you have been victorious," she says without any hint of familiarity.

Hephæstion lets go of the handle of his sword and bends his head and Rošanak glides the wreath around his neck.

Her scent mixes with the scent of fragrant flowers and fills his senses. For a moment, he thinks about pulling her into his arms and kissing her.

Woof!

The moment passes quickly.

He looks down at Peritas with envy and then lifts up his head to look at her.

She was more loyal to the damn dog than she was to him!

"Yes, Queen Roxana. We were victorious," he says formally.

Rošanak smiles and nods and glances back at the young Hindu Prince and smiles again. She turns around and rejoins the other Hinduya women, and they all walk back noisily toward the palace. Rajah and the young Hindu Princes and the rest of the younger children start to follow them.

Peritas mixes with the other palace hounds and follows the crowd excitedly.

Hephæstion stands there for a moment, not quite sure what to do. The interpreter approaches him, points to the palace and says politely in broken Persian, "Guest quarters have been prepared for you, Commander, if you wish to stay at the palace."

Hephæstion's eyes trail Rošanak disappearing with the rest of the Raja's family into the palace walls.

"Thank you."

The interpreter nods politely. "You are invited to feast with the Great Rajah in the main palace, when the sun has set. A servant will come for you."

LATER

Feast of victory… flowers and food and women and children, nosily eating and talking…

Hephæstion looks around. The tiresome interpreter is sitting close to him, trying to entertain him. He nods politely without having heard a word of it.

The large hall of the palace was filled with the sizeable household of Raja Poros. Raja's Chief Wife was seated next to him, chatting away. His remaining sons were sitting next to their wives, surrounded by their own children.

Roshanak sat surrounded by a couple of Raja's younger wives and her own women, with the young Indian Prince sitting close by.

After the feast, the center of the large hall is emptied and cleaned for the dancers, who dance to the voice of a singer, with their bangles and foot jewelry clicking in the scented fragrant air.

Hephæstion looks over and the young Hindu Prince was now sitting next to Rošanak, both of them whispering and talking and laughing. Hephæstion bites his lip and tries to hide his anger.

He was a man and he could easily see by the way the two of them whispered and talked and laughed that there was more than politeness between them…

He had been campaigning hard for two months in the sweltering heat to conquer more lands for the Raja, while she was being entertained by a handsome Indian Prince under the cool shades of the palace trees and on the cool sheets of the palace beds.

His anger rises. He picks up his wine cup and drinks it whole and then looks back at the dancers, grinding his teeth, trying even harder not to notice Rošanak, who had not even once looked at him.

LATER

Warm night.

Hephæstion tosses and turns restlessly in his hot bed and finally sits up. He gets to his feet, walks over to the table and grabs the wine flagon, pours a full cup of rice wine and drinks it whole, and then another full cup.

He was the master of his body… master of his pleasures…

The rice wine runs through him rapidly and makes him miss her even more. He puts down the wine cup and goes back to bed, looking up at the shadows the flame of the night candle was making on the ceiling of his gilded bedroom.

Since that rainy night he had bedded her on the banks of River Hydaspes, he had tried hard to forget her.

He had lost control and had been disloyal to Alexander and had dishonored himself.

She was a mistake not to be made again…

But now, he was lying awake in his bed, consumed by the thoughts of her… filled with anger and doubt…

Had she taken another lover and forgotten all about him so quickly?

Was he so easy to forget?

Ah! Women!

Life was so much easier in the company of men of honor!

He gets out of bed again and starts getting dressed.

He was going to find her, even if he had to go room to room… even if he had to tear the whole palace apart… brick by brick… stone by stone…

The Indian palace had no real security, no guards posted inside the palace anywhere. Now that there was peace between Raja Poros and the Makedonians, the palace was no different than the houses that surrounded the palace.

He grabs his Persian dagger and silently heads for the palace courtyard.

LATER

Middle of the night… cloudy…

Sleepy palace…

Hephæstion enters the palace's inner courtyard quietly and looks around trying to guess which bedroom belonged to Rošanak. He hears hushed voices approaching and hides in a fold of darkness. A pair of women are talking in low voices, laughing and chatting.

The voices slowly die down, with quiet footsteps parting in different directions.

In an instant, he decides to grab the woman coming in his direction and force her to take him to Rošanak. The shadow of the woman passes by him in the darkness and he quickly steps behind her. With one hand he covers her mouth and with the other hand he pulls her to him and holds her tightly. The woman struggles and finds it useless, so she stops motionless and surrenders. He quietly whispers in her ear. "Roshanak!"

The woman points to one of the rooms opening into the inner courtyard.

Hephæstion presses harder against her mouth and nose and she faints and goes limp in his arms. He gently lays her down on the ground and moves swiftly toward the room the woman had indicated.

He climbs into the room through an open window and kneels on the floor for a few moments, until he can see better in the darkness. He quietly approaches the bed and listens to the quiet sound of breathing. His heart beats faster in his chest. All the candles are burned out and it is too dark to see the face of the woman.

He stands there for a few moments undecided, then takes a step and almost stumbles over something soft on the floor. He gains his balance on the floor and sees a pair of eyes staring back at him in the darkness. His pulse quickens.

The moonlight slowly streams through the window and illuminates the room.

Hephæstion takes a deep breath and lets it out and quietly whispers, "Peritas."

Woof! softly…

"It is just me. Go back to sleep."

Peritas wags his tail with familiarity, stretches down on the floor and goes back to sleep.

Hephæstion gets to his feet quietly and looks at the woman on the bed, now drenched in the moonlight.

It was Roshanak… sleeping utterly naked on the bed.

He drinks her like wine with his eyes and then without even thinking he bends and wraps her gently in the bed linen, lifts her up and carries her quietly out of the room.

Peritas rolls and sleepily gets up on his four legs and follows Hephæstion quietly, wagging his tail.

LATER

Rošanak lays in a deep sleep in Hephæstion's bed, wrapped in bed linen.

He bends and smells her breath. Her breath smells like wine. He grinds his teeth.

Soon, Raja would know she had been taken and everyone would be looking for her.

And she was drunk… loaded with wine… like Hellene whores!

He gently shakes her and calls her name, "Roshanak…"

Soft breathing…

He shakes her harder, "Roshanak!"

Rošanak slowly opens her eyes and sees him and narrows her eyes trying to remember. "Hephæstion?"

"You are loaded with wine!" Hephæstion says scornfully in a low voice, leaning on the edge of the bed.

She looks around and pushes herself up on his bed, disoriented. Her head hurts, her head spins. The room looks unfamiliar. "Where am I?"

"In my room."

"In your room?" She looks around. "Why? Where is Abi-Samar?"

"I— wanted to talk to you—"

"Talk to me? In the middle of the night, like this? Are you mad?"

"Have you been with him?"

Rošanak sits up on the bed and looks at Hephæstion, still sleepy with wine.

"Who?"

"The Indian Prince— have you bedded him?"

"How dare you!"

"Did you forget me so quickly?"

"Forget you?"

"Just tell me!"

"You! You regretted bedding me! You left me! You wished to be forgotten!"

"I—"

Rošanak wraps the bed linen around her tighter and starts to get to her feet, pushing him away.

"You? You, what!? You took all I had to give… and gave me nothing in return… you left me… and now you have taken me from my room in the middle of the night… like a common thief… demanding an accounting of my heart! How *dare* you!"

"This is not your home!"

"No? Where is my home then?"

Silence.

Hephæstion does not answer. He holds his head in his hands. His head pounds.

For nearly two months, he had stayed away from her and had thought about how he was to treat her when he saw her again… what to do if she was with his child…

… what to do if she threatened to tell Alexander…

He had imagined her crying night and day, missing him… but he had never thought of her simply forgetting him root and branch… and finding another lover, while he was trying to find ways to get rid of her.

And now that she had no use for him, he desired her even more.

It no longer mattered why he desired her… only that he did.

Was he not a good lover?

"I am happy here."

"Is this what you want? To be a mistress of an Indian Prince?"

"What I want—" her voice softens… she murmurs. "What I want… is to go home! I want to celebrate No'rouz with my fathers and my mothers and with my brothers and their wives and children… and with my sister and her husband and their children… I want to have a husband of my own… and my own children about me… I want a big noisy house full of love and laughter and happiness…"

Rošanak pauses and takes a deep breath.

"But I have no home…" She closes her eyes. "Damn Alexander to eternal darkness! Because of him, I have a husband who sleeps with his dagger… I have a lover who sleeps with his honor… and I sleep with my loneliness…"

"Roshanak…"

"This is the happiest I have been… these women love me as if I was one of their own kin…" She points around. "I have been treated with more kindness as a hostage here than I have been treated by the entire Makedonian lot, being married to their bloody king." She mocks Hephæstion. "And I would be lucky to be a woman of the prince… not a virtuous virgin, deserving of becoming a wife…" She pauses and takes a deep breath. "And yet he is willing to marry me and have me as a wife."

"You are already married!" he grunts.

Rošanak looks at Hephæstion and then starts walking toward the door.

"I see more of Peritas than I see of Alexander! Alexander cares nothing for me… tell him I died! Tell him I caught black fever… was bitten by a snake… drank bad water… fell off a wild horse… trampled by a mad elephant… anything… He trusts you! He will believe you! Are you not his lover?"

Hephæstion gets to his feet quickly and walks toward her and takes her hand.

She stops.

He pulls her back toward him and embraces her tightly.

"I am your home!"

Rošanak pulls away.

"Let me go! You are no better than Alexander! No! You are worse!"

Hephæstion bends his head and holds her tight and seals her mouth with a soft kiss. Rošanak resists and pulls away. Hephæstion holds her tighter and kisses her again harder. He rests his head on the side of her head. She feels his warm breath on her neck.

"I am your home! I—" Hephæstion's voice trails off and he lets go of Rošanak abruptly.

Rošanak looks up and Abi-Samar is holding a dagger at Hephæstion's throat. Rošanak is startled. "Ah!"

Hephæstion moves slightly and Abi-Samar tightens his grip on him.

Rošanak whispers quietly. "Do they know I am here?"

"No, My Lady. I saw Peritas sleeping outside the bedchamber."

Rošanak looks back at Hephæstion and demands quietly.

"Swear to one of your gods that you will make peace with Abi-Samar, if I order him to release you! That you will not harm him with your bloody pride!"

"To which god?"

"Swear an oath to Apollo!"

"I swear to Apollo that I will forgive Abi-Samar for holding a dagger to my throat!"

Rošanak eyes Hephæstion. Wine evaporates… she hears him… loud and clear… "Swear by Styx!"

Hephæstion grinds his teeth and resists.

Abi-Samar presses the sharp dagger harder against Hephæstion's throat.

"By Styx! I will not harm your protector!"

"You think me a fool? Loaded with wine? Ha? Say his name!"

"I have said enough!"

"You have, have you? You are the one who taught me your ways… you are the one who said I needed no more tutoring! Say his name, or he will cut your lying throat where you stand!"

Hephæstion grinds his teeth. The dagger digs in his throat.

"Abi-Samar… by Styx… I will not harm Abi-Samar!"

Rošanak narrows her eyes at Hephæstion and then waves her hand and orders Abi-Samar. "Release him!"

"My Lady, are you sure?"

Rošanak looks back at Hephæstion and then at Abi-Samar.

"Yes. Release him. He is bound by his oath to his gods. He is more fearful of his gods than your dagger. He will keep his word."

Abi-Samar removes his blade and steps back.

Hephæstion reaches and rubs his sore neck where the dagger had been resting.

Rošanak speaks quietly to Abi-Samar. "Go back to my room quietly and quickly bring me something to wear."

Abi-Samar looks at Hephæstion for a moment and hesitates.

"Abi-Samar!"

Abi-Samar hears her and then relents. He sheathes his dagger, bows his head and turns around and quietly leaves the room, closing the door behind him.

"He was just protecting me!"

"Does he put a dagger to the Indian Prince too, when he visits you at nights?"

Rošanak looks intently at Hephæstion.

He was jealous!

"You have sworn a sacred oath not to harm him!"

"You care for everyone more than you care for me!"

Rošanak takes a deep breath.

"You care nothing for me! There has been not a word from you, since—"

Rošanak stops her words and turns around and walks to the window. She leans out and looks at the moon.

Hephæstion looks at her. His anger evaporates and he fills with longing.

He walks over and puts his arms around her, holding her tight and whispers into her ear. "Look into my eyes and tell me you do not care for me and I will do as you wish!" He kisses her neck. "I will tell Alexander that you died… took poison… heart-sick after losing your child…"

Rošanak leans back into Hephæstion and rests her head on his heart.

Hephæstion bends his head and kisses her neck again.

There is a soft knock on the door. The door opens and closes.

Rošanak pushes back a tear. "I care nothing for you!"

"Tell me again!"

"Chandrâ is not old like you… he is not bound to Alexander like you! His ancestors are Aryas. He will rule this land one day!"

Hephæstion suddenly grunts and lets go of Rošanak and turns around swiftly.

"I said I will not harm—"

Rošanak turns around and is startled to see Hephæstion and Chandrâguptâ standing eye to eye, holding their sharp daggers at each other's throats.

"Ah!" Rošanak moans miserably.

Chandrâguptâ growls at Hephæstion in accented Persian. "How dare you seize my betrothed!"

Hephæstion growls back in accented Persian, "Your betrothed?" He points to Rošanak with his free hand. "She is Alexander's wife!"

Chandrâguptâ narrows his eyes at Hephæstion fearlessly. "And that gives you the right to seize her naked in the middle of the night from her bedroom and bring her to yours?"

Rošanak pleads with both of them. "Stop this madness! Put down your daggers!"

They both ignore her and tighten their grips on their sharp golden daggers.

Rošanak walks over and grabs the blade of Hephæstion's dagger with her hand. "Hephæstion, please, withdraw your dagger!"

"No!" Hephæstion growls.

Rošanak grabs the blade of Chandrâguptâ's dagger with her other hand and pleads. "Chandrâ, please, lower your dagger!"

"No!" Chandrâguptâ growls.

Rošanak squeezes the two blades with her hands. Sharp blades cut into her palms. Blood starts to drip from her hands.

Hephæstion and Chandrâguptâ look with horror and disbelief at the blood dripping from Rošanak's hands.

"Roshanak, are you mad? Have you lost your reason? Let go of our blades!" Hephæstion yells at her.

"Roshanak! Release the daggers!" Chandrâguptâ yells at her.

"Do not yell at her!" Hephæstion yells at Chandrâguptâ.

"I do what I like! You think I am one of those army idiots you command?" Chandrâguptâ yells back at Hephæstion.

Heat rises.

Rošanak finally lets go of the blades. Both blades are stained with her blood. She rests her bloody palms on top of Hephæstion's and Chandrâguptâ's hands, still tightly gripping their daggers, and then withdraws her hands. She looks at her blood staining the two men's hands for a moment and then quietly says, "Go ahead and kill each other. You both have my blood on your hands, and that is all either of you will ever have of me!" She then turns around and heads for the door and leaves the room quietly.

Her blood stains the mayûxa.

Abi-Samar is waiting for her by the door, holding a saree. He sees blood on the white linen wrapped around her. Peritas stands up and stretches and rubs himself against Rošanak's legs worriedly, smelling her blood.

Rošanak's legs fold under her. She passes out.

Abi-Samar quickly catches her mid-air and silently rushes her back to her room.

Peritas follows them back to Rošanak's bedroom and lies down quietly on the floor by the bed, watching, as Abi-Samar lays her unconscious body gently on her bed and looks at her hands.

Abi-Samar grabs a cotton linen and soaks it in the golden water bowl next to her bed and starts washing her cuts and curses under his lips. He drops the linen in the water bowl, turns and walks over to her chest and takes out a jar of sacred bitter salve. He brings it back and rubs the sacred salve on her cuts, then rips the soft linen with his dagger and wraps her wounded hands tightly with strips of cool cotton.

Peritas turns his nose into all the sadness and misery of his mistress. He whimpers and spreads himself quietly on the floor by her bed, watching over her.

HEPHÆSTION'S TENT. ROYAL ARMY CAMP
2 DAYS LATER
MID-DAY

Alexander To Hephæstion,
Greeting. Come back and bring her with you. Farewell.

Hephæstion reads the order from Alexander once more and then closes and folds the note.

He had moved out of the Palace of Raja Poros and back into his own tent at the Makedonian army camp.

He had been brooding and impossible, yelling orders left and right.

His men had widened the circle around him, staying clear of his path of anger.

A royal messenger from the Royal Army Camp of Alexander had brought astonishing news that Alexander and the Royal Army were planning to head back toward River Indus and he and his men were to join up with them and sail down the river together.

The royal messenger had elaborately described how the Makedonians had refused to go further up country from the banks of River Hyphasis and no winning words from Alexander had persuaded them to change their minds. And how Alexander had stayed in his royal tent for three days brooding without the Royal Army bending.

Even all the kingsmen of Alexander had remained silent this time… well, all except for old Koinos, who had spoken for the Makedonians. He had said:

"Alexander, we have come to the ends of the earth against the will of our gods.

"We want to go home to our wives and children before it is too late.

"Let your mother have a look at you while she still can.

"There is nothing up country but more warlike tribes and man-eating snakes and fighting elephants and hellish heat and unbroken rain…

"We do not want to die on strange lands under strange skies ruled by other gods.

"Sir! A man should know when to stop!"

Hephæstion closes his eyes.

Old Koinos should have taken his own wise counsel!

At the end, the royal messenger had mentioned that Alexander had also ordered him to bring back "his wife"!

He had thanked the royal messenger and sent him to rest and eat and return to the King, acknowledging receipt of his royal orders.

The face of Alexander rushes into Hephæstion's eyes along with old oaths and older memories.

He knew how much Alexander wanted to push further into India to conquer all the lands to the edges of the Great Ocean that encircled the whole world as Aristoteles had always told them… it was the only victory that would have convinced Alexander that he had finally surpassed his own father in fame and glory.

He bites his lip hard.

He had to get to Alexander quickly, well before his wrath burned what was left of the Royal Army.

It was after the Battle at Issos that Alexander had changed… the Great King had been defeated and his Royal Family had fallen into the hands of Alexander along with his royal tent and his royal bow and arrow and chariot too. The royal tent of the Great King was bigger and more magnificent than the entire Palace of Archelaos at Pella.

He had seen the change in Alexander as they walked into the tent, when Alexander had looked around in amazement and said:

"So, this is what it means to be a Great King!"

War to punish the Persians and avenge the burning of Athenai by Xerxes some one hundred and fifty years before their time had suddenly turned into a war of conquest… an unquenchable thirst to become a Great King and to rule the world… all of it!

An impossible dream had turned into a possible reality with the first true victory.

Then Alexander had become consumed by the thoughts of Darius… he was sleeping in his bed, bedding his queen, wearing his Persian Purple, and spending his golden gold. He had tried hard to bend Darius to his will… writing him letters, demanding to be called The Great King, refusing to ransom his Royal Family, treating Sisygambis better his own birth mother, calling her: Mother… and Darius had remained defiant.

Worse— he had utterly ignored Alexander!

Alexander wanted to do to Darius what Achilleos had done to the Trojan Hektor… but Darius was not Hektor. He had remained elusive and had not engaged Alexander and Alexander had stewed in his blood with anger and fury… and the wrath of Achilleos.

And when Darius was killed by his own nobles, Alexander's dream of conquering Darius had been lost, along with the rightful ascension to the Persian throne.

Drinking was what dulled the pain of the unspeakable massacres in their wake… they had not conquered an ancient Empire, they had butchered it and they all knew it, all too well… and the more blood they shed, the more blood they had to shed to keep the Empire from slipping from their slippery grasps.

The Persians had won the war by losing a few battles.

Hephæstion takes a deep breath and smiles to himself.

… Relieved that he was ordered back… just like the Makedonians, he was tired too… when they had left to conquer the Persian Empire years ago, no one had ever imagined that Alexander would never stop.

… And pleased that he was ordered to bring Roshanak back with him. Now he could just drag her along with him and separate her from her Indian Prince lover. He would be simply carrying out the order of the King and her husband and it was all very honorable. And if she was to refuse, he had enough Horse and Foot with him to siege the Palace of Raja Poros and take her by bloody force, dead or alive, and that was all very honorable too.

Hephæstion gets to his feet and leaves his tent and heads toward the palace to inform Rajah Parvataka that he and the Makedonians were leaving the next day to join King Alexander, who was no longer planning conquests further up country, and that the hostaged Queen of Alexander was to be returned to him, as it was agreed to between Alexander and the Rajah.

They were not coming back…

INSIDE the PALACE

LATER

Air scented with sadness…

The sparkle of the palace is masked by the sound of sorrow.

A woman is crying sadly.

As he makes his way inside the palace, Hephæstion hears voices from the palace courtyard. He follows the sounds.

The courtyard is crowded with Rajah's women and children standing in a circle, hovering around something on the ground. The women quietly open a path for him and pull the children out of his way.

In the center of the palace courtyard, Rošanak is kneeling down, cradling the body of Peritas, crying.

Hephæstion is taken off guard.

Abi-Samar, standing over Rošanak next to Mâr'at Bani Âriyânnâz, sees Hephæstion. He walks over to him and quietly says, "Commander, Peritas died early this morning."

Hephæstion forgets all his anger in the blink of an eye.

Honor and pride quietly surrender to love and compassion.

He had hand-picked and trained Peritas for Alexander years ago after their victory at the Battle of Chæronea. The hound had lived well beyond his time in her good care.

He looks down at Rošanak and then at Abi-Samar and quietly says, "We are leaving tomorrow to join the King and the Royal Army. Pack everything and set up Queen's tent in my camp tonight. Send a couple of my men to meet me by the palace doors."

Abi-Samar bows his head slightly and says, "Yes, Commander," without hesitation. He leans forward and whispers into Mâr'at Bani Âriyânnâz's ear.

Hephæstion kneels down and puts his arms around Rošanak.

Rošanak turns her head and looks at Hephæstion with teary eyes and moans sadly, "Peritas is dead!"

"He was old," Hephæstion says gently. "We will bury him as Alexander would have."

"Do not burn him!" Rošanak moans, caressing Peritas' body.

"We will bury him by the river. We will tell Alexander he was properly honored," Hephæstion says gently in a tender, comforting voice.

Hephæstion slowly lifts Rošanak to her feet.

The women of Rajah whisper and point with their eyes to Rošanak and Hephæstion.

He whispers to her. "Alexander has sent for us. We are leaving."

Rajah Parvataka and his sons and an interpreter make their way through the circle of women and children and face Hephæstion.

"Raja, the King is returning to River Indus. He is not going further up country.

"We are leaving to join up with him and the rest of the Royal Army tomorrow," Hephæstion says politely.

The interpreter quietly interprets for Rajah.

"Alexander will not push further inland?" Rajah Parvataka asks, raising his eyebrow.

The interpreter interprets for Hephæstion.

"No."

Rajah Parvataka narrows his eyes and reads Hephæstion's face.

"Alexander has asked that his Queen join him, as we have honored our commitments to you and have expanded your territory."

The interpreter quietly interprets for Rajah.

Rajah Parvataka looks at Hephæstion holding up Rošanak. He notices her both hands are wrapped in white linen and wonders.

The Nandâ Prince had left the palace early the day before without saying a word.

"My Dear Daughter, do you wish to stay here?"

The interpreter quietly interprets for Rošanak.

Hephæstion narrows his eyes and locks his gaze fiercely on Rajah. Anger pours back into him.

Gods had opened another gap for him… he had enough men with him to engage the warriors of Raja over his refusal to release the royal hostage to him.

He could kill her after the battle and tell Alexander that she had taken an Indian lover and had dishonored him, and rid himself of his passion for her… he could not remain under her spell, if she was dead!

And Alexander was in a murderous mood and would forgive her death as a necessity.

Only if he could let go of her… only if he knew how to let go of her…

He lets go of Rošanak, just in case he needs to reach for his sword. He whispers in Rošanak's ear in Attik quietly threatening her. "Baktria is heavily guarded… ten thousand Foot and three thousand and five hundred Horse, all under the command of Alexander… and thirty thousand boys are hostages…"

Rošanak's face folds in pain.

Rajah Parvataka notices. He eyes Hephæstion carefully.

Even though they were allies now, he would have liked nothing better than to throw the arrogant Makedonian mlechchha to his fighting elephants and let them crush him and the rest of his men under their merciless heavy feet to avenge the death of his son… and his men…

"Do not fear, Roshanak! You are like my own daughters! I will protect you as I protect them. The Nandâ Prince has openly declared his royal intention of marrying you honorably."

"Your words are hostile to us as your friend and ally." Hephæstion politely forces the words through his teeth, glaring at Rajah eye to eye. "The Queen is already wedded to the King."

Rošanak stands on her own feet, aching with uncertainty.

"I thank you for your kindness, Rajah." Rošanak finally says, holding back tears. "I think it is best that I leave."

Hephæstion breathes and relaxes his hands.

"You can stay, if you wish, My Daughter," Rajah offers again, carefully eyeing Hephæstion. His young sons step closer to their father.

As an old satrap of the Persian Great Kings, he was obligated to defend the Royal Women of the Empire.

But he was a practical man… nothing was more important than ridding his ancestral land of the murderous invaders… the sooner they all left, the better!

"I thank you for your hospitality on behalf of the King," Hephæstion interrupts, gazing fiercely at Rajah. "The Queen will stay in her own tent tonight in my camp. We will leave early tomorrow morning to join the King."

Rajah looks at Hephæstion and then back at Rošanak and then nods.

"Very well."

The women of Rajah surround Rošanak with warm hugs and kisses.

Rošanak bids them farewell.

Hephæstion kneels and gently picks up Peritas' lifeless body and heads out.

Rošanak follows him, wiping her tears.

….

Abi-Samar and the servants have the Queen's tent already set up by the time Hephæstion and Rošanak arrive at the army camp, having buried Peritas somewhere along the river.

Rošanak walks into her tent without a word and disappears.

NIGHT

Moonlit night… warm and luminous… with a cooling breeze…

In the middle of the night, Hephæstion stands in front of his tent, restless. The army camp is quiet and the air is cooler. He looks around. Even some of the night guards were falling asleep on their feet.

The old Kalyana is walking around the army camp as usual with his young interpreter following him. His eyes find Hephæstion and he walks over quietly and stops and says a few words to him.

The young Hindu interpreter interprets in broken Persian.

"My teacher, Kalyana, says to tell the Queen that her hound will be reborn."

The old Kalyana then points to the skies and says a few more words. The interpreter interprets.

"My teacher, Kalyana, says man is born of the Sun…"

Hephæstion looks up at the moon and then back at the old Kalyana.

"My teacher, Kalyana, says man is like the equinox… the spring equinox and the autumn equinox. The upper half thinks and the lower half desires. To unite the upper half and the lower half, ancient gods created woman, born of the moon.

"Without a woman, life is not possible… as the moon follows the sun, women follow men… women too desire men, just as men desire women… my teacher says!"

Old Kalyana nods his head and says a few more words.

"My teacher, Kalyana, says it is bad karma to refuse a woman who comes to the bed of a man willingly when she desires him… it is not forbidden by the ancient gods that when a woman is neglected by her husband, another man should worship her…"

Hephæstion narrows his eyes at the old Kalyana wordlessly.

The old man mumbles a few more words, nodding his old head knowingly.

"My teacher, Kalyana, says that bedding the wife of another man who longs to be bedded is part of the worship of the ancient love god."

Hephæstion eyes old Kalyana intently. The old man speaks a few more words again and points with his finger toward Rošanak's tent next to his tent.

"My teacher, Kalyana, says, find the light in the sea of darkness!"

A few more words are spoken.

"My teachers asks: is the Queen not very beautiful?"

"Yes, very beautiful," Hephæstion says miserably and looks back at old Kalyana. But the old man and his young interpreter continue their walk silently and disappear into the darkness of the night.

Hephæstion draws a deep breath.

Hellenes locked away their women and killed adulteresses and Indians made an art of seducing the wives of other men!

He was half-Makedonian and she was half-Persian and they were in India on the edges of the world and they were now ruled by the Indian gods…

The world was broken…

And he was one of the men who had broken the world…

And Makedonians had refused Alexander…

Where were the golden gods of gold and glory leading them?

He looks at Rošanak's tent and then looks down at his restless feet and commands them to walk back into his empty tent and go to sleep. But his feet refuse him flatly and remain standing where they are. He looks back at her tent.

Sleep had become impossible after the night he had bedded her. Her scent had remained on his pillow and taunted him mercilessly every time his eyes had become heavy with sleep. And now she was just a few steps away.

Was her heart calling him back to her?

Or was Aphrodite standing next to him, urging him to her bed?

What if old Kalanos was right and his desire for her was not forbidden in the eyes of the Indian gods who ruled over India?

Maybe that was why the Makedonians had refused Alexander… maybe their own gods had not followed them all the way to the edges of the world.

Who was he to disobey the will of the Indian gods?

He looks around.

Camp is still quiet.

His feet start heading toward Rošanak's tent. The rest of him follows his feet. He relents. He quietly enters her tent and almost falls over something big in the darkness, barring the entry.

"Ah!" He catches himself and finds himself eye to eye with a pair of large black eyes locked on him.

Abi-Samar stares into Hephæstion's eyes without blinking.

Hephæstion stares back at Abi-Samar and both men slowly get up to their feet, with their eyes locked on each other. They are almost eye to eye. Hephæstion forgets his oath and his hand reaches for his dagger, but Abi-Samar bows his head and then turns around and silently exits the tent.

Hephæstion takes a deep breath and lets go of his dagger. He looks back in the direction of the tent flap. It is quiet again. He waits for a moment and then steps quietly past the curtain shielding the private bedchamber in the back of the tent. He enters the bedchamber and stands over Rošanak.

It is the first time he has entered her private bedchamber. A small candle burns by her bed. She is curled up in his old bed, sleeping wrapped around a pillow.

After her own bed was soaked in her blood during the birthing of her firstborn, he had given her his own bed… and she had been sleeping in it since then.

All she had on her skin were the two white strips of linen covering the wounded palms of her hands… the rest of her body was covered by the dim light of the candle… her naked body glowed in its soft light.

He quietly disrobes and lies down next to her and kisses her bare shoulder.

Rošanak turns her head and opens her eyes and looks at him for a moment, then turns her head back, ignoring him.

"I heard you calling me to you," Hephæstion sweetly whispers into her ear in Persian. "Have you not tormented me enough already?"

"No!" Rošanak tries to ignore him.

"You are my undoing, by the gods." Hephæstion whispers, kissing her neck and tenderly caressing her naked body.

"Go away!"

Hephæstion kisses her neck again and whispers sweetly. "I told you once: No matter where I go I always come back to you, and I meant it!"

"Go away!" Rošanak says with tears in her voice. "Go crawl in bed with your honor. Leave me to my loneliness!"

"I am lonely for you…"

Hephæstion rolls her gently toward him and kisses her wrapped palm.

The thought of her palms bleeding from the cuts of blind merciless sharp daggers torments him.

His voice loads with longing and desire for her.

"Why are there tears in your eyes, if you do not care for me?"

"My tears are for Peritas."

"Lucky dog! Old Kalanos told me to tell you that Peritas will be reborn!"

Tears stream from the corners of Rošanak's eyes.

Hephæstion tenderly kisses the tears on Rošanak's face.

"Do I have to die first before you will think of me in your bed with tears in your eyes?"

Rošanak bites her lip. Hephæstion kisses her mouth.

"Shall I go and leave you free to mourn?"

"Yes…"

Rošanak raises her hand and sweetly caresses Hephæstion's smooth face.

He was her undoing too…

Hephæstion smiles and pulls her closer and kisses her tenderly.

All was forgiven…

Rhyton of night fills with the sweetness of kisses and sacred utterances and spills carelessly into the platter of dawn…

EARLY DAWN

"Who are you writing to?"

"My mother."

"Read it to me," Hephæstion asks quietly from her bed.

Rošanak, sitting at the small table in her bedchamber, looks at him hesitatingly, pulls the thin linen wrap tighter around herself, then looks down at her letter and starts reading quietly in Persian:

"A letter from Rošanak to Farânak, my beloved mother.

"In the year 233 after Kuruš the Elder, in Month 4, Garmapada, 27 days passed, in Year 5 of Alexander:

"May the Wise Lord and Divine Ânâhitâ bless my mother and keep her in good health.

"May my mother be well and her heart be happy.

"Alexander finally defeated Rajah Parvataka, one of the most powerful Hindu Rajahs. Alexander is allowing the Rajah to continue to govern his own old satrapy, as he did before the battle with Alexander.

"Alexander has even conquered more lands for Rajah to rule over. Now Alexander and Rajah Parvataka are friendly allies. I have been staying at the Palace of Rajah for a while. It is truly a beautiful palace, with doors made of pure gold, and a magnificent library housed in a separate building as great as the palace itself.

"Rajah gave Alexander a magnificent golden sword, jeweled with precious rubies, and offered one of his daughters to Alexander as a wife. Alexander, of course, declined the daughter. He kept the golden jeweled sword.

"Chief Wife of Rajah gave me a hundred golden bangles and a few Hindu silk gowns, as she heard my royal gowns were destroyed in a fire last year, and she gave me some beautiful jewelry for my feet too!

"The Hindu Royal Women are beautiful and kind and wrap themselves expertly in their fine bright-colored silks. They favor adorning their wrists with many fine gold bangles over the thicker Persian bracelets and armlets that we wear. It must be the heat. I am wearing my new Hindu gold bangles as I write this letter. My wrists feel heavy with the weight of the gold. I am also dressing in the manner of the Hindu Women, wrapped in a sheer purple silk saree, which is more suitable to this torrid heat."

She pauses and looks at her wrists.

Her wrists were free of jewelry. The palms of her hands were wrapped with clean linen to cover her new honor wounds. She was naked and wrapped in cool linen.

She glances at Hephæstion and then looks back at her letter and continues.

"How is my horse, Šâru, doing? Alexander's horse, Bukephalas, was wounded in the battle with Rajah Parvataka and died. Alexander was so grief-stricken, he named a city Bukephala, after Bukephalas. I wonder if he will name anything after me, when I die. My spaka, Peritas, died yesterday."

She pauses and looks up at Hephæstion and takes a deep breath. She looks back at her letter and continues.

"I miss Persian food. Hindu food is spicy and Hindu spices do not agree with me. Alexander eats everything. He does not care as much for food as he cares for wine.

"I have not seen Oštana for two months, so I have no news of him. He is with the main Royal Army.

"May the Wise Lord and Divine Ânâhitâ bless Dârâ and Nimâ and keep them in good health. And Thukrâ, too.

"May the Wise Lord and Divine Mithrâ bless Abû and Itâna and keep them in good health."

Rošanak finishes and looks at Hephæstion.

He looks at her intently without words. His eyes ask the questions.

"What would you have me tell my mother?" Rošanak says quietly.

Hephæstion looks at her wordlessly.

Rošanak continues quietly, "… that my son is dead… my husband is bedding a eunuch… and that… I… I am an adulteress?"

She takes a deep breath and closes her eyes. "The Wise Lord knows of my wretchedness… my mother can be spared the shame!"

"Are you ashamed of me?"

"No. I am ashamed of me…"

In FRONT of ALEXANDER'S ROYAL TENT. RIVER VIPÂŠ
YEAR 11 of ALEXANDER, MONTH 12, HYPERBERETAIOS
YEAR 5 of ALEXANDER, MONTH 6, KARBAŠIYAŠ
A MONTH LATER
AFTERNOON

Hot and steamy.

"Hephæstion, wait!" Ptolemaios yells, rushing quickly toward Hephæstion.

Hephæstion stops and turns around. Ptolemaios stops short of the royal tent and waves Hephæstion toward him. Hephæstion grinds his teeth and then relents and walks over to Ptolemaios.

"Did the messenger tell you what happened?"

"Yes." Hephæstion takes a deep breath and looks back at Alexander's royal tent. "How is he?" he asks quietly.

"Crazed as a caged lion! Talk to him, please!"

Hephæstion takes another deep worried breath.

"Old Koinos only advocated the cause of the men," Ptolemaios says. "You know yourself the old man will follow the King anywhere! He condemned his own kinsman, Philotas, to death in front of the whole Assembly to please the King!" he adds quickly.

"Yes," Hephæstion nods tiredly.

"The men… they are not refusing the King, they are just worn out… many are sick with fever… their wives and children are sick with the same fever too… some have died. Their weapons rust before they are done cleaning them and their clothes are rotting on their bodies… and the rumors about hordes of elephants waiting to crush them further up country… and tribes of warlike men… giant snakes and this wretched heat and rain…" Ptolemaios says in a low voice. "Men are building twelve giant altars by the River Hyphasis to mark how far he got up country."

"I heard."

"He has not admitted anyone to see him for days. He has been waiting for you."

Hephæstion looks back at Alexander's royal tent.

"Old Koinos… when he removed his helmet at the Assembly and approached the King to speak, he had tears in his eyes."

"I will talk to Alexander."

"I wish we had stayed in the Two Lands… that was the only place that opened her arms to us. Tell him we should go back to the Two Lands."

"Tell him yourself! I hate cats!" Hephæstion grunts impatiently and turns and heads toward Alexander's tent.

Two Lands crawled with scrawny cats and Ptolemaios was the only one who liked the strange creatures.

ALEXANDER'S ROYAL TENT

Hot and steamy inside the royal tent.

"Alexander!"

Alexander turns and rushes toward Hephæstion and seizes him by his shoulders… his powerful fingers dig into Hephæstion's flesh.

"Tell me, Hephæstion! Do you want to go home too?"

Hephæstion is taken off guard.

His mind empties for a long moment, trying to think where home *was… the memories of his former life before Roshanak's love had found him, tasted like sweet pure wine mixed with bitter tainted poison.*

He was her home… and she was his home… there was no other home!

"Home?" Hephæstion thinks quickly on his feet. "… to… Persis?"

Alexander stops and gives Hephæstion a straight look, eye to eye, for a long moment, then takes a deep breath and relaxes and lets go of him.

"Yes— you are right! Home is Persis, is it not?" Alexander shakes his head and smiles to himself. Relieved.

Heavy anger and rage become lighter… more bearable…

"Yes… Home is not the lands of our fathers, it is where we desire to be… Pella has not been home since we left it behind years ago," Alexander says truly. "My father was right when he told me the UpLands were too small for me… that I should conquer another kingdom for myself."

Air cools.

"Yes!" Alexander nods and eagerly repeats to himself. "Let them go to wherever they want to go… Persis is calling us home… that is what the omens mean. We have been in India far too long, for almost two years now. We have been victorious and now we should head home to Persis… Old Kalanos said that the Empire should be ruled from the center, not from the edges. Persia is the Axis of the Empire!"

"Where was Krateros when all this happened with the Royal Army?"

"I had sent him to build two fortified cities on the banks of the River Indus, so we can secure the rear of the Royal Army as we move down the river."

Alexander pauses and takes a deep breath.

"Did you— bring her?"

"Yes."

"Is she with you?"

"No— I left her at the army camp by the River Indus."

"Is she… well?"

"Yes."

"Did she ask about me?"

Silence.

THIRTY-OARS GALLEY. BANKS of RIVER SINDHU
YEAR 12 of ALEXANDER, MONTH 2, APELLAIOS
YEAR 5 of ALEXANDER, MONTH 8, MARKAŠANAŠ
MID-DAY

"Whoaa!" Rošanak cries out, startled, as she slips on the wet floor of the thirty-oars galley and falls backward into the rushing River Sindhu.

"*Rowshanaaakk!*"

Mâr'at Bani Âriyânnâz screams, bending down after her.

All the men turn their heads toward the noise.

Alexander and Hephæstion and the kingsmen, just arriving at the river bank, quickly dismount their horses.

Mâr'at Bani Âriyânnâz points desperately to the river with her whole body and screams wordlessly.

"Roxana!" Alexander screams and starts running toward the rushing river, forgetting his wounded ankle.

Hephæstion starts running toward the river, following Alexander.

He should have learned how to swim.

The rest follow quickly behind. They all look at the churning river. There is no sign of Rošanak.

Mâr'at Bani Âriyânnâz twists in pain.

Nearchos, an Islander, a Kretan, a man born to the sea, jumps into the rushing river and he too disappears from sight.

Alexander, so careless of himself in the face of danger and death, pales at the thought of losing Rošanak to the mad river, of never seeing her alive again. He starts after Nearchos. Perdikkas and Ptolemaios pull him back.

Tense moments pass amidst shouts and screams.

The head of Nearchos emerges from the river further down the banks. He yells at the top of his voice, "I need a sharp knife! Quickly! She is caught below on tree branches!"

Everyone runs down the river banks toward Nearchos. He hangs tightly to a tree branch as the water rushes furiously around him.

Hephæstion quickly unsheathes his short Persian dagger and tosses it to Nearchos. Nearchos catches the dagger mid-air and disappears back into the water.

Krateros quickly unsheathes his Makedonian dagger and jumps into the mad river after him and he too disappears.

Anxious moments stretch… forward and backward…

"Father-Zeus…" Alexander holds his breath, invokes his gods under his breath and offers a sacrifice.

> *"Zeus-Father, Please hear me…*
>
> *"… save my Queen… only you can command Hades to spare her life…"*

Hephæstion closes his eyes. He had always left it to Alexander to pray to the gods and offer sacrifices. He utters a silent prayer under his lips.

"Hear me, Poseidon, Lord of the Sea, Shaker of the Earth, in the name of the one you love… do not grudge my love for her… bring my beloved back to me safely!"

Mâr'at Bani Âriyânnâz coils into herself, choking with sobs.

And then, further down the river banks, Krateros pulls himself out of the raging river slowly, dragging Rošanak's body behind him with one arm, holding his dagger in the other, with Nearchos pushing her out from behind.

They all rush toward them.

Krateros, dripping wet, slowly lowers Rošanak's limp body on the banks of the river.

Her lips purplish… her gown ripped by tree branches and sharp daggers… her body, half-naked, cut and bloodied from sharp branches of trees, lies motionless.

A voice whispers.

"Is she dead?"

Alexander's eyes fill with tears. He drops to his knees carelessly by her body and calls her. "Roxana…"

Hephæstion stands motionless, unable to move or breathe or think or pray.

Nearchos drops the dagger on the ground, pushes everyone away, and kneels down by Rošanak's body and starts shaking her violently. Her ivory skin has turned the color of faded skies. Nearchos rolls Rošanak on her belly and starts pounding on her back fiercely.

"Nearchos!" Alexander yells at him angrily.

Nearchos ignores Alexander and continues pounding her.

"Ah!" She gasps suddenly and throws up a bellyful of water and coughs.

Nearchos sighs with relief. He lays her down gently on the ground and yells, "No women on any of my ships from now on!"

Hephæstion makes a fist, turning his knuckles the color of snow. He takes a step forward. Perdikkas grabs his arm and holds him in place and gives him his dagger. He then grabs a Hellene cloth from one of the men standing nearby and kneels down to cover Rošanak's half-naked body from manly eyes.

Alexander's body fills with air. He lifts her up and pulls her to him and holds her tightly.

"Roxana!"

Rošanak coughs and more water spills out of her mouth.

ROŠANAK'S TENT

LATER that NIGHT

"Are you well?" Alexander asks Rošanak tenderly in a low voice.

"Well enough!"

Rošanak stretches her back and feels her aching bones.

Nothing like almost dying to purge ghastly ghostly memories…

Living was sweet…

"They say Nearchos pounded on my back to pour life back into me."

"Yes."

"If it had been someone else, he would have broken all my bones!"

Alexander smiles.

Nearchos was not much taller than he, but a lot leaner and weaker…

"Yes."

Silence.

A long moment passes.

"Who pulled me out of the river?"

"Krateros."

"Krateros? Can he swim?"

"No."

Silence.

Another long moment passes.

"I sacrificed to Zeus and Poseidon for your health this evening," Alexander says as he eyes her tenderly, "a bull to Zeus and a golden cup full of pure wine to the river."

"Thank you, My Lord."

He looks at her for another moment and lingers, waiting for a sign. Then he relents and gets up and walks hesitantly toward the tent flap.

He limps slightly and his head tilts a little more than usual to the left.

Rošanak notices.

In the heat of the night, Alexander is wearing just a tunic and sandals.

Rošanak sees the new scars of an arrow wound on his right limping ankle. His neck and shoulder bear another purplish stone mark.

"My Lord should be more careful. His fearless ancestor, Achilleos, was killed by a single arrow to his unprotected heel," Rošanak says softly.

Her voice floats like a cool breeze in the warm air, reaches him quickly and beckons him back to her.

Alexander hears her heart and turns around and stands motionlessly, looking at her intently.

Her Attik had improved even more since the last time he had seen her four months ago, when he had left her with Raja Poros as a royal hostage.

Then he looks down at his ankle and points, and says quietly, "I got this when we were sieging—" He pauses. He does not remember where. Then he points to his neck. "This one, a stone, from Sangala Siege. Krateros got an arrow wound." He says it proudly.

Rošanak's heart softens.

"But I have done Achilleos one better. I have married a beautiful Persian Princess who cares for me. Her love has bathed my entire body… no part left carelessly unprotected."

His voice, full of sweetness and longing for her, fills the cup of her heart till it runs over.

Rošanak gets to her feet and picks up a small jar of sacred oils from her table and beckons Alexander to her.

Alexander walks back, slightly limping, and sits back down on the couch.

Rošanak kneels down in front of him on the carpet, loosens the sandal off his foot and tenderly rubs his injured ankle with the sacred oils mixed with za'farân. His tender skin turns golden yellow. Scent of mint and lavender fills the tent.

A little lower and the arrow would have shattered his ankle… and made him lame for life, like his father.

"At your late age, you should let your warriors do the fighting!" Rošanak says softly, with a half-smile loaded with concern for him.

Alexander hears her and smiles back at her.

The fire from the candle danced softly on her face. There were so many small cuts and bruises on her face and arms from the tree branches in the river… and when she had been pulled onto the riverbank, he had seen many more cuts on her half-naked body, now sheathed in a sheer Indian gown… and still she looked so beautiful.

He leans into her slightly and gently caresses the small cuts on her face with the tips of his fingers.

She rubs more sacred oils on his neck and shoulder with the tips of her fingers. Her fingers tremble.

"Were you scared?" Alexander asks quietly.

"Yes…"

He reaches and caresses the small cuts on the top of her breasts, heaving under her gown.

Her skin beat and pulsated like a living heart under his fingers… like it used to…

He pulls her into his arms and kisses her face wordlessly.

She does not resist him.

The small jar falls soundlessly on the carpet and spills.

"What happened at River Hyphasis?" she gently whispers into his mouth.

"My men refused to go further up country… warlike tribes… fighting elephants… giant snakes… relentless rain and heat…. they said they wanted to go home… they said they missed their wives and children…" He whispers back quietly into her mouth, kissing her.

"And their King… does he miss his Queen too?"

"More than his men miss their wives," he says sweetly.

"Any man refusing the command of the King and his royal wishes should not live to see another rising sun," she whispers gently into his ear.

He pulls her closer to him. "Any man? What about his Queen?"

"Her too…" she whispers back.

He smiles and pulls her closer to him and wraps her tenderly in his kisses and whispers old love words in her ears.

MIDDLE of the NIGHT

"Ah!"

The point of a sharp Persian dagger pushes into Hephæstion's throat in the darkness as he is about to enter Rošanak's tent.

"Commander," Abi-Samar whispers and withdraws his sharp dagger and sheaths it.

Hephæstion straightens and narrows his eyes at him, his temper rising.

Sacred oath or not, one day soon he should do away with the troublesome eunuch!

He always had the point of his sharp dagger pushing on his throat!

"The King is with the Queen."

Abi-Samar bows his head, turns around and quietly walks away.

Hephæstion stands there motionlessly for a moment. His face creases and folds with pain.

He should have left her with her Indian Prince… it would have been less painful than to lose her back to Alexander… again…

He did not need to beg her and plead with her to return to Alexander… the very moment Alexander laid eyes on her and beckoned her back to him, she went running…

Alexander was like the Sun in the center of the heavens and she was the Moon of his Sun… even with the thickest clouds in the skies, the shining Sun always knew the shimmering Moon was revolving around his orbit…

Yes…

Alexander would notice if a wife went missing… if the only wife went missing…

ROŠANAK'S TENT. ROYAL ARMY CAMP
YEAR 12 of ALEXANDER, MONTH 3, AUDNAIOS
YEAR 5 of ALEXANDER, MONTH 9, ÂÇIYÂDIYA
A MONTH LATER
MID-DAY

"Roxana!"

Perdikkas rushes into Rošanak's tent, roughly pushing Abi-Samar out of his way.

Rošanak is sprawled on the carpet crying. She coils into herself at the sight of Perdikkas and moans.

The news that Alexander had been killed while attacking the Mâlavâns had already reached the camp of the Royal Army followers.

She covers her face in her hands. "No!"

Perdikkas kneels down next to her and takes her hand.

"Roxana, get up! Come with me!"

Rošanak looks at Perdikkas in horror. "Perdikkas!"

He was covered in dried blood.

"Alexander…" Perdikkas says faintly.

Rošanak blanches. Words utterly fail her; her mind darkens with grief.

"He is not dead! But he has taken a bad arrow wound— his lung is pierced."

"Ah!"

Throbbing silence.

Perdikkas takes Rošanak's hand and pulls her to her feet, mumbling, "No time to waste… coming in the carriage… it might be too late already!"

Perdikkas pulls Rošanak behind him and thunders at Abi-Samar.

"Pack her carriage and bring it down to the main Royal Army Camp. The King has been gravely wounded."

Abi-Samar bows his head slightly. "Yes, Commander."

One of his men is holding the reins to Perdikkas' horse. Perdikkas jumps on and pulls Rošanak up behind him mindlessly. He grabs the bridle and gallops away as fast as he can.

ALEXANDER'S ROYAL TENT. ROYAL ARMY CAMP. NEAR TOWN of MÂLAVÂ
SETTING SUN

"Damn you!"

Rošanak cries softly on the pillow, her tears falling freely.

She was not blessed with his love… she was cursed with it!

Alexander lay unconscious a hair's breadth away from her, his chest wrapped tightly in white cloth.

Fresh blood stains the snowy white cloth, like the breast of a dove bloodied by an arrow. The side of his neck is wounded and purplish from a new blow.

He breathes slowly… every breath weighed and measured painfully…

"You love me tenderly and leave me carelessly when I get with child."

Tears fall.

"Damn you! Every time I push you out of my heart, you get yourself mortally wounded by a sword or an arrow or a spear or a stone… and crawl right back into my heart, and lie in a death sleep in my arms, just to remind me how much I love you!"

Alexander breathes slowly, painfully.

Rošanak reaches and plays with a lock of Alexander's hair.

"If you are so eager for death, just swallow a mouthful of poison and be done and end my misery!"

Alexander breathes more slowly.

"You rush recklessly in pursuit of your glory and take a wound, and your men turn into barbarian blood-thirsty beasts."

Rošanak takes his hand and brings it to her lips and kisses it and pulls it to her heart. Her heart pounds with utter sadness against Alexander's hand. Her bitter scolding comes to an end.

"Do not leave me…" she pleads softly.

In FRONT of KING'S TENT
LATER
EVENING

"Hephæstion!" one of the Makedonians cries out in anguish.

"King is dying!" another one moans with tears.

"Gods help us!" another one cries out desperately.

Hephæstion hurls himself off his horse and runs toward the small tent displaying the royal standard. He forces his way through the Makedonians who have surrounded the tent.

A haunted, desperate silence hangs in the air.

Fear and grief dance hand in hand on the faces of the fearless men.

Perdikkas is standing in front of the royal tent, covered in dried blood.

"Perdikkas!"

Perdikkas looks around in a daze and locks eyes with Hephæstion. He takes a deep breath and grinds his teeth and looks back at the tent.

"Roxana is with him."

"How bad is it?"

"Bad!"

Hephæstion pierces Perdikkas with his fierce eyes.

"Barbed arrow… cut through his armor and right into his right lung. He lost a lot of blood…" Perdikkas closes his eyes. His brow creases and folds. He touches his forehead with his fingers. His hands are blackish with dried blood.

"What happened?"

"When he got to the Town of Mallians, he thought it was already taken. So he and his royal guards wrenched a gate from its hinges and pushed their way into the town without waiting for me and my men…"

Perdikkas pauses and takes a breath. "He thought the men were not following his orders quick enough… so he charged up the ladder himself first and stood up there on the crown of the wall all alone… the royal guards rushed behind him in fear for his life and the ladder broke under them… a piece of the broken ladder flew and hit him hard in the neck. Men were standing below outside of the walls, yelling at him to jump backward into their arms, but instead he jumped forward inside the wall, right into the folds of the enemy, bleeding from his neck."

"Damn fool!" Perdikkas grinds his teeth.

Hephæstion twists his lips, tempted to scold Perdikkas.

But Perdikkas was right… what Alexander had done was not heroic… it was pure madness…

"Finally some men made their way to him. Habreas, Peukestas, Leonnatos, Aristonous… Habreas was killed at once, when an arrow broke his face. The rest are all wounded… Aristonous took an arrow in the arm… Peukestas was pierced three times with arrows and Leonnatos is half-dead, battered by heavy stones to his neck.

"Peukestas protected Alexander as long as he could with his old shield. If my men had not finally broken into the walls, they all would have been slaughtered!"

Perdikkas pauses again and catches his breath. "They brought him back on Peukestas' old shield… he was bareheaded… his helmet had been shattered by stones… he was bathing in his own blood in the middle of the old shield…"

Hephæstion narrows his eyes in pain.

"When he came to his senses, he ordered us to pull the arrow out of him… but the arrow was barbed… it was firmly planted inside of his chest… everyone knew it could not be removed without causing more damage. Cursed Indians…"

"Perdikkas!"

"Old Kritoboulos was afraid to touch him… he feared that if the King died in his hands, the Makedonians would rip him apart limb from limb. The men slaughtered the Mallians… to the last man, woman and child… when they heard rumors that the King was dead… I could not stop them… I tried…"

Hephæstion closes his eyes and rubs his forehead with his fingers.

"Alexander was in unspeakable pain… so, I invoked the gods and took out my Persian knife and cut the wound open… and Kritoboulos pulled out the arrow… his blood gushed out… air too… blood mixed with air… mortal blood. No idiot flatterer around the battlefield to liken his mortal blood to ichor from the immortal gods!"

Perdikkas closes his eyes in pain and then opens them to look at his bloodied hands. "This is his royal blood! If he dies, his blood is on my hands."

"Perdikkas… go wash the blood off your hands." Hephæstion puts his hands on Perdikkas' shoulders. "The old shield of Peukestas was the shield of Achilleos we took from Troia, when we crossed into Asia. Achilleos protected Alexander with his shield, or he would have died already!"

Perdikkas looks at Hephæstion with dismay.

Hephæstion looks around at the Makedonians and grunts, "Return to camp!"

No one moves.

Hephæstion shakes his head gloomily and enters the tent.

INSIDE KING'S TENT

Quiet.

Rošanak is sitting by Alexander's bed, resting her head on his pillow.

Hephæstion takes a deep breath and closes his eyes.

His gods were punishing him…

Two loves were slipping through his fingers… both at once…

Hephæstion approaches the royal bed quietly and gently puts his hand on Rošanak's shoulder. His hand trembles.

Rošanak reaches and gently touches the tips of Hephæstion's fingers.

Hephæstion gently lifts his fingers to her face and bathes his fingers in her rolling tears.

Rošanak closes her eyes as her heart unravels.

The Wise Lord was punishing her…

Two lovers were slipping through her fingers, a king and a kingsman… one following the other…

She prays quietly.

"I worship the Wise Lord…

"I invoke the Heaven… the boundless time…

"I invoke the Divine Mithrâ, Protector of Brave Warriors…

"… watchful and wakeful…"

ALEXANDER'S ROYAL TENT. MAIN ROYAL ARMY CAMP. BANKS of RIVER SINDHU
7 DAYS LATER
MID-DAY

"Ah!" Hephæstion sighs quietly in pain and clenches his powerful fist around Rošanak's hand, without letting go. Her fingernails dig into the palm of his hand, almost drawing blood.

"What do they want? To make sure he is still alive, so they can kill him themselves?" Rošanak growls, as she watches Alexander from the tent flap.

Alexander slowly dismounts from his horse and walks slowly and deliberately toward the royal tent. Makedonians flock to him, throwing flowers at him and shouting blessings in their mother tongues, their voices echoing on the banks of the River Indus.

Rumors had shrouded the Royal Army.

He had slept for four days, passed out in pain. His men had thought him dead… the Royal Army had started to unravel.

So, in spite of Roxana's pleading, he had ordered the army wound-healer to wrap his chest as tight as he could and load him onto a thirty-oars galley. He had sailed down the River Indus in full view of his men to arrive at the main Royal Army Camp.

His men had not believed their own eyes… they thought it was his dead body lying in state on the ship. So he had ordered a horse brought to him and had ridden from the galley to his royal tent on a horse, letting his men come close and see him and touch him and tell others that he was alive.

The horse ride was agonizing… only his Bukephalas had known how to carry him when he was wounded and in pain.

He had never been in so much pain… ever… each breath was counted carefully… and taken only if absolutely necessary…

Where was Roxana? Where was Hephæstion?

If the bloody sons of Hades had obeyed his command and had followed him up country, this would not have happened. His pain and his defeat were their fault… all of it!

The men of Darius had abandoned him at Gaugamela and the Persians had put Darius to the sword for his defeat, and the Makedonians had refused him at River Hyphasis and now he was near death…

And now they were blessing him in his mother tongue… sons of Hades and bloody whores… Did they think he would forget their disobedience over a bloody wound?

Hephæstion watches Alexander's every move from the royal tent.

"Discipline will break in a blink of an eye if the men think him dead. They butchered all the Mallians to the last… even women and children. They love him… they go mad whenever something happens to him," Hephæstion says quietly, holding on to Rošanak's hand.

Rošanak grinds her teeth in worried anger.

Makedonians loved anyone who satisfied their lust for blood and gold…

"They should love him less… they are killing him!" She does not even notice Hephæstion is holding her hand.

"He knows what he is doing. He can bend death to his will to keep his men."

"Go bring him in! Please! Before he bleeds to death where he stands!"

Hephæstion lets go of her hand and looks around the royal tent.

All the kingsmen were boiling in their blood for the danger Alexander had foolishly taken upon himself to capture another worthless fortress.

Hephæstion signals Perdikkas and they both walk out of the royal tent.

Alexander then steps inside the royal tent and both men follow him.

The tent flap closes.

"Roxana…" Alexander moans and folds and passes out in pain.

Fresh blood seeps through his tunic.

Rošanak pales with horror and misery.

ALEXANDER'S ROYAL TENT. ROYAL ARMY CAMP. BANKS of RIVER SINDHU
YEAR 12 of ALEXANDER, MONTH 4, PERITIOS
YEAR 5 of ALEXANDER, MONTH 10, ANÂMAKA
A MONTH LATER
MIDDLE of the NIGHT

Warm steamy night. Sound of water flowing in the river.

Thick clouds are beclouding the moon and the little stars.

Alexander is sleeping deeply, his chest wrapped up tightly with fresh linen.

Rošanak is passed out by his bedside from heat and exhaustion.

A royal servant is fanning Alexander with a long palm leaf to chase away the flies and heat.

Hephæstion enters the royal tent quietly, takes Rošanak's hand gently and puts a letter, sealed with the Bakhtrian Satrapal Seal, in her hand and whispers gently into her ear in Persian. "Roshanak, a letter from Baktra! This should cheer you up, my beloved Queen!"

Rošanak opens her eyes, sits up, smiles tiredly at Hephæstion, breaks the Satrapal Seal carelessly and reads.

> *A letter from Pêhâtu Uxšiyârta to Dukšiš Rošanak:*
> *In the year 233 after Kuruš the Elder, in Month 8, Markašanaš, 7 days passed, in Year 5 of Alexander:*
> *May the Wise Lord and Divine Ânâhitâ bless my daughter and keep her in good health.*
> *My beloved daughter, it is with greatest sadness that I am informing you that your mother, my beloved sister, our beloved Queen- Mother, Dukšiš Farânak, has died due to sudden illness.*
> *I have formally assumed the care and administration of the Baktra hadiš, until your safe return. I have also assumed the care of Dârâ and Nimâ, the Royal Sons of your late sister, Dukšiš Parânak.*

"Matar..." Rošanak utters quietly under her breath. she shifts her body and re-reads the words quickly. She forgets to breathe... then quickly reads the rest.

> *By the favor of the Wise Lord, we have dutifully observed and performed all the religious rituals.*
> *Her body is now resting alongside her beloved sons – your brothers.*

May the Wise Lord bless my blood sister, the beloved Dukšiš Farânak
and grant her soul passage into the Land of the Eternal Light.
Θukrâ died a day after your mother. The same Angel of Death who had
come for your mother, took her too. We buried her next to your mother.
I know it is what you would have wanted for her.
Itâna is well. Dârâ and Nimâ are growing up and their childhood has
ended. Let me hear news of you quickly.
By the order of Pêhâtu Uxšiyârta, Dâtamithrâ wrote this letter.
SEAL of SATRAP of BAKHTRIŠ

"Thukrâ…" Rošanak moans. She feels light-headed. She rubs her fingers on the broken seal at the end of the letter. She loses her voice.

It was real. Her father's old seal… when he was the Satrap of Bakhtriš…

She slowly rises to her feet and re-reads the letter again quickly.

Lightning flickers in the sky.

BOOM!

Rošanak jumps, startled.

BOOM!

Another loud clap of thunder and lightning and then rain starts to pour again.

Rošanak opens her hand and the letter flies out of her hand and falls to the ground. She grabs her belly and twists in pain. "No."

The heavens were mourning the death of her mothers with their mournful tears…

Hephæstion jumps and grabs her quickly before she hits the ground.

She starts to bleed; blood drips on the letter on the ground.

Hephæstion lifts her up and puts her on a silver couch and yells at the royal guards urgently, "Go fetch Kritoboulos at once!"

He quickly picks up the bloodied letter from the ground, kneels down next to Rošanak and holds her hand and looks at the letter desperately.

Her red blood runs and smears the black words.

What was in the damn letter?

He should have had it read and interpreted before carelessly giving it to her.

He had learned the spoken tongue but not the written tongue… he had never thought there would be anything written in Persian that he would want to read.

His father was right when he had counseled him to learn the written words too.

Rošanak fades into mourning.

Two mothers dead and another child…

More love leaving carelessly for the Land of the Eternal Light…

She was left behind on dirt and earth…

ALEXANDER'S ROYAL TENT. ROYAL ARMY CAMP. BANKS of RIVER SINDHU
YEAR 12 of ALEXANDER, MONTH 5, DYSTROS
YEAR 5 of ALEXANDER, MONTH 11, SAMIYAMAŠ
A MONTH LATER
MID-DAY

"Come back home with me to Baktra," Uxšiyârta pleads in a low voice with Rošanak. "He will not survive this!"

Rošanak looks at him. Her face folds in anguish.

Uxšiyârta had come to see her when the news of Alexander's arrow wound had reached him in Baktra… after he had sent her the news of the death of her mothers.

"Roshanak," Hephæstion says under his lips.

Rošanak turns her head toward Hephæstion.

She had taught Hephæstion a few words of Bakhtrian herself… the Bakhtrian tongue was close enough to the tongue of the Persians and Hephæstion had heard enough words to string them together and understand Uxšiyârta…

"He is healing," she says faintly.

"He is dying!"

Rošanak looks at Alexander and then at Uxšiyârta.

Uxšiyârta did not understand the nature of Alexander.

Alexander was made of stubborn metal… he was invincible… the grave wound would have killed any other man, but not Alexander… he would live until the day he willed it otherwise.

She takes a deep breath and asks quietly, "My mother?"

"It was quick…" It pains him to talk about it.

Rošanak closes her eyes and pushes back tears. "Thukrâ?"

"She just went to sleep and did not wake up…"

A tear falls.

"The boys?"

Uxšiyârta puts his hand on her shoulder kindly. "The boys are well cared for… they are growing up fast… they miss you!"

"I doubt they even remember me…" Rošanak says quietly under her breath.

"Itâna is still an idiot… just older."

"Oxyartes," Alexander says with a faint voice.

"Alexander."

Alexander takes a painful breath. "I hear Baktria is in revolt again… against me…"

Rošanak interprets hesitatingly.

Uxšiyârta nods his head confirming.

No use denying it…

Alexander was in no shape to return to Bakhtriš himself and the Makedonians had already turned on him once, as Oštana had told him.

No doubt they still remembered the three years of bloody fighting and sheer misery and the dreadful taste of eating their own animals in Bakhtriš and Sughud.

If Alexander had not married his daughter, their blood would still be spilling on the dirt of Bakhtriš and Sughud!

Alexander closes his eyes.

He was in no shape to go back to Baktria... nor did he wish to... he only wished to move forward to see the unseen... not to go back...

"I am sorry to hear about my mother... was she given an honorable burial worthy of the mother of my Queen?"

Rošanak winces as her eyes fill with tears. His kind words get caught in her throat as she interprets.

"Yes. My sister was buried according to the customs of her king and husband and her faith," Uxšiyârta replies.

"Good." Alexander takes another painful breath. "I wish to appoint you to the Satrapy of Paropamisadai."

Rošanak interprets quietly.

"Yes, Alexander."

He had no intention of ever leaving his ancestral homes and lands. But, no use turning down the meaningless royal gift openly. Everyone knew that all his satraps were no more than Makedonian tribute collectors. They all lived like prisoners in fortified fortresses in fear of the locals... easily corruptible with enough gold and wine. And if any of the bloody invaders were foolish enough to leave their prisons without their bloodthirsty guards and armies, the locals would cut off their heads and their manhoods and put them on spears for display and throw the rest of their wretched bodies to the vultures!

Even the wild dogs did not touch the dead of the Makedonians... only the vultures had a taste for them. The Makedonians had eaten the raw flesh of their own animals and they had hunted and eaten sacred beasts and their bodies had become untouchable to the faithful. But there were always enough dead Makedonians to keep the vultures happy.

Vultures were the subjects of the Lord of the Darkness... they ate anything dead!

Alexander passes out in pain once again.

Hephæstion eyes Alexander and then looks at Uxšiyârta with his tired eyes.

He had been sleeping in Alexander's royal tent since Alexander had been wounded, according to the ancient customs of the Makedonian Kings.

And he was in no mood to let her slip through his fingers again!

He would tie her to a tree and post guards to watch her night and day, if he had to!

She was royal property!

Hephæstion leans forward and whispers discreetly in Rošanak's ear. "There are ten thousand Foot and three thousand and five hundred Horse in Baktria... and thirty thousand Baktrian boys are hostages to ensure the peace will keep in Baktria and the Queen will stay with the King."

Even though some had been killed here and there...

Rošanak closes her eyes in pain.

ALEXANDER'S ROYAL TENT. ROYAL ARMY CAMP. BANKS of RIVER SINDHU
YEAR 12 of ALEXANDER, MONTH 9, PANEMOS
YEAR 6 of ALEXANDER, MONTH 3, ØÂIGRACIŠ
4 MONTHS LATER
MORNING

A painful breath…

And then another one…

Alexander puts his hand on his side.

The arrow wound still hurt, after all these months… every breath was still counted carefully… as usual, Roxana had rubbed healing salve on his wound and had wrapped his chest tightly with clean linen that morning… but the pain in his side was nothing compared to the restlessness in his feet.

He had not come to India to lie down in bed day after day to recover and regain his strength… He had come to conquer and to see the Ocean!

But the size of his Royal Army was also slowing him down.

It was no longer a Royal Army, but a traveling Royal City on feet… with hungry mouths that had to be fed. The multitude of camp followers now outnumbered the multitude of his fighting men.

The shade of Darius was mocking him. He had laughed at the size of Darius' Royal Army at Gaugamela and gods had punished him by giving him a bigger one.

Another painful breath…

Alexander closes his eyes.

"Young man," the old Pythia of the Oracle of Apollo at Delphi had told him once, "you are invincible!"

Was he still invincible?

Dioxippos of Athenai, a Hellene, victorious at Olympian Games, had defeated the Makedonian Korrhagos…

He had consented to a single battle between the two in the heat of a drinking feast in his honor and the unarmed, naked, short Hellene had easily beaten the tall Makedonian in full arm and armor!

And he had to consent to false charges of theft against the Hellene to stop the rumors that Makedonians were no longer invincible. Dioxippos had killed himself in shame!

Well, the damn Hellene should have known better than to test the benevolence and patience of an ailing Makedonian king!

Alexander opens his eyes.

Another painful breath…

Roxana had been traveling with him since his arrow wound, staying with him in the royal tent. She had lost another child of his… no one had said anything to him, not even Hephæstion… but he could see it in her eyes…

He would take the honor wound and she would bleed instead…

And he had seen her desire for him again in her eyes and had felt it in her tender intimate caresses… but he could not bed her without feeling his own mortality…

His body had never been in this much pain before. It had been months since the arrow wound and he was still in tormenting pain.

He opens his eyes and looks down at the maps on his royal table and thinks.

Both halves of the Royal Army could reach Karmania in a few months… no longer than a full season… and that was all that he needed.

His body was made of hammered metal… by the time they got to Karmania, he would be as he was before… and he could take her in his arms and satisfy her desire for him and his desire for her, without dying in the act himself… and he would see the Ocean on the way!

"Alexander, shall we come back later?" Krateros asks.

Alexander looks around at his kingsmen, standing around the royal table, patiently awaiting his command. He eyes Hephæstion.

Krateros was more capable in battles, but he needed Hephæstion more, and Hephæstion and Krateros would eventually kill each other, if they were not separated for good…

"Krateros with Polyperchon as his second-in-command will take the Makedonian Horse, some of the archers, the men of Meleagros, Attalos, and Antigenes… all the elephants and all the Makedonians no longer fit for good service, to Karmania through Arachosia and Drangiana."

Kingsmen look at each other.

That was the larger part of the Royal Army.

"Oxyartes will take over the Satrapy of Paropamisadai."

He was trustworthy. His love for Roxana was greater than his hatred for him.

Another painful breath…

"Eumenes, send orders to all the other satraps that they are to come before me in Karmania."

"Yes, Alexander."

"Nearchos will lead the fleet down the River Indus under my command— and no women on any of the ships. Hephæstion has the rest of the Royal Army moving on the right bank of the river as deemed more favorable by the advance scouts."

Krateros glares at Hephæstion with naked contempt.

Alexander was giving the command of the best of the HighLanders under him to Hephæstion, while he was given the care of the damn elephants and the sick and wounded back to Karmania…

Alexander catches the hostile looks exchanged between his two kingsmen.

Another painful breath…

"Krateros, you will also take some of baggage train and the Royal Army camp followers and— the Queen."

Krateros eyes Alexander.

… and the care of the damn women and children!

"Roxana?" Hephæstion says out loud without thinking.

Alexander turns his gaze on Hephæstion and growls.

"The Queen."

"You are sending Roxana back with him?" Hephæstion asks again.

Alexander nods briefly and then looks around.

"You all have your orders. Dismissed!"

The royal tent empties. Hephæstion stays behind.

"Alexander!"

"I heard you the first time, Hephæstion."

"She has been in my care since we crossed into India."

"I know."

"Then, why change?"

"We can move faster without her."

"She only has two carriages. She is not any slower than the rest of the Royal Army camp-followers."

Another painful breath…

Hephæstion's voice softens up.

"Let her stay with you. I will take full responsibility for her safety. I will make sure she moves with the rest of the Royal Army— ahead of them even, if you wish it!"

Alexander closes his eyes and puts his hand on his side.

Her presence was more painful than her absence… a constant reminder of a love that could not be had without unspeakable pain. Every time he had tried to bed her, his chest wound had opened up and had bled all over her.

And he had to see to the discipline of the Royal Army…

"It is only for a season… maybe even shorter. We will follow in the footsteps of Scylax of Karyanda who sailed down the River Indus at the order of the First Darius. Once we reach the Ocean, we sail back to Persis, as he did—"

"Alexander, please!"

"No."

"Then keep Krateros with you. Let me take them to Karmania. Krateros is more useful to you campaigning back to Persis."

Alexander opens his eyes and looks at Hephæstion.

"In all the years you have known me since the old days at Mieza, how many times have I ever changed my mind?"

Silence.

"I will assume the full responsibility for two thirty-oars instead of one!"

"No!"

"Three!"

"No!"

"Please! Alexander! Reconsider! He hates her! He will kill her on the way to Karmania!"

"He has earned the honor to guard the Queen. He has no cause to harm her. He jumped into the raging river to save her life without a care for himself."

Hephæstion considers Alexander carefully and then he reads it in his eyes.

He knew Alexander better than anyone… even better than Alexander knew himself…

It was not to reach the Ocean faster without her… it was to avenge his lost glory!

Alexander never tolerated any opposition to his absolute rule…

… he had always ruthlessly removed all those who had opposed him and all those who ever could.

All the rival Argead males executed… All the men of Philip… Attalos, Parmenion and all his sons… Amyntas… all dead…

Old Koinos who had spoken for the Royal Army at the River Hyphasis had been quietly seen to… a poisonous snake had found its way into his bed… there were so many snakes in India… he should have taken better care…

And the formidable One-eyed Antigonos was left behind on the western edges of the Empire by the sea to keep the roads clear for communications right after the victory at Granikos… cut off from the King and Court and Campaign.

Alexander would eventually see to the old Antipatros and the One-eyed Antigonos too… when the time was ripe…

And the Black Kleitos speared…

And the royal boys stoned to death by the Makedonians and he himself had seen to Kallisthenes after the death of the firstborn of Alexander…

But this time, his Makedonians were the ones who had refused him… and had not repented…

His men… His army… His Royal Army!

Hephæstion leans back in his chair and sinks into tormented silence and horror.

Alexander never changed his mind and he never forgot an insult or a disobedience…

He forgot nothing… ever… he remembered everything…

Alexander was planning to punish the whole of the Royal Army for refusing to obey him and to follow him to conquer the rest of India!

And Krateros was not a man to agree to and then stand by obediently and watch the King severely discipline the Royal Army.

Alexander was planning mass murder to bend the Royal Army to his will… and he was sparing Roxana.

He did not want Roxana to know how ruthless and merciless and murderous he could be when he was not absolutely obeyed.

He wanted Roxana to think well of him… he wanted to shield his Queen and Wife from the naked brutality of her King and Husband.

He closes his eyes. Pain paints on his face.

And he could never leave Alexander, knowing all too well that leaving the King meant abandoning the Queen as well…

HEPHÆSTION'S TENT

DAYS LATER

MID-DAY

"Commander, our carriage is full and My Lady sent me to ask you if there is room in your baggage for something of great value to her that she cannot leave behind."

Hephæstion looks up.

Lady Ariana was standing before him, asking him quietly in Persian.

Hephæstion looks around at his barren tent and feels his empty heart.

"I have plenty of room for anything the Queen desires to carry back to Persia."

He calls Philippo over.

"Philippo can go with you and bring back anything she wishes me to carry for her in my care."

"No need, Commander. I have brought it with me." Mâr'at Bani Âriyânnâz bows and speaks softly in Persian.

Hephæstion looks around her.

"Ah! Where? I do not see any servants with you."

Mâr'at Bani Âriyânnâz bows her head again, extends her right hand and slowly opens her clenched fist.

"Here it is."

Hephæstion looks down at the palm of her hand. She is holding a gold ring. He picks it up and looks at it.

It was a golden lion coiled around a man's ring.

He looks at her, full of questions that could not be asked.

Mâr'at Bani Âriyânnâz reads his eyes and takes a deep breath and hesitates.

"The ring belonged to a man she loved and lost a long time ago."

Hephæstion eyes the golden lion ring.

"She wishes you to carry it for her safely back to Persia… she wears it to bed at night on a golden chain close to her heart."

Hephæstion swallows hard and tries the gold ring on his fingers. The ring slides on his fourth finger and settles comfortably.

A sacred ring to watch over him and take him back to her safely…

A charmed token from a beloved to a lover…

Mâr'at Bani Âriyânnâz bites her lip and mumbles fretfully.

"This ring is all she has left of him… if anything happens to it…"

Hephæstion clenches his fist and reassures her confidently.

"This ring is safe with me. I will see to it and I will see her in Karmania."

Mâr'at Bani Âriyânnâz lingers for a moment, hesitatingly biting her lip, then bows her head and turns around and leaves quickly without looking at Hephæstion.

Sun gets warmer.

Three

III

AXIS of EMPIRE

On the WAY to the SATRAPY of KARMÂNA. PERSIA
4 MONTHS LATER
SETTING SUN

Autumn winds scattering the golden leaves.

Air heavy with tension.

"Return the woman to me in exchange for your men and I will let you all go free!" Krateros says with a powerful voice, accustomed to high command.

Blood seeps through the white linen covering the deep arrow wound on his left thigh.

Words are interpreted.

"Who is she?" The Persian rebel asks with contempt.

Krateros narrows his eyes at him. Without even looking at all the swords and arrows pointed at him, he sneers at the Persian rebel.

"She belongs to me!"

"She is dead."

"Then bring me her dead body!"

"If she is worth that much to you dead, then what is she worth to you alive?"

Krateros ignores him and looks at the Hellene and Persian rebels surrounding him.

"I will release all your men, if you deliver her to me alive by the sunrise— if you do not deliver her to me by then, I will kill all the prisoners and raze all the lands with no mercy."

The rebels look at each other.

A Hellene speaks, "We keep our heads while we keep her. When we give her up, we lose our life."

Krateros glares at the rebels.

"Keeping her will not help you overcome the powers of the Royal Army."

He stands up, ignoring the terrible pain in his bleeding leg.

"You have until the sunrise!"

....

ROYAL ARMY CAMP. SATRAPY of KARMÂNA. PERSIA
YEAR 13 of ALEXANDER, MONTH 4, PERITIOS
YEAR 6 of ALEXANDER, MONTH 10, ANÂMAKA
3 MONTHS LATER
NIGHT

"Alexander!"

Rošanak jumps out of her carriage and runs to Alexander, embracing him and showering his face with missed kisses.

They said he had died crossing the Desert of Emptiness…

Alexander laughs and holds her tight in his arms.

He was still weak.

The Desert of Death had extracted a heavy price.

He could barely walk as he left the edges of the deadly wasteland.

And the pain in his chest had never left him. The wound had turned into a scar with throbbing pain underneath… but the joy of seeing her was greater than the pain in his body…

He had counted the days.

"Roxana!"

ROYAL ARMY CAMP
2 DAYS LATER
AFTERNOON

"I prayed for you, by Zeus! I knew you were more cunning than the Desert of Death!"

Alexander excitedly greets Hephæstion and his men personally.

Hephæstion looks around discreetly for Rošanak, but there is no sign of her.

"No one is more cunning than the Mother Earth. I just had to make good on a promise."

"Yes! You promised to follow me and you did!"

"Yes."

"Take a bath and clean up and eat with me and the rest of the kingsmen tonight."

"Krateros? and— his men? Everyone— that was in his care?" Hephæstion asks cautiously.

"Krateros is here. He arrived two days ago– and well before you. The baggage train is arriving tonight."

Alexander does not answer his question.

Knowing well Hephæstion cared nothing for Krateros, only for the Queen…

HEPHÆSTION'S TENT

LATER that NIGHT

Scent of yâsmin in the air.

Hephæstion returns from the night meal with Alexander and his kingsmen.

Almost all the kingsmen had survived the death trap.

He sorely missed old faithful Philippo who had died in the desert after the death of his wife. But his tent had been set up as usual by a couple of new servants and a big basin of warm water was waiting for him as he had ordered it. The last time he had bathed was nearly two months ago.

If there was a drop of water, it was for drinking, no matter how tainted and foul.

Candles burning in a tall candleholder dimly light his tent.

He caresses the surface of the water gently with his fingers like the soft skin of a beloved. A small fire burns under the water basin, keeping the water warm.

He walks over to the small table by his bed and picks up the pure silver water jug, takes a few sips and savors each drop. He puts down the jug, takes a deep breath and touches the golden ring hanging from a sturdy leather strap around his neck.

His tent smelled like jasmines…

After two months of smelling death and burning corpses, everything smelled like jasmine.

He undresses and steps into the water basin and loses himself in the comfort of the warm water.

Alexander enters Hephæstion's tent quietly and stands by his bathing basin.

Hephæstion smells him and opens his eyes to look at him. "Alexander…"

"I stayed a whole day in the water when we first got here. So much water— I could not bear to part with a drop of it…"

"Yes…"

"Everyone has gone to Krateros' tent for more wine and women."

"Krateros has more reason to feast than me. He did not lose most of his men to the sands of death."

Alexander pulls a chair over and sits down. A royal guard steps forward quickly, but Alexander dismisses him. "I never thought crossing the desert would take such a toll. If our supplies had reached us as planned, we would have made it through and looked better for it than Kuros did, who had only seven men left with him after he crossed it… even Queen Semiramis survived it. Are we lesser men than that Babylonian woman?"

"No…"

"Eumenes says I lost sixty five thousand… lots of my men, almost all of the camp followers… merchants, tradesmen, women… almost all of the women and children… he counts people as he counts his gold and silver!"

"I know. I burned the corpses that you had left behind— the ones not already swallowed by the desert sands. The smell of burning the dead was as bad as the stench of Death herself."

A moment passes quickly in silence, both desperately eager to forget the stench of death and the sound of dying.

"Get out of the water. Good Persian wine is waiting for us."

"I have had my fill of wine for tonight."

"Wine dulls my pain. I was almost glad, suffering from thirst and hunger crossing the Desert of Emptiness. It made me think less of the pain in my chest… and my neck…" Alexander pauses and takes a deep breath.

"Roxana— Did she—" Hephæstion finally relents and asks cautiously.

Alexander smiles.

"She ran to me when Krateros finally got to Karmania two days ago. She gets more beautiful with the passing of each day. Her beauty torments my eyes. The more she looks like Aphrodite, the more I feel like Hephæstos, dwarfish and disfigured."

Hephæstion takes a deep breath. Relieved.

Alexander closes his eyes.

"No part of my body, front or back, has been left without a wound or a scar… every kind of weapon known to man has left its mark upon my body… scarring on my chest from the barbed arrow looks horrid and still hurts as bad, as I walk and breathe… my ears still ring from the stones that crashed into my neck and face and I can no longer hold my head up straight. I still limp from the arrows that tore into my ankle and legs in India."

Hephæstion closes his eyes. He knows Alexander's every wound by heart as if they were his own.

"Aphrodite loved Hephæstos, his limp and all. She never left him."

"Yes," Alexander laughs. "But away from the eyes of the dwarfish ugly Hephæstos, she was bedding the tall handsome Ares."

Hephæstion looks away.

"When Krateros refused her invitation and sent her word that Makedonian highborn women did not share meals with men, she pushed away his guards and unexpectedly walked into his tent while he was eating and told him that she was Persian, not Makedonian, and he had dishonored her and had dared him to write to me and ask how she should be treated. Krateros thought better of throwing her out of his tent and sheepishly invited her to eat with him."

"Krateros sure knows how to treat the Queen."

"With all his bark, Krateros took good care of her." Alexander pauses.

"They told me that when she came down with fever and was too sick to travel, he stayed behind with her until she was better. Imagine that! He spent seven months with her— more than I have ever spent with her, since I wedded her. Well, at least he no longer speaks ill of her to my face."

Hephæstion closes his eyes and tries to think of a slow and painful way to kill Krateros… Maybe the Makedonian rack… pull him apart limb by limb and feed his bloody carcass to wild dogs…

Let Hades have the bastard! All of him! Flesh and bones! Devour him whole!

Alexander takes a deep breath.

"I took the Lands of the Persians by the blood of my men. She is taking my men one by one by her sweet beauty, spilling no blood." Alexander leans forward in the chair, closer to Hephæstion. "Krateros told me that he saw her every night, praying before her fire altar. He had a translator listen to her and bring back her words to him. Do you know what she was saying to the burning fire?"

"No."

"She said: *My Lord, please keep the king and my lover safe from mortal harm. Please keep the Lands and Waters of my beloved Persis safe from famine and the conquering armies.*"

Alexander leans back in the chair and smiles.

"I never know if she prays for my health— or my death!"

Hephæstion closes his eyes in pain. "Is she— well now?"

"Well… and happy to be back in Persia… as I am."

Alexander slowly stands up. "Are you coming?"

"No!"

"I will tell Krateros that you will host the next drinking feast, when you have gotten your fill of water!"

"Tell him what you like!"

Alexander smiles, eyeing Hephæstion unguardedly.

"Ah! Speaking of Hephæstos, Roxana had asked Krateros, the first night she had eaten with him, if you were related to Hephæstos— something about you looking yellowish and disfigured, with a limp."

"I am glad to know the Queen thinks so highly of me."

Alexander laughs.

"Apparently Krateros had laughed so hard, he almost knocked the flagon of wine off the food table. Krateros then volunteered to personally teach her everything about the Hellene gods. She says she likes Hermes, the messenger of the gods… she calls him the Divine Protector of the Persian Royal Couriers… I wonder if Krateros told her that Hermes is also the god of manhood."

Hephæstion sinks further into the water basin, hiding his anger.

He did not want to know what she thought of Hermes.

Her life had gone on so well without him for all these months…

"If you change your mind, come later."

"I am not coming!"

Alexander shrugs his shoulders and leaves the tent.

Hephæstion closes his eyes and tries hard to force the faces of Rošanak and Krateros eating and laughing out of his head. Anger and jealousy grips his heart.

Damn Krateros!

MIDDLE of the NIGHT

Well beyond midnight.

The noise of revelry in the Royal Army Camp is beginning to die down as the wine and food and sleep wrap around the Maka Desert survivors and the Royal Army Camp dwellers.

Everyone glad to still be alive, after so many had died.

Hephæstion has finally fallen asleep in his warm water basin. The scent of orange blossoms fills his senses. He takes a deep breath half asleep and fills his lungs with old memories of Rošanak. He feels a soft caress on his hand and slowly opens his eyes. The blurry shape by his bathing basin starts to sharpen as he slowly wakens. His body fills with air and happiness at the sight of her.

"Roshanak…" Hephæstion softly whispers.

Rošanak empties the rest of the scented oil into the water basin and drops the small bottle into the water.

They both watch it sink below the surface as the bottle drinks and fills with precious water.

She looks at Hephæstion, slowly reaches and gently touches the golden ring dangling from an avastâ strap around his neck, resting on his chest in the bath water.

You have come…

And the land of the lions and the lizards…

… has turned into a Persian Paradise under your feet…

"I lost weight in the desert… it became too loose on all my fingers… I was afraid it might fall off and be swallowed by the sand, so I wore it around my neck! Closer to my heart." Hephæstion whispers in Persian.

Rošanak bends down her head and softly kisses Hephæstion's hand which is resting on the edge of the bathing basin. Her hair falls on his hand and in the water. He raises his hand and caresses her hair and face. Happy tears openly fall on her face. He pulls her face toward him and kisses her mouth with hunger.

Her heart skips a beat. She prays silently in her heart.

My Lord, please forgive me…

… they said they had all died in the Desert of Emptiness.

"Most of my men died in the desert. Do you know how I survived two months with no water and no food?"

Rošanak shakes her head wordlessly with tears falling on her face and into his bath water.

Hephæstion smiles and moves his head closer to her face and drinks her tears.

"I remembered those days in India when you kept me alive on love alone by denying me food and water…

"When I was thirsty— almost every moment of every day I would remember the taste of the raindrops I drank from your skin the night I claimed you in my tent in India. And the memory of those raindrops quenched my thirst.

"And when I was hungry— almost every moment of every day I would remember the taste of your mouth the first time I kissed you blindfolded in your tent in India. And the memory of your kisses fed my hunger."

Hephæstion gently runs his wet fingers through her silky yâsmined hair.

"And when the smell of death filled my body, I closed my eyes and remembered the scent of jasmine in your hair… and the scent of orange blossom oil on your skin."

He caresses her soft lips with the tip of his finger.

"The love sighs from these lips swallowed the sound of dying in my ears."

She kisses the tip of his finger.

"I would have died in the Desert of Death, if you had not loved me in the Land of Seven Rivers."

Rošanak leans forward and kisses Hephæstion's lips.

Hephæstion whispers into her mouth.

"I am getting out of the water and when I do, I am going to hold you tightly in my arms, so you can feel how my heart is beating for you… so I can feel your beauty bleeding into my blood…"

Her heart melts.

"Go now, if you do not desire my love… if you remain, neither god nor man may come between our bodies…"

She kisses his face again.

He kisses her back.

Her kisses were a wordless tongue he understood completely.

ROYAL TOMB of KURUŠ the ELDER. PÂRSÂKATA. PÂRSÂ
YEAR 13 of ALEXANDER, MONTH 5, DYSTROS
YEAR 6 of ALEXANDER, MONTH 11, SAMIYAMAŠ
FOLLOWING MONTH
MID-DAY

Whoever you are, from wherever you have come,
for I know you will come.
I am Kuruš, who founded the Empire of the Persians.
Grudge me not therefore, this little earth that rests under my body...

"... You who bless me, may a Great King bless you," Rošanak whispers quietly under her breath, hushed as if she were uttering sacred words of prayer.

All the Persians knew by heart the words on the golden table upon which the golden casket of Kuruš the Elder rested...

... in his Royal Tomb in Pârsâkata, the Land of the First Tribe of the Persians...

... the most royal of all noble Persian tribes... the First of the Persians...

Rošanak slowly gets out of her carriage and bends her knees and bows her head low toward the Royal Tomb that had been built inside the ancient sacred Âyadana of Divine Goddess Ânâhitâ.

All that was now left of the ancient âyadana were tall white columns, slowly bending their stony knees to the ravages of hanatâ...

She walks slowly into the sacred grounds and sits on a wooden bench in the blooming sweet-scented heavenly gardens surrounding the sacred âyadana columns of the Tomb of Kuruš the Elder.

A light breeze brushes against her and passes quickly.

She felt slightly unsettled... unwell... weary...

They had been traveling back toward the heartland since Karmâna and before that since Hind and she had not been feeling well for the past month.

Traveling in the carriage was making her sick!

A small stream dances under her feet and rolls toward a large water basin.

It was early spring and No'rouz was in the air... approaching fast...

She looks around her.

Alexander dismounts his horse and heads for the sacred tomb.

She breathes in the fragrant air.

The heavenly Persian gardens surrounding the remains of the sacred âyadana of the Royal Tomb of Kuruš the Elder were filled with sweet spring flowers and bees and butterflies... golden daffodils and purple irises and white narcissus and purple violets... yâsmin vines knotted through the gardens scented the air seductively.

Wild spring flowers planted by the Guardian Angels of the Wise Lord stretched beyond the Persian gardens.

They said Kuruš himself had planted many of the plants and trees and flowers himself, with his own royal hands. He loved gardening and working the earth… they said he had declared once that no work was more honorable than working the dirt… making earth bloom and blossom… that gardeners were beloved of all gods.

Every single flower and flowering bush and plant and tree had been blessed by the Wise Lord himself to keep faithful watch around the Royal Tomb of his beloved Great King… renewing every year with the blessed coming of the new year in spring.

The sweet-scented pure air refreshes her. Butterflies fly all around her; one lands quietly on her lap.

Her own gardens in Baktra were now in full bloom…

She looks at the rolling water in the stream below her feet and remembers her beloved blood sister and utters a prayer.

"Divine Ânâhitâ, bless my sister…"

She closes her eyes and smiles sadly.

In former years in Pârsâ… she could not have been more than ten years old… she had lain around a murmuring stream in the royal gardens of Pârsâ Palaces, together with her blood sister and her royal sisters, the Royal Daughters of the Fourth Artakhšaçâ and the Third Dâriuš…

It was No'rouz and the royal gardens of Pârsâ were filled with spring flowers, blooming everywhere… and blossoming apple trees too…

Her beloved blood sister, Parânak, had sweetly uttered an old poem:

"Lie down beside the rambling stream,
And watch the dead leaves floating by…
… and know that…
This is a sign…
… of the fleeting nature of life…"

The Royal Daughters had laughed playfully and had splashed Parânak with cool water from the rambling stream.

She rests her head on the wooden bench and slowly drifts.

Life was so sweet in the former days… before it had turned so bitter…

When Parânak had died of grief, she had thought of this poem, imagining her sister floating away like a dead autumn leaf on the ebbing stream of life.

"Rošanak?"

Rošanak opens her eyes and looks up at the Persian standing in front of her.

The man bows his head and says urgently in a low voice, "You might not remember me. I am Aršana, the head of the Pârsâkata Tribe, second brother to your royal father."

Rošanak gathers herself respectfully and slowly tries to stand up.

"Mâr Bani Aršana."

"Rošanak. Sit down and listen to me carefully. There is not much time!"

"My Lord?"

"The Bâbiruviya eunuch— Alexander's wretched lying greedy whore— has accused me of robbing the Tomb of Kuruš the Elder, because I gave him no golden gifts."

Rošanak slowly sits down and holds her breath. Lines appear quickly around her eyes.

Aršana looks around urgently and hurriedly continues in a hushed voice.

"Everyone has sworn a sacred oath of secrecy. No one will talk. Everyone will take the secret to their graves, before telling the wretched Makedonian invaders."

Rošanak's voice fails her.

"My Lord?" faintly.

"The Royal Purple Robe of Kuruš and his Royal Scepter and Royal Bow and Quiver of Arrows and his Sacred Cup were removed from his Royal Tomb and taken to Bakhtriš in haste, after Dâriuš was put to the sword by the noble heads of the Seven Persian Families in the old village of Øara in Parøawa, close to the City of a Hundred Gates, the ancient capital of Parøawa— and everyone swore an oath of loyalty to Bayasa, your father, under the throne name of the Fifth Khšâyaøiya Artakhšaçâ."

Rošanak's heart skips a beat. And then her heart starts beating faster, pounding restlessly in her chest.

Dear God!

"There is no time to mention all the names of the nobles of the Seven Persian Families. Everyone knows who they are. One was your own father. We are all bound to an ancient blood oath that our fathers took after the death of Kuruš the Elder— to never, ever let another Persian King die in the hands of our enemies!"

He shakes his head with deep regret.

"First, we all tried desperately to reason with Dâriuš, hoping to avoid disaster— but he had lost his heart after the death of Setâreh.

"He was getting desperate to gain the release of the rest of his Royal Family. He was afraid that Alexander would rape his Royal Daughters as he had raped his Royal Wife. No Persian King had ever raped a Royal Woman of the fallen lands they had conquered, as a right of conquest— never!

"Mâr bîti Ariâbarzâna had already died defending Pârsâ and Mâr bît šarri Tiršata was in the hands of the enemy."

He looks away in despair.

"We were all consumed by grief and guilt and shame. The Makedonian King had refused to ransom any of our women and children who had fallen into his hands at Issos, not even the women of Artâvazda who were personally known to him. We all knew what the enemy men were already doing to our women— and we all knew how they treated young boys of their own race—"

"—no one thought they would treat our sons any differently— better to let our sons die honorably in battle than let them live to become whores of such wretched men!"

He looks back at Rošanak.

"We had no other choice!" he says in a low, haunted voice.

He looks around cautiously and continues, lowering his voice even further.

"Bayasa offered himself as the substitute king to take upon himself all the bad omens for the Great King, but Dâriuš refused him. We all knew what Alexander wanted the most was the head of Dâriuš. He had not accepted the fair offer of ransom and had turned down the offer of peace and lawful marriage alliance.

"After a secret Rite of Ascension, your father assumed the Persian Crown as the rightful heir to the Royal Hakhâmanišiya. Your father died as a king by the swift blade of one of the Persian nobles in his royal service, before his body was torn to pieces by Alexander's men— the noble turned the blade on himself afterward. The Great King was dead before he was tied to those tall trees. Royal Fire was doused in all the sacred âyadanas across the Lands by the order of the Âtravaxš of this temple to mark his death." He points with his head to the crumbling Âyadana of Divine Goddess Ânâhitâ.

"The Seven Nobles and the Zarathuštra Athravans have hidden the Royal Purple Robe of Kuruš and the rest of the sacred kingly objects, so the Makedonian could never succeed the Great Kings to the Persian Throne."

Rošanak's eyes well up and her tears begin to fall.

Aršana shakes his head again with dismay.

"It was all agreed and decided among the Seven Nobles after the defeat at Black Eagle. But we foolishly waited too long and hoped it would all come to pass. What we could not agree to as the Nobles of the Seven Families, we understood all too well as husbands— and fathers of young sons and daughters.

"We should not have waited so long! May the Wise Lord have mercy on us, when he judges us on the final Judgment Day— for we not only lost our women and children— we lost his Empire on Earth to his evil enemies!"

Words fail Rošanak.

Aršana takes a deep breath and looks around in utter misery.

"We all used to hunt lions around here when we were young. Who would have thought then that it was our wretched fate to decide the death of our own brother by our own hands one day."

He looks up at the heavens with tears in his eyes.

"Our fathers watch us and weep!"

He pauses, swallows hard and looks back at Rošanak and bows his head.

"I am a dead man— I have failed the Wise Lord and I have failed the Great King— but no matter what happens to me, remember this. If you have a son and he is raised a Persian and he reaches manhood, the Nobles of the Seven Persian Families and the Zarathuštra Athravans and Maguš will support him and his royal bloodline and will acknowledge his blood ties to the Hakhâmanišiya—"

"—even though he is a half-breed and carries the blood of the enemy king."

Heavens fill with mercy.

....

Alexander looks around.

Years ago when he was in the City of the Persians, he had not come to honor the Tomb of the Great Persian King who by all accounts was the first of all the Great Kings. Kuros was the Great King he had always tried to surpass.

The Royal City itself had surrendered and the treasury had been emptied… but he was warned by all, even by Aristandros and the seers from the Two Lands, not to walk on these sacred grounds or he would incur the wrath of the divine goddess who protected the Tomb of the Kuros the Father.

The omens had been unfavorable for four months and then they had burned Persepolis and had left for Ecbatana to hunt Darius to his bloody end…

Alexander looks up.

The modest white limestone tomb inside the remains of the sacred temple pulsated with timeless royalty, with tall jasmine vines tightly embracing the tall gray-white columns of the sacred temple wrapping around the Royal Tomb.

Alexander climbs the six broad limestone steps, ignoring his painful body, and walks into the small chamber through a low and narrow entrance.

He gasps with disbelief.

All that was inside the Royal Tomb was a gold casket, resting on a golden table with a golden inscription… dead bones scattered on the ground…

A tall Babylonian bends his head low and follows Alexander inside and interprets the inscription on the golden table for him.

> *"Whoever you are, from wherever you have come, for I know you shall come.*
> *"I am Kuros, who founded the Empire of the Persians.*
> *"Grudge me not therefore, this little earth that rests under my body."*

Alexander touches the golden inscription on the golden table with the tips of his kingly fingers. He stands there for a moment as anger builds in him and then turns around and leaves the Tomb. He walks down the tall steps and yells at the royal guards, "Bring me the new satrap and the guardians of the Royal Tomb!"

The royal guards quickly stand to attention and obey.

Alexander beckons Deinokrates, the Rhodian Architect.

"I want this Royal Tomb restored. Ask Hephæstion for all the gold you need."

"Yes, Alexander."

Alexander turns and demands angrily from Aršana and the athravans.

"The Tomb of Kuros has been desecrated! His bones scattered all around! Where are all the offerings in his Royal Tomb?"

Rošanak's legs weaken.

Aršana bows his head politely. "King Alexander, the tomb is generations old, many items have been lost over many years past."

Alexander narrows his eyes at Aršana.

"My eunuch told me that the Royal Tomb was filled with gold and golden treasures."

"King Alexander, Kuruš the Elder liked simplicity. He preferred the beautiful Persian gardens around his tomb to hoards of gold heaped inside it!" And he speaks the truth.

Alexander yells angrily at the top of his voice.

"Where is his Purple Robe? I heard rumors that you have taken the Sacred Robe of the Great Kings to prevent me from ascending to the Throne of the Achæmenids!"

Aršana bows again politely.

"King Alexander! My enemies have filled your kingly ears with false rumors." And he lies with a golden tongue.

Alexander orders his royal guards. "Bring him to Persepolis! I will judge him there, on the ruined site of his own ancestors!"

Aršana steps back.

"King Alexander— I—"

"Alexander, please!"

Rošanak takes Alexander's arm and quietly pleads with him.

"Orsines is the noble head of the Persis Tribe!"

Alexander ignores her plea, pulls his arm away from her and grunts angrily, "If he is innocent, he has nothing to fear from my justice!"

More than half of his satraps had revolted in his absence and he meant to make an example of all of them! And not just the Persians… his own men too… all running wild while he was in India… gold and power had turned them all into thieves and liars! He had already ordered all the satraps to disband their satrapal armies and by his orders all the troublesome mercenaries were to return to Hellas under the Exiles Decree. None was to remain in Asia to cause more trouble for him.

Even lame Harpalos, his own noble boyhood friend he had left guarding the royal funds at Babylon had stolen five thousand talents of royal gold, bought a thousand Hellene mercenaries and had fled to Athenai with his whore in fear for his life, when the Makedonian envoys have arrived in Babylon to inform him that the King was alive and was returning to Persia with the Royal Army.

And Orsines was not even appointed by him! He had declared himself the Satrap of Persis without the knowledge or permission of the King.

No one was to be spared… no matter how much the Queen wept and begged and pleaded on her delicate half-Persian knees!

PÂRSÂ RUINS. FOOT of the MOUNTAIN of MERCY
YEAR 13 of ALEXANDER, MONTH 5, DYSTROS
YEAR 6 of ALEXANDER, MONTH 11, SAMIYAMAŠ
DAYS LATER
AFTERNOON

One hundred and eleven long limestone steps to the top of the terrace…

Haunted silence…

Rošanak slowly dismounts her horse. Her eyes widen… her mouth opens even wider… her jaw drops… her skin goes ghostly white… her heart skips a beat and then another… her knees soften… her body fails to obey her grief… not even a single tear…

Life vanishes…

Heavens sink into utter darkness…

Pârsâ was dead… utterly destroyed… the stench of death hung over the blackened carcasses of the beloved city of the Persians… even the ridges of the mountains around Pârsâ were cloaked and shrouded and veiled with the cloth of death…

Splendid sky-high columns that once kissed the face of the heavens were now humble dust and broken-faced stones… tiled walls of lions and bulls and lotus flowers were now ruined heaps of rubble and wreckage.

At the foot of the Mountain of Mercy, there had been no mercy for the beloved Pârsâ.

Rošanak bleeds tears.

"No! My Lord! No!

"O Alexander… What have you done?"

Was the wrong of one king washed by the wrong of another king?

How was evil weighed and measured and avenged?

World vanishes…

She closes her eyes. Being alive fills her body with unspeakable pain and shame.

> *"My Lord… how could this be?"*
>
> *"My Lord, what did the Persians do to deserve this?*
>
> *… Please, My Lord, tell me… I want to know…"*

She screams in silence.

The Athenian Themistokles had said of Athenai a few generations back:

> *"Suppose that Athenai was abandoned and only her temples and ruins of the buildings remained. Surely as time passed, men who came upon it would find it hard to believe that we who once lived here, were ever powerful."*

What would he have said if he had seen the burned and blackened Pârsâ?

The Great King had taken him in after the same Athenians had exiled him for saving Athenai and had gifted him cities in the Lands by the Sea for his bravery in battle.

Wind howls…

Scent of kapautaka lotus flowers fills her body…

Joyful drum beats… beating in the distance…

She opens her eyes.

Her eyes widen… again…

> *"Hurry up, Rošanak. If we do not get to the Apadâna Hall by the sunrise, we will miss No'rouz with the Great King!" Utâna says hurriedly as he runs past her quickly, racing up the Great Stairway.*
>
> *Persian royal guards stand proudly in their magnificent arm and armor, glinting gloriously with golden bits catching all the early rays of the golden morning sun.*
>
> *"You are Royal Daughters! Do not run up the stairs like the daughters of the women of the royal court!" Farânak says in a hushed voice to Parânak and Rošanak and takes Parânak's hand firmly.*

Rošanak's rosy gown flows in the dusty wind blowing across the desolate stony steps. Her childhood memories dance around her.

> *"Rošanak! A whole year of bad fortune, if you miss No'rouz!" Utâna yells at the top of his voice from the top of the Great Stairway.*
>
> *Rošanak is ten. She smiles brightly. She pushes the kapautaka lotus flower into her belt, pulls up her gown and starts hurrying after Utâna. Her brothers run past her.*
>
> *She yells, "Wait for me!"*
>
> *"Be lazy! Be late! Be unlucky for a whole year!" Utâna yells, his voice starting to fade.*
>
> *She yells at the top of her voice, "Utâna! Wait for me! I am coming! Do not leave me behind! Wait!"*
>
> *Her mother bellows after her, shaking her head side-to-side with dismay. "Rošanak!" Her voice trails off.*
>
> *"No one has ever been punished by the Great King for running around on No'rouz!" Bayasa comforts Farânak, as they walk up the Great Stairway.*
>
> *"Your daughter has no dignity! If Dukšiš Setâreh and Ummi Šarri Sisygambis see her running around like a wild beast, they will be all too eager to remind me how dignified and gracious their Royal Daughters behave in the Royal Court of Dâriuš!"*
>
> *Bayasa laughs.*
>
> *"Just remind them that you have borne me three splendid sons!"*
>
> *Farânak glows.*

Rošanak runs past the Apadâna. The Apadâna is too big and she is too small. All the Ten Thousand Anauša could fill the Apadâna Hall.

She runs faster.

Everything glitters with gold and happiness.

This is the first No'rouz in the third year of the Third Dâriuš, the new Great King of the Persians and the brother of her father of a different mother and father.

He has finally crushed the rebellion and brought Mudrâya back into the folds of the Empire and the spirits at the Royal Court are high.

Rošanak crashes into the Golden Throne Hall, the splendid Hall of One Hundred Columns.

The hall is filled with the Royal Family and the Nobles of the Seven Persian Families and the Kinsmen and Kindred… and the Kingsmen… the whole world… all who matter… with all that matters.

She folds in half and catches her breath and looks around hurriedly.

The golden hall is packed with golden people murmuring with anticipation, but there is no sign of Utâna and her blood brothers.

The royal guards eye her under their stern brows.

She straightens and quickly pulls out the kapautaka lotus flower and walks straight into the glinting glowing golden hall, heading as straight as a Persian arrow for the Royal Throne.

She can see the Great King. The Third Dâriuš is sitting on the golden Persian Throne with its silver feet of lions, wearing the sacred Royal Purple Robe of Great Kings, embroidered with golden griffins. His wounded right ankle is wrapped tightly with white linen. Dukšiš Sisygambis and Dukšiš Setâreh and her royal sisters, Setâreh and Dripeyti are all standing faithfully behind the Third Dâriuš. Mâr bît šarri Tiršata is too young to attend such an important event.

She elbows her way through the gold-scented royal line. She quickly walks in front of the next noble in line and bows down and sinks to her knees before the Great King. The noble gives her a shocked look and sneers discreetly.

Hushed silence.

The palace eunuchs and royal guards stir forward.

Dâriuš sees her and leans forward, favoring his wounded ankle. He raises his hand and declares, "A Royal Daughter!"

The palace eunuchs and royal guards step backward.

Dâriuš smiles and beckons Rošanak forward.

She smiles brightly and gets to her feet and approaches the Great King.

Dâriuš extends his right hand to Rošanak. She bows low and kisses his hand and offers him the kapautaka lotus flower.

Dâriuš takes the fragrant lotus flower, smells it and smiles, beckons her closer and points with his eyes. "Rošanak, see all those in the royal line?"

Rošanak timidly looks behind her and then looks back at the Great King and nods shyly.

"Only the most beloved Queen of the King can approach him before all!"

Rošanak nods understandingly and her face warms. She looks down at her feet, embarrassed.

Dâriuš laughs and teases her.

"Next time you cut in front of everyone else in line, I will have to take you as a wife!"

Rošanak blushes and giggles. Her whole body tingles and warms with the thought of marrying the Great King one day.

Dâriuš beckons one of palace eunuchs. The palace eunuch approaches quickly kneeling before the Great King with a magnificent silver chest. Dâriuš reaches inside the chest and pulls out a beautiful golden Manyâkâ and gives it to Rošanak.

A royal gift from the Great King.

Rošanak looks happily at the golden necklace.

"Do you like it?"

Rošanak nods her head eagerly and answers wordlessly with glinting eyes.

Dâriuš smiles.

"Remember, Rošanak… the Royal Women are the guardians of the Great Kings of the Lands and Waters and the most beloved ba^{n}daka of the Kings of the Persians." He points with his eyes to the palace eunuchs and royal guards. "They are all your subjects! When you are a Royal Woman, command them fearlessly as such, at the pleasure of the King!"

Rošanak smiles and nods her head. Her golden earrings dangle in the golden air.

That was the command of the Great King she was to live by…

"Good! Now go see your royal grandmother! She misses you!" Dâriuš smiles and points with his eyes. "And no running. Royal Daughters sway like airy mountain breezes… they do not run like wild Nisâya horses!"

Rošanak bows down again. She looks at her hands for another glimpse of her golden gift, and then looks up again.

"Ah!"

Everything has turned into ash and dust.

She is standing on a barren stony terrace. She turns around quickly. Everything has vanished. She turns around one more time and then again…

Blackened ashes swirl around her on the blackened terrace…

Her body fills again with pain…

That was the last No'rouz celebrated at Pârsâ...

If she knew then what the gods of other lands had fated for Pârsâ, she would have chained herself to the tall columns and burned in the sacred fire along with the rest of Pârsâ when the angel of death had come.

She takes a step forward.

Crunch!

She takes a step backward startled.

Crunch!

She quickly looks down at her feet. Apadâna Terrace is covered with pavastâ, broken fragments of clay tablets... broken pieces of the most beloved Empire... the Broken Empire!

She looks around her, utterly despondent... she screams tearfully at the top of her voice:

"Where were the Arštibara... the One Thousand Royal Bodyguards of the Great King... the bravest of the braves... noble sons of the Seven Persians?

"Where were the Ten Thousand Anauša?

"Where were the valiant Warriors and the Zarathuštra Athravans?

"Where were the Guardian Angels of the Wise Lord?

"Where were the Protectors of Pârsâ?

"Where was the Wise Lord?"

She opens her hand and the golden necklace slides and falls out of her hand onto the stony ground of the once grand terrace.

"Manyâkâ..."

She sinks to the ground, carelessly scraping her knees, and desperately sifts through the blackened ashes and broken fragments for her kingly gifted golden necklace.

Careless fool!

How could she have dropped the precious golden gift from the Great King?

She searches and searches and searches... but there is nothing but ashes and dust and broken clay fragments beneath her fingers. A sharp fragment cuts her finger.

Life to Death... Death to ash... Ash to dust... Dust to dust... Dust to wind...

She has finally lost all her reason. She stands up and wipes her blackened hands and bloody finger on her once rosy royal gown.

"Ah!" Her heart nearly stops.

In front of her, on the barren Apadâna Terrace, three Royal Women were standing. All dressed in royal purple gowns... all splendidly golden crowned... their faces covered with mournful veils of sorrow...

Behind them, on the barren steps, stood all the Royal Women of the Persians... all dressed in royal colors... crimson and purple... their faces also shrouded with veils of sorrow...

Rošanak immediately bows low and sinks to her knees and tries to hide her blackened bloody hands in the folds of her rosy gown.

A haunting voice dances into the desolate wind calling to her… with a tongue more ancient than hers.

"Rošanak, Royal Daughter of King Artakhšaçâ and Dukšiš Farânak. Roxana, Queen of the Lands of the Bitter Sea..."

Rošanak cannot breathe.

"These sacred grounds are the realms of the Great Kings and their Beloved Queens."

Rošanak's eyes well with tears. The haunting words fall like dusty rain on her dusty head.

"By the favor of the Wise Lord, no mortal may ever live where the Divine Persian Kings hold immortal Royal Court."

"The destroyer of Pârsâ and the Lands and the glorious palaces of the Persian Kings is cursed by his own deeds! He will not see his seeds take root in the Lands of the Persians."

"Leave Pârsâ to the Persians."

"Go to the HighLands of the Barbarians, Queen of the UpLanders."

"Look now and despair... Do not return here."

"We command you in the name of Auramazdâhâ, who is the beginning and the end. Who sees what cannot be seen by the eyes of the mortals."

"NO!" Rošanak closes her eyes and moans in anguish.

She opens her eyes.

A Great King stands before her, holding a royal bow. A quiver full of arrows with golden tips are hanging from his shoulder.

A pair of golden lions are circling them.

The lions leap…

He swiftly pulls out a handful of golden arrows and shoots the lions… one after the other…

One of the golden lions falls dead at her feet. His blood splatters on her dusty rose gown. Red blood of the golden lion stains the royal rose…

The Great King looks at her with a piercing gaze and cloudy face.

"I am Dâriuš, the Great King, the King of Kings, the King in Persia… the King in all the Lands… By the grace of Auramazdâhâ, I built this city. I built it secure and beautiful and adequate, just as I meant to.

"Now our beloved Pârsâ is a ruin, the lair of lions and leopards and lizards."

Rošanak looks down at the dead golden lion bleeding at her feet. She looks up.

Another Great King stands before her, holding a royal scepter. He opens his arms wide.

"I am Khašâyârša, the Great King, Son of Dâriuš, the Great King, the King of Kings, the King in Persia. Behold the palaces within this city of Pârsâ, which I built and which my father built. What is seen is all that we built by the favor of the Wise Lord."

"May the Wise Lord protect me and my Kingdom… and what was built by me and what was built by my father."

Mâm Auramazdâ pâtu utamai xšaçam…

She holds her breath.

King Khašâyâr-šan… the Commander of Heroes… as splendid as she had always imagined him to be…

Rošanak feels warm… she looks around.

Unbearable heat…

Fire…

Everything is burning and blazing around her… the magnificent tall cedar columns start to fall all around her, nearly crushing her. She falls to her knees, raising her hands over her head to shield herself from burning falling timbers… pleading faintly…

"My Lord! Please! Forgive me! Please!"

Silence…

Everything vanishes again…

A sandstorm rages through the desolate ruins.

Her horse rears and runs away.

She covers her face with her hands. Her face blackens with burnt ashes. Blood smears on her face. She moans. "No! My Lord! I implore you! Please be merciful! I beg you! Please! Spare my lover!"

Wind howls…

Rošanak gets to her feet. She looks around for a sign, a sign from the Wise Lord, but it is just the faceless wind scattering the blackened ashes on and around the Apadâna.

She cries.

"My Lord! Please! Forgive my deeds… Judge me by my words and my thoughts! Do not banish me from the Lands of my royal ancestors!"

She begs and pleads and prays.

"Divine Ánâhitâ! Shield me from the evil that surrounds me!"

Wind howls…

"Roxana!"

She turns toward the voice of Alexander. He is approaching her. Hephæstion is walking behind him. They are both wearing plain long white robes, Shrouds of the Dead. She covers her mouth with her hand and cries.

"No!"

"Roxana!"

Rošanak feels a sharp pain in her belly. She grabs her belly, twists in pain, sinks to the ground carelessly and rips her dusty rose gown, scraping her knees again.

"No! My Lord! No!"

"Roxana!" Alexander rushes toward her.

She twists in pain on the barren stony ground of the Pârsâ.

Alexander kneels down next to her.

Hephæstion catches up hurriedly.

"She is bleeding!" Alexander points to the drops of blood on the ground, shaking his head with dismay.

Hephæstion bends down and lifts her up quickly and shelters her in his arms. He turns and puts her on his horse and rides down the steps… all one hundred and eleven of them.

Alexander lingers for a moment and looks at the blood where Rošanak had been standing. He closes his eyes in pain.

He should never have brought her here.

Her forgiving words in Baktra were the words of a young girl, ignorant of reality.

Even he himself could not bear to look at what he had done with his own hands.

His blind wrath had brought such devastation to the people and the lands he had meant to rule.

The Babylonian seers had divined that the Persians would curse him for the burning of Pârsâ with their every breath.

The Magi had cursed him for all eternity for the burning of the sacred words of the God of the Persians.

He was the son of a god, cursed by the lips of the sons of men.

ALEXANDER'S ROYAL TENT. EDGE of PÂRSÂ RUINS
LATER that NIGHT

"The Queen…" The Old Persian Healer talks quietly to Alexander's back.

Hephæstion interprets his Persian words for Alexander's ears.

Alexander is leaning on the bed post, watching over Rošanak.

Rošanak is sleeping in his royal bed in the royal tent, tossing and turning restlessly.

"King Alexander!"

"Alexander!"

The Old Persian Healer puts his hand on Alexander's shoulder.

"I am sorry!"

Alexander does not move.

"The Queen has miscarried… again!"

Hephæstion's face folds in pain.

He did not even know she was with child again.

Neither did Alexander, from the look on his face.

Was it his?

Or was it Alexander's?

He looks at Alexander's eyes.

There was no need to interpret.

He understood all too well the sorrowful tone of the voice of the old wound-healer.

The Old Persian Healer lowers his voice.

"She needs rest! She is too weak! She has lost a lot of blood. More traveling right now might cause her mortal harm!" He whispers. "Your Highness! Are you hearing me? The Queen needs to heal! If she gets with another child, it could be fatal not only for the child, but for the Queen as well!"

"Alexander, Roxana needs to heal! She needs rest! If she gets with another child, it could kill her!" Hephæstion quietly interprets.

Alexander takes a deep breath and closes his eyes.

"We will rest at Susa!"

"Alexander!"

Silence.

"Alexander, please!"

Silence.

Four

MURMURS

ROYAL PALACE. ROYAL CITY of ÇÛŠÂ. ROYAL LANDS at ÛVJA
YEAR 13 of ALEXANDER, MONTH 6, XANDIKOS
YEAR 6 of ALEXANDER, MONTH 12, VIYAXANA
MID-DAY

This Palace which I built at the Royal City of Çûšâ,
its ornamentation was brought from afar...

Rošanak runs the tips of her fingers on the Royal Dipî carved on the massive palace doors at the Royal City of Çûšâ, Ša-ša-an, the old city of the old Elam-tu.

The naucaina timber was brought from Labnâna...
The yaka timber was brought from Gandâra and from Karmâna.
The gold was brought from Sparda and from Bakhtriš... the lapis-lazuli and carnelian was brought from Sughuda. The turquoise from Uwarazmiy, the silver and ebony from Mudrâya, the ornamentation from Yaunâ, the ivory from Kûša and from Hinduya and from Harahuvatiš.
The stone-cutters who wrought the stone, those were Yaunâ and Spardiya.
The goldsmiths were Mâda and Mudrâya.
The men who wrought the wood, those were Spardiya and Mudrâya.
The men who wrought the baked brick, those were Bâbiruviya.
The men who adorned the wall, those were Mâda and Mudrâya.

I am the Great King... King of Kings...
King of all the Lands and all the People...
aita tya kartam ava visam vašnâ Auramazdâhâ.

Rošanak looks around again and lingers by the giant gates of the royal palace.
This was her first time in the royal palace at the Royal City of Çûšâ.
The old palace murmured with haunting sorrow... as if she knew her beloved son, Pârsâ, had died... burned to ashes... blackened with shame of captivity... bent to his knees by gasta hainâ. The First Dâriuš had lived in the Çûšâ royal palace while Pârsâ was being built. They said that the First Dâriuš loved the royal palace at Çûšâ the most, but even the old palace of the old Elam-tu knew that Pârsâ was the Axis of the Empire... its heart... and blood... and pulse... its flesh and bones... the Kingly Palace of all royal palaces, loved by the King of all Kings... and by the God of all gods... God of all kings... the Wise Lord...

Rošanak takes a deep breath and enters the royal palace silently with soft feet of sorrow. Palace guards and eunuchs bow low as she passes through the tiled hallways.

Faithful Persian Anauša forever stood guard silently on the walls of the royal palace at the Royal City of Çûšâ.

Even they knew Pârsâ had died.

They had heard the heartbreaking tears of the First Dâriuš falling on its black ashes when Pârsâ was burning… and they hung their heads low with the sorrow of their beloved king… eyes downcast and heavy… and their tiles, the color of the summer skies, had turned blackish like the color of a mourning heart… even the pure gold in their arm and armor refused to glint in the thousand rays of the sun and the hundred flickers of the fiery torches…

She takes another deep breath of pain.

Abi-Samar had arrived before her and had prepared her quarters.

Her grandmother and all her royal sisters had resided in the Queen's Quarters since they were left behind by Alexander in former years, and Abi-Samar had ordered the palace eunuchs to prepare the royal rooms on the top story of the old palace for her.

She wanted to be close to her royal kinsmen and kindred.

Alexander was to stay in the royal tent on the other side of the old palace.

She rests her tired hands on her aching belly for a long moment. Her heart stops and then starts again.

She was empty again… empty of life… empty of hope…

Her ancestral queens had fiercely demanded and her body had obediently handed them the seed of Alexander…

She was a Royal Woman… her body had remained faithful to the Great Kings, even though her heart had surrendered to the new king…

She closes her eyes in pain and then beckons Mâr'at Bani Âriyânnâz.

"Please go see my royal grandmother and my royal sisters. Ask them if I could be admitted to see them this afternoon."

Mâr'at Bani Âriyânnâz hesitates and bites her lip wordlessly.

"What?"

"Dukšiš, they should be coming to pay their respects to you, as the Queen Consort."

Rošanak eyes Mâr'at Bani Âriyânnâz and then looks away tiredly.

Her body still throbbed from her long journey in the carriage from Pârsâ. And she had not slept much since her haunted visit there…

She was aching and tired and weary, but it was unthinkable not to pay her respects to her royal grandmother immediately.

"She is my grandmother. It is my duty."

"Yes, Dukšiš."

ROYAL QUARTERS of DUKŠIŠ SISYGAMBIS
AFTERNOON

Rošanak enters the quarters of Dukšiš Sisygambis and her royal sisters in the royal palace of Çûšâ, followed by Mâr'at Bani Âriyânnâz and several palace eunuchs. In the Queen-Mother's antechamber, a pair of older Persian noble ladies are sitting on silver couches, chatting away. A few more are playing takh'teh nard.

One of the Persian noble ladies rushes to Rošanak and bows her head and dismisses the palace eunuchs and guides her toward the Queen-Mother's royal room. Mâr'at Bani Âriyânnâz silently remains behind.

"We were told that you had arrived, Dukšiš. The Queen-Mother is having a good day today. She might even remember you! Her memory of others fails her now and then."

Rošanak smiles wearily and nods and enters the royal room. The noble lady quietly announces her and then leaves, closing the door behind her softly.

The curtains are drawn, shading the golden royal room from the ruthless rays of the glaring sun. A young girl plays the santoor in a corner, filling the room with scented sadness.

Dukšiš Sisygambis is reclining on a large silver couch listening to the sound of the murmuring music.

Rošanak walks softly and kneels on the luxurious silky carpet in front of the old Ummi Šarri. "Grandmother."

Dukšiš Sisygambis looked a lot older than Rošanak remembered. She looked broken and painted with the pain of shame… all of her hair was now as white as the snow on the mountains of Bakhtriš. Her pale skin had not seen the rays of sun for years…

Dukšiš Sisygambis looks at Rošanak blankly with no sign of recognition in her sad big brown eyes.

Silence.

Then Dukšiš Sisygambis narrows her eyes at Rošanak and pushes herself up from the silver couch and sits straight. She leans forward and takes Rošanak's face in her old hands.

"O Child… Let me look at you! How you have grown!"

Rošanak kisses the rose-scented hands of her old grandmother holding her face, pushing back tears. "Grandmother."

She tasted like home. She tasted like her own mothers.

"O Yes… I remember well when you put your small arms around my neck during No'rouz, when you were a mere child, no more than seven years of age… and you kissed my face with honeyed sesame sticky lips and declared me your grandmother, just as I was to your royal sisters."

Dukšiš Sisygambis looks at the musician and dismisses her with a discreet nod, then looks back at Rošanak. She leans forward and kisses Rošanak's face.

She tasted like her daughter… she tasted like her youth…

Rošanak raises her hands and wraps them around Ummi Šarri's hands, and gently turns her head and kisses Sisygambis' rose-scented wrinkled hands again.

Dukšiš Sisygambis smiles and keeps Rošanak's face firmly in her hands.

"O Those eyes! Axšaina! Color of the old forests adorning the mountain ridges that circle the Sea of Varkâna, bathed generously in deep skies. You have your father's eyes."

Rošanak pushes back tears and nods. "Forgive me!"

"Why? What have you done?"

Tears roll down Rošanak's face unguardedly.

"My father…"

"O Child… Your father was a Royal Son… he did his duty. He did what I would have done had I been born a man!"

"Mâr Bani Aršana— he was executed while I lay in waste," Rošanak moans.

Everything was like a faded dream since Pârsâ…

Her heart had broken again and when it was sewn back together by the wound-healers, bits and pieces were missing… left on the Âpadâna Terrace… lost…

"His honorable death in the hands of his enemies was his blessed fate!"

"The old athravans… the Watchers of the Tomb of Kuruš were tortured when I—" She puts her hand on her belly.

"The Wise Lord protects his own faithful subjects! They were released and all have gotten well again."

"Grandmother…"

"Your mother wrote to me before your royal wedding and asked for my blessing!" Dukšiš Sisygambis leans forward and kisses Rošanak's face again, and wipes her tears with her old rose-scented hands.

"I sent you a royal purple gown for your wedding. Did you like it?"

"Yes. It was the most beautiful gown I had ever seen!" Rošanak nods and smiles.

It was the gown she had worn to the Âyadana of Divine Ânâhitâ that night… the one her father had torn up and wrapped her bloody wrists with… her mother had made cushions out of the rest of it later.

Dukšiš Sisygambis smiles. "You miss your beloved mother, yes?"

Rošanak nods wordlessly resting her head gently in the Ummi Šarri's lap.

She was tired… lost… she needed her mother… she needed a mother…

She wanted to crawl into a soft warm bed with cool pillows and have her mother bring her a plate full of Persian sweets and tell her old stories of Great Kings and their Queens… just like the days when she was a child…

"I have no one left to love me! My mothers! My sister! My life! All gone! My royal sisters shun me! They have ignored all my letters!"

Dukšiš Sisygambis caresses Rošanak's soft silky yâsmined hair.

"Setâreh and Dripeyti love you… as do I. You did what you had to do."

She takes a deep breath. "It has been nine years since that fateful day when we all came under the care of the Makedonian Conqueror. I am an old woman. Sooner or later the Wise Lord will remember his old heartbroken servant and will call me back to him to face my sorrowful judgment. But my girls, my beautiful granddaughters… they have to endure the sins of their father for an eternity longer."

She pauses and take a short breath, and then another.

"Their shame is greater than their love… they have to live with the shame that their own father lost his divine glory and lost the Empire… and will roam the Land of the Eternal Darkness for an eternity, shunned by his royal ancestors… spurned by his own fathers. Their shame has hardened them."

"The Makedonian King has been kind to me. He punished my King-Father, but spared his family… what was left of them! He wedded me in front of my mother and my kinsmen and kindred. I was not raped and shamed." Rošanak speaks quietly in her grandmother's lap.

Tears fill the old eyes of Dukšiš Sysigambis.

Her Royal Daughter Setâreh was raped and shamed in the bed of the same king.

"I knew the Makedonian would one day claim the Right of the Conqueror and take my virgin girls according to the custom of his ancestors. I showed him kindness… trying to delay the inevitable… the thought of him touching my virgin daughters makes my blood run cold! I pray for their death before they are forced to lay in the sinful bed of the same man who lay with their blood mother!"

Rošanak pushes back tears.

"He will be kind… he will not force himself unwanted upon my royal sisters!"

Dukšiš Sisygambis caresses Rošanak's hair gently, comforting her and herself.

"Whatever will be, will not be your doing! It is all in the hands of the Wise Lord! The Wise Lord has favored the Makedonian in the arts of war… but has not blessed him with a rightful son and heir! All he has is a bastard son born from a half-breed whore with the blood of a traitor to the Great King. His blood will disappear with his death and Âryânâ will be reclaimed by the Persians!"

Rošanak tears up again.

"It is me! I am the one with the blame! My womb is a wasteland. It kills any manly seed planted in it! I will die childless and will be forgotten… as I am cursed by the ghosts of my royal ancestors!"

"Nonsense! Your royal bloodline goes back to the First Dâriuš himself! It is the Makedonian whose seed is cursed by our royal ancestors."

Old Dukšiš closes her eyes in pain of utter shame.

"I wish my womb had expelled my firstborn, before he could bring such shame to his blood mother! It is I who is cursed, not you! My name will be forgotten in my beloved lands… no mother will ever name her daughter after me, remembering that it was I who brought into this world the man who lost our beloved Lands and Waters to a cursed barbarian half his years!"

"Grandmother! I will remember you!"

Eyes of the old Dukšiš fills with tears. "No, Child… I wish to be forgotten!"

She looks away. Her old face creases and folds… and becomes older.

"The blessed is Kîanuš, the Royal Mother of the First Dâriuš. When the mothers name their sons Dâriuš, they are honoring her Royal Son— not mine! I pray to the Wise Lord every day to strike the name of my son from the pages of the Book of Kings and all the Royal Journals and Royal Archives and Royal Storehouses!

"I told Artašatu, my son, to take the kingly name of Dâriuš, when he came upon the Throne of Lands and Waters of the Persians, hoping that the First Dâriuš will be the royal sun guiding his kingly path."

"Grandmother, the Great King was always kind to me." She takes a deep breath and comforts the old Dukšiš with kindness. "Even the Angels of the Wise Lord can be attacked by the Demons of the Lord of Darkness."

Rošanak narrows her eyes and thinks for a moment.

"The Eclipse of the Moon!" she says, nodding, remembering an old tale from childhood. "Ancient Chaldæans used to say that the Eclipse of the Moon happened when Nânna, the Bâbiruviya Moon-God was vanquished by the Seven Evil Demons."

Old Dukšiš shakes her head in dismay with teary eyes. "Child!"

Rošanak persists.

It was a tale that Abi-Samar had told them all many times when she was a child.

It was the tale of his favorite Bâb-ilim god, Nânna… the one his blood mother had told him about when he was a child growing up in Bâb-ilim… an ancient tale passed from mother to son…

"The Seven Evil Demons forced their way into the secret chamber of creation and seized Nânna, the Moon-God, and took him from the Seven Heavens and the Four Quarters and the Six Dimensions. When the night came, the sky remained dark and the Moon-God did not sit shining on his heavenly throne…"

Utâna used to pretend he was Nânna, the Moon-God, and the rest of them were the Seven Evil Demons stealing away the Moon-God from the Vaults of the Heaven. Whenever Abi-Samar told the story… Abi-Samar was all the other gods.

"Enlil, the King of the Gods, called to Adad, the Storm-God, and told him to call to Êa, the God of Waters, and tell him that Nânna, Son of Enlil, was bedimmed in the heavens. When Êa heard of this, he cried and all the waters of the world were filled with his tears of sorrow. Êa called his firstborn son, Marduk the Warrior-God, and said to him, *Go, Marduk! Rescue Nânna!*"

Old Dukšiš closes her eyes, pushing back tears, not hearing a word.

"I know Artašatu did not run from battle, as the Makedonians claim he did! His men left the battlefield after he was taken to safety when he was wounded… as he wrote to me with the account of his battles, asking for my forgiveness.

"But I was so angry… I cursed him instead with my words stretching to the seven corners of the heaven. He should not have left us behind to fall into the hands of the hainâ!"

She remembers.

"He was such a handsome boy when he was young and even more tall and handsome when he grew into manhood… and yet, when he became a Great King, he became a king not worth dying for."

Rošanak's eyes well up again and she says quietly, "Grandmother, many men died in many battles for the Great King… all my brothers from the same mother and father… my lover… my brothers from another mother and father… all their faithful and friends… Battlefields were watered with their blood from one side of the battlefields to the other side! The unfaithful speak ill of our dead because they are no longer alive to defend their own cause! All liars are cursed to Hell!"

Old Dukšiš closes her eyes and mumbles and rambles under her old breath to herself.

"The Makedonian is small in stature… his feet did not even touch the floor when he first sat on the Persian Throne here in Çûšâ… one of his men pushed a golden table under his feet. A poor palace eunuch was killed when he wept after seeing the table of a Great King resting under the feet of the enemy conqueror. All the athravans prayed night and day for the Makedonians to leave, and to leave us to our misery!"

She pauses and shakes her head and talks to herself. "But the short Makedonian was born to the sword. He is what my son should have been! What kind of a mother bears a son like my son?"

Rošanak kisses the rose-scented, tear-bathed hands of the old Ummi Šarri. "Grandmother!"

"My beloved Setâreh cursed Artašatu when she found him in bed with a wretched eunuch! Men take no notice when they are cursed by women… but the Wise Lord hears all who cry out to him when they are wronged! She died without ever forgiving him!"

"Grandmother!" Rošanak embraces her grandmother and bites her lip, thinking of her own misery.

She had cursed Alexander for bedding the same wretched eunuch.

Old Dukšiš pulls back from her in pain. "I have not seen my grandson, Tiršata, for a year now. Alexander tells me that he is in the Lands Beyond the Sea, being trained as a Makedonian hamarana-kara."

Old Dukšiš pauses and shakes her head. "But I know in my heart that my poor grandson is dead, so he could not raise his claim to the Persian Crown and Throne of his King-Father. What king has ever left a crowned head and a head worthy of a crown untouched? My own father put to the sword all my brothers who could have risen against him!"

"No!" Rošanak coils into herself in horror and pain.

"All I have left now are my two granddaughters. Soon the Makedonian will claim them too and take them from me!" Old Dukšiš points to her royal gown with her old fingers. "That is why Royal Women of the Kings wear royal purple, the color of the blood of their Kings… so we always remember that the kingship is watered and wrapped in our own blood."

"No!" Rošanak covers her face.

Old Dukšiš looks at Rošanak with pity.

When the Makedonian had claimed Setâreh and had shamed her and had gotten her with child, Setâreh had cried blood for nine months.

She had tried everything to rid her body of her shame, the unborn bastard of a hainâ… potions and spells… but nothing had worked… the poor cursed bastard had clung to her womb as the cursed Makedonian father had clung to the Lands of the Persians…

When the bastard son of the Makedonian was born to her Setâreh, she had taken him from her and had held the newborn bastard in her arms and had pressed his small head firmly to her old breasts until the Wise Lord had finally taken pity on him and had taken him from her.

And then the Wise Lord had taken pity on her Setâreh too and she had never awakened after birthing the wretched bastard… Setâreh had mercifully bled to death… her dying blood had washed away her living shame.

"You too one day will bury your child wrapped in your own blood!"

Rošanak closes her eyes in pain.

She had already buried one son…

Dukšiš Sisygambis takes a deep breath and leans further back on her silver couch and looks away.

Her Royal Son had failed his Royal Ancestors…

Her Royal Son had failed his Royal Mother…

Her Royal Son had failed his God.

He had lost his Royal Woman,

And his Crown Prince, the Royal Son of the Royal House,

… and all the Royal Sons…

And his Royal Mother and Royal Daughters,

And the Empire of his Royal Ancestors… all the Lands and Waters that were bestowed upon his royal blood by the Wise Lord.

But by the grace of the Wise Lord, her Royal Son had died a Great King… without ever admitting defeat in hands of the evil enemies…

… her son had died a Persian…

ROYAL QUARTERS of ROYAL DAUGHTERS
FOLLOWING DAY
AFTERNOON

"Sons of bloody filthy whores! Worshippers of adulterous murderous gods! I curse them all! They are a horrid plague unleashed across our magnificent Lands! I hope they all die!" Setâreh bellows at Rošanak.

Rošanak's eyes widen. She leans back on her couch.

"Setâreh!"

"This was one of our royal palaces. We once lived here as Royal Daughters.

"Now we all live here as captive women, at the mercy of the barbaric Makedonians, who have invaded our Lands and have put all our men to the sword and have raped all the women. Men who have plundered and sacked and burned Pârsâ, the beloved Royal City of our royal ancestors. The most holy of the all the Royal Cities of the Persians."

Setâreh eyes Rošanak with anger and pain and rages on heatedly.

"Alexander offered us his protection when we were captured after the Battle of Issos. We were abandoned to the will of the conquering Makedonian Army. When our beloved mother died of her shame and a bleeding broken heart, Alexander gave her a fine funeral, befitting of a fallen Queen." she says cuttingly, "I wish we had all died at Issos!"

Rošanak leans forward on her couch.

Setâreh ignores her and continues her rage.

"All the books and scrolls of the Royal Archives and all the Royal Journals at the Royal Storehouse of Royal Documents in Pârsâ have been burned to ashes by these godless barbarians! *Book of Varusanka*, royal records of our splendid ancestors, holy books of our faith have vanished, as if they never existed! Wisdom of ages, light of our eyes… gone! All gone!"

"Setâreh," Rošanak says softly, trying to appease her.

Setâreh ignores her again and continues raging, "Is it not better to die and be remembered as we were, than to be alive and forgotten as we are? Is it not better to have died and never witnessed the disgrace that our fathers brought upon us and lost the Lands that we have loved since the day we were born and see our blood mother shamed and raped and dead?"

"Setâreh!"

Setâreh finally looks straight at Rošanak with blazing eyes.

"You married the man who murdered our father for the Throne of Persia!"

"Setâreh!"

"Our Bakhtrian sister freely married the man who had murdered her own father and brothers for the Throne of Persia!" Dripeyti says bitingly.

"Your own blood sister would have disowned you," Setâreh says harshly.

Rošanak becomes pale. Her head starts to ache. Unforgiving spoken words are like pointed Persian arrows that quickly found their marks.

It was the first time she had seen Setâreh and Dripeyti in years.

She had written to them from the Sughud Didâ and then again after she had wedded Alexander. She had pleaded with them, "Please, write to me! Let me hear from you!"

They had never written back to her…

Setâreh and Dripeyti were no longer the young royal sisters she remembered. They had grown tall and beautiful and they had turned bitter and ugly.

They had been tutored expertly in Attik by Hellene tutors and they carelessly mixed and wove their Attik and Persian words when they spoke.

They had lost the scented softness of their Persian and they had gained the foul harshness of Attik… worst of two worlds… without the beauty of either…

They spoke harshly like the men around Alexander.

They said what they meant and they meant what they said… that was not the tongue of the Persians… they had lost the golden tongue of their mothers… the royal tongues of their royal ancestors…

… they had lost themselves.

Rošanak softly pleads with her royal sisters.

"Dukšišbe! Please! We are sisters! We used to play together when we were all children! I love you!"

"We are not sisters! We are the whores of the Makedonians! Captive women of men who have murdered our fathers and our kinsmen and have raped our mothers and sisters and have destroyed our Lands!"

"They call her the Queen!" Setâreh says mockingly. "The Queen of the Pârsâ Ruins from Bakhtriš!"

"Please! Past is past! Let us be good sisters! Let us bury the old wounds along with the dead!"

"And let us bury the treacherous Makedonians along with the old wounds!" Dripeyti says bitterly.

Setâreh nods in agreement with her royal sister, mocking Rošanak with royal tongue. "Yes! Good Sister, Rošanak! Let us do as you command us!"

"Dukšišbe!"

Silence.

Rošanak sinks back into her couch.

Dripeyti leans forward.

"Rošanak, Alexander always talks about his glory! Do you know what will be most glorious?"

Rošanak looks at Dripeyti wordlessly.

Dripeyti says bitterly, "To pile up all the bloody conquerors on one giant pyre and burn them all alive, while we all stand and watch! Damn the sacred fire! Let them burn! Let them die! Their dim-witted historians can write about how gloriously those wretched invaders died and burned and went to their cursed Hades!"

Bitter silence.

KING'S ROYAL QUARTERS
DAYS LATER
SUNSET

"LEAVE US!"

Alexander screams at the royal guards.

The large royal room empties quickly and becomes small. The weight of deafening silence lowers the lofty golden ceiling down close to the golden floor.

Alexander reaches and locks his powerful fingers around Rošanak's neck and pulls her closer to him. He is white with wrath.

Rošanak looks like a small prey caught in the powerful jaws of a deadly lion. She moans in pain. "Alexander." Her voice trails off, the air in her body draining away.

Alexander tightens his fingers around Rošanak's neck.

"Call my name again and I will rip your tongue out with my bare hands!" he screams in a harsh cold voice she has not heard before. His sharp tongue cuts her like a sharp sword, makes her bleed.

"Alexander…"

Alexander throws her on the floor. She lands hard on her side and moans in horrible pain.

Alexander clenches the hilt of his golden dagger with all his anger and takes a step toward her. His eyes blaze blood red with rage, his knuckles whiten with deep anger, his chest wound pulsates with pain, his pain screams through his teeth. "Do you think I am a fool? Did you think I would not find out?"

Rošanak pulls back from him slowly, crawling on the golden floor. "Alexander," her words break, "please… forgive me…"

Alexander lets go of his dagger and kneels down next to her on the floor and grabs her shoulders and pulls her back close to his face.

"Do you think I will be merciful and kill you and send you to Hades?"

"Alexander…" Rošanak weeps and pleads.

"You will probably charm him too, blind his eyes with your beauty. He will probably toss Persephone right out of his house in favor of you. Hades the Unseen will make you his Queen of the Underworld."

"Alexander…"

"I said do not call my name!"

"Alexander."

"No! I will not be merciful!" Alexander throws her back on the floor and rises to his feet and looks away, knowing well that looking at her would make him angrier. He draws in a painful breath. His chest fills with more pain than air.

"Is this my reward for loving you?" He growls. "Move and there is only war!"

Rošanak moans silently. Sharp pain shoots through the whole of her body.

"Please, Alexander." She tries to catch her breath. "Please! Do not take your wrath out on my Baktrians, punish me instead."

Anger pushes back pain.

Alexander bends back down and grabs Rošanak's shoulders again and pulls her toward his face. His angry fingers dig sharply into her soft flesh.

Her body starts to bleed and bruise under her ivory skin.

"Your Baktrians? *Your Baktrians*?"

Alexander tightens his grip on Rošanak.

"They are my men now! My successors! My warriors! Not yours! No one even knows you!" He rages, pulling her face closer to his, and the rest of her follows obediently.

"I am marrying Stateira!" he says, as though declaring a death sentence.

Stunned silence.

Alexander lets go of Rošanak. Her body folds and she falls down hard on the golden floor in front of him. He gets to his feet and screams again.

"Hephæstion will marry Drypetis, and Krateros will marry Amastris!"

"No!" Rošanak's eyes widen. Her blood runs cold.

"And all, ALL of my kingsmen, all the LowLanders and the HighLanders," he yells, "will be given a highborn Persian bride!"

"No!"

"You are ordered to attend the weddings and bear witness!"

"No!"

"I command you as the Lord of Asia and your King and Husband!"

"Just kill me!" Rošanak moans in pain.

Alexander takes a deep breath, too angry to think; his arrow wound pounds and throbs.

"I told you I would not be merciful!"

Rošanak lies on the golden floor crying.

"If you refuse my royal order, I will have your hair chopped off, cover you from the top of your head to the bottoms of your feet in black ashes from Persepolis and have your naked body dragged to my wedding, bound and bleeding in heavy chains!"

Rošanak weeps.

Alexander straightens and clenches his fists with anger. He turns around and leaves.

Rošanak weeps.

QUEEN'S ROYAL QUARTERS
FOLLOWING DAY
SUNRISE

"GET OUT!"

Hephæstion thunders at Mâr'at Bani Âriyânnâz as he storms like a dark cloud into the Queen's Quarters, unannounced, looking as if he has not slept in days.

Rošanak is lying face down on a pile of large luxurious silk pillows on the Persian carpet, hugging a big pillow, crying softly.

Hephæstion looks again fiercely at Mâr'at Bani Âriyânnâz who is standing back by the wall trembling and biting her lip and wringing her hands, worrying about Rošanak.

"Get out!" Hephæstion yells again angrily at her in Persian.

Mâr'at Bani Âriyânnâz goes white with fright, looking at Hephæstion, holding in her breath.

"I said: *GET OUT!*" Hephæstion screams at her.

Mâr'at Bani Âriyânnâz's legs fail her and her face grows alabaster white. She loses all her breath and words. She leans back, melting into the golden wall.

"Hephæstion!" Rošanak yells at him. "Leave her be! Your quarrel is with me!"

Hephæstion looks down at Rošanak, blazing with anger and then grabs Mâr'at Bani Âriyânnâz's hand. He drags her to the massive doors and pushes her out and closes the doors behind her. He looks around. His eyes find their mark. He walks swiftly to a heavy wooden chest and pushes it forcefully against the massive doors with his foot.

"There! I do not want that wretched eunuch of yours to force his way in here and put a bloody dagger to my throat again, before I kill you!" Hephæstion yells in red anger.

Rošanak grabs the pillows, trying to shield herself against Hephæstion's rage.

She had not seen him this angry since that night in Hind.

Hephæstion marches back to her, bends down and clutches her shoulders and pulls her to her feet. His powerful fingers dig painfully into her delicate shoulders. He shakes her violently.

She moans in pain and drops the pillow to her feet.

Hephæstion notices the purplish marks of Alexander's fingers around her neck and her shoulders.

He could have easily crushed her neck, if he had pressed any harder… he had killed a ferocious lion single-handedly in Baktria with the same bare hands.

He digs into her; his own anger is no less.

"Krateros?" Hephæstion screams into her face in pain and anger.

"He was dying!" she says faintly, sobbing.

"You should have let that bastard die!" Hephæstion rages at her.

Rošanak closes her eyes and bites her lip, holding in her breath.

"He saved my life!"

"He should have let you die! How could you? Tell me! I want to know!"

"Hephæstion…" She moans softly, sobbing.

Hephæstion curses and screams. "I brought you here from Persis. You were in my bed every night for two months and you said nothing to me!"

"Hephæstion…"

Hephæstion breathes fire. "Do not say my name! I hate you! I never want to hear my name passing through your lying lips— ever again!"

"Hephæstion… please…"

"Lying is evil? Ha?" He growls. "Any man who trusts a woman with his heart is nothing but a damn fool!" Hephæstion pushes her away roughly; she loses her legs and falls back down on the hard floor on top of the soft pillows.

"Alexander should have you hanged!"

"Hephæstion…"

"Right after cutting off that bastard's head in front of your eyes!"

"Hephæstion…"

"I forgave you that Indian Prince. I was wrong! I should have put you to the sword then and there myself, and cut off his head and taken it to Alexander!"

Rošanak pushes the words out of her lips. "Where were you when he shielded me from the rain of arrows?"

Then she softens her voice and pleads with him, "Hephæstion… please… you know nothing about how it feels to be utterly lonely and alone and useless… forgotten… utterly abandoned by everyone… Alexander… you… not even Peritas… days stretching into nights… months stretching into seasons…"

"No?" Hephæstion's voice softens. "I know nothing about being lonely? Am I not lonely enough for you? Am I not enough for you?"

Hephæstion quietly kneels down in front of her, looking into her teary eyes.

"You gave me your ring! I lived through the Desert of Death to bring it back to you!"

"Do you think my heart is so small that it only has room for one?" Rošanak cries softly. "There is no one left to mourn me when I die! My mothers, my sister, my brothers, my father… all gone! Dârâ and Nimâ no longer remember me!" she says sadly, weeping.

"I… I will mourn you… after I kill you!" Hephæstion grinds his teeth and shakes his head and growls. "Alexander—"

What more could he tell Alexander… that his Queen was unfaithful to her lover too?

"Alexander? What about Alexander? He loves me not! He named a city after Peritas and another after Bukephalas. I am less than a dog and a horse to him! How can he demand my love in private when he shames me in the full rays of the sun by kissing a wretched whore in front of his men," Rošanak says bitterly.

Hephæstion's voice softens.

"Alexander… he loves you… as much as he can love any woman."

He breathes in pain. "He kissed all the victors at the games… the damn eunuch was one of the victors…"

"He cares nothing for me. He only cares for himself and his own glory."

"Roshanak…" he says her name.

"Kill me or go away and leave me be!"

Hephæstion takes a deep breath, breathing in more pain and revenge.

"Kill you? No! Why should I? I will take another woman to bed! One of the Royal Daughters of Darius! That will be the only punishment that will make you suffer as I have!"

"No!"

"Alexander and I will marry the Royal Daughters of Darius! We will have children, related by blood of our Persian wives!"

"Nooo!"

"I do not want you to die! I want you to suffer!"

Hephæstion gets to his feet painfully, kicks the heavy wooden chest away from the giant doors and storms out.

The wooden chest crashes into a column and cracks. Golden room quakes.

Rošanak weeps.

ROYAL ROOM
DAYS LATER
SETTING SUN

Hot… tension builds…

"I will not utter the sacred words!" The old Âtravaxš, the supreme head of all the Zarathuštra Athravans in the Royal City of Çûšâ, declares defiantly to Dukšiš Sisygambis.

"Union of a man and a woman is holy, sanctified by the utterance of the sacred words of the Wise Lord. It makes no difference if the man is a king. Marriage is *not* a damn Hellene play for the amusement of the ignorant masses!" the old Âtravaxš declares with disdain.

"They are Makedonians, not Hellenes," Rošanak says quietly, "except for half of Hephæstion and the whole of Eumenes and Medeios. Lysimachos is Thessalian."

The old Âtravaxš turns his head, considers Rošanak for a moment, and then asks cuttingly, "Which one burned Pârsâ and the Avestâ?"

"Makedonians did to avenge the burning of the City of Athenai in the name of Hellenes."

"Then Makedonian or Hellene makes no difference! They are both cursed by the lips of the Wise Lord for burning his sacred words!" The old Âtravaxš pauses and then points to the royal audience hall. "This is an abomination, mocking the Laws of the Wise Lord! Not a blessed wedding ritual!"

Persians worshipped the Wise Lord.

Their Great Kings were vessels of the Wise Lord.

The Wise Lord and the Lord of Darkness had battled since time immemorial for the soul of men.

The Persian Wars were to destroy the evil of the Lord of Darkness and to enforce the will of the Wise Lord upon the Lands and Waters of the Persians…

Their faith was being tested again…

Some of the words are interpreted for Chares, the king's chamberlain, pacing outside the royal room nervously. He twists in the hallway in desperation and begs frantically. "Roxana, please! Tell them the King has commanded this! He wants to marry, as his men do!"

Rošanak eyes the dim-witted chamberlain dispassionately and then looks out of the window at the mountains.

Alexander had no intention of marrying as his men did, when he had wedded her…

Chares looks fearfully into the royal audience hall behind the heavily gilded draped curtains.

The royal audience hall in the Palace of Susa was sparkling with looking glass and candles and flowers… brides and grooms were garmented and jeweled, waiting outside the hall, and no mage to marry them!

Alexander would have him hanged if the weddings did not come to pass according to the customs of the Persians as he had willed it!

"Roxana, please! By gods! What shall I do?" he asks again, almost in tears.

Rošanak shrugs her shoulders. She wears her unbearable pain on the tip of her tongue. "Have the grooms cut the bread loaves on the food tables in the Tent of a Thousand Silver Couches for the wedding feast with their swords, just as their fathers did when they married their mothers."

Chares shakes his head with dismay and nervously enters the royal room and pleads again. "By gods! Alexander wants a Persian wedding! Why are they refusing the King?"

Someone asks the athravans.

One of them answers directly to Dukšiš Sisygambis in Persian, ignoring the King's Makedonian chamberlain altogether.

"Dukšiš Sisygambis, today is most unlucky for a holy union of a man and a woman. One of the diviners of the King picked the wedding day without any counsel from us."

"Holy Union is one man and one woman," another one adds.

The old Âtravaxš says quietly, "Even if we were to overlook the multitude of grooms and brides, the barbarian King has sent word that he will not kneel down before the Wise Lord, nor will any of his kingsmen, and the Persian brides will not stand." He shakes his head.

Dukšiš Sisygambis breathes pain and bites her lip.

Everyone at the royal court knew that the Queen had fallen out of favor with the King shortly after arriving at the Royal City of Çûšâ, but no one knew why.

The palace eunuch had heard the screams of the King behind closed doors, but did not know the meaning of his harsh words… rumors had spread that the King had ordered the weddings to punish the Queen… and she had remained guarded and secluded in her quarters until the day of the forced wedding ritual…

But she knew that like all the Great Kings before him, the Makedonian was not a man to allow the Royal Daughters to fall into the hands of his rivals.

She had pleaded with him on her old knees and he had not wavered from his intent to marry her granddaughters. His path was set by the Lord of Darkness…

Old Dukšiš considers Rošanak discreetly, defiantly dressed in royal purple against the order of the King.

Her granddaughter looked the way everyone felt… utterly wretched.

She had tried to hide the faded purplish marks on her neck and shoulders with layers of golden necklaces, piled high… she was about to topple over with the weight of the gold around her neck and the weight of the pain in her heart…

"If they were to be wedded by the customs of the barbarians?" Dukšiš Sisygambis asks quietly.

"The grooms will be wedded in the eyes of their own gods and the brides will be unwedded in the eyes of our Wise Lord," the old Âtravaxš says confidently, without any hesitation.

And they all knew well what that meant.

Dukšiš Sisygambis closes her old eyes in torment.

Dishonor!

Utter Shame!

Without the utterance of the sacred words by the Âtravaxš, her beloved granddaughters were to be raped like all captive women in their wedding beds!

She could not stop the forced marriage alliances but she could keep the Royal Daughters and the noble women of the Seven Families of the Persians from being raped and shamed at the hands of their captors in front of the Wise Lord.

Chares starts to pace again anxiously back and forth across the royal room, rubbing his hands together nervously.

Dukšiš Sisygambis eyes the dim-witted chamberlain who dares to stand in her presence insolently without bending his knees and sighs to herself, thinking of her own wretched misery.

She then beckons the old Âtravaxš over to her and pleads with him quietly.

"Will the Wise Lord be utterly offended if the brides and grooms were to both sit down on chairs?"

The old Âtravaxš shifts side-to-side uncomfortably, thinking to himself.

"Chairs?"

Dukšiš Sisygambis points to the king's chamberlain with her eyes.

"Your Holiness, the Wise Lord knows all too well I do not command you as a queen… as you can see with your own eyes, I am no longer one, nor deserving of any mark of royalty or any honor given the mother of the king. I beg of you as a grandmother… with all of our men defeated and dead and dying, has there not been enough shame heaped upon our women already?"

"Well…"

"As you know… even though it is forbidden to utter her name again…" Dukšiš Sisygambis pauses mournfully and then says her name in a hushed voice, "My granddaughter, Dukšiš Amastris, took her own life, choosing the Land of the Eternal Darkness over the bed of an enemy invader."

Silence.

"Will the Divine Ânâhitâ wish her humble flock of virgins to be raped and shamed by these barbarians in their wedding beds?"

Silence.

"These men could have just taken our women without a lawful marriage."

The old Âtravaxš takes a deep breath and looks at the others and finally relents and bows his head to the old Dukšiš.

"Very well Dukšiš, they can all sit on chairs."

Dukšiš Sisygambis beckons the Chief Eunuch of the royal palace at Çûšâ.

"Bring chairs, one for each bride and groom."

Rošanak pushes back a tear, disappointed.

She had cursed the weddings under her breath all the days and nights since she was told of them… wishing they would not come to pass… that they would be struck down by divine lightning delivered through the hands of the Divine Ânâhitâ herself.

She had sacrificed milk and honey and wine and heaps of precious Arabâya incense.

Dukšiš Sisygambis beckons one of her noble Persian ladies.

"Go tell all the brides that I have ordered them to sit on chairs during the sacred wedding ritual."

"But Dukšiš—"

Dukšiš Sisygambis gives the noble Persian lady a sharp look.

"Yes, Dukšiš!"

Dukšiš Sisygambis then beckons the king's chamberlain.

"Go tell the King that his royal mother begs of him and his kingsmen to sit on chairs during the wedding ritual. Tell him to come and see his royal mother if his view of this is different from that of his royal mother."

Chares sighs with relief and walks away.

LATER

Alexander and his kingsmen grooms enter the royal audience hall and sit down on chairs according to their rank. Alexander and a handful wearing royal purple, the rest wearing their ancestral scarlet cloaks.

The Royal Daughters and the rest of the Persian brides, all wearing white, enter the royal audience hall from the other side of the hall, are directed to their assigned grooms and sit down on chairs next to them.

The old Âtravaxš stands in front of them. He quietly asks the athravans behind him, "How many are there?"

"Ninety one, Your Holiness, including the Lord of Asia," a young athravan says quietly.

The old Âtravaxš shakes his head and utters under his breath,

"Tell the other athravans that we will not tie the hands of the brides and the grooms together. These unions are cursed, they will not last. Even Dukšiš Sisygambis cannot bargain with the Wise Lord!"

"Yes, Your Holiness."

Rošanak looks at them from afar.

Alexander and Setâreh, the older Royal Daughter of the Third Dâriuš…

Setâreh, a good head and shoulder taller than Alexander… even seated on a chair… and cold as the ice crowning the mountains of Bakhtriš.

Alexander, seated so far away from her… yet it felt as if he was twisting a golden dagger straight into her heart.

Hephæstion and the beautiful Dripeyti, the younger Royal Daughter of the Third Dâriuš.

The beautiful Dripeyti, as tall as Hephæstion… colder than ice… and sharper than the edge of a Persian dagger.

Krateros and Amastris, Daughter of Hukhšaqra, the Royal Brother of the Third Dâriuš.

Amastris, tall and Persian… Krateros… HighLander… pale… limping… still suffering from the arrow wounds at Harahuvatiš he had suffered for her.

She takes a deep breath. The bride of Krateros was of royal blood but not a Royal Daughter. Amastris, the Royal Daughter of the Fourth Artakhšaçâ, had taken poison when she was told of her fate. She says a prayer under her lips for Amastris, as she looks at the next couple.

Perdikkas and a golden honor wreath and Madumîtu, Daughter of Âtrupâta, the Satrap of Mâda…

Ptolemaios and Artâkama, Daughter of Artâvazda, the cursed traitor, from his Persian wife…

Eumenes and Artone, half-breed Daughter of Artâvazda, from his Hellene wife…

Nearchos and the Daughter of Barsine…

Well, at least Alexander had not allowed Barsine to come to her own daughter's wedding… he knew well that there were limits to his kingly wrath, if he ever meant to keep the Queen to his bed… punishing his wife behind closed doors for her deeds was his right as her wedded husband, but dishonoring the Queen in the royal court was dishonoring the King himself…

Seleukos and Apâma…

She blesses Apâma and Seleukos under her breath.

Seleukos was lucky. The girl favored him and he loved her… it was a love match.

He had seen her in Bakhtriš, when she had bravely gone to the Royal Army Camp to plead for the return of the head of her father.

Seleukos had persuaded Alexander to honor her wishes and had given her father an honorable burial… and had treated her well ever since… Apâma had always remembered…

Hushed silence.

The old Âtravaxš starts the wedding ritual.

"I say to you, marrying brides and bridegrooms. Impress then upon your mind: May you enjoy the life of good mind by following the laws of the Wise Lord. Let each one of you clothe the other with righteousness. Then assuredly there will be a happy life for you.

"May the Wise Lord grant you a progeny of sons and grandsons, prosperity, heart-ravishing love, bodily strength and long life."

Words are interpreted loudly.

"Marrying brides and grooms. May you enjoy a virtuous life by honoring the gods. Let each one of you be a comfort to the other. Then there will be a life of virtue for you. May Zeus grant you many sons and grandsons, prosperity and bodily strength and honor."

The wedding ritual finishes. Drums start to beat.

Dukšiš Sisygambis quietly leaves for her quarters.

Alexander smiles at the wedding couples.

Rošanak looks at Alexander for a long moment and then leaves the great royal audience hall quietly for the wedding feast, followed by the royal guards.

... her heart ached... all she wanted was to find a grave somewhere...

TENT of a THOUSAND SILVER COUCHES
WEDDING FEAST
EVENING

"We are all dead!" Dripeyti announces bitterly, sipping her sweet wine.

"Embalmed like the ancient Pharaohs of the Two Lands! Dressed up in our finest virgin white silks and gold jewelry! Whores on display for the pleasure of our Makedonian captors!" Setâreh adds bitterly and drinks more sweet wine.

"Dead all the same! Vultures pick at our rotting flesh!" Dripeyti bellows.

"Dripeyti!" Rošanak hisses and looks around the crowded wedding feast and eyes Hephæstion sprawled on a golden couch, drinking deep with Alexander.

He neither heard them nor cared much...

Dancing drums start to play.

Rošanak takes a deep breath and takes a sip of her wine.

By the order of Alexander, all the Royal Daughters, she and Setâreh and Dripeyti, were seated on the silver couches together, with their husbands sprawled on golden couches nearby... drinking...

It was not a mark of honor... it was to shame her more by her own words... the small ugly half-breed Persian sitting with the tall beautiful pure Persian Royal Daughters... feeling like a fool dressed in Persian purple in a sea of snowy white Persians...

Amastris walks over and sits next to Rošanak.

Setâreh draws closer to Rošanak. "Do not flatter yourself with royal purple. This is not your punishment. It is our fate. They taught us their tongue so we know we are forced to wed and bed these men as the prizes of their victory over our men. We are nothing more to them than their captive women, and our sons will be nothing more than their bastards. Their love is for beardless boys and their lust is for our precious gold and for the strong thighs of each other."

Rošanak looks away coldly.

If only they knew...

"Setâreh! Dripeyti! Sheath your sharp tongues!" Amastris says discreetly, sipping her wine. "This is neither the time nor the place for such foul words."

Dripeyti and Setâreh ignore Amastris, sip their wine and speak openly.

"They are not honoring us by marrying us, they are dishonoring our men by denying them their own beloved women," Dripeyti says bitterly. "Sons of Hades are doing what causes the most pain and shame and misery for our men."

"Âryânâ will be free of their plague soon enough!" Setâreh says bitingly, casting her eyes around. "They are their own worst enemies. Like their own ancestors, they will tear each other apart in pursuit of their own flaming glory."

Rošanak sinks back into the silver couch.

She had been utterly jealous of the Royal Daughters of the Third Dâriuš... jealous of her royal sisters wedding and bedding her men.

... but they were more wretched than she in their own misery...

They were consumed, devoured whole by their own hatred... whatever Alexander and his kingsmen were to find in their wedding beds tonight was not going to be love or desire or madness... nor alliances of any kind...

Their hands had not been tied!

Only Apâma had persuaded one of the athravans to tie her hand to Seleukos...

Dripeyti and Setâreh drink more wine.

Amastris leans closer to Rošanak and whispers in her ear. "Ignore them! Their unbridled royal tongues will be their undoing. I would have married a two-headed demon to get out of this golden Hell away from their royal spitefulness!"

Rošanak looks at Amastris with aching heart, burning hot under her cold skin.

She was not married to a demon. She was wedded to Krateros, her HighLander.

ROŠANAK'S BEDCHAMBER. QUEEN'S ROYAL QUARTERS
MIDNIGHT

The dreaded night has come. Finally.

And the sky has fallen on the Little Star.

Rošanak is in bed, softly crying.

The royal palace at Çûšâ was getting quieter... no doubt the brides and grooms had retired to wedding bedchambers to take pleasure in each other...

Love or not, a wedding bed was a bedding bed...

And Alexander was in bed bedding her sister, Setâreh...

She gets out of her bed restlessly and walks over and opens the window. She fills her lungs with the cool air of the night and wipes her face of her tears. She rubs the old scars of the old cuts on her wrists and the faded cuts in the palms of her hands.

If Uxšiyârta had not come upon her that fateful night at the âyadana, like Amastris, she would have surely died of her own doing.

Was the Land of the Eternal Darkness any worse than the blazing fire that was now burning through her soul, consuming her whole?

She tries to think of something more dreadful to keep her mind from what was going on behind the closed doors of the wedding bedchambers of her men. The face of her old teacher, Kalyana, the old Hinduya Brahman, sitting peacefully, surrounded by fiery flames, passes before her eyes.

Her mind wanders.

She kneels on the bare floor, pleading with Kalyana, "Please, Holy One… I beg of you… Reconsider your death… Dying on a day of your choosing will banish you to the Land of the Eternal Darkness."

"My teacher, Kalyana, thanks you for your kindness, but his path is set."

"No! Please! Do not desecrate the sacred fire with the burning of your flesh."

"My teacher, Kalyana, says that the dead flesh desecrates the sacred flame. He will be alive when the fire is set upon him."

"Alexander, how can you allow this to be?" she pleads with Alexander.

Alexander says nothing.

"Hephæstion, please stop this!" she pleads with Hephæstion.

"The fate of the Indian Sage is in the hands of his own gods."

She cries bewildered.

"My teacher, Kalyana, says that the sadness of his young pupil the Queen in the old City of the Elam-tu will soon pass. In the Gathering Place of the ancient Mâda Kings, sadness will seed life, as one love passes and old love rekindles the flames of sacred wedded desire."

"Your teacher still talks in riddles… surely his gods do not wish him to suffer the burn of fire on his living flesh."

"My teacher, Kalyana, says that the fire will wrap around him, as a lover embraces the beloved and becomes one with the Heaven."

"Please!" Rošanak begs.

"My teacher says there is but one Master, with many names… the Master of the World, the self-created creator of all who existed before creation, who faces in all directions… Master of the Heaven, who has no master… beginning of the world, endless and without beginning…

"My teacher says he regretted his oath to his Master once and then he saw in a dream that for his impudence, he was destined to one day follow in the footsteps of the richest and most powerful conqueror on earth and see for himself that the Conqueror and the Conquered were the same in the eyes of his Master.

"My teacher, Kalyana, says he will see you by the Gate of Gods, between the low lands of the two ancient rivers," the young Brahman tells Alexander quietly.

Rošanak shakes her head and pushes back a tear.

Old Kalyana had sat for hours motionlessly on his funeral pyre in the full view of the entire Royal Army, while fire devoured him slowly.

The Royal Army had raised the fierce battle cry of their ancestors and had pounded on their shields with their swords in his honor. Neither she nor Alexander nor Hephæstion nor Krateros could have watched it with their own eyes.

Nearchos had told her later that the old Kalyana never cried out in pain or even moved. He had looked as if he was locked in a long rapturous embrace with a fiery lover. He had said the smell of burning living flesh was no different than the smell of dead warriors burning on funeral pyres.

The mournful memory makes her feel even more sad and lonely.

Old Thukrâ had taken away her fear of all men.

And the old Kalyana had given her a small window to the pleasures to be had with such men…

Hephæstion had abandoned her for his honor after that rainy night and day of love in Hind. Her silent lips had no one to talk to and her eyes had heaps of tears to shed… so, she had wept with shame at the feet of the old Kalyana who had stayed with her at Rajah Parvataka's court.

She would have obediently kept herself for the sacred wedded bed of her King-Husband, but after the death of her firstborn, there was no sacred wedded bed to keep to. She was broken and Alexander had gone back to his old ways for his bodily comfort, and she had cursed him and wept and wept and wept…

She was sick at heart and so he had cured her body… the old Kalyana had patiently gifted her with the knowledge of desire… with the sacred rules of love.

The meaning of the sacred writings in the small illuminated k^e^tâb he had given her had taught her the ancient ways of love and pleasure between men and women. Not just how to bed a wedded husband obediently to beget a child, but how to bed a lover to satisfy awakened hungry mortal desires.

He had told her the secrets her mothers had never told her… he had given her the taste of pleasure… he had taken away her shame of her body and of having taken a lover, and had given her Hephæstion back to her… and more.

He had said to her,

> *"A lover is like a burning candle in a darkened night,"*
>
> *and,*
>
> *"All men are alike in love and desire…"*

… and so they were.

Utâna… Alexander… Hephæstion… Chandrâ… Krateros…

Her teacher had told her that she was the moonstone that made the sun whole and that her King-Husband was bound to her, as were her lovers… that Hephæstion would come back to her and he had… Krateros too… like fluttering moths taking eager shelter in the comforting flames of the flickering fire…

In the world of the chaste old Hindu Brahman, life was about the sacred union of man and woman… there was no Land of the Eternal Light in the life after, if there was not pleasure and love in the life before.

And so he had joined with his own lover in a fiery embrace at the end of his own life of contemplation and suffering and virtue…

Mayûxa turns quietly.

The massive doors to her royal bedchamber quietly open.

She feels a blast of cool air entering the warm bedchamber. She turns and looks at the massive doors as Alexander enters the room and the doors quietly close behind him. Her eyes widen.

Stunned silence.

"Alexander?"

Alexander walks over to her by the window and wraps his strong arms around her and holds her tightly, slightly trembling. "Roxana."

"Alexander? What are you doing here? It is your wedding night!"

"Roxana— do you love me?"

Rošanak turns her head toward the window.

"Alexander, go back to your new bride."

"Roxana… do you love me?"

"No!"

Alexander starts kissing Rošanak's neck. "Roxana…"

She pulls away.

"I said: *No*."

"She begged me to kill her— she said she preferred a grave next to her birth mother to my bed! She called me the *Cursed*."

"You must have misunderstood her."

"No! Her Attik is perfect. She said it was a mortal sin for a man to bed the mother and the daughter of the same mother! She repeated it a few times to make sure I heard her!"

"Go back to her— enjoy the punishment you had planned for me."

"Roxana…"

"Go… eat and drink of her until you no longer can walk!"

Alexander starts pulling her toward her bed.

"It is a marriage alliance to appease the Persian Nobility and reduce their hostility to my rule and no more."

Rošanak eyes him.

She was not one of the countless who were swayed by his royal words… she knew his heart… he had married to punish her by his own words…

"As was our marriage." She pushes him away.

"No! I married you because I desired you!" He pulls her back.

"Alexander. Go back to your bride."

He caresses her body intimately.

"You wore royal purple to my wedding."

"So you could see what I looked like underneath."

Regret dances on Alexander's face.

He touches her face, feels her tears.

She pushes away his hand.

"I have not come empty-handed. I have brought you a golden royal gift."

Rošanak looks at Alexander.

His hands were empty.

"Ten thousand of my men have Asian wives. I will gift you their unions. I have decreed that all the children born of their unions are now legitimate. All the women are to receive a generous dowry from the royal funds, and the debts of their husbands paid from the royal funds too."

Her heart softens.

The warm room fills with another cool breeze from the window.

In the flicker of the candles, Alexander sees the faded purplish mark of his fingers around her delicate neck and shoulders. He caresses the painful marks gently with the tips of his fingers.

"Your neck… does it still hurt?"

"No. I only feel pain when my heart is marked."

He pulls her delicate gown off her body.

She turns toward him and stands naked in the flicker of the candles. The deep black and blue marks on the other side of her body had truly turned the color of royal purple.

Alexander closes his eyes. His face creases with pain and remorse. He drops his wedding robe on the floor and undresses himself with no words spoken.

Rošanak looks at his naked body in the light of the glowing candles. Her heart softens.

Old honor wounds were adorned by new honor wounds… wounds upon wounds…

The long jagged scar from the barbed arrow in Hind looked as heartbreaking as ever… throbbing with ceaseless pain. Half of his chest was the same color as her bruises.

Alexander pulls her toward him and holds her in his arms and whispers, "Forgive me…"

Rošanak yields softly to his embrace. "Alexander."

Old Kalyana was right after all…

He was bound to her…

> *The King and his Royal Woman…*
> *Wife-Queen and Kingly-Husband…*
> *The lion devouring the bull… again…*
> *Sun eclipsing the beclouded little star…*
> *Autumn pulling the spring rose petals in his wake…*

ROYAL QUARTERS of DUKŠIŠ SISYGAMBIS
A MONTH LATER
OÛRARÂHARA
EVENING

"Grandmother."

Dukšiš Sisygambis beckons Rošanak forward and she sinks into her grandmother's generous lap. Old Dukšiš lovingly caresses her long silky hair.

When her son had declared her A Royal Daughter at the Festival of No'rouz, when she had walked up to him so carelessly as a child, he had, by his own royal proclamation, made her the substitute daughter for his own Royal Daughters.

And after her royal father had assumed the Persian Crown with the blessing of the Nobles of the Seven Persian Families, she had become the last Royal Daughter.

Rošanak had faithfully taken the misery that was to befall on the Royal Daughters of Dâriuš to herself, saving them the shame of becoming whores of the barbarians… by offering herself in return… an offering that had been accepted by the Heaven.

"We are leaving for Hagmâtâna soon," Rošanak says quietly. "Setâreh and Dripeyti will stay here with you. But Amastris will accompany her husband."

Dukšiš Sisygambis kisses the face of Rošanak in gratitude.

Even a few more months with her beloved granddaughters were sweeter than life itself.

"When you get to Bâbiruš, tell your eunuch to prepare the Royal Palace of Queen Amytiš for you. It is a beautiful small palace in the middle of the Persian gardens, hanging in the heaven that King Nabû'Kudra'Cara built for Amytiš, the Royal Daughter of the Mâda King. It is a secret hidden palace jealously guarded by the palace eunuchs for the pleasure of the Royal Women of the Great Kings."

"Yes, Grandmother."

Dukšiš Sisygambis eyes her for a moment, then lowers her head slightly and whispers quietly into Rošanak's ear. "Rošanak, listen to me!"

Rošanak senses the intrigue and hesitation in her grandmother's old voice.

"Grandmother?"

"Rošanak, shield your heart. What is foretold will come to pass!"

All the Royal Cities of the Lands were as connected as they had ever been since the days of Kuruš the Elder… royal orders and news and rumors traveled fast in the skin bags of Persian pirradaziš on the Royal Roads. Everyone in the Empire knew that the prophecies had only turned darker since they were first foretold.

And more curses were uttered throughout the Lands…

Rošanak closes her eyes and takes a deep breath.

She was tired of all the prophecies and curses and omens and signs…

"Yes, Grandmother," she says in a soft obedient tone to appease the old Dukšiš.

"When you get to Bâbiruš, there is an old Chaldæan. His name is Kudurru. He was the pupil of Kidinnu.

"Kidinnu was ordered to follow Alexander, from Bâbiruš, when we were there after the Battle of Issos. The old Chaldæan Master foretold his fortune and it displeased the King immeasurably, and when Kidinnu did not bend to Alexander and did not change his unfavorable divination, Alexander had him put to the sword after the death of Dâriuš.

"When needed, seek him out and listen to what he has to say. Listen to all his words carefully and do what he tells you to do and do it well and with great care. Do you hear me, my daughter?"

"Yes, Grandmother."

Dukšiš Sisygambis hears it in the tone of Rošanak's voice and shakes her old head with dismay. She was not listening to her.

Persians were the gardeners of the Persian pleasure gardens… they knew that even on the driest plains of the Lands of their ancestors, Persian purple violets always bloomed after being buried under months of merciless ice and snow…

They were of an ancient race… most noble… their nâmanâfa went back thousands of years… They had fought wars before… they had lost and they had won… they were the first to worship the Wise Lord… and they were the first Empire Builders…

She whispers patiently into Rošanak's ear.

"Remember my daughter, the Persians worship the Wise Lord and there are no other gods.

"Our faith is being tested, so we must remain faithful and never stop resisting foreign gods and foreign kings, and never stop calling upon the Wise Lord from mountains and caves and valleys and plains… from this side of the mountains to the other side of the mountains… from this side of the ocean to the other side of the ocean… from this side of the deserts to the other side of the deserts… our voices, thunder loud and crystal clear, must break the silence of the night in mountainous caverns and echo and remain… all in the praise of the Wise Lord."

She pauses and says quietly, "Alexander can never become a Great King. Do you hear me, My Daughter?"

"Yes, Grandmother."

The old Dukšiš shakes her head and sighs to herself.

The girl was not listening…

Just as Alexander had not heard her when she had told him in her imperfect tongue that he could never become a Great King.

Now that the battles were lost, there was no need for the Persians to offer up more blood on battlefields than the red sea of blood they had already sacrificed… they would do what their ancestors had done since their early days. They would wait until the next Great King rises and proclaims himself… and deny all the pretenders what they desire the most: the Persian Crown and Throne… even if it took thousands of years.

It was not enough to win the battles and win the war and claim the Royal Women… the Persian King had to be Persian, son of a Persian, son of another Persian, son of Hakhâmaniš…

... an Ârya...

When the cursed Spartan Klearchos had not heeded the command of the Younger Kuruš at Kuniša, thinking he knew better than the Son of the Royal House, and the battle was lost and the head of the Younger Kuruš forfeited in defeat, the ignorant Spartan mercenaries had offered to make Âriyâ, a Kingsman of the Younger Kuruš, the next Persian King and he had laughed in their rude faces.

Âriyâ had told the Spartan that his blood was not royal enough, he was not born to purple... that the Persian Nobles of the Seven Families would never agree to call him Great King and bend their knees to him...

Alexander could never become a Great King... even if he razed all the Lands and killed all the people and married all the Royal Women... He was not Persian.

The Great King had to be Persian, son of a Persian, Son of Hakhâmaniš ... Worshiper of the Wise Lord... Whisperer of the sacred words of the Wise Lord... the Protector of the Divine Glory.

Kingship of the Great Kings was by the favor of the Wise Lord...

Alexander could never become a Great King.

The girl was lovesick...

Alexander had gone back to her right after the weddings, without even touching her granddaughter, and all that fell into her ears afterward were his words alone... she was not hearing her any longer.

"Persia belongs to the Persians," the old Dukšiš mumbles under her breath and sighs to herself. "No Persian will ever call Alexander *Great King.*"

ROYAL FEAST of HARMONY. FORTRESS CITY of ḪÛVJIYA on RIVER TIGRÂ
YEAR 13 of ALEXANDER, MONTH 11, GORPIAIOS
YEAR 7 of ALEXANDER, MONTH 5, TURNABAZIŠ
4 MONTHS LATER
NIGHT

Sounds of lutes and harps… and loud singing…

"Nine thousand?" Alexander asks half-smiling.

"Yes, Sir!" Chares says confidently.

Alexander looks around him.

The number was unquestionably an exaggeration… closer to three thousand, maybe a few more. His cooks and his wine pourers exaggerated just like his commanders and his historians. His sharp eyes estimated the number, friend or enemy, with a keen glance. His victories in battles were indebted to his discerning eyes.

Roxana always said: Chares could not count!

He starts to count his men in his mind.

He had left some men back at Susa… and had sent many to rebellious satrapies…

More than a few had died along the way too…

But still it was a good number… half Makedonians and half of them HighLanders… the rest mostly Persians… and some Baktrians… and others… all his subjects… the best warriors from all his lands.

And the Makedonians thought of themselves as his kinsmen now…

He smiles to himself.

He could count his true kinsmen on the fingers of his two hands and no more.

He had dismissed ten thousand Makedonians from his Royal Army at the Assembly of Makedonians, when he had reached Opis a few days back…

They had asked to go home in India… they had stolen his glory and his victory in India from him…

Worse! The had disobeyed his orders… he had nearly died of the bloody wretched arrow wound in India and he still felt the pain!

And so he was sending them home as they had wished… with enough gold and silver to make them the envy of their kinsmen.

Yet, instead of gratitude and blessings, they had yelled and shouted at him… they had demanded that all of the Makedonians be discharged from his Royal Army.

They had told him to take his god-father, Ammon-Zeus, on his next campaign… and his new boys from Baktria…

Ungrateful bastards! Sons of Hades and filthy whores!

Almost none of them even knew where Persia was or who the Persians were when they had followed him into Asia, greedy for gold and fame and to avenge the cause of the Hellenes. Athenians would not even permit most of them to worship at the same Temple of Athena, before they had become the Masters of the Hellenes…

Even to this day, the Hellenes thought the Makedonians were the Barbarians of the North… the Barbarian UpLanders.

Demosthenes had said that Philip was not only not Hellene, he was not even a barbarian from some worthwhile place like Persia who could be hated with respect. He had called Philip a plague from Makedonia… a place where Hellenes could not even buy a good slave.

They only kept their tongues to themselves because sharp Makedonian swords were now pointing at their soft Hellene throats!

He considers his kingsmen, seated all around him in the order of their ranks.

Where would the Makedonians be without him?

So, he had grabbed thirteen of them single-handedly with his bare hands and sent them to be hanged for their insolence.

And then he had shouted back at them:

> *"Under my command, no man has ever fallen with his back to the enemy!*
>
> *"I eat as you eat. I marry as you marry. I wake earlier than you and keep watch that you may sleep longer!*
>
> *"You said you were sick for your homes… so, GO HOME! Go then and when you reach your homes, tell your kinsmen that you abandoned Alexander, your King, and left him in the care of the Persians, whom you yourselves had defeated!*
>
> *"GO and remember that you treated me worse than I treated you!"*

So, he had dismissed them all and had given all their ranks and posts and honors to the Noble Persians!

… to Hystanes, son of Oxyartes, Brother of Roxana…

… and to Hydarnes and Artibules, sons of Mazæos…

… and to Autobares and his brother Mithrabæos…

… and to Sisines and Phradasmenes, sons of Phrataphernes…

And to sons of Artabazos…

All under the command of Hystaspes, the Baktrian Commander, a kinsman of Oxyartes.

Alexander rubs his face and sips his pure wine.

His skin still felt the harsh skin of the Makedonians as they had all come forward to kiss his face as kinsmen do… and now they were all loaded with wine, singing the songs of victory at the top of their voices… Makedonians and Persians.

He glances at the men around him.

What a sight!

None could tolerate the other, just a few days ago… now they all sang and drank together like long lost blood kinsmen.

He sips his pure strong wine.

The only kiss he truly desired was from the only lips he wanted to touch his face… the soft lips of his Queen.

A Persian kiss… A kiss from the one most beloved…

He closes his eyes. An old memory rushes into his eyelids.

The night before his first wedding... balmy... he kissed her nervously after walking her from her temple back to the palace... full of worries that she might change her mind about marrying him freely... and dishonoring him publicly...

Women were fickle like the gods...

He lingered in the gardens wondering what to do... he carelessly picked a red rose from the fragrant rosebushes lining the pathway. A sharp thorn pricked his finger... he dethorned the rose and smelled it. It smelled sweet like her. Then he turned back.

She was standing on the terrace of the main palace watching him, looking like a goddess of the heavens bathing in the light of the moon. He looked at her and filled with desire. Then he walked back toward her, up the steps, stopping and looking at her again. He gently pushed the thornless rose behind her ear. She looked right into his eyes, took his face into her hands and pulled him closer and kissed him. Her kiss swallowed his fear.

He opens his eyes and glances around.

Look at them!

The hard, brave, disciplined Makedonians his father himself had trained, the ones he had brought with him when he had left the UpLands, had turned into flawed, unruly, disobedient children.

After he had dismissed them all, they had stood at the Assembly like rooted trees and finally they had flung their arms on the ground in front of his royal tent and had stayed there calling and begging and crying for him for three days...

Fine warriors, they were, surrendering their arms like that and begging for quarters...

Any true-born Makedonian commander would be ashamed to go into a battle with them! They would probably try to drown the enemies with their tears instead of slicing their throats and shedding their blood with honor.

When he had finally taken pity on the wretched horde, Kallines had said with tearful eyes that all they wanted was to kiss him.

"Persians kiss you!" he had said, "but no Makedonian has ever tasted that high mark of honor!"

Alexander sips his pure wine and smiles to himself.

Yes... they were all his kinsmen now... but none was his equal.

How could all men be brothers, when his own brother was a half-wit bastard?

He would not even allow Arrhidaios to come to one of his drinking feasts, for fear he might become sick and embarrass him in front of his kingsmen...

But Arrhidaios was harmless otherwise and was allowed once in a while to follow him some mornings and put a handful of incense in fire altars. He liked the crackling sound of incense pouring into the fire.

How could he have ever thought that Philip would make Arrhidaios his heir?

Alexander looks around him and nods.

His kingsmen had been flattering him with their stories and he had not been listening... he was so tired of the same old stories... told and retold again... night after night...

He takes a deep breath and drinks more pure wine.

The same ten thousand Foot were to be dismissed again tomorrow… and another one thousand and five hundred Horse too. They were as unfit for service after the Feast of Harmony as they were before it.

He should let them march up country by themselves, as the Ten Thousands had done a few generations back… and see if they could do the Hellenes and Spartans one better.

He only kept and promoted men based on their merit, not on how well they sang his praises at drinking feasts… or performed the kiss of the kinsmen.

Persians and Baktrians and others had proven themselves to him… the battles they had lost were lost by the Persian fools who had commanded them into battle… the warriors themselves were worthy to serve any king!

Even the best of warriors failed without worthy leaders!

His boys, his successors, had finally arrived at Susa and they had not disappointed. The thirty thousand Baktrian boys he had trained like Makedonians for four campaigning seasons had turned out as good as his Makedonians— in the days when they knew how to fight! No! Better… and much finer-looking… they all shaved their faces as his kingsmen did… not a rough beard among them!

They were his heirs… his inheritors…

If other kings had a handful of sons to their names to fight for the kingdoms of their fathers, he had thirty thousand… with them, he would conquer all there was left to conquer… and more…

What was the use of having a son of his own blood? To hate him and wish him dead, as he had his own father?

No… he needed no other sons to fly at his throat and count his days to the last…

"Enjoying the Feast?" Hephæstion sits down to the right of Alexander. "Chares says nine thousand, but he is exaggerating as usual."

Alexander looks at Hephæstion for a moment. Hephæstion's golden earrings of Chiliarchos glint in the light of the flickering torches.

He wore it well, as if he had been born to it… just like all the noble Seven Persians before him.

The Second Man in the Empire after himself… the sole commander of all the Makedonian Horse… The highest mark of honor bestowed upon an old love who had never failed him… even with Roxana between them… and who could blame him?

They were so much alike… both hit with the same arrow of Eros…

Roxana…

Growing up, neither had ever thought that they would find worthy women to love…

They used to say gods had not created women worthy of great warriors and Aphrodite had heard them and had punished them for their arrogance. She had sent Eros to hit them with his arrows and mischievous Eros had shot them both with the same arrow… they had not only found love with a woman, they had both found love with the same woman.

And now he was bound to him more than ever… they were now more than friends and kingsmen and old lovers… they were kinsmen, connected by the blood of the Royal Daughters of Darius…

He breathes deep.

The palace eunuchs had told him that Hephæstion had not spent any time in his wedding chamber either… his new bride had thrown a glass goblet at him which had missed him and hit the wall and shattered… a sharp broken piece flying into his face… Hephæstion had left his virgin bride at Susa even though he was ordered to bring her with him… and he had decided to overlook his disobedience…

Well… now that he was the Second-in-Command, more jealous eyes were on him, just waiting and watching for anything to break him. He would not dare go near the Queen again without risking his head… and hers…

And so he had ordered Hephæstion to take Roxana and the bulk of the Foot and the Horse, while he himself had sailed down with the Fleet and then up the River Tigris, where the Fleet, the Foot and the Horse had reunited and had moved up to Opis.

He turns his head and looks to his left.

But the other one, Krateros, he could not forgive. A man not just a friend to the King… but a good friend to the Queen as well…

The tall tale Krateros had told him after reaching Karmania, bringing with him only a handful of Persian and Hellene rebels to hang… how he had treated the Queen with honor during the whole journey and how he had nursed her back to health from Black Fever… and how he had believed every word of his lies like a damn fool!

A thought crosses his mind, but it is quickly dismissed. He looks back at his kingsmen around him and smiles.

His new kinsmen had given him a perfect gap in the battle formations of his enemy in their utter ignorance… and he always knew how to make the most of a golden moment, gifted by the gods themselves… he felt it in his bones…

"Krateros!" Alexander says loudly, raising his pure wine cup.

Krateros, lightly loaded with wine, raises his pure wine cup to Alexander.

"To the King!"

Alexander gets to his feet and walks over to Krateros.

Krateros sobers up hurriedly and gets up to his feet, as swiftly as he can manage. His bones fill up with pain.

Arrow wounds of a few months back, suffered gladly to protect his Queen, still ached…

"Krateros, the most Makedonian. The most loyal of all my kingsmen. The Friend of the King who saved the life of the Queen. The man I love as dearly as my own life."

Krateros eyes Alexander carefully and holds his breath.

These kinds of proclamations by Alexander never ended well… someone usually ended up dead on the ground…

The kingsmen start to quiet down. They all eye Alexander quietly, cautiously, listening to every word from his lips.

After Alexander, loaded with pure wine, had speared the Black Kleitos right in the heart for criticizing him, they had all learned to thread more carefully at drunken feasts around Alexander and to count and measure their words cautiously.

Thirteen dead Makedonian bodies still dangled from tall posts in plain view… hanged for angering the King, who was quicker to anger as time went by. Bodies were left to rot and reek in the heat for days by the order of the King… none was to be buried.

Alexander's commanding voice echoes in the stillness of the perilous air.

"All the Makedonians, HighLanders and LowLanders, who are going back home, will travel under the command and protection of Krateros— so they all know how I feel about them!"

Voices and sounds hush quickly.

Krateros goes pale, undetected in the flush of the unmixed wine.

He had married Amastris, Daughter of the Brother of the Third Darius in Susa, as Alexander had ordered for his punishment.

He should have known that Alexander was not done punishing him…

And now this…

Alexander was so much better than him in warfare… he never missed an opportunity to exploit a weakness in his enemies… or in his own men. His eyes always searched for a gap to drive a wedge though… and his eyes always found their mark… never missed… there was always a gap!

"Krateros has been in poor health from the wounds he suffered marching up country to reach Karmania." Alexander looks at Krateros intently, half-smiling, pleased with the ease of ridding himself of Krateros. "So, Polyperchon will go with him, as his second-in-command! Just in case something happens to Krateros on the way home!"

Alexander smiles and savors his own words.

It was a long way back to Pella… and an even longer way from his Queen…

Polyperchon sits up on his couch. His ears stand at attention.

Kingsmen eye each other. They had all come unarmed, as Alexander had ordered them. This was to be a peaceful Feast of Harmony.

Krateros is pale with anger.

Alexander's words were sharper than the edge of any sword ready to kill and slaughter. He had just been banished from the royal court… so swiftly… and bleeding him dry with no drop of blood shed. Alexander was taunting and torturing him in front of his men… with the highest mark of honor, no less, knowing all too well that he was not a man to ever dishonor the Queen or himself publicly.

"All the Makedonians bound for home will leave their Asian women and children behind in my care." Alexander looks at his men intently and says mockingly, "No need to carry back grief to the wives at home, taking half-breed campaign children to the Makedonian wives, so greatly missed while in the arms of their native women of Asia."

Did they think he was going to let them take his children with them?

They were the children of his Royal Army, bound to him… loyal to him and to him only! None would ever refuse any of his orders! Ever!

Silence.

"Krateros, do not forget to take your beloved Persian wife with you and when you get to Pella, by gods, relieve old Antipatros and have him bring me more UpLanders for the Royal Army."

And if you refuse, I would like nothing better than to hang you right next to the other thirteen rotting rebels who dared to question my command!

Alexander looks around intently.

Hushed silence swallows all the sounds.

Not even the flattering tongue of Anaxarchos had a ready silvery word to say… finally outflanked by the King… both right and left…

Was he not the one who had said, after he had killed the Black Kleitos in his rage that: he was of Zeus and like him, he was all powerful… that what the King did was just… that the King was the law.

As Zeus, so his son, son of Zeus-Ammon!

Alexander smiles and sips his pure wine and glances at Hephæstion.

"Poor Antipatros could use a break from my mother!"

He would deal with old Antipatros too, if he ever dared to show his face in his royal court! He was tired of hearing about his constant quarrel with Olympias… one tear from her eyes washed away the sin of all her meddling in the affairs of the old Antipatros.

Terrified silence.

Kingsmen and kinsmen exchange cautious glances with each other and smile uneasily, masking their true faces.

What had been done to Philotas and Parmenion and the Black Kleitos was a lot more merciful than what was happening to them…

They were being relieved of their command posts and their ranks, slowly… one by one… replaced by the Persians. The same men they had come to conquer had become their rivals… soon to become their masters…

Who was now the conqueror and who was the conquered?

The reason they were seated closer to Alexander was because he did not speak a word of the tongue of the Persians, not because of his love for the Makedonians. But the Persians were becoming fluent in the tongue of their new king.

Death was more welcome than losing honor like that…

Who would be marked next after Krateros? The one most capable after Alexander…

If Krateros was expendable, so was everyone else…

Well, everyone except for Hephæstion… who had just been elevated above all to the second-in-command when all the rest had been brought down lower.

Blood starts to run cold… as cold as the unmixed wine in the mixed cups of harmony.

QUEEN'S ROYAL QUARTERS. ROYAL PALACE. ROYAL CITY of HAGMÂTÂNA
SATRAPY of MÂDA
YEAR 14 of ALEXANDER, MONTH 1, DIOS
YEAR 7 of ALEXANDER, MONTH 7, BÂGAYÂDIŠ
FEAST of MITHRÂKÂNNA
3 MONTHS LATER
NIGHT

"They say…
Men…
Live and die for the love of:
God…
… Glory,
… or Gold…
"Not me, My Beloved.
All I need,
All I want,
is:
You…
a loaf of bread…
… and a cup of wine…"

The old poet finishes his poem and bows generously and sits back down on the floor.

The old eunuch bows his head and discreetly interrupts, quietly whispering, "Dukšiš Rošanak."

Rošanak looks at the old eunuch with displeasure.

"Dukšiš Rošanak, the Ša Rêš Šarri is outside. He is requesting an audience," the old eunuch says, bowing down to his knees, pointing with his old hands.

Rošanak raises an annoyed eyebrow and then looks away.

"Tell him to go away."

The old eunuch bows down lower and shifts side-to-side uncomfortably, pleading anxiously with his eyes. "But Dukšiš, he is insisting."

She leans forward and picks up her wine cup, takes a sip and tastes every drop.

"This is a Banquet of the Queen, in honor of Divine Mithrâ. Tell him to go to the naked drunken barbarian feast the King is hosting for his own men in the royal quarters, if he desires a royal audience."

Alexander and his kingsmen did not drink wine to take pleasure from the milk of dates and grapes and honey… they bathed in it, until dead bodies were pulled out of their drinking feasts…

"Please Dukšiš… he is in arms."

Rošanak eyes the old eunuch.

The poor man looked desperate… the sort of man who was scared of his own shadow. But then again Ša Rêš Šarri was a man who could strike fear in the heart of any mortal, even battle-hardened Makedonians sheathed in full arm and armor.

Ša Rêš Šarri had utterly abandoned her after the weddings at the Royal City of Çûšâ… not even one word to her in all these months…

Could a lover have more cause to anger than a husband?

And now that what was left of the Royal Army had gathered in the Royal City of Hagmâtâna, the old gathering place of the Mâda Kings at the crossroads of the Empire, the Queen had not much use for the arrogant former lover.

"Tell him to go away!"

"Please, Your Highness!" The old eunuch starts to sink to the bottom of the black sea of panic and despair.

She eyes the old eunuch for another long moment.

The seven-walled ancient Palace of Hagmâtâna was shrouded in doom and gloom and grief… it was the last royal palace the Third Dâriuš had stayed in after his disastrous defeat at the Battle of the Black Eagle.

And the lavish banquets for Alexander and his kingsmen hosted by Âtrupâta, the Satrap of Mâda, and the father of Madumîtu, the bride of Perdikkas, had not helped to lift the dark and dismal and dreary mood of the ancient palace.

Parmenion, one of the old kingsmen of Alexander, had captured and occupied the ancient Royal City and the old palace after Dâriuš had left it.

Parmenion had been put to the sword by the order of Alexander, his head cut off in the middle of the ancient palace gardens and sent to Alexander in Bakhtriš.

The palace had not been purified and blessed by the Zarathuštra Athravans and the Maguš afterward and the palace eunuchs and all the cooks and maids and servants and gardeners and guards and all the rest saw blood and death and ghosts in every corner of it… everything was an evil omen! A mouse running from one side of the palace to the other side was a demon sent by the Lord of Darkness himself to spy on the mere mortals… obedient subjects of the Wise Lord!

Worse! The ancient Royal City of Hagmâtâna was infested with throngs of Hellene actors and dancers and singers who had followed Alexander from the Royal City of Çûšâ to entertain the royal court for fame and food and fortune, and another barbaric ignorant bunch who had come to compete in royal summer games in the middle of the Mâda winter… who ran around shamelessly naked in the ancient palace gardens, dripping with olive oil!

And she had to listen to the poor gardeners all day lamenting the destruction of their beloved gardens under the feet of the hated enemy barbarians…

… and hear cooks and maids and servants crashing into the precious palace furnishings this way and that, trying to cast their eyes away from the nakedness of shameless men…

All the Persians carried small skin bags on their belts filled with sacred salts and herbs to ward off the evil demons. They constantly cursed the Makedonians under their breath and threw sacred salt over their shoulders and into the eyes of anyone who was unfortunate enough to be walking behind them.

… more broken furnishings!

And after the sack of the ancient Âyadana of the Divine Ânâhitâ in the Royal City of Hagmâtâna by the Makedonians a few years back when the enemy army was pursuing Dâriuš, the Zarathuštra Athravans prayed continuously around the palace fire altars for the wrath of the Wise Lord to strike the demon Makedonians like a bolt of lightning and turn them into pillars of salt and stone!

Rošanak looks around and then beckons Mâr'at Bani Âriyânnâz.

"Where is Apâma?"

"She is sick again, Dukšiš. She has been throwing up all day!"

Rošanak narrows her eyes and bites her lip with envy at the reminder.

Apâma had easily gotten with child on her wedding night and was now either frequently sick or blessedly happy!

"Dukšiš, the Ša Rêš Šarri is still waiting outside!" the old eunuch says again cautiously.

Rošanak takes a deep breath and finally relents.

"Very well. Show him in. I will tell him to go away myself!"

The old eunuch lets out a sigh of relief and bows generously to the ground.

"Thank you, Your Highness!"

Hephæstion enters the banquet hall in the Queen's Quarters following the old eunuch and looks around, searching.

The banquet hall was decorated luxuriously in orange silk, the color of the rising sun, with the royal funds he had provided for the Queen, who now saw fit to make him wait endlessly behind palace doors.

There were no silver couches… the guests, mostly Women of the Queen, were sprawled on the Persian carpets on the palace floor, resting on large cushions.

A few female musicians played santoor.

Melancholy.

Hephæstion's eyes search swiftly across the crowded banquet hall and find their mark. He makes his way to Rošanak warily through the groups of lounging women.

"My Lord? Have you lost your way to the drunken feast of your king? The old eunuch mistakenly assumes that you desired an audience with me!" Rošanak says in Attik, pointing to the old eunuch without even looking at Hephæstion, taunting him coldly.

Hephæstion looks down at her.

She had not spoken one word to him since Susa and now she was mocking him publicly.

"Send them away!" Hephæstion growls in Attik.

He was coming from another lavish drinking feast of Alexander's given in the honor of Atropates, the Satrap of Media, the father of the bride of Perdikkas from Susa.

They were treated honorably by the fathers of some of their brides from Susa to Ecbatana… it was the brides who wanted nothing to do with most of them.

And he was loaded with pure wine… and he missed her in his bones… and his pain had finally become unbearable…

And she was as cold in revenge as she was warm in love…

"My Lord?"

Hephæstion sinks down to his knees next to her on the soft carpet.

Women of the Queen eye him curiously and whisper quietly.

"I said: Send them away!"

"Why, My Lord?" Rošanak says, high and cold, taunting him cruelly.

"I am the Second-in-Command of the Empire! And I order it!"

Rošanak smiles without looking at him. She signals with her hands. A pair of young girls rise up and start dancing slowly to the sound of santoor.

She had no use for his arrogance… or for him. She had pleaded with him with her words and her eyes in the Royal City of Çûšâ and all the way to Hagmâtâna and he had closed his eyes and his ears and his heart to her… not even the smallest crack for her to crawl back in…

And now that pure wine was mercilessly sieging his tainted heart, he had come back expecting her to open her folds and grant him her favors!

No! Not asking… with soft whispered words pouring secretly at her feet… but demanding arrogantly, with harsh words spoken openly in front of her women!

Hephæstion looks at the young dancers and then back at Rošanak. His eyes plead with her with words that his lips cannot easily say…

Forgive me…

Rošanak ignores his pleading eyes and tightens her words and her voice.

"My Lord, when you speak to me, you are not speaking to a barbarian whore. You are speaking to *Your Queen*."

"Damn you!" He moans in pain and mumbles. "Ecbatana is haunted—"

Shades of Philotas and Parmenion were eating away at him…

Father and Son!

For insulting Alexander and Olympias, Parmenion had killed Attalos, the husband of his own daughter, in exchange for keeping his rank and his men when Alexander had become King…

Philotas had betrayed and shamed Alexander to his father over the Pixodaros marriage alliance…

Alexander had waited and waited until the gods had gifted him with a minor plot against his life, and Alexander had skillfully woven Philotas and Parmenion into the whole cloth of a murder conspiracy against him…

So, he and Krateros and Koinos had tortured Philotas brutally…

... to extract a damning confession of his guilt and the guilt of his father... something to ensure the Assembly would not question their guilt nor rise against Alexander for killing his own kingsmen. They had bound his eyes and stripped him naked and burned and lashed and torn him to his bones... until he had finally relented and asked them what they wanted him to say to stop the torture and let him die in peace. He knew they were not going to let him live... Philotas had tears in his eyes... weeping that he had brought death to his own father by his careless deeds... and had cursed Alexander and the rest of them for their part in plotting against them.

The broken voice of Philotas continued to haunt him...

"... Father, you will die with me and because of me..."

It had made him think of his own father, Amyntor, and how much he loved him... he would have died on the Makedonian Rack himself to avoid bringing dishonor and harm to his father in any way!

He had called Philotas "unmanly", accusing him of feeling pain like a woman.

The evil he had done in Baktria to please Alexander had come back looking for him in Ecbatana.

Rošanak mocks him with a gracious tongue.

"Perhaps My Lord wishes to take his dark demons and white ghosts and return to the drunken red feast that is hosted by his king, and the thousands of his mortal worshipers, and the naked Hellene singers and dancers and actors."

"Damn you!"

She was more skilled at torturing him than he was at torturing Philotas. He had stopped after he had broken Philotas, but she had never stopped tormenting him with her love. She used the same tongue he had taught her himself to burn his soul.

Then he softens his voice. "Can you not see how lonely I am for you?"

"No. I just see an arrogant fool heavy with pure wine," she says with a sharp tongue, masking her anger.

Hephæstion fingers the golden hilt of his dagger.

Rošanak looks away unconcerned.

"An arrogant fool with a sharp Persian akinakês loaded with Persian wine—"

"Damn you!"

"My Lord, the splendid Persian wines are not for reckless drinking fools. Perhaps you should water your wine like your elders and ancients—"

"Did you not tell me once that your kingdom was mine to do with what I like?"

"For good, not for evil!"

Hephæstion leans forward, sinks into her and drops his head in her lap.

His ears had faithfully recorded every word she had ever said to him, even when he himself did not remember.

He tries again.

"Did you not tell me once that you would grant my every wish and love me?"

"No!"

Hephæstion sinks further into her lap.

She was right to mock him so cruelly… he had been such a fool for staying away from her for so long. He had not punished her for her excess, he had punished himself for his arrogance and foolishness!

Rich beyond what he had ever imagined…

Powerful beyond all other men… after the King…

And what he wanted the most was what he could never have.

Rošanak looks at him and her heart softens…

An arrogant fool with a Persian dagger loaded with Persian wine… who missed her…

… wearing the golden earrings of a Ša Rêš Šarri…

… commanding Arštibara, the first one thousand of the ten thousand Anauša, the noblest of all the nobles… the bravest of all the brave warriors…

… the Keeper of the King…

The man second only to the Lord of Asia himself in all the Lands…

The man second only to the King himself in the Queen's bed…

Rošanak waves her hand. Everyone bows low and disappears quickly.

Hephæstion rambles in torrid pain. "Philotas is here… and Parmenion… and Nikanor and Hektor…"

Rošanak gently puts her hand on his brow. He is burning up.

Ah! How she had missed the arrogant fool!

The lover had more cause to anger than the husband… the King-Husband took what was his by right, but the lover was gifted the royal favor of the Royal Woman freely.

He missed it more when it was taken away…

Hephæstion quietly moans and noticeably twists in pain.

"Philotas said that I tortured him to death because I was angry that he brought young Hektor to Alexander to be his beloved."

Rošanak runs her fingers gently through his hair. She relents.

"My Lord, you look ill."

Hephæstion ignores her.

He was not ill… he was bitterly lonely for her sweet love… her kingdom once won by his sword was now lost to his arrogance!

"Your Lord is not here! Your Lover is!" he utters quietly.

Her voice softens. She forgets his transgressions.

"Hephæstion, you are loaded with wine. You are burning up!"

"Not enough wine in the world to clothe us with the glow of righteousness!' Hephæstion says mockingly in Persian.

"Hephæstion, you have been drinking too much pure wine!" Rošanak says worriedly.

Hephæstion takes a deep breath and says quietly, "Drunk or sober, I forever seek the beloved in the house of eternal love!"

Rošanak's heart skips a beat.

He had at last mastered her tongue…

Silence.

"Perhaps it is best to have the royal healer look in on you," she says faintly, fingering his golden earring.

"No!" Hephæstion protests, mixing Persian and Attik words in his mouth and in his mind. "It is not something a damn wound-healer can cure."

It was the price he had paid to Alexander to keep her alive and it was a bargain he had meant to keep… He had paid the price willingly…

Old Kalanos was right and Aristoteles was wrong about love: there was true love among men… but love between a man and a woman was the perfection of true love.

With all the pain and misery she had caused him, all he could remember was the sweetness of her love… she was his perfect love… and for that he would have paid any price that Alexander demanded of him…

Rošanak sinks back into her soft cushions and then gently pushes him away and slowly gets up to her feet, knees slightly trembling along with the rest of her murmuring body.

She could love him again and he would leave her again…

What was the use of it all?

The bitterness of his absence had become greater than the sweetness of his embrace…

The remedy for her broken heart had become worse than her broken heart…

She was tired of crying herself to sleep night after night over him.

"I will walk you to your quarters."

Hephæstion staggers up to his feet, slowly. His head spins around the banquet hall.

"I… will accompany the Queen. My… Queen."

PALACE HALLWAY
MIDNIGHT

"Ahhh!" Hephæstion feels a sharp pain in his belly and stumbles, as they are leaving the Queen's Quarters.

Rošanak grabs him quickly.

A Mâda Palace Guard runs over.

"Hephæstion!"

Hephæstion twists and moans in pain. "It feels as if I have been stabbed."

Rošanak orders the Mâda Palace Guard. "Send for my royal healer at once! Bring him to my quarters! Go quickly!"

The Mâda Palace Guard bows his head, and rushes away.

Rošanak gently holds on to Hephæstion. "Hephæstion! Put your arm across my shoulder! Lean on me! My healer is on his way!"

Hephæstion bends over in piercing pain. He walks along, holding on to her, without resisting.

Rošanak beckons a palace eunuch and they carry him back to her royal quarters.

Hephæstion collapses on a feathery silver couch.

Rošanak touches Hephæstion's forehead.

He was burning hot like a smoldering fire altar, heaped with sacrificial incense offerings.

Rošanak orders the palace eunuch to bring over a bowl of scented cool water and clean linen. The palace eunuch quickly obeys, and places them on a small table next to her. She waves her hand and the eunuch quickly steps back and disappears from view. She dips the hand linen in the scented water bowl and wipes the sweat on Hephæstion's brow. Dripeyti's pitiless words haunt her.

"Let him die! Let them all die!"

Rošanak softly calls him. "Hephæstion…"

Hephæstion opens his eyes. Pure Persian wine is devouring him slowly. He is burning hotter than the summer sun. He forgets his Persian tongue. He mumbles and whispers in Attik, "Roxana! I wish I had listened to you! We should have run away!"

Tears flow on Rošanak's face. Her heart softens. "Hephæstion."

"Let us play dice tomorrow! I will let you win again!"

Rošanak bends; her tears bathe his hand as she kisses it. "You still owe me a few hundred golden archers!"

"She hates me! We never had a wedding night!" Hephæstion rambles feverishly. "She put a Persian dagger to her heart! She told me that she will plunge the dagger straight into her heart if I ever went near her— if I ever touched her! She said she would rather taste death than taste me— she threw her bloody wine cup at me—"

Rošanak gently caresses the faded scar on his face from his wedding night.

"Alexander ordered me… I promised him… I took an oath… I swore by the gods… he said our half-breed royal children would be kinsmen. If only he knew. If only he knew how much we want to be loved by the one we love."

"Hephæstion…"

"I… I have always loved you!"

"I have always known…" Rošanak softly cries.

It is painful for him to speak.

"From the moment I saw you walking down from the Sogdian Rock Fortress. Your hair caught like the feathers of a raven, in the winds of fortune, flying in the favored sky." Hephæstion catches his breath. The words are searing his insides. "I was such a fool! We should have run away!"

Rošanak holds on to his burning hand, gently caressing his burning face.

"Save your strength, Hephæstion. My healer is coming."

Hephæstion takes a lock of Rošanak's hair in his hand and rambles.

"You, you look so much like her. Her long raven hair scented with jasmine and those sweet starry nights in Baktria."

"Hephæstion."

"Do you ever think of me?"

"Hephæstion—"

"You said you hated me, do you still hate me?"

"I—"

"You see Alexander's broken body, do you see my broken heart?"

"Hephæstion—"

"Do not forget me!" Hephæstion pleads softly.

There is a soft knock on the golden door.

Rošanak is startled at first, then remembers and starts to get up and gently lets go of Hephæstion's hands.

"Do not leave me!" He clasps her hand tightly in his hand and pulls her back down close to him.

Her long yâsmin-scented hair falls around his face.

He whispers sweetly, words breaking. "Kiss me before I go!"

She gently kisses his face. "Hephæstion," and tries again to get to her feet, but he holds her hand tighter and pulls her closer.

She feels his hot breath on her warm face. He smells like sweet wine, his body burning hotter than the smoldering sun.

She fingers his golden earring and leans into his face and gently kisses his lips.

He closes his eyes and kisses her back hungrily and fills her mouth and drinks her like a cup of pure wine.

Rošanak cannot breathe for a moment.

The kiss had brought back the sweet memory of the first time they had kissed, like lovers, and so many stolen kisses afterward…

"Will the gods forgive me for all the evil I have done?" he moans in pain.

She loses her words. She kisses his hand instead. Her tears fall on his hands.

"You saved my firstborn from the fire of his father."

He squeezes her hand tightly for a few moments longer, remembering the kind deed that had bound her to him, and then lets go.

She looks at Hephæstion. He has passed out. Her tears bathe his face.

Another soft knock on the golden door.

Rošanak gets up and wipes her tears and signals the palace eunuch to open the door.

Her Old Persian Healer, disheveled and breathing fast, steps inside.

"Dukšiš."

He is holding his bag of sacred herbs and oils. "I came as fast as I could!" the old man says quickly, catching his breath. "Are you in pain?"

Rošanak points to the silver couch and says in a low voice, loaded with worry, "It is Hephæstion!"

"Hezârapatiš?"

The Old Persian Healer goes white, drops his bag of cures unconsciously to his feet and takes a step backward.

Hezârapatiš had put a dagger to his throat at Pârsâ asking him under pain of death why no woman had ever gotten with his child.

He had told Hezârapatiš that when a man did not beget a child, it was the fault of the woman and he should bed another woman!

He could still feel the point of the sharp dagger digging fiercely into his fleshy old throat.

He could not even curse him under his breath, as he knew Hezârapatiš understood the tongue of the Persians.

Rošanak grabs him and pulls him forward. The old man pleads.

"Dukšiš… please… summon one of their own wound-healers."

"I have summoned you!"

"But, Dukšiš… please… they kill their wound-healers!"

"And I will kill you if you refuse!" She snaps at him.

"Dukšiš!"

"You have taken a sacred oath to heal the sick and the wounded. Do what you are sworn to do!"

The Old Persian Healer takes a deep breath, relenting, and reluctantly walks over to Hephæstion's side and examines him. Hephæstion has lost his senses.

Moments pass, stretching to eternity.

"Was he drinking?"

"Yes!"

He examines Hephæstion's eyes and tongue.

"Hezârapatiš! Hezârapatiš! Can you hear me?"

Silence.

The Old Persian Healer feels Hephæstion's forehead. "Hmmm…"

"It is just too much wine, right?"

The Old Persian Healer scratches his beard and his face distractedly.

"I am afraid not!"

Rošanak pleads. "He was at the royal games! He must be just exhausted?"

The Old Persian Healer shakes his head. "I cannot be certain!"

"Are you ever certain of anything?"

"Yes! I am certain he is sick!"

She tries again. "By the favor of his gods, he will get better! Right?"

The old man looks at her carefully and then shakes his head side to side.

"Everything is possible by the favor of the gods! Hmmm… His body is burning up! Let us take him to the bath and immerse him in warm waters. I can think more on the way!"

Rošanak quickly beckons the palace eunuch.

"Summon the palace eunuchs. Tell them to prepare a warm bath for Hezârapatiš."

The palace eunuch bends in half and rushes away hurriedly.

Moments later, a pair of Mâda Palace Guards lift up the unconscious Hezârapatiš and carry him toward the bath.

"Please! Be gentle!" Rošanak begs desperately.

Rošanak and the Old Persian Healer anxiously follow the Mâda Palace Guards.

QUEEN'S ROYAL QUARTERS
2 DAYS LATER
MIDDLE of the NIGHT

Šuttu…

"Forgive him!"

"No! He abandoned me! He must suffer!" Rošanak says stubbornly.

"You have been stubborn as a mule since the day you were born!" her father says with a smile, tapping lovingly on her forehead. "It is that Bakhtrian blood of your mother in you!"

"He burned Pârsâ."

"Nothing kings and men build lasts forever… what man builds, nature takes… Pârsâ would have crumbled and faded into dust… now its star is woven tightly with the stars of Alexander and his men from the Bitter Sea… it will never be forgotten… it will be remembered to the last man in the Lands and all the Lands Beyond the Sea."

"Father!"

"Forgive a heart that is bound to you so hopelessly… you tamed his weary heart and his wild nature… he has kept faith with you all these years… there is no other woman in his heart but you… only you.

"Have mercy and let him go in peace to his gods and atone for his sins in Hamestagan… set him free…"

"No!"

"He showed mercy to your firstborn."

"And I prayed for him when he got sick."

"You are everything to him."

"He is nothing to me!"

….

"Rošanak… Rošanak!"

Mâr'at Bani Âriyânnâz shakes Rošanak in her bed. "Rošanak, wake up!"

"Manâ Pitâr." Rošanak calls out to her father longingly.

"Rošanak, it is me, open your eyes!"

Rošanak's eyes, happy with sleep, refuse to listen and obey.

She had come to live like a candle… dead during the day… alive during the night…

Mâr'at Bani Âriyânnâz shakes her harder and calls her louder.

"ROŠANAK!"

Rošanak slowly opens her sleepy eyes, unwilling to let go of the dream still roaming around her heart.

"What?" she says quietly.

"Hezârapatiš has collapsed!"

A bolt of lightning straight from the hands of the Hellene Zeus hits Rošanak in the head. She sits up in her bed quickly.

"Hephæstion?"

"A palace eunuch saw him, after he entered his room. He had fallen face down on the carpet. The palace eunuchs have bathed him and rested him in his bed by the order of his own wound-healer."

Rošanak pushes away the soft blanket, jumps out of the bed and carelessly pulls a warm Persian Purple robe around her. She rushes out of her bedroom and desperately races through the deserted Hagmâtâna Palace hallways.

Mâr'at Bani Âriyânnâz runs after her.

QUARTERS of the HEZÂRAPATIŠ. HAGMÂTÂNA ROYAL PALACE
MITHRÂKÂNÂ
RISING SUN

Waking dream…

"Hephæstion, take the hand of any woman and if you call her by her rightful Persian name, she has to grant you your heart's desire," Lady Ariana says playfully.

The Women of the Queen laugh and whisper softly, surrounding him.

He stands motionless in the middle of the moving circle of women.

He only cared about her name.

He reaches and takes the hand of Rošanak and whispers sweetly,

"Be Roshanak!"

"What does your heart desire?" Lady Ariana asks agreeably.

He pulls Rošanak closer to him and gently whispers, "A kiss!"

The Women of the Queen laugh and Lady Ariana dismisses them quickly and quietly. She leaves the tent herself after everyone else leaves.

He brings Rošanak's hand to his nose.

He was a hunter… he could find her in a multitude by her scent…
and her voice… she was accented and scented like no other…

"Roshanak," he calls her.

She breathes softly without a word.

He pulls her closer and kisses her face softly, still blind-folded. She remains within his arms… his lips move slowly across her face with small kisses, until they find her soft full lips and linger with pleasure.

Her skin beats nervously under his lips.

He presses his clean-shaven face into her soft skin. She raises her hands and removes the blind-fold and cups his face into her hands. He leans into her face and kisses her mouth slowly, taking his time. He pulls back and looks at her.

"Do not leave me!" she whispers sweetly in Persian.

He smiles and puts his arms around her, pulling her trembling body tightly against his body and kisses her again once, and then once more.

"No matter where I go, I will always return to you…"

….

Hephæstion opens his eyes. Rošanak's head is resting on his bed by his side. He is holding her hand. He reaches and caresses her hair with longing…

… so close and a world away…

What was living without ever having her again…?

"Roshanak," a loved voice calls to her.

Rošanak opens her eyes and lifts up her head. Her dream disappears quickly, like a wisp of smoke from a fire altar.

"Hephæstion…"

"Roshanak…" He calls her again, and his voice fades into the heavens.

He tightens his hand powerfully around her hand and then lets go and drops his hand.

"Hephæstion?"

Silence.

"Hephæstion!"

Utter silence.

Not even the sound of labored breathing… Nothing…

"HEPHÆSTION!" She screams in pain. Then she moans, as she realizes…

"Nooooooo!" Then she shouts at the Persian royal guards watching by the door. *"Find Alexander!"*

A Mâda royal guard rushes away hurriedly.

Her scream echoes around the bedchamber and shatters like delicate Persian kâsaka against the stony palace walls.

The ancient Palace of Hagmâtâna shakes and quivers and folds.

The Angel of Death had finally arrived at the Royal City of Hagmâtâna, the ancient gathering place of the ancient Mâda and Pârsâ… where the HighLanders and the LowLanders and the Persians had now come to gather…

Unwanted and unwelcomed…

… answering the call of the Holy to feast on the body of the enemy warriors.

She had started with the Ša Rêš Šarri, the Hezârapatiš, the Second to the King, the one most loved by the King… the gate-keeper of the King, without whom all the gates to the King were laid wide open… like a golden sword without a golden scabbard… left in the rain to rust and dust.

Death had come to Hagmâtâna…

… and had summoned the last Ša Rêš Šarri to her kingdom first…

The Gathering Place of the ancient Mâda Kings had become the Assembly of dead Makedonian warriors…

YEAR 12 of ALEXANDER, MONTH of PYANEPSION,
in the ARCHONSHIP of HEGESIAS at ATHENAI
YEAR 14 of ALEXANDER, MONTH 1, DIOS
YEAR 7 of ALEXANDER, MONTH 7, BÂGAYÂDIŠ
DAY 16: MITHRÂKÂNÂ, DAY of the DIVINE MITHRÂ
MORNING

So died Hephæstion, Son of Amyntor, descendant of ancient Hellenes.

Ša Rêš Šarri, Hezârapatiš, Framâtar of Arštibara, the first one thousand of the ten thousand Anauša, Second-in-Command of Alexander, the Lord of Asia.

On Mithrâkânâ, the Autumn Equinox, the day of the Divine Mithrâ, Angel of Light and Goodness and Strength on Earth… Angel of War… Proclaimer of the Rising Sun, Protector of all Warriors…

In the arms of his beloved, Rošanak, a Persian Royal Woman…

… who whispered upon his passing,

"Hephæstion, the fire that never dies, burns in my heart."

The Sacred Royal Fires were extinguished all across the Lands of Alexander, the Lord of Asia, by the order of Alexander himself…
Since time immemorial, the sacred Royal Fires had been put to sleep only after the death of a Great King and reawakened after the accession of a new Great King…

And the Royal Fires remembered…

Ša Rêš Šarri had died… a Kingsman had died…

OUTSIDE of HEPHÆSTION'S BEDCHAMBER
3 DAYS LATER
EVENING

Torchlit palace hallway.

"Please! Have mercy!" Rošanak quietly pleads with the old Âtravaxš.

A pair of younger Zarathuštra Athravans and Maguš stand a few steps back, listening intently.

Two Persian royal guards stand at attention, flanking the doors to Hephæstion's death chamber.

A mourning wreath, the color of the darkest night, adorns the center of the gilded doors.

Perdikkas, Ptolemaios, Aristonous, Leonnatos, Lysimachos, Eumenes, Medeios, Seleukos and other kingsmen aimlessly pace the palace hallway from one end to the other with long faces loaded with agony and worry.

Perdikkas walks over and gently takes Rošanak's arm. He pulls her back away from the door and warns her quietly.

"Do not go inside! He is in a murderous mood! He has ordered the damn healer hanged for his incompetence!"

Rošanak narrows her eyes at Perdikkas and asks hesitatingly, "Which one?" with a quivering voice.

"The Hellene."

Rošanak takes a deep sigh and shakes her head and pushes back a tear and reclaims her arm gently from Perdikkas. "Tonight is the third night of his passing… he cannot remain as he is without receiving his Rite of the Dead! His soul will be trapped between Heaven and Hell forever."

Perdikkas shakes his head side to side with dismay. "You go in there and you will be trapped between Alexander and Hephæstion!"

She bites her lip and turns around and continues pleading with the old Âtravaxš. "Please!"

"My Dear Dukšiš. What you ask is impossible." The old Âtravaxš refuses her flatly.

Rošanak pleads again softly, pushing back tears. "Please! I beg of you! All his own men will do is hold games and run around naked in races trying to win golden wreaths!"

"As I said, they are barbarians. We cannot perform the Rite of the Dead for a barbaric heathen. Our prayers will be of no use to a murderous enemy."

Rošanak closes her eyes and takes a breath. The words of the old Âtravaxš sear her bleeding heart. "It is evil to speak ill of the dead!" she says quietly under her breath.

She had never doubted that all her dead had crossed into the Land of the Eternal Light. That they had all been received honorably by her royal ancestors.

But what was to happen to the soul of Hephæstion?

Did he have any noble ancestors of his own to claim him? Did they know where to come looking for him? Would they know where to find him? He had died so far away from the lands of his fathers.

How could she know so little about him?

She had listened countless times to the beat of his heart, but had never heard the song of his ancestors…

"He was Ša Rêš Šarri, second only to the Lord of Asia in all the Lands."

"That does not entitle him to our prayers."

"Please! If not at my request, then do it by the order of the King!"

The old Âtravaxš narrows his eyes at her. "My Dear Dukšiš. I serve the Wise Lord, not the Lord of Asia. The Makedonian King has no dominion over the servants of the Wise Lord."

… and neither have you!

"And we warned the King, but he took no heed of our counsel. He ordered all the Royal Fires doused until after the funeral. Lands are without a king."

"Please! The King is alive and he will kill you, as he has so many others for disobedience!"

"Life and Death are by the favor of the Wise Lord!"

"Please!"

Tears fall on Rošanak's face.

"Has there not been enough noble blood spilled already?" she begs. "If not by the pleading of the Queen, nor by the order of the King, then please do it out of mercy to a noble warrior who died far away from the Lands of his noble ancestors."

"My Queen, the sacred words are for the faithful. Not for these invading barbarians."

"Does the Wise Lord not love all who live on the Lands of the Persians?"

The old Âtravaxš looks at her and takes a deep breath.

"No!"

"Please!"

The old Âtravaxš shakes his head side to side.

"May the Wise Lord reduce the blood-thirsty demon gods of these invaders into viperous serpents and scorpions and crumbled dust and scatter them on the burned steps of Pârsâ and over the ashes of Avesta! May the Guardian Angels of the Heaven walk on the bones of their demon gods on the Day of Judgment!"

Rošanak sighs regretfully and then relents. "Then please just wash his body and anoint him with sacred oils."

A tear rolls down her cheek.

"He restored many temples of the Divine Goddess Ânâhitâ across the Lands."

The old Âtravaxš narrows his eyes at her.

"They are the men responsible for the destruction of our sacred temples in the first place. If they had not ruined our temples, there would have been no need to restore them! Sacking of the sacred Âyadana of Divine Ânâhitâ in Hagmâtanâ was not enough for these godless men! The greedy heathens tried to scrape the gold and silver off the sacred temple columns!"

"One should always honor the dead." Rošanak bites her lip and shakes her head with sadness. "If I had died on strange lands beyond my ancestral home, I would have wanted a holy man of their gods to bless me and say a prayer over my dead body."

The old Âtravaxš considers Rošanak and he also finally relents.

"Very well, we will prepare his body, but we will not pray for his soul. If he had a soul, that would be the concern of his own godless gods."

"Please… say something over his dead body… recite a poem… tell an ancient story… or say a prayer. The King knows not a word of our Persian tongue, not even my name. But he is not without hearing either… he will know… and he will punish with no mercy!"

INSIDE HEPHÆSTION'S BEDCHAMBER

Mournful silence…

Cold as death… no… colder… much colder…

Hephæstion lays dead on his bed.

The window is wide open, the curtain sways in the chilly mountain air of Hagmâtâna. The Royal Fire is doused and dead in the fire altar; a torch bathes the room in flickering fiery light. The bedchamber is haunted and quiet; no longer a bedchamber, it is a death chamber.

Alexander is slumped in a tall chair, watching over Hephæstion's dead body.

There is a soft knock on the door.

"Go away!" Alexander growls.

One of the doors quietly opens, Rošanak softly walks in and the door quietly closes behind her. She stands silently for a moment and looks at Hephæstion's dead body, holding in her breath. His words whisper loudly in her ears, *"Do not forget me!"* Another tear rolls down her face.

Alexander turns his head and sees her.

Her grief shrouded her face like a veil of sorrow…

He looks back at Hephæstion's body, heavy with guilt, loaded with pain.

When he had decided to marry her, he had expected his old lover to quarrel with his wife or just ignore her. Who would have thought Hephæstion would fall madly in love with her instead… that she would become more to him than anyone?

And who would have thought he would drink himself to death over her? They were invincible LowLanders, their warrior blood was mixed with unmixed wine since birth.

Rošanak takes a deep breath and turns her head and looks at Alexander with teary eyes, making no effort to hide her grief.

He, too, was heavy with grief… his eyes melting away in tears…

… sitting in Hephæstion's room for three days, grieving… not allowing anyone to go near Hephæstion's body.

He had forbidden all his kingsmen to enter his death chamber on pain of death…

He had banned her and her old Persian wound-healer from Hephæstion's bedside and had sent him a Royal Army Healer instead…

What did an army wound-healer know about mending broken hearts?

He needed her love poured into his soul and her sacred prayers poured into his ears…

Well… at least he had only hanged the army wound-healer and had spared her old healer…

She takes another deep breath. Grief lines around her eyes deepen. She reads Alexander's face like a folded piece of old precious parchment.

Love or Guilt… it made no difference… neither brought back the dead… there was no cure for death…

Rošanak wipes her tears and walks slowly and kneels on the carpet by Alexander's chair.

Cut locks of his unruly lion mane are scattered everywhere on the floor. His flaxen hair that used to glimmer and glint like the fields of honey-golden wheat in the rays of sun, now looks like a harvested wheat field sleeping under the winter cold.

Alexander eyes her for a long moment and then looks back at Hephæstion's body, exhausted.

He felt sick…

He had not slept or had anything to eat or drink since Hephæstion's death… only wine.

His mind races.

In Babylon, when he had become the Lord of Asia, they had brought him a highborn woman caught bedding a lover… they told him it was the ancient Law of Babylon, the Code of Hammurabi, that such a tainted woman should be tied to her lover and both thrown to their deaths into the raging River Euphrates. But her husband loved her and had forgiven her and wished her back, and had begged for the mercy of the King… only the King could have spared her life against the ancient Laws of Kings. And so, he had spared the life of the woman, and let her husband do with her as he would.

And he had spared the life of his own Queen too… when he had discovered that she had been bedding a lover… his own best friend and old lover no less…

In Karmania, after the drinking feast in the tent of Krateros, he had gone back unannounced and unexpected to see to Hephæstion and had found him in bed sleeping deeply wrapped around the naked body of a woman…

He had not seen the face or the rest of the woman, but he had smelled the sweet scent of jasmine on a lowly Hellene himation that was tossed carelessly on a wooden chair…

How many Hellene women had made it to Karmania after the march through the Desert of Death and how many of them bathed in the luxurious royal scent of jasmine, other than his own Queen?
What should have he done?
As a king… or… as a man?
Tied up Roxana and Hephæstion together and flung them into the Persian Waters?
or…
Caught the lovers in a hammered bronze net, invisible to the eyes, and called all his royal court to gather as judges and witnesses… just as Hephæstos had caught the cheating Aphrodite and Ares and had shamed them in front of all the Olympians.
All the other goddesses had not looked upon the naked lovers, but all the gods had laughed and winked and nudged… Hermes had even offered to change places with Ares… Ares had totally refused… he preferred to be tied painfully to Aphrodite in a bronze net and shamed nakedly in front of all the gods than be free of her!
or…
Divorced her by simply saying: "You are not my wife!" and returned her to her kinsmen… and then have to send for her later when he missed her beyond reason?
So instead, loaded with wine and pain, in front of his men, he had reluctantly kissed his young eunuch who had won a dance contest during the royal games thinking news of it would make them both jealous… and neither of them had taken any notice of it… And that was before he even knew about her and Krateros… if he had known, he would have let Hephæstion and Krateros kill each other in Karmania.
Just as Zeus had chained Titan Prometheus to the peak of an ancient mountain on the other side of the Hyrkania Sea to make him suffer endlessly in utter cold and loneliness for stealing fire from the heavens, he had punished Hephæstion in Susa for stealing Roxana from him by chaining his old lover to himself, promoting him to the highest rank above all others and giving him a Persian wife… and Roxana was the raven eating out Hephæstion's heart every day, tormenting him with no mercy…
He had even ordered Hephæstion to take her from Karmania to Persepolis… but she had gotten with child again. He was relieved when she had lost her unborn again in Persepolis, not knowing whose it was, and he had finally decided to separate them for good in Susa… and then had ordered him to bring her to Ecbatana, knowing well this time his eyes were on them both…
As a woman, Roxana had proven no less troublesome than Pandora.
He could have the Queen hanged for treason against the King… but what was the use? He still would love her bitterly to his grave… as he had found out in Susa.
Nothing she had ever done had lessened his love for her… hurting her hurt him more than her… he could not destroy her without destroying himself; she was half of his heart. So just as hope was all that was left in the Jar of Pandora, he had kept hope that she would willingly come back to him and that she would think him more worthy of her love than all her other lovers…

The poisonous love arrow Eros had brutally wounded him with in Sogdiana was still firmly lodged in his heart… and made him bleed with the pain of love every time he looked at her. There was no remedy for love… just endless bitter pain… and yet he preferred a hopeful, painful life with her to a hopeless painless life without her.

Rošanak gently takes his hand and kisses it.

"Alexander…"

He pulls his hand away without looking at her and grunts quietly.

"Leave us!"

"Alexander! Please! It has been three days. Hephæstion must be given his rites to let him pass through to the Land of the Eternal Light by dawn of the fourth day!"

Alexander looks away and growls cuttingly, "He is not your concern!"

There was no Eternal Light after death for the mortals… all dead men just went to the dark and dreary House of Hades… but if one were a god, one would enjoy the pleasures of Mount Olympus…

Rošanak takes a quiet deep breath and looks at Hephæstion. She then reaches and gently takes the empty wine cup out of Alexander's hand and puts it on the floor, and takes his hand in her hands again and caresses it tenderly. He does not pull away from her soft touch. She narrows her eyes and searches her memory.

Hephæstion had told her once that when Alexander sank into darkness, all that could reach him were words of Homer or Euripides… he knew all their written words by heart… and only Homer, when his mood was the darkest…

And now his mood was the darkest she had ever seen…

Her mind tosses and turns.

Alexander had killed one of his own kingsmen, a man who had saved his life at the Battle of Granikos no less, for speaking a line from Euripides' Andromache in a drunken feast in Bakhtriš.

She had never seen Alexander that loaded with wine.

What line of that play could have pushed him to the edge of such murderous rage?

She desperately tries to remember.

Time slowly disappears… leaves the room… vanishes in grief…

She absently remembers the lines from Andromache she had rewritten to tease Hephæstion and to show him her mastery of Attik. It had amused him, made him laugh. He had said she was no longer in need of his tutoring.

> *Darius: Loosen her chains! Untie her hands!*
>
> *Alexander: No! I have a right to her!*
>
> *Darius: Why have you come to the Lands of the Persians? Are the HighLands and LowLands of Makedon, lands of your own fathers, not enough for you?*
>
> *Alexander: I came for your gold!*
>
> *Darius: Take the worthless gold and set her free!*
>
> *Alexander: She is my captive woman! I took her from Baktria!*

Darius: She is my son's royal gift!
Alexander: What is his is mine and what is mine is mine!
Darius: For good, not evil… not for murderous wrath!
Alexander: You will never take her from me!
Darius: Coward! What right have you to a place among men? He stole your wife. You knew she was unfaithful. But when she fell back into your hands, you spared her life. At the sight of her nakedness, you dropped your shield and surrendered… then you dropped your sword that was raised to kill her. You filled up with manly desire for her instead!
Krateros: Alas! What evil now reigns in the Lands! Men shed their blood and King claims their glory! The king is but one man among ten thousand to wave his sword… he does the work of one… he wins more glory than all… he wins all the glory for one!

Her mind wanders.

I, Andromache, was once of a proud race of the free… married to Hektor, Royal Son of the House of Priamos, the King of the Trojans… his worthless brother, Paris, stole Helene, a naked Spartan wench… the Hellenes came for her…
I watched Achilleos kill Hektor and tie his body to his chariot and pull his royal body in the dust around the heavy walls of Troia… My infant son, Astyanax, begotten by Hektor, was hurled down the tall Towers of Troia by the merciless Hellenes who sacked and burned the Palace of King Priamos.
I was pulled by my hair and taken to Hellas in chains as a captive woman and given to Neoptolemos, Son of Achilleos, as his prize of war… I bedded my enemy!
Alexander is the blood of my blood! Alexander is the blood of ancient Âryâs…

She takes a deep breath.

No… reciting the virtues of the Queen on the deathbed of her dead lover might harvest the same murderous fate at the hands of her grieving Kingly-Husband…
Homer, then!
She had read Homer to please Hephæstion, but the words were old and dusty and dead and mostly forgotten… finally she pulls worn and faded words out of her thin failing memory…

"Alexander, was Hephæstion ever left unattended without care in his life as he is now in his death? Did the shade of Patroklos not come to Achilleos after his death and ask his beloved to give him his burial rites and release him from mortal life? Did he not ask Achilleos to give him his fire and let him pass through the Gates of Death?"

Cold dead silence.

Alexander runs his fingers through his shorn hair wordlessly, avoiding her eyes.

"So much for Homer... he gives me no aid..."

Rošanak mumbles to herself in Persian and looks around desperately, then leans over and picks up the small dagger resting carelessly at Alexander's feet and cuts off a lock of her hair. She gently pulls Alexander's hand toward her and puts the dagger and the lock of her hair in his palm.

"Alexander, I accept whatever punishment that will satisfy the King. Take your dagger and cut all of my hair and spill all of my blood and take whatever else of me that will gratify you and your gods and release the body of Hephæstion to the men of god for his death rites." She takes a deep breath and pushes back a tear. "Did you not ask me to release the body of our firstborn to the fire yourself? Did I not obey your command?"

Alexander turns his head toward Rošanak and his heart finally softens. He accepts her peace offering. He lets go and the dagger silently falls on the carpet. He keeps the lock of her hair firmly in his fist. "I will never see him again. If only I could just hold him near one more time, stay up all night and drink and talk about the days when we were young!" He looks intently at Rošanak and mumbles in pain. His eyes become loaded with tears. "Roxana, who can I turn to now? Who can I trust with my life now? My men love me for their King! He loved me for Me!"

"Alexander—"

"I have never feared death! I have never understood all the tears shed over the dead!"

"Alexander."

"I understand now! There is this pain in my body, worse than the arrow wound from India." He moans in pain. "How can anything hurt so much? It started in my heart," putting his hand on his heart, "and then it spread like wildfire all over my body."

Rošanak kisses his hand.

"I keep calling his name, but he does not answer me..."

Tears fall on Rošanak's face. "Alexander, Hephæstion was blessed by your gods, because he was loved!"

Alexander looks at her and goes quiet.

Yes... he was loved not just by his gods... he was loved by his Queen too...

Rošanak lets go of Alexander's hand, gets to her feet and walks over quietly to open the door. She then steps away and leans against the wall, steadying her trembling knees.

The Zarathuštra Athravans enter the room quietly.

Alexander's eyes follow them wordlessly.

They quietly approach Hephæstion's body.

A palace maid quietly enters the death chamber with a tray of food for the living, sets it next to Alexander's chair and bows and leaves quickly.

The aroma of food fills Alexander. There is bread and cheese and milk and honey on the tray. Without a care whether the food has been tasted for poison or not, he reaches and takes a piece of bread and eats it. He drinks some milk. Life slowly pours back into him.

The athravans slowly undress Hephæstion and start washing his body.

Mercifully the cold mountain air had kept his dead body from spoiling quickly…

The old Âtravaxš eyes the Lord of Asia under his old brow for a long moment.

The gods of the Lord of Asia were no different than other gods. They had given him a true friend and then had taken him away to inflict the greatest agony and misery on the arrogant king…

He then utters an old Bâb-ilani story quietly in Persian.

"It is a story as old as time. Long before the Great Kings, Gilgâmeš, the King of Uruk, son of a goddess and a man, two parts divine and one part mortal, became a tyrant. As the divine right of the kings, he demanded the virginity of every maiden on her wedding night:

I enter first the chamber of the virgin bride, then may the groom, after I leave!

"His people became afraid of him and cried out to their gods. The gods of Bâbiru heard their cries, but instead of punishing Gilgâmeš in haste, they divined that the king was lonely and sent him Enkîdu, a man himself equal to Gilgâmeš, one part divine, two parts mortal, to become his true friend. And then they took him away.

"When Enkîdu died, Gilgâmeš mourned his death and cried out to his gods:

My beloved is dead. I weep over him day and night. I will mourn him as long as I live and breathe.

"And Gilgâmeš learned that not even a king had the power to bring back the dead to life. For the first time, Gilgâmeš felt his own mortality and again cried out to his gods:

Must I die too? How can I find the man, who became immortal in the hands of the great gods, to ask him how I might become immortal too?"

Another athravan enters the room, lights the fire in the small fire altar and scatters a handful of incense on the dead embers and prays. The scent of Arabâya incense fills the room. The athravan leaves the bedchamber with Hephæstion's death clothes.

Alexander looks on.

The athravans wash and dry Hephæstion's body three times with scented rosewater. Then they anoint his body with sacred scented oils. Another athravan enters the death chamber carrying a white robe.

Rošanak looks at the white robe and looks at Alexander. She takes a deep breath and bites her lip and pushes back a tear.

On the barren Apadâna terrace of Pârsâ, she had seen Hephæstion wearing a long white robe… and Alexander too…

A pair of palace servants bring clean scented clothes for Hephæstion and lay them gently on the foot of the death bed and leave the room. Another palace servant brings in Hephæstion's Makedonian body armor, his breastplate and his burnished leg guards, his arm and armor, all polished to perfection.

The athravans clothe the body of Hephæstion in his own cleaned scented clothes and armor and then they cover him with the white robe. They quietly leave the room and close the doors behind them.

The fire burns gently in the small altar. The room becomes quiet again.

Alexander stands up and walks over to Hephæstion's body. He picks up Hephæstion's arms and carefully lays them on his body and says quietly, "Farewell, Hephæstion! Peace be with you in the dark where Hades commands!"

More tears roll down Rošanak's face.

Alexander turns and walks toward the door. He stops and stands in front of Rošanak. He reaches and touches the tears on her face and then leans forward and gently rests his forehead on her forehead. "Roxana…"

Rošanak whispers tearfully, "I will offer blood sacrifice to the Wise Lord tomorrow in the early dawn, the fourth day of his death, before his soul leaves the land of mortals! You can have him for his funeral afterward!"

Alexander turns back and looks at Hephæstion once more and shakes his head. "Very well."

Rošanak takes Alexander's hand. He turns his head toward her.

"Will you honor him by burning him in a casket of hammered gold and silver?" she asks faintly.

She could not bear to see him burn…

Alexander eyes her for a moment and thinks on his feet.

A casket of gold and silver, covered with arms dedicated to him, would be glorious.

Alexander nods quietly, "Hephæstion would like that," and then leaves the room, leaving Rošanak alone.

The room becomes empty and quiet. The sacred fire crackles and burns slowly in the altar. The flame of the torch moves this way and that way in the cold air from the window.

Rošanak rests her head against the wall for a long moment, tears falling. She closes her eyes.

Dripeyti was utterly right! They were not sisters!

She was glad his damn arrogant wife was left behind in the Royal City of Çûšâ and was utterly forgotten… she could not have endured her there… his wedded wife was not his bedded wife… their hands were not tied together… the only gift of the wife to the husband on their wedding night was a Kâsaka cut close to his eye…

No! His wife cared nothing for him… she bitterly hated him… his death would have pleased her so! If she had heard of his death, she would have braved the icy snowy passes from Çûšâ to Hagmâtâna just to throw more dead trees on top of his funeral pyre and watch him burn hotter!

Rošanak opens her eyes and wipes her tears, pushes away from the wall and walks up to Hephæstion's body.

She hesitates for a moment and prays under her breath.

"My Lord, please forgive me."

It was forbidden to touch the dead… only the Âtravaxš and the Maguš and the Zarathuštra Athravans could touch the dead body and then purify themselves by ritual prayers later.

She narrows her eyes. The light of the torch flickers on his face.

His soul was still on earth… still in the death chamber… until the early dawn of the following day, the fourth day of his death. Tonight was the night that his soul regretted dying… the night before the morning of his First Judgment…

Mortal sin or not… she could not help herself…

She takes a deep breath. She then gently reaches and caresses Hephæstion's cold lips with the warm tips of her fingers and remembers him and tears run down her face like a river.

The lips that had kissed her a thousand times… and a thousand times more… had lost their kisses…

She gently takes the tips of his firm fingers into her hand. The words from Homer that he had made her read to teach her his tongue rush into her mind.

She kneels down by his body and talks to him quietly under her breath.

"Hephæstion, remember when I said *Ilias* was old and cruel and dusty and bloody, and you wrote these lines and gave them to me and made me read these words to you?"

She clears her throat and pushes back tears.

"The wrath of Alexander, the blistering fury that brought unspeakable pains unto the Persians. When the heavenly beauty, Roxana, the captive Persian girl, the share of Alexander from the Persian Wars, saw Hephæstion dead on his bed, she wept. She said: *My Hephæstion, dear to my heart, as wretched as I am, you were my protector. My three brothers, my father, and my childhood lover, all were dead when Alexander took my ancient fortress and captured me. But you saw me wedded to Alexander, not shamed, given a wedding among the Makedonians.* You said to me: *There is no shame in royal bonds. I will not let any harm come to you.* Now I am left behind to mourn your death."

Tears.

"Why have you gone and left me?" she weeps.

"Come back and teach me more!" she begs.

"Come back and finish writing on my skin," she pleads.

Rošanak pulls out a white silk thread from the fold of her royal gown and wraps it around Hephæstion's wrist, tying a knot, and takes one of his golden earrings, then bends and kisses his cold hand and remembers more.

> *Hephæstion stood… unarmed and unguarded… his eyes covered and tied with a piece of silky soft cloth. He reached and took her hand and whispered sweetly:*

"Be Roshanak!"

"What does your heart desire?"

Hephæstion pulled her closer to him and gently whispered, "A Kiss!"

He pressed his smooth face into her soft skin…

His body pulsated with desire against hers…

"Do not leave me!" she whispered sweetly.

"No matter where I go, I will always come back to you…" he whispered back, making a promise… he then pulled her trembling body tightly against his body and kissed her again…

Tears pour out of her heart.

… I have always loved you…

… Kiss me before I go…

Cold mountain air rushes recklessly into the dimly lit death chamber. The fire torch flickers and fights the merciless mountain air to stay alive.

Rošanak turns her head and looks through the open window.

Dark clouds were gathering around the pale moon…

She looks back at Hephæstion.

A soft knock on the door.

A slow twist of mayûxa.

A young Zarathuštra Athravan dressed in a snow white heavy winter robe quietly enters the room and closes the door behind him.

Rošanak turns her head and looks at him through the veil of tears.

The young Zarathuštra Athravan walks over quietly and stands by the death bed of Hephæstion and utters quietly,

"Only the Wise Lord judges. Mysteries of God are hidden from mortal eyes. The Lord of Darkness inflicts ninety nine thousand nine hundred and ninety nine diseases on the Wise Lord, and still at the end he will be forgiven."

Rošanak eyes him wordlessly.

He takes a deep breath and then offers a short prayer for the dead warrior:

"A^{h}uramazdâ^{h} said unto Zaraøuštra:

"When I created Miørâ, I created him worthy of sacrifice, worthy of praise…

"I made him the most powerful of all that I created…

"… the Protector of all Warriors…

"… the Protector of Order and of Fidelity and of Oath…

"Warriors should approach him with honor and reverence…

"… offer him songs of praise worthy of being heard…

"No one should break a covenant with a follower of Mithrâ…

"… with a follower of Truth…

"A^{h}uramazdâ^{h} spoke these words to Zaraøuštra…"

Aête zî vâcô Ahurô Mazdâ frâmroat Zaraøuštrâi…

He takes a deep breath.

"The Wise Lord will be victorious at the end and all men will renounce the Lord of Darkness and will worship the Wise Lord and will become purified. On the Day of the Last Judgment, Man will be restored. He is made for life and not for death. He will neither grow old again nor will he ever die, he will live forever and will act according to the Laws of the Wise Lord."

He pauses and then looks at Rošanak and then continues quietly.

"Great is the glory of *A*^h^uramazdâ^âh^… Great is the glory of the Holy *Z*araøuštra."

The haunted death chamber fills with the grace of god.

More tears.

Rošanak leans forward and kisses the hands of the young Zarathuštra Athravan with unspeakable gratitude.

May the Divine Ânâhitâ bless you with warrior sons…

May the Divine Dên await you with an armful of fragrant yâsmin…

May the Bridge of Chinvât widen under your blessed feet…

OUTSIDE of HAGMÂTÂNA ROYAL PALACE
7 DAYS LATER
MIDDLE of the NIGHT

Terrified silence… Winter cold… Moonless night…

Rošanak takes a deep breath and signals with her hand.

Embalming was not a custom of the Persians…

There were no Mudrâya embalmers in the royal court and camp nor any in Hagmâtâna and none that could be dispatched to Hagmâtâna. The winter cold and snow season had already started and the mountain passes in and out of Hagmâtâna in all directions had begun to close one after the other.

Alexander had finally decided to burn the body of Hephæstion according to their customs before it became corrupted and despoiled.

Death-eating maggots cared nothing for a man or a king… by the order of the gods, they ate up the body of the dead after the fourth day of passing… the cold of the mountain air was no barrier to the marching maggots!

So, Hephæstion had been laid in a hammered golden casket and covered with a thin layer of wax according to the customs of the Persians and then packed in sacred salt and spicy scented myrrh. He was to be burned on a magnificent pyre on the eleventh day of his death.

And his body was exchanged for that of a dead LowLander who had died a few days before and the golden casket was re-sealed with the Royal Seal of Dâriuš, the royal seal her father had sent to her before his death. And Hephæstion's body was quickly covered with another thin layer of wax and was put in a humble wooden casket and packed with precious sacred salt and spicy scented myrrh…

The young Zarathuštra Athravan and Abi-Samar load the lowly wooden box with Hephæstion's body heaped with sacred salt and scented myrrh into the back of the covered carriage. Rošanak looks on anxiously as the men secure the wooden box and pull down the back flap and tie it to the carriage posts.

Mâr'at Bani Âriyânnâz stands inside the palace doors, anxiously looking out for anyone coming their way.

They all knew that if they were caught, Alexander would show no mercy!

The plain wooden box disappears from sight. The blessed young Zarathuštra Athravan, sympathetic to her tears, bows to Rošanak, turns around in haste and quietly disappears back into the belly of the ancient Hagmâtâna Palace.

Rošanak feels anxious and doubtful. Her heart flutters restlessly, confidence leaves her cold.

Is this what Hephæstion would have wanted for himself?

The Realm of the Dead of the Hellenes, the House of Hades, was a dark and misty place with five rivers: River of Sorrow, River of Lamentation, River of Fire, River of Forgetfulness, and River of Hate…

Had he already paid the ferryman Charon with golden Persian archers to take him across the River of Sorrow? Had he stopped and drunk from the River of Forgetfulness on his way to the Gates of Hades? Had he already forgotten her?

"Abi-Samar."

"My Lady?"

"Abi-Samar… I… fear for your safety…"

"Everyone will be watching the burning of the great funeral pyre… even the palace guards will abandon their posts to see the magnificent spectacle."

Abi-Samar pauses, taking a deep breath. "And my passage documents are all in order, all signed by Eumenes, the Royal Secretary, himself. The body is that of my brother, taken back to Bakhtriš for proper burial by his kin."

Rošanak pushes back tears and pulls the heavy robe tighter around her. "Passes are iced."

"Not any worse than icy passes in Bakhtrian mountains!"

"Abi-Samar… I…" She pauses… "Maybe we should take him to the funeral pyre… let him burn by the custom of his ancestors…"

Abi-Samar looks searchingly into Rošanak's face. Her eyes glisten with tears in the darkness of the night. Heavy snow clouds brew overhead.

"He never told me… what I should do… with his body… I never thought he would… die too… and leave me… he survived bloody battlefields to die in bed!"

Abi-Samar looks intently at Rošanak, consumed by doubt. "My Lady, dawn is approaching. I should leave soon."

"What shall I do? He said to me once that… no matter where he went… he would always return to me…"

Abi-Samar takes Rošanak's hand, kisses it and whispers, "I am not a man who would ever know the sweet love of a woman but, if I was such a man blessed with your love as he was, I would want to be near my beloved in life and in death."

Rošanak closes her eyes and thinks for a moment. She takes a deep breath and opens her eyes and looks at the carriage again.

Abi-Samar lets go of her hand and looks at her quietly. "I would bury his body next to that of your firstborn."

Rošanak bites her lip hard. She tastes her own blood in her mouth. She turns her head back and looks at Abi-Samar. "I free you from your oath to me. Live as a free man for the rest of your days, with my gratitude. Do not come back!"

Abi-Samar bows to Rošanak graciously. "My Lady, I have served you freely, since the death of your father. I am bound to you by my own free hands. I wish to serve a Royal Woman. It is my honor to serve the Queen of the House of the King."

His words catch her by surprise. She nods and takes Abi-Samar's hand for a moment and then lets go.

"Give this to the old Zarathuštra Athravan for the Divine Goddess Ânâhitâ," Rošanak says quietly, and gives him a small skin bag full of golden archers.

"Ask him to say a prayer in remembrance of all my loved ones."

"Yes, My Lady."

"Wait." She hesitates and then reaches and unclasps the gold chain from around her neck and puts the chain and the golden lion ring into Abi-Samar's hands and quietly whispers, "Leave this with his body."

ROYAL LANDS OUTSIDE of ROYAL CITY of HAGMÂTÂNA
FOLLOWING DAY
MID-DAY

First heavy snow of the winter season.

Fires roar to the heavens.

The entire funeral pyre of Hephæstion is in flames, a golden casket heaped with the dedicated arms of Alexander and his kingsmen.

Royal guards stand ready to douse the flames with large barrels of wine.

Alexander and all his kingsmen are standing and watching.

The smell of burning wood and burning flesh fills Rošanak's senses.

Blissful heavy snow had closed all the passes into and out of the Royal City of Hagmâtâna right after Abi-Samar had left.

All sounds are drowned in the roar of the fire.

The snowy sky above darkens with the smoke. Ashes and snow fall like rain from the sky. The veil of sorrow shields Rošanak's face from black ashes.

It had come to pass…

A nameless LowLander was burning… polluting the sacred flames…

While Hephæstion's body was on its way to the tomb of her ancestors...

If she had let Hephæstion burn in the sacred fire, he would have been lost to her... her royal ancestors would surely take kindly to a man who had loved her well...

If only Alexander knew...

She had even covered the golden casket with one of her precious royal purple robes, before all the arms that were dedicated to him were heaped on it...

Rošanak looks around feeling bitter and mumbles to herself.

"Lying bastards!"

She was right to rescue the body of Hephæstion from the mockery of his enemies. The men who had made the biggest dedication of their arms to Hephæstion were the ones who hated him the most... or feared him the most... or had seized the death of Hephæstion as an opportunity to get closer to the living Alexander.

Eumenes, the bloody Kardian, looked so grief-stricken, as if his entire clan were roasting on fire!

Was he not the one who had quarreled with Hephæstion bitterly, when Hephæstion had flung his whore from his room and had given the room to a Hellene flute player?

And afterward he had refused to obey Hephæstion, when he had become the Second-in-Command and the Guardian of the Royal Journal.

She glances at Alexander. Alexander stands close to the burning pyre, rooted to the snowy ground like a tree, breathing in and bathing in the blackened ashes.

"How is Abi-Samar these days?"

Rošanak looks around, startled. "Oštana!"

"Little Sister."

Rošanak looks at Oštana for a moment, distracted, and then looks back toward the blazing pyre.

"Did you think I would not keep my eyes on you, just because you are angry with me?" Oštana leans forward and whispers into her ear.

Rošanak glares at Oštana with annoyance. "What do you want, Oštana?"

He smiles and leans forward and lifts her veil of mourning and kisses her face.

"Do not worry, Little Sister. Your secret is safe with me! We made sure that Abi-Samar got out of the city before the high pass closed."

A handful of Bakhtrians always kept watch in the dark to make sure she was safe among the enemy invaders. They all knew she had been bedding the former lover of the King.

Why not?

She was lost to the Bakhtrians and the Persians once she was bedded by the Makedonian who did not share their faith.

But her sacrifice had saved the lives of so many... and for that she deserved whatever comfort and happiness she could find.

Her tall and fine-looking lover was a lot like Utâna. He was everything her King-Husband was not. Her lover was a man the Makedonian himself had once desired.

Unlike the Persian Kings, the Makedonian was not much to look at.

He was just half a head taller than her, with a head that was always bent to his left.

His hair was always disheveled and he did not have a beard to shave.

His fair skin burned easily under the Persian sun.

His body was visibly scarred and torn and his forehead slightly bulged over his fearsome eyes. And it was the blazing gaze from those eyes of different colors that struck fear in the hearts of men.

The Makedonian looked half-man, half-demon… and sounded like one too… his harsh voice could kill the living and raise the dead.

He could not think of a man he hated more.

The Makedonian had not won an empire… the Persians had lost it! But it was hard to fault the Persians with all he had seen of him and his men… their sheer brutality and greed had no bounds… no one had ever seen men like them.

On the battlefield, they were not warriors, they were butchers… they killed whatever they touched… death was their shadow… cities and towns and villages had simply vanished in their wake. Off the battlefield, they were just thieves…

Rošanak looks at Oštana and lets out a breath, relieved.

Oštana eyes Rošanak with sadness.

He missed the times he used to visit her in her tent to talk about their long dead brothers. She had gotten angry with him when he had spoken ill of her king-husband to her face, and had thrown him out of her tent in Hind. And yet she had faithfully continued to send him food from her royal table to make sure he was well taken care of.

Oštana reaches and takes her hand.

"The pain of losing a lover never goes away… but it becomes easier to live with…" he says under his breath, comforting her.

She pushes back a tear and squeezes his hand.

Oštana takes a deep breath and looks up at the skies.

The mountains and the falling snow reminded him of his beloved Bakhtriš.

And of his blood brothers… older one dead… younger one protected…

And his dead lover, still alive and living well in his heart…

If the cursed invaders had all burned along with Pârsâ, it would have saved the Persians the trouble of burning them on wood piles later.

"The King ordered all the Royal Fires in all the Lands to be doused after the death of his old lover, not to be re-awakened until after the Royal Funeral," Oštana utters under his lips quietly as he watches the roaring flames. He smiles to himself with satisfaction.

Everyone knew the Bâb-ilani Prophecy.

The Makedonian was mourning his own death.

It had been seven years… His days were now numbered and counted… weighed and measured…

There was to be sweetness in the revenge for the blood of his lover and for Utâna, his blood brother… and for all his brothers of different fathers… and all his kinsmen…

BANQUET HALL. ROYAL PALACE. ROYAL CITY of HAGMÂTÂNA
YEAR 14 of ALEXANDER, MONTH 4, PERITIOS
YEAR 7 of ALEXANDER, MONTH 10, ANÂMAKA
LONGEST NIGHT of the YEAR
WINTER SOLSTICE of DAYGHÂN
NIGHT

Fire roars in the fireplaces. Santoors playing.

Hephæstion would have liked this gown, Rošanak thinks to herself, as she enters the Persian Feast in the honor of the Winter Festival of Day'ghân, wearing a heavy crimson red silk royal gown.

It was almost the color of the standard that was raised in front of his men... the old Regiment of Hephæstion...

She looks around.

Everything bathes in the color of blood. The banquet hall in the Palace of Hagmâtâna is decorated with crimson color, the banquet tables are covered with fruits and nuts, large bowls are filled with pomegranates and watermelons.

A royal court story-teller is telling the old love story of Zariadres and Odatis again. He stops and bows, and then continues with her leave.

All that was missing was... the Hezârapatiš...

Yes, Hezârapatiš was bitterly missed by the lonely Dukšiš...

She sinks into a silver couch wearily.

A Queen had to attend all the damn festivals... even when she felt like crawling into a cave somewhere and disappearing from the Lands... altogether...

Well, at least all the bloody Hellene singers and dancers and actors and whores who followed Alexander like mice following a sack of barley, hoping for droppings of gold wreaths, had been banished from the palace during the mourning period. The noises of drunken singing had vanished and the magnificent old palace of the Mâda Kings and the summer palace of the Great Kings at Hagmâtâna had been purified by the Zarathuštra Athravans and had regained its royal dignity.

Still... she would willingly suffer them all, if they brought her lover back with them.

She would gladly grant every one of them a golden garland...

Rošanak looks around again mindlessly.

Apâma had given birth to a healthy baby boy. She was happy for Apâma and sad for herself... envious...

Hephæstion was right... all newborn babies looked alike!

She swallows hard and picks up a rhyton full of red wine and looks at it in the shimmery lights of the hall... the color of the blood of warriors.

She sips her sweetened wine and whispers in Attik, "To Hephæstion, as we remember our heroes, so they remain immortal in our mortal hearts!"

"To Hephæstion! A Divine Hero!" Alexander says in a quiet voice.

Rošanak is startled. She almost drops the rhyton of wine in her lap.

She had not even noticed Alexander. She did not even know Alexander was still at Hagmâtâna.

The last she had seen him, he was covered with dead ashes at the funeral.

The last few months, since the death of Hephæstion, had been lost in a blur of utter sadness… loaded with guilt… heavy with regrets, for words left unsaid…

…for love left unspent…

She had recklessly said she had no more use for him and his gods had heard her and had taken him from her…

Alexander had ordered Eumenes to write to Dripeyti and inform her of the passing of her husband… and that she was not permitted to marry again… ever… by the order of the King.

Alexander sips his strong wine and looks at her from the corner of his eyes.

She had avoided him since the funeral of Hephæstion… she had blamed him for his death. He blamed himself for Hephæstion's death too…

He had put his Second-in-Command in charge of the welfare of his Queen in Susa.

He had kept the two of them close enough and far away… and made them both pay dearly for betraying him…

But it was he himself who had come to suffer the most… losing both loves together, after the sudden death of one…

Rošanak straightens and smiles.

"My Lord, I thought you would be at the banquet for…"

"I was told that you were celebrating the birth of your Sun-God, God of Warriors."

"Yes… Divine Mithres…"

"It is the festival Hephæstion would have attended on behalf of the King."

"Yes."

"I miss Hephæstion…"

Rošanak hears the sadness of loss in Alexander's voice.

They had both lost when Hephæstion had died…

What use was it to guess who had suffered more?

She looks at him and then reaches and touches the tips of his fingers gently.

The tips of his fingers were burning with old memories of lost loves…

His chopped up hair had grown back and now it was fully kissed by the rays of the moon…

"I miss him too!" Rošanak whispers quietly.

Alexander leans forward and gently plays with her hair, the shorter locks she had cut off in mourning for Hephæstion on his death bed.

He whispers, "I sent envoys to the Oracle of Ammon-Zeus at Siwah. I asked them if Hephæstion could be granted divinity. They said that he could be worshiped as a Hero."

"I heard." She nods sweetly with a smile.

"Do you think he would have liked that?"

"Yes… Hephæstion would have liked that…"

Yes, he would have… remembrance was the only remedy for death…

A man, two-thirds mortal, one-third divine, three-thirds remembered…

ROŠANAK'S BED CHAMBER. QUEEN'S ROYAL QUARTERS
MIDDLE of the NIGHT

Snowing outside.

Night has quietly wrapped around the Hagmâtâna Palace.

Another Festival of Day'ghân has come to pass.

Rošanak is restless. She cannot sleep. She walks over and leans against the window in her royal bedchamber, feeling lonely and anxious.

She missed Alexander more than ever…

Seeing him at the festival had stirred up sweet old memories and had flamed the fire of bodily desires… but he had left the festival wordlessly without beckoning her to him as he used to…

It had been too long…

Life was for the living… love was for the living…

They had both lost love…

She rests her warm head on the rim of the cold window.

Shimmery snowflakes dance slowly on the other side of the window. The rim of the thick window is colder than the winter air outside. The fireplace in her bedchamber glows.

She reaches for the snowflakes. The tips of her fingers touch the elaborate glass of the window.

"Alexander…" she whispers sadly.

She takes a deep breath.

Who could blame the candle for flaring and flickering and flaming when kissed by the friendly fire?

She thinks for a moment, then turns around and grabs her royal robe, quietly leaves her bedroom and heads for the royal quarters of the king on the other side of the palace.

KING'S ROYAL QUARTERS
LATER

Sleepy palace… flickering torches…

Rošanak approaches the royal bedchamber of the king.

Persian royal guards are guarding the massive golden doors to the King's bedchamber.

Rošanak stands before the Guards and the doors.

The Guards bow their heads and open the doors silently for the Queen Consort and then quietly close the doors behind her.

Even though the Queen was not summoned by the King to his bedchamber, it was the ancient custom of the Persians: the Queen-Mother and the Queen-Consort always had access to the King, without being summoned, unless the King had another wife or a woman of the court or a lover in his bed.

And as the King was alone; the door to his bedroom had opened up obediently for the Queen…

Alexander's royal bedchamber is warm and quiet.

The burning fireplace glows in the darkness.

Rošanak takes off her royal robe, drops it on the floor carelessly, walks to Alexander's royal bed and stands there by his bedside watching him sleep deeply and listening to him breathing deeper.

The burning wood in the fireplace crackles and crumbles and roars and tumbles.

Rošanak turns her head and looks at the fireplace, startled.

Alexander wakes up and turns and sees a smallish shadow by his bed. Quickly without thinking, he grabs his golden dagger from under his pillow and swiftly puts it on the shadow's throat.

It was the same jewel-crusted, golden-handled, lion-headed Persian dagger he had cut his wedding loaf and his finger with and that he had kept under his pillow all these years.

She stands motionless, soundless, voiceless.

The sharp tip of the golden dagger glints and slides smoothly and rests in the hollow of her throat.

Slight pressure on the golden handle of the golden dagger… the sharp tip of the sharp dagger pricks her throat… red blood rushes to the surface of her ivory skin. The god of the golden dagger tastes her blood and accepts her blood offering.

The fire flickers on Rošanak's face. Her old emerald earrings sparkle seductively in the flicker of the fire.

"Roxana…"

Wine and sleep swiftly pour out of Alexander, wake and worry quickly pour in.

He carefully pulls his sharp dagger away from her throat and drops it.

The bloodied-tip golden dagger falls silently on the Persian carpet covering the floor.

He reaches and puts the tip of his finger on the small blood cut and presses it tightly. Her heart pounds and pulsates under the tip of his trembling finger.

"Forgive me…" he whispers silently, filled with regret.

She gently pushes his hand away and slides her winter gown off and embraces his naked warm body with desire. She pulls his head to her heaving naked breasts and runs her fingers tenderly through his unruly mane and kisses the top of his head. His familiar scent fills her body… like a late afternoon summer downpour from the belly of the thickly clouded heavens.

He puts his arms around her tightly and rests his head on her naked breast, listening to the familiar sound of her beating heart. Her familiar scent fills him up.

He had missed her… this was the first time she had come to him… and she had come freely without being beckoned… or ordered… or summoned…

She sweetly whispers his name; her voice mixes with the crackle of the crackling fire. "Alexander."

"Roxana."

"I have missed you."

"Roxana."

He feels the warmth of her trembling body.

Hope returns… Desire rekindles… Old buried love comes hurrying back…

A love lost…

Another love regained…

Like Aphrodite who had never left Hephæstos, she had always remained with him.

He eagerly pulls her naked body down into his empty lonely bed, licks the blood off her dagger honor cut, kisses her neck and whispers her name again. "Roxana…"

"Alexander…" She willingly pulls him back into her heart.

The memory of the old Kalyana whispers quietly into her ears:

"The King needs to be loved softly…"

Five

ECLIPSE of the SUN

TEMPLE of DIVINE GODDESS ÂNÂHITÂ. ROYAL CITY of HAGMÂTÂNA
The NIGHT before NO'ROUZ
FESTIVAL of FRAWARDIGÂN

Crackling Arabâya incense. Flickering fire altar.

Honoring the ancestors, remembering the dead, whispering sacred words of Avesta under the breath.

"I worship the Wise Lord…"

Pushing back a tear…

"This I ask you, My Lord, tell me truly,
Who is the Creator, the Wise Lord of Righteousness?
… and who is the Destroyer, the Dark Lord of Wickedness?
Who sets the path for the sun, the moon and the little stars?
… and who makes the moon first wax and then wane?
Who, My Lord?
… all this and more I wish to know, My Lord…"

Taking a deep breath…

"This I ask you, My Lord, tell me truly,
Who holds the earth below and the sky above from falling?
Who created the Lands and the Waters?
Who created the wind and the clouds?
… the rain… and the Royal Fire?
Who, I wonder, My Lord?
All this and more I wish to know, My Lord…"

Rošanak pauses and then continues. "Divine Ânâhitâ, the Mother Goddess, who makes the seeds of all men pure, who makes the womb of all women pure for bringing forth…"

She closes her eyes, another tear falls on her face.

What was the purpose of her life? If not to bear fruit and bring forth sons?

"Roshanak… are you crying again?"

"Ah!" She opens her eyes. She looks around, startled.

There was no one in the âyadana, except for her and an old athravan.

She was losing her reason… going mad… hearing voices…

She takes a deep breath and puts another handful of Arabâya incense in the silvery fire altar. Hephæstion's loved voice whispers again in her ear softly.

"Women are a mystery to men… even Queens to Kings…"

"What shall I tell Alexander?"

"The truth… tell him the truth…"

"He would leave me again…"

"He never goes very far, does he?"

KING'S ROYAL QUARTERS. HAGMÂTÂNA PALACE
YEAR 14 of ALEXANDER, MONTH 7, ARTEMISIOS
YEAR 8 of ALEXANDER, MONTH 1, ADUKANAIŠA
FESTIVAL of NO'ROUZ
SUNRISE

"I worship the Wise Lord, who made the light and the dark, the morning and the noon and the night, who keeps the sky from falling."

The fallen little star had been restored back to the starry skies…

"The Wise Lord who created the sky and water and earth and plants and animals and man."

Rošanak pauses and looks up at Alexander and smiles at him.

"I am with child," she utters softly like a sacred prayer.

"May the Lord of Asia accept the love of his First Wife as the first tribute of the people of his Lands on the New Day at the start of the Persian New Year."

And then she leans over and kisses his hand and looks up and smiles, again.

Alexander eyes her.

This one was his…

"May the gods help us!" Alexander says quietly, taking a deep breath.

Breathing deeply still hurt…

FOLLOWING DAY
MID-DAY

"Alexander left for Babylon this morning," Perdikkas tells Rošanak in a low voice. "He will pass through the Land of Kossæans in the mountains on his way."

Silence.

Perdikkas eyes Rošanak cautiously. "The mountain passes out of Ecbatana are still iced with snow. I am to take you and Hephæstion's bones to Babylon when the snow melts and the passes re-open. Alexander did not want to endanger you and his unborn child by taking you along on his campaign."

Rošanak puts her hand on her belly and leans over and smiles at Perdikkas.

"It is a son… begotten on the night of the birth of the Divine Mithres… a most lucky day…"

She had felt the very moment Alexander had gotten her with child… and this time she wanted the child more than she wanted Alexander.

Alexander could go all the way to the Kingdom of Qin, Land of the Phoenix and the Dragon, on the other side of the farthest edges of Bakhtriš, without her missing him…

… well, maybe not that far.

Perdikkas eyes her with pity.

With all her beauty, her body was unlucky… a wasteland ruled by Hades…

After the death of her firstborn, no seed had ever taken root in her weak womb…

Alexander should have married a sturdy Makedonian.

GATE of GODS. ROYAL CITY of BÂB-ILIM. BÂBIRUŠ
YEAR 14 of ALEXANDER, MONTH 7, ARTEMISIOS
YEAR 8 of ALEXANDER, MONTH 1, ADUKANAIŠA
YEAR 8 of A-LEK-SA-AN-DAR who is called ALEXANDER, MONTH 1, NÎSANNU
MID-DAY

"Alexander!" Nearchos rushes toward Alexander, waving his arms in the air.

Alexander raises his hand and the royal guards come to a halt and wait for Nearchos to reach them.

The first time he had approached Babylon almost eight years ago, after the Battle at Gaugamela, Mazæos, the Satrap of Babylon, had come forward and received him and his Royal Army with his sons and had surrendered Babylon to him whole.

Bagophanes, the Guardian of the Royal Treasury, had strewn the road into the city through the Gate of Gods with flowers and had burned precious Arabian incense and exotic scents in silver altars in his honor…

Now, Mazæos and Bagophanes were both dead…

He was warned by the old insolent Chaldæan not to return to Babylon if he touched a Royal Daughter; the same man who had foretold the death of Mazæos and Bagophanes.

There was no magic in foretelling the death of Mazæos and Bagophanes… they were traitors to their own king… how long were they to remain loyal to him?

He had the old Chaldæan put to the sword for his insolence.

And there was no royal ceremony to welcome him back into Babylon… no long lines of Babylonians offering him tributes… no lions and leopards and chanting priests… just Nearchos, appointed the New Satrap of Babylon for bringing the Fleet safely back to Persia and for saving the Queen, followed by a train of gloomy Chaldæans in their long white robes adorned with golden stars.

And there was no Hephæstion riding behind him… his bones were coming later in a golden casket, traveling again with Roxana… one last time.

Nearchos reaches Alexander and bows his head and catches his breath.

"Alexander, welcome to Babylon, the Gate of Gods."

Alexander eyes the Chaldæans following Nearchos guardedly.

The Chaldæans bow their heads, anxious to talk to him.

Alexander looks back at Nearchos wryly. "Unfavorable omens?"

"Alexander, please listen to them, before entering the city. They want to talk to you."

Alexander beckons the Chaldæans. They approach, bowing, with their interpreter. "What do your stars foretell of my destiny now?"

Bêl-rimanni, the Chaldæan, bows and says, "The Lord of Asia, it is wise not to enter Bâb-ilim, with your back toward the rising sun."

The interpreter interprets for Alexander.

"What about the gate on the other side of Babylon?" Alexander asks.

"My Lord, the lands around the gate facing the setting sun are covered with flood waters and muddy marshes this time of year."

Words are interpreted.

"Is the temple of your gods not complete?"

Bêl-rimanni bows again and says formally, "No, My Lord. The rebuilding of the E-sag-ila, the great temple dedicated to the Bâb-ilim supreme god Marduk, next to the large temple tower E-temen-an-ki, is not yet complete."

Alexander eyes Nearchos and then looks at the Chaldæan tiredly.

"Why is the Babylonian temple not complete? I ordered the reconstruction when I first came here— eight years ago."

Bêl-rimanni bows lower.

The Lord of Asia did not know much about Asia and the old ways of the Lands.

"My Lord, we are Chaldæans… Watchers of the Heavens… Diviners of Celestial Omens… the Temple of E-sag ila is served by the Temple Enterers of Bêl Marduk. We are not the keepers of the temple funds, nor the builders of the sacred temple."

"Alexander, the reconstruction has been slow. They say it will be completed by next year," Nearchos says cautiously.

"I am told the Babylonian temple will be complete within a year," Alexander says to the Chaldæans.

Bêl-rimanni bows again. "Golden-honey ants cover the foundation of the new temple… the Temple of E-sag-ila will not get built!"

Alexander narrows his eyes at the Chaldæan.

Golden ants?

Fools! Did they not know he was the Lord and Master of Asia?!

The Chaldæans wait for the interpreter and exchange glances.

"Antalû." Bêl-rimanni points to the sun. "An Eclipse of the Sun is foretold for the day 29 of month of Nîsannu. The King will die within a year."

The interpreter interprets for Alexander.

A voice says, "Babylonians are doom worshippers. Your father, Zeus-Ammon, will shield you from any evil within the walls of Babylon."

Alexander takes a deep breath and closes his eyes for a silent moment of remembrance.

Just as Achilleos knew his death was near after the death of Patroklos, so was his death near after the death of Hephæstion…

Blood curdling sounds closer to Babylon.

Alexander narrows his eyes and looks up at the skies.

Ravens were fighting each other high in the skies over Babylon… a few start falling, bloodied and dead, to the ground not too far from him…

Ravens were unlucky omens… signs of forthcoming chaos and clash and conflict…

Alexander finally worries. He looks back at the Chaldæans and asks quietly.

"How can such misfortune be avoided?"

Bêl-rimanni bows again and considers the Lord of Asia under his brows.

A-lek-sa-an-dar,
Take heed of the great gods! Listen to my words!
As Bêl Marduk destined the fate of Gilgâmeš,
So has he fated you for kingship and no more…
He has given you lordship over men,
He has given you victory on the battlefields…
And the blood of countless brave warriors…
and the dust of many great cities…
But he has granted you only one godly part… a part of the rebel god…
The part thirsting for immortality…
…you are not fated for eternal life…
…you are fated for eternal thirst for immortality…
Nergal, the god of destruction, awaits you…
His spirit lurks in the marshes around the Gate of Gods…

"Return to the Gathering Place of Mâda, Lord of Asia. Do not enter the Gate of Gods."

"The Queen is heavy with child… she is already on her way… traveling back to Ecbatana will be too tiring for her."

He was not going back to Ecbatana. The shade of old Parmenion had taken his Hephæstion from him in the ancient place of the gathering of the Persians.

Bêl-rimanni eyes the Lord of Asia in despair and bows again.

Not just the Eclipse of the Sun, but Nêbiru was standing inside the House of Nânna, the Moon-God… another grave celestial omen. The King was to die within a year.
Their old master, Kî-Nabû, the chief diviner of the royal court, was certain of it.
The Lord of Asia did not understand their words of warning.
He made light of the god of death who was sitting on his shoulders.
Just as Bêl Marduk had weighed and measured King Nabû Nâ'-id,
He had weighed and measured A-lek-sa-an-dar…
And both had been found wanting…
What more could be said without angering the great gods?

"My Lord, please reconsider."

Words are interpreted, as spoken.

"No."

"Then camp here My Lord, and wait until a substitute king is chosen by the Temple Enterers of Bêl Marduk, so he takes upon himself the evil omens of Heaven and Earth." Bêl-rimanni bows again.

"Do as you please. I will circle the city and enter through the gate facing the setting sun."

"Alexander, the prophecy…" Nearchos says with dismay.

Alexander shrugs his shoulders. "I accept the omen! So be it! The best prophecies are those that come true!"

ENTRANCE GATES. ROYAL PALACE of the SECOND NABÛ-KUDURRÎ-ÛSUR
ROYAL CITY of BÂB-ILIM
YEAR 14 of ALEXANDER, MONTH 8, DAISIOS
YEAR 8 of ALEXANDER, MONTH 2, OÛRAVÂHARA
YEAR 8 of A-LEK-SA-AN-DAR, MONTH 2, AYYÂRU
LATE NIGHT

"… ša ekalli?"

Rošanak turns around, bracing her tired back with her hands on her sides, and looks at the smallish man standing before her addressing her carelessly, calling her *woman of the palace… mistress of the king*. He does not recognize her. She is dusty and travel-stained and her rounded belly plainly declares the unborn child inside.

A Queen traveled queenly, as Ăriyânnâz was always quick to remind her.

"This way," the small man says in broken Persian and points to the hallway behind him.

She narrows her eyes at him with displeasure.

She was tired to the bone…

She had come earlier than the rest of the Royal Army with a handful of royal guards, in hope of a warm bath and a comfortable bed, and had arrived in the middle of the night. The road from the other side of the mountain had brought them directly to the formidable outer fortified walls of Bâb-ilim and then to the inner massive bronze doors guarding the Gate of Gods. She had entered the city through the Gate of Ištar and had passed the glazed guardian lions and bulls and dragons and had come straight to the Royal Palace of Nabû'kudra'cara, which was hard to miss next to the golden gate, being the largest palace she had ever been to…

… now that Pârsâ was blackened and burned to ashes…

The ancient palace glinted in gold and silver and lapis lazuli, crushing mere mortals with its immensity… and bedazzling and seducing all the kings and queens it had hosted from time immemorial with its intoxicating beauty…

A familiar voice interrupts and bellows in the large entrance hall, uttering Bâb-ilani words… words she understands.

"Issi Ekalli! Mârat Šarri, Aššat Šarri!"

She turns around slowly and looks at Abi-Samar. Then she smiles and relaxes.

She had so many questions… but they could all wait for a quiet moment when there were not so many eyes on them…

Abi-Samar bows his head low.

He had returned from Baktra safely where he had taken Ša Rêš Šarri's body to be put to rest in King Artakhšaçâ's rock-cut burial tomb next to her firstborn, and had then come back directly to Bâb-ilim, the city of his birth, to prepare her royal quarters.

The small man whitens like a ghost, sinks to his knees and drops to the ground before her and babbles in accented broken Persian. "Your Highness! Please! Forgive me! I am your humble servant!" His words become faint. "No royal messenger has come tonight to announce your royal arrival. We were not expecting you for a few more days!"

"Is Mâr'at Bani Âriyânnâz following you?" Abi-Samar asks quietly.

Mâr'at Bani would have insisted on a royal ceremony to properly welcome Issi Ekalli into the royal city of Bâb-ilim according to the royal court customs, if she was traveling with her. She would not have allowed the Queen to arrive carelessly unannounced.

"No. She was sick with fever. I left her in Hagmâtâna," she replies wearily.

An older man in an elegant embroidered robe rushes forward and bows, barring the small man behind him from her tired eyes.

He had carelessly insulted the Persian Royal Woman… Palace eunuchs had lost their heads for a lot less…

Abi-Samar graciously introduces the old man.

"Issi Ekalli Rošanak, may I present the oldest brother of my father, Abi-Enši-Marduk, the Chief Eunuch of the Palace of Nabû-Kudurrî-Ûṣur."

The Chief Eunuch bows lowly and graciously.

"Issi Ekalli Rošanak. We have been expecting you!" He bows lower. "Welcome to the House of the King, on the Foundation of the Heaven on Earth."

He discreetly points to the smallish man behind him with his eyes, bowing lower. "Elnuškira."

Abi-Samar quietly translates. "He is the keeper of the palace doors at night."

"Your Highness, please forgive him and spare his life. I assure you he will be lashed for his insolence!" the Chief Eunuch pleads quietly.

Rošanak looks at the Chief Eunuch and then turns to Abi-Samar and whispers quietly in an anxious voice, unable to tolerate the burden of ignorance a moment longer.

"The matter of Hezârapatiš…?"

Her face wrinkles with pain for a moment.

"It has been seen to, My Lady, just as you ordered it!" Abi-Samar says in a hushed voice, bowing his head.

She takes a deep breath and nods her head, relieved. She waves her hand and dismisses the royal guards who had accompanied her to the palace. She then turns back to the Chief Eunuch. "Abi-Samar does honor to the House of his Fathers. Are my quarters ready?"

The Chief Eunuch bows low and points to the golden curtains next to the other side of the palace entrance gate. "Yes, Your Highness, this way."

Palace maids quickly pull away the curtains revealing a dimly-lit passageway behind them.

Rošanak wearily walks down the passageway and then stops at the end by the steps leading upward.

The Chief Eunuch and Abi-Samar follow her. A few palace maids and servants follow invisibly behind them. The small man quickly disappears in the belly of the giant palace.

"As Abi-Samar, the son of my brother, conveyed your wishes, all the furnishings have been replaced. If they are not to your liking, Your Highness, we will replace them again at once," the Chief Eunuch says in a flattering voice, eager to please the new Queen of the House of the King.

Rošanak slowly and silently walks up the stairs and finally reaches the top. The Chief Eunuch bows quickly and steps forward and opens the massive doors, bows again and steps back.

Rošanak steps outside. Before her a wide stony sky bridge stretches from this side of the main giant palace toward the small garden palace, nestled among the splendid Persian gardens, stretching into the heavens.

A hanging Persian garden, planted, root and branch, in the sky… with a splendid garden palace built by the Bâb-ilu King, the Second Nabû'kudra'cara for the love of his Mâda Royal Woman, Amytiš, the Royal Daughter of the legendary Dragon King, King Ištu-Vigu… the Niyâka of Kuruš the Elder…

Indeed the paradayadâ built on the foundation of Heaven on Earth!

The fragrant scent of the spring flowers and exotic trees fills her senses. Torches light the sky bridge from one side all the way to the other side.

She had dreaded coming to Bâb-ilim.

It was the surrender of Bâb-ilim to the Makedonians that had cracked the vessel of the Empire and the crack had gotten wider and wider… until the vessel had utterly shattered.

She wanted to remain at the royal palace at the Royal City of Hagmâtâna. Even though Hephæstion's bones were not there, his memories and his scent still lingered in the air. After Alexander had left for Bâb-ilim, she had slept many lonely nights in Hephæstion's old bed… even though his old room was purified by the athravans, his old bed and pillow still smelled like him.

A giant lion statue marked the earth where the body of a dead nameless warrior had been burned in the name of Hephæstion…

Alexander hated Hagmâtâna for taking Hephæstion but he would have come back to see his son, once he was born!

The Chief Eunuch leans forward and quietly whispers, "No one has entered this splendid Palace of Queen Amytiš but Persian Royal Women and their Kings. The Lord of Asia and his men were mostly interested in the Royal Treasury and Bâb-ilani wine and women when they first stayed in the royal palace. Harpalos, the Guardian of the Royal Funds, who stayed in the main palace with his many harimtu, was lame and could not walk but a few steps and could not climb the stairs. We covered the passageway to the Garden Palace with heavy curtains and put powerful spells to guard against the intruders. It has remained hidden until now."

He bows low and points with his hand.

"Ašar lâ amârim… a place that cannot be found…"

Rošanak looks at the shimmery jewel hidden between the old flowering and fruiting trees.

That was why the wretched Harpalos had been born lame. So he could not climb the tall steps and desecrate the most precious jewel in the Palace of Nabû'Kudra'Cara with his wicked bloody whores…

Rošanak relaxes and takes a deep breath and the stench of her long journey starts to fade, as her body fills up with scented flowers and murmuring falling waters.

> *"Come! See my beloved city…" the old Sumerian Scribe, Sîn-Lêgi-Unninni, had written about the ancient city of Uruk.Ki, not far from the other side of Bâb-ilim, in former days… a thousand years ago…*

She looks around. Sweet air fills her tired body.

Do not all scribes write lovingly about their beloved cities?

> *"Come… See my beloved city!*
>
> *Come!*
>
> *Walk up the stony steps… older than time immemorial…*
>
> *See how her palaces glint like honey gold in the rays of the blazing sun,*
>
> *And like hammered silver wrapped in the shimmer of the moon…*
>
> *See the beautiful temples… built on the other foundation of Heaven on Earth…*
>
> *… with sky-glazed tiles, dotted with bits of golden gold…*
>
> *Their great walls touching the clouds in the heavens…*
>
> *Walk in the gardens and the orchards and the bazaars on this side or that side of the great rivers…*
>
> *Smell the freshly baked breads and taste sesame cakes sweetened with golden date-honey…*
>
> *Listen to the sensual whispers of lovers in the secret hidden places…*
>
> *… and hear their hushed sighs uttered with pleasure in the rapture of their union…*
>
> *… and hear the sweet murmurs of fresh water rolling gently in spring streams…*
>
> *Great gods have built my great city…*
>
> *And have filled it with joy and with delicious fruits… filled with lusciousness and ripeness and sweetness…"*

She smiles.

The Chief Eunuch takes a deep breath, relieved.

"The Garden Palace of Amytiš… This Palace is the Jewel in the Crown of all the jeweled palaces in Bâb-ilim…

"Even more beautiful today than in the days of Queen Amytiš, for the love of whom the Second Nabû-Kudurrî-Ûṣur built this palace and these heavenly gardens. All the flowering and fruiting trees were brought here from the Lands of the Persians.

"The palace and the gardens are shielded from the hot winds from this side of the desert lands. The winds from the other side of the lowlands bathe the gardens in cool air and take away the smell of the city," the Chief Eunuch speaks proudly, starting to walk on the sky bridge backwards, bowing.

Rošanak follows him, enchanted. The Garden Palace glints in the light of the torches, beckoning her into her fold.

"You can walk from your royal bedchamber right onto the terrace, and just a few steps to the water basin with healing powers." The Chief Eunuch waves his arms in the air. "In the heat of Bâb-ilim, nothing is more delightful… none of the other palaces are built this way."

The Chief Eunuch opens the massive doors into the small garden palace and bows and points inside.

Small torches light the hallways inside the palace. Fragrant sacred incense glows lazily in small silvery fire altars, guarding the hallways, waiting patiently to bless the new Royal Woman.

"How was your journey, My Lady?" Abi-Samar asks quietly, following her inside.

"Long!"

"Shall I summon the palace cook to prepare a night meal for you, My Lady?"

Before Rošanak answers, the Chief Eunuch approaches a massive set of golden doors, pushes them open and walks inside.

Rošanak forgets everything and follows the Chief Eunuch inside. The royal bedchamber has been awaiting her for days. A massive royal bed, with silver feet shaped like lions, rests majestically in the middle of the royal room, covered with snowy white, cool soft scented linen.

Delicate gossamer silver netting hangs from the tall ceiling, falling gently around the royal bed, glinting in the low light of flickering candles.

A golden bowl filled with golden peaches and pears and plums and pomegranates from Persia on a golden table next to the bed scents the bedchamber sweetly. Another bowl is filled with golden apricots from Armina.

"This royal bed was made for Aššat Šarri Pur-ru-uš-iš, the Queen Consort of the Second Da-ri-a-muš. They say she had begotten her favorite Royal Son, the Younger Kurrašu, in this bed." The Chief Eunuch proudly points to the bed posts and walls. "Sacred amulets to protect the royal unborn and keep away evil Demoness Lamaštu."

The Chief Eunuch then walks and opens the silver doors to the terrace, and cooler, fragrant air lazily enters the royal bedchamber. He pushes the silk curtains away and points to the terrace.

"The bathing basin, My Lady."

He then points to the lush greens around the basin. "Only the great gods can gaze upon you in this water basin, made of pure marble from Yaunâ. It is well-hidden from the eyes of the mortals."

Rošanak walks onto the stony terrace dotted with stony basins overflowing with more fragrant flowers. The air feels cooler and softer; water gently falls and murmurs and rolls into a shimmery water basin a few steps away with another Persian garden stretching behind it, filled with date palms and pomegranate trees. She extends her right hand to the Chief Eunuch and he bows low and gladly kisses her royal hand.

"Please have my belongings sent here, when they arrive with the Royal Army." Rošanak asks softly.

"Yes, My Lady." The Chief Eunuch bows and leaves the room quietly and closes the door behind him.

"Abi-Samar."

"Yes, My Lady?"

"Please let the King know that I have arrived safely and I do not wish to be disturbed for a few days."

"Yes, My Lady."

Rošanak starts to undress.

Abi-Samar hesitates.

"What is it?" Rošanak stops and asks tiredly.

"The King has been absent from Bâb-ilim for eight years and now that he is here, he has refused to take part in the Akîtu Ritual of the New Year."

Rošanak closes her eyes.

Abi-Samar continues quietly. "Bâb-ilani nobles have come from all the corners of the Land between Twin Rivers to attend the Akîtu Ritual and Royal Festivities with the King of the Lands. But the King is too busy receiving the nakaru envoys and then his own kingsmen and then the satraps and the rest. The nobles have been waiting for a month. Akîtu Ritual was to be honored and celebrated in the month of Nîsannu."

"Have the temple priests of Bêl Marduk spoken to the King?"

"Yes."

Rošanak takes a deep breath.

Alexander was not a man to submit to the Ritual of Akîtu.

"I will speak to him."

"Thank you, My Lady!"

Abi-Samar bows his head and then turns and quietly leaves the royal bedchamber. Massive doors close behind him.

Blessed silence.

Rošanak drops her dusty and travel-stained gown on the carpet and walks on the terrace and into the shimmery warm water basin.

A palace maid quickly gathers her dusty travel clothes and disappears.

The silvery moon and the warm water bathe her in comfort.

She looks up at the moon.

A piece of moonlight breaks and falls and shatters all around her.

World fades.

Maybe that cursed traitor Mazdâyâ, now long dead and forgotten, had opened up the Gates of Bâb-ilim to Alexander, not for a handful of cursed gold and silver, but because he could not bear to see his beloved Royal City burned and razed to the ground… the city he had come to think of as his home… the city of his wife… where his children had been born… every bend and corner filled with a memory…

She closes her eyes and sinks into the shimmery water basin. Warm water wraps around her like the loving arms of a long lost lover.

After the bloody destruction of Ṣurru, everyone knew what Alexander would do to a city that did not submit to him willingly and quickly. If Bâb-ilim was to be sieged as the Third Dâriuš had commanded it and if the city had fallen to Alexander, all of this that now surrounded her body lovingly would have been heaps of ashes and dust…

It was the nature of Alexander to destroy what did not bend to his will…

Who could fault the lion for ripping apart the bull?

But it was also the nature of the Persians to preserve the beauty of the Lands that were entrusted to them by the Wise Lord for safe-keeping.

Those who had cursed the Persian Satraps for not burning the lands and the homes and the palaces and the gardens to stop the invaders, had not seen the Lands and the Homes and the Palaces and the Gardens of the Persians…

Who could fault the gardeners for protecting their beloved gardens?

Only wretched demons, worshipers of the Lord of Darkness, destroyed beauty on earth!

Persians worshipped the Wise Lord… protected the beauty bestowed upon them by his benevolence…

It was their sacred duty… no duty was more sacred than caring for the earth and the Lands on Earth…

No sin was more contemptible that burning the bountiful land…

Everyone knew that satraps who took great care of their satrapies were rewarded generously by the Great Kings and those who were neglectful, were punished severely…

Great Kings hanged men who intentionally desecrated the Royal Lands.

She sinks into the water basin.

Water murmurs.

TEMPLE GROUNDS. E-TEMEN-AN-KI. ROYAL CITY of BÂB-ILIM
YEAR 8 of A-LEK-SA-AN-DAR, MONTH 2, AYYÂRU
DAY 16: KING at ROYAL COURT. UNFAVORABLE
BÊL DID NOT COME OUT of E-SAG-ILA
NABÛ DID NOT COME TO BÂB-ILU
MID-DAY

Warm day in Bâb-ilim.

"Alexander, the Memorial Monument for Hephæstion!" Deinokrates, the Rhodian Architect, points with honor to the wooden model resting on the sacred E-temen-an-ki Temple grounds.

Alexander walks around the model of the Hephæstion's Memorial and listens intently.

He had gone to Bisitun on the way to Ecbatana with Hephæstion and they had seen the Tombs of the First Darius and Xerxes cut into the rocks high up the mountains.

He had told Deinokrates that for Hephæstion he wanted something more magnificent than any memorial and monument ever built in honor of the Great Kings.

Deinokrates describes the lavish memorial building with excitement:

"Five stories. Layers like a Babylonian step pyramid.

"Golden prows of fifty-oar galleys on the bottom, with standing and kneeling archers and warriors.

"Topped with tall flaming torches with flying eagles spreading their wings over snakes.

"Then a royal hunt in Persian gardens, and the battle of the Hellenes and Centaurs, topped with golden Persian lions and bulls from Persepolis, crowned with Makedonian and Persian arms.

"On the top of the memorial, hollowed siren statues big enough for singers to slide into and sing laments for Hephæstion on solemn occasions.

"It will cost ten thousand talents, maybe more," he says.

Alexander smiles.

Truly magnificent… ten thousand talents… well worth the gold… more than anyone had ever spent on a memorial to a lover…

Hephæstion would have liked it.

Sun gets warmer, afternoon begins.

Rošanak closes her eyes.

It was so hot…

… even under the white linen shade the palace servants were holding over her head.

She opens her eyes and looks at the model.

The hideous structure was the very definition of excess… Hephæstion, who had lived simply, almost like a Brahman, would have been utterly embarrassed…

Persian Kings were buried in modest tombs cut into rocks, high in the belly of the mountains, after receiving their religious rites… with their royal bows and a quiver full of arrows…

Makedonian funerals were entertainment for the multitudes…

What kind of people held funeral games with drunken idiots to honor their dead?

Court chamberlain said three thousand dancers and singers and actors had come from all over to compete in the funeral games for Hephæstion in Bâb-ilim.

Some of them had made their way with the Royal Army behind her carriage when she had come to Bâb-ilim from Hagmâtâna with Perdikkas.

"Do you think Hephæstion would have liked this?" Alexander asks Rošanak.

"Only if he does not have to come and visit it in the middle of summer, Alexander," Rošanak says irritably. "Lizards fry in the sun of Babylon crossing the streets."

The unborn had gotten bigger inside her… she felt hot and heavy and irritated… and she rarely slept much with her heavy load…

She could feel the hot sweat brewing and beading under her heavy breasts…

They were never in the right royal city in the right time of the year… they were in Çûšâ in spring, Hagmâtâna in winter and now in Bâb-ilim for summer. Alexander had grown used to going wherever he wanted, whenever he pleased. Bâb-ilim was not the royal city to be in during the scorching months of summer.

Alexander walks away annoyed.

He should have thought better of getting her with child again. She was always sweeter and more agreeable when she desired a child than when she was heavy with one.

Temple priests of Bêl Marduk stand quietly, farther away, looking grim.

Abi-Samar bows his head and pleads quietly with Rošanak, horrified. "This is sacred temple grounds, My Lady. The Foundation of Heaven on Earth, since time immemorial. All belongs to Bêl Marduk and the great gods of Bâb-ilim.

"E-temen-an-ki is the House of the Foundation of Heaven on Earth— and Temple of E-sag-ila, what is left of it, is the House of Bêl Marduk."

He points with his head to the Bêl Marduk temple priests. "Êrib-bêt-ili, the Bêl temple enterers, are the most powerful men in Bâb-ilim after the King. They have told the King that no monument could be built on these sacred temple grounds to honor a man."

Rošanak glances at the Bêl temple priests and looks back at Alexander and the scores of men surrounding him, like dogs eager to flatter and please their master, bent on outdoing each other in honoring Hephæstion.

They all hated Hephæstion when he was alive; he himself would have thrown all of them off the Bâb-ilim Walls.

To them Hephæstion was no longer a man, but a ghostly rope to bind them tightly to Alexander.

When they were in Hagmâtâna, Alexander had written to Kleomenes, the Collector of the Royal Tributes and the Keeper of the Royal Funds at Mudrâya, and had ordered him to build a new temple in honor of Hephæstion and in exchange, he would turn a blind eye to all the complaints of the Mudrâya against Kleomenes.

And now he had decided to have a memorial built in Bâb-ilim, the new center of the Empire, right in the middle of the sacred grounds of the Temple of E-temen-an-ki… to house the bones of Hephæstion…

She looks around the walled temple grounds.

It was by far larger than the entire Palace of Nabû'Kudra'Cara… it was a city unto itself filled with a sea of farmers and shepherds and carpenters and blacksmiths and merchants.

"Have the Bêl temple enterers offered the King another site?" she asks impatiently.

Abi-Samar nods his head with dismay. "Yes. As there is no other land unbuilt within the walls of Bâb-ilim, the memorial could be built on hallowed grounds next to the sacred Bît Akîtu on the other side of the Walls of Bâb-ilim. But the King told the Bêl êrib-bêt-ili that the Oracle at Siwah had decreed that Hezârapatiš can be worshipped as a Divine Hero and his memorial next to the Temple of E-sag-ila will be a house of worship. He told the êrib-bêt-ili that they will all be put to the sword if they do not submit to his desire and release the sacred temple lands to him for the temple of a divine hero."

Rošanak looks at Abi-Samar.

He knew better than anyone that the only man who could talk to Alexander truthfully about such delicate matters was the man whose dead body he himself had carried to the tomb of her ancestors… the man the memorial was meant to remember… the man for whom the temple was to be built for his worship…

Hephæstion was no more…

"Only Hephæstion could have told Alexander he had gone mad and still keep his life and his head and his tongue."

Abi-Samar looks at Rošanak with a heavy heart.

First, the Men of the Race of Wrath had come and had brought their gods with them…

… then they had burned Pârsâ, the Holiest City of the Persians… and then they had built temples to honor their own gods.

Now, their king had declared war on the great gods of Bâb-ilim.

And the êrib-bêt-ili of Bêl Marduk had lost no time in cursing the Lord of Asia and all his kingsmen and all his men to Bêl Marduk…

This was what the heavenly stars had foretold many years ago…

The battle between the will of the great gods and the will of the mortal king had begun again…

GARDEN PALACE of QUEEN AMYTIŠ
PALACE of the SECOND NABÛ-KUDURRÎ-ÛSUR
DAYS LATER

Warm day in the palace garden… water murmurs…

"I worship the Wise Lord, more eternal than eternity—"

"My Lady!" Abi-Samar interrupts Rošanak grimly.

Rošanak turns and look at Abi-Samar with annoyance, with her hands supporting her sides.

He knew never to interrupt her during sacred prayers.

Fear is carved on Abi-Samar's face.

"A-lek-sa-an-dar—" Abi-Samar calls the King, Alexander, by his common name.

Rošanak's eyes widen. Her arms go limp and fall motionless at her sides.

Wind blows and her hair dances in the warm breeze.

She looks at Abi-Samar, her eyes asking questions, her lips silent with fear.

"The Chaldæan Prophecy." Abi-Samar's face creases. "A-lek-sa-an-dar was sailing down stream, by the tombs of the ancient Aššûr Kings in the Lands of the Reeds. He was wearing a sun hat of his fathers tied by a string. A wind blew off his hat and the Persian Purple he was wearing underneath."

Rošanak's knees soften. Blood drains from her face.

"The Persian Purple landed on one of the ancient tombs… the hat was caught by one of his men and was brought back to him… after the man had worn it on his head… to keep it from wetting… the Persian Purple was rescued by another man… he too wore it on his head to keep it from wetting…" he says miserably.

He cared nothing for the Makedonians… he cared about her and her fate was woven into their cloth…

Rošanak slowly embraces a tree and rests her head on a branch.

"Who was the man who caught the Persian Purple?" she asks faintly, dreading the knowledge.

Abi-Samar looks at her with heavy heart.

"He was given a biltu of silver and then beheaded… the Bêl temple enterers told the King that he should not leave untouched the head who had worn the royal mark of the kings."

"Who?" Rošanak asks again faintly.

"One of the fighting men, a Phoenician. They say he gave the Persian Purple to one of the kingsmen, to Si-lu-ku, the husband of your second sister, Apâma."

"Seleukos?"

"Yes, My Lady."

"Seleukos—"

She closes her eyes and grabs her belly.

The Persian Purple of the Great Kings was passed onto another man… to a man married to Apâma, the daughter of one of Alexander's fiercest enemies, Spitâmaneh… her second sister of other father and mother, who was now heavy with her second child…

Alexander was no longer the Lord of Asia…

All was lost…

How could this be?

The new king was not even of royal blood, nor a noble… just a warrior, a common man… Seleukos was not even one of Alexander's close kingsmen.

"Abi-Samar, the Chaldæans… are they worthy of their standing?"

"Yes, My Lady… They are the Watchers of the Heavens."

"Find me the Chaldæan, the pupil of a known Chaldæan, whom Alexander had put to the sword for his prophecy, the one who was taken into royal court, when Alexander first passed through Bâb-ilim. Ask Abi-Enši-Marduk. He should remember who the Chaldæan was."

"Yes, My Lady." Abi-Samar lingers for another moment.

Rošanak eyes him wearily. "What else?"

"A tamed ass kicked the ferocious lion of the palace in the head and killed it!"

"Oh!"

ROYAL PALACE of the SECOND NABÛ-KUDURRÎ-ÛSUR
DAYS PASS
ROYAL BANQUET
NIGHT

Another warm Bâb-ilim night.

"Alexander." Medeios approaches Alexander after the farewell feast for Nearchos. "Night is young. Wine is cold and women are without virtue," he says enticingly, pointing toward his tent.

"Who is there?"

"All of your nearest kingsmen and dearest friends!"

Alexander takes a deep breath.

No… not all of his nearest and dearest friends… the one most loved was missing…

"Perdikkas, Leonnatos, Lysimachos, Peukestas, Eumenes, Ptolemaios," Medeios says counting the kingsmen. "Nearchos and Peithon too— and Chares has gotten us loads of cold pure Babylonian wine!"

Alexander looks toward the Royal Army Camp beyond the walls of the palace.

He had heeded the omens… the Eclipse of the Sun had come to pass as foretold… a substitute king had been marked by the temple priests and had been put to the sword, after wearing the royal crown and sitting on the royal throne… his men had cleared the earth for rebuilding of the Babylonian temple and for the building of the Temple of Hephæstion… and he had entered and left and returned to Babylon unharmed…

Lonely moments pass in the heat of the night.

He takes a deep breath. His body fills with pain.

Hephæstion was gone…

He was in need of Roxana and she was heavy with child…

He looks back at the massive Babylonian palaces all around him.

He was to leave Babylon for Arabia in a few days to punish the Arabs for ignoring him. He had ordered them to come before him and worship him as their Third God and they had ignored him. The Land of the Fertile Crescent was his as the rightful successor of the Great King.

The Arabs used to send a thousand talents of Arabian incense to the Great Kings before him, but they had never sent him an embassy or shown him any marks of honor or their customary tribute and the time was now ripe to water their lands with their blood.

Alexander shakes his head and follows Medeios to his tent.

Wine was a blessing and a curse… it was healing him and killing him… it made him forget the painful wounds in his body and made him remember sweet loves long lost…

GARDEN PALACE of QUEEN AMYTIS
LATER
BEFORE DAWN

"I wrote to Darius. I told him: *I crossed into Asia, wishing to punish the Persians!*" Alexander says feverishly.

"Do you see him?" Alexander leans over and gently shakes Rošanak in bed. She opens her eyes unwillingly, still filled with sleep.

She is heavy with child. He is heavy with wine.

"Do you see him?"

"See who?" Rošanak asks sleepily.

"Him! The Younger Kuros!"

"No! I am not loaded with wine like you!"

"You do not see him, because he is not here! He is in the royal quarters!"

"Alexander. Go back to your bedchamber!"

"I saw him first in a dream when I was a boy. He commanded me to follow him to Persia, defeat the Persians, and avenge his blood."

Alexander crawls into bed naked next to her and puts his heavy arms over her swelling tender breasts. His wet hair is dripping on the pillow. His body is hot. He rolls on his back, twisting in pain.

"He said— He said I was not a god— just a man, son of a man— mortal by all accounts!" Alexander rambles on feverishly.

Rošanak pushes his heavy hand off her aching breasts. "Alexander… Go… Sleep off the wine!" she says irritably.

"He said… there is no Zeus… No Achilleos… No Herakles…"

"And there will be no Roxana, if you come to my bed loaded with wine every night!"

"He said… my gods were invented by faithless storytellers… He said there is just one god… one with no name… the nameless god…"

"Alexander… go to sleep!"

Alexander passes out.

His body feels like a burning sun next to hers. She touches his forehead with the tips of her fingers. She finally worries. "Alexander?"

Silence.

Rošanak calls him louder, shaking him gently. "Alexander!"

Alexander opens his eyes, unsettled, looking beyond her.

"Philip yelled at me in front of Philotas. He said I deserved to have that barbarian Pixodaros for a kinsman… the man who was the servant of the Great King. He said I deserved to marry the lowborn daughter of a servant of the King."

He closes his eyes in pain and starts to drift.

"He ordered me to take my troublesome mother and get out of Pella. He said he would not tolerate a son who had the blood of that Molossian snake-worshipping witch in him… He said I was a bastard begotten by one of her cold-blooded snakes…"

He passes out in pain.

"Alexander…"

Silence.

Rošanak calls him again, shaking him gently. "Alexander!"

Alexander moans, "Hephæstion…"

Silence.

Painful breathing.

Then he starts to moan and ramble again. "I am a god!"

Rošanak leans back, irritated, pushes him away and mumbles under her breath. "You should have wedded your half-Hellene whore, if you wanted to be a god, not a Persian Royal Daughter!"

Alexander passes out again.

Rošanak ignores him.

All men thought they were gods' gift to women…

If she had been given a choice, she would have kept Peritas instead!

GARDEN PALACE of QUEEN AMYTIŠ
3 NIGHTS LATER
MIDDLE of the NIGHT

Heavy breathing.

"I was kneeling in front of Batis by the walls of Gaza, bound in heavy chains. I could not move. Batis looked down at me with sheer hatred just as he had when he was brought before me after I captured Gaza. He said nothing."

Alexander moans in pain, feverish and hallucinating again.

"They drove metal nails through my ankles as Batis looked on. Batis tied my chains to his chariot and dragged me around the walls of Gaza while my father watched with blazing eyes. I said nothing."

Alexander catches his breath.

"The Oracle of Zeus-Ammon told me… gods had fated two destinies for me.

"I could wage war for the Empire of the Persians and die young gloriously and become immortal. Or I could go back to Makedonia and die of old age in my bed and become utterly forgotten."

Rošanak looks at Alexander, holding her rounded belly, her heart drenched in grief and sorrow.

Alexander had crossed the River Ufrâtû and had rested at the cleaner, cooler and quieter side of the river for a few nights and had gotten better. Now he was back to this side of the river and he was worse.

"Like Achilleos, I chose to die young with undying fame."

Alexander passes out on Rošanak's bed, dripping with hot sweat.

"Alexander?"

Silence… heavy labored breathing…

"Alexander?"

She feels his body. It is warmer than the mid-day Bâb-ilim sun. Her heart sinks into her knees.

"Hephæstion…" she utters mindlessly, expecting a swift reply…

She takes a deep breath and pushes herself out of her bed and walks out of her bedchamber and summons one of the palace eunuchs. "Send for my healer at once! Wake him up! Bring him here! Go quickly!"

Rošanak puts her hand back on her belly, as the palace eunuch rushes away. She walks back to her bed and sits on the edge, close to Alexander.

"Ah!" She feels the unborn kicking restlessly, sensing her fear. She puts both her hands on her belly, rubbing it, comforting the unborn. She moans softly, pleading. "My Lord! I beg you! Please spare my son!"

"The Scythian Chief told me: *Who are you? Why have you come here? What dealing do you have with us? We wish to live our lives ignorant of who you are!*"

Silence.

"Hephæstion, remember?" Alexander asks feverishly and moans.

Rošanak closes her eyes, her heart aching.

"Hephæstion…" Alexander moans and passes out again

There is a soft knock on the door. She slowly gets to her feet and walks to the door and opens it.

Her Old Persian Healer, disheveled, breathing fast, clutching his bag in his hand, enters the room hurriedly.

"Rošanak! My Lady! I came as fast as I could!" He pauses and takes a deep breath and points. "Those damn steps!"

He catches his breath and looks at her intently. "Are you in pain?"

"It is the King!"

"The King?"

"The King… he is burning up with fever!"

The Old Persian Healer goes deathly white with fear, drops his bag of cures unconsciously at his feet and takes a step backward. He loses his tongue.

The King had the hainâ wound-healer hanged after the death of the Hezârapatiš.

If the King himself had not forbidden him to care for the Hezârapatiš, his own old body would have hanged next to the other poor wound-healer…

Men died… women and children too… it was the law of the Wise Lord…

Rošanak looks at him and takes a deep breath, then puts her hands on her sides and returns to Alexander's bedside.

The Old Persian Healer stands motionlessly for a moment, then takes a deep breath and relents and reluctantly walks over to the side of the King and examines him carefully.

The King was soaked in his own hot sweat.

The deep, long scar on his chest had turned black.

Moments feel like an eternity.

"Was he drinking?"

Rošanak eyes the old man tiredly.

What a question!

Everyone at the royal court knew that Alexander drank wine like water…

"I do not know. His men brought him back from the other side of the river tonight. He ordered them to bring him here."

The Old Persian Healer shakes Alexander.

"Your Majesty… Your Majesty… can you hear me?"

Silence.

"He does not know the Persian tongue."

The Old Persian Healer feels Alexander's brow. "Hmmm…"

He might not understand the Persian tongue but he was not deaf… he should respond to someone yelling into his ears and shaking him!

"It is just too much cold wine in this heat!" Rošanak utters in denial.

The Old Persian Healer looks at her wordlessly, thinking. "Hmmm… he is certainly ill but I cannot be certain of the cause or the severity."

Alexander twists in pain in his sleep and moans in his mother tongue.

The Old Persian Healer looks at Rošanak, hiding his worries.

"I will stand watch over him. You need to rest!" He points to her belly. "You have lost your unborn twice! Or three times… chances of losing this one are high too!"

"Please tend to the King! I am well!"

The unborn kicks again, harder.

"Ah!" She bends and folds in pain.

The Old Persian Healer looks at Rošanak, worried and conflicted.

He was committed to heal the sick and the wounded… but the care of a Royal Woman of the Lands was by far more important than caring for a brutal conquering invader…

Those men had their own wound-healers…

And they hanged their wound-healers when their sick and wounded died!

Men died… even with the best of care from their wound-healers… it was the Law of the Wise Lord and the Law of Nature… even the young and the healthy died… and the King was not young and he was not healthy. Yes… even the Great Kings died.

"You can rest on the couch. If it is bad wine and the King is cured by the morning, you have not missed your good night's rest. If the King remains sick, you will need to be well rested to deal with the malady of an ailing king!"

Rošanak bites her lip and relents. She walks over to the soft silvery couch and lies down, watching Alexander and softly crying, holding on to her belly.

The Angel of Death had followed the King from the Gathering Place of the Mâda Kings to the Gate of Gods…

She had taken the gate keeper of the King first… and now she was flying over the head of the King… playing with him, like a Persian cat playing with a palace mouse…

Death was the only outcome of such deadly games…

CHALDÆAN QUARTERS. ROYAL CITY of BÂB-ILIM
FOLLOWING NIGHT

"Ah! Come in!"

Kudurru narrows his eyes in the dim light of the flickering clay lamp and then nods and says in low accented Persian, gesturing with his old hands toward the inside of his small brick house. "It is such a pleasure to have Your Royal Highness honoring my humble house."

Rošanak looks around for a moment hesitatingly.

The old Chaldæan was famed and had rich patrons. He lived in an old house not too far from the Palace of Nabû'Kudra'Cara, on the other side of Kunuš-kadru, the Processional Way, on a street named "may the enemy not have victory". It was close to the Libil'hegalla waterway, which kept the house cool and well-watered in the evenings.

She takes a deep breath and bites her lip and then enters the old house following the old Chaldæan with Abi-Samar following cautiously, closing the small wooden door behind him.

"I am so pleased that you have come to visit me here. That palace has more eyes and ears than some gods." The old Chaldæan stops.

"The eunuch can wait in the courtyard," he says absently, with a voice accustomed to being heard by kings and nobles and the moneyed of Bâb-ilim, powerful men with powerful desire to know heavenly secrets beyond what their own eyes and ears saw and heard and told them.

Abi-Samar puts his hand on the handle of his Persian dagger guardedly.

Rošanak waddles awkwardly and stops in the middle of the small fragrant treed courtyard by the maltaku, the old murmuring water clock, and turns and questions Abi-Samar with her eyes.

Abi-Samar glares at the old Chaldæan for a moment, annoyed, and looks around and then yields and bows his head slightly and stands motionlessly in the middle of the small courtyard.

The Chaldæan was old and his small house was quiet… his slaves were well-hidden from view… and he had no cause to harm her…

Rošanak turns and follows the old Chaldæan inside the old house, holding on to her sides.

Kudurru passes through a small humble bedroom and walks into a larger room, covered floor to ceiling with dusty clay tablets and rolls of old parchment and papyri and skin. He pushes away some old clay tablets on his crowded wooden table and puts the clay lamp down and considers her for a moment. The warm scent of burning sesame oil fills the room.

He had seen her from afar when she had come to the temple grounds of E-temen-an-ki with her King-Husband to view the plans for the memorial building of the dead Hezârapatiš.

The unborn had gotten heavier inside her since that day…

And her eyes too had gotten heavier with a certain uncertainty…

"I have been expecting you!" he utters with an air of authority.

Rošanak slowly turns her head and looks at the old Chaldæan intently.

Kudurru points up toward the sky above with his old fingers and nods.

"Yes… it was written in the skies a long time ago."

Rošanak looks up. Through a small opening in the ceiling, little stars shine brightly.

"Little Star! Yes! Sit! Sit!" Kudurru eagerly points to a small chair next to his crowded table.

Rošanak slowly lowers herself into the chair, favoring her belly, sitting uncomfortably on the edge.

"Plunging into the clean warm waters in the Gardens of Šarratu Amytiš will ease your heavy load," Kudurru says paternally and points to Rošanak's belly discreetly with his head.

Rošanak puts her hands on her belly and nods her head politely.

"Mâru or Mârtu?" Kudurru mumbles to himself. He looks around on his table and picks up a star chart and looks at it. "Ah! Nânna is surrounded by a tarbâșu and Šarru stands in Nânna." He smiles and nods. "Mâru… it is a boy!"

Kudurru picks up a cup and pours something into it from a tall massîtu and offers it to Rošanak.

Rošanak looks at the cup hesitatingly. Her mouth feels dry and parched.

Her old wound-healer had forbidden her to ride in a litter and ordered her to walk everywhere for easy birthing. She was thirsty after her long walk from the palace in the warm night, but had no taste for wine… wine only made her thirstier and she could only swallow a few drops at a time… there was only room for the unborn in her swelling belly and not much for anything else…

Kudurru moves the cup in his hand and says agreeably, "Nurmû… the blood of Pomegranate. Is it not what the boy inside of you has been craving?"

Rošanak looks at the old man.

Her grandmother had told her to seek the old Chaldæan in Bâb-ilim. Alexander was relentlessly sick and suffering… and the old Chaldæan was her last hope.

She leans forward slightly and takes the cup graciously.

She takes a sip of the sweetened sour pomegranate juice and looks around the dimly lit room.

Kudurru considers her for another long moment.

The great gods of Uruk.Ki, Anu, the father of gods, and Aruru, the mother of creation, had sent Enkîdu to Gilgâmeš, when the people of Uruk.Ki had cried out to them for justice…

The Wise Lord of the Persians had sent a Royal Woman to A-lek-sa-an-dar, to tame the wild man in him and to exact revenge. The fatal wound to his ancient warrior ancestor had been delivered to his unprotected heel… the fatal wound to the Lord of Asia had been delivered to his unprotected heart… the only place in his whole body not protected by his gods… not covered with metal… not shielded from love.

Just like Gilgâmeš and Enkîdu… and like all men, the King from the Lands by the Bitter Sea with an indestructible body had a destructible heart.

All kings were men first… before they were kings of all… the Lord of Asia was a mortal man… clay mixed with royal warrior blood… and bits of the soul of the ancient rebel god…

And she had marked his heart expertly… no arrows, no poisons, no spears, no swords, no weapons of any kind…

It had taken the conqueror from the other side of the seas eight cycles of the sun to conquer the Lands of the Persians… it had taken the Persian Mar'at Šarri but a fleeting moment to conquer the heart of the conqueror… bent him to his knees to claim her… for love or peace… it mattered not to the great gods in the Heaven… they gave him her heart and then took it away to make him suffer bitterly.

The Great King had offered A-lek-sa-an-dar the wrong Mar'at Šarri… this one was the one who was fated for him by the great gods and stars.

But his master, Kidinnu, had faithfully forewarned the Lord of Asia…

But instead of gold and gratitude, A-lek-sa-an-dar had shown the blade of a sharp sword to his master, for telling him what the little stars had foretold for him: that he was not to die a warrior's death, by the sharpened tip of a sharp sword… or a king's death by the sweetened taste of bitter poison… but a man's death of a broken heart… in a broken body… a shattered clay vessel… releasing another bit of the soul of the ancient rebel god…

She had begotten a son in a single moment of his passion and had shunned him afterward…

Kudurru sits down on a tall chair behind his wooden table and shakes his head. He looks up to the stars and points and curses under his old lips.

"Damn Harṭibu!"

"My Lord?"

Kudurru is startled for a moment.

Her voice was like a gentle spring stream running in the foothills of forests the colors of her eyes. Her voice was scented with intoxicating musk.

It was that assured royal calmness that had tamed a wild and ferocious king… a man one part divine, one part wrath, one part king… a heavenly voice soothing the endless pain of the rebel god… caged in the painful mortal clay.

"My Lord?"

"Ah! Yes! Harţibu… those priests at the Oracle of Ammon in Mudrâya… instead of looking up at the stars, they crawl into the belly of the shifting sands for answers that only heavenly bodies are meant to reveal to mortal men."

They said that the Oracle of Ammon was a navel fastened by emeralds and when an answer was sought from the Têrtu, the priests brought out the jeweled navel in a golden boat with silver cups hanging from both its sides.

The Oracle of Ammon was a great golden tub that clicked and clacked like a dancing Bâb-ilani priestess of earthly delights!

"Each heavenly body is a god…" Kudurru nods to himself and continues, "Sun is Šamaš, Moon is Nânna, the eight-pointed star is Ištar…"

Rošanak slowly takes a sip of her sour pomegranate juice and eyes the old Chaldæan discreetly.

Was this the same man her grandmother had counseled her about?

He seemed half-mad!

"Will I rule the world?"

"My Lord?"

"Everyone, king and man alike, always asks the same question from the Oracle of Ammon and the answer has always been the same, for hundreds and hundreds of years. *YES! If it is the will of the gods!* If one becomes a king, the oracle is true and if one does not become a king, the oracle is true! After all who knows what is the will of the gods?"

Rošanak takes another sour sip of souring juice, still eyeing the old Chaldæan carefully.

"Am I begotten by a god?"

"My Lord?"

"The other question everyone asks that oracle!" The old Chaldæan nods with certainty.

Rošanak narrows her eyes at the old man.

"As if the great gods have any need of sons begotten by snake-worshipping priestesses."

Rošanak's face folds.

The old Chaldæan pauses and looks at her.

She doubted his words… it was written on her eyes…

"Kidinnu, my master, told the King from Iš-ku-du-ru, what the great gods in Heaven had fated for him and how to appease the great gods."

Rošanak narrows her eyes again and looks at the old Chaldæan intently without any words.

"But, what he heard displeased him so much that he had my old master put to the pitiless sword when he stood fast to his words. Men from the Lands by the Sea are restless children with young gods only children could be dazzled with."

Kudurru nods with a sigh and then points to the clay tablets behind him and says knowingly, "My master knew… yes… thousands of years of watching the heavens… observing every movement. You gaze upon the Sun and the Moon and the Heavenly Stars long enough, they will bend down their heavenly lips and whisper their godly secrets into your mortal ears."

"The Prophecy, My Lord…" Rošanak asks quietly.

Kudurru takes a deep breath. "Ah! The Prophecy! Yes!" He shakes his head mindlessly. "Not just prophecies… curses too!"

"Curses?"

"Yes… many… old and new… some harmless, others powerful…"

Rošanak breathes deep. Her head begins to spin around the disorderly room.

Kudurru looks around on his crowded table and pushes some old clay tablets around, searching, and then carefully pulls out a stack of parchment hidden under a clay tablet, tied together with a golden thread, wipes off the dust from the top and offers it to Rošanak. "Here!"

Rošanak hesitates and then reluctantly leans forward in her chair and takes the dusty bundle.

Kudurru says quietly, pointing with his eyes to the bundle. "Read!"

Rošanak eyes him, searching. "The one foretold about the Lord of Asia?"

Kudurru nods his head and points again with his old finger.

"As I said! Not just one… many…"

Rošanak takes a deep breath and slowly pulls at the golden thread and opens the tied bundle and looks at the first parchment on top. It was written in Aramaic. Old and faded. She starts reading, slowly, carefully, every word.

These are the words of one named Šamaš-nâsir, a wise and competent sipîrû ša ûqu, scribe of the people:

> *And then shall come to the happy Lands of Asia,*
> *A man, unknown, clad in crimson cloak,*
> *Ferocious, fiery, outlandish, unrighteous…*
> *From him a thunderbolt raised into light.*
> *And whole of Asia shall bear an evil yoke,*
> *And many a murder will the damp soil drink.*
> *He will court the Unseen One.*
> *And his own blood shall be destroyed,*
> *By the blood of those he wills to destroy.*

Her heart starts to crumble.

She reads the next parchment underneath.

> The Demons of the Race of Wrath will spill the blood of the righteous with frenzy... they will bring famine and pestilence to the Lands of the Persians...
> For six thousand years the Wise Lord and the Lord of Darkness will fight...
> Many cities will be destroyed... dark chaos will fall like black rain...
> Where there is abundance of corn and barley, there will be loads of death and dust...
> At the end, the righteous will prevail upon the wicked...
> The Great Gods will cast the Rebel God into Hell...
> The Good is purified by fire and the Evil is consumed by it.
> Men of the other side of the seas are children of the Men of this side of the seas... begotten in time immemorial... West is seeded by the East...
> Sons will remember the fathers of their fathers...
> Fathers will bless the sons of their sons...
> Darkness will be undone...
> East will save the West...
> A new age of the Wise Lord will settle over the Lands...
> The Lands will be happy again.
> The Wise Lord is a peaceful God.
> He will forgive the Lord of Darkness, if the Lord of Darkness begs for his mercy... begs for forgiveness...

She reads the next faded parchment.

> *A man will come to the golden Lands of the Persians...*
> *... unlike any other...*
> *His wrath will water the Lands with blood,*
> *Earth shall drink the blood of man and woman and child...*
> *But the race he means to utterly destroy,*
> *Will utterly destroy him...*
> *He leaves behind a root,*
> *And a tree of many branches,*
> *Infested with maggots...*
> *The maggots shall rule,*
> *... until they are destroyed too,*
> *By his own son and the sons of his son...*

She looks up and shakes her head with heavy heart.

Then she looks down and reads the next parchment reluctantly.

Greed for glory makes him wander the world.
He kills the living... he burns the Lands.
... but...
He is not long for this world.
Death is his shadow.
Dirt is his pillow.
He will die in the lands of his enemies.
He will be buried and unburied and buried again...
His enemies will walk on his dead bones.

She bites her lip and reads the next parchment.

More of the same…

… and many more written in tongues, both old and young, she could not even read…

She looks up, pushing back tears in her eyes. She puts her hand on her belly with misery.

She was carrying the unborn of a cursed king…

Then her soft ears close defiantly to the harsh words.

Meaningless words by faceless and nameless men…

"There are always murmurs of doom in the air about kings," she says with heavy heart, taking a deep breath. "They say when the Younger Kuruš and the Second Artakhšaçâ fought for the Crown and the Throne of the Persians, the Lands were filled with prophecies worse than these.

"The royal court of the Second Artakhšaçâ had even spread wretched lies about his own most royal ancestor, Kuruš the Elder… a royal king forsaking the royal blood of his kingly ancestors, all because his own blood brother, the Younger Kuruš, spoke of going back to the ways of the elders, back to the noble traditions that had made the Persians great!

"The Great King denied his own royal bloodline to his own kingly-fathers and said Kuruš the Elder was a commoner, a lowborn subject of Mâda King Ištu-Vigu! He lied! His own royal ancestors cursed his blood."

And nothing was worse than lying.

Kudurru considers her again for another moment and sees her pain in her teary eyes and hears it in her trembling voice.

Who could blame her?

These were harsh cruel words about the father of her unborn son.

He casts his eyes and searches on his crowded table for a moment and then slowly pulls out another dusty clay tablet.

"Ah! Here it is."

He pulls the lamp closer and starts reading it loud enough to be heard.

"This was foretold when the Judeans were brought to Mât Akkadî, Bâb-ilim of the old, many generations ago, by the Second Nabû-Kudurrî-Ûṣur.

> *"The Men of the LowLands Between the Twin Rivers, the River Tigrâ and the River Ufrâtû, the ancient Watchers of the Heavens, will be abandoned by their own gods...*
> *Enlil and Marduk will hide their shame in heavenly dark clouds...*
> *Nânna will become forever bespeckled...*
> *Mât Akkadî... so ancient... so storied... so glorious... so wealthy... will be abandoned...*
> *Fields of wheat will turn into fields of dust...*
> *Old Mât Akkadî will be buried and forgotten under the shifting sands of time..."*

Kudurru looks up and nods.

"Everyone laughed at this prophecy. They said Bâb-ilim was the center of the world for three thousand years and it would remain the center of the circle for the next three thousand years!"

Rošanak bites her lip.

Kudurru picks up another clay tablet and nods.

"I like this one better. It is about the fate of the Muṣru. It was foretold by the Ma-gu-uš." And he then starts reading slowly.

> *"Mudrâya... so old... so storied... so wealthy...*
> *Remetj have been nothing but trouble from the beginning for the Persians. The Wise Lord had called unto them over and over and they had turned a deaf ear... they had utterly tried the patience of the Wise Lord... when their ancient gods had died away, they had started to worship cows and snakes and beetles...*
> *Where there is light... there is also darkness...*
> *If there were no such men, how would the Lord of Darkness amuse himself until the Day of the Last Judgment?*
> *The Second Ka^{m}bujiyâ who had first brought the Two Lands of ancient Mudrâya, Ta-Mehu and Ta-Shemau, under the sway of the Persians and had honored all their ancient gods and ancient ways, was wrong! He should have skewered the damn fattened Apis Bull and eaten it with a rhyton full of splendid strong Persian wine!"*

"Oh!" Rošanak narrows her eyes.

Her back aches and throbs.

"Here is another one from the Ma-gu-uš.

"The Wise Lord will send the Anointed One...
A man most beloved and most gentle, not born to the sword but born to the cloth, born to a blessed Virgin from Beyond the Rivers, the Land of the Phoenicians, the old Persian Xšâna...
Three Ma-gu-uš will follow the path of the little stars stretched across the shifting sands of the deserts and will bear him joyous gifts upon his sacred birth... incense from Arabâya and gold from Bakhtriš and myrrh from Makran Desert..."

Rošanak leans back in her chair. The unborn pushes up against her heart. Another swift kick. She folds and holds her belly and then straightens.

"Surely something can be done... or undone..." she says faintly.

Kudurru scratches his gray beard mindlessly.

Hmmm... one was missing... where was the one about her?

He leans over his crowded table and searches through the heaps of papyri and parchments and skins, and pulls out a skin and brings it closer to the light of the lamp and reads quietly.

"The Last Royal Daughter will come...
... to the ancient âyadana, built by the Second Royal Son of the House...
... the one with body marked for divine sacrifice...
... she will offer sacrifice worthy of being heard...
... she will pour incense into the sacred fire altar...
... the old silver one... that holds the spilled blood of the First Holy...
She will bend her knees and will pray with tearful eyes...
... to Divine Ânâhatâ... the ancient Mother Goddess...
... she will pray with the tongue of her mothers... her blood mixes with her tears...

> *"... hear my voice and strike those who have desecrated your temple... those who worship the Lord of Darkness and do not obey the laws of the Wise Lord..."*

The ancient mother goddess will hear her prayers.
... She will accept her golden blood offerings...
... She will grant her wish..."

Rošanak's face folds in pain of remembrance. A tear falls.

So that was the other prophecy...

She was the one who had cursed Alexander and his kingsmen with her own words... the words from the lips of her own blood mother had cursed the blood father of her own unborn... the seed of Alexander...

She had cursed carelessly and her goddess had heard faithfully.

Kudurru glances at her intently under his old brow and then leans forward and puts a small bundle wrapped in golden linen in front of her and very carefully opens it and points to it wordlessly.

Rošanak leans forward in her chair and looks at the small clay fragments, all cracked and broken and bound together, sitting like priceless jewels in the middle of the golden linen cloth.

"The words of Da-ri-a-muš, the first Great King. Ummi Šarri Sisygambis sent this one to me, bundled fragments from Par-ri-sa-a-a. It was in every royal room of every royal apadâna and dacara and hadiš and takara in Par-ri-sa-a-a; not a prophecy, a curse! A powerful one, from a Great King, beloved of the God of the Persians," Kudurru says quietly.

Rošanak leans slightly forward in her chair and looks at it with reverence.

Pavastâ… clay tablet fragments from Pârsâ…

Fragments… all cracked and broken like her…

The tips of her fingers burned with desire to touch the commands of the Great Kings.

She carefully lifts up a cracked fragment and brings it closer to her heart and reads it.

She reads it carefully once and then once more and then once again. Her royal kingly ancestor, the First Dâriuš himself, the Great King, was speaking to her from beyond his grave, commanding her.

Dâriuš the King says:
If you behold these words and destroy them,
and do not protect them as long as there is strength to you,
may the Wise Lord strike you…
… may he utterly destroy you.

"Is Pârsâ unburned?" Kudurru asks quietly.

Rošanak's face lines and folds.

Now, the old Chaldæan was mocking her…

It was one wrong deed that could never be undone…

Like death… it was forever…

Kudurru shakes his head and says quietly, "The Lord of Asia, the blood of the blood of First Ka-ši-ar-šâ, was summoned by the Royal Son of the House, Mâr Bît Šarri Ku-raš, to avenge the death of his grandfather… the Eagle… the Standard… flying over A-lek-sa-an-dar. It was the spirit of the Younger Ku-raš who guided his path and shielded his mortal life.

"But A-lek-sa-an-dar grew arrogant and forgetful… he thought all was his own doing… he broke faith with the Younger Ku-raš in his arrogance and ignorance and burned Pârsâ, the City of the Persians, the beloved city of the Younger Ku-raš and sealed his own fate with his own drunken hands.

"Heavenly bodies that have foretold his fate have not changed direction… it is… as it was… as it has been… as it had been foretold… eight years of kingship and no more. He was warned and he did not listen… he did not heed the command of the royal owners of the apadâna and dakara and takara and the hadiš. He feasted at the generous royal table of the Great Kings and then burned down their tables and their homes and their palaces and murdered the faithful and left them for the death-eating vultures!"

And that was all that needed to be said…

He leans back.

Unlike the great gods, there were no golden statues honoring the Supreme God of the Persians… just sacred words of sacred utterings uttered in front of sacred fire altars.

The Supreme God of the Persians cared nothing for the stones and bricks and columns that were raised to his glory either… but he cared that his sacred words had been razed by unbelievers… by the clay men of the rebel god… by his evil twin.

It was foretold since the time before time that he would utterly destroy the rebel god… unless the rebel god knelt down at his godly feet and repented and asked for godly mercy.

He takes a deep breath. His old mind wanders.

After the Lord of Asia had taken sacred temple grounds to build a monument to a dead man… on the landed property of the great gods… the omens had become even more dreadful. The êrib-bêt-ili, the priests of Bêl Marduk, had finally cursed the Lord of Asia… and the mighty Bêl Marduk had heard them…

He shakes his head mindlessly.

When his old master had forewarned the priests of Bêl Marduk, they had ignored him… they had called him an old Star Chaser!

At first the young conqueror had come in pursuit of his own glory… and the êrib-bêt-ili were given promises of rebuilding of Temple of E-sag-ila and their gold was left untouched and the temple tributes and duties were forgiven… and as long as the temple priests could trade wheat and wine and wood and wool for gold to keep as their own, they had turned a blind eye to other deeds of the Lord of Asia.

But they had finally taken notice when the Lord of Asia had come back for the sacred lands of the great gods and had brought with him dead bones to be worshiped like the great gods… he had brought the rebel god to the sacred grounds of the great gods of old…

"The Demon of Death has come for him and all men born of clay turn to dust when Death comes calling on them," he says, shrugging his old shoulders.

Rošanak's face furrows and folds in anguish.

The old Chaldæan scratches his forehead with his old fingers. His eyes narrow.

"They say a creature was born to a Bâb-ilani woman a few days back… upper half, man; lower half, five wild beasts: a lion, a wolf, a panther, a dog and a wild boar. The man part had died and dried while the beasts still kicked and lived. The Chaldæans divined that the upper part was A-lek-sa-an-dar, and the lower wild beasts were his kingsmen.

"I did not see it with my own eyes but I know the Chaldæans. The Chaldæans gave the creature to the Bêl êrib-bêt-ili, who burned the creature on the golden altar as sacrifice to Bêl Marduk."

Rošanak closes her eyes for a long moment. Then she opens her eyes, pushes back a tear, leans forward and puts her drinking cup on the table and rests her hands on her belly. She listens as Kudurru continues.

"All the men of the old gods know what has been foretold… the Chaldæans and the Maguš and the Brahmans and the Judeans… even some of the Muṣru Priests… The blood of the royal father was spilled for the kingship of the Royal Son… Pârsâ was burned… royal blood of the rightful Mâr bît šarri spilled… the Sacred Fires were smothered… the Persian Purple has flown to another head…"

"Surely there must be something that can be done… more precious offerings to the gods…"

"Great gods are enraged and cannot be appeased with fragrant incense and burnt meat."

Rošanak tries again.

"There must be something to soothe the heart of angry gods."

Kudurru wordlessly shakes his head side to side with dismay.

"Another substitute king?" Rošanak pleads.

Silence.

"Dinânu?" Kudurru mumbles to himself and narrows his eyes at her.

Bâb-ilim was to be the new center of the Empire of A-lek-sa-an-dar, the Lord of Asia… the old center of a new world.

When the Lord of Asia had told the êrib-bêt-ili of Bêl Marduk that he planned to build a ziq-qur-rat tomb in honor of his dead kingsman right next to the half ruins of the Temple of E-sag-ila, the priests of Bêl Marduk had begged and pleaded in vain to change his mind.

And when they found the Lord of Asia unbending, they hurled new powerful curses at him for intending to desecrate the sacred temple grounds of the great gods.

This was beyond what a substitute king could take upon himself…

Not even the Persians had ever trampled on the sacred temple grounds of the great gods of Bâb-ilim…

The Great King, Ka-ši-ar-šâ, had taken the golden statue of Bêl Marduk from the Temple of E-sag-ila to punish Bâb-ilim for rising against him and had brought the wrath of Bêl Marduk upon himself… but he had left the sacred temple ground undisturbed, and the Persians had never brought their own gods into Bâb-ilim nor forced the People of Bâb-ilim to worship other gods than their own.

But Bâb-ilim was doomed either way… if the sacred temple grounds were desecrated, the great gods of Bâb-ilim would unleash their wrath upon the city and its people… if they were to resist A-lek-sa-an-dar, the Lord of Asia, then they would suffer his kingly wrath… and so they had decided to curse A-lek-sa-an-dar and his men and take their chances with the great gods. It was the price Master Kinninu had told them they would have to pay when the êrib-bêt-ili had betrayed the Great King Dârius̆ and surrendered Bâb-ilim to A-lek-sa-an-dar without a battle.

They had thought that heaping precious incense and slaughtered oxen upon the sacrificial altars would fool the great gods!

And the ancient great gods were not fools of the young temple priests!

Silence breaks.

"Worthless for the King. By his own royal orders, all the sacred temple fires were doused for the funeral of the second man in all the Lands, signaling the death of a reigning king. Not even a single candle burned in any of the sacred temples of all the Lands…

"Three times the sacred fires have been doused and yet no king has ascended to the throne, no Sacred Rite of Ascension, no one wears the Royal Purple Robe of the Elders… Lands have no kings!"

Kudurru leans backward and mumbles to himself quietly. "Royal Water, water from River Ulai, has been cursed too. The Maguš cursed the Royal Water after the burning of Pârsâ and the temple priests of Bêl Marduk cursed it again after the sacred grounds of the Temple of E-temen-an-ki were desecrated. Royal Water is poison to the Lord of Asia. A king can live without wine, but can a king live without water?"

Rošanak covers her mouth, pushing frightened words back into her trembling throat.

It was the same water she had been drinking, too…

Rošanak slowly pushes herself up from her chair, trying to catch up with her heart… she feels as if her heart is trying to leave her body.

How could anyone be more wretched than she? For loving a man who was so cursed by all the Great Kings and their Royal Women and by all the men of the gods and by all the Persians!

She utters quietly. "Should not a brave warrior die honorably in battle?"

"When the days of a king are numbered and counted, it matters not to the great gods if he dies in battle or in bed!"

She puts her hand on her belly with dread.

"But for the Royal Son…" he says faintly, thinking.

"My Lord?"

Kudurru scratches his gray beard for a moment and then leans forward and points at Rošanak's belly and says, "His chart is long… his blood is royal and he is blessed by his royal ancestors," offering a faint ray of hope.

Rošanak lets out a relieved breath and bows her head slightly and turns toward the door. Then she stops and looks back at the old Chaldæan, with another question in her heart. "What do the stars say about—?"

The old Chaldæan reads her eyes.

He had seen her star chart too.

She was born in the Year 16 of Third Ar-tak-šat-su, who was called Artakhšaçâ, Month 3, Sîmannu, the month of the Moon-God Nânna, seven days passed, on the Day of the Moon… at the moonrise… under a half-waxing moon… the month was not full…

It was the year the Third Ar-tak-šat-su himself had led the Royal Army against the Second Nekhthoreb to end the rule of Muṣru as foretold by the Celestial Omens and divined by Kidinnu, his old master, the chief Tupšar E-nû-ma Anu Êa Bêl…

The Little Star belonged to the Moon-God since the day she was born…

"Your Royal Ancestors have not looked heartlessly toward the man who loved you best and was sent into their care by your sacred prayers."

Rošanak takes a deep breath and nods and looks up at the little stars through the small window in the ceiling.

Kudurru leans forward and puts a small delicate glass bottle on the wooden table close to Rošanak.

The King was heading for the land of no return… er ṣet lâ târi…

"It is foretold that he will linger in death sleep for a long time… but there is no need for a royal king of royal blood of an old Royal House to suffer needlessly long in great pain of death."

Rošanak walks back toward the crowded table and eyes the small kâsaka bottle and considers it for a short moment in the dim light of the lamp.

There was no need to ask what was in the bottle…

… she knew… half of her was from the mountains of Bakhtriš… and the other half was the granddaughter of Dukšiš Purušâtu.

She picks up the small bottle and holds it tight in her hand, and turns and heads for the door. Then she stops halfway.

She had forgotten something…

She turns around and looks at the old Chaldæan, who was looking back at her.

She was a Royal Woman… wife of the king… Âriyânnâz always followed her and paid for whatever she desired… Hephæstion had always given her whatever was necessary from the royal funds.

She had come alone and had no golden archers with her, not even a small silver šiklu.

And Abi-Samar carried only his sword, not gold, with him.

She takes a step toward the old Chaldæan hesitatingly.

Her golden emerald earrings dance and dangle and move with her feet. She takes a deep breath, relieved. She takes another step and stands before the wooden table, removes her earrings and looks at them lovingly for a short moment in the light of the dim lamp, then leans forward and puts them down gently on the ancient curse of the First Dâriuš etched on the pavastâ fragments from Pârsâ.

She had no more use for them, with the skies falling on her… and the world ending…

"Please accept these as a token of my gratitude."

Kudurru looks at her and then looks down at the ancient curse cradling the glinting earrings.

The old love earrings of Mâr'at Bani Mândâna… the beloved of the Younger Ku-raš, the Royal Son of the House…

A small black scorpion pushes himself up between the wedges of the clay tablets and strolls across the emerald earrings.

Kudurru leans forward and flicks the scorpion away from the beautiful earrings. "Zuqaqîpu…" He then nods and says, "May your god bless you in the Assembly of the great gods and put abundance in your path."

Rošanak nods and takes a step back, bows her head slightly and turns around and quickly leaves on heavy feet.

Kudurru looks up at the starry skies above.

There were so many little stars in the heavens… the Watchers of the Heavens did not know the names of many of them. Men knew even less… but they all shined brightly just the same… little stars were the candles that lit the heavenly nights… the heavenly messengers who took the prayers of the mortals to the ears of the great gods…

They were the bright goddesses of the night.

He raises his hands and starts to pray:

"O Ištar, queen of all men, guide of all men,
iltu Ištar šar-ra-ti kul-lat da-ad-me muš-te-ši-rat te-ni-še-e-ti,
O lady, your rank is majestic, above all the great gods,
iltu Bêlti šu-pu-u nar-bu-ki eli ka-la ilâni ṣi-ru,
Anu, Êa and Bêl have raised you high, among great gods they have given you dominion.
ilu Anu ilu Êa ilu Bêl u ul-lu-u-ki ina ilâni u-šar-bu-u be-lu-ut-ki.
You came to me in a dream and said to me: You made an offering to me.
Let me hear your prayer that I may fulfill your heart's desire…
I pray unto thee, lady of ladies, goddess of goddesses,
Šiptu u-sal-li-ki be-lit be-lit-e-ti-ilat i-la-a-ti,
pity me and listen to my prayer,
ki-niš nap li-sin-ni-ma ši-mi-e tas-li-li,
look upon me, O my lady, and accept my prayer…"
a-mur-in-ni-ma iltu bêlti-ia li-ki-e un-ni-ni-ia…

GARDEN PALACE of QUEEN AMYTIŠ
FOLLOWING MORNING

Soothing murmur of cool running water…
Cool shade of fruit trees…
Lovely scent of fragrant flowers…
Eyes heavy with sleep…
Belly heavy with child…
Haunting words turn into dreamy visions…
Šuttu…

Divine Assembly of God and Angels…

The Lord of Darkness had secretly gathered the young gods of the Lands of the Middle Sea and the Bitter Sea and the old gods of the Two Lands and the great gods of the Lands between the Twin Rivers in council and had intrigued against his old archenemy, the Wise Lord and his Divine Angels and Archangels…

And together they had driven the armies of the enemies of the Wise Lord against his most faithful subjects, the Persians… they had bathed in the blood and had feasted on the flesh of the brave Persian warriors as they lay rotting on the battlefields across Âryânâ, their own Lands.

The Wise Lord breathed the scent of the eternal sacred fire reaching to the Heaven… it smelled new… different… dark…

So he called the Divine Assembly of seven of his Angels and asked them: What was scenting the eternal sacred fire?

And Atar, the Angel of Fire, bowed and replied:

"My Lord, it is the mournful scent of Pârsâ burning!"

And Mithrâ, the Angel of Sun, bowed and replied:

"My Lord, it is the scent of brave Persian warriors dying!"

And Ânâhatâ, the Angel of Waters, bowed and said:

"My Lord, it is the scent of captive Persian women and children weeping!"

And Khvarənah, the Divine Glory, bowed and said:

"My Lord, it is the scent of your sacred wise words burning in the fires of Pârsâ which the noble Persian warriors gave their blood in battles to protect, and their women and children have been raped and sold as captives for their devotion to you!"

And the Wise Lord asked his seven Divine Angels in council: Who had waged war against him and his Persians?

Atar, the Angel of Fire said:

"My Lord, Alexander, Son of Philip, King of the Lands by the Bitter Sea."

Mithrâ, the Angel of Sun said:
"My Lord, the Uplanders, Men of Alexander."
Ânâhatâ, the Angel of Waters said:
"My Lord, the Men of the Lands of the Middle Sea."
Tištryâ, the Angel of Rain said:
"My Lord, the young Olympian gods of the Mount Olympus."
Mâha, the Angel of Moon said:
"My Lord, the old gods of the Two Lands."
Vanu, the Angel of Wind said:
"My Lord, the great gods of the Lands between the Twin Rivers."
Khvarənah, the Divine Glory said:
"My Lord, the rebel god… the Lord of Darkness!"

….

The Wise Lord summons Alexander.

Alexander goes to his fate…

The long shimmery Bridge of Chinvât sways gently before Alexander's feet on the Day of the First Judgment… it stretches from this side to the other side beyond where mortal eyes could see.

Gleaming dogs guard the Bridge of Chinvât faithfully…

A long line of old women are holding Alexander's House of Songs… records of all his mortal deeds written faithfully on heavenly cloth…

The Divine Sraoša, one of the Three Heavenly Judges, asks:

"Thoughts?"

An old woman reads out loud:

"I am godly!"

The Divine Rašnu, one of the Three Heavenly Judges, asks:

"Words?"

Another old woman reads out loud:

"I accept Asia from my gods!"

The old woman continues:

"It is divine to live with courage and die with everlasting fame!"

Alexander steps on the Bridge of Chinvât… the sacred bridge starts to narrow under his feet.

The Divine Mithrâ, one of the Three Heavenly Judges, asks:

"Deeds?"

Another old woman reads out loud:

"Ancient city of Thebai destroyed, 20,000 dead…

"Siege of Ṣurru, 8,000 massacred, 30,000 sold in slave markets…

"Siege of Gaza, 10,000 killed… all women and children sold in slave markets…

"Battle of Granikos, 25,000 dead…

"Battle of Issos, 100,000 dead…

"People of Samaria annihilated…

"Battle of Black Eagle, 300,000 dead… more sold in slave markets…"

The old woman catches her breath and continues:

"Persian Gates, 25,000 dead…

"Bît Par-ri-sa-a-a, City of Persians, sacked, 150,000 killed… all the women raped…

"Sacred Pârsâ burned…

"100,000 verses of Avesta written in gold on 12,000 sacred skins of sacrificial oxen, burned when Pârsâ burned…

"Tribe of Branchidæs annihilated…

"Kurtaø… City of Kuruš… 8,000 killed… 15,000 sold into slavery…

"100,000 Bakhtrians and Sughdians killed…

"Battle of Vitastâ… 16,000 dead… 9,000 captured… 8,000 wounded…

"Massacre at Sangala… 17,000 dead… 70,000 captured…

"Mâlavâns slaughtered whole…

"65,000 dead in the Desert of Emptiness… men and women and children…"

The Bridge of Chinvât under Alexander's feet narrows more… becomes no wider than the sharp edge of a Persian sword…

The Wise Lord asks Alexander:

"Who are you?"

"I am Alexander."

"Whose are you?"

"I am son of Zeus-Ammon, son of god, a god…"

"A demon is not a god."

The sharp edge of the Persian sword cuts into the bottom of Alexander's feet… the sword becomes bloody… blood drips…

drip… drip… drip…

Alexander struggles and staggers and falls into the jaws of Hell.

Angra Mainyu, the Lord of Darkness, mocks Alexander without pity:

"Why did you eat the bread of A^h^uramazdâ^h^ and do my work?

"Why did you not recognize your own master and accomplish my will instead?"

….

"Ahh!"

"Your Highness!"

Rošanak is shaken out of her nightmare. She opens her eyes hesitatingly and looks at the Old Persian Healer. Her heart pounds.

"No matter which dark demon is ailing the King, Haoma can expel the evil!" the Old Persian Healer says with confidence, nodding his head. He bows and hands a cup of precious golden-honey Haoma to Rošanak.

"Ah!" The small cup slides out of Rošanak's sleepy fingers and the delicate cup cracks and crashes into bits and pieces on the ground all around them. Watery honey-golden Haoma splatters over her royal purple gown.

Rošanak sits motionlessly looking at the broken cup and the spilled Haoma.

Palace maids rush over and clean every broken bit and piece carefully by hand.

The Old Persian Healer bows and looks miserably at the wasted sacred Haoma. "Dukšiš, shall I prepare more Haoma for the King?" he asks quietly with dismay.

Rošanak wells up with tears and looks away.

Sacred Haoma had spilled…

Alexander was no longer the King in all the Lands… the Persian Purple had passed to another head…

The Divine Glory of Kingship had left the King…

All was lost…

All that was left was a Great Conqueror caught in the jaws of the powerful ancient curses of the Greater Kings!

"No. He says he wishes no healing brew. Leave him in the care of his own wound-healers."

"But, My Lady…"

Rošanak gives a sharp look to the Old Persian Healer.

"Yes, Dukšiš." The old man quickly bows low and leaves quietly.

Rošanak reclines into the soft pillow supporting her back and closes her eyes… her gown wet with Haoma, her heart wet with woe, one drying faster than the other in the high heat of the Bâb-ilim sun.

She did not need the Zarathuštra Athravans and the Hindu Brahmans and the Chaldæans to whisper words of darkness and despair and doom into her ears…

No ancient prophecies or old curses…

She could see it with her own eyes… it was in his eyes… one eye the color of the early morning dawn and his sword, the other the color of a mournful night and his wrath, both turned the reddish bloody color of royal purple…

Alexander was neither the king nor the man who had wedded and bedded her years ago… he had changed. After the death of Hephæstion, Alexander had slowly divorced his reason and had wedded his wine… he and his kingsmen were men of war and wine… and now that there was less war, there was more wine.

The dazzling, gleaming Crown of the Great Kings was a murderous, pitiless, ruthless seductress… She had beckoned and seduced and used Alexander, just as easily as she had beckoned and seduced and used all the other Vîsa Puça… all the Sons of the Royal House of the Hakhâmaniš… all to the last man… and her lap was more desired than the lap of any mortal Royal Woman by the Sons of the Royal House of the Persians.

A King, one-third man, one-third wine, one-third wrath… three-thirds captive…

A King, a prisoner of his own passion for the Persian Crown… now abandoned by her.

Then the Lord of Darkness had slowly found his way into Alexander's wounded soul through the arrow wound in Hind and through the tongues of the wicked royal court flatterers, desirous of royal favors… and there was no one left to tell Alexander the truth of the Wise Lord… Hephæstion, the gate keeper of the King, had died in Hagmâtâna… lost in the Place of Gathering.

The King was wrapped in the golden lies of the Lord of Darkness…

The Lord of Darkness had tempted Zarathuštra with fame and wealth in return for abandoning the Wise Lord and the Truth, and the prophet had repelled him by uttering sacred words of sacred prayers:

"Never shall I renounce the worship of Ahuramazdâh!"

Zarathuštra was put to the sword by enemy invaders… his holy throat cut and his holy blood spilled into a silvery fire altar in Baktra, and the Sacred Fire had burned blood red since that day in remembrance, and never doused until the âyadana was sacked…

The Dark Demon Lord knew many tongues and he had finally spoken the tongue of Alexander… words he understood completely. The Lord of Darkness had whispered into his ears that he too was a god, son of a god, begotten by a god, godly like gods… immortal and invincible… and that he too was deserving of worship and sacrifice like gods… and Alexander had believed the Lord of Darkness… and the Dark Demon had finally claimed him whole.

A King, one-third wine, one-third wrath, one-third god… three-thirds tormented tyrant… and gods had no need of mortal wives and sons…

And she was bone weary… weary of traveling behind the Royal Army… she wanted to stay at Hagmâtâna until her son was born… and then raise her Son-Prince as a Royal Son of the House should be raised.

Alexander was never satisfied… the more he had, the more restless he was…

As long as Alexander lived, she was tied to a carriage on a never-ending road in search of more glory in the fettered service of the Lord of Darkness… all alone with Hephæstion dead and Krateros banished…

She was tired of it all…

Alexander could be a god if he so desired and the gods could have him if they too so desired… it was all the same… it was all the manly mortal madness of a king…

He was as his gods had made him…

A King… one-third god, one-third wine, one-third wrath… three-thirds dying…

KING'S ROYAL QUARTERS
ROYAL PALACE of the SECOND NABÛ-KUDURRÎ-ÛSUR
DAY 27: KING at ROYAL COURT. UNFAVORABLE
AKÎTU FESTIVAL DID NOT TAKE PLACE
MID-DAY

Sky looks like a parched lake.

Alexander is dying…

And he knows it in his mortal bones…

He had seen it in Roxana's eyes… and had heard it from her silent lips. Unlike the days and nights and midnights she had whispered into his ears and had kept to his bedside when he had taken that bloody arrow wound in India, she had no sacred words to utter softly in his ears this time… no eyes tearing at his bedside… no lips pleading in his heart…

The fever, starting like a flicker of a candle, had finally become a full raging inferno. Just as Pârsâ had burned, so was he now burning…

… and his nightmarish dreams had become even more haunting.

He had bathed in cool waters daily… and had performed his daily sacrifices to his gods… all of them. He had eaten a little… not much…

He had reviewed the twenty thousand warriors, mostly Persians, that Peukestas had brought to Babylon for him. He had promoted his men and had filled empty ranks in his Royal Army… but still no one to the rank of the Keeper of the King. That forever belonged to Hephæstion.

Perdikkas had been the Chiliarchos and the Commander of the Makedonian Horse since Hephæstion's death and that was enough.

He had played dice with Medeios and had heard the details of his next campaign to Arabia from Nearchos… and had told Perdikkas and the Royal Bodyguards and all his kingsmen and the commanders of the Royal Army to remain close in the palace, and the rest of the Royal Army to stay close beyond the palace walls.

There was no longer comfort in sleeping… just unbroken nightmares.

He could no longer command his fingers to write…

His lips move silently… "Roxana…" No one hears him. He closes his eyes in pain.

And now he had finally lost his words and his voice… he could no longer will his lips to speak.

And his eyes were flickering like a candle caught in a warm breeze.

His flanks were finally turned by the Unseen One… both right and left… the center had fallen too…

… stay or move… there was neither war nor peace… there was only death…

He had cheated the Gordian Knot… but the knot of death was not as easily fooled.

He once had stood between the old philosopher, Diogenes, and his sun…

… now nothing stood between him and his death.

He was caught in the jaws of a powerful dragon who intended to keep him… as his prize of war.

In India, he had asked a Brahman:

"How long should a man live?"

… and the Brahman had said to him:

"Until death becomes more desirable than life."

The Crown and the Throne of the Persian Great Kings were forever lost to him. His kingsmen and satraps conspired against him persistently and disobedience and mutiny had plagued his Royal Army. With constant throbbing pain sieging and burning his body, death had finally become more desirable than life.

Hades, the Unseen One, had patiently waited for him for eight long years… by the Gate of Gods of Babylon.

He had lived fearlessly with unbounded glory and in death everlasting fame would be his.

A living god resigned to tasting death…

A long string of Makedonians are still waiting to enter the palace of the dead old Babylonian Kings to see the dying young Makedonian Alexander.

The one and the last Lord of Asia…

Dying in bed… not like a warrior king on a battlefield somewhere, by the thrust of a sharp sword, or a swift arrow, or a long spear… but like an old man from a failing mortal body that no longer obeyed his kingly commands.

Palace eunuchs busy themselves nervously and fortify Alexander with multitudes of large soft white pillows.

What a disaster!

A dying king!

No king had died in bed in Bâb-ilim in their living memory… the Lord of Asia was dying with no living sons… who will come after him?

Bêl êrib-bêt-ili had requested an audience with the Lord of Asia and had not been admitted to his presence… he had played dice instead with some of his own men… which had infuriated the Bêl priests!

Everyone in the palace was murmuring afterward that the êrib-bêt-ili of Bêl had called the King, "bêl lâ ilim… man without god…" and had said that the King had sinned against the great gods of Bâb-ilim and that the great gods of Bâb-ilim had inflicted him with a dying disease, and they had refused to pray for the health of the King or sacrifice to Ninisina, the divine patron goddess of healing.

And they were all caught between the powerful priests of Bêl and the powerful Lord of Asia!

What was to be done?

Alexander takes a painful breath.

His Makedonians were waiting.

They had shouted first and then begged and cried to see him, fearing him dead already, and his kingsmen had finally relented…

They had opened the massive palace doors and had let his men enter…

And they had all come, one by one, unarmed, unguarded, to see him one last time.

And none had uttered a word as they entered the old palace of old kings.

They had all passed by his bed silently… mournfully… they all knew he was dying too.

It was so quiet…

And so hot…

And so dark…

The candles of his eyes were burning out…

Hephæstion…

Where was Hephæstion?

Was he coming later?

Where was his Roxana?

Roxana…

Roxana…

Roxana…

Sun is fading at the end of a long hot summer day.

Finally the last of the Makedonians leaves.

Alexander slowly sinks back into the multitude of pillows behind him, like the warm bleeding sun sinking into the cool comforting ocean, burning the sky all around him.

All his kingsmen are knotted around his royal bed, like hunters watching a dying lion.

Perdikkas bends and takes Alexander's hand in his hand.

Leonnatos finally leans closer and asks grimly, "Alexander, to whom do you bequeath your Empire?"

Alexander closes his eyes. His face folds with pain.

He was taking his Empire with him…

It was his Empire…

Won by spear…

Watered by blood…

Woven by sedition…

Perdikkas clenches his fist around Alexander's signet ring tightly and bends his head forward and asks quietly, "Alexander, who shall succeed you?"

Alexander moves his lips in pain but utters no sound.

A candle burning twice as bright… finally all burnt and spent…

Perdikkas leans closer and puts his ear close to Alexander's mouth.

Silence.

Twilight mournfully follows the body of the dying sun.

Little stars bend to their knees in the darkened skies.

Šamû îrup.

GARDEN PALACE of QUEEN AMYTIŠ
FOLLOWING NIGHT

"The King—"

Abi-Samar bows his head and whispers in a hushed haunted voice, "They say the King is dead. His men have all left the royal bedchamber. The death chamber is empty of the living."

Rošanak wipes her eyes and looks at Abi-Samar. She takes a deep breath and bites her lip. She pushes herself up from her silver couch and gets to her swollen feet and stands uncertainly, bracing her sides with her hands.

Her heart was beating so loud in her ears that she was not certain she had heard all the words that had carelessly slashed through the mournful veil of silence… words that should not have been spoken.

Her back hurt from the weight of her unborn and still she had a few more months before birthing. She felt as heavy as a Hindu war elephant.

Being with child was a high price to pay for having a son!

A warm night breeze fills the room.

She closes her eyes and listens to the hushed quiet of the palace.

Palaces always murmured… but even the singing garden birds had turned silent…

When the dreadful news of the death of her blood brothers had finally reached the palace at Baktra, the screams of her blood mother had cracked the glass windows in her bedchamber.

"But it is so quiet."

"The palace eunuchs do not know what to do. There is no one to command them," Abi-Samar continues with a heavy heart. "Bêl erib-bêt-ili have sent word that the King had sinned against the great gods of Bâb-ilim and they have forbidden the palace eunuchs to mourn him unless they wish the wrath of the great gods upon them. He was a stranger in the Lands from the lands with strange gods. The royal mourning reserved for kings was given to Hezârapatiš when the Sacred Royal Fires were quenched in all the temples all through Bâbil and beyond by the royal order. Everyone wishes he had died in Muṣru where he was liked, not here. They will start mourning and wailing for him, if you command it as the Queen of the House of the King. They cannot refuse your royal order." Abi-Samar speaks plainly, in a low voice, barely audible.

"No! Not yet!"

Rošanak dips a hand linen in the water bowl next to her bed and wipes her eyes and face and neck and shoulders and in between her breasts to cool down. She then drops the hand linen carelessly next to the water bowl, picks up the small bottle, and heads for the door, with an empty expression on her face.

A palace maid quickly opens the door for her.

Abi-Samar follows her as she slowly waddles toward the sky bridge, and then slowly down the steps toward the main palace maze where the King's royal quarters lay patiently waiting.

KING'S ROYAL QUARTERS
LATER

Pleasant wind… unpleasant air…

Quieter than death…

The royal quarters at the other side of the Palace of the Second Nabû-Kudurrî-Ûṣur had sunk behind a veil of silence.

Heaps of precious Arabâya incense burn lavishly in small altars along the maze of inner courtyards and hallways leading to Alexander's private royal quarters. There is no sign of the kingsmen or the royal guards or the royal boys who normally linger and lurk around in such late hours, half-asleep. Palace guards and palace eunuchs have all vanished into the shadows, biding their time until they could safely come back and blend seamlessly into the royal court of the next king.

Rošanak and Abi Samar reach Alexander's royal bedchamber on the other side of the throne room. Rošanak catches her breath and stands motionlessly and wordlessly, looking at the massive doors in front of her with eyes heavy with tears and sorrow.

She dreaded the death that was hiding behind the massive closed doors, waiting for her.

Knowing for days that he was surely dying had not lessened the pain of losing him.

There are no palace guards to open the doors. Abi-Samar shakes his head in dismay, curses under his lips and quietly presses on the giant heavy doors. They are not locked, and yield and obediently surrender to Abi-Samar's firm touch.

Rošanak takes a deep breath and then waddles inside on heavy feet. The great royal bedchamber is hushed and dimly lit by small candles, flickering in the warm night breeze coming through the open window… filled with the scent of burning candles and Arabâya incense and death.

On the old royal bed where her ancestral Persian Kings had once slept, Alexander's body lay still, covered waist down by soft white linen. His head resting on a single pillow, his eyes closed, his honor wounds purpled and blackened…

The palace eunuchs had removed the bedding for the Hezârapatiš and had arranged Alexander's body as straight as a Persian arrow.

She stands still and looks at Alexander for a moment. Her heart beats with grief and regret and sorrow.

Great King Khašâyâr had permitted his great-grandson who had come back home to his Lands to die in the bed of his ancient royal ancestors…

The ancient Bâb-ilani golden vines of the sycamore fig tree, the eternal Tree-of-Life, wrapped around the giant bedposts, heavy with rubies and emeralds, were guarding a dying king…

Rošanak steps toward the royal bed and rests her head on the golden bedpost. Her heart fills with old love at the sight of his lifeless body.

How could he die before her? He was so strong and she was so weak.

She then notices a small hand moving a palm-leaf fan back and forth over Alexander's body. She follows the small hand to a face that is staring at her with blazing hateful eyes. She recognizes the vile wicked face. Blistering anger breaks inside of her.

It was the eunuch… the one Alexander had kissed in front of his men… he was dressed like the palace servants and was wasted and unkempt and unwashed. The evil wretch looked more like the whore of Hades than the whore of Alexander.

"What are you doing here?" Rošanak demands cuttingly.

"I am watching over the body of my master," the eunuch, Bagaya, says tearfully in a soft, almost womanly accented voice.

She stares at him for a moment, forgetting herself.

It was the first time she had heard his strange voice… a soft voice of a half-woman coming from the lips of a half-man…

Itâna was right. The eunuch was not Persian, and there was not a mark of the royal slave on his forehead or palace slave on his wrist… he was meant for the royal bed.

She closes her eyes and takes a deep breath.

Alexander had only a handful of bed companions… and they had all come and gone here and there, but he had only kept two loves in his heart… beloved of one and lover of the other… and it was always Hephæstion he had called for in his deep sleep or in his deep pain. His heart was no different than his empire… old ancestral land, ruled by Hephæstion, his first lover, and vast new conquered land, ruled by her, his last beloved… and the two powerful xšaçapâvans of both lands had made peace between themselves from the beginning by the desire of the King himself, knowing well enough that neither could win the land of the other without breaking the heart of the King and shattering the whole of the Empire in half. And so after peace, they had knotted in love too… it was only after the King himself had grown jealous and had pulled apart the two obedient rulers under his command that disaster had befallen him.

Alexander had ripped his own heart… and one half had swiftly died of boundless grief for losing the other half… and the King could not survive with just half a heart.

What more was there to say?

She comes back to herself, opens her eyes, and straightens and looks away.

Time was short… She had no time to waste with the miserable creature before her now.

"Queen Consort overlooks the King's indiscretions," Âriyânnâz always reminded her.

"Leave!" Rošanak orders the eunuch firmly, as she steps closer to the royal bed and gently takes Alexander's hand and looks at his face.

His hand was limp and soft and warm.

Her heart skips a beat. Hope returns.

She leans slightly forward and gently puts her other hand over Alexander's naked heart. His body too is soft and fresh.

The old Chaldæan was right! Even though her anxious fingers could not detect a beating heart… Alexander was still trapped in his mortal body in a death sleep, alive inside, dead to the world around him.

His death was forthcoming; but it had yet to come…

A growling voice slices like a dagger through her thoughts. She turns her head toward the repulsive creature.

"Do not touch him!" the eunuch moans quietly in accented Persian, throwing himself over Alexander's body. "Leave him be!"

Rošanak takes a step back. Her anger starts to rise.

She might not have fully understood the barbarian Makedonians, but she utterly understood palace eunuchs who were bound by sacred oaths to the crown to honor the Queen Mother and the Queen Consort above all. The eunuch had forgotten who he was!

"I have summoned Princess Setâreh from Susa Palace. She will be here soon enough to assume her rightful place next to her Lord!" the eunuch says in an arrogant voice, mixing accented Persian and Attik words together.

"You?" Rošanak finds her voice again and thunders at the eunuch. "By whose authority have you summoned our royal sister to the court?"

"By my own authority!" the eunuch cries defiantly, brandishing a royal signet ring on one of his fingers. "You are not worthy of my master!"

"Shut your filthy mouth, you bloody isinnû! You are speaking to the Queen!" Abi-Samar roars furiously at Bagaya and grabs him.

"Ah!" The eunuch cries in pain as Abi-Samar seizes his bony body by his long hair and drags him off Alexander's body down to the dark floor at Rošanak's feet.

"Ah!" Rošanak holds her heavy sides in pain.

The unborn royal son had made himself remembered again by a kick inside her belly… and then another…

What should she tell her unborn son? That his father was dying?

Rošanak holds her breath for a moment in pain and then lets it out. She narrows her eyes with contempt at the insolent eunuch down at her feet.

"I have not been unsympathetic to your miserable being. Your manhood slashed to pay for the sins of your disloyal ancestors to the Crown and the Throne of the First Dâriuš, forced into pleasing the desires of men more wretched than yourself—

"But you are not only disrespectful toward the Queen Consort, by your evil words and your evil deeds, you have brought death to noble men of the highest royal blood. Mâr Bani Aršana was the head of the Pârsâkata Tribe. Did you think the Persians would forget his execution caused by your greedy treacherous words? You are a contemptible, evil, wicked creature, a disgrace to the royal court eunuchs, and your deadly mouth has uttered its last evil words!" Rošanak thunders and then points to Abi-Samar with her head.

Before Bagaya can open his mouth again, Abi-Samar wraps his powerful hands around Bagaya's throat and with a swift and hard squeeze crushes the eunuch's voice. Bagaya falls to the floor, grabbing his throat in choking pain.

Rošanak points to his hands.

"And your deadly hands have written their last evil words!"

Bagaya clasps his hands together without thinking.

Crunch!

The sound of breaking bones shoots across the heavy quiet of the royal bedchamber like a broken arrow.

Abi-Samar lets go of Bagaya's hands and the eunuch twists in pain silently on the floor.

Rošanak looks at Abi-Samar and says quietly, "Give me the stolen royal ring. Cut off his nose and ears. Put him in a box and take him to the kinsmen of Mâr Bani Aršana in Pârsâkata. Let them decide his wretched fate."

Bagaya folds in fear and starts to crawl away on the floor.

Abi-Samar puts his strong feet on the bony back of the crawling eunuch and holds him still in place like a small insect. He then looks at Alexander for a quick moment and then casts his eyes away.

The great gods of Bâb-ilim had finally spit on the arrogant mortal king.

Even the great A-lek-sa-an-dar had proven no match for the great gods.

Unconquered was finally conquered!

"My Lady, I think it is better for me to stay and protect you. The bloody isinnû can be seen to later. The air is growing dangerous with treacherous men. I fear for you," Abi-Samar says quietly.

"Will the palace eunuchs keep faith with me while you are gone?"

"Yes! You are the Queen of the House of the King heavy with his royal child. Brother of my father, Abi-Enši-Marduk, will see to it!"

"Good! Tell him to look for the Royal Daughters of King Dâriuš."

"Yes, My Lady."

"Now go. And remember me in your prayers to your Lord Marduk."

Abi-Samar hesitates for a moment and then bows his head, bends down and grabs Bagaya's hand and pulls the signet ring off his crooked broken finger and hands it over to Rošanak.

Rošanak takes the royal ring and wipes off the blood and looks at it.

"Take this back to my bedchamber and leave it with the rest of my jewelry." Rošanak hands the royal signet ring back to Abi-Samar.

Abi-Samar bows his head and takes the ring. He bends down and grabs Bagaya by his hair, dragging him out of the royal bedchamber.

"Wait!" Rošanak calls him.

Abi-Samar stops. He turns around, hoping that she has changed her mind. "My Lady?"

Rošanak picks up a silver casket resting on top of the golden table next to the royal bed and opens the top. Alexander's old book of *Ilias* sleeps quietly inside the silver casket of old Persian Kings. She runs the tips of her fingers on the old avestâ cover and then closes the top.

Did it know its master was dying?

"Take this with you. Leave it in my bed chamber, next to my jewelry box."

Abi-Samar walks back, dragging the eunuch behind him.

He takes the silver casket and bows his head. "Yes, My Lady."

Rošanak unleashes the full weight of her grief and pain and points to the eunuch whimpering at her feet.

"Burn the mark of royal servitude on his filthy forehead, so everyone will know he is a slave of the royal crown, punished for his insolence. He deserves no mercy."

"Yes, My Lady." He bows his head again and turns around, dragging the eunuch behind him. He leaves the bedchamber and closes the door behind him.

Sounds die down. The room becomes quiet again.

Rošanak looks back at Alexander. She waddles forward again, slides off her silk slippers and slowly lies down on her side on the royal bed next to him. She rests her forehead on the side of Alexander's head.

At last… finally… utterly alone…

It is the first time the two of them are alone together since Baktra, without anyone lurking in the shadows or behind closed doors.

She takes a deep breath and closes her eyes.

No Hezârapatiš… no Kingsmen… no Generals and Commanders and Warriors…

No Royal Boys, no Royal Guards, no Royal Bodyguards, no Companions…

No HighLanders, LowLanders, UpLanders, FlatLanders, MainLanders, Islanders, NorthLanders or TwoLanders…

No Horse nor Foot nor Fleet… no Nobles, Satraps, Governors, Ambassadors, Treasurers, Couriers, Messengers, Envoys… no diviners, seers, philosophers, brahmans, sages, historians, flatterers, geographers… no poets, singers, dancers, actors, entertainers, boxers… no wand-bearers and wine-pourers… no harpists and flutists…

No Mothers, Sisters, Wives, Mistresses, Lovers or Whores… no bloody eunuchs…

… no one!

Just man and wife…

King and Queen…

And utter peaceful silence.

She raises her hand and gently plays with his unruly hair and utters tenderly, "Alexander…"

The sweet memory of her tender wedding night pours into her heart without warning… how his hand slightly trembled as he claimed her for the first time… the sweet eager feel of his desire for her… and how her body trembled with desire for his touch…

She sees a slight movement in his lashes. She closes her eyes and takes a deep breath and a tear falls on the pillow.

His once golden hair was now almost the color of silver… like the color of freshly fallen snow on a field of harvested golden wheat… the color of the night he had gotten her with child in Hagmâtâna.

"Forgive me… your kingsmen came and took you from my bed and brought you back here… I should not have let them… I should have kept to your bedside… prayed for your life…"

Another slight movement of his lashes.

"This is the royal bed of Xerxes. I thought you would be better cared for with your great-grandfather watching over you."

She leans forward and kisses his face tenderly again and takes his hand gently and rests it on her belly. "What shall we name him?" The unborn kicks.

Silence.

Rošanak puts her arm over Alexander's body and holds him tightly.

"I saw Hephæstion in a dream… he said to me, *Do not worry! I will be waiting for him.*"

Another tear falls on the pillow. Thoughts of him suffering in horrible pain pierce her heart and make her bones shiver.

She slowly pulls out the small bottle hidden between her breasts. She opens the top gently and moistens her finger with the colorless liquid and gently rubs it on Alexander's lips. The liquid slowly seeps into his closed mouth.

"Remember the first time you kissed me?" she whispers lovingly. "All I could think about today was the night before our wedding night when you were waiting for me outside my temple."

She sees another tiny movement in his lashes. She gently rubs more liquid on his lips with trembling fingers. "Poppy juice… it will ease your pains…" She rubs more on his lips. She touches his body; it starts to cool down.

"I still have the rose you gave me that night… I dried it… I put each petal between the pages of a book Hephæstion gave me… the petals kissed and scented the pages with fragrant bloody lips… it looked as if the rose petals had bled into the words… as if the words had bled…"

Another slight movement of his lashes…

She rubs more poppy juice on his lips and pleads with all her heart.

"You said you would give me whatever I ask of you. Take me with you!"

How could he refuse her? Her hand was tied to his hand… she was his…

Tears pour like rain.

She closes her eyes. An unbearable burning pain starts in her heart and spreads through her whole body like wildfire.

"I am coming with you. You are not leaving me behind this time. Your gods took Hephæstion from me… they will not take you too without taking me!"

Land of the Eternal Darkness was living in a body when all love was lost…

Another warm breeze fills the room.

A candle flickers and dies.

She rubs some poppy juice on her own lips. Its sweetness is like nothing else she has ever tasted.

She licks her fingers and starts to drift into darkness…

YEAR 14 of the THIRD ALEXANDER, MONTH of TARGELION,
114th OLYMPIAD in the ARCHONSHIP of PHILOCLES at ATHENAI
YEAR 14 of ALEXANDROS, MONTH 8, DAISIOS, DAY 28
YEAR 8 of ALEXANDER, MONTH 2, ΘÛRAVÂHARA
YEAR 8 of A-LEK-SA-AN-DAR, MONTH 2, AYYÂRU, DAY 29
EVENING

So died Alexander, Son of Philip, descendant of the ancient Âryâs and Hellenes. King of Makedon, Son of Ra, Pharaoh of Ta-Mehu and Ta-Shemau, Beloved of Ammon, Lord of Asia.

In the arms of his beloved queen, Roxana, a Persian Royal Woman…

… who whispered upon his passing,

"Alexander, the darkness you see is the flame of eternal fame."

They say she was the only woman he ever loved…

E-SAG-ILA. TEMPLE of BÊL MARDUK. E-TEMEN-AN-KI TEMPLE
ROYAL CITY of BÂB-ILIM
YEAR 8 of A-LEK-SA-AN-DAR, MONTH 3, SÎMANNU, DAY 1
NIGHT

"Here it is, Father."

Bêl-rê'ušu silently walks into the candlelit room wearing a white robe adorned with golden stars. He bows his head respectfully and quietly puts the clay tablet on the wooden table in front of his father. He straightens and stands obediently in front of him.

Kî-Nabû eyes his son proudly under his snow white brow.

His son was finally mastering the art of his fathers. He was now an Ummânu. And he was learning the tongue of the foreign king too… his mother would have been proud.

He draws a deep breath and reluctantly leans forward in his old worn chair, pulling the flickering candle closer, and tries hard to read the latest entry in the Book of Heaven. His eyes fail him. He finally relents, leans backward in his chair and points to the clay tablet.

"Read it to me."

Bêl-rê'ušu leans forward and obediently reads the clay tablet for his father.

E-NÛ-MA iltu ANU iltu ÊA iltu BÊL…
When the great gods Anu, Êa and Bêl
established the bounds of Heaven and Earth in council…

Year 8 of A-lek-sa-an-dar who is called Alexander, Month 2, Ayyâru
Day 29: The King died.
Clouds were in the sky.

Kî-Nabû rubs his eyes and scratches his white beard, thinking for a long moment. He slowly leans forward again.

"Where is the commentary?"

"There is none, Father. There were thick clouds above. We kept watch all night, but no one could see the moon. It remained well hidden behind the clouds until it disappeared before dawn."

"Nânna hid his face?"

Kî-Nabû shakes his head and closes his eyes and shifts uncomfortably in his chair. He leans back and rests his old bones on older wood and nods.

"The moon was not seen in the heavens… unfavorable… the great gods have not changed their inauspicious plans for the Lands…"

"O Ištar, let thy great mercy be upon me…"

iltu Ištar ta-ai-ra-tu-ki rab-ba-a-ti lib-ša-a eli-ia…

A warm breeze lazily enters the hot room.

Kî-Nabû opens his eyes, shakes his head and mindlessly mumbles to himself.

"Prophecy is fulfilled. The King is dead. Age of darkness begins.

"Qurun šalmât ummânâtīšu… I see a pile of corpses."

He then leans forward in his chair and pulls a wine cup closer to him with his trembling fingers.

Bêl-rê'ušu quickly steps forward and picks up a half-empty massîtu of date-wine and pours a cup for his father. Kî-Nabû takes a sip and puts the wine cup down on the wooden table and looks up.

"Šarratu—"

"Father?"

"Have you seen her?"

"Yes, Father."

"Is she as beautiful as they say she is?"

"She might be, hard to tell, Father," Bêl-rê'ušu says, "She is heavy with child. Master Kudurru says her eyes are arqu, green like an old rainforest in late spring. He says her voice is like a jar full of rare wild honey."

"Old Kudurru?" Kî-Nabû asks, surprised.

They were old friends, equal in rank and position… two ṭup-šarru, celestial diviners. Both had learned their art of reading the heavens from Master Kidinnu… they had seen good times and they had seen bad times, together when they were young.

But old Kudurru used his knowledge to serve the moneyed and the powerful, whereas he himself had remained in the service of the great gods of Bâb-ilim.

One served the kings… the other served the men of the kings…

"Yes, Father."

"Immati?"

"She had gone to see him, when Šarru got sick. He is still in favor with Ummi Šarri Sisygambis."

Bêl-rê'ušu leans slightly forward.

Old Kudurru had sworn a blood oath to avenge the death of Master Kidinnu…

"I remember—" Kî-Nabû shakes his head, mumbling, trying to remember.

Had the heavenly clouds hidden the celestial omens?

Bêl-rê'ušu interrupts worriedly. "Palace eunuchs say Šarratu has been sleepless since Šarru got sick. They say that her name was the last word that crossed the lips of the dying Šarru. Šarratu might not survive the death of Šarru."

"I have seen her celestial chart," Kî-Nabû says, nodding, without elaborating. He draws another deep breath, cloudy and distracted, and points to his right.

"Sit down, My Son."

Bêl-rê'ušu quickly sits down and turns over the clay tablet in front of him.

"I am ready, Father."

"Record my words on the ṭuppu exactly as I speak them: My father Kî-Nabû spoke the following words on day 1, month 3, Sîmannu."

Bêl-rê'ušu obediently starts writing warily on the other side of the clay tablet:

MÂ BÂRÛTU
Divination

As it was foretold, so it came to pass.
For eight years, a king from iš-ku-ud-ra exercised kingship.
He conquered the Persian Royal Army. He called himself the Lord of Asia.
A son will be born to the King of his Persian Queen.
His son will raise an army. Marduk and Nabû and Nânna will go at the side of his army. He will bring about the demise of the armies of his fathers from the Lands beyond the Bitter Rivers.
The people who have been unfortunate will become fortunate once more.
The Lands will be happy again.
Ibbi mâti itâb.

Kî-Nabû stops and draws a deep breath.

"That is all I have to say about this matter. Now read it back to me."

Bêl-rê'ušu puts down his tablet marker and reads all the written words faithfully. He then looks up at his old father, anxiously waiting for his blessing.

"Yes, it is in good order… nothing is missing." Kî-Nabû nods and says quietly, pointing to the clay tablet.

He then lifts his head and looks out the dark window again. His old memory fades. He mindlessly rubs the deep lines on his forehead and says, "Bêl-rê'ušu, take this tablet to Kênu-nâ'id and tell him that Kî-Nabû, your father, said that this tablet should be kept with the other tablets in the royal archives forever!"

"Yes, Father," Bêl-rê'ušu says obediently and takes a deep breath, relieved. He leans forward, picks up the hardening clay tablet and utters a quiet prayer under his lips.

"Guide my footstep in the light, that among men I may gloriously seek my way."
Šu-te-ši-ri kib-si nam-riš e-til-liš it-ti amêlûti lu-ba-'sûki.

"Wait," Kî-Nabû says, pointing to the old table in front of him. "Do you see the Amulet of Tašmêtu? The one carved on a moonstone?"

Bêl-rê'ušu looks around the crowded table.

Winged Sun of Šamaš… Crescent Moon of Nânna… Lightning Fork of Adad… Eight-pointed Star of Ištar…

Ah… Amulet of Goddess Tašmêtu, beloved of the great god Nabû.

"Yes, I see it, Father."

"Take it to the palace yourself tonight and give it to Abi-Enši-Marduk, the Palace Chief Eunuch. Tell him Kî-Nabû said to purify her bedchamber again and tie the sacred amulet and flowers of yellow za'farân to the bedpost of the Šarratu.

"Tell him to purify her bath water with threads of red za'farân."

Kî-Nabû draws another deep breath. "Let goddess Tašmêtu stand between the Šarratu and demoness Lamaštu, who is lurking in the marshes, waiting to steal the breath of the mâr bît šarri. Tell him Kî-Nabû said to pick the yellow flowers at moonrise from the side of the royal garden of Šarratu facing the sun. Scent of za'farân flowers will soothe her and will help her sleep deep."

"Yes, Father. Anything else?"

"Hasânu."

Bêl-rê'ušu puts the amulet in the fold of his white robe and smiles gratefully for his father's blessing. He bows his head and silently leaves the chamber.

Kî-Nabû closes his eyes in pain, his face creases and folds, his mind wanders.

Bâb-ilani were finally being punished for surrendering the Gate of Gods freely to the enemy armies of the foreign king and foreign gods.

What did they think would happen to them, when they broke faith with the Great King? Did they think that the great gods would turn a blind eye to their treachery?

Bâb-ilim, the city of his ancestors, was to become deserted and forgotten by the sons of Bâb-ilani, faded from the memory of men, abandoned by her great gods. Bâb-ilim would become dust under the feet of enemies of the great gods of Bâb-ilim, under the feet of the armies of the rebel god…

And this too was already foretold…

Great gods had spit on Bâb-ilim…

Great gods had spit on him too and had long forgotten him.

He could no longer see the little stars, the goddesses of the night, with his own eyes.

Kî-Nabû reaches for his wine cup and swallows another mouthful. The sweet date-wine tastes bitter in his old mouth.

He was miserable… he missed his wife… he had named a little star to the left of the Eight-pointed Star of Ištar after her… hûd ibbi…

He utters a quiet prayer.

> *"How long, O Ištar, will you be angry, your face be turned away?"*
>
> *a-di ma-ti [iltu] Ištar zi-na-ti-ma suh-hu-ru pa-nu-ki?*

A cooler breeze lazily fills the hot room.

A candle flickers in the breeze and dies.

Kî-Nabû takes a painful breath and opens his eyes. He lifts his wine cup to his lips and drinks the rest of the sweet wine to the last drop and then leans back again in his chair.

A comforting voice quietly whispers to him from a light, "It is your time."

The wine cup slips and slides out of his hand and onto the floor, and shatters into bits and pieces. He slumps into his old worn chair and disappears into the darkness of the night.

Slowing, his old soul separates from his old body.

The great goddess had heard his heartfelt prayers and had finally granted him hišihtu… his heart's desire… his beloved wife was waiting for him by the Gates of Arallû…

Six

SON and FATHERS

KING'S ROYAL QUARTERS
ROYAL PALACE of the SECOND NABÛ-KUDURRÎ-ÛSUR
YEAR 8 of A-LEK-SA-AN-DAR
YEAR of NO KING, MONTH 3, SÎMANNU
DAY 2: A STAR STANDS LEFT in FRONT of the MOON
NIGHT

Massive doors push open forcefully.

"Ahhh!"

Rošanak opens her eyes from deep sleep… startled… disoriented…

Men are pouring into Alexander's royal bedchamber, surrounding the royal bed.

"Ah!"

She had fallen deeply asleep next to him and the time had passed carelessly…

How long had she been there?

She screams faintly in fright and holds on tighter to Alexander.

Alexander was dying and his men had finally come to kill his half-Persian wife and his half-breed son.

She feels his body. His skin feels cool to her touch.

Was Alexander dead?

Was she left behind again?

Her heart fills with pain.

"Nooo!"

Her scream echoes across the massive royal bedchamber, cutting through the angry voices around her, and bounces off the swords and spears and helmets of the men and hangs over the massive royal bed cradling a dead king.

The kingsmen rushing back from the Assembly had not seen her until now. They stop motionless on their feet for a moment and look at her, shocked.

Rošanak is lying on her side on the royal bed next to Alexander, favoring her unborn child.

The unborn they had been debating in the Assembly of Makedonians.

More men in arms rush into the royal bedchamber. Chaos and confusion follow in their footsteps.

Suffocating hot air… angry voices… screaming and shouting and yelling…

A powerful voice commands, "Shut the bloody doors!"

Everyone turns their heads back toward the giant doors as the royal boys noisily pour into the royal bedchamber behind the kingsmen and close the giant doors behind them. They start pushing pieces of heavy golden furnishings against the massive doors to bar the entry of the men following them.

Another voice growls, "Under siege by our own men!"

Another voice yells, "There are too many of them! Doors will not hold! Guard the King!"

The royal boys rush and circle the royal bed, two layers deep, with their swords drawn.

Rošanak hides her face in Alexander's shoulder.

Were they going to spill her blood right there? Turn her and her royal unborn into grave offerings for their dying King?

BANG! BANG! BANG!

The royal bedchamber shakes.

Her thoughts are interrupted by the deafening noises of men shouting outside the giant doors of the royal bedchamber, pressing against and hammering on the doors with their swords and shields like blood-thirsty beasts.

The massive doors surrender and break and shatter…

More men pour into the royal bedchamber… all in arms…

Rošanak looks at the treacherous faces of the men all around her and then closes her eyes with contempt. The repugnant smell of their sweaty bodies makes her sick and unsettles her heavy belly… she cannot breathe… she hides her face in the soft pillow.

They were blood-thirsty barbarians of the Lands Beyond the Sea, not civilized people of the Lands… they cared for nothing but themselves… they would slaughter their own blood mothers and wives and children if it brought them more Persian gold and glory.

A long eternity unfolds in a brief moment.

A spear flies across the royal bedchamber, pierces the massive golden Tree of Life close to Rošanak and hits the bedpost. The bedpost shatters. A piece of ancient royal wood flies and hits her in the face.

She screams, terrified. "Noooooo!"

More spears fly across the room.

One hits Leonnatos in the shoulder… another hits Perdikkas in the arm… another scratches Lysimachos… a few more find their marks and cut and pierce the kingsmen and the royal boys. Their blood splatters on the royal bed and the body of Alexander and stains Rošanak's gown.

She hurriedly leans over and tries to wipe the warm blood from the cold body of Alexander with her trembling fingers. The blood smears on his skin. More blood splatters…

"Alexander!" Rošanak finds her voice in her throat, and screams at the top of her voice.

No matter what they were going to do to her, it was willed by the Wise Lord.

But she was going to die honorably like her royal brothers!

She was a Royal Woman!

Everyone in the royal bedchamber finally notices her.

She pushes herself up on the bed and yells with the authority of a Royal Woman, "Where are the royal guards? How dare you all break in the royal bedchamber like this and spill common blood on the royal body of the King?"

Then she forgets, and without thinking she shouts, "Where is Hephæstion?"

Her voice carries over the chaos and startles and rattles the men. She rolls to her other side slowly and gets out of the bed with difficulty.

The forgotten empty kâsaka bottle rolls carelessly off the folds of her gown and falls on the floor. She steps on the kâsaka and it shatters and cuts the bottoms of her feet. Bits and pieces of broken kâsaka dig into her skin. Her feet bleed. She mindlessly walks on them, pushing the royal boys away from her path and moans, "What kind of godless beasts are you?"

The men are shaken and take a step backward. Their hot blood starts to cool at the sight of her.

The angry voices start to die down as she waddles painfully in the sea of armed and armored men all around her… her body and gown splattered with spilled blood… blood running from her feet…

"Sheath your swords!"

Perdikkas screams the order with authority, pushing the royal boys out of his way and making his way to Rošanak. His commanding voice echoes and carries across the packed royal bedchamber. He sheaths his own sword slowly, blood dripping unheeded from a spear cut on his left arm.

Their men were in a murderous mood! Ready to kill anyone who got in their path, just as they had every time they had thought Alexander was wounded or dead… and now Alexander was dead.

Perdikkas sees the tips of sharp swords and spears just a hair's breadth away from Rošanak's body. He cringes at the thought of her body brushing against the sharp blades pointed toward her, tearing her and ripping the unborn king.

He remembered how Alexander had carelessly jumped off the steps at Fortress of Opis, unarmed and unguarded, and had made his way through the angry multitude of Makedonians, grabbing thirteen of them and ordering their immediate executions, without anyone even thinking of making the slightest move against him.

The men start to lower their swords.

Perdikkas puts his hand on Rošanak's shoulder, protectively reassuring her. "Roxana, I am here."

Rošanak feels the powerful hand on her shoulder and recognizes Perdikkas' voice behind her.

"A king must be buried by his successor… it is our ancestral law." Perdikkas mumbles under his breath. He is tired, but glad for the break in the violence that had started earlier during the Assembly of the Makedonians, which had been heading toward a shameful bloody massacre among the LowLanders and the HighLanders, the Foot and the Horse, before Alexander's body had cooled.

He and the kingsmen were outnumbered and caught off guard by the fighting that had broken out in the Assembly.

He should have known better…

"He is not dead!" Rošanak moans.

Silence, heavy with hope.

The men instantly look toward Alexander's body lying motionlessly on the royal bed, splattered as usual with blood of battle, covering his honor wounds.

He had cheated death and had lived through much worse! Maybe this time too!

"Alexander will have their blood for their insolence!" Rošanak cries, pointing with her head.

Her words pierce through the men who all too well knew Alexander's wrath. They murmur words that Rošanak does not understand.

Where they asking for her blood?

The men retreat further. Some are choked up and ashamed of themselves. They look over at Alexander's body, which appears to be wrapped in a bloody peaceful sleep.

She was right to scorn them for breaking into their king's royal bedchamber... armed and armored for battle with their helmets on and swords and spears drawn... trying to kill his kingsmen.

Peukestas makes his way through the men and stands next to Perdikkas and also tries to shield and protect Rošanak just as he had shielded Alexander in Hind. "Roshanak, Alexander meant a lot to his men. They got a little heated at the Assembly... and lost their heads... but we will remedy the damage, when the blood starts to run cooler," he gently tells her in Persian.

Perdikkas gives a fierce look sideways at Peukestas.

He could have spoken in Attik, so the men could have understood him.

He pushes Peukestas back and takes Rošanak's hand.

Another voice breaks from the back... behind the wall of men and swords and shields.

"Roxana, I have come to bury Alexander. He is dead, you know!" Arrhidaios says cheerfully.

Men turn their heads and eyes and look at Arrhidaios scornfully.

Someone grunts roughly in a hushed voice, "Be silent!"

Rošanak's eyes follow the voice across the royal bedchamber and find Arrhidaios, wearing Alexander's old ancestral crimson robe, standing among a group of men with hard and lined and cracked faces... she does not recognize any of them.

She shakes off Perdikkas' hand and pushes her way on bleeding feet through the men still firmly grasping their shields and swords, and stands in front of Arrhidaios.

"Arrhidaios."

She looks gently into his face and asks as calmly as she can, "Arrhidaios, where are you planning to take the body of Alexander for his burial rites in the middle of the night? Ha? You want to burn your brother like a common thief on the pile of old ashes left over from other pyres?"

Arrhidaios looks confused. He looks at the men around him, who are all looking away, avoiding eye contact with him.

"Where shall we burn Alexander?" Arrhidaios asks, still cheerful.

Shameful silence…

There is no response, except for the sound of men slowly lowering their shields and sheathing their swords and removing their helmets.

Air so thick with tension that it could be sliced with their swords…

"Now, Arrhidaios, this robe belongs to Alexander. We will have one made just for you, in a color you like!" Rošanak reaches and taps Arrhidaios gently on the head, as if talking to a small child.

Perdikkas looks on in astonishment.

No man there would even think of patting that dim-witted boy on the head, like a dog, without fearing that their fingers and hands and heads would be immediately chopped off!

Arrhidaios nods approvingly. "Maybe in the color of tree leaves? I really like trees! Like your eyes! I want a robe in the color of your eyes!" Arrhidaios declares cheerfully, nodding.

"Very well… one royal robe in the color of my eyes," Rošanak says as she pushes the men around Arrhidaios away, reaches gently and unclasps the robe around Arrhidaios' shoulders and pulls the royal robe from his back.

Perdikkas holds his breath and clenches his fist and locks his eyes on Meleagros and his men, his fingers getting ready to grab his sword.

She was doing what he and all the kingsmen wished they had done themselves.

"Aristonous!"

Heavy breathing…

"Where is Aristonous?" Rošanak asks again firmly.

"Aristonous!" Perdikkas grunts loudly.

"Roxana, I am here!" A young commander, a new kingsman, stands to attention and announces himself.

"Aristonous, please take Arrhidaios back to his room," Rošanak asks wearily.

"Arrhidaios, have you had your night meal yet?" Rošanak asks kindly.

"No, Roxana! These men," Arrhidaios points openly with his fingers, "interrupted me as I was about to eat my meal! I am hungry!"

"Aristonous, please make sure Arrhidaios has a good meal, with extra sweets for dessert!" Rošanak says kindly, reaching and gently removing the kingly Persian Purple hanging miserably on Arrhidaios' forehead, begging to be rescued and respected.

"Thank you Roxana! Will you come and play with me later? Alexander just gave me a new board game from the Two Lands!"

"Arrhidaios, go with Aristonous. I will come to see about you when I can. Go now!"

Perdikkas nods discreetly in the direction of Aristonous, keeping his eyes firmly on Meleagros and his men.

She had separated the fool from his bloody supporters without shedding another drop of blood.

Aristonous steps next to Arrhidaios and points with his hand, "This way, Sir!"

"The King stays with us!" Meleagros growls and steps forward.

"No! I am going to eat my night meal with extra sweets, as Roxana said!" Arrhidaios says cheerfully and looks at Rošanak.

She nods approvingly and forces a smile. Arrhidaios then turns toward Aristonous and grabs his arm. A handful of royal boys circle them.

Rustling of men and swords…

A voice says, "The King does what he wants to!"

The Makedonians open a pathway for them without hesitation.

The Queen was kin to the brother of Alexander. And she was kind to him.

And Aristonous was the kingsman of Alexander himself. Alexander trusted him with his life. He wouldn't harm the brother of the King… the new king.

Royal boys always followed the king…

Rošanak takes the old royal robe and the Persian Purple and slowly walks back to the royal bed.

Perdikkas follows her, shielding her… she spreads the Makedonian royal robe over the bloody body of Alexander, covering him up to his shoulders. Perdikkas grabs a corner; a drop of blood from his honor wound drips carelessly on Alexander's face. She reaches and wipes the fresh drop of blood from his royal face with her fingers.

A pair of the royal boys jump to their feet and help pull the old robe across the royal bed, arranging it ceremonially over the body of their King.

Rošanak rubs the fresh red blood between her fingers mindlessly.

The old Chaldæan was wrong!

It mattered whether the King died in battle or in bed…

Alexander had died in bed, but he had died with warrior blood on his royal body… covered not with his own blood, but with the blood of honor wounds of his kingsmen.

He had died with high marks of honor… befitting a king.

He had died a great king…

A King, one-third Makedonian, one-third Persian, one-third darkness, three-thirds loved by his men…

She wipes her bloody fingers on her gown and leans over Alexander's body. She arranges the locks of his hair on his forehead, ties the Persian Purple around his head and quietly utters,

"Like the fire that never dies…"

Perdikkas looks around the room and eyes the men carefully.

Gloom had begun to settle. The men around Meleagros who had started the bloody vicious encounter had quietly pulled away from him, distancing themselves in front of Alexander… they had lost the day and they all knew it.

The gap in their line was opened up easily by the Queen. This was the woman Alexander had married.

"No one will disturb the royal body of the King, until funeral arrangements are made, according to Makedonian customs!" Perdikkas declares with authority, eyeing everyone in the royal bedchamber. Heads nod in agreement.

He needed time… his mind raced… he was so tired… he had not slept in days…

"Making funeral arrangements will take time— we should summon the embalmers from Aigyptos to preserve the body," Ptolemaios says quietly.

Everyone considers Ptolemaios' words.

Why not?

Alexander was considered a god in the Two Lands and embalming could keep his body from despoiling until they could decide what was most befitting for their King.

Men nod their heads in agreement again.

"Very well. Eumenes, send a messenger to Kleomenes. Have him send the Royal Embalmers from the Two Lands to Babylon swiftly," Perdikkas orders, firmly turning his head toward the Royal Secretary.

"Yes, Perdikkas," Eumenes nods in agreement.

"No! He is not dead!" Rošanak moans under her breath.

Men start to leave the royal bedchamber, most with tears in their eyes.

At last, in their eyes she had become Alexander's Queen…

No longer the campaign wife, the Baktrian barbarian whom Alexander had married to force peace on the satrapies on the furthest edges of the Empire… but the mother of his unborn son… a legitimate heir to the throne… the mother of their next king.

"I can take you back to your palace," Perdikkas says, gently pulling on her hand, trying to get her out of there safely, and himself too.

No one would try to kill him while she was his shield… carrying the unborn of Alexander in front of her.

Rošanak slowly turns back to face the men.

To her palace?

She closes her eyes and takes a deep breath.

She was so tired… she wanted them all to leave… she wanted to crawl back into Alexander's bed and die with him.

She should have drunk what little was left of the poppy juice herself, instead of carelessly falling asleep thinking there was time…

The royal bedchamber starts to empty.

Air starts to return to the room.

Rošanak opens her eyes and looks around.

It becomes quiet again.

Most of the LowLanders and HighLanders have left the royal bedchamber already, with only Perdikkas, Ptolemaios, Peukestas, Leonnatos, Lysimachos and Seleukos and a few other kingsmen staying behind, and a few teary-eyed royal boys lingering by the broken doors aimlessly, not knowing what to do.

She slowly braces herself against the massive royal bed.

She feels another swift kick inside her belly to her side.

"Ah!" The unborn is restless… feeling the death of his father. She grabs her belly and sits on the edge of the royal bed to catch her breath. The bottoms of her cut feet burn and sting. She fills with regret.

Why had she rubbed almost all of the poppy juice on Alexander's lips? A bottle full of it… why had she not saved any for herself?

"The Assembly will change their minds about Arrhidaios, once they take the measure of him," one of the royal boys says indignantly, breaking the haunted silence.

All the kingsmen give him a look that makes the royal boy step further away from them.

Another royal boy carelessly jumps in, agreeing, all too eager to make his mark with Alexander's kingsmen. "Yes! Once he addresses the Assembly, everyone will see he is dim-witted… not a man born to the sword! I hear his attendant does not even let him use a knife to cut an apple!"

"Order!" Perdikkas thunders in the room.

The royal boys all fall in line and stand at attention instinctively without thinking.

"Good! I was beginning to think the whores of Darius were guarding the body of our King!"

The royal boys look down at their feet, embarrassed.

"Go have your bloody wounds looked at by the wound-healers." Perdikkas orders the bleeding royal boys.

The wounded boys obey and start leaving the room with heavy feet.

The kingsmen linger, none willing to leave the room before the others.

Rošanak tries to stand up… another kick… she folds and grabs her belly in pain and sits back down on the edge of the royal bed. "No!" she silently moans.

"Once the Son of Alexander is born, I will go back to the Assembly and ask them to select a regent for the Boy-King!" Perdikkas pushes the words out through his teeth.

"You all should have supported my proposal to rule the kingdom in common… now, if it is a girl, we are stuck with that half-witted idiot for a king!" Ptolemaios grunts.

"Leonnatos, go see the wound-healer before you bleed to death standing around here." Perdikkas grunts.

"Just a scratch," Lysimachos sneers, "compare to the one I got from that ferocious lion during the royal hunt!" wiping the blood off his own wound.

"Ferocious?" Leonnatos ignores the pain in his bleeding shoulder and glares at Lysimachos. "The damn lion was old and lazy. Otherwise he would have eaten you instead of just playing with your shoulder."

The royal bedchamber feels warmer with heated words.

"Alexander is dead!" Rošanak utters under her breath and closes her eyes. Her face folds. Her legs feel wet and warm.

She felt heavier… loaded with more trouble…

She was now utterly alone… left behind again…

Abi-Samar was right! She should have told him to come back for her. Getting rid of that damned eunuch could have waited! Maybe he had come back for her and was trampled to death or killed by the Makedonians who had forced their way into the royal bedchamber.

Men turn their eyes back on her.

Reality becomes heavy and scents the warm air.

She pushes up again and stands up, forgetting her painful feet. Her head starts to spin around the warm room.

Seleukos looks with horror at the edge of the royal bed where she had been resting.

A circle of fresh blood stains the white sheets, matching the crimson color of the old ancestral robe stretched over Alexander's body.

"His blood is on my hands!" Rošanak moans in Persian.

She had denied him Haoma and sacred prayers of healing… she had left him to his fate… and he had gone to his fate… painlessly loaded with poppy juice…

"Roxana!" Perdikkas grinds his teeth.

She was unraveling like the thread of a golden ball…

Rošanak cries and moans and points to Alexander's body.

"My suffering is before me… Zeus. May she who caused all this suffering not escape her punishment."

"Roxana," Perdikkas says quietly.

She knew her Medea… the book he had given her in India…

Seleukos catches Perdikkas' eyes and points with his head to the blood stain.

Rošanak takes a small step away from the royal bed.

Now, the red blood stain is visible to all the kingsmen standing around it.

Her gown and the bed are all soaked in her blood…

The kingsmen look at her in horror.

They all knew about the fate of her firstborn and her many losses. They had all at one time or another thought Alexander should have married a strong Makedonian woman who could bear healthy sons. Kings should not marry for love… just to beget healthy sons and heirs… but now it was all too late…

Alexander was dead and the last of him was dying inside of her.

Rošanak rambles in Persian. "His judgment now rests with the Wise Lord. If he has done good, he will roam in the Heaven with the kings and divine heroes. If he has done evil, he will roam in the darkness until eternity. He shall not reap except what he has sown."

Rošanak pleads quietly in Attik. "I ask no mercy for myself… all I ask is to be allowed to bury the body of Alexander, performing my last duty to the King."

The kingsmen look at each other… uncertain of what to do with her.

"SIR!"

Another royal boy strides into the room, dragging an old man covered in blood behind him. He pulls the man into the middle of the room and holds him up by the neck.

The old eunuch is breathless and looks scared out of his mind.

Everyone turns and looks.

"This filthy barbarian reported that he saw the naked bodies of two highborn women thrown into an old well, by the walls on the other side of the palace."

"No!" Rošanak grabs the bed post and moans silently.

"The Palace Guards pulled out the bodies… no one knows who they are… they are naked and their bodies are broken and torn. He says they were the Royal Daughters of Darius."

"WHAT?" Peukestas pushes his way forward, pulls out his Persian dagger and points it at the old man's throat and questions him in Persian, grabbing him by the shoulder.

"Tell me what you know, and I will let you live! Lie and I will kill you right here and now!"

The old man shakes with fear and says trembling in broken Attik, "We were bringing the Royal Daughters to the palace as ordered by the King. A group of men attacked us… angry and screaming… men in arm and armor… they cut up all the eunuchs first and then turned on the Royal Daughters—"

Peukestas lets go of him. The old eunuch drops to his feet.

"I was covered under their dead bodies. They thought I was dead too… My Ladies were virgins… Royal Daughters of the Great King! They screamed and cursed the wretched men in their own tongues… the barbarians suffocated My Ladies first, to silence their piercing curses and screams, tore off their royal gowns and then took their turns with their lifeless bodies… the horrid beasts did not care… they passed the naked dead bodies around to each other like spoils of war…"

The kingsmen look at each other with dismay.

Discipline had broken…

Their men had turned into wild beasts in their grief…

"Noooo!" Rošanak starts to go down on her knees. Her head spins… her eyes darken.

She had forgotten all about her royal sisters… their blood was on her hands too…

"They were virgins… not even violated by their own husbands!" The old eunuch cries.

Another painful kick.

Rošanak grabs her belly in pain.

"Alexander, forgive me …" she utters quietly.

Alexander had finally punished her for all her wickedness. He had taken Setâreh with him to his grave and had left her behind and he had taken Dripeyti for Hephæstion.

Perdikkas quickly turns around and grabs her mid-air as she starts to collapse.

Her warm blood mixes with his, dripping from his wounded arm…

The royal boys still in the royal bedchamber look on with terror at the sight of Alexander's wife, bleeding.

No doubt they will all be accused of killing her and her unborn child, should she die that night!

"We will all be accused of killing the Son of Alexander… to gain the royal lands for ourselves!" Ptolemaios shakes his head with dismay and says loudly the thoughts floating in the air above all their heads.

Seleukos pushes Peukestas and the old eunuch out of his way and starts walking fast toward the broken doors, pushing his way through the stunned royal boys, determined to save the life of the Queen and her unborn, the kinsmen to his own wife and son. "We have to take her to the royal healer now!" he says urgently. "I know the quickest way to his quarters through the palace maze." He grabs one of the royal boys by the neck and yells at him: "Run to the end of the hallway and then turn right, two doors down and tell the royal healer that we are on our way." He orders a few other boys. "Go with him. Break down the door and wake him up if you have to. RUN!"

Perdikkas orders the royal boys, as he follows Seleukos carrying Rošanak in his arms, "Guard Alexander with your life! Not a word about Roxana to anyone or I will personally run a spear through everyone of you!"

Broken pieces of the giant doors splinter and crack under his sandaled feet.

The royal boys nod tearfully.

"One of you find the palace eunuchs and have them change the bloody sheets on the royal bed and personally watch them burn the sheets." Perdikkas' voice trails off in the palace hallway. "Guard the bodies of the Royal Daughters… until I get back…"

Blood drips from Rošanak.

CROWN of the OUTER WALLS. ROYAL CITY of BÂB-ILIM
FOLLOWING NIGHT

Night smolders like the Royal Fire.

Perdikkas grinds his teeth, thinking to himself, standing on the massive crown of the Walls of Babylon, watching the shadows leaving the city gates under the cover of the cloudy moonless night.

All the kingsmen of Alexander were worthy warriors!

Alexander was not just a great king, he was a king served by great men… all had sworn an oath of loyalty to have the same friends as the King and the same enemies as the King.

Alexander was not just favored by the goddess of fortune… he was favored by men who were favored by fortune and excellence in art of war…

All warlike and battle-hardened! All born to the sword... sharpened to perfection by years of constant conquest...

Horse and Foot trained by Philip to perfection... the best army in the world... all brave and fit and disciplined... until the death of their king.

Kallisthenes had cheated such men of their meed of glory and now that the King was dead, sooner or later all the kingsmen would want their deeds to shine in the rays of the sun...

And as gods had fated, it was sooner rather than later.

The Royal Army had not lasted even one whole day after the death of Alexander... it had broken into bits and pieces almost instantly.

Alexander was not just a king, but the peg that had held the entire Makedonian Royal Army in a massive Gordian Knot and now that the Alexandrian Knot had been unraveled by his death, the Royal Army was becoming unhinged. He was like a vessel that kept the army within itself and now that the vessel was broken, everything inside was spilling out in all directions... mostly murderous directions.

Horse and Foot had turned into two giant beasts ready to tear each other apart.

And now that he was dead, all his kingsmen wanted to be the next Alexander... wanted to have what he had... wanted to rule like he had ruled.

Damn Leonnatos was even starting to tilt his bloody head to the left now and displaying his shoulder wound like a standard flying over his head! If he had not taken honor wounds shielding the wounded Alexander in India, where would he be now?

A few commanders and royal guards and royal boys surround him, watching the movement of men and horses out of the city, along with frightened multitudes who did not want to get caught between the grinding deadly jaws of the fracturing Makedonians.

By his orders, Leonnatos had finally straightened his damn head and neck, wrapped his bloody shoulder securely, and was quietly leading the LowLander and HighLander Horse out of Babylon.

The mahouts were taking the fighting Indian elephants out from another gate.

The Foot was in for a big surprise when they woke in the morning! They would be under siege by the Horse!

Had the idiots not learned anything from years of campaigning with Alexander?

The strongest always ruled all!

Babylon has sunk into near haunted silence. The people of the city had simply vanished into houses and walls and shops, waiting and watching and praying... it is so quiet that Perdikkas can hear the murmur of River Euphrates as it rushes and rolls and coils through the middle of the city.

Damn fool!

Who else, he had thought, would the Makedonians pick to lead them?

He was the most senior... the strongest... the Second-in-Command to Alexander after Hephæstion had died in Ecbatana.

He was the only one of the high command who was known to both the Foot and the Horse. He had started as a commander of a Foot regiment before becoming a Horse commander. Alketas, his brother, was still a commander of the Foot.

According to their ancient customs, he was the one who had watched over Alexander day and night without closing his eyes for a moment when his fever had taken a turn for the worst, just as Hephæstion had watched over Alexander in India after his arrow wound. Other kingsmen had gone to the sacred temple grounds to pray for Alexander. Alexander himself had given him his signet ring on his deathbed before he had lost his tongue and his words.

He could hardly keep his eyes open by the time they had all gathered in the Assembly to decide the fate of the conquered lands.

He had thought his competition would be other kingsmen, other members of the high command. Who would have thought that the damn rough Makedonians would even consider a half-wit fool to succeed Alexander, suggested no less by an unknown man in the Assembly?

No one had even remembered or mentioned Arrhidaios when all the kingsmen had quickly met in council to consider all options after the unexpected death of Alexander.

Half-witted Arrhidaios had always been an army camp-follower… Alexander never allowed him anywhere near the Royal Army…

He takes a deep breath and grinds his teeth.

What a bloody mess!

He had shown weakness by hesitating in the Assembly… his mind had clouded and he had given in to the insane desire to be asked to lead the LowLanders and the HighLanders, and the LowLanders had treacherously turned on him.

He knew better!

Those men only understood the tongue of absolute power… the tongue Alexander had spoken so well all his life…

Well, lesson learned!

It was not a mistake he was planning to repeat. Makedonians turned murderous without a king… they had already butchered the Royal Daughters of Darius.

Every time they had thought Alexander was dead, they had gone mad and had massacred the multitudes beyond all reason… fearing they could never find their way home without him…

No one understood better than Alexander the thirst of the Makedonians for blood and gold… he shared in their taste for blood… to gold, he was indifferent…

The Makedonian Royal Army was a beast that Alexander's father had forged by melting arms and armor and blood into each other… it was a beast that lived to feast on flesh and blood and gold… just as the Royal Kingsmen drank pure wine, the Royal Army drank pure blood.

Alexander always turned a blind eye when the Royal Army turned into royal butchers. He had even encouraged unnecessary massacres whenever the army drifted away from him… it was the way he ensured their loyalty to him… loyalty watered by blood.

No man, woman or child would be spared if the LowLanders and the HighLanders broke apart fully and decided to march up country back to Makedonia!

They would spill every drop of blood on their way home!

First, he needed to bring the Royal Army back securely under his command, before they started to destroy the whole of Asia and drown the Empire in blood.

All else had to wait.

Perdikkas narrows his eyes at the shadows below.

Who could he rely on?

Alketas and Attalos and Polemon were kinsmen… Aristonous and Eumenes and Medeios and Myllenas and Seleukos had given him their right arms…

Leonnatos and Lysimachos and Peithon and Ptolemaios were all kingsmen and wanted satrapal commands…

Old Antipatros and the One-eyed Antigonos were far away…

Krateros… hmmm…

An unfamiliar accented voice quietly breaks in the darkness.

"You sent for me, Hezârapatiš?" Oštana asks formally in accented Attik.

The heat of Babylon, heavy with tension, weighs down the air and presses on their shoulders.

Perdikkas turns around and looks at Oštana and considers him for a moment.

"Roxana has collapsed and the Royal Daughters of Darius are dead."

Oštana looks Perdikkas straight in the eyes. His eyes widen in the darkness, the veins in his neck start to throb with hate and anger.

So, it was true! Bastards!

Rumors about Rošanak and the fate of the Royal Daughters had already reached the camp of the Persians and Bakhtrians.

All palaces had eyes and ears.

"The Makedonian Horse are loyal to King Alexander and his unborn, if your sister bears a son." Perdikkas eyes Oštana carefully. "Foot has broken from Horse and they have declared themselves for Arrhidaios, brother of Alexander, the only other son of Philip still living."

Oštana looks at Perdikkas intently.

He wanted to grab Rošanak in the midst of all the chaos and take her back to Baktra and protect her at any cost…

The Bakhtrians would support him… Persians too… none cared anything for the son of Alexander, but they all cared about the Royal Son of the Royal Daughter… with the blood of Royal Hakhâmanišiya.

But he knew his sister was not likely to survive such a journey in her advanced months… she had already started to bleed and purge.

Perdikkas turns back and points to the shadows leaving the city gates and continues. "Makedonian Horse are leaving the city tonight and will siege Babylon tomorrow, cutting food and provisions into the city to force the Foot to a compromise. Arrhidaios is a dim-witted bastard incapable of leading a Royal Army— not acceptable to the nobles of Horse."

Oštana takes a step forward and looks down at the movement below and listens wordlessly.

Alexander had just died and the Makedonians had already started to turn on each other... the external war of conquest had turned into the internal war of succession...

Without a king, the Makedonians were like a giant snake cut in half that still slithered and bled and moved unpredictably...

The Wise Lord was wise indeed... He had simply broken the invaders in half and had set them upon each other. With the same fury they had killed the Persians and the Bakhtrians, they will now kill each other.

The blood of his blood brother and his brothers and his lover and his king and father were being avenged by Makedonians themselves.

The Heaven had demanded fiercely and the Earth had finally relented...

Good!

Perdikkas narrows his eyes.

Hystanes was the only Baktrian who had become one of Alexander's kingsmen, trusted by Alexander because of Roxana. Was he trustworthy?

"What are the Persians and Baktrians planning to do?" Perdikkas looks at him and asks directly, without attempting to hide his concern.

Oštana eyes Perdikkas carefully and considers him for a long moment.

He was the most experienced Kingsman of Alexander.

A man who could easily separate truth from lie...

Black clouds of a bloody storm were brewing and swirling all around him, yet being in the center of it all, he was strangely calm... in control... cool in the heat of chaos...

Blood had dried and darkened on the wide white linen wrapped around his left arm...

There were rumors that all of Alexander's kingsmen had barely escaped with their lives on the night of the Makedonian Assembly... many were wounded that night in the struggle among the Makedonians for the control of the Royal Army.

And Perdikkas had shielded and protected Rošanak so far.

There was no need to provoke and disaffect him so quickly.

Time was now on the side of the Persians and the Bakhtrians.

And he had surely already talked to the commanders of the regiments.

Oštana straightens and speaks truthfully.

"Neither Persians nor Bakhtrians care who rules the Makedonians!"

Wise men should not get in the way of fools who were so eager for servitude in the Land of the Eternal Darkness, in the wretched company of the Lord of Darkness...

When maddened war elephants charge each other, wise men should get out of their way! Unless bloody fools wanted to be trampled to death by giant beasts!

"We will not take sides between the Makedonian Horse and Foot."

Let them massacre each other!

"Good."

Perdikkas nods his head, satisfied with the straight reply. He hears what he wanted to know.

"Then Persians and Baktrians should leave the city tonight to avoid getting caught in the middle of the Makedonian Horse and Foot. Any man who wants to leave the Royal Army, should go tonight and disappear. I will not look for them, unless they raise against me. Those who decide to stay, will keep their ranks and pay in the Royal Army, as it was under Alexander."

Oštana narrows his eyes at Perdikkas, startled.

"You are releasing all the hostages, Hezârapatiš?"

"Yes— with the condition that they will leave and go back to their homes— that they will not fight against me."

Oštana thinks for a moment. "And what of my royal sister?"

"I am staying inside the palace for now and will keep watch over the Queen. The best of Horse is protecting the unborn king and his mother. I need a small hand-picked group of loyal men to return the bodies of the Royal Daughters to Queen Sisygambis."

"I will see to it, Hezârapatiš."

The Royal Daughters of Dâriuš were his kindred… there was no question that it was his absolute duty and Perdikkas knew it! He was testing him.

"Good."

Oštana straightens.

"Hystanes?"

"Yes, Hezârapatiš?"

"I would like you to stay with the Royal Army and serve under me directly, when the Queen births her son. She and her Son-King will need protection."

"And if she bears a Royal Daughter?"

Perdikkas looks at Oštana, reading his young face in the dark.

A lot could happen between now and when she had the child…

"She will be free to return to Baktria, with her daughter. You have my word."

"Very well."

"You should leave for Susa as soon as possible. When you return, come back and report to me directly."

"Yes, Hezârapatiš."

"Hystanes!"

"Yes, Hezârapatiš?"

Perdikkas hesitates for a moment.

"I think it is best not to pain Queen Sisygambis with the details of the death of her granddaughters. Their bodies have been washed and anointed and blessed and wrapped by the temple priests. Just tell the Queen-Mother that I swear by Styx that those who were responsible will be seen to, when this is all over."

Oštana's face folds in pain.

The wretched rumors were true…

"Yes, Hezârapatiš."

"Dismissed."

Oštana turns around and disappears into the darkness.

Perdikkas narrows his eyes and then summons Seleukos over and points. "Post guards all around the river tonight and close all the docks. No one is to leave the city by the river tomorrow, once we siege Babylon!"

"Yes, Perdikkas."

Perdikkas turns his head and looks toward the sacred E-temen-an-ki temple grounds in the distance.

Smoke was still rising from the remains of Hephæstion's Memorial, shrouding the massive temple, almost the size of a mountain, behind it…

After the death of Alexander, the foundation of the Memorial had mysteriously caught fire and everything had been burned to the ground… it had burned for days until nothing was left.

The temple priests had said that the sacred temple grounds had been desecrated by the unholy temple and the great gods of Babylon had sent divine lightning to burn and purify the temple grounds.

Divine lightning… hmmm… what kind of fool did they think he was?

But the temple priests were the least of his troubles.

He takes a deep breath of the burning air.

Well, he was planning to purify the Royal Army quickly, and the ancient Makedonian Purification Ritual was no less brutal…

He looks up at the smoky skies.

He had asked the Assembly if they wanted him to continue with the plans Alexander had left behind and they had said: NO!

The Memorial to Hephæstion was one of those plans… costing ten thousand talents… already a thousand talents burned to ashes…

And one of the most unnecessary… there was a stone lion in Ecbatana marking Hephæstion's ashes and his bones had been buried in the palace grounds and that was enough honors for an old friend.

The other plan was the campaign in Arabia… the men who had been dispatched by Alexander in advance to survey the route and the lands had told the Assembly that compared to Arabia, the Desert of Emptiness looked like a Persian garden!

He turns and looks at the last of the shadows leaving the city gates.

Nothing mattered until the Royal Army was made whole again and purified!

The Royal Army was all that mattered.

He could not be the Commander of the whole Royal Army, if the Royal Army was not whole!

GARDEN PALACE of QUEEN AMYTIŠ
DAYS LATER
EVENING

Sound of soft breathing.

Warm air bearing down… a small breeze blowing…

Perdikkas opens his eyes wearily and shifts his body in the massive golden chair that once belonged, he was told, to King Nebuchadrezzar himself.

Every bone in his body was exhausted… he could not remember the last time he had slept comfortably in a comfortable bed. First, he had kept watch every night over the dying Alexander, and then over the dying Roxana…

The chair was brought for him from the main palace into the Queen's bedroom by the palace eunuchs, who had deemed the other chairs in her room too small for him after he had fallen asleep from exhaustion and the chair he was sitting on to watch over Roxana had broken under him. He was a good head and shoulder taller than Alexander and packed with lean muscle.

He looks worriedly at Rošanak sleeping quietly in her bed.

She had been hanging in a death sleep without waking for days, but her bleeding had finally stopped mercifully after the first day. The royal boys had dragged the Chief Eunuch of the palace into the royal healer's room at the palace that fateful night and the Chief Eunuch had in turn rallied the entire palace in the care of the dying Queen. Her own eunuch had disappeared mysteriously…

Her bedroom, which opened to the luscious Persian gardens of Nebuchadrezzar, was scrubbed clean twice and filled with tubs of orange trees to sweeten the air.

Temple priests and Chaldæans had brought charmed amulets to protect the Queen from all the demons and demonesses.

They had drawn a magic circle around her bed and had chanted a powerful spell to protect her and her unborn.

Perdikkas looks outside. The doors to her bedroom are left open for scented air from the cooler gardens. The sun is setting into a pool of crimson red, blending into pure blackness.

Roxana cannot die!

She was carrying the last of the Argeads… HighLanders were always ruled by Argead Kings…

He shakes his head with dismay.

Alexander had left her in his charge. He had trusted him with his unborn Son-King!

He had favored him with the highest mark of honor…

And now the Queen was dying too!

He had made it crystal clear to the Hellene and Persian healers who had been gathered to care for her, that if she was to die, they would be all piled high on the funeral pyre for Alexander's Son-King and burned alive!

A couple of the wound-healers had slipped away under the cover of darkness, and to keep the rest, he had ordered all their families to be rounded up as hostages.

He was the last person in the Empire who would benefit from the death of the unborn, but there were plenty of kingsmen envious of his position who would twist the death and make it seem entirely his fault— even those who would never submit to be ruled by a half-breed Persian, should the Boy-King live!

Krateros was one of them!

And the old Antipatros…

He leans back in his massive chair and runs his fingers through his unkempt hair.

The BOY!

Most of the men always said, "If it was a boy…" but all the palace women, courtiers and nobles and servants called the unborn "The Son of Alexander" with utmost certainty.

Roxana herself had told him in Ecbatana that she was carrying a son… something about the way she was craving pomegranate. Her mother, the beautiful woman he had met in Baktria, apparently had consumed an orchard full of pomegranates when she was heavy with Roxana's brothers.

Women were strange creatures! Eating four seeds of pomegranate had condemned Persephone to the House of Hades in the Underworld for four months out of the year, and Roxana eating bowls full of pomegranate seeds was to produce a male heir for the Empire!

Perdikkas leans forward in the enormous chair and takes his head in his hands and takes a deep breath.

Who was he fooling?

He cared for her.

Even with all the chaos and madness that was swirling around him…

He remembered everything about her, since he had watched her with envy nursing Hephæstion back from the edge of the House of Hades in India, and later Alexander… when he was ripped open with the Mallian arrow and his dagger!

He was devoted to Alexander and to the Royal House of the Argeads… but the girl was wasted on Alexander.

Krateros knew by now and would soon come back for her and for Alexander's son.

Perdikkas leans back in the massive chair, looks out at the darkening skies and takes a deep breath. Being so close to the gardens makes the air cooler and sweeter.

If Krateros had been standing next to him when Alexander was dying, would Alexander still have given him his royal signet ring, or would he have chosen Krateros instead?

He himself was one of the kingsmen absolutely loyal to Alexander who had immediately chased and swiftly killed the assassin of Philip.

When a king was dead, all that mattered was who would succeed him to the kingship… who killed the king and why was for damn philosophers to argue over… not for the men of the sword who had an army to command… and they all knew Alexander was worthy of their loyalty. Philip had left him in charge of the army in the UpLands when Alexander was no more than sixteen and he had earned the respect of the men.

When Alexander had given away the entire royal property to his kingsmen before leaving for Asia, he had asked Alexander, what was he keeping for himself? And Alexander had said: "HOPE!"… And he had returned his share of the royal lands to Alexander and had said: "That, I will share with you!" Had Alexander remembered that when he had given him his royal ring?

Others had returned their shares too… enough to give Alexander seventy talents and thirty days of provisions when they had crossed into Asia… an empty treasury and a debt of two hundred talents had turned into heaps of hope!

He bites his lip.

Krateros had become the Second-in-Command of the Royal Army after old Parmenion was put to the sword… well-liked, cool-tempered and almost as good-looking as Hephæstion and almost as competent as Alexander— although Hephæstion hated Krateros and Krateros did not particularly care for Hephæstion either!

But Roxana… she had been in the care of Krateros for over seven months when Alexander had sent Krateros back to Persia up country. He always suspected that the reason Hephæstion had grown intolerable and impossible heading down River Indus was not because the men had mutinied at River Hyphasis… it was because Alexander had sent Roxana back with Krateros… Hephæstion had been both worried and jealous…

And all those rumors… when they had finally reached Karmania…

Seven months was an eternity… and a lot could happen in seven months…

Perdikkas looks back at Rošanak. Someone has lit small candles by her bed. A young maid fans her with a large palm-leaf.

Her own noble lady had taken ill the day before, overcome by the heat, utterly exhausted from keeping faithfully to her bedside night and day.

He looks around. A young palace eunuch is sitting on a small chair by the door, about to fall asleep. Her old Persian wound-healer was slumped in another chair, sleeping and snoring.

"Idiot!" Perdikkas grunts angrily under his breath. He stands up and heads for the wound-healer to wake him up. The scent of yellow saffron flowers makes him sneeze.

A good omen, sent by Zeus.

He kisses the tips of his fingers and then senses he is being watched.

His senses had always been keen, from years and years of being a warrior, an instinct once learned and always used… it came like second nature to him.

He turns and looks over at Rošanak.

She was awake. And she was watching him.

He forgets about the Persian wound-healer, walks over to her bedside and pushes away the sheer netting around her bed, then leans over and calls her quietly. "Roxana."

Rošanak closes her eyes. She feels dazed, weary and watery and heavy. She opens her eyes. Her belly is as loaded with child as ever. She tries to remember.

"Alexander…" she moans quietly.

Had he gone ahead and had left her behind again?

Perdikkas gently touches the fading bruise on her face, then dips a white hand linen in the water bowl next to her bed and wipes her forehead with the cool scented linen.

"How do you feel?" His voice mellows and softens.

"Where is he?"

"Still in his room…"

Her eyes darken with pain and horror.

His body had been left unburied, against the Laws of the Wise Lord.

"What will become of his body?"

"Embalmers from the Two Lands… they have been sent for."

Rošanak closes her eyes. Her face wrinkles with grief.

Alexander was really dead…

She takes a deep breath.

Embalming was against the Laws of the Wise Lord, too.

She pushes the painful thoughts out of her head.

It did not matter…

Body was just an empty vessel… it was the soul that mattered…

Smoldering Bâb-ilim heat… intolerably hot…

Rošanak breathes in warm air and pulls back the cool white linen. A silky sheer nightgown reveals her naked body underneath.

Perdikkas tries to look away.

He turns his head and sees the old wound-healer and beckons the palace eunuch, who walks softly toward him and bows, awaiting orders.

Perdikkas just points to the snoring wound-healer.

It was useless to say anything, as no one in the palace spoke his tongue anyway.

The palace eunuch walks back quietly and shakes the Old Persian Healer.

The old man rises and walks drowsily over to Rošanak's bedside. He puts his hand over Rošanak's belly and feels the unborn and then rubs her belly under Perdikkas' watchful eyes.

He whispers to her in Persian, pointing with his old eyes to Perdikkas, "He has taken all my family hostage, thinking I would flee from your royal care in the middle of the night! I cannot even answer the call of nature without two armed guards on each side of me!"

Rošanak takes a deep breath painfully and lets it out.

"Do not just stand there idly… wash her royal feet and put more salve on them!" The Old Persian Healer says to the palace eunuch, who walks back to the foot of the bed softly and starts to wet and wash and rub Rošanak's feet with cool, scented water.

"The cuts on the bottom of your feet are almost healed. I used the salve that old Polydoros gave me." The Old Persian Healer speaks quietly to Rošanak and then looks at Perdikkas. "Queen and her unborn are healing."

Perdikkas looks at him wordlessly.

The Old Persian Healer shakes his head and walks around and takes Perdikkas' hand and puts it on Rošanak's belly.

Just like the dead king, this one was tongueless too.

The palace eunuch looks startled and then looks away and continues rubbing her feet with cool scented water. The Old Persian Healer, catching the eunuch's scornful eyes, grunts under his breath, "He has threatened to kill me and my family if the unborn dies!"

Perdikkas feels the unborn moving inside her.

"In the former days, the Persian Kings would have cut off the hands of any man who touched the naked body of a Royal Woman without her leave, before impaling him," Rošanak says quietly.

Perdikkas pulls his hand back.

"You have threatened the lives of all the palace wound-healers and have taken their families as hostages… you have forbidden them to sleep and eat and answer the call of nature… so he just wants to make sure that you know the unborn is still alive," Rošanak continues faintly.

"I…" Perdikkas twists his lips.

Rošanak waves her hands and dismisses everyone.

The young palace maid lays the palm leaf fan down gently and disappears into the garden. The palace eunuch stands up, uncertain for a moment, and then speaks quietly under his lips in broken Persian and then bows and leaves the bedchamber.

"He said the Bêl Temple Priests have prayed for me and offered sacrifices to Nintu, their ancient goddess of childbirth, the mother of all the little ones," Rošanak says faintly.

The Old Persian Healer stands by her bedside looking undecided. He pleads quietly, "Dukšiš… please…"

"Go. I will talk to him," Rošanak replies quietly.

The old healer shakes his head and turns and walks out of the bedchamber and closes the door quietly behind him.

The room becomes quiet. Only Perdikkas remains.

"My royal sisters?"

"The savages who— well, they will be seen to! I will throw them to the fighting elephants, when we purify the Royal Army. I will see to Meleagros who started the bloody mess about succession, when the Boy-King is born!"

Or sooner…

Meleagros was the dim-witted Foot commander who had fallen out of favor with Alexander in India. Loaded with wine, he had praised Alexander for finding a man who was worth a thousand talents of silver even if it had meant coming all the way to India, after Alexander had given that amount to Omphis. Alexander had spared his life, but had never given him a higher command post. Instead he had mocked Meleagros openly and had said that jealous men tormented themselves with their own jealousy.

Alexander should have handed him the same justice he had given to the Black Kleitos…

Well, he would see to him… when the time was ripe.

His days were numbered…

Meleagros could not even hide in a sanctuary to save his cursed carcass from vengeance. There was no mercy for the men who had broken his Royal Army!

Rošanak eyes Perdikkas for a moment.

She found no pity in her heart for the men who had killed and then raped the dead bodies of her royal sisters, the last of the Royal Daughters… they should be hanged and quartered.

What kind of beasts rape dead women? Virgins no less! Never known the intimate touch of a man… not even their own husbands…

She takes a deep breath and closes her eyes.

She had hated them when they were wedded to Alexander and Hephæstion in the Royal City of Çûšâ… but they were still sisters… bound to each other by ancient royal blood. Their blood was on her hands… as if she had killed them herself… she had utterly forgotten about them and now they were dead.

"Good," she says bitterly, and then beckons Perdikkas and takes his hand and puts it back on her belly.

"Here!"

Perdikkas feels a kick, and puts his other hand on her rounded belly instinctively, feeling the unborn with both hands.

He then relaxes and smiles for the first time in a long time.

"A good, strong kick! Yes! It is a boy!"

Rošanak lets go of his hand.

Perdikkas has never touched the rounded belly of a woman, loaded with child. He is awed and amazed.

Life living and kicking in the middle of chaos and madness and death…

"Release the hostages."

"I…" Perdikkas bites his lip.

"You may leave now…" Rošanak wryly dismisses him.

Perdikkas stands back, uncertain and slightly offended.

It starts to rain outside. Air slightly cools.

He turns his head and listens to the rain falling.

Rošanak pushes herself out of her bed, braces herself against the tall bed post and catches her breath. The Bottoms of her feet are sore from the healing cuts.

"Roxana, what are you doing?"

She ignores him and slowly heads for the gardens.

He curses under his breath and then follows her outside.

She walks slowly toward the water basin. Rain gently falls, breaking the heat of the night. She stops and drops her gown and stands naked on the edge of the water basin.

He stands, startled, and looks at her. From the back, her rounded belly is hidden from his eyes. Torches flicker on her body. Her body is pure ivory, with her long raven hair billowing down over her shoulders.

Her naked body was more beautiful than the statue of the Aphrodite of Knidos, carved in pure Parian marble from the Island of Paros by the hands of Praxiteles of Athenai. The naked statue was so famous that when they were boys, they had all gone to Knidos to see it for themselves… it stood seductively in the midst of a great garden surrounding the sacred temple of the goddess… grown men had tried to make love to it and had stained the pure white marble goddess yellow with their manly seeds…

Rošanak slowly steps into the water basin and immerses herself in the warm water, disappearing from view.

Perdikkas is startled again and rushes forward and kneels by the edge of the water basin searching for her.

Rošanak's head pushes gently through the surface of the water. She rests her head against the ledge of the water basin, the rest of her body covered by the water. Raindrops fall on her wet face.

Perdikkas yells at her in a low voice.

"Have you lost your reason? Get out of the water!"

"Still here?" She opens her eyes and looks at him and then closes her eyes again. "Speak or leave!"

"You have been dying for days," Perdikkas says with utter frustration, "now you are bathing in the rain, as if nothing has happened!"

"Days? How many days?"

"Seven days! Get out of the water!"

She fills up with pain.

Seven days… she had failed in her royal duty to her Kingly-Husband… he had died and no one had offered sacrifices to the Wise Lord on the fourth morning of his passing… had his own gods come for him?

"Did you offer blood sacrifices on the fourth day of his passing?"

"Are you mad?"

"Did anyone remember?"

"The whole world is broken! Bleeding and killing cows can wait! Get out of the water!"

Rošanak breathes in the familiar scent of za'farân in the warm bathing water.

"The warm za'farân water eases my back pain… it lightens my heavy load."

No one had performed the Rite of the Dead… it was her duty and she had failed.

Perdikkas takes a deep breath and runs his restless angry fingers through his wet hair distractedly. "I will be the regent for your unborn son— if he is a boy."

"A son is a boy!" Rošanak mocks him wearily.

"If anything happens to you, there is no telling what the men will do!" Perdikkas ignores her and mumbles to himself.

"Why? I am the same barbarian I was before Alexander died," Rošanak says quietly. "It would be far better if men gave birth to their own sons and there were no women. How happy men would be then."

"Stop this nonsense at once! Medea was a heartless bitch! I should never have given you the damn book! Get out of the water and go lay down on your bed like a virtuous queen!" Perdikkas grates his teeth, ordering her.

"Or what?"

"Please!"

"Go away!"

Rošanak sinks back into the water basin and disappears.

Perdikkas waits impatiently for a moment.

Rošanak emerges again. She opens her eyes and takes a deep breath and closes her eyes again.

"Does Krateros know?" she asks quietly.

"Yes!" Perdikkas forces the word out through his teeth grudgingly.

"Is he coming back?"

"I did not come here to discuss Krateros with you!"

"Then, why did you come?"

"I—" Perdikkas loses his words and finds new ones. He looks up at the rain. Raindrops fall into his eyes; his face is wet and washed with rain. His voice softens and lowers.

"I am leaving the palace tonight— I just wanted to make sure you were well cared for."

Rošanak looks at him blankly.

"The Makedonian Horse is sieging Babylon. The Foot wants Arrhidaios to succeed Alexander. The Horse will never agree to be ruled by a dim-witted bastard who cannot lead the Royal Army— he throws up at the sight of blood— they all know how Philip felt about the boy. If Philip wanted his dim-witted bastard to rule his men and his lands, he would have said so— he would not have kept it a bloody secret. And if Alexander thought Arrhidaios could become a king, he would have killed him a long time ago."

Perdikkas pauses and catches his breath. "The Foot is camped inside the city and they outnumber the Horse. Eumenes and Medeios and a few Thessalians are talking to both sides. Until we can hammer out an agreement with them from a position of strength, nothing will change. The HighLander Horse are loyal to Alexander and his Son-King!"

Rošanak listens to him without hearing a word.

"It has been a few days, but should not take long. The Foot either has to take to arms or take to a compromise! There has already been an attempt on my life, so I have to leave the city and join the Horse. I am leaving Aristonous and a small group of royal guards to protect you. They all have taken a sacred oath to protect you with their lives. No harm will come to you! If you need to contact me, they can get your words to me. You can trust them. They are men of honor."

As Perdikkas speaks, his words begin to fade in the rain.

"Your own eunuch has disappeared," Perdikkas says quietly.

Rošanak rests her head on the edge of the water basin. Rain washes her face.

"I ordered him to take the whore of Alexander… the eunuch who had wrongly caused the death of the Persian Governor of Persepolis with his lies, after we returned from India… to his kinsmen… to settle the blood feud."

Perdikkas wipes the rain from his eyes and raises his eyebrow.

"Why did you not ask me to see to him?"

She ignores him and breathes in the rainy air.

"Something is burning. What is burning?" she mumbles quietly to herself.

"Memorial for Hephæstion— it caught fire and burned to the ground after the death of Alexander."

She closes her face.

That must have finally appeased Abi-Samar and the Bêl Temple Enterers.

And then she remembers again. "Perdikkas?"

"Yes, Roxana?"

"My royal sisters… the Royal Daughters…"

"We sent their bodies back to Queen Sisygambis. Your Brother, Hystanes, took them home— as you asked."

"I did?"

"Yes— before you fell into darkness."

"My poor grandmother… I must go to her…"

"Ah!"

"What?"

Perdikkas hesitates for a moment.

"Roxana, Queen Sisygambis died two days ago. The royal messenger just brought word this morning. She died swiftly after burying the Royal Daughters. They said she died of grief over the death of Alexander!"

"No!" Rošanak closes her eyes in pain and sinks lower in the water.

Her poor grandmother had finally died of grief over the death of her grandson and granddaughters… she had died when there was no longer a reason for her to live… all her blood had died…

"I thought Alexander loved me…"

She takes a deep breath and continues under her breath, talking to herself. "I thought he gave me his seed as a royal gift, not for an heir for himself, but because he knew how much I had always wanted a son," she says bitterly.

Alexander had known all his life who he was… that is why he did not have a burning desire for sons.

Alexander was the beginning and the end unto himself. He had no need of a father or a son. There was no one who could have gone before or come after him… ever…

What he had done throughout his life, was just a measure of himself against himself and his gods and nothing more… All was done for the glory of himself… Nothing was done for the glory of his gods or his men or his lands…

And he had died without naming a city after her…

Tears mix with raindrops.

Well, he had not named a city after Hephæstion either…

She starts to burn. "But I was wrong! Alexander hated me. He took Stateira with him, and left me here utterly alone."

Alexander and Hephæstion had died and had taken the Royal Daughters of the Third Dâriuš with them… neither of them loved her…

She was utterly forgotten…

"Roxana— Alexander loved no other. He was planning to take you with him to Arabia. I was the one given the task of protecting you, as Hephæstion had before me."

She closes her eyes and pushes back a tear. "You should have let me die!"

"Roxana, please!"

"The son I always wanted is unlucky, he brought death to his own father."

"Roxana!"

"Tell me, which unborn has ever lived long enough into manhood to inherit the throne of his dead father? Which boy-king has ever reached manhood to become king? Where is the Crown-Prince… the son of the Third Darius?"

"Roxana! Please!"

"Medea was not a heartless bitch… she loved Jason and he turned on her… she should have taken a lover… bedded the best friend of Jason…"

Perdikkas looks at her, exasperated. "Roxana!"

He wanted to pull her out of the water basin and slap some sense into her…

Talking to her was more consuming than dealing with Meleagros and those idiots in Foot. At least they understood the tongue of a sharp sword or the thrust of a blunt sarissa pushed against their worthless carcasses.

Could the unborn breathe under so much water?

He takes a deep breath and says quietly, "I have released all the Persians and Baktrians from the Royal Army."

Rošanak opens her eyes and looks at him for a moment and then sees him for the first time.

He was only a season older than Hephæstion, but he seemed older… a lot older…

His face was broken with lines… the whole world was weighing on his shoulders… He was being measured against greater men.

His left arm was wrapped tight with snow white linen… now all wet in the cooling rain… an honor wound from that shameful night when Makedonians had broken into the royal bedchamber with murder in their hearts, bent on spilling kingsmen's blood…

"You have?"

"Yes!"

"Why?"

His voice softens and bends. "I did not want to fight two hostile Royal Armies at the same time. Makedonians are the most dangerous now and the ones who need my attention most."

"And the Persians and Baktrians?"

"They can attack the splintering Makedonians. But that could reunite the Makedonians and if I was a Persian, I would let the Makedonians tear each other apart, without any harm coming to my own men. Why waste good blood after dead blood already marked for the House of Hades?"

"You are not Persian!"

Rošanak eyes Perdikkas.

Perdikkas eyes Rošanak.

"I have to leave," Perdikkas says quietly and lingers on his knees for a moment longer in the rain.

"Then leave…" Rošanak closes her eyes and utters quietly.

Perdikkas gives up and straightens to his feet. He is now thoroughly soaked from the rain. His head feels cooler. He takes a deep breath and looks around.

The calmness inside the Garden Palace was such a world apart from the chaos that was raging outside… she seemed like a goddess living on Mount Olympus, oblivious to the fate of the wretched mortals down below.

Another uncertain moment passes in the rain.

"Perdikkas?" Rošanak says faintly.

Perdikkas bends down quickly and kneels by the water basin, uncertain that she had even called to him.

"Yes?"

"Your arm wound?"

"It is healing."

"Divine Mithres is the protector of all warriors. I will pray to him to watch over you."

Perdikkas looks at her for a moment, etching every line of her face into his memory.

He had never thought of anyone praying for him.

His Median wife loathed him and his brother was an idiot and he had not seen his sister since he had left for Asia with Alexander.

If he died in the bloody chaos, there was no one to see to him… no one to bury him… no one to mourn him… he would die unburied and unmourned… his glorious deeds all forgotten.

His enemies were dangerous, ruthless, murderous men. They had tried to kill him once and they were going to try again… and if they got to him, they would come for her afterwards. He had seen what those bastards had done to the Royal Daughters of Darius… how they had clawed into them… he was not going to let the same fate happen to Roxana. He had told her in India that he would protect her with his honor and he had meant every word!

If he was going to die that night, her rain-and-tear-washed face was the face he wanted to remember with his last dying breath.

He looks at his hands, at the two rings on his fingers. One, the golden royal signet ring Alexander had given him on his death bed, and the other, an old ancestral ring. He takes off his old ancestral ring and offers it to her. His voice mellows and softens and blends with the rain.

"This is Nike, Goddess of Victory. My father gave this to me when I came of age, on his death bed, before he died. It is my ancestral ring. Wear this for me until I return."

Rošanak considers Perdikkas for a moment in the rain and then slides her hand out of the water and takes the ring.

Perdikkas wraps his powerful fingers around her small wet hand and holds it for a moment. He anchors himself in her.

"I am sworn to your keep. I will come back for you," he says quietly, squeezing her hand in his hand.

He forgets his weary wounded body… life pours down on his exhausted head like soothing rain.

She closes her eyes and swallows hard. The ring of victory digs into the palm of her hand. She accepts his oath and the rest of him.

Where there was darkness, there was also light…

More tears mix with raindrops.

He lets go of her hand, gets to his feet and looks at her for another moment, and then turns around and leaves silently in the rain.

She sinks back into the warm water basin, filled with tears pouring down from the heavens.

GARDEN PALACE of QUEEN AMYTIŠ
BEGINNING of the REIGN of PI-LIP-SU who is called ARRHIDAIOS
YEAR 1 of the THIRD PHILIP, MONTH 3, AUDNAIOS
YEAR 1 of PI-LIP-SU, MONTH 9, KISILÎMU
KING at ROYAL COURT. DAY is GOOD
MID-DAY

"Nikaia?" Rošanak says softly, continuing to play with the infant Alexander without looking at Perdikkas.

"Yes, daughter of Antipatros," Perdikkas says quietly. His brown eyes darken, disappointed with her lack of interest.

He was hoping for something, anything, a sign.

"And what of Madumîtu, your wife?"

"I returned her to her father with honors months ago after Alexander died—while I was caring for you. She is free to marry anyone of her own choosing—and I gave her father the upper territory of the Satrapy of Media. The territory will be called Media Atropates."

"I see."

"I never touched her! I swear by the gods!"

His bride had started crying when he had entered the bridal chamber after the wedding and then had tried to hide under the marital bed. So he had left her to her tears and had gone to drink pure Persian wine with Hephæstion and other HighLanders who had also been shut out of their marital beds by their Persian brides.

What idiot wanted to bed a woman who cried and cursed her husband in her marital bed? In any tongue?

He did not even remember what she looked like!

Rošanak eyes him under her long lashes.

He tries again.

"Old Antipatros is still the regent ruling in Makedonia. A marriage alliance with his daughter will make us allies."

"Does her face favor her father?"

Perdikkas grates his teeth in frustration.

"Sister of Kassandros. His hair was on fire, or seemed to be, when he came to see Alexander in Babylon. Sister of Iolaos, the red-headed cupbearer. You like red-headed women?" Rošanak says wickedly, taunting Perdikkas.

"Auburn!" Perdikkas says through his teeth, looking at the infant Alexander who has fallen asleep again cradled in her soft arms.

No one slept as much as the Boy-King… he was either suckling her full breasts or sleeping within her soft cradling arms or mindlessly answering the call of the nature… what a life!

Is that what he had done, when he was that size?

He did not remember much of his own birth mother… she had died before he was old enough to remember her. He was raised by his birth sister.

"It is a marriage alliance, not a love match!" He bites his lip in anger and plays with the old ring on his finger.

She had returned his ancestral ring of Goddess Nike to him, after he had purified the Royal Army and returned to the palace.

He had meant for her to keep it…

"Then well-matched, My Lord." Rošanak laughs quietly while handing the sleeping infant Alexander to a Bâb-ilani târîtu.

"May the marriage alliance be a lucky one!"

Perdikkas grinds his teeth and reluctantly looks away from her heaving breasts under her royal gown.

"Do not call me Your Lord!"

"What shall I call you then?"

"Perdikkas!"

"Yes, My Lord!"

"Aristoteles!" Perdikkas grimaces and bites his lip loaded with frustration, trying hard not to slap her.

Rošanak raises her eyebrow in the air and eyes Perdikkas intently.

"You are marrying him too, My Lord?" She taunts him with half a smile.

"He died!"

"Huh… like a beast or a plant?"

"He killed himself by drinking poison."

Silence.

She narrows her eyes and lays back on her couch.

The wretched old man who said all non-Hellenes should be treated like slaves, had not died a man… he had not even died a beast or a plant… he had died a demon.

By taking his own life, the coward had died in the service of the Lord of Darkness… that was the fate of a man who thought men did not need gods.

If he had heard the call of the Wise Lord, instead of babblings of philosophy, the Wise Lord might have taken pity on him and let him die as a man.

Her mind drifts.

What a Great King Alexander would have become if he had been educated at the Gate of the King in the Persian Royal Court by royal tutors, instead of catching flies listening to that starry-eyed philosopher sitting in a darkened cave in Mieza.

Kings did not need philosophy… they needed to ride a horse well and shoot an arrow better and tell the truth always and dispense King's Law and Justice mercifully.

No more and no less…

Silence.

GARDEN PALACE of QUEEN AMYTIŠ
YEAR 1 of the THIRD PHILIP, MONTH 6, XANDIKOS
YEAR 1 of PI-LIP-SU, MONTH 12, ADDÂRU
KING at ROYAL COURT. MONTH is GOOD
EVENING

"Kleopatra?" Rošanak asks with a curious smile.

"Yes, daughter of Queen Olympias. Sister of Alexander by Queen Olympias," Perdikkas says quietly. "With her hand in marriage, comes Makedonia as her dowry."

Fool! She knows who Kleopatra was. She was married to her brother.

"What about her two children?"

"She is leaving them with Olympias."

"And what about the other one, Nikaia?"

"I will send her back to Pella to her father."

"I see." Rošanak raises an eyebrow, smiling playfully.

"Being the regent to my Son-King has certainly made you the most desirable man in the whole of Asia, and with such lovely noble Makedonian ladies too."

No Persian Royal Daughter, once gifted, was ever sent back! It was the most precious gift a Great King could bestow on a man… any man!

There were bloody battles fought when the Great King had declined to gift a Royal Daughter to a powerful satrap or a noble of the Seven Persian Families.

"Phila—" Perdikkas mumbles and grunts, trying hard not to slap her.

"Ah! Another one? You will soon need a larger palace for all your wives."

"She is the one Krateros is marrying— another daughter of Antipatros. A woman of exceptional quality," Perdikkas says vengefully, looking straight at her for her reaction.

Rošanak's eyes narrow and darken for a moment, and then she dismisses it and slips back under a mask of indifference.

A woman of exceptional quality?

She must be ugly as hell! If she was beautiful, they would say she was beautiful! No one would care much about her other exceptional qualities!

Krateros had sent her a golden apple once with a note that said:

> "To the fairest, Greeting.
> Paris turned down offers of power and wealth and wisdom and gave the golden apple of Eris to Aphrodite for the promise of the most beautiful wife in the world…"

She had eaten the golden apple and tossed the note in her silver jewelry box.

"Who could have divined that the death of Alexander would bring such a marital boon for the kingsmen of Alexander and the lovely daughters of Antipatros?" Rošanak says with a forced smile. "Is she not the oldest one, meant once for Alexander? The one a season younger than Olympias?"

"Phila is generous and kind and a counsel to her father, not ruled by mad passion!" Perdikkas grunts and grumbles. His fingers beg him to strangle her.

Rošanak takes a deep breath, feeling relieved.

The passionate Krateros was marrying a passionless woman.

A warrior of Homeric beauty with a virtuous woman.

His bed was to be empty of passionate love…

Let living without having a beloved be his reward and his punishment!

"Well-matched," she says dismissively.

Perdikkas grabs Rošanak's arm. "Must you be so cruel?" he says in quiet frustration and anger.

"Let go of me!" Rošanak tries to shake him off.

Perdikkas loosens his grip on her, but just as she is about to walk away from him, he pulls her back into his arms and kisses her, hard, taking his time, and then pushes her away and walks out of the royal room, leaving Rošanak breathless.

Stunned silence.

She leans against the wall, taken completely by surprise, and rests her head. She touches her lips.

Her heart was beating faster… her lips were throbbing… her body felt warmer…

She had sometimes seen a glimpse of his desire for her in his eyes, but he had always kept his feelings well-hidden behind a mask of hammered metal.

That rainy night he had given her his ring… and when she had returned the ring, he had not insisted that she keep it as a sign of his desire for her… but what now?

She touches her breasts.

She had weaned her son after three months of taking him to her breasts, when her own milk had dried up. She had regained her old womanly body soon afterward.

Her mind wanders.

Perdikkas had kept to her bedside until her son was born.

For days after the birth of her son, all she could do was cry. She had drowned in a huge basin of bottomless melancholy, and the more she had cried, the more the tears had come. She had wanted a son all her life and when she had finally given birth to one, she could do nothing else but cry. She had let Alexander die, and then she had felt alone and ashamed and guilty and regretful. Her firstborn had died just after a day, taking half of her heart with him. Her secondborn was born early too and she was so fearful that she would lose this newborn too, that she had not even asked to see him.

Perdikkas had watched her in quiet desperation for days. Nothing had worked with her. She was not receiving anyone, not even Âriyânnâz who had been with her for so many years.

He had the palace eunuchs guarding her doors dragged away by his own men, so he could get in to see her himself. Her son had not taken to a wet nurse and he was slowly starving to death.

Finally on the fifth day, Perdikkas had walked into her bedroom with her crying infant son, had forced the baby into her arms, pulled out his dagger and told her that if she was waiting for her infant son to die, she no longer had to wait… he would kill the infant right then and there as he lay crying in her arms.

And his harsh words and the glint of the sharp dagger had brought her back to her reason and she had taken her infant son to her arms and to her breasts full of milk.

Perdikkas had wreathed the whole palace with olive twigs according to his ancestral customs to signal the birth of a son to Alexander.

On the tenth day after birthing, he had offered sacrifices in the morning to his gods and to Alexander and had hosted a feast at night for all the kingsmen and Makedonian commanders of the Royal Army, Horse and Foot warriors alike, where her Son-King was presented formally to his men and given his royal name, his father's name… Alexander Aigeos, the Fourth Alexander.

She takes a deep breath.

She only had Utâna for one stolen night, with a sweet memory that had to last her a whole lifetime.

Alexander… her body would quiver with utter pleasure just in anticipation of his love… her heart would beat faster at the sound of his voice… he had given her the most pleasure and had extracted the most pain… she had bled out more tears over him than the skies had unloaded in a lifetime.

Hephæstion had done Alexander one better… he had learned her tongue and had whispered sweet Persian poetry and intimate love words into her ears while bedding her. Her moments with Hephæstion were stolen moments, never whole but sweet all the same… Alexander always lurked in the shadows somewhere, not seen, but always felt.

Chandrâ…

Krateros…

Perdikkas… She felt safe with him… he was another HighLander…

She had not been wrong about him… he had remained true to his words from those days back in Hind and had always kept faith with her.

He had stood by her side and had sat by her sick bed after the death of Alexander and had stood up for her Son-King before the Assembly of Makedonians… even before he was born. And he had been like a good father to Alexander since the day her son was born to her… and had never given her a reason to worry.

KING'S ROYAL QUARTERS
YEAR 1 of the THIRD PHILIP, MONTH 6, XANDIKOS
YEAR 1 of PI-LIP-SU, MONTH 12, ADDÂRU
FESTIVAL of FRAWARDIGÂN
3 NIGHTS before the PERSIAN NEW YEAR

"If you, My Lord, are the Son of God... Why... so, am I!" the other old Hindu Brahman had declared to Alexander. "I desire nothing that you can give me. I fear no exclusion from any blessings which may be yours... Hind is enough for me while I live!"

Rošanak remembers, a bit of a golden memory comes into her eyes.

Uxšiyârta had heard from the Hindu in the satrapies on the other side of Bakhtriš that a new king had become the ruler of Hind... one called Chandrâguptâ... and he had rid Hind of the invading Makedonians...

He always said he would rule over Hind one day!

Did he remember her? Did he ever think about her?

Rošanak takes a deep breath and then waves with her fingers, and Abi-Samar opens the giant doors to the royal bedchamber.

The aroma of sacred salts and myrrh pushes out into the hallway and wraps around her.

Scent of death...

Rošanak stands motionlessly for a moment. And then she takes a candle from Abi-Samar and walks into the darkened royal bedchamber.

A massive golden sarcophagus lay in the middle of the room. All the royal furnishings that used to fill the royal bedchamber had long since been removed... the giant broken doors mended... just a dead king in a golden casket remained...

Guarded by eternal silence... Packed away with fragrant myrrh... and sacred salt...

She hesitates for a moment.

It was a mortal sin to look upon the dead... she had not even looked at Hephæstion, after the fourth day of his passing...

The dead belonged to the Wise Lord... and to him alone...

But it was the Festival of All-Souls and his Persian soul was expecting her.

She hesitates for another moment, searching for courage in the far corners of her beating heart. Then she steps inside the room and Abi-Samar closes the massive doors quietly behind her. She walks softly toward the majestic golden casket, almost as majestic as the royal bed he had died in, the royal bed of Xerxes, his Royal Persian ancestor.

She takes a deep breath and then looks inside.

The candle flickers slowly on the face of Alexander; a drop of melted wax falls on her hand and burns her. She bites her lip in pain.

He looked as if in a deep sleep, lying on a bed of sacred Mudrâya salt... his lionish tangled honey-golden mane, turned silver, never looked more tamed.

His face had aged and darkened and hollowed and wrinkled. His body was covered with his golden arm and armor and a white robe edged with Persian Purple.

In death, he looked more peaceful… rested…

He was and was not Alexander…

"Alexander…"

She forgets her burning hand and whispers softly, almost expecting him to stir and smile and pull her close to him and kiss her tenderly.

Silence.

"Why did you leave me behind?"

Silence.

"Alexander… your son is splendid… his eyes… both… are as pale as the color of the sky at dawn…"

Silence.

Her eyes fill with tears.

The old Hinduya Brahmans were wrong! They had told Alexander that in his death, he would possess only as much of the earth's dirt as he was standing on…

Alexander, who had conquered all the Lands, in his death had been denied even less of the Lands than any mortal… king or man…

In life, Alexander was always in motion…unbound by gods and men…

In death, her King-Husband was bound… a golden lion caged in a golden chest…

Where were those gods he had sacrificed to all his life? Why had they not come for him?

Had they not told him he was the godly son of one of them at the Oracle at Siwah?

A tear falls.

"Alexander… give your son your blessings and speak well of him to your gods!" Her voice ripples with sadness.

Silence.

Now she understood why it was a sin to look upon the dead.

It was not to guard the dead but to shield the living… from the pain of seeing a lover… still loved… beyond the grave… a love that could not be returned in kind.

She opens her other hand and looks at it in the light of the candle.

She had not brought Alexander Arabâya incense, nor Persian sweets, nor Bakhtrian gold, nor Bâb-ilani flowers…

She had brought him something far more precious… a lock of Hephæstion's golden-brown hair, tied with a shimmery white thread…

She places her precious offering on Alexander's armor; a tear falls next to it.

Blessing them both… as they themselves would have liked to be blessed…

She pulls the white robe up. Alexander disappears from her mortal eyes.

"Divine Mithrâ, Protector of Noble Warriors,

Here lies a warrior who was once a king. His final judgment rests with his gods.

If he has done good, he will roam in the Heaven with the kings and divine heroes.

If he has done evil, he will roam in the darkness until eternity.

He shall not reap except what he has sown… and for the burning of Pârsâ…"

SMALL AUDIENCE HALL
ROYAL PALACE of the SECOND NABÛ-KUDURRÎ-ÛSUR
FOLLOWING DAY
MID-DAY

"To the King and My Lord, from your faithful subjects, Lâbaši-Marduk and Nabû-Nâdin-Šumi:

"Good health to Your Majesty! Peace be upon My Lord. May the great gods Nabû and Marduk and the great goddess Nânâ bless Your Majesty. May the royal rule of Your Majesty be as pleasant as cool water and sesame oil.

"Fire broke out on day 13 of month Šabatu, during the night, in the Temple of Nânna. We went to see about it and by the favor of the great gods, everything in the temple is safe and in good order, but the temple priests have run away. Kinâ, the son of Ibašši-ilu who was the temple guard, has also run away. There is no one left in the temple to serve the sacrificial meals to the gods and no one to stand guard. From the days of old, since the time of the Great Flood, Nânna, the Moon-God, has been worshipped by men here.

"May My Lord act quickly and send instructions about this matter.

"Much rain has fallen this year and the wheat and barley crops will be plentiful for the autumn harvest. My Lord should be happy about this great blessing."

The Bâb-ilani Royal Court Scribe finishes reading the letter and bows his head and stands ready to write down words of immense wisdom to be uttered shortly by the man who spoke for the Kings.

He had a library full of such immense words of wisdom and kingly instructions in his head that could be carefully suggested when needed to the One with Raised Head above all other heads. The Royal Archives in the Palace of the Second Nabû-Kudurrî-Ûṣur were full of the wise wisdom of the ancient kings.

Perdikkas closes his eyes.

He missed his life as a warrior… the rush of battles and charge of horses and the clash of swords… the thrill of the unknown… the wind on his face… the blood on his sword… dead enemies in his wake.

Now his life as the highest in command was no different than the life of a court secretary, knotted with slippery alliances and sticky words and pieces of sealed parchment.

The line of people who wanted to see him was endless too… how did Alexander ever see to all these hordes who all wanted something from him?

Perdikkas opens his eyes and wryly glances at the tall stack of parchment and papyrus sitting on the long table of the Royal Secretary, patiently awaiting his attention on behalf of the Kings, and the row of court scribes sitting behind the tables, tending to the endless letters. He takes a deep breath.

All the requests ended with: "Let My Lord send instructions quickly about this matter or that matter."

He discreetly eyes the Royal Court Scribes who are discreetly looking at him.
All too ready and eager to respectfully tell him how to behave like one of their great ancient kings, how Sargon and Ashurbanipal and Nebuchadrezzar and Kuros and Darius ruled justly by the favor of the great Babylonian gods.
Some of the court scribes could read ancient words written some two thousand years before they were born. And none ever failed to mention that, every time a gap opened in his mind… in their eyes, he was just a warrior from the Lands Beyond the Sea… someone who had to be taught kingship, with tales of great kings and what made kings great… they all thought he was an idiot and an outsider with no royal blood!
He takes another deep breath.
He wanted to be riding a horse leading men into battle, not sitting on a silver couch sending instructions about missing temple guards.
He was a warrior…
…forced to worry about farmers and fishers and fowlers and shepherds… beast keepers and bee keepers and horse handlers… brickmakers and brickburners and canaldiggers and carpenters and stonecutters… jewelers and potters and sandalmakers and scentmakers and shopkeepers and spinners and weavers… bakers and brewers and butchers and cooks and confectioners and oilpressers… advocates and bankers and merchants and wound-healers… dancers and singers and musicians… diviners and fortunetellers and magicians and seers and storytellers… kaššâpu and kaššâptu… astronomers and astrologers and mathematicians… muppišu and muppištu and muppišânu… architects and builders and surveyors and sweepers… ambassadors and couriers and envoys and messengers… accountants and administrators and auditors and scribes and tribute collectors… âšipu and bârû and hassu and kalû and narû and ṭupšarratu and ṭupšarru… the immigrants and the natives and the settlers…
…priests and priestesses and slaves and whores… the poor and the moneyed…
… and the gods of Babylon and Borsippa and Nippur and Sippar and Uruk.ki…
In one of the small palaces, a small army of old mistresses of Great Kings long dead and gone still lived along with a small army of their eunuchs oblivious to the world around them, and he was called to their quarters whenever they quarreled… there were even written laws to deal with the intrigues of the women of the royal court.
This was not the life he was fated to live!
Moments pass slowly waiting for a reply.

"My Lord, shall I send a message to Nanâ-Êriš by the order of Your Majesty, to dispatch new temple priests and temple guards to the Temple of Nânna?" The Royal Court Scribe bows his head low and suggests politely.

"Yes," Perdikkas grunts.

"Your Majesty is most wise." The Royal Court Scribe bows again and writes down the official words and seals the letter.

"Who is next?" Perdikkas asks the Royal Secretary wearily without even looking up.

An old eunuch steps forward quietly and bows low and discreetly interrupts in broken Attik. "Your Lordship, the Queen is requesting an audience."

Perdikkas looks up, surprised. "The Queen?"

"Yes, Your Lordship! Issi Ekalli Rošanak." The old eunuch nods with an air of urgency and bows again and points to the giant audience hall doors. "Her Royal Highness is waiting on the other side of those doors."

Perdikkas narrows his eyes, looking in the direction the old eunuch is pointing.

He had not seen her since he had kissed her… nor had she sent for him… she had completely ignored him. Had she come to officially complain about him, the Man, to him, the Regent?

"Clear the royal audience hall!" Perdikkas orders the royal guards cautiously.

Whatever she wanted did not require a full royal court with eyes and ears and witnesses.

The royal audience hall quickly empties.

"Show her in."

"Yes, Your Lordship!" The old eunuch bows and leaves on soft feet.

Rošanak enters and before he calls her name, she bows softly and kneels down before him.

"Rox— ana—" Perdikkas is caught off guard.

He had seen the bow of the head and the bend of the knees done by the Persians and others so often. He had even done it himself, toward Alexander and Alexander only, when he was alive… but this was the first time Roxana had treated him with such high marks of honor.

He stands up quickly, not sure what to do or say.

"My Lord." Rošanak looks up at him, still kneeling down on the floor.

"Roxana, you do not have to—"

Rošanak softly interrupts. "My Lord. I have come to ask a favor of you."

Perdikkas' knees go weak with uncertainty.

Did she want another regent for her Boy-King because of his impropriety toward her?

He sits back down on his tall golden chair and puts on his mask of absolute authority.

It did not matter what she wanted.

Who would listen to her?

He had already pushed all the kingsmen of Alexander to the edges of the Empire and he was now the highest authority in the whole of Asia! And significant matters of guardianship and regency were decided by the kingsmen of Alexander, not by women.

She was just the mother of the Boy-King and no more… she had no say in such important affairs of the Empire.

He ruled over Babylon and he ruled over her.

Babylon had ten gated quarters and twenty-four great streets and forty-three great temples of great gods and more than nine hundred temples of other gods and each house had a household god, and multitudes from all over the Empire lived in the great city… she was just one woman.

"Yes?"

"I ask not as a queen for the punishment of those who have committed the act of treachery," she pauses and eyes him carefully, and then continues softly, "but as a mother of a son myself… whose life you yourself spared."

Perdikkas' eyes widen.

"Festival of All-Souls started the day before today and will last until the sun sets three days hence, before the rays of the sun bring forth the New Year of the Persians."

Perdikkas eyes her wordlessly.

Damn Persians never got to the point quickly and painlessly… not concise and precise like the Hellenes… nor direct like the HighLanders… their tongues sprawled endlessly like their endless lands… even when they spoke other tongues.

Rošanak quietly continues. "It is when the souls of the dead, old and young, come to receive their rites from their descendants and their beloveds." She pauses and looks at him and takes a deep breath. "All the Royal Women of Tiršata, the Crown-Prince, son of the Third Darius and Queen Stateira, are all dead." She pauses for another moment. "So, as a mother and their kindred and their blood, I ask that the bones of the Crown-Prince be placed next to the bones of his kingly-father, so his young soul knows that he is not forgotten by the living when he visits his kinsmen to receive his Rite of Hospitality."

She looks straight into Perdikkas' eyes.

"As a Royal Woman, I leave the judgment of those who killed the guiltless Crown-Prince to their own gods. His dead bones are of no threat to anyone and will not lay a claim to the Lands of his ancestral fathers!" She pauses and takes a deep breath. "I beg of you, as the Guardian of King Philip and the Regent of King Alexander and the Guardian of the Monarchy and the Regent of the Kingdom, on their behalf."

Perdikkas loses his words.

He knew the Boy-Prince was dead. Alexander had ordered it before the weddings in Susa, to be carried out right after the weddings.

The Boy-Prince, almost fifteen, had grown up kingly and warlike, even in captivity, even separated from Queen-Mother Sisygambis, and it was just a matter of time before the Persian Nobility would acknowledge the Boy-Prince as the rightful heir to the Persian throne of his royal father and his royal ancestors.

Oxathres, the brother of Darius, was dead too… he was seen to quietly by Peithon while crossing the Desert of Emptiness, by the order of Alexander.

Rošanak softly gets up to her feet and approaches him, bends and reaches and kisses his hand and then turns and leaves without another word spoken.

His heart bends into his knees.

This was how Alexander must have felt, when the first Persian knee was bent in his honor. How could any man... any man... resist wanting to become the Great King of the Persians? And when the man was already the King of the Persians, how could he resist wanting to become a god?

GARDEN PALACE of QUEEN AMYTIŠ
LAST DAY of FESTIVAL of FRAWARDIGÂN
MID-DAY

"Perdikkas sends greeting to Queen Roxana!" The royal boy says directly with a mark of honor in his voice. "He sent you this message." He leans over and presents the note in his hand to Rošanak.

Rošanak takes the note. "Thank you."

The royal boy hesitates and shifts his weight from one leg to the other.

"Anything else?"

"Ah! No! Just, Perdikkas asked me to wait for you to read his note and take back any message from you."

Rošanak eyes the royal boy curiously for a moment.

Makedonians had no head for tactfulness.

She then relents and breaks the royal seal and reads the note.

> Perdikkas to Queen Roxana, Greeting.
> Your wish has been carried out.
> The men who committed the wicked deed have been seen to.
> That I did for my own sake. Farewell.

She closes and folds the note and takes a deep breath.

He had written the note himself... he had honored her request and had honored her in his note and had not even used any of his own honor titles in the note. But why had he sent a boy to carry his private message?

"Do you have a message for the regent?"

"No."

The royal boy hesitates again. "Perdikkas said that you might have a message for him, after reading his note."

"No. No message."

"Very well." The royal boy shrugs his shoulders and turns around briskly and leaves the royal room.

Rošanak prays under her lips for the dead Crown-Prince.

Tears fall. And another prayer for Perdikkas.

"I worship the Wise Lord... He guides whom he will unto his light..."

KING'S ROYAL QUARTERS
YEAR 1 of the THIRD PHILIP, MONTH 7, ARTEMISIOS
YEAR 2 of PI-LIP-SU, MONTH 1, NÎSANNU
BEGINNING of the REIGN of A-LEK-SA-AN-DAR, who is called ALEXANDER
YEAR 1 of the FOURTH ALEXANDER, MONTH 1, NÎSANNU
DAY 1: KINGS at ROYAL COURT. COMPLETELY FAVORABLE
NIGHT

Restless night…

"Forget her!" Perdikkas grunts as he paces up and down in his royal bedchamber late at night, grinding his teeth. He stops in the middle of the room and puts his hands on his waist.

The Persian Festival honoring the start of the New Year was tomorrow. The palace eunuchs and the palace maids and the palace servants had been rallied by Roxana to set up the Garden Palace of Amytiš. And even after he had sent that note to her earlier in the day, no invitation had been received by the Regent to attend the Persian New Year Festival with the Queen… the most important festival of all Persian celebrations.

He sits down restlessly.

Why should he care?

It was just another damn festival of the Persians and he was a true-born HighLander!

He was the Captor and she was the Captive… the Guardian and the Guarded… the Successor and the Mother of the Boy-King…

And he already had enough troubles elsewhere!

He stands up and starts pacing again.

Alexander had been dead for almost ten months…

He stops and pours a full cup of the dark date-sweet Babylonian beer that the temple priests had been sending over daily, the same beer that was offered to Babylonian gods, and drinks half.

He had brought the Royal Army under his command, had purified it and had pushed all the kingsmen of Alexander to rule their own satrapies far away from Babylon.

Meleagros was put to the sword the day after the army was purified, right inside the sacred Babylonian temple he had taken refuge in to escape his wretched fate.

Leonnatos had already died bleeding in battle raising the Siege at Lamia, helping the old Antipatros, who was held up by the Hellenes who had revolted almost immediately after the news of the death of Alexander had reached Athenai. Leonnatos had never made it to the bed of Kleopatra, who had offered him her hand in marriage and Makedonia as her dowry.

Good! One less man to plot against him!

He had ordered Krateros to go to the aid of the old Antipatros now that Leonnatos was dead, and Krateros had sent him a sharp reply saying that they were equals and that he was not taking any damn orders from him.

He shrugs his shoulders and drinks more dark sweet beer.

Well, let Krateros tell old Antipatros he was too busy sitting on a silver couch wearing a purple robe playing king in Kilikia to go to Makedonia to help him kill the troublesome Hellenes!

Ptolemaios had put Kleomenes to the sword when he had gotten to the Two Lands and had planted himself firmly there, root and branch, fortified with the mountains of gold Kleomenes had squeezed out of the damn TwoLanders.

Lysimachos was grumbling again that Thrake was too small for him, and that the One-eyed Antigonos was eyeing it with his good eye to add to his own bigger satrapy.

Hmmm…

The One-eyed Antigonos was also slowly building an army, thinking he did not know of it. He was one of Philip's old men. To rid himself of his father's man, Alexander had quickly left Antigonos behind at Phrygia after the victory at Granikos with the charge of keeping the roads back to the UpLands clear. He was not a man to be counted on as an ally… if Alexander did not trust him to keep him close in the royal court, neither could he!

Peithon, who had been sent with a small part of the Royal Army to subdue the rebellious Hellene mercenaries who were left in Baktria by Alexander, had finally returned after killing them all. He had given the order to kill all the rebels to Peithon himself in front of the entire Royal Army… and when Peithon had wavered, his men had disobeyed him and had put the three thousand troublesome Hellenes to the sword for their loot… preventing Peithon from creating an army of the Hellene mercenaries for himself. He had given Peithon the other half of the Satrapy of Media for his troubles.

Eumenes had left for Kappadokia and Paphtogonia to bring the region under his own command as the new satrap. He had commanded his idiot brother, Alketas, to help Eumenes. Eumenes was his link to Olympias and as the regent to her grandson, it was wise to ensure the good will of the troublesome old queen-mother. He had ordered the One-eyed Antigonos to help Eumenes and he had ignored his command… one more reason to eliminate Antigonos when the time was ripe.

And Seleukos was patiently following him around the royal court in Babylon as his Second-in-Command. Someone lesser had to be assigned to his old post.

Not peace… but not all-out civil war yet either…

But war was the nature of the Makedonians… Peace was for women. Sooner or later, they all missed the smell and taste of the blood and battle in their bones.

The Boy-King had lived through his first year and now he was formally one of the 'Kings' along with the dim-witted Philip Arrhidaios and he was the regent to the purple-bundled Boy-King and the guardian to the dim-witted king.

Krateros was elected the Guardian of the Kingship of Philip Arrhidaios and since Krateros was in Kilikia and Arrhidaios was in Babylon under his personal command, the guardianship meant nothing, but sounded impressive enough!

He had offered to send Arrhidaios to Krateros and Krateros had ignored him. Krateros did not want to be saddled with him either.

Well…

He stops and touches his face and hesitates.

He had bathed and shaved twice. He had chewed on the skin of sweet lemons. He had even anointed himself all over with sacred oils of Babylonian Kings that were enchanted with magical spells to make their women powerless in their kingly presence…

The court eunuch had said: 'Eat bread, drink beer, anoint yourself and speak to great gods daily and like gods you will get your heart's desire!"

He drinks the rest of his dark date-sweet beer and puts down the cup and rehearses his lines one more time in his head, his hard head hurting with too many soft words.

He was the Regent and the Guardian of the Kings in Asia… that meant something!

He was the Supreme Commander of the Royal Army…

He was almost a king… and Roxana treated him as if he was a lowly royal boy, from a fresh crop of young royal boys from the HighLands of Makedonia, who did not know any better!

Antipatros had sent his daughter to marry him.

Kleopatra was coming to marry him with the blessings of Olympias.

And Roxana treated him like one of the palace eunuchs, even though he had honored her the most… he had kept her father in command of his old satrapy and had promoted her brother to serve directly under him with honors.

He walks toward the doors to his royal bedchamber. He pushes the heavy doors open forcibly and walks into the fiercely lit hallway maze of the old Babylonian palace.

He had first moved into the old palace after he had arrived in Babylon as the chiliarchos and then closer to the royal quarters when Alexander had gotten sick with fever, and then moved right into the royal quarters after the Royal Army had reconciled months ago. He was better protected within the old palace walls… and was closer to both Kings.

It was wise to be cautious… Makedonian kingship was watered with the royal blood of Argeads… just as Persian kingship was watered with the royal blood of the Achæmenids…

He bites his lip.

Damn girl!

Queen or not, she will treat him with respect!

She will not dishonor him like this!

Just as she used to invite him to her table in India, she will invite him to all her Persian festivals and her feasts and all the damn Banquets of the Queen… no matter how insignificant… so he could turn them down promptly as a good HighLander!

How could he turn down the Queen's invitations and be known as a true HighLander, if the damn Queen never invited him to anything?

He hears heavy footsteps behind him. He stops and turns around.

A pair of royal boys were following him closely. He raises his right hand.

"Go back and guard my room."

The royal boys look at each other with uncertainty. "But, Sir! You are not in your room!"

"That was a direct order, not a request," Perdikkas thunders. "Present yourselves to me tomorrow for disciplinary action!"

The royal boys hang their heads low, disappointed, and turn around and head back, dragging their feet.

"Move! Or go back and have the next watch take your place!" Perdikkas grunts impatiently.

The royal boys straighten and walk away quickly, to avoid suffering more of his anger later.

Perdikkas considers them for a moment.

The royal boys had aged after the death of Alexander.

Everyone had!

The royal court Barber had told him that snow had started to fall on his own hair!

Perdikkas shakes his head and runs his fingers through his freshly snowed hair. It still felt the same to his fingers. He shrugs his shoulders and turns around and heads for the steps to the second story. A palace door-keeper bows low and opens the palace doors for him. He steps out and stops in the middle of the sky bridge to the Garden Palace and looks up for a moment.

It was a beautiful night, a silvery crescent moon, and lots of little stars…

He hesitates and thinks about going back to his room.

He was the most powerful man in Babylon. He was the most powerful man in the Empire! In the whole of Asia!

He was treated like a king… He was a king!

King of Babylon… King of the Lands… King of the Black-headed People…

… until the head of the small-headed Boy-King got big enough for a crown.

He could summon a temple full of Priestesses of Astarte to entertain and pleasure him!

The High Priestess of the Temple of Astarte had sent him words inviting the King to come and take pleasure in her fruits of passion, in her perfumed bed of delight, covered with snowy sheets of cool linen…

She had sent him a small statue of a naked priestess offering up her breasts…

"Hmmm…" He takes a deep breath and pushes the image out of his eyes. His thoughts return to Rošanak and his legs move him forward on the sky bridge. He passes two royal guards and enters the Garden Palace and stops in front of Rošanak's bedroom. An armed palace eunuch is guarding the golden door to her bedroom. The palace eunuch recognizes Perdikkas. The two eye each other for a moment and then the palace eunuch narrows his eyes and thinks for a moment to himself, and then bows and opens the door to the bedroom of the Queen for the man who spoke for the Kings of the Lands.

GARDEN PALACE of QUEEN AMYTIŠ
QUEEN'S BEDCHAMBER

Fragrant darkness.

Scented softness.

Perdikkas steps inside the familiar room and the golden bedchamber door quietly closes behind him. He looks around.

Her bedroom was quiet and dimly lit by small candles.

Arabian incense burned slowly in a silver fire altar by the door. The door was left open as usual to the outside garden, hidden behind long golden curtains that swayed softly in the night breeze. Sheer silvery netting suspended from the high ceiling wrapped around her massive bed, keeping the flies from disturbing her while she slept.

A palace eunuch had told him that the Boy-King was now kept to his own room by his nursemaids at night by the order of the Queen, and only brought to her if he was sick…

He stands there quietly for a moment.

Everything he has rehearsed evaporates from his thoughts instantly, like morning dew in the first rays of the hot Babylonian sun.

He hesitates.

He should have come himself the day before instead of sending her a note carried by a royal boy.

She had probably thought he had dishonored her by sending him. Maybe the royal boy had not conveyed his message to her properly.

She had come to him at the royal court. He should have gone to her in her Palace Garden. He should have asked her directly… he should have expressed an interest in the native customs of the Boy-King… as was proper for the Regent.

Rošanak raises her head and sees Perdikkas and then lays her head back down on the soft feathered pillows.

She knew he would come, even before he did.

Perdikkas slowly walks to the side of her bed and looks at Rošanak who is looking at him quietly through the sheer blur of the netting.

She was sleeping utterly naked and utterly beautiful and utterly alone.

And he had come in arm and armor, dressed for battle… wearing a breastplate and a sword.

But it was too late… there was no retreat… no place to go… nowhere to fall back to…

If she screamed, his head might just roll on the floor, swiftly removed from his body by the armed palace eunuchs, sworn to guard the Persian Queen according to their ancient customs.

Or worse… he would look like a fool heavy with wine trying to bed the sleeping Queen… even though he was stone cold sober.

Or maybe the old palace eunuch was right after all and the Babylonian magic love potions were indeed magical. Then it was gold well spent.

He quietly drops his arm and armor on the floor. From a conquering commander, he is transformed into a simple warrior at the end of a long siege, surrendering his arm and armor and seeking quarters from the victor.

He takes off his clothes and drops them on top of his arm and armor.

He pulls aside the netting and crawls into bed next to her naked body.

Her soft silky skin was more soothing than cool raindrops in the hot Babylonian shade… he did not think skin could be this soft… her hair jasmined…

Rošanak raises her hand and gently caresses Perdikkas' face.

His body too, was full of battle scars and honor wounds.

The fragrant scent of her skin fills his head. He lowers his head closer to her face.

Her face was clean and fresh and unadorned… like that rainy night…

And she was luminous… bathed in seductive beauty with tenderness and grace… governed by Aphrodite…

A faded purplish bruise marked her lower lip where he had kissed her a few days ago… his hard kiss had purpled her soft lips…

He gently caresses the purplish blood mark with the tip of his finger.

She kisses the tip of his finger.

He smiles and lowers his head and kisses her marked lips slowly and tenderly. He tastes her mouth for the first time… the taste of her mouth mixes with the taste of date-sweet beer in his mouth.

She tasted sweet… sweet like buttery honeyed sesame… like a plate full of Persian sweets… as he had always thought she would… he had kissed her all over so many times in his dreams… awake or asleep… and so many more times after that fateful rainy night… it had given him hope…

She feels his pulsing body under his clean smooth skin and senses his manly desire for her pressing strongly against her body. She reaches and gently caresses the battle scars on his arm and the faded wrestling bruises on his chest with the soft tips of her fingers.

His body beats and pulsates with powerful desire to completely possess her. He takes the tip of her sensuous breast in his lips while his hand glides down her soft body and caresses her intimately.

She felt like soft honey butter… melting willingly under his warm wanting fingers…

She closes her eyes and softly sighs.

No words spoken.

What was there to say?

This was a tongue they both understood all too well.

The care of the Royal Woman had passed on from one conquering king to another…

GOLDEN CHAMBER of BÊL MARDUK TEMPLE. CROWN of E-TEMEN-AN-KI
DAY 12: FESTIVAL of AKÎTU. FAVORABLE
MIDDLE of the NIGHT

Late night… warm breeze…

Long delicate golden curtains sway back and forth, keeping out the early heat of the season and the wandering dragonflies.

Perdikkas pours golden honey-sweet beer in a tall lion-headed golden goblet and drinks some.

Babylonians had as many different beers as they had gods and temples. He had tried beer reluctantly at first. Alexander did not like beer, so no one drank beer in his court.

The Chief of the Royal Court Scribes had told him that if he drank beer and did not like it, he could throw him in the River Euphrates as punishment and let him sink or swim to the banks of the river… he had quoted an ancient proverb:

"He who does not like beer, does not know what is good."

Fortunately for the Chief of the Scribes, he had liked beer.

He leans back in his tall golden chair with golden feet and looks over at the massive golden bed in the center of the golden sanctuary and smiles. Rošanak is softly sleeping. He listens to the sound of her quiet breathing and sips his beer… he had kept her up all night the past few nights, bedding her.

He had honored the Festival of the New Year with the Persian Queen when the first golden rays of the golden sun had hit her Garden Palace, in the center of the beautiful Persian gardens on the first day of the vernal equinox.

She had told him he will have good fortune for the entire year, for celebrating the Persian New Day.

His body had already bathed in that good fortune in her sweet body.

And then he had honored the Akitu Festival of the Babylonians for twelve days and nights… they said it was the first time in many years that Akitu was celebrated with the Kings of the Lands themselves present in Babylon…

Enuma Elish, the Story of Creation, was enacted by the temple priests and priestesses, no different than a Hellene play, in front of the moneyed nobility of Babylon and all the free-born members of the popular assembly of Babylonians and anyone who had been lucky enough to enter the sacred grounds of the Temple of E'temenanki.

They said when the Babylon was created, the Babylonian great gods had decreed the fate of men and the fate of Babylon… the temple priests said it was an act that had to be repeated every year at the beginning of the New Year to ensure the continuation of the favor of the Babylonian great gods upon Babylon… and upon the King…

Then, he had gone to Borsippa to accompany the statue of Nabu, the son of Lord Marduk, back to Babylon.

And then, he was initiated in the inner golden sanctuary of Lord Marduk by the temple priests… he had been stripped naked and they had inspected his body to make sure he was as clean as the statue of the Lord Marduk.

It was fortunate that no one but the King could enter the inner sanctuary in the E'sagila Temple of Lord Marduk… no one saw him get slapped painfully by the Priests of Lord Marduk before being crowned on behalf on the Kings for the New Year. The temple priests had not slapped him more than once to fill him with tears and humility before their gods… no doubt fearing for their own lives when they had seen the angry murderous look in his eyes. He had taken an oath that he had not sinned against Babylon and that he was planning to protect Babylon for the new year. The temple priests had resigned themselves to singing longer sacred hymns to pain and purify him… and then they had clothed and crowned him on behalf of the Kings.

"Do not fear!
Worship gods every day… Lord Marduk listens to the words of warriors…
He will destroy your enemies… He will bless you forever…
…you will get your reward…
Great gods will not let you fall, until they do…"

Afterward, everyone in Babylon saw him follow the statues of Lord Marduk and his son Nabu and other gods down the Processional Way, then taken in great ceremony to the Akitu House in golden chariots outside of the city walls in a great garden on the other side of Babylon, as all kings had done since time immemorial.

Babylonians had all knelt to the ground in adoration as he and the gods had gone by. Babylon was filled with music and singing and dancing… everyone heavy with wine and song, singing:

"The great gods are satisfied… the kings are happy… the palace is merry…"

They were still celebrating the New Year down below throughout the temple grounds and all throughout the Royal City of Babylon… singing…

"Celebrate day and night… eat and drink… dance and play… make love…"

It was a small price to pay to ensure Babylon remained loyal to him for another year, while he reined in the bloody LowLanders and HighLanders.

A golden warm breeze fills the golden sanctuary and flickers the golden candles.

The room glitters; almost everything in the inner sanctuary is made of gold. Even the shimmery netting around the bed is made of pure gossamer gold.

Rošanak sighs quietly in her sleep and tosses and turns in the massive golden bed.

Perdikkas drinks more honey-sweet beer and listens to the sweet sound of harps coming from the temple grounds below and smiles to himself.

They said… to ensure the fertility of the lands, the Babylonian Kings took Astarte, the High Priestess of Ishtar, to bed for a sacred marriage rite between the gods and the kings at the end of the New Year Festival of Akitu.

The Kings were a fool and an infant, so after he had returned to the city after taking the Babylonian gods to the Akitu House, the temple priests were ready to marry him ritually to the most beautiful woman in Babylon on behalf of the Kings…

The Queen would not have taken kindly to him bedding a high priestess after bedding her. So he had told the temple priests that he would only bed the Queen and they had relented and ordained the Persian Queen the High Priestess of Ishtar in an elaborate temple ritual…
Even the temple priests knew that the Persian Queen was the most beautiful woman in all of Babylon.
And the Queen had agreed to it, after the temple priests had told her that the Goddess Ishtar, goddess of men and divinity of women, was the protector of the kings and the wife of Nanna, the Babylonian Moon-God.
He had spent an entire afternoon earlier that day on top of the Temple Tower, in the most sacred golden sanctuary of Lord Marduk himself, sacrificing to the Babylonian gods by bedding the Queen… the sacred union of a man and a heavenly goddess…
According to the faith of Babylonians, they were now ritually married.
She had read to him from a parchment translated from an ancient clay tablet as the High Priestess of Ishtar and his bride:

> *"My King, put your earrings on me.*
> *Let me give you pleasure in my garden.*
> *Let me make you happy.*
> *Come here and embrace me.*
> *Sustain yourself with my body.*
> *Spend your desire on me.*
> *The king who is loved by the goddess forgets his fear and sorrow."*

And afterward the fertility of the Lands was abundantly secured for the coming New Year… through the love of a mortal for a goddess… and the love of a goddess for a king.

He looks at her and thinks for a moment longer and then leans forward and writes slowly and deliberately with golden ink on golden parchment:

> Perdikkas, Regent to King Alexander Aigeos,
> Guardian to Third Philip Arrhidaios,
> Regent of the Kingdom, Guardian of the Monarchy,
> to Krateros, Greeting.
> If you want her, come and get her. Farewell.

He leans back in his golden chair and reads the note again to himself.
Everything he wanted to say to Krateros was contained in those few words.
And that was all that needed to be said… no more and no less…
And they both knew well what that meant…
It was not just about kingship… it was about her…

Trojan wars would not have happened if Helene had not been so beautiful... if she was not beautiful, Paris would not have abducted her in the first place.

Men never fought bloody wars over homely women...

And those who said Alexander never loved her... married her just to subdue the Baktrians... did not know Alexander nor her. It was the thought of seeing her again that had kept them alive through the wretchedness of the Desert of Emptiness. He had heard Hephæstion call her name in his restless starving sleep. Alexander had a small likeness of her painted by Apelles on a small stone amulet and encircled it with an inscription with his name and an ancient Persian spell to bring him health and glory, and had tied it to his arm... to guide him back to her.

He had thought marrying Kleopatra would make him a king... but he had been foolish. He was already a king... he possessed the Queen of Alexander...

What idiot would leave the bed of a wondrous beauty like her for that of a woman who looked like Philip without a beard?

All Kleopatra could offer him was Makedonia... for the men of Alexander who had seen the world, Makedonia looked small and far away from the heart and the pulse and the blood of the true Empire...

He leans forward and puts the note on the golden table and drinks more honey-sweet beer.

Alexander himself did not want Makedonia or a Makedonian wife, why should he?

Like Alexander, Asia was enough for him too.

Krateros could have Makedonia... or float face down in the middle of the Bitter Seas for all he cared!

True HighLander! Right!

Well, Krateros, the most HighLander of all, started to wear the Persian Purple right after Alexander had died. He never wore anything Persian when Alexander was still alive... now all he wore was Persian, all but the Royal Crown...

Still planted in Kilikia like a damn tree, root and branch, Krateros had been wearing a Persian Royal Robe he had looted from Persepolis and had been preparing an army. The old worn out Makedonians Alexander had sent with Krateros to go home and retire were still some of the best trained warriors in the Royal Army... most had been trained by Philip himself... and they were all now loyal to Krateros.

It would be an unforgivable mistake to underestimate Krateros... he was one of the best... he would not engage in battle until he was ready for conquest. No Makedonian would think seriously about facing Krateros in battle... his Royal Army of Makedonians was useless against Krateros... they would all drop their arms and armor at the sight of his bloody helmet.

He gazes at Rošanak sleeping in the golden bed and then smiles to himself and nods and pours himself more honey-sweet beer. Sounds of drums and harps and lutes dance in the golden air around the golden room.

But like any man, Krateros could be tortured and bent with jealousy… the Rack of Jealousy was a lot more painful than the Makedonian Rack and he meant to strap Krateros to that rack with his words and pull him apart piece by piece!
He would tell his man who was to deliver his message to Krateros to mention that he was bedding Roxana.
That she was now freely his ritual bride… according to the customs of the Babylonians.
As for Kleopatra… he would make Kleopatra the governor of Sardeis… that should keep her busy. He would send Eumenes to her with his message… the clever Kardian knew how to talk that woman into anything… he knew her well from the days when he was Philip's Secretary. She could marry someone else and give them the lands of Makedonia.

He finishes the rest of his honey-sweet beer and puts down his golden goblet. He seals the note with Alexander's royal signet ring, blows out the golden table lamp, pushes himself up from the golden chair and heads for the golden bed.

He crawls into the bed next to the golden Persian High Priestess of Ištar and pulls the sheer shimmery golden netting around them.

The world disappears in a thick cloud of thin gold.

A dragonfly flies into the sanctuary and then flies out again.

He reaches and runs his fingers gently on her naked back a few times. Her body is covered with golden purplish traces of his passion and pleasure. He bends and kisses her love marks, her delicate skin so easily bruised.

A Royal Court Scribe had translated some Babylonian love words into Attik for him for his wedding night. His fingers write the love words on the body of his Akitu bride.

"Rise…
Be my life…
Bless me and let me bless you…
You are my beloved wife…
Let me hear the blissful beating of your heart…
… and let me make love to you…
… in your delicious lap made for loving…
My love will pour out of you…
Your love is sweet…"

Rošanak wakes up and rolls back toward him and looks at him for a moment and then wraps her golden legs around him.

He leans forward and stretches over her soft scented body.

The old body of the worldly king joins with the golden body of the heavenly goddess.

GARDEN PALACE of QUEEN AMYTIŠ
QUEEN'S BEDCHAMBER
DAYS PASS
NIGHT

Whisper of the spring winds.

Murmur of water flowing in and around the Persian gardens.

Perdikkas quietly pushes a small ornate silver box across the carved table, without a word.

Rošanak narrows her eyes at him and then picks up the small box and opens the top. Her old emerald love earrings glint in the flicker of the candles.

Her heart skips a beat.

The emerald earrings she had given to the old Chaldæan…

She looks up at him wordlessly, searching.

Was he testing her?

He looks at her intently and then finally relents.

"I thought it might be something you would like."

Rošanak looks at her old earrings and then looks back at him and relaxes.

He was just trying to put his earrings on her.

Blind fool!

He must have seen her wear those so many times… Alexander had given them to her in Takšiçila… Men had no eyes for such womanly things.

"A palace eunuch told me an old Chaldæan was selling these… he said they belonged to Queen Semiramis!"

Rošanak looks down at her old earrings.

Queen Semiramis… ha! These were pure Persian, made for a Royal Woman of a Great King!

Perdikkas looks at her for a sign, anything, feeling like a fool.

He had wasted too many feelings on matters of too little importance.

He had sent an old ring he had found lying around in his room to Kleopatra and Eumenes said she was still wearing it around her neck like a gift from the gods.

He would strangle that old eunuch who had persuaded him to spend a small fortune and buy the earrings, saying, "Well, of course Your Lordship must put your earrings on the Queen. How else would the royal court know who is the most beloved of the King?"

"I paid a king's ransom for it!" he says calmly, but his fingers tapping nervously on the ornate table betray him.

And an extra golden darik for an ancient charm to bring good fortune to the one who would wear them!

Rošanak finally smiles and slowly takes off her cornered golden earrings and dons the old emerald forest ones.

The face of Alexander showering her neck with his warm kisses the first time she had put on these earrings passes slowly before her eyes.

Her favorite earrings!

If these earrings could talk… love kisses they had seen… love words they had heard…
She had worn them that night in Hagmâtâna when Alexander had passionately gotten her with her Son-King…
The last time she had seen her beloved love earrings, a black scorpion was trying to make love to them on top of a broken fragment from Pârsâ.
The old Chaldæan knew what these earrings meant to her. He wanted them to find their way back to her ears, so they could sing old love songs into her ears whenever she missed Alexander. That was why he had brought them back to the palace… instead of selling them to one of the Banking Houses of Bâb-ilim.
Even though Alexander was cursed, he was also loved by his Queen and the mother of his Son-King… he was in her blood… his sweet wordless kisses were written on the skin of her heart.

Perdikkas finally relaxes and smiles and leans back in his chair.

"They say— that Alexander put your hand in mine and gave you to me as a bride on his death bed," he says quietly, testing the waters carefully, searching for the gap in the enemy line.

"They do? And where was I when this happened?" Rošanak says wickedly, playing with her emerald earrings.

"Will you marry me, if I asked you?"

"When you ask me, I will think about it!"

"Will you marry me?"

"No!"

"You said you would think about it!"

"I did!" she says with a smile.

"Why not?" he grunts.

"Why should a Queen marry a Regent?" she taunts him.

Perdikkas leans back in his chair and thinks for a moment or two.

Krateros was a regent too… was she thinking about him?
He, like everyone else, had heard the rumors after Karmania. Everyone had whispered and winked and smiled… but no one really knew. It was a mysterious scandal shrouded in secrecy… damn Krateros himself had never even opened that big mouth of his and spilled the secret tale.
If there had been nothing to the rumors, would Alexander have sent Krateros away from the royal court?
Whatever it was, Hephæstion somehow knew and the knowing had driven him to the edges of drunken madness in Ecbatana…
Her own voice always changed whenever she mentioned his name.

He straightens and thinks better of it.

What was the use of knowing? It would change nothing!
She was his bride by the Babylonian customs.
And her taste was still sweet in his mouth.
That was enough for him.

Another one of the Royal Court Scribes, who used to translate Hellene documents for the Great Kings, had started to translate some Babylonian poetry into Attik for the man who spoke for the Kings.

He remembers what a Babylonian warrior-poet had written once long ago.

As a Commander,
advance against my army,
and I shall withdraw to the bedroom…
As a Warrior,
march against my line,
and I shall retreat to bed… to our bed…

He eyes her for a moment longer.

She was wearing his earrings…

She knew what that meant…

He gets to his feet and walks over to her, pulls her out of her chair and lifts her up in his arms and carries her to her bed.

REGENT'S TENT. ROYAL ARMY CAMP. SATRAPY of KISSUWADNA
YEAR 3 of the THIRD PHILIP, MONTH 8, DAISIOS
YEAR 4 of PI-LIP-SU, MONTH 2, AYYÂRU
YEAR 3 of the FOURTH ALEXANDER, MONTH 2, AYYÂRU
2 YEARS LATER
MID-DAY

"Cursed Ptolemaios has stolen the body of Alexander!" Perdikkas grinds his teeth angrily.

"How can anyone steal the body of Alexander? His golden casket was heavier than an Indian war elephant. His funeral carriage was followed and protected by his royal guards… it was pulled by sixty-four slow mules," Rošanak says, stunned.

Perdikkas bites his lip.

He should have known!

He should have burned Alexander's body on a royal pyre right after his death and put his ashes and bones in a golden box and bury it.

Who would have thought Ptolemaios was capable of such a deed? He was not a great warrior, but he was generous with spending stolen gold…

"The men I had sent to bring back the body have failed! Ptolemaios was waiting with all his men for the funeral procession. They told the royal guards that Alexander had ordered Ptolemaios on his deathbed to take his royal body to Two Lands and bury it close to the Oracle at Siwah. He opened up the royal funds of the Two Lands and bought Arrhidæus and the royal guards with gold and gifts and promises. I will hang those bloody traitors when I get my hands on them!"

Silence.

"Alexander never said anything to anyone about being buried in the shifting sands in the middle of nowhere! He would have wanted a monument like the one he had ordered for Hephæstion for himself."

Silence.

"If I had gotten my hands on the damn One-eyed Antigonos before he had run away to the old Antipatros in Pella to spread lies about me, I would have hanged the traitor with no mercy with my own bare hands too!"

Silence.

"I am taking the Royal Army to reclaim the body of Alexander."

Rošanak looks away.

"We will leave for the Two Lands tomorrow and we will find supplies along the way. I know the region. We were there with Alexander when the Two Lands surrendered."

"Tomorrow?"

"Yes. Tomorrow. And I am taking both Kings with me."

"Both Kings?" Rošanak narrows her eyes at Perdikkas. "Perdikkas, what use is a three year old boy on an armed campaign?"

"Makedonians will be persuaded to fight other Makedonians, only if they have their Kings with them."

Rošanak takes a deep breath, feeling anxious, sounding disappointed.

"Perdikkas, you promised me that we would return to Babylon after Eumenes was established as the Satrap of Kappadokia and Paphlogonia. Please let us return to Babylon and celebrate Akitu Festival. The Lord Marduk Priests have not given you their blessings for the New Year. Let your men go to the Two Lands to face Ptolemaios. Two Lands is drenched in evil… it is the realm of the Lord of Darkness."

"This is necessary!" Perdikkas grunts.

"Poor Alexander is teething and he is suffering! Following an army is not a life for a Royal Son. He needs to be raised like a king, at the Gate of the King, in a palace with royal tutors and wise men, not like a campaign child in a carriage dragged behind the Royal Army!"

"Still teething? Alexander is three years old! You think I know nothing about my son!" Perdikkas yells at her, pointing around as if the Boy-King was playing in the room. "How is he supposed to lead an army, if he grows up in a palace with a horde of eunuchs?"

Rošanak gives him a sharp look, annoyed.

He was as ignorant as Alexander about Persian customs. But there was no use arguing with him. He would just order her Son-King brought to him so he could count all his teeth for himself.

"You promised me! That was two years ago! We left Babylon just to establish Eumenes in Kappadokia, then to punish Antigonos in Phrygia, and we have been on the road since! I do not even know where we are anymore! Armina, Kappadokia… Pisidia… Larada or Isaura… Kilikia… nor do I care!"

She knew!

Perdikkas and the Royal Army had been spilling blood ever since they left Babylon, all in the name of her Son-King!

Perdikkas had defeated Âriyârta, the Satrap of Katpatuka, in battle and for all his troubles he had suffered a serious sword wound, while Âriyârta and all his court and kinsmen who had never submitted to Alexander had returned home and killed all their wives and children and set their city and themselves on fire, leaving behind nothing but ashes for the conquerors.

And since then they had been trekking in the old Lands of the Younger Kuruš… following almost in his footsteps, when he had taken the Hellene mercenaries to fight his Royal Brother for the Persian Crown and Throne.

They were not that far from Issos where her blood brothers had died on the fields of battle… it pained her to be in that part of the Lands.

Stench of rotting death hung in the air… like the bitter smell of rotten fruit…

Perdikkas narrows his eyes at her and grunts through his teeth.

"Only cowards and jackals and pigs send their men to their death without going with them!"

"Please!" Rošanak softens her voice and pleads.

"You do not understand!" Perdikkas sneers at her.

Rošanak yells back. "What do I not understand? Tell me! I want to know!"

Perdikkas softens his voice.

"Roxana, a king must lead his men to battle himself. If Darius had been at Granikos, things might have been different for Alexander and the Persians. Only the Great King could have stopped Alexander at Granikos. He was the only one who could have understood what the prize of war was. Alexander had nothing and had everything to gain and did, and Darius had everything and had everything to lose and did! Instead of relying on his own two eyes, he relied on the flattering words of the idiot kingsmen and nobles around him." He speaks in a quiet voice, reflecting on his own mistakes.

Rošanak looks at him with eyes widened.

"Perdikkas!"

Perdikkas straightens.

"When his men lost at Granikos, Darius was merciful to his commanders who had survived the battle. He should have hanged and quartered them all! Then the rest of his men would have known that he would have done the same to them if they too lost the next battle. That is what Alexander threatened he would do at Granikos, if we lost to the Persians."

Rošanak shakes her head with dismay. "That was different!"

"It is all the same! Men need commanders who suffer their pain... all of it... Commanders need men who obey their orders no matter what."

Perdikkas tries to persuade her. His voice softens and mellows.

"Roxana, I am the Commander of the Royal Army. My men look to me to lead them in battle. How could my men respect me and obey my orders, if I do not lead them to take back the body of their dead king?"

Silence.

"How do you think I brought the entire Royal Army under my command?"

Silence.

"After I purified the Royal Army according to our ancient rites, I walked unarmed and unguarded to the middle of the filed, marked by the blood of a hound on four corners, and demanded the Foot to give up the men who had started the bloody fight between the Horse and the Foot. And they all obeyed me without any hesitation and handed over all the men responsible, knowing well what would happen to such men."

Perdikkas pauses and takes a deep breath, remembering the bloody execution.

"They saw with their own eyes that I was not afraid of anything, that they could rely on me to lead them into battle with the same boldness. Those men would abandon me if I do not fight Ptolemaios for the body of their Alexander."

Rošanak shakes her head and tries again.

"Let Ptolemaios have the body! What good is a dead body to anyone? It is just an empty vessel. It is the soul that matters… and only gods are deserving of worship and sacrifice. Let the damn Two Landers bend their knees and pour libations and worship what is mortally left of Alexander. It is no worse than that white Apis Bull they worship in the Two Lands! Two Landers are worshippers of cows and lies!"

Perdikkas shakes his head angrily and yells at Rošanak.

"When I die, what will you do with my bones? Are you going to shrug your shoulders and throw my body to wild dogs and say, *who cares, it is just an empty vessel?*"

"Perdikkas!" Rošanak yells back.

Perdikkas takes a deep breath and steadies himself. "We are Makedonians! The new king entombs the dead king."

Rošanak raises her voice. "You are ruling Asia. No one in Asia cares anything about your Makedonian ways!"

"The Makedonians care."

"Then let those who care go after Ptolemaios."

Perdikkas takes a deep breath. "I care! I have given Olympias my word that I will return Alexander to her!"

Rošanak demands angrily. "What about your words to me?" She eyes him, hurting, pushing back tears. "Am I less than Olympias in your eyes? Just a Barbarian to bed who is not worth keeping your words to?"

Perdikkas looks away grimly.

His heart hurt… his head hurt more…

He heard her pain… he read her face… but he could not help himself.

He had to forcibly drag her from Ecbatana to Babylon by the order of Alexander, when she was heavy with child. She had locked herself in the old bedchamber of Hephæstion. He had to order the royal guards to break down her doors and he had to grab her himself and throw her over on his shoulders and carry her down to her carriage, as no one in the royal palace dared to touch the royal body of the Queen. She had thrown anything she could grab at him and had kicked him and had pounded on his back with her angry fists and had screamed and yelled and cursed in his ears in several tongues.

But she had taken to Babylon after she had returned to the land of the living and the Boy-King was born to her.

She had come to like the palace life… her little Garden Palace hidden in the cool Persian gardens, shielded from the stench of life and the intense heat of Babylon.

And she had come to like the life in the big city and Babylon was the biggest city she had ever been to… she liked the bakeries and the confectioneries and the markets and the shops and the taverns and the temples and all the madness.

And Babylon was maddening, brimming and boiling and simmering with multitudes from all the Lands of the Empire.

He was not just passing through, he was the Regent for the Empire.
He was responsible for everything and everything was a lot to be responsible for… from all the banking houses to all the houses of delight.
He was not tempted by the Priestesses of Ishtar any longer… he had spent plenty of time in their pleasurable laps and had learned many love secrets the first time they had come to Babylon and stayed for a month… when they were all glorious conquerors… young and tireless and full of desire for everything new… rich with gold and glory beyond their wildest dreams…
Hope had been rewarded by heaps of gold and wine and women…
But he was not needed in Babylon. Royal Administrators governed everything, as they had since the times when the Persians were the masters of Asia… nothing in Babylon had changed much except for the king. And in Babylon, the king was always in need of divine forgiveness, through the benevolent hands of the bloody Babylonian temple priests.
He looks back at her tenderly.
She was more beautiful now than the first time he had bedded her… life had been ripe with sweetness with her… the first time in his life that he had a family of his own…
a wife and a child to care for… and an Empire to run…
Just as that tavern-keeper had told King Gilgamesh:

> *"Love the child who holds your hand… let your wife enjoy herself in your lap… sleep in peace beside your wife…"*

And he had taken better care of her, since she had become his… but he hated the palace life… sitting around on a silver couch with silver feet all day long and answering petitions and sending instructions…
He hated honoring the golden statues of strange gods and hated even more kneeling down naked in front of the native temple priests and getting slapped during the Babylonian New Year Festival.
Why could he not just pour some libations and throw some incense in the fire altars and sacrifice some cows?
He had agreed to it at first, thinking it was similar to the Persian New Year… eating loads of Persian sweets and receiving sweet Persian kisses from the Persian Queen all over his body. He had done it in the first year, because he had just started bedding her and he wanted to act like a King who was worthy of bedding a Queen and a Goddess.
It did not matter that the entire ritual took place in the golden sanctuary inside the belly of Temple Tower under the crown of the house of gods which was made of pure gold… and no one was permitted inside during the Ritual of Akitu, except the golden gods and the old temple priests and the naked kneeling bleeding king…
He was tempted to slash the throat of the temple priest who had slapped his face… that was why kings were stripped of their arms and armor before they entered the golden temple… to spare the lives of the idiot temple priests at the hands of the furious kings!
He knew and that was enough!
How could the Great Kings have tolerated such a humiliating ritual?

Alexander was never slapped in the face to be called a king! He would have put all the Babylonian temple priests to the sword first and then impaled their bloody bodies as a warning to others!

He grinds his teeth.

She had obediently followed Alexander from Baktria to Babylon… why could she not follow him the same way from the Lands between the Twin Rivers to the Two Lands?

Why could she not just accept his nature?

He was born to the sword.

Achilleos and the Myrmidons were calling him home… unto the battlefields… for more glorious deeds.

Rošanak hesitates for a long moment.

They said if the dead were not buried properly, they would torment the living.

But the wellbeing of the living Son-King came before the burial of the dead King-Father.

"Let Olympias demand his body from Ptolemaios. Let Ptolemaios be the one who denies her the bones of her dead son!" Rošanak pleads.

"You do not understand!"

Rošanak narrows her eyes at him.

She understood!

The dazzling gleaming glinting Crown and Throne of the Great Kings had beckoned and seduced and used Perdikkas, just as easily as she had beckoned and seduced and used Alexander… and all the rest… the seductress of kings was not the kind of hainâ who could be easily defeated by a roll of the dice.

Rošanak takes Perdikkas' hand and pleads again quietly.

"Please Perdikkas… this place haunts me… let us go back to Babylon! Do not think well of the Two Lands… it is a bloody grave for the Persians… the evil of Two Lands is well-matched with the evil of Ptolemaios. Leave them both to your gods and walk away!"

Perdikkas shakes his head side to side and steals his eyes away from her wordlessly.

"Please listen to me! There is no dishonor in returning to Babylon to honor the gods and receive their blessing for the New Year."

Silence.

She finally gives up. She lets go of his hand and gets up to her feet and storms out, yelling at him angrily. "You are right! I do not understand! I do not want to understand your barbaric ways!"

"Roxana!"

"Go wrestle in the precious Makedonian sand you carry around with you!"

Angry words fly into the wind.

Wind blowing…

"Roxana!"

Gone with the blowing wind…

"ROXANA!"

QUEEN'S TENT. ARMY FOLLOWERS CAMP. NEAR PORT of SAND. TWO LANDS
YEAR 4, FIRST MONTH of SHOMU, under the MAJESTY of the THIRD PHILIP
YEAR 3, FIRST MONTH of SHOMU, under the MAJESTY of the FOURTH ALEXANDER
DAWN

Tap! Tap! Tap!

Rošanak opens her eyes.

Baby Alexander is standing by her bed, slapping her gently on the face with his small hand.

"Âmma."

She smiles at him sweetly. "Alexander, what is it? Are you hungry?"

The Boy-King smiles brightly and waves a wooden toy lion in the air.

"Purkas!"

Rošanak reaches and taps the wooden toy lion on the head.

"Yes, Perdikkas gave this to you."

"Âmma! Get up! Come play with me!" Baby Alexander babbles sweetly.

Rošanak looks around. A small lamp burns low on a small table near her bed. There are no rays of sun filtering through the cracks of the tent. Alexander's nursemaid is hovering nearby. Rošanak dismisses her by a wave of her hand and runs her fingers around Baby Alexander's face gently and plays with the dark locks of his unruly hair.

"It is too early, Alexander. Sun is still sleeping!" She taps softly on the bed. "Come and lay down here next to me and I will tell you a story. We play with Purkas later."

Baby Alexander starts climbing into her bed holding his wooden toy lion firmly in his hands.

Rošanak pulls him up gently and rests his head next to hers on the soft pillow.

"Grrrrrrr!"

Rošanak laughs softly.

"I think the lions roar, like this: RRROOOAAARRR!"

"Rrrrrrrr!"

Baby Alexander imitates her and laughs happily and waves his wooden toy lion over his head.

Rošanak pulls him away from the edge of the bed and braces him securely within her arms.

"How about the story of *The Brahman and the Heavenly Wisdom*?"

"No!" Baby Alexander shakes his head side to side.

Rošanak looks at the wooden toy lion and points.

"Then, how about the story of *The King of Cats and the Battle of Mice*?"

"Šarru Purkas!" Baby Alexander nods his head eagerly, waving his wooden toy lion.

Rošanak nods and starts the story:

"O Great King, I heard once there was a cat who lived in the City of Karmâna, when the city was ruled by your great father, Alexander, the Lord of Asia. He was known as the King of Cats by all the cats who lived in the city. He looked like a golden lion… hmmm… let me see… just like this one!" She points to the wooden toy lion.

Baby Alexander laughs and shakes the toy lion in the air.

"Yes! He had sharp teeth and long whiskers and a pink tongue and a big belly the size of a big Persian drum." She playfully taps on his belly with her fingers. "And bellowed like this, MEOW!"

"Meeoww!" Baby Alexander imitates her and laughs.

"On sunny days, he walked around the city proudly with his chest like a shield and his tail like a standard waving in the air behind him. On rainy days, he slept. He fiercely fought with all the other cats to show them he was the king of them all. On starry nights, he slept. On starless nights, he hunted and caught and ate mice!

"Like this!"

She grabs Baby Alexander and tickles him and he laughs heartily.

"One long hot summer day, the King of Cats pushed through the cellar door and went down into the cool dark wine cellar and slept behind the big wine barrels.

"A young mouse came out of his hole and did not see the sleeping King of Cats and jumped on a wine barrel and started dancing and singing: *O where is that fat old ugly cat, who calls himself the King of Cats? Is he hiding because he is scared of me? I would cut off his head and gut his fat belly and stuff his old skin with straw!*

"The young mouse sang louder and louder and danced faster and faster. The King of Cats woke up from all the noise and listened patiently with his eyes closed. Then the young mouse got careless and fell off the big wine barrel and right into the sharp claws of the King of Cats!"

She starts whispering and gazes at him tenderly, as he slowly gets heavy and falls into sleep, still holding on to his wooden toy lion with his small fingers.

"The King of Cats roared like a lion: *Cut off my head and stuff my skin with straw, ha?* The young mouse trembled and cried and begged: *O King of Cats, forgive me! I was drunk! I am the humblest of all your humble servants!* The King of Cats roared again: *You are a liar too!* And he ate the mouse!"

She takes a deep breath and covers him with cool linen and kisses the top of his small head.

"and that is how the story started—"

He had never stayed awake long enough to hear the whole story.

Her mind drifts. She looks at the wooden toy lion.

Perdikkas had given him the toy before they left for Mudrâya and Alexander loved Perdikkas like a father.

If it hadn't been for Perdikkas, she was not sure what would have become of them.

Baby Alexander snores.

She leans over and kisses his head again and lays awake watching him sleep.

She could not imagine her life without him. Her every breath was knotted with love for him!

She thinks of her blood mother. In happiness and in sadness, she always used to tell her, *"Wait until you have children of your own!"*

And now after all these years, she finally had a child of her own and she finally understood.

Children were both a blessing and a curse, Heaven and Hell, knotted together, like two faces of the same golden archer!

Rošanak takes a deep breath and lets it out wistfully and the wooden toy lion catches her eyes again and the face of Perdikkas emerges from it.

Once Perdikkas had claimed her, he had almost forgotten all about Kleopatra. And Kleopatra had ended up confined to the Palace at Sparda, becoming in name the governor of Sparda, under the protection of the One-eyed Antigonos.

Old Antipatros had taken the return of his daughter as the refusal of the alliance and had aligned himself with Krateros and Ptolemaios who had both accepted his gifted daughters… and now they were all fighting fiercely among themselves for the Lands of the Persians… and the Lands Beyond the Sea… none accepted another head raised above their head.

Krateros… they say his wife had borne him a son… named after him…

Did men love sons begotten by women they did not love or want? Was this the way of the HighLanders?

Rošanak closes her eyes and breathes in deeply.

She had a small silver box full of Krateros' letters, since he had been sent off from Hûvaja by Alexander.

How he had begged her to wait for him… how he had pleaded with her… that his wounds had finally healed and his body had finally mended in Kilikia, that he was now whole again and finally worthy of her.

"Why do you not write me a letter with your own hands?
Why do you not send me a message from your lips?
Why do you not forgive me in your heart?"

He had promised her all of the Empire… and a wedding bigger than the one at the Royal City of Çûšâ!

He had honorably divorced Amastris, the daughter of Hukhšaqra, the Royal Brother of the Third Dâriuš. He had even found her a new husband… one she had chosen for herself… Dionysios, the tyrant of Herakleia Pontika, the man she had met many years ago in the court of the Third Dâriuš. He had sworn to Zeus and Apollo that he had never even touched her. He had been ordered by Alexander to wed her and take her with him.

His men were treating him like a king.

They said he was dressing just like Alexander, without a Persian Purple, wearing a royal purple robe and receiving everyone sitting on a silver couch.

With his loot of the Persian gold, Krateros had commissioned the old Lysippos to build massive bronze statues of the first glorious royal lion hunt in Sidon where he had saved the life of Alexander… and to display them close to the Oracle of Apollo at Delphi.

She smiles to herself.

Alexander would have liked that…

Then she bites her lip.

Well, what did it matter any more?

Perdikkas had truly surprised her. Unromantic by nature, he had become her most enduring lover. She did not know what to expect of him at first. His men feared him and for good reason. He was shrewd and tough and unforgiving… the kind of a kingsman and a commander who could survive around Alexander, who did not tolerate imperfection in his kingsmen or himself. But away from the harsh and relentless world that was closing in on Perdikkas from every direction, within the walls of her bedroom, he had been gentle and loving, almost tender.

He had no use for Persians or poetry or words, sweet or bitter… he just wanted her… and nothing kept him from her bed, not even the cycle of the moon, obeyed by her body faithfully… when her body was forbidden, not to be touched by a man.

When in Bâb-ilim, he would come to her bed late at night when he was finally caught up with the Empire's never-ending affairs and would leave early at dawn to review and drill the Royal Army. And sometimes he would come to her unannounced and unexpectedly, when the heat of the Bâb-ilim sun got unbearable, and bathe and bed her in the cool water basin in the middle of her Persian gardens, shaded by fragrant fruiting trees. After bedding her, he liked to sleep on top of her, covering her body like a heavy comfortable blanket on cold winter nights, even in the intense heat of Bâb-ilim… he liked to sleep to the sound of her beating heart.

He was not discreet… all the royal boys knew and all the palace in Bâb-ilim. She was a widow, and he did not command attention like Alexander nor was he handsome like Hephæstion, nor was he a king with jealous lovers, or wives, or mistresses… so no one talked… or cared much.

He had added the Lands that were needed to securely bridge the Lands of the Persians to the Lands of the Bitter Sea… and she had followed him along the Royal Road when he had gone to settle Eumenes in Katpatuka and then down to Pisidia and then to Kissuwadna… and she had come with him all the way to Mudrâya to reclaim the body of Alexander.

Rošanak opens her eyes.

The sun is beginning to rise and the tent is getting lighter.

Perdikkas had taken the Royal Army along with Arrhidaios downstream days ago, leaving everyone else behind in the base camp between the City of Ammon near the Port of Sand, at the mouth of the Great River Pirâva and the Fort of Camels downstream.

Her mind drifts.

She shudders to herself thinking about the barbaric wife of Arrhidaios who was sleeping in a tent not too far from hers. The eyes of that girl burned bright red like her hair, night and day, with undiminishing hatred for her and her son, completely and wholly possessed by the demons of the Lord of Darkness.

Poor Arrhidaios! Alexander had not seen fit to give him a Persian wife in the Royal City of Çûšâ... only his kingsmen were given the gift of Persian noble women. She remembered Alexander saying he was not even sure Arrhidaios knew what to do with a woman! Maybe the sweet lap of a good woman would cure whatever it was that ailed poor Arrhidaios.

But what was Alexander thinking when he had decided to have Arrhidaios marry this manly evil creature? Surely he did not hate his poor half-brother that much? The girl did not even bathe or scent herself... she smelled and her body was covered with unseemly hair... if she knew how to draw a bow, she could have cut off her right breast and joined the Amazons! But the manly girl had no breasts to cut off! That was probably why she was so mean and manly! They said her mother was an Illyrian warrior who had trained her like a warrior. A woman warrior did not need to be manly. The wretched girl was a creature that belonged neither to the Assembly of Men nor to the Kingdom of Women.

She curses the wretched creature under her breath.

The Illyrian Amazon Bitch desired to rule over Lands that she had not shed any of her own blood to conquer. She just wanted the Lands of Alexander's Son-King, won by the blood and spear of his Kingly-Father, to be gifted to her on a silver platter.

Not as long as Perdikkas watched over the inheritance of her Son-King with an iron fist!

Her thoughts quickly return to Perdikkas.

Perdikkas was a light sleeper...

Unlike Alexander who slept dead to the world before battle, Perdikkas paced back and forth, tossed and turned restlessly, not out of fear, just anticipation... eager to measure up to Alexander's golden fame... and his golden glory.

She quietly gets out of bed and pulls a light cover over her son.

She missed Perdikkas.

They had exchanged harsh words when he had decided to go to war over the stolen body of Alexander. She had denied him the pleasure of her bed to force some sense back into his thick head and he had utterly ignored her.

She had sent him Alexander so he would find his way back to her, and he had ordered Aristonous to return the Boy-King, to avoid seeing her altogether.

She had sent him words that she was not feeling well, so that he would come and see to her and sit by her bedside and hold her hand as he had in Babylon after the death of Alexander, and he had utterly ignored her...

And now she was heavy with guilt.

Fool!

Just like Hephæstion, he had wasted so many nights and days… so many moons and stars… being a stubborn willful fool to get his own way with her!

Although his eyes had always wanted her love, his lips had never asked for it. And she had never offered him any… and now he was heading into a battle with Ptolemaios.

And battles were not games of strategy, nor outflanking moves… they were cradles of death, seas of blood and bones of the dead and dying. They were graves of the brave warriors.

And she hated Ptolemaios… he was the man who had taken her father to Alexander in chains all cut and torn up and bloody. Older by ten years than Alexander, he was cunning and ruthless… what he lacked on the battlefield, he packed with treachery.

Rošanak pulls a royal robe around her carelessly and summons the nursemaid forward. "Watch him," she orders, pointing to Baby Alexander.

She then walks toward the antechamber of her tent.

Abi-Samar was either there or in front of her tent, as he had been when she had followed Alexander around.

She walks into the antechamber and calls softly, "Abi-Samar."

"Yes, My Lady." A comforting voice replies quietly and quickly in the dimly lit antechamber.

"Abi-Samar, when is the battle?"

"Tomorrow or the day after, My Lady."

"How far is the Royal Army camp from here?"

"They have camped close to the Fort of the Camels. No more than half a day's ride by a fast horse."

"Bring me a horse."

"My Lady?"

"I will not go far!"

"But, My Lady!"

"Please! Just do as I ask!" Rošanak says, pleading.

Abi-Samar resists. "Battle grounds are no place for a Queen."

"Please! I have to see him!"

"Then, I will go with you and protect you!"

"No! I want you to guard Alexander!" Rošanak says firmly.

"Very well. Then I will call the royal guards to take you."

"No! I will be faster without them."

"But, My Lady…"

"Please… I swear I will be careful," Rošanak says persuasively and then takes a deep breath. "If that Illyrian Amazon Bitch comes anywhere near Alexander, cut her to pieces with no mercy!"

"Yes, My Lady." Abi-Samar bows his head worriedly and leaves the tent quietly.

REGENT'S TENT. ROYAL ARMY CAMP. NEAR MEN-NOFER
BANKS of GREAT RIVER ITERU
LATER that DAY
SETTING SUN

Men nod in agreement and leave the Council of War in Perdikkas' tent.

Perdikkas sips his wine and looks again grudgingly at the crumpled parchment note in his hand. The envoy who had delivered the note earlier that evening had said it contained everything. It was a very short note. He puts down his wine cup and opens the note and reads it again.

Krateros to Perdikkas,
I am coming for her.

No titles of honor… no greeting… no farewell.

Just man to man… regent to regent… kingsmen of Alexander… equals in arms… childhood friends. Both HighLanders, Princes from the HighLands of Makedonia.

Two bitter enemies… going back to the days when Alexander had left them both in charge of the Royal Army in Tyre and had gone to Arabia with Hephæstion to attack the Arabians who had killed Makedonians and taken some Makedonian prisoners back to Arabia. He had wounded Krateros in his leg unintentionally, when his spear meant for a mongoose they were chasing to pass the time and relieve the boredom had hit Krateros instead. Krateros had accused him of trying to kill him and had never forgiven him. And everything had gotten worse between the two of them when he had gotten closer to Hephæstion.

There could be only one man left to possess the Queen and the whole of the Empire and wear the Persian Purple… and they both knew it well!

One head had to wear the Royal Persian Purple… and to a king no one was a kinsman… kingsman… or a friend!

Perdikkas holds the note over the flame of the candle and mumbles to himself, "She is mine!" The small parchment catches fire and quickly burns to a crisp.

He picks up another sealed letter and breaks the royal court seal and starts reading:

To the King and My Lord, from your servant, Bêl-rê'ušu, from Bâbilu:
In Month 4, Du'ûzu, 9 days passed, in Year 4 of Pi-lip-su:

Your Majesty gave me an order before you left Babylon: "Berossos, keep watch for me and tell me whatever the stars tell you."
Now I am writing to Your Majesty.

God of War has turned around and started moving. He is moving forward in Scorpion. That is an unfavorable omen. Your Majesty should not go out, until we see how the God of War moves and stands.
War is imminent if Scorpion remains dark.
The new moon stands low and has become visible at night. This is a favorable omen. A fine gift from a distance will come to Your Majesty and will make Your Majesty happy.
May there constantly be rain from the heavens during your reign.
May the great gods Marduk and Nabû and the gods Your Majesty invokes grant good health and happiness to Your Majesty for long days and many years.

"Hmmm… I am in the middle of a war and the fool wants me to stay in my tent!" Perdikkas grunts and holds the note over the flame of the candle. The small parchment catches fire and burns quickly. Burnt ashes fall over the ashes from Krateros' note.

He bites his lip.

Every bone in his body missed that heartless girl!

He wanted so much to get her with child… a son… a half-brother to the son of Alexander… he had tried for over two years… but her weak body had not taken to his strong seeds.

Phila had already borne Krateros a son.

He had baskets of pomegranates sent to Roxana wherever they were… he was prepared to reconquer any land in all the Persian Lands if they ever ran out of pomegranates! Bloody wars had been fought for a lot less!

If he had gotten her with his child, then Krateros would no longer have a claim to her… and she would not leave him for Krateros ever, if she had borne him a son.

If she was the mother of his child, she would not deny him the favor of her bed…

Damn girl!

He missed her bitterly… the sound of her soft accented voice… the sound of the beating of her accented heart.

He even missed seeing her tent right next to his.

The last months had been so lonely, after she had thrown him out of her bed and his stupid pride had gotten in his way and had not let him waver and go back to her and make her his again. She had been angry with him before, but it never lasted more than a day or two before she would beckon him back to her tent and comfort him in her sweet lap…

Armed eunuchs had started guarding her tent after they had left for the Two Lands, saying she feared for her life from the bloodthirsty wife of Arrhidaios. Her head had started hurting day and night for no reason and she had caught every ailment known to man or woman, just to avoid seeing him.

But she had dutifully sent the Boy-King to his tent regularly, so he had no cause to visit her in her tent…

He would have looked like an idiot in front of his men, if he had tried to storm her tent in the middle of the night to bed his own wife!

He takes a deep breath.

He missed his Boy-King too! He had left a few royal guards to protect Alexander from Adeia… if the LowLander Bitch was foolish enough to try to harm him in his absence, they had orders to arrest her immediately or to kill her with no mercy.

He had told the royal guards that he had counted all the hair on the small head of the Boy-King himself and if any hair was missing when he got back to the camp, he would put all of those responsible to the sword!

The Boy-King was no longer an unborn or a mute purple bundle with eyes… he babbled and stumbled and waddled.

The Assembly would not tolerate a mere woman plotting against the Son of Alexander! More than half of his men had Asian wives and their sons looked more or less like the Boy-King. They would stone Adeia to death themselves if she caused him any harm!

And if anything happened to the Boy-King, Roxana would be lost to him for good.

She would never forgive him. Alexander would never forgive him. He would never forgive himself.

He leans back in his chair.

Well, a son could begotten with Kleopatra when the time was ripe. As they all used to tell Alexander, marriage and begetting a son had nothing to do with desire and pleasure… and he had never listened either. Eumenes had taken her gifts when she had arrived at Sardeis and had kept her interested in him. He had visited her there himself, leaving Roxana at the army camp and her looks had not changed much… just older…

He looks at the candles on the table and his mind sifts through the burned ashes.

Damn Krateros… the note he had sent him was just a few words, but his letter to Roxana that he had intercepted a few months back, was pages long… he had quoted Euripides and Pindar to her.

… and like Aphrodite, with your silvery body,
you will welcome me when I return to you.
… over our bed, the love goddess would cast her spell…

“Hmmm…”

Who cared for all that romantic nonsense and who knew Krateros was capable of twisting and quoting the boy-loving Pindar to a woman?

He must have been writing to her long before one of his damn letters had fallen into his hands… and she had never mentioned anything to him.

What else had he written to her? While Phila was waddling with Krateros' child, he was writing love letters to his Roxana.

He had sent Eumenes to deal with Krateros, knowing full well that Eumenes was not a match for him. But Eumenes was a Kardian and dispensable. It was just a temporary measure, long enough to get rid of the conniving, deceitful, scheming Ptolemaios first.

He takes a deep breath and grinds his teeth together.

By Styx, he was going to hang Alketas, his idiot brother, for disobeying him again! Being his brother did not mean he could disobey his direct commands in front of the whole Royal Army! Alketas was the one who had talked him into agreeing to marry Nikaia… then Alketas had made a mess of things, when he was sent to see to that Illyrian Bitch, Kynnane and her daughter!

How difficult was it to kill two women, one of them no more than fifteen, for men who had conquered an Empire for Alexander?

And now Alketas had refused to join forces with Eumenes, claiming Makedonians would not fight the old Antipatros and Krateros with a Hellene lording over them, and had disappeared disobediently somewhere up on the other side of Kilikia in the mountains.

Makedonians will fight anyone for their pay!

He would see to Alketas himself. He would have his brother lashed first, and then hanged and impaled and his body thrown to the wild dogs!

He leans forward and blows at the ashes. The ashes scatter around the table. He picks up his wine cup and drinks it down. His thoughts return to Rošanak.

Roxana was wrong to be angry with him… this was something that had to be done… it was necessary. And he was the man who had to do it! It was his duty! He was the one who had succeeded Alexander!

After Ptolemaios had stolen Alexander's funeral carriage on its way back to the old capital of Aigai to be entombed, he had taken it to Memphis instead and had given it a Pharaoh's burial. They all knew Makedonian kings were entombed by their successors. Getting the body of Alexander back was worth sacrificing Eumenes…

When Alexander had died in Babylon, Olympias had written to him and had ordered him to return his body to her for royal burial. Roxana knew that. He had shown her the queen-mother's letter. He had promised Olympias that when the funeral carriage was ready, he would send Alexander's body back to her… it was a promise that he meant to keep.

By stealing and burying the body of Alexander, Ptolemaios had declared himself king to the Makedonians and had fearlessly challenged his rightful regency… it was not a war he could step away from.

Yes… he could visit Kleopatra in Sardeis again for a few moments when he was back up country to deal with Krateros. He would not even have to look at her… it would be just like any another matter that the King had to tend to himself… an instruction given by the King of the Dark-headed People in person…

Roxana would come back to him when Kleopatra was heavy with his child... and Krateros was dead. Where else could she go? He was the King and she was the Queen.

He pours more wine in his cup and takes a sip and bites his lip.

Damn girl!

When he had sought her and told her that she was his wife and could not refuse him, she had flung a pomegranate at his head!

When he had cut an olive loaf in half with his Persian dagger and had given her a half, she had thrown her half out of the tent for the birds... and when he had called her a barbarian, she had flown into a rage and had flung the other half of the olive loaf at his head and had cursed him in her mother tongue.

She said she wanted a marriage contract with witnesses and seals and a large wedding feast big enough for the entire city of Babylon... not that Akitu ritual nonsense!

Well... marrying her according to the Babylonian ritual had seemed like a good idea. Divorcing her for refusing him would have been a better idea! He should have complained to the Babylonian temple priests that the High Priestess of Ishtar was refusing to open her sweet lap to the advances of the King of the Dark-headed People to ensure the fertility of the lands! If the crops failed and there was to be famine in the Empire, it would all be completely Queen's fault for not yielding to the intimate embrace of the King!

"Hmmm..."

But he could not bring himself to be harsh with her... a disapproving look from the corner of her forested eyes melted all the metal in his arm and armor...

He takes another sip of his wine.

He had missed her so much that he had even thought of deliberately getting hurt in one of his wrestling matches, just so that she would come back to him and nurse him back to health, as she had done faithfully after his sword wound in Kappadokia.

"Sir, you have a visitor," the royal boy interrupts and announces formally, standing straight in front of Perdikkas.

Perdikkas looks up at the royal boy and growls at him with displeasure.

"I said no interruptions! That meant no visitors!"

He had not even heard the damn boy come in.

"Sir!"

"Why are you still here?"

"Sir, you might want to see this visitor— a Persian! He says you would be interested to hear what he has to say."

"Where are the guards?"

"Outside, Sir!"

Perdikkas narrows his eyes, considers the royal boy for a long moment, and then takes a deep breath and relents.

A distraction...

Well, it could help pass the time. He could not sleep before battle anyway.

"Search him and bring him in unarmed."

The royal boy nods and waves in the visitor. "Come in."

Perdikkas looks at the smallish visitor, dressed in old Persian trousers and a tunic, face and head wrapped up with cloth, concealing his identity. He looks across the table. His sharp sword lies flatly on the table, within easy reach.

He dismisses the royal boy, keeping his eyes firmly on his visitor.

"Leave us."

"Yes, Sir!" The royal boy nods his head knowingly and quickly leaves the tent.

"Show your face!"

The visitor unrolls the turban around his head and face, releasing a shower of long silky raven hair to fall on her shoulders and down her back. A pair of familiar emerald earrings glitter in the light of the candle, accentuating her forest green eyes.

Perdikkas smiles, gets up to his feet quickly and wraps his arms around Rošanak with hunger, pulling her into him, trembling with happiness.

She had forgiven him! Finally…

He had never whispered in her ears… he had never wanted the gods to become envious, as they had been with Alexander…

And she had never said anything to him…

But she had come to him at last and nothing else mattered!

The Babylonian Diviner was right… a most valuable gift had come for the King from a distance.

"I should bathe first. I have been riding." Rošanak whispers softly, slightly trembling.

Perdikkas holds her tightly in his arms. He seals her mouth with a hungry kiss.

She was bathed with tenderness… showered with forgiveness… scented with love…

Reality slowly fades… a candle lazily flickers…

"How is my Son-King?" he asks, whispering in her ear.

"He misses his father," she says sweetly.

He pulls her closer and kisses her again and whispers. "No more than his father missing his wife."

When all this was done, and the body of Alexander had been delivered properly to his queen-mother and honorably buried in the ancient burial site of the Makedonian kings, by him, his successor, he meant to marry her according to her customs… and raise her Boy-King as his own.

He would take her back to Babylon and let her live sweetly in her golden Garden Palace… with himself living sweetly in the palace of her garden…

She could have a marriage contract and witnesses and seals and a wedding feast for the whole of Babylon and all the people from Across-the-River too…

And maybe even one day he could tell her that he loved her and no other…

QUEEN'S TENT. ARMY FOLLOWERS CAMP. NEAR PORT of SAND. TWO LANDS
ROŠANAK'S TENT
5 DAYS LATER
MID-DAY

"Perdikkas," Ptolemaios says wryly, lowering himself carefully into a chair in front of Rošanak, "is dead."

Rošanak looks at him without blinking an eye. His broken nose from long ago makes his words sound harsher and his years seem older.

She was told a day or so ago by Oštana, who had made his way back from the Royal Army Camp after he had found the bruised and bloodied body of Perdikkas in his tent. She had lost all track of time afterward…

Oštana had hurried back to guard his sister and his kinsman, the Fourth Alexander, the Boy-King. That was what Perdikkas would have wanted him to do, had he lived.

Oštana had told her what had happened on the day of the battle, long after she had left the Royal Army Camp early in the morning, returning back to the base camp. He had brought her the ring of Goddess Nike. Perdikkas had ordered him to take the ring to her, should anything happen to him, and he had obeyed his orders… his blood had dried on the ring… after three years, the Goddess of Victory had finally failed Perdikkas in Mudrâya, in the Great River watering the Two Lands. Mudrâya had defeated Perdikkas as she had defeated so many Great Kings before him.

Her head spins. Her body numbs.

The assault on the Fort of the Camels had failed and the following day Perdikkas had taken the Royal Army upstream to an island across from Men-nofer. Oštana said he had stayed close to Perdikkas but some two thousand of his men had died in the strong currents of Great River Iteru trying to reach the damn island… some had been eaten alive by crocodiles downstream.

The battle was lost to Ptolemaios and his men and Perdikkas had been killed by his own kingsmen the very same night when he had returned to his tent, bloodied and bruised, the typical Makedonian reward for losing in battle. A good reason why the Makedonians fought so mercilessly and killed so many; there was no other way if they meant to keep their own heads.

Oštana had said to her that according to the Makedonians themselves, it was Peithon who had treacherously betrayed Perdikkas and had taken gold from Ptolemaios to murder him.

She bites her lip. She tastes her own blood.

She had fallen asleep for a while and had awakened when Perdikkas had left her body in the middle of the night to prepare for battle. When he had seen her awake in the light of a burning candle, he had come back to bed and had made love to her once more, taking his time, spending all his desire on her…

When she had heard about his death, she wondered if he had heard the footsteps of Hades in his bones that night and had given her all the love that he had left in him…

"No use taking a gift of love to the House of Hades," he had whispered in jest, "Hades could have my bones and no more…"

His love was for her… his bones for Hades…

Her skin still bore the purple marks of his passion… if she had known it was their last time together, she would have stayed awake all night long with him…

"They asked me, of course," Ptolemaios continues undaunted, "afterward, at the Assembly, to become the next regent for the Joint-Kings!"

"Krateros?" Rošanak asks with a hollow voice, "is he coming?"

"Ah! Yes—"

Ptolemaios looks as if he had just remembered something important.

"You probably have not heard yet. I just heard it myself!"

He deliberately lingers on each word and looks slyly into her eyes, probing.

Did she know how close she had come to feeling the full force of Alexander's wrath?

There were hushed rumors about her and Krateros after they were all reunited in Karmania. But Krateros himself had said nothing to anyone… silent as death!

And by that he had spoken volumes. Krateros was a man who had always talked… he had taunted Hephæstion mercilessly over Roxana in India… but in Karmania… nothing… silence.

Krateros was the most able commander after Alexander… loved by both the Horse and the Foot. Just hearing his voice on the fields of battle was enough to bring the Makedonians under his absolute command. He was not a man Alexander could easily have rid himself of over a woman without a bloody bloodbath.

Eumenes had told him in confidence that Hephæstion had spent a whole day, stretching well into the next sunrise, alone with Alexander in his royal bedchamber in Susa, unarmed and unguarded, pleading for the life of Roxana.

Krateros was truly hated by Hephæstion and that had finally tipped the scale with Alexander.

Spared but not forgiven…

Alexander had unleashed his anger at her immediately when he had ordered the weddings in Susa to punish her… or to free himself of her spell, to make her suffer his pain. Hephæstion and Krateros were ordered… the rest were persuaded. Alexander had given the daughter of the brother of the Third Darius to Krateros… not to honor him but to make Roxana weep… and she had. Her punishment had been more brutal than what had been handed to Philotas or the Black Kleitos … they had died at the end of their suffering… she had lived to suffer more.

His kingsmen had agreed to be gifted with Persian brides, imagining the women were all like Roxana. Except for Seleukos and Nearchos and a handful of others, they all had divorced their Persian wives before Alexander's body had gone completely cold.

They could not rid themselves of their Persian wives fast enough!

He himself had sent his Susa bride, the sister of Barsine, back to Barsine in Pergamos immediately. What use was it to stay married to the sister of an old mistress of Alexander… Alexander did not even care for Barsine when he was alive.

But even in the midst of his darkest wrath, Alexander loved Roxana.

At the Susa weddings, she had disobeyed his royal order and worn royal purple as the Queen Consort. They had all held their breaths not knowing what Alexander would do, but he overlooked it. According to the Susa palace eunuchs, he had returned to her on his wedding night to the Daughter of Darius. Both Daughters of Darius were virgins untouched by men until their horrid deaths… they said…

Alexander had sent Krateros away from the royal court after Opis… back to Makedonia to relieve the old Antipatros as the new regent, even though Krateros was sick, his body broken with Persian arrows when he had taken half of the Royal Army to Karmania up country.

And they all knew what that meant…

Roxana had been finally forgiven and spared but Krateros was exiled back to Makedonia to die on the way or to be forgotten once he got there. Alexander loved her too much not to forgive her and who could have blamed him? There were many great Makedonian commanders who had become greater under Alexander's command… the funeral games since Alexander's death had proven that.

But there was only one Roxana. And no man ever, even in their darkest days or their drunkest moments, had ever bragged publicly: "I had her, too…" If they had, they had taken their secrets to their graves with them, like some precious charmed amulets from Aigyptos wrapped to their bodies to ward off evil after death…

If Perdikkas had wedded her formally, bloodier wars would have broken out sooner. The kingsmen of Alexander would have eventually tolerated all the marriage alliances to the ugly daughters of Philip and Antipatros… but none would have allowed another to marry the one most beautiful… the one loved by Alexander himself… not even the One-eyed Antigonos, who had never seen her.

There were rumors that Alexander had bequeathed Roxana to Perdikkas… but that was not true. The rumors were started by Perdikkas himself who was the shrewdest of all the kingsmen of Alexander. He had told everyone that Alexander had given her to him on his death bed along with his signet ring… he was bedding her and he had walked away from the daughters of the old Antipatros and Philip.

He was slowly becoming the Regent, not to the half-Makedonian Son of Alexander, but to the half-Persian Son of Roxana. The Lands of the Persians were the largest part of the Empire and all that mattered according to some… and Persians were half of his Royal Army.

Soon Perdikkas could have made himself the Regent of the Persian Boy-King and the Royal Keeper of the Persian Crown and Throne with a full Royal Army of Persians, something Alexander himself had started at Opis. Perdikkas had to be stopped, if the rest of the kingsmen of Alexander wanted to keep what was theirs by right of conquest!

They had all agreed. And so they had all joined their forces against him. He himself had been planning and preparing and waiting for two years to join Perdikkas in battle across the Two Lands.

Perdikkas had to die!

Ptolemaios finally breaks the silence.

"Krateros is dead too!"

Stunned silence.

The words prick like sharp thorns from a rose bush as they tumble carelessly into her ears. She mindlessly touches her ears, wondering if blood was dripping from them.

It was surely just a lie... Ptolemaios was not always truthful... she had cursed him and his sickly Hellene Mistress, Thaïs, so many times and both still lived and breathed and intrigued.

How could any man be so wretched to take such pleasure in her pain?

"It seems both Krateros and Perdikkas died on the same day," Ptolemaios continues, narrowing his eyes, trying to reconcile the dates in his head shrewdly, maybe a day or two apart. "Most unfortunate!" He shakes his head.

If the word of Krateros' death had come a day sooner, no one would have dared touch Perdikkas. He would still be alive!

"How—?" Rošanak says faintly, not sure if the word actually left her mouth.

"Eumenes, the damn Hellene, as it turns out, is even more cunning in battle than any of us ever thought," Ptolemaios says carefully, concealing a hint of admiration. "As you know well yourself, he was the Secretary of Alexander, and of Philip before Alexander. He had not seen much battle, except in India after you left with Krateros. He mostly just wrote about them. Well, one never knows what men are capable of, until gods glance at them favorably and whisper in their ears."

Rošanak looks at Ptolemaios, her eyes creasing and folding at the corners, bearing the full force of her unbounded grief.

"Krateros underestimated Eumenes," Ptolemaios nods with regret.

"He defeated the bloody Persians and was defeated by a damn Hellene. You would have thought being the Second-in-Command to Alexander during all those bloody battles would have taught him never to underestimate his enemies! Not even the damn Hellenes!"

Ptolemaios pauses and takes a deep breath. "They say he fell from his horse and was killed by some nameless Thrakian horseman near Kappadokia."

Rošanak forgets to breathe.

How could a noble who was born to horses fall from his horse in battle?

Krateros was as good on a good horse as a Bakhtrian! He was good even on a Makedonian horse!

She looks around the tent, desperately trying to remember where she had put all his letters.

"But fortunately one of the commanders of Eumenes recognized Krateros and defended his fallen body with his shield. So, his body was not desecrated after his death."

Rošanak fills with a short breath and pushes up to her feet.

"You must be tired after a victorious battle," she says politely. "I should not keep you from important feasts and banquets in your honor!"

Ptolemaios looks at Rošanak. He hears her hatred for him in her soft accented voice.

She had never brought him close to her when Alexander was alive. It was Alexander who had included him in some of her Persian feasts... no invitation had ever come from her directly and he had always noted it and remembered bitterly. She was even kind to that half-wit Arrhidaios, whom she visited from time to time...

Hatred for him was in her eyes. He was the executioner of her father and she had never forgotten or forgiven. That was why when the Makedonians killed one, they killed all their kinsmen too in fear of a blood feud. Nothing was more important than to avenge the death of a kinsman.

If she had been nicer to him, he would have seized the chance to become the regent for the Boy-King, but he knew better. Just as Olympias had poisoned Alexander with hatred for his father, she would poison the Boy-King against him, and he would have to start sleeping with a dagger under his pillow in fear for his life and all his work raising the Boy-King would be for nothing!

Thaïs, his Hellene Mistress, could not even pass by her tent in the old days. Roxana had ordered her eunuch to cut Thaïs into pieces for the burning of Persepolis if she ever got close to her. When he had complained to Alexander, he had just shrugged his shoulders... his Hellene mistress could not hold a candle to the King's Persian little star. Thaïs swore that Roxana had cast a dark spell on her in India, after she had started suffering from headaches and fainting spells that never went away.

Ptolemaios slowly gets up to his feet.

"I declined, of course, becoming a regent," Ptolemaios looks around for Alexander's son. "Aigyptos is enough trouble."

Rošanak eyes him tiredly.

"May I hope to see the King, Son of Alexander, before I leave?" Ptolemaios asks politely. "It has been a while and they say he is growing up."

"He is teething. Maybe during your next visit?" Rošanak replies properly.

"Yes, well then, if there is anything you need— the King, Son of Alexander and his royal mother are always welcome in Alexandria."

"Thank you."

Ptolemaios glances at her again.

Even all broken, she was still so beautiful.

The wondrous beauty of the Persian Royal Women had always tormented the eyes of the Makedonian men... among all the women of the Empire... as Alexander himself had said once...

Did she know he was a good lover? Far better than Alexander and all his other kingsmen? He had only bedded women all his life.

Ptolemaios finally loses control.

He moves closer to her and tries to persuade her to his cause.

"Alexandria will be beautiful! Temples, gardens, theaters, stadiums, gymnasiums, the sea, the river, the harbor, the marketplace. Alexander himself picked the site, bathed in mild sea breezes, away from harsh sea winds, and designed the whole city in the shape of a Makedonian cloak. He drew the city on the black sands of a rocky piece of land with white flour and named it Alexandria after himself.

"When birds came and ate all the flour, Aristandros said that Alexandria will be a nursing mother to all men. Ships will come from every city bringing wares to sell. Palaces built with beautiful rare Aigyptos marble, houses built with stone. It will never burn to the ground. I am planning a library, the biggest in the world, it will have every book ever written! You would love it!"

A king who owned the Men of the Words could write himself well into the histories of the Men of the Sword…

He knew the nature of all men… historical accuracy was of no great importance…

The multitudes wanted to be entertained with tales of glorious deeds, not taught the wretchedness of bloody history.

Everyone knew that the LowLanders and the HighLanders wanted the gold… they did not care who had it before it glinted and glittered in their own hands.

Blood easily washed off silent stolen gold!

"Yes, I am sure," Rošanak says politely in a low voice.

She preferred Hell to the Two Lands of the wicked Mudrâya! They had done nothing but cause endless trouble for the Great Kings.

And now the blood of her noble lover and the protector and regent of her Son-King had spilled on the Lower Lands of the Two Lands.

May that fat Apis Bull devour all the Mudrâya traitors whole!

Ptolemaios tries again.

"My treasury is full and overflowing with gold. I will build the Boy-King the biggest palace in Alexandria. Anything you like will be yours for asking!"

He had married that ugly Eurydike, the oldest daughter of Antipatros… and even the Apis Bull was more attractive than that woman.

Antipatros was old and Eurydike was useless after the death of her father… and Kassandros, her brother, was unlikely to make anything of himself. If Kassandros had been worth anything, Alexander would have tolerated him for a while, as long as he was useful, just like Philotas, and then seen to him too.

Even all who hated Roxana bitterly admitted freely that she was the most beautiful of all the women they had ever seen… and there were not that many men of Alexander who hated Roxana herself.

Mostly they hated that Alexander had not married earlier…

… and begotten a Makedonian heir to secure the kingship… but even he himself doubted that Alexander ever wanted a Makedonian heir.

Women were jealous and envious of Roxana and hated her for how easily she had tied Alexander to herself with her beauty. Even the same women who hated her fashioned themselves after her, hoping to tie their husbands and lovers to themselves, as she had. Even Thaïs wore fragrant flowers under her Hellene gowns as Roxana was rumored to do… even as she constantly cursed "the Persian Sorceress" under her lips.

Scent makers did as much business as the sword makers in the Royal Army market after Alexander had wedded her… maybe more, as they demanded the same price for a small bottle of their wares as men paid for their big swords… knowing well that no matter what they charged, the women of the camp would pay willingly to be scented like the Queen of Alexander. She was hated and imitated all the same.

Rošanak nods again politely. "You are a most generous man."

Ptolemaios bows his head slightly, waits for a moment longer, then relents and gives up and turns toward the tent flap.

"Ptolemaios?"

The name spoken softly with golden politeness races across the warm tent and grabs Ptolemaios off guard and pulls him back to her.

Ptolemaios turns around and takes an eager step toward Rošanak.

"Yes, Roxana?"

"There is one thing, I would like to beg of you," Rošanak says quietly. Her voice turns soft and womanly again.

Ptolemaios looks at her surprised.

Beg?

"Yes, Roxana, anything!" Ptolemaios says readily.

"Perdikkas—"

"Yes?"

"Will you grant him the favor of an honorable funeral?"

"Of course, Roxana, his body was burned with all honors of his rank, as Alexander himself would have done. All the dead were treated with due honors, on both sides, as befitting of Makedonians fallen in battle! No duty is more sacred than honoring the dead fallen in battle!" Ptolemaios answers too quickly to a request most unexpected.

"His bones—" Rošanak says faintly, trying to keep her face from peeling off.

"Yes?"

"What will become of his bones?"

Perdikkas was already burned and there was nothing more to do for him, than honor his bones, as he would have wanted for himself.

"His bones? We will bury all unclaimed bones in Aigyptos!"

Rošanak takes a deep breath. "May I beg you— for his bones?"

Ptolemaios considers her for a moment.

It was the last thing he had expected her to ask of him.

"I wish to take him back to Babylon, when I return. We were happy in Babylon," Rošanak mumbles, as if talking to herself.

Ptolemaios takes a deep breath and considers her for a long moment.

She owed her life to Perdikkas.

That fateful late afternoon in Babylon, after Alexander had died, all his kingsmen and high command had gathered in council quickly to avert disaster with the Royal Army and to decide the fate of the Empire of Alexander.

No one believed Alexander would die, until he did!

It was Perdikkas who had freely spoken for her and the unborn son of Alexander.

He himself had advocated for the Council of Kingsmen to rule the Empire jointly in common… no man higher than another… all equals in arms… and no one had liked his ideas. They all wanted a king… Kingship was what they had known all their lives… and they saw no reason for a change.

And so they had all accepted what Perdikkas had proposed… to wait for her to give birth and then gather in council again and decide.

That fateful night, few nights after the death of Alexander, when they had all taken sanctuary in the royal death chamber in fear of being killed by their own men, she had cooled the heated blood of many with her words and her voice and her loaded belly… she would not have seen the morning sun, if it had not been for Perdikkas… he had been fiercely loyal to her.

Perdikkas was not a king… his brother Alketas should have given Perdikkas his burial dues, but he was fighting alongside Eumenes… and both were his enemies now. Eumenes and Alketas and all of the supporters of Perdikkas had been declared outlaws and condemned to death by the Assembly. None would be coming for the bones of Perdikkas any time soon… they had to worry about the fate of their own living flesh, before the dead bones of their kinsman and commander. His sister had been killed right after Perdikkas himself and Attalos, married to the sister of Perdikkas, was with Alketas.

He did not know if Perdikkas still had any other living kinsmen in Makedonia who would care. He himself only cared about the body of Alexander, already in his possession in Memphis.

Would she ask for Alexander? And if she did, what would he say? Perdikkas had commanded him to return the body of Alexander… so many men had died on both sides…

But she was the Queen… she could order him…

"Very well, I will have his bones delivered to you."

"Thank you," she says faintly. "If you still wish to see Alexander, I will have his nursemaid wake him and bring him."

Her soft words catch and capture him with surprise.

She had practiced an art so effortlessly Persian. He had given her a gift and she had reciprocated graciously in kind with a bigger gift… just as Alexander used to do.

"No need to disturb the Boy-King." Ptolemaios bows his head slightly and turns around, and then stops and turns around again, raising his finger in the air.

"Ah! I knew I had forgotten something," he says triumphantly.

"Alexander had ordered a temple for Hephæstion to be built in Alexandria, the best site right on the harbor, on a beautiful small island, facing away from the sun, bathed in cool air. When the Temple of Hephæstion is finished, it will host the body of Alexander instead. Since we buried the bones of Hephæstion in Babylon after the death of Alexander, when his memorial burned to the ground. There were more pressing matters at the time." Ptolemaios pauses and looks intently at Rošanak for a moment and then asks quietly, "Do you think Hephæstion would mind?"

"Hephæstion would not mind," Rošanak says softly, as if in a dream. "I think Alexander will be happy in the House of Hephæstion, in the Lands of the ancient pharaohs who accepted him as one of their own. He was loved there."

Rošanak closes her eyes for a moment, pushing back tears.

Ptolemaios is stunned silent.

Rošanak opens her eyes and quietly asks, "Alexander— is he properly buried?"

They said if the dead were not buried at all, their tormented soul would bring pestilence and death upon the living…

"Yes, Roxana. He is buried with other Aigyptos pharaohs in Memphis!" Ptolemaios says confidently.

"You will not burn his royal body, will you?" she asks faintly.

"No!"

He was more valuable dried than burned.

She takes a breath, relieved. "It would have pained me unspeakably to see his royal body burn in the sacred fire," she says quietly and looks more kindly at Ptolemaios. "I thank you for taking the royal body of my much-loved King-Husband to rest with his chosen ancestors." And she means it.

She reaches and picks up a small silver box from a table and offers it to him. "I meant to leave this with Alexander, when he reached the end of his last journey home." She wipes a tear quickly from the corner of her eye.

Ptolemaios takes the small silver box and opens it slowly.

A lock of her raven hair, tied with a shimmery white thread… kept from her wedding night in Baktria…

It was the only time he had ever seen Alexander bend his knees… to marry her according to her customs… a sight only a handful of his most intimate kingsmen had witnessed with their own eyes. He would have never believed it if he had not been there himself.

"Will you see to it that it rests with Alexander in the House of Hephæstion?"

A silvery-leaved olive branch extended graciously…

"Yes," Ptolemaios says quietly.

A gift of forgiveness generously given to an old enemy who had wished it more than once.

He becomes wordless. He feels small.

This was why Alexander had always loved her and no other afterward.

He knew Alexander had fallen in love with her the moment he had seen her walking down from the Sogdian Rock behind the Baktrian Oxyartes.

She had walked past them without even looking at them… her silky raven hair had floated in the air, caught in a sudden gust of wind and like a net had caught Alexander's heart in the blink of an eye. Even Alexander had not known himself until he had seen her again in his tent later, when she was summoned to his presence. Never at a loss for words, he had lost his tongue at the sight of her. He had seen Hephæstion's eyes as she had walked by… and he too had felt it in his bones… new love had eclipsed old love…

And just like that, he suddenly knows in his bones that this is the last time he is laying eyes upon her alive, and the idea strangely pains him.

She seemed painfully out of place… desert without sand… fish without water… goddess without worshippers… a part of a world that had disappeared whole when Alexander had died… a little bright star caught in the sharp rays of many powerful suns in the light of day.

The olive branch is accepted. Ptolemaios lingers for a moment longer and then bows his head gently. "Health and prosperity to Queen Roxana."

Rošanak stands still for a few moments until Ptolemaios leaves her tent. Then her legs fold under her and she crumples completely on the Persian carpet, face down, bleeding tears.

Ignorant fools! The curse of the First Dâriuš had finally taken them all…

> θâtiy Dâraya-vauš Xšâyaθiya:
> Thus spoke Dâriuš the King:
> If you shall behold my palaces and destroy them and not protect them as long as there is strength to you, may the Wise Lord strike you…
> May he utterly destroy you!

Alexander and his kingsmen had not heeded the command and the curse of the First Dâriuš, the Great King, the King of Kings… they had burned his beloved Pârsâ… and had sealed their own fates by their own hands…

Just as all the Persian Royals and Nobles of the Seven Families had died all around the Third Dâriuš at Issos and Black Eagle, all the men of Alexander, his kingsmen, most worthy, had fallen one by one, all becoming grave offerings for Pârsâ…

Hephæstion… the most worthy before Alexander…

Then Alexander…

And then the rest…

Leonnatos… Perdikkas and Krateros… all dead after Alexander.

LATER

Mâr'at Bani Âriyânnâz holds Baby Alexander in her arms and peeks through the curtain, looking miserably at Rošanak. She knows by the sound of her tears that Rošanak is sinking back into herself.

If it had not been for Perdikkas, Rošanak would have simply died after Alexander, and now Perdikkas was dead too.

She whispers quietly in the baby's ear and then gently puts him down and pulls away the curtain.

Baby Alexander waddles to his mother's side, clutching his wooden toy lion and drops himself down on top of her and taps her on the head.

"Âmma!"

Rošanak quickly wipes her tears and raises herself and forces a smile and pulls her Son-King into her arms and kisses him wordlessly.

Baby Alexander pushes his wooden toy lion into her lap to cheer her up.

"Âmma, Purkas loves you!"

Rošanak tears up again.

She knew Perdikkas had loved her. A love she had been too stubborn to admit freely, until it was too late… and now he was dead… without ever hearing a love word poured into his ears late in the nights.

She kisses Baby Alexander again and holds on to him tighter.

Damn fool!

He had always been too proud to ask for her love… he had just assumed that she did not love him… he had died never knowing. She would not have left him for Krateros, because he had become a father to her Son-King, and her Son-King loved him… as the only father he had ever known.

It was not true that unlike Persians, the Makedonians were hard and indifferent to children, that they spent all their nights in drunken feasts. Perdikkas used to carry Alexander on his shoulders and toss him up in the air and make him shriek with laughter. He would talk to him in his own mother tongue, wanting to make sure Alexander learned the tongue of his ancient fathers from the other side of the seas, and not just the tongues of the Hellenes and Persians and Bakhtrians.

After months of bedding him, it was obvious that she could not get with his child.

The Wise Lord had only meant for her to have sons with Alexander and no other… she had prayed and sacrificed to Divine Ânâhitâ and nothing had grown in her womb.

Perdikkas would have wanted to have a son of his own body sooner or later, and would have taken Kleopatra to bed. Then she would have become the childless wife of a king and soon forgotten, and that was something she could not have lived with.

Damn HighLander…

She looks down. Alexander has fallen asleep in her arms, snoring softly, blissfully ignorant of the death of his father. She rocks him gently in her loving arms.

Tears flow, like a sea of rain pouring out of a passing summer cloud.

BAZAAR. 3PARADAYADÂ. ACROSS-the-RIVER. SATRAPY of AΘURÂ
YEAR 3 of the THIRD PHILIP, MONTH 11, GORPIAIOS
YEAR 4 of PI-LIP-SU, MONTH 5, ÂBU
YEAR 3 of the FOURTH ALEXANDER, MONTH 5, ÂBU
MID-DAY

"Little bastards! May the *Two-Horned One* get you!" the old woman cries angrily in broken coarse Attik, pointing her bowed finger at the young boy who had stolen a piece of fruit from her stand and had run away and disappeared into the crowded market. "The bloody men! They rape the women on the way to their wretched glory and now their bastards are everywhere… making trouble for everyone… their dim-witted mothers should have left them out for the jackals to feed on when they were born!" The old woman grunts and shakes her head side to side. "Men and their glory and their greed!"

She mumbles to herself, rearranging the fruits in her stand. "Honor wounds! Ha! Let them carry their bastards inside their bellies for nine months and give birth from a hole the size of their mouths and then sing about how honorable are the insignificant sword cuts on their arms and legs!"

She turns her eyes to the highborn woman passing by her fruit stand. "Lady! Buy some love fruit, Lady… dark, luscious, sweet figs, or some hot, sweet, plump dates for your man to inflame his passion for you and keep him strong in you all night long!"

"Mother, I have no man," Rošanak says sadly.

"A Lady who looks like you never lies down in her bed alone! No need to bargain with an old woman, Lady! My fruits are the best! Go look around the whole market! You will come back to me, and by then the juiciest and ripest and sweetest fruits will be all gone!"

"I am cursed by my face!"

"I am cursed by mine too!" The old woman sighs and points to behind her fruit stand. "I came here with a Makedonian I met at Miletos, but I got heavy with child and could go no further. So I was left behind here to live or die. Now I have five mouths left to feed, all begotten by the Makedonians and Thrakians and Hellenes who found me irresistible on their way to conquer the lands between the Two Rivers and the Lands of the Persians."

She shakes her head side to side with regret.

"When Persians were our masters, we paid our tributes to their tribute collectors and complained to our gods! Our gods sent us the *Two-Horned One* to free us! Now we pay five times more for corn and seven times more for barley and the same men who collected the tributes for the Persians, now collect the same tributes for the Makedonians. Not enough left even for a small cup of date wine!"

The old woman points and continues.

"That woman over there used to be a Priestess of Ishtar. She fled from the Lands between the Two Rivers when Babylon surrendered. She sells potent love potions, if you need a man to fill your body at nights.

"But if you need a child to fill your arms during the day, take one of mine."

Rošanak looks at the old woman with dismay. She had always easily gotten with child… and as easily lost them… and the old woman had five and was giving them away.

"Mother, you will give away your child to me freely?"

"Aye! By the gods! You do not have any of your own, do you?"

Rošanak steals away her eyes and looks down at her feet.

"Better to give them to someone who can keep their bellies full of barley and meat and wine… than to see them suffer in pain of hunger. Take one of the girls… they will make good maids… or take one of the boys and raise him decently. The Persian Great Kings used to give all the mothers silver shekels when they bore girls… and a gold darik for sons. No more! Those days are gone when the mothers were loved by their Great Kings!"

"Mother…"

"Do not be stingy, Lady! That beautiful gown covering your flesh and bones, Lady, could feed all of my brood for a whole year with enough left over for a jar full of grape wine!"

Rošanak bites her lip. She is wearing just a simple plain Hellene himation. She kneels down on the ground by the children.

One of the boys was almost the size of her Alexander, with unruly honey-golden hair. He looked more like Alexander, the Kingly-Father, than Alexander her Son-King.

She reaches and plays with the boy's golden hair. The boy turns his head up and looks at her. He is filthy from the top of his head all the way down to the bottoms of his feet, his flesh sticking close to his bones.

Her own Royal Son had never sat on dirt… he had never gone hungry… he had all that a child could want and more…

"What do you call this one?"

"Alexandros."

Rošanak looks up at the old woman.

"My youngest boy… he had no father to name him, so I did. And I sacrificed to Goddess Artemis when he was born and prayed that my boy would share in the fortunes of Alexander, the Great Conqueror, his namesake."

Rošanak pushes back a tear. "How many years has he seen?"

"Four… maybe five… who can remember years, when life is spent hand to mouth… day to day…"

Rošanak eyes the boy.

He was almost the same size as her three-year old Son-King.

The old woman bends down and gives a small sliver of an apple to each of her children.

The boy takes a small sliver and bites into his share and then offers the rest to Rošanak and smiles at her brightly.

Rošanak tears up with shame.

She had been given so much by the gods and yet she was overflowing with such misery, and the little boy had been given nothing and he seemed so happy with a sliver of an apple for his mid-day meal. She was cursed with gardens full of all sorts of fruits and he was blessed with a sliver of an apple.

QUEEN'S TENT. 3PARADAYADÂ

FOLLOWING DAY

"What is all that noise?" Rošanak asks Mâr'at Bani Âriyânnâz.

"The poor boy has never been given a bath in his whole life. He is wedded to all the dirt on his filthy body. He is screaming as if the Makedonians were torturing him on a rack! He sounds like a Mudrâya cat who has fallen into a tub of sacred water!" Âriyânnâz says with dismay, shaking her head side to side.

Rošanak bites her lip.

It was all a whim… she had not planned it or thought about it at all. Alexander had no playmates since they had left the Royal Palace of the Second Nabû'kudra'cara in Bâb-ilim.

She had given the old woman at the old bazaar a golden archer. She wanted two manû for the boy, and she only had a golden archer with her… so she had also given the old woman her words in exchange for the boy: she had promised his blood mother that the boy would be well-fed and well-cared for… and she had promised her that he would not be cut as a eunuch and sold in the slave markets.

She did not have the heart to return the poor boy… no matter how troublesome.

She takes a deep breath and bends down and grabs a discarded wooden toy on the carpet, and walks into the private chamber of her tent where the filthy boy was being given a clean warm bath.

"Alexandros, look! A toy cat!" she says softly to the poor boy, pulling the strings of the small wooden toy. The head of the wooden toy cat moves side-to side… the limbs move up and down… "Here… take it."

She waves the wooden toy cat in front of the boy's face. The boy slowly stops crying and his eyes light up; he reaches for the toy and takes it. Rošanak starts to wash the boy's hair gently, as he sits obediently in the small silvery water tub and plays with his first toy.

"My Lady, the new regent is here… outside the tent. He is requesting an audience with you," Abi-Samar says quietly, bowing his head.

Rošanak looks at Abi-Samar and then back at the boy. She dreads meeting the new regent. A man she had heard about from Alexander and Perdikkas, the man who had more red-headed sons and daughters than dogs had fleas and fruits had flies… ugly daughters… ugly daughters with exceptional qualities. Krateros had married one of them.

She should have been nicer to Ptolemaios so that he had accepted the regency… at least he was one of the kingsmen of Alexander she knew!

"Tell him I am resting."

"My Lady, he is… *very old*… he might not live long enough to see tomorrow…" Abi-Samar says quietly.

"Life and death are by the favor of the Wise Lord." She shrugs her shoulders.

"My Lady…" Abi-Samar's brow creases.

"Oh, very well… bring him back here."

Abi-Samar bows and disappears and reappears with the new Makedonian regent.

"Queen Roxana," old Antipatros says formally with a tone, declaring how much he disapproves of her.

Rošanak turns her head and considers him discreetly.

He was indeed old and not much taller than Alexander… his hair long and snowy white, wearing a simple cloak, leaning on a tall walking stick. He looked like the old Artâvazda without the splendid Persian clothes… more like an old beggar in a bazaar. They said this was the first time he had crossed into Asia.

"My Lord."

Old Antipatros narrows his eyes at her. He had just visited the dim-witted Arrhidaios and his troublesome child-wife and found the haughty tongue of the barbarian queen no more pleasing.

The boy plays with the wooden toy cat in the water tub and splashes old Antipatros carelessly.

"Alexandros, be careful with that!" Rošanak gently scolds the boy.

The boy looks up and smiles.

Old Antipatros looks at the boy.

He had not seen Alexander since he had left for Asia years ago. Ptolemaios had told him that Alexander's son did not favor his father and looked like his barbarian mother. But to his old eyes, the boy in the tub full of soapy water looked a lot like Alexander, with an easy smile. Even wet, the boy's hair looked like the mane of a lion.

His heart softens.

"The eunuch told me that you were bathing Alexandros. I can come back later."

"My hands are soiled, but my ears are free, My Lord."

His heart hardens at the dismissive tone of her voice.

Philip had meant to fill his empty treasury with Persian gold when he planned the invasion of Persia, not to fill his Makedonian throne with a half-breed Persian.

"Abi-Samar, please bring a chair for the regent," Rošanak says kindly, washing the boy's hair.

"I prefer to stand," old Antipatros says in a deep voice. His authority carries across the tent.

He will not be looking up at her from a chair…

... nor will he ever bend his knees to anyone... least of all to a woman, and a barbarian, no less...

"As you wish, My Lord." Rošanak narrows her eyes at him.

He was too old to stand... but she knew better than to indulge the Makedonians with kindness... they thought kindness was weakness.

"It has been decided that I will be the new regent for the Two Kings."

"Yes, My Lord."

"I am leaving for Phrygia soon with the Royal Army and the One-eyed Antigonos. It is my wish that the Kings accompany me to Phrygia and from there to Pella until I make further decisions."

Air leaves the tent.

Rošanak stops, motionless, and goes pale.

"Pella?"

"King Philip and his wife, Eurydike, have agreed, enthusiastically, if I may add, to accompany me."

That troublesome Adeia almost had him cut to pieces by the men of the Royal Army a few days ago with the same enthusiasm!

The boy splashes in the water tub and splatters Rošanak.

She looks down at her wet gown, trying to think.

Her Son-King had to be raised a Persian to be worthy of the Persian crown and throne...

"Alexander would have wanted his son to grow up in the Lands of the Persians," she mumbles.

"Then the King should not have died!" old Antipatros sneers at her cuttingly.

"You are free, of course, to accompany your son, or remain in Asia. I will see to it that you are provided for from the royal funds as the mother of the Boy-King." Old Antipatros shifts his weight and moves his walking stick to the other side. "It is the will of the Makedonians that your son will be raised in the land of his fathers, not among the conquered barbarians."

She narrows her eyes at him with disdain.

Defeated in battle did not mean conquered!

His thorny words cut and bloody her ears and make their way into her body. She quivers with unspeakable pain.

Leaving the Lands of the Persians...?

Her life was tied to the Lands of the Persians... like an unborn tied tightly by a life cord to the belly of her mother...

Rošanak picks the boy up out of the tub of water without thinking. Mâr'at Bani Âriyânnâz wraps a white linen around him. He starts to cry. Rošanak grabs the boy back from Mâr'at Bani Âriyânnâz and holds him tightly in her arms.

Alexander, her Son-King, was napping in her bed, ignorant of all the wicked common kingsmen who were deciding his fate, against the wishes of his King-Father... and royal mother... and royal ancestors...

The boy starts to cry louder, missing the scent of his own mother and sensing the sea of fear ebbing and flowing in the strange woman holding him. Rošanak holds him closer and kisses his face and rubs his back gently, instinctively. The boy calms and quiets down and puts his small head on her big shoulder.

"Should you decide to accompany your Son-King to Pella, the slaves at the Pella Palace will see to your needs." old Antipatros looks around. "Eunuchs and Barbarians will not have an easy life in Pella. It is best if they are left in Asia."

Rošanak's knees start to fold under her. Alexandros has fallen asleep on her shoulder and feels heavier.

"My Lord, if there is anything else…"

"No. Nothing else!"

LATER

A single candle flickers in the tent near Rošanak's bed.

She could flee with Alexander to Baktra with the help of Oštana… Uxšiyârta and her kinsmen would protect her… they would fight for her Son-King…

The Lands of Alexander were breaking up. She could travel from 3Paradayadâ to Bâb-ilim on the Royal Road and then on to another Royal Road, from Bâb-ilim to Baktra. They could travel on horses… sleep in the resting houses along the Royal Road. There were still a few Persians and Bakhtrians left in the Royal Army who were loyal to her and her son… they could see to the travel documents and give them protection along the way…

Or… she could persuade Seleukos to become the regent for her son. He would let her go to Baktra… or to any royal palace in the Lands. Old Antipatros could rule in the name of Arrhidaios…

Poor Arrhidaios… Alexander had asked her to watch over his dim-witted brother and she had been kind to him, even without being asked. He was her kinsman too… all families had dim-witted kinsmen. All of Alexander's blood were her kinsmen, even the dim-witted one… one did not choose one's kinsmen and kindred!

She could persuade Arrhidaios to command old Antipatros to leave her and her Son-King behind in Asia… but the wicked Eurydike had isolated poor Arrhidaios and had filled his head with wicked lies in her mother tongue.

Rošanak tosses and turns in her bed; her belly could not feel any worse if she had eaten a basket full of ripe sweet cherries in the heat of summer… cherries always gave her a nasty belly ache. She coils and twists around herself in pain.

She looks over at Alexander, her Son-King, sleeping quietly in her bed, still fiercely clenching his wooden toy lion in his hands. Next to him, the boy, Alexandros, also slept quietly, clenching the wooden toy cat in his fingers. Both were oblivious to the gods who were conspiring against them.

She cautiously rolls out of bed, wrapping her arms around her body.

Damn Hephæstion for dying…

… none of this would have come to pass, if she had been sweet to him…

She walks into the next chamber and in her forgetfulness, she falls over Abi-Samar and lands on the carpet. "Ahh!" Rošanak moans in pain.

"My Lady?"

"Ah!"

"Are you not well, My Lady? Shall I summon the royal healer?"

Rošanak starts to cry. "I am well… I am just dying…"

"My Lady?" Abi-Samar says worriedly in a low voice. "Shall I wake Mâr'at Bani Âriyânnâz?"

"No!"

Abi-Samar takes a deep breath and sits up.

Damn the Makedonian for dying and leaving her like this… unarmed and unguarded… among these wild beasts… The men who had died looked almost civilized compared to the creatures who were left behind to fight over the Persian Empire…

Rošanak sits up and wipes her face. "The new regent wants to take Alexander back to the land of his fathers."

"My Lady?"

"He said he cared nothing if I went too or not."

"These men are no better than beasts!"

"We can escape to Baktra."

"Yes…" Abi-Samar says hesitatingly.

And Rošanak hears it in his voice.

"What shall I do?" Rošanak tears up again and puts her head on her knees, crying. "Alexander… he never would have gone back to the land of his fathers… had he lived, by the favor of the Wise Lord, his Son-King would have been raised… Persian…"

"Yes… My Lady!" And he means it and she hears it in his voice too.

"And I… How can I survive in the lands beyond the Lands of the Persians… if those lands were blessed by the Wise Lord, they would have become one of the Lands of the Persians long ago… Not even the Wise Lord looks with favor beyond the Lands of the Persians," Rošanak sobs.

Abi-Samar takes a deep breath.

"I am forsaken no matter what I decide. I cannot separate from my own flesh and blood. If I take him to Pella, it will anger his Kingly-Father and my royal ancestors, and if I keep him here, it will cause another bloody war."

"Men will die anyway… at least dying for the king and the kingdom is a noble cause."

Rošanak looks at him through blurry eyes.

Damn all the men who were so eager to kill or die… as if their lives were their own and meant nothing to the women who loved them so…

She was a dreadful Queen… if she was to ever rule the lands, she would forbid men to die! And if they did not obey her royal command, she would put them all to the sword!

QUEEN'S TENT
FOLLOWING DAY
EARLY DAWN

"I worship the Wise Lord."

Rošanak prays by the light of a dying candle, tears flickering in her teary eyes. The boys are still in her bed, heavy with sleep.

"The Wise Lord is the light of the Heaven and the Earth…
Light upon light…
The Wise Lord guides whom he will unto his light…
The Wise Lord is the knower of all things…
… the knower and the known…
… the knower of what cannot be known…
Please My Lord, guide my path…
What shall I do?
What shall I do?"

Tears fall gently on her face.

Her eyes catch a glimpse of an unfamiliar chest in the corner of the tent. She wipes her tears and gets to her feet and walks over and bends to look at it closely in the dim light.

"Ah!"

Ptolemaios had sent over the bones of Perdikkas, as he had agreed to.

The name of Perdikkas was written on the top of the Mudrâya chest in three different tongues. An old wooden chest full of bones was all that was left of a man she had come to care for…

A mortal kingsman who had bedded and wedded her as a divine goddess…

The face of Perdikkas steps into her eyes, demanding: *"When I die, what will you do with my bones? You are going to shrug your shoulders heartlessly and throw my body to wild dogs and say it is just an empty vessel? Ha?"*

She bites her lip. She slowly opens the chest and then closes it.

His bones were already anointed with sacred oils and wrapped in fine Mudrâya linen.

He had asked so many women to marry him and yet he had died wifeless and childless and landless and crownless, with no one of his own blood left to tend to his memory.

If it was she who had died instead, he would have taken her body back to Bakhtriš, to be buried in the tomb of her ancestors, even if he had to walk all the way and carry the damn heavy chest on his bare back.

She kisses his name. Her tears fall on the top of the chest; one of the names wets and smears and runs.

An old chest full of burned bones was filled with memories of a mortal king who had thought she was a heavenly goddess… a man who had filled her lonely bones with his eager desire.

Damn the HighLander for dying…

MIDDLE of the DAY

Old Antipatros enters Rošanak's tent, followed by a pair of royal guards.

Mâr'at Bani Âriyânnâz is giving Alexander a bath in the private back of the tent. Alexandros is playing on the ground with his wooden toy cat, his clean unruly honey-golden hair about his face, looking like a baby lion playing with a tiny mouse.

Old Antipatros points to the boy and orders the royal guards, "Take him."

One of the Guards picks up the boy. Alexandros sneezes and coughs and starts crying.

Rošanak jumps up and yells at the Old Antipatros. "Antipatros! What do you think you are doing? Tell them to put him down!"

"I have come for the King. As I said, we are all leaving this afternoon for Phrygia with the One-eyed Antigonos."

The royal guards leave the tent quickly.

Alexandros screams and cries, frightened.

Rošanak goes after them and runs into two more royal guards entering the tent, holding on to Abi-Samar. Abi-Samar struggles.

"Release him!" Rošanak growls at them.

"If you decide to accompany your son, you should pack your carriage," old Antipatros says calmly.

Rošanak eyes him with hatred.

Mother of Alexander was right! Alexander should have done away with him and his red-headed brood long ago.

Old Antipatros signals the royal guards and they release Abi-Samar. He reaches for his Persian dagger. The royal guards reach for their Makedonian swords.

Rošanak hurls herself in the middle of them. "No!"

Old Antipatros nods and the royal guards sheath their swords and step back. He looks around and then leaves the tent followed by the royal guards.

The tent becomes quiet.

Abi-Samar stands motionlessly, uncertain of what to do.

Mâr'at Bani Âriyânnâz quietly enters the room, holding Alexander, who has fallen asleep in her arms after a warm bath.

Rošanak walks over and takes Alexander and rests him gently on her shoulder and walks around the tent, caressing his back softly, her heart full of love for Alexander, her eyes full of worries for Alexandros.

The poor boy had caught a cold after his first bath; he was not used to being bathed and cleaned and scented.

No one speaks.

Silence.

Rošanak breaks the silence and speaks softly in a low voice so as not to wake the sleeping Alexander.

"Abi-Samar, go find Oštana and bring him to me! Do not get caught in the nasty claws of the Makedonians again!"

Abi-Samar hesitates for a moment and narrows his eyes at her with shame and then quickly turns around and leaves the tent silently.

Rošanak speaks softly in a low voice into the ears of the sleeping Alexander, holding back her tears.

"Oštana and Âriyânnâz and Abi-Samar will take you back to Bakhtriš to my Abû, Uxšiyârta, my father, and to my brother, Itâna. They will teach you to ride a horse and draw a bow and speak the truth… and you will learn prayer and poetry… and about the Laws of the Persians and the Justice of the Great Kings:

> *"Reward the right and punish the wrong, sustain the weak and restrain the strong!"*

She closes her eyes and pushes back a tear. "And I will come as soon as I can."

"Rošanak, the barbarians already have the boy. Let them go. We will all go back to Baktra together," Mâr'at Bani Âriyânnâz says quietly.

Rošanak gently caresses Alexander's back. The face of Alexandros runs into her eyes again, sneezing and coughing and offering her his meager mid-day meal with a free smile.

How he had cried for her when they were taking him out of her tent!

How frightened he was!

How sick he was! Poor lonely motherless child!

Antipatros was not a man to be cuddling and comforting a small frightened sick boy.

She had taken him from his mother and had given her her words and a gold archer… she had to keep her promise or gods would become angry and punish her Alexander for her deeds…

Abi-Samar returns with Oštana.

"Rošanak."

"Oštana, do you still have travel documents from Perdikkas permitting you to travel anywhere in the Lands freely and well-provisioned?"

"Yes," Oštana says quietly, narrowing his eyes at her.

"The old Chaldæan told me that a substitute will protect my son, he will take upon himself the bad omens meant for my Son-King. I thought he was mad… who would do bloody harm to a blameless boy?" Rošanak whispers quietly not to wake Alexander. "All the kingsmen of Alexander still living would know that boy old Antipatros has taken with him is not the blood of Alexander… and they will all come looking for him, soaking the Lands in more blood… they will not look at him that closely, if I am there."

"But, Rošanak—" Oštana grunts.

Rošanak interrupts Oštana quietly, "If the old Chaldæan was right, the poor boy has already taken on the bad omens meant for my Son-King… I will come back… by the favor of the Wise Lord…"

"Rošanak…"

"Oštana… tell me my son will live to see the No'rouz next year and the year after in the care of these wretched men. You worship the Wise Lord and the truth! Tell me and I will believe you! Tell me!"

Oštana looks down at his feet.

He knew the years of the Boy-King without Perdikkas were now numbered and counted. He had come to respect the men of the enemy… there was not a soft bone in their hard bodies. The best of them, the most noble born to the sword, all had died quickly; within two years after the death of their king, they were all dead… just like all the Persian Nobles who too had died all around their Great King on the fields of battle… just like his own beloved.

None was left… all were lost… love was lost…

Everyone was dead and dust…

"Oštana, for the love of your brother and mine, if you care anything for me at all, I beg you, please take my Alexander and Âriyânnâz and Abi-Samar and return to Bakhtriš undetected. We could not even get to Bâbiru if I was to go with you."

Tormented silence.

Rošanak holds Alexander tightly and kisses his small face and head and smells him; he smelled naturally sweet like his blood father.

She was unlucky… not favored by fortune…

She could bring nothing but death to her own Son-King… the son born from her own body— the mixing of two ancient royal bloods in the vessel of his small royal body.

Tears bathe her eyes.

"This will all come to pass— These men care nothing for me… as soon as Alexandros is settled with his new kinsmen, I would leave. I will be home by next No'rouz."

Oštana looks down at his feet, avoiding her teary eyes.

It was all in vain… all was lost… all over again…

Seven

LANDS without KINGS

ESTATE of ANTIPATROS. PELLA. MAKEDONIA
LANDS by the BITTER SEA
MONTH of HEKATOMBAION, DURING the ARCHONSHIP of APOLLODORUS at ATHENAI
YEAR 4 of the THIRD PHILIP, MONTH 9, PANEMOS
YEAR 5 of PI-LIP-SU, MONTH 3, SÎMANNU
YEAR 4 of the FOURTH ALEXANDER, MONTH 3, SÎMANNU
FULL-MARKET TIME

Sunny and mild.

"Good day, Polyperchon."

Polyperchon abruptly stops, surprised. He quickly turns around and walks back, retracing his steps. He passes by the line of people waiting to see the old Antipatros and then he grabs Rošanak's arm gently and pulls her out of the long line.

"Roxana, I mean Queen Roxana, what are you doing standing in line?"

"I wish to speak with Antipatros."

"You are the Queen-Mother. He is the Regent to your Son-King. You summon him to come and see you and the Boy-King. You do not come to see him."

"Yes. I sent word a few days back. But my Attik tongue is sadly inadequate with the noble Makedonian ladies he has assigned to my care."

Polyperchon eyes her for a moment.

Krateros had sworn him with a sacred oath for her protection on the way to Karmania.

He was bound by his honor to his oath and to his word given to his old commander.

"Come with me."

Polyperchon guides Rošanak up the short stairs and past the guards and into the house of the old Antipatros, just a few steps away from the Palace of Archelaos.

Old Antipatros is reading a long document. He rubs his old eyes and looks up and sees Polyperchon.

"Good day, Antipatros."

"Polyperchon, when did you return?"

"Last night." Polyperchon turns and points to Rošanak. "Queen Roxana wishes an audience with you."

Antipatros' old eyes roll from Polyperchon to Rošanak, who is standing blurry a few steps behind his line of sight.

Rošanak takes a few steps forward and comes into sharp focus and bows her head slightly. "My Lord."

Old Antipatros pushes himself up from his chair slowly. His white brow creases and folds. His old bones crackle.

"Queen Roxana, I will come to you, if you summon me."

"Thank you, My Lord."

Old Antipatros slowly sits back down in his chair and glares at her impatiently.

Damn Persians and their civil tongues. Philip had the cunning and the patience to deal with them when Artabazos and his barbarian brood were at his court in exile.

He himself preferred the strong tongue of the Makedonians, or the precise tongue of the Hellenes.

And what did she want now? He had a kingdom to run. He was too old and too busy to be nursemaid to a barbarian queen and a boy and a half-wit bastard and his Makedonian bitch, a thousand times worse than troublesome meddling Olympias!

He was saddled with the royal baggage, because the One-eyed Antigonos was too Makedonian. He had refused to take the Kings and their women along with him when he was ordered to capture Eumenes and what was left of the outlawed Royal Army who were still loyal to Perdikkas and put them all to the sword. Alexander's men who had followed him through Asia had no hesitation dragging the royal baggage along with them behind the Royal Army… but the One-eyed Antigonos was planning to leave them at his court in Kelainai with his wife. Even though Antigonos himself was the one who had rescued him from being stoned at the hands of the Makedonians by the provocation of the Royal Bitch Adeia, and knew how dangerous she could be, left on her own. Gentle Stratonike, wife of the One-eyed Antigonos, was no match for the malevolent warrior girl.

The troublesome girl had the blood of Philip and an Illyrian. She was raised by her mother like a warrior. She had killed a wild boar with her own hands.

That was why he had dragged the Kings back to Pella with him. And because Kassandros had persuaded his old ears that the One-eyed Antigonos could not be trusted with the Kings as the Regent and wanted to be more than a Regent.

He should have brought back only the half-barbarian boy and the half-wit bastard and left their women back in Asia to live or die on their own.

"May I speak with you, since I am already here, My Lord?"

"Yes, please sit down, and I am not Your Lord."

Rošanak takes another step and sits in front of the heavy desk hiding most of old Antipatros from view.

"I will be outside, Antipatros," Polyperchon says officially.

"Polyperchon, no need to leave on my account," Rošanak says graciously.

"Stay, Polyperchon," old Antipatros says, almost ordering.

He wanted to make her unannounced and unexpected and unwelcomed visit short. Shorter if gods were favoring him today.

"Antipatros, the noble ladies you have assigned to look in on Alexandros and me have been very kind to us."

"Yes?"

Rošanak regards the old man cautiously.

All the kingsmen of Alexander who had not followed him into Asia were intolerably rude and barbaric.

None had breathed the cultured and cultivated and polished air of the Persians… they had all remained sadly ignorant in their old ancestral ways.

She had almost persuaded the dying old man to leave her behind in Sparda with the One-eyed Antigonos, but the One-eyed Antigonos was ambitious and cunning and so the old Antipatros had thought better of leaving her behind and had dragged her to Pella with him… along with Alexandros and Arrhidaios and the Illyrian Amazon bitch.

Old Antipatros had quickly married off Phila, the wife of Krateros, to Demetrios, the fifteen year old son of the One-eyed Antigonos, even before the body of Krateros had cooled in Katpatuka… surely, well matched! A homely woman of exceptional character in her third decade of life with a beautiful dazzling boy half her age… Phila had come to live in the court of the One-eyed Antigonos and the sight of the cold virtuous woman, once married to Krateros, was painful to her eyes.

Medeios had remained in the court of the One-eyed Antigonos.

The faithful Aristonous had followed her to Pella and had been keeping an eye on her and Alexandros out of loyalty to Alexander and Perdikkas with no pay from the royal funds.

The kingsmen who had been chosen for Alexandros at the 3Paradayadâ had disappeared back into the Royal Army. Guarding a child every day was not honorable duty… not desired by warriors.

"Would it be possible to assign one of the old kingsmen of Alexander to guard Alexandros?"

Old Antipatros narrows his eyes at Rošanak, considering her request carefully.

"Why?"

"Arrhidaios is a gentle man, a man-child. I have known him for many years now, but his wife is hostile to Alexandros."

Old Antipatros takes a deep breath and looks at Polyperchon.

Adeia had already tried once to rule in the name of the half-witted Philip Arrhidaios.

If the Royal Bitch could provoke the Royal Army, his own men no less, to almost tear him into pieces for their back pay when he had reached Triparadeisos, what could she do to a four year old boy?

"This is Makedonia, Queen Roxana. We have laws here. You and the Boy-King are fully protected."

Polyperchon tires from listening to the two quarrelling with polite tongues.

"I can assign the task to Aristonous, one of the Royal Bodyguards of King Alexander who came back to Pella with you, forgiven for serving under the command of Perdikkas. And I can look in on the Boy-King and the Queen-Mother from time to time myself," Polyperchon says politely.

"Good. Anything else?"

Rošanak gracefully gets up to her feet. "Thank you, Antipatros." She bows her head slightly and heads for the entrance and then stops and turns around. Old Antipatros is still glaring at her.

"Anything else?" Old Antipatros grunts.

"Perdikkas—"

Rošanak cautiously plants a seed and then takes a deep breath and waits for it to take root.

"Yes?"

"I will understand if you cannot grant my request."

"What?"

"Ptolemaios kindly gave me his bones."

Old Antipatros looks at Polyperchon and back at Rošanak, puzzled. "Yes?"

"I meant to take his bones to Babylon for burial. But after Triparadeisos, we came here— and I brought his bones with me." Rošanak stops and considers old Antipatros for a moment and then continues, "Would it be possible to send his bones to Orestis, the HighLands of his fathers, for a proper burial?"

Old Antipatros raises his thick white eyebrows and leans back in his chair, his body heavy with pain from his many years.

That was why the barbarian had come to see him.

He looks at Polyperchon and back at Rošanak. He thinks of Nikaia, his daughter, for a moment.

Well, Nikaia already had been married to Lysimachos and Perdikkas had not touched her.

Rošanak waits patiently for an answer.

"Polyperchon, take a few men and go with Queen Roxana and collect Perdikkas' bones. Take the bones to Orestis and give them to his kinsmen for proper burial."

"Yes, Antipatros."

"Perdikkas was a prince of royal blood, born to the last of the royals who ruled the HighLands of Orestis," old Antipatros says under his lips.

"Thank you."

"Anything else?"

Rošanak eyes Antipatros. "Would it be possible to bury the bones of Perdikkas in ancient Aigai, where your men of royal blood are buried?"

Old Antipatros narrows his eyes at her.

"No! Only the Royal Argeads are buried in Aigai."

Rošanak nods and bites her lip.

"Anything else?"

"No. Will you come to share a meal with us soon?" she asks politely.

Antipatros pushes himself up to his feet. "Yes, Queen Roxana. I look forward to seeing the Boy-King again," he answers graciously.

Rošanak bows her head slightly.

It was just well-mannered conversation… a date none intended to keep.

Old Makedonian men did not eat with their women, much less Persian women, nor with children, not even with boy-kings!

PLUM ORCHARD. PALACE of ARCHELAOS. PELLA
A MONTH LATER
AFTERNOON

Mild breeze blows.

"I am a bad mother!" Rošanak mumbles to herself sadly.

That was why she had been banished to this wretched place… in this wretched land…

Pella, the largest city in Makedonia, was smaller than the smallest city in Asia.

The royal tent of the Great King that had fallen into Alexander's hands was bigger than the palace she was given. Pella felt even smaller amongst the Makedonians who were rude and deliberately unkind to her; they spoke in their own mother tongue to her, even if they knew Attik well. Alexander was treated better by the Persians as an invader than she was treated by the Makedonians as the rightful Queen-Mother.

Her curiosity was well satisfied. He would have never returned from Persia to Pella…

Pella was just too small for Alexander… he must have heard the whispers of the ancient Persian nomads roaming the vast plains of Âryânâ in his bones all his life…

Rošanak sighs as she wanders down through an old weathered stone pathway to the end of the plum orchard scenting and shading the rear of the Pella palaces.

The Illyrian Amazon had gone to see about the house of her dead mother and was not expected back for days. Alexandros was sleeping, watched by a Hellene nursemaid and she was feeling restless. She felt more dim-witted than Arrhidaios for abandoning her own Son-King.

What kind of a mother abandons her own son for the boy of another woman?

And she missed Âriyânnâz and Abi-Samar too… they had been with her since the day of her birth… she had never been separated from them… they were so much a part of her life that she hardly thought of them. It was their fate to serve her Son-King now, as they had served her then.

The plum tree blossoms shower her with delicate white petals. She stops and looks around. The breathtaking beauty of the old orchard fills her body. Her mind wanders back to her own gardens in Baktra.

Oštana had safely taken her Royal Son home to Baktra.

When asked by the ever watchful Guardians of the Royal Roads, he had said that the boy was his own blood son from a campaign wife who had died in Mudrâya and he was taking him back to his kinsmen to be raised properly. The boy was missing the arms of his mother and had cried a lot, but eventually the tears had stopped.

Their journey from the 3Paradayadâ to Baktra had been long but uneventful.

Her Son-King was now safe with her kinsmen, hidden away from the barbaric blood-thirsty Makedonians.

She wraps her arms around her body.

Her arms ached to hold her own son… her lips longed to sing him old lullabies to put him to sleep… her face yearned for his sweet small kisses…

She looks up.

Heavens were heaping more fragrant white plum blossoms on her head, beckoning her attention.

She smiles bitterly.

She should have moved to the middle of this blissful fragrant orchard to get away from the dreaded palace…

The ancestral home of Alexander was violent and disturbing to her eyes. The walls and floors were painted and tiled with images of naked men violently hunting and hacking and slaughtering wild beasts; a repulsive statute of Philip, the father of Alexander, stood in the middle of the large hall on the ground floor, watching her constantly. The old Antipatros told her that Philip had been lame in one leg and blind in one eye, but the evil man was hideous even in his perfected form. No wonder Alexander had come to think of himself as fathered by a god. Evil Philip… the servant of the Lord of Darkness who had plotted the demise of the Persians. Every time she passed by the damn ugly statue, she cursed that hideous wretched man under her breath for all the blood on his hands.

Everyone knew that the demon king had not plotted against the Persians for revenging Hellenes, as Persians and Hellenes had made peace and had lived for generations like quarrelling kinsmen… he had come for the Persian gold, like a common thief… and like a common thief, he had died by the blade of a worthless boy-lover… and no doubt had gone straight to the Hell of Hellenes in the House of Hades!

No king was ever hated more by his own Royal Son than Philip was hated by Alexander… and no blood father hated more by his blood son.

She had sent polite words to the Illyrian Amazon offering her the statue of her grandfather, but the wicked bitch had ignored her generous gift… even Arrhidaios had gotten sick and fallen to the floor twitching and twisting uncontrollably at the sight of the statue of his own blood father. Poor Arrhidaios, who had to live in the other palace with his Illyrian Amazon keeper… not worthy of being called his wife, as she had never bedded him!

Lysimachos had told her once that Kleopatra looked just like her father. She had thought Lysimachos was mocking her, but Lysimachos was not a light-hearted man… no wonder Kleopatra was still sitting in the Palace of Sparda waiting for a husband! Royal Daughters were meant to be beautiful… not ugly, lame, one-eyed creatures of torment.

When they were in Sparda with the old Antipatros, she could have gone to see Kleopatra for herself, but she had thought better of it… it was Kleopatra who should have come to see her.

Even the red-headed homely daughters of old Antipatros had ended up in the bed of Alexander's kingsmen.

They said Alexander never arranged a marriage alliance for his blood sister… well, Alexander loved beauty and he knew full well what his blood sister looked like.

And they said Alexander never arranged marriage alliances for the Persian men and the Makedonian women. Well, those who said that had not seen the homely Makedonian women who did not shave or scent themselves… even Alexander had not married one himself.

She takes a deep breath and bites her lip.

Ah! And then on one of the palace walls there was a shameful painting by Apelles, the official painter of the royal court, of a naked woman sitting on a bed with two men standing nearby gazing at her, with naked plump children flying overhead.

When Aristonous had told her that it was a painting of her and Alexander's wedding night with Hephæstion as the best man, she had quickly removed it to storage, hoping moth and mold would devour the damn painting.

She stops. An old iron-edged wooden gate stands ajar between the palace orchard and the grand estate adjoining it in the back. Vines loaded with grapes drape over the old stone walls. Bees dance drunk around the dark sweet grapes. She peeks through the old gate cautiously; it opens to another plum tree orchard.

She had never thought it important enough to ask old Antipatros who lived there.

Then she shrugs her shoulders with indifference.

It did not matter…

She ties a long white thread around an old plum tree next to the old gate and makes a wish to go home. She steps back and then takes another curious peek into the orchard beyond the old gate.

It was quiet and peaceful… with muted sounds of happy dogs playing not too far in the distance… She missed Peritas, her old faithful hound…

She leans on the old gate and thinks about going back. The gate creaks and moves slightly forward and stops. She steals in without thinking and stops and raises her hands toward the heavens, trying to catch white petals in her hands.

It was the first time she had left the palace grounds in a long time… there was rarely a reason to leave the palace these days.

She takes a deep breath and then turns around to head back to the palace.

Whoever lived there had no desire for her company, like the rest of the Pellians… or they would have come to visit her in her lonely palace…

"Who are you?"

A familiar voice startles her.

Rošanak turns around and searches for the source of the voice and her eyes find a tall man standing in the middle of the blossoming orchard. Her eyes lock on their mark… and then her eyes widen and she forgets to breathe.

Hephæstion, silver-haired and unshaven and older, was staring straight at her.

Without thinking, she steps toward him eagerly.

"Hephæstion?"

The tall man looks at her intently for a moment and then smiles and nods.

"I am Hephæstion, too. Who are you?" he repeats.

"I am Roxana," Rošanak says, hesitating.

The man steps closer to her, reaches out and takes her face into his rough hands and looks at her intently.

"Ah!" Rošanak blushes slightly.

White petals fall from the blossoming plum tress and dance around them idly in the breeze.

Moments slowly pass.

"I thought so." He takes a deep breath and lets go of her face and smiles.

"I am Amyntor. Hephæstion was my son, my only son."

Rošanak's eyes widen.

Hephæstion's father?

Amyntor points to the two palaces behind her. "I heard you had come. I should have come to pay my respects," he says shaking his head. He speaks pure Attik; it is his mother tongue.

He reaches calmly and wipes off the white petals sticking to her face and one on her nose and smiles. "It has been a cold year. The plum trees have bloomed and blossomed late into early summer." He eyes her carefully. "What shall I call you, Queen Roxana, Queen, or Roxana?" He asks directly, without a hint of disrespect.

"Roxana," Rošanak says faintly.

Hephæstion's father…

"Ah! Good. That would have been my choice too."

Amyntor points to his house. "I am glad you have come to visit me. The house would have been in better order, if I had known you were coming. Will you come in?"

"I should go back. I do not wish to intrude on your privacy."

Amyntor ignores her golden politeness. He listens to her searching eyes.

"You look just as Hephæstion described you," Amyntor says as he turns around and starts walking toward his house. "Come!"

Rošanak follows him wordlessly. He walks up a few steps and enters his house.

HOUSE of AMYNTOR
INSIDE

"Oh!" Rošanak sighs with surprise as she enters the house.

The house was almost as large as the Palace of Archelaos. But unlike the palace, the huge audience room, in spite of its large size, felt comfortably familiar.

One of Hephæstion's old standards in faded crimson hung high from the ceiling. There were books everywhere, on top of splendid pieces of Persian furnishings. Half-opened books spread across well-worn couches. Splendid Persian furnishings and wise Hellene books mixed and mingled easily and effortlessly… none seemed offended by the presence of the other… both glad for the agreeable union.

Things and books were wiser than men and men…

Hephæstion himself had lived simply and sparsely… but it seemed that he had sent his share of the loot of the Persian Palaces back to his blood father.

"Will you have some wine? It is all that I can offer you. My slaves have gone to the market."

"Persian wine?"

Amyntor smiles effortlessly. "Oh! No! Hephæstion sent me a few carefully wrapped flagons, which I drank a long time ago. Last one, after I heard Hephæstion… well…"

He had drunk himself unconscious for days when the news of the death of his only son had finally reached him.

Separated by the sea and by the lands and rivers and mountains and deserts, the father and son had remained close in heart and closer by words.

A treasured bond only broken by wretched death.

Amyntor walks into another room and returns in a few moments with a flagon of wine and a pair of silver cups. He puts the cups down on the magnificent Persian table in the middle of the room and fills them with wine.

"I live alone— except for a handful of slaves, who take care of me and the house and the estate." He offers her a silver cup of red wine.

Rošanak takes the cup and takes a sip. It is pure wine, unmixed and untainted.

"You like it pure, right? Or shall I water it?"

"Pure." Rošanak smiles graciously and nods her head.

Amyntor nods and says with a smile, "Aristophanes wrote: *Those pitiless Persian hosts! They forced us to drink sweet wine, wine without water, from golden cups!*"

Rošanak eyes him intently.

Amyntor sips his wine and points to a stack of old books on the floor.

"A line from one of the comedies Aristophanes wrote!" He takes another sip. "I used to water my wine… an old Hellene custom… my father drank his wine watered." He pauses. "I wanted to be able to carry my wine pure when Hephæstion came home…"

Home…

The word hangs in the air for a long moment.

This… was Hephæstion's home…

And Hephæstion was her home by his own words…

"Was his funeral magnificent?" Amyntor asks quietly.

Rošanak is taken by surprise. She loses her words for a moment, then she nods and says faintly, "Yes… all the Royal Fires were doused… his funeral was befitting of a king!"

Amyntor smiles and nods and waters his wine from a jar on the table and takes another sip.

"That is what Alexander wrote too. He said it was the most magnificent funeral pyre in living memory. He said he had ordered a monument to be built to the memory of Hephæstion.

"Perdikkas wrote and said that the memorial had burned to the ground after the death of Alexander in Babylon."

Amyntor pauses remembering, and points to something behind her.

Rošanak turns her head and looks behind her.

On a beautifully carved and gilded side table sat a splendid Persian silver box with the golden feet of a golden lion.

She walks over and runs her fingers lovingly on the markings on top of the old silver box.

"You can read the inscription, yes?"

Rošanak nods and puts down her wine cup and runs her fingers over the old carved dipî and reads in Persian.

"I am Artakhšaçâ, the Great King, King of Kings, King of the Lands and Waters.

"Son of Khašâyar-šâ, Son of Dâriuš, the Great Hakhâmanišiya King, in whose house this chest was made."

She translates to Attik for Amyntor:

"I am Artaxerxes, the Great King, King of Kings, King of the Persians.

"Son of Xerxes, Son of Darius, the Great Achæmenid King, in whose house this chest was made."

"It belonged to the First Artaxerxes?" Amyntor asks, raising an eyebrow.

"Yes."

"The Persian Great King guards the letters from my son," Amyntor smiles and says proudly.

Rošanak looks down at the old silver chest and touches it again.

It was holding Hephæstion's letters. He used to write heaps of letters and more during the cold months of winter… some were written on her naked back late at night, as she lay sleeping in his bed. Alexander too… they both liked to write letters.

Oh, what would she give to read those letters…

She looks around. "You have so many books. Are you a writer?"

Amyntor smiles and shakes his head. "No. Just a lover of books!"

He walks over and puts his hand on top of the silver chest.

"Have you brought any Persian books with you? You can teach me how to read your tongue," he says eagerly and points to some of his books. "Even in the best of Attik, there are Persian words."

Rošanak shakes her head side to side. "Persian books? Books burn. Alexander burned many Persian books when he burned Persepolis. He burned the ancient sacred words of the Wise Lord."

Amyntor takes a deep agonizing breath. The thought of his own son burning books and burning temples pains him right down to his old bones.

He had written long letters screaming at Hephæstion for the shameful deeds committed by their hands…

No god ever favored those who destroyed the house of another god!

Rošanak hides her pain and shrugs her shoulders.

"We used to commit our prayers and our poems to writing… but now what we love the most we commit to our memories. Memories do not burn like books… they live as long as we live."

"Prayer and poetry? What about the accounts of your kings… your heroes… your battles?"

Rošanak sips her pure wine and smiles.

What was prayer and poetry then?

"We Persians only care for the Wise Lord to know of our accounts… and the Wise Lord knows everything… our thoughts and our words and our deeds… good and evil… all recorded by the Recorder of Deeds in our House of Songs. The Royal Scribes used to record the affairs of the Great Kings and the Lands in the Royal Journals for the Royal Libraries and Royal Storehouses… but they were mostly burned too by the ignorant Makedonians."

He eyes her curiously. "But—"

Rošanak pauses and eyes Amyntor and then continues, "Your gods are too young… and too numerous… too forgetful… and you have no angels… so your gods do not remember your thoughts and words and deeds… so you have to write them down yourself to remind them after your deaths… and read them to your gods from the top of your voices!"

She points to the books. "The Wise Lord does not judge us by what we say about ourselves. He judges king and man alike. But they say he loves Persian poetry… they say even gods are moved by words of love. They say raindrops are tears of the Wise Lord when he is moved by hearing Persian poetry.

"That is why all Persians are poets… not writers… Persia is the paradise of the poets…"

How could men who did not worship the Wise Lord and did not love women and wine and poetry and horses and dogs and gardens ever understand the Persians?

Amyntor raises his eyebrows, astounded.

Wise men should not leave it to their enemies to write their histories.

"But you will be forgotten!"

"How can we be ever forgotten… as long as the Wise Lord remembers us?"

Amyntor narrows his eyes at her.

All that wasted time…

He should have gone to see her when she had first arrived at Pella…

He had always liked the Persians… that was why his father had been exiled from Athenai years ago… they had called him 'A Lover of Persians'.

Looking at her, that insult seemed more like flattery…

"Hephæstion spoke the tongue of the Persians. He knew Persian poetry!" Amyntor declares proudly.

Rošanak looks back at Amyntor. Her ears burn with remembrance.

She knew! He had poured them into her ears late at night… along with his love…

"He said it was a small price to pay for the love of a beautiful barbarian."

"Ah!"

Rošanak closes her eyes in pain and takes a deep breath, pushing back tears.

Amyntor quickly puts down his wine cup and takes her hand and holds it.

"Oh, no, My Dear, no! I did not mean you! Please forgive me! I am an old hermit… sometimes I forget myself… my old tongue gets careless!"

"No. It is all my own fault. I should not have so rudely intruded upon you. Thank you for the wine." Rošanak gently pulls her hand out of Amyntor's clasp and bows her head slightly and heads quickly out of the house and runs back to the wretched palace, crying.

Hephæstion's father had called her a barbarian!

Amyntor watches her with dismay as she disappears from sight and curses himself under his lips.

How could he be so bloody careless?

Bad beginnings made for bad endings!

PALACE of ARCHELAOS
2 DAYS LATER
AFTERNOON

Knock! Knock!

The Thrakian slave girl knocks on Rošanak's bedroom door.

Rošanak opens the door wearily.

She slept longer… sometimes to mid-morning and went to sleep earlier at nights to make her days shorter in the barbaric land…

"Queen, there is someone here to see you," says the girl in coarse, accented Attik.

Rošanak thinks about asking who, but she doubts she can understand the words of the Thrakian slave girl.

It did not matter much anyway. No doubt another one of those unbearable barbaric Makedonian women, the old Antipatros was fond of torturing her with their company. A few women had shown up the day before, wanting to teach her how to spin yarn! Probably the same women who had been sent to her grandmother, Ummi Šarri Sisygambis, to teach her how to spin wool after the Royal Women of Dâriuš had fallen into the hands of Alexander. Her poor royal grandmother had cried for days.

The old Antipatros had a Persian sense of humor.

"Very well. I will come down in a few moments."

"Yes, Queen." The Thrakian slave girl nods and leaves. The door closes.

Rošanak makes her way downstairs unhurried and unadorned and unpainted.

Since the red-headed Illyrian Amazon married to poor Arrhidaios insisted on calling herself: "Eurydike," she had told the slave girls to call her: "the Queen".

She was not quite sure what the slave girls called her when she had first arrived at the palace. It had taken her some time to teach the Thrakian girls a few words that she could at least understand without calling on old Antipatros or Aristonous or one of Alexandros' guards to translate for her.

"Good Day, Roxana," Aristonous says, bowing his head slightly.

"Aristonous." Rošanak smiles and nods.

Aristonous looks around and then hands her a folded parchment. "A letter came for you yesterday from Persia."

Rošanak smiles and takes the letter with Oštana's seal. "Thank you."

Aristonous looks around again and then steps closer to Rošanak and says in a quiet voice, "One-eyed Antigonos has defeated Eumenes in Kappadokia. Eumenes is sieged in the Fortress of Nora on the border of Kappadokia, by Antigonos."

Rošanak bites her lip with dismay.

She hated Eumenes for quarrelling with Hephæstion and for causing the death of Krateros. But Eumenes was still loyal to Perdikkas and to the cause of her Son-King… and for that he was marked for death by the other kingsmen…

"I am leaving for Dodona in Epiros tonight to take news of Eumenes to Queen Olympias. I will return quickly. Two of my kinsmen will be guarding the palace until I return. Old Antipatros and Polyperchon know nothing of my connection with Queen Olympias."

Rošanak nods hesitatingly. "I will not betray your secret."

Aristonous nods and looks around again. "I think it is best if you do not leave the palace until I return."

Rošanak takes a deep breath and nods, resigned.

That was just as well… she had no place to go anyway…

Aristonous turns around and leaves.

Rošanak lingers for a long moment and then bites her lip and swallows hard and tightens her fingers around her letter from home.

No matter where she was, storm clouds always danced above her head… and every day the distance between her and her Son-King was getting longer…

She turns around with a heavy heart and heads for the steps back to her bedroom on the second story, pushing back a tear.

"Greeting, Roxana."

She nearly jumps, startled, and then turns around quickly. Her eyes widen and tighten. "Amyntor?"

"I came in through the back of the palace," Amyntor points. "Will you forgive me?" he speaks politely, bowing his head slightly.

He had shaved his gray beard and cut his silver hair shorter… and had bathed in scented waters, anointed himself with scented oil and had sweetened his breath.

"Yes… of course." Rošanak nods graciously.

"Good," Amyntor says, relieved, as he kneels down on the floor.

Rošanak looks at him curiously.

He opens the top of a small basket resting on the floor at his feet and gently picks up a small sleepy golden puppy. "A month old! From the same stock as Peritas. I thought the Boy-King might like a loyal friend," Amyntor says with a smile. "Hephæstion once wrote that Peritas took sanctuary with you in his old age. He said you loved dogs."

Rošanak's eyes brighten with pure joy and she smiles sweetly and nods, "Yes," and quickly pushes her letter into the fold of her gown. She kneels down on the floor next to Amyntor and moves her face close to the golden puppy. The sleepy puppy opens his sleepy eyes and fawns indifferently and sniffs her. He fits in the palm of Amyntor's friendly hand. Rošanak looks into Amyntor's eyes and her smile brightens and widens.

Amyntor looks at her directly and smiles at the face of the woman about whom his son had written stacks of letters.

Rošanak gets up to her feet and calls out loudly. "Alexandros! Alexandros! Come down! Alexandros!"

A door upstairs sways open and Alexandros runs out, followed by his nursemaid. He recklessly rolls down the stairs and ends up on the floor in front of Rošanak's feet. She bends down to her knees and picks him up and shows him the golden puppy.

"Alexandros, look! A puppy!" she says excitedly, forgetting her troubles.

Amyntor gently brings the golden puppy closer to Alexandros. Alexandros leans forward and pushes his small face carelessly into the face of the small puppy. The puppy fawns again and opens his eyes and licks Alexandros' face. Alexandros breaks out in happy laughter and throws down his wooden toy cat.

New love eclipses old love…

Rošanak puts Alexandros back on the floor and Amyntor carefully puts the puppy down next to him. Alexandros and the golden puppy start rolling around on the floor together, pawing and playing. She smiles and shares openly in the pure delight of the child. It is the first act of kindness anyone has shown them since they left the Lands for Pella.

"Your father had a hound just like this one, Alexandros. His name was Peritas," Amyntor says kindly to the Boy-King.

"Pertoss!" Alexandros yells out, laughing. The boy and the puppy roll around playing, crashing here and there into the furnishings.

Rošanak closes her eyes and fills her lungs with the laughter of Alexandros. Her body fills with bittersweet happiness. She prays under her lips that her own son, Alexander, is also happy in Baktra, growing up free among horses and dogs and mountains. She reaches and takes Amyntor's hand and kisses it gratefully.

Was kindness not mightier than the sword?

Amyntor is caught off guard. Youth pours back into his old body without any warning.

This was how the Persian Queen had conquered the mighty conqueror.

HOME of AMYNTOR. PELLA
A MONTH LATER
NIGHT

Smoldering fire… flaming softly in the fireplace…

Amyntor walks back into the living room.

The room had turned quiet, with only the crackling of the dried old logs in the fireplace occasionally breaking the comfortable sleepy silence.

Roxana and Alexandros and Pertoss had all fallen asleep sprawled in front of the large fireplace on the skins of lions Hephæstion had sent him from the royal hunts across the Persian hunting grounds in Asia.

There were lots of golden lions in Asia… they said the Royal Persian Princes had to kill a lion with their bare hands to become Great Kings.

He smiles to himself and makes his way to his old couch, puts his watered wine cup next to it on a small table and reclines on the couch, holding a small book in his hands.

In former days, the couches in his house had served their share of royals and nobles… Philip and his kingsmen used to come and drink strong wine and talk freely away from the eyes and ears of the Palace of Archelaos and the meddling Queen Olympias. Then Hephæstion and Alexander used to stretch and talk endlessly on these couches after they had been called back from Mieza by Philip. And then after they had all left for Asia, it had become just him and his old dogs and his many books and his watered wine… and then just him and his wine after his dog had died… and now the tradition was carried on by the Persian Queen-Mother and the four year old Boy-King…

He takes a sip of his watered wine.

Pure wine made him fall asleep… and since Hephæstion was no longer coming home, he had started to water his wine again.

He glances over at his house guests, feeling grateful to Eurydike, Arrhidaios' wild bride, who had finally scared Roxana out of the Palace of Archelaos and into his house at the counsel of Aristonous and other Royal Bodyguards.

Roxana and Alexandros and Pertoss, the puppy, had come to visit and stayed longer and longer each time. Alexandros liked the dogs and the horses and had taken to following him around the estate. He had started to teach him how to ride a horse… it was good to have a young boy in the house again… it reminded him of Hephæstion when he was that age. Hephæstion's mother had died before he had sent him to Mieza at Philip's request to accompany Alexander, then the Boy-Prince.

Now, he had become the keeper of Alexander's son, Alexandros, the Boy-King…

That was last month and he had gotten so used to them, he had quickly forgotten what his life was like before the Persian Queen-Mother and her Son-King had drifted into his house and into his heart.

Alexandros slept in Hephæstion's old room with Pertoss... just as Alexander used to, with Peritas stretched sleeping at their feet.

And Roxana...

"What are you reading?" Rošanak says drowsily, standing next to the old couch.

Amyntor looks up at Rošanak.

His hearing was not what it used to be... he had not even heard her coming up to him.

He looks at the book in his hand.

"Xenophon the Athenian. He wrote a book about leading the Ten Thousand out of Persia. He called it *Anabasis*, the March Up Country, the march inland from the Middle Sea. He should have called it *Katabasis*, Journey Back," he mumbles.

"Eight thousand!" Rošanak says, looking at the book. "They were some thirteen thousand Hellenes and Spartans in the service of the Younger Kuros. Some died at the Battle at Kunaxa, some died on the way back. The remaining warriors marched through the Lands to the Lands by the Sea. Eight thousand and a handful survived."

She shakes her head. "Hellenes cannot count! The seven thousand at Hot Gates were counted as three hundred and the eight thousand who marched up country under the watchful eyes of the Royal Army of the Second Artaxerxes, were counted as ten thousand! Persian children can count better than Hellene historians."

Amyntor smiles.

Rošanak sits down casually next to Amyntor.

"Polydoros, my family healer, was a Hellene from Erchia. He taught me Attik. He forced me to read *Kyropædia.*"

"We used to have an old ancestral estate in Kolonos near Erchia. It was close to the Temple of Hephæstos. I do not remember much about it, but I hear it is still beautiful, full of olive trees. It was taken from my father when we were exiled. With the Exiles Decree of Alexander, I will go back one day and reclaim it when all the fighting ends. My old kinsmen have been watching over it for years, hoping it would become ours again—"

"Will you take me with you? I wish to see Athenai. Polydoros said Athenai is beautiful."

Amyntor smiles and nods.

"Yes, I will take you. Athenai is beautiful, you will like it. The Parthenon sitting high looking over the city, the Marketplace, the Academy— my father was a citizen, before we were exiled for advocating alliance with the Persian Great King and against the Spartans."

Rošanak smiles and leans over and picks up Amyntor's wine cup and takes a sip and then puts the cup to Amyntor's lips. Her body carelessly brushes against his. Amyntor takes a sip and feels his heart pounding.

Rošanak takes another sip of wine and leans over and puts the cup back on the table and reclines next to him on the couch. Her feet brush against his.

"Your feet are like ice!"

"Sorry."

"Do you ever wear anything warm on your feet?"

"Yes… when I remember…" Rošanak curls up her toes and laughs playfully.

Amyntor feels warmer.

His body was beginning to boil over sitting next to her, and hers was cold as ice!

Amyntor makes room for her and puts his arm around her and Rošanak nestles within his arms like a little girl, eager for a tall story. She rests her head on his shoulder.

"Poetry and prayer? Huh…" Amyntor mumbles distractedly under his breath.

"Poets are Lords of Words!" Rošanak nods her head. "On the Day of Final Judgment, Great Kings and Poets stand first before the Wise Lord."

"What about the historians?" Amyntor eyes her curiously.

Rošanak laughs and asks wickedly. "Like Kallisthenes or Herodotos?"

"Yes."

"Persians speak the truth. There is no amount of gold or land that would persuade a Persian to write lies like Herodotos. No Persian knows *The Persians* Herodotos wrote about! Their own mothers do not even recognize them."

She points to the book in Amyntor's hands.

"Read to me… I like Xenophon… his account of the past warms me up."

But not Herodotos! He would make her blood boil with anger!

Amyntor takes a deep breath and opens up the book.

Rošanak sees notes written all around the edges of the pages. She fills with remembrance and smiles and whispers, "Hephæstion's notes."

"No. Mine. I write notes along the edges when I read a book."

"Ah!"

"Like most boys, Hephæstion did not like to read much when he was young. So, I used to write notes for him on pages of books, telling him what was important for him to pay attention to, what everything meant. Hephæstion liked that. When he left for Asia, I continued to send him books with my notes and when he read the books, he wrote notes about my notes and returned the books to me. So, we always talked together, even when he was far away."

Rošanak's heart skips a beat.

She reaches and touches the familiar notes on the opened papyrus page with the tips of her fingers.

They were his notes… She had read and had added her own notes to them, when Hephæstion was tutoring her in Attik.

Amyntor was the one who had been reading her notes, when Hephæstion had sent the books back home to his father…

She had known Amyntor almost as long as she had known Hephæstion…

Amyntor starts reading to her:

"… when an eagle appeared upon his right and flew on ahead of him, he prayed to the gods who watch over the Lands of the Persians to conduct him on with favor and grace…

"… it was mid-afternoon when the two royal armies clashed… younger Kuros did not have his entire army in full line of battle…

"Younger Kuros charged at his Royal Brother with his 600 Horse… they routed their enemy and his 600 pursued them… all that was left about him were his closest kingsmen… then Younger Kuros caught sight of his Royal Brother and charged at him, yelling: 'I see the King!'

"Someone thrust a spear violently under his eye… Younger Kuros fell… his loyal men leaped from their horses and threw themselves on his royal body. The Great King ordered his men to cut the throats of the faithful kingsmen of the Younger Kuros over his royal dead body…

"So died the Younger Kuros…

"… of all the Persians who came after the Elder Kuros, the most royal and the most worthy to be king, as all agree who are reputed to have known Younger Kuros himself. When he was still a boy, and being educated with his royal brother and other boys, he was considered the best of them all in everything… he was the greatest lover of horses… he was most fond of hunting…

"… Friends he made and found loyal, he treated well, no man better, as all agree… when he received good wine, he often sent some to a friend with a message: 'I have not drunk such good wine for a long time, so I send you this. Please drink it up with your friends!' He would send half of all things he liked to his friends saying: Kuros liked this and he wanted you to have a taste…"

Amyntor pauses and takes a sip of his watered wine and quietly reads the note Hephæstion had written along the edges and smiles to himself: "I doubt the Younger Kuros did the same with his beloveds as he did with his wines and all things he liked… sending his beloved around with a note that said:

"Here is the woman I love best and I want you to have a taste."

Amyntor pauses and looks at Rošanak. She has fallen asleep on his chest. He looks over and Alexandros and Pertoss are both softly snoring by the fireplace. Rošanak feels heavier with sleep in his arms. He smiles to himself and continues reading the book:

"Some said his common prayer was:

May I live as long as I am able to go one better with friends and enemies.

"When he died, all his kingsmen and companions died all around him fighting to protect his royal body…"

Amyntor stops. He closes the book and closes his eyes and listens to her quiet breathing. He breathes in her scent.

Her hair smelled of sweet night-blooming jasmine…
He had not held a highborn woman in his arms for longer than he cared to remember…
His passion for Hephæstion's mother had cooled after she had gotten with child and was not rekindled after his son was born.
He had no taste for young boys and there were always a few slaves who had seen to his needs, and his needs had become fewer with the passage of time.
He was certain she was the one Hephæstion had agonized over in his letters. He had never mentioned her by name… even though it was not the custom to write of highborn women by their names, Hephæstion used to write to him about everything and everyone by name… but who else could it have been? She had appeared in his letters shortly after Alexander had married…
At first, he was glad for his son, finding a beloved after Alexander… but the new love was a secret torturous love… it had burned his soul and tormented him day and night… and had haunted his dreams.
He had not written much after he had married in Susa… just that he had married one of the Royal Daughters of the Third Darius by the order of Alexander… he had not even mentioned the name of his bride.
The gods had gifted Alexander and Hephæstion a true beauty, Roxana, *a bargain for which they had extracted a heavy price.*
But the Persian Queen, sleeping quietly in his arms, unaware of him as a man, was blameless. Who could fault her for the men who had fallen for her freely?
Men always fought over women… from the first man and first woman to the last. Even Homer had held Helene blameless for causing the Trojan Wars and all the deaths in her name.
And like all those women in the stacks of books all around him, her troubles were not of her own doing; they were sent by jealous envious gods.
"I just want her to love me!" Hephæstion had written in frustration once.
And now the same gods had sent her to him… and he felt no different about her than his son had felt… so late in life too. She had brought the flame of bodily desire back to his old body… old embers of his passion he had thought were no longer burning, long buried under the ashes of age, now silently burned and smoldered for her relentlessly…
The gods were cruel and vengeful!
Athenian writers always warned the Hellene men about the Royal Women of the Achæmenids… how they were driven by passion and emotions and manipulated the Great Kings and scattered chaos and turmoil and ruin in their path!
Well… Great Kings were men and Athenian writers were fools!
Who did not wish to be ruined by such passionate beauties?

HOUSE of ANTIPATROS. PELLA
A MONTH LATER
EVENING

"Greeting, Antipatros."

Old Antipatros looks up slowly. His age has finally caught up with him, passing eighty years.

"Amyntor."

"It has been a while."

Old Antipatros reclines back on his couch. He has been expecting him.

"I am dying," old Antipatros says, eyeing Amyntor carefully under his brow.

Their relationship had always been cordial even though they had not spoken since the Lamian wars.

Amyntor was a Hellene and he was true-born Makedonian. Philip had many kingsmen and warriors and men of the sword… but only a handful of men of words… and Amyntor was one of them. Amyntor had served Philip well as an advisor and intimate of his royal court. Even in exile, he had trusted high connections deep in Athenai that had proven very useful over the years. He was completely trusted by Philip and Philip was no fool. His grand estate bordered the royal palace with gates always left open, as a high mark of honor, so Philip and Alexander could visit as they pleased. His son was loved the most by the King. Amyntor had raised a better son than he had.

Amyntor reclines on a couch next to Antipatros, considering him intently.

The old man was hearing the call of his ancestors in his old bones.

Old Antipatros shifts slightly on his couch. Pain fills his old brittle bones.

"I hear Queen Roxana has taken sanctuary in your estate."

"The Queen-Mother and her Son-King are welcome in my humble house any time."

Old Antipatros narrows his eyes at Amyntor and says quietly, "I know two queens cannot live peacefully under the same golden crown."

"It is not for her own sake; she fears for the safety of the Boy-King!"

Old Antipatros takes a deep breath. It hurts. "All the successions in the Royal House of the Argeads have been dipped in a sea of blood!"

"None between a young girl and a four year old boy!"

"The Royals settle the succession among themselves!"

"Antipatros, how is a four year old boy supposed to defend himself against a sharp blade pointing at his throat by the merciless hands of a warrior girl? She can kill a wild boar with her bare hands! The boy is no taller than her knees, and half of half the size of a wild boar, with soft baby teeth!"

Amyntor leans forward on his couch.

"I am sure you have already told the troublesome girl that the Makedonians will never be ruled by a woman! Even Alexander had told his own mother the same, when she had wished to rule in his absence, as his regent, in your place."

Amyntor's words find their mark.

Slaves bring food and wine.

Old Antipatros takes a deep breath and reclines back on his couch and closes his eyes. His old face creases and folds.

The Royal Bitch had become even more troublesome than Olympias.

And she had gotten bolder since knowing he was dying.

"The Barbarian Queen should return to the palace."

"Will you see to the safety of the Boy-King?"

"The girl is the blood of Philip— his granddaughter, no less—"

"She is the daughter of Amyntas with a blood feud to avenge."

"She will obey the Laws of the Makedonians."

"And if she does not? Who will bring back the dead from the House of Hades? You?" Amyntor says sharply.

Old Antipatros looks at Amyntor with blazing eyes.

Amyntor slowing sips his wine and softens his words. "Antipatros, you served Philip well. You served Alexander better, even though he was younger and more difficult and had fiery meddling Olympias for a mother!"

Everyone knew that if the old Antipatros and the Royal Army he commanded had not immediately supported the right of Alexander to the throne of Makedonia after the murder of Philip, Alexander may never had become the King.

Philip had divorced Olympias before marrying Kleopatra and had called Kleopatra, Eurydike, honoring her above all his wives. He meant to disinherit Alexander, once Eurydike had borne him a prince... pure Makedonian. Alexander had pushed his King-Father to the edges of his kingly limits, with his intense passion to become a glorious king and with an intensely passionate mother who would have done anything to see her son become a king!

Amyntor leans back on his couch and his lined face folds with pain.

"We are old men, you and I. We both know well that no boy-king that young will ever live long enough to rule the Makedonian kingdom, or any kingdom, with or without the troublesome girl to start a succession war."

Amyntor was nearing sixty...

His voice softens. "Like you, I wish Alexander had begotten a proper son-prince before he had left for Asia. A full Makedonian. But things being as they are, shall we let the Boy-King die under our watch? The only legitimate son and heir of Alexander? What will people say of us as Men of Honor then?"

Old Antipatros leans back and takes another painful breath. "I will protect the Boy-King with my last breath, but I fear even my own son, Kassandros, cannot be trusted when Hades gets me."

"We can only do what we can, Antipatros."

"Amyntor?"

"Yes?"

"We— you and I— we both served Philip well."

"Yes."

"What I did was to keep Makedonia under my protection. It was what I had done since the days of Philip! It was all I had done since the days of Alexander! Garrisoning Athenai and punishing all the Hellene rebels after the Lamian War was necessary!"

"Yes," Amyntor says dismissively, sipping his wine.

Like most of Philip's men, old Antipatros was a man born to the sword.

"I will assign a few more men for the protection of the Boy-King."

"Good!"

"You know Kassandros. Take the Boy-King to his grandmother, if all else fails. Olympias is the only one who cares the most about him. She is the only one who can delay the inevitable."

Amyntor looks at Antipatros surprised.

It must have taken all of his pride to admit something like that to him.

Alexander and Kassandros utterly hated each other. Kassandros was the only noble son of fighting age who was left behind in Pella when Alexander left for Asia… he did not even take Kassandros as a hostage to ensure the good behavior of old Antipatros in his absence… and that had made the blood of Kassandros bitter beyond cure.

And they both knew all too well no boy-king had ever lived long enough to claim the blood-covered throne in Makedonia… ever. Philip himself was first the regent for the five year old boy-prince, Amyntas, the son of his own king-brother after his death in battle, the father of Adeia, the troublesome wife of Arrhidaios. Once Philip had secured his own position with the Makedonian Royal Army, the boy-prince had been forgotten and Philip had started to rule in his own name. Alexander had ordered the death of Amyntas once he had come to power after the death of Philip, but had spared his wife and daughter, the same daughter who was now holding a sharp sword pointing at the throat of the Boy-King, the Son of Alexander.

What chance did the Boy-King have to live beyond childhood in the brutal Royal Court of the Argeads?

Their Boy-King was marked for the shades by powerful men and his years were numbered and marked and counted faithfully… even Alexander had known on his deathbed that his Son-King would never live into manhood.

Amyntor sips his wine and half-smiles. "If I outlive you, I will!"

Old Antipatros looks at Amyntor and softens his words.

"Would you like me to pay for their expenses from the royal funds while they reside at your estate?"

The Boy-King was safer with Amyntor than with his kingsmen.

"No, old friend—" Amyntor takes a deep breath and puts down his wine cup. He smiles and gets to his feet, eager to return home.

He was wealthy beyond his dreams… Hephæstion's booty from the splendid Palaces of the Persians…

"Hephæstion has already seen to it."

HOME of AMYNTOR
ANOTHER MONTH PASSES
LATE NIGHT

In the middle of another haunted lonely night…

How could this be?

Rošanak coils into herself and looks at the crackling fire in the fireplace, feeling the warm tears on her cold face. The desolate harsh reality of her life has finally seeped into her bones.

The sweetness of sleep eluded her like most other nights… she could not remember the last time she had slept without any care all through the night.

All the men around her had died…

Three blood brothers and all their companions…

Utâna and all his hadâbarâ…

The Great King and all the Faithful, too…

Alexander, Hephæstion, Krateros, Perdikkas…

A whole generation of splendid men had simply vanished.

Clay to dust… Dust to dust… Dust to wind…

They had all lived as though they would never die…

And they had all died as though they had never lived…

And none had loved her enough to take her with him.

Her life with each of them had been like a passing rainy cloud on a hot summer day…

And when the hot sun had chased away all the rain clouds, she was left behind in the midst of her enemies… forgotten… fated with worse than death…

She would give up her life gladly if one of them came back for her.

She rests her head on her knees.

She was twenty-four and her life as a woman was now over.

Her body no longer obeyed the cycle of the moon.

It had ebbed after the death of Perdikkas and Krateros…

… and it had not flowed again.

She had sinned wickedly against the Laws of the Wise Lord.

She had bedded Perdikkas during her forbidden cycle, the seven days a month when her body was forbidden to be touched by a man, and now she had been utterly punished for her sins.

Her womanhood had been the grave offering for Perdikkas, who was the lover most desirous of getting her with his child.

All she was now, was the Queen-Mother of a half-breed Son-King hidden far away from the murderous claws of the Makedonian LowLanders and HighLanders.

She missed everything about Persia… sights and sighs and sounds and scents… the scented air of the Persian gardens, the soothing sounds of Persian poetry and prayer… the taste of Persian food and wine, even the taste of its earth and dirt!

Amyntor steps into the large room and fills with sadness.

What would his life be like without her and the Boy-King?

He had just nursed her back to health from a harsh winter chill and it was not even full winter yet.

Right in front of his eyes, she was slowly wasting away… homesick…

Amyntor takes a deep breath and looks at Rošanak from across the dimly-lit room.

Polyperchon had come to see him after the old Antipatros had died and made Polyperchon his successor on his death bed… and the two men had discussed it over some serious pure wine.

Unlike Hephæstion, he had no political ambitions and knew Polyperchon from when he was one of Philip's kingsmen. Polyperchon was a good man to follow orders… but came up short as a man-in-command… came up short in every way following in the footsteps of the old Antipatros… not the sort of a man who could rise to the occasion…

He had told Polyperchon that the Queen-Mother was not a royal prisoner, unless marrying their king and begetting a son was now considered a crime, and that she was free to live anywhere and he himself had no desire to become regent for the Boy-King.

But the old Antipatros had ordered Polyperchon to always keep the Kings with him, so Polyperchon had resisted at first. Finally Polyperchon, heavy with wine, had relented and the matter was decided. Polyperchon had agreed that his Estate was on Royal Land and to consider the House of Amyntor as a part of the Palace, as old Antipatros had done before him and the old gates between the two regal estates were left wide open to make it so.

Amyntor grabs a warm blanket from the couch and walks over and sits silently next to her and covers her with the blanket.

Crying again… Why do women always cry?

She looks at him through her blurry tears, shivering.

She was so lonely, her body ached. She missed the intimate touches of a lover… and the comfort of loving arms to hold her and hold on to her late at night.

All the men around her now were Makedonians who either disregarded her or tolerated her… and Polyperchon had refused her heartfelt pleading to let her return to Persia, even when she had offered to leave Alexandros behind in his care. "The Boy-King needs his mother!" he had told her firmly. Did he think she did not know that?

How would she ever return to her Son-King? To the Lands of her ancestors?

How would she ever get home?

He looks at her feet, peeking through her nightgown, and shakes his head.

She was bare-footed again.

He reaches and starts rubbing her icy feet with his warm hands.

She brushes away her tears.

"This is Pella, not Persepolis. You are just recovering from a bad winter chill. You will catch your death like this!" he says tenderly, full of concern for her.

She gently leans forward and puts her head on his shoulder and quietly utters, "You worry too much about me."

"Yes…" Amyntor says quietly, warming up her feet. His warm hands instinctively start to slowly move up her cold legs.

She takes no notice of it.

"I was born and raised in Baktria, not Persepolis. I have seen colder. Pella is not that cold." Rošanak pulls closer to his warm body.

His body was warm and comforting, just like Hephæstion's. And he smelled familiar too… like Hephæstion! He was the other side of Hephæstion.

Amyntor takes a deep breath and his body fills up with her sweet scent and his heart fills up with the pain of desire.

She was so close, right in his arms, and yet so far away…

He had tried so hard to think of her as a daughter and of himself as her guardian… as the Protector of the Queen-Mother… but he had failed miserably!

When Philip had married Kleopatra, a beautiful young girl less than half his age and a commoner, he had thought him a fool… he had thought to himself, how could a girl that young be satisfied with the body of an old man… even if the man was a king?

He was now older than Philip was then… and Roxana was not that much older than Philip's Kleopatra. And he desired her as a man desires a woman in every way… just as Philip had desired Kleopatra… but Philip was a King and could order any woman to his bed.

He was just a man… and she was a beautiful young Queen-Mother who could tempt any man to her bed…

And every moment he desired her more and more, and not having her was becoming even more painful! His old bones ached for her young body!

He closes his eyes.

And if he was to tell her of his desire for her, and if she was to find him an old fool, and if she was to judge him harshly and if she was to scorn him and leave? What then? How could he live shame-faced without her and without his honor?

His life had been so simple before she had stepped into his heart and settled so comfortably! Now, his entire life was completely wrapped around her…

Philip's shade was laughing at him… mocking him now as he had mocked Philip then…

"You should go back to your palace— you and Alexandros," Amyntor says abruptly, pushing her away.

"Why?" Rošanak says, startled. "What have we done to displease you?"

"Nothing! They can take better care of you in the palace. Here it is just me, and the horses and the dogs and two slaves— not a royal palace befitting a queen."

"Has Alexandros been too noisy?"

"No!"

"Have I done something wrong to offend you?"

"No!"

"Are we too costly to keep?"

"No!"

"Then why? Alexandros and I… we like it here, with you and the horses and the dogs… and all the books… I swear by Styx I will start wearing warm socks and I will not get sick again!"

"I want you to leave!"

"Why? Tell me the truth and I will get the boy and we will leave tonight!"

"No reason—" Amyntor says faintly and starts to get to his feet.

Rošanak reaches and takes his hand and kisses it.

What would her life be like in Pella without him?

The Amazon would eat her and her boy alive!

Amyntor pulls his hand away.

Rošanak's eyes fill with tears. "Hephæstion…" she utters quietly.

"I am not Hephæstion!" Amyntor grunts with dismay through his teeth.

Rošanak looks at Amyntor, hurt… tears flow.

Her tears break his resolve.

Amyntor takes a deep breath and sits back down and dares to take a chance.

"Do you think it is easy to watch a woman you desire day after day wasting away, loving a ghost, even if that ghost happens to be the shade of your own son?" he says in quiet desperation.

Rošanak is startled. She looks intently at Amyntor.

Could he not see in her face that her body was barren and unfruitful and worthless?

"You… desire me?"

"No!" Amyntor lies in haste. "I am too old for you—" He softens his voice. "You came here to be close to his memory. It was you he was in love with, the one he wrote about endlessly."

Rošanak takes a deep breath and lets it out silently, not denying, nor evading.

"Do you want his letters? Is that why you came to me?" Amyntor points to the silver box, wrapped in darkness, his voice quivering. "Take them and go back to the palace!"

Rošanak looks at Amyntor, bewildered.

"I came here because I saw kindness in your eyes for me and for Alexandros and heard gentleness in your voice." She turns away and rages quietly. "Damn Antipatros for dragging me to this forsaken land of faithless savages! I was free as long as I was his prisoner! And now that idiot Polyperchon lords over me! If Alexander knew how his kingsmen would treat me after his death, he would have killed me himself to be merciful!"

Amyntor fills up again with desire for her. His reason returns to him slowly.

She lowers her voice and says quietly, "I loved Hephæstion… and Alexander… and I utterly took the punishment that your gods had planned for me… and my own gods heaped more punishment on me after your gods were through with me."

Rošanak pushes herself up to her feet. "I would be glad for your love, if you were not thinking of me as the woman in those letters. A part of that woman died when Hephæstion died… another part died with Alexander… I am not in love with a ghost… you desire a dead woman… I am flesh and bones and if you cut me with your sharp words, I will bleed all over you!"

Rošanak starts to walk away and Amyntor reaches for her hand and pulls her back toward him.

"Roxana." He calls her with longing.

Rošanak stops.

Amyntor's voice softens.

"I am not taken with the woman in those letters— she belonged to my son— and to him alone!"

Amyntor pulls her hand toward his lips and kisses the tips of her fingers.

"As long as I was in the Lands of the Persians, I knew I was safe… I was a Royal Woman… I was protected by blood ties and by my divine goddess and by my god. Here, I am utterly alone. I am called a barbarian and treated with contempt even by lowly slaves… and I am forced to live next to a wretched evil girl, an Illyrian Amazon, a sworn enemy, who will not be satisfied until she bathes in the blood of my son."

She eyes Amyntor tenderly. "I came here to your good house to get away from evil… I do not fear death… I fear evil…

"And that girl, Adeia, is pure evil. She has never spoken my name out loud… she intends evil upon me… her eyes told me when I first saw her that she meant harm for me and my Son-King, because he stands in her way of becoming a queen. I had dreams of seeing Alexandros with his throat cut… with life bleeding out of him… and she was the one wielding the dagger. My dying dreams stopped when I came here. I could sleep here… I left those ghastly dreams back in that ghostly palace."

She points to the silver box of old letters. "Burn those letters, if you wish!"

Unguarded tears fall.

"Hephæstion found me when I was utterly lost and he lost me to no other but himself. On his death bed, he told me he loved me and that is enough for me. I will not ask for more."

Amyntor bites his lip and says in a quiet voice, "I am too old for you!"

"Do you think your years make you older than me? I lived with Alexander, every wound on his body, every plot against his life, every rumor about his lovers… my dead firstborn… all those times apart added years to my life. A woman is glad for what is in the heart of a man for her. Love grants powers that nature denies."

She takes a deep breath.

"It is not I who sees you too old, it is you who sees me too young!"

Amyntor pulls her closer to him and kisses her hand longingly.

Rošanak sits back down next to him.

The fire roars in the fireplace.

"Gods are everywhere. I will take you and Alexandros to the Temple of Apollo tomorrow. The Temple of Artemis is nearby too," Amyntor says quietly.

Rošanak leans against him and puts her head on his shoulder.

Amyntor starts warming up her feet again wordlessly, his warming caresses grow stronger and more intimate.

The weight of years lifts from his shoulders, desire hardens his body.

Rošanak leans forward and kisses his perfect face tenderly.

Come…

Mix fire with water…

… and fill the cup of spring again…

… with the sweet pure ice wine of winter…

Drink, while you live!

Time passes…

Life passes…

… once dead, the cup is broken…

… the fire is doused with water…

He kisses her back, his lips find her mouth, the rest of him finds its mark too.

HOME of AMYNTOR
MONTHS LATER
NIGHT

Warm bed…

Words falling on the pillows…

"As I told you before, you will like Athenai. The Parthenon, high on the hills of Acropolis, the Academy— well, you are a woman and cannot enter the Academy, but we can go to the Marketplace, and we can go see a play, if you dress like my companion," Amyntor whispers into Rošanak's ear.

Rošanak looks at Amyntor. Her eyes widen with excitement.

"Parthenon?"

"Athenai was garrisoned by Antipatros after the Lamian War, but we can still enter the city. I have many connections there. My Athenian citizenship was restored after Alexander became King and it was extended to Hephæstion. Demades, Archon of Athenai, thought it useful to have a direct link to Alexander through me. Hephæstion had the ear of Alexander and put it to good use to ask for mercy for the Athenians. We will travel in plain clothes, no one will look at an old man and his companion. We will go once I know the roads are safe— the damn wars have torn up the lands. I will buy you new clothes when we get to Athenai."

Rošanak leans forward and kisses Amyntor's face.

"You are not old and I am not your companion."

"My barbarian mistress then," Amyntor says playfully.

Rošanak pinches him.

"Ouch!"

"And what about Alexandros?"

"We send him to Polyperchon. His wife can look after him. We tell them the Queen-Mother is sick again and needs to rest."

Rošanak laughs. "You are wicked!"

"That is how Philip and I journeyed undetected into Athenai a few times."

"Why?"

"To visit Hellene brothels!"

"Which one of you dressed like the companion of the other?"

Silence… then a quiet laughter…

"Ouch!" Rošanak moans and rubs the tip of her breast and then laughs.

….

> "Impressive!" Rošanak says admiringly.
>
> *Parthenon was even more beautiful than Amyntor had described… sitting high on a hill presiding majestically over the City of Athenai, amidst old forest groves… under skies the color of the deep sea… white marble columns painted the color of the sun…*

… its splendid beauty was truly breathtaking… worthy to be admired, all the same… even though splendid Pârsâ had burned in its name.

She looks up and across.

Multitudes walked around the sacred grounds…

The statute of warrior Athena stood tall in the middle of the high temple grounds, waiting silently for sacrifices from her worshipers.

"Did I not tell you?" Amyntor whispers proudly into her ear. "Erekhtheum, built in the honor of Erekhtheos, founder of Athenai, is my favorite!" he says wistfully, pointing with his hand to the beautiful smaller temple on the other side of the Parthenon, with a row of stony painted maidens holding up the temple roof.

Athenai had grown even more beautiful in the years he had been gone. And his eyesight was not what it used to be. The Lamian War had mercifully been fought close to the City of Lamia in Thessalia.

His old connections had quietly brought them into Athenai. Years of famine and Lamian War had finally broken the spirit of Athenai, but Acropolis was as beautiful as ever.

Amyntor starts walking up the marble steps leading toward the Parthenon.

Rošanak takes another look in the direction of the Temple of Goddess Nike next to the sacred gateway into the Parthenon and says a prayer under her lips for Perdikkas. She then turns around and steps up following Amyntor.

"You are a Barbarian!"

Rošanak turns around quickly, startled. The harsh words are coming from an old man sitting on the steps of the Parthenon. She looks around. She is the only one close to the old man. She looks at his face; it is scarred by a sword slash, right through his eyes.

The old man was blind…

"How can you tell?" Rošanak says in a low voice in perfect Attik.

"I am blind— not deaf!" The old blind man says cuttingly, seeing without eyes.

Rošanak narrows her eyes at him and then shrugs her shoulders and turns and starts walking up the steps after Amyntor who was already half way up.

"You must be beautiful." The old blind man says, undaunted, hungry for conversation.

Rošanak stops and turns around and considers him for a moment and then ignores him and walks up another step.

"The man who brought you here— he must have been in exile for a long while!"

Rošanak turns around and steps down. "How—"

"I said: I am blind, not deaf! He sounds excited like a little boy seeing Parthenon for the first time!"

"And your blindness makes your tongue twice as sharp?" she says cuttingly, without a hint of pity, and the old blind man hears it in her voice and smiles.

"I made my way back to Athenai after Alexander ordered all the cities to take back their exiles. His order was proclaimed during the Olympic Games the year before he died. But my home is gone, it was given away when I was exiled, so I live on the steps of the goddess, telling old stories."

He pauses and then puts his hand on the step he is occupying. "Sit by me and I will tell you the story of the Trojan Wars. It was the story Alexander liked the best! Homer was blind like me."

Rošanak turns and looks at the old blind man. "I know the story of the Trojan Wars."

"Yes— you have read it, but have you heard it as it was meant to be heard, told by the voices of men who are descendants of the Hellenes who fought the Trojans?"

The old blind man feels the hesitation in her feet.

"What do you look like?"

"Like Helene."

The old man laughs.

"You do not sound like a Spartan either."

Rošanak relents.

"I am Persian!"

"Ah!" the old blind man says half-smiling. "I thought so!"

"How?"

The old man bellows again remorsefully, pointing to his eyes with pride wrapping around his old words. "Are you blind? I was not always blind like this. When I was a young man, I was a Hellene mercenary in the service of the Great King at Susa!"

Then his voice softens.

"You speak Attik like the Athenians, accented but pure and perfect, not like the tongue of the common people, tainted with the smell of real life, nor like a Hellene mistress, speaking to please a man. Like a woman who is used to speaking into the ears of the men of the sword who like to listen to her voice no matter what she says, even if she says nothing or speaks about nothing. My face does not repel you, you have seen worse. There is no pity in your voice for me. You just see me as a warrior with an honor wound on my face. The last woman who saw my face ran screaming and crying," the old blind man says wryly, touching the old scars on his face.

A silent moment passes.

"I saw the glorious Persepolis and the jealous gods took my sight for it!"

Rošanak's face folds.

"It is all in ruins now… all razed to the ground… blackened and burned and doomed," she says quietly with sadness. "It must have pleased the Hellenes… they must have written comedies about it, laughing at the Persians, or worse… written tragedies!"

The old man takes a deep breath.

"MainLanders are lovers of beauty— unlike the UpLanders of the North. I cried when I heard Persepolis had burned.

"Hellenes do not wish Persians destroyed, they want to be their equals… or better yet, have Persians envy the Hellenes. Xerxes burned the Temple of Athena and angered the Hellenes to the depth of their souls. Burning of Persepolis will end no differently, it will anger Persians and their calls to their gods will come back to haunt the Hellenes. The Hellenes are as wretched as the Persians now… both bent to the will of the Barbaric UpLanders of the North! Freedom of Hellenes was the grave offering for the dead at the Battle of Chæronea."

"Hellenes started it all generations past, when they first submitted their Earth and Water to the Elder Kuros, and then thought better of it and lied about it later," Rošanak says bluntly. "The Wise Lord called the Hellenes unto him… He sent his beloved king, the King of the Persians, Xerxes himself, born to the sword, to carry his message and the Hellenes arrogantly killed the Great King's envoys… and bent their knees only to gold and war…"

"Roxana!" Amyntor calls her from the top of the steps.

"He loves you," the old blind man says gently.

"He does not!"

"I said: I am blind, not deaf! It is in his voice— he is even jealous of an old blind warrior taking a meager handful of your attention, but he is also secure in your affection for him!"

Rošanak gets up to her feet and says loudly, "I am coming!"

"And you love him," the old man says gently. "Your voice is full of tenderness for him. He must be a good lover."

Rošanak turns and narrows her eyes at the old blind man.

He mumbles to himself quietly. "The burning of Persepolis was entirely dishonorable. No Athenian will ever sink that low, to praise such a shameful act committed in their honorable names, not by their brave warriors but by the hands of a wretched whore! Hellenes know all too well that their own free ways burned along with Persepolis!"

Rošanak steps down and bends her knees and takes the hand of the old blind man in her hands.

The scent of yâsmin in her hair fills his old warrior body. He says quietly in her face, "I had a Persian lover when I was in Susa. A woman who smelled like baked bread and Persian sweets."

A sharp pain travels across Rošanak's heart.

"I told her I was going back for her but my face was cut— my eyes— I became as I am. I thought she could never desire a useless blind man. I did not want her pity!"

Rošanak's eyes fill up with tears.

"Women do not pity men they love!"

He hears the tears in her voice. "Can I touch your face?" the old man says longingly, remembering the woman he had once loved. He has not touched a woman in years.

She pulls his coarse old hands to her soft face.

His coarse hands map her face softly. The tips of his fingers see her face, her wet tears seep into his parched skin.

Skin softer than the breast of a dove… lips made for kisses… lots of kisses… tears… like hallowed drops of rain falling on a desert on a cool night…

"You look nothing like a Spartan."

"Roxana!" Amyntor calls her again.

"You look like Persepolis!" the old blind man says quietly.

"Coming!" Rošanak shouts up toward Amyntor.

Then she leans forward and asks quietly, "Does your honor wound on your face still hurt?"

"No— it never did," he says, with old pain dancing around in his old voice.

Rošanak leans closer and gently kisses the sword slash on the eyes of the old blind man.

Divine Mithrâ… The Protector of all Warriors…

….

"Ah!" Rošanak opens her eyes. Her heart is racing.

The room is dark and quiet.

Amyntor kisses her bare shoulder and wraps tighter around her, covers her with the warm blanket and whispers, half-asleep. "Just a dream… go back to sleep…"

A tear falls on the pillow.

The old blind Hellene in her dream looked just like the One-eyed Antigonos…

What would have been her fate, if she had remained at his court under his protection in Asia?

Her mind wanders. She feels anxious and restless. Old deeds haunt her.

From the 3Paradayadâ, she and Alexandros had followed the Royal Army to Kelainai, the center of the old Satrapy of Phrygia where the One-eyed Antigonos had been left in charge by Alexander in former years. They had stayed in the old palace of the Younger Kuruš.

The One-eyed Antigonos had refused to take orders from the younger Perdikkas and had fled to old Antipatros when Perdikkas had summoned him to answer for his disobedience toward the Kings. He was the man who had told the old LowLander about Kleopatra and the old Antipatros had taken offense at the news…

Antigonos was a big man… tall and imposing and one-eyed. Alexandros had burst into tears when he had first seen the One-eyed Antigonos… the slash wound closing his one eye had frightened the poor boy and had embarrassed her in front of him… and when he had laughed, his thunderous laugh had terrified the boy even more!

But they said he had only bedded his only wedded wife since he had married her and his own sons had real affection for their warrior father. His eldest son, Demetrios, followed his father as a shadow followed a man.

She had seen Demetrios admitted to the presence of the One-eyed Antigonos even carrying an unsheathed sword in his hands… that was the measure of affection of a father for a son and a son for a father among the barbarian UpLanders.

She had gotten a good glimpse of Phila, the red-headed virtuous passionless widow of Krateros who was now married to the young Demetrios, a passionate boy half her age. And she had seen Krateros, the Son of Krateros, whom Phila had brought with her to live in Asia with her new husband's kinsman, the One-eyed Antigonos. The boy resembled his warrior father with deep brown eyes…

She was jealous and envious of Phila, who had so easily forgotten Krateros… the virtuous woman of exceptional character was already heavy with the seed of a beardless youth. She had kept mostly to herself, as she was missing her own Son-King, cut off from all she had known and loved…

The One-eyed Antigonos, like most Makedonians, had no taste for the Lands of the Persians beyond the Lands by the Sea, but the Lands by the Sea were still closer to the Lands of her ancestors than the wretched Pella.

She missed Persia desperately… just like Queen Amytiš had missed her home at Mâda surrounded by tree-covered mountains.

And just as Queen Amytiš had taken comfort in the beautiful Persian gardens and the Garden Palace that King Nabû'Kudra'Cara had built for her in Bâb-ilim, she had taken comfort in the House of Amyntor… and in his bed.

But a home away from home… was never home…

Rošanak takes a deep breath.

She had not said a word when the old Antipatros had finally decided to return to Pella and take the Kings with him, rather than leaving them with the One-eyed Antigonos in Asia.

She had no desire to live in the same court as Phila and her son by Krateros, especially without her own Son-King by Alexander to cling to. And Barsine, the half-Hellene mistress of Alexander, lived not too far away in Pergamos with her bastard son.

And Phila was relieved to see her leave too. Poor Phila… Demetrios had many lovers even at his young age and made no attempt at secrecy. It was not a love match, as most Makedonians were not loving people… just another marriage alliance to bind the old Antipatros to the One-eyed Antigonos. Phila had taken great care to turn the dead Krateros into a man who had never lived: a true HighLander who hated Persians and their customs.

That was the woman of exceptional quality Krateros had married and gotten with his seed… a woman who had wiped the truthful accounts of Krateros from the Royal Journal and had written accounts of a man she had wished him to be… the truth of the true HighLander had turned into lies in the hands of a virtuous wife.

Even Krateros would not have recognized himself in the righteous words of his wife.

She closes her eyes and willfully banishes the old painful memories.

She had begged Polyperchon and he had finally relented and had written to Queen Olympias to come to Pella and become the guardian of Alexandros and prepare him for kingship. No one had challenged Alexandros as the son of Alexander.

But Queen Olympias had refused… not because she thought Alexandros was not the son of Alexander, but because Eumenes had advised her to wait for the outcome of the funeral games among the kingsmen of Alexander.

She bites her lip in the dark.

If Olympias would agree to come to Pella and take over the care of Alexandros, she could quietly find passage over the waters and return to Persia… and back to the care of her own Son-King…

Alexandros did not need two queen-mothers to guide his path. And Olympias would be glad to be rid of her… as she had always counseled Alexander. Olympias could do no worse for Alexandros than she had done for Alexander.

And if she made it to Seleukos, who was now the Satrap of Bâb-ilim, he would protect her. He was her kinsman… he was married to her second sister, Apâma, who was heavy with child again…

Rošanak closes her eyes and moves deeper within the arms of Amyntor, wrapped around her in deep sleep, breathing warmly on her naked shoulder.

Amyntor kisses her shoulder in his sleep and caresses her naked breasts without waking, like an old habit.

Another tear falls on the pillow…

But what about Amyntor?

He had taken her under his protection and into his bed and to his temples to worship the gods of the lands… he had taught her the words of wise Hellenes she had not known before… Pella had become a fragrant plum orchard in his loving arms.

She felt torn between her two worlds… one of blood, the other of love.

The arms of her Son-King were calling to her from the Lands of the Persians.

And the arms of Amyntor were holding her tightly in the Lands by the Bitter Sea.

Would Amyntor abandon his home and his life and his gods and the dream of returning to the land of his ancestors one day and come with her to Persia? Would he come to love her Son-King, once he met him? What would she do, if he decided to stay behind?

How could she leave Amyntor behind?

Life in his house and in his arms had been so peaceful… as life should be…

She rolls around and lies on her side and rests her head on the pillow quietly, watching Amyntor sleeping. The light of a small candle flickers on his quiet face.

The life she always dreamt about with Hephæstion, she had found with Amyntor… a quiet comfortable peaceful life without all the glitter and intrigue and madness of the royal court and camp and campaign…

He was not Hephæstion, but he was so much like him in so many ways… and a kinder and gentler and sweeter soul… quiet and full of words. Like her, he loved books and dogs and horses and he had been a father to Alexandros… and like her, he had no taste for a life knotted with blood and battles.

And he was a good lover, too… more patient with her and more loving and more forgiving… never in a rush… he was all hers…

Her heart fills up with tenderness and her body fills up with longing for him again. She moves her face closer to him and kisses his face and reaches and starts caressing his body seductively and softly, whispering his name, waking him up in the middle of the night, like a candle calling the moth to her flame.

"Amyntor…"

Awake…
You are the pure wine,
And I am the fluted silver rhyton…
I see you and I become empty.
You pour into me…
… and when you pour into me,
I fill up with poetry…

Amyntor awakens and opens his eyes and looks at her and then smiles and pulls her closer to him. His body fills up with strong thirst for her. His pure wine slowly fills her empty rhyton and spills over.

It was sweet to be desired in the middle of the night by his beloved…

QUEEN'S TENT. ROYAL ARMY CAMP. CLOSE to PELOPONNESUS
MONTH of METAGEITNION DURING the ARCHONSHIP of ARCHIPPOS at ATHENAI
YEAR 5 of the THIRD PHILIP, MONTH 10, LOIOS
YEAR 6 of PI-LIP-SU, MONTH 4, DU'ÛZU
YEAR 5 of the FOURTH ALEXANDER, MONTH 4, DU'ÛZU
A MONTH LATER
MID-DAY

Warm air filled with tension.

"The Royal Bitch has allied with Kassandros and has started a succession war! She has written to Polyperchon in the name of Philip and has told him to hand over the Royal Army to the wretched Kassandros, as the new Regent for the King. She has sent a letter to the One-eyed Antigonos informing him of the change." Aristonous grinds his teeth and says in deep anger, "Polyperchon should never have left Adeia and Arrhidaios alone in Pella! He was warned by the old Antipatros never to turn his back on that troublesome girl. He was not at Triparadeisos and had not seen how she had provoked the Royal Army to murderous anger for their back pay!"

Amyntor leans back into his chair. He listens to sounds coming from the open window. Rošanak and Alexandros play noisily with the dogs outside. His face folds.

Idiot Polyperchon had absorbed the Persians' love of luxury, but none of their cleverness…

Old Antipatros had raised his son all too well. Old Polyperchon was no match for the ruthless Kassandros.

Aristonous continues, shaking his head. "Perdikkas was right! He should have not hesitated to do away with her. He should have thrown her on top of the funeral pyre of her warrior mother."

"What is to be done now?" Amyntor asks quietly.

"There are many who are still loyal to the Son of Alexander, almost all of the Horse. The nobles will only submit to a legitimate king begotten by Alexander."

Amyntor closes his eyes, dreading the news.

Makedonians were fickle!

They had remained faithful to the Argead Royal Houses, but they were greedy too! With wars raging in Asia among the old kingsmen of Alexander, they had started to join anyone who paid them more for their swords and services.

"Does she think they will ever be ruled by a woman? Alexander himself used to say that Makedonians will never be ruled by a woman! Not even his own Queen-Mother!" Aristonous says mockingly.

"Let Queen Olympias deal with Adeia."

"Queen Olympias—" Aristonous shakes his head. "She will need an army, and Molossians hate Makedonians!"

"True— but she is the Mother of Alexander and the Makedonians still remember him well."

Aristonous grinds his teeth. "I had sent a messenger to Polyperchon for further instructions. He has ordered us to leave for Epiros before Kassandros returns to Makedonia. Olympias cannot refuse her grandson now… the life of the Son of Alexander is now openly threatened by Philip Arrhidaios through the hands of his treacherous wife, if the Boy-King returns to Makedonia."

OUTSIDE of PALACE at DODONA. NEAR ORACLE of ZEUS. EPIROS
MONTH of BOEDROMION, DURING the ARCHONSHIP of ARCHIPPOS at ATHENAI
YEAR 5 of the THIRD PHILIP, MONTH 11, GORPIAIOS
YEAR 6 of PI-LIP-SU, MONTH 5, ÂBU
YEAR 5 of the FOURTH ALEXANDER, MONTH 5, ÂBU
DAYS LATER
AFTERNOON

"Your grandmother is a queen. You will approach her respectfully and address her properly, as Amyntor has taught you!"

Alexandros nods with the mischievous smile of an excited six year old boy. "Yes, Mother!"

Rošanak takes a deep breath and asks again. "Alexandros, you will remember everything I have told you? Yes?"

"Yes, Mother!"

"Very well," Rošanak says hesitantly. "Go."

Alexandros smiles again and starts running toward Queen Olympias, yelling, "Grandmother!" and waving his arms in the air with Pertoss running and barking after him and faithful Aristonous following both of them like a shadow. Alexandros' unruly golden hair flies around his face like a golden standard, shining in the sun.

"Grandmother!"

Queen Olympias pushes back a tear.

Alexandros crashes into Queen Olympias and hugs her tightly.

Rošanak takes a deep breath and bites her lip.

Her own Son-King would have acted like a Royal Son… not like a wild boy from the high hills…

"He is only six," Amyntor whispers into Rošanak's ear.

"He is a king."

"He is a boy!"

Rošanak pales. Her knees weaken, her heart beats faster. She remembers the cruel letters Olympias had written to Alexander about her, telling him to rid himself of her.

What if she was truly a snake-worshipping sorceress?

What if she could see the boy was not her grandson… not her blood… not of royal blood… a commoner… a substitute Boy-King… just a boy with no father of his own… the son of a poor woman of common blood… a fruitseller in the Bazaar of the 3Paradayadâ…

Could she feel it in her bones?

And if she did, could she pull down the moon and destroy what was left of her?

"Come. She is not a Persian Queen. She was the Queen-Mother. Now you are the Queen-Mother. She should be worrying about pleasing you," Amyntor says with a guarded smile.

He knew all too well how intimidating Olympias was… grown men paled at the thought of having to deal with her.

She had made poor Antipatros blaze with anger at the mere mention of her name. She had questioned everything the old Antipatros had done as the Regent and had written to Alexander to accuse and complain and meddle in affairs of the kingdom that were no business of hers…

They had all gone to the Oracle at Dodona in the morning and sacrificed generously to Zeus praying for divine courage to face her.

Rošanak hesitates for a short moment.

"I told you, if she smells fear in you, she will make your life miserable," Amyntor whispers in a hushed voice. "She is a woman who sleeps with snakes in her bed. She is not like the women you know."

Rošanak takes a deep breath and masks her face.

Queen Olympias smiles and bends her knees and hugs Alexandros tightly. "Alexandros!"

"Grandmother! Am I as handsome as my father?"

Olympias smiles. "No!" Olympias says hugging him. "But I might change my mind after you bathe and wash your dusty face and hair and body, and I can see what you look like!"

Alexandros laughs confidently and points to Pertoss proudly. "This is Pertoss! Amyntor gave him to me, when I was just a little boy! A long long time ago!"

Olympias looks up at Amyntor and the barbarian woman she has been dreading to meet. "Amyntor."

Amyntor bows his head slightly.

"Queen Olympias, you look as ravishing as ever."

They had not spoken for years. Hephæstion and Alexander were lovers when they were young men and Olympias had done nothing but try to separate the two.

Hephæstion despised her.

Alexander might have been blameless and ignorant of the death of his father, but the blood of Philip still dripped from the hands of Olympias… that was why the old Antipatros could never bring himself to tolerate the murderous woman.

Old Antipatros was loyal to the Argeads and to Philip himself… and truthfully none of Philip's old men could tolerate her.

She had gold-wreathed the dead body of Philip's assassin and had burned his body over the ashes of Philip. If she had not been the mother of Alexander, she would have been torn into pieces by Philip's men with no mercy.

Old Antipatros used to say Olympias would have murdered all twelve Olympian gods, if that was the price she had to pay to make her son King.

"This is Queen Roxana." Amyntor points respectfully to Rošanak and introduces her.

Olympias nods and extends her right hand to Rošanak.

"How was your journey, Roxana?"

"Too long, Grandmother!" Alexandros interrupts and pulls on Olympias' gown. "I rode half way on a horse, all by myself!" He points with his fingers to a small Makedonian horse. "On that giant horse!"

Olympias smiles and takes his hand.

It was good to have a piece of her beloved Son-King return to her at last after so many years. His blood had finally returned to the lands of his ancestors.

TENT of QUEEN OLYMPIAS. ROYAL CAMP. VILLAGE of EUIA
BORDER of EPIROS and MAKEDONIA
MONTH of HEKATOMBAION, DURING the ARCHONSHIP of DEMOGENES at ATHENAI
YEAR 6 of the THIRD PHILIP, MONTH 10, LOIOS
YEAR 7 of PI-LIP-SU, MONTH 4, DU'ÛZU
YEAR 6 of the FOURTH ALEXANDER, MONTH 3, DU'ÛZU
MID-DAY

"Do with the Makedonian Bitch what you will. I care nothing for her. Perdikkas should have seen to her!" Rošanak says, taking Olympias' hand.

It was Adeia and her cursed Illyrian mother who had forced themselves into a world of powerful men who had no use for either of them… and it was she who had caused all the bloody vicious troubles.

Instead of being a wife in the bed of poor Arrhidaios and begetting a Royal Son, she had worn manly clothes and the arm and armor of the Foot and had brought some thousand old Makedonians to the border between Makedonia and Epiros to engage in bloody battle with an old queen and a six year old boy.

All the wretched chaos and death, so she could call herself a bloody queen and rule in the name of poor Arrhidaios over lands to which she had no claim.

"Perdikkas was the only man who had taken the true measure of her. Right after she had forced Arrhidaios to wed her, Perdikkas had told her that he would throw her to the fighting elephants in front of the entire Royal Army if she ever caused him any trouble." Rošanak shakes her head.

The Makedonians remembered well how the Royal Army was purified after the Foot and Horse had cracked in Bâb-ilim after the death of Alexander and the Makedonian Amazon had kept her wretched mouth shut as long as Perdikkas was alive.

She ill-treated Arrhidaios and had never taken him to her bed.

Poor Arrhidaios.

And now the Illyrian Amazon was caught in the claws of Olympias and had sealed the fate of Arrhidaios along with her. Olympias had them both entombed alive in a hut, while pondering the manner of their wretched demise.

Rošanak pleads with Olympias.

"But please spare Arrhidaios! What good will come of killing a dim-witted man-child? He does not understand any of this! He thinks it is all a game. He thinks Funeral Games are the Foot and Horse races he remembers from the days of Alexander, and the victor will get wreathed and cheered by the multitudes! He does not understand that the prize of these games is his head on a spear!"

Olympias ignores her pleadings.

Amyntor steps forward and tries to help Rošanak up to her feet.

He remembered all too well the rumors about how Olympias had brutally killed Eurydike and Europa, the young wife and newborn daughter of Philip…

She had roasted Europa over a cooking fire, forcing Eurydike to watch. Roasting a newborn girl, who had no claim to kingship, alive over a smoldering fire had repulsed even Alexander himself, when he was told of his mother's bloody deed!

He had asked Hephæstion if the bloody rumors were true and he had not denied the rumors. Putting a man to the sword was at least honorable.

Olympias was as hard as the Makedonian men. She was not a woman his soft Persian could even begin to understand, nor a woman many men could understand either.

"Roxana—"

Rošanak pushes him away gently and tries again, with tears in her eyes.

"Alexander would have seen to him, if he had been troublesome! He traveled safely with Alexander in his good care for all those years. He has no honor wounds. His body has never been touched by a sword or by a woman, he has never been initiated into manhood! He will not get any women with child and heir! What use is killing him? It was that cursed Illyrian Amazon who started it all!"

Olympias looks away with blazing eyes, ignoring Rošanak, her heart burning with passionate hatred and fury and rage.

Her Son-King had died young and no one had been punished for it!

How could a young son made of godly metal just die, if his death had not been woven with the treachery of mortal men?

Arrhidaios and the bloody bitch were nothing! They would never have gotten past the Makedonian Assembly… they could have been seen to quietly with the same poison that had killed her Son-King.

It was the sons of Antipatros that she meant to destroy… Iolaos was already dead but Nikanor was in her hands and Kassandros would be next!

Amyntor eyes Olympias and bends down and whispers quietly in Rošanak's ear. "Get up! She will not change her mind!"

"That is not our way! Sons of Antipatros must die for poisoning Alexander!" Olympias says with fury.

Rošanak looks back at Olympias with teary eyes.

Amyntor was right! Alexander had gotten his fighting genius from the seed of his father, descendants of Khašâyâr and Herakles… but his deeds of utter cruelty and madness, those he had inherited from the blood of his mother… from the cruel Achilleos.

And both in battle and blood, Alexander had done all his royal ancestors one better.

She tries again. Her face wrinkles with pain.

"Alexander was not poisoned! He went to his fate, as it was foretold!"

Olympias looks away.

It was her duty and right of blood to avenge the death of her Son-King.

Rošanak closes her eyes. Her head spins.

No… Alexander was not poisoned… nor was it the wine or the wounds.

He drank the water… the sacred water from the River Ulai…

The water sacred only to the Great Kings of Hakhâmanišiya… the water cursed by the Zarathuštra Athravans and by the Babylonian Temple Enterers and by all the mothers whose sons had died needlessly in worthless wretched wars.

She was telling the truth… but who would believe her?

Olympias was desperate to believe that her beloved Son-King had died of something heroic, like Achilleos, felled by the poisoned arrow of Paris… or Hektor in the hands of Achilleos… her ears had been deafened to the sound of truth! She was in the cruel clutches of the Lord of Darkness.

Dying from drinking sacred water was not heroic… not Homeric… not glorious… not worthy of Son-Kings.

She opens her eyes and looks at Olympias through her tears.

What could she possibly tell her to persuade her to spare the life of poor Arrhidaios?

Whatever she said to her did not matter…

Since her fate had been woven into the same cloth as her captors, she had come to understand that what mattered the most to the Persians did not matter at all to the Makedonians… not to Alexander, not to his kingsmen and not to his mother.

Persians cared about the truth… they lived and died by the truth… it was the command of the Wise Lord. Lie was the source of all evil, the true weapon of the Lord of Darkness… Men of the Lands lost their tongues and their hands and their heads if they did not tell the truth!

But to the Makedonians, what mattered most was glory and gold… they cared nothing about the truth of gods.

They had been raised for generations on evil lies…

Lies told by their own ancestors and by the Hellenes… lies told by Herodotos… and by Aischylos and all the rest… those wicked men who called themselves writers of histories…

Lies to entertain the multitudes and the multitudes wanted to be entertained, not saved.

And so they had believed the lies because the truth was not as glorious… as the truth held a looking glass to their own treachery.

They wanted to believe that the Persians and all who were not Hellenes were less than human… to make it easy for their armies to kill all their men and rape and enslave and butcher multitudes of guiltless women and children for pleasure and profit and revenge… and so they had all believed the lies, until the wicked lies had become their virtuous truth.

They wanted to raise sons like Alexander who cared for nothing but his own personal glory… and they did not want men like Alexander who had come to love and exalt his enemies, the Persians.

How could men be brothers, if one worshiped the Wise Lord and the truth and the other bent his knees to the Lord of Darkness and treachery?

No… all Olympias wanted was to revenge her blood, and her hatred for old Antipatros and his sons knew no bounds…

And poor Arrhidaios was just small prey caught in a trap set for big foxes.

Olympias was going to kill him, no matter what anyone would say.

Rošanak straightens and gets to her feet and wipes her tears.

The only good thing she had ever done in her life was to send her Son-King, the son of her body, to her kinsmen to be raised like a Persian… to learn to honor the truth above all else… and learn the Law of the Great Kings and their merciful justice, away from such hard and wretched people, who worshipped gold and lies and golden lies. Truth was not in their nature… the only tongue they understood was the golden tongue of the Lord of Darkness.

Rošanak takes a deep breath.

Well, even the lying wicked historians died too and were taken before the Wise Lord for their judgment… even they had to stand shame-faced before the gods while their deeds, recorded by the Recorder of Deeds, were read out loud by old women holding their Houses of Songs.

And who would bend their knees and sink low and kiss the ground before the Wise Lord, seeking mercy for the lying historians?

They too were flung into Hell by the Angels of the Wise Lord for all their lying mischief… the Wise Lord was merciless to liars, kings and men and historians alike.

Olympias considers Rošanak for a moment.

If the ignorant Persian was a Makedonian, she would know what must be done.

How could her Homeric son have wedded such a Trojan weakling?

She shakes her head in anger and finally leans forward in her chair and sneers at Rošanak.

"Do you think if that blood-thirsty girl had carried the day, she would have been merciful with my Alexandros? Ha? Do you think that bastard Arrhidaios would have bent his knees to her and begged for mercy for Alexandros, because he was just a Boy-King of six? Because he was not initiated into manhood? Her mercy would have been to put Alexandros to the sword at once in front of your ignorant eyes, with Philip's dim-witted bastard watching and cheering!"

Olympias then turns her head and points to a handful of Thrakian mercenaries standing in the back of the room and beckons them forward.

"Put the dim-witted bastard of Philip to the sword!"

She narrows her eyes at Rošanak and then looks back at the Thrakian mercenaries and orders:

"The girl is of royal blood, so I will be merciful. Give her a sturdy rope and a sharp sword and a cup of strong poison. Let her choose her own manner of death!"

ROYAL HALL. FORTRESS at PYDNA. MAKEDONIA
MONTH of GAMELION, DURING the ARCHONSHIP of DEMOGENES at ATHENAI
YEAR 1 of the FOURTH ALEXANDER, MONTH 4, PERITIOS
YEAR 6 of A-LEK-SA-AN-DAR, MONTH 10, TEBÊTU
NIGHT

Frosted windows.

A snowstorm rages outside.

Rošanak sits close to the fireplace, looking into the roaring flames. Thessalonike is keeping Alexandros occupied, reading books.

The siege in Pydna had stretched into winter.

Kassandros had returned to Makedonia with his men after the deaths of Adeia Eurydike and Philip Arrhidaios and had forced Olympias and her court and camp to seek refuge in the Fortress at Pydna at the foot of Mount Olympus, hemmed in by the river. The men who had promised aid had been cut off by the army of Kassandros, both by land and by water, and the supplies they had been expecting never came.

Their food rations had been cut to one meal a day.

All of them, Olympias, Alexandros, Thessalonike, young Deidameia and Amyntor and some of Olympias' kinsmen and kindred had been spending most of their days in the small audience hall to conserve what little firewood they had left.

Some of the Molossian kinsmen of Olympias who had followed her from Dodona and most of the servants and slaves were granted permission to leave the fortress and return to Dodona to prevent everyone else from starving faster. They had taken Neoptolemos and Kadmeia, the son and daughter of Kleopatra with them.

Kassandros only wanted Olympias and had allowed those who wanted to leave to pass through the siege barriers unharmed.

Olympias sits down by the fire next to Rošanak.

"Thessalonike's mother, Nikesipolis, was the most beautiful woman Philip married. She was from an old line of witches from Pheræ in Thessalia," Olympias says, pointing with her eyes, and smiles. "Poor Thessalonike has no taste for men. If her mother was alive, she might have conjured up some magic potion to make her daughter more womanly."

Rošanak looks at Thessalonike for a moment and then looks back at the fire.

Thessalonike was modest and quiet.

"She is good with Alexandros."

"I raised her as my own, after her mother died a month after birthing her… if she was not the daughter of Philip, no one would give her a second look!"

Rošanak's mind wanders.

The endless days and nights in the Fortress of Sughud, when sometimes she and her mother would sit by themselves in front of a warm fire and murmur about the women they knew…

At the time, living in the mountains at the Fortress of Sughud compared to the Palace at Baktra had seemed like being in a prison. She never thought she would look back on those days warmly, but now thinking about them made her feel less cold and hungry.

"When Alexander was pursuing my father, my mother and I and the rest of the kinsmen and kindred were sent to the Fortress of Sogdian Rock, under the protection of the brother of my mother and his kinsmen," Rošanak remembers quietly. "My mother and I used to sit by this great big fire at night and talk about all the women we knew. My mother was a Baktrian Princess and she was never fully accepted by the Royal Women of the Persian Court, and she knew it! She felt the humiliation in her bones all her life! The Persians treated me the same."

Olympias glances at Rošanak. "I was always treated like a barbarian wife of Philip, too." She takes a deep breath. "Philip was charming when we first married… I was young and he was a warrior-king… but he slowly turned into a beast. He used to come to bed heavy with wine, reeking of other lovers… and he expected me to take him in with open arms. I was glad for having Alexander… he was born a king!"

Rošanak looks at Olympias. The flames flicker on the lines on her old face.

The evil snake-worshiping sorceress she had been so terrified of was just an old woman. Just another wretched Royal Woman… who had done her best for her Son-King.

Rošanak loses all her fear of Olympias.

"My mother was the most beautiful woman I knew. Her eyes were the color of golden honey… and my sister took after her." Rošanak looks back at the fire and pulls her royal robe tighter around her. "My father used to say… instead of the *Luminous Star*, they should have named me the *Bony Forest-eyed Cat*. My mother and my sister were inseparable… they looked like sisters. I used to run around after my fathers and my brothers… my brothers used to complain to my fathers that one day I would catch my death with one of their arrows, as I ran through the fields where they used to ride and hunt. My birth father had laughed and said that was just as well, since I was too ugly and bony to catch the eyes of the handsome Persian Royal Sons of the House of the Great King."

Olympias looks at Rošanak, amused.

After Alexander had died, she had been in no great hurry to meet his barbarian wife. She just wanted her grandson, the blood of Alexander. But now, after all this time, the barbarian woman Alexander had married, was just a girl…

With all the world at his feet and all the women of the world in his grasp, Alexander, the lion-hunter, had caught a scrawny little half-breed Persian cat for his bed.

ROYAL HALL

DAYS PASS

"Spartans are evil!" Amyntor declares with authority.

All heads turn toward Amyntor who is sitting between Alexandros and Deidameia, reading them a book.

Alexandros and Deidameia laugh quietly.

"No one will dispute that, Amyntor," Olympias says with authority. "Alexander hated them to the last man."

Amyntor continues reading to keep the children occupied with words, as food was becoming less and less. "Xerxes ordered Mardonios to tell the Athenians that his orders from the Great King were: first to restore to Athenai her territory, and secondly, to allow her to choose in addition whatever other territory she wished, and to enjoy her liberty. *Let Athenai but come to terms with the Great King.* Mardonios had his instructions to rebuild the temples which had been destroyed by fire. He had entrusted this mission to the First Alexander of Makedonia, your great grandfather, who was related to the Persians by blood and had a relationship with the Athenians. The Spartans threatened the Athenians that they would not send an army to assist them, if they made peace with the Persians, so the Athenians refused Mardonios. But the Athenians told the Spartans that if they ever turned them down, the Athenians would take their chances with the Persians."

Amyntor pauses.

Alexandros thinks for a moment and then gets to his feet and walks over. "Mothers, can you help us settle a debate?"

Olympias and Rošanak look up at him and almost together they smile and nod agreeably.

The boy was aging beyond his years… he was approaching seven in the hurried eagerness of a six year old…

"Amyntor and I are debating which one is more important: Honor or Strength?"

Rošanak glances over Alexandros' shoulder to Amyntor. Amyntor nods and smiles proudly.

"Which one do you value more over the other? Honor or Strength?"

Olympias and Rošanak look at Alexandros and then look at each other.

He was too young to know.

"His belly has had too much bread today!" Rošanak whispers to Olympias.

Olympias smiles and indulges Alexandros.

"Alexandros, Honor and Strength are both important and indispensable to a king. A great king must possess both to rule wisely!"

Rošanak eyes Olympias.

Without a belly full of food and wine, honor and strength were just useless words.

Then she relents and nods in agreement, "Your Grandmother is right. But a Great King must also have Heart!"

Alexandros persists. "But Mother, which one do you pray to gods that I have most? Honor or Strength?"

Rošanak gives a look to Amyntor. He shrugs his shoulders.

"Alexander had both in equal measure!" Olympias says confidently.

Alexandros patiently looks at his mother for an answer.

Rošanak tries not to think about her hunger. She relents and words pour out.

"You need enough strength to string your bow and use it honorably, and you need enough courage and wisdom to always speak the truth."

Alexandros looks confused. His mother sometimes babbles.

Deidameia pulls his hand and whispers in his ear and Alexandros gives up and they go back to Amyntor.

Amyntor glances at Rošanak discreetly and sighs.

He missed her bitterly… the last time he had slept well was wrapped around her, before they had left for Dodona to seek protection with Olympias.

Olympias points with her eyes at Amyntor. "His son, Hephæstion, and my Alexander…"

Rošanak turns her head and narrows her eyes at Olympias.

"Amyntor withdrew from the court when Alexander and Hephæstion left for Asia. I always wanted Alexander to marry and beget a son quickly. But Alexander had Hephæstion— and they were close.

"To show his continued affection for my son and his contempt for me, Hephæstion sent me a letter from Persia and wrote with an arrogant royal air:

> "To Queen Olympias, from Hephæstion, Greeting.
> Stop quarrelling with us. Not that in any case we shall much care.
> You know Alexander means more to us than anyone. Farewell."

Rošanak closes her eyes for a moment. Hephæstion is writing the letter.

He liked to sip wine and write in the middle of the night… when it was peaceful and quiet in his tent. So many nights she had awakened in the middle of the night and had quietly watched him write letters sitting at his wooden table by the light of a lamp or a few candles. Sometimes he would catch her watching him and bring the parchment and lay it on her naked back and continue writing, teasing her… sometimes he would read his letter out loud to her… Some of those letters were now sleeping quietly in the silvery box of the Great King in the House of Amyntor…

Rošanak opens her eyes and looks at Amyntor and then back at Olympias.

The poor woman knew the boy she had raised but not the man he had become.

In birth, Alexander belonged to his mother… in death, he belonged to his wife.

Hephæstion too… she remembered the boy and did not know the man.

Olympias knew nothing of the torn up men and their honor ridden bodies who had held her and had held on to her tighter than tight night after night trying to forget who they had become… remembering who they used to be.

Both of them had bathed in enough blood and had drunk enough wine to be remembered as men… not boys…

They were men to be remembered as they were by those who knew them well.

Rošanak looks back toward Amyntor, praying for wisdom.

Olympias continues, "I told Alexander marriage had nothing to do with love, it was about alliances and heirs and empires. I told him he could take anyone he desired to bed, as long as his kingship was secure with sons. Even half-breed sons with barbarians were better than no sons at all!"

Rošanak bites her lip and looks back at Olympias for a moment. The reckless words cut deep and blood starts to pour.

Amyntor had told her that Olympias could sometimes be utterly cruel… just like her snakes, she could deliver a nasty viperous bite without warning.

She breathes in deep pain.

So many lonely nights she had cursed herself for not listening to her blood mother when she had told her not to go to that cursed feast, dressed in that tight crimson dress, beckoning trouble and courting disaster!

If she had only listened to her beloved mother, Alexander would have passed through Bakhtriš without ever seeing her.

She would have married a noble of the Seven Persian families— they had not all died after all. She would have had sons and horses and dogs… and a loving husband… a life she was born to live… a life she would have preferred for herself.

Certainly a life without being subjected to daily insults from faithless barbarians and the snake-worshiping mother of her dead King-Husband.

"My mother told me once that the Mother of Alexander raised him well. He was true to his friends, generous to his men, deadly to his enemies, respectful to women, kind to animals, and… he loved his Queen…" *and a Kingsman…*

Rošanak gets up to her feet slowly.

"My mother called Alexander King, and treated him as one. I think Alexander, the King, would have liked his beloved Queen-Mother to treat his Queen-Consort well with her words… even if not in her thoughts. And Alexander, the man, would have been pleased if his mother treated his wife and child, as he himself would have."

Olympias eyes Rošanak, stunned.

What had she said to make the Persian so angry?

FORTRESS at PYDNA
DAYS PASS
MIDDLE of the NIGHT

"Ahhhhhhh!"

The loud scream cuts through the quiet night.

Rošanak jumps out of bed and grabs her robe and a candle and rushes to Alexandros' bedroom. "Alexandros? What is it?"

"Sssss… Snake!" Alexandros says as he pulls closer to the edge of his bed, pointing with his small fingers.

Olympias, Amyntor, Thessalonike and a few others pour into the bedroom behind Rošanak.

Rošanak looks to where Alexandros is pointing.

A small black snake was coiled in the middle of his bed.

One of Olympias' damn snakes had escaped from her room and had found its way into Alexandros' bedroom and had crawled into his bed…

Rošanak looks at the snake in the light of the candle and shakes her fear away, remembering how Abi-Samar had fearlessly handled the snake that had fallen on Hephæstion in Hind. She puts down the candle, sits on the edge of the bed and offers her arm to the snake fearlessly. "Şerru." The black snake moves slowly and coils around her arm. "This little one? Nothing to be afraid of! This is a *Snake of Fortune*, bringing good omens. It means you will survive the Siege of Pydna," Rošanak says confidently without a mark of fear in her voice.

"Really?" Alexandros asks, edging back toward her, eyeing the black snake wrapped around her pale arm.

"Yes!"

Rošanak rises slowly and extends her arm toward Olympias, without looking at her. "Snake is the sign of Zeus… it means Zeus himself is guarding you… protecting you from your enemies!"

Olympias takes her snake quietly without saying a word.

"Alexander was never afraid!" Rošanak says as she walks back to Alexandros.

"Never?"

"Never!"

"You want to come to my bedroom and we can read about Alexander?" Olympias asks quietly.

Alexandros looks at Rošanak and she nods her head approvingly, without looking at Olympias.

Everyone returns to their bedrooms and the fortress becomes quiet again.

Rošanak waits in her room until all waking sounds fade into silence and then quietly makes her way downstairs and sits down by the dying fireplace, shivering and tearing. Amyntor follows her quietly. He sits down next to her and covers her with a warm blanket. Rošanak looks at him through her tears, shivering. He looks at her feet, peeking through her heavy nightgown and shakes his head.

Bare-footed again!

He reaches and starts rubbing her cold feet. He scorns her tenderly.

"You will catch your death like this! No matter where you were born!"

She gently leans forward and puts her head on his shoulder and utters quietly, "Amyntor…"

"We should have stayed in Pella and taken our chances with Kassandros!" Amyntor says regretfully while warming up her feet. His warm hands start to move up her cold legs. "I have missed you…" he whispers softly in her ear. "My bed is cold and empty without you!"

Rošanak pulls closer to him and nestles in his arms.

His body is warm and comforting and the fortress is cold and frightening. "Amyntor…" she whispers quietly and starts kissing his face silently.

Amyntor pulls her closer to him and kisses her face softly, his loving caresses growing stronger and more intimate. He whispers quietly into her ear, "Come… Lay with me in my bed tonight…"

"Olympias… fortresses have so many eyes and ears…"

Amyntor starts to get to his feet. He pulls her up with him. "What will she do? Write to Alexander and complain? Enough people have died by her treacherous hands and venomous words."

Rošanak looks at him, uncertain, and looks up at the bedrooms on the second story.

She missed him… she missed eating sweet grapes and ripe plums from his orchard while he read to her from his beloved books… she missed sleeping in his arms at night… she had not slept a night soundly after they had left his house in Pella.

Amyntor pulls her into him and whispers, "Olympias be damned. This is all her doing. Instead of making a friend of old Antipatros, she made a bitter enemy of him. When she captured Arrhidaios and Adeia, instead of showing them mercy, she showed Arrhidaios the blade of an Thrakian dagger and sent Adeia a rope and a dagger and a cup of poison and ordered her to kill herself by the weapon of her choice. Even Alexander could not tolerate her. He always said Olympias extracted too high a price for nine months of lodging in her belly. He never summoned her to him. He preferred Queen Sisygambis, the Mother of Darius, to his own birth mother.

"Hephæstion wrote to me that Alexander lavished more jewelry on Sisygambis than on Olympias. Olympias used to boast about all the booty Alexander sent her. Foolish woman did not know how much Alexander had kept back in the royal treasuries. She got a few purple robes, some silver plates and some Persian carpets and a few sacks of grain… when there were 180,000 talents of gold and silver piled up in the royal treasuries of Ecbatana and Babylon. Everyone knew that that thief Harpalos lavished more of the royal funds on his whores than Alexander did on Olympias."

Rošanak laughs quietly for the first time in a long while.

"I can take you here by the fireplace, if my bed does not suit you," Amyntor says firmly with longing, and puts his arms around her and pulls her to him.

They might not survive the siege… Hades was watching and waiting…

Men already had slaughtered and eaten most of the horses and other animals in the fortress…

Olympias was a queen without an army and Kassandros had his army and all the time in the world and he was a patient man…

All the men who were still in the fortress knew that once the last bit of the food was gone, Olympias had to surrender to Kassandros and take whatever terms he was willing to offer and he was not likely to offer her any mercy after what she had done to his brothers and his men…

Her hatred for old Antipatros had sealed their fate at the hands of Kassandros.

"Come!" Amyntor pulls her into his arms. "I will not sleep alone tonight!"

He no longer just desired her… there were no words in his mother tongue to describe how he felt for her. One could say that he loved her… a borrowed word from her Persian Poets… the way Persians meant it… what Hellenes called Madness.

She was more than air to him… if this was madness, then he was mad for her!

Men who said: "Wise men do not fall in love," were all fools!

Yes… his madness was a blessing sent by the gods… he had been sick with her sweet madness for nearly three years now… he wished he had been mad all his life…

His bed was empty… he needed her.

What was tormenting him was not his own suffering, but hers. Her soft curves had been slowly melting away and her hard bones were quickly showing under her pale ivory skin.

He had resigned himself to stolen hurried moments with her in dark blind corners against cold watchful fortress walls since they had joined the court and camp and campaign of Olympias and he was tired of it.

It did not suit him to take her in secret… he wanted to hear her soft sensuous sighs when she raptured in his embrace late at night… he was proud of his love for her and grateful that she had returned his mad affection. He missed those sensuous nights back in Pella when she used to wake him up in the middle of the night, desiring his body… and the early mornings when he would wake her up, thirsting to fill her empty wine cup… and the lazy pleasant afternoons when his hard body easily found her sweetness under shady plum trees in his orchard, after the Boy-King had fallen into deep sleep in Hephæstion's old room, exhausted from running after dogs and horses…

His needs were simple: he wanted to fall asleep next to her every night and wake up next to her every morning and take pleasure from her whenever he desired her, day or night.

Olympias could go to Hades, if she did not like him bedding Roxana…

Rošanak starts to follow him to his room.

Olympias could go to Hell, if she did not like Amyntor bedding her…

Olympias cared nothing for her… she thought of her not as a beloved daughter, the Royal Wife of Alexander entrusted to her hands for safe-keeping, but as a hapless tiresome campaign wife picked up in the backwoods of Bakhtriš.

Olympias did not care much for Kleopatra either… she hardly spoke of her own blood daughter and her children were quickly forgotten, after they had left the fortress.

She was desperate for a good night's sleep without thinking the sky might fall on her at any given moment, and that was only to be had in the bed of Amyntor. He watched over her, just as Hephæstion used to… she knew she was safe with him… and well-loved and much wanted.

Her needs were simple: she wanted to fall asleep in his arms at night and wake up with his tender touches desiring her in the early mornings when the first rays of sun kissed the face of early dawn.

His gentle love was her only blessing in that wretched hard land of cold people.

STEPS OUTSIDE of FORTRESS at PYDNA
A MONTH PASSES
SUNRISE

Dawn breaks.

Unbearable cold and hunger…

The ghosts of the dead haunting the desolate fortress…

Rošanak, wrapped in a thin wool blanket, weeps quietly sitting on the cold stony steps, leaning against the stone walls. She is beyond cold and hunger.

She had been keeping Alexandros wrapped up in a multitude of blankets, forcing him to sleep longer, so he would feel his hunger less.

But still…

Everyone was down to one very thin slice of hard bread a day… but Olympias has been making sure somehow that Alexandros had three slices. Olympias always cursed Leonidas under her breath… her kinsman who had nearly starved Alexander in his childhood… and because of him, Alexander had never grown tall, as the rest of the Makedonians. Olympias was determined that her grandson would not suffer the same fate as her son.

Even the extreme cold could not chase away the stench of death. All the animals, except for Pertoss, had died of starvation or been killed and eaten… and death was flying over the head of Pertoss too…

Most of the large war elephants, brought to Makedonia by Krateros as prizes of war from Hind, had starved from a diet of sawdust and air. The one or two remaining were near starvation too… their thick tough skins hung loose on their massive bones. And no one could eat them after they died— their death stench was the worst!

The bodies of the dead were piled high in a ditch below the walls… there was not any wood left to burn the corpses. There were rumors that some of the men were making meals from the flesh of the dead.

She had promised the mother of Alexandros that she would provide for her son and now the poor boy was cold and hungry and starving again… all because of her foolishness.

But Alexandros never complained… Amyntor had read to him about the life of Alexander and all the hardship he had lived through with his men and the boy felt bound by his young honor to suffer in silence and make his father proud.

The silence of the morning breaks.

Incomprehensible words fill her ears. She looks in front of her; her vision blurred by tears and cold and hunger.

A few armed warriors were standing in front of her waving their hands.

She shudders with fear and pulls the blanket tighter around her and leans further away into the walls and moans.

Their Men of Words had wiped her clean from their Royal Journals…

… they had called her a barbarian dancing girl…

… worthless and weak and wretched…

They had called her Kingly-Father the Bakhtrian Slayer of the Third Dâriuš.

They had called her Royal Mother a whore.

Now… their Men of the Sword… had come… to eat her!

"No!" Rošanak moans faintly, too terrified to even pray

A comforting voice wraps warmly around her. "Take it," Amyntor whispers, lowering himself next to her and pulling his double cloak tighter around him.

Rošanak turns her head toward him.

He, too, was showing signs of suffering from severe cold and hunger, his hair whiter in the light of the pale winter sun, his body leaner, closer to his bones…

"Take it!" Amyntor repeats confidently. He turns his head and says a few words to the men standing in front of them. They step closer.

Rošanak pulls away, frightened.

"They have brought half of their own food for Alexandros."

Rošanak looks at Amyntor and then at the men. Her eyes widen… stunned… tears stream down her face. "What?"

"They are offering half of what they have to their King!"

The men step closer and drop bread bits into her lap.

She looks down at her lap. Her lap fills up with old dried up bread bits. She looks up.

There were tears in the eyes of the old warriors of Alexander.

She reaches and takes the coarse hands of the old warrior closest to her.

She feels ashamed to her bones.

She had always thought of common Makedonians as senseless and brutal beasts.

They had left a trail of blood in their wake across all of the Lands of the Persians and beyond.

But just like most men she had known all her life, next to unspeakable cruelty the LowLanders and the HighLanders were also capable of true kindness…

Her heart softens.

"King Alexander used to say that in his Makedonians, he had heirs and sons and kinsmen… he used to say: He was not without heirs, when he had all of you!"

Amyntor translates elaborately for the Makedonians.

Rošanak's lap fills with more bread bits.

….

Rošanak walks back hurriedly into the cold hall holding her heavy gown close and empties her gown on the wooden table in the center of the room. The table fills with bread bits.

Everyone rushes over.

"The men have offered half of their daily food to Alexandros," Amyntor says, pointing to the breaded table.

Olympias' eyes widen.

Rošanak pours some wine into a bowl and dips two bits of hard dried bread into the wine and puts it in front of Alexandros. "Eat, Alexandros! Eat!"

She then dips a piece of bread in wine and puts it down in front of Pertoss, too weak to even beg with his eyes. He licks her hand and then the piece of bread and eats it slowly… savoring it like a fine piece of roasted meat.

Rošanak hurriedly counts on her hands and then quickly counts out and separates portions of the hard bread bits and orders one of the Thrakian slaves. "Go bring a clean linen— the cleanest you can find, and a basket too. Go!"

The Thrakian slave girl runs toward the kitchen.

Everyone eyes Rošanak.

The Persian had finally gone mad and lost her reason from hunger.

The Thrakian slave girl returns with a piece of cloth and a basket. Alexandros looks at her, weakly eating his wine-soaked bread bit… life slowly draining from his small body.

Rošanak puts the small pile of the old bread bits in the middle of the cloth and wraps it up tightly. She then piles the rest in the basket. She looks over at Alexandros. He has finished his last bit of bread… his eyes asking for more.

"Alexandros, come here."

Alexandros gets up obediently and walks to Rošanak.

She kneels on the floor in front of him and pulls him close and speaks softly to him. "Alexander was loved by his men, because in their eyes he always shared in their troubles, even though he was their king."

"Yes, Mother."

"When Alexander and his men were all suffering from unspeakable thirst in the Baktrian deserts, two men brought him a few drops of morning dew that they had managed to capture in their bronze helmets, with lots of trouble. He thanked them and then poured the dew drops down into the sand… there was not enough for everyone in the Royal Army Camp and Alexander chose to suffer from thirst as much as his men did."

"Yes, Mother. Kallisthenes has written about that."

"I know you are hungry and it hurts… but so is everyone else. You can do no less for your men out there than Alexander did for his men."

Alexandros looks at Rošanak… eyes widening…

Rošanak picks up the basket and takes Alexandros' hands. "We are going to go out there and you will thank each man for their good service to you and your grandmother, and you will give him a bit of bread."

Alexandros' face brightens up.

He was walking in the footsteps of his father…

They were His Men out there!

Rošanak looks around and then calls, "Thessalonike, you can come with us and translate."

Alexandros had picked up a few coarse Makedonian words here and there, but not enough to talk to grown men. And she knew even less…

"I will go with him," Olympias says quietly, gently taking the bread basket from Rošanak.

Rošanak looks at Olympias for a long moment. Their eyes meet and speak.

Amyntor was right. Olympias was not a woman she had ever understood or loved, but she had easily taken to her son and had quickly become his beloved grandmother and deserved her public respect.

"Go, Alexandros. Go with your grandmother. Go. It is the wish of your birth mother that you share in the fortune of Alexander."

Olympias looks at Rošanak kindly. Her heart softens.

"Thessalonike. Come. You can carry the bread basket. It is too heavy for Alexandros." Olympias hands the basket over to Thessalonike. Life had been draining slowly out of her old body too.

"I will go with you too, Alexandros!" Deidameia says firmly.

Rošanak looks at Deidameia.

She was a year or two older than Alexandros and the daughter of Aiakides, the nephew of Olympias. Olympias had betrothed her to Alexandros in a small ritual to keep up their spirits and Deidameia was now following Alexandros like a shadow around the fortress, night and day.

They all wrap up warmly and leave the cold hall with Pertoss following Alexandros weakly, wagging his tail slowly.

It becomes quiet. A small fire crackles in the fireplace.

Rošanak looks at the bundled cloth holding the small pile of hard dried up bread bits on the table longingly, turns and stares into the fire and then walks over and kneels in front of the fireplace and prays quietly.

Fire was fire… she did not need a fancy silver altar to pray to the Wise Lord.

Amyntor walks over and kneels down next to her and embraces her gently in his arms.

She leans back into him and cries softly. She is beyond hunger.

"We will all starve to death!" she moans quietly.

Amyntor holds her tightly and looks at her tenderly.

All this was his doing… it was at his counsel that Roxana had fled to Olympias with the Boy-King… and she had never even once complained.

What would he tell Hephæstion if she died in his care? What would he tell himself?

"We might!" Amyntor whispers gently in her ear. "But we will die honorably with the good will and blessing of all the men out there in the fortress."

His gentleness calms her anxious fears.

"Men and their honor…" Rošanak shakes her head and pushes herself up to her feet.

Amyntor stands up.

"We are utterly alone in this house." Rošanak whispers quietly and reaches for Amyntor's hand and caresses the tips of his fingers.

She is unwashed and unshaved and unscented and she does not care.

"I prefer that you love me well before you rush to your honorable death."

Amyntor takes her hand and pulls it up to his lips and smiles sweetly, slowly pulling her to him.

She smelled like a slice of heaven.

"We will go back to Pella when this is all done. I will never let you out of my sight or out of my house again!"

Rošanak embraces Amyntor.

"When this is all done, promise me that you will take me back to my Persia."

… and to my son…

Amyntor holds her tightly and kisses her starving face with hunger.

"By Styx, I will take you anywhere you want to go when this bloody siege is over, I promise, by the gods!" And he means it…

Anywhere in the whole world to keep her safe from all who wished her harm.

ROYAL HALL. FORTRESS at PYDNA
MONTH of ELAPHEBOLION, DURING the ARCHONSHIP of DEMOGENES at ATHENAI
YEAR 1 of the FOURTH ALEXANDER, MONTH 6, XANDIKOS
YEAR 6 of A-LEK-SA-AN-DAR, MONTH 12, ADDÂRU
EARLY SPRING
MID-DAY

"Kassandros sends greeting to Queen Olympias," the Makedonian Envoy from Kassandros declares flatly, standing straight. "But he regrets that your terms are not acceptable. He demands unconditional surrender of the fortress and all your arms! Any man surrendering freely will be given quarters and food and released unharmed."

The Makedonian Envoy clears his voice and continues rudely. "Kassandros also demands the unconditional surrender of Aristonous and all his men at the Fortress of Amphipolis."

Olympias grinds her teeth, too weak and cold to stand.

Hieronymos had finally written her a letter after his wounds had healed, telling her how his kinsman, Eumenes, had been put to the sword by the One-eyed Antigonos after the Makedonian Silver Shields had turned him over to the old commander in exchange for their wives and children and their loot that had fallen into the hands of Antigonos during the Battle at Gabiene.

Eumenes was starved for days before he was executed. Had he been born a Makedonian, he might have escaped his fate as a Hellene, caught in powerful Makedonian claws.

The worthless Polyperchon had fled to Peloponnesus and disappeared.

Aiakides had been expelled from Epiros by Epirotes, who had allied with Kassandros.

Everyone still alive at the Fortress of Pydna was near death by starvation.

The last of all the war elephants had finally died.

All the men who would have helped them had fallen.

All the men who could have helped them had turned their backs.

Aristonous was her last hope and Kassandros knew it.

May the Son of Hades fall on his own sword!

"Will Kassandros guarantee the safety of Aristonous and his men if I order them to surrender?"

"Yes." The Makedonian Envoy looks at Olympias with contempt and grunts.

Lying to a woman was not lying.

Two of his sons had been put to the sword by her, when she had defeated Adeia Eurydike and the Third Philip at the Euia border. If she had given quarters to the defeated Makedonians, they might have joined and supported her in remembrance of Alexander and Philip… against Kassandros. Foolish woman had not even asked for an oath from Kassandros and words unguarded by gods meant nothing.

Olympias leans forward and writes a note to Aristonous with trembling hands, ordering him to surrender to Kassandros, and seals it and hands it over to the Makedonian Envoy.

Kassandros was a wretched beast… no better than his father. By ordering Aristonous to surrender, she had just sealed his fate and the fate of those still loyal to her.

Her only chance now was to appeal to the Assembly of Makedonians and wait for Polyperchon and Aiakides to make new allies and raise a new Royal Army.

The Makedonians would never agree to stone the mother and wife and son of Alexander to death.

The Makedonian Envoy takes the sealed note and looks around.

"Kassandros has ordered all the men still in the fortress to leave with me if they wish to be given quarters. Any man remaining in the fortress will be tried in front of the Assembly for treason."

"Very well."

"Food will be delivered to the fortress this afternoon."

He turns around and leaves.

ROYAL HALL
DAYS LATER
AFTERNOON

"I wish to return to Asia with my son, in the care of the One-eyed Antigonos," Rošanak says faintly, still weak from extreme hunger and cold.

"I am the new Regent for the Boy-King. He stays in Makedonia with his mother," Kassandros says dismissively… bluntly… cuttingly…

"Then I wish to return to Pella with my Son-King. Your father, Antipatros, had agreed that we could live in the House of Amyntor. Amyntor left with your envoy a few days ago," Rošanak says faintly, controlling the fear and anger in her voice.

Kassandros narrows his eyes at Rošanak.

Amyntor… the worthless Hellene… the father of Hephæstion, bloody lover of Alexander…

"Amyntor, yes…"

He raises his eyebrow and deliberates slowly.

"Old Amyntor was ambushed by faceless men on his way to the Assembly."

Rošanak's knees disappear under her. She steadies herself against the large table.

She had persuaded him to leave with the Makedonian Envoy so that he could return to Pella and write to One-eyed Antigonos and Lysimachos and Seleukos for their help.

He had wanted to stay with her and Alexandros.

She had sent her lover to his death.

She had killed Hephæstion's father.

"I will punish the men who killed Amyntor without cause, when we capture them of course, as it is the Law of Makedon," Kassandros says flatly as he rises to his feet.

Rošanak feels faint and light-headed and heavy-hearted. Her eyes load up with unbearable pain.

Breathable air quickly leaves the room.

Rošanak struggles for a gasp of air and then slowly gets up to her feet, marks him with her eyes and utters quietly under her breath:

"May I live as long as I can go one better with friends and enemies."

There was nothing more to say…

Kassandros narrows his eyes at her and then turns and stalks out the door.

He would put the wretched barbarian and her half-breed son to the sword immediately once the control of Makedonia was firmly in his grasp.

He had hated her from the moment he saw her in Babylon at the royal court, when he had gone to negotiate with Alexander in place of his father.

Anything that Alexander had touched must be completely destroyed.

Men always took the women of their enemies… it was their ancient custom since the days of the Trojan War… it was the right of conquest. But he hated Alexander so much that he could not even bring himself to look at his barbarian wife, let alone rape her… he could see the face of Alexander painted on her face, and the sight of her made him sick.

He preferred the plain poor Thessalonike to the perfumed proud Barbarian… the wordless Makedonian to the wordy Persian…

Marrying Thessalonike would make him heir to Philip's throne and that was what he wanted.

Foolish Olympias had done him a good service by getting rid of Adeia and Arrhidaios. Why be a Regent to a Fool and a Boy, when he could become a King?

ROYAL HALL. FORTRESS at PYDNA
MONTH of HEKATOMBAION, DURING the ARCHONSHIP of DEMOKLEIDES at ATHENAI
YEAR 1 of the FOURTH ALEXANDER, MONTH 9, PANEMOS
YEAR 7 of A-LEK-SA-AN-DAR, MONTH 3, SÎMANNU
LATE SPRING
MORNING

Angry sounds approach the fortress.

"Please let me go with you!" Rošanak takes Olympias' hand in her hand and pleads with her desperately.

Olympias nods and gently caresses Rošanak's face and says with confidence, "They will not harm me. I am the Mother of Alexander! Even the men of Kassandros ordered to kill me did not dare touch me when they came for me last month… not even for the promise of gold."

"Stay here with Alexandros." Rošanak pleads with Olympias. "I will go out with Thessalonike and see to their demands. Thessalonike can translate for me if they speak in their mother tongue."

Olympias smiles kindly and gently caresses Rošanak's hair.

"When Alexander told me that he had married a princess of a satrapy on the far edges of the Empire, I scorned him… I told him that he was the Lord of Asia… that he should only marry the daughters of the Persian King, if he was to marry a barbarian."

Rošanak's eyes well with tears.

The angry sounds outside grow nearer.

"That was a long time ago."

Rošanak looks back toward the door anxiously and then looks back at Olympias with pleading eyes.

"Yes," nods Olympias. "But not so long that it cannot still be remembered."

The shouting angry voices outside grow angrier.

"All mothers think their sons are great. But my Alexander was truly gifted. He could see in people what others could not see! That was what made him a great conqueror… he saw the strengths and weaknesses of his enemies and made the best and most of it."

Olympias takes a deep breath and lets out a sigh.

"I was envious of you. He was so far away from me and you were there with him. He became angry with me when I scorned him for marrying you! He wrote to me that he had married you to please himself, not his mother!"

"What are those noises?" Alexandros interrupts, walking into the room half-asleep.

"It is nothing. Go back to bed, Alexandros," Rošanak says quickly.

"I am not sleepy!" Alexandros says, running and hugging Olympias' legs.

"Listen to your mother, Alexandros." Olympias says gently, smiling and caressing Alexandros' unruly hair.

"No! I want to stay with you!" Alexandros says stubbornly, looking up at Olympias.

Olympias laughs and bends down and kisses Alexandros' head.

"Stay with your mother. I will be right back. I will show you some of the letters your father wrote to me when he was campaigning in Asia!"

Alexandros resists and sulks.

"I am a big boy, Grandmother! Let me go with you!"

"You are much bigger than your father was when he was your age!" Olympias laughs and hugs him tightly. "But you still have to listen to your mother!"

Alexandros smiles half-heartedly and lets go of her reluctantly.

Olympias embraces Rošanak and whispers into her ear. "I feel the gods are smiling at me. Among all who surrounded Alexander, I am holding the one he loved the most." The old queen finally spares a few kind words.

....

Finally, deadly silence…

The horrid sound of the killing mob has finally stopped.

Everything has become hauntingly quiet outside of the deserted fortress.

Alexandros trembles in Rošanak's arms. She gently pushes him into Thessalonike's lap and gets up to her feet.

The broken faces and bloody bodies of the royal boys who were stoned to death on the way to Hind rush into her eyes.

"Ah!" Her belly twists in pain. She wraps her hands around her belly and bends over. She feels sick.

Thessalonike and Alexandros look at her, scared.

Rošanak straightens. Her knees shake and her heart pounds nervously.

"Keep him here!" she tells Thessalonike firmly, pointing to Alexandros.

Thessalonike nods timidly and puts her arms around Alexandros.

Alexandros resists and insists, "I want to go with you! Let me go with you!"

"Alexandros, please! Listen to me! Stay here with Deidameia." Rošanak points to Deidameia standing behind him.

"No! I am not a child!" he yells defiantly. "Do not treat me like one!"

"Alexandros!"

"No!" He screams and stomps his foot down hard.

Rošanak loses her temper and looks at Alexandros angrily and points.

"No? Very well! Go! Go, see what evil looks like! Go on! Go!"

Alexandros frees himself from the holding arms of Thessalonike, pushes the door open and runs outside. Deidameia quickly runs after him.

Rošanak bites her lip and stands silently for a moment, looking at Thessalonike wordlessly. Her knees shake and shudder.

Thessalonike shakes her head quietly and moans. "It is the law of Makedon. Those condemned by the Assembly are stoned to death."

Rošanak yells at her, pointing with her fingers, "Is this what you call civilized? Then, I am honored to be called a Barbarian! We Persians honor our mothers, we do not stone them to death in public!"

Thessalonike pulls further away from Rošanak, without uttering a word.

Rošanak takes a deep breath.

"It is the mother of Alexander broken into bits and pieces out there!" She turns around angrily, takes another deep breath and walks outside.

Alexandros is standing motionless, chained with fear, a few steps in front of the old gate of the old fortress. His face is ghostly white… Deidameia looks whiter than newly fallen snow.

Rošanak catches up with Alexandros and stands next to him, looking at what he is looking at. Before their eyes, a few steps away, Olympias lies dead on the ground in a pool of blood and flesh and bones.

Rošanak puts her hand on Alexandros' shoulder and quietly says, "Go back inside."

Alexandros, whiter than a ghost, looks up at her with tears in his eyes.

She wipes his tears.

She had yet to tell him about Amyntor's wretched fate. She had yet to tell herself…

He had been asking about Amyntor day and night and she had been evading and hoping Kassandros had lied just to torment her.

She reads the new painful markings on his young face.

Death had moved out of the wordy pages of old histories and had found a human face…

The face of a loved grandmother…

He was no longer a child…

The Unseen One had taken his childhood along with his grandmother.

"Go on. Go back inside."

Alexandros turns around quickly and grabs Deidameia's hand and runs back into the old fortress, as fast as his shaky legs can carry him, pulling her along with him.

Rošanak's knees weaken.

With the death of Amyntor all hope of love was lost…

With the death of Olympias all hope of life in that wretched land was now lost too.

She slowly kneels down next to the dead body.

Olympias is unrecognizable, except for her long white hair, drenched in blood. Stones have reduced her body to a heap of broken flesh and bones in a sea of blood.

Rošanak's body fills with pain.

She had witnessed two stonings in her life…

The first one had taken the lives of a handful of young royal boys, and a Royal Son… her firstborn.

The second one had taken the life of a queen… the mother of Alexander.

If gods had told Alexander that his own blood mother was to die such a wretched bloody death… what would he have done?

He had destroyed the splendid House of Hakhâmanišiya…

And he had suffered the ultimate punishment for his troubles… he had destroyed the Argeads too… his own ancestral Royal House…

He had destroyed himself!

He had destroyed his own mother!

Rošanak covers her face and cries out in Persian, "*My Lord*, please… do not let me die here like this in this forsaken place at the hands of these barbarians! Look what they have done to this old queen! If this is what they do to the mother of their Alexander, what will they do to me?"

She pleads.

"My Lord, please forgive this old queen's deeds that can be forgiven. She was loved by her son, the King. She died not on the day of her fate. Let her go to the care of her ancestors."

She mourns for the fate of Olympias and for her own fate.

Fearful voices whisper around her.

She finally looks up with teary eyes. The Thrakian slave girls are gathering around the dead body. She slowly gets to her feet and wipes her tears and points to one of the Thrakian slaves and orders, "Go to the room of your mistress and bring me her royal robe."

The Thrakian slave girl stands there unmoving, rooted in fear, her eyes locked with horror on the broken body.

Rošanak yells at her, "Go! Or by your Zeus, I swear, you will taste your death at my hands!"

The Thrakian slave girl turns around and runs back inside, terrified.

Rošanak looks at the others.

"Go back inside and get your belongings and leave while you can! There is nothing but death here! Tell everyone you see on your way that Queen Olympias, the mother of Alexander, is dead!"

The slave girls turn around and run back into the old fortress.

Rošanak kneels back down again, gently caresses Olympias' bloody hair, and cries. The Thrakian slave girl comes running back, clutching a crimson royal robe. Rošanak gets to her feet and takes the old royal robe and covers Olympias' body and her dignity with it.

Thessalonike steps out of the old fortress, covering her mouth with her hands.

Rošanak looks at her with contempt.

How could someone so weak be related to Alexander by blood?

"Write to Kleopatra and tell her that her birth mother is dead!"

Familiar pounding sounds of the hooves of horses approach.

Horses neigh loudly.

Rošanak turns around and looks in the direction of the sound. The ground under her feet shakes.

Kassandros and his men were coming to bathe in the blood of their enemy…

Hate and anger starts to build in her throat.

Kassandros and his men stop and dismount their horses. He approaches with authority and stands over Olympias' broken body. He kneels to lift the royal robe covering the body.

Rošanak quickly kneels and pulls the old royal robe back gently and says at the top of her voice, "Makedonians! Look! Here is the body of the mother of Alexander! Is this what you have come to take pleasure in?"

Kassandros and his men take a step backward. The men look in horror at the broken body of a woman they themselves had refused to kill.

Kassandros looks at Rošanak and says flatly, "We had no hand in this!" He looks as empty as he did when he had told her of Amyntor's death.

"No?" Rošanak says, narrowing her eyes.

"The Assembly condemned her to death. It was the will of the Makedonians!"

Rošanak looks at the men. "Did Alexander not allow everyone accused to be heard in the Assembly, if they chose?" She points to the body and asks, "Who spoke for the mother of Alexander?" She says louder, demanding, "Who among you served with Alexander?"

The Makedonians look at each other awkwardly and murmur.

"This," Kassandros points to the body, "was done by those who had a blood feud with her, the kinsmen of those she had slaughtered in Euia, not by men in my army. The kinsmen of the dead must avenge them."

Rošanak looks at Kassandros and his men and shakes her head with dismay.

It was obvious why Alexander hated Kassandros so much.

Kassandros had no honor. And he had no gods.

"I told Queen Olympias to leave the fortress, as it was not safe for her and she refused. I tell you the same. As you can see with your own eyes, it is not safe for you here or in Pella. You and your son are to go to the Fortress in Amphipolis to live in safety under my guarded protection." Kassandros announces, trying to silence her.

They were now his prisoners!

Rošanak hears his unspoken words from his hateful eyes. She kneels down and gently covers the broken body with the old royal robe and gets to her feet.

"Who among you will give the mother of Alexander her burial rites?" Rošanak asks quietly.

The Makedonians murmur.

They all knew the curse of the dead upon the living who left their bodies unburied and denied them their burial rites… a royal body no less…

Rošanak's face folds in pain.

They had killed the mother of Alexander…

… and now they were going to deny her the honorable burial due a queen according to their customs…

"Are there any men here who cherish their mothers?"

Silence.

"Are there any men here who cherish their fathers and their sons?"

Silence.

"I will not repeat what men who knew King Alexander remember. As they all remember well that to their King no duty was more sacred than honoring the dead fallen in battle. And the King himself always honored his birth mother."

Silence.

Rošanak shakes her head with a mourning heart. She looks at Kassandros with blazing eyes and marks him again and curses him again under her breath.

May your gods fate you with a shameful death.
May the land under your feet curse you day and night.
May the sky over your head darken with fury and hail.
May all words be like thorns in your ears.

She sits back on the ground and puts the bloody stones back on the edges of the old robe, hemming in the broken body, and then gets to her feet and turns around and steps back into the old fortress like a ghost.

LATER
MIDDLE of the NIGHT

Flickering lamp… smell of olive oil burning…

Rošanak searches through Olympias' room hurriedly.

Mercifully, the damn snakes had died long ago and had been eaten during the siege.

She opens an old ornate cedar chest, loot from one of the Persian palaces that Alexander had sent to his mother. She pulls out a Persian royal robe and looks at it in the dim light of the flickering lamp in the room. It was an old royal robe that once was worn by a Persian Royal Woman.

"This one," she mumbles under her breath to herself.

She looks inside the chest and picks up a small silvery box. She opens the top. It is packed with old letters. She looks at the royal seal on the letters; it is the Makedonian seal of Alexander. She opens the letter on top. An unseen hand clutches her heart tightly. It is a letter from Alexander to his mother.

Alexander to Olympias, my mother, Greeting…

His memory comes rushing back like a rain storm forcing through the walls of old clouded memories. She closes her eyes and pushes back a tear. She had given all the letters Alexander had written her to Âriyânnâz to take back to her beloved Baktra to keep safe for her until she returned.

His voice whispers softly in her heart… "To my beloved Roxana…"

She folds the letter without reading it and puts it back in the silver box and closes the top and then picks up another box. It is filled with the splendid Persian jewelry of old Persian Royal Women. She closes the top and looks into the chest one more time.

"Ah! A Persian dagger!"

She secures the dagger and the jewelry box and the box full of letters in the middle of the Persian royal robe and bundles it. She gets up to her tired feet and turns down the lamp and leaves quietly.

OUTSIDE of the FORTRESS at PYDNA
LATER

Moonless night… haunted…

Rošanak wraps her royal robe tightly around her and pulls the bundle tightly into her chest. The night air is strangely cold for late spring, as if knotted with the chill of dead winter. She looks around. The grounds outside of the fallen old fortress are hauntingly empty and quiet.

No doubt the men of Kassandros were still watching the old fortress carefully.

Sudden rustling noises on the grounds…

She closes her eyes for a long moment and drowns in the darkness of fear and then opens her eyes and straightens.

Just wild animals lurking in the shadows, smelling the death in the air… eager for a taste of it.

Olympias was dead… and all the queen's men were dead. All that stood now between her and death in this land forsaken by the Wise Lord was time…

She must do her duty in whatever time she had left.

As her beloved mother had always told her: "With royal blood comes royal duty."

"We brought what we could find!" Thessalonike whispers quietly in Rošanak's ear, standing next to her.

Rošanak looks at her with trepidation. Her resolve ebbs and flows for a few moments.

"We should hurry!" Deidameia whispers impatiently.

Rošanak turns and looks at the young girl. "Go back inside, Deidameia. Go stay with Alexandros. Thessalonike and I will see to this!"

"Alexandros is sleeping." Deidameia raises her voice defiantly. "You cannot stop me! I am going with you! She is my blood!"

"Let her come!" Thessalonike says quietly. "She can keep an eye out for the men of Kassandros."

"Very well." Rošanak relents and takes a deep breath and nods her head, and all three women walk quietly toward the dead body of Olympias.

They all kneel down next to the body, surrounding it.

Three Royal Women, a half-Persian, a half-Makedonian and a young Molossian, had come to bury the body of the fourth Royal Woman, Olympias.

The heavy stones hemming the edges of the old royal robe have kept the dead royal body from being desecrated by the wild animals.

They all hesitate for a moment, none eager for the bloody task at hand.

Then Rošanak bites her lip and takes a deep breath and pushes herself forward and starts removing the stones one by one. Thessalonike and Deidameia start clearing the stones too. Rošanak hesitates. Thessalonike slowly lifts back the old bloodied robe.

They all pull back in horror for a moment, looking at the heap of flesh and bones and clotted blood before their eyes and smelling the sickening stench of death.

In the dark of the moonless night, the broken dead body looked more horrid than it had in the light of day.

"Hurry!" Deidameia urges in a trembling voice, turning her eyes away from the broken body.

Rošanak straightens out and flattens the old bloodied royal robe on the ground next to Olympias. Together they heave the dead body over it and pull the edges of the robe over the body. The dead blood of the old queen covers their hands. They heap all that they had brought with them on the body of Olympias. They get to their feet and start pulling the robe over the rough ground toward the groves.

The small body of the queen, loaded with death, had stiffened and seemed as heavy as a Hindu war elephant!

A few steps away, once they clear the edge of the ancient groves, they lay the body down and pick up the axes and shovels and start digging into the hard ground.

The ground was still sleeping from the harsh winter and did not yield easily to the pounding of small women…

"Ahh!" Deidameia gasps and drops her shovel and pulls back, looking behind Rošanak and Thessalonike. Her eyes widen with fear.

Rošanak and Thessalonike hurriedly turn and look behind them.

"Ahh!"

They all freeze with fear. Their pulses quicken.

The shadows of a few men surrounded them.

Men of Kassandros!

Rošanak closes her eyes. Her heart pounds like a fist against her chest. She cannot breathe.

Dear God! Is this where she was going to die?

A few frightening moments hang in the cold dark air and then pass overhead.

Rošanak thinks about the old silver box full of golden jewelry, but quick words have abandoned her terrified tongue. Her body trembles and shakes in naked fear; her heart beats in her throat and in her ears.

Then the faceless men bend down and without a sound take the axes and shovels from their hands and push them aside, and begin fiercely digging the ground.

The hard ground yields easily to harder men… and offers up a shallow grave swiftly.

The men drop the axes and shovels and disappear into the darkness, and are gone as soundlessly as they had come.

A secret honorable act of kindness for a dead queen by men who still remembered her Kingly-Son… their mothers had raised them right.

Was it not such deeds done by faceless men, without an eye for reward in coins or words, that separated them from the faceless demons of the Lord of Darkness?

The Royal Women catch their breath, finally. Their faces are pale with fear and cold. They all get to their feet quickly and pull the old royal robe with the body of Olympias heaped on it into the shallow grave.

Rošanak puts the silver box of golden jewelry at the feet of Olympias and the silver box with letters from Alexander on her broken bloodied chest.

A son's words of love to seep into the heart of his mother…

Heart to heart…

An eternal bond unbroken by death.

Rošanak's tears fall on the box.

Had Uxšiyârta remembered to put her own letters to her beloved blood mother with her, when he had buried her?

Did her blood mother know how much she had loved her and how much she had missed her?

If she had known that the last time she had seen her blood mother was to be the last time she saw her alive, she would have told her how much she loved her!

Had her blood mother died thinking she loved Thukrâ more?

Well…

She loved them both… she had two mothers… Love was not weighed and measured by scales of heart…

"Roxana, hurry!" Thessalonike urges quietly.

Rošanak takes a deep breath and wipes her tears with the backs of her hands and then puts the Persian dagger on top of the old letters. She covers the body of the Molossian Queen with the purple robe of a Persian Royal Woman and then looks around worriedly.

No doubt there were still men and beasts watching them in the dark shadows of the ancient groves… there was gold in the grave and the scent of gold always tempted faithless men who had no respect for the graves of the dead…

She runs the tip of her finger over the sharp edge of the Persian dagger, her royal blood marks its lips.

"Here lies Olympias, the mother of King Alexander, the wife of King Philip, daughter of King Neoptolemos. A Molossian Princess by birth, a Makedonian Queen by marriage, a Royal Mother by fate.

"Any man who desecrates her grave… her gods, her Son-King, and this bloodied dagger will see to him!" Rošanak says loud enough for the ears of the men unseen, her voice shaking and trembling.

Even if they did not understand her tongue, they would know by the tone of her voice that the grave was marked and protected by powers far beyond their own.

The Royal Women look around them cautiously.

Eerie, creepy sounds of the ancient groves meet their ears and nothing else.

Rošanak rests the bloodied dagger on top of the royal robe. Then they quickly cover the grave with the cold dirt that the faceless men had dug.

Olympias disappears into the womb of the earth.

Rošanak closes her eyes in pain.

Now, when Kassandros comes for her own blood, perhaps someone would take pity on her and bury her bones, so her dead body would not become desecrated by men and beasts…

"Remember this place!" Rošanak tells Deidameia quietly, pointing around. "Tell your men where the body of their queen is buried. Tell your father to bury the body of his kindred according to the customs of their gods."

Deidameia nods her head dutifully in the dark.

Rošanak looks up at the heavens.

> *"My Lord! Tell the gods of Alexander to tell him that his Royal Wife honored the body of his Royal Mother… the body of her own kindred… the mother of the father of her Royal Sons…*
>
> *"Divine Mithrâ… the Protector of all Warriors… here lies the royal mother of a conquering king… who loved and honored his birth mother like a loyal Persian son until his last mortal breath…"*

She slowly gets to her feet, her face washed with tears. She presses the dagger cut on her finger to keep the blood from flowing and prays under her lips.

> *"Divine Ânâhitâ… the Protector of all Women… grant me this favor…*
> *Please deliver Amyntor to his gods, as he himself would have wanted…*
> *His son knew how things should be done… he always honored the dead…*
> *Do not let the body of his father become dishonored by men or beasts…*
> *… let marigolds and violets grow where his blood was spilled…"*

FORTRESS at AMPHIPOLIS. BANKS of RIVER STRYMON. MAKEDONIA
MONTH of BOEDROMION, DURING the ARCHONSHIP of SIMONIDES at ATHENAI
YEAR 6 of the FOURTH ALEXANDER, MONTH 12, HYPERBERETAIOS
YEAR 12 of A-LEK-SA-AN-DAR, MONTH 6, ULÛLU
5 YEARS LATER
SETTING SUN

Oakata…

Men were fools of fortune!

Rošanak puts down Alexander's old worn out copy of *Ilias* and looks out at the rolling river pouring into the shifting waters of the Bitter Sea.

They said a blind poet had written Ilias… Homer had blamed the gods for the treacheries of men… but men, as the Wise Lord had decreed, were free to choose…

Hephæstion was right all along; Ilias was not a tale of love, it was a tale of death. Hellenes had no words for love… just honor and revenge and war and death.

And poor Helene… everyone spoke of her wondrous beauty… no one spoke of her wretched loneliness… and in her own wretched loneliness, Rošanak had finally understood Helene.

A Spartan, Helene was stolen by the worthless Paris from the arms of the brutal Menelaos and taken to the Lands by the Middle Sea on the edges of the Persian Empire. The Divine Ânâhitâ had pitied the poor woman and had sent her Hektor, who was the noble brother of worthless Paris but nothing like him. Handsome and brave, he had taken Helene under his generous protection. It was Hektor whom Helene had loved and lost, not Paris… Paris was a fool!

The blind poet should have known that.

He should have sung about the rage of Helene, not Achilleos. Achilleos had lived in the blink of an eye and had died in a moment of glory… he should have worn Persian boots to protect his unprotected heel from the arrow of Paris! Paris was not even half as good as a Persian archer!

Helene had walked bare-footed through all her years in captivity, wearing pieces of cloth too meager to even cover her naked breasts.

Poor Helene had gone on living and living and living… Her daughter, Hermione, begotten by Menelaos, the brutal Spartan, was so ashamed of her bloodline that she had conspired to kill her own blood son.

Achilleos was a weakling compared to Helene! The wrath of Achilleos was like a flicker of a candle… the rage of Helene was like the flames over Pârsâ!

"Mother! Look at me!"

Rošanak leans out of the window in her room and turns her head down toward the voice.

Alexandros waves, smiling at her from the stony banks of the river below, with Pertoss, still limping and chasing after birds at his old age.

She smiles and waves back.

Time had passed quickly…

Like swift Nisâya horses racing over the vast plains of Pârsâ… and all the Lands.

Alexandros had grown up to near manhood in the five years following the deaths of Olympias and Amyntor. The loss of his grandmother and his father had marked the end of his childhood. His voice flickered between the shallow voice of a boy and the deep voice of a man and the price was the memories of the people and lands and years gone by. By the account of his blood mother, he had seen thirteen or fourteen years by now… but was still shorter and smaller than other boys his age. His young body still bore witness to years of starvation, first as a young child growing up and then the torment of the Siege at Pydna. Mercifully, the gods of his ancestors had taken away his painful childhood memories… he only remembered fragments… and his only companion, Pertoss, was still as loyal to him as Peritas had been to Alexander.

But even poor Pertoss was broken after the Siege of Pydna and walked with a limp on his four old legs.

After the deaths of Amyntor and Olympias, Alexandros had grown more quiet. Other than his size, he looked no different from the other boys at the Fortress of Amphipolis. He had outgrown his old royal clothes soon after they were sent to the fortress and she had to clothe him like all other boys his age after Kassandros had denied them all marks of royalty.

Almost everything of value she had brought with her to Amphipolis had been sold or bartered or bribed to ensure Alexandros got better food in his belly and warmer clothes on his back, and some secret arms training to keep his spirit strong from some of the older guards who were still mindful of his namesake and had served under Alexander in Asia. And there was not much else for Alexandros to do in this wretched fortress anyway, and no boy had ever entered manhood without knowing how to draw a bow or wield a sword… it was gold well spent…

Her emerald necklace too was gone… a token of Alexander's love…

Alexander had stayed in Amphipolis before crossing into Asia and wanted to build a temple there, but that surely must have been a different place than this one… the Fortress at Amphipolis was utterly forgotten by the gods.

A dark cloud crosses her heart. She takes a deep breath.

Amyntor…

After the death of Amyntor, she had grown more quiet herself. When they had separated and stayed apart on account of Olympias, he had started to write her letters… and while they were sieged in the Fortress of Pydna, he had written her sweet poetry. She had put those precious letters in his baggage to keep them from falling into the hands of Kassandros when Amyntor had left Pydna Fortress with all the other men after the siege had ended. All those love words were now lost to her… all she had left of him, aside from precious love memories in her heart, were the notes he had written for her along the edges of the Royal Journal she had been keeping, still talking to her beyond his grave.

She slept with the journal under her hard pillow, fiercely guarded, for fear of losing those last bits of him too… "Poetry is better than gold," he used to say to her often, "… like air, it belongs to all men, poor or moneyed…"

She takes a breath and curses Kassandros under her lips.

She had tried hard not to think of Amyntor, lest the grief and guilt of losing him drive her to bitter madness…

So she only thought of him on rainy days and starry nights and in early spring when the old Heaven made love to the young Earth and made everything clean and new. He used to say all men were like flowers in a meadow… spring brought forth many flowers growing in the same meadow… all meant to live together peacefully…

She looks up at the sky. The sun is beginning to fall into the sea, dark clouds gathering in the distance…

She had done the best she could for Alexandros… could his own blood mother have done any better?

Rošanak gently caresses the top of the small silver jewelry box that was filled with the ashes of Pârsâ mixed in with the fragments of her life. Her thoughts wander to her own Son-King.

What did the son of her body, Alexander, look like?

Was he growing up handsome and tall like her fathers and brothers?

Or…

Was he favored by the looks of his blood father?

She takes a deep breath.

As long as Aristonous was alive, he had sent her letters back to the Lands of the Persians, without asking any questions. He had remained faithful to Alexander and had treated her and Alexandros like members of the Royal House of Argead.

But Kassandros had killed Aristonous when he had surrendered his arms and armor and the Fortress at Amphipolis by the order of Olympias. Kassandros had replaced him with one of his own men by the time she had been banished to Amphipolis… a man named Glaukias, and he was loyal only to Kassandros and hated Alexander as much as he did, or liked the gold of Kassandros more. It did not matter much, one was no better than the other… like Amphipolis, Glaukias was godless.

But much to her surprise, it was Thessalonike who had kept faith with her all these years in Amphipolis. After the death of Olympias, Kassandros had forced Thessalonike to marry him, to tie himself not to Alexander but to Philip. Poor wretched girl, who could not bear the intimate touch of a man, had been forced to bed the most wretched of all men… and had borne him three sons… two of them born together!

And she loved the last son the best and favored him over the others. He had torn her body at birth and had ended her fertility and Kassandros had no more cause to bed her. She had named him Alexandros.

Because of Thessalonike, Kassandros had taken all the Molossian kindred of Olympias to the borders of Epiros and had released them to their men without ransoming them or harming them… and she had paid slaves to rescue Pyrrhos, the infant son of Aiakides, and hide him from the blade of Kassandros.

Thessalonike had kept connected to all the kingsmen and men who were still loyal to Alexander and to the Molossians and had given them news of her and Alexandros.

The One-eyed Antigonos had always demanded that Kassandros free her and Alexandros and let them live among the Makedonians with full honors and marks of royalty and had openly accused Kassandros of murdering Olympias… and other voices had murmured that the Boy-King should be taught the skills needed to become a king.

Thessalonike had given her news of the Antipatrids and the Lagids and the Seleukids and the Antigonids and the Lysimachians.

And Thessalonike had even managed to give Amyntor an honorable burial according to his customs and bury his bones with honors… and had sold or given away what was left of his furnishings and horses and dogs. His books she had kept. His house had caught fire one night in early autumn and all that was left of Hephæstion and Amyntor had burned and afterward what remained of the house had been abandoned… and then there was no one of their blood left to care about their cause.

All the letters of Hephæstion were lost in the fire too…

Thessalonike had been kinder to Alexandros than Kleopatra.

She had written to Kleopatra after Olympias had been stoned to death and after Kassandros had exiled her and Alexandros to the Fortress at Amphipolis, but Kleopatra had never responded. Eumenes must have told Kleopatra about her and Perdikkas, but why should she have cared? Kleopatra cared nothing for Perdikkas… she had just wanted a husband to make into a king. Was it her fault that Perdikkas had cared for her? If he had wanted Kleopatra, how hard would it have been to get loaded with wine and cut a loaf of bread in half and take a bite?

Thessalonike had come to see her as often as she could and always brought little gifts for Alexandros, and books… lots of books… all from Amyntor's old house before it had burned… Euripides and Plato and Sophocles and Xenophon and others, all with his notes around the edges.

Olympias had been like a mother to Thessalonike, and she had always remembered the kindness Olympias and Alexander had shown her, kindness that was not wasted on her as on so many others.

She looks down at the river again. Winds have picked up. A young guard is approaching Alexandros.

Alexandros had reached that age when, according to the customs of the LowLanders and the HighLanders, young men took older men as lovers… and so he was beginning to get attention from the older men around the fortress who wanted to become his lover and initiate him into manhood and were beginning to compete for his favors…

That was not a custom of the Persians.

She was glad she had left her own blood Son-King in the Lands of the Persians in the care of her kinsmen.

"Alexandros, come inside. It is getting dark!"

Alexandros waves back at her and Rošanak returns to her small desk by the window and looks down at her letter.

Thessalonike had told her that before Eumenes died, he had finally sent the bones of Krateros to Phila for burial.

Just like Perdikkas, Krateros too had finally come home to be buried in the HighLands of his ancestral fathers as he had always wanted for himself.

Nearchos had pleaded with the One-eyed Antigonos for the life of Eumenes... Nearchos and Eumenes were kinsmen, tied by the blood of Barsine at the royal weddings at the Royal City of Çûšâ. Nearchos had returned to Pergamos to his wife after Eumenes was put to the sword, and had taken the bones of Eumenes for his wife and children to bury. He was ashamed of having served a man like the unforgiving One-eyed Antigonos, but had returned later to serve Demetrios.

And Peithon, who had betrayed and stabbed Perdikkas for gold and later betrayed Eumenes to the One-eyed Antigonos... he too was killed by Antigonos for his good service to him on charges of plotting a rebellion. The bloody betrayer finally betrayed in blood... death justified... a reward well-deserved... for a man who had the blood of a king on his bloody sword.

She hears footsteps and turns her head slowly and sees her Thrakian slave girl bringing in a night lamp. Rošanak smiles at her kindly and turns her head back toward the view of the sunset through the window.

She had bribed Glaukias generously for a small room with a window overlooking the Bitter Sea. She had gifted his wife with Olympias' old royal robe that she wore to her sacred religious rites... and the wife had talked her husband into a generous favor for the forgotten Queen-Mother...

She takes a breath of the fresh salt air and then looks down at her letter and continues reading.

A letter from Rošanak to Alexander, my beloved Son-King:
In the year 248 after Kuruš the Elder, Month 6, Karbašiyaš, 17 days passed, in Year 12 of the Fourth Alexander:

I send you much greetings of love and peace and prosperity. May the Wise Lord and Divine Mithrâ bless my Son-King and keep him in good health. May my Son-King be well and his heart be happy.
I have not written for far too long! I think about writing often, but writing to you only makes me miss you more, so I do not write as often as a mother should to her beloved son. But today I am at peace and thinking of you fills me with pure joy.

Glaukias says the Wars of the Successors have finally come to an end and there is much hope for peace and an end to the bloodshed. Glaukias says a peace agreement was agreed to among the kingsmen of your Kingly-Father in the last month of the last year, right before the Festival of No'rouz, and finally signed and sealed early this summer.
Ptolemaios keeps Mudrâya. Lysimachos keeps Thrake. One-eyed Antigonos and Kassandros are to remain high commanders of the Makedonian Royal Army, Kassandros in the UpLands and One-eyed Antigonos in the Lands by the Sea.
The peace agreement names you as the sole ruler of the entire Empire of your father when you come of age in six years. By the favor of the Wise Lord, maybe once peace rules the Lands again, Kassandros will finally free me from the Fortress of Amphipolis and let me return to Persia.
This year come late summer, after the Festival of Tirgân, you will be thirteen years old. Mâr'at Bani Âriyânnâz tells me that now you are taller than your father was at the peak of his manhood and still growing taller. She says that even with the sky gray eyes of your father, you look a lot like my youngest brother when he was your age and he was the most handsome of all my brothers.
I would give my life to look upon you now and see the man you are becoming from the young boy I remember, barely three years old who cried for my arms in 3Paradayadâ, more than nine years ago. I know that you too do not remember me as I was. This is the way of the world and not your fault or mine. You live your days dreaming of becoming a king and I live mine dreaming of the days I used to be a queen. As I grow older, the memories of my youth are as fresh as ever in my mind, whereas my life in exile in the UpLands seems already forgotten.
The small Ketâb I have been writing for you is almost finished. I will send it to you as a gift to honor the day of your birth to me. Mâr'at Bani Âriyânnâz tells me that like all Persian boys, you excel with the bow and arrow and command a horse better than your older brothers, Dârâ and Nimâ, when you play the game of chogân.
She also tells me that you do not apply yourself as much to reading and writing and prefer the Art of War. I hope one day you will master the art of reading my Ketâb without the assistance of a Tippirâ, as most of what I have written is just to be shared between a mother and her beloved son.

She looks up.
She had not taught Alexandros her tongue.
What use would it have been to teach him the tongues of the Great Kings?

She bites her lip and looks down and reads.

> *Be kind, when you read my Ktâb, as I have not made any attempt to make you think better of me than I am.*
> *I am not as skilled a writer as those court scribes who write magnificent Royal Journals to be read in the Royal Court and to be preserved in the Royal Archives of the Royal Libraries. I just write what is in my heart.*
> *I loved your father the best I could, as it is never easy to love a King who has spilled royal blood.*
> *Alexander used to say that all men loved him for their King and only one man loved him for Alexander. Good or bad, your father was much loved by his mother, as you are much loved by me.*
> *Till the end of time, mothers will name their beloved sons Alexander, remembering how much you and your father were loved by your mothers!*
> *And men will name their sons Alexander, hoping that their sons grow up fearless and invincible and kingly.*
> *I wish I could tell you that your father and I fell in love under the starry skies of Baktra, where he shined like a victorious King in his glorious arm and armor and I sparkled like a jewel in the crown of a Persian King. But the truth is that we took an oath in the Baktra Hadiš stables in front of our aged horses to bring peace to the Lands, and we both kept to that oath.*
> *I did love your father and loved him well the first year we were married, but it was not to last. Bakhtrians revolted when we crossed into Hinduya and a group of royal boys, sons of noble families of the UpLands, sent to serve their King, none older than you are now, banded together and conspired to kill your father, when we were celebrating our first Festival of Mithrâkânâ together.*
> *Your father's heart turned and he was never fully trusting of men afterward.*
> *You are my only Son-King, but not my firstborn, as your older brother was born after the attempt on the life of your Kingly-Father and lived only a day, before he was called back by the Wise Lord.*
> *Should he had lived by the favor of the Wise Lord, he would have been named Alexander. His innocent soul waits for me by the Bridge of Chinvât, as he will share the same judgment as that of his mother.*

She pauses and swallows hard and looks up.
Hephæstion… according to Amyntor, today was his birthday. He was born a day's ride from Amphipolis and his mortal body was buried about a day's ride from where her Son-King lived now.
She had never asked him if he was the one who had burned her beloved Pârsâ.
She had loved him too well to want to know with certainty.

What would she have done, if she had known with utmost certainty?
Did the blame for such a merciless act not rest with the King himself?
It no longer mattered why Pârsâ was burned… only that it had burned in the hands of the invaders… with the blessing of their king…
Alexander had burned the inheritance of his blood sons.

She wipes her tears and starts reading again. She wants to finish her letter. Thessalonike would see to the letter the next time she came to see her and Alexandros.

> My Keţâb is not a full accounting of your father, as he was a famous king and conqueror and many will write about him to elevate him to eternal light or damn him to eternal darkness. It is just what I know of him and our brief lives together, as I know not much of what went on before he stepped on the Lands of the Persians, only what he saw fit to tell me.
> No matter what is told by the storytellers, just know that he looks upon you from wherever dead Makedonian Kings are and when he does, his heart is filled with pride to claim you as his royal blood and his son.
> And know that his love that was lost to me for the years after your blood brother died in his arms, found me again in our last year together, and you were begotten with much love and wanting.

She pauses and caresses the cover of her K^{e}tâb on the table with the tips of her fingers.

Amyntor was right. Women should not leave the telling of the accounts of their men to their sworn enemies.
It was Amyntor who had persuaded her to write her K^{e}tâb, a private Royal Journal, when they were at the Fortress of Pydna to keep her mind off starvation.
Every night, he had lovingly read every word she had written.

She pushes back a tear and starts reading again.

> My desire is for you to remember those who are not so well remembered.
> My father who would have loved to sit you upon his knees and tell you stories of his younger years when he hunted lions with his royal brothers on the plains they lovingly called *the Cradle of the Persians*, and the stories of my beloved royal ancestors who will hear of my good words through the winds that bring such news and through the Divine Goddess Ânâhitâ, the protector of all women, and may they forgive me my captive life and let me return to my beloved home!
> My beloved mother, may her soul be happy in the Land of the Eternal Light, always told me that one can only pray for the King and the Lands of the Persians.

Then, I am the most blessed of all mothers! As when I pray to the Wise Lord, I pray for both of my Kingly-Sons. And when I pray for you, my beloved son, I pray for your life to be long, and for your days to be filled with love and for the world that surrounds your mortal body to be filled with peace.
May the Wise Lord and Divine Ânâhitâ and Divine Mithrâ bless Abû and Oštana and Itâna and Dârâ and Nimâ and keep them in good health.
May the Wise Lord make your heart merciful.

ROYAL SEAL of DUKŠIŠ ROŠANAK

Rošanak looks up. The sun has set.

Where was Alexandros?

He no longer listened when she called him.

He thought he was too old now to mind his mother.

She gets to her feet and picks up her small jewelry box and walks toward the open window. The fortress is strangely quiet.

She calls out again, "Alexandros!"

A dog barks and snarls and then yelps. Then quiet.

A shadow walks quietly into Rošanak's room. He picks up the letter and the little book on the small table and puts them in the fire altar. The fire quickly devours the letter and slowly dances around the small book. He then approaches Rošanak quietly from behind.

Rošanak is deep in her thoughts and does not hear the cautious footsteps.

Wind whistles…

Fresh blood splatters on Rošanak's gown.

She turns and pulls back in horror, as Glaukias staggers and falls on the floor in front of her, blood gushing forth furiously from his cut throat. Her fingers forget the silver box in terror and it slides and falls out of her hand carelessly and hits the floor. The top opens and the dark ashes spill all around her.

Her voice utterly fails her.

A bloody blade shines in the dim light of the night lamp and the man holding the dagger slowly steps out of the darkness toward her.

Rošanak's eyes widen with fear.

"Who are you?" She forces out the words in Persian, forgetting her Attik tongue in her utter fear.

A tall young man, wearing trousers, emerges fully out of the darkness and guardedly steps toward her. She pulls back on weak knees.

"This man meant to kill you!" he says in a low throaty voice in accented Persian.

Another young man emerges from the darkness and approaches the Persian and whispers quietly in his ear. The Persian looks back at Rošanak and takes a deep breath and says quietly, pointing, "Your son— my men did not get to him in time."

Rošanak covers her mouth and the color of life drains from her face. She runs to the window, but the darkness has wrapped around the Fortress at Amphipolis and the moon and the stars are still hiding in the belly of the Bitter Sea. She turns around and rushes out the door and runs down the steps.

The faded sun is hemmed in by the coming darkness.

The Fortress at Amphipolis was empty… utterly deserted…

She pauses for a moment and looks around.

The guards at the fortress were not careless…

She looks around again in bewilderment.

Where were all the guards?

And all the women and children of the guards who crowded the fortress day and night?

Had they all gone to the temple of one of their gods to offer him the blood and breath of her son as godly sacrifice?

She rushes outside. She looks around again and her searching eyes find their target. "Ah!"

Blood everywhere!

Alexandros was lying in a pool of his own blood.

Pertoss lay dead in a pool of his blood too.

Another man was standing over the body of a guard, lying on the shore next to Alexandros in a pool of blood.

She runs to Alexandros and sinks down on her knees quickly and calls him. Her knees scratch and scrape on hard stones.

"Alexandros!"

Blood pours out of Alexandros' slashed throat, his eyes closed.

"Alexandros!"

She bends her head closer to him in the darkness of the night. She begins to see in the dark shadows. Her eyes start to crack in horror… her heart begins to shatter in pain…

Salt air leaves the sweetness of the night.

This was neither a knee scraped… nor an elbow bloodied…

It was a cut… deep… ear to ear… side to side…

His last words pour back into her ears. "Mother, look at me…"

She looks closer and then talks softly and rapidly to Alexandros.

"No, it is not that deep. Alexander had survived worse wounds— his arrow wound in Hind was worse, but he survived it.

"Hephæstion and Krateros and Perdikkas had survived arrow wounds and spear thrusts and sword cuts and knifed-chariots too.

"One-eyed Antigonos has a sword slash right through his eye, remember? Alexandros, you can survive this! It is just an honor wound! All the LowLanders and HighLanders have honor wounds. You will command their respect when you heal with a fierce scar on your throat!"

She hastily puts her hands on his throat, trying to push the blood back into his body, keeping his life from escaping through his wound. Warm blood gushes and pours and wraps all around her fingers.

"Alexandros!"

She pleads with the men. "Help me! Please! He is not dead."

The men say nothing. They know she knows the truth.

She presses harder on his throat… more blood pours out, and streams out of the corner of his mouth…

She desperately yells in vain, "Call the guards! Find a wound-healer!"

She did not know how to mend him!

How does a mother mend a dead child?

Silence.

She calls him again, and again, and again.

Silence.

She screams his name.

"ALEXANDROS!"

Silence.

Her voice leaves her.

His birth mother had prayed that her son share the fortune of Alexander and now the fortune of Alexander was bleeding out of her poor Alexandros.

She pulls the lifeless body of Alexandros into her arms and holds him tightly and kisses his face and weeps. His blood pours on her gown, smears on her face. She rocks the body back and forth in her arms.

What kind of a man cuts the throat of a boy and his dog, too?

Did they think poor Pertoss would ask for the bloody throne of Makedon, after his Master was put to the sword?

The men stand quietly circling her and the bleeding boy. The Persian kneels down next to Rošanak and puts his arms around her and holds her for a moment and says quietly, "We could not come any sooner, didâ was crowded."

The salt air bathes in the chill of bitter death.

The wind picks up and begins to blow.

The Persian looks up at the skies up above.

Dark clouds were gathering… covering the waning moon…

If they did not leave soon, the sea would soon become impassable with storm and treacherous winds…

One of the men bends his knees and whispers something quietly.

The Persian whispers in Rošanak's ear, "We have to go!"

Rošanak caresses and kisses and holds the head of Alexandros.

She bleeds and cries and moans.

"Nooo! Cursed barbarians! How could they kill a blameless child?"

"We have to leave!" The Persian stands up and repeats firmly in Persian.

Rošanak holds Alexandros tighter in her embrace. She mumbles in her mother tongue.

"I have to bury him, those barbarians will burn him."

The Persian shakes his head and quietly says, "They will burn you along with him, if we do not leave now!"

Rošanak sits motionlessly, bloodied. "Leave us!"

"We are not leaving you behind," the Persian tells her and then motions to his men and orders firmly, "Bring her."

The men step forward and take Rošanak's arms and start lifting her up to her feet. She pulls Alexandros up with her.

The Persian pulls the body of Alexandros away from her. "Leave him. They will find his body and the blood in your room and think you both dead."

"Nooooooo!" Rošanak moans and resists letting go of Alexandros, crying, pleading.

The Persian pulls the body away from her again and Rošanak finally lets go of Alexandros. The Persian gently lays Alexandros back on the ground and heads back toward the fortress. The men carry Rošanak back into the fortress, following the Persian. Back in her small room, he hands her some slave clothes.

"Wear these and give me your bloody gown."

Rošanak mindlessly follows his order. The men turn away from her nakedness as she drops her bloody gown to her feet carelessly and pulls the drab slave clothes over her head.

The Persian picks up the gown and wipes the blood on her hands with it and then gives it to the other man and points to the dead body of Glaukias.

"Throw his body and the other one off the cliff into the river. Throw this by the body of the boy."

The other man takes the bloody gown and grabs and pulls the dead Glaukias behind him and disappears down the steps.

The Persian orders Rošanak quietly. "You have to leave everything behind."

Rošanak looks blankly down on the room. Her mind empties.

She had nothing left…

What did she own that was more precious than the life of a child… forever lost?

What did she own that could not be left behind?

All that mattered now was the safety of her Son-King in Bakhtriš.

After all these years, her poor son had finally taken the faith of her Son-King upon himself… The substitute son had died to save the Son-King…

The ashes from Pârsâ and the dried rose petals and plum blossoms swirl gently on the floor in the night breeze coming from the open window.

She kneels down and grabs her silver box and starts sweeping the floor with her hands. She scoops up as much of the ashes as she can and pours them back into the box. The red blood on her hands mixes with the dark ashes. She scoops up some more, mindlessly.

The Persian impatiently looks at her and then turns around and heads down the stairs. The other man searches the room. He notices a half burnt book in the small fire altar and grabs it. The fire had gone out, smothered by the weight of the book.

The sacred fire knew… the son of a king had died…

He shakes out the ashes from the edges of the book and pushes the book into a small skin bag hanging from his belt.

Rošanak gets to her feet wordlessly and clasps the small silver box tightly in her hands.

Which gods had taken her child from her?

Whose gods shall she curse?

From whose gods shall she demand justice?

To whose gods shall she pray for his soul?

She mumbles under her breath, tears pouring out.

"My Lord… please have mercy… please… he was a good son… he loved his mother… and his dog… he loved horses and swords and books… he rode horses well and he spoke the truth… he was innocent… I claim him as mine… He was my son…"

Her voice abandons her again mercilessly. Words drown in tears.

… My Lord… please send him to the care of my ancestors…

… please… My Lord… I beg of you… please… please…

Her mind empties.

All the Sons of the House had died…

Lands were without Kings…

Tears stop.

Night becomes darker than a mournful heart.

World darkens.

The man pulls the small silver box out of her hand, secures the top and pushes it in his skin bag. He takes her hand and pulls her along with him out of the deserted fortress and out of the deserted town in the blindness of the darkened night to a small boat waiting for them by the river. His firm hand digs into her soft arm. Her body bleeds underneath her skin.

Heaven vanishes.

The moon rushes and hides behind stormy clouds.

It starts to rain.

Life starts to wash away.

It pours.

MOON and the PEACOCK

IMPERIAL PALACES of PÂTALIPUTRÂ. LAND of SEVEN RIVERS
YEAR 13 of the FOURTH ALEXANDER
YEAR 12 of SAMRÂT CHANDRÂGUPTÂ, MONTH of CAITRA, R'TU of VASANTA
6 MONTHS LATER
MORNING

Unfamiliar hushed murmurs…

Rošanak slowly opens her eyes awakened by a small army of serving girls.

They bathe her, clothe her in a silky soft saree the color of young forest groves, color and paint her face and deliver her to a short fleshy old man, leaning on a tall walking stick, waiting for her patiently at the entrance to the Quarters of the Imperial Women of the Court.

The old man bows his head to her and speaks quietly in a tongue she does not understand.

Rošanak looks at him blankly.

Where was this place?

Was she dead?

Where was Divine Dên?

The old man points in the direction of a large palace and repeats his unfamiliar words.

Rošanak narrows her eyes at him and looks at him, dazed.

He finally gives up and reaches and takes her hand and pulls her along with him.

Rošanak follows him, reluctantly.

They walk through a beautiful garden, cross through a large gate, follow the paved pathway to a great palace, walk up a few tall steps and enter the palace. The old man leans on his walking stick, catches his breath and points to a set of massive doors and mumbles. He lets go of her hand and she follows him quietly without words. They reach the heavily guarded giant doors.

The guards open the giant doors. The old man leaves his walking stick with the guards and enters the audience hall, trailed by Rošanak.

Rošanak stops and looks around quickly. The audience hall is large and spacious and luxuriously appointed with brilliant silk brocades and gilded golden furnishings. Her searching eyes find a king sitting on a large and ornate gilded throne in the middle of the court.

Quiet murmurs.

The men around the King look at Rošanak and whisper quietly among themselves. The woman walking into the Imperial Audience Hall on her own feet, clothed and painted and bedecked and bejeweled, bears little resemblance to the half-dead creature who was brought into the Imperial Palace a few days ago in a heap of slave rags.

The old man bows low to the King and points to Rošanak and mumbles a few words respectfully, then bows again and steps back.

The King beckons her.

Hesitatingly, Rošanak takes a few steps forward and bows her head and looks discreetly at the King.

He looked familiar. But he was sitting too far away for her to be certain.

The King starts to speak in accented Persian and the large court quiets down quickly.

"My warriors were ordered to bring you and your son to me unharmed."

His words are quietly translated for the court.

The voice…

His voice brings long forgotten memories into Rošanak's ears.

So, she was not dead after all.

She discreetly looks down at the palms of her hands without thinking. The cuts on her palms from a night long ago were mostly faded and forgotten. She looks up, listening.

His kingly voice carries on the hushed air of the golden audience hall.

"They failed!" the King thunders. "They are to die!"

Rošanak's eyes widen.

The King points to his other side and Rošanak's eyes follow the direction of the King's hand and locks on the three men standing at attention, with a row of guards standing behind them. His words are translated for the court.

She looks at the men for a moment.

The men stood at attention, stripped of their arms and armor, and their hands were fettered and bound in heavy chains in front of them. Yet, they all looked loyally at their king without moving an eyelash.

She narrows her eyes at them.

They were the same men who had rescued her from the Fortress at Amphipolis.

She had traveled with them from Amphipolis to wherever this place was for months, and yet she did not even know their names or anything about them. All she knew was that one of the men was a Persian… the rest was a blur of boats and horses and endless roads…

She hears the voice of the Persian in her head.

"… they will burn you along with him, if we do not leave now!"

Rošanak looks back at the King.

Seated high on his golden throne, covered in rich jewels and rich clothes… his features had deepened as he had grown older and more handsome and kingly.

His clear voice and his harsh words had gained the authority of a true king.

She had wronged him in those former days and he was not a man to forgive and forget.

She bows her head and speaks politely in Persian.

"My Lord, no one will ransom me… or my son, had he lived."

The King narrows his eyes at her, searching.

"Ransom you?"

Rošanak gasps with uncertainty and points with her eyes.

"I… was brought here by these men… am I not your captive woman… to be ransomed… or kept as a hostage?"

"Captive? Hostage?" the King thunders. "The authority of my Empire does not depend on netting Persian Royal Women!"

The King takes a deep breath and thinks for a moment and then leans forward and declares: "I am the one who freed you from those who had held you captive."

He points to outside of the palace. "I have a thousand imperial warriors behind these walls standing ready to take you anywhere you wish to go, and protect you till the end of your days. And a thousand imperial servants that will carry enough gold and silver that you will never want for anything."

He pauses and narrows his eyes at her. "I ensure your safety within my Empire. In lands beyond my borders, your safety will be in your own hands."

Rošanak stands quietly and looks at the King and then looks at the warriors behind him and the Brahmans on this side of the King and the prisoners on the other side and the guards all around.

The King leans back in his golden throne and points again to the chained prisoners. "You can choose how these men are to die, as they failed to rescue your Royal Son! I gift you their warrior blood for his royal blood!"

Rošanak looks back at the fettered prisoners. She feels the weight of the eyes of the whole royal court on her shoulders. Her knees weaken.

She had known the world when she was the Royal Woman of Alexander… powerful men had kneeled to her and gifted her and flattered her to gain the royal favor of her King-Husband.

When she was in Pella, she had written to those men and had asked for their help to return to Persia and they all had ignored her and turned their hard backs on her… none had replied to her… she had been left utterly alone.

By the time she had been caged in Amphipolis, there was no one left to help her… most had died by the same swords they had lived by… it was just poor Alexandros and her… and the faithful Thessalonike.

And just moments before the blade of a dagger was to meet her throat, these strangers had come for her… men who had no cause of their own to come to her aid… and had rescued her…

… like Angels down from the clouds… all by the favor of the Wise Lord…

A moment too soon for her and a moment too late for her Alexandros…

Unforgiving fate was not to be delayed for one or hurried for the other…

Anxious court murmurs.

She looks back at the King and bows her head and gently speaks.

"My Lord, I thank you for your kindness. Please forgive me my ignorance, as I am unfamiliar with your royal court and your customs."

She takes a deep breath and continues quietly, "The death of my son was his inescapable fate, ordained by the gods of his Kingly-Father. He was destined to share in the fortune of Alexander from birth."

She points to the fettered prisoners.

"As for these noble warriors, I beg you to forgive them and spare their lives and restore them their honors and their swords and their women and allow them to serve you well as they already have. If my ignorant words do not please you, My Lord, then I beg you to let me suffer their fates along with them."

Her words are translated for the court.

Quiet relieved murmurs.

She straightens and looks straight at the King.

The King leans back in his golden throne and consider her intently.

An old Brahman approaches discreetly and whispers quietly in the ear of the King.

The King looks at her for another moment and then looks around at his court and then at the chained prisoners and then leans forward and speaks to the court in his own mother tongue.

The guards step forward and unbind the hands of the chained prisoners.

The prisoners look at the King and bow their heads low to him.

They become his warriors again…

She bows her head to them, acknowledging them with gratitude. She then looks back at the King who is looking at her intently. She bows to him and asks his permission to leave.

"My Lord, is there anything else?"

The King leans back in his golden throne. "Nothing else."

Rošanak bows her head and steps back and heads for the massive doors.

The King beckons one of the warriors standing on his side and speaks to him quietly. The warrior bows his head to the King and follows Rošanak out of the audience hall.

Rošanak exits the audience hall and the palace and starts walking down the steps. She looks at the beautiful gardens stretching before her eyes.

She had not taken much notice of all the beauty around her when she was rushed before the King.

The air smelled sweet from the fragrant beds of flowers stretching endlessly under shady trees. If there was a difference between these gardens and the Persian gardens of the Lands of her ancestors, she could not tell with any certainty.

She steps on the smooth stones that pave the garden paths. She is barefooted and the stones under her feet are flat and pleasantly cool to touch. She stops and looks down at her feet.

She had no idea where she was or where she was going. There was no sign of the old man who had rushed her among the palaces and pathways to the presence of the King. Palace gardeners were busy tending to their gardens and took no notice of her.

There was no one around to show her the way.

She was lost… utterly lost…

Rošanak looks around and sees a small latticed pavilion next to the pathway nearby, covered with climbing nightblooming yâsmin, with elaborately carved wooden benches.

She makes her way to the small pavilion and sits on a bench and leans back and closes her eyes, trying to remember.

And with the slow return of her memory, pain grips her heart.

She takes a deep breath and her body fills with death and foul air.

Alexandros was dead!

She bites her lip, pushing back dammed tears.

Her poor blameless child!

Her innocent boy had become the ultimate substitute son-king and had finally taken the fate of her Son-King upon himself.

Love for her dead son fills her heart.

She should have taken his bloody body and his cut throat to the Assembly of the Makedonians and screamed for justice!

She should have seen to his honorable burial…

She should have seen to his murderers…

She takes another deep breath and her body fills with life and fragrant air.

Alexander was alive!

Tears roll down her face, as the face of her own Son-King fills her eyes. She remembers crossing through Bakhtriš, the Land of her ancestors… the Land of a Thousand Cities… and the beloved jewel city of Baktra by the River Bakhtruš.

The Persian had reluctantly let her go to the Temple of Divine Goddess Ânâhitâ to pray after she had begged for days on the way to Baktra and once she had entered the sacred âyadana, she had stolen away hurriedly through the back door of the âyadana and had quickly melted away into the streets of Baktra she used to know so well.

Everything had changed.

Alexander had gifted her the hadiš when they had wedded… and the new Satrap of Bakhtriš had built himself a bigger, more golden palace on the other side of the river…

Nothing had changed!

Air was scented with the sweet scents of childhood… golden apricots and peaches drying lazily in the spring sun on the brick rooftops…

She had made her way through the old bazaar and the unmarked hidden pathway through the old pistachio grove behind it and past the old cracked walls behind the mulberry trees and overgrown wild berry bushes into the Baktra hadiš.

She had feasted on sweet white mulberries and had covered the slave rags on her body with a piece of stolen cloth from the old bazaar. She had quickly arrived at the hadiš in early morning, right after the break of dawn and followed the sounds coming from the chogân field.

And there, she had stepped right back into her own youth.

Young men covered head to foot in oxen skin, riding magnificent white Nisâya horses, were noisily playing chogân. They looked liked her blood brothers and her brothers and their hadâbâra, playing in the coolness of the early morning before the blistering heat of the coming sun.

She had stood there by the side of the chogân field, looking at the young men… her eyes searching desperately for her blood son… almost expecting a happy three year old boy running eagerly into her open arms… calling to her: Âmma, come play with me!

Oštana had written to her that each noble of the Seven Persian Families had sent a noble son the same age as Alexander to be his hadâbâra.

The ball was suddenly hit forcefully outside of the chogân field, landing somewhere in the berry bushes close to where she was standing.

One of the young men had galloped toward her and leaped down from his white horse, running carelessly into the thorny bushes searching intently for the missing ball, taking no notice of her.

One of the other riders had yelled out to him impatiently:

"Hurry up, Alexander!"

And other riders had joined in and yelled out to him, laughing:

"Yes! Alexander! Hurry! Before we all die of old age here!"

"Your father would have conquered the Sakâ women and begotten a child by now!"

And they had all laughed and her heart had nearly stopped, as her eyes turned swiftly toward the young man who was still searching intently for the missing ball in the wild berry bushes.

He had found the ball and was running back toward his horse who was standing obediently waiting for him.

He had swiftly brushed past her, wreathed with leaves and carelessly scratched and bloodied with thorns, and had turned and looked at her with a light-hearted smile, displaying the ball victoriously in his hand, and then he had jumped back on his horse and had galloped back toward the others.

His eyes, his smile, his face… they were etched forever in her eyes!

Those splendid eyes the color of sky at dawn!

He had his father's eyes… half of his father's eyes…

And all the brightness of his father's smile…

The rest of him was Persian! Tall and fair and handsome with long dark unruly hair carelessly falling around his face.

Her son was the perfection of his father… he was effortlessly Persian Royalty…

Son-King of the Royal House…

Šar Šarrâni A'lek'sa'an'dar… Khšâyaøiya Alexander… Sunki Alexander… Basileos Makedonôn…

He was what had always remained outside of his father's grasp and his mother's too…

He was one-half Makedonian and one-half Persian and three-thirds Persian…

All Persian!

She takes a deep breath and bites her lip as tears fill her eyes.

She had never intended this… any of it…

Alexander wanted to be the Persian Great King… he wanted a Persian son… he did not wish his son to grow up in Makedonia.

She had done what the Kingly-Father would have wanted for his Son-King.

The substitution in 3Paradayadâ was only meant for a short while, until she had taken the bones of Perdikkas home for burial, had seen the birthplace of Alexander and left Alexandros in care of Olympias, and had returned to the Lands.

How could she have known that the planned months in the Lands by the Bitter Sea would bitterly stretch to an unplanned eternity and her own blood Son-King would grow up without her care and come to know only her name and no more of her?

But Alexander had willed everything in his life while he had lived and maybe this was the will of Alexander too, after all…

Their blood son had lived most of his life where his blood father had fallen in love with his blood mother… and where they truly had been filled with love for each other and happy for a short while away from the eyes of the world… he had been raised on the same field playing the game of kings that his father and his mother had played so many times, and so many more times had made love under starry skies…

Her son was home…

"Dukšiš?"

The voice of a man calling to her in Persian interrupts her thoughts. Rošanak opens her eyes. His word drips into her ears. Rošanak looks at him, searching. No one has called her that for an eternity and longer.

Her father was the first she remembered calling her Dukšiš… Royal Daughter.

The man kneels in front of her, looking worried. He bows his head and stands up, when she looks at him.

He stood tall and handsome and stately with fair skin weathered in the rays of the sun and brown eyes, looking like the men she had grown up with.

He was Persian, too…

"I am Ârash, son of Mâr Bani Ârtafarnâ."

Rošanak wipes her eyes quickly and slightly bows her head.

"My Lord?"

"May I have a word, Dukšiš?"

Rošanak sits up and straightens and points to the other wooden bench.

Ârash sits down. A serving girl appears out of nowhere with a tray of cold drinks. Ârash picks up a cup and offers it to Rošanak.

Rošanak takes the cup and takes a sip. The cool taste of sweetened mango and lemon juice brings back sweet memories of her stay in Rajah Parvataka's household.

"You have been lifeless for almost five days. You need to get back your strength," Ârash says in a fatherly tone, encouraging her to drink more.

Rošanak drinks a little more, trying to think.

"Five days?"

"Yes— we did not know if you were in death sleep or just plain exhausted." Ârash nods, sipping his drink. "You were traveling for almost two seasons, covering five times the distance Alexander covered when he crossed the Desert of Emptiness below Karmâna."

Rošanak drinks a little more and tries to remember. "Where am I?"

"You are now in the Imperial Palace of the Imperial City of Pâtaliputrâ, the Imperial Capital of Chakravarti Samrât Chandrâguptâ, the first Emperor of the Mauryan Dynasty."

Rošanak looks down at her palms again and mumbles, "Chandrâ?"

Emperor…?

What was an Emperor?

"Yes. The Emperor who drove the Makedonian invaders out of Hind and united all the Lands and the People of the Land of Seven Rivers."

Rošanak looks at Ârash intently, without a word.

A Hinduya Great King?

He continues. "I was a warrior from the Seven Noble Families in the Royal Army of the Third Dâriuš, the Great King."

He remembers painfully. "We were sent to Pârsâ to guard the Royal City and the royal funds by the Great King under the command of Ariâbarzâna, the Royal Son of the House. No one thought the invaders would move beyond the Royal City of Çûšâ to Pârsâ— Pârsâ was sacred, the City of the Wise Lord, protected by the Wise Lord and by powerful athravans—

"We defended the ancient Persian Gates through the mountains and almost defeated the enemies.

"Alexander had to leave his dead warriors and retreat. But the enemy found a traitor who knew the ancient mountain passes. Alexander crossed over our heads through icy mountain passes in full darkness and fell behind our lines. Wolves were howling all around us in the darkness, but the enemy men were so blinded by their thirst for our gold that they were fearless.

"Ariâbarzâna with a handful of horsemen and less than five hundred foot warriors fell back to Pârsâ but traitor Tiridâta closed the city gates and the Royal Son and most of the Persian warriors were annihilated before the city walls by the thousands and thousands of Makedonian invaders who fell on us. Then he opened the city gates to our enemies."

He pauses and curses Tiridâta under his breath.

"Those few who survived the bloody massacre trekked to Hagmâtâna in the dead of winter over the icy mountain passes. When the Great King was put to the sword by the Seven Nobles, we joined the armies of your father. After he was betrayed and killed, a handful of us made our way to the Hindu Satrapies of the Great King, first to Harahuvatiš and then to Takšiçila in the Satrapy of Gandâra."

He nods and continues.

"When we heard that Samrât was planning to overthrow his father, the last Nandâ King, and take over his kingdom, we made our way to him and pledged him our arms and our loyalty."

Ârash takes a deep breath and sips his cold drink and looks at Rošanak who is eyeing him intently. "As Samrât said, there are a thousand imperial warriors within the city walls standing ready to take you anywhere you wish to go along with a hundred biltu of gold and a thousand biltu of silver. The Emperor has put me in charge of taking you and settling you, as you desire."

Rošanak puts down her drink on a small wooden table between the wooden benches and looks down for a moment, thinking.

Showing up in Baktra with a thousand imperial warriors would surely not go unnoticed to Kassandros and the rest of the kingsmen of Alexander.

They meant to kill her Alexander and they would try again, once it became known that they had failed.

Her presence meant certain death for her son… she would offer up her own life gladly to shield her only Son-King from such evil men!

She then looks up.

"I cannot accept such a generous gift from your Emperor."

Ârash smiles.

"Samrât is as rich as the Persian Kings. The Hindu Satrapies used to send in a tribute of three hundred and sixty biltu of gold dust each year to the Royal Treasury at Pârsâ."

Rošanak thinks about Baktra and her Son-King.

She had nothing… nothing left… she had even less than the dead… the dead had caskets and graves and tombs… she did not even own the gown on her back or the paint on her face…

All that was left to her was an old body that had become the grave for her soul.

She had nothing… and she desired nothing…

What she desperately craved was… forgiveness… not armed and armored warriors… not mules loaded with gold and silver…

She narrows her eyes and then looks away from Ârash and says quietly, "What good is gold and silver to a Royal Woman with no Royal Husband and no Royal Sons?"

Ârash looks at her with pity.

She was famous to those who had heard of Alexander. And everyone had heard of Alexander, the King who had appeared over the skies of the Lands of the Persians, like a storm cloud heavy with thunder and lightning and hail and fury.

Like all the conquerors of old, he had left unspeakable death and destruction in his wake after leaving the lands of his ancestors.

Among all the women in his path across the Lands he had passed, he had married one woman for love… her… a half-Persian Royal Daughter.

"There is no rush for your answer," he says quietly.

"I… have nowhere to go," she mumbles quietly.

Ârash leans back in his wooden bench and considers her words for a moment. He then stands up. "Please wait for me here." He quickly turns around and heads back toward the Imperial Audience Hall.

Rošanak closes her eyes and drifts again. The face of her Son-King fills her eyes again.

His life seemed as it should have been all along… a Persian Royal Son living a Persian life…

What she had written in her letter to him long ago was meaningless… it was good that her letter had been burned.

Her Son-King did not know her as his mother and she would never become more than the woman who had given him birth… he had long passed the years when his blood mother would have been of any use to him.

As Alexander used to say, "Gods always get even with the mortals!"

A living life for her Son-King was a life that no longer included his blood Queen-Mother.

The gods of his blood father had extracted their godly price!

A price she had willingly paid… to keep him safe…

And a price she was willing to pay henceforth to keep him hidden and to keep him alive.

Her body fills up with sweet air and bitter remembrance.

At first, she had thought about disappearing in Baktra and watching her Son-King live from afar… but that would have been much too painful. So she had finally returned to the âyadana to face her fate with the Persian and the rest of them.

She had prayed in the Temple of Divine Goddess Ânâhitâ after she had left the old Hadiš. Âyadana was as she had seen it last… restored to its former glory and standing proudly overlooking River Bakhtruš.

She had run the tips of her fingers on the inscription that Hephæstion had added to the sacred statue… his words spoke to her from beyond the grave.

ALEXANDER, THE LORD OF ASIA,
RESTORED THIS SACRED TEMPLE
FOR THE LOVE OF HIS QUEEN, ROXANA OF BAKTRIA.

She had read the words of love Utâna had carved for her too… more than once… and they still sounded as sweet as the first time she had read them.

Other lovers had carved the names of their beloveds and their own names next to the words of love… and why not? His words were their words… all lovers spoke the same tongue in the worship of their beloveds…

She hears her own voice praying.

A man's voice interrupts her prayer. She opens her eyes. Ârash is standing before her.

"Dukšiš, please follow me."

Rošanak hesitates for a moment and then gets to her feet reluctantly and steadies herself and starts following him.

He continues talking, "You can stay here. You will be safe here from the Makedonians. The Imperial Palaces of Pâtaliputrâ are in the heart of the Imperial City of Pâtaliputrâ. The Imperial City is built on the old fort of Pâtaligramâ, defended by timber walls, with sixty and four gates, and five hundred and seventy towers— Ah! And a deep moat, filled with waters from the River Sona. The Imperial Palaces were inspired by the Palaces of the Persians— especially the ones in the Royal Cities of Çûšâ and Pârsâ, with gilded columns adorned with golden vines and silver birds, amidst pure Persian gardens with water basins and fish ponds and exotic trees and fragrant flowers."

He points to the Imperial Palaces and continues. "No one can enter the palaces without a permit."

They reach a gated wall within the gardens of the Imperial Palaces, guarded by female imperial guards.

Ârash speaks to one of the female imperial guards who quickly disappears inside the gated quarters.

A few moments pass quietly.

The female imperial guard returns with a short fleshy old man, panting and sweating and out of breath, walking with a long walking stick.

Ârash smiles and points to the old man. "This is the Quarters of the Women of the Emperor. Kayvârtâ, who brought you to the imperial court earlier, is the Chief Eunuch who is responsible for the Imperial Women. He acts rough to protect the Imperial Women, but he is a good man. He reports to Samrât every morning about the status of the Women of the Imperial Court. No man can enter these guarded walls but the Emperor himself, or by his imperial orders."

Ârash loudly greets the Chief Eunuch with a big smile and shows him his golden imperial permit and speaks to him in a tongue Rošanak does not understand.

Kayvârtâ examines the golden imperial permit carefully and then waves at the female imperial guards to open the guarded gate.

Ârash and Rošanak walk inside, followed by Kayvârtâ and a few female imperial guards, fully armed and armored.

"I know a little Sanskrit, enough to get by. Samrât speaks Persian from his young days traveling in the Lands of the Persians," Ârash says as they follow the Chief Eunuch.

"I will find you some noble ladies who can speak Persian to keep you company. My own wife died years ago."

Inside the gated quarters, a cluster of smaller palaces are connected by pathways and arranged like petals of flowers around a central lotus and lily pond in a vast fragrant garden with Ašoka trees, bearing lovely blood-orange flowers.

Some of the Women of the Imperial Court are out in the fragrant gardens, enjoying the day.

Kayvârtâ points to one of the small palaces and mumbles under his breath and they all follow him.

Six or seven serving girls stand waiting by the doors and at the sight of Rošanak, they all smile and bow and clear the pathway.

Rošanak walks into the small palace followed by Ârash, Kayvârtâ and the serving girls, with the female imperial guards entering last. Rošanak remembers the inside of the small palace from earlier in the morning.

The serving girls all line up around Rošanak, admiring their own hand in bringing her back to life.

Kayvârtâ mumbles under his breath and sits down exhausted in a golden chair by the gilded doors. A serving girl brings him a cup of mango juice.

Ârash looks around and starts talking again, "Samrât gifts you this small palace. This is where you have been cared for. It used to belong to the Chief Wife of Samrât, Queen Durdhara, the Royal Daughter of the last Nandâ King and the Queen-Mother of the Crown-Prince Bindusâra. She was his second wife.

"His first wife died before Samrât came into the Throne of Magadha. The second wife also died a few years ago. These small palaces are now mostly lived in by his single Royal Daughters, the wives of the Crown-Prince and the Royal Sons, a handful of mistresses and some older women from the previous Nandâ Royal House."

He looks at Rošanak for a reaction, but she just looks around without any words. Ârash continues, "The Third Dâriuš had many Women of the Royal Court to seal his position with his powerful satraps, the same ones who fell into the hands of Alexander and his men at the battle at Issos, along with the Royal Women of Dâriuš."

Silence.

He nods his head. "I do not know how many mistresses Samrât has— but no wives!" he declares reassuringly and then points to the serving girls, "There are seven serving girls, all trained to take good care of the woman of this small palace. They all stay here. All share small rooms in the back. If they do not please you, there are hundreds of girls in the Imperial Palace that you can choose from."

He turns and looks at Rošanak and says quietly, "They bathed you every day and dripped sweetened mango juice down your lips, by the order of the Samrât's healers."

Rošanak looks at the serving girls and smiles and they all bow and laugh quietly and murmur.

Ârash continues, "There is a cook," and he mumbles to himself, "I can find you someone who can prepare Persian food. There are no sweet figs in Pâtaliputrâ— but there are lots of sweet mangos!"

He then points toward one of the rooms and continues, "By the order of the Samrât, the old furnishings were all removed and new furnishings were brought in before you arrived.

"The furnishings in the bedchamber are the best. Samrât chose them himself. The rest of the furnishings here are adequate; most were brought here from the imperial storage, to fill the small palace."

Rošanak looks around at the lavish golden furnishings that Ârash was calling adequate.

The palaces at Pella looked like lowly horse stables compared to this small residence.

Her room at Amphipolis was probably less appointed that the rooms of the serving girls in the back.

Kassandros had taken cruel pride in stripping them of all marks of Royalty.

He had given her one slave girl to tend to her needs in Amphipolis and no more.

Ârash looks at Rošanak and hearing no response, he continues, "We can go to the imperial storage and you can pick anything you like— and the imperial palace carpenters and ornament makers can make you anything that is lacking in the imperial storage."

Rošanak nods and quietly says, "Thank you."

The serving girls laugh quietly when they hear her talk. This is the first time she has uttered any words in front of them.

Kayvârtâ gives them a sharp look and grunts.

Ârash looks at Rošanak and tries to think of what he has forgotten.

"Ah! There is an army of seamstresses who can make you whatever you like to wear and Imperial Jewelers— what else?" He mumbles to himself. "This is your palace by the order of Samrât. The gold and silver biltu that the Samrât has gifted you will be recorded in the Imperial Treasury as yours and you can draw upon those personal funds, for whatever is not a part of the household budget for the Imperial Palaces."

He remembers.

"The Emperor, Samrât Chandrâguptâ, has beckoned you to join him for the night meal tonight. I will come for you after the sun sets on the horizon."

Rošanak nods her head slightly.

Ârash bows his head and turns toward the door. He hesitates for a moment and then turns around and takes a step back and quietly says, "When Samrât first brought up the mission to rescue you and your son, no one at the Imperial Court was in favor of it, including myself. Alexander was long dead and according to the Imperial Eyes and Ears, the Makedonians were too busy killing each other over control of the Lands by the Seas that Alexander had conquered to worry about returning to Hind."

He leans forward and quietly says, "Samrât has five hundred thousand foot warriors, twenty five thousand horses and eight thousand fighting elephants under his imperial command."

He leans back and smiles confidently. "All part of the standing army, getting paid regularly. We will make maggot food out of any invading enemy army that crosses our borders.

"The Imperial Army is managed by an Imperial War Council, run by thirty noble members of the Warrior Caste— I am one of the council members. What happened at Issos and the Black Eagle will not happen here!"

Ârash pauses and suppresses a painful memory and then continues. "So, instead of decreeing it, the Samrât proposed it to his imperial warriors and offered it as a challenge. The reward would be honor by the Samrât with higher ranks in the Imperial Army for the commanders and double pay for each of their men, if they were successful— and the punishment for failure would be death."

Rošanak looks at him and waves the serving girls away. They all bow and disappear from view.

Kayvârtâ has almost fallen asleep on the chair and the female imperial guards are standing by the doors.

Ârash continues, shaking his head. "Same old story… while the older warriors, who had fought in many bloody battles with the Emperor, saw the mission as fruitless, the younger warriors saw a glorious adventure in the making.

"The men you saw this morning were the warriors who had volunteered and with their men they set out— about a hundred of them. They made the long journey as fast as the Persian asa-bâra and pirradaziš. Most of their men were posted at intervals between here and the Land by the Bitter Sea, Beyond the Lands, with the responsibility to get fresh horses and supplies and secure the rear and keep a communication line back to the imperial base.

"They all returned to the last man and brought back first hand reports about strengths and weaknesses of our borders and the Lands Beyond the Sea. And— they heard talk of plans to reclaim Alexander's conquests in Hind from the kingsmen of Alexander."

Ârash takes a deep breath and continues. "Samrât was furious with his warriors— the way he thought they had dragged their feet and dragged your half-dead body into the Imperial Court. He said he should have gone himself!"

He bites his lip and continues. "In the judgment of the Emperor, his warriors had utterly failed him. They had been too cautious, they had not been fast and bold enough to be victorious. Your son was dead and you were caught in the claws of death. Samrât was blinded by anger and declared the mission a failure. The entire Imperial Court pleaded with him and he forgave the men, but left the fate of their warrior commanders in your hands, should you live. He said the failure was the failure of the commanders and not their men, who had followed orders. They were all to die, if you had died!"

He nods to himself, relieved. "By the favor of the Wise Lord, you came to last night and spared the lives of the noble imperial warriors this morning. One of the warriors was the third son of Samrât. Kingship regards neither son nor father, they say."

Rošanak looks at Ârash, her eyes widen.

He nods and continues, "One of the other two was my firstborn son!"

He bows his head and then turns around and leaves without any more words.

One of the female imperial guards quickly nudges Kayvârtâ who jumps up to his feet from sleep and they all follow Ârash out of the small palace.

The serving girls run back into the room and point with their hands and babble. Rošanak follows them, still thinking about what Ârash had told her.

The Persian who had saved her life was his firstborn son.

She walks on the terrace, overlooking the lush gardens, where the serving girls had set up a mid-day meal table for her.

Was she now a Woman of the Imperial Court?

TERRACE. PRIVATE IMPERIAL PALACE of SAMRÂT CHANDRÂGUPTÂ
LATER that NIGHT

Rošanak walks on the golden terrace, glinting in the light of the dancing torches, following Ârash with soft jeweled and bangled bare feet.

The night had cooled the air and huge golden bowls dotting the surface of the golden terrace were filled with fragrant night yâsmin and white lilies.

female imperial guards and serving girls surround the Samrât, who is sitting crossed-legged on an embroidered silk cloth spread on the golden terrace floor, bathed and bare-chested and dressed simply in a white dhoti, twisted and tied at his waist, void of all the imperial jewels he was adorned with earlier at the Imperial Court. He looks a lot more like the young prince Rošanak remembers.

Ârash bows low and respectfully announces Rošanak.

"Samrât, Dukšiš Rošanak, the Persian Royal Woman, as you have summoned her."

Chandrâguptâ looks at Rošanak intently for a moment and then beckons her to sit down.

Rošanak steps forward, bows her head, and kneels down and sits on her knees before him on the silky spread.

Chandrâguptâ points to one of the serving girls, who steps forward bowing low and puts a folded piece of parchment in front of Rošanak. Chandrâguptâ points to the parchment silently and with authority.

Rošanak leans forward hesitatingly and then picks up the folded crumpled letter and looks at it intently.

Dried blood stains the parchment.

She looks at Chandrâguptâ nervously and then takes a deep breath and slowly opens the letter. The letter is in Attik. She slowly reads it.

> *Kassandros, Ruler of Makedonia, to Glaukias, Commander at the Fortress of Amphipolis, Greeting.*

She pauses for a moment. Her hand trembles with anger and grief.

She then reluctantly continues reading.

> *Truce has been established and peace has been made between us, Lysimachos, Ruler of Thrake, Ptolemaios, Ruler of Aigyptos, and Antigonos, Ruler of Asia Minor. Antigonos and his men are again asking for the release of the prisoners you are holding in Amphipolis Fortress.*
>
> *We thought it best to send you Perpelaos to speak further on this matter with you and inform you of our orders regarding the prisoners. He brings copies of the Peace Agreement which we have made and of the Oath.*
> *We think it is best if you take the Oath which we have sent.*
> *Farewell.*

She closes her eyes for a long moment and bites her lip and then reads the letter again and tosses and turns the words in her eyes.

… our orders regarding the prisoners…

She rubs the tips of her fingers on the seal and then folds the letter and puts it back down in front of her and looks at it thinking.

What about Seleukos?

He was not mentioned… was he not a part of the murderous Peace Agreement?

She takes a deep breath.

Had Seleukos remained faithful to the blood of Alexander? Or had he died too?

She eyes Chandrâguptâ discreetly.

No doubt he already knew what was in the letter.

Chandrâguptâ waves his hands and Ârash and the female imperial guards and the serving girls disappear from view. He leans forward and says in a low voice, "The man who was about to kill you, had this letter in his possession. It is his blood on the letter."

kingsmen of Alexander were a bunch of murderous rats who had fallen into a Persian sack full of gold and grain and glory… they were not going to surrender their lands and rules and powers to a powerless boy-king.

Who would have? No one would!

Rošanak looks back at the dried darkened blood tainting the parchment.

Blood of the treacherous Glaukias…

Chandrâguptâ takes a deep breath.

"A copy of the Peace Agreement that was sent to all the satraps and governors and allies and friends of the kingsmen of Alexander, fell into the hands of my Eyes and Ears in the Town of Scepsis by the Sea.

"My War Council reviewed the Peace Agreement completely. In their collective opinion, kingsmen of Alexander had made a fleeting peace, worn out by war. They had divided his Empire among themselves.

"Like any division of land, those who got less will want more, and those who got more will want all, eventually. All my Imperial Ministers agreed that the kingsmen of Alexander had agreed to the hidden words, to what was not written in the Peace Agreement— they had all agreed wordlessly to the death of the Boy-King.

"Chanâkya said that *Kassandros to rule in the Lands of the Bitter Sea, until the Boy-King becomes old enough*, meant that the Boy-King would never come of age and become old enough."

Rošanak closes her eyes in pain.

What a fool!

She had thought peace meant peace. Peace agreements of the Great Kings were always sealed with marriage alliances with the Royal Women…

When Glaukias had told her that peace had been made among the kingsmen of Alexander, he had neglected to mention that the peace agreement was sealed with the blood of her son and she was too ignorant to hear the buried swords in his spoken words…

No wonder the Common Peace of the Great Kings had never lasted long with such wicked men from the other side of the seas. They were not peaceful men… they were not men of honor… they were liars!

The dried blood on the announcement of the Peace Agreement was the blood of Alexandros… and the ink was her blood…

Chandrâguptâ leans slightly forward. "I wish my men had reached your son sooner. They got to him right after— well—" Chandrâguptâ pauses. "But the man who killed your son paid with his own blood for his treachery."

Rošanak pushes back a tear.

"The Boy-King died quickly. He did not suffer. He is reborn." Chandrâguptâ speaks to her compassionately in a low voice.

A tear rolls down Rošanak's face.

It took months for women to bring forth sons and years to grow them into men and it took just a sudden moment and a sharp sword to make a short end to all that work.

"Brahmans say life is infinite… Death leads to rebirth…" Chandrâguptâ says quietly, eyeing Rošanak. "Kalyana, the Brahman must have told you." He asks, "How did old Kalyana die?"

"He burned himself in the old Royal City of the Elam-tu," Rošanak says quietly, tears dancing in her voice. "He said the pain in his body was sickening his soul."

Chandrâguptâ nods knowingly.

"Ah! Then it was his time. He is probably already reborn too."

Rošanak looks at him wryly.

A few long moments pass in silence.

"Do I look much different from the days you knew me?" Chandrâguptâ leans forward and asks curiously in a low voice.

"As do I from the days you knew me…" Rošanak replies in a teary voice.

Chandrâguptâ smiles and looks at her intently. "Then I must look far better than I used to!"

Rošanak straightens and half-smiles politely and nods, and gently wipes away her tears with the tips of her fingers.

Chandrâguptâ waves his hand and a pair of serving girls appear quickly with plates of food.

Rošanak looks at the food on her plate with indifference.

After the siege at Pydna, where she had nearly starved to death, her belly had shrunk and her appetite for food had almost disappeared. That was probably why she had survived the punishing journey from Amphipolis to Pâtaliputrâ and the days she had collapsed without much food or water in her.

Her body had learned to live on air alone…

Chandrâguptâ narrows his eyes and says assuringly, sensing her reluctance, "The food has been tasted."

Rošanak nods and looks reluctantly at her plate again.

Chandrâguptâ leans toward her and brings a spoon full of cooked rice to her mouth. "You must eat. You were lifeless for almost five days. I was worried that you might die without coming back to—"

He pauses and takes a deep breath and moves the spoon closer to her mouth. "There are no hot spices in this!"

Rošanak opens her mouth and takes a small bite.

Chandrâguptâ smiles. "Remember how you almost choked on spicy food I fed you at the table of Rajah Parvataka?"

Rošanak smiles and nods with remembrance and takes another small bite.

"I told my cook to make the food free of spices as you like it. But you must learn to eat Hindu food spicy or our summer heat will surely kill you!" Chandrâguptâ grins and continues, "The Emperor will be displeased if that happens!"

"Would you have killed your own son, on my account?" Rošanak asks quietly.

Chandrâguptâ is taken back with surprise.

Ârash must have told her about the condemned warriors she had spared that morning… that was why beautiful women were so valuable as the Eyes and Ears for the Empire… men readily told beautiful women secrets that they would not spill under the pain of torture and death to other men.

He heaps more cooked rice on the spoon and takes a bite himself.

"The warriors who volunteered for the charge, knew well the reward for success and the punishment for failure."

He heaps more rice on the golden spoon and brings it to Rošanak's mouth. She leans forward and takes another small bite to appease him.

"Kings must do what they promise."

Chandrâguptâ puts down his fork. "Strong warriors will not follow weak kings!" he says with absolute certainty.

Then he considers her for a long moment. Her thoughts were written on her folding face. "What you want to know in your heart is how Alexander would have treated his own son— had he lived."

Rošanak looks at Chandrâguptâ and bites her lip and holds in her breath.

"Do you really want to know?" Chandrâguptâ asks curiously.

Rošanak gazes at him intently, without uttering a word. He reads her eyes.

"Very well," Chandrâguptâ takes a deep breath and says quietly, "he would have hated his son if he was weaker than himself and would have hated him even more if he was better than himself! Gods have always seen to it that great kings have lesser sons and great sons have lesser fathers to humble the mighty at their feet!"

"No!" Rošanak leans back in dread.

"My father was the last King of Nandâ Royal House. I was born to him from a beautiful serving girl in his royal court. I grew up to be a man better than my father. He called me a bastard of lowly birth because of my mother and condemned me to death. I took the name of my mother for my name, Maurya... Peacock..." Chandrâguptâ says in a low voice, shaking his head side to side.

Rošanak covers her mouth in disbelief and closes her eyes.

"When you saw me at the Court of Rajah Parvataka, I had narrowly escaped death and had fled to Gandâra. There I met a Brahman, by the name of Chanâkya, who taught me how to take power and become an Emperor!" Chandrâguptâ takes a deep breath and continues. "That is what Alexander lacked, someone to teach him how to be a king— all he knew was how to be a conqueror."

Another long moment passes.

"Kings grow gold and lands and people... they build roads and canals and cities... they plant and irrigate and harvest... the welfare of their people is their own welfare. Conquerors kill and raze and sack... Men bless the kings and curse the conquerors!"

He pauses and eyes her.

"Now eat!" Chandrâguptâ says firmly, bringing another spoonful of cooked rice to Rošanak's mouth.

Rošanak bites her lip. Chandrâguptâ shrugs his shoulders and eats the cooked rice himself.

"You said you wanted to know!" Chandrâguptâ takes another bite. "And I told you!" he tells her with old familiarity.

"What is virtue for a man, is vice in a king! And what is virtue for a king, is vice in a man!"

Rošanak covers her face in her hands.

Chandrâguptâ looks at her for a moment and then waves his hands.

The serving girls appear quickly and take away the plates. Another serving girl brings golden cups filled with fragrant wine.

Chandrâguptâ takes a golden cup of wine and sweet-talks Rošanak.

"Have some fragrant wine. You used to like it! Remember?"

Rošanak sits motionlessly.

Chandrâguptâ tries again. "You are making me look bad in front of my subjects! Everyone obediently obeys my commands!" He leans forward and whispers sweetly, "If you do not obey my words, I will have to have my Imperial Guards shoot you with their sharp arrows!"

Rošanak puts her hands on her lap and looks at him irritably and replies stubbornly. "You dragged me here all the way from Amphipolis, so you could have the pleasure of killing me yourself?"

Chandrâguptâ leans back and laughs, shaking his head, and drinks his fragrant wine. "I can order my Imperial Warriors to return you to your Makedonian executioners, if being here with me does not please you."

Rošanak takes a deep breath and pushes herself up and bows her head and turns around and leaves in haste without a word. She brushes carelessly against Ârash as she leaves the golden terrace.

Ârash looks at her, startled, and runs quickly to Chandrâguptâ and bows his head. "Ah! My Lord, shall I… follow her?"

"No!" Chandrâguptâ laughs and drinks the other golden cup of fragrant wine. "Let her be! She is as fearless as ever! The years have not changed her at all! That is why men cannot get her out of their blood! It is easier to defeat a formidable army in pitched battle than getting her to heed!"

"My Lord?"

"Make sure she has whatever she desires!"

"She does not seem to desire much!"

"She will. Her heart is buried under the frost of the Lands Beyond the Sea. The warmth of Hind will make her bloom again. She will open like a fresh lotus flower."

Chandrâguptâ looks at Ârash and thinks for a moment and then beckons him to sit down.

Ârash bows his head and sits down crossed-legged in front of the Emperor.

"How many seasons have you been joined with me now?"

Ârash adds up the years in his head. "Fourteen years, My Lord."

Chandrâguptâ nods and waves his hand.

Serving girls bring more golden fragrant wine.

Chandrâguptâ picks up his golden wine cup and sips it slowly.

Ârash takes a sip of his fragrant wine.

Chandrâguptâ considers him for a moment and then leans slightly forward and says, "This is for your ears only!"

"Yes, My Lord!" Ârash bows his head respectfully with anticipation.

Chandrâguptâ considers him for another moment and then relents. The restless words in his mouth and on his lips are too impatient to be held in check any longer.

He waves away the serving girls and the female imperial guards and they all withdraw. He takes another sip of his fragrant wine and says in a low voice, "The battle at River Vitastâ between Rajah Parvataka and Alexander was a bloody mess!"

Ârash's ears stand to attention.

"I still think Rajah Parvataka lost the battle, but won the war!"

"My Lord?"

"If Rajah Parvataka had not been wounded, he would have won the battle too. His fighting elephants frightened the Makedonians to their bones. So many men were stomped and flattened by his fighting elephants, that those who were there said that it was impossible to recognize the dead. They were all crushed into a bloody field of blood and flesh and bones! It was such a bloody massacre that no one who was there will ever forget it!"

He takes a deep breath.

"No death is more honorable for a warrior than dying in a battle... but massacres are pure evil... they offend the gods!" Chandrâguptâ says, sipping his wine slowly. "I was in Gandâra then. My own father had condemned me to death, my first wife had been poisoned with poisonous food meant for me, and I had fled the Nandâ Royal Court in fear for my own life, vowing not to tie my hair until the destruction of my father. That was where I met Chanâkya and my life changed.

"I heard it all from Rajah Parvataka himself. Alexander had sent Rajah Âmbhi to settle with Rajah Parvataka when blood was pouring out of him and still Rajah Parvataka had declined to submit to his old enemy. So, Alexander came himself. When it was all agreed to, Alexander left his wife with Rajah Parvataka as a sign of his words and their alliance, until he returned from capturing the rest of Hind.

"That is when I met Alexander. I told him about the Nandâ Royal Court of Magadha Kingdom and the riches by the River Ganga. I offered to help him overthrow my father, in exchange for leaving me in charge. I told him all of Hind was within his grasp, only a few days march straight through well-watered and well-peopled lands. But he rejected me and told me I was too young and he was not in need of my help. I told him he would fail without me and he grew angry and asked Rajah Parvataka to imprison me for my insolence."

He takes a deep breath.

"I was young and foolish then!"

He shrugs his shoulders and sips his fragrant wine.

"I fell asleep exhausted after meeting with Alexander and a giant tiger came and licked the sweat off my face and left without harming me.

"Those who saw this with their own eyes told Rajah Parvataka and he took the omen and only held me for a day and then released me on the condition that I stay in his court for a while as his guest, so he could keep an eye on me. He said I was a prince of royal blood protected by the sacred heavens. He was a great Rajah."

Chandrâguptâ nods his head. "First I thought to myself that I did not taste good enough even for a tiger to eat me!" He smiles in remembrance. "That is when I met the Wife of Alexander. The Makedonians called her *the Bakhtrian*, but one look at her, and everyone knew she was Persian of royal blood. She looked a lot like the Royal Wife of Dariush, but not as tall and arrogant. She was a few fingers shorter than Alexander."

Chandrâguptâ narrows his eyes, remembering. "She was barely eighteen years old then. Her dark green eyes and her sweet smile could melt the oldest ice on the highest peaks of the living mountain god Himalâya, the Abode of Snow. That, I thought, was the favorable omen. I fell in love with her."

"Ah!" Ârash utters in surprise.

"Yes!" Chandrâguptâ nods, smiling. "Both of us were hostages at the Court of Rajah Parvataka. Alexander had dragged her with him from the land of her royal ancestors like a court slave and she was glad to be away from those barbarians who treated her like a woman of their king and not a Royal Woman!"

Chandrâguptâ pauses and then points to the inside of his Imperial Palace. "That long bow that is enshrined in my Private Palace is the one I used to shoot Alexander."

"Ah!" Ârash looks in the direction of the private palace, his eyes wide and startled.

"When Alexander declined to assist me, he became my enemy, and as Chanâkya always says, *Any man who is not a friend, is an enemy!* I had to do everything I could to drive him out of Hind, before I could go after my father's Kingdom.

"Two kings cannot sit on the same throne. I could not fight two enemies at once. My father had two hundred thousand foot warriors and six thousand fighting elephants. So, I went after Alexander who was the weaker one. As Chanâkya always says, *You make peace with the king equal to or greater than you and make war upon the weaker king.*"

Chandrâguptâ sips his fragrant wine slowly, tasting every drop.

"Chanâkya had joined the camp-followers of Alexander undetected. He had served the Hindu satraps of the Great King and was fearless. He used to say: *All Hindus look the same to those ignorant barbarians.* Under the guidance of Chanâkya, the Hindu women who had lost their men in the battles and were taken from their families and villages and tribes by the men of Alexander by force, started to spread rumors about vast rivers and thousands of fighting elephants and warlike men and man-eating snakes waiting for Alexander and his men further inland.

"They planted the mighty seeds of fear in the heart of his fearless Royal Army. Those men, who had faced only two hundred elephants on the banks of River Vitastâ, lost their fighting spirit quickly when they imagined facing thousands of elephants and a sea of giant snakes. They started to believe every word once they saw a giant snake in the forest who had swallowed a sleeping man whole!"

"Thousands of fighting elephants were not just rumors," Ârash says quietly.

Chandrâguptâ smiles. "They call Alexander *Unconquered*, but he was defeated by his own men, terrified of our fighting war elephants. He had to turn back from the banks of River Vipâš, when his men dropped their arms and refused to go any further inland!"

He pauses and narrows his eyes and sips his fragrant wine.

"When he sent back for his wife, I no longer had a reason to wait. I traveled with a handful of warriors faithful to my cause in advance of his army, when he started down River Sindhu, warning the tribes in his path. Towns and cities emptied quickly and women and children were sent away into the mountains and further inland for safe-keeping. Those who ignored our warnings paid for it with their lives. The brave Mâlavâ warriors and Brahmans vowed to stand their ground and fight him face-to-face, so we joined with them and waited for the barbaric invaders."

He takes a deep breath.

"He had not expected so much resistance— every step of the way on this side of the River Sindhu we offered him resistance. Even those who submitted to him initially raised arms against him as soon as he had passed through their Lands. When the Makedonians reached the Mâlavâ Fortress, they were dragging their feet. They had marched day and night for days in pursuit of the Mâlavâ and had killed all who had fallen into their murderous hands. I could see from afar that the Makedonians were bone weary from marching and killing.

"Alexander had not even rested his men long enough to wash the blood from their hands and their arms and armor. All of a sudden, I saw a lone figure standing on the wall of the Mâlavâ Fortress, urging his men forward. He was wearing a feathered helmet and golden armor, holding a golden sword and a lion shield in front of him. I knew from a distance he was Alexander."

A moment passes in remembrance.

"I still remember how I rested that long bow on the ground, pressed on it hard with my left foot and released the barbed arrow with all my might. Crack! It cut right through his golden armor and pierced his royal body!"

"Ah!" Ârash says, stunned.

No one at the Imperial Court ever talked of this… only that the Emperor had saved Hind from the invaders and had pushed them out by force in a most befitting manner! His fearless deeds were likened to that of Varaha, the incarnation of Lord Višnu…

… just as godly Varaha had rescued the Earth, imperial Samrât had rescued Hind.

Chandrâguptâ shakes his head side-to-side. "My aim was off! And fortune was with him that day! Just a finger more that way and the arrow would have ripped through his heart, instead of merely puncturing his lung, as I found out later!"

He takes a deep breath and continues in a deep voice.

"His men went mad and put to the sword the whole of the Mâlavâ tribe to the last man and woman and child and impaled all the Brahmans. We blessed and burned all their bodies later and buried their bones, so they could all be reborn. It was well worth it.

"The killing of the Brahmans angered all the Hindus beyond reconciliation and alliance with the invaders. Everyone became his enemy and my ally, all at once! When I heard he did not die and recovered well enough, I had to come back. We followed him this time and when I found out he planned to go back to the Lands of the Persians through the Desert of Emptiness, the gods had given me my second chance.

"There was a well-known ancient path through the desert to Karmâna with adequate food and water that all the Hindu guides knew, but I had taken the measure of Alexander face-to-face. He always wanted to do what they told him could not be done! So, by my command, the Hindu guides told him that there was a shorter path through the dry Death Desert but no one had ever lived through it. That was the path he took!

"Immediately after Alexander took for the Desert of Death, his fleet was pushed into the sea and into unfavorable sea winds by Hindu warriors. He lived through death but he was closer to death than ever when he reached the other side of the desert.

"Some of his warriors had died on the way from thirst and hunger and their bodies were abandoned. Almost all of his army camp followers and all the women and children died in the shifting sands and rolling rain waters from the mountains. The desert was strewn with dead bodies.

"My men burned and buried the dead women and children they could find, but left their dead men unburied to deny them rebirth for the killing of all the Brahmans."

He takes a deep breath. "He had asked the Brahmans, before putting them to the sword, why they had stirred trouble and had provoked the Hindu Rajah against him and they had told him, *Because we wanted him to live with honor and die with honor!*"

He pauses again and shakes his head.

"I knew that arrow wound in Mâlavâ would soon kill him. He was marked for a certain death the day my arrow pierced his body."

Chandrâguptâ points proudly with his head to the bow. "I had killed elephants and tigers and lions with that bow. Alexander was just a man!"

He sips his golden fragrant wine.

"I had to make a choice then: go after a kingdom or go after her.

"I chose to become an Emperor! I worked hard to forget her and I did. She was just a woman, I told myself. An Emperor could have a thousand women if he wishes! And more." He pauses and closes his eyes.

"There was only one man who had come to realize that among all that Alexander had conquered, she was the precious jewel, not the worthless gold and lands and palaces, and he was willing to die for her!"

Another pause.

"I had forgotten all about her in my heart, or so I thought, until last year, when I heard the reports from my Eyes and Ears that the men who had fought for years to possess her and her Son-King had made peace among themselves to rule until her son became of age. I knew then that the peace was to be sealed with her blood and that of her son. All the men around her who would have spoken for her must have died. I just could not let those barbarians spill her royal blood on the lands beyond the Lands of the Persians."

Chandrâguptâ leans forward and speaks quietly. "Your son had strict orders to either save her or kill her, and bring back her body to be buried in Bakhtrish in the tomb of her ancestors alongside her royal kinsmen. She had confided to me once that she never feared her own death, just feared her body to be desecrated by the men who were not of her faith. Her captors burned their dead in fire that was sacred to her faith. The bodies of her brothers who had died in the wars of King Dariush were lost to her and the body of her father was torn apart to a thousand pieces by the men of Alexander, denying him an honorable death and the royal burial due all Kings!"

A man never knows how deeply he is in love with a woman until he looks her death in the eye.

Ârash looks at Chandrâguptâ astounded; his voice and words fail him.

The reason he was so harsh with his warrior was because she was more to him than the wife of an old enemy… he loved her.

It was why he had sent them in the first place.

Chandrâguptâ finishes his fragrant wine and gets up to his feet.

He held his wine better than any man.

Ârash scrambles to his feet quickly.

"She is to be treated as one of the Imperial Women of mine, with all due honors, not a Woman of the Imperial Court. You will see to it that she becomes familiar with all the customs of my Imperial Court."

"Yes, My Lord." Ârash utters quietly, bowing his head.

Chandrâguptâ nods and turns around and walks quietly into his Private Imperial Palace.

TERRACE. PRIVATE IMPERIAL PALACE of SAMRÂT CHANDRÂGUPTÂ
A MONTH PASSES
NIGHT

Starry night…

"I am here, My Lord. You summoned me?"

Rošanak walks on the expansive golden terrace on soft bare-footed feet.

Chandrâguptâ dismisses everyone and the terrace empties and becomes intimate. "Yes."

He beckons her to him on the floor and points to an ornate box in front of him. "This box of yours has been in my care for many years and I wish to return it to you."

Rošanak narrows her eyes at the box. The box does not look familiar. She kneels down on the soft silky spread before Chandrâguptâ and leans forward and opens the box and looks inside.

It was filled with beautiful golden jewelry. A jeweled golden dagger with dried blood on the blade slept protectively on top of the glittering jewels.

She looks up at Chandrâguptâ wordlessly, blankly.

Chandrâguptâ eyes her, relieved.

The color of life had finally returned to her face.

He then reaches and picks up the bloodied dagger and holds it before her eyes. "Remember this?" he asks in a searching voice.

Rošanak narrows her eyes at the dagger and then she remembers. Silent tears fill the cups of her eyes.

"Still sharp after all these years." Chandrâguptâ gently rubs the tip of his finger on the edge of the golden dagger.

"It is your blood— you said that was all I will ever have of you."

Chandrâguptâ puts down the golden dagger on the silky spread in front of him and then points to the golden glinting jewelry in the box.

"When you left me, you sent back to me all the jewelry I had gifted you. I could not bear to see these on any other woman, so I threw them in this box and put the bloodied dagger on top of them and locked the box away, until you just opened it."

He pauses and takes a deep breath and looks at her intently.

Tears silently fall on Rošanak's face. She reaches and gently touches the jewelry with the tips of her fingers and then sits back and looks at him.

Chandrâguptâ speaks quietly. "I swore that night to myself that one day I would be a great emperor— greater than Alexander— greater than the Persian King of Kings— and then I would bend you to my will— I would bend you to your knees— that one day I would have all of you and not just a few drops of your dried blood on a golden dagger, as you had promised me!

"I vowed to possess all that you loved and destroy all whom you loved. Now that you live right here in my imperial palace, you are farther away from me than ever before… your knees bent, your heart unbent…"

Rošanak takes a deep breath and casts her eyes down.

Chandrâguptâ draws closer to her. "I sent you a letter and declared my love for you and asked that you send for me, when you were free of him. But you never did.

"When I heard about the peace agreement, I knew they would unquestionably kill you and your son. Men of the sword cannot give up true power of kings, once they have gotten a taste of it in their blood! So, I forgave you and sent for you, even though you never sent for me— not even a small letter from you in all those years, telling me that you were still alive. Did you ever think well of me and of the times we spent together when we were young?"

"That was many years ago," Rošanak says quietly.

He asks her, searching. "There is no one here but you and me. Tell me, do you not remember those blistering nights we used to sit by the lotus pond in the palace of Rajah Parvataka and dip our feet in the cool scented waters? I told you stories about the days I had traveled in the Lands of the Persians. Do you not remember those sweet nights when we kissed tenderly under starry skies, and our embraces had grown intimate?"

Rošanak slowly leans forward and picks up the bloodied golden dagger and puts it back to sleep on top of the golden jewelry in the box and closes the top wordlessly.

She fills up with pain.

"That woman died years ago."

Promise of life,
Pain of death,
… only one thing is true…
… the rest is lies…
Life passes…
The flower that once was…
… is no more
She is no more…
God is perfect…
She is the imperfection…
… the false thread in the true Persian carpet…

PALACE of CHIEF WIFE. QUARTERS of the IMPERIAL WOMEN
IMPERIAL PALACES of PÂTALIPUTRÂ
ANOTHER MONTH PASSES
MID-DAY

"From the Emperor, Dukšiš."

Ârash bows his head and points to a rolled palm leaf on the table.

Rošanak looks at the palm leaf and then looks up at Ârash, puzzled.

"What is it?"

"Ah!" Ârash reaches and picks up the palm leaf, unrolls it and looks at it.

"It is the imperial list of the daily activities of the Samrât."

Rošanak looks at the palm leaf again.

What did that have to do with her?

Ârash continues, pointing to the palm leaf. "Since you cannot read it, I will read it to you. It says here: Samrât wakes up early— as you already know."

He pauses and eyes her for a sign, and then looks back at the palm leaf and continues reading. "Then, after contemplating the affairs of the Empire while taking a bath, he receives the Council of his Imperial Ministers and makes any decisions that need to be made immediately. Then the Samrât receives the Crown Prince and the rest of his Imperial Sons in the presence of his Imperial Ministers—"

He quickly skips a few lines. "Then he receives the imperial healer and the imperial head gardener and the imperial chief cook. Ah, and then he hears a full report from Kayvârtâ, the Chief Eunuch in charge of the Imperial Women of the Samrât."

He eyes Rošanak discreetly and then clears his throat and continues reading. "Then Samrât moves to the public audience hall where he receives the people of the Empire and listens to their causes… then after a light mid-day meal and a short rest, he attends to more affairs of the Empire… the state of the Imperial Funds—"

Rošanak interrupts graciously.

"It is very considerate of the Emperor to inform me."

Go away!

Ârash looks at her tactfully and then gets to the point.

"In the afternoons, Samrât plays dice with his Nobles, or a game of chatrang or two, reviews his Imperial Army and visits the imperial elephants and the imperial horses in the imperial stables."

Rošanak nods graciously, trying to hurry him along.

Ârash continues with the authority granted to him by the Emperor, undaunted by her impatient prodding.

"When the sun goes down, Samrât takes a bath with a few favorite mistresses and then eats his night meal with a few Women of the Imperial Court."

Rošanak stands up nodding and smiling, while graciously showing him to the door. "The Emperor certainly keeps busy!"

Go away now!

"After the night meal, when the sky becomes dark, Samrât engages in star gazing on his private imperial terrace with an Imperial Woman—"

"Yes, how exciting!"

"You have been ordered to join the Samrât when he gazes at the night stars!"

"What?"

Rošanak stops, startled, and then she laughs unguardedly.

"I thought I heard you say that I am ordered to star gaze with the Emperor!"

"Yes. You heard correctly." Ârash nods his head, pointing to the palm leaf in his hand. "Here, it is so written— right here! Ah! And you are also summoned to night meals, as the food-taster for the Samrât!"

Rošanak's eyes widen.

"Your Emperor wants me to taste his food and then, if I live through it, sit around his private terrace and gaze at the night stars with him?"

"Yes." Ârash nods tactfully. "Also, you will be summoned to any imperial meetings and imperial feasts, where you will be the personal interpreter to the Samrât, for the tongues you are familiar with—"

Rošanak breaks into laughter.

Ârash had been jesting with her to brighten her mood.

Ârash looks at her intently and then bows his head and says tactfully but firmly, "I assure you, Dukšiš! The command of the Samrât is not a laughing matter!"

Rošanak stands there looking at him, as the smile disappears from her startled face.

"Summoned to stargazing! Surely, Your Emperor is not serious!"

"Very serious!"

The Samrât had thought with confidence that her iced-over lake would melt quickly at the first sunny sight of him… and when he had finally gotten tired of waiting and waiting for her to melt and bloom, he had simply ordered her to his presence.

Ârash looks at her seriously. "I can come for you every night, or you can go by yourself to the Private Imperial Palace of the Emperor after the sun goes down."

"I will go alone. Thank you," she says faintly.

"As you wish, Dukšiš."

Ârash bows again and walks out of the terrace.

TERRACE. PRIVATE IMPERIAL PALACE of SAMRÂT CHANDRÂGUPTÂ
LATER that NIGHT

New moon.

Another starry night.

"My Lord, I am here to taste your food, as you have commanded me," Rošanak says quietly, bowing her head slightly and kneeling down on the terrace floor. She looks up at the heavens and points with her head. "And for stargazing afterward."

Chandrâguptâ smiles and beckons one of his female imperial guards.

The female imperial guard bows and puts down a rolled piece of golden cloth in front of the Samrât.

Chandrâguptâ opens the golden cloth ceremonially. A glinting jeweled golden dagger rests between the golden folds of the immaculate cloth.

He looks up at Rošanak and beckons her closer and quietly points to the gleaming dagger. "The bloody ghost that was haunting this noble dagger has been washed away. The splendor has been restored to my splendid imperial dagger!"

Chandrâguptâ waves away the female imperial guards. They bow their heads and step back into the shadows. Chandrâguptâ looks down at the golden jeweled dagger and then picks it up admiringly and runs his fingers on the sharp blade and remembers.

"He looked straight at me. He had no fear in his eyes. Then— he looked and saw the blood on his own dagger. He pulled back his dagger from my throat and rubbed his fingers on the blood and then looked intently at the blood on the tips of his fingers. He looked at the dagger soaked in blood and he saw his own face on the blade. What I saw in his eyes then— was pain. He did not fear this dagger still pointing at his throat. He feared that you had meant what you had said. He reminded me of Kâma Šastra, the Knowledge of Desire."

One never knows how deeply a woman is in love, even when one is her lover…

He pauses and eyes Rošanak for another moment and then continues, "When I entered his room that night— I could not hear what was being said. I just knew from the tone of your voices that love was being spoken, the way you were standing nestled within his arms… the way he held you and whispered gently in your ear. I unsheathed this dagger and silently stole into his bedroom—

"I can still feel the envy and jealousy that gripped my heart. I knew then that I had come upon you when you had already given away your heart to another."

He looks into her darkening eyes.

"Earlier that night, at the festivities, he pretended not to see you, yet never took his eyes off you, even though he never looked at you, and he knew you never looked at him. He knew you were taunting him and the rage was bleeding him worse than any sword cut."

Chandrâguptâ takes a deep breath and puts the golden dagger down in front of him and then reaches and takes her hands and looks at the old faded scars on the palm of her hands, hardly perceptible to unsuspecting eyes. He rubs the tip of his finger gently on her old scars.

"If you had not marked those sharp blades with your red blood, one of us would have died that night. Only the gods know whose life was spared that night."

He lets go of her hands.

"My Empire stretches from the other side of River Sindhu to this side of River Ganga, from the abode of the snowy mountains to the shores of the watery oceans, won more by wits and words than with war. It is bigger than the Empire Alexander conquered… that means nothing to you?"

Breathless silence.

Chandrâguptâ looks at her intently for a moment and then says wryly, "Go now… if you do not desire my company… you neither have to taste my food nor gaze upon the stars with me! I can summon any of the women of my court or any woman in my Empire to take pleasure in my company! *Any woman!*"

Rošanak takes a deep breath, pushing back tears, and then pushes herself up to her feet and bows her head slightly and leaves the hard terrace wordlessly on soft feet.

A single woman… a purple rose wounded by a heap of thorns…
A wet lake without a drop of rain water…
Deaf to the sweet songs of the nightingales,
Only hearing the torturous cries of the kites and crows…
Looking away from the World and saying to it:
… Be not!
… naiy!

IMPERIAL PALACE GARDENS. IMPERIAL PALACES of PÂTALIPUTRÂ
A YEAR PASSES
NIGHT

Full moon…

Warm night… mild breeze…

Sounds of joyful revelers dancing and singing, sound of soft feet running.

Rošanak quickly turns a corner and then another corner and hides in the shadow of one of the Imperial Palaces.

The murmuring voices of the women following her draw near and pause and then trail off in the other direction.

Soothing silence wraps around her.

She takes a deep sigh of relief and steps out of the long shadows.

Finally… Blessed silence…

She looks around.

No'rouz was coming and her heart was restless and her body was sleepless again.

And she was lost as usual in the maze of Pâtaliputrâ palaces and had no idea where she was.

There were so many palaces inside the walled imperial palace quarters that it was hard to keep them straight even in the thousand rays of the blazing sun.

She walks around. She has wandered into the belly of a great garden.

Small candles light the pathways and fragrant flower beds. The air smells sweet. A shimmering pond murmurs silently in the center of the garden, covered with pink petals and snowy and sapphire lotus flowers.

An ancient sycamore fig tree of life spreads splendidly over the lotus pond.

She stops and lingers and fills her cup with fragrant air. She strolls toward the murmuring lotus pond and lies down on the edge of it and touches the fragrant lotus flowers and caresses the cool skin of the scented water.

Her heart whispers into the night,

"*You…*
a bit of bread and a cup of wine…
and then,
let whatever is to come,
come…"

The murmuring soothing water easily seduces her.

She closes her eyes and drifts into blessed sleep.

The ancient tree of life spreads lower and stands guard over the sleeping little star.

PRIVATE IMPERIAL GARDEN
PRIVATE IMPERIAL PALACE of SAMRÂT CHANDRÂGUPTÂ
LATER that NIGHT
FESTIVAL of SPRING

Late night…

The full moon hangs low in the night sky and glows, looking close enough to be touched and loved.

Little stars flicker like the candles of the heavens.

Chandrâguptâ steps on his quiet private terrace and looks over his murmuring private gardens. He looks up at his private starry skies and takes a private restless breath.

His life was incomplete!

He had just returned from the Festival of Spring honoring the ancient love god and there was neither love nor pleasure in his life!

As the love god was burned to ashes by the supreme god in his former life, his love life was in a heap of burnt ashes!

His body ached for hers… he dreamt of holding her and touching her and kissing her lips and caressing her shaded umbrella of kâma late at night…

He had caught a glimpse of her earlier at the Festival of Spring, but as usual, she had left too quickly for him to summon her to him…

In former days, when he had first seen her in the Palace of Rajah Parvataka, days were long and nights were longer and seducing the wife of another king was a pleasurable game… she was a sweet forbidden fruit and the wife of a great conquering king and she was lonely!

Like all the princes of the Nandâ Court, he was fully skilled at the Rules of Desire and the Sixty-four Arts… all of them!

In those days, he had kissed her tender lips and had tasted the tips of her young breasts and had touched her deep navel late at night when the rest of the palace and the whole sky were sleeping deep.

He had thought to himself that seducing her the second time around would be much easier… he had saved her life, after all, and had set her free… he was an emperor…

And he had been wrong!

He curses the ancient love god under his breath.

The ancient love god was mocking him for his arrogance!

He had done everything to seduce her and bring her back to his bed freely… to live like a bee on the petals of her lotus…

Jewelry, Flowers, Fragrant Wine, Poetry, Threads of Pearls and Precious Za'farân, Sweet Cakes… Love Potions… Scents and Sacred Oils…

And she had ignored all his affectionate advances…

Even sleeping lotus buds left a little corner of their mouths open at night for sleepy bees to crawl into the center of their soft fragrant petals and anchor for the night.

No! Not her!

She was shut tighter than the golden doors to the Imperial House of Jewels!

She did not even know he still existed! And he was the damn emperor and her damn life and death was by his imperial favor!

She had made a lowly beggar out of a mighty emperor!

He should have her flogged publicly for refusing her emperor and her master!

Kâma Sûtram was useless!

Even the blessed Moon, the goddess of all the heavens, was now pitying him, bending down from the heavens, reaching for him, Chandrâguptâ, the Protector of the Moon, to comfort him in her silvery arms…

He did not want the pity of the Moon, he wanted the pleasure of the Little Star!

He gazes at the moon for a moment longer and sighs restlessly and then starts to turn around when the shadow of a woman lying down by his private lotus pond catches the corner of his eye with surprise and displeasure.

His anger builds and rises…

His Private Imperial Palace and Private Imperial Gardens were private… forbidden to all his women, unless they were summoned by him.

He used to visit the quarters of his women in the evenings and bathe with them and take pleasure of one or two or three of them before returning to his private palace…

But he no longer desired any of them… his manhood had fallen one night and had refused to rise again at the naked sight of any of his women… So he had stopped visiting the quarters of the Women of the Imperial Court a long while ago.

There were murmurs and mutterings in his Imperial Court behind his back that he was no longer favored by the ancient love god and no longer followed his ways.

Worse! He had even started to have doubts about his manhood himself!

Was he still a whole man, if there were no women in his bed?

Or was he now half of himself?

He fills up with heartless wrath and rage…

The rumors about his manhood had been started by his own damn women!

And now one of them had dared to come and visit him in his private palace, unexpected and uninvited and unwelcomed, to test his manliness and laugh at him!

He beckons one of his female imperial guards and points to the trespasser and yells,

"Kill her!"

It was imperial justice to kill a disobedient trespasser! Even if the trespasser was one of the women of his imperial court!

The female imperial guard hesitates.

Chandrâguptâ narrows his eyes at her with surprise.

His female imperial guards were fearless.

They had killed ferocious tigers with their long bows and arrows. No man dared cross their lines when they protected him in public, unless he desired a certain death.

None had ever hesitated to carry out any of his imperial orders… none had ever dared disobey him.

He was no longer just half of himself to himself, he was now half an emperor to his subjects!

He had to prove himself all over again!

He orders her again furiously,

"Shoot her!"

The female imperial guard hesitates again.

Anger cooks and rises and flies over his head.

He steps across the imperial terrace with imperial fury and grabs the long bow and arrow from the female imperial guard and pushes her away. He rests the bow effortlessly on the terrace floor and aims and presses on it hard with his left foot. He nocks the barbed arrow to the bowstring, draws and releases it with all his might and let it fly, all in one flawless motion.

Wooosh!

The arrow soars high over the fragrant garden and descends low and finds its mark swiftly.

Thump!

The full moon hides her face in pity under a sliver of a dark cloud.

He grabs another arrow angrily and storms down the terrace steps and toward the woman and then stops motionless under the ancient wishing tree.

He stops breathing for a moment and his knees go soft… he steadies himself against the weeping wishing tree… his fury fades away, he becomes pale as dust, white as ash.

The female imperial guards quickly run down the terrace steps following the Samrât and head for the lotus pond.

Chandrâguptâ raises his hand quickly and they stop obediently and wait for his command. He then dismisses them with a quick wave of his hand.

Private imperial air leaves the private imperial garden… moonlight leaves with the moon…

Paradise becomes Hell…

It was his Anuragini…

She was motionless, with her hand floating in the golden lotus pond…

He closes his eyes. He dares not look.

By his own bloody hands, he had expertly marked and shot and killed the woman he had been trying so hard to seduce!

He had saved her from her bloody fate in the hands of her former enemies and had condemned her to worse by his own hands!

Wrathful death by the raging hands of an old lover who still utterly desired her.

Her voice quietly whispers to him…

"Did you bring me here, to kill me yourself?"

He prays desperately with all his heart.

"Is there a god? Is god here?"

He despairs… without even thinking, he invokes the ancient love god under his breath… his imperial heart loses the arrogance of his imperial crown…

"Kâma…

"Kâma… Are you here? Are you still here? Please hear me! I have sinned! The sinful arrow of the slayer has slain a beloved…"

Bow and arrow slip and fall out of his hands silently on a fragrant flower bed drenched in the mournful darkness of the night.

He moans…

"Vain is the Emperor!

Forgive the arrogance of an arrogant fool, My Lord! Forgive me!

I am the trespasser… the one who has failed to protect my beloved in my care…

I am the one who must die!"

He covers his teary eyes with his trembling hands. He pleads with all his heart under the ancient wishing tree.

"Kâma… You are the prayer and I am the worshipper… bodiless god, take your body again and save her! Grant me her life… undo the wrong that cannot be undone by man and let me love her in your sacred worship… she and I, we both used to honor your ancient ways… I will return to the worship of your way of love… man is only half of himself without a woman… even less with a heart full of anger… or take me from me and set me free… my life for hers… take away my empire… burn me into ashes… do with me as you will…"

He goes down hard on his softened knees and sinks into the roots of the ancient wishing tree and covers his eyes again and takes a deep mournful breath and prays again quietly.

Seven times and then seven times more…

Tears flow mournfully…

His tears drench the roots of the weeping wishing tree…

The ancient sycamore fig tree of life weeps for him…

Night passes slowly… stars and shadows move from one side of the sky to the other side…

He finally opens his mournful regretful shameful eyes and gets to his feet and hopelessly takes a few steps on weak knees toward her. He anchors himself down by her side on the edge of the lotus pond and narrows his sharp eyes and looks intently… hoping… praying… searching…

Private fragrant air returns to the private fragrant garden… shimmer returns to the lotus pond…

Hell becomes Paradise…

He takes a deep breath of life and hope.

His prayers had been answered…

There was no blood…

She was sleeping deep, breathing quietly, sheathed in the light of the higher full moon.
His arrow rested a hair's breadth away from her head and had pinned her raven hair to the edge of the golden lotus pond.

"There is god!"

He offers a quiet heartfelt prayer of thanks under his breath and slowly pulls the barbed arrow by the side of her head out of the grey stone and looks at its twisted tip for a short moment and then throws it away quickly into the garden out of sight.

He gazes at her face in the light of the full moon for a long moment.

His heart murmurs and pounds and pulsates.

The ancient love god had mercifully forgiven him…

Kâma had descended from the high Heaven to gaze upon the face of his beloved Roshanak bathing in the light of the Moon-goddess and had found her worthy and the arrow had bounced off Kâma and had only claimed a chunk of the beloved's raven hair.

Hair would grow back.

The ancient love god had accepted his heartfelt prayers and a lock of her mâlati-scented hair as a worthy offering and had spared her life in his eternal service…

Whispering voices approach, breaking the quiet of the late late night.

He narrows his eyes and looks up, startled.

A pair of serving girls were approaching his private lotus pond with soft feet.

He raises his hand.

The serving girls stop motionless for a moment in fright and then nervously bow and turn around and quickly disappear toward the Quarters of the Imperial Women.

It becomes quiet again.

Moonlight returns, higher with the silvery rising moon.

He looks back at her. Sweetness returns to his tongue… love returns to his heart… his cup fills with the grace of the ancient love god.

He lowers his head and quietly whispers into her ear, "Roshanak…"

She takes a deep breath in her sleep.

"It is cruel how you shamelessly torment the love god with your beauty."

Life kisses Rošanak's face. She opens her eyes lazily, heavy with sleep, and looks at him and then closes her eyes again and murmurs.

"I felt a shot in the dark heart!" she says sleepily.

"Then, I had a dream. My son and his dog were running and playing in the Valley *of the* Kings… my son saw me and ran to me and said to me that he was well… that he was with his fateful gods… and with his faithful dog… he said my constant grieving for him was grieving him for me. He said the world was a bazaar… it gave this and it took away that… he said to me, *May my mother become happy again!* and that I should no longer mourn him, so that his soul could be blissful… then I heard you calling me… commanding me back to you…"

Then sleep evaporates quickly.

She opens her eyes wide and sees the darkened face of Chandrâguptâ above her, close to her face, immersed in the light of the moon, smiling at her.

"Ah!" she gasps and tries to get up. Her body is sore from sleeping on the hard grey stone.

He takes her hand gently and pulls it toward him, loaded with hope and longing.

"Stay…"

Rošanak eases back down on the edge of the pond and mumbles softly… her hand falls back into the blessed and purified lotus pond.

"I… Forgive me… I lost my way… those women were following me around… I lost my way trying to escape from them… they were trying to take me back to the festival of their ancient love god…"

How could she honor the love god when there was no love in her heart?

He fills with unguarded happiness.

He loved the sound of her voice… when she spoke openly… softly… woman to man… the way she used to talk to him so long ago… not formally, like Imperial Woman to Emperor.

He becomes truthful… his tongue reclaims the thirst of a lover for the beloved… nearly departed…

"Nothing is as intoxicating as a love song… or the captivating gaze of a beautiful woman… and the soothing murmur of her soft voice."

"Ah!" she says softly.

He smiles and continues whispering, filling her ears with his grateful words. "If my Eyes and Ears had not told me about the peace agreement between the men of Alexander, you would have been lost to me forever."

She narrows her eyes at him and asks quietly… for the first time.

"Why did you come for me?"

"I…" he looks at her tenderly, "I wanted to see if it could be done," he says truthfully and takes a deep breath. "Alexander had come all the way from the other side of the seas to Hind. I wanted to see if I could go all the way from Hind to the other side of the seas, following the roti pieces he had left on his path. I wanted to go myself, but my ministers would not hear of it! So, I sent my warriors!"

Soft breathing…

"Brahmans say: *Body is just an empty temporary vessel… wrapped around the eternal soul…*"

He lifts her hand out of the golden lotus pond and brings it to his lips and kisses it tenderly.

She does not pull away her hand… she lets her wet hand rest in his dry hand.

"I remembered how I once was so fond of this vessel that wraps perfectly around your soul."

He gently kisses her hand again. "I did Alexander one better… Alexander came and lost his life and lost his Lands of the Persians. I went and found the Persian Woman I loved and kept my Empire!"

She breathes in his words… her heart softens… she starts to melt, at last…

"My first wife died eating the poisoned food I shared with her unknowingly. My first son was born after his mother died. My heart was an empty vessel until I met you in the court of Rajah Parvataka.

"Kalyana told me that three men were bound to you— a Conqueror and a Warrior and an Emperor. In those days, I thought I was the Warrior… but now I know I am the Emperor." He takes a deep breath and continues gratefully, "Nothing ever happens by chance in the heavens… when I first saw you, you were a Little Star… now you have grown into a Full Moon… and I am the Protector of the Moon… it was always meant to be… I was favored by the gods when I found you then, and again tonight!"

She reaches and softly touches his face.

"I am not the woman you once loved…"

He draws closer to her face and gently kisses her forehead.

She was scented with the sweet night mâlati he had gifted her… just as she was the first time he had met her…

He breathes her in…

"No… and I am not the man you left behind…"

"It has been so long… I have forgotten what it means to be loved… my beauty left me a long time ago…"

She could not even remember the last time she was loved by Amyntor… a few hurried moments in the dark the night before Olympias had finally surrendered the Fortress at Pydna to Kassandros… Both starving and weary and spent, more desirous of bread than love… thinking they were to see each other again soon in Pella… thinking love could wait…

It was so long ago… her memory had long since faded.

She had not even looked at herself in a looking glass for years, dreading what she would find staring back at her.

The Hindu serving girls washed her body with warmed honey and crushed fruits and salts and oils and bathed her in cool yâsmin-scented waters and clothed her in soft silky sarees and lined and painted her face every day.

She was not sure what beauty the Emperor saw in her ugliness…

"It ran away with my youth!" he smiles truly.

A gentle unexpected rain starts to fall.

Drops of rain pass through the ancient sycamore fig tree of life and kiss her face and rest peacefully on her eyelashes.

He slowly lies down next to her and stretches over her, keeping the rain away from her. His body gets wet and drips down on her.

Her saree gets wet.

He whispers fragments of old Hindu love words in her ear, woven with his sweet kisses.

"Lady of the Moon,

You have at last drawn near to me...

You have come home, in your coming...

Like a bird back to her nest,

High on a sycamore fig tree...

Leaving the crow for the tail of the Peacock...

I prayed by Kalpa Vrikša,

And the divine wishing tree granted me my wish...

... you... the desire of my heart..."

His desire for her drips into her heart...

Her dry body accepts the cool wet raindrop offerings from his wet body. Her heart opens up to him. She reaches and caresses his smooth chest with the tips of her fingers, her fingers get wet... the dry bed of the old river fills with rainwater...

His body flames with burning desire... he slowly unwraps her wet saree and lowers his head and kisses her lower lips tenderly and caresses her naked wet body in the gentle falling rain. His body hardens and rises... he bridges with his burning golden rod over her melting lake in the cooling rain in the worship of the ancient love god...

Kâma...

I offer you my worship...

Accept it...

As a victor accepts victory...

Moon waxes into the auspicious house of the seventh sign.

She sighs softly with pleasure under him.

He catches his breath and becomes whole again. He becomes himself again... he becomes better than himself.

The ancient love god accepts the love offering.

More cooling rain pours after the torrid heat of love.

Night lingers longer till dawn.

His life was complete.

TERRACE. PRIVATE IMPERIAL PALACE of SAMRÂT CHANDRÂGUPTÂ
YEAR 15 of the FOURTH ALEXANDER
YEAR 14 of SAMRÂT CHANDRÂGUPTÂ, MONTH of BHÂDRAPADA, R'TU of VARSÂ
MONTHS LATER
NIGHT

Almost full moon.

Hot and sultry… sleeping under the stars…

"You wish to… marry me?" Rošanak asks, startled, as she wraps the cool cotton linen around her body.

"Yes!" Chandrâguptâ catches his breath and says with a smile.

"Why?"

"Why not?"

"But, I already sleep in your bed."

"Then you can make your decision based on facts gathered by your own senses."

"At my age? I am barren and old enough to be a grandmother."

She was thirty four years of age… olden…

"I am already a grandfather. Eleven children already born to my sons and daughters and a few more on the way."

He was thirty nine years of age… youngish…

"All the men who have claimed me have died!"

Chandrâguptâ raises his eyebrow and eyes Rošanak curiously.

A hive was always full of sweet wild honey…

And lots of bees always buzzed around an open fragrant lotus…

He knew of two, a number he could live with.

She had taken a lover because her husband had been busy raging through Asia.

It was the duty of the husband to keep his wife satisfied so she would have no cause to seek her womanly pleasures in other manly arms.

How could Alexander keep a captured empire in his grasp, when he could not keep a wedded wife to his bed?

And he was not a mere man… he was a Samrât… an Emperor!

And to the eyes of the lover, the beloved was perfect in her every lovely imperfection.

"I would take my chances!"

"Why?"

"Why not?"

Rošanak narrows her eyes, considering him.

"I asked you for your hand many seasons ago. Hindus like long courtships and consult the stars for favorable celestial omens. I have known you for—" he pauses and counts on his fingers— "fifteen years, and the stars have just become favorable."

Rošanak laughs.

Chandrâguptâ points to his gardens.

"I found you breaking into my private palace and sleeping by my lotus pond in the middle of my private garden. I ordered my Imperial Guards to shoot you and they disobeyed me, so I took the omen and took you to my bed instead."

He had finally caught her like a golden butterfly in a net he had spread for her made of ancient prayer and pure spun sugar.

And once she had been caught in his sugary net, he had no intention of setting her free… ever.

"I gave you your own palace… silk sarees… jewelry… loads of za'farân… heaps of sugar… bottles of sweet night mâlati scent… armed guards… multitudes of serving girls… and to show your gratitude, you moved right into my private palace and took over my private gardens and all my peacocks… and stole my favorite horse!"

He had ordered the serving girls to bring her belongings to his Private Imperial Palace from the Palace of the Chief Wife before she had awakened in his bed in the morning following their first night joined together.

All she had of her own was a small book, half-burned, and a small silver box, filled with dark ashes… a pair of emerald forest earrings… a pair of old, golden manly rings… and one earring of a Persian warrior…

"You would never find a husband with your dowry! I am stuck with you!"

Everything else belonged to him, provided by the imperial staff funded by the imperial funds of the Samrât himself. The most worthwhile investment he had ever made had been returned to him with many benefits.

More smiles.

"You are already a load of trouble…"

Previous Karma running its course through his current rebirth, no doubt…

"… and you steal the linen in my bed with no regard for me! Men have been punished severely for stealing a lot less from the Samrât! You have taken everything!" He plays with the linen wrapped around her naked body.

He did not tire easily and never slept much and he liked watching over her while she slept, tossing and turning and snoring like a tigress.

He too was making his decision based on facts gathered by his own senses.

More smiles.

He pulls away the linen, stretches over her body again and whispers sweetly, "You are like an invading army. The only way to stop you is either to kill you or to marry you!"

Rošanak laughs.

Chandrâguptâ smiles unguardedly. "Do you desire to rule my Empire?"

He lowers his head closer to her face, looking at her with deep desire.

Rošanak laughs harder and shakes her head *No* side to side.

He finally relaxes, slowly rolls on his back, keeping her firmly with him. "Then, I wish to give you the only valuable I have left in my possession."

Her hair falls around his face. She whispers playfully as she kisses his lips, "What is more valuable than your Empire, My Lord?"

He plays with her soft hair and caresses her naked back and smiles lovingly. "Me! I wish to give you all of myself!"

"Ah!" Her green eyes smile warmly.

"You are, indeed, more valuable than the whole of your Empire!"

Chandrâguptâ beams.

She eyes him in the light of the moon.

He was serious.

Her eyes become cloudy for a moment and she slightly pulls back.

He gently draws her back into his arms and reads her eyes like a palm leaf.

"I promise I will not die before you," he whispers as he wraps around her, "and I promise you will never burn in a fire."

PRIVATE IMPERIAL AUDIENCE HALL
NEXT MORNING

"Marry her?" Chanâkya says, stunned. He looks at Chandrâguptâ intently.

The woman was a widow… and she was not a taruni any longer either.

She was polluted and tainted and used.

If she was a good Hindu woman, she would have lost her desire to live and would have faithfully burned herself to death on the pyre of her dead husband.

She was already married to the mlechchha Alexander, when the Samrât first laid eyes on her many moons ago… and had tried to seduce her with his blessing.

Seducing a woman was no different than conquering a kingdom.

Chandrâguptâ narrows his eyes at Chanâkya and gives him a sharp look.

Chanâkya straightens out and takes a deep breath.

He had spoken rashly and unguardedly.

Samrât had proven himself worthy in battle… he had conquered five kings and five kingdoms.

He had taught him well how to become a greater king, a Chakravarti Samrât, and he had been a masterful pupil. He had surpassed his Brahman teacher long ago.

And not even he could now risk losing the affection of the Samrât.

In the circle of powerful men, nothing was more potent and divisive than a beautiful woman. He should have counseled him to keep away from the wife of another king!

The eyes of the two men meet halfway in the middle of the private audience hall for a few more silent moments and ponder their long journey together.

Pupil and Teacher… Emperor and Chief Brahman Minister…

One, a man of god and knowledge… the other, a warrior king…

Bonded by affection and friendship and history…

Bound by an Empire.

Silence hangs and lingers between them.

Chandrâguptâ is the first to give ground.

"She is the daughter of the last Persian Great King… a Royal Woman of the Persians… from the same Warrior Caste as I am," he says persuasively.

He did not wish to sever the ties to his old teacher… unless it was absolutely necessary. His teacher had served him well; they had birthed a splendid Empire together.

"She does not share your faith," Chanâkya says, thinking.

"God resides in the heart of all. She worships the Wise Lord of the ancient Âryâs… the same Âryâs who came to Hind and brought their gods with them," Chandrâguptâ says firmly. Then he softens his voice. "I was blessed with the love of two faithful wives and I have a Crown-Prince and many sons from my wives and women of the court."

And she was barren…

"I do not know if my love for her is a blessing or a curse, but I intend to find out by wedding her."

Chanâkya leans forward and asks quietly with old familiarity, "Why do you wish to marry her now after all these years? She is a widow… she could just live quietly in the Imperial Court as your favorite woman. A rose in the garden can give pleasure… it is her thorns that wound."

"Persian Royal Daughters are not roses! They are not raised to be the favorite women of the court… they are brought up under the care of the Great Kings to become Royal Women of their Lands. Through their royal bloods, their Great Kings have ruled for generations."

Chandrâguptâ leans back and says quietly, "Do not think of Hindu sugar as a mere plant… think of its intoxicating sweetness."

Chanâkya leans back in his chair. His face folds.

The Empire was not just won by his wits and words… it was won by the wars led by the Samrât… both necessary to maintain a prosperous wealthy Empire.

"You can wed any woman of the Warrior Caste in all of Hind."

Chandrâguptâ takes a deep breath and says quietly, "My first wife was the daughter of the brother of my mother who had protected my life in the Court of Nandâ. My second wife, the daughter of the brother of my father, fell in love with me and picked me in the svayamvara ritual. I was her choice."

He takes another deep breath and speaks the truth.

"I know she is not perfect like a goddess… but who knows why a man loves and desires one woman above all the rest? Why one face looks easier on the eyes… why one voice sounds easier on the ears… why one kiss tastes the sweetest… why one glance opens the Gates of Hell and another opens the Gates of Heaven. And who knows why one woman stays in the heart of a man for so many years, while others come and go? Her scent lingers in the folds of his body… and never fades…"

Chanâkya intently listens to Chandrâguptâ as he continues.

Kayvârtâ had told him that the Samrât had not bedded any of his Women of the Imperial Court after bedding her.

"This one… she is that one woman for me… she is my choice. I have taken a sacred oath to love her with my every breath. I want to walk with her and lead her around the sacred marriage fire. I wish her to be bound to me in the eyes of the ancient love god and in all the heavens."

TERRACE. PRIVATE IMPERIAL PALACE of SAMRÂT CHANDRÂGUPTÂ
FOLLOWING DAY
MIDDLE of the DAY

Warm air scented with fragrant flowers…

"The future of the Enlightened One was foretold twice."

The young Buddhist Monk nods and speaks quietly to Rošanak.

"They said he would either become a great king, known through all the lands… or he would become enlightened and set the people of the Land of Seven Rivers free from ignorance… if he was to embrace the pleasures of the world, he would become a King… and if he was to renounce the pleasures of the world, he would become the Enlightened One…"

The young Buddhist Monk pauses and catches his breath and waits for his words to be interpreted for Rošanak and then continues, "His kingly father shielded the young prince from the mortal world by keeping him inside his royal palaces.

"The young prince never set foot outside the golden gates of the royal palaces of his kingly father. His life was well protected from living…

"When the Royal Prince was twenty nine years old, he wished to see what lay beyond the walls of his father's royal palaces. He ventured out into the world and witnessed the Four Sights:

"First he saw Old Age,

… then, Disease,

… and, Death…

"And finally he saw a monk carrying a begging bowl. He was told the monk had denounced the pleasures of the world in search of truth and happiness… and there and then the Royal Prince resolved to do the same."

The young monk stops and catches his breath.

The words are interpreted for Rošanak.

She looks at the young Buddhist Monk intently.

Šiyati?

She had never known a prince who had walked away from a throne… a Persian Vîsa Puça had always valued the Crown and the Throne of the Lands of the Persians above all else… and all the Persian Royal Sons had always intrigued to become the next great King of Kings.

Royal Sons had spilled a sea of royal blood to become the Great Kings of the Lands… it was all there was… it was all that mattered…

And here was a Royal Prince who had denounced a kingly crown and throne for truth and happiness…

Truth was the law of the Wise Lord…

Kingship was the law of the Lands…

… but what was happiness?

Was it just another old dead word written in ancient markings with its true meaning long lost and forgotten from the memories and tongues of living men?

Or…

Was there truth in happiness?

… was there happiness in truth?

She narrows her eyes and tosses and turns the words backwards and forwards in her heart.

What had tormented her most for years and had kept her up at nights tossing and turning and wondering, was what she had done to her own Son-King.

Was she right to let her Son-King choose his own kingdom for himself?

… or had she thoughtlessly stolen the Crown and the Throne of the Lands from her own Son-King, by her own careless, foolish, selfish deeds?

Was an inheritance so washed and watered by the blood of the men of the Lands worth the gold and the glory the King-Father had left for his Son-King?

Even a king-father had not fared all that well in forcing the path of his Enlightened Son from the path that the heavens had intended for him…

Her mind starts to dissolve… like a ball of golden spun Hindu sugar.

Her Son-King was alive and he was splendidly Persian…

… but was he happy? Was he meant to be?

Was he destined to become a king? Or was he meant to become happy?

What was the path that the heavenly stars had charted for her Kingly-Son?

An unfamiliar voice pulls her out of her rambling thoughts. She turns her head around toward the voice.

Chief Brahman Minister Chanâkya was standing on her private terrace.

He utters a few words with authority and everyone hurriedly gets to their feet and leaves. The terrace empties and becomes private. He sits down in front of her on the silky carpeted terrace, dispenses with the usual imperial court pleasantries and speaks to her directly.

"The Samrât is intent on wedding you," Chanâkya says quietly in broken Persian and considers Rošanak under his purposeful brow for a long moment.

The Samrât had been bedding her for months and his passion had not yet cooled for her and she was not with his child… she could be barren… or too old to even get with child! Then what good could come of such a useless union?

Rošanak looks at him wordlessly.

The dark-skinned smallish man was the Chief Brahman Minister of the imperial court. Chandrâ valued his advice and his wisdom and his words.

She had met him once at the Palace of Rajah Parvataka when he had come to see Chandrâ. He had taken no notice of her then…

And he had taken no notice of her in the Imperial Court of the Samrât either.

He spoke carefully, as he had lost some of his teeth at a young age… but he spoke with cunning and intelligence and wisdom and forbearance, and when he spoke, her shrewd Emperor listened… and so did everyone else at the Imperial Court.

They said he had always stayed a step ahead of the treacherous assassins and had saved the life of the Samrât by his watchfulness several times. There was always an assassin lurking in the shadows wishing to shorten the life of her Samrât.

The Chief Brahman Minister was the most powerful man at the Imperial Court of the Emperor, after the Samrât himself.

He had not even sent words prior to his visit… he had just come unannounced.

"He asked the Brahmans to bless the wedding, as you are not of the same faith as the Samrât."

Rošanak looks at Chanâkya intently, listening to every word carefully.

His words were heavy with his love for the Emperor and the Empire.

"What is your wish?" he asks her directly.

Her eyes widen. "My wish?" she asks in a hushed voice.

No one had ever asked her what she wished… what she wanted… she had always done her duty… what was expected of her as a Royal Woman…

"Yes. What is your wish?" he repeats.

Rošanak takes a deep breath and straightens herself.

"I wish…"

She pauses for a moment and then sweetens her voice with golden spun Hindu sugar.

"The Samrât asked for my hand in marriage when we first met in the Palace of Rajah Parvataka many years ago. He was a young warrior and I was already wedded… a marriage alliance to save the lives of my warrior people from certain death and utter destruction. I will gladly stay with the Samrât as his ba^{n}daka for as long as he desires me. I would be dead, if he had not sent for me."

She looks at Chanâkya and then bows her head slightly and utters quietly, "I would give my life willingly, the very moment the Samrât becomes desirous of it. He is the Great Emperor and I am his loyal ba^{n}daka… I will never disobey his imperial command!"

Rošanak takes a deep breath and straightens and says with devotion, "May the treacherous dagger of an assassin take my life instead of my Samrât."

Chanâkya narrows his eyes at her and thinks for a moment.

The throne was secure with many princes already, and a Crown-Prince too, and if she was barren, then what harm could come from such a pleasurable marriage?

She was not chaste and virtuous as a wife should be, but she was still a Persian Royal Woman worthy of a Persian King and it was best to keep the Samrât happy in bed, so he could concentrate on the affairs of the Empire.

Power and pleasure were knotted like Heaven and Earth…

Dharma Śastra and Artha Śastra rested on the pillars of Kâma Śastra…

After all, satisfaction and salvation were the goals of living, and nurturing of desire and pleasure was the main mission of life.

If a man did not first cross the gates of desire and pleasure and satisfaction, he had no right to the take the second step toward the god and salvation… a man could only wish for salvation when his desires were utterly satisfied.

And the Samrât had not wedded again after the death of his second wife; he had been wifeless for a few years now… it was not fitting for a Samrât to be without a wife… as all the Imperial Court Nobles fashioned themselves after the Samrât himself, weddings had declined in the Imperial Court over the last few years… nobles without wives were not as wedded to the Imperial Court as the wedded nobles were… wives tied the nobles more obediently to the Imperial Court and the Emperor than gold!

"Women must be purified before a wedding ritual. Will you be willing to bathe in the River of the Goddess Ganga? River Ganga is sacred… it descends from the Heaven to purify the Earth… it will purify your body and wash away your sins and will lighten your heart of pain, if you bathe in it."

Rošanak looks at Chanâkya discreetly.

She had done the work of a Royal Woman all her life…

Were all her sins written on her face with dark markings? And all her pain too?

Was her face that easy to read?

Did her face speak that loudly, betraying her deep secrets so carelessly?

Was it time to leave the past behind?

Was she willing to? Could she?

"Yes… if you wish it, so be it…"

BANKS of RIVER GANGA
FOLLOWING NIGHT

"Anuragini," Chandrâguptâ whispers sweetly into Rošanak's ear, "in the beginning, there was nothingness swimming in an ocean of darkness… in the beginning, there was no worship of love, and no existence in the nothingness swimming in an ocean of darkness… then came the world without love… the Lord of Beings absorbed the world, and the loveless world was thus destroyed and then purified and created again with love…

"And when the world was destroyed by the burning flames, its blackened ashes fell into the sacred rivers and the sacred rivers emptied into the vast ocean… and the cycle of rebirth started." He points to the expansive River Ganga stretching wide before their eyes.

She had told him she had agreed to the purification ritual and about her desire to bathe in the River Ganga and he had brought her to the Sacred River late at night when it was less crowded.

Rošanak takes a deep breath.

Had the blackened ashes of Pârsâ fallen into the sacred ocean too?

Amyntor used to say that Alexander was neither man nor god… he was the fire of nature that had burned old forest groves so new trees could take root and grow…

The female imperial guards clear a path to the sacred River Ganga and array themselves on both sides of the path with their bows and arrows drawn.

The scent of burning incense fills the heavy air of the warm night.

Chandrâguptâ takes Rošanak's hand and starts walking toward the sacred river. People bow their heads and clasp their hands together and whisper blessings as the Samrât passes by. Rošanak walks barefooted with Chandrâguptâ into the sacred river. The warm water wraps around them.

Chandrâguptâ floats a white lotus wreath on the river, an offering to the Goddess Ganga.

Rošanak looks up.

The moon was full.

She breathes nervously and fills her body with the warm scented air of the night.

This was harder than she had imagined…

It was not just a walk into a watery river…

It was a walk backward into the known river of her past…

And a walk forward into the unknown river of her future…

And the wise Chief Brahman Minister knew it!

That was how the clever old Brahman had always stayed a step ahead of the multitudes of foolish assassins!

She lets go of Chandrâguptâ's hand and takes a step forward, clutching the small silver jewelry box from her past in her hands. She unlocks the box and opens the top and takes one last look.

Ashes kneaded with old memories…

Dried up petals of a Bakhtrian rose and plum blossoms from the UpLands…

… dried rose petals from the night before her wedding to Alexander…

… and dried plum blossoms from the House of Amyntor…

An old ancestral ring protected by the Goddess of Victory…

… the golden earring of Ša Rêš Šarri…

… a small baby tooth…

Fragmented memories buried in a handful of blackened ashes from Pârsâ.

She takes a deep breath and picks the small baby tooth, the gold earring and the old ring out of the box and holds them tightly in her fist and then closes her eyes and empties the rest into the wind.

The ashes and petals swirl in the night air and fall into the River Ganga and dance on the skin of the river and then slowly disappear into the belly of the sacred waters.

She opens her eyes and drops the small silvery box into the sacred river too and watches it as the watery mouth of the sacred waters opens and hungrily devours it, and it too disappears quickly in the dark waters.

She prays quietly under her lips, trying to summon up all her courage.

"*My Lord*, forgive me my sins… I pray to thee… help me, as I take refuge in thee…"

She takes a deep breath. Tears fall on her face.

It was hard to give up the fragments of her past that were the whole of her life once.

She had been a captive woman since the day the Fortress at Sughud had fallen into the hands of Alexander… that was most of her life.

No Royal Woman had ever become a captive woman since the day Kuruš the Elder had brought all the Lands under the sway of the Persians… ever.

Eternal curses on those men who had lost the Empire to the enemy… lost the Lands of the Persians… lost the inheritance of their noble fathers and sons, and brought such shame to their women.

She takes a deep breath.

But to say that she had not loved Alexander was a lie too…

And lies were the source of all evil.

He had treated her with affection and sweetness and tenderness.

She had cursed his kingsmen who were like a murderous plague on the Lands…

… but not Alexander… never Alexander.

He had loved her in his own way… and he had loved her well.

He was the father of her sons and cursing him was no different than cursing her own sons… and her own blood… and she knew all too well the power of curses.

And there was nothing but love and tenderness in her heart for the kingsmen of Alexander who had loved her and protected her when she was amongst them… they all had burned like sacred fire with desire and love and passion for her…

None had dishonored her in public or in private.

More tears fall on her face.

"Divine Ânâhitâ, when the Lands of the Persians fell to the armies of our enemies, you protected me. You shielded me from the evil that surrounded me. You put love in the hearts of Alexander and his kingsmen for me. When they killed all around me, not a single man raised his hand against me. I traveled to the Lands of the Bitter Sea on the other side of the Lands of the Persians and crossed the sea without fear, obeying your order.

"Now I am here, without a hair on my head being harmed. My Son-King has safely been raised a Persian in the Lands of his royal ancestors, away from men who wish him dead."

She takes a deep breath.

"Divine Ânâhitâ, I saw you in a dream. You said to me: *Fear not! I am with you! Wherever you go, I will go with you.* Wherever I went, you went with me… wherever I am, you are already there…"

She takes a step further into the sacred river, her hand tightly fisted guarding the small baby tooth and the gold earring and the old goddess of victory.

She prays with all her heart and soul…

"Divine Ânâhitâ, forgive me… wash away the shame of captivity from my body… make me whole… make me worthy…"

She was praying for forgiveness, but there was no forgiveness in her heart for the men who had killed her son.

She had thought Olympias was mad when she had burned with rage over the death of Alexander… and had mercilessly killed poor Arrhidaios and the bloody Amazon… and all the rest.

She had thought Purušâtu was cruel when she had mercilessly tortured the Karian who had killed her Royal Son, the Younger Kuruš, and had gouged out his murderous eyes with reddened iron and had poured molten metal into his throat…

If she had gotten her hands on Kassandros, she would have done Olympias and Purušâtu one better!

She takes another step into the river. Fish swim around her. Her legs disappear under her into the watery river. Her wet saree weighs heavy on her body. She closes her eyes. A tear falls on her face.

But she wanted to be free of the past… free of the pain…

The past was like golden chains around her wrists… it had never let the cuts on her body and her heart and her soul to mend and heal and scab over…

Could the sacred waters of the Divine Ganga really wash away her sins of captivity? Free her from her golden chains and fetters? Wash away the blood of a dying son from her living hands?

All the royal and noble women who had been forced into wedding the Makedonians had been released of their wedded bonds when Alexander died… they had all wedded the remaining men of the most noble Seven Persian Families… but not her… she had remained a captive of those wretched men until Chandrâ had come for her…

What right had she to a place among women?

What good had she ever done in her life to deserve happiness?

Why had everyone around her died while she had lived?

Why had she lived?

Prayer mixes with tears… and falls like rain…

"My Lord, please forgive me my sins… I pray to thee… please help me, as I take refuge in thee… please forgive me…"

What she desperately needed more than anything else… was forgiveness.

She wanted to be forgiven… wanted to know that she was forgiven…

Forgiven by all her fathers and mothers and brothers and sisters…

…forgiven by Alexander and all the men who had loved her…

…forgiven by her sons… forgiven by Alexander and Alexandros…

Forgiven by her God… forgiven by all gods…

"*My Lord*, please forgive me… please hear me… from my unworthy lips to your merciful ears… may all lips be silent who do not speak of thee…"

She starts walking further and further into the sacred river. Shimmery moonlit water wraps tighter around her… and draws her in deeper and deeper.

She tearfully prays silently under her breath.

"Great is the Wise Lord,
Baga Vazarka Auramazdâh,
Who created this earth, who created this sky,
haya imân bûmim adâ haya avam asmânam adâ,
Who created man,
haya martiyam adâ,
Who created happiness for man…
haya šiyâtim adâ martiyahayâ…
There is no other god…"
Baga aniya naiy astiy…

She opens her clenched fist under the skin of the sacred waters… the small baby tooth washes away… the winged goddess of victory leaves her… a fish swallows the gold earring… The sacred water pulls her in further… swallows her whole… dousing the flame of the smoldering grief and shame in her heart…

She disappears completely into the belly of the sacred river… becomes utterly immersed under the sacred waters.

Was the silvery moon just beclouded by the black clouds?

… or had it utterly left the orbit of the heavens?

Was the moon lost?

Chandrâguptâ stands there for a moment and then quickly rushes into the deep river after Rošanak. A few of the female imperial guards rush to follow the Samrât. Chandrâguptâ reaches her who is floating face down in the river. He grabs her powerfully with his two hands and pulls her back out of the sacred water and shakes her fiercely and calls her. "Roshanak!"

Rošanak is motionless within his arms. He pulls her closer to him and holds her tightly, trying to force life back into her limp body.

"Roshanak!"

A moment stretches to eternity.

He embraces her firmly and kisses her face and whispers into her mouth, "Anuragini, you are a gift to me from the gods, my Anumâti, the Divine Blessing of the Moon, and I am the Protector of the Moon, your protector… Come back to me… Follow my voice back to the land of the living. Stay with me!"

He kisses her again and again and holds her tighter and tighter.

She suddenly takes a deep breath and starts coughing and purging water.

He breathes again, relieved.

She had finally given up living in the past… with ghosts… and guilt… and shame.

The little star had washed away in the sweet waters of the sacred river.

IMPERIAL AUDIENCE HALL. IMPERIAL PALACE of PÂTALIPUTRÂ
DAYS LATER
MID-DAY

Glittering Imperial Court.

"Any type of marriage is acceptable, if it pleases the groom and the bride," Chanâkya declares confidently.

His Warrior-Pupil had powerfully wrested Hind from the clutches of the invaders…

… his Brahman-Teacher could do no less than to honor his Samrât as it was most befitting of a great Warrior-Emperor, now that his beloved woman was cleansed and purified by bathing in sacred waters.

The Imperial Court Brahmans and the Imperial Ministers all nod their heads in agreement.

Chandrâguptâ smiles, relieved, and eyes Rošanak discreetly for her reaction, as the words are interpreted for her. She glances at him with smiling eyes.

He had decided to hear the decision of the Brahmans and the Council of Ministers in his Imperial Court along with her.

There was no telling what he would have decided, if they had not agreed to bless the matrimony… maybe they would have all added to their cycle of rebirth!

"We have decided that the Lady of the Moon is Hindu for the sake of the Hindu Wedding and the Ritual of Saat Phere, and can hence wed His Imperial Majesty, Chakravarti Samrât Chandrâguptâ, in a manner befitting of a Great Emperor," Chanâkya continues.

Chandrâguptâ regards his Imperial Court.

The Imperial Court Brahmans nod their heads with approval.

The Imperial Council of Ministers nod approvingly too.

More smiles.

Chanâkya continues. "And since the Lady of the Moon has no blood relatives in Hind, the wedding ritual will be shorter."

More smiles.

IMPERIAL PALACE of PÂTALIPUTRÂ. LAND of SEVEN RIVERS
YEAR 15 of the FOURTH ALEXANDER
YEAR 14 of SAMRÂT CHANDRÂGUPTÂ, MONTH of ÂŠVINA, R'TU of ŠARAD
IMPERIAL WEDDING
SETTING SUN

Sacred Fires smolder regally in giant golden basins.

Fragrant incense burns lavishly in the Sacred Fire.

The entire Imperial Palace glints in gold and sparkling murmurs… bathes ankle deep in intoxicating white mâlati and pink lotus petals…

The Brahmans sing sacred hymns.

The Groom and the Bride are garlanded and jeweled and scented; the hands and feet of the bride are hennaed and painted.

Chandrâguptâ rises from his golden seat and extends his right hand to Rošanak and takes her right hand into his.

Chanâkya bends and ties the end of Chandrâguptâ's golden dhoti to Rošanak's purple saree. The knot signifying the bond of sacred marriage.

Chandrâguptâ and Rošanak step to the right and walk around the Sacred Fire seven times for the Seven Sacred Steps.

With each step, he utters sacred words to her, making seven sacred promises to be fulfilled in their married life.

His voice slightly trembles with excitement, only detectable to her ears.

Her golden ankle bangles tinkle in his ears.

Step One:

"With god as our guide, take the first step with me to live with honor and respect. Walk with me so we gather pure and blessed food."

Step Two:

"Let us be happy and enjoy life. Walk with me so we grow together in strength."

Step Three:

"Let us share joys and pains together. Walk with me so we grow together in riches."

Step Four:

"Let us not forget our elders and ancestors. Walk with me so we grow in happiness by sharing our joys and sorrows."

Step Five:

"Let us honor all acts of charity and kindness. Walk with me so we grow a family together."

She stops for a short moment.

Her hand trembles slightly, her fingers flicker, her knees weaken.

He holds her hand firmly in his hand and squeezes it confidently and pulls her along with him to the right.

She follows him with obedient hennaed feet.

Step Six:

"Let us live a long and peaceful life. Walk with me so we grow in joy of life."

Step Seven:

"Let us be friends with love and sacrifice. Walk with me so we grow in friendship. Let me not be severed from your friendship. Let your friendship not be severed from me."

He stops and takes her hands into his hands and tenderly wraps his fingers around hers and squeezes.

"Rani."

He pauses and points to the sacred fire with his head.

"This sacred fire is witness to our marriage. I am now yours forever, as you are joined with me in this seventh blessed step—

"—so may you be a source of divine blessing. May you be devoted to me for life," he says sweetly as he finishes the Ritual of Seven Steps of the Imperial Wedding.

He puts the red mark of wedding on her forehead.

She puts a palm full of blessed parched rice into the sacred fire.

The rice crackles and dances in the fire.

And thus the wedding ceremony was finished.
Samrât Chandrâguptâ married Rošanak… a Persian Royal Woman…
… according to the customs of the Hinduya…

IMPERIAL WAR COUNCIL. PALACE of PÂTALIPUTRÂ
YEAR 18 of the FOURTH ALEXANDER
YEAR 17 of SAMRÂT CHANDRÂGUPTÂ, MONTH of MÂGHA, R'TU of ŠIŠIRA
3 YEARS LATER
MORNING

Sun breaks through the clouds…

"It is confirmed, Your Imperial Majesty." one of the Imperial Eyes and Ears says confidently, bowing his head. "Seleukos Nikator, the Ruler of the Lands between the Two Rivers, is finally planning to follow in the footsteps of Alexander into Hind. They claim the Makedonians never relinquished the old Persian satrapies that Alexander had conquered by spear in Hind. They say he is planning to recapture all those abandoned lands in Hind that the Lord of Asia had conquered in former days."

Chandrâguptâ narrows his eyes and leans forward in his golden chair.

"In the footsteps of Alexander, ha?"

The man nods respectfully. "Yes, Samrât."

Chandrâguptâ shakes his head. "Then he is a bloody fool! Alexander himself followed in the footsteps of the Persian Kings!"

Then he smiles and leans back in his golden chair.

"Alexander conquered nothing in Hind!" he says with absolute confidence. "Like a child, he hastily took a bite of a hot roti, burned his mouth and discarded the rest."

Chandrâguptâ pauses and points. "Like a mystic angry river god, he burst forth from the belly of the Abode of Snow, tossed and turned and hurried across the Lands on the other side of River Sindhu, and emptied into the shifting sands of the Desert of the Emptiness. The people he slaughtered are already reborn and are more fruitful… the towns he destroyed, I have already rebuilt, bigger and better… and all those men he left behind, we put to death and burned and returned their flesh to their gods and tossed their bones in the dirt."

He leans forward and asks Mahâsenâpati, his Great General. "How many fighting elephants are under my command now?"

"9,000, Your Imperial Majesty!"

Chandrâguptâ smiles.

Mahâsenâpati continues, "690,000 warriors under your command, Your Imperial Majesty. 600,000 on foot, 30,000 on horse, 24,000 on chariots and 36,000 on fighting elephants— a mahout and three archers to each elephant and a driver and two archers to each chariot."

Chandrâguptâ smiles and nods and says, "Those are very favorable numbers!"

Mahâsenâpati smiles and bows his head low with pride.

"Indeed, Your Imperial Majesty!"

BATTLEFIELD. BANKS of RIVER SINDHU. SIND
MONTH of ŚRÂVANA, R'TU of VARSÂ
MONTHS LATER
MORNING

Thunderclouds…

Deafening noise…

Fighting elephants…

A thousand of them… all painted in war colors with massive tusks as white as the crown of the Himalâya mountain god on the ridges of the Abode of Snow. All arrayed three layers deep in a line standing on this side of the River Sindhu, right across from the Royal Army of Seleukos and his men, arrayed on the other side of the River Sindhu. All loaded with flowers and rice wine in their giant bellies, all ready to pierce and stomp and toss their hated enemies.

Chandrâguptâ eyes them from his magnificently adorned Nisâya Horse, a sweet gift from his beloved Samrâjni.

He was eager for battle… eager for the victory of his splendid Imperial Army, with splendid warriors and chariots and horses and elephants.

When Alexander had come years ago, Hind was divided… he had only faced a handful of small quarrelling Rajahs on the edges of the sacred Land of Seven Rivers.

Now Seleukos was facing a Warrior-King…

No! A Warrior-Emperor, ruling over more lands and people than Alexander had conquered in his entire mortal life.

In the Battle at River Vitastâ, Alexander's last big battle, Makedonians had faced only two hundred fighting elephants.

Rajah Parvataka had known that the only way to counter Alexander and his ferocious army was to hold the river with his small forces against them and keep the enemy army to the other side of the raging river. He also knew that with the size of Alexander's army, that was only possible as long as the river remained uncrossable. So he had waited for Alexander to make the first move of the Battle.

And given time, Alexander had found a way to get half of his men across the heaving and swelling river under the cover of monsoon rains concealing the clatter of arms and men… leaving the other half facing Rajah Parvataka's Army Camp downstream. When the battle was finally joined, Rajah Parvataka had been caught between two halves of Alexander's army, like a mere mortal caught in the deadly jaws of a ferocious striped ice tiger. The battle was lost the moment Alexander's army crossed the River Vitastâ.

It was not a mistake that an experienced battle-hardened Emperor was likely to repeat!

A commander Alexander had left behind had killed Rajah Parvataka and stolen his elephants, and had left for his own lands years ago.

So, he had not even let Seleukos and his enemy army cross the River Sindhu to get to River Vitastâ.

He meant to keep the enemy army from even crossing into his Empire!

River Sindhu was the border he meant to keep between him and the enemy armies.

Chandrâguptâ takes a deep breath.

Alexander had taught him how to think fast on his feet with his feet listening only to his belly. Like Alexander, he never waited for anything.

He would have liked to face Alexander in battle himself and crush him with the might of his Imperial Army and make a gift of his head to his Samrâjni… but it was not to be… he knew none of Alexander's men were his equal in arms…

An Emperor only fights another Emperor!

Well, at least he was the one who had finally prevailed and kept the sweetest and most precious prize of all Alexander's conquests: His beautiful half-Persian wife.

Alexander had lost more by victory than he had gained by war.

He looks around.

As Chanâkya always said: "The one superior in power shall wage the war!"

He raises his hand and gives the signal.

All the war elephants raise the battle cry and stomp their feet once, at the command of their mahouts. The ground trembles and shakes and moves under their massive feet…

The sound thunders and screams and deafens…

….

Across the River Indus, Seleukos clenches his fists and grinds his teeth.

Clouds were heavy and dark, signaling the coming monsoon rains.

His horses were already going mad with fear, hearing and smelling the fighting elephants on the other side of the river.

He was there when the Makedonians had refused to march up country in India under Alexander, and he knew the ones he was commanding now had not grown any more courage to face fighting elephants and warlike Indians and giant snakes than the ones who had refused Alexander— and Alexander was the master at getting his men to follow his command absolutely… everywhere… except in India!

Some of his men remembered all too well the bloody ancient ritual of purification of the Royal Army at Babylon, when Perdikkas had thrown three hundred of the Makedonian Foot rebels to the fighting Indian elephants— all were trampled and crushed and stomped to death under the feet of the massive war elephants while the whole Royal Army watched in sheer shock and terror…

… and those who remembered had told the rest…

IMPERIAL TENT. IMPERIAL ARMY CAMP. RIVER SINDHU
FOLLOWING DAY

Rainy day.

"Seleukos Nikator wishes to be a friend to the King of India."

Words are interpreted.

Silence.

Chandrâguptâ narrows his eyes and looks at the Makedonian Envoys and then at Rošanak.

"Bloody cowards! Alexander would have put these men to the sword himself, if he was alive! Just one generation after Alexander, and his men have forgotten how to be fighting warriors and die with honor on the fields of battle. And the idiots belittled the Persians who had lasted powerfully for ten generations after the First Dariush. His rule did not even last one generation after his own death!"

"What is the Conqueror prepared to offer the Emperor of India?" Rošanak asks the Makedonian Envoys in Attik.

The Makedonians were young and arrogant LowLanders and she had never laid eyes on them before.

The Makedonian Envoys eye her cautiously.

She knew their second tongue well.

"Seleukos Nikator offers the Satrapies of Paropamisadai and Areia and Arachosia, all the Lands this side of River Indus, to the King of India, as the mark of his friendship."

"Seleukos is offering you Gandâra and Haraiwa and Harahuvatiš, most of the old Hindu Persian Satrapies, this side of the River Sindhu, My Lord," Rošanak quietly interprets.

"The fool has come all this way to offer me my own lands?" Chandrâguptâ asks mockingly.

"He can be a valuable ally, My Lord. If he holds the Bakhtrian side of the lands, all the other enemies have to defeat him first, before crossing into the imperial territories," Ârash says quietly, bowing his head.

Rošanak looks down. Old memories heartlessly haunt her.

Seleukos had been Perdikkas' Second-in-Command. They said he was one of the men who had plunged their swords into his noble body after they had lost to Ptolemaios in the Battle for the Body of Alexander.

But the Persian Purple had passed to his head. Still… he had not signed the unwritten death agreement for her Son-King.

And he was a kinsman… still married to Apâma.

Chandrâguptâ looks at her intently and then looks at his men.

"The sleep cycle of Lord Višnu is about to start soon," one General says.

"They are not worth wasting our arrows," another General says.

"Or our elephants—" another one says.

"What about Maka Desert?" another one asks.

Chandrâguptâ leans back on his golden throne, taking a deep breath, and shakes his head.

He finally understood why Alexander had not taken to him many years ago… just like himself, Alexander was unwilling to elevate another man, untested in battle, to his own royal kingly rank… and why Dariush had not taken to Alexander at first…

All to risk in losing and nothing to gain in victory.

Dariush was a real king with a real empire to rule. Alexander was just a wild boy commanding a horde of savage barbarians with long spears.

How was the Great King to know that a handful of men could do such harm to his beloved empire?

Who would have thought that a handful of men with no right of blood were foolish enough to attack the mightiest empire on earth in the first place?

And as for Alexander… his true greatness was in understanding what really mattered on a battlefield and not listening to any of the fools around him once his mind was set on what needed to be done.

He leans further back and fills up with pity.

What had finally killed Alexander was not his wounds… he had finally understood what all kings already knew… that his own men would never accept and obey him as the Persians had accepted and obeyed their Great Kings…

"My Lord, I hear Seleukos and my sister, Apâma, have beautiful daughters," Rošanak says quietly.

Fruitful Apâma had borne Seleukos healthy sons and daughters.

Chandrâguptâ turns his head and looks at her and reads her eyes.

A marriage alliance?

"Tell your ruler to come to me himself, in friendship if he wishes, or in arms with as many men as he wishes, and I will decide then," Chandrâguptâ says to the Makedonian Envoys. Rošanak interprets.

Silence.

Makedonian Envoys look at each other and then acknowledge. "We will take your reply back to Seleukos Nikator." They turn and leave the imperial tent.

FOLLOWING DAY
MIDDLE of the DAY

Stormy rain clouds.

The air is heavy with the smell of danger and intrigue, and of men and horses and elephants.

Seleukos Nikator has come to see Samrât Chandrâguptâ and he has come alone— in arms— but alone, with an interpreter in tow, crossing the River Sindhu in a boat with his horse, still wet from the river crossing. He dismounts his horse and removes his bronze helmet and follows the guards toward the imperial tent.

Chandrâguptâ eyes Seleukos as he approaches the tent. He beckons one of his interpreters and steps outside, unarmed.

Seleukos knew Roshanak and it was best not to carelessly display a queen believed to be dead in front of a former subject and kinsman.

Chandrâguptâ approaches Seleukos with his interpreter and stops in front of him. He reads Seleukos' face. Seleukos looks pale from sailing on the raging river. Chandrâguptâ smiles and opens his arms, and points. "The River Sindhu has changed course slightly since the days of the Great Alexander."

That was over twenty campaigning seasons ago.

Both were older men now… much older…

Seleukos was wearing his years on his creased face and in his white hair.

Interpreters eye each other carefully and interpret faithfully.

"And it seems it has birthed many more fighting elephants." Seleukos smiles and nods.

Chandrâguptâ laughs and beckons one of his guards. "Bring us fragrant wine."

Attendants bring fragrant wine in tall golden goblets.

Chandrâguptâ takes a wine goblet and takes a sip of the fragrant wine and then offers the goblet to Seleukos. Seleukos reaches and takes the wine goblet and takes a sip. Chandrâguptâ smiles and takes the other goblet of fragrant wine and takes another sip and eyes Seleukos intently.

He did not remember him from the days of Alexander. He must have been a junior commander following orders of others above him.

But Samrâjni knew him well and she had told him all about Seleukos. He was one of the few who had kept his Bakhtrian wife, second sister of Samrâjni, after Alexander died. He had sons… two half-breed Bakhtrian-Makedonian sons… and he had marriageable daughters… two of them.

And he did not lack courage, coming to see him alone.

"Come, Seleukos. We can review my Imperial Army and talk about the old days and Great Alexander."

Seleukos sips his pure wine and considers Chandrâguptâ.

The Indian King was not armed… but heavily guarded.

His armed guards carried the same long bows and arrows that had nearly killed Alexander in India.

Seleukos follows Chandrâguptâ.

"The first time you were here, the rains had come earlier and had lasted longer," Chandrâguptâ says, pointing to the rain clouds in the sky above.

"But no less hot and misty," Seleukos says, nodding his head.

Chandrâguptâ smiles.

Poor Makedonian must be roasting like a lamb in his heavy metal armor in this torrid heat.

Seleukos looks out at the sea of men and horses and arms arrayed behind the curtains of fighting war elephants.

Alexander had defeated the formidable Persian Army at Gaugamela…

But he was not Alexander and the Indian King was not Darius.

Chandrâguptâ reads Seleukos' face, a common tongue of warriors that did not need to be interpreted.

Chandrâguptâ sips his fragrant wine and beckons one of his Imperial Guards.

"Summon the Crown-Prince!"

The Imperial Guard bows and steps away in haste.

"Your men said yesterday that as new friends, you will recognize our joint borders at the mountain ridges in Hindu Kush, where Alexander first crossed into Hind, and at Maka Desert on the other side of the River Sindhu where he left Hind."

As Chanâkya always said:

"Whoever is superior in power can break the agreement of peace… later… when the time was ripe!"

And:

"It was absolute power that brought about peace between any two kings… no piece of iron that was not blood-hot would combine with another piece of hot iron!"

Seleukos thinks for a moment and carefully observes the Indian Imperial Army and Chandrâguptâ.

He was taking more territory than he had offered to give— but who could claim dominion over the Desert of Death, except Hades?

"Yes." Seleukos agrees.

Chandrâguptâ smiles and points to his son, the Crown-Prince, who has caught up with them. He bows to his father.

"My Son, Crown-Prince Bindusâra."

Bindusâra acknowledges Seleukos.

"I hear you have sons and daughters with your noble Bakhtrian wife."

"Yes. The King is well-informed!" Seleukos nods his head.

Chandrâguptâ smiles with imperial confidence.

"I have a thousand fighting elephants with me."

And eight thousand more in reserve…

Seleukos looks at Chandrâguptâ.

"I will gift you five hundred of them. A small wedding gift, when my son, Crown-Prince Bindusâra, marries one of your half-Bakhtrian daughters."

Seleukos looks at the interpreters and then back at Chandrâguptâ, trying to mask his interest.

"Five hundred?" he asks.

"Yes."

"Five hundred?" Seleukos asks again.

"Yes, five hundred," Chandrâguptâ says with importance, making much of it, smiling and eyeing Seleukos intently.

Poor Seleukos!

The father of the new bride of the Crown-Prince did not know how much massive war elephants ate or drank or he would not be so grateful for the generous gift!

He would have to conquer new lands and waters on the other side of his lands just to feed his hungry and thirsty wedding gifts with gigantic bottomless bellies!

Samrâjni was right… Mlechchha did not know how to count.

Seleukos looks back at the fighting elephants, still standing, arrayed for battle on the banks of the River Indus, and then smiles.

An honorable gift indeed… not even Alexander had more than two hundred fighting elephants under his command.

The One-eyed Antigonos and Ptolemaios and Lysimachos had no fighting elephants… and they were the ones he aimed to stomp and subdue.

And Kassandros had no war elephants either… the elephants that Krateros had taken with him to Makedonia long ago and left there had all starved to death during the Siege of Pydna.

And he had two daughters of marriageable age. An honorable marital alliance.

The Crown-Prince looked like the Indian King when he was his age… no less handsome.

"My daughter Apâma is as beautiful as her Baktrian mother. She will make a good bride for your son, the Crown-Prince!"

"Good! Nothing bonds men like the blood of their women!"

Seleukos nods in agreement.

Thunder and lightning roar in the distance.

Chandrâguptâ looks up at the stormy skies and then looks back at Seleukos and points to his magnificent imperial tent.

"Return with your men tomorrow night and we will seal the marriage alliance with a feast in your honor, Father of the Bride. Dress more lightly if the heat troubles your men."

Come unarmed!

Seleukos nods in agreement.

Chandrâguptâ smiles and extends his right arm to Seleukos.

Seleukos takes the right arm of Chandrâguptâ with his right arm and seals the alliance.

IMPERIAL AUDIENCE HALL. PALACE of PÂTALIPUTRÂ
YEAR 20 of the FOURTH ALEXANDER
YEAR 19 of SAMRÂT CHANDRÂGUPTÂ, MONTH of ÂGRAHÂYANA, R'TU of HEMANTA
2 YEARS LATER
MID-DAY

Imperial Court murmurs…

"No one knows for certain, but there were always rumors that Kassandros poisoned Alexander, by the order of old Antipatros, his father, aided by Aristoteles! They say the poison was the color of water, deadly cold as ice, distilled from a rock in the district of Nonakris in Arkadia. Kassandros took it to Babylon in the hoof of an ass, as no other vessel could safely hold the deadly poison! His brother, Iolaos, the cupbearer of Alexander, mixed it in his unmixed wine to hide its bitter taste and gave it to Alexander during a drunken feast in Babylon hosted by Medeios, the Thessalian, who was the lover of Iolaos." The young Makedonian Ambassador, Megasthenes, speaks with a scent of intrigue spicing his voice.

His words are interpreted discreetly for the Samrât and for the Ministers and for the Brahmans… and for the Imperial Sons and the Nobles and the rest of the Imperial Court, all by Imperial Scribes and Imperial Interpreters trained skillfully by Samrâjni herself in the tongue of the Yaunâ.

Chandrâguptâ narrows his eyes at the young Makedonian.

What about his arrow that had pierced Alexander's chest in the Fortress of Mâlavâns?

Alexander was not a king who would have died of old age in bed!

He looks around the Imperial Court with annoyance. "Samrâjni."

Where was his Rani?

She knew the tongue of the Yauna better than anyone else!

She knew not just the meaning of their words, but the meaningful intent knotted with their words.

"What happened to the wife and son of Alexander?" the Samrât asks curiously.

"No one knows for certain, but there are rumors that they were poisoned by the order of Kassandros after the peace agreement among the old kingsmen of Alexander was signed. But their bodies were never found. Glaukias, Commander at the Fortress of Amphipolis, who was their keeper, disappeared mysteriously one night and his wife claimed that Alexander's barbarian wife bewitched her husband and he ran away with her."

Words are interpreted. Chandrâguptâ glances at Chanâkya and nods.

Massive golden imperial doors open and the Imperial Court Chamberlain bows low and announces:

"Her Imperial Majesty, Samrâjni Anumâti."

Chandrâguptâ smiles and leans back.

Rošanak quietly enters the Imperial Audience Hall and makes her way gracefully toward Chandrâguptâ, bows her head generously, smiles and sits down on a silky cushion on the silky soft carpet next to his throne.

She feels his gaze on her feet and tactfully leans forward and rearranges her silky saree around her legs, discreetly covering up her Persian sarbalâ and her weather-worn oxen-skin riding boots.

Rošanak then discreetly eyes the young Makedonian Ambassador from Seleukos who had returned again to the Imperial Court and rolls her eyes and then gives a discreet unhappy look from the corner of her eye to Samrât.

Ay! More tales of Gold Ants!

There was no burning need for her to be summoned to the Imperial Court… Samrât should have had one of the Imperial Court Interpreters translate for him.

The Makedonian's account of Hind was no better than that of Herodotos who had written that Hind had gold-digging ants which threw up gold dust in the Desert of Sands… Gold Ants smaller than a dog but larger than a fox!

And a heap of other nonsense to widen the eyes of green Hellenes, who did not travel much beyond Hellas, with false wonders of faraway lands.

Was Hind not wondrous enough without false Gold Ants throwing up gold dust?

Chandrâguptâ eyes her tenderly.

He had not seen her since the early dawn of the morning and he had missed her!

As usual, instead of spending all day making herself beautiful like a normal Samrâjni, an Empress, she had been riding one of his horses when one of his ministers had finally found her somewhere in the vast pastures around the Imperial Palace to summon her to his Imperial Court to talk to the idiot Makedonian Ambassador sent by Seleukos.

The size of his imperial stables had doubled since he had wedded her… she was fond of gifting him splendid Nisâya pure-bred horses from Mâda, paid for by Imperial Funds from his own Imperial Treasury, no less… and then she rode them herself!

She trained them herself properly, and always claimed: "Only a Persian can train a Nisâya horse!" All the imperial grooms followed her around the horses and stables and listened spellbound to her every word! If only his warriors listened to him like that!

And not to mention the fortune she spent in feeding the imperial horses green food and not dry hay!

It was fortunate the Samrâjni was not too fond of riding war elephants… she did not like their beastly scent.

And it was also fortunate that she looked utterly beautiful, painted and bedecked or unpainted and plain… and always tasted sweet in his imperial bed this way or that way…

Chandrâguptâ looks discreetly around Rošanak.

Lately, a few parrots had taken to her and followed her around yelling broken Persian love words in the middle of his dignified Imperial Court, which made everyone laugh.

He did not want to start talking and be interrupted by her damn talking parrots!

Whatever the Samrât whispered in the ears of the Samrâjni in their private imperial bed late at night to gain her sweet favors, was not for the ears of the Imperial Court!

Well, at least the damn parrots were no immediate danger to the lives of the Imperial Court around him.

Parrots did not eat people!

A few years back, the Samrâjni had taken a liking to an orphaned striped ice tiger cub with one eye the color of the sky at dawn, the other the color of the night sky… she was utterly convinced he was Alexander reborn… and no one in the imperial court, not even Chanâkya, had the heart to tell her that since Alexander was not burned or buried, he was not yet reborn… the ferocious tiger cub had come to think of her as his own mother and did not care to share her with anyone.

Finally, after the damn cub had clawed his arms and legs when he and Samrâjni were making love, mixing rice with sesame, one of their favorite Sixty-four Arts positions, the Brahmans had declared the cub sacred and had sent him away to a far-off temple!

Well… initially the tiger cub had proven very useful and had ripped a pair of assassins apart when they had slipped into the imperial bedchamber, intending to kill the Samrât as he slept.

When the word had gotten out that the Samrât was protected by a sacred ice tiger while he slept, the assassination attempts on his life had stopped, which had made the Samrâjni happy as they did not have to change imperial bedrooms around his Imperial Palaces every night.

She was a creature of habit and liked to sleep in the same imperial bed every night.

And she never failed to mention at least once a day how it was her ice tiger who had saved his life!

He looks around the court one more time.

Good! No sign of her damn talking parrots!

He straightens.

"If the strings of a lute are too tight, they will break. If the strings of a lute are too loose, they will not play. Only a properly strung lute plays sweet music. Strings of Alexander were too tight— they finally broke!" Chandrâguptâ says with imperial confidence.

Samrâjni eyes the Samrât tenderly.

Samrât was very fond of lutes! But he sounded infinitely wiser talking about them than playing them… a Hindu lute in the hands of the Protector of the Moon sounded like a dying Mudrâya cat stretched mercilessly on a Makedonian rack, pleading for mercy or death!

Great Kings and Emperors should only engage in heroic deeds like hunting ferocious lions and tigers and killing the enemies of the Lands… and if there was nothing to kill, they should spend their time playing dice games and chaturangam and gambling on horse races! Playing the lute was not dignified for a Great King or a Conqueror or an Emperor… even Alexander could not play the lute or sing!

"Well, Kassandros might not have poisoned Alexander, but he poisoned Alexander's half-breed son and his barbarian wife and hid their bodies!" Megasthenes repeats with the absolute authority of an idiot.

Rošanak quickly turns her head toward the Makedonian and narrows her eyes at him.

The unobservant Makedonian Ambassador continues with an air of importance, feeling all eyes on him. "And he talked the old Polyperchon into killing the half-Rhodian mistress of Alexander and her bastard son!"

"Barsine?" Rošanak asks in a hushed, stunned voice.

Eyes and Ears of the Emperor had always kept them in touch with the news of the Lands of the Persians.

Kleopatra had been killed by the One-eyed Antigonos in Sparda three years after the death of Alexandros, when she had finally decided to leave for Mudrâya and marry Ptolemaios.

The thought of Kleopatra standing before Alexander in the House of Hades and having to answer to him, had brought a sad smile to her grieving heart: "How did you treat my wife and son, sister?"

But the wretched deaths of Barsine and her son must not have meant much, or had happened secretly on the other side of the Bitter Sea… or no one thought it important enough to give a report of it to her Samrât.

Chandrâguptâ eyes the Makedonian and then looks back at Rošanak curiously.

Imperial Interpreters continue to translate discreetly for the Samrât and the Imperial Court.

Megasthenes looks surprised.

"Yes. Barsine and her son, Herakles. Polyperchon summoned them to Makedonia, a year after the death of the Fourth Alexander, to put Herakles on the throne of his father and then had them both put to the sword when Kassandros offered him a deal for their blood, promising to restore to him his large estate in Pella and giving him the command of Peloponnesus and one hundred talents."

Rošanak takes a deep breath and closes her eyes. Her face folds in pain of remembrance.

She had not thought about Barsine for years.

She had had nothing but contempt for Barsine and Alexander knew it… not jealousy, because Barsine was Alexander's mistress once and had borne him a bastard son, but because she was the daughter of Artâvazda, the wretched traitor to her King-Father.

Barsine's daughter and sisters were given to the Makedonians at the wedding ritual at the Royal City of Çûšâ, when Alexander was furious with her over Krateros and had arrayed the kinsmen and kindred of his old mistress before the Queen to punish the Queen publicly…

Alexander did not even think enough of Barsine to make her one of his Women of the Royal Court… not even a royal mistress kept at the royal court… she had remained no more than his first youthful indiscretion.

And Alexander himself had sworn to her by his gods that Herakles was not his after he had returned to her bed. Even though rumors had murmured through the royal court during the Çûšâ weddings, with the kinsmen of Barsine at the court.

Had Barsine dared to think that the throne of Makedonia belonged to a bastard son… a son never acknowledged by his father? The barbaric Makedonians had no more regard for Barsine and her half-breed bastard son than they did for the Queen and the rightful Son of Alexander born to purple.

But still, she was a mother too… she knew what a bleeding, dying son looked like… what mother wished to see the son of another mother cut to pieces like that?

All bleeding dying blameless sons, were the sons of all mothers.

Had the wretched Polyperchon at least given them an honorable burial?

Her breath tightens. The bleeding throat of the dead Alexandros fills her eyes more swiftly than a Nisâya horse.

She had tried hard for so many years to bury the bloody memories of her past somewhere so deep they could never be found again, but just a few careless words had easily found their mark in her heart: there he was, her poor child, his cruelly cut throat bleeding all over her memories again.

She pushes back a tear and curses Polyperchon under her trembling lips.

Polyperchon was another forgotten man whose company neither Hades nor the Lord of Darkness was looking forward to.

As Amyntor had once said to her during the Siege of Pydna: "The wretched Polyperchon was the biggest mistake the old Antipatros ever made. He had left a jackal to match wits with a fox— Kassandros. In trying to preserve the Royal House of the Argeads, the old Antipatros had ended up utterly destroying it through the hands of his own Kassandros. Had the old man not taken good measure of his own bloody son?"

Well, not all the Argeads were dead… the Son of Alexander lived…

She stops herself cold.

But the Son-King of Alexander was her son too… his royal blood was her royal blood and that of the Persian Great Kings… not an Argead, a Royal Hakhâmanišiya.

Seeded by Alexander and fathered by Perdikkas and then raised by Uxšiyârta and Oštana and Itâna…

Raised a Persian!

Yes… all the Royal Argeads of the blood of Alexander had died.

"Alexander suffered from desires. He was filled with yearnings to be a god!" the Makedonian Ambassador declares confidently, secure in his knowledge of Alexander.

Rošanak, stunned, wills away her tears and looks up again and narrows her eyes at Megasthenes. "Yearnings— desires?"

Alexander had died nineteen years ago. But his memory still lived brightly in her heart. And like all memories, death and distance had made the love stronger and the hate dimmer.

He was dead… and it no longer mattered how he had died… only that he had died.

The King-Father of a beloved Son-King must remain clothed in the kingly light…

No man should cast a shadow on the glory of the Kingly-Husband and the King-Father… ever…

Megasthenes eyes her for a brief moment.

Another strange Indian custom, to allow women in the Imperial Court.

It was good fortune that men never cared to read about women.

"Yes!" Megasthenes nods. "He wanted to be worshipped like the gods," he says flatly in a dismissive tone.

Rošanak hears the raw arrogance in his voice and her temper rises like steam from a well-cooked roti.

Chandrâguptâ takes notice of the heat rising from the top of her voice. He leans forward slightly and eyes the Makedonian discreetly and then leans back in his throne.

The young fool looked seriously committed to his cause.

He could stop her with a glance, but that surely meant incurring her private anger later… and heaps of begging in private to regain her lost favor!

The Makedonian was not worth it!

"Did you know Alexander?" Rošanak asks the Makedonian.

"No, but—"

"But what?"

"I have read all about him and have heard many stories. Everyone knows about Alexander. Kallisthenes, Ptolemaios, Nearchos, and Aristoboulos—Eumenes, Chares, Onesikritos. They all have written about him! Others too."

Rošanak takes a deep breath and closes her eyes and her body fills with pain.

Even the dim-witted court chamberlain had dared to write about Alexander.

And Ptolemaios, still trying to bathe in the light of the deeds of Alexander.

If Alexander had known that men like Ptolemaios and Chares would one day write lies about his deeds, he would have hanged them all before he had died in Bâb-ilim.

Everyone knew that Kallisthenes had written to please Alexander, to glorify his deeds for the Hellenes and the LowLanders and the HighLanders… not truth but heroic words to please a young conquering king. Had he lived, he might have lifted the wrap of flattery and falsehood from what he had written and let the rays of truth bathe the true deeds of Alexander.

Even Alexander himself had finally lost the taste for all the lies that had been written to flatter him. He had told Choerilos of Iasos in front of everyone that he preferred to be the Thersites of Homer than the Achilleos of Choerilos.

Then she thinks better of it.

Others could read lies about Alexander written by his own kingsmen.

He himself mostly read his old worn out copy of Ilias that his old teacher had annotated for him… a beloved book that was sadly lost the night Alexandros was put to the sword…

"Although, as my benefactor Sibyrtios, the Satrap of Arachosia, always says, one should not believe anything that Eumenes wrote about Alexander! Eumenes was a lying Kardian!" Megasthenes adds with an arrogant air of blind conviction.

Rošanak raises an eyebrow.

Everyone knew that Sibyrtios was a friend of Peukestas and that Peukestas hated Eumenes…

But what could have Eumenes written that was worse than the rest?

His intense hatred of Hephæstion was no secret in the royal court of Alexander.

When Hephæstion had become the Hezârapatiš and the Second-in-Command of the Empire in the Royal City of Çûšâ, Eumenes used to quarrel with him constantly, as Alexander had set Hephæstion above him in all matters of the royal court. He was so worried that Alexander might suspect him of poisoning Hephæstion, that the tight-fisted Kardian was the first to dedicate his costly arms to Hephæstion after his death in Hagmâtâna; he had even given a thousand manû of his own funds toward the cost of Hephæstion's funeral.

Eumenes was loyal to Olympias and was the one who had told Olympias not to rush to the aid of Alexandros and his barbarian mother! He was the one who had filled the ears of Olympias with promises of a Royal Army to fight for the cause of the Boy-King and so promised, Olympias and the rest of them had foolishly ended up besieged and nearly starved to death by Kassandros and his bloody men in the Fortress of Pydna.

And he was the man who had filled the head of Perdikkas with talk of wedding Kleopatra. But he was also the man Perdikkas had always relied on and he too had remained faithful to Perdikkas to the end. Even she herself had asked Uxšiyârta to support Eumenes in his battle with the One-eyed Antigonos and Uxšiyârta had sent both Foot and Horse to Eumenes for the bloody battles fought near Aspâdâna.

She takes a deep breath.

Hephæstion… Those who had written about Alexander, had not written well of him. Because he had not butchered armies of men and raped multitudes of women, her Hephæstion was called dim-witted and dull and incompetent!

And Perdikkas too… they had called him ambitious and harsh and ruthless. They had forgotten how he had saved the life of her Son-King and had made the Royal Army whole again and had kept them from needless massacre.

No… she did not need to read all those accounts to know that they had all lied. They had started their vicious lies when Alexander was still alive and dying.

Out of jealousy, ignorance, wickedness, wretchedness or plain stupidity, they had turned the love Alexander had come to have for the Persians into something shameful.

They had called him: "a decadent Asian King… a tyrant"… they had called her "a lowborn Bakhtrian dancer"…

And worse… they had erased Alexander's love for her and Hephæstion out of his life.

Alexander had chosen to be a Persian King… he had conquered many kingdoms and Persia was what he had come to claim as his own.

He had remembered what Persians had forgotten themselves, what this Great King did or that Great King said… not even Persians were all that Persian. And that was the truth that his historians had tried for years to bury under the blackened ashes of their wretched lies.

Did they think that the sun was to remain clouded forever?

Why all the lies? What Alexander was— all that he was— was it not enough for men to remember him by?

She takes a deep breath and controls her anger and utters words weighed and measured and fitted for an Empress.

"Alexander was a King. The Lord of Asia. Victorious in battles. He wore the Golden Purple of the Persian Kings… he sat on the Persian Throne… he wedded a Persian Royal Daughter… he did deeds worthy of remembrance."

"Ah!"

She ignores Megasthenes and continues. "Only the gods will see to his judgment!" She narrows her eyes at the Makedonian. "And the Wise Lord will judge him wisely as he would judge any king or man… on his own words and his own thoughts and his own deeds… not by the clouded words of other men… or lies…"

Had the men who had followed him, done him one better?

His men were the ones who had been rightly foretold as the Men of the Race of Wrath… the demon beasts who had been unleashed on the Lands of the Persians by the Lord of Darkness. What could have Alexander done without his men?

Funeral games for Alexander were not foot races or horse races or chariot races for golden wreaths… they had become wars among his kingsmen to annihilate each other from the face of the earth for the possession of the Lands of the Persians!

The words are discreetly interpreted for the imperial ears of the Samrât.

For a brief moment, Chandrâguptâ feels sorry for the poor Makedonian and watches his Empress as she fearlessly cuts through the young man with her sharp words.

It was not her doing. The tongue of the Persians was like a sharp sword wrapped and rewrapped a thousand times in soft silk and the tongue of the Yaunâ was not meant for softness at all. The Makedonian had not even realized how he was being cut into pieces by the beautiful Samrâjni.

She was born a Royal Woman. It was her duty to defend the deeds of her first husband and king and the father of her son.

The first time he had bled with jealousy over other men in her life, he had lost her… and he was not a man to make the same mistake twice.

He was secure in her love for him and the others in her past had died… and reborn… and no longer mattered… he was a practical man… he was an Emperor!

Megasthenes looks over at the Samrât who is eyeing him. "Did you know Alexander, Empress Anumati?"

"No— no one knew Alexander."

Megasthenes eyes her carefully and then ignores her.

Just another troublesome woman…

He turns his attention to the Emperor and takes out a sealed papyrus from his skin bag.

"Seleukos Nikator sends you greeting and wishes to inform you of the false claims that his enemies are spreading about him. Here is a copy of the false Will of Alexander."

Rošanak's eyes widen.

An Imperial Court Scribe takes the document from Megasthenes and presents it to the Samrât. The Samrât breaks the seal and looks at the document briefly and then points the document to Samrâjni. The Imperial Court Scribe bows and takes the document and presents it respectfully to Samrâjni.

Rošanak takes the document reluctantly and reads it:

The Will of King Alexander, Son of King Philip

She looks up, surprised, and then looks at Chandrâguptâ and utters quietly, "It is the Will of Alexander."

She looks back at the document and reads the rest.

"A list of all the Persian satrapies and their satraps— and the hands of his sisters to his kingsmen… and…"

Her eyes narrow. She reads the lines over again.

… her hand to Perdikkas…

And some nonsense about Olympias to live anywhere she wanted and Rhodians of all the multitudes in the Lands entrusted with the Will of Alexander…

Alexander cared nothing for the Hellenes and cared even less for the Rhodians…

Written by a faceless Olkias, who claimed that he had been at the drinking feast hosted by Medeios and by Alexander's deathbed…

Who was Olkias?

Her eyes widen wider, utterly stunned.

In all her years with the LowLanders and the HighLanders, they had called her the Barbarian wife of Alexander, the illiterate Sughdian commoner of low birth, the dancing girl Alexander had married to force peace on Bakhtriš and Sughud…

Now that they had thought her dead, they called her the loving and faithful wife of Alexander, mother of his legitimate heir… and a demon of the Lord of Darkness who had taken the mortal soul of Alexander with a last kiss…

Ay!

Her body fills with pain. Anger starts to simmer in her royal blood. She looks at the remaining words on the next sheet.

A list of the men who had gone to the drunken feast of Medeios in Bâb-ilim before Alexander had become feverish and fatally ill… Perdikkas and Lysimachos and Leonnatos… Ptolemaios and Nearchos and Meleagros… Seleukos and Peukestas and Peithon and others…

Perdikkas and a few others, mostly dead, declared innocent of poisoning Alexander.

The rest stood accused of Alexander's blood on their hands…

The rumors of poisoning had started long after Alexander had died.

It was because of those false rumors that Olympias had turned her wrath on the Sons of Antipatros. Those lies had shed the blood of many… and had destroyed what was left of the royal blood of Alexander.

Her blood starts to boil and spill over.

No… It was not enough to slander Alexander…

All his kingsmen had assumed the Golden Purple and were calling themselves Kings, after they had ordered the death of her Son-King!

What a shameful travesty!

Kingship was a divine duty… a sacred honor…

It was bestowed upon worthy men by the favor of the Wise Lord!

It was inconceivable to think that men had tied the Golden Purple around their own heads themselves by their own hands and had declared themselves King!

They were neither heir to Alexander nor heir to their own ancestors… men without roots… men without ancestors… men without royal blood… heads so unworthy of golden crowns…

They were kingsmen who had royal blood on their hands!

She slowly folds the parched papyrus and hands it back to the Imperial Court Scribe and straightens.

"Nothing, My Lord, just lies."

She wanted to take the document to Amyntor and show him how words were twisted and turned into lies… this time not against the Persians, but against the Makedonians… the LowLanders and the HighLanders alike.

The Lord of Darkness cared nothing for mortals… he wanted the blood of all of them… the blood of all mortals tasted the same… looked the same… spilled and splashed and splattered the same…

Chandrâguptâ eyes her and hears the wordless anger in her voice.

Nothing was worse than a lie to his beloved Persian.

No offense was worse than lying.

And he had never lied to her… he had just not told her everything… that was not lying!

Megasthenes looks up at the Emperor.

"What is certain, of course, is that Seleukos Nikator was a close companion of Alexander when he conquered the Persians and married their women to his men and mixed the Makedonians and the Persians in the cup of friendship!"

Rošanak pushes up to her feet.

Defeated in battle did not mean conquered…

Persians lived and died by the favor of the Wise Lord…

Once the dust of the battles had settled, it was the conquerors who had been conquered by the Persians and their ways.

"Persians are as they have always been… timely and timeless… eternal… the most splendid of all mortals, by all accounts," she says confidently with the authority of her rank, and continues to eye Megasthenes.

"Alexander drank his wine unmixed. He did not water his wine and he did not water Persians with the Makedonians!"

The only mixing had been done in the vessel of Alexander himself… born a LowLander Prince, died Lord of Asia…

She quickly bows her head low to Samrât, "My Lord," and turns around and leaves the Imperial Audience Hall on soft feet, without asking to take leave of the Imperial Court from the Emperor.

"Samrâjni."

Chandrâguptâ narrows his eyes at her with surprise.

Rani had never left his Imperial Court without his leave, no matter how disagreeable the dealings of the Empire.

The Imperial Court murmurs.

Chandrâguptâ looks at her vanishing trail, raising his eyebrow.

Persians always made much of themselves.

They thought of themselves greater than every one in their empire in every way.

Their kings had grown accustomed to being the Kings above all other Kings… to rule over all other lands… to be the masters of all…

Confident of their exalted place at the feet of their gods.

Confident of their own perfection.

Confident of their manliness and strength.

Confident of the splendor of their women.

Then Chandrâguptâ smiles.

Why not?

Persians were the first of firsts…

They were the riders of splendid horses… the builders of the First Empire…

The gardeners of earthly gardens… and the wine makers to the celestial heavens.

There would have been no Alexander, Lord of Asia, without the Great Kings before him… he only took with blood what the Persians had knotted together with peace.

Yes… Persian Kings were the most splendid of all mortals and the splendid Persian Royal Women were the most costly to maintain, by all accounts…

No need to ask who were the Persians or where was the Empire of the Persians… everyone knew.

Their empire had spread everywhere, like a banyan tree… wherever great men desired to become Great Kings, and wherever Great Kings desired to build Great Empires.

Wherever Great Kings ruled justly by the Laws of the Medes and Persians over Great Empires of many men and of many races walking in the footsteps of Kuruš the Founder… there were the Persians.

The gardeners had become the gardens, growing great kings!

Chandrâguptâ rises to his feet.

The Imperial Court rises and bows low.

Chandrâguptâ beckons Chanâkya forward.

"I am spending the rest of the day with the Samrâjni."

"Yes, Samrât— but your imperial calendar is full for today, as usual."

Samrât waves his hand and all the men following him all stop quickly.

"My plans just changed. I must deal with an urgent matter immediately!" Chandrâguptâ says as he walks down the steps and approaches Megasthenes.

"You have come to our Imperial Court under very favorable stars. Samrâjni Anumâti used to have an ice tiger who ate people who insulted Alexander or the Persians. She is half-Persian."

Words are interpreted.

Megasthenes becomes a little pale.

"I share the view of my Empress. A man who just wages war for the sake of war is not worthy of respect. But a man who wages war for the sake of war and is victorious is worthy of remembrance. Alexander will be remembered for his great conquests, but the Great Kings will be remembered for how magnificently they lived and ruled."

Chandrâguptâ pauses and takes a deep breath.

"The Great King extracted a heavy tribute from Alexander for the Empire. He forced Alexander to give up his own fathers and ancestral lands and people if he wanted to claim the throne of the Great Kings. And so, the Persian Alexander avenged the Persians before his death, by killing most of his own men himself."

Megasthenes finally loses his tongue.

Chandrâguptâ beckons Ârash to him.

"Send your men to Nisâya and have them bring back a hundred more white Nisâya horses. My birthday is coming up soon and Samrâjni is no doubt looking for a suitable gift for me."

"Yes, My Lord."

Chandrâguptâ turns around and leaves the Imperial Audience Hall quickly, heading for his Private Imperial Palace, followed by his female imperial guards.

The splendid Persian Samrâjni was in tears by now and he was just the man to make her feel better!

She was probably summoning her female imperial guards at that very moment to bring back her ice tiger to eat the poor insolent Makedonian Ambassador.

And then he would have to send more war elephants to Seleukos along with the bones of the idiot Makedonian Ambassador to keep his kinsman happy…

Well… maybe the sacred ice tiger could eat her parrots afterward for dessert.

BÎT MÂR ŠARRI. BÎT UMASUPITRÛ. BAKTRA. SATRAPY of BAKHTRIŠ
YEAR 22 of the FOURTH ALEXANDER, MONTH 1, ADUKANAIŠA
DAY 7: AMURDÂD, DAY of IMMORTALITY
YEAR 21 of SAMRÂT CHANDRÂGUPTÂ
2 YEARS LATER
WEDDING
SETTING SUN

"Alexander, Son of Alexander and Rošanak, do you accept Rošanak, Daughter of Itâna, of your free will as your wife?"

"Yes."

"Rošanak, Daughter of Itâna, do you accept Alexander, Son of Alexander and Rošanak, of your free will as your husband?"

"Yes."

"May the Wise Lord grant you a progeny of sons and grandsons and prosperity and heart-ravishing love and bodily strength and long life."

Beat of the ancient wedding drums…

Wall to wall bliss… lips clad with blessings and laughter…

Joyful murmurs knotted with fragrant flowers…

Tears of happiness stream down Rošanak's face.

The manly voice of a blood son… known to the heart, strange to the ear.

The kingly face of a son… careless of his own worldly fame and fortune…

Temples that had been dedicated in his name…

Gates to the cities that had been built in his name…

Men who had ruled in his kingly name:

King Alexander
Malkâ Alexander
Wyšpsy Alexander
Basileos Alexandros
Miššaputra Alessander
Khšâyaθiya Alexander
Šar Šarrâni A'lek'sa'an'dar
Pharaoh of Ta-Mehu and Ta-Shemau…

Even though the Eyes and Ears of the Samrât had brought news that the Mudrâya refused to call the city that Alexander had founded by the name of Alexandria… they still called it Raqed in their native tongue… the building site.

Maybe after so many years, the Mudrâya had found the rule of their Makedonian liberators no different than the authoritarian rule of the Persian Kings before them…

Rošanak utters a blessing under her lips for Alexander and talks to him as if he was standing right next to her.

"Alexander, look at our son marrying as we did!"

"Any king would be proud of such a splendid son." Chandrâguptâ whispers into Rošanak's ear softly.

She had never told him about her blood son… he had just seen the intense desire on her face to go back to the land of her ancestors. When the news of a certain wedding in Baktra had reached the Imperial Court by the Imperial Eyes and Ears, she had restlessly started to climb the palace walls… and so they had come, bearing gifts and blessings.

And now looking at the Groom, he could tell why his beloved Persian wanted to come… the tall Royal Son-King favored the Persian looks of his Imperial Mother.

He could have been their Imperial Son… he could have been his son… he could have been the heir to his Empire… he could have been his love child, as he himself was one…

Gods had given him many children but they had never blessed him with a love child…

He breathes deep.

So, that was why his Persian Royal Woman had so easily forgiven the blood feud… and then who was the other boy who had died in his name long ago?

Old Kalyana was her teacher…

He had thought all along that she had been merciful, as the teachings of the Brahmans had taught her:

"When the soul has been released for rebirth,
Why weep over the broken empty vessel left behind?"

But he was wrong!

She had spared the life of his warriors… because the butchered boy was not her blood son.

Rošanak smiles and cries.

Even to this day, she knew nothing about what had happened to the dead body of Alexandros… the thought of his young bloody body left unburied and unloved and unmourned in the pouring rain on the sandy stony edges of Amphipolis haunted her eyes and tormented her soul on moonless nights.

She utters a quiet prayer for Alexandros under her lips and then takes a deep breath and discreetly wipes her eyes.

One of the Imperial Eyes and Ears had reported that a Bakhtrian Noble with the namesake of Alexander was to be married in the old house of the Son of the King at the old estate of the Crown-Prince in Baktra.

The old house and the old estate had gotten their names from the second Vîsa Puça of the Lands… Mâr Šarri Bârdiyâ, the Son of the Royal House, the Royal Son of Kuruš the Elder, who had built the old house in the old estate in the years long past.

The Samrât and the Samrâjni had quietly left the Imperial Palace at Pâtaliputrâ with a small number of female imperial guards in plain clothes and had made their way to the Bît Mâr Šarri in Bît Umasupitrû at Baktra.

The wedding ritual and festivities were open to all who wanted to come and bless the blessed union of brother and sister of different fathers and different mothers.

Now that there was peace between the Samrât and Seleukos, the journey was uneventful.

Pâtaliputrâ was now connected to Bakhtriš directly and safely by the longest Imperial Road through Mathurâ and then the upper valley of the River Sindhu, passing bountiful fields of rice on both sides of the road.

She had slowly gotten used to the colder air as they had traveled from the warmer Pâtaliputrâ to the cooler Baktra. It was the first time they had left Pâtaliputrâ in a long while.

Pâtaliputrâ had become the most splendid city, even surpassing Bâb-ilim and Alexandria by all accounts… not a city built by slaves… a city built by artisans and builders and gardeners.

And Apâma, the daughter of Apâma and Seleukos and the wife of Bindusâra had borne him a son, almost three years old now, whom the Emperor had named Ašoka… Without Sorrow… beloved of the gods.

Apâma's blood mother had died and Ašoka had no other grandmothers, and the Boy-Prince had come to think of her as his grandmother, just as she had taken Sisygambis to be hers. And the years with him were almost as sweet as the few years she had with her own Son-King… some days even sweeter… it was hard to be away from the Boy-Prince for too long!

Samrât always told her that she was spoiling the Boy-Prince who could become a Samrât one day… but she could not help herself… she just loved him! She did not want to die with love left unspent in her heart for a child…

The more she loved, the more she could love!

She had been stingy with her love for Alexandros. She had kept her love in her heart, to gift it to her own Son-King, when she retuned to him in Bakhtriš. And the days had stretched into months and then years and years afterward and by the time she had found her way back home it was too late… everything had come to pass without her.

And when Alexandros had died so bloodily, she had died too… and then she had become consumed with guilt and grief and hate and shame… her heart had shrunk to the size of the smallest grain of sand or salt… no… smaller…

She had taken refuge in a golden grave and had shunned the whole world… but old love had come looking for her and had found her dying on the edge of a shimmering lotus pond.

And when she had been blessed and cherished and purified again by unbounded love, love of an Emperor no less, her heart had grown as vast and as deep and as giving as an ocean.

It was the ocean that Alexander had desired but never reached in his mortal days… maybe he would find it when he was reborn again.

Her life with Chandrâ had been bathed in the everlasting light of love.

"Ummi šarri."

An unfamiliar voice interrupts and beckons her gently, flattering her with an old honor title, the Mother of the King.

"When I said I hated you, I did not mean it!"

Rošanak turns around slowly and looks at the man standing behind her, in faded Persian Purple. She narrows her eyes trying to remember.

He looked tall and handsome and vaguely familiar.

"Come now! Have I changed that much?" the man asks quietly, begging for recognition in her eyes. He adds with a scent of lightheartedness, "I look more grown up now without my lucky frog."

"Itâna?"

The man smiles.

"Itâna!"

Rošanak smiles and opens her arms and embraces him tightly and warmly kisses his face. Her heart fills up with familiar happiness and spills over.

Brother and sister… connected by hearts… reunited after so many years spent apart.

"When they said you had died, I did not believe it!" Itâna whispers softly, his voice quivering with happiness. "I thought when someone you love dies, you are meant to feel their passing through your bones— and I felt nothing!"

"Itâna…"

"I knew you would come home for the wedding!"

Rošanak smiles and nods.

"I thought after my brother died, your love and care had passed on to me for safe keeping— but fortune had other plans for you."

Heavy with happiness and wine, his childhood love for her, the guarded secret long kept locked up like royal funds, pours out of his heart.

Rošanak leans over and kisses Itâna's face again and lets go of him.

She should have known…

But he used to be such a bloody idiot!

He used to hide his frog in her bed when they were in the Sughud Didâ, which would scare her half to death when the damn frog jumped out at her when she pulled the bed covers back.

"He does his royal ancestors proud— on both father and mother bloods." Itâna says, pointing with his head to young Alexander. "Mâr Šarri is the best archer in the whole Bakhtriš— and my daughter, Rošanak, worships the grounds he walks on."

He had raised the Boy-King like his own, after Uxšiyârta and Oštana had died fighting Hellene mercenaries years ago.

Faithful Abi-Samar had died… and beloved Âriyânnâz too…

His blood daughter loved her blood son just as he had loved his sister… but with a love that was returned in abundance.

His sister had never taken any notice of him! All they ever did was argue and quarrel when they were young. She had always treated him as if he were an idiot and would hit him on the head without any cause!

She used to hurl his lucky frog at his head when they were sieged at the Sughud Didâ! The last time he had left her his lucky frog to sing to her and keep her bed warm at night, she had threatened to roast it and eat it if he did it again!

Rošanak turns her head back toward the Bride and Groom and smiles, pushing back tears of joy. Her hands slightly tremble with happiness.

He had named his daughter after her!

Who would have thought he had any sense when he was growing up like reeds and weeds? And who would have thought that he was the one destined by the hands of faith and by the will of the Wise Lord to raise her Son-King into manhood and gift him his own blood daughter?

She had always cursed him under her breath for losing the Sughud Didâ with his arrogant, careless, childish words. It was during the Siege of the Fortress at Pydna that she had finally realized that Alexander would have sieged Sughud Didâ just as Kassandros had sieged Pydna Fortress… until everyone had died of starvation or gone mad and jumped from the high walls to the low depths and killed themselves in utter desperation. With his arrogant words, Itâna had saved the People of the Sughud Didâ.

Her blood mother was right all along… Alexander would have found a way into the ancient fortress, even if it had taken him the rest of his mortal life and the blood of his entire Royal Army.

Her blood mother was always right… even if she did not have a thousand eyes!

As the old Sumerian proverb said:

"Treat the words from your mother as if they were words from gods!"

Itâna smiles and continues with pride. "Alexander used to say that he was fathered by Zeus-Ammon. Well, his own son fared better than his father— his Royal Son was born with the blood of Great Persian Kings through the royal blood of his Royal Mother— not with the seed of foolish thunder-bolt-wielding foreign gods!"

Itâna points to the other side of the wedding banquet hall.

"Dârâ and Nimâ and their wives and children."

Rošanak looks and her eyes widen with happiness.

The Boys who used to bang their heads on her knees had grown tall like Cyprus trees and handsome just like their blood father, the beloved husband of her sister.

And now they had children of their own who came up to their knees.

"So much has changed…" Rošanak says, taking a deep breath.

"Nothing has changed…" Itâna says with a smile. He looks around and smiles again.

"As Utâna used to say to me: *Defeated in battle does not mean Conquered!* We live as we have always lived. We worship the same god and speak the same tongue. Mountains are the same and so are the deserts… wine is sweet and horses are swift! What more does a man need, than a few horses, some oxen, a house, a good wife and some children, and a dog to watch over everything?"

Alexander and his men had not understood Persians at all!

Persians had Great Kings or they had no kings!

The enemies left behind in garrisons were mostly dead; those still living were tribute collectors who lived behind heavily guarded walled towns, with heavy arms to protect themselves against the rightful owners of the lands. The garrisons and towns Alexander had built to subdue the natives had turned into prisons for his own men… everyone knew that Alexandria here and Alexandria there were prisons for the men Alexander had left behind.

"All the dead are blessed and buried, the traitors shamed and purged, the broken alliances of the Nobles of the Seven Persian Families mended and reknotted. The Persian gardens are all replanted, watered by the blood of our enemies. We have gone back to our riding and hunting and feasting and our wine and our women. We still have prayer and poetry… and drink it with the sweet milk of luscious grapes. We are watching and waiting… when savage armed and armored invaders bent on total destruction charge our way, we just step aside and let them pass through."

He takes a deep breath. His face folds in remembrance.

"As Oštana used to say: *Once the bloody Makedonians ran out of Persians to kill, they started killing each other!* Soon, they will all turn to dust. They will all die and leave their sons and their gold and their bones on our lands. We will raise their sons as our sons with the memories of our fathers… the names of the invaders will all be forgotten in all the Lands!"

Itâna catches his breath and then smiles wickedly and whispers, "Yes, I am now old enough for women and wine."

Rošanak smiles.

Itâna points with his hand to a tall handsome man on the other side of the banquet hall.

"Dârparna says that Persians take care to have good words and good thoughts and good deeds, so when they die they can go to the Land of the Eternal Light and drink milk and honey every day and bed beautiful virgins!"

Itâna pauses and smiles.

"Dârparna says that is why the Makedonians are so bloodthirsty— they have no good words and no good thoughts and no good deeds and when they die they all go to some dark hell and flutter around some damn foul river like blind bats until the end of time."

Rošanak smiles.

And the Hinduya were all reborn.

As Chanâkya always said: "Alexander had passed through muddy lands like clear water!"

Just like her, the one good deed Alexander had done in his mortal life was the splendid son he had gotten with her… so all else that Alexander had done in his life had been for nothing? Just water passing through many lands… making muddy waters?

Itâna straightens and points with his head to Dârparna.

"Dârparna says that gold is not a substitute for God!"

Rošanak eyes Dârparna, amazed, and then looks back at Itâna and smiles.

Who would have thought the arrogant, awkward fools would become confident and handsome and wise? Both of them!

They must have married and bathed in the love of good women… women better than themselves!

Who had been brave enough to gift these fools their beloved daughters?

"Dârparna says that every ruler from Bakhtriš to the Lands by the Sea still proudly claims kinship with the Great Kings, while the Makedonians seek guidance from the old thrones your King-Husband used to sit on," Itâna says lightheartedly and smiles brightly.

"Come. I will take you to them." He reaches and takes Rošanak's hand and points to the Bride and whispers, loaded with hope. "Her mother died years ago. She could use a mother."

Rošanak pulls back her hand gently. Her heart murmurs nervously.

It had been so many years…

What kind of a mother would she be?

The Son-King she loved more than her own life had grown to know only her name and remembered nothing more of her; the son who had come to love her as his mother as the memory of his blood mother had faded and forgotten, had died a wretched death alone.

"Does he remember me?"

"He went to the Temple of Divine Ânâhitâ, before dawn broke today, and remembered you to the divine goddess."

Happy tears bathe Rošanak's face.

She had gone to the same blessed âyadana after the sunrise to pray for her Son-King's happiness.

"He took his bride as the son of his blood father and his blood mother— proud of both— and uttered the name of his mother under his breath when the old athravan uttered the sacred words."

Itâna leans forward and whispers wickedly, "He does not know the tempestuous Rošanak of Utâna carved on the back of the divine statue in the âyadana is his own blood mother!"

Rošanak smiles and bites her lip and her ears redden slightly.

Some secrets about mothers were best kept beclouded away from their sons and the sun of a thousand rays…

"He remembers his mother as a gentle sweet woman with a soft voice who told him stories and he remembers a giant tossing him up in the air.

"His eyes darken and he mixes strange words into his Persian tongue when he is victorious at games or rages with anger!"

"Ah!" Rošanak's eyes widen.

After all these years, her son remembered Perdikkas, the man who had been a father to him when he was born, and some of the words of his mother tongue he had taught him so patiently!

The Divine Mithrâ, Protector of all Warriors, had gifted her son with the eyes of one father and the words of the other…

Her son remembered his fathers.

"Rani." Chandrâguptâ calls her back to him.

Rošanak and Itâna turn their heads toward the commanding voice. Rošanak smiles tenderly at Chandrâguptâ.

Itâna eyes him carefully.

Tall and weathered and worldly… clean-shaven… with silky long hair down his back… and with a definite air of Royalty. Even without any visible royal insignia, the stranger was splendidly confident in his own greatness.

With a multitude of female guards behind him, weaving easily into the sea of wedding guests, circling him and watching every move and hearing every sound.

Itâna looks back at Rošanak, with surprise. "He does not look Makedonian!"

"He is not!" Rošanak smiles.

… and that was all that needed to be said!

Itâna looks back at the stranger.

A king or a prince, no doubt… his sister had always attracted men to her who were splendidly larger than life.

His sister had been well hidden and guarded and protected from the living by a kingly-man in some garden paridaiẓa somewhere!

"You have done well for My Alexander, Itâna. May the Wise Lord keep you and bless you. May my Alexander give your Rošanak many sons and give you many grandsons!" Rošanak leans into Itâna and kisses his face again.

"Do you not want to see him?"

"There is no need. He lives in my eyes, Itâna."

She pauses. "Itâna?"

"Yes, Rošanak?"

Rošanak takes off her old emerald love earrings and puts them in the palm of Itâna's hand and folds his fingers around them.

It was all that she had left of Alexander… and of Perdikkas…

A worthy gift from a blood father and a father…

Old love passing on to the new lovers.

“His father gave these to me. Please give them to your beautiful daughter— tell her that the Father and the Mother of her Husband give the Bride all their blessings… and wish her many sons and grandsons… gifted with royal blood of all their ancestors from this side and that side of the dividing seas!”

She reaches and pulls out an old golden ring from the fold of her gown.

The old golden signet ring of Alexander taken from Dâriuš… the one Abi-Samar had wrested from the broken fingers of the wretched eunuch.

The one that had not been sacrificed to the sacred River Ganga.

The divine mark of mortal kingship…

The golden signet ring of the King-Father belonged to the Son-King… it was not hers to discard… it could not even be sacrificed to the gods… the royal ring of the father was the inheritance of the son.

And now it was returned to the hands of its rightful owner… to do with as he pleased.

“And give this to my Alexander— tell him he was born to Persian Purple, tell him his King-Father left him the Empire that he had won by his spear… and that the Empire of his King-Father was lost.

“Tell him his Queen-Mother left him her royal blood of the Great Kings, which can never be lost. Tell him this is the golden key to a new Empire he can conquer for himself, if he is desirous of one!”

Chandrâguptâ eyes Rošanak intently and takes a deep breath and smiles to himself, and reaches and firmly takes Rošanak’s hand into his hand.

The Emperor of the Peacocks beckoning the Empress of the Moon back to his golden empire…

She turns her head and smiles at him sweetly.

He squeezes her hand confidently.

Goddess Ganga had finally melted and washed and taken the last of the Little Star… now only the luminous Full Moon remained in the starry skies shining on earth… bound to the ancient love god… bound to Kâma… and to the Emperor…

She was finally all his.

TERRACE. PRIVATE IMPERIAL PALACE of SAMRÂT CHANDRÂGUPTÂ
PÂTALIPUTRÂ. LAND of SEVEN RIVERS
YEAR 25 of the FOURTH ALEXANDER
YEAR 24 of SAMRÂT CHANDRÂGUPTÂ, MONTH of CAITRA, R'TU of VASANTA
FESTIVAL of SPRING
SUN SETTING

What is the color of happiness?

Rošanak smiles and leans against a golden column on her private terrace overlooking her gardens, clutching a piece of parchment in her hand, looking up at the reddening golden skies.

Her forty-four years had been longer than the years of her beloved blood mother, who had died at thirty-nine, and Thukrâ who had died at forty.

She utters a sacred prayer under her breath for her beloved mothers... both of them...

Life was sweet...

She was a grandmother of three now.

Just like all the other Persian royal and noble women who were freed from captivity and forced marriages after the death of Alexander... all had married into the Seven Noble Persian Families with the blessings of the Zarathuštra Athravans and had gotten with children... lots of children... and grandchildren.

The blackened ashes of Pârsâ had indeed fallen on the Lands and into the Waters of the Persians as her Chandrâ had once told her, and the rebirth and renewal had started a long time ago...

Dakata...

And No'rouz was coming. Jiyamna was the birthday of Samrât... he was to be fifty.

She smiles again to herself.

Rošanak, the daughter of Itâna, had borne her Son-King, Alexander, two Royal Sons born together a year after their wedding and she was heavy with child again...

... maybe a daughter this time... a Royal Daughter...

Her bloodline that was almost utterly destroyed by Alexander, was now booming and blossoming and flourishing... that too by Alexander...

And the mothers had named their blood daughters after her...

She was remembered... she was not forgotten... she was forgiven...

She looks over and not far from her, her first grandson, the Boy-Prince Ašoka, plays noisily with a small golden toy monkey on the private terrace.

He was almost six years of age now and spoke three tongues... from his mother, he had learned Bakhtrian and Attik and from his father, he had learned Sanskrit...

... and she had taught him a few words of Persian.

And he frequently corrected her words... with the absolute authority of a child!

She beams and takes a deep breath and looks over her fragrant gardens filled with golden sapphire and snowy peacocks.

The Divine Mithrâ had patiently taken all the wretched invaders who had crossed into the Lands of the Persians… one by one…

The old One-eyed Antigonos was dead… he had fallen in the battle against Seleukos and Lysimachos. Seleukos had put the fighting war elephants gifted by the Samrât to good use.

Phila… her husband, Demetrios, the golden son of the One-eyed Antigonos, had dishonored her publicly by marrying Deidameia, the Molossian royal girl who was once betrothed to her Alexandros in former days. And Krateros, son of Krateros and Phila, had grown up and become a man in the service of his younger brother. Both she and Phila were mothers to sons who never knew their glorious blood fathers…

And Polyperchon was dead too… finally.

"Rani." Chandrâguptâ walks on their private imperial terrace and puts his strong arms around her tightly and kisses her face and sweetly whispers, "Are you sure you do not wish to come with me to the Festival of Spring to honor Kâma, the Love God?"

"Kassandros is dead!" Rošanak says smiling, holding up the letter in her hand.

She had cursed Kassandros and his bloodline the day he had told her about the death of Amyntor… a man much loved and remembered…

And again when Olympias had been treacherously murdered,

And again after Alexandros was brutally murdered with no mercy…

… and Pertoss too… the poor lame spaka…

"Kassandros? Finally, after all these years?" Chandrâguptâ nods and smiles with satisfaction.

She had told him all about Kassandros once on a moonless night with sadness pouring out of her with her tears… and he had listened and always remembered.

"He died a horrid death, eaten alive by flesh-eating maggots, as written in the latest letter to you from Seleukos." Rošanak shows the letter in her hand to Chandrâguptâ.

"Alexandros and the Mother of Alexander," she pauses for a short moment in remembrance, "and the Father of Hephæstion are all finally avenged." She speaks with sad satisfaction rippling through her voice.

Thessalonike was finally free of Kassandros too… she was probably the only other woman who had bled and shed a tear for Alexandros, once his death had become known. She had named the son she loved best after Alexandros…

The letter said that her firstborn son, Philippos, had died a month after his father of the same sickness.

Poor Thessalonike… the cursed blood of the father had poisoned the innocent blood of the son. All his wretchedness had brought nothing but misery to himself and death to his firstborn son… all for the sake of stealing a kingship that was not his.

Hades, the Unseen One, finally had Kassandros in his pitiless clutches.

She bites her lower lip wistfully.

Maybe Thessalonike had remembered Olympias and Alexandros and had forgotten to put a coin in the mouth of the corpse of Kassandros for Charon, the Ferryman of the Dead, and Kassandros was to wander by the edge of River Styx forever… fluttering like a blind bat, never crossing over to the Fields of Reeds, with the blessed of his ancestors… forever hungry for a taste of pale yellow asphodel flowers growing in the Meadows of the Blessed…

"More reason to celebrate!" Chandrâguptâ kisses Rošanak's neck with desire.

Rošanak smiles and nods.

Ptolemaios was still ruling in Mudrâya…

And Lysimachos was still ruling Skudra. Nikaia, his wife, had died and he had married Amastris, her royal sister, after her second husband had died. Lysimachos had divorced her a year later and married the young daughter of Ptolemaios in his late years, but had cared for Amastris enough to avenge her death when she had drowned on a day not of her fate…

Neither Ptolemaios nor Lysimachos cared anything for the heartland of the Persian Empire. The Lands were safe from their invading armies.

And Seleukos had remained a faithful ally and kinsman to her Samrât… the blood father of the blood mother of the Boy-Prince Ašoka. After the death of Apâma, he had taken a young daughter of Lysimachos to bed.

"All I want to do tonight is to gaze upon my namesakes!" Rošanak nods and points toward the sky, smiling.

Chandrâguptâ hesitates for a moment and then relents reluctantly.

"I allow it this one time only! Samrâjni has to honor the ancient love god obediently or he will become angry at her and take away her sweet love juices and that would make her Samrât utterly miserable!" Chandrâguptâ kisses her lower lip again and whispers in her ear intimately.

By the grace of the ancient love god, his hot passion for her had remained like a burning fire under the sacred ocean, never doused by the waves ebbing and flowing and rolling on the watery surface…

"Stay with me!" She leans forward and kisses his face tenderly and whispers intimate love words in his ear seductively.

He smiles and considers it for a moment, and then sighs and whispers back in her ear intimately, "I have to go to the Festival of Spring— but I will not stay long. Wait up for me! And I will worship the ancient love god in your sacred temple all night long!"

Rošanak smiles and caresses his hands.

He kisses her and lets go of her and turns around and heads for the Festival of Spring, followed by his imperial followers and female imperial guards.

A nursemaid picks up Ašoka and brings him over to Rošanak. Ašoka puts his arms around her neck and kisses her face sweetly with sugary sticky lips a few times and the nursemaid takes him away, back to his blood mother.

Rošanak turns around and calls to Chandrâguptâ, "Chandrâ."

He stops and looks back at her tenderly while she walks up to him and listens to the tinkle of her golden ankle bracelets dancing in the air. The letter falls out of her hand and drops carelessly on their private imperial terrace.

Rošanak reaches and takes his hands into hers and sweetly whispers, "All these years… I have been very happy here with you."

"I know!"

Chandrâguptâ smiles confidently and pulls her back tightly into his arms and kisses her mouth again passionately and lingers for a long moment.

Rošanak lets go of him and Chandrâguptâ and his imperial followers and female imperial guards disappear from her eyes inside the belly of the palace. Rošanak turns around and walks back to the private terrace and leans back on the golden column and looks up at the skies, blood bleeding now into purple.

Breezy air becomes quiet and peaceful.

She fills her body with the fragrant purple sky.

She had forgiven Ptolemaios long ago, when he had kept his words to her… he had kept the royal body of Alexander in full honors…

The Eyes and Ears of the Samrât who had traveled to Alexandria had brought back news that Ptolemaios had built a Sema in the middle of Alexandria where all the roads met and had laid to rest with all kingly honors the golden casket of Alexander… watched over and guarded faithfully by the marble statues of his gods.

All the roads in Alexandria led to Alexander, the founder of Alexandria.

And the Temple of Hephæstion had remained his… all his…

A road led straight from the Sema of Alexander to the Temple of Hephæstion on the breezy small island…

From Alexander to Hephæstion, Greeting…
From Hephæstion to Alexander, Farewell.

What they both wanted above all else was to be remembered and she had remembered them well every year during Frawardigân, the Festival of All-Souls, along with all her kinsmen and kindred…

She had remembered Alexandros and Amyntor and Krateros and Perdikkas to the gods… they were dry bones and empty vessels and sweet and bittersweet and sad memories… her soul was full of their remembrance and their kisses.

They said women rubbed the Stone Lion of Hephæstion in Hagmâtâna for luck in getting with child!

She smiles unguardedly to herself.

Hephæstion would have liked that!

Even though their own passionate union had not borne any fruit… maybe other women would be more fortunate than she had been…

A splendid snowy peacock leisurely struts on the private imperial terrace and arrays his long shimmery feathers behind him and smugly demands to be noticed by the Empress of the Peacocks. His snowy feathers drink the goldish purple of the sky.

Rošanak waves her hand and dismisses a pair of scribes seated on her private imperial terrace, still writing on precious parchment and palm leaves. They get to their feet quickly and bow their heads low and leave quietly.

The Empress of the Peacocks then smiles at the golden snowy peacock still waiting on her and then follows his flying purplish feathers as he drifts down into her fragrant gardens and sits by the shimmery lotus pond, which is murmuring silently, dotted with snowy lotus flowers, under the ever watchful old eyes of the ancient sycamore fig tree of life.

It was no longer her way to dwell too much on death and dying… she had freely given, and the sacred Goddess Ganga had willingly taken, her grief and shame and sorrow…

The world was filled with pain and misery and loss and lies and death… but it was also filled with love and wonder and mystery and truth and rebirth…

The world was wondrous…

…filled with true wonders… from this side of the lands to the other side of the seas…

If the world was not so wondrous, why would the Lord of Darkness be so hungry to steal it away from the Wise Lord?

And she had taken much to the teachings of the followers of the Enlightened One… and had easily made room in her heart for his compassionate wise words right next to the words of the compassionate Wise Lord…

She beams.

With the permission of her Samrât, her small court was always filled with Brahmans and Monks and Priests and Poets and Scribes.

She had put the gold and silver her Samrât had gifted her to good use… she had paid scribes to write Persian poetry and prayer and even the kingly accounts of her royal ancestors, the Great Kings and their Royal Women. And the promise of the golden gold and the silvery silver had brought to her court many scribes with knowledge of the ancients and tongues of silk and sugar to rhythm and rhyme.

What was left of the half-burnt k^e^tâb she had started years ago was rewritten to become a book of a thousand Persian stories in their expert hands… Hezâr Afsâna…

… one story each in remembrance of all her brothers and their companions who had served in the Aarštibara… the first One Thousand Royal Bodyguards of the Ten Thousand Anauša… the bravest of the braves.

It was all for her Son-King and his Royal Sons and Royal Daughters, so they too would remember what was always remembered among the Persians from time immemorial.

It was for Amyntor too, who had learned her tongue just as Hephæstion had before him, and had done his son one better… he had written her sweet poetry in Persian.

A fragrant spring breeze…

She takes a deep fragrant breath. Her heart sparkles like the little stars in the heavens. She looks at the skin of the shimmery lotus pond; little stars were sparkling on the silky platter of water too.

Hind was neither Pârsâ nor Bakhtriš... a land on this side of the ancestral Lands of the Persians. But if she had to choose any land other than the Lands of her royal ancestors to live in, Hind was her choice.

The Hinduya had taken her to their hearts as one of their own Royal Women... they had generously blessed her with their prayers and adorned her with wreaths of yâsmin and bangles of gold and had touched her sarees for good fortune. She was not judged... weighed or measured... nor was she ever called a barbarian... she was simply the Samrâjni their Samrât loved... and his happiness was their happiness.

And the Emperor had loved her best, in her advanced age, barren and with all her multitudes of imperfections... and since the day he had claimed her as his wife and then his empress and half of himself, she had been devoted to him.

He had never asked about her life that had come before theirs... and the men who had shared her bed and body. He had never interfered with the part of her heart that was not his. And he had held her tight within his loving arms when the memories of her former days haunted her dreams in the middle of the moonless nights.

He had forgiven and spared her ice tiger who had so carelessly ripped into his arms and legs, and had sent him to be cared for by the Brahmans in a beautiful sanctuary in the ancient forest-groved mountains on the other side of Pâtaliputrâ.

He had built her silver fire altars in the Imperial Palace of Pâtaliputrâ, so she could freely pray to the Wise Lord from anywhere in the imperial palace... God and guardian angels were everywhere!

And in return she had honored his gods and had celebrated all the Hindu feasts and festivals and holy days and had gone on royal hunts as his Empress... honoring everything from the Festival of Spring in the honor of the ancient love god, to the births of gods, to his birthdays, to the passing of Brahmans, to celestial omens... even the sleep cycle of Lord Višnu.

He had celebrated the Festival of No'rouz with her every spring to honor the beginning of the Persian New Year, and she had celebrated the Festival of Lights with him every autumn to honor the arrival of the Hindu New Year.

He had never left her bed... nor had she ever left his...

They both had kept faithfully to their marriage bed and to their wedding oaths... even in the nights when to ward off treacherous assassins they had to sleep in a new bedchamber every other night, like the ancient Persian nomad highlanders of the other side of the Abode of Snow...

She had eagerly mastered the ancient Sixty-four Arts to please her Samrât... and had gladly forgotten most of them...

... as Samrât always said: When there was mad burning passion in full thrusting motion, there were no rules of love and desire!

Moon kisses the face of the sky.

Rošanak looks up and smiles again to herself.

Samrât had given her only two commands: to taste his food and to stargaze with him…

And he had always taken the first bite of his food himself and given the second bite to her… which then had left only stargazing. And Hind had such beautiful skies dotted with shimmery little stars… bigger than any other little stars… except for the little stars sewn to the skies over the Lands of the Persians.

She takes a deep breath of life.

Her childhood years were sweet…

Her youth was sweet… and then bitter…

Her years with Alexander and his kingsmen were bittersweet and bitter and bittersweet…

Her life with Chandrâ was too short…

Grrrrrrr!

Rošanak puts her hand on her heart, feeling her happy heart beating and racing, and then looks down at her feet and smiles.

Her ice tiger was growling and rubbing himself smoothly against her shimmery silvery, purple-edged saree-wrapped legs, demanding her attention.

He had returned home to his adoptive mother to celebrate another Festival of No'rouz with her… all good Persian sons always returned home to their mothers for No'rouz! They knew it would be a whole year of bad fortune to miss No'rouz at home!

And all Persian sons loved and never stayed away from their mothers, even if it meant to disobey the orders of an Emperor!

Tears of the Empress-Mother always washed away the wrath of the Emperor-Father.

Grrrrrrr!

> "Son ice tiger to my sweet mother, greeting… may gods bless my mother and keep her in good health… your heart called unto me and I came… still obedient to your command…"

She reaches and sinks her delicate fingers into his soft snowy furry skin and calls his name.

"Alexander…"

Purrrrrrr!

A pair of strong loving arms wrap around her tenderly. She leans back into him and whispers, "Back already?"

"I never left you…" A familiar voice from many suns and moons ago, whispers sweetly into her ear, in pure Persian.

A soft, shimmery white thread slowly wraps loosely around her right wrist.

… Remember the song of the nightingale… abandon the beauty of the peacock…

… return to the garden of roses…

… My beloved… be the melted ruby in my wine cup…

"Ah!" His sweet silent words drip into her eager ears, and like pure sweet wine pour straight into her heart.

She smiles and lovingly plays with the shimmery white tie around her wrist. His manly scent fills the vessel of her heart and runs over. Familiar warm scent of fragrant musk knotted with orange blossom oil and yâsmin brings back so many long lost precious memories. Her body murmurs with happiness.

The first hand tied… the first oath honored… an old promise fulfilled… at last…

He had said to her that night:

"No matter where I am, you live in my heart… I will come back for you."

And he had written it with golden ink on the beating skin of her murmuring heart…

"The moon is full tonight… it neither waxes, nor wanes…" he softly whispers into her soft ear.

"I asked My Beloved, what kind of moon is this… that neither waxes nor wanes?

"And she said to me, she said:

"It is magic… beyond what you know…"

"Then… I asked the Wise Lord… I said to him… O Please My Lord, tell me… I beg you… I wonder… I want to know. Who is the Creator who commands the moon to neither wax nor wane? All this and more I wish to know…

"And he said to me, he said:

"It is sacred… beyond what you could know…"

Rošanak smiles sweetly. Her heart flickers and flutters and flows.

He kisses her neck.

"What is man without woman? Lover without the beloved? Heaven without little stars?"

She caresses his strong tender arms and hands that embrace her so lovingly. Her trembling fingers find their mark. She rubs the tips of her eager fingers over the old familiar golden lion ring on his finger. She softly utters his name carved eternally on the skin of her heart. "Utâna…"

Utâna holds her tighter. She nestles within his warm tight embrace. He kisses her neck and shoulders. "Rošanak…"

Rošanak smiles and raises her hand and sees his face with the happy tips of her fingers and whispers, "Little Star says to the Moon-God: Stay as you are and there is love between us!"

Utâna takes her right hand and kisses her scarred wrist and lovingly whispers back her name. "Rošanak…"

In the blood of my heart,

… the seed of your love was planted and watered with the beat of every breath…

Yesterday dead and tomorrow unborn…

This moment is sweet…

… today… is all there is…

The ice tiger lays down silently and spreads massively on the ground at her bangled, bedecked, bejeweled and hennaed bare feet.

Rošanak looks up at the starry skies and her heart fills with sweet wine and spills over… beloved becomes one with the lover…

She closes her eyes… full moon becomes a full circle of sunny silver…

Embrace of the first lover… the one most loved…

The one remembered forever and a day… the one never forgotten…

Sweet voice of her true lover calling her back unto him…

Moon-god beckoning the Luminous-star back to the Vault of the Heaven to sit by his side… and shine until the end of time…

From this world to that world which lies beyond the Bridge of Chinvât…

By and by…

This is how the Eternal Light must feel…

Like the sacred fire under the living ocean that never dies…

Like the eternal light which is not the Sun…

… and yet it is of the Sun…

… of the Sun knotted with the Moon….

TERRACE. PRIVATE IMPERIAL PALACE of SAMRÂT CHANDRÂGUPTÂ
LATER that NIGHT

Full moon.

Fragrant night. Fresh breeze.

"Rani."

Silence.

Chandrâguptâ dismisses the imperial followers and female imperial guards and walks on his private imperial terrace alone. The terrace is sparkling as usual in the light of the full silvery moon and golden torches. His eyes look around for his beloved Persian.

"Rani, I am back." he calls her again softly.

Silence.

"Roshanak, where are you?"

Spring was in the air… the birds sang sweetly around the gardens, romancing the fragrant flowers… water whispered warmly in the shimmery fragrant lotus pond…

The ancient wishing tree danced this way and that way in the cool breeze.

He strolls across the flickering murmuring private terrace and looks for her in her beloved gardens. Then his eyes find their mark.

Roshanak was sleeping peacefully, by the fragrant shimmery lotus pond, full of golden lotuses… sheathed in the light of the full moon… dusted with petals from spring blossoms… with the tips of her painted fingers floating on the skin of the pond…

The same place he had first claimed her many years ago.

It was her favorite place to sleep in the garden, waiting for him… she was a creature of habit… she was rooted there… nothing he had done over the years, short of telling her the truth, had made her move to another place…

He smiles and walks down the terrace steps, calling her again.

"Rani."

The Emperor of the Peacocks beckoning the Empress of the Moon…

"Roshanak."

Silence.

Then he stops motionless on his moving feet. His heart loses a quick beat and then another.

A giant ice tiger lay on the ground at her feet in the darkness.

Air leaves his body. He is unarmed and the female imperial guards are far away.

No longer a cub… the ice tiger could rip him to pieces with a slight move of his massive paw… but it was too late… like a blind man he had stumbled and walked straight into the claws of danger and death…

He gathers himself swiftly and then takes another cautious step toward her.

The ice tiger lifts his massive head and looks at him indifferently and then lays quietly back down on the cool dark fragrant ground.

Chandrâguptâ looks around the giant ice tiger. There is not a drop of blood that he could see in the dark. He takes a deep breath, relieved, and calls her again, "Rani."

The ice tiger growls quietly without moving.

He steps between the growling ice tiger and the whispering lotus pond and lowers himself cautiously next to her, caresses her back gently and calls her softly, "Roshanak, wake up! I am back!"

The ice tiger does not move; neither does Rošanak.

The ancient sycamore fig tree of life hangs his head lower and murmurs and mutters in the flickering night breeze.

Chandrâguptâ's eyes close in denial. He takes a deep breath and then opens his eyes and pulls her gently toward him. Her yâsmined hair falls carelessly forward around her face and her head drops down to her chest.

She was scented with early spring orange blossoms… a delicate shimmery thread wrapped loosely around her limp right wrist…

The mighty ice tiger whimpers with sorrow and spreads lower on the cool dark ground.

Fog lifts. Mist clears.

Then, in a beat of a heart, Chandrâguptâ knows, feels it in his aching bones.

The faithful son ice tiger had breathed the scent of her death and had come home to honor his dearly loved mother one last time.

"Nooo," he moans in pain.

He had made a promise to the ancient love god and the ancient love god had remembered and he had forgotten… how could he have forgotten? His life with her had passed like a blink of an eye… a beat of the heart… pulse of a kiss…

As years had passed by, he had told himself, it was just a dream… all a dream… his aim was off again… his hand had flickered… his arrow had missed her all along…

She had died on the same place he had marked her for death years ago.

The ancient love god who had tasted the sacrificial offering of her mâlati-scented hair and had come back for her again every year to receive her words of worship… had come back again and this time he had taken all of her with him for dishonoring him and missing his sacred Festival of Spring.

Fragrant air leaves the Hindu gardens. Clouds wrap around the full moon.

"Anuragini…"

He pulls her cold body closer into his warm arms and embraces her tightly. His tears flow freely. He prays and prays and prays, with all his heart and soul.

He knew she was marked for death… he should have stayed with her… he should have held on to her tighter… prayed more… fought the ancient love god to keep her…

…fought all the gods to keep her…

What was more to him than his Rani?

Emperor of the Peacocks had failed…

Empress of the Moon had eclipsed…

Cool night breeze writes the story of the Luminous Star on the leaves of the ancient sycamore fig tree.

O Great King, I heard once there was…

"Roshanak…"

Sadness wraps in silence.

Mournful heart slowly bleeds out in woeful tears.

I prayed by Kalpa Vrikša,

And the old wishing tree granted me my wish…

…And then took it away… took it all away…

Old wishing tree of life weeps.

Eyes of Nine Heavens weep.

Emperor weeps.

Crown becomes heavy, a golden burden…

Life becomes incomplete, imperfect, intolerable…

YEAR 25 of the FOURTH ALEXANDER. MONTH 1, ADUKANAIŠA
YEAR 24 of SAMRÂT CHANDRÂGUPTÂ, MONTH of CAITRA, R'TU of VASANTA
JOURNEY HOME
NIGHT

So lived and so died the Luminous Star and the Full Moon by the favor of the Wise Lord.

Rošanak, the Royal Daughter of the Fifth Artakhšaçâ, the last of the Great Kings of the Hakhâmanišiyâ of Pârsâ.

Queen Roxanâ, beloved wife of the Third Alexander, the King of Makedonia and the Lord of Asia…

… and the royal mother of the last of the Argeads of the UpLands…

… the beloved mother of the Fourth Alexander, both sons…

… and the beloved adopted mother of Alexandros.

Samrâjni Anumâti, beloved wife of Chandrâguptâ, the first Samrât of the Mauryans of Hind…

… the beloved adopted mother of an ice tiger…

… and the beloved grandmother of Ašoka.

Moon was full. There were little stars in the sky.

By all accounts, she was the loveliest woman in all the Lands of the Persians and in all the lands on this side and on that side of the Lands of the Persians …

They say…

When Samrâjni Anumâti died, Samrât Chandrâguptâ returned her body to her beloved Son-King with full honors. He then relinquished his crown and throne and renounced the mortal world and became a Jain follower and followed Bhadrabâhu, a Jain Holy Man, to the lowlands on this side of the rising and falling mountains, and fasted to death in a cave in Sravana Belgola… nestled between two steeply rolling hills, hemmed in between the height of the silvery moon and the depth of the black earth.

A sacred striped ice tiger followed Chandrâguptâ to his last days and guarded his cave until the early dawn of the fourth day of his death and then disappeared back into the ancient forest groves of the ancient mountains on the other side of the watery lowlands.

The Imperial Peacock died in a manner most befitting a Great Emperor of Men… beloved of all gods.

As is was foretold… so it all came to pass…

World broke…

The curse of the Younger Kuruš took the Third Dâriuš and the Fifth Artakhšaçâ, the blood of the Second Artakhšaçâ, and all their faithful.

The curse of the First Dâriuš took the Third Alexander and all his kingsmen.

Third Dâriuš and Third Alexander… both cut from the same kingly cloth… one took and the other one gave… both lost a Great Empire jointly… both utterly destroyed by the ancient curses singly… both forever cursed under the lips of the Persians… in all the Seven Heavens and Four Quarters and Six Dimensions… till the end of time… and the last of the little stars with no names.

Wars of the common men replaced the Common Peace of the Great Kings…
An era of Great Kings and Great Conquerors came to pass…
And they were no more…

And all that remained were words etched on clay fragments, written on parchments and papyri and palm leaves, and on the sacred skins of sacrificial oxen, with blood and gold and ink and golden ink.

And the Royal Women?

They too were obedient to the laws of their beloved Great Kings… their royal blood mixed with the blood of the Nobles of the Seven Persians, bloomed and blossomed into the next great monarchies of the Persian Kings…

And what of all that Persian gold?

All that golden gold that was stolen from the royal funds of the Great Kings stored in the Royal Cities of Sparda and Bâb-ilim and Çûšâ and Pârsâ and Pârsâkata and Hagmâtâna… on the backs of camels and mules and men… soured in the bellies of the invaders and thieves and traitors.
The golden beast carelessly unleashed, devoured the souls of men and the hearts of kingdoms whole.
And then the Wise Lord replaced it all and more with blackened gold, the royal blood of the Great Kings, hidden in the belly of the earth deep beneath the Lands of the Persians, clinging faithfully to the old bones of the mother goddess… as a child clings to the love of his mother… not easily taken away… by camels and mules and men.

Everything changes…
And everything remains the same…
Nothing changes…

Men of the West still lust after the blackened Persian gold and the glory of the Great Kings… Men of the East still worship the Wise Lord…
East and West are still knotted in mortal combat…
Clay to clay… dust to dust… rebel god rages against the great gods…

Sons spilling the blood of their fathers…
Fathers shedding the blood of their sons…
Brother killing brother…
Women wailing and weeping…
Lands burning and dust scattering…

The prophecy remains unfulfilled…

It is… as it was… as it has been…

But those who say: "Nothing lasts!" are wrong.

Love blooms and sweetens and lasts… and soothes the anger of the rebel god…
… and even angry great gods of council are moved with whispering words of love…
… with sweet utterances of lovers… with sacred words of prayer…
… with sacrificial offerings of poetry…
Love lasts…

Sun sets,
And Moon rises… again…
… by and by…

Glossaries

Fragments ⸜ 721

1

GODS and MEN ⸜ 733

2

PERSIANS ⸜ 758

3

UPLANDERS ⸜ 760

4

PEACOCKS ⸜ 762

5

TIMELINE ⸜ 764

6

WORDS ⸜ 772

7

SOURCES ⸜ 785

Scribe's Note ⸜ 801

When a world ends, words remain...

LANDS and PEOPLE
DAHYÂVA

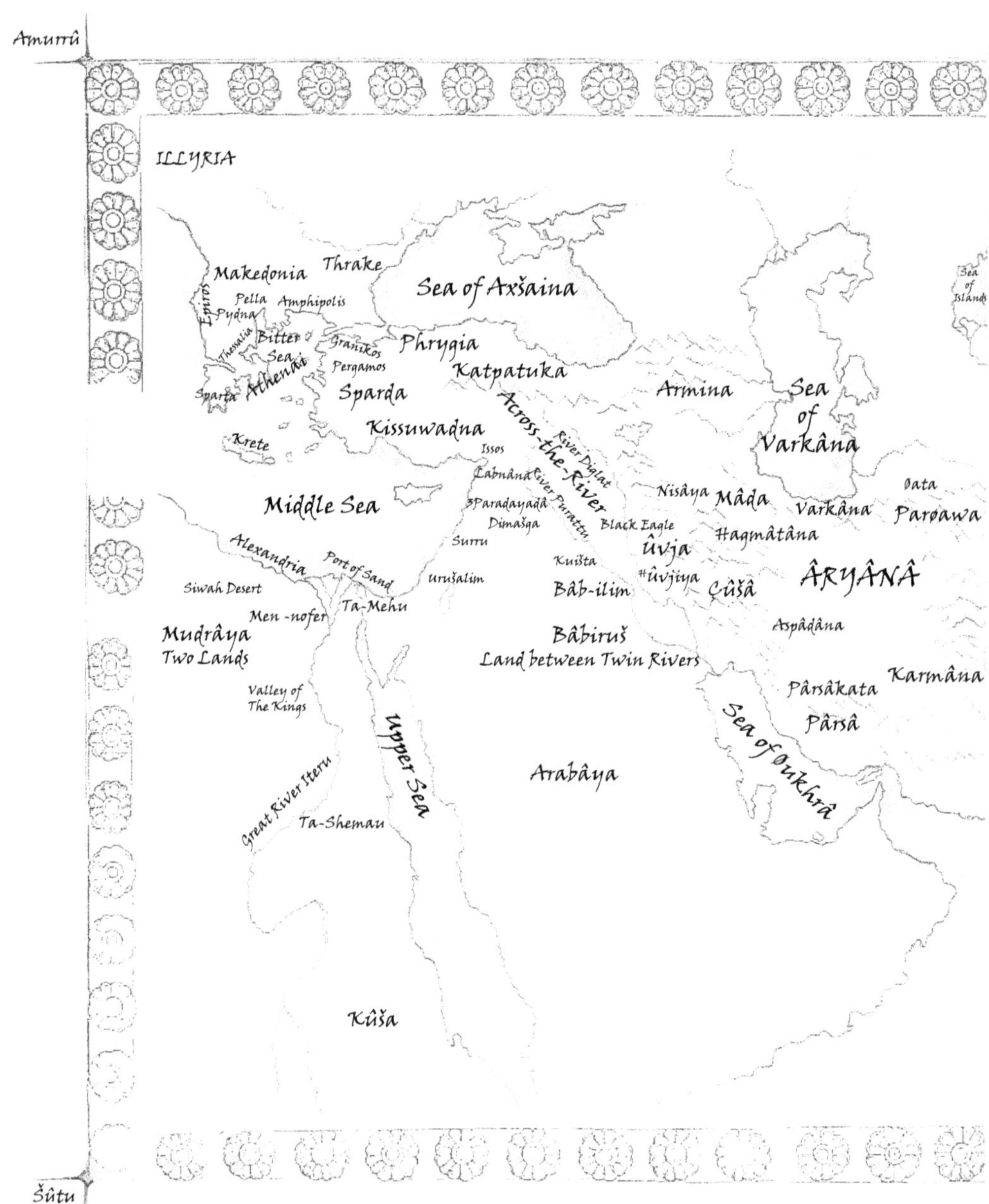

Then...

In the year 261 after the Second Kuruš

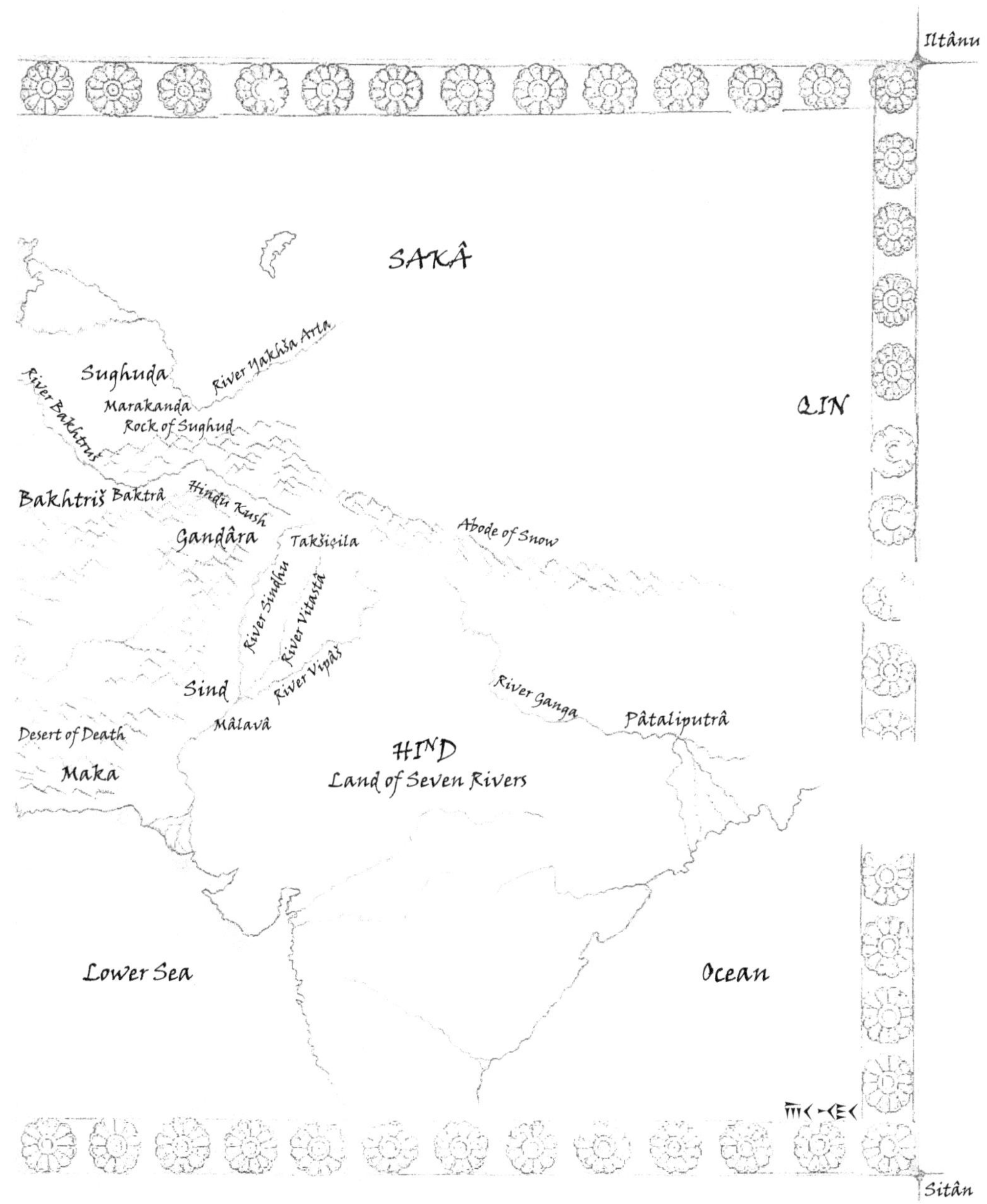

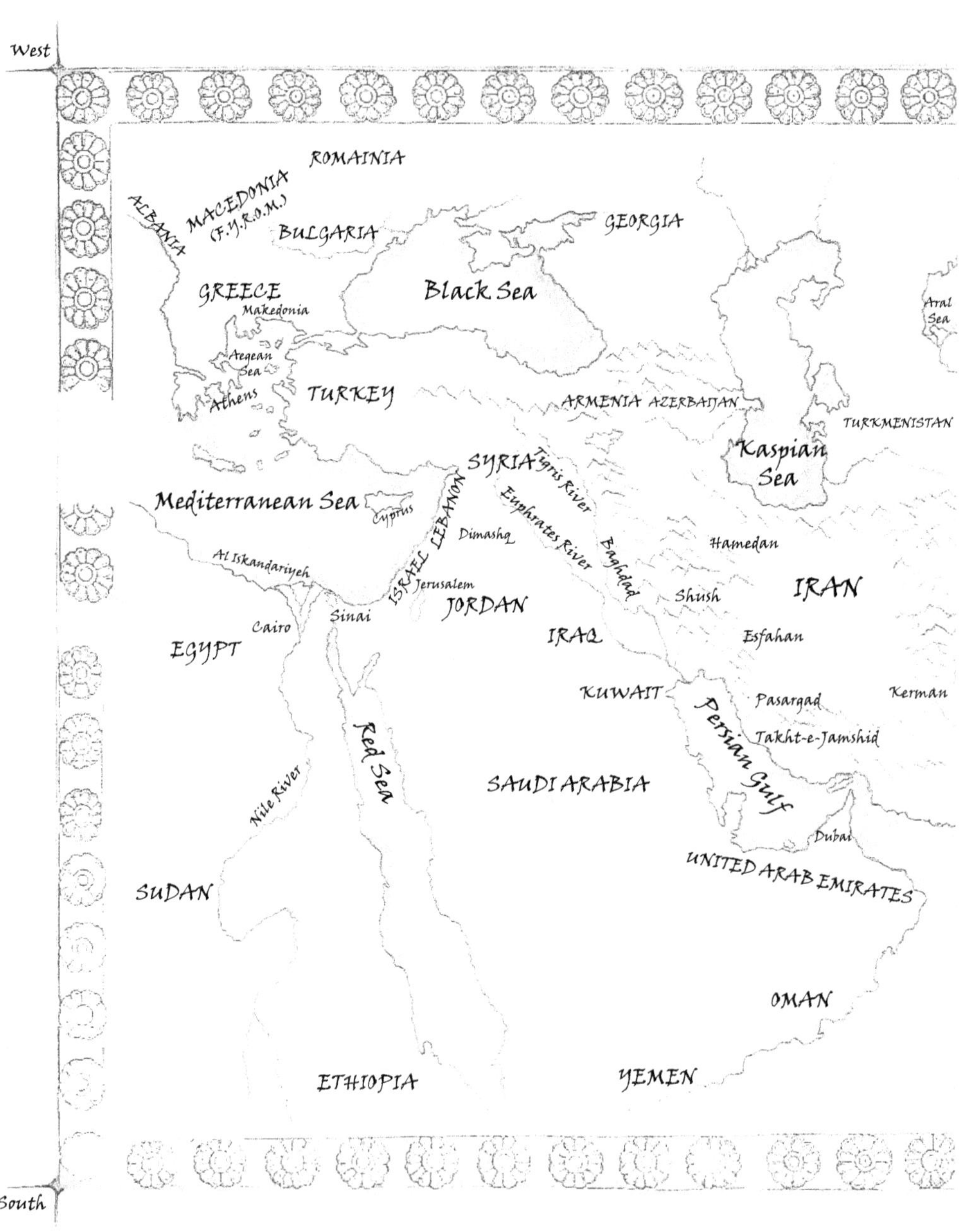
West
South
ROMAINIA
ALBANIA
MACEDONIA
(F.Y.R.O.M.)
BULGARIA
GEORGIA
GREECE
Black Sea
Makedonia
Aral
Sea
Aegean
Sea
Athens
TURKEY
ARMENIA
AZERBAIJAN
TURKMENISTAN
SYRIA
Tigris River
Kaspian
Sea
Mediterranean Sea
Cyprus
LEBANON
Euphrates River
Dimashq
Hamedan
Al Iskandariyeh
ISRAEL
Jerusalem
Baghdad
Shush
IRAN
Sinai
JORDAN
Cairo
IRAQ
Esfahan
EGYPT
KUWAIT
Pasargad
Kerman
Persian Gulf
Takht-e-Jamshid
Red Sea
SAUDI ARABIA
Nile River
Dubai
UNITED ARAB EMIRATES
SUDAN
OMAN
ETHIOPIA
YEMEN

And...

In the year 2007 Common Era

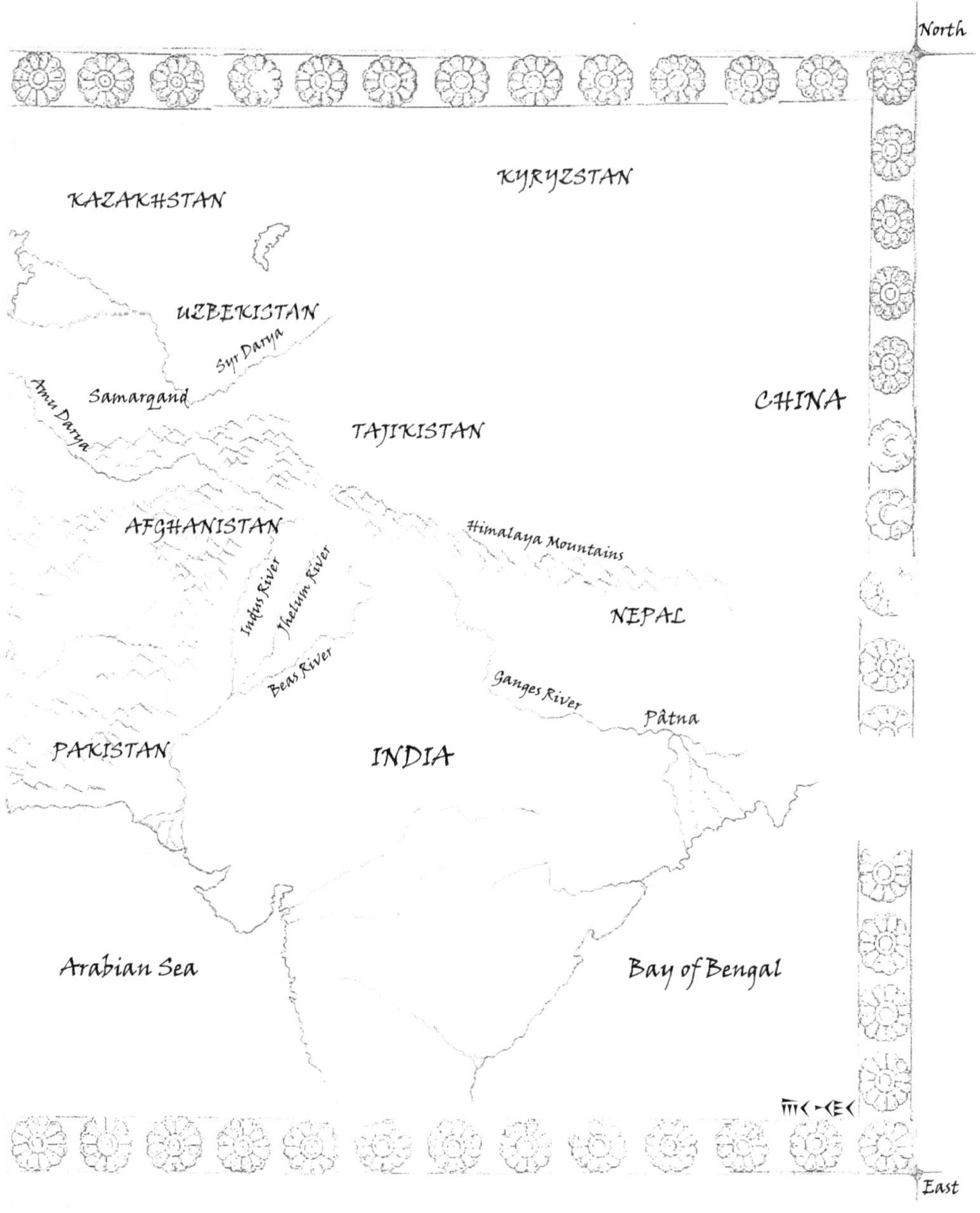

LANGUAGE
HAZÂN

Marking	Letter	Marking	Letter	Marking	Number	Marking	Symbol
	A		a		1		.
	B^{a}		b		2		,
	C^{a}		ç^{a}		3		-
	D^{i}		d^{a}		4		
	E		e		5		
	F^{a}		f		6		
	G^{u}		g^{a}		7		
	H^{a}		h		8		
	I		i		9		
	J^{i}		j^{a}		10		
	K^{u}		k^{a}				
	L^{a}		l				
	M^{i}		m^{a}				
	N^{u}		n^{a}				
	Ø		ø				
	P^{a}		p				
	Q		q				
	R^{i}		r^{a}				
	Š^{a}		s^{a}				
	T^{u}		t^{a}				
	U		u				
	V^{i}		v^{a}				
	W		w				
	X^{a}		x				
	Y^{a}		y				
	Z^{a}		z				

PRONUNCIATION

Letter	Sound	Letter	Sound	Letter	Sound
A	Axis	B	Beauty	Ş	Tsunami
Â	Army	C	Celestial	Ţ	Tether
E	Eternity	Ç	Chalice		
Ê	Eagle	D	Dawn		
I	Imperial	F	Faith		
Î	Evening	G	God		
O	Omen	H	Home		
U	Utter	J	Journey		
Û	Universe	K	King		
		KH	Khan		
		L	Luminous		
		M	Mother		
		N	Noble		
		P	Persian		
		Q	Queen		
		R	Rosemary		
		S	Sycamore		
		Š	Shimmer		
		T	Time		
		Ø	Thread		
		V	Violet		
		W	Woman		
		X	Khayyam		
		Y	Young		
		Z	Zodiac		

CALENDAR

SEASON	MONTH	PERSIAN	BABYLONIAN	
SPRING	March/April	Adukanaiša Vernal Equinox No'rouz	Nîsannu Akîtu Festival	1
	April/May	Øûravâhara	Ayyâru	2
	May/June	Øâigarciš	Sîmannu	3
SUMMER	June/July	Garmapada Summer Solstice Tirgân	Du'ûzu	4
	July/August	Turnabaziš	Âbu	5
	August/September	Karbašiyaš	Ulûlu	6
AUTUMN	September/October	Bâgayâdiš Autumn Equinox Mithrâkânâ	Tašrîtu	7
	October/November	Markašanaš	Arahsamnu	8
	November/December	Âçiyâdiya	Kisilîmu	9
WINTER	December/January	Anâmaka Winter Solstice Day'ghân	Tebêtu	10
	January/February	Samiyamaš	Šabâtu	11
	February/March	Viyaxana	Addâru	12

CALENDAR

SEASON	MONTH	EGYPTIAN	
FLOOD of NILE	First of Akhet	Dhwt	1
	Second of Akhet	Pa-n-ip.t	2
	Third of Akhet	Hwt-hwr	3
	Fourth of Akhet	Ka-hr-ka	4
WINTER GROWTH	First of Proyet	Ta-'b	5
	Second of Proyet	Mhyr	6
	Third of Proyet	Pa-n-amn-htp.w	7
	Fourth of Proyet	Pa-n-rnn.t	8
SUMMER HARVEST	First of Shomu	Pa-n-hns.w	9
	Second of Shomu	Pa-n-in.t	10
	Third of Shomu	Ipip	11
	Fourth of Shomu	Msw-r'	12

CALENDAR

SEASON	MONTH	HELLENE		MAKEDONIAN	
SUMMER	June/July	Hekatombaion	1	Loios	10
	July/August	Metageitnion	2	Gorpiaios	11
	August/September	Boedromion	3	Hyperberetaios	12
AUTUMN	September/October	Pyanepsion	4	Dios	1
	October/November	Maimakterion	5	Apellaios	2
	November/December	Posideon	6	Audnaios	3
WINTER	December/January	Gamelion	7	Peritios	4
	January/February	Anthesterion	8	Dystros	5
	February/March	Elaphebolion	9	Xandikos	6
SPRING	March/April	Mounichion	10	Artemisios	7
	April/May	Thargelion	11	Daisios	8
	May/June	Skirophorion	12	Panemos	9

ARCHONS of ATHENS

YEAR	ARCHON	EVENT
1st Year of Alexander III	Euainetos	Year 1 of Third Dâriuš
2nd Year of Alexander	Ktesikles	
3rd Year of Alexander	Nikokrates	
4th Year of Alexander	Niketes	
5th Year of Alexander	Aristophanes	
6th Year of Alexander	Aristophon	
7th Year of Alexander	Kiphisophon	Death of Third Dâriuš
8th Year of Alexander	Euthykritos	Death of Fifth Artakhšaçâ
9th Year of Alexander	Hegemon	
10th Year of Alexander	Chremes	
11th Year of Alexander	Antikles	
12th Year of Alexander	Hegesias	
13th Year of Alexander	Kephisodoros	
14th Year of Alexander III 1st Year of Philip III	Philokles	Death of Alexander III
2nd Year of Philip	Archippos	
3rd Year of Philip	Neaichmos	
4th Year of Philip	Apollodoros	
5th Year of Philip	Archippos	
6th Year of Philip III	Demogenes	Death of Philip III
1st Year of Alexander IV	Demokleides	
2nd Year of Alexander	Praxiboulos	
3rd Year of Alexander	Nikodoros	
4th Year of Alexander	Theophrastos	
5th Year of Alexander	Polemon	
6th Year of Alexander IV	Simonides	Death of Alexandros

CALENDAR

SEASON	MONTH	INDIAN	
AUTUMN		ŠARAD	
	September/October	Âšvina	1
	October/November	Kârttika	2
WINTER		HEMANTA	
	November/December	Âgrahâyana	3
	December/January	Pausa	4
COOL		ŠIŠIRA	
	January/February	Mâgha	5
	February/March	Phâlguna	6
SPRING		VASANTA	
	March/April	Caitra	7
	April/May	Vaišâkha	8
SUMMER		GRIŠMA	
	May/June	Jyaistha	9
	June/July	Âšadha	10
RAINS		VARSÂ	
	July/August	Šrâvana	11
	August/September	Bhâdrapada	12

1

GODS and MEN

GODS
BAGÂHA

DEITY	ORIGIN	
𒀭	Akkadian	Dingir God Divine
𒀭𒀭	Akkadian	Gods Divinity
Adad	Babylonian	Great god Son of Anu and Ki God of weather, rain and storm, thunder and lightning
Aešma	Zoroastrian	Demon of wrath and fury
Ahura Mazda A^{h}uramazdâ^h Auramazdâhâ U-ra-ma-az-da	Zoroastrian	Wise Lord God of the Aryas Protector of kingship Creator of the truth
Ahurani	Zoroastrian	Goddess of fertility
Ama.Ka	Akkadian	Mother goddess
Ammon	Egyptian	Supreme god Father of pharaohs
Anâhatâ Ânâhitâ Anaitis	Zoroastrian	Goddess of waters and fertility
Angra Mainyu	Zoroastrian	Lord of Darkness, Dark Lord Ahriman Evil Lie Demon Destroyer
Anointed One		Holy Prophet Yeshua Jesus of Nazareth Jesus Christ
Anšar	Babylonian	Great god Husband of Kišar Father of Anu, Êa and Enlil
Anu	Babylonian	Great god Son of Anšar and Kišar Husband of Ki Father of Adad, Šamaš, Nêbiru and Ninisina God of heaven
Anunnakkî	Babylonian	Old gods
Aphrodite	Hellene	Daughter of Zeus and Dione Wife of Hephæstos Lover of Ares Goddess of romantic and erotic love

Apis Bull	Egyptian	Sacred bull Manifestation of god P'tah
Apollo	Hellene	Son of Zeus and Leto Brother of Artemis God of healing, purification, prophecy, poetry and music God of light and truth
Apsû	Babylonian	Sweet water First father
Ares	Hellene	Son of Zeus and Hera God of war
Artemis	Hellene	Daughter of Zeus and Leto Sister of Apollo Goddess of hunt
Arûru	Babylonian	Mother of creation Mother goddess
Ašaivanuhî	Zoroastrian	Goddess of marriage
Asklepios	Hellene	God of medicinal arts
Atar	Zoroastrian	Angel of fire
Athena	Hellene	Daughter of Zeus and Metis Goddess of wisdom and invention
Bêl Bêlu	Babylonian	Lord Master Bêl Marduk
Bêlet balâti Bêlet ilî	Babylonian	Goddess of creation
Brahma	Indian	God of creation
Dam-ki-na	Babylonian	Great goddess Consort of Êa Mother of Marduk
Dên	Zoroastrian	Angel Greets the souls of the blessed with flowers
Dionysos	Hellene	Twice-born Son of Zeus and Semele God of wine and intoxication
Êa	Babylonian	Great god Son of Anšar and Kišar Brother of Anu and Enlil Husband of Dam-ki-na Father of Marduk God of water, wisdom and magic Creator
Enlightened One	Buddhist	Buddha
Enlil	Babylonian	Great god Son of Anšar and Kišar Brother of Anu and Êa Husband of Ninlil Father of Nânna and Ninurta God of earth

Ereškigal	Babylonian	Great goddess Sister of Ištar Consort of Nergal Goddess of underworld
Eris	Hellene	Goddess of discord
Eros	Hellene	Son of Aphrodite God of love
Ganga	Indian	Water goddess of purification
Hades	Hellene	Son of Titan Kronos and Rhea Brother of Zeus and Poseidon Husband of Persephone God of the dead and the underworld
Helene	Hellene	Goddess of light
Hephæstos	Hellene	Son of Zeus and Hera Husband of Aphrodite God of fire and blacksmiths
Hera	Hellene	Daughter of Titan Kronos and Rhea Wife and sister of Zeus Sister of Hades and Poseidon
Herakles	Hellene	Son of Zeus and mortal Alkmene Founder of Olympic Games
Hermes	Hellene	Son of Zeus and Nymph Maia Messenger of gods God of cunning and sexual prowess
Igîgî	Babylonian	Young gods
Ishtar Ištar Astarte	Babylonian	Great goddess Goddess of love and war Queen of Heavens
Kâma	Indian	God of love and desire
Khvarənah	Zoroastrian	Divine glory
Ki	Babylonian	Great goddess Consort of Anu Mother of Adad, Šamaš, Nêbiru and Ninisina
Kišar	Babylonian	Great goddess Consort of Anšar Mother of Anu, Êa and Enlil
Lahâmu	Babylonian	Male great god
Lahmû	Babylonian	Female great god
Lamassu	Babylonian	Protective Angel
Lamaštu	Babylonian	Female demon who steals the lives of unborns and newborns
Lord of Darkness Dark Lord	Zoroastrian	Ahriman Evil, Lie Demon Destroyer
Mâha	Zoroastrian	Angel of moon

Marduk Amar-utu	Babylonian	Great god Son of Êa and Dam-ki-na Husband of Zarpânîtu Father of Nabû Supreme god of Babylon
Medusa	Hellene	Female demon with snake hair Gorgon
Mithrâ Miørâ Mithres	Zoroastrian	Angel of sun and light Protector of warriors, order, fidelity and oath One of the three divine judges at First Judgment
Mu-um-mu	Babylonian	Deity
Nabû	Babylonian	Great god Son of Marduk and Zarpânîtu Husband of Tašmêtu God of wisdom Patron of scribes
Nânâ	Sumerian	Great goddess Goddess of love and war
Nânna	Babylonian	Great god Firstborn son of Enlil and Ninlil Brother of Ninurta God of moon
Nêbiru	Babylonian	Great god Son of Anu and Ki Jupiter
Nergal	Babylonian	Great god Husband of Ereškigal God of the dead and destruction God of the underworld and pestilence
Nike	Hellene	Daughter of Titan Pallas and Styx Goddess of victory
Ninisina	Babylonian	Great goddess Daughter of Anu and Ki Goddess of healing
Ninlil	Babylonian	Great goddess Consort of Enlil Mother of Nânna and Ninurta
Ninsûna	Babylonian	Great goddess Consort of Lugal-Banda Mother of Gilgâmeš
Nintu	Sumerian	Great goddess Goddess of childbirth
Ninurta	Babylonian	Great god Son of Enlil and Ninlil Brother of Nânna God of war Saturn
Pandora	Hellene	Both a goddess and the first woman

Pârvatî	Indian	Mother Goddess Wife of Lord Šiva
Persephone	Hellene	Daughter of Zeus and Demeter Wife of Hades
Poseidon	Hellene	Son of Titan Kronos and Rhea Brother of Zeus and Hades Husband of Amphitrite God of the sea
Qi-in-gu	Babylonian	Great god Rebel god
Ra	Egyptian	Sun god
Rašnu	Zoroastrian	Angel One of the three divine judges at First Judgment
Šamaš	Babylonian	Great god Son of Anu and Ki God of sun God of justice, seeing all things from heaven Sun
Šiva	Indian	God of destruction and creation Destroyer of the world, so the world can be recreated
Sraoša	Zoroastrian	Angel One of the three divine judges at First Judgment Greets and watches over the souls at death
Tašmêtu	Babylonian	Great goddess Consort of Nabû
Ti'âmat	Babylonian	Salt water Mother of Creation
Tištyra	Zoroastrian	Angel of water
Vanu	Zoroastrian	Angel of wind
Varaha	Indian	Manifestation of Lord Višnu
Višnu	Indian	God of creation with power to repel death
Wise Lord	Zoroastrian	God of the Aryas Ahura Mazda, A^{h}uramazdâ^{h}, Auramazdâhâ U-ra-ma-az-da Protector of kingship Creator of the truth
Zaraøuštrâi Zarathuštra	Zoroastrian	Holy Prophet
Zarpânîtu	Babylonian	Great goddess Consort of Marduk Mother of Nabû
Zeus	Hellene	Son of Titan Kronos and Rhea Brother of Hades and Poseidon Husband of Hera Supreme god of Hellene Pantheon Father Lord King

PEOPLE
KÂRA

NAME	VARIATION	ORIGIN	
1st Dâriuš Da-ri-a-muš Darius	Dârayavauš	Persian	Great King The First Dâriuš, 522-486 BCE
1st Khašâyar Ka-ši-ar-šâ Khašâyâr-šan Xerxes		Persian	Great King The First Khašâyar, 486-465 BCE Son of First Dâriuš
2nd Artakhšaçâ Artaxerxes		Persian	Great King The Second Artakhšaçâ, 404-359 BCE Brother of the Younger Kuruš
2nd Dâriuš Da-ri-a-muš	Darius Dârayavauš	Persian	Great King The Second Dâriuš, 424-404 BCE Husband of Purušâtu Father of Second Artakhšaçâ and the Younger Kuruš
2nd Kambujiya Kambujiya	Kabujiyahya Kam-bu-zi-ia Kambyses Cambyses	Persian	Great King The Second Kambujiya, 530-522 BCE Son of Second Kuruš
2nd Kuruš Kurrašu Ku-raš Kuruš the Father Kuros the Elder	Kûrauš Cyrus II	Persian	Great King The Second Kuruš, 559-530 BCE Founder of Hakhamanišiya Dynasty
3rd Artakhšaçâ Û-ma-su Artaxerxes		Persian	Great King The Third Artakhšaçâ, 359-338 BCE
3rd Dâriuš Artašatu Darius Dariush		Persian	Great King The Third Dâriuš, 336-330 BCE Son of Astâna and Sisygambis Father of Ariâbarzâna Husband of Setâreh Father of Setâreh, Dripeyti and Tiršata
5th Artakhšaçâ Artaxerxes Bayasa Bessos	Bessus	Persian	Great King The Fifth Artakhšaçâ, 330-329 BCE Cousin of Third Dâriuš Husband of Farânak Father of Parânak and Rošanak Grandfather of Dârâ and Nimâ
Abi-Enši-Marduk		Babylonian	Chief Eunuch of the Palace of Nabû-Kudurrî-Ûṣur
Abi-Samar		Babylonian	Eunuch Protector of Rošanak

Achilleos	Achilles Achilleus	Hellene	*From Iliad by Homer* Son of Peleos and Thetis Hellene Hero in the Trojan War
Ada		Karian	Queen Daughter of Hekatomnos Sister and wife of Idrios Sister of Pixodaros Adoptive mother of Alexander III
Adeia	Adea Adeia Eurydike Adea Eurydice	Makedonian-Illyrian	Daughter of Amyntas IV and Kynnane Wife of Philip III
Aiakides	Aeacides	Molossian	King of Epiros Nephew of Olympias Father of Deidameia and Pyrrhos
Aischylos	Aeschylus	Athenian	Writer of Tragedies, 525-465 BCE
Alexander III A-lek-sa-an-dar	Alexander Alexandros A-lik-sa-an-dar Eskandar Iskandar Sikandar	Makedonian-Molossian	King of Makedon, Lord of Asia The Third Alexander, 336-323 BCE Son of Philip II and Olympias Brother of Kleopatra Half-brother of Thessalonike and Arrhidaios Husband of Rošanak Father of Alexander IV Husband of Setâreh Father of Herakles
Alexander IV A-lek-sa-an-dar Alessander	Alexander	Persian-Makedonian	The Fourth Alexander, 323-305 BCE Son of Alexander III and Rošanak
Alexandros			Adopted son of Rošanak
Alexandros I		Molossian	King of Epiros Brother of Olympias Husband of Kleopatra
Amastris	Amestris Amastrine	Persian	Royal Daughter Daughter of Hukhšaqra Wife of Krateros Wife of Dionysios of Heraklea Mother of Klearchos and Oxathres Wife of Lysimachos
Âmbhi Omphis	Taxiles	Indian	Rajah Ruler of the City of Takšiçila
Amyntor	Amyntoros	Hellene	Noble Father of Hephæstion
Amytiš		Median	Royal Woman Daughter of Ištu-Vigu, King of Mâda Wife of Nabu'kudra'cara
Anaxarchos	Anaxarchus	Hellene	Anaxarchos of Abdera Philosopher in the royal court of Alexander III

Andromache		Trojan	*From Iliad by Homer* Wife of Hektor Captive woman of Neoptolemos Mother of Molossos
Antigonos "The One-eyed"	Antigonus Monophthalmos An-ti-gu-nu-su	Makedonian	Kingsman of Alexander III Son of Philippos Husband of Stratonike Father of Demetrios Assumed the title of king in 306 BCE
Antipatros	Antipater	Makedonian	Kingsman of Philip II and Alexander III Son of Iolaos Father of Kassandros, Iolaos, Eurydike, Nikaia, and Phila Regent of Makedonia
Apâma	Apâme Abbamuš	Bakhtrian-Persian	Daughter of Spitâmaneh Wife of Seleukos Mother of Apâma, Laodike and Antiochos I Queen
Apâma	Apâme	Bakhtrian-Makedonian	Daughter of Seleukos and Apâma Sister of Laodike and Antiochos I Wife of Bindusâra Mother of Ašoka
Apelles		Hellene	Son of Pytheas Royal court painter of Alexander III
Ârash		Persian	Son of Ârtafarnâ Noble of the Seven Persian Families Commander serving Chandrâguptâ
Ariâbarzâna	Ariobarzanes	Persian	Royal Son Son of Third Dâriuš Half-brother of Setâreh, Dripeyti and Tiršata Grandson of Sisygambis Cousin of Rošanak Commander of forces protecting Pârsâ
Aristandros	Aristandrus Aristander	Hellene	Seer and interpreter of dreams and omens for Alexander III
Aristoboulos	Aristoboulus Aristobulus	Hellene	Engineer in the army of Alexander III Historian Wrote about Alexander III
Aristonous	Aristonus	Makedonian	Kingsman of Alexander III and Alexander IV Son of Peisæos Supporter of Perdikkas
Aristophanes		Hellene	Writer of Comedies, 445-385 BCE
Aristoteles	Aristotle	Hellene	Son of Nikomachos Uncle of Kallisthenes Philosopher, student of Plato Tutor of the young Alexander III

Âriyânnâz Ariana		Persian	Tutor of Rošanak Noble Lady of the Seven Persian Families
Arrhidæus		Makedonian	Son of Alexandros Builder of Alexander's funerary carriage
Arrhidaios Philip III	Arrhidæus Arridæus	Makedonian	The Third Philip, 323-317 BCE Son of Philip II and Philine of Larissa Half-brother of Alexander III, Kleopatra and Thessalonike Husband of Adeia Eurydike
Aršana Orsines	Orxines	Persian	Noble of the Seven Persian Families Head of the Pârsâkata Tribe of the Persians
Artâvazda Artabazos	Artabazus	Persian	Royal Son Father of Artâkama, Artone, Barsine and Kophen Father-in-law of Mentor and Memnon Appointed the Satrap of Bakhtria by Alexander III
Ašoka		Indian	Samrât, 272-232 BCE Son of Bindusâra and Apâma Grandson of Chandrâguptâ Grand son of Rošanak
Aššur-bâni-apli	Ashurbanipal	Assyrian	Assyrian King, 668-627 BCE
Atossâ		Persian	Royal Woman Daughter of Second Kuruš Wife of First Dâriuš Mother of First Khašâyar
Âtrupâta Atropates	Atropatos	Median	Satrap of Mâda Âtrupâta Father of Madumîtu Father-in-law of Perdikkas Noble of the Seven Persian Families
Bagaya	Bagoas	Babylonian	Eunuch
Bardiyâ		Persian	Royal Son, 522 BCE Son of Second Kuruš
Barsine		Persian-Hellene	Daughter of Atrâvazda Half-sister of Artâkama Sister of Artone and Kophen Wife of Mentor Wife of Memnon Mistress of Alexander III Mother of Herakles
Batis	Babemesis	Arab	Commander of Gaza
Bêl-re'uša Berossos		Babylonian	Son of Kî-Nabû Priest of Bêl Marduk Wrote *Babyloniaka*
Bêl-rimanni		Babylonian	Chaldæan Diviner Pupil of Kî-Nabû

Bindusâra	Vindusara Amitra ghâta Amitrochates Sindhusena	Indian	Samrât, 298-272 BCE Son of Chandrâguptâ Husband of Apâma Father of Ašoka
Briesis		Trojan	*From Iliad by Homer* Captive woman given to Achilleos
Chanâkya	Kautilya	Indian	Chief Brahman Minister of Chandrâguptâ Wrote *Ârtâshastrâ*
Chandrâ Chandrâguptâ	Sandrocottus	Indian	Samrât, 322-298 BCE Husband of Durdhara Father of Bindusâra Grandfather of Ašoka Husband of Rošanak
Chares		Hellene	Chares of Mytilene Court chamberlain of Alexander III
Dârâ	Dâriuš	Persian	Royal Son Son of Parânak Brother of Nimâ Grandson of Fifth Artakhšaçâ and Farânak Nephew of Rošanak
Dârparna		Persian	Friend of Itâna
Deidameia		Molossian	Daughter of Aiakides Betrothed to Alexander IV
Deinokrates	Deinocrates	Rhodian	Architect of Alexandria Architect of the Memorial for Hephæstion
Demosthenes		Athenian	Son of Demosthenes Politician and Orator Opposed Philip II and Alexander III
Dripeyti Drypetis		Persian	Royal Daughter Younger daughter of Third Dâriuš and Setâreh Sister of Dripeyti and Tiršata Half-sister of Ariâbarzâna Granddaughter of Sisygambis Cousin of Rošanak Wife of Hephæstion
Durdhara		Indian	Princess Daughter of the brother of the last Nandâ King Wife of Chandrâguptâ Mother of Bindusâra
Enkîdu		Babylonian	*From the Gilgâmeš Epic* Sent by the great gods to tame Gilgâmeš

Eumenes		Kardian	Kingsman of Alexander III Royal Secretary to Philip II and then to Alexander III Husband of the sister of Barsine Writer of the Royal Journal
Euripides		Athenian	Writer of Tragedies, 480-406 BCE
Europa		Makedonian	Infant daughter of Philip II and Kleopatra Eurydike Killed by Olympias
Farânak		Bakhtrian-Persian	Royal Woman Sister of Uxsiyartâ Wife of Fifth Artakhšaçâ Mother of Parânak and Rošanak Grandmother of Dârâ and Nimâ
Frâda		Bakhtrian	Head gardener of Baktra Palace
Gilgâmeš	Bilgames Gilgamesh	Babylonian	*From Gilgâmeš Epic* Fifth King of Uruk.Ki
Glaukias	Glaucias	Makedonian	Commander of the Amphipolis Fortress
Ha-am-mu-ra-pi Hammurabi		Babylonian	Babylonian King, 1792-1750 BCE Wrote *code of Hammurabi*
Hakhâmaniš A-ha-ma-ni-iš	Achæmenes	Persian	Founder of Hakhâmanišiya Clan
Harpalos	Harpalus	Makedonian	Kingsman of Alexander III Son of Machatas Appointed the Keeper of the Royal Funds by Alexander III
Hektor	Hector	Trojan	*From Iliad by Homer* Son of King Priamos and Hekuba Brother of Paris Husband of Andromache Trojan Hero, killed by Achilleos
Helene	Helen	Spartan	*From Iliad by Homer* Daughter of Zeus and Leda Wife of Menelaos Her abduction by Paris caused the Trojan Wars
Hephæstion Hephaistion		Makedonian-Hellene	Kingsman and intimate friend of Alexander III Son of Amyntor Promoted to Second-in-Command to Alexander III Husband of Dripeyti
Herakles	Herakles	Makedonian-Persian	Son of Alexander III and Barsine
Herodotos	Herodotus	Karian	Herodotos of Halikarnassos Historian Wrote *Histories*

Hieronymos	Hieronymus	Kardian	Kinsman of Eumenes Historian of the Successors of Alexander III
Hukhšaqra Oxathres		Persian	Royal Son Son of Astâna and Sisygambis Younger brother of Third Dâriuš Father of Amastris Kingsman of Alexander III
Iolaos	Iolaus Iollas	Makedonian	Kingsman of Alexander III Son of Antipatros Brother of Kassandros, Eurydike, Nikaia, and Phila Cup-bearer of Alexander III
Itâna	Itanes	Bakhtrian-Persian	Lastborn son of Uxsiyartâ and Parmys Brother of Utâna and Oštana Cousin of Rošanak
Kallisthenes	Callisthenes	Hellene Olynthes	Nephew of Aristoteles Philosopher and historian Wrote *Deeds of Alexander*
Kalyana Kalanos	Calanos	Indian	Brahman and Philosopher Tutor of Rošanak Followed Alexander III from India to Susa
Kassandros	Cassandros Cassander	Makedonian	Son of Antipatros Brother of Iolaos, Eurydike, Nikaia, and Phila Husband of Thessalonike Father of Philippos, Antipatros and Alexandros
Kayvârtâ		Indian	Chief Eunuch of Quarters of Imperial Women in the Palace of Pâtaliputrâ
Khabbabash		Egyptian	Rebelled against Third Dâriuš
Kidinnu	Ki-di-nu Cidenas	Babylonian	Chief Watcher of Heavens Chief Astrologer
Kî-Nabû		Babylonian	Chief Scribe of Celestial Omens Watcher of Heavens Astrologer Diviner Pupil of Kinninu
Kleitos "The Black"	Kleitos Melas Cleitus	Macedonian	Kingsman of Alexander III Son of Dropidas Brother of Lanike Killed by Alexander III in Bakhtria
Kleopatra	Cleopatra	Makedonian-Molossian	Daughter of Philip II and Olympias Sister of Alexander III Half-sister of Thessalonike and Arrhidaios Wife of Alexandros I of Epiros Mother of Neoptolemos and Kadmeia

Kleopatra Eurydike		Makedonian	Last wife of Philip II Niece of Attalos Mother of Europa Killed by Olympias
Koinos	Coenus	Makedonian	Kingsman of Alexander III Son of Polemokrates Advocated returning back to Makedonia when the Makedonian army mutinied in India
Krateros	Craterus	Makedonian	Kingsman of Alexander III Son of Alexandros of Orestis Husband of Amastris Husband of Phila Father of Krateros
Kritoboulos	Critobulus	Island of Kos	Physician Treated Alexander III's arrow wound in India
Ktesias	Ctesias	Hellene	Ktesias of Knidos Physician of Second Artakhšaçâ Wrote *Persika* and *Indika*
Kudurru		Babylonian	Astrologer Diviner Pupil of Kinninu
Kuruš Ku-raš Kuros "The Younger"	Cyrus	Persian	Royal Son Son of Second Dariuš and Purušâtu Brother of Second Artakhšaçâ
Leonnatos	Lenonnatos	Makedonian	Kingsman of Alexander III Son of Anteas Member of Lynkestian Royal House
Lysimachos	Lysimachus	Thessalian	Kingsman of Alexander III Son of Agathokles Husband of Nikaia Husband of Amastris Husband of Arsinoë II Assumed the title of king in 305 BCE
Lysippos	Lysippus	Hellene	Royal court sculptor of Alexander III
Madumîtu		Median	Daughter of Âtrupâta Wife of Perdikkas
Medeios	Medeius Medius	Thessalian	Kingsman of Alexander III Son of Oxythemis of Larissa
Megasthenes		Hellene	Ambassador of Seleukos Sent to the Imperial Court of Chandrâguptâ Wrote *Indika*
Meleagros	Meleager	Epirote	Kingsman of Alexander III Son of Neoptolemos Caused the breakup of the Makedonian army after the death of Alexander III

Memnon		Rhodian	Brother of Mentor Second husband of Barsine Son-in-law of Artâvazda Appointed the Commander of the mercenary army in Asia Minor by Third Dâriuš
Menelaos	Menelaus	Spartan	*From Iliad by Homer* King of Sparta Husband of Helene
Nabû'kudra'cara Nabû-Kudurrî-Ûşur Nebuchadrezzar	Nabû-Kudurru-Ûşur Nebuchadnezzar	Babylonian	Babylonian King The Second Nabu'kudra'cara, 604-562 BCE Husband of Amytiš for whom he built the Hanging Gardens in Babylon
Nabû-Na'id	Nabonidus Nabunaita Nabonides	Babylonian	Last Babylonian King, 556-539 BCE Overthrown by Second Kuruš
Nakhthoreb	Nectanebo	Egyptian	Last Egyptian Ruler of the 30th Dynasty Overthrown by Third Artakhšaçâ in 343 BCE
Nearchos	Nearchus	Kretan	Kingsman of Alexander III Son of Androtimos Admiral of the Makedonian fleet Husband of the daughter of Barsine Wrote about the naval expedition
Nikaia			Daughter of Antipatros Sister of Kassandros, Iolaos, Eurydike, and Phila Wife of Lysimachos Mother of Agthocles, Euridike and Arsionë
Nimâ Neema		Persian	Royal Son Son of Parânak Brother of Dârâ Grandson of Fifth Artakhšaçâ and Farânak Nephew of Rošanak
Olympias	Polyxena Myrtale Stratonike	Molossian	Queen Daughter of Neoptolemos Sister of Alexandros I of Epiros Wife of Philip II Mother of Alexander III and Kleopatra Adoptive mother of Thessalonike Grandmother of Alexander IV
Onesikritos	Onesicritus	Hellene	Kingsman of Alexander III Son of Philiskos Wrote *Education of Alexander*

Oštana	Hystanes Uštanu	Bakhtrian- Persian	Middleborn son of Uxsiyârta and Parmys Brother of Utâna and Itâna Cousin of Rošanak Kingsman of Alexander III and Perdikkas
Parânak		Persian- Bakhtrian	Royal Daughter Older Daughter of Fifth Artakhšaçâ and Farânak Sister of Rošanak Mother of Dârâ and Nimâ
Paris	Alexander	Trojan	*From Iliad by Homer* Son of King Priamos and Hekuba Brother of Hektor Abducted Helene and caused the Trojan Wars
Parmenion	Parmenio	Makedonian	Kingsman of Philip II and Alexander III Son of Philotas Father of Philotas, Nikanor and Hektor Beheaded in Hagmâtâna by the order of Alexander III
Parvataka Poros	Puru	Indian	Rajah of Paurava Left in command of his satrapy by Alexander III and his rule was expanded to neighboring lands
Patroklos	Patroclos	Hellene	*From Iliad by Homer* Intimate friend of Achilleos
Peithon		Makedonian	Kingsman of Alexander III Son of Krateros Supporter of Perdikkas
Perdikkas	Perdiccas	Makedonian	Kingsman of Alexander III Son of Orontes of Orestis Member of the Orestis Royal House Brother of Alketas and Atalanta Second-in-Command after the death of Hephæstion Regent for Philip III and Alexander IV
Peukestas	Peucestas Peukestes Peucestes	Makedonian	Kingsman of Alexander III Son of Alexander of Mieza Learned Persian language and was given the command of the Citadel at Pârsâ by Alexander III
Phila			Daughter of Antipatros Sister of Kassandros, Iolaos, Eurydike, and Nikaia Wife of Krateos Mother of Kratros Wife of Demetrios Mother of Antigonos and Stratonike

Philip II	Philippos Philippus Pi-lip-su	Makedonian	King of Makedon The Second Philip, 360-336 BCE Son of Amyntas III Husband of Philine Father of Arrhidaios Husband of Nikesipolis Father of Thessalonike Husband of Olympias Father of Alexander III and Kleopatra Husband of Eurydike Kleopatra Father of Europa
Philotas		Makedonian	Kingsman of Alexander III Son of Parmenion Commander of the Companion Horse Tortured and killed in Bakhtria by the order of Alexander III
Polydoros	Polydorus	Hellene	Physician of Fifth Artakhšaçâ and his family
Polyperchon	Polypercon	Makedonian	Kingsman of Alexander III Son of Simmias Second-in-Command of Krateros Appointed Regent for Philip III and Alexander IV by Antipatros
Praxiteles		Athenian	Son of Kephisodotos Sculptor in marble and bronze, 375-350 BCE Sculpted the first nude Aphrodite
Priamos		Trojan	*From Iliad by Homer* Trojan King Husband of Hekuba Father of Hektor and Paris
Ptolemaios	Ptolemaeus Ptolemy	Makedonian	Kingsman of Alexander III Son of Lagos Assumed the title of King in 305 BCE Wrote *History of Alexander*
Purušâtu Pur-ru-uš-iš	Parysatis	Persian	Royal Woman Wife of Second Dâriuš Mother of Second Artakhšaçâ and the Younger Kuruš
Rošanak Roxana Rauxšanâ	Roxane Rhoxane Rauxšnâ Rošan	Persian-Bakhtrian	Royal Daughter Younger daughter of Fifth Artakhšaçâ and Farânak Sister of Parânak Aunt of Dârâ and Nîma Cousin of Utâna, Oštana and Itâna First wife of Alexander III Mother of Forth Alexander Third wife of Chandrâguptâ
Šarru-kîn	Sargon II	Assyrian	Assyrian King The Second Sargon, 721-705 BCE

Seleukos Si-lu-ku Nikator	Seleucus	Makedonian	Kingsman of Alexander III Son of Antiochos and Laodike Husband of Apâma Father of Antiochos, Apâma, and Laodike Husband of Stratonike Assumed the title of king in 305 BCE
Semiramis	Semmuramat	Assyrian	Assyrian Queen, 823-811 BCE
Setâreh	Stateira	Persian	Royal Woman Niece of Sisygambis Wife of Third Dâriuš Mother of Setâreh, Dripeyti and Tiršata
Setâreh	Stateira	Persian	Royal Daughter Older daughter of Third Dâriuš and Setâreh Sister of Dripeyti and Tiršata Half-sister of Ariâbarzâna Granddaughter of Sisygambis Cousin of Rošanak Second wife of Alexander III
Sisygambis	Sisyngambris	Persian	Royal Woman Aunt of Setâreh Wife of Astâna Mother of Third Dâriuš Grandmother of Setâreh, Dripeyti and Tiršata Grandmother of Ariâbarzâna Grandmother of Rošanak Adoptive mother of Alexander III
Spitâmaneh Spitamenes		Bakhtrian-Persian	Noble of the Seven Persian Families Father of Apâma Supporter of Fifth Artakhšaçâ
Thaïs		Athenian	Mistress of Ptolemaios Started the fire that burned Pârsâ during a drunken feast
Thalestris		Scythian	Queen of the Amazons
Themistokles	Themistocles	Athenian	General, 524-459 BCE Created Athens' naval power Exiled in 471 BCE and ended up in the royal court of First Artakhšaçâ
Thessalonike	Thessalonice	Makedonian-Thessalian	Daughter of Philip II and Nikesipolis of Pheræ Half-sister of Alexander III and Kleopatra and Philip III Wife of Kassandros Mother of Philippos, Antipatros and Alexandros

Tiršata		Persian	Crown Prince Son of Third Dâriuš and Setâreh Brother of Dripeyti and Setâreh Half-brother of Ariâbarzâna Grandson of Sisygambis Cousin of Rošanak
Thukrâ	Øukrâ Thukhrâ	Persian	Head cook of Baktra Palace
Utâna	Otana Huttâna Otanes	Bakhtrian-Persian	Firstborn son of Uxsiyartâ and Parmys Brother of Oštana and Itâna Cousin of Rošanak
Uxsiyartâ	Oxyartes	Bakhtrian-Persian	Noble Brother of Farânak Brother-in-law of Fifth Artakhšaçâ Husband of Parmys Father of Utâna, Oštana and Itâna Uncle of Parânak and Rošanak Appointed the Satrap of Gandâra by Alexander III
Xenophon		Athenian	Son of Gryllos, 428-354 BCE Served in the Hellene mercenary army of the Younger Kuruš Wrote *Anabasis*

PLACES
AVASTÂYA

PLACE	DESCRIPTION
3Paradayadâ Triparadeisos	3 joined royal Persian gardens and hunting grounds in Assyria
Abode of Snow Himalâya	Himalaya mountain range in northern India
Across-the-River Aøurâ Athura	Persian Satrapy of Assyria Land of the god Aššur in the Upper Tigris River
Aigai Aegæ	Capital of Makedonia before Pella
Alexandria Al Iskandariyeh	City of Alexandria in Egypt founded by Alexander III
Amphipolis	Makedonian seaport Old Thrakian town of Ennea Hodoi on the east bank of the Strymon River
Arabâya	Saudi Arabia
Arba-ilu Arbela	City of Assyrians, between tributaries of Tigris River, near the site of the Battle of Gau Gamela
Armina	Persian Satrapy of Armenia
Aryânâ Persia	Land of the Âryâs Land of the Nobles Iran
Aspâdâna Gabiene	City in the heartland of Persia, near the site of Battle of Gabiene City of Esfahan
Athenai	City-state of Athens
Attika	Territory of Athens
Bâb-il Bâb-ilim Bâb-ilani Bâb-ili Bâb-ilu Bâbiru Babylon Bêl-êpuš	Gate of God, Gate of Gods Capital of Babylonian Monarchy One of the five Royal Cities of the Persian Empire Site of the Hanging Gardens
Bâbiruš	Persian Satrapy of Babylon Land between Euphrates and Tigris Rivers Babylonia
Bagistâna Bîsutûn	Place of Gods Site of the rock-cut inscription of First Dâriuš in Persian Satrapy of Media
Bakhtriš Bakhtria Bactria	Persian Satrapy of Baktria Land of a Thousand Cities
Baktra	Capital of Satrapy of Baktria, located on the banks of River Bakhtruš

Bitter Sea	The Aegean
Black Eagle Gau Gamela Gaugamela	Site of the Battle of Gau Gamela in Assyria near the City of Arbela
Borsippa	City of Babylonians southwest of Babylon
Chæronea	Site of the Battle of Chæronea in Thebes
City of Ammon	City at the easternmost mouth of the Nile River in Lower Egypt, forming a natural barrier into Egypt Pelusion, Pelusium
Çûšâ Susa Ša-ša-an Shush	Royal City of the Elamites One of the five Royal Cities of the Persian Empire
Diglat Tigrâ Tigris	Tigris River
Dimašqa Damaskos Damascos	City in Babylonia City of Dimashq
Dodona	Site of the small palace of Molossian Kings in Epiros Site of the oldest Hellene Oracle
Epiros Epirus	Kingdom bordering Makedonia
Erekhtheum	Temple of Erekhtheos on the Acropolis in Athens
Fort of Camels	Town in Lower Egypt close to Nile River
Fortress of Âriâmazda Rock of Ariamazes	Fortress in the Persian Satrapy of Sogdiana
Fortress of Sisimithrâ Rock of Sisimitres	Fortress in the Persian Satrapy of Sogdiana
Fortress of Sughud Rock of Sughud Rock of Sogdiana	Fortress in the Persian Satrapy of Sogdiana
Gandâra Gandhara Paropamisadai	Persian Satrapy of Paropamisadai
Gaza	City in the Persian Satrapy of Phoenicia between Babylon and Egypt
Gordium	City between the Greater and Lesser Phrygia
Granikos	Site of the Battle of Granikos
Hagmâtâna Ecbatana Hegmataneh	Royal City of the Medes One of the five Royal Cities of the Persian Empire Summer residence of the Great Kings Meeting place City of Hamedan
Halikarnassos Halicarnassus	Capital of the Persian Satrapy of Karia

Harahuvatîš Arachosia	Persian Satrapy of Arachosia
Harriwa Areia	Persian Satrapy of Areia
Hellespont	The narrow strait between Asia and Europe
Hindu Kush	Mountain range in Central Asia
Hinduš Hind Hi^{n}duš Hi^{n}d	India Land of Seven Rivers
^{H}Ûvjiya Opis Û-pe-e	City of Elamites on Tigris River
Illyria	Kingdom bordering Makedonia
Ipsos	Site of Battle of Ipsos in the Persian Satrapy of Phrygia
Iš-ku-ud-ra Iš-ku-du-ru Skudra	Makedonia and Thrake
Issos Issus	Site of the Battle of Issos
Iteru Pirâva Great River	Nile River in Egypt
Karmâna Karmania	Persian Satrapy of Karmania City of Kerman
Katpatuka Kappadokia	Persian Satrapy of Kappadokia
Kelainai Celanæ Celainai	Capital of the Persian Satrapy of Phrygia
Kissuwadna Kilikia	Persian Satrapy of Kilikia Mountainous region in the Southern Asia Minor
Krete	Island in the Middle Sea Crete
Kuniša Kunaxa Cunaxa	Site of the Battle of Kuniša
Kunuš-kadru	The Processional Street in Babylon
Kûša	Ethiopia
Labnâna	Lebanon
Lamia	City in Thessalia, site of the Lamian War between the Athenians and Makedonians
Land of Seven Rivers	India
Land of the Calm Mornings	Korea

Land of the Phoenix and the Dragon	China
Libil'hegalla	'May it bring prosperity' Water canal from Euphrates River to irrigate gardens and orchards in the City of Babylon
Lower Sea	Arabian Sea
Mâda Media	Persian Satrapy of Media
Maka Makran Desert of Death	Persian Satrapy of Gedrosia
Makedonia Uplands	Makedon, Makedonian, Macedonia
Mâlavâ	Town of the Mâlavâ Tribe close to River Sindhu
Marakanda	Samarkand, Samargand City on the Silk Road in the Persian Satrapy of Sogdiana
Men-nofer Memphis	Capital of Lower Egypt
Middle Sea	Mediterranean Sea
Miletos	Port City in the Persian Satrapy of Lydia
Mudrâya Muşru Two Lands Aigyptos	Egypt
Nippur	City of Sumerians
Nisâya	Mountainous region close to Ecbatana renown for their horses
Nonakris	District of Arkadia where allegedly poison was harvested for killing Alexander III
Øara	Village in the Persian Satrapy of Parthia where Third Dâriuš was killed
Ocean	Mythical body of water surrounding the world
Oracle of Ammon	Oracle in the Oasis of Siwah in the desert
Parøawa Parøava Parthia	Persian Satrapy of Parthia
Pârsâ Par-ri-sa-a-a Persepolis Persis	City of the Persians One of the five Royal Cities of the Persian Empire The religious and ceremonial capital of the Persian Great Kings that was burned by Alexander III, and never rebuilt
Pârsâkata Pârsâgada Pasargadæ Pasargad	First Royal City of the Persian Empire City of the Pasargadæ Dwelling of the Persians Site of the Royal Tomb of Second Kuruš
Parthenon	Temple of Athena on the highest part of the Acropolis in Athens
Pâtaliputrâ	Capital of the Mauryan Empire near the confluence of the Ganges and Sona Rivers

Pella	Capital of Makedonia and largest Makedonian city located near the Lydias River
Peloponnesus	Island of Pelops, connected to mainland Hellas by the Isthmus of Korinth
Pergamos Pergamon	City in the Persian Satrapy of Lydia
Phrygia	Persian Satrapy in Asia Minor
Pisidia	A mountainous region in Southern Asia Minor
Purattu Ufrâtû Euphrates	Euphrates River
Pydna	Small town in Makedonia close to the Middle Sea
Qin	China
River Bakhtruš	Amu Darya Oxus River Longest river in Central Asia
River Ganga	Ganges River in India
River Sindhu Indus	Indus River in India
River Strymon	River surrounding Amphipolis on three sides
River Vipâš Hyphasis	River Beas in India
River Vitastâ Hydaspes	River in India Jhelum River, Jihlam River
River Yakhša Arta	Great Pearly River, River in Central Asia Jaxartes River Sur Darya
Rock of Arnos Fortress of Âvarana	Fortress in the Persian Satrapy of Paropamisadai Sanctuary of the Heavens
Royal Road	Network of roads connecting all the Royal Cities and royal residences of the Persian Empire, running from Susa to Sardis, secured by rest houses and guard posts
Sakâ	Northern lands beyond the Lands of the Persian Empire
Sea of Axšaina	Sea of Turquoise Black Sea
Sea of Islands	Aral Sea
Sea of Øukhrâ	Red Sea Persian Gulf
Sea of Varkâna	Sea of Wolves Kaspian Sea
Seleukia-in-Tigris	Capital of Seleukos on the left bank of Tigris River built on the site of Opis in Babylonia
Sind Indus Valley	Lands of River Sindhu
Sippar	City of Sumerians City of Akkadians

Siwah Desert	Site of the Oracle of Ammon in Egypt
Sparda Sardeis Sardis Lydia	Persian Satrapy of Lydia Capital of the Persian Satrapy of Lydia
Sparta	City in Lacedæmon
Sughud Sughuda Sogdiana	Persian Satrapy of Sogdiana
Takšiçila Taxila	Capital of the Persian Satrapy of Paropamisadai
Ta-Mehu	Lower Egypt
Tarsus	Capital of the Persian Satrapy of Kilikia
Ta-Shemau	Upper Egypt
Thebai Thebes	Chief city of Boeotians in Hellas
Thermopylæ	Narrow pass between the Uplands of Makedonia and Mainland of Hellas
Thessalia	Thessaly Vassal kingdom of Makedonia renowned for their cavalry
Thrake	Kingdom bordering Makedonia
Troia Troy	City of Ilion, site of the Trojan War
Tyre Ṣurru	Rock Coastal city of Phoenicians renowned for the Tyrian purple dye
Ulai Choaspes	River Choaspes in Elam
Uplands	Makedonia
Upper Sea	Red Sea
Uruk.Ki	City in Babylon Home of Babylonian Hero and King, Gilgâmeš
Urušalim	Jerusalem
Ûvja Ûwja	City of Elamites on Tigris River
Uwarazmiy Chorasmia	Persian Satrapy of Chorasmia
Varkâna Hyrkania	Land of Wolves Lands bordering the Caspian Sea
Yaunâ Hellas	Greece

PERSIANS

The HAKHÂMANIŠIYA
559 – 329

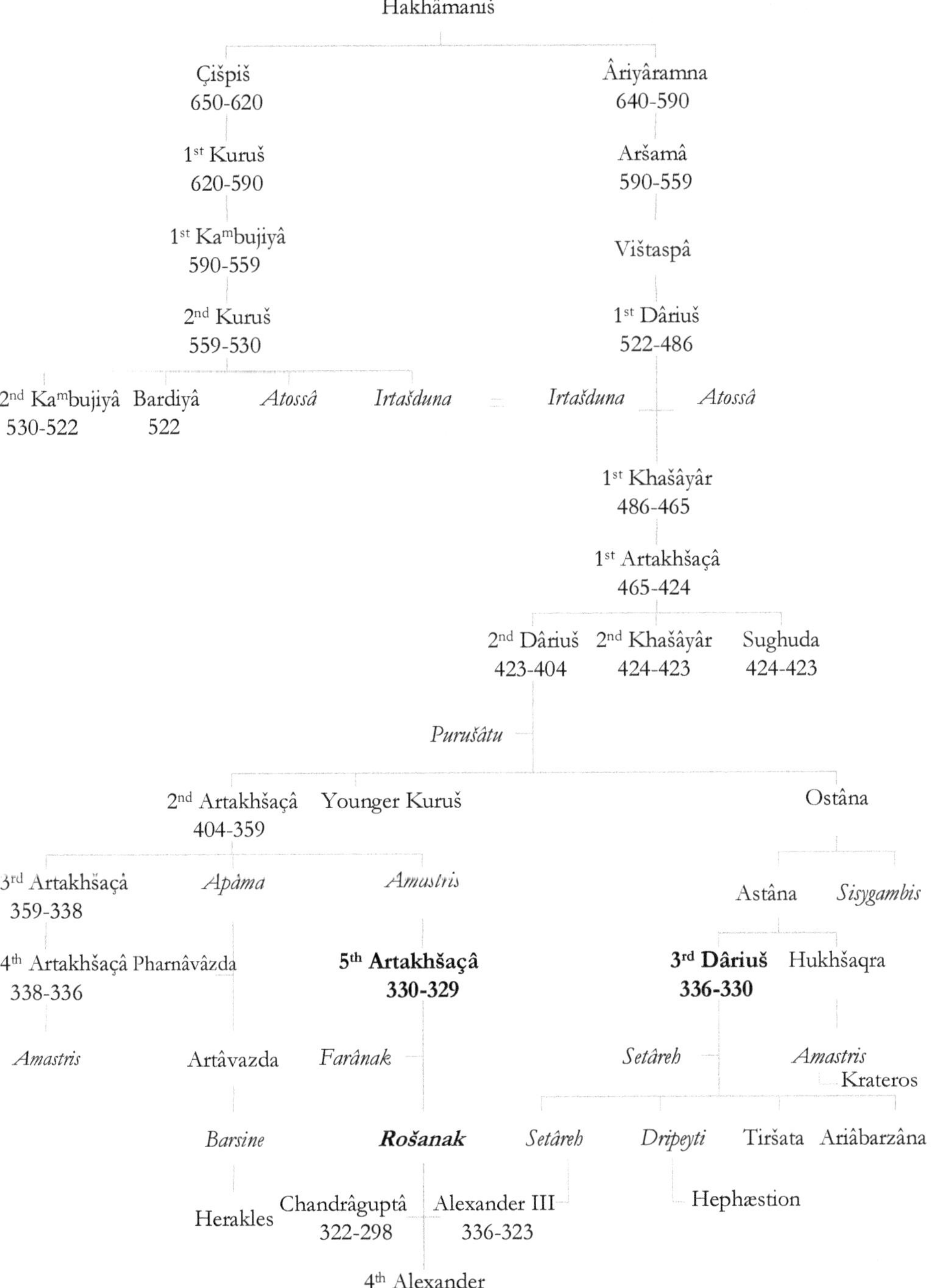

UPLANDERS

The ARGEADS
497 – 311

Amyntas I

Alexander I
498-454

Perdikkas II
454-413

Amyntas

Menelaos

Archelaos
413-399

Aeropaos
398-395

Arrhidaios

Amyntas II
395-394

Orestes
399-398

Amyntas II
393-392

Pausanias
394-393

Amyntas III
393-370

Ptolemaios
367-365

Alexander II
370-367

Perdikkas III
365-360

Philip II
360-336

Nikesipolis

Olympias

Philinna

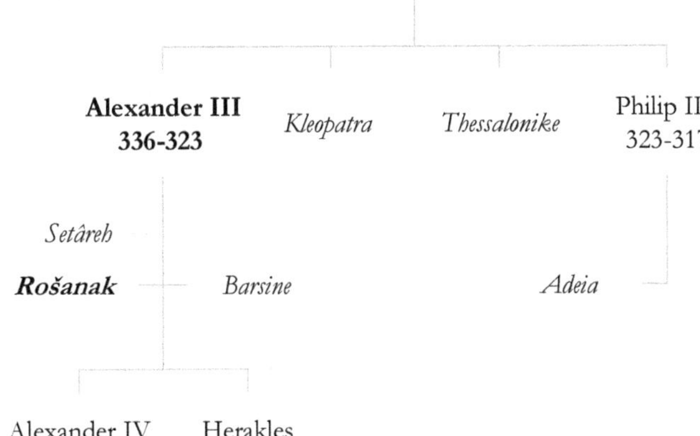

4

𒐏

PEACOCKS

THE MAURYANS
322 – 185

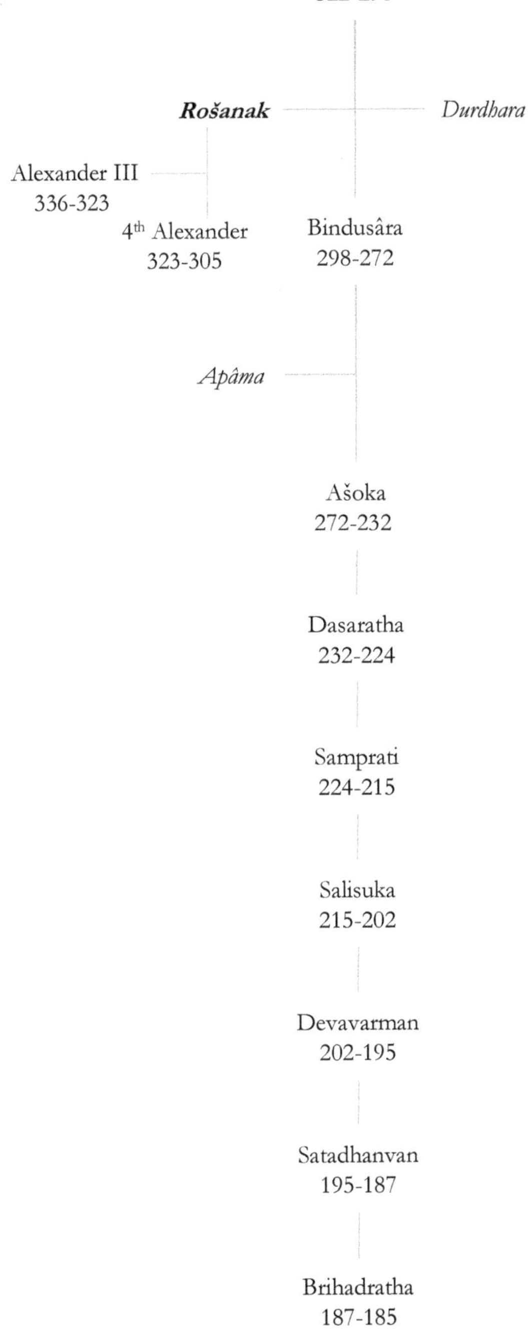

TIME LINE

HISTORICAL TIMELINE
Before Common Era

DATE	SIGNIFICANT EVENTS
336	Philip II of Makedon attacks the Persian Empire by sending an advanced Makedonian army across Hellespont into Asia Minor, under the command of Parmenion and Attalos. Artašatu ascends to the throne of the Persian Empire as Third Dâriuš of Hakhâmanišiya, after the death of Fourth Artakhšaçâ. Alexander, son of Philip II, secretly offers himself to Pixodaros, Satrap of Kardia, one of the western satrapies of the Persian Empire, for a marriage alliance with his daughter, instead of his half-brother, Arrhidaios. His advisors are exiled by Philip, when he finds out. Philip is murdered by Pausanias, a bodyguard, at Aigai during the wedding feast of his daughter Kleopatra to her uncle, Alexandros I of Epiros. Alexander becomes the King of Makedon as Alexander III, succeeding his father, and is confirmed as the leader of the League of Korinth, uniting the Hellenes against the Persians. Khabbabash revolts against Dâriuš and declares himself Pharaoh of Upper Egypt.
335	Dâriuš reasserts Persian rule over Egypt. Alexander crushes revolts and uprisings against his rule in Thrake and Illyria. Alexander crushes revolt and destroys the city of Thebes. Olympias, Mother of Alexander, murders Eurydike Kleopatra, the last wife of Philip, and her infant daughter, Europa. Alexander orders the death of Attalos, uncle of Eurydike Kleopatra. Aristotle returns to Athens from Makedonia and opens a school of philosophy.
334	Alexander crosses into Asia with the Makedonian Army. Alexander is victorious at the Battle of Granikos against the armies of western satraps of the Persian Empire. Arsites, the Persian Satrap of Phrygia, commits suicide after the defeat at Granikos. Dâriuš appoints Memnon of Rhodes as the commander of the western satrapal armies fighting the Makedonian invasion. Mithrâna, the Satrap of Lydia, betrays Dâriuš and surrenders Sardis to Alexander. Alexander disbands his fleet. Alexander sieges and captures Miletos. Alexander sieges Halikarnassos. The City of Kardia surrenders to Alexander. Alexander captures Lykia, Pamphylia and Phrygia. Alexander appoints the One-eyed Antigonos as the Satrap of Phrygia. Memnon initiates a naval campaign against Alexander.
333	Memnon dies of illness. Alexander becomes ill at Tarsus after bathing in River Kydnos. Alexander unravels the Gordian Knot. Alexander is victorious at the Battle of Issos and captures the Royal Family of Dâriuš. Parmenion captures Damascos along with the wives and children of the Persian Nobles, including the noble women and children of Artâvazda.
332	Dâriuš offers to ransom his Royal Family. Alexander refuses to ransom the Royal Family of Dâriuš and keeps them captive. Alexander sieges Tyre. Tyre falls after seven months. Alexander sieges Gaza and executes Batis, the Arab Governor of Gaza. Persian fleet collapses. Alexander enters Egypt.

331 Mazakes, the Satrap of Egypt, surrenders Egypt to Alexander.
Alexander becomes the Pharaoh of Egypt and visits the Oracle of Ammon in Siwah Desert.
City of Alexandria in founded by Alexander in Egypt.
Dâriuš moves the Persian Royal Army from Babylon to Gau Gamela.
Moon eclipses.
Setâreh, wife of Dâriuš, dies at childbirth, before the Battle of Gau Gamela.
Alexander is victorious in the Battle of Gau Gamela and declares himself the Lord of Asia.
Dâriuš retreats to Ecbatana.
Mazdâyâ, the Satrap of Babylon, surrenders Babylon to Alexander.
Bagophanes, the Treasurer of Babylon, surrenders the Royal Treasury to Alexander.
50,000 talents of gold fall into the hands of Alexander.
Aubulites, the Babylonian Satrap of Susa, surrenders Susa to Alexander. 40,000 talents of gold fall into the hands of Alexander.
Agis III, King of Sparta, fights against the Makedonians and is defeated and killed by Antipatros in the Battle of Megalopolis.
Alexandros I of Epiros, uncle-husband of Kleopatra, is killed, campaigning in Italy.
Olympias leaves Makedonia for Epiros.
Alexander campaigns against the mountain tribe of Uxians.
Alexander captures the Persian Gates.

330 Tiridâta, the Treasurer of Persepolis, surrenders the Royal Treasury to Alexander.
120,000 talents of gold and silver fall into the hands of Alexander.
The Army of Alexander sacks Persepolis.
Gubarû, Governor of Pasargadæ, surrenders the Royal Treasury of 6,000 talents to Alexander.
Alexander burns Persepolis during a drunken feast four months later.
Dâriuš retreats further toward Baktria.
Alexander reaches Ecbatana in pursuit of Dâriuš, dismisses the Hellene allies and leaves Parmenion and Harpalos behind in Ecbatana.
Dâriuš is executed by the Persian Nobles in Parthia. His body is sent back to Susa by Alexander for royal burial.
Bayasa, the cousin of Dâriuš and the Satrap of Baktria and Sogdiana declares himself the Great King and assumes the throne name of Fifth Artakhšaçâ.
Philotas, son of Parmenion, is tortured and killed by stoning after the Assembly of the Makedonians finds him guilty of plotting against Alexander.
Parmenion is beheaded in Ecbatana by the order of Alexander.
Famine rages in Greece.

329 Alexander captures Samarkand, Capital of Sogdiana.
Artakhšaçâ is captured and executed by the order of Alexander.
Satibarzaneh, the Satrap of Areia, revolts against Alexander and is captured and executed.
Spitâmaneh revolts against Alexander in Baktria and Sogdiana.

328 Alexander captures Rock of Ariamazes.
2,500 Hellene Mercenaries are massacred by Spitâmaneh.
Kleitos, "the Black", is killed by Alexander during a drunken feast in Baktria.

327 Spitâmaneh is betrayed and killed by the Scythian tribes and his head is sent to Alexander.
Alexander captures the Rock of Sogdiana.
Alexander marries Rošanak.
Alexander unsuccessfully attempts to introduce proskynesis, the protocol of the Persian Royal Court, in his court.
Alexander captures the Rock of Sisimitres.
Alexander invades the Indus Valley.
Seven royal boys, sons of Makedonian nobility, are found guilty of plotting the murder of Alexander by the Makedonian Assembly and are stoned to death by the army.
Kallisthenes is accused of encouraging the royal boys to plot against Alexander and is eventually killed.
First son of Alexander and Rošanak dies in India shortly after birth.

326 Alexander splits the Makedonian Army. Hephæstion and Perdikkas command half of the Army to Gandhara through the flatlands, while Alexander campaigns in Swat Valley with the rest of the Makedonian Army.
Alexander enters the City of Taxiles, the capital of Gandhara, and is received by Rajah Âmbhi.
Alexander is victorious in the Battle of Hydaspes in India, facing Rajah Parvataka and 200 fighting elephants.
Alexander and Chandrâguptâ meet. Alexander orders Chandrâguptâ to be detained.
The Makedonian Army mutinies at the River Hyphasis in India and refuses to go further inland, forcing Alexander to return to Persia.
Koinos who publicly supports the action of the Makedonian Army dies within days.
Alexander appoints Nearchos as admiral of his fleet and starts sailing down the River Sindhu toward the Ocean.
Alexander receives a near fatal arrow wound during the siege and attack on the Mâlavâ Indian Tribe.
The Makedonian Army massacres the Mâlavâ Tribe.
Nearchos guides the Makedonian fleet down the River Indus.

325 Hellene mercenaries and unfit Makedonians left behind in the Satrapy of Baktria revolt against Alexander.
Alexander divides his army again. Krateros is sent back to the Satrapy of Karmania with half of the army. The rest of the Makedonian Army moves down the River Indus with Alexander.
Alexander marches through the Gedrosian Desert and reaches Karmania with heavy casualties.
Nearchos guides the Makedonian fleet through the Persian Gulf to Babylon.
Nearchos and the fleet arrive in Karmania.
Krateros arrives in Karmania, bringing a handful of Persian rebels for execution.
Harpalos steals 5,000 gold talents from the Royal Treasury of Babylon and flees to Athens.
Alexander orders the execution of the Persian and Makedonian satraps who have revolted against his rule during his campaigning in India.
Hukhšaqra, brother of Dâriuš, disappears.

324 Alexander and his men marry ninety-one Persian royal and noble women in Susa. Alexander marries Setâreh and Hephæstion marries Dripeyti, the Royal Daughters of Dâriuš. Krateros marries Amastris, the Royal Daughter of Hukhšaqra, brother of Dâriuš.
30,000 Baktrian and Sogdian Youth trained by the Makedonians arrive in Susa and join the Armies of Alexander.
The Makedonian Army mutinies at Opis, as the Makedonians who are deemed old and unfit are dismissed by Alexander to return to Makedonia. They demand that all the Makedonian Army be dismissed.
Alexander dismisses the entire Makedonian Army and replaces them with the Persians.
The Makedonian Army asks for forgiveness.
Alexander forgives the Makedonian Army and hosts the Feast of Harmony in Opis.
10,000 Makedonian infantry and 1,500 Makedonian cavalry unfit for military service are sent home with Krateros, with Polyperchon as Second-in-Command after the Feast of Harmony, with orders for Krateros to replace Antipatros as the Regent of Makedonia.
The young son of Dâriuš disappears.
Alexander issues the Exiles Decree and orders the Hellene city-states to allow the return of the exiled Hellenes.
Hephæstion, Alexander's Second-in-Command, dies in Ecbatana from heavy drinking.
Perdikkas becomes the Second-in-Command of Alexander.
Kleopatra leaves Epiros for Makedonia.
Harpalos is killed in Crete.
India revolts against Alexander and the Makedonians are either executed or repelled from India.

323 Alexander campaigns against the mountain tribe of Kossæan, on the way to Babylon.
Perdikkas brings the main Makedonian Army and Hephæstion's bones from Ecbatana to Babylon.
Kassandros, son of Antipatros, arrives in Babylon to negotiate with Alexander on behalf of Antipatros.
Alexander dies at Babylon, on June 10th, a month short of his 33rd birthday.
Royal Daughters of Dâriuš are murdered.
Sisygambis, mother of Dâriuš, dies in Susa, a week after the death of Alexander.
The Makedonian cavalry and infantry break up after Alexander's death, unable to agree on a successor to lead the army. Makedonians agree to wait for the birth of Alexander's unborn child, as suggested by Perdikkas.
The First Settlement at Babylon names Arrhidaios, half-brother of Alexander, King.
Perdikkas becomes the guardian for Arrhidaios, who becomes the king as Philip III.
Alexander's Generals take satrapal commands.
Ptolemaios is appointed the Satrap of Egypt in the First Settlement at Babylon.
Perdikkas purifies the Makedonian Army after the army is reunited.
Alexander IV is born to Rošanak two months after the death of Alexander III.
Majority of the forced marriages at Susa are dissolved. Seleukos remains married to Apâma.
Kleopatra offers to marry Leonnatos.
Lamian War between the Athenians and Makedonia breaks out immediately after the death of Alexander is confirmed.
Athenians occupy the pass at Thermopylæ against the Makedonians.
Antipatros is defeated in Thessaly and is sieged in Lamia.
Hellene mercenaries in Baktria revolt again.
Perdikkas sends Peithon to Baktria to deal with the rebellious Hellenes.

322 Infant Alexander IV becomes Joint-King along with Philip III, with Perdikkas becoming the Regent for the Two Kings.
Peithon crushes the rebellion in Baktria and kills all the rebellious Hellenes.
Perdikkas invades Kappadokia and executes Âriyârta, the Persian Satrap, and establishes Eumenes as the new satrap.
Perdikkas invades Armania.
Antigonos betrays Perdikkas and flees to Pella and joins Antipatros.
Aristotle is charged with impiety, leaves Athens and dies at Chalkis, in Euboea.
Leonnatos reaches Lamia and dies raising the Siege of Lamia.
Krateros returns to Makedonia and joins forces with Antipatros.
Antipatros and Krateros are victorious in the Battle of Krannon against Athenians.
Athens is garrisoned by the Makedonians.
Democracy is abolished in Athens.
Demosthenes, the Athenian Orator, commits suicide to avoid falling into the hands of Antipatros.
Ptolemaios kills Kleomenes, the Treasurer of Egypt.
Aiakides, nephew of Olympias, becomes the King of Epiros.
Eumenes takes a marriage proposal from Perdikkas to Kleopatra. Kleopatra accepts and leaves for Sardis.
Chandrâguptâ Mauryan becomes Emperor in India, uniting the northern India and Indus Valley, creating the first Indian Empire.

321 Krateros marries Phila, daughter of Antipatros.
Perdikkas invades Pisidia.
Kleopatra and Nikaia arrive in Sardis.
Kynnane, daughter of Philip II, and her daughter, Adeia, cross into Asia, claiming Adeia is betrothed to Philip III. Alketas, brother of Perdikkas, kills Kynnane in front of the Makedonian Army. The Makedonian troops are outraged and demand that the wedding take place. Philip III marries Adeia.
Antigonos returns to Asia Minor.
Antipatros and Ptolemaios form an Alliance.
Ptolemaios marries Eurydike, daughter of Antipatros.

320 The sarcophagus of Alexander on its way to Makedon for burial is diverted and taken to Egypt by Ptolemaios.
Antipatros and Krateros cross into Asia Minor.
Polyperchon is left in command of Greece and Makedonia.
Antipatros, Krateros, and Antigonos wage war on Perdikkas.
Perdikkas marches on Egypt to reclaim the body of Alexander and dispatches Eumenes to face Krateros.
Perdikkas is killed in Egypt near Memphis by his own officers after defeat in the battle with Ptolemaios.
Krateros is killed by the army of Eumenes.
Antipatros, Antigonos, Ptolemaios, Seleukos and Lysimachos meet at Triparadeisos in Syria and agree to the new list of satrapal commands.
Antipatros becomes the new Regent for the Two Kings.
Seleukos returns to Babylon.
Phila, widow of Krateros, marries Demetrios, the fifteen year old son of Antigonos.
Lysimachos marries Nikaia, Daughter of Antipatros, after she is returned by Perdikkas.

319 Antipatros returns to Makedonia with the Two Kings.
Antipatros names Polyperchon to succeed him as the Regent for the Two Kings, bypassing Kassandros, his own son. Kassandros is named the Second-in-Command to Polyperchon.
Antipatros dies in Pella.
Kassandros escapes from Makedonia.
Antigonos defeats Eumenes in Kappadokia.
Eumenes is besieged by Antigonos at the Fortress of Nora on the border of Kappadokia.

318 Antigonos campaigns in Pisidia.
Kassandros joins Antigonos.
Eumenes is captured and then released by Antigonos.
Polyperchon campaigns in Peloponnesus.
Eumenes allies with Polyperchon and winters in Babylon.
Polyperchon returns to Makedonia.

317 Artâvardiya, the Persian Satrap of Armenia, frees Armenia from Seleukos.
Adeia starts the Succession Wars in Makedonia by declaring against Polyperchon, naming herself Queen to rule on behalf of Philip and orders Polyperchon to hand over the Royal Army to Kassandros as the Regent for Philip.
Antigonos campaigns against Eumenes.
Kassandros allies with Adeia and attacks Makedon.
Rošanak and her son Alexander IV join Olympias.
Olympias, Polyperchon, Rošanak and Alexander IV return to Makedonia.
Olympias is victorious in the Battle of Euia against Adeia.
Philip III and Adeia are captured and executed by Olympias.
Olympias executes Nikanor, brother of Kassandros, and 100 of his supporters.
Aristonous captures and defends the Fortress at Amphipolis.
Kassandros controls Athens.
Kassandros sieges Olympias at the Fortress of Pydna.
Eumenes and Antigonos face each other near Esfahan in the heartland of Persia.

316 Eumenes is betrayed by the Makedonian Silver Shields and is executed by Antigonos.
Antigonos executes Peithon on suspicion of plotting against him.
Kassandros defeats Polyperchon.
Fortress of Pydna falls. Kassandros captures Olympias.
Olympias is stoned to death by the families of the men of Kassandros executed in Euia.
Kassandros takes control of Makedonia and marries Thessalonike, half-sister of Alexander.
Aristonous surrenders the Fortress at Amphipolis to Kassandros, and is killed.
Kassandros declares himself the Regent for Alexander IV and confines Rošanak and Alexander IV to the Fortress at Amphipolis.
Antigonos rejects demands from Ptolemaios, Lysimachos and Kassandros to divide his loot.
Seleukos flees from Babylon.

315 Kassandros restores the City of Thebes.
Kassandros gives Philip III and Adeia a formal funeral.
The Makedonian port city of Thessalonika is founded by Kassandros in the name of his wife.

314 Antigonos promises freedom to the Greek City-states.
Kassandros, Lysimachos, Ptolemaios, and Seleukos march against Antigonos and his allies.

313 Ptolemaios moves his capital from Memphis to Alexandria and transfers the embalmed body of Alexander to a temple in Alexandria.

312 Ptolemaios and Seleukos are victorious in the Battle of Gaza against Antigonos, who is captured but is immediately released.
Antigonos returns to Phrygia.
Seleukos invades and settles in Babylon.

311 Kassandros and Lysimachos negotiate for peace with Antigonos.
Ptolemaios sues for inclusion in the peace negotiations.
Seleukos is excluded from the peace negotiations.
Demetrios, son of Antigonos, attacks Seleukos in Babylon.
Seleukos moves his capital from Babylon to Seleukia-in-Tigris.
Antigonos, Ptolemaios, Lysimachos and Kassandros agree to the Peace Agreement, 'Peace of Dynasts', and name Alexander IV to succeed his father when he comes of age at 18.
Kassandros secretly orders the death of Alexander and Rošanak.

310 Antigonos campaigns against Seleukos in Babylon.

309 Polyperchon brings Herakles, the illegitimate son of Alexander to Makedonia, as the next heir to the Argeads.
Polyperchon murders Herakles and his mother Barsine, when Kassandros offers him the command of Peloponnesus.

308 Kleopatra offers to marry Ptolemaios.
Kleopatra is murdered in Sardis by the order of Antigonos.
Ptolemaios makes peace with Kassandros.

307 Kassandros and Demetrios war against each other.
Demetrios controls Athens.

306 Menelaos, brother of Ptolemaios, is defeated and captured by Demetrios in the Battle of Salamis. The naval power of Egypt is destroyed during the battle.
Antigonos declares himself and his son, Demetrios, joint kings.

305 Seleukos declares himself king and takes the title of Nikator.
Seleukos concedes all the Indian Satrapies to Chandrâguptâ in exchange for 500 elephants and a marriage alliance.
Ptolemaios declares himself king of Egypt.
Lysimachos assumes the title of king in Thrake.

304 Demetrios raises the Siege of Rhodes.

303 Demetrios succeeds against Kassandros.
Seleukos sends Megasthenes as ambassador to the court of Chandrâguptâ.

302 Lysimachos marries Amastris.

301 Antigonos is defeated at the Battle of Ipsos against Lysimachos and Seleukos, and is killed.
Pâtaliputrâ, capital of the Mauryan Empire, becomes the largest city in the world, taking the lead from Alexandria, capital of Ptolemaic Egypt.

300 Demetrios resumes war against Lysimachos.
Lysimachos divorces Amastris and marries Arsinoë II, daughter of Ptolemaios.
After the death of Apâma, Seleukos marries Stratonike, daughter of Demetrios.

299 Ptolemaios and Lysimachos form an alliance.
Seleukos and Demetrios form an alliance.

298 Kassandros dies in Makedonia from consumption.
Chandrâguptâ abdicates his throne and becomes a Jain monk.
Bindusâra ascends to the Mauryan throne.

6

WORDS

WORDS
DIBBÎ

AS USED	VARIATION	MEANING
[illegible]		Wedding night
’		Glottal stop
…		Pause Omission of words that are untranslatable
….		Break
300		“The Three Hundred” Elite Spartan warriors fighting alongside Spartan Kings Elite Theban Sacred Band of warriors
Abû		Father Uncle
Acropolis		High city Citadel
Agora		Hellene marketplace
Ahriatiš	Ah-ri-a-ti-iš	Forever, for the rest of time
Akinakês		Short stabbing Persian sword with characteristic scabbard
Akîtu Akitu	Akiti	Babylonian Festival of New Year during the first eleven days of the month Nîsannu
Akkadian		Language of Babylonians and Assyrians Script used for writings of Âryâ, Elamite and Babylonian
Amâru		Behold!
Amazons		Race of Scythian female warriors
Amêlûtu		Mankind
Amma		Mother
Amurrû		West
Anâku		I
Anauša		The Ten Thousand Immortals Persian elite warriors
Anîna		Listen! Hear me!
Antalû		Eclipse Alignment of Earth, Sun and Moon
Antigonids		Antigonid Dynasty, named after the One-eyed Antigonos
Anumâti		Divine favor
Anuragini		Beloved
Anzû		Monster Lion-headed eagle
Aøuriya		Assyrian Eastern Monarchy

Apadâna		Palace Columned hall
Apkallu		Divine Sage
Arad-šarrûtu		Slave of the Crown
Arallû		Land of No Return Underworld
Aramaic		Written language commonly used for administrative purposes in the Persian Empire
Arašni	Arašan	Cubit
Archon		Ruler Athenian year named after the ruler
Arštibara		Elite One Thousand Royal Bodyguards of the Ten Thousand Immortals
Ârta		Truth
Artha Šastra		Treatise on statecraft, economics and military strategy Science of politics
Âryâ		Noble Written language created in the court of the First Dâriuš for imperial monumental inscriptions
Âryânâ	Ariyana Iran	Land of the Âryâs Land of the Nobles
Asa-bâra		Horse rider
Ašipu		Incantation singer
Asp'asta		Alfalfa Green horse food
Aspa		Horse
Aššat Šarri		Wife of the king
Assembly		The People passing decisions on major questions
Assyria		Eastern Monarchy
Athravan		Priest Keeper of the Sacred Fire
Âtravaxš		Supreme Priest
Attik	Attic	Of Athens Language of Athenians
Ava Stâya		Places
Avastâ		Leather
Avesta		The sacred book of the Zoroastrian religion According to legend, two copies existed by the time of Alexander III; one copy was burned in the fires of Pârsâ; the other copy was sent to Athens and disappeared
Axšaina		Blue-green, turquoise

Âyadana		Place of worship Sanctuary Place of the sacred fire
Azdâkara		Herald
Bâb-ilim Bâb-ilani Bâb-ilu		Babylon
Bâbiruviya		Babylonian Eastern Monarchy
Baga		God
Bagâha		Gods
Bâji		Marker
Ba^{n}daka		Faithful and loyal subject of the Great King
Baru		Omen interpreter
Bârûtu		Divination
Basileos		King Archon
Bašmu		Viper, snake
Belilit		Elamite month of August/September
Bêt rimdi		Bath room
Biltu	Talent	Weight and measure 67 pounds, 1 biltu=60 manû
Bît mâr šarri		King's son Prince
Bît Ṭuppi		School
Bît umasupitrû		Estate of the Crown-Prince
Book of Heaven		Astronomical Diaries
Brahman		Member of the highest caste of Hindu
Brātar		Brother
Bridge of Chinvât		Bridge of Judgment The holy bridge between Earth and Land of the Eternal Light, crossed after death in Zoroastrian religion
Bukephalas	Bucephalus	Alexander's favorite horse
Bukru		Firstborn son
Bûmi		Empire Land
Captive woman		Prisoner of war
Chakravarti		Imperial
Chaldæan		Babylonian astrologer Eastern Monarchy
Chatrang Chaturangam		Chess

Chiliarchos	Hezârapatiš	Commander of the elite One Thousand in the Persian Royal Army
Chiton		Hellene tunic for men
Chogân		Polo
Code of Hammurabi		Ancient Law of Babylonians from 18th Century BCE
Common Peace	King's Peace	Peace imposed by the Great Kings to end wars
Companion Kingsman	Hadâbâra Hetairoi	Nobles close to the king who accompany him
Dabâbu		Speak!
Dahyâva		Lands and People Country
Dakara		Palace
Daraniya		Gold
Darik	Archer Daric	Royal gold coin showing an archer issued from the time of First Dâriuš
Dâta		Law
Dauštar		Friend
Day'ghân		Festival of Dayghân celebrated on the longest night of the year, marking the victory of the sun over the darkness
Dharma		Universal law Righteousness
Dharma Šastra		Knowledge of virtuous living
Dhoti		Indian men's garment Piece of cloth wrapped around waist and legs
Didâ		Fortress
Dipî		Inscription
Dukšiš		Royal Woman Royal Daughter Princess
Dukšišbe		Royal Women Royal Daughters
Duppu šarrute		Art of writing
Dup-šîmâti		Tablet of Destinies
ê		Don't
Eastern Lion		India
Elamite		People of Elam-tu Written language used for the clay tablet from Pârsâ
Elam-tu		Elamite
Elnuškira		Door keeper of the royal palace
Enlightened One		Buddha

E-nu-ma eliš Enuma elish		Babylonian story of Creation
Êrib-bêt-ili		Temple Enterer Priest
E-sag-ila	E'saglia	Supreme Temple of Bêl Marduk
E-temen-an-ki	E'temenanki	Ziggurat Stepped temple pyramid in Babylon
Exiles Decree		Decree of Alexander III ordering the Hellene city-states to allow the return of the exiles to their homes
Fragment		Broken piece of clay, leather, parchment or papyrus Summary or quotation of a lost author in the works of the surviving author
Framâtar		Commander
Frawardigân		Festival of All-souls, honoring the dead
Full market Time		Mid morning
Gasta		Evil
General	Strategoi	Highest military command
Girtablitû		Demon
Gordian Knot		An intricate knot tied by King Gordios of Phrygia with the prophecy that whoever undoes the knot will become the next ruler of Asia
Hâ'iru		Lover, husband
Hadâbâra		Royal companion
Hades		Hell Underworld
Hadiš		Palace
Hainâ		Enemy Army
Hakhâmanišiya	Achæmenid	Eastern Monarchy The First World Empire founded by Second Kuruš Of the clan of Hakhâmaniš
Hamarana kara		Fighter
Hamestagan		Purgatory
Hanatâ		Old age Lapse of time
Haoma		Ancient plant sacred to Zoroastrian religion with hallucinogenic properties
Harimtu		Whore
Harṭibu		Egyptian priest
Hasânu		Take care Be well
Hazân		Language Tongue
Hellas		Greek-speaking world

Hellene		Greek The name of ancient Greeks
Helots		Native Hellene slaves of Sparta
Hezâr Afsân^{a}		A thousand stories
Hezârapatiš	Chiliarchos	Commander of the Elite One Thousand in the Persian Royal Army
HighLander		Makedonian from the Highlands of Makedonia
HighLands		Steppes
Himation		Hellene tunic for women worn like a cloak
Hinduya	Hi^{n}duya	Indian
Hišihtu		Heart's desire
House of Songs		Tablets that record the deeds of the living for the day of judgment according to the Zoroastrian religion
Hûd ibbi		Joy of heart
Huso Huso		Sturgeon fish
Hussanni		Remember me!
Ilî mušîti		Prayer to the gods of the night
Ilias		Iliad Hellene epic attributed to blind poet Homer
Iltânu		North
Imhullu		Evil wind
Immati?		When?
Iran	Âryânâ	Land of the Âryâs
Isinnû		Male prostitute
Issi Ekalli		Queen of the Palace Queen of the House of the King
Ištânu		North wind
Išutu		Womankind
Jiyamna		Last day of the month
Kalpa vrikša		Wish fulfilling divine tree Banyan tree
Kalu		Cult singer
Kâma Šastra		Knowledge of desire
Kâma Sûtram	Kâma Sûtra	Rules of Love Sixty-four Arts
Kapautaka		Blue Sapphire
Karbašiyaš		Persian month of August/September
Karka		Karian

Karma		Law of cause and effect Every action has consequences that influence how the soul is reborn
Kâsaka		Glass
Kaššâptu		Sorceress
Kaššâpu		Sorcerer
K^{e}tâb		Book Journal Written text
Khav'jar		Caviar
Khšaçâ		Empire Royal command Power
Khšâyaøiya		King
Kingsman		High command of the royal court Companions of the king
Kukku		Cake
Ku-li-li	Kulilu	Dragonfly
Lagids	Ptolemies	Ptolemaic Dynasty, named after Ptolemaios
Lands		Empire
League of Korinth		Alliance of Hellenes, except for Spartans, forged by Philip II for the purpose of attacking the Persian Empire
Lie		False, Chaos Disorder of the World according to the Zoroastrian religion
Light of the heaven		Naked
Lû		Let
Lumâšu		Constellation
Mâ		Thus
Mâda	Mede	Eastern Monarchy, 728-550 BCE
Magadha		Indian Kingdom
Mage Maguš Ma-gu-uš		Priest
Mahâsenâpati		Indian General
Mâhyâ		Month
Mâlati		Jasmine
Mâlavâ	Malloi Malli	Indian Tribe
Maltaku	Mukanzibtu	Water clock
Manâ pitâ		My father
Mannu		Who?

Manû	Mina	Silver 5 golden dariks=1 silver manû, 60 manû=1 biltu of silver
Manyâkâ		Necklace
Mâr Banê		Full citizen of Babylon
Mâr Bani		Noble
Mâr Bît Šarri		Royal Crown Prince
Mâr Bîti		Prince Son of the House
Mâr'at Bani		Noble Daughter
Mâr'at Šarri		Royal Daughter of the King
Mar'utu		Daughter
Mârtu		Daughter
Mâru		Son
Massîtu		Wine pitcher
Matar		Mother
Mayuxa		Doorknob
Mê		Universal laws created by the great gods governing all aspects of life What is needed for a civilized life
Miššaputra		Elamite King
Mithrâkâna		Festival of Mithrâ celebrated on the autumn equinox for six days
Mlechchha		Invader Foreigner
Molossian		Royal House of Kingdom of Epiros
Muppišu	Muppištu Muppišânu	Practitioner of witchcraft
Mušhuššu		Dragon
Naiy		Not
Nakaru		Foreign
Nâmanâfa		Genealogy
Nâmeh		Book
Naru		Singer
Naucina	Naucaina	Cedar
Nâyaka		Indian commander
Nêšu		Lion
Ni-Pišta		Written words
Niyâka		Grandfather
No'rouz		Festival of Persian New Day celebrated on the vernal equinox

Nudimmud		Creator Name of great god Êa
Nurmû		Pomegranate
Oracle of Ammon		Diviner of Ammon-Ra in Siwah Desert
Øakata	Thakata	Time passes Passage of time
Øanuvaniya	Mâhişu	Archer
Øukrâ Øukhrâ Thukrâ		Red
Øûrarâhara		Spring time
Paradayadâ Paridaiza	Paridaida	Garden, Park, pleasure spot Paradise
Patikara		Picture
Pavastâ		Clay tablet
Peace of Dynasts		Peace Agreement among the Successors of Alexander III, naming Alexander IV to succeed his father when he came of age at 18
Pêhâtu		Governor
Persian Purple Golden Purple		Royal purple cloth diadem worn around the head Color of Persian purple
Persians		Tribe of Âryâs who migrated to Pârsâ on the Iranian plateau
Phalanx		A column of heavily armed foot warriors
Pirradaziš		Royal Couriers of the Royal Road
Piru		Ivory
Pit		Fig
Pitar		Father
Proskynesis		Persian royal court custom of bowing and blowing a kiss to the Great King
Puça		Son
Pythia		Priestess of Apollo at Delphi
R'tu	Rtu	Season of Indian lunar year
Ra'âmu		Love
Rani		Queen
Remetj	Rekhyt	People of Egypt Egyptians
Rošanak Nâmeh		Book of Rošanak
Roti		Indian bread
Royal boys		Young sons of Makedonian nobility serving as royal pages in the court of Philip II and Alexander III
Royal City		Capital Residence of the Great King

Royal tent		Large tent with comforts of a royal palace, such as throne, bath, furnishings…
Ša ekalli		Woman of the palace
Šakku		Demon Seven-headed serpent
Šamallû		Apprentice of astrology and astronomy
Šamû îrup		Sky darkens
Šâr erbetti		Four Winds
Ša-Rêš-Šarri		Second to the King Grand Vizier
Šarratu		Queen
Šarru		Double star, Regulus King
Šastra		Timeless knowledge
Šemû		Hear me!
Šeššišu		Six times
Šiklu	Šiqlu Shekel	Silver coin; Smallest unit of currency 60 šiklu=1 manû, 60 manû=1 biltu, 1 golden darik=20 silver šiklu
Šimtu		Destiny
Šiyâti		Happiness
Šu-gu-ra-a		Awesome stillness
Šuttu		Dream
Šûtu		South
Saat Phere		Wedding vows during each step of Hindu wedding
Sacred Band		A Theban warrior unit of 150 pairs of male lovers
Saguš		Saturn
Saiyma		Silver
Sakâ Scythia		Scythia, Scythian
Sakâtu		Be silent!
Samrâjni		Indian Empress
Samrât		Indian Emperor
Santoor		Dulcimer Persian string musical instrument
Sapattu		Full Moon
Sarbalâ		Persian trousers
Saree	Sari	Indian women's garment Piece of cloth wrapped around the body in various ways
Sarissa	Sarisæ	Makedonian spear 15-18 feet in length
Satrap	Khšaçapâva	Protecting the Kingdom

Satrapy	Khšaçapâvan	Protector of Kingdom
Seleukids		Seleukid Dynasty, named after Seleukos
Sema		Mausoleum
Şerru		Snake
Sipîru		Scribe writing on parchment and papyrus
Sipîru ša ûqu		Scribe of the People
Şît libbi		Offspring, child
Şitân		East
Sixty-four Arts		Kâma Sûtra
Slave		Prisoner of war
Spaka		Dog
Spardiya		Sardian
Stâna		Carved niche in the wall
Styx		Great oath of the Hellene gods One of the mythical rivers in the Hades across which Charon ferries the souls of the dead
Substitute king		When a bad omen predicted the death of the king, a substitute was chosen for the king by the temple priests to take on the bad omen to himself. After the substitute king died, the king would resume his kingship
Summâq		Milled dried leaves of the nonpoisonous sumac plant
Sunki	Sunkina	King
Svayamvara		Bride's choice
Sycamore tree		Fig tree
Takara		Palace
Takh'teh Nard		Backgammon
Tarbâşu		Halo
Târîtu		Wet nurse
Taruni		Woman between the age of 16 and 30
Têrtu		Oracle
Threading		Using two fine long threads to remove hair
Tippirâ	Tuppira	Persian scribe
Tirgân		Festival of Tirgân celebrated on the first day of summer Rain festival in honor of Tištyra, Zoroastrian Angel of Water
Toth Totote		Thunderer Sound of salpinx, Makedonian war trumpet
Truth		Proper order of the world according to Zoroastrian religion
Ţup šarratu	Ţup-šar-ra-at	Female scribe
Ţup šarru	Dup šarru	Scribe on clay tablet
Tupšar Enuma Anu Enlil		Scribe of the Celestial Omens

Ub-šu-kkinna	Ubšukkinakku	The divine assembly hall
Ugallu		Demon
Ulûlu		Babylonian month of August/September
Umasupitrû		Crown-Prince
Ummâni dannuti		Senior scholar of astrology and astronomy
Ummi šarri		Mother of the King
Uridimmu		Mad dog
Ušâru		Penis
Uvâmaršiya		Suicide
Ûvjiya	Susian	Elamite
Varusanka		Benefactors of the King Widely renowned
Vîsa Puça	Viøa Puça	Son of the Royal House Prince
Wane		Gradual decreasing of the illuminated surface of the moon
Wax		Gradual increasing of the illuminated surface of the moon
Wyšpsy		Sogdian King
Xšaçapâva Khšaçapâva	Satrapy	Protecting the Kingdom
Xšaçapâvan Khšaçapâvan	Satrap	Protector of Kingdom Protector of King
Xšâna		Domain
Yâsmin		Jasmine
Yaunâ	Ionian	Hellene Greece
Za'farân		Saffron
Zarathuštra Zaraøuštra	Zartušt Zoroaster	The Prophet of Zoroastrian religion
Zibbâtu		Pisces
Zoroastrianism	Zarathušthian	Monotheistic religion of the ancient Persians that believes in a single supreme god who created the world
Zuqaqîpu		Scorpion

7

𒐛

SOURCES

SOURCES
NI-PIŠTA

General

100 Great Kings, Queens and Rulers of the World, edited by John Canning (New York: Taplinger Publishing Company, 1968)

Bartlett, John: *Familiar quotations: a collection of passages, phrases, and proverbs traced to their sources in ancient and modern literature*, 10th edition, revised and enlarged by Nathan Haskell Dole (Boston: Little, Brown, and Company, 1929)

Brosius, Maria: *Ancient Archives and Archival Traditions* (New York: Oxford University Press, 2003)

Campbell, Joseph: *The Oriental Mythology: The Mask of God* (New York: Penguin Books USA Inc., 1962)

Durant, Will: *Our Oriental Heritage, The History of Civilization*, Part 1 (New York: Simon and Schuster, 1954)

Eastern Wisdom, edited by C. Scott Littleton (New York: Henry Holt and Company, 1996)

Everyday Life in Ancient Times (Washington, DC: The National Geographic, 1951)

Ferrill, Arthur: *The Origins of War: From the Stone Age to Alexander the Great* (London: Thames and Hudson, 1985)

Finley, M. I.: *Ancient History, Evidence and Models* (New York: Elizabeth Sifton Books, Viking, 1986)

Foucault, Michel: *The History of Sexuality*, translated by Robert Hurley, Vols. 1 & 2 (New York: Vintage Books, 1990)

Frazer, Sir James George: *The New Golden Bough* (New York.: S.G. Phillips, Inc., 1972)

Glover, Lady Elizabeth Rosetta Scot: *Great Queens: Famous Women Rulers of the East* (London: Hutchinson & Co. Ltd., 1929)

Hanson, Davis Victor: *Ripples of Battle* (New York: Double Day, 2003)

Hawkes, Jacquetta: *The First Great Civilizations* (New York: Alfred A. Knopf, 1973)

Herman, Zvi: *People, Seas, and Ships*, translated by Len Ortzen (New York: G.P. Putnam's Sons, 1967)

Images of Women in Antiquity, edited by Averil Cameron and Amélie Kuhrt, revised edition (Detroit: Wayne State University Press, 1993)

Jidejian, Nina: *Tyre Through the Ages* (Beirut: Dar El-Mashreq Publishers, 1969)

Levy, Jean-Phillippe: *The Economic Life of the Ancient World*, translated by John G. Biram (Chicago: The University of Chicago Press, 1967)

Nietzsche, Friedrich Wilhelm: *Thus spake Zarathustra*, translated by Thomas Common (Mineola: Dover Publications, 1999)

Rawlinson, George: *The Seven Great Monarchies of the Ancient Eastern World*, 3 Vols. 2nd edition (New York: A. L. Burt, Publisher, 1870)

Smart, Ninian: *The World's Religions* (Cambridge: Cambridge University Press, 1998)

The Ancient Near East, edited by James B. Pritchard, Vols. I and II (Princeton: Princeton University Press, 1958, 1975)

The Arabian Nights, translated by Hussain Haddawy, based on the text edited by Muhsin Mahdi (New York: W. W. Norton & Company, 1990)

The Arabian Nights II: Sindbad and Other Popular Stories, translated by Hussain Haddawy (New York: W. W. Norton & Company, 1995)

The Arabian Nights: Tales from a Thousand and One Night, translated by Sir Richard F. Burton, introduction by A. S. Byatt (New York: The Modern Library, 2001)

The Bible and the Ancient Near East, edited by G. Ernest Wright (Garden City: Doubleday & Company, Inc., 1961)

The History of al-Tabarí, Vol. IV, The Ancient Kingdoms, translated and annotated by Moshe Perlmann (Albany: State University of New York Press, 1987)

The Seventy Wonders of the Ancient World, edited by Chris Scarre (London: Thames and Hudson Ltd., 1999)

The Sibylline Oracles, Books III-V, translation by Rev. H. N. Bates (New York: The Macmillan Company, 1918)

The Statesman's Yearbook 2008: The Politics, Culture and Economics of the World (New York: Palgrave McMillan, 2007)

The Tree of Life, edited by Ruth Smith (New York: Viking Press, 1942)

The Works of Josephus, with a Life Written by Himself, translated by William Whiston, A.M., Vol. 2. (New York: A. C. Armstrong & Son, 1897)

Warry, John: *Warfare in the Classical World* (Norman: University of Oklahoma Press, 1995)

Encyclopedias

Encyclopaedia Iranica, edited by Ehsan Yarshater, 12 Vols. (New York: Columbia University Press, 1974-)

Jordan, Michael: *The Encyclopedia of Gods* (New York: Facts on File, 1993)

Marzolph, Ulrich and van Leewen, Richard: *The Arabian Nights Encyclopedia*, 2 Vols. (Santa Barbara: ABC-CLIO, Inc., 2004)

Merriam-Webster's Encyclopedia of World Religions, Wendy Doniger, consulting editor (Springfield: Merriam-Webster, 1999)

The Cambridge Encyclopedia of the World's Ancient Languages, edited by Roger D. Woodard (Cambridge: Cambridge University Press, 2004)

Maps

Atlas of Classical History, edited by Richard J. A. Talbert (New York: Routledge, 1985)

Grant, Michael: *Atlas of Classical History, from 1700 BC to AD 565*, 5th edition (New York: Oxford University Press, 1994)

Hammond Atlas of World History, edited by Geoffrey Barraclough, 5th edition edited by Richard Overy (Maplewood: Hammond, 1999)

National Geographic Atlas of World History, edited by Noel Grove (Washington, D.C.: National Geographic Society, 1997)

Oxford Atlas of World History, edited by Patrick K. O'Brien (New York: Oxford University Press, 2002)

Oxford New Concise World Atlas, 2nd edition (New York: Oxford University Press, 2006)

The Complete Atlas of World History: Prehistory and the Ancient World, edited by John Haywood (Armonk: M. E. Sharpe, Inc., 1997)

The Harper Atlas of World History, revised & updated (New York: HarperCollins Publishers, 1992)

The Times Atlas of World History, edited by Geoffrey Barraclough (New Jersey: Hammond Inc., 1978)

The Times Atlas of the World, 10th Comprehensive Edition (New York: Time Books, Random House, 1999)

Astrology

Ancient Astronomy and Celestial Divination, edited by N. M. Swerdlow (Cambridge: The MIT Press, 1999)

Barton, Tamsyn: *Ancient Astrology* (London: Routledge, 1994)

Brown, David: *Mesopotamian Planetary Astronomy-Astrology* (Groningen: Styx Publications, 2000)

Oppenheim, A. Leo: *The Interpretation of Dreams in the Ancient Near East* (Philadelphia: The American Philosophical Society, 1956)

Reiner, Erica: *Babylonian Planetary Omens*, Vols. 1&2, in collaboration with David Pingree (Malibu: Undena Publications, 1975 & 1981)

Reiner, Erica: *Astral Magic in Babylonia* (Independence Square: The American Philosophical Society, 1995)

Reiner, Erica: "The Use of Astrology", *Journal of American Oriental Society,* Vol. 105, No. 4. (Oct-Dec., 1985), pp. 589-595

Links

Avesta: www.avesta.org

Briant, Pierre: www.achemenet.com

Encyclopaedia Iranica: www.iranica.com

Hegmataneh: www.hegmataneh.ir

Iran Chamber Society: www.iranchamber.com

Lendering, Jona, Livius: www.livius.org

Pergamon Museum Berlin, Museum of the Ancient Near East: www.smb.spk-berlin.de/smb/sammlungen

Persepolis: www.persepolis.ir

Persepolis Fortification Archive Project: persepolistablets.blogspot.com

Susa: www.susacity.com

The British Museum, Forgotten Empire: www.thebritishmuseum.ac.uk/forgottenempire

The Circle of Ancient Iranian Studies: cais-soas.com

The Oriental Institute of the University of Chicago, Persepolis and Ancient Iran: oi.uchicago.edu/museum/collections/pa/persepolis

Assyrian

Contenau, George: *Everyday Life in Babylon and Assyria,* translated by K.R. and A.R. Maxwell-Hyslop (New York: St. Martin's Press, 1954)

Dougherty, Raymond P.: "Writing upon Parchment and Papyrus among the Babylonians and Assyrians", *Journal of the American Oriental Society*, Vol. 48. (1928), pp. 109-135

Fales, F. M. and Postgate, J. N.: *Imperial Administration Records*, State Archives of Assyria, Vol. VII (Helsinki: Helsinki University Press, 1992)

Grayson, Albert Kirk: *Assyrian and Babylonian Chronicles* (Winona Lake: Eisenbrauns, 2000) reprinted from 1975 J. J. Augustin edition

Hunger, Hermann: *Astrological Reports to Assyrian Kings*, State Archives of Assyria, Vol. VIII (Helsinki: Helsinki University Press, 1992)

Livingston, Alasdair: *Court Poetry and Literary Miscellanea*, State Archives of Assyria, Vol. III (Helsinki: Helsinki University Press, 1989)

Nissinen, Martti: *References to Prophecy in Neo-Assyrian Sources*, State Archives of Assyria Studies (Finland: University of Helsinki Press, 1998)

Parpola, Simo: *Assyrian Prophecies*, State Archives of Assyria, Vol. IX (Helsinki: The Neo-Assyrian Text Corpus Project, 1997)

Parpola, Simo: *The Standard Babylonian Epic of Gilgamesh*, State Archives of Assyria, Cuneiform Texts, Vol. I (Helsinki: Helsinki University Press, 1997)

Roux, Georges: *Ancient Iraq* (Cleveland: The World Publishing Company, 1964)

Smith, Sidney: *Early History of Assyria to 1000 B.C.* (New York: E. P. Dutton and Company, 1927)

Babylonian

Bertman, Stephen: *Handbook to Life in Ancient Mesopotamia* (New York: Oxford University Press, 2003)

Biggs, Robert D.: "The Babylonian Prophecies and the Astrological Traditions of Mesopotamia", *Journal of Cuneiform Studies,* Vol. 37, No. 1. (Spring, 1985), pp. 86-90

Black, Jeremy and Green, Anthony: *Gods, Demons and Symbols of Ancient Mesopotamia* (Austin: University of Texas Press, 1992)

Burstein, Stanley Mayer: *The Babyloniaca of Berossus* (Malibu: Undena Publications, 1978)

Contenau, George: *Everyday Life in Babylon and Assyria,* translated by K.R. and A.R. Maxwell-Hyslop (New York: St. Martin's Press, 1954)

Dougherty, Raymond P.: "Writing upon Parchment and Papyrus among the Babylonians and Assyrians", *Journal of the American Oriental Society*, Vol. 48. (1928), pp. 109-135

Dubberstein, Waldo H. and Parker, Richard A.: *Babylonian Chronology, 626 B.C.–A.D. 75*, 4th Printing (Province: Brown University Press, 1971)

Geller, M. J.: "Babylonian Astronomical Diaries and Correction of Diodorus", *Bulletin of the School of Oriental and African Studies,* University of London, Vol. 53, No. 1. (1990), pp. 1-7

Englund, R. K.: "Administrative Timekeeping in Ancient Mesopotamia", *Journal of the Economic and Social History of the Orient*, Vol. 31, No. 2. (1988), pp. 121-185

Gilgamesh: A Reader, edited by John Maier (Wauconda: Bolchazy-Carducci Publishers, Inc., 1997)

Grayson, Albert Kirk: *Assyrian and Babylonian Chronicles* (Winona Lake: Eisenbrauns, 2000) reprinted from 1975 J. J. Augustin edition

Harper, Robert Francis: "Babylonian Penitential Psalms", *The Biblical World*, Vol. 23, No. 5. (1904), pp. 358-365

Heidel, Alexander: *The Babylonian Genesis: The Story of Creation*, second edition (Chicago: University of Chicago Press, 1951)

Hunger, H. and Sachs, A. J.: *Astronomical Diaries and Related Texts from Babylonia I: Diaries from 652 B.C. to 262 B.C.* (Vienna, 1988)

Jacobsen, Thorkild: *The Treasures of Darkness: A History of Mesopotamian Religion* (New Haven: Yale University Press, 1976)

King, Leonard William: *The Seven Tablets of Creation*, Vol. 1 (London: Luzac & Co., 1902)

Lambert, W. G.: *Babylonian Wisdom Literature* (Oxford: Clarendon Press, 1960)

Lambert, W. G. and Millard, A. R.: *Atra Hasîs: The Babylonian Story of the Flood*, with the Sumerian Flood Story by M. Civil (Winona Lake: Eisenbrauns, 1999)

Late Babylonian Astronomical and Related Texts, copied by T. G. Pinches and J. N. Strassmaier, prepared for publication by A. J. Sachs with the co-operation of F. Schaumberger (Providence: Brown University Press, 1955)

Leick, Gwendolyn: *A Dictionary of Ancient Near Eastern Mythology* (London: Routledge, 1991)

Leick, Gwendolyn: *Sex and Eroticism in Mesopotamian Literature* (London: Routledge, 1994)

Leick, Gwendolyn: *Who's who in the Ancient Near Eastern Mythology* (London: Routledge, 2002)

Leick, Gwendolyn: *The Babylonians: An Introduction* (London: Routledge, 2003)

Letters From Mesopotamia, translated by Leo A. Oppenheim (Chicago: University of Chicago Press, 1967)

Marcus, David: *A Manual of Akkadian* (Lanham: University Press of America, Inc., 1978)

Mitchell, Stephen: *Gilgamesh* (New York: Free Press, 2004)

Myths from Mesopotamia: Creation, the Flood, Gilgamesh, and others, edited and translated with an introduction and notes by Stephanie Dalley (New York: Oxford University Press, 1989)

Nemet-Nejat, Karen Rhea: *Daily Life in Ancient Mesopotamia* (Connecticut: Greenwood Press, 1998)

Neugebauer, O: Studies in Ancient Astronomy. VIII. The Waterclock in Babylonian Astronomy", *Isis*, Vol. 37, No. ½ (May 1947), pp. 37-43

Oates, Joan: *Babylon*, revised edition (New York: Thames and Hudson, 1986)

Oppenheim, A. Leo: *Ancient Mesopotamia: Portrait of a Dead Civilization*, revised edition, completed by Erica Reiner (Chicago: The University of Chicago Press, 1964, 1977)

Oppenheim, A. Leo: "A Babylonian Diviner's Manual", *Journal of Near Eastern Studies,* Vol. 33, No. 2. (April, 1974), pp. 197-220

Parker, Richard Anthony and Dubberstein, Waldo H.: *Babylonian Chronology 626B.C.-A.D.75* (Providence: Brown University Press, 1956)

Reiner, Erica: *Babylonian Planetary Omens*, Vols. 1 and 2, in collaboration with David Pingree (Malibu: Undena Publications, 1975 & 1981)

Reiner, Erica: *Astral Magic in Babylonia* (Independence Square: The American Philosophical Society, 1995)

Reiner, E. and Güterbock, H. G.: "The Great Prayer to Ishtar and its Two Versions From Boğazköy", *Journal of Cuneiform Studies*, Vol. 21. (1967), pp. 255-266

Rochberg, Francesca: "Babylonian Horoscopes", *Transactions of the American Philosophical Society,* New Series, Vol. 88, No. 1. (1998), pp. i-xi + 1-164

Saggs, H. W. F.: *Everyday Life in Babylonia & Assyria* (London: B. T. Batsford Ltd., 1965)

Saggs, H. W. F.: *The Greatness that was Babylon* (New York: Frederick A. Praeger Publishers, 1969)

Sperl, S.: "The Literary Form of Prayer: Qur'ân Sura One and a Babylonian Prayer to the Moon God", *Bulletin of the School of Oriental and African Studies*, University of London, Vol. 57, No. 1. (1994), pp. 213-227

Thompson, Reginald Campbell: *Late Babylonian Letters* (London, Luzac and Co., 1906)

Tigay, Jeffrey H.: *The Evolution of the Gilgamesh Epic* (Wauconda: Bolchazy-Carducci Publishers, Inc., 2002)

Wallis Budge, E. A.: *Babylonian Story of the Deluge and the Epic of Gilgamish* (London: British Museum, 1920)

Baktrian

Holt, Frank L.: *Alexander the Great and Bactria* (Leiden: E. J. Brill, 1988)

Holt, Frank L.: *Thundering Zeus, The Making of Hellenistic Bactria* (Berkeley: University of California Press, 1999)

Holt, Frank L.: *Into the Land of Bones* (Berkeley: University of California Press, 2005)

Rawlinson, H. G.: *Bactria, The History of a Forgotten Empire,* reprinted from the edition of 1912 (New York: AMS Press Inc., 1969)

Egyptian

Empereur, Jean-Yves: *Alexandria: Jewel of Egypt* (New York: Harry N. Abrams, 2002)

Ions, Veronica: *Egyptian Mythology* (New York: Hamlyn, 1965)

Mertz, Barbara: *Red Land, Black Land: Daily Life in Ancient Egypt*, revised edition (New York: Dodd, Mead & Company, 1978)

Murray, Margaret A.: *The Splendor that was Egypt*, revised edition (Mineola: Dover Publications, Inc., 2004)

Mysiliwiec, Karol: *The Twilight of Ancient Egypt: First Millennium B.C.E.*, translated by David Lorton (Ithaca and London: Cornell University Press, 2000)

Parker, Richard A.: *The Calendars of Ancient Egypt* (Chicago: The University of Chicago Press, 1950)

The Oxford History of Ancient Egypt, edited by Ian Shaw (New York: Oxford University Press, 2000)

Wood, Margot Miller: *Shortcut to Progress: Religious Matrix of the Egyptian Calendar and Number Glyphs* (San Francisco, 1973)

Hellene

A Garden of Greek Verse, images and verse selected by Yvonne Whiteman (Los Angeles: J. Paul Getty Museum, 2000)

Abbott, Jacob: *Histories of Cyrus the Great and Alexander the Great*, with revisions and an appendix by Lyman Abbot (New York: Harper and Brothers, 1880)

Acts of Love: Ancient Greek Poetry from Aphrodite's Garden, selected and translated by George Economou, introduction by Wendy Doniger (New York: The Modern Library, 2006)

Aeschylus, translated by Richard Lattimore, Vol. 1 (Chicago: University of Chicago Press, 1953)

Badian, Ernest: *Studies in Greek and Roman History* (Oxford: Basil Blackwell, 1964)

Brill's Companion to Thucydides, edited by Antonios Rengakos & Antonios Tsakmakis (Leiden: Brill, 2006)

Bryce, Trevor: *The Trojans and Their Neighbors* (London: Routledge, 2006)

Bulfinch, Thomas: *Bulfinch's Mythology* (New York: The Modern Library, 1993)

Bury, J. B., and Meiggs, Russell: *A History of Greece*, 4th edition (New York: St. Martin's Press, 1983)

Cantor, Norman: *Alexander the Great: Journey to the End of the World* (New York: Harper Collins Publishers, 2005)

Carney, Elizabeth Donnelly: *Women and Monarchy in Macedonia* (Norman: The University of Oklahoma Press, 2000)

Carney, Elizabeth Donnelly: *Olympias: Mother of Alexander the Great* (New York: Routledge, 2006)

Cartledge, Paul: *Agesilaos and the Crisis of Sparta* (Baltimore: The John Hopkins University Press, 1987)

Cartledge, Paul: *The Greeks: Crucible of Civilization* (New York: TV Books, 2000)

Cartledge, Paul: *The Spartans* (Woodstock: The Overlook Press, 2003)

Casson, Lionel: *The Greek Conquerors* (Chicago: Stonehenge, 1981)

Chamoux, Francois: *The Civilization of Greece*, translated by W. S. Maguinness (New York: Simon & Schuster, 1965)

Dalby, Andrew: *Rediscovering Homer: Inside the Origins of the Epic* (New York: W. W. Norton & Company, 2006)

Diodorus Siculus, *Library of History*, 12 Vols., translated by C. H. Oldfather and edited by C. B. Welles (Cambridge: Harvard University Press, 1954)

Euripides, *The Complete Greek Tragedies*, Vol. 3, edited by David Grene and Richard Lattimore (Chicago: The University of Chicago Press, 1959)

Garrison, Daniel H.: *Sexual Culture in Ancient Greece* (Norman: University of Oklahoma Press, 2000)

Grant, Michael: *The Ancient Historians* (New York: Charles Scribner's Sons, 1970)

Grant, Michael: *The Classical Greeks* (New York: Charles Scribner's Sons, 1989)

Graves, Robert: *The Greek Mythology*, 2 Vol., revised edition (London: Penguin Books, 1960)

Greeks and Barbarians, edited by Thomas Harrison (New York: Routledge, 2002)

Greek Historical Inscriptions: From the Sixth Century B.C. to the Death of Alexander the Great in 323 B.C., edited by Marcus N. Tod (Chicago: Ares Publishers, Inc., 1985)

Green, Peter: *Xerxes at Salamis* (New York: Praeger Publication, 1970)

Hanson, Davis Victor: *A War Like No Other: How The Athenians and Spartans Fought The Peloponnesian War* (New York: Random House, 2005)

Hanson, Davis Victor: *Wars of the Ancient Greeks* (New York: Smithsonian Books, 1999)

Herodotus: *The History of Herodotus*, translated by George Rawlinson, edited by Manuel Komroff (New York: Tudor Publishing Company, 1956)

Herodotus: *The History*, translated by David Grene (Chicago: The University of Chicago Press, 1987)

Hirsch, Steven, W.: *The Friendship of the Barbarians: Xenophon and the Persian Empire* (Hanover: University Press of New England, 1985)

Hogan, James: *A Commentary on the Complete Greek Tragedies: Aeschylus* (Chicago: The University of Chicago Press, 1984)

Homer: *Iliad*, translated by Robert Fitzgerald (New York: Doubleday, 1974)

Homer, *Readings on Homer*, edited by Don Nardo (San Diego: Greenhaven Press, 1998)

Hornblower, Simon and Spawforth, Antony: *The Oxford Classical Dictionary* (New York: Oxford University Press, 1996)

Oates, Whitney J. and O'Neill, Jr., Eugene: *The Complete Greek Drama*, 2 Vols. (New York: Random House, 1938)

Pindar: *Olympian Odes, Pythian Odes*, edited and translated by William H. Race, 2 Vols. (Cambridge: Harvard University Press, 1997)

Pindar: *The Odes of Pindar*, translated by Richmond Lattimore (Chicago: University of Chicago Press, 1976)

Peddle, John Griffiths: *Sardis in the age of Croesus* (Norman: University of Oklahoma Press, 1968)

Plutarch: *Plutarch Lives*, translated by John Dryden, edited with preface by Arthur Hugh Clough (New York: The Modern Library, 2001)

Plutarch: *The Life of the Great Alexander*, translated by John Dryden (New York, 2004)

Pritchett, William Kendrick: *The Greek States at War*, Vol. 1 (Berkeley: University of California Press, 1971)

Pritchett, William Kendrick: *Essays in Greek History* (Amsterdam: J. G. Gieben, Publisher, 1994)

Quennell, Marjorie and C. H. B.: *Everyday Things in Ancient Greece*, revised by Kathleen Freeman (London: B. T. Batsford Ltd, 1954)

Rosenmeyer, Thomas G.: *The Art of Aeschylus* (Berkeley: University of California Press, 1982)

Schein, Seth L.: *The Mortal Hero* (Berkeley: University of California Press, 1984)

Scott, John A.: "The Gesture of Proskynesis", *The Classical Journal,* Vol. 17, No. 7. (April, 1922), pp. 403-404

Shipley, Graham: *The Greek World After Alexander, 323-30 BC* (New York: Routledge, 2000)

Stadter, Philip: *Arrian of Nicomedia* (Chapel Hill: The University of North Carolina Press, 1980)

Stobart, J. C.: *The Glory That Was Greece*, revised by F. N. Bryce (New York: D. Appleton, Century Company, Inc., 1935)

Strabo: *Selections from Strabo*, with an introduction on Strabo's life and works, by H. F. Tozer (Oxford: Clarendon press, 1893)

The Cambridge Illustrated History of Ancient Greece, edited by Paul Cartledge (Cambridge: Cambridge University Press, 1998)

The Complete Writings of Thucydides: The Peloponnesian War, the unabridged Crawley translation with an introduction by John H. Finley, Jr. (New York: The Modern Library, 1951)

The Oxford History of Greece and the Hellenistic World, edited by John Boardman, Jasper Griffin and Oswyn Murray, (Oxford: Oxford University Press, 1986, 1991, 2001)

Toynbee, Arnold: *Some Problems with Greek History* (London: Oxford University Press, 1969)

Translated Documents from Greece and Rome: Archaic Times to the end of the Peloponnesian War, edited and translated by Charles W. Fornara (Baltimore: The John Hopkins University Press, 1977)

Translated Documents from Greece and Rome: From the end of the Peloponnesian War to the Battle of Ipsus, edited and translated by Philip Harding (Cambridge: Cambridge University Press, 1985)

Translated Documents from Greece and Rome: The Hellenistic Age from the Battle of Ipsos to the Death of Kleopatra VII, edited and translated by Stanley M. Burstein (Cambridge: Cambridge University Press, 1985)

Vrettos, Theodore: *Alexandria* (New York: The Free Press, 2001)

Waterfield, Robin: *Xenophon's Retreat, Greece, Persia, and the End of the Golden Age* (Cambridge: The Belknap Press of Harvard University Press, 2006)

Wells, C. Bradford: *Royal Correspondence in the Hellenistic Period* (New Haven: Yale University Press, 1934)

Wells, C. Bradford: *Alexander and the Hellenistic World* (Toronto: A. H. Hakkert Ltd., 1970)

Xenophon: *Anabasis*, translated, W. H. D. Rouse (Ann Arbor: University of Michigan Press, 1958)

Xenophon: *Hellenica: A History of My Times*, translated by Rex Warner (Suffolk: Penguin Books, 1979)

Xenophon: *Xenophon*, translated by Carlton L. Brownson, revised by John Dillery (Cambridge: Harvard University Press, 2001)

Xenophon: *The Education of Cyrus*, translated and annotated by Wayne Ambler (Ithaca: Cornel University Press, 2001)

Young, Philip H.: *The Printed Homer* (North Carolina: McFarland & Company, Inc., Publishers, 2003)

Indian

Basham, A. L.: *The Wonder That Was India*, 3rd revised edition (New York: Taplinger Publishing Company, 1968)

Chattopadhyaya, Sudhakar: *The Achaemenids in India* (Calcutta: Calcutta Oriental Press, 1950)

Gopal, Lallanji: *Chandragupta Maurya*, translated by O. P. Tandon (New Delhi: National Book Trust, India, 1969)

Hart, George L. III: *The Poems of Ancient Tamil* (Berkeley: University of California Press, 1975)

Kâlidâsa: *Kâlidâsa's Kumârasambhava, The Origin of the Young God*, translated by Hank Heifetz (Berkeley: University of California Press, 1985)

Mallanaga, Vatsyayana: *Kamasutra*, translated by Wendy Doniger and Sudhir Kakar (New York: Oxford University Press, 2002)

Smith, Vincent A.: *The Early History of India: From 600 B.C. to the Muhammadan Conquest*, 4th edition revised by S. M. Edwards (Oxford, 1962)

Strong, John S.: *The Legend of King Aśoka* (New Jersey: Princeton University Press, 1983)

Thapar, Romila: *Early India: From the Origins to AD 1300* (Berkeley: University of California Press, 2002)

The Complete Kâma Sûtra, translated by Alain Danièlou (Rochester: Park Street Press, 1994)

Judean

Aramaic Documents of the Fifth Century B.C., abridged and revised edition by: G. R. Driver (Oxford: Oxford University Press, 1965)

Jewish Documents of the Time of Ezra, Translated from the Aramaic by A. Cowley (New York: The Macmillan Co., 1919)

Moreen, Vera Basch: *In Queen Esther's Garden: An Anthology of Judeo-Persian Literature* (New Haven: Yale University Press, 2000)

Makedonian

Alexander the Great: A Reader, edited by Ian Worthington (London: Routledge, 2003)

Arrian, *The Campaigns of Alexander*, translated by Aubrey De Sélincourt (London: Penguin Books, 1958)

Badian, E.: "The Eunuch Bagoas", *The Classical Quarterly*, New Series, Vol. 8, No. 3/4 (1958), pp. 144-158

Billows, Richard A.: *Antigonos the One-Eyed and the Creation of the Hellenistic State* (Berkeley: University of California Press, 1990)

Billows, Richard A.: *Kings and Colonists: Aspects of Makedonian Imperialism* (Leiden: E. J. Brill, 1995)

Borza, Eugene N.: "Fire from Heaven: Alexander at Persepolis", *Classical Philology*, Vol. 67, No. 4. (1972), pp. 233-245

Borza, Eugene N.: *In the Shadow of Olympus: The Emergence of Makedon* (New Jersey: Princeton University Press, 1990)

Borza, Eugene N.: *Makedonika*, edited by Carol G. Thomas (Claremont: Regina Books, 1995)

Bosworth, A. B.: *Conquest and Empire: The Reign of Alexander the Great* (Cambridge: Cambridge University Press, 1988)

Bosworth, A. B.: *Alexander and the East* (New York: Oxford University Press, 1998)

Bosworth, A. B.: "Perdiccas and the Kings", *The Classical Quarterly*, New Series, Vol. 43. (1993), pp. 420-427

Bosworth, A. B.: *The Legacy of Alexander: Politics, Warfare, and Propaganda under the Successors* (New York: Oxford University Press, 2000)

Bosworth, A. B., and Baynham, E. J.: *Alexander the Great in Fact and Fiction* (New York: Oxford University Press, 2000)

Briant, Pierre: *Alexander the Great: Man of Action, Man of Spirit*, translated by Jeremy Leggatt (New York: Harry N. Abrams, Inc., 1987)

Brill's Companion to Alexander the Great, edited by Joseph Roisman (Leiden: Brill, 2003)

Brunt, P.A.: "Persian Account of Alexander's Campaign", *The Classical Quarterly*, New Series, Vol. 12, No. 1. (1962), pp. 141-155

Cartledge, Paul: *Alexander the Great: The Hunt for a New Past* (Woodstock: The Overlook Press, 2004)

Crossroads of History: the Age of Alexander, edited by Waldemar Heckel and Lawrence A. Tritle (Claremont: Regina Books, 2003)

Dodge, Theodore Ayrault: *Alexander* (Cambridge: De Capo Press, 1890)

Doherty, Paul: *The Death of Alexander the Great* (New York: Carroll & Graf Publishers, 2004)

Engles, Donald W.: *Alexander the Great and the Logistics of Macedonian Army* (Berkeley: University of California Press, 1978)

Errington, R. M.: "From Babylon to Triparadeisos - 323-320 BC", *The Journal of Hellenic Studies*, Vol. 90. (1970), pp. 49-77

Fuller, John Frederick Charles: *The Generalship of Alexander the Great* (Cambridge: Da Capo Press, Perseus Book Group, Reprint of 1960 Edition)

Grainger, John D.: *Seleukos Nikator, Constructing a Hellenistic Kingdom* (New York: Routledge, 1990)

Green, Peter: *Alexander the Great* (New York: Praeger Publishers, 1970)

Green, Peter: *Alexander to Actium: The Historical Evolution of the Hellenistic Age* (Berkeley: University of California Press, 1990)

Green, Peter: *Alexander of Makedon, 356-323 B.C.: A Historical Biography* (Berkeley: University of California Press, 1991)

Green, Peter: *The Hellenistic Age* (New York: The Modern Library, 2007)

Hamilton, J. R.: *Alexander the Great* (Pittsburgh: University of Pittsburgh Press, 1974)

Hammond, N.G.L.: *The Genius of Alexander the Great* (Chapel Hill: University of North Carolina Press, 1997)

Hammond, N.G.L. and Griffith, G.T.: *A History of Makedonia*, Vol. 2 and 3 (Oxford: Oxford University Press, 1979 & 1988)

Heckel, Waldemar: *The Last Days and Testament of Alexander the Great* (Stuttgart: Franz Steiner Verlag Wiesbaden GMBH, 1988)

Heckel, Waldemar: *The Marshalls of Alexander's Empire* (New York: Routledge, 1992)

Heckel, Waldemar: *The Wars of Alexander the Great, 336-323 BC* (New York: Routledge, 2002)

Heckel, Waldemar and Yardley, J. C.: *Alexander the Great: Historical Sources in Translation* (Oxford: Blackwell Publishing, 2004)

Heckel, Waldemar: *Who's Who in the Age of Alexander the Great* (Oxford: Blackwell Publishing, 2006)

Jouguet, Pierre: *Macedonian Imperialism and the Hellenization of the East*, translated by M. R. Dobie (New York: Alfred A. Knopf, 1928)

Justin: *Epitome of the Philippic, History of Pomprius Trogus*, translated by J. C. Yardley with introduction and explanatory notes by R. Develin (Atlanta: Scholars Press, 1994)

Lane Fox, Robin: *Alexander the Great* (London: The Dial Press, 1974)

Lane Fox, Robin: *In Search of Alexander* (Boston: Little, Brown and Company, 1980)

Lane Fox, Robin: *The Classical World* (New York: Basic Books, 2006)

Lerner, Jeffrey D.: *The Impact of the Seleucid Decline on the Eastern Iranian Plateau* (Stuttgart: Franz Steiner Verlag, 1999)

M'Crindle, John Watson.: *The Invasion of India by Alexander the Great, as described by Arrian, Q. Cutis, Diodoros, Plutarch and Justin* (Westminster: A. Constable and Co., 1896, 1972)

Macurdy, Grace Harriet: *Hellenistic Queens* (Baltimore: The John Hopkins Press, 1932)

McKechnie, Paul: "Diodorus Siculus and Hephaestion's Pyre", *The Classical Quarterly*, New Series, Vol. 45, No. 2. (1995), pp. 418-432

Pearson, Lionel: *The Lost Histories of Alexander the Great* (Chicago: Scholars Press, 1983)

Quintus Curtius Rufus, *The History of Alexander*, translated by John C. Rolfe, 2 Vols. (Cambridge: Harvard University Press, MCMXLVI)

Quintus Curtius Rufus, *The History of Alexander*, translation by John Yardley with an introduction and notes by Waldemar Heckel (Harmondsworth: Penguin Books, 1984)

Renault, Mary: *The Nature of Alexander* (New York: Pantheon Books, 1975)

Saunders, Nicolas J.: *Alexander's Tomb, The Two Thousand Year Obsession to Find the Lost Conqueror* (New York: Basic Books, 2006)

Sherman-White, Susan and Kuhrt, Amélie: *From Samarkand to Sardis, A new approach to the Seleucid empire* (Berkeley: University of California Press, 1993)

Simpson, R. H.: "The Historical Circumstances of the Peace of 311", *The Journal of Hellenic Studies*, Vol. 74. (1959), pp. 25-31

Stoneman, Richard: *Alexander the Great*, 2nd edition (New York: Routledge, 2004)

Sushko, Alexander: *Gavgamela* (Chicago: University of Chicago, 1937)

Tarn, Sir William W.: *Alexander the Great*, 2 Vols. (London: Cambridge University Press, 1948)

The Cambridge Ancient History: Macedon, 401-301 B.C., Vol. 6, edited by J. B. Bury, S. A. Cook, and F. E. Adcock, 3rd Impression (Cambridge: University Printing House, 1964)

The Greek Alexander Romance, translation: Richard Stoneman (London: Penguin Books, 1991)

Warry, John: *Alexander 334-323 BC: Conquest of the Persian Empire* (Westport: Praeger, 2005)

Wood, Michael: *In the Footsteps of Alexander the Great: a Journey from Greece to Asia* (Berkeley: University of California Press, 1997)

Worthington, Ian: *Alexander the Great: Man and God* (Harlow: Pearson Longman, 2004)

Persian

Abbott, Jacob: *Histories of Cyrus the Great and Alexander the Great*, with revisions and an appendix by Lyman Abbot (New York: Harper and Brothers, 1880)

Allen, Lindsey: *The Persian Empire* (Chicago: University of Chicago Press, 2005)

Arberry, A. J.: *Classical Persian Literature* (London: George Allen & Unwin LTD, 1958)

Badian, E.: "Darius III", *Harvard Studies in Classical Philology*, Vol. 100. (2000), pp. 241-267

Beny, Roloff: *Persia: Bridge of Turquoise*, essay and anthology by Seyyed Hossein Nasr (Boston: New York Graphic Society, 1975)

Birth of the Persian Empire, edited by Vesta Sarkhosh Curtis & Sara Stewart, Vol. 1 (London: I.B. Tauris, 2005)

Briant, Pierre: *From Cyrus to Alexander: A History of the Persian Empire*, translated by Peter T. Daniels (Winona Lake: Eisenbrauns, 2002)

Brosius, Maria: *Women in Ancient Persia: 559-331 BC* (Oxford: Oxford University Press, 1996)

Brosius, Maria: *The Persians: An Introduction* (New York: Routledge, 2006)

Cook, J. M.: *The Persian Empire* (New York: Schocken Books, 1983)

Ctesias: *Persica by Ctesias of Cnidus*, summarized by Photios, translated by J. H. Freese, www.tertullian.org

Culican, William: *The Medes and Persians* (New York: Frederick A. Praeger, 1965)

Curtis, Vesta Sarkhosh and Canby, Sheila R.: *Persian Love Poetry* (London: The British Museum Press, 2005)

Dandamaev, M. A.: *A Political History of the Achaemenid Empire*, translated by W. J. Vogelsang (Leiden: E. J. Brill, 1989)

Dandamayev, Muhammad A.: *Iranians in Achaemenid Babylonia* (Costs Mesa: Mazda Publishers, 1992)

Dandamaev, Muhammad A. and Lukoniv, Vladimir: *The Cultural and Social Institutions of Ancient Iran*, English edition by Philip L. Kohl with the assistance of D. J. Dadson (Cambridge: Cambridge University Press, 1994)

Davis, Dick: *Epic and Sedition: The Case of Ferdowsi's Shahnameh* (Fayetteville: University of Arkansas Press, 1992)

Eddy, Samuel K.: *The King is Dead* (Lincoln: The University of Nebraska Press, 1961)

Farrokh, Kaveh: *Shadows in the Desert: Ancient Persia at War* (Oxford: Osprey Publishing, 2007)

Fennelly, James M.: "The Persepolis Ritual", *The Biblical Archaeologist,* Vol. 43, No. 3. (Summer, 1980), pp. 135-162

Ferdowsi Toosi, Hakim Abol-Ghasem: *The Shâhnâma of Firdausi*, done into English by Arthur George Warner and Edmond Warner (London: K. Paul, Trench, Trübner, 1905-1925)

Ferdowsi Toosi, Hakim Abol-Ghasem: *In the Dragon's Claws: the Story of Rostam & Esfandiyar, from the Persian Book of Kings*, translated & introduced by Jerome W. Clinton (Washington, DC: Mage Publishers, 1999)

Ferdowsi Toosi, Hakim Abol-Ghasem: *Shâhnâmeh: The Persian Book of Kings*, translated by Dick Davis (New York: Viking, 2006)

Ferdowsi Toosi, Hakim Abol-Ghasem: *The Shâh Nâmah of Firdusî: The Book of the Persian Kings*, translated in prose and verse by James Vere Stewart Wilkinson (London: Oxford University Press, 1931)

Ferdowsi Toosi, Hakim Abol-Ghasem: *Shâhnâmeh: Fathers and Sons*, translated by Dick Davis (Washington, DC: Mage Publishers, 2000)

Ferdowsi Toosi, Hakim Abol-Ghasem: *Shâhnâmeh: Sunset of Empire*, translated by Dick Davis (Washington, DC: Mage Publishers, 2004)

Flowers from Persian Poets, edited by Nathan Haskell Dole and Belle M. Walker, Vol. 1 (New York: Thomas Y. Cromwell & Co., 1901)

Frye, Richard N.: *The Heritage of Persia* (Cleveland: The World Publishing Company, 1963)

Hafez Shirazi: *Robaiyyat of Hafez Shirazi*, translated by Richard Francis Burton, 1891

Hallock, Richard T.: *Persepolis Fortification Tablets* (Chicago: University of Chicago Press, 1969)

Hekmat, Forough: *Folk Tales of Ancient Persia* (Delmar: Caravan Books, 1974)

Hinnells, John R: *Persian Mythology* (London: Chancellor Press, 1985)

Holland, Tom: *Persian Fire* (New York: Double Day, 2005)

Iskandarnameh, A Persian Medieval Alexander-Romance, translated by Minoo S. Southgate (New York: Columbia University Press, 1978)

Jackson, Williams, A. V.: *Persia Past and Present* (New York: The Macmillan Company, 1906)

Kent, Roland: *Old Persian: Grammar, Texts, Lexicon*, 2nd edition, revised (New Haven: American Oriental Society, 1953)

Landinsky, Daniel: *I Heard God Laughing: Rendering of Hafiz* (Oakland: Dharma Printing Company, 1996)

Levy, Reuben: *Persian Literature* (London: Oxford University Press, 1923)

Nezami of Ganjeh: *Makhzanol Asrâr: The Treasury of Mysteries*, translated by Gholâm Hosein Dârâb (London: Arthur Probsthain, 1945)

Olmstead, A. T.: *History of the Persian Empire* (Chicago: The University of Chicago Press, 1948)

Omar Khayyâm: *Rubâiyât of Omar Khayyam*, rendered into English verse by Edward Fitzgerald (New York: Garden City Books, 1952)

Parker, Richard A.: "Persian and Egyptian Chronology", *The American Journal of Semitic Languages and Literature,* Vol. 58, No. 3. (July, 1941), pp. 285-301

Pavry, Bapsy: *The Heroines of Ancient Persia* (Cambridge: At the University Press, 1930)

Payne, Robert: *The Splendor of Persia* (New York: Alfred A Knopf, 1957)

Persian Literature, Columbia Lectures on Iranian Studies, edited by Ehsan Yarshater (Albany: State University of New York Press, 1988)

Pourafzal, Haleh and Montgomery, Roger: *The Spiritual Wisdom of Haféz: Teachings of the Philosopher of Love* (Rochester: Inner Traditions, 1998)

Rumi, Jalâl-al-Din Balkhi: *The Essential Rumi*, translated by Coleman Barks (New York: Harper Collins Publishers, 1995)

Rypka, Jan: *History of Iranian Literature* (Holland: D. Reidel Publishing Company, 1968)

Sa'adi Shirazi, Sheikh Muslih al-din: The Bustan of Sa'adi, Iran Chamber Society

Sa'adi Shirazi, Sheikh Muslih al-din: The Golestan of Sa'adi, Iran Chamber Society

Shahbazi, Shapur A.: "Irano-Hellenic Notes 3: Iranians and Alexander", *American Journal of Ancient History*, New Series, Vol. 2, No. 1. (2003), pp. 5-38

Stolper, Mathew: *Entrepreneurs and the Empire: Murašû Archive, the Murašû Firm, and Persian Rule in Babylonia* (Belgium: Nederlands Historisch - Archaeologisch Instituut Te Istanbul, 1985)

Studies in Persian History: Essays in memory of David M. Lewis, edited by Maria Brosius and Amélie Kuhrt (Leiden: Nederlands Instituut Voor Het Nabije Oosten, 1998)

The Cambridge History of Iran: The Median and Achaemenian Periods, edited by Ilya Gershevitch (Cambridge: Cambridge University Press, 1981)

The Forgotten Empire: The World of Ancient Persia, edited by John E. Curtis and Nigel Tallis (Berkeley: University of California Press, 2005)

The Hand of Poetry: Five Mystic Poets of Persia, translation from the Poems of Sanai, Attar, Rumi, Saadi and Hafiz by Coleman Barks (New Lebanon: Omega Publications, 1993)

The Poetry of Nizami Ganjavi: Knowledge, Love, and Rhetoric, edited by Kamran Talattof and Jerome W. Clinton (New York: Palgrave Publishers, 2000)

Tolman, Herbert Cushing: *A Guide to the Old Persian Inscriptions* (New York: American Book Company, 1893)

Wheeler, Mortimore: *Flames Over Persepolis* (New York: Reynal & Company, Inc., 1968)

Wiesehöfer, Josef: *Ancient Persia: From 550 BC to 650 AD*, translated by Azizeh Azodi (London: I.B. Tauris Publishers, 1996)

Wilber, Donald: *Persepolis: The Archeology of Parsa, Seat of the Persian Kings* (New York: Thomas Y. Crowell Company, 1969)

Yarshater, Ehsan: *The Lion & the Throne*, translated by Dick Davis (Washington, DC: Mage Publishers, 1998)

Zimmern, Helen: *The Epic of Kings: Stories Retold From Firdusi* (London: T. Fisher Unwin, MDCCCLXXXIII)

Sumerian

Crawford, Harriet: *Sumer and the Sumerians*, 2nd edition (Cambridge: Cambridge University Press, 2004)

Kramer, Samuel Noah: *Cradle of Civilization* (New York: Time, Inc., 1967)

Lambert, W. G. and Millard, A. R.: *Atra Hasîs: The Babylonian Story of the Flood*, with the Sumerian Flood Story by M. Civil (Winona Lake: Eisenbrauns, 1999)

Woolley, C. Leonard: *The Sumerians* (New York: W. W. Norton & Company, 1965)

Zoroastrian

Avesta, Khorda Avesta: Book of Common Prayer, digital edition, Joseph H. Peterson, 1995

Boyce, Mary: *A History of Zoroastrianism*, Vols. 1 and 2 (Leiden: Brill, 1975)

Boyce, Mary: *Zoroastrians: Their Religious Beliefs and Practices* (London: Routledge & Kegan Paul, 1985)

Clark, Peter: *Zoroastrianism: An Introduction to an Ancient Faith* (Brighton: Sussex Academic Press, 1998)

Dhalla, Maneckji Nusservanji: *History of Zoroastrianism* (Bombay: The K. R. Cama Oriental Institute, 1963, 1985)

Mehr, Farhang: *Zoroastrian Tradition* (Costa Mesa: Mazda Publishers, Inc., 2003)

Sacred Books of the East, Vol. 4, translated by James Darmesteter and L.H. Mills, edited by Max Müller, revised edition (New York: Collier, 1900)

The Zend Avesta of Zarathustra, translated from the Zend, by Edmond Bordeux Szekley (British Columbia: International Biogenic Society, 1990)

COMPANIONS
HADÂBÂRA

Jinny Antone
Kian
Mary Jo
Belinda Hui
Sunnie
Kathy Lum

BENEFACTORS
VARUSANKA

Atul Asthana
Archer
J. C.
Larry King
Susan Shankle

All this has been done by the will of the Wise Lord.
aita tya kartam ava visam vašnâ Auramazdâhâ.

Neither Histories... nor history...
One-third history, one-third legend, one-third myth,
three-thirds fiction...

So let me neither exalt my royal ancestors nor defame their enemies, for that is vain...
Splendid men are worthy of splendid enemies...
... one hand washes the other...
... in words as in life, there must be understanding and sharing of all that one is capable of understanding...

May Auramazdâhâ protect me and what is done by me,
and what was done by my fathers.

𐎭𐎠 𐎴𐎹𐎢𐎽𐎣

The story of the Persians is yet to be written...

God King Country Earth